Grace,

Thank you so much
for hosting my ~~first~~
book signing!

Mary Singer
Dec 11, 1999

MOTHER *Flies* HURRICANES

E.M. Singer

MOTHER *Flies* HURRICANES

AVIDIA
CASCADE PRESS

Published in the United States by Avidia Cascade Press, PMB 33, 2650 NE Highway 20, Suite G, Bend OR 97701

ISBN 0-9674677-0-5

Foreword

*W*hen the author's British mother-in-law and I were pilots together in Britain's Air Transport Auxiliary during WWII, the events of this novel, which seem so dramatic today, were just routine.

We Americans, arriving in early spring of 1942, were struck by the strength of local communities. Air, sea, and ground combat was getting all the press, but combat was not the only arena of heroism.

"Loose Lips Sink Ships" brought many a pub chat to silence, and may have made local folks seem unfriendly. They did not respond to interest shown in their lives or their work. "Mend and Make Do" in practice uncovered remarkable ingenuity among the working populace. "Carry On" covered for dreadful losses, and individuals did not miss a day at their jobs in tank, munitions, or aircraft factories.

Recently I heard from a gentleman, now around 70, who in 1942 had come from school to an assignment with the ATA at our Pool as a Cadet helper, to fly with us when operation of an aircraft required more than one pair of hands. He appeared to be about 15 years old at the time. The impact of events upon children, who were sent to sponsor families in the US, was upsetting. Others had their schools moved to isolated, non-target areas. These disruptions to young lives would be called "traumatizing" today. They were borne with the traditional stiff upper lip by British families.

The author has done her research well, and has brought to life again the temper of those times. Her story emerges from the perspective of a nine-year-old schoolboy, whose parents are both pilots: his father in the RAF and his mother in the ATA. How the progress of WWII changes this family, and everyone involved with them, makes a story full of historical interest as well as the excitement of individual struggles to survive.

Roberta Leveaux
Former ATA Pilot

Acknowledgements

*E*very endeavor is a journey, and I have been blessed in having so many helping hands along the way.

I am grateful to my "readers," who perused the early drafts of my manuscript and gave me suggestions, corrections, and very constructive criticism: Tiffany Bolling, Loran Booth, Sarah Cornwell, Meg Franklin, May Groff, Paul Moore, Barbara Munro, Andrew Rideout, and Jane Meissner. A double helping of gratitude goes to Barbara Munro for assistance in proofreading; also to Meg Franklin, who valiantly carried on with her proofreading mission, despite the fact that her county was declared a disaster area in the wake of Hurricane Floyd. Thanks also to Amy Beech, Carolyn Tabor, and Terry Shumaker for proofreading, and a very special thanks to Pamela Thomas for assistance in obtaining resource materials.

I could not have accomplished anything without a chorus of "encouragers": Ann, Beth, Claudia, Dan, Darylee, Lura, Mel, Michael—and my best friend, my mother.

Thanks to Sue Myers at Bookmasters, Larry Jackson at Heidelberg Graphics, and Paula Lawyer for their professional assistance, and to Pete and Aprille Chadwell of Dynamic Arts for a terrific cover.

I am grateful to my children for their patience, insights, and cyber-assistance. My deepest appreciation, love, and adoration go to P.J.: my technical advisor, cultural consultant, aviation expert, military historian, research assistant, copy editor, critic, and cheering squad—without whom this book would never have been written.

I owe the greatest debt of gratitude to the men and women of the Air Transport Auxiliary, who shared their memories and friendship with me, and gave me their trust and blessing in this endeavor. They include: Ruth Ballard, Lettice Curtis, Maggie Frost, Annette Hill, Joy Lofthouse, Yvonne MacDonald, and Veronica Volkersz. A very special thanks to Diana Barnato Walker, Commodore of the ATA Association, for graciously critiquing the ATA "bits" in my manuscript, and to Ed Heering, Roberta Leveaux, and Philip Rogers for their enthusiastic and unflagging support. I am grateful to Pauline Gower's son, Michael Fahie, for giving me an early draft of his mother's biography, *A Harvest of Memories*, which provided a wealth of information and inspiration in the unfolding of this story.

Of course, the responsibility for any errors, inaccuracies, or shortcomings is mine alone.

It is my hope in writing *Mother Flies Hurricanes* that the "Forgotten Pilots" of the ATA will always be remembered for their dedication, courage, and contribution to the Allied victory in WWII. It is to them that this book is dedicated.

E.M.S.
October, 1999

Out of the chill and the shadow,
Into the thrill and the shrine;
Out of the dearth and the famine,
Into the fullness divine.

Margaret E. Sangster

Chapter 1

*F*or Andrew Hadley-Trevelyan, the Second World War began on March third, 1940. This particular day would not be remembered to history, except for the fact that it marked a milestone of sorts, for exactly six months earlier England had declared war on Nazi Germany. Other than that, no notable events occurred in the world.

At the time, to Andrew, the incident that occurred on that day seemed just a momentary fright. It would not be until much later that he would remember this day as a turning point in his life.

Before that day was all the innocence and ease of his childhood. He believed that nothing could touch that safe, pleasant world he inhabited, a world he thought would last forever.

After that day, fear became his companion and tormentor.

For it was on the third of March, 1940, the day before his ninth birthday, that Andrew first began to be afraid for his father.

Though the war had begun a half year earlier, it had not had much of an effect on Andrew's life, other than providing a few annoyances and some measure of excitement. The voice of a weary man marked its inception. Andrew vaguely remembered Prime Minister Chamberlain sadly informing his countrymen that a state of war existed between England and Germany on September third, 1939, two days after Germany's invasion of Poland.

At the time, Andrew didn't give it much thought. He was mildly amused by the strange sort of euphoric panic that gripped his country during the days following the announcement of war. Bomb shelters were dug, buildings were boarded up and sandbagged, and a nationwide black-out was ordered. Fleets of silvery barrage balloons sailed above the cities and major ports. Posters appeared everywhere with the stern admonition: *Hitler will send no warning, so always carry your gas mask!* Andrew's mother had gotten him a gas mask that had a Mickey Mouse face and ears on it, much to his annoyance. He protested that he was *not* a baby, and that he would rather be *gassed* than wear a babylooking mask, so his mother exchanged it for a plain black, mature version.

As a final precaution, an evacuation from the cities to the countryside of children, pregnant mothers, and handicapped people was organized. This was the most unpleasant thing that Andrew had experienced thus far, for a motley gaggle of slum children descended upon Greycliff, the family estate of Andrew's mother in Northumberland. Andrew was spending, as usual, the last week of his summer holidays there, and he would never forget the sight (or the smell!) of the appalling assortment of filthy, bedraggled children from the East End of London. There were seven of them, all from the same family, ranging in age from three to twelve.

They were ushered into the front hall at Greycliff by a worker from the Women's Voluntary Service, all of them huddled together like sheep in a thunderstorm. The younger ones whimpered and sobbed; their older siblings were wide-eyed with wonderment and terror. They had name-tags around their necks, and gas masks in cardboard boxes slung over their shoulders. With grimy hands they clutched their meager belongings, which were wrapped with brown paper and equally grimy string. And to Grandmother Howard's consternation, these urchins had been *sewn* into their clothes!

They were lice-infested. They refused to sit at the table for meals. They grabbed handfuls of food and squatted on the floor to eat. The younger ones screamed in terror when they heard a toilet flushing. The older ones were stunned speechless to discover hot water coming out of a tap. They had never even seen a toothbrush, and regarded this bizarre implement with undisguised contempt. They wet the bed, leaving poor Maria, the maid, mounds of acrid laundry to be dealt with in the morning.

They constantly whined about wanting to go back to London, saying it was just "'Orrible, 'orrible, being away from 'ome."

What with the little ones defecating under the stairs and the older boys picking the lock on the liquor cabinet, it was all Andrew could do to keep his distance from them until, to his immense relief, he was able to leave for boarding school a few days later. As he carried his gas mask in a smart tweed satchel and his belongings in a nice leather suitcase, he felt rather superior to this sniveling bunch of cry-babies. After all, it didn't bother him in the least to be setting out to spend the better part of the next nine months at his boarding school, Askew Court, away from his mother and father, as he had been doing for the previous two years. Mercifully, the evacuees (or *filthy vackies*, as Mrs. Beaton, the cook, called them) all returned to London by Christmas.

After the frenzy and fear of autumn, when everyone expected bombs to start raining down on English soil and great battles to be fought on the continent as the Nazis sought to conquer and subjugate everything in their path, the war, such as it was, sputtered into a spooky sort of stand-off which was dubbed the "Phony War." The Germans sat tight on the possessions which they had already acquired, but made no more aggressive moves. They glowered behind their Siegfried Line, a series of pillboxes, gun emplacements, and minefields on their border with France. The French likewise glowered back behind their similarly fortified counter-deterrent, the Maginot Line.

England sent an army to France, the British Expeditionary Force, or BEF, and an Advanced Air Striking Force composed of twelve bomber squadrons of Blenheims and Battles. In addition, four fighter squadrons of Hurricanes were sent as the Air Component to the BEF. And it was at this point that the war, for Andrew, changed from being a minor annoyance, like the gas mask perpetually slung over his shoulder, to being a marvelous affair. For his father, who was a fighter pilot in the RAF, was sent to France soon after Christmas as a replacement in one of the Hurricane squadrons. Andrew bragged about him to his schoolmates: "My father flies Hurricanes! He's the best pilot in the RAF! He's going to shoot down more Nazis than anyone, once the war really gets started, that is!" For he, like almost everyone else, was itching for the British forces to have "a go at the Huns."

What was the point in having a war if it was only a phony one!

Such were his feelings and thoughts until that morning in March.

Andrew was home from boarding school at Armus House, the Hadley-Trevelyan family estate in Berkshire, enjoying the break between winter and spring terms (or Hilary and Trinity, as his father called them, using the Oxford appellations). He was having breakfast with his mother and his Aunt Jane, his father's twin sister, and they were discussing preparations for Andrew's birthday the following day.

Andrew knew that the form for tomorrow's celebration would be much the same as that of his previous birthdays. His father, who had said that he would be arriving in the afternoon (barring an unexpected outbreak of hostilities, of course, and Andrew hoped that the Phony War would not turn into an *unphony* one, at least not this day!) would present Andrew's mother with a bouquet of roses, one for every year of Andrew's age. Her face would beam with a joyous smile. Then Andrew's father would whisper something in her ear and she would break into that glorious lilting laugh that was reserved only for him. They would gaze at each other with *that look*, and then smile at one another, as if they shared a private joke. They would look at Andrew as if he had done something wonderfully pleasing, no matter that he was just standing there grinning at them. Then his father would say to him, "March forth, and open your presents!"

Andrew had always thought how wonderful it was that his birthday was so easy to remember. It would be a bit more difficult to remember one's birthday if it was, say, January twentieth or November twelfth. His father's birthday was October the tenth: ten-ten-ten, (he was born in 1910), almost as easy to remember. His mother's birthday, however, was April eighth, a little more difficult to recollect, until Andrew made up a little saying: One ate (eight) cake for (four) one's birthday, and adding eight and four made twelve, the year his mother was born: 1912. A little contrived, perhaps, but it did the trick.

Andrew spread some orange marmalade on his toast and wondered what his father was going to give him for a birthday present. Perhaps a new pair of boxing gloves, or a book about aeroplanes, or a chess set of his own.

"Would you like some more tea, Alice?" Aunt Jane asked Andrew's mother.

"Just a bit, thank you," Andrew's mother replied. "Do you expect Roger will be able to stay for more than a few days?"

"I do hope so. You two have got a lot of catching up to do," Aunt Jane teased.

Then it happened. As Aunt Jane was pouring the tea, a spasm of fear and dread tore across her face, her hand jerked, and she dropped the teapot, which shattered with a loud crash.

"Jane—?" Andrew's mother looked at her, bewildered. Aunt Jane looked, terrified, back at her. Andrew's mother gasped, and her voice dropped to a horrified whisper as she uttered one word: "*Roger—*"

Andrew's heart seemed to drop into his stomach as he witnessed the scene. That his father and Aunt Jane seemed to possess an extraordinary sort of communication between them was not a revelation to him. He had always been aware that they seemed to know each other's thoughts and feelings, even when far apart. Two years ago, for instance, Andrew had been on a picnic with his parents. They had been throwing crumbs to a squirrel and laughing at its antics when, all of a sudden, worry had crossed his father's face like a swiftly moving cloud.

"It's Jane—something's happened," he'd said to Andrew's mother. And a few hours later, a cable arrived from France to inform them that Aunt Jane and her husband had been in a car accident. Aunt Jane had been injured slightly, but Uncle Marc had been killed.

And so it was that Aunt Jane returned to Armus House to live with Andrew (when he was home from boarding school, that is), his father and mother, Aunt Gwen, Gram, and Freddie, who was a cousin of Andrew's father. Freddie did not reside at Armus House all the time, as his shipping business required him to spend most of his time in London or Southampton.

"My father—what's happened to my father?" Andrew blurted.

The look that his Aunt Jane gave him sent a chill up his spine: a terrible look of horror and sorrow and guilt. She jumped to her feet and, without a word, dashed into the drawing room. Andrew's mother followed her.

Andrew sat frozen to his seat for a moment, waves of cold fear breaking over him like surf. Hearing his Aunt Jane's voice from the drawing room, he got up and walked over to the double doors, now shut, which separated the drawing room from the dining room. He had long ago discovered that there was a good size gap between the doors, starting about three feet up and continuing almost to the top, perfect for hearing and observing all sorts of interesting conversations and goings-on. He peered through the crack.

"...It's all right, it's all right," Aunt Jane was saying. "He was very frightened—now he's angry—"

"Is he hurt?" Andrew's mother asked, her arms around Aunt Jane.

"No, no. He's fine, oh, but I've never known him to be so angry!" Aunt Jane looked distressed now, as if someone were screaming obscenities in her ear. "Oh Alice, I'm sorry—I've upset you and Andrew. Andrew—!"

Andrew scurried back to the table and sat down. Seconds later, the doors opened and Aunt Jane dashed towards him and enfolded him in an embrace.

"Is my father all right?" he asked.

"He's fine, he's fine," Aunt Jane assured him. "Oh darling, I'm so sorry. I didn't mean to scare you."

"Is he still coming for my birthday?"

"I know he'll do his best to be here, don't you worry!"

Andrew tried to finish his breakfast, but, relieved as he was that nothing had happened to his father, he found he wasn't hungry anymore.

"Damned wooden propellers." Andrew's father stabbed at a piece of ham.

"So it just disintegrated on you in mid-air?" Uncle Robert asked. Uncle Robert, who was married to Aunt Gwen, Andrew's father's younger sister, was also a pilot. He was in the Fleet Air Arm and flew Swordfish, or "Stringbags" as they were affectionately dubbed, since they were capable of being crammed full with an incredible variety of things necessary to do battle over His Majesty's seas.

"Fortunately I had enough altitude to glide back to base. And fortunate, as well, that the Jerries weren't around. Well, this month we're getting a batch of new Hurris with metal propellers, metal wings too."

"The Spits were designed with metal wings, and they're far superior to the Hurris," Uncle Robert said. "It would make sense to send them to France, wouldn't you say?"

"Stuffy Dowding doesn't want any of his precious Spitfires to get too far from home." Freddie grabbed a roll. "He's like an old miser who wants to keep his pennies locked away from everyone else. He doesn't want anybody to lay a finger on his precious Fighter Command. Why they didn't retire him years ago is a mystery to me." Freddie usually was able to find some way to denigrate the Royal Air Force in general, and Fighter Command in particular. He reserved his most scathing remarks for Fighter Command's Commander in Chief, Air Marshall Hugh Dowding.

"...as I said, it was a mistake to make the RAF a separate branch of the service," Freddie went on. "Now these upstart chiefs with wings on their chests think they can call the shots! It makes more sense to have your air component tied to the Army or the Navy, as it is in the case of the Fleet Air Arm being under the Royal Navy, or like it was in the Great War with the Royal Flying Corps as part of the Army. How can one expect cooperation with all these egos running around, and the army not being able to control the fly-boys? It makes for nothing but chaos, pure and simple."

"It's a good thing that the RAF isn't hamstrung to a bunch of bureaucrats who think that the next war, if God forbid there is to be a next war, is going to be fought like the Great War was," Andrew's father said. "If anyone has taken a good hard look at what happened in Spain, and in Poland, it should be convincing enough to see that thinking in the same old grooves of military strategy is suicidal, pure and simple. The Nazis were able to conquer Poland in just four weeks with their blitzkrieg—they threw the Polish defenses into complete chaos—"

"Throwing Polacks into complete chaos isn't all that difficult to accomplish, dear boy," Freddie snorted. "Stupid bloody peasants, mounting charges on horseback against German tanks! We never should have thrown our lot in with Poland, especially without knowing if we could count on Russia's support if those stupid Polacks tried to provoke a war with Germany. Furthermore, we should have reconsidered our position after Germany and Russia signed that non-aggression pact in August. What did our illustrious leaders think those two were going to do, play skittles? Poland was properly trounced, that's all there is to it. Their army was a joke from the start—"

"The blitzkrieg technique would make mincemeat of any army not prepared to meet it." Andrew's father dished up a serving of carrots. "It throws all the old ideas of warfare out the window. It's exactly what the word means: a lightning war, using high-speed tanks, dive-bombers, and fighter planes. Air power is the key, and the Nazis have made good use of theirs. Air power, above all else, and how effectively it's employed, will be the decisive factor from now on."

"The idea of the dashing fighter pilot, dueling in the skies far above the battles of ordinary mortals, is a charming notion, but completely impractical," Freddie retorted. "Using aircraft for bombing and reconnaissance is useful, to be sure, but the activities of the Air Force need to be controlled by the tacticians on the ground. To have a bunch of hot-shot pilots going off half-cocked, looking for trouble, is absurd and wasteful. All those aerobatics and fancy flying are nice for air shows, but not the least bit useful when it comes to fighting a real war. Why, if Trenchard had had his way, we wouldn't have any fighter forces, anyway. Strategic bombing is the *only* practical use in which airpower can be effectively employed. As they say, the bomber will always get through."

Andrew's father glared at Freddie. "Trenchard was right to fight for the existence of the RAF as a separate service, and thank God he was Chief of Air Staff. But he was wrong in believing that bombers alone would win a war, though I'll admit that putting forth that argument to the politicians at the time ensured the survival of the RAF. But the bomber *won't* always get through, not if your opponent has enough fighter planes to intercept them. And if your opponent sends his bombers to attack *your* country, you'll need fighters to defend yourself. Fighters are essential for both defense and offense, and the side that has the best fighters, and the best fighter pilots, has a decisive advantage, perhaps the *ultimate* advantage.

"Dear boy, are you and your band of Merry Men going to save the realm single-handedly? Careful, Roger—your armor is blinding us. I must send a memo to His Majesty to henceforth disband the army and navy—after all, what need do we have of soldiers and guns and ships at sea, what with Fighter Command to impress our enemies with thrilling air shows?"

"It's not a show, Freddie. To downgrade the importance of home defense—"

"The best defense is to hit the other fellow first."

"You're wrong Freddie. Defending yourself *from* attack is vital—"

"Defense doesn't win a war."

"But it keeps you from losing it. And if you're knocked out before you have a chance to fight back, winning is an impossibility, pure and simple. In boxing for instance, it's just as important to defend yourself from a knock-out punch as it is to deliver one—"

"You're not boxing at Oxford anymore, dear boy. This is the real world. If you had applied yourself to your studies instead of wasting your time flying and boxing you might have come out with enough intelligence to understand that there's more to life than doing fancy aerobatics or dancing around a boxing ring."

"More wine, Freddie?" Without waiting for a reply, Andrew's father refilled Freddie's glass.

"Nice Chardonnay." Freddie took a sip. "At least you're able to pick out a good bottle of wine, Roger, on occasion."

It used to bother Andrew when his father didn't give Freddie a verbal clouting at conversational junctures such as these, until his father explained: "It's no use sinking down to his level. If you decide to start slinging mud, you're going to get just as filthy as the other fellow. There's a time to fight fire with fire, but most of the time you can win just by taking advantage of your opponent's weaknesses. Freddie has already persuaded himself that he can win by attacking others, and I'm not going to sink to his level, or try to persuade him to change his ways. The Americans have a clever saying: 'Never teach a pig to sing; it wastes your time and annoys the pig!' Freddie usually starts getting obnoxious when he knows he's losing an argument, and since he's determined to drink himself into insensibility anyway, I figure it's best to put him, and us, out of misery as soon as possible.

Andrew watched as his father surreptitiously refilled Freddie's glass again while Freddie argued with Uncle Robert about another subject that never failed to arouse his anger.

"...why the hell anyone thinks we should fight a war with Germany anyway! The Germans are reasonable people, and they're quite willing to sit down with us and sort things out. Hitler doesn't want a war with England! If our politicians have any sense at all they'll see to it that Churchill is given the sack. He's already started stirring things up! Yes, given the sack or at least sent far enough away that he can't cause any trouble! The Australian outback would be nice, perhaps India or Burma—I'd like to see Winnie stew in some God-forsaken place. A pity we don't have the American colonies anymore—North Dakota or Kansas would suit him just fine—"

Uh-oh, thought Andrew. Now that he's started in on America he'll *never* shut up and I'll have to wait *forever* for my party.

"...and furthermore the place is rotten with wogs! All Micks, Dagos, and Polacks in the east, Chinks and bean-eaters in the west, and nothing but bugger-all in the middle! Too many coloreds and Jews running around—the Jews run everything there, you know. The place is positively stinking with foreigners! The Yanks let anyone and everyone in, all the odds and sods from every fourth-rate country on earth—"

"Why don't we go to the drawing room? A bit of sherry would do just fine, now, don't you think?" Gram said.

Freddie broke off, turned to her, and smiled. "Marvelous idea, darling Vickie."

Andrew rolled his eyes. Once Freddie started calling Gram "Darling Vickie" it was only a matter of time before he would be draping himself around her and slobbering sweet nothings in her ear. A glass of sherry should finish him off, though. For all the vast quantities of liquor he consumed, Freddie had never developed a tolerance for the stuff—thank God!

Once in the drawing room, Andrew's father poured the sherry, offering Freddie a sip first in order to get his opinion as to whether or not it was fine enough to be served on this special occasion.

"Splendid, splendid," Freddie pronounced. He downed the rest of the glass in one gulp.

He's so potted he wouldn't know if it was horse pee, Andrew thought. He watched as Freddie proceeded to lay his arm across Gram's shoulder in a not-so-nephewly way, his eyes bleary and his legs starting to sway like barrage balloon cables in a high wind. Then he began to nuzzle her neck.

"Here Freddie, why don't you sit for a bit?" Gram guided him to a chair, where he plopped down. Andrew's father handed him another glass of sherry, and winked at Gram.

Gram rolled her eyes and Andrew fumed. Freddie's behavior towards her had always irked him, even though he was secretly pleased that his grandmother was still one to turn heads. She was only in her late forties, just a few years older than Freddie, but looked positively ten years younger. She had only been seventeen when she'd been married to Grandfather Hadley-Trevelyan, who had been more than thirty years older than her at the time. He'd died of a stroke four years later. She had married again, this time to a man whom Andrew referred to as Grandfather Denniston. He was killed in the Great War in 1918. It seemed strange to Andrew that the man his father called "Dad", or "My father" was this stepfather; Grandfather Hadley-Trevelyan, of whom Andrew's father professed to have no recollection, was referred to more formally as "Father". Andrew wondered how his father could think of a man not really his father as "Dad".

How could a man who is not your father, your flesh and blood, really care about you?

Freddie's head was starting to loll, and Andrew's father and Uncle Robert nodded to each other. With a practiced motion, they hauled Freddie away from Gram and escorted him into the study, where he was unceremoniously deposited on the couch. Andrew followed this entourage at a close distance, relieved and gleeful that Freddie was finally out of commission. He was glad, first of all, that Freddie would not be around to spoil his birthday party. He was also a little afraid of Freddie when he started getting really nasty. It reassured Andrew to see him in such a torpid condition; it was rather like seeing a ferocious beast caged. It was annoying, too, that Freddie bothered Gram; but if that wasn't bad enough, Freddie's lecherous proclivities had lately taken a most disturbing turn: Ever since Andrew's father had joined the RAF, Freddie had been eyeing Andrew's mother in the same sort of way, albeit not quite so playfully or obviously.

There was nothing glaringly inappropriate about Freddie's behavior. It was quite subtle, but there none the less: the discreet admiring glances, the somewhat effusive compliments, the more-than-cousinly way he kissed her hand, the way he always seemed to be trying to find an excuse to touch her, whether it was putting his hand on hers or his arm around her shoulder, or playfully smoothing back a lock of her hair or brushing off an imaginary piece of lint on her clothing. Of course, Freddie did not indulge in this behavior when Andrew's father was around! Andrew's mother would always gently, but firmly, remove the offending appendage from her person, without creating a scene, of course, although Andrew wished she would.

I wish she would just smack him, just give him a good, hard slap right across the face or better yet, a swift kick in the—

"Go back to the drawing room, old chap." Andrew's father winked at him.

Andrew dashed back to the drawing room. His mother gave him a kiss on the forehead. "Well, I wonder what your father's up to?"

They did not have long to wait. In a few minutes the doors to the dining room flew open, and Andrew's father stood there, a joyful smile on his face and a bouquet of nine roses in his hand. Andrew's mother laughed that wonderful laugh as she accepted it. They kissed, and then Andrew's father grinned at him and announced: "March forth, and open your presents!"

"Stand back a little more, Andrew. Now hold the plane out a little so the wings will show." Andrew's father focused his camera.

They were outside. Andrew held his favorite present, a wooden model Hawker Hurricane that his father had given him. It had a propeller that really spun around, and was painted exactly like the real thing: brown and dull green camouflage, with RAF roundels on the wings and fuselage, and red, white, and blue stripes on the tail. Andrew remembered the first time he had seen a real Hurricane, at the Hendon Air Display in 1936, where it had first been shown to the public along with another new fighter plane: the Supermarine Spitfire. He had been breathless with wonder at the sight of these wonderfully modern-looking planes—how sleek and powerful they appeared next to the ungainly biplanes! Both of them were capable of speeds of over 300 miles an hour—incredible to think that something could go that fast! After watching a thrilling aerobatic display, Andrew's mother, who was a pilot also, had exclaimed, "I'd like to put one of those through its paces!" Andrew's father had smiled at her and replied, "I'm sure you could show it a thing or two!" When his father had joined the RAF, Andrew was thrilled to find out he'd been assigned to a squadron equipped with Hurricanes.

"Hold it, now—oh, wait the film's not advanced. Wait a sec—"

Andrew, tired of holding the stiff pose, lifted the plane high above his head and made it soar through the sky in a half-loop, finishing up with a Immelmann: a half-roll at the top of the loop so that the plane turned right side up and flew straight. He made a loud whirring noise to accompany the maneuver. Then he felt his father's hand on his shoulder.

"Aren't you going to take my picture?"

His father smiled. "I already did."

"Can we go to town now?"

"Certainly!"

Andrew ran back to the house, holding the Hurricane aloft as he made it dive and soar.

"Bring it in for a landing," his father laughed.

Andrew obliged, and gently set the plane down on the lawn.

"Perfect three-pointer." His father put his arm around Andrew's shoulder as they walked into the house. "Well, shall we have Thomas drive us in the Bentley, or do you want to go in the MG?"

"The MG!"

"Well, wash up and we'll be on our way!"

Andrew ran upstairs to wash his hands. It had been a wonderful birthday so far, everything perfect, except for Freddie's behavior (which was to be expected; and he had been disposed of quite easily) and for the fact that Mrs. Tuttle, the cook, had made carrot cake for his birthday, which Andrew detested.

"It's my birthday—why do we have to have carrot cake?" he'd complained.

"It's your father's favorite," Aunt Gwen had told him. "We wanted to have something special since he was able to make it home for your birthday."

"But I hate it!" Andrew had made a show of picking out the shreds of carrot with his fork, which didn't leave much in the way of cake left to consume. No matter, his father had promised to take him to a nice restaurant in town for tea, and he would be allowed to get whatever sweets he wanted.

After insisting that his father put the top down on the MG, Andrew settled himself into the passenger seat. He liked to watch his father drive. He could be a race car driver, Andrew thought, as he watched his father deftly shift gears and turn corners so expertly.

The wind lashed his father's dark hair. *The same shade of brown as mine*, Andrew thought. He delighted in sharing this particular feature with his father. Andrew's mother had red hair, and while it looked very attractive on her, Andrew considered that he himself would look horrible with red hair. Besides, he had never known a boy with red hair who had not been thoroughly obnoxious. Leaning back against the seat, he regarded his father's profile: the straight nose and high cheekbones; the firm jaw, clenched ever so slightly with concentration; the gray eyes crinkled with keen attention; the look of complete assurance on his face. The sight of him, completely intent on his task—it was the same look his father had whenever he was absorbed in anything, be it flying, boxing, driving, whatever—gave Andrew a feeling of such pleasure and security that he imagined no harm could ever come to either of them.

There's nothing he can't do—and do well!

They arrived at the restaurant and were shown to a table next to a window overlooking the Thames. Andrew's mouth watered at the thought of the scrumptious desserts he would soon be devouring: iced cherry tarts, trifle piled high with whipped cream, perhaps a chocolate truffle or two. The waitress brought a tray of desserts for their inspection and Andrew saw, to his dismay, that the fare was quite unexciting: fruit tarts (no icing), gingerbread with raisins for garnish, and walnut cakes (no icing either, just a walnut on top.)

"Don't you have anything sweet?" he grumbled to the waitress.

"Sugar's been rationed since January, you know," she replied.

After making a show of his distaste for each item, Andrew settled on the walnut cake. His father selected an apple tart.

"Don't worry, Andrew. I've brought along a little something extra." His father winked at him.

"Chocolates?"

"Eat your cake—no, don't wolf it down. I'll have to eat them all by myself if you choke to death!"

Andrew devoured his cake, took a sip of tea, and sat straight up with anticipation. His father reached into his jacket as if he were about to present a treasure of exceptional value and, with a flourish, presented a small, bright red box to Andrew.

Andrew opened it and saw that it contained, much to his delight, six chocolates: three dark and three milk chocolate, of varying shapes and sizes. He proffered the box to his father, who selected a medium-sized oval piece of dark chocolate.

"Orange cream," his father pronounced, before taking a bite.

He was right.

"Raspberry jelly," Andrew said, selecting a large square milk chocolate. He bit into it. "Vanilla. How do you know what's inside?"

"Oh, grown-ups learn to see through things. Just takes practice." There was a twinkle in father's eye.

"No you don't! But how do you do it?"

"It's a state secret. I've been sworn to secrecy by His Majesty—personally."

"No you haven't! Please, please tell me!"

"Well, since you're so persuasive, I shall. There's a little swirl on the top of each candy, and each swirl is different, depending on what's inside. You can tell by the shape, too. He pointed to one with a long, narrow loop, like a lower-case cursive L. "That one's lemon."

Andrew bit into it. "You're right."

His father pointed to the other pieces: "Chocolate, cherry, coconut."

Andrew offered his father another piece, but he declined. He watched Andrew select another chocolate; then his face grew serious.

"It would be so easy," he said, "If you could tell what was inside a person just by looking at the outside. You would see a big "E" tattooed on a person's forehead and you would know he was evil—wouldn't that be nice? Trouble is, it's not that simple. The bad people aren't going to let on right away that they're bad. Look at what happened in Germany, for instance. At first, Hitler seemed like such a wonderful person. He promised to make Germany great again. He gave the people hope, and pride in themselves and in their country. That sort of thing is very—" his father pursed his lips, as if he were searching for just the right word. "Persuasive, I guess you could say. He told people what they wanted to hear, and after that, it was easy to tell them anything."

"The Germans should have known that Hitler was evil. He even *looks* evil!"

"Sometimes it's very obvious from the way a person talks and acts that he's a bad sort; other times, though, you have to observe and listen carefully. If anyone tries to tell you that you have to hate someone else—that is, because of *what* that person is, not *who* he is—beware! Also, don't judge a person too quickly and assume he's bad just because he's a little different. It would be nice, too, if all the good people had a special mark on them to show that they're good. It's just as easy to misjudge a person as bad, when he really isn't, as to think an evil person is really good. Give everyone a chance, at least, but look beneath the surface and don't be deceived by appearances."

"The Germans are bad, all of them!"

"It seems that way, doesn't it? Most of the Germans are following Hitler blindly; they're good people wasted on a bad cause. Some Germans are against him, but they're afraid to speak out. The Nazis often do horrible things to people who disagree with them."

"They're *all* bad! If they let a man like Hitler run their country, then they all *must* be bad! Hitler's the evilest one of all. He's crazy too! He foams at the mouth and chews the carpet when he gets mad—that's what everyone says."

His father tried to suppress a smile. "Well, that's something I would have to see to believe. Don't believe something just because everybody says it's so. Besides, merely doing those things—if in fact, those reports are true—doesn't necessarily mean a person's evil. Strange perhaps, and deserving of pity, but not wicked. But when someone says it's necessary to annihilate an entire group of people, like the Nazis think they ought to do with the Jews and with anyone who doesn't fit in with their concept of their "Master Race, that's when you can tell he's evil. If he tells you that you should hate a group of people just because they're different, he's wrong, and you shouldn't listen to anything else he has to say. Don't believe him, don't follow him, and above all, don't let him control you." His face was very serious; then he smiled. "Class over, old chap. Uh-oh—" He picked up a piece of candy and held it up. "Unidentified bogey, two o'clock high." He whirled it through the air, glanced at it, and announced, "We have a positive identification: chocolate covered cherry—coming in for a landing!" He popped it into Andrew's open mouth.

Andrew smiled as the tangy-sweet taste of chocolate and cherry delighted his taste buds. He washed the last two pieces of candy down with his tea, and asked, "What kinds of planes do the Germans have?"

"Three types of bombers, all twin-engined: Heinkels, Dorniers, and Junkers 88s. They also have a single-engined dive-bomber, the Junkers-87, or Stuka."

"What kinds of fighters do they have?"

"They have two different kinds: the Messerschmidt 109, which has a single engine, and the ME-110, which is twin-engined."

"The Hurricanes are better than the German fighters, aren't they?"

"The Hurricane's a good bus—you saw it yourself." Andrew's father smiled briefly, took a quick sip of tea, and replaced his cup in the saucer with a careful, deliberate motion. He looked out the window, his expression now very serious.

"Did you shoot down any Jerries?" Andrew asked.

"We shot down one plane a few weeks ago."

"Did you capture any of them?"

"There was one of the crew who survived, yes."

"Did he say 'Heil Hitler' and make that funny thing they do with their arms, you know, hit their chest and stick their arm straight out?" Andrew demonstrated the motion. "I think it looks rather ridiculous, don't you?"

His father smiled, but it was a smile only with his mouth, not with his eyes. "No, he didn't. He was a young boy, maybe eighteen or nineteen. He was scared."

"What happened to him? Did you have him tortured? That's what the Nazis do. They torture people, then they kill them. Sometimes they just kill them. They hang them or shoot them or drop bombs on them. Any time we capture any Nazis, we ought to torture them, so they'll know what it's like and stop doing such bad things."

"I don't think that's a good way to impress people. Besides, once they're captured, they're not going to be doing any more harm."

"We should punish them, then. Make them suffer for all the bad things they've done."

His father folded his hands and brought them up to his lips. He was silent for a moment; then he spoke in a low voice. "It's one thing to call to account the leaders and those people who deliberately do cruel and inhumane things. But if we inflict our fury on our enemies after the fighting's over, then we haven't solved anything. We've just sown the seeds of hatred that will result in future conflicts. Look what happened after the Great War, when the Treaty of Versailles imposed a burdensome debt on the German people, one that bankrupted their economy and impoverished them. Some of the provisions of the Treaty were intended to make sure that the Germans could not raise the threat of military force; other things simply rubbed their noses in defeat. People here are wondering how the Germans could follow a man like Hitler. Well, he promised to deliver them from the despair and destitution that was their lot. Desperate people do desperate things."

"But the Nazis are doing horrible things—there's no excuse!"

His father smiled tenderly at him. "See to it then, that *you* never hurt anyone out of any pain or despair in your own life."

"I'm not ever going to feel like that! If you just make up your mind that nothing can trouble you or hurt you, then nothing will."

Andrew's father looked as if he wanted to say something, but he laid his hand on Andrew's and looked at him with an enigmatic look—somewhat disturbed, somewhat pleased. Then he sighed, and spoke.

"I can understand how some people wanted to punish the Germans and make them pay for all the devastation and suffering and loss of life in the war. When I found out that my father had been killed, I wanted to kill every last German, just to make them pay for it. It took a long time to get over that rage, and to realize that mere retaliation doesn't accomplish anything."

"But he wasn't your *real* father, was he? I mean, I know you can feel sad when someone you know dies, but you can't have felt as badly as if he had been really your father!"

"He was the only father I ever knew. A father is someone who takes care of you, watches out for you, raises you, teaches you. He taught me how to box, in fact. Well, the basics, at least. I was only about five at the time. A father doesn't necessarily have to be someone who's related to you by blood."

Andrew considered this. "Well, I suppose since you didn't know your real father, then Grandfather Denniston was the next best thing. But it's not as if you really belonged to him, surely? If he had been your real father, then you would have felt like—" Andrew stumbled, trying to think of exactly what he wanted to say, not daring to say what he really meant:

I could never, ever feel that anyone else could be my father...Never!

"...Be that as it may, how could anyone not see that our government's promise last March to support Poland against Germany was the height of folly and short-sightedness? How could the Germans not view that as a threat?" Freddie set his glass of brandy down and glared across the table at Aunt Gwen.

"German aggression just had to be stopped, and it was time someone made a stand," Aunt Gwen countered.

Freddie savagely sliced a roll. "We didn't have any objections to Germany's expansion before. Why did our illustrious leaders all of a sudden start getting shirty over a bunch of stupid Polacks?"

"We should have opposed Hitler from the very first. At the time, though, people believed that Hitler would be appeased by being allowed some territory, but that turned out not to be the case—"

"On the contrary, dear girl, it wasn't until *after* we promised to support Poland that Hitler invaded it. It was *we* who made the first aggressive move, and it was just as good as challenging the Germans to a fight. And since it was impossible for us to give any real protection to Poland, especially without Russia's cooperation, the Germans knew it was an empty bluff, and they called it."

"I'm afraid you're right, Freddie," Andrew's father said.

Freddie raised an eyebrow in mock surprise. "Roger, dear boy, you flatter me!"

Andrew's father ignored Freddie's sarcastic remark. "We should have secured Russia's backing before promising to defend Poland, though that would have proved difficult, to say the least. It was impossible for us to protect a country completely surrounded by hostile territory. And we hadn't done anything before that to oppose Hitler's aggression. In fact, we positively encouraged Hitler to expand eastward, in order to divert danger from the West, and that didn't endear us to the Soviet Union. Furthermore, we cold-shouldered the Russians when they offered to cooperate with us to stop German aggression after Austria was annexed, and ignored their proposal to join with them to defend Czechoslovakia from Nazi demands. The Russians were even excluded from the Munich conference—"

"Roger, have you suddenly developed a soft spot in your heart for the Bolshies? You consider Hitler a ruthless dictator—Stalin makes him look like a Boy Scout! Look at Finland! Not to mention the fact that Stalin has murdered millions of his own countrymen. Look at what happened in the Ukraine! He's already had most of his army officers executed. And don't forget that he betrayed us by signing that non-aggression pact with Germany."

"Betrayed? After we had turned a blind eye to Germany's expansion eastward? The Russians were faced with either fighting alone against the Germans, or making peace with them."

"Peace?" Freddie snorted. "You weep for your stupid Polacks, and think the Nazis are the villainous conquerors, but the Russians attacked Poland from the East. Half of Poland is under Soviet domination, the damned place split right down the middle."

Andrew's father sighed. "Poland was just a pawn. Our offer to aid Poland was noble, but ill-conceived. But I don't believe this so-called peace between Germany and Russia is going to last. Neither side really trusts the other."

Uncle Robert spoke. "Well, now that the BEF is in France, I don't expect the Germans are going to be causing any more trouble, at least in the West."

"I quite agree, Robert," Freddie said. "The Germans are reasonable people; they just needed a little breathing space. Eastern Europe is quite sparsely populated, and the land there could be more efficiently cultivated to provide enough for Germany's needs."

"What about the needs of the people who already live there?" Aunt Jane asked. "Did it ever occur to anyone that the people already inhabiting the place might have some objections to being conquered?"

"Dear Jane, there's enough to go around! The Germans are perfectly willing to co-operate with those who would be willing to work side-by-side with them. Eastern Europe has been nothing but a hotbed of trouble. Everybody there hates everybody else, and they spend more time fighting each other than they do taking care of the business of running their countries and growing enough food to feed their own peoples. Why, look what happened in Czechoslovakia! The Slovaks wanted to be free from the Czechs so Hitler just stepped in and—"

"Invaded their country."

"Put a stop to all the squabbling is more like it. Those people just need a firm hand, that's all. All the Germans want to do is just order up the continent—"

"Never confuse order with tyranny, Freddie."

"Jane—" Freddie shook his head and smirked. "Jane, Jane—being married to that Frog certainly soured you on Germans, I must say—"

"Freddie, I will not have you saying a word against Marc," Gram said.

Freddie smiled at her. "Of course, darling Vickie." He turned again to Aunt Jane. "Jane, don't you know it's very unbecoming for you to constantly flaunt your superior intellect? Men don't like women who are too smart for their own good, and I fear that you may scare away any eligible suitors. You know, it's high time you considered getting married."

"She *was* married," Aunt Gwen pointed out.

"I mean *again*," Freddie countered. "You don't want to be alone for the rest of your life, do you Jane? How do you ever expect to find a husband if you keep parading your intellect like that?

Aunt Jane glared at Freddie. "When I am good and ready, I shall place an advertisement in the *Times*: *Twits and imbeciles need not apply.*

Andrew tried to stifle the burst of laughter that he felt starting to erupt, but he failed to check it: It bubbled out of him in a loud chortle. He tried to mask it by pretending to cough, but he gasped and started to choke. Then he doubled over and *really* started coughing. His father, seated next to him, gently pounded his back. "I say, old chap, are you all right?" He bent over so his face was next to Andrew's. Andrew saw that he also was trying to suppress a smile. Andrew's coughing subsided, and his father rubbed his back.

Uncle Robert spoke. "Well, what's happened, for better or worse, has happened. And to try to set things right might cause more trouble. As it is, the Germans haven't made any more aggressive moves—they're afraid to. They wouldn't have a chance against either the BEF or the French army; certainly not against both combined. France is secure—they have the best army on the continent, and the Germans wouldn't dare attack across the Maginot Line." He looked at Andrew's father, as if for confirmation, but received no encouraging response.

Freddie smiled. "Oh, the war will be over by Christmas! The politicians will get their fill of blustering and posturing—Winnie will be sent to cool off in the tropics—and the soldier-boys, *and* the fly-boys—" Freddie winked at Andrew's father, "will quit all this damned foolishness."

"All right, hold still so I can get your gloves laced up." Andrew's father pulled at the laces on Andrew's boxing gloves and tied them securely. "Remember to always make sure the laces are tied just right, so they won't cause an eye injury to your opponent—there. Now, practice some left jabs while I get mine on."

Andrew's father held out his hands and Thomas laced on his gloves while Andrew shadow-boxed against the far wall in the conservatory.

"Good! That's a good on-guard stance. Now, rotate your left shoulder a bit more forward, and remember to drive your fist forward in a straight line. Terrific! Again—now, don't turn your shoulder away before you deliver your punch; you don't want to—"

"I know, I don't want to telegraph to my opponent what I'm going to do."

"Right. Don't raise your fist either—keep your opponent guessing. Now let me see some straight rights—" His father watched proudly as Andrew delivered a series of punches to his shadow counterpart. "Great! Remember to move your left hand back at the same time to protect your chin—good show! You've been practicing!"

"I practice every day at school. Mr. Nugent had a speed bag installed in the gymnasium. I need new gloves, though."

"Those should do you for another few months. Maybe you'll find some new gloves under the Christmas tree. All right, come here. Let's see you do an alternate right and left hook."

His father knelt down. Andrew stood in front of him, got into an on-guard position, and delivered a right hook at his father's gloved hands, following through immediately with a strong left hook.

"Excellent—you're keeping the angle of arms held perfectly. Just snap your right arm a little more. Use your shoulder muscles—again! Good! Now, let's try something new. I'll show you a left uppercut." Andrew's father stood up. "I'll do this in slow motion first. I'll start with a straight right—now watch. I follow through, I bend my knees a bit, dip my body to my left. See, my left elbow is close to my side. Now I rebound: I rotate to my right; my legs and body straighten up, and my left fist drives upwards." He demonstrated again, this time a little faster. "Now, let's see you try it. Do it slowly first."

Andrew delivered a straight right. His father coached him along with the new maneuver: "Remember to bend your knees and drop your body slightly to the left. You're like a spring, ready to recoil. That's good! Now, left elbow close to your side, and face the palm of your fist upward—excellent! Now, drive your left fist upwards—good! Again!"

Andrew's father had him repeat the movement a few more times. "Excellent! Now try this—" He got into an on-guard position; then demonstrated: "A straight right, a straight left, now a right uppercut." He repeated the sequence again. "Now you can do a series of straight lefts and right uppercuts, a whole routine, alternating the combination from both sides. You're lucky you're ambidextrous. You're just as strong and coordinated with your left arm as you are with your right. That will really throw your opponents off guard!"

Andrew smiled. He was so glad that his father wasn't upset about this aberration; on the contrary, he was delighted. Andrew had started out left-handed, and his parents had not discouraged this trait at all (though Grandfather Howard had vigorously protested that they should). Upon going to boarding school, however, every effort was made by Andrew's first year instructor, Mr. Quinton, a gloomy and sullen man, to change Andrew's "sinister" proclivity. Andrew had acquiesced to Mr. Quinton's demands, mainly because Mr. Quinton had such bad breath that Andrew hated to have him lean over and admonish him. He found that, with a little practice, he could write just as well with his right hand as his left. The same held true for him in sports and other activities as well. He could throw and catch a ball with either hand, and bat at cricket too. Andrew's parents were dismayed to find that he had been forced to use his right hand, but Andrew had reassured them: "I haven't forgotten how to use my left hand, and now I can do everything with both hands!"

And it had indeed proved an advantage. His present instructor and house-master, Mr. Nugent, allowed Andrew to use either hand in class, sometimes even smiling at Andrew when he chose to use his left.

"We left-handed people have a different way of looking at things, I think." Mr. Nugent had told Andrew's parents when they visited with him before Andrew started in his class. "We tend to see things from a different perspective. It's a kind of intelligence that doesn't fit into the preconceived ideas of traditional thinking. In fact, I rather look on it as a special insight that should be encouraged." Andrew's parents had been delighted by Mr. Nugent's views, and by the subsequent reports of Andrew's progress in class: excellent writing skills, a keen intelligence in puzzling out problems that left the other students stumped, an extraordinary ability to see through to the core of a complicated assignment. "Most students, and even some teachers," Mr. Nugent told Andrew's parents, "Simply see education as a regurgitation of facts. Andrew thinks things out, which is a refreshing and delightful thing to see."

"...All right, do a few straight right-left uppercut combinations," Andrew's father said. "Then switch to straight left-right uppercuts."

Andrew executed several straight rights alternating with the left uppercuts, but when he threw a straight left he leaned his body too far forward and nearly fell over. An explosion of cackling laughter burst into the room.

"Andrew, dear boy, you fight like a girl!" Freddie stood in the doorway to the hall, a glass of brandy in his hand.

Andrew tensed; he would have hurled himself at Freddie if his father had not caught him.

"Quite the testy little pugilist, isn't he? Just teach him how to do some fancy aerobatics, Roger, and see to it that he neglects his studies as well. He'll take after his old man!"

Andrew's father threw Freddie a sharp glance, then squatted down and wrapped his arms around Andrew. Andrew tried to twist out of his father's grasp. Freddie smirked, and Andrew's rage erupted in a quick right jab, followed by a powerful straight left—straight at his father, who fell backwards with a stunned look on his face. Andrew watched, horrified, and flew at him to try to break his fall.

His father managed to twist sideways, and landed unhurt. Andrew was reassured to see him get right back up; then he heard another explosion of laughter from Freddie. "You could always rent him out for prizefights, Roger—save you the expense of sending him to Oxford. Not that it did you any good—"

Andrew shot across the room and sprang at Freddie, fists flying and an unearthly howl ringing in this ears. At first Andrew couldn't quite figure out where the sound was coming from, then was horrified to realize it was coming from himself. He was just as appalled to find himself pummeling ferociously at Freddie. The brandy glass sailed through the air and shattered against the far wall of the hallway; Freddie's hand went around Andrew's throat and Andrew delivered a savage kick, which just missed Freddie's crotch. It wasn't through any lack of skill that Andrew's aim was off; Freddie just managed to twist away at the last moment. Andrew, flailing away at Freddie, felt the powerful hands tighten on his throat.

"That's enough!" His father's sharp voice was enough to make Andrew drop his fists at once. Freddie flung him off like a rag doll. Andrew watched as his father approached Freddie.

I hope he knocks him into next Sunday, Andrew breathed to himself. *I hope he kills him—*

"Quite the little guttersnipe you have there, Roger." Freddie brushed his smoking jacket, as if it were contaminated.

Andrew's father glared at Freddie.

Kill him, kill him—

"Get out, Freddie," Andrew's father said quietly.

Freddie narrowed his eyes at Andrew's father; then he smiled that smirky smile again. "With pleasure, dear boy."

Andrew and his father watched as Freddie sauntered down the hall. Andrew's father then put his arm around Andrew and drew him back into the conservatory. He motioned for Andrew to sit on the wicker sofa in the corner.

Andrew plopped down on the sofa. His father sat by his side and took a deep breath.

"I can see that your opponent had better not make the mistake of getting you angry." He smiled at Andrew and put his arm around his shoulder. "If you could learn to channel that anger, you'd be quite a formidable boxer. Now, remember what I told you yesterday about not believing someone, if that person tells you to hate people because of what they are?"

Andrew was perplexed. He expected to be admonished for his behavior, but what was his father getting at?

"You became enraged when Freddie said you fought like a girl. Freddie was taunting you, but it was the same as if he had told you that girls are weak and stupid. And you, by getting insulted, affirmed his opinion." His father paused. "Hate begins when you despise someone else. Someone convinces you, or you convince yourself, that a particular group of people is inferior, and deserving of contempt. Do you see what I mean?"

Andrew bit his lip. "I think so."

"I'll tell you what I believe. I think if we gave women just as much of a chance at things as the men have, they'd prove themselves to be equal, or even better, than men at almost everything: in intelligence, skill, reasoning. The only disparity you'd see would be in anything that takes physical size into account." He grinned at Andrew. "I'll tell you something—Jane used to beat me at running until I started getting taller than her!"

"Really?"

"Really. And she used to tutor me in mathematics too. When we'd come home from school on holiday, she'd sit down with me and help me with my lessons. She not only had an incredible memory; it was amazing how she could glance at a page in a book and remember it almost word for word. She learned things so quickly too: mathematics, history, languages. I used to struggle with French and Latin, but she could speak and write them as if she had learnt them as a child. After taking one year of German, she could speak it like a native, too. She learned Italian in a few weeks one summer; she hired a tutor, then went to Rome for a few weeks to polish up her accent, and came back chattering fluently." He chuckled. "She decided it would be fun if I took her out to dinner, and she played the part of an eccentric Italian countess. We went to a restaurant in London and she was positively smashing—screeching in Italian and gesturing wildly—she had all the waiters scurrying around in terror!"

"Crikey! I would have loved to see that! Do you think she'd do it again, sometime?"

Andrew's father smiled. "It was quite a sight. She had everybody convinced—sorry, I'm getting off the subject. The point is, don't ever think that women are inferior."

"Well, you don't see any women boxing, or playing cricket or rugger or soccer."

"They aren't given the chance, that's all. I'll tell you a secret if you promise not to breathe a word of it."

"Promise!"

His father lowered his voice. "I'm teaching your mother to box."

"*You're teaching Mum to—*"

His father put his gloved hand over Andrew's mouth and grinned. "Mum's the word. She doesn't want anyone to know, but I know you can keep a secret." He winked at Andrew.

"Can I watch sometime? I'd love to see her—"

"No, I don't think she'd feel comfortable with an audience, though she's quite good. Especially with those left hooks. She has a pretty mean right uppercut too."

"I can't imagine Mum boxing!"

"Well, she's very good. She's good at anything she puts her mind to—like flying, for instance. She's one of the best I've seen. She's better than most men who have twice the flying time she has. She learns quickly, is clever, capable, decisive—"

"But you're better!"

"That's because I have more training and experience. If she could do a course at Central Flying School, she'd be tops."

19

"Well, then, why doesn't she?"

"Because they don't allow women there."

"They should."

"Quite right, old chap. Now, we need to talk about another matter. I know that Freddie made you angry, but there's no excuse for how you behaved. You know I've told you, time and time again, that the reason I'm teaching you how to box is to give you some useful skills so that you can enjoy a sportsmanlike competition with others, keep physically fit, and, as a last resort, be prepared if you need to defend yourself. Not to go bullying—"

"I wasn't bullying! He's bigger than me—"

"Or brawling—"

"I wasn't brawling!"

His father smiled. "You could have fooled me." His face turned serious again. "I know you were angry, but—"

"He was saying nasty things about you! He was saying that you're stupid and all you know how to do is box and fly and—and, it's not true! You graduated at the top of your class at Oxford!"

"Who told you that?"

"Aunt Jane. She said that they only allowed people with top grades into the Flying Club, and that Freddie knows that, too. So he's lying! You should just—just—"

"Give Freddie a thrashing?"

"Yes!"

"Because it's not worth it, old chap. It wouldn't change him. He'd believe that the earth was flat if it suited his purposes."

"But he's wrong!"

"In this instance, force isn't going to change anything."

"If you believe that it's wrong to use force, then why are we at war with the Germans?"

"I didn't say that it was always wrong. If you need to protect yourself, or if you have to stop someone from hurting another person, then it becomes necessary. If I thought that Freddie was going to hurt you, or someone else I cared about, I'd figure out a way to stop him. Physical force might be necessary, then again, sometimes there are better ways to go about things. Freddie's all bluff and bluster, anyway. It's usually easy to get the better of him."

Andrew considered his father's words and smiled. "Maybe I should have just refilled his brandy glass."

His father beamed at him and gave him a playful, gentle punch on the shoulder. "That's the form, old chap!"

Aunt Jane tucked Andrew into bed. "Now darling, don't try to wait up for your parents. They won't be back until late."

Andrew threw his arms around her neck and nuzzled his face into her hair—the same dark brown in color as his father's, but long and a little wavy. Her face was strikingly attractive, though not conventionally pretty, with features that were almost identical to those of Andrew's father: the same high cheekbones, straight nose, and firm mouth. With short hair and a slightly broader face she would have almost been his double; yet, those same features were imbued with a kind of enchanting allure when set in her face. Her eyes were china blue in color, sparkling with keen intelligence and steady with self-assurance.

"What's the matter, Andrew? Are you still upset about Freddie?"

Andrew nodded. "I just hate it when Freddie gets nasty like that. I wasn't really mad at him for teasing me for stumbling—well, yes I was, a little. But when he started talking about Dad—the way he smirked about him boxing and flying and saying that's all he knows—"

"You know that's not true—"

"Well, why doesn't Dad act, you know, really smart and clever when he's around Freddie."

"Act like a pompous twit, you mean? Like Freddie?"

"Well, not exactly like Freddie, but—"

"Some people do nothing with their education except flaunt it at others. They can't hold a conversation without dropping a bunch of Latin phrases, or ostentatiously parading what little intellect they have, or asking a bunch of rhetorical questions—"

"What's that?"

"Rhetorical? Oh, that's a type of question that's really not a question at all. One only asks it to make a point, not to elicit information. Sometimes it's used for effect, to make people think, but I think it's often overused. It's rather a verbal smirk, most of the time. Your father will ask a question to find out information. He listens to other people and always wants to learn something new. To him, a conversation with someone is a exchange of knowledge, not a display of one's intellect or cleverness. While you were at school, we had a guest here from America, a correspondent. He and your father were up half the night talking. Your father was fascinated with what this man had to tell about America: what it looks like, what the people are like, how it's different from England. Your father told me that he learned more from that man than from all his reading at school—"

"America! Crikey, I almost forgot!"

"Forgot what?"

"I made him a present! It's a leather bookmark. Mr. Nugent went to America last summer and he brought back some leather and tools and he taught us how to make things—I made a bookmark. It's in the top drawer of my dresser."

Aunt Jane looked through the drawer and found it. "Oh, it's lovely! Your father will be delighted."

"I'm afraid I might forget to give it to him tomorrow. He's leaving so early. Could you wake me up when he comes home?"

"No, they'll be late. Look, there's a little hole at the top. Why don't we get a piece of string, and tie it around your wrist. He'll wake you up tomorrow morning to say good-bye, and it'll be right there, so you won't forget to give it to him." She undid one of

Andrew's shoelaces and looped it through the bookmark; then she tied the whole thing around Andrew's wrist.

"There! Now you won't forget."

Andrew regarded Aunt Jane's invention with delight. He so much enjoyed being with her and he didn't want her to leave—not yet. His face turned serious. "Why was this correspondent in England?"

"He was concerned that America's isolationism is great mistake. He wanted to write a series of articles about England's opposition to Germany, and why it was important that the United States ally itself with Britain."

"Does everyone in America believe in this isolationism?"

"Evidently, most do. They think it would be bad for America to support England."

"Why?"

"Well, I think that people in America believe they would be left in peace if they didn't get involved in a war with Germany or support countries who oppose the Nazis. I think most Americans are resentful that their country got dragged into the Great War and they don't want that to happen again. They want to be left in peace and they see their country as vast and rich enough in natural resources to stand alone."

"Are they?"

"Almost, but not quite. They could feed and house and clothe all of their own people with what they have, but they couldn't fight a war if they were entirely dependent on their own resources. One of the interesting topics that this man and your father discussed was that a nation, nowadays, needs to have certain things to fight a war, or defend itself. For example: iron, copper, aluminum, petroleum, rubber, wool, cotton. A nation either needs to have these things, or access to them. The United States is fortunate in that it has most of these commodities, but not all. For instance, rubber. If you didn't have rubber, what would you make your automobile and aeroplane tires out of? If you don't have tires for aeroplanes, you can't have an air force. If you don't have an air force, you can't defend yourself from aggression. That was the key to Germany's successful invasion of Poland: air superiority. Cut off from the rest of the world, the United States could probably survive, but it would be at the mercy of any other nation determined to invade it."

"Can't they see that what happened in Poland and Czechoslovakia could happen to them?"

"I think they would like to believe that it wouldn't."

"That's stupid."

"Well, you have to understand their point of view. America is a nation largely made up of people, or descendants of people, who emigrated from other lands to escape wars, political conflicts, persecution, or oppression. Quite often, the monarchs or noblemen would decide to have a war, and they'd send the peasants off to do the fighting. Is it any wonder that people would want to get away from that? All they wanted to do was live in peace—to be able to have lives free from fear and violence. They don't want to see the United States running all over the world, policing everybody and becoming embroiled in every single conflict in every corner of the globe. They lost over fifty thousand men in the Great War, and they don't want a repeat of that."

"That's nothing—we lost almost a million!"

Aunt Jane glared at him. "Don't ever think that anyone else's sacrifice is insignificant. The fact that the United States lost fewer men than Britain is no consolation to the families who lost their loved ones."

"Sorry."

Aunt Jane smoothed back his hair. They were silent for awhile; then Andrew spoke.

"Can't the Americans see that this is different? Hitler is an evil man, eviler than the Kaiser, more evil than a *hundred* Kaisers!"

"I don't think most Americans see that yet. That's why this correspondent was so anxious to convey this very point to his readers: He sees the danger of the United States waking up too late to the realization that it's foolish to think that what is now going on in Europe is simply a squabble between nations that are far away. And I also think that many Americans don't want to ally themselves with Britain."

"Why?"

"Well, the United States started out as a British colony, and the Americans fought their Revolutionary War against us. Even though that was more than a hundred and fifty years ago, I think Americans still are a bit resentful of the fact that they had to fight a war to be a free country. Maybe not openly resentful, but it is the cornerstone of their history as a people, and they're not going to forget it. After the Revolutionary War, there was the War of 1812. And during their Civil War, only eighty years ago, our country aided the Confederacy. Many Americans don't like the idea of us having colonies all over the world. I think that a great many American people feel that, even though the United States and England are not enemies any more, they still are not quite ready to be friends." She looked thoughtful for a moment; then she leaned over and kissed Andrew on the cheek. "History lesson over, darling. It's past your bedtime. Good night."

Andrew gave her a hug. "I hope you stay here always and always. I liked going to France in the summer to visit you when you were married, but I didn't get to see you the rest of the year, except when you came home at Christmas. I hope that if you get married again, you'll stay in England."

Aunt Jane smiled. "I hope so, too."

"I think Freddie's wrong—I mean, that you won't get a husband because you're smart. Why should that matter? Why would someone want to marry someone who's *stupid?*"

Aunt Jane thought about that for a moment. "Well, I think that sometimes, men think that if they have a wife who is less intelligent, it makes them appear smarter by comparison."

"That's ridiculous! I should think it would be very tiresome to have a wife who's stupid!"

"Oh, you do?" Aunt Jane smiled.

"Yes. I wouldn't want a wife who was stupid, because then I would have to do everything, and I wouldn't have any fun. If I wanted to play chess, and my wife was the only one around, if she couldn't play chess—well, what could I do? Just sit around and do nothing! I'd want her to understand what I was talking about, so we could discuss things, like we do, like Mum and Dad do. And when we used to fly in the Puss Moth, Mum flew the plane sometimes so that Dad and I could sit together in the bench seat and talk. That's nice, isn't it?"

"Yes, it is."

"I'm afraid that if you get married, you'll go away again."

"Not necessarily. Aunt Gwen got married and she didn't go away."

"But she's in London most of the time!"

"That's because she works there, not because she's married. Besides, all she has to do is catch the train, and she's here."

"All the same, I'm afraid that you'll go away if you get married again. If you do get married, could you please marry someone who doesn't live so far away and then I could see you as often as—I *know!* You could marry Mr. Nugent! Oh, that would be *grand!* Then you could come to live at Askew Court with him, and you'd be right downstairs from me! Oh, he's ever so nice—you'd like him! He let me write with my left hand, remember? He has his rooms on the first floor—I've only seen his sitting room, but it's quite nice. It has lots of pictures of the places he's travelled to—"

"Andrew, thank you for your concern, but I am not at the moment looking for a husband, nor do I require any assistance if I should decide to do so. When I am good and ready, I shall—"

"Place an advertisement in the *Times*: 'Twits or imbeciles need not apply'*!*" Andrew laughed.

"Exactly!"

Andrew scowled. "Freddie's a twit. No one wants to marry him! No one even likes him! His girlfriends just pretend to like him because he has lots of money."

"Sad, isn't it?"

"No it isn't. He doesn't deserve to have anyone like him! Why can't we divorce him? There's a boy in one of the Infant's classes at school, Willie Dunkley, whose parents got divorced, and now they don't live with each other anymore. His father moved out of their house and Willie says—" Andrew mimicked Willie's excited twittering—"'My daddy has lots of new mummies, a different one every time I visit him! And my mummy's got a new daddy for me, only he's too young to be my daddy!'"

Aunt Jane regarded him with a solemn look on her face. "I think that's very sad."

Andrew tried to evince a serious expression. "Well, it's not funny about your parents getting divorced, I suppose. After all, when you get married to someone, you promise to be with that person forever, 'till death us do part'—that's what you say, right?" Realizing that the discussion had gotten off track, he repeated his original query: "Why can't we divorce Freddie? It's not like we ever promised that he would be a relative. That way, he couldn't live at Armus House anymore."

"He is tiresome, isn't he?"

"He's a bloody twit!"

"Andrew, I do not want you using language like that."

"Well, he's a gigantic, monumental twit—the biggest twit in England! If we could put Freddie in a bomber and drop him over Germany, with no parachute, which I think we ought to do, he'd be the biggest twit in Germany! I hate him! Why can't we divorce him and send him away?"

"You can divorce a spouse, but not a relative. And this is Freddie's house too."

"He's a monumental, gigantic, nasty, horrible, colossal twit. He doesn't *deserve* to be liked!"

Aunt Jane gave him another hug. "I think that *one* little boy would like to have a *long* discussion about that into the wee hours of the night, but it's well past that little boy's bedtime—"

"He's a colossal, whacking great twit, and he *doesn't deserve* to be liked!"

"Nice try, Andrew, but bedtime is bedtime."

"You always say that!"

"Because it's true. It can wait until morning."

"No it can't!"

Aunt Jane narrowed her eyes at him. "Bedtime is bedtime." A smile played at the corners of her mouth. "No exceptions."

"What if the house is on fire?"

Aunt Jane rolled her eyes. "Well then, *that* would be an exception."

"What if Hitler knocked on the door and wanted to come to dinner?"

"I would say, 'Bedtime is bedtime, no exceptions.'"

"What if he said, 'If you invite me to dinner, I promise not to start a war, and it will be all your fault if you refuse.'"

"Bedtime is bedtime!"

"What if Freddie said, 'I promise to stop being a twit if you'll let Andrew stay up late'—what then?"

"Freddie stop being a twit?" Aunt Jane rolled her eyes again.

"What if—"

She put her hand over his mouth. He responded by chattering away in muffly protests and throwing her wild-eyed glares.

"Bedtime is bedtime—good night, sweet prince." She kissed him on the forehead, shut off the light, and departed to his playful babblings.

Andrew felt a kiss brush his forehead. Even though his eyes were closed and the black-out curtains pulled shut, he sensed that it wasn't night anymore. He opened his eyes.

His father was in uniform. "Morning, old chap." He took off his cap and set it on Andrew's head.

"Dad!" Andrew put his arms around his father's neck and pulled him down beside him. His father slipped one arm under Andrew's back, and Andrew snuzzled his face against the embroidered RAF wing over his father's left pocket.

"What's this?" Andrew's father felt the leather bookmark.

"Oh, it's a present for you. It's a bookmark. I made it in school. Aunt Jane tied it around my wrist so I wouldn't forget to give it to you." Andrew sat up and held his wrist out to his father so that he could untie it.

"It's smashing. And you made it?"

"Yes—see? It has your initials on it." Andrew pointed to the "R.H." carved into the leather. That's a RAF roundel at the bottom. I wanted to make a plane, but I'm not very good at drawing. The roundel was easier."

"It's marvelous, old chap. Who taught you how to make it?"

"Mr. Nugent. He went to America last summer with a friend. They stayed in a place called Colorado with his friend's aunt. She has a cattle ranch. Mr. Nugent said it was positively grand. He said it's the most magnificent place he's ever seen, even though it's not green at all like England. They have these incredibly high mountains and wide-open spaces. He says it's like looking at forever."

"America's a wonderful country, from what I've heard. I'd like very much to visit it someday. Maybe we'll go together."

"Freddie's been there, lots of times. He says it's nothing but bugger-all. Is he wrong?"

"Freddie only sees what he wants to see. If you make up your mind you're going to hate something before you even see it, than you'll probably hate it."

"Where will we go in America? It's so huge! Mr. Nugent says it took over a week to drive to Colorado from New York City. He says that America is such a big country that they have four different time zones. When his friend called his aunt from New York, it was two hours earlier in Colorado!"

"It's a vast country, that's for certain. There's a lot to see."

"Will we go by ship or by plane?"

"Maybe both. We'll fly over, take a ship back. Or perhaps do it the other way around."

"It's too bad we don't have the Puss Moth anymore. We could fly that to America."

"The Puss Moth has a range of only three hundred miles. It would be tricky to figure out how to get it across the Atlantic."

"Jim Mollison flew a Puss Moth across the Atlantic."

"That's right, he did."

Andrew snuggled against his father's chest again, and a soft moan escaped his lips.

"Andrew, what's the matter?"

Andrew took a deep breath. "I'm sorry about yesterday afternoon, about hitting you, I mean. I didn't mean it. I was angry at Freddie."

"I know. It's all right."

"I'll never, never do anything to hurt you again, I promise."

His father gave him that jaunty *I know, old chap* look. Andrew smiled at him, then ran his hands over the blue-gray fabric of his uniform, his fingers skimming over the gold buttons, down the sleeve, and tracing around the light blue band in the middle of the black braided ring around the cuff—the insignia of a Flying Officer.

"Is the war going to be over by Christmas, Dad? That's what everyone says. They say it will last only another few months."

"I hope so, Andrew."

"Do you *think* so?"

"Perhaps. Maybe old Hitler will decide to go back to being an architect."

"No, he won't!" Andrew's emphatic assertion produced a look of consternation on his father's face. Andrew explained: "He wasn't an architect, he was an artist. He drew buildings. Rather badly, too."

His father's face beamed with pride. "Right you are, old chap. Maybe he'll decide to go back to drawing buildings."

"I had a wonderful birthday."

"Next year you'll be double-digits, old chap. It'll be a very special birthday, for sure. You'll have a positively smashing time!" His father took back his cap and started to get up. Andrew grabbed his hand and laced his fingers tightly with his. His father smiled and squeezed his fingers in return.

"Chin up, old chap. Bye."

"Bye."

His father gently slipped his hand out of Andrew's, winked at him, and was gone.

Andrew plopped back onto the pillow. If only the war would be over by Christmas!

The war would not be over by Christmas.

It would last not just a few months, but five long years.

After it became apparent that the conflict was to be desperate and protracted, it occurred to Andrew that his father might have been dissembling. Then again, Andrew reasoned, who could possibly have foreseen how things would turn out?

He didn't want me to worry, that's it. And how could he have known what would happen?

For that matter, not even Andrew, in his wildest imaginings, could have envisaged the appalling devastation and misery the war would unleash upon his country, and upon the rest of the world, and how it would chart a bizarre, bewildering course for him. It would shatter the peaceful, secure world he had always known and take every one of his family from him, in one way or another—some temporarily, some forever. He would always remember this spring holiday not so much as a pleasant and happy experience, but as the very last time all of his family were together.

His father was right about one thing, though.

On Andrew's next birthday, he *would* have a positively smashing time.

Chapter 2

"The balloon's gone up!"

Andrew could not help but picture in his mind a huge balloon (*red*—why did he have such a vivid image of it being *red?*) flying skyward, but he knew what it really meant: The Phony War had finally turned unphony. He greeted the news with mixed excitement and trepidation.

Now we're going to give the Huns a thrashing! The boast was on everyone's lips. Andrew and his schoolmates, to a large extent cut off from the rest of the world by their sheltered boarding school existence, took the snippets of information that filtered in, and constructed a grandiose scenario of British victories on the continent. *We're in it now! We're really in it now!* was the continual refrain.

The news of the German invasion of the West came on the heels of the resignation of Prime Minister Chamberlain; Winston Churchill succeeded him as head of a coalition government, bringing all of the political parties—Liberal, Labour, and Conservative—into a cooperative union. The news of this was not in the least dismaying to Andrew's schoolmates: What the country needed was a strong hand at the helm, and Churchill was just the one to "trounce the Huns." Andrew privately rejoiced, knowing that Churchill's elevation to power was bound to infuriate Freddie.

A few days later, Mr. Nugent gathered Andrew and his classmates into his sitting room so they could hear the new Prime Minister's message to the House of Commons, spoken by a newsreader on the BBC:

I have nothing to offer but blood, toil, tears, and sweat. We have before us an ordeal of the most grievous kind. We have before us many, many long months of struggle and suffering. You ask what is our policy? I will say. It is to wage war, by sea, land and air, with all our might and with all the strength that God can give us; to wage war against a monstrous tyranny, never surpassed in the dark, lamentable catalogue of human crime. That is our policy.

The goal of this thrilling new policy was emphatic and simple:

It is victory, victory at all costs, victory in spite of all terror, victory however long and hard the road may be; for without victory there is no survival.

The bits about grievous ordeals, about terror and long hard roads, about blood, toil, tears, and sweat fell through the minds of Andrew and his school chums like fine grains of sand through a sieve. The huge chunks retained by them were the words *victory,* *victory!* No doubt about it: the Huns are *really* going to get a thrashing now!

Two of Andrew's roommates, James Martin and Nigel Willoughby-Ramsbottom, had brothers in the BEF, and John Gordon-Fairweather's father flew Fairey Battles in the Advanced Air Striking Force. The talk in the dormitory was impassioned and elated, leaving their two remaining roommates, Gregory Thomas and Arthur Popham-Goode, envious of the close association that their friends had with the battles now raging on the continent:

"My brother says the Huns have all old men in their army; mostly veterans from the Great War who shake so badly when they hold their guns that they can't hit a cow at twenty paces!"

"My father's going to bomb the stinking Huns. They'll start running all the way back to Germany, run away like cowards just like Hitler did in the Great War!"

"My dad says Hurricanes and Spitfires are better than the German fighters any day! The RAF can trounce the Luftwaffe as easy as kiss your hand—it'll be a piece of cake!"

The news from the outside world was exasperatingly vague, however: reports of German paratroopers dropping into Holland, fragmented accounts of fierce fighting in Belgium, and lots of talk about German troop movements through the Ardennes, which Nigel Willoughby-Ramsbottom scoffed at:

"It's the stupidest thing the Jerries could do. My brother says that if the Germans ever even tried to get their army through there, let alone tanks, they would get so bogged down they'd be like flies in jam!"

News came of the bombing of Rotterdam, the fall of Holland, the entrance of the Germans into Brussels, and the breakthrough of the German army into France at Sedan. Andrew's schoolmates were not in the least dismayed by what they affirmed were "temporary setbacks." The problem, they agreed, was that as Holland and Belgium had been neutral, and the BEF had not been there at the time of the German advance, it was to be expected that the Germans would meet ineffective resistance. Once the Germans tried to fight in France, though, they would meet with stiff opposition.

"Those filthy Huns are no match for the BEF!" James Martin and Nigel Willoughby-Ramsbottom agreed.

News of the attacks by British bombers on Germany also boosted morale. As John Gordon-Fairweather put it, "The Huns will get a taste of their own medicine now. They'll be *begging* us to let them surrender!"

As more reports filtered through of the German's push through France, Andrew started to have some doubts about the optimistic expectations of a speedy rout of the German Army: *If the Germans are taking such a beating, why are they still advancing so rapidly?* He remembered how swiftly the Nazis had conquered Denmark and most of Norway in April. Was this to be a repeat performance? He thought it best, though, not to express these reservations to his friends.

On May 21st, German troops reached Le Crotoy, a seaside resort on the Channel coast. Andrew knew it well: He and Aunt Jane used to spend a few days there after

Andrew's arrival at Calais for summer holiday, before going on to Paris. Uncle Marc's sister, Evelyne, had a summer cottage there. Even after Aunt Jane was widowed, she and Andrew still went on holiday to France every summer, spending most of the time at Evelyne's. Andrew was upset at the thought of Germans in a place he knew so well, and worried about Evelyne and her family. One of Evelyne's sons was Andrew's age and they used to play together at the beach. Andrew's schoolmates, not as familiar with French geography as Andrew was, did not see the disturbing significance of this event: It meant that Germans had managed to divide the Allied armies in two. The BEF was now trapped, cut off from the main French force in the south.

Andrew was seated outside Mr. Harris's office one afternoon, waiting to ask permission to use the phone to call home, when he heard Mr. Nugent's voice:

"Shall I tell him?"

"No, his mother is coming tomorrow afternoon to pick him up, and she wants to break the news to him. She knows he'll take it badly, and she wants to be with him," Mr. Harris answered. "Just have his things packed and ready to go. Best to have it done while the students are at afternoon classes, so the boy won't get suspicious. Give the students some written work to do. Mr. Quinton said he would look in on the class while you're out."

Andrew's heart lurched, and he held his breath as he moved a little closer to the door.

"Losing a family member is bad enough, but from what I gather, they were particularly close," Mr. Nugent said.

Brother or father? Andrew wondered.

"...terrible, terrible, a boy that age growing up without a father...."

Andrew stood frozen at the door, his heart pounding. That could only mean it was either his own father or John Gordon-Fairweather's...wait, one of the other boys in his class, Colin Kirknewton, had a father in the BEF—perhaps it was his! Andrew hated the idea of wishing evil on someone else, but what had happened wasn't his fault, and there was nothing wrong with wanting the person he cared most about to be safe, was there? Well, *someone's* father was dead, and he hoped to God it wasn't his.

He heard Mr. Nugent bidding Mr. Harris farewell, and shot out of the room like a fox fleeing a pack of hounds.

The next morning, Andrew found it impossible to concentrate on his studies. The Latin verbs seemed to blur on the pages and he felt oddly disassociated from everything around him.

Please God, please, don't let it be my—

"Andrew? I asked if you could give us a translation of the sentence I just pointed out." Mr. Nugent looked at Andrew.

Andrew's mouth hung open.

Please, please get mad at me for not paying attention.

Mr. Nugent never got mad at anyone for not paying attention, though.

Please, this time! At least tell me I shouldn't daydream. Make me translate a whole page as punishment...please! If you don't rebuke me, I'll know—

Mr. Nugent's gaze rested for a moment on Andrew; then he glanced away and repeated the question to James Martin.

Andrew slumped in his chair, weak with fear.

Class was dismissed, and he somehow forced his legs to trudge to the dining hall with the rest of his classmates.

At lunchtime, there was none of the usual animated discussion that Mr. Nugent so enjoyed. He kept silent for the most part, talking quietly, if something needed to be said. The other boys sensed that something was amiss, and were subdued as well. Andrew tried to eat, but the food tasted like sawdust in his mouth.

*Just because Mr. Nugent didn't get upset with me for not paying attention doesn't mean that it was my father who was...*Andrew could not even think the horrific thought. *I need to be sure...I need to find out—somehow.* Then he had an inspiration.

After lunch his class lined up to receive their daily spoonful of cod liver oil, administered by Mrs. Bunch, the cook. Andrew was third in line, behind George Garton-Ward and Arthur Popham-Goode. When his turn came, he tightened his lips together and shook his head. Mrs. Bunch admonished him, "Come now, Andrew, it's good for you. Open up."

"No, I shan't. It's horrid stuff!" Andrew snatched the spoon from her and flung it across the room.

Mr. Nugent, who had been finishing his tea as the boys were waiting to receive the foul-tasting concoction, said softly, "I think that will be enough for today, Mrs. Bunch. I can't see that missing their medicine for one day is going to do any serious harm. Boys, you're dismissed."

Wild cheers greeted his pronouncement—wild cheers from everyone, that is, except George and Arthur, who had already been forced to ingest the vile liquid, and from Andrew, who suddenly felt sick with terror.

Mr. Nugent would have certainly gotten upset with me for doing that. He would have said something to me, at least...He didn't say a word...He didn't even glare at me....

After mathematics lesson that afternoon, Mr. Quinton popped his head in the door and nodded to Mr. Nugent.

"Class, please turn to page 264 in your geography texts and answer questions one through twenty," Mr. Nugent said.

Then he was gone.

Andrew picked up his pencil and tried to concentrate on the questions.

"How many times have you been told, Andrew, we use our right hands here." Mr. Quinton leaned over his shoulder. Andrew smelled his foul breath and switched his pencil to his right hand. Harry Peel, seated next to him, pinched his nose and crossed his eyes as soon as Mr. Quinton turned away. Usually Andrew would have found Harry's antics funny, but today he was not amused. Harry gave him a quizzical look, shrugged, and turned back to his work. Mr. Quinton left the room, returned every ten minutes or so, and finally, at three o'clock, dismissed the class.

Andrew dashed back to his dorm. He ran up the first flight of stairs to the second floor, where Colin Kirknewton shared one of the smaller rooms with Charles Provis. Maybe Mr. Nugent was in there, after all. Andrew tiptoed down the hall. He tapped on Colin's door; no answer. He opened the door a crack and peeked in: No one was there. His heart sinking, Andrew clambered back down the hall and climbed the stairs to the third floor, where he shared the large, dormered room with John Gordon-Fairweather and their four other roommates.

The door was shut. Andrew heard the soft, squeaky sounds of drawers being opened and closed.

It's John's father...it has to be....

He stumbled down the steps and trudged outside. He was walking down the narrow, winding drive leading to the main road when a taxi sped by. Andrew turned and raced after it, trying to discern the identity of the lone female figure in the back seat. She was wearing a hat—damn! If only he could see if she had his mother's wild mop of auburn hair!

He ran as fast as he could, even though he felt a knifing pain in his side and his lungs screamed with exertion. He couldn't keep up. The car turned the corner and, by the time Andrew caught up with it, it was already parked in front of his dormitory. He caught a glimpse of the woman, just the back of her, entering the front door, Mr. Nugent behind her.

Andrew raced up to the building and arrived just as Mr. Nugent was about to shut the door. "You can use my sitting room—" Andrew heard him say.

"Mr. Nugent!" Andrew nearly shrieked as he stumbled up the front steps.

Mr. Nugent turned; the woman did, too.

Andrew almost collapsed with relief.

"Mrs. Gordon-Fairweather! Um, hullo...."

John's mother barely nodded at Andrew. Her eyes were distant and her mouth was set into a tight line.

"Andrew, would you be so kind as to get John?" Mr. Nugent said gently. He stepped away from Mrs. Gordon-Fairweather and whispered, "Just tell him that I need to speak with him; don't mention that his mother is here."

Andrew nodded. He ran to the playing field, elation coursing through him. As he approached his classmates, however, he was stabbed with a feeling of sadness. He saw John kick a soccer ball and laugh as it sailed over the heads of the other boys.

"John!"

"What is it?" John called out cheerily.

Andrew tried to keep his voice even and nonchalant. "Mr. Nugent wants to talk to you. He's at the dormitory."

John gave the other boys a wave, and sauntered off. Andrew watched him, burdened by the knowledge that John's world was about to be shattered. He felt a special kinship with John, as both their fathers were pilots in the RAF. How often they had bragged to one another of their fathers! They had argued good-naturedly about the relative merits of Fighter Command versus Bomber Command, and each of them had pictures of the planes of their favorite respective services tacked over their beds: John had Battles, Blenheims, Hampdens, Wellingtons, and Whitleys; Andrew had Hurricanes and Spitfires.

"Andrew, do you want to play?" Gregory Thomas asked.

"No." He didn't offer his friends an explanation. Relieved as he was that his father was still alive—at least no word to the contrary—he still felt heavyhearted. *No word to the contrary....*

He broke into a run. *Just because I haven't been contacted...yet. Maybe there's been word and they're coming to get me—*

He arrived at Mr. Harris' office. Mrs. Harris, who sometimes acted as school secretary, was sitting in the outer office.

"Mrs. Harris—may I please use the phone? I need to call my mother."

"I'll give it a try, Andrew, but...." Mrs. Harris's voice trailed off as she noted Andrew's anguished expression. "Some of the other boys have been wanting to contact their families—just can't seem to get through." She tried to place the call, listened at the receiver, and shook her head. "Sorry, all the lines are still tied up."

Andrew walked back outside. The bell at the dining hall rang: tea time. Maybe a nice, hot cup of tea would do right now....

Tea didn't help; neither did supper, which he could barely gag down anyway.

That night, he lay awake in bed long after the other boys had gone to sleep. After tossing over for the hundredth time, he finally got up and tiptoed down the stairs to the first floor. He knocked on Mr. Nugent's door.

A muffled voice called, "Who's there?"

"It's me—Andrew."

A few moments later, the door opened. Mr. Nugent, bleary-eyed, was still tying the sash on his bathrobe. He looked down at Andrew and gently asked, "What is it, Andrew?"

Andrew's voice came out as a strangled rasp. "John's father was killed, wasn't he?"

Mr. Nugent knelt down and put his hand on Andrew's shoulder.

"Yes, he was."

"I just want to ring my mother. She'll still be awake. She stays up late reading when my father's not home—" Andrew's voice caught in his throat.

"All right, let me get changed and get the keys to the office. Why don't you have a seat?" Mr. Nugent indicated the reading chair by the window; Andrew remained standing. "It'll be just a minute," Mr. Nugent whispered. He went into his bedroom and returned after a few minutes, dressed in his trousers and an old sweater. He took his jacket off a clothes peg and handed it to Andrew: "Here, why don't you wear this. It's a bit nippish outside."

They walked in silence to the office. Mr. Nugent tried to place the call, listened with consternation at the receiver, and shook his head. "I'm sorry, still can't get through.

What with the mess in France...." He caught himself, and looked apologetically at Andrew.

"Is it that bad?" Andrew's voice quavered.

"It would seem so." Mr. Nugent looked away for a moment. "Andrew, just because John's father was killed—I know you're fearing the worst, but...." He paused again, and seemed to be searching for the right thing to say. "Your father flies Hurricanes, doesn't he?"

Andrew nodded. Mr. Nugent went on. "I think he'll be all right. The Hurricane's a terrific aeroplane, and a good pilot can turn circles around the German fighters. John's father was flying Fairey Battles—damned plane is too slow and underpowered, not very much in the way of firepower either. They should never have sent them into battle against the Germans—" He broke off, looking sorry for what he'd just said. "Andrew, please don't mention anything about what I just said to John."

"Oh, no, I won't, I promise," Andrew reassured him. "I didn't know you knew a lot about aeroplanes."

"Well, it's a hobby of mine. My uncle was a pilot in the Great War, so I'm fascinated by them. I must admit, though, that I dread flying."

"You do?"

Mr. Nugent smiled. "I love to look at planes from the ground, however. Did you see the Hendon Air Display in 1936?"

"Yes, my father brought me."

"The sight of those Hurricanes and Spitfires was just marvelous, don't you think? Did you see the aerobatics they did—wasn't that the grandest thing you've ever seen? I do like the look of the Spitfire: Those wings make it look alive, as if it had a soul of its own. The Hurricane is a terrific aeroplane as well: a good solid construction, highly maneuverable—" He put his hand on Andrew's shoulder. "Why don't we go back to the dormitory?"

They walked back through the darkness. When they arrived at the house, Mr. Nugent asked, "Would you like to have some cocoa? I keep some in a flask. Sometimes I have trouble sleeping, too."

Andrew nodded. They went into the sitting room, and Mr. Nugent poured two cups of cocoa. They sat down together on the settee. Andrew took a sip, and said, "I gave my father the leather bookmark. He liked it very much."

"You put his initials on it, didn't you? And the RAF roundel at the bottom?"

"Yes. I told him that you brought the leather and tools from America." Andrew took another sip of cocoa. "He says he wants to go to America someday—that we could all go there on holiday, I mean. What's it like there?"

"Oh, it's grand! Such a huge country, and so much to see! And it's all so different, everywhere. New York is amazing—such tall buildings, higher than anything you could imagine! We motored through, let's see, New Jersey, Pennsylvania. We saw some of their Revolutionary War sites. Americans take that all very seriously, you know. Would you like some more cocoa?"

Andrew shook his head.

Mr. Nugent went on. "We passed through two states that began with an 'I'—let's see, Indiana, Iowa?—no, Illinois. So much farmland—I'm sure America could feed the whole world! We stopped in quite a few little towns along the way—it was so much fun chatting with people. One day we met a man who had fourteen sons—can you imagine that? That's as many students as are in our entire class! All different sizes, of course, and all of them had names starting with 'J': There were John and James and Jonah and...oh yes, the twins, Jeremiah and Jedediah. We asked them if they wouldn't mind if we took their photograph, and they were just delighted. We bought lollipops for all of them—they thought it was quite a treat! They call them 'suckers.' Well, they invited us for dinner, and the table was positively piled high with...."

Mr. Nugent's voice seemed very far away, and the next thing Andrew knew, he was in his own bed and Gregory Thomas was calling for him to wake up.

"Andrew, do you know what happened to John?" Nigel Willoughby-Ramsbottom asked.

"He went home. His mother came yesterday."

"Lucky sod!" Arthur Popham-Goode said.

"Why did he go home?" Nigel's eyes were full of apprehension.

Andrew shook his head. He knew that if he said *I don't know,* Nigel would suspect him of lying. But he didn't want to be the bearer of bad tidings, either. He turned away.

"Andrew, get up," Gregory said.

"Oh, all right!" Andrew flung himself out of bed and glared at his roommates.

At breakfast, Nigel picked at his food in silence. Andrew noticed that James Martin and Colin Kirknewton were unusually quiet also. When they were dismissed, Nigel stayed behind. Andrew peeked though the dining room window on his way to class and saw Mr. Nugent listening sympathetically to Nigel, whose face was tear-streaked and distressed.

Mr. Nugent was a few minutes late to class; Nigel did not come at all. At lunchtime, two more places were vacant: James's and Colin's. Mr. Nugent dismissed classes early that afternoon, and organized a boxing practice instead.

"Would you like to help out, Andrew? I could use an extra coach," Mr. Nugent said to him. Andrew shrugged. He knew that it would be good to get his mind off things, but he didn't feel much like boxing.

"Tell you what, why don't you just stay for about twenty minutes—work with Harry on his left jabs. If you want to leave after that, it's all right."

Andrew nodded. He worked with Harry for awhile; then, George Garton-Ward asked for some help on left and right hooks.

It was no use: He really wanted to be alone, so he nodded at Mr. Nugent and left.

As he wandered across the playing field, he saw a soccer ball lying off to the side. He walked over and kicked it back onto the field. After regarding it ruefully for a moment, Andrew trudged over to it and, with a great effort of will, forced himself to shuffle it along with his feet.

All of a sudden, the ball was kicked away from him. Andrew experienced a stab of annoyance, thinking it was one of his classmates teasing him. He turned, and saw a flash of grey-blue—

The figure in the familiar RAF uniform, now several feet ahead of him, gave the ball a swift kick, sending it flying into a skyward arc. The figure turned, and laughed, and Andrew threw himself into his father's arms.

"They should have given Winnie the sack when they had the chance—that pompous, warmongering loudmouth is determined to get us into a war with Germany." Freddie downed the last drop of brandy from his glass, which Andrew's father surreptitiously refilled. "He's like a punch-drunk fighter, asking for a thrashing. Trouble is, he's going to be sitting tight in a cozy little bomb shelter. It's the rest of us who are going to be getting the thrashing."

"More peas, Freddie?" Gram asked. Freddie took the serving bowl from her, piled the peas onto his plate, and launched into another tirade.

"Winnie loves the Frogs, that's the trouble. We should have never sent the BEF to France—"

"Freddie!" Gram was indignant.

"Sorry, darling Vickie," Freddie smiled. To Jane he said, "Please don't take it personally dear—you know I always had the highest regard for Marc. After all, he was not your typical Fro—Frenchman."

"How frightfully decent of you to say so, Freddie. All I can say is that you're not a typical Englishman, either." Aunt Jane ladled a spoonful of potatoes onto her plate. Andrew put his napkin up to his mouth to conceal his grin. He loved it, positively *loved* it, when Aunt Jane gave it back to Freddie.

"The BEF was there before Churchill became Prime Minister, Freddie," Andrew's mother pointed out.

Freddie gazed adoringly at Andrew's mother, as if she had said something wonderfully profound, instead of merely pointing out the obvious. "You're quite right, Alice—" He set his knife and fork down, folded his hands, and gazed at her. Andrew became alarmed. Up until this moment, Freddie had only shown this kind of attention to his mother when his father was away, but now...It seemed like it was a challenge of some sort.

"...Tell me, Alice, what sort of position do you think our government should take, now that Hitler has control of the continent?" Freddie's voice was low, his words measured.

"The same position that we've had for the last nine months: We are in a state of war with Germany. We gave Germany the choice after they invaded Poland. If they had chosen to withdraw, we would not have declared war, pure and simple."

Andrew hoped that Freddie would point out that England had stood idly by while Germany had annexed Austria and invaded Czechoslovakia. *Come on, Freddie!* Andrew wished that he could shoot a thought at someone like a bullet: *Ask her why we didn't show the least bit of concern then.* Then she would say: "Well, we should have stopped Hitler then." Then he would start in on how the Germans were so reasonable and civilized and how sensible it would be to cooperate with them instead of throwing our lot in with a bunch of wogs and Frogs, which would *really* get her worked up—

"But it was we who antagonized Germany in the first place," Freddie murmured.

"How? By pledging to support a nation that didn't want to be invaded? If that's belligerence—"

"Not belligerence, just an unwise decision at the time—didn't you say so, Roger? Noble, but ill-conceived, wasn't it?" Freddie raised his eyebrows as he glared at Andrew's father.

Andrew felt his heart lurch. Andrew's parents looked at one another; then as if by some prearranged signal, both of them simultaneously broke into smiles.

"I did say that, didn't I?" Andrew's father said.

"We'll discuss it later," Andrew's mother said in a low voice. She looked at Andrew's father very seriously for a moment, but it was a pretend serious look, not a *serious* serious look. Then a smile spread across her face.

Andrew breathed a silent sigh of relief. Freddie took another sip of brandy and glared at Andrew's father. With utmost care, he set his glass down.

"Well, Roger, permit me to congratulate you on your promotion. Flight Lieutenant, is it? Jolly good show." The last three words were said with so little enthusiasm that Freddie could just as well have been mumbling in his sleep. "Though I still say the old man would roll over in his grave if he knew you were RAF. If you were so keen on flying planes you should have joined the Royal Navy, like Robert. The Navy—now that's a fine career for an ambitious young man—and you *are* an ambitious young man, aren't you, Roger?" Freddie narrowed his eyes ever so slightly. "Experience in sailing ships—that's the ticket to a brilliant career in whatever field you might choose. You could even work for me someday, Roger old boy."

"Thank you, Freddie, I shall make a note of your generous offer," Andrew's father said coolly.

"Well, Flight Lieutenant, now, is it?" Freddie poured himself another glass of brandy. "What's after that—no, no, let me guess. I've been making an effort to swot up those clever little names the RAF chooses to give its ranks. Group Captain?—no, wait, I've got it—*Squadron Leader*—what a nice ring that has! Squadron Leader Hadley-Trevelyan! Wouldn't it be nice to have your own command? Just think, you'd be doing your fancy aerobatics and everyone would be following you—wingtip to wingtip. Oh, I think it would be positively splendid! And you'd get to yell 'Tally-ho' when you spotted a Jerry. Isn't that the form? Or can anyone, regardless of rank, yell "Tally-ho!," provided he's the first one to spot the Jerry? Do you ever get into fights with one another over who saw—"

"Flight Lieutenant is fine for now."

"Oh Roger, you're so modest and unassuming! I find that quite charming. Wouldn't it be nice, though, to have your own command?"

"Sorry to disappoint you, Freddie. Even if I attained the rank of Squadron Leader,

I wouldn't have my own command, anyway. No one over the age of twenty-six can command a squadron."

"Shocking!" Freddie evinced mock outrage. "Why Roger, you must be positively *crushed!* To think that a man of your ability and experience is denied his own command merely because he's too *old!*

"Really Freddie, you should talk—you're forty-five—" Gwen said.

"My dear, I don't desire a career in the RAF. Running a shipping business is quite exciting enough for me. Now your Robert wouldn't have that problem in the Navy, would he? That's the problem with the RAF—just a bunch of young upstarts, wanting to run everything. Except for Stuffy—he's a fossil, isn't he? It's no doubt one of his silly rules. He was due for retirement months ago, and it's obvious his career is on the wane. He was passed up for Chief of Air Staff a few years ago, wasn't he? Well, that's because he doesn't know how to get along with anyone—it's as simple as that. He's a pain in the arse and nobody likes him. Stuffy doesn't know how to play the game, how to please his superiors, and that's a quick way to end a career, isn't it? Why, he even refused Churchill's request to send more fighters to France— did you know that?"

"It's not in his power to refuse," Andrew's father rejoined. "He simply pointed out, given the loss of Hurricanes by that time, which was May 15, that at the present rate of wastage there would not be any Hurricanes left at all in two weeks, either in France or England. He saw defending Britain as the top priority, and that draining off our fighter strength to remedy the situation in France would leave our nation defenseless. In light of what happened in France, it was a wise action. The War Cabinet decided to accept Dowding's warnings, and made a decision to support his recommendation."

"Winnie still overruled it and sent more fighters to France, though. That should have given Stuffy the hint that his Prime Minister doesn't think very much of his opinions."

"Dowding doesn't really care what people think of his opinions—and I'm glad he doesn't. He put his request to the Air Ministry, and thank God they finally saw reason and kept the fighters at home. As far as Dowding is concerned, Fighter Command, not his own political advancement, is the top priority. He fought for better equipment, better training; he made sure we got armor plating and bullet-proof windshields in our fighters."

"Oh, I heard about that," Freddie snickered. "Stuffy got quite a laugh when he said that if bullet-proof windshields were good enough for—"

"Chicago gangsters, they were good enough for Fighter Command." Andrew's father glared at Freddie. "He's *right.* And he's right to put the defense and security of the home base above all else. If you don't have that, then nothing else matters. Fighter Command is the linchpin of our nation's survival, and Dowding will fight tooth and nail against anyone who would dare undermine it or make it subordinate to anything else. And if he steps on a few toes in the process, then those toes deserve to get stepped on."

"Well, it looks like Stuffy's been stepping on quite a few toes, dear boy. His throne is a bit shaky, I fear. He's not only making enemies with his superiors; his subordinates are not too pleased with him either. I have it on good authority that Leigh-Mallory has vowed, and I quote: 'To move heaven and earth to get Dowding sacked.' He was quite miffed when Stuffy put Park in command of 11 Group—"

"That's because Park is the best man for the job. He and Dowding know how to work together."

"But Leigh-Mallory has command of 12 Group—that's right next door. I don't see he and Park cooperating very well with each other. And Leigh-Mallory has it in for Stuffy's job, I've heard. Oh, we're going to see exciting things happening in Fighter Command, that's for certain."

"I'm sure that everyone realizes that the important thing is defending our country from the Germans," Andrew's father said tersely.

"Dear boy, how can one expect the little people to do their jobs properly when the big boys can't get along?"

"More brandy, Freddie?" Gram asked.

"Thank you, Vickie darling." Freddie downed his drink in one gulp. "Well, I must say, things are getting a bit dodgy in France, aren't they?" He glared at Aunt Jane.

"Freddie, I would prefer that we talk about something else right now," Gram said.

"Oh, I just wanted to reassure Jane that everything's going to be just fine. Not to worry, old girl. I'm sure Marc's family is all right. I don't think the Germans are interested in imposing any sort of tyrannical rule in France, despite all the nasty rumors that are floating around."

"The Nazis invaded France with tanks and dropped bombs on people. Those are not nasty rumors," Aunt Jane snapped.

"My *dear*, it was merely a show of strength. Hitler just wants the cretins who are running our government to realize that an alliance with Germany would be to our advantage, and that nothing will be gained by fighting a silly war. If the French cooperate, they have nothing to fear. All the Germans want to do is order up the continent, quiet the rabble, so to speak. Europe has been in such an infernal mess, everyone squabbling with everyone else: imbecilic peasants, Wogs and Frogs creating chaos, Bolsheviks churning up trouble. Hitler was the only one willing to put down the Communist menace. The only thing he wants is for Germany to have a place in the scheme of things. We have nothing to be afraid of—Hitler admires the English! He envisions a mutually beneficial Anglo-German alliance, and sees the British Empire as having a stabilizing influence. All Hitler wants is for Germany to have its rightful place in the world. We get to keep our colonies, Germany gets to retake theirs. We work together as allies, not fight one another."

"What Hitler wants is no interference in his plan to subjugate the entire world, either by outright conquest or by cowing the rest of the world into acquiescing to any and every demand." Aunt Jane retorted.

"Which is exactly what the British Empire accomplished, dear Jane. You wail about the beastly Germans, who merely want the same spoils of conquest as the British Empire acquired through invasion and intimidation over the past four centuries. Do you think we politely asked the inhabitants of our prospective territories if they wouldn't mind being conquered and exploited? All that rot about Pax Britannica—it was nothing more than gunboat diplomacy! England has already done what the Germans are being condemned for attempting now. There's no difference—the Germans have just arrived at the game a little late."

"There *is* a difference, Freddie. What the Nazis want is tyranny, pure and simple. They want to exterminate anyone who doesn't fit in with their concept of a master race, anyone who disagrees with them, anyone they see as undesirable: Jews, the weak and disabled, trade unionists, socialists. What if the Nazis suddenly decide that the English people aren't pure enough for them? If you dehumanize one group of people, you dehumanize everyone."

"We have never proposed wholesale slaughter of entire peoples," Aunt Gwen added. "Or shutting them up in concentration camps—"

"Proposed? Oh, no, we're too civilized to blather about it, or to brag that we're a "Master Race." We implicitly assumed it all along, no need to advertise. Wholesale slaughter just happened to be an unfortunate side effect of our civilizing influence on the world. As for concentration camps, the British were the originators of that particular concept, during the Boer War, I believe—isn't that right, Roger?" Freddie turned and glared at Andrew's father.

"Correct as usual, Freddie." Andrew's father said dryly. There was an uncomfortable silence.

Freddie cleared his throat. "Well, the Germans are just trying to follow in our footsteps. For instance, this new blitzkrieg technique. Everyone is positively wailing that it's such a ghastly, unfair way to fight a war, and who originated the concept, at least in theory? The British! The Germans merely took very good notes! Isn't that right, Roger?"

"Correct again, Freddie."

Freddie narrowed his eyes at Andrew's father. "Roger, dear boy, I do believe you don't like to admit I'm right, do you?"

"Correct, yes; right, no. I will admit that you're correct in some of your evaluations as to British conduct and intent in establishing its empire. I do agree that we have not always been noble or civilized or even decent in our dealings with the countries we have subjugated. But I don't think you can compare what we did with what the Nazis propose to do."

Aunt Jane spoke. "If our country allies itself with the Nazis, merely because it seems the expedient thing to do, then we're no better than they are."

Freddie snorted. "Jane dear, you are taking things much too seriously. I do say, you're beginning to sound like Winnie, and he a tiresome old windbag, isn't he? All this blathering about 'soul destroying tyranny' and 'long dark nights of barbarism'— he does run on, doesn't he? All this talk of war! Don't you think it would be better for children to grow up happy and carefree, rather than have all this talk of war threatening their young, innocent lives?" He smiled at Andrew.

Andrew glared back at him. *Since when have you been so concerned about me having a happy, carefree life?*

Andrew looked at his father. His father smiled.

"Well, old chap, why don't we take a walk? Finish your lunch, first."

Andrew gobbled up the rest of his meal. To get away, away from Freddie, away from the talk of war—better yet, just to spend time alone with his father! Since coming home last night, his father's time had been taken up by other...things. Andrew had awakened early, but his parents did not emerge from their room until after ten o'clock. He read through all the *Addie and Hermy* ("The Nasty Nazis") comics that Thomas had saved for him. Then Aunt Jane played chess with him to pass the time. By the time his parents sat down to breakfast, he was ready for elevensies, so he had tea and scones with them. Mrs. Tuttle used a precious egg to make Eggs Benedict for Andrew's father, which he shared with Andrew.

As he followed his father out of the room, Andrew glanced at the Grandfather clock in the corner: three o'clock, time enough to spend at least two or three hours alone with his father until tea time. Perhaps they could go to town for tea—

"Why don't we have Mrs. Tuttle pack us a snack to eat for tea?" his father suggested, as Andrew got his rucksack organized. "We'll take a flask of tea along, and have a picnic. We can stay out until evening. I'll tell everyone we'll have a late supper alone together, all right? Just the two of us, old chap!"

His father got his rucksack packed with a blanket, a flask of tea, a canteen of water, and other hiking essentials. "Here, you pack the food in yours, Andrew. Be sure to take your canteen, too, and a sweater, in case it gets chilly."

"Are we going to visit Charlie's grave?"

"I was thinking of stopping there. Let's cut some roses from the garden to bring to him."

It always struck Andrew as rather poignant the way his father always talked about his brother Charlie as if he were alive and capable of being delighted by gifts and attention; in reality, he had been dead for twenty-one years, as long as Grandfather Denniston.

"Let's put a bit of baby's breath around the rose-buds—there, isn't that lovely?" Andrew's father arranged the bouquet and wrapped the stems in some paper.

"Well, let's be on our way." They walked together down the well-worn path, Andrew's father holding the flowers in his left hand and Andrew's hand in his right. The day was gloriously sunny and the countryside blazed with the brilliant green of the late spring foliage. A gentle breeze played at their faces, and the chitter of birds provided gentle music to accompany their footsteps.

"Is it really that bad in France?" Andrew asked his father, after they had walked along in silence for awhile.

His father sighed. "It looks as if it won't be easy to battle the Germans back." He was silent for a moment; then, in a swift motion, picked Andrew up and clasped him to his chest in a tight embrace. Andrew wrapped his arms around his father's neck and pressed his face against his cheek. After the fear and terror of the day before, Andrew's soul soared with joy at the feeling of his father holding him close, holding him as if he could never let go. He wanted to plead with his father not to ever go away again, but he knew that it would only make him troubled and distressed. He wriggled down a bit, so his head was resting on his father's chest, and listened to the soft heart-beat, so steady and soothing.

They stood together for a long, long while, wrapped in the tranquillity and loveliness of the gentle spring day. It seemed impossible that a war was going on little more than a hundred miles away. Each beat of his father's heart; each even, gentle breath lulled Andrew into a sweet, secret rapture. If only his father didn't have to go away so soon, if only this moment could last forever....

After a long, long while, he felt his father draw a deep breath, heard a low, soft moan—of what? Joy, anguish, sadness, fear? Andrew tensed, thinking that his father was about to let him go, so he tightened his arms around him and pressed his face against his father's shoulder.

"How long will you be home?" Andrew whispered.

"I think for a few weeks. Then I'll be rejoining my old squadron."

"We're not going to have a war against Germany, are we?"

His father was silent for a long time; then he looked skyward, and spoke softly. "I wish that there could be a way to put things right again without having a war. Anything is possible. What is not possible is giving in to tyranny." He sank to his knees, and repositioned Andrew so that he was cradling him in both arms. Looking up at him, Andrew felt the boundaries of his own self fall away, felt the fringes of his soul weave into his father's spirit: Their fears, their pain, their hopes, their love for each other tangled together in a nexus of joy and dread.

"Andrew, I wish I could make the world a safe, wonderful place for you, free from fear, free from evil. I would give everything, *everything* for that. Do you understand?"

Andrew nodded and closed his eyes, so that his father could not see the tears that were welling up; but as he squeezed his eyelids shut the tears sprang out and splashed down his cheeks. As he felt his father's gentle kiss grace his forehead, Andrew was transported into blissful remembrance of the countless times his tears, whether from scraped knees or nightmares, had been so gently dealt with. Any physical pain, any distress of soul, could be eased simply by his father's touch. A whirlwind of fierce joy and paralyzing dread tore through him. If only it were possible for his father to somehow be in two places at once: Away, doing the things that were necessary and right to protect the England they both loved, and at the same time always by Andrew's side—

It was as if Andrew's wish had somehow backfired onto himself, for suddenly he felt as if he were two people, in two different places at the same time. One self was still wrapped in his father's arms; the other self seemed to be floating upwards, as if in a dream, looking down at the small boy being comforted by...the man looked up, and Andrew screamed in horror, for the face was not his father's face. Not a dream it was, but a nightmare, a waking nightmare, even though he was fully aware of his father really holding him, now shaking him gently, speaking to him in an agitated voice, pleading with him to realize that everything was all right, *all right*—

Andrew opened his eyes and stared at his father, though his vision was still blurred by tears. He ran his hands over his father's face, trying to engrave upon his memory the feel of his father's features, trying to eradicate the image of that unfamiliar face staring up at him. Even as he sought to drive that vision away, he was unable to recollect precisely what the stranger's face had looked like, or if he had even had a distinct perception of the visage at all. All he knew, all he could remember, was that it was not his father's face.

He continued to glide his fingers across his father's face, in touches that were half explorations, half caresses. It was as if they were the only two people on earth; that if somehow the rest of the world had suddenly ceased to exist and the two of them were the only two beings left alive with nothing, nothing left at all, it wouldn't matter, not one bit. If it were somehow possible to make time stand still, that would only make everything even more sublime: to always, always see his father's face close to his, to touch him for eternity, to feel his arms around himself forever.

As if his father could somehow read Andrew's thoughts, he said in a low, soft voice, "When I first held you in my arms, just after you were born, I thought that I would never be able to love you more than I did at that moment. I wanted you to always stay little, so that I could snuggle you in my arms forever. I wished that time could stop, and that you would forever be so tiny and precious. Well, you grew, and I was just thrilled with every new thing you did—your first smile, your first step, your first word—it was 'da', I remember—" He looked at Andrew, love shining in his eyes. "Then I realized that I could never love you less the more you grew, only more. Now it seems as if that overwhelming love I felt the first time I saw you was just the beginning—" Even though he had been looking at Andrew the whole time, the expression on his face now was more intense, as if he, too, were trying to engrave this moment on his memory. He continued, his voice almost a whisper, "But I will always remember that day."

Andrew closed his eyes and felt himself floating in a sublime, serene, free-fall into sweet unawareness of everything except his father's arms around him.

A feathery sensation against his face brought Andrew to consciousness. He opened his eyes, and his father's face was still looking down at his.

"How long have I been asleep?"

"About an hour."

"I guess we ought to go see Charlie."

His father smiled, and Andrew stretched out his arms and legs and arched his back.

"You remind me of a contented cat stretching out by the fire," his father laughed.

"If I were a cat, what would you call me?"

"Andrew, of course—you'd still be Andrew."

"Why did you call me Andrew?"

He was surprised by the loud burst of laughter from his father. "Someday I'll tell you."

"No, now."

His father pursed his lips, and said, "You were named after a good friend of mine.

Everyone called him Sparky, because his last name was Sparks, but his first name was Andrew."

"Why did you laugh?"

It seemed as if his father were trying to think of an explanation that was a cover for the real reason. Finally he said, "Sparky was a real character. He was friendly, always had a smile on his face, but at times he could be a bit forgetful."

"What sort of things did he forget?"

"Next question please."

"Did I ever meet him?"

"You were too little to remember. He came to every one of your birthday parties until you were four. Then he joined the RAF and was sent overseas."

"Where is he now?"

"In Singapore."

"Did he have red hair?"

"Why yes, he did. Do you remember him?"

"I remember somebody with red hair giving me an airplane ride at my birthday party. He held me up high in the air. He gave me a model plane—it was a de Havilland Giant Moth."

"So you do remember!"

"I remember that Mum laughed and laughed when she saw what he'd given me. Why?"

"Oh, Sparky's uncle owned a Giant Moth and sometimes Sparky would borrow it and we would all go on holiday. I guess your mother was remembering some of the times we had." His father looked at the sky. "Well, we should be on our way. Let's have our picnic with Charlie—what do you say?"

"Super!" Andrew knew that having a picnic with Charlie meant spreading out their picnic blanket by Charlie's grave, as they often did, and leaving a biscuit or a piece of fruit for him. Whenever they would return, they would find the offering gone. Andrew always knew that it had probably been taken by a hungry squirrel or field mouse, but it was nice to think that Charlie was aware of their gift and appreciated it, all the same. Andrew liked to imagine him looking down from a cloud in heaven and being delighted each time he saw Andrew and his father visit his final resting place on earth. For some reason, Andrew always thought of Charlie as being perpetually three or four years old, even though he had lived barely a day, and even though he would now be a grown man if he'd survived.

They arrived at the small cemetery, which was tucked away behind a grove of trees, and headed straight for "Charlie's Playground", which was a wrought-iron enclosure around Charlie's grave. Andrew always found cemeteries rather dreary, spooky, places, but once inside Charlie's Playground he felt that he was in an oasis of carefree happiness.

Andrew's father closed the gate behind them and spread the blanket out on the grass. Andrew walked up to the headstone and traced his finger along the carved lettering:

Charles Denniston
Born 13 August, 1918
Died 14 August, 1918
May the Angels Always Keep Thee

At the top of the headstone a carving of three angels, looking like cherubs on a Valentine's Day card, presided over the solemn words, but the angels' faces were full of joy and impish delight. Andrew liked to think that they were Charlie's playmates up in Heaven, and that one of them always kept a look-out for visitors. "Can I give the flowers to Charlie?"

"Of course." Andrew's father handed him the bouquet. Andrew held it up next to the angels' faces; he imagined they would tell Charlie how nice it smelled. Then he set the bouquet down at the base of the headstone.

His father had already unpacked both rucksacks and had their picnic things spread out. He poured the tea into two metal cups. Andrew seated himself and picked out a cucumber sandwich. He munched it, then sipped his tea; his father did likewise.

"Mrs. Tuttle packed some raisin scones and some peaches, too," his father said. "And I brought along a special treat."

Andrew knew that something wonderful was still packed away in his father's rucksack. "Eat everything else, first," his father admonished.

Andrew grabbed a peach and bit into it.

"Did you know that Charlie was going to die when he was born?"

"No, although I knew that my mother was upset when she sent for the doctor, because she said it was too soon for him to be born."

"You always told me he was too little to survive."

"Well, yes. A baby grows inside its mother, just as you're growing now. If it's born before it supposed to be born, it's too little."

"But how does being too small keep it from living?"

"I think that Charlie couldn't breathe very well. I remember the doctor saying something like that. His breathing sounded funny, sort of like little grunts. I held him for a few minutes and tried to tell him to take deep breaths. I thought he could understand me, because he did seem to be trying to breathe faster. But the doctor said he didn't understand me, and that he was probably breathing faster because he heard my voice, that's all."

"Did he know that you were his brother?"

"No, newborn babies aren't aware of things like that. It takes awhile for them to understand the world around them. When you were born, you looked at me as if you knew that I had to be someone special, but you couldn't quite figure things out. You looked a little bewildered, and even though I wanted you to always be small enough to fit in my arms, I couldn't wait for you grow a little and recognize me as your father."

"When did I do that?"

"Oh, it wasn't all at once. You started to focus more and more when you looked at either me or your mother; then you started to smile when you saw us. Then you laughed and started calling me 'da' and your mother 'mum-mum'"

"I remember calling her that. Grandfather Howard didn't like that. He wanted me to call her 'Mummy' or 'Mother'."

At the mention of Grandfather Howard, his father's face turned solemn. He ate the rest of his sandwich in silence.

Andrew was sorry he'd brought up the subject of Grandfather Howard, for he knew that his maternal grandfather had never approved of his daughter's choice in a husband; for whatever reason Andrew was not quite sure. He'd barely acknowledged Andrew's father even to his face, and always referred to him as *that man* behind his back.

"I'm glad he's dead—I never liked him!" Andrew blurted.

"You shouldn't wish for people to be dead just because you don't like them."

"I didn't say that I wanted for him to be dead; I'm just glad that he died, that's all. I would be glad if Hitler were dead."

"Your grandfather wasn't like Hitler."

"Well, I still didn't like him. I wished that we didn't have to go visit him."

"You were his only grandchild, and it was right that you should see each other."

"When I'm a grandfather, I'm not going to be like that. Do you think he was mean and scary when he was a little boy?"

"Oh, I don't think he was mean and scary, just somewhat formidable."

"He was too mean and scary! He always glared at me, as if he didn't like me at all."

His father's expression changed from consternation to distress. Andrew flung himself into his arms, hugged him with all his strength, then pulled him down so that they were lying against each other, his father's face snuggled in his chest. He stroked his father's hair—the texture, he knew, was much like his own: straight and thick, and the color was almost the same as his: dark brown, the color of chocolate....

"Where's my surprise?"

His father laughed. "You have to promise to share it."

"I will."

His father reached into his rucksack and pulled out a Cadbury bar. "I'll show you a special way to eat it." He handed it to Andrew. "Take a bite of chocolate, and a bite of peach, and chew them together."

Andrew tried it. "It's very good. They each taste better when they're together."

"They do, don't they? Often, things that are different make each other even better when they're together."

They washed down their confection with a drink of tea. Andrew's father refilled their cups from the flask.

"Well, let's polish off those scones," his father said. "Shall we give one to Charlie?"

"Of course."

As Andrew selected a scone and placed it next to Charlie's headstone, he wondered what it would be like to have brothers and sisters. Without ever being told, he knew

46

the subject of having children, specifically *if* and *when* and *how many*, was not the sort of matter one broached with anybody, even with one's own parents. For whatever reason, he was an only child, and he somehow sensed it would always be so. Not that he was all that upset about it, for he knew that he was very special in his parents' eyes. Having a sibling would mean that his parents' affections would be...divided. Perhaps a cousin or two would be nice. He was sure that Aunt Gwen and Uncle Robert wanted to have children someday, and maybe Aunt Jane would remarry, and have children too. Cousins...then he remembered—Freddie!

"Why did you agree with Freddie this afternoon, about the concentration camps and all?"

"Because he's right."

"He's a twit!"

"Sometimes twits can be right."

"Is he right about England being just like Germany and doing such terrible things?"

"Partly. We did build our empire by gunboat diplomacy, most of the time. We had far superior weaponry; England has been at war, or has lived with the threat of war, for most of the last eight centuries, since William the Conqueror. And for hundreds of years before that there were waves of invaders: Celts, Romans, Saxons, Vikings. So we had already developed quite sophisticated weapons with which to defend ourselves, or attack our enemies. The peoples that we conquered were not quite so—" His father paused. "I don't like to use the word 'advanced', because being able to kill others more easily or efficiently does not seem to be advanced. 'Proficient' is more like it. We were not always decent or kind, either. Some people were, sometimes; others were horribly cruel and selfish. Some saw England's expansion as having a noble intent, a civilizing influence; others used it as an opportunity to exploit and oppress the lands that were under British rule. Sometimes people were better off being under 'Pax Britannica,' most of the times they were worse off."

"Freddie doesn't really care about the people who got conquered by us anyway. He thinks that anyone who isn't English is a wog. Like he says, 'The wogs begin at Calais.' He complains about other people being bigoted—he's the worst bigot of all."

His father raised an eyebrow. "You noticed!"

"Well, he is, isn't he?"

"Quite right, old chap."

"And he's a twit, too—a stupid, foolish, pompous twit! He always acts as if he knows it all, but he doesn't know—know—."

"His head from a hole in the ground!"

"What?" Andrew giggled at the novel, yet hilariously appropriate, analogy.

"Oh, it's an American saying."

Andrew smiled, and repeated his father's observation. "That's right. He doesn't know his head from a hole in the ground. So you do think Freddie's ignorant?"

"I'll admit he's clever, but he's unwise."

"How can he complain about England having an Empire when he's made piles of money in his shipping business? If we didn't have our Empire, he wouldn't be rich."

"Sometimes Freddie plays devil's advocate to make his point."

"What does that mean?"

"He takes the opposite point of view for the sake of argument, or to make his point, though he may not necessarily believe in that view, or not entirely agree with it."

"What do you mean?"

"He wants to convince us that what Germany is doing now is exactly what we did. In some respects, there are similarities, and some of his arguments are valid. In England's overseas expansion, there were evil people, pursuing evil ends by evil means. Freddie doesn't care at all about the people who were subjugated unjustly, and he doesn't for a moment believe that the British Empire is a bad thing; he has profited quite handsomely from trade with our colonies. He thinks that there was nothing wrong with what we did in acquiring our colonies and possessions, and that the Nazis are exactly like us, and have every right to do what they are doing."

"Do you think the Empire is a bad thing, or that we were wrong to get all of our colonies?"

"Wrong? Yes—I've thought about it a long time and I think that we were wrong. The colonies we possess now are not ours to keep, Andrew."

"But if the colonies are set free, our Empire will be nothing!"

"If there is always an England, and England is free, then that's all that matters." He smiled at Andrew. "We were never meant to possess forever what we had attained, but I believe our Empire will ensure the survival of freedom in the world, and after that it must be set free. I believe that it was given to us in trust, to be used for a special purpose, and then it must be returned to its rightful owners."

His father pressed his fingertips together. "For instance, take the United States. It started out as an English colony, but then the Americans wanted to be free. There were many people in England who thought it would be to England's advantage to keep America as a colony, but the Americans won their war of independence. I think that America having her freedom was the best thing for both countries. The American people are dynamic, resourceful, energetic, and I don't think they would be like that if they were still living as British subjects. They want to be linked to us, but not under our control. And that, I think, is the way things should be: two nations, free of each other, and yet joined by ties that are deeper and stronger than coercion and domination. We speak the same language, and Americans are similar to us in some ways, but very different as well. I think the differences are complimentary. Remember how good the chocolate and peaches tasted together? You said they were better together than they were alone. Well, that's what happens when two peoples bring into a partnership their differences, because it makes each better than they would be alone."

"Do you think the Germans are like us?"

"No." His father's voice, though strained, was emphatic. "There is something fundamentally different—for all our faults, for all the wrong we've done to people who should be allowed to be free—" His voice broke off, and he looked off into the distance for a long, long while. Then he turned to Andrew. "Our way of life, our government, what we are as a people, allows for good, for fairness. Our political system has evolved over the centuries to give everyone a voice, a say in how the country is run. It has, I believe, the ultimate goal of fairness for everyone—even though, in practice, we often do not treat people fairly, and there is bigotry and unkindness in abundance. But the essential difference is that the Nazis see bigotry and cruelty as the goal of their rule, and hatred as an official state policy. They teach their children in school to hate—to hate Jews, to hate anyone who is not of their 'Master Race.' Freddie believes that mere snobbery and the Nazi's program of persecution of the Jews are the same. Both spring from intolerance, but it is not merely a question of degree. Snobbery may still allow for a 'let live' course, but the Nazis do not propose a 'let live' policy in their dealings with others. They see hatred, oppression, and cruelty as the means to their ultimate goal. It's one thing to have pride in your country; it's another thing altogether to hate those who are different from you. Do you understand?"

Andrew nodded. His father went on. "What we have here in England is not perfect, but I believe it is essentially good and right. It's something worth preserving, it's something worth fighting for, and even though we may have to fight alone, it's something we must do. I want you, and your children, and your children's children, to grow up free, and to know what is right and good."

"*Crikey*—you're already making me a grandfather!" Andrew laughed.

"Come on, old man!" His father tousled his hair. "It's getting late—we'd better be getting back."

A few nights later they were blessed with warm, dry weather and a clear sky. After supper, Andrew and his parents, laden with blankets and pillows, set out to spend a few hours star-gazing. They climbed to a small hill a little ways from Armus House and piled several thick woolen blankets on the ground. They then arranged the pillows at one end and slithered into the bedding, snug as "bugs in a rug," his mother laughed. Andrew, nestled between his parents, thought he was the snuggest bug of all. He knew he should pay attention to his father's astronomy instruction, for he wanted to be a pilot someday and knowing stellar navigation was important. He was able to keep his eyes open for awhile; then his father's voice lulled him to that blissful state halfway between consciousness and sleep.

"...Polaris, Ursa Minor, Ursa Major, Hercules, Cygnus...."

Someday, he promised himself, he would try to stay awake so that he could learn not only the names, but the appearances and whereabouts and other particulars about these brilliant pinpoints of light. *Someday....*

Something, someone was nudging him: Time to get up and walk back to Armus House. Then he realized he was back in his own room, in his own bed. There was a sliver of daylight around the blackout curtain. He opened his eyes a crack, and saw a blur of blue-gray—

He sat bolt upright. His father, dressed in his RAF uniform, bent over him.

"I thought you said you were going to be here for a few weeks!" Andrew blurted.

"Something's come up," his father whispered.

"No!"

His father sat down beside him. "It's important." His arms went around Andrew's trembling body, and held him tight as the sobs erupted in a torrent of anguish and fear.

"All right, old chap, it's all right. I wish that I had a bit more notice about this."

"About what?" Andrew sputtered.

His father's reply was to hold him even more closely. Andrew's sobs turned to soft groans. His father kept silent until Andrew's trembling and anguished utterings ceased.

"When will you be coming back?"

"Soon, I hope."

Andrew buried his face in his father's neck, knowing that it would be pointless to implore him to stay. Finally his grip slackened, not from lack of desire to have his father remain, but from the knowledge that their parting was as inevitable as the rising of the sun on this new day.

If only his father's return could be so assured!

His father kissed him gently on the forehead, and pressed his cheek against Andrew's for an eternal, but all too brief, moment.

Andrew closed his eyes as his father left the room. He tried to drown out the soft sounds of his father's footsteps down the hall by taking deep, rapid breaths. The panic within him raked his soul, and he hurled himself out of bed and dashed to the window.

He yanked back the blackout curtain and saw his father walking down the front steps towards the car and waving at Thomas to dispense with the formality of opening the door for him. It was almost an involuntary gesture, for Andrew's father never wanted to have the door held open for him, anyway.

Look up, please look up!

His father paused, and Andrew held his breath. His father turned his head, then looked up at Andrew. He winked and made a casual salute, as if to assure Andrew that everything was going to be all right.

He got into the car, and Andrew watched as it receded down the drive. His father looked out from the back window until the car turned the corner at the front gate and disappeared from view.

Chapter 3

"*A*ndrew, hurry up! We don't want to miss the train."

"Yes, Mum," Andrew called down the stairs.

"Did you pack your schoolbooks?"

"Yes, I did."

"Good, we'll get some of your studying done on the train. I promised Mr. Nugent that you would keep up with your schoolwork while you were away. Did you do your geography lesson last night?"

"Yes, I did."

"What about your French and Latin homework?"

"That too."

Andrew finished packing his school things in his suitcase and set it outside his door. Then he remembered that Mrs. Tuttle had promised to send him off with some treats to eat on the train, since he would miss elevensies. He ran down the backstairs to the kitchen; perhaps he could convince her to put a few more raisin scones in the package. His mother had promised that they would go out to lunch in London, as they had a two hour wait between train connections. Even allowing for the time journeying between the two stations (Andrew had always known them as "The Station to go to Armus House" and "The Station to go to Askew Court and Greycliff") they would still be able to enjoy a somewhat leisurely meal.

He found Thomas in the kitchen, sipping a cup of tea.

"Remember to save me the *Addie and Hermy* comics," Andrew reminded him.

"Promise," Thomas said.

"Would you like more apple tart, love?" Mrs. Tuttle asked Thomas.

"Yes, dear. Hope they never start rationing apples!"

Mrs. Tuttle gave Thomas a peck on the cheek as she dished up another serving of apple tart. Andrew always liked to visit with Thomas and Mrs. Tuttle for, though they'd been married for twenty-five years, they often acted like newlyweds. He liked to think that his parents would someday be like this, an old married couple still delighting in one another, though he could never imagine his mother plump like Mrs. Tuttle, nor his father with Thomas's wrinkles and stiff gait. He knew that Thomas had been injured in the Great War, so Andrew supposed he must have walked like this when he was a young man, too.

"Oh, I don't doubt that Lord Woolton would find a way to ration the sunshine!" Mrs. Tuttle chirped in her thick Cornish accent. "Would you like some apple tart, Andrew?"

"Just a bite—we'll be leaving in a few minutes."

Mrs. Tuttle gave him a small piece of tart on a saucer and Andrew proceeded to wolf it down. "Could you please pack a few extra scones for us, Mrs. Tuttle?" he said between mouthfuls. "You make the best scones in the world!"

"Learning how to flatter the ladies at such a tender age, really Andrew!"

"Andrew!" His mother stood in the kitchen doorway. "I've been looking all over for you! Come on, chop, chop! We'll be leaving in ten minutes."

"Yes, Mum." He heard her sprint up the front stairs.

Mrs. Tuttle handed Andrew a glass of milk, which he downed with one gulp. She then blotted his mouth with her apron. He gave her a quick hug and dashed out through the dining room to the front hallway. The door to the study was open and he heard Freddie's voice within.

"...Well, I suppose that we have no choice about it, Maurice. Just my luck for the army to get itself in a tight spot right now, but I suppose we have to do our bit. It might prove advantageous to put on a show of being patriotic right now. Well, you handle the details—just don't bother me for the next few days. You can leave any messages with Helena."

There was a pause; then Freddie's wheezy chuckle shattered the silence. "Why Maurice, you dirty old man! Whatever gave you the idea I was planning on debauching some innocent young thing? You know me better than that!" Another wheezy chuckle. "You know very well, I don't prefer the *innocent* types!" Freddie then roared with laughter.

"...How did you guess, old boy? A marvelous stroke of luck: He was called back to his old squadron, and she'll be in London for a few days while the boy is finishing up his examinations at school. Seems like there *is* a bright spot in this whole nasty business after all. So while Roger is off terrorizing the Luftwaffe, I'll be—well, not letting a valuable opportunity slip by. As they say, all's fair in love and war, and there is a war going on right now, or so the politicians tell us!" Silence; then another explosion of laughter. "Why Maurice, sometimes you surprise me! You *can* be a lecherous devil on occasion, can't you! Cheerio!"

Andrew leaned against the wall, weak with dismay. The sound of Freddie shuffling some papers startled him out of his stupor, and he dashed up the stairs.

He got his suitcase, clumped down the stairs, and called to his mother, "I'll be waiting by the front door, Mum."

"Andrew! I've got your treats all packed." Mrs. Tuttle's voice boomed from the kitchen. Andrew left his suitcase by the front door and dashed down the hall.

"Here's a package of gingersnaps. If you're a mite peckish before your examinations, these'll help."

"Thanks awfully."

"Now give us a hug." Mrs. Tuttle opened her arms wide. Andrew gave her a hug and was enfolded in a strong embrace.

"Mind yourself, Andrew."

She held the door open for him, as both his hands were occupied.

"I'll get the car." Thomas gave his wife a peck on the cheek and slipped out the back door.

Andrew rounded the corner to the front hall and what he saw sent a spasm of terror down his spine: His mother was backed against the wall, trapped by Freddie's outstretched, rigid arms to either side of her. His palms were firmly flattened against the wall and his face was very close to hers. He spoke in a low, crooning voice.

"Alice, I'm so worried about you being all alone in London. It would really ease my mind if you would stay at my place. After all, you never know what might happen, and there *is* a war on, you know."

Andrew's mother glared at him. "I'm sure the Gestapo hasn't taken over Hyde Park yet. Don't worry, if any Nazis try to bother me, I shall give you a call. Now I must be going, Freddie."

"Alice, you know I'd be worried sick about you, all alone. You never can tell what might happen to a defenseless, attractive woman in a big city. And Roger's gone off and left you on your own again. I would never forgive myself if something happened to you."

"I've been on my own in London many times. I'm perfectly capable of taking care of myself!"

"I'm sure you are." His voice was a malevolent murmur. He pressed his body close to hers, reached into his pocket, and pulled out a key on a gold ring. He dropped it into her jacket pocket. Andrew stared at the scene, chilled and mesmerized. Freddie's mouth brushed hers; she turned her head away and struggled against him.

"*Mum!*" Andrew's shriek shattered the silence, startling Freddie. Andrew's mother took advantage of his discomfiture by throwing him off so that he nearly fell backwards.

"Mum," Andrew tried to make his voice sound firm, but steady.

What to say, what to say?

"Mum...Thomas is getting the car."

She crossed to him, and nodded. "Do you have your suitcase ready?"

"It's by the front door." Andrew tried to focus his attention on his mother but he couldn't help but see, over her shoulder, Freddie's savage stare.

Andrew's mother paid for their tickets and they went outside to wait for the train. She glared down at the track. Andrew slipped his hand in hers, and felt her fingers tighten. Then she turned to him and smiled. "Not to worry, darling, Freddie just likes to bother people. It's a game to him."

Andrew nodded, trying to smile, but he still felt a knot in his stomach. This was something more than a game.

"Here comes the train, Andrew. Do you have your ticket?"

"No, you took both of them and put them in your pocket."

"Oh, that's right." As she reached into her pocket, a startled look erased the smile. She pulled out Freddie's key.

"Damn him!" She flung the key over the tracks. It glinted in the sun as it soared skyward and fell into the field beyond.

Andrew's mother carried his suitcase and her overnight bag towards the platform. Andrew hurried along behind, clutching his packages of treats. The station was quite crowded, and there was more than the usual buzz of noise in the air. Andrew heard two words: "Dunkirk" and "BEF" repeated over and over again.Dunkirk? He knew it was a place in France, on the Pas de Calais, some twenty miles to the east of Calais. Had there been some sort of victorious battle? Were the Germans being beaten back from the sea? The excited hubbub around him seemed to confirm his guess. There was a shout of "Here it comes!" and Andrew and his mother were swept along by the throng of people out to another platform. There were hundreds of tiny Union Jacks fluttering in the air all around them, and a cheer went up from the crowd as a train pulled in. Over and over he heard the words: *Dunkirk* and *BEF*.

It must be some great victory, it must be!

"What is it, Mum?" Andrew tugged at his mother's sleeve. In contrast to the people around them, she seemed dazed and dispirited. Maybe she was still upset about Freddie.

The flags were waving in a frenzied celebration of red, white, and blue, and the roar of the crowd was deafening.

"Mum, we won, didn't we? Didn't we?"

As the train pulled by them, Andrew expected to see the smiles of conquering heroes. Instead, he saw the windows crowded with faces: grimy, stubbled, weary, desolate faces; faces etched with grief and strain; some tear-streaked, some impassive, some expressionless with exhaustion. All betrayed a legacy of defeat, not victory.

The train halted and the faces looked out at the crowd. Small parcels and various items of food—biscuits, fruit, bottles of juice—now appeared scattered among the Union Jacks and were conveyed by outstretched arms to the sad, disheveled, tired figures in the carriage. Andrew's mother turned to him.

"I'll buy you an extra treat for lunch, darling." She then took the two packages from his hands, stepped forward, and offered them to a pair of arms hanging outside the train window.

Andrew heard a hoarse, "Thank you, mum."

She stepped back and Andrew could see that her face was wet with tears.

...A miracle of deliverance, achieved by valour, by perseverance, by perfect discipline, by faultless service, by resource, by skill, by unconquerable fidelity, is manifest to all....

"Nigel, would you please turn up the volume on the wireless?" Mr. Nugent said.

...We must be very careful not to assign to this deliverance the attributes of a

victory. Wars are not won by evacuations. But there was a victory inside this deliverance, which should be noted....

Andrew knew that he should be listening to the Prime Minister's speech; but his mind bounced back and forth between the scratchy voice on the radio and his own worries.

...It was gained by the Air Force. Many of our soldiers coming back have not seen the Air Force at work; they saw only the bombers which escaped its protective attack. They underrate its achievements. I have heard much talk of this; that is why I go out of my way to say this. I will tell you about it....

Why hadn't his mother called?

This was a great trial of strength between the British and German Air Forces. Can you conceive a greater objective for the Germans in the air than to make evacuation from these beaches impossible, and to sink all these ships which were displayed, almost to the extent of thousands? Could there have been an objective of greater military importance and significance for the whole purpose of the war than this? They tried hard, and they were beaten back; they were frustrated in their task. We got the Army away; and they have paid fourfold for any losses which they have inflicted.

What does he mean by losses? Injured and killed, or just killed?

All of our types—the Hurricane, the Spitfire, and the new Defiant—and all our pilots have been vindicated as superior to what they have at present to face. When we consider how much greater would be our advantage in defending the air above this island against an overseas attack, I must say that I find in these facts a sure basis upon which practical and reassuring thoughts may rest. I will pay my tribute to these young airmen....

The Prime Minister's voice was drowned in static, then bobbed up in clear, emphatic tones.

The great French Army was very largely, for the time being, cast back and disturbed by the onrush of a few thousands of armoured vehicles. May it also be that the cause of civilisation itself will be defended by the skill and devotion of a few thousand airmen?

Andrew looked around the room at his classmates gathered around the radio. John Gordon-Fairweather had not returned; Colin Kirknewton was missing also. Those who remained sat motionless, listening intently to the impassioned voice over the airwaves.

They could very well have been a still-life tableau. Mr. Nugent sat in his easy chair, head bowed, hands folded, his knuckles pressed against his forehead.

Nevertheless, our thankfulness at the escape of our Army and so many men, whose loved ones have passed through an agonising week, must not blind us to the fact that what has happened in France and Belgium is a colossal military disaster....

That's putting it mildly!

We must expect another blow to be struck almost immediately at us or at France....

Attack?

I would observe that there has never been a period in all these long centuries of which we boast when an absolute guarantee against invasion, still less against serious raids, could have been given to our people....

Invasion?

...We shall not flag or fail. We shall go on to the end, we shall fight in France, we shall fight on the seas and oceans, we shall fight with growing confidence and growing strength in the air, we shall defend our island, whatever the cost may be, we shall fight on the beaches, we shall fight on the landing grounds, we shall fight in the fields and in the streets, we shall fight in the hills; we shall never surrender, and even if, which I do not for a moment believe, this island or a large part of it were subjugated and starving, then our Empire beyond the seas, armed and guarded by the British Fleet, would carry on the struggle, until, in God's good time, the New World, with all its power and might, steps forth to the rescue and the liberation of the old.

"What does Mr. Churchill mean, the New World—does he mean America?" Simon Inskip asked.

"I'm sure he does," replied Mr. Nugent.

The radio went staticky. "Please turn the wireless off, Nigel," Mr. Nugent said.

"But America wants to be neutral," Andrew pointed out.

"Things can change," Mr. Nugent said.

"Right, Belgium and Holland were neutral—*that* changed," countered Keith Vincent-Hill.

"Sometimes things can change for the better," Mr. Nugent replied. "Look what happened at Dunkirk! It seemed certain that the BEF was lost, but over three hundred thousand British and French soldiers were brought back to England, James's and Nigel's brothers among them."

"Have you heard anything about Colin's father?" Andrew asked.

"Not yet," Mr. Nugent said.

"Mr. Nugent?" Charles Provis spoke softly.

"Yes, Charles."

Charles bit his lip, then blurted: "If Mr. Churchill says that he doesn't believe for a moment that we're going to be subjugated and starving, then why does he say that the New World is going to rescue us if we are?"

The question had been in everyone's mind anyway, and a dozen pairs of eyes stared earnestly at Mr. Nugent.

"I think that Mr. Churchill is saying that even if it seems as if things are at their worst, that all will turn out best in the end. Even if things seem hopeless, we should not give up hope—that's what I think he means. Miracles can happen. Remember what he said: 'The British army seemed about to perish upon the field or be led into ignominious captivity.' Now look what happened! Most of the BEF—over two hundred thousand men, plus over a hundred thousand French soldiers—are safe in England!"

"But they had to leave most of their rifles behind," Duncan Paget said. "How can they fight a war without guns?"

"Not just guns," Andrew added. "Ammunition too, and tanks and trucks and things. Bags of stuff!"

"It's the men who are important. Guns and equipment can be replaced—people cannot be."

"Where are we going to get the guns from?" George Garton-Ward asked.

"We'll get them from somewhere. Mr. Churchill has asked America for help."

"America doesn't want to help us—they're neutral," Andrew countered.

"Things can change. It may appear that we're very much alone, but we still have our Empire, and I believe that America will help us eventually."

Andrew's mother came to get him a few days later, bringing the welcome news that his father was safe.

"Is Dad coming home soon?"

"Not right away, darling. He may come home in a few weeks."

"Why can't he come home now? He was supposed to be home for two weeks, and he had to leave after only a few days. They should let him come home right now."

"Andrew, they can't let everyone go at once. Don't worry, you'll see your father soon."

"He's all right, isn't he?"

"Of course, he's all right." Her voice had an almost imperceptible edge to it. There was something, too, about her demeanor which gave Andrew the distinct impression that, though she was not dissembling, she was not being entirely truthful either.

They journeyed home, the usual two train trips bracketing the ride on the Underground. Excited talk swirled around them.

"Thank God we're alone now!"

"Bloody Frogs—we're better off without 'em!"

"It's just us for the finals, and we've got the home ground advantage!"

Then it happened.

As they were about to board the train at Paddington Station, a man came hobbling up. Andrew saw that his left trouser leg was pinned up above the knee and that he was missing his right arm as well.

The man glanced their way and, in that instant, a terrible premonition settled on Andrew: His father, dismembered just like that, hobbling and lurching about, a mere vestige of a man.

Upon their arrival at Armus House, Andrew found the atmosphere vaguely tense, as if everyone were keeping a secret from him. Gram and Aunt Jane greeted him warmly enough; Freddie glowered, which was to be expected, but Andrew could not shake the feeling that something was amiss.

"Can I phone Dad?" Andrew asked his mother at tea.

"Oh no. I'll leave a message for him to give you a ring."

"He's all right, isn't he?"

"Andrew, I've told you—he's fine."

"What's the matter with Aunt Jane?"

"She's not feeling well. She wanted to rest for the afternoon. She'll be down for supper."

"Andrew?" Aunt Jane stood in the doorway. Andrew rushed to her and threw his arms around her. He was afraid to repeat his query as to his father's well being, so he simply looked up at her, silently imploring her to either reassure him, or else reveal whatever terrible truth was lurking behind the silence. She closed her eyes and kissed him on the forehead.

"Miss Jane, would you like some of my cherry-pear compote?" Mrs. Tuttle stood in the doorway to the kitchen, wiping floured hands on her apron.

"No, thank you, Mrs. Tuttle, tea's just fine."

Aunt Jane sat down and Andrew's mother poured her a cup of tea. They smiled at each other, tense, tremulous smiles. Their eyes were troubled and distant. Andrew, worried as he was for his father, was somewhat calmed by the bond between them. When he remembered how his father had been treated by Grandfather Howard, and how the very air at Greycliff seemed to be charged with tension whenever he went there with his parents, Andrew was glad for the harmony that reigned at Armus House. His mother never resented the bond between Andrew's father and Aunt Jane; in fact, though she seemed to enjoy everyone's company (except Freddie's of course), she was particularly close to Aunt Jane, especially now that Andrew's father was away most of the time. And Aunt Jane seemed to bask in the love that Andrew's parents had for each other: It seemed to be somehow affirming and comforting after losing her husband so tragically.

Aunt Jane sipped her tea.

"I think I did well on my examinations," Andrew said.

"Oh, I'm glad!" Aunt Jane smiled a little too brightly at Andrew. "Why don't we read to each other after tea? Would you like to read Mark Twain or Rudyard Kipling?"

Andrew shrugged.

"When I last talked with him, your father mentioned that he was reading *Huckleberry Finn*, and that it was quite enjoyable," Andrew's mother suggested.

"Since when does he have time to read?"

Andrew's mother and Aunt Jane glanced at one another, an unspoken consultation that left Andrew even more disquieted. Then Aunt Jane spoke.

"Things have been rather quiet since Dunkirk; no one knows what the Germans are up to. But Fighter Command still has to be ready in case anything happens. They can't send everyone home at once, you see." She forced a smile. Seeing that Andrew was still not assuaged by her explanation, she went on. "I'll try to get a message to your father and ask him to call you, all right?"

Andrew nodded; Aunt Jane kissed him on the forehead and left. While she was in the study, Andrew picked at his food.

"Darling, nothing is going to be gained by your not eating properly," his mother admonished. "Your father wouldn't want to see you wasted away when he comes home."

"That's right, Master Andrew." Mrs. Tuttle stood over Andrew, proffering a tray laden with potato pie, sausages, and carrot flan.

"You'll be nothing but skin and bones if you keep this up, and wouldn't that upset your father!"

"I hate carrots," Andrew grumbled.

"Just eat a little," his mother soothed. "You need your vitamins."

Aunt Jane returned. "No promises, Andrew, but your father will try to call soon." She rubbed Andrew's back. "Now, eat your food and afterwards we'll read to pass the time."

"Did Dad say that it's been quiet at the squadron?"

"Andrew, I didn't talk to him; I left a message."

"Who did you talk to?"

"Andrew, eat your food."

"Did the person you talked to say the Germans haven't been causing trouble?"

There it was again: that quick, collaborative glance between Aunt Jane and his mother. This time his mother spoke: "Andrew, they're not going to tell *everyone* who calls what the Germans have been up to. Now eat your food."

Andrew picked at his meal, listlessly shoving morsels of food into his mouth. That task finished, he settled down with Aunt Jane in the drawing room to read *Huckleberry Finn*. They alternated reading aloud, Aunt Jane doing the odd chapters and Andrew doing the even ones. He was reading Chapter 4, and was at the part in which Jim was telling Huck's fortune with the magic hair-ball, when the phone jangled. Racing out, he almost ran into Lucia, who was coming from the kitchen to answer it, as it was her duty to greet callers.

"Sorry, I'll get it," Andrew gasped. He flew into the study and grabbed the phone on the third ring.

"Hullo—hullo!"

"Andrew, have you taken over Lucia's job?" his father laughed.

"Dad!" Andrew gulped with relief. "Are you all right?"

"I'm just fine, old chap. How are you?"

"I'm fine, but I've been ever so worried. Are you sure you're all right?"

"Just fine."

"When are you coming home?"

"Can't tell right now—soon I hope. Things are a bit disordered right now, but I'll have a better idea in a few—" His father was interrupted by a voice, a *woman's* voice. A crackly, crunchy sound emitted from the receiver, followed by muffled conversation, his father's low voice alternating with the sharp, female voice.

"Dad, *Dad!*" Andrew almost screamed into the receiver.

"It's all right, old chap."

"Who was that?"

"Who was who?"

"That woman you were talking to."

"Oh, she was just letting me know that, um, she needs to use the phone."

"She was very rude—she didn't call you 'Sir'; she called you Mr. Hadley-Trevelyan. Who is she?"

"Andrew, are you trying to convince me that you should get a job as an interrogator for any captured Germans?"

"No, but—"

"How are things at Armus House?"

"Um, fine. Aunt Jane and I were just reading *Huckleberry Finn*. And Thomas has joined the Local Defence Volunteers. He says they have to drill with broomsticks and golf clubs and pitchforks, since they don't have any guns, and that they're learning how to disable vehicles in case the Germans invade. They can put crowbars through the wheels and pour sugar into the petrol tanks. They can also make grenades out of kerosene."

"Ingenious!" his father chuckled. Then he added, "And how are you?"

"I miss you. If you can't come to see me right away, can I come to see you?"

"Afraid that's not possible, old chap."

"Why? I came to visit you at your squadron last year—lot's of times!"

"Things are different now. Tell you what—I'll call you every day until I'm able to get away. Would after teatime be all right?"

"Yes, I'll be here, promise!"

"Fine! Well, I have to—"

"Dad!"

"What?"

Andrew's mind fumbled around for the right words to say. It wouldn't do to ask his father point blank if he was still at his squadron; Andrew was quite sure that he wasn't, even though everyone seemed to imply that he was. "Seemed to,"—but they hadn't outright affirmed anything for certain, except that he was just "all right".

"Dad, can we go for a walk when you get home?"

"Sure, old chap."

"Can we have a boxing practice?"

"We'll see—I have to go now. Be good. I'll ring tomorrow after teatime. Bye."

"Bye, Dad." A muffled click; then the line went dead. Andrew hung up the receiver, his heart pounding.

A walk—*Sure.*

Boxing—*We'll see.*

The news from France is very bad, and I grieve for the gallant French people who have fallen into this terrible misfortune. Nothing will alter our feelings towards them or our faith that the genius of France will rise again. What has happened in France makes no difference to our actions and purpose. We have become the sole champions now in arms to defend the world cause. We shall do our best to be worthy of this high honour. We shall defend our island home, and with the British Empire we shall fight on unconquerable until the curse of Hitler is lifted from the brows of mankind—

"Why don't we have the curse of you, Winnie, lifted from the brows—" Freddie sneered.

"Shhh!" Aunt Jane hissed. She turned up the radio.

...We are sure that in the end all will come right.

"Why is Aunt Gwen coming home with Dad?" Andrew asked Aunt Jane as she selected records to play on the gramophone in the dining room.

"I told you, she got off from her job to meet him in London. Why are you fussing about them coming home together?"

"I'm not fussing—I'm asking."

"Andrew, please ask Mrs. Tuttle if she wants me to set out the soup bowls." Lucia, who was setting the table, smiled at him.

He trudged into the kitchen and stood in a trance by the stove, watching Mrs. Tuttle stir the soup.

"What is it, Andrew?"

"Um, I forgot." He clumped out to the dining room and asked Lucia to repeat her query. "Soup," she reminded him. He shuffled back to the kitchen and gazed into the steaming pot of vegetable soup.

"Lucia wants to know if we're having soup," he said.

"No, I'm making gunpowder for the LDV," Mrs. Tuttle told him.

"What?"

"Andrew, have you gone daft or blind?"

"What do you mean?"

"What does it look like I'm doing?"

"Cooking."

Mrs. Tuttle set down the spoon on the stove, turned to Andrew, and gave him a big hug.

"What's the matter?" Andrew asked.

"You are, you silly monkey." She squeezed Andrew again. "You're worried about your father, aren't you? Hasn't everyone told you? He's just fine!"

Andrew nodded. Mrs. Tuttle cupped his face in her hands and declared in a loud voice, "He's fine. Now tell Lucia that we're having soup."

Andrew nodded again, wandered out the door to the hallway, and trudged up the stairs to his room. Throwing himself down on the bed, he at last allowed his forebodings to give way to tears, which trickled unchecked down his cheeks. His father, one-armed, an object of pity, needing to have even the simplest tasks done for him. Not able to box, or—an even more revolting though assaulted Andrew. What if his father had lost both arms? He thrashed about on the bed, trying to drive the revolting images from his mind.

No, *no, NO*....

He squeezed his eyes shut, then opened them and stared at the ceiling for a moment. He let his gaze travel down to the window, which overlooked the front drive. He had always enjoyed having such a lookout, for he could see all manner of comings and goings from this most excellent vantage point. The sunlight streamed in through the window, illuminating the dust into sparkly swirls. The faint music of the gramophone, a tinkly piano solo of a Gershwin melody, filtered through the walls.

At least he's alive, he's alive....

The crunch of tires against gravel startled him and sent him flying to the window; if his feet managed to touch the ground in the twelve feet between his bed and the window he was not aware of it. Andrew forced himself to look at the scene: Thomas holding the door open, the uniformed figure slowly emerging. Andrew saw one arm jut out, now the other....

Andrew's mother now appeared. She raced down the steps and towards the car, her golden-coppery mass of wild curls flinging about, creating a joyful banner heralding her mad dash to the laughing figure with outstretched arms—arms that enfolded her, hands that held her face close and stroked her hair—

"*Dad!*" Andrew's joyous shriek banished every fearful imagining into oblivion. In the twinkling of an eye, it seemed, he was outside in the sunshine, ready to fly into his father's arms. A hand caught him in mid-leap.

"Let them be together for a second." Aunt Jane held him fast. Andrew's heart nearly burst with exhilaration and relief as he watched his parents kiss: not a polite, playful peck, but an eager, exultant outpouring of love and joy and rapturous delight.

"There, Andrew, now you can greet your father." Aunt Jane released him. His father at the same time gently let go of Andrew's mother, dropped to one knee, and held his arms wide. Andrew flung himself against him and buried his face in his shoulder. His father's arms went round him.

"Sorry, old chap," his father murmured. "I'm just a little tired. I hope you don't mind if I don't pick you up."

Andrew collapsed again against his father as waves of bliss coursed through him.

"Come now, dear boy, Hitler *let* our army get away. No doubt about it." Freddie downed his wine and refilled his glass. He pointed the wine bottle across the table at Andrew's father in an indifferent offer to fill his glass as well, and was met with a wordless refusal. He continued. "What other explanation is there? He ordered his tanks to halt ten miles from Dunkirk."

"What possible reason could Hitler have for wanting the BEF to get away?" Aunt Gwen stabbed at a slice of ham.

"Dear girl, precisely what I've been saying all along: Hitler *wants* to make peace with us. He let the BEF be evacuated as a gesture of goodwill. He doesn't want to fight us; he could have annihilated our army, but he didn't want to rub our noses in defeat."

"I don't think so, Freddie," Aunt Jane said.

"What's your theory, Jane dear? Do you think the Germans were too afraid to fight? Afraid of going in for the kill after they had completely surrounded the BEF—come now!"

Andrew's father pressed his palms together. "I think the swiftness of the German advance through France took even Hitler by surprise. I don't think he or his generals ever expected it would be quite that easy, that the British army would be cut off, and they were a little nervous. For one thing, the area around Dunkirk is quite marshy, not very good country for tanks to fight in, and I think Hitler was terrified at the thought of his armored divisions getting bogged down there. I believe that conquering France was his primary objective and he wanted to save his tanks for the final thrust."

Freddie snorted. "It's true that Hitler wanted to trounce the Frogs, but he could have wiped out our army as well. Piece of cake. France was merely a show of strength. He wants to make peace with us, and that is precisely why he let our army get away. This whole fiasco was nothing more than a game—"

"The Luftwaffe was not playing games, Freddie. They were bombing and strafing our men on the beaches, and sinking the boats that were trying to evacuate them."

"Well, Hitler was just letting Goering have a bit of fun, that's all."

"Goering may be a pompous twit, but I think he managed to convince Hitler that he could destroy the British army with his Luftwaffe. That's why Hitler didn't send the tanks against our army."

"It's obvious, dear boy, that you refuse to see this as a gesture of conciliation. Hitler has made it clear all along that he admires the English, and he wants to work together with us for peace and order, not fight us." Freddie threw his napkin down in disgust. "Churchill's the problem. Winnie loves the Frogs, though they've shown nothing but contempt for us. We never should have allied ourselves with them. Doing so was a slap in the face to Germany."

"We were allied with France before Churchill came to power," Andrew's mother pointed out.

"Churchill may not have been in power, but he was still a troublemaker. Now that he's got a crown on his head, he's determined to foist his hatreds and belligerent proclivities onto the British people, with no thought at all of the consequences. All of that blather about fighting on beaches, fighting on the landing grounds, fighting in the streets—did you know that—" Freddie broke into that annoying wheezy chuckle. "After Winnie had finished his speech, he covered the microphone with his hand and muttered 'And we'll hit them over the head with beer bottles, which is about all we've got left.'"

"Freddie, *really!*" Gram said.

"Vickie darling, do you doubt me? I have it on good authority. Maurice's cousin works at the BBC."

"I don't think Mr. Churchill would—"

"*Mr.* Churchill is nothing but a brandy-swilling, cigar-chomping, boorish, bombastic, tin-plated despot with delusions of grandeur," Freddie snapped. "And if he's not stopped, he's going to get us all killed."

"Freddie..." Gram threw a wary glance in Andrew's direction. "I don't thing we should be discussing this in front of—"

"And why shouldn't we?" Freddie glared at Andrew. "It's the children who are going to inherit the mess their elders make of the world, and if they can learn from the mistakes of the past, they won't repeat them in the future."

Andrew bit his lip and stared down at his plate, conscious that all eyes were upon him. There was an interminable silence, which was finally broken by Freddie taking a quick gulp of wine and setting his glass down with a thump. "Speaking of mistakes, the biggest error Winnie has made thus far is that he expects America will help us, and that delusion will be his fatal undoing, and ours. He loves the Yanks just as much as he loves the Frogs, and his misplaced affections will prove disastrous. The French whine about how we've failed them, but it was our alliance with France that nearly proved fatal to us, had it not been for Hitler's mercy. And America is not going to lift a finger to help us if we're stupid enough not to make peace with Germany."

"The Americans have promised to help us, Freddie," Aunt Gwen said. "President Roosevelt gave a speech a few days ago, didn't he? He promised to—to—"

"'Extend to the opponents of force the material resources of this nation.'" Andrew's father pronounced.

"Hah!" Freddie hooted. "Well, Rosie's political career is finished, that's for certain. The American people won't stand for it—not one person in twenty there wants the United States to aid Britain. Oh, Roosevelt might find a way to send us some obsolete, useless equipment as a token of support, and most Americans might not object to selling supplies to us, for a price, that is. I think that the United States is going to sit back and watch, and profit handsomely in the meantime. The Yanks are very clever about not missing a trick, and they'll pick up the pieces in the end."

"Things can change," Andrew's father said.

"Right, things *can* change. For one thing, this happens to be a presidential election year in Yankland, and Winnie's friend is going to find himself out of a job. And if Hitler chooses to invade us, we might go down fighting, but we'll go down, and any help that Winnie expects to be forthcoming from the Yanks will come too late."

"Hitler could never expect to invade us by sea," Gwen rejoined. "Even if he did manage to get his army across the Channel—which would be impossible anyway because he doesn't have the proper boats to do the job—the RAF and the Royal Navy would cut it to ribbons. Besides, we have our troops to beat back any enemy soldiers who did manage to get onto the beaches—"

"What are they going to fight them back with—Elizabethan pikes and broomsticks? If the Germans have air superiority, invasion will be a piece of cake," Freddie declared.

"They *won't* have air superiority," Andrew's father said.

"Oh no, not if you can help it, dear boy," Freddie scoffed. "Oh, Roger, I don't intend to disparage your marvelous Fighter Command; after all, you boys really put on a jolly good show over Dunkirk, at least that's what Winnie tells us. What did he call you, now? Noble knights, that's it! He compared the pilots of Fighter Command to the Knights of the Round Table and the Crusaders—charming! You can tell your grand-children all about it! But face facts, dear boy, Fighter Command is no match for the Luftwaffe. That was proven in France."

"Nothing was proven in France. It was just an opportunity to learn from our mis-takes."

"Ever the optimist, Roger. Sorry to disappoint you, but everyone knows that the ME-109 is far superior to the Hurricane and Spitfire, and the ME-110 is the best fighter plane of all, with its high speed and long range. And look how the Stukas made mince-meat of everything on the ground. Our Royal Air Force doesn't stand a chance."

"If Goering thinks that his Luftwaffe is going to beat the RAF, he's in for a nasty shock."

"Oh, Roger, do you know something we don't know? Tell us, please—it's not on to keep secrets. If the RAF is going to trounce the Luftwaffe, at least let us know how, and with what, they intend to do it."

Andrew's father eyed Freddie with contempt.

"Dear boy, keep your secrets, then," Freddie snapped. "It's no secret that the Yanks are going to elect a new president this year, and that Jew-loving Roosevelt is going to be out of a job. We should be able to dispose of our Prime Minister so easily, the Yank-loving megalomaniac. Well, what can one expect—he's half-Yank himself!"

"Churchill?" Aunt Gwen exclaimed.

"Yes he is, a half-breed, didn't you know? His mother's American. In fact, she's part American Indian. One-sixteenth Iroquois, to be precise. God help us! Wonder what other mongrel bloodlines he's got! Pity it wasn't the other way around!"

"What do you mean?" Aunt Gwen asked.

"Well, if his mother had been English, and his father American, it'd be the Yanks who'd be stuck with him! America!" Freddie spat the word with disgust. "Land of wogs, mongrels, and half-breeds; from sea to shining sea infested with gangsters, corrupt politicians, tobacco-spitting cowboys, and inbred, imbecilic hillbillies. They're going to sit tight, and pick up the pieces when it's all over. Mark my words, the Yanks will not give us one penny in aid, and not one drop of American blood will be spilled on European soil."

After lunch, Freddie stumbled off to the study while everyone else withdrew to the drawing room. Sitting on the sofa, nestled against his father, Andrew listened to everybody's reassurances about the ability of Britain's armed forces to repulse an invasion by the Nazis.

"Europe was one thing—wide open for attack; it was a piece of cake for the Nazis to attack in any direction." Aunt Jane said. "Poland is like a giant soccer field—no natural boundaries to deter any aggressor. And France, well, the Germans violated the neutrality of Belgium and took a gamble on the Ardennes. So as France and Poland each shared such a long land boundary with Germany, theirs was a difficult position from the start. We're protected by the sea."

"So was Norway," Andrew countered.

"Norway was different," Andrew's father said.

"How?"

"Well, for one thing, we're prepared. We're expecting the Germans to attack. Hitler's chief weapon was surprise." Andrew's father closed his eyes and slumped backwards.

Aunt Gwen got up and took Andrew by the hand. "Come on, Andrew. Let's let your father rest for awhile."

"What's the matter?" Andrew said, alarmed.

"Just a bit tired, old chap," Andrew's father reassured him. "And Mrs. Tuttle's cooking is so wonderfully filling—the wonders she does, even with rationing! I'm just going to relax a bit and let my lunch digest."

"I think the wine was especially strong, too," Aunt Jane said. "I'm feeling a bit light-headed myself. It certainly put Freddie out—thank God he managed to haul himself off to the study on his own, for a change."

Andrew's father nodded absently and Andrew suddenly remembered: His father had not had wine with his meal, just water.

"Come on, Andrew." Aunt Jane put her hand on Andrew's shoulder. "Let's play a game of chess." She led him away. Andrew's mother, Gram, and Aunt Gwen followed.

Aunt Jane set up the chessboard in her room. Andrew tried to concentrate on the game, but after fifteen moves, Aunt Jane leaned back, folded her arms, fixed her eyes on Andrew for a moment, then glared at the board. Andrew looked at the board and saw that he was about to be checkmated in two moves.

"Andrew, are you letting your squiffy old aunt win?" Aunt Jane gently teased.

"You're not old—twenty-nine isn't old. And you're not squiffy, either. Neither is Dad."

"Well, we're exactly the same age, that's true, so if he's not old, then I'm not either.

"That's not what I meant. Dad's not squiffy. He didn't drink any wine."

Aunt Jane looked tenderly at Andrew. "Your father just needed to rest, that's all." Seeing as that failed to reassure him, she prompted, "Why don't we read some more of *Huckleberry Finn*?" She glanced about her room. "Oh dear, I think I put it back in the library."

"I'll go get it," Andrew volunteered.

"All right—I'll stack up the pillows on my bed."

Andrew ambled down the hall, down the stairs, and into the front hallway. Freddie's snores emanated from the study, and the distant voices of his mother, Gram, and Aunt Gwen filtered out from the conservatory at the far end of the hall. He was about to open the door to the library when he glanced behind him at the closed door to the drawing room.

I'll just open it ever so quietly—I just want to see him!

He crossed the hall, stood for a moment by the drawing room door, and slowly turned the doorknob. Peeking in, he saw his father's form slumped on the sofa: He was lying on his back, his face slack and expressionless. Tiptoeing over to him, Andrew gazed at his motionless form. He seemed so peaceful, so free of worry and care....

Something was wrong. It registered on Andrew's brain as something different from what he remembered when he had left the room just a little while ago. What?

What?

Andrew systematically surveyed his father from head to toe, and his sense of disquiet increased. Think! *THINK!* He felt as if he were looking at a puzzle in an activity book: *What is the difference between these two pictures?*

Then he realized: At dinner, his father had been wearing a shirt that was light grey, a color that matched his eyes. This shirt was—

Red!

No, not completely red—the bottom part of his right sleeve was the same light grey as before. Andrew watched in horror as the crimson stain seeped downward; then his gaze swept up to his father's face. It was very, very pale, and Andrew's knees trembled as he realized how very still his father's body was. Absolutely motionless...horribly, horribly bloodstained.

A rushing noise filled his ears, the room swirled around him; he heard shrieks, and realized they were his own. His legs collapsed under him, and he felt himself tumbling into a numbing darkness.

Chapter 4

Someone was singing softly, in a foreign language—French. The melody was familiar, a lullaby Andrew remembered from distant childhood, and the voice was familiar, too. He felt a hand brush his forehead and stroke his hair; then his face was pressed against someone's shoulder as he was clasped in a tender embrace. The singing stopped, and Andrew fretted, for he wanted it to continue.

"There, there, you've had a terrible shock," Aunt Jane soothed.

"*Dad!*" The vision of his father's body, still and bloodsoaked, jerked Andrew to full consciousness. "He's dead, he's *dead!*" he screamed.

"Not at all, old chap." His father's voice broke though his cries. "Just a little scratched, that's all. I'm fine."

Andrew twisted around to see his father slumped in a semi-reclined position on the sofa as Aunt Gwen hovered over him. She pressed a blood soaked-towel against his shoulder. Andrew's mother knelt next to him, her arm slipped under his head so that it was cradled gently.

"Mum, get me some more towels, please." Aunt Gwen turned to Gram, who was standing next to Andrew's mother.

"What the bloody hell was all that yelling about?" Freddie stood in the doorway, glowering.

"Sorry to disturb your nap, Freddie," Gwen said. "Can't have a homecoming without a little excitement." Freddie, blanching at the sight of Andrew's father, made a quick exit.

"If you feel like fainting, Freddie, find yourself a place where you won't do too much damage on your way down," Aunt Gwen called after him. "And don't go spewing all over the place either—one mess is enough!"

"Gwen, you're positively awful," Andrew's father said. "Are you that nasty with all your patients? You no doubt terrorize them into getting better!"

"Gwendolyn the Ghastly, that's what they call me," Aunt Gwen replied. "Well, be thankful that I'm an angel of mercy, because they wouldn't have released you so soon had I not sworn to minister to you. And now look what you've done—gone and made a bloody mess all over the place! Matron would have my head if she heard about this!"

"You're an angel, that's for certain, Gwen." Andrew's father smiled at her. Then he looked at Andrew and his face filled with remorse. "Andrew, I'm sorry. I should have told you, but I didn't want you to worry."

Andrew squirmed out of Aunt Jane's embrace and stumbled over to his father. He stood, swaying slightly, still feeling a bit stunned and dazed. "I thought you were dead," he whispered.

"I'm all right, really. It's just a flesh wound, that's all."

"More towels." Gram handed Aunt Gwen a stack of hand towels.

"I should have had you change the dressing right after lunch," Andrew's father told Gwen. "I shouldn't have dozed off like that."

"Those pain pills made you a bit groggy, that's all." Gwen held the towel against his shoulder. "Looks like the bleeding's stopped, but just lie there awhile, then we'll get you into the kitchen so I can put a new dressing on you. Perhaps we can press Freddie into service—"

"Freddie needs more assistance than I do in getting around right now—leave him be." Andrew's father sat up a little more and took a deep breath. "I'm just fine. Let's go." Winking at Andrew, he swung his legs to the floor. He then stood, slowly but deliberately, and walked unaided to the doorway. Gram, Aunt Gwen, and Andrew's mother followed him.

Andrew slumped against the couch and tried to stifle a sob. Aunt Jane's arms went around him. He turned and burrowed his face against her shoulder.

"There, there, darling, everything's all right," she soothed.

"I thought he was dead. There was blood all over him—" Andrew hiccupped, his voice then breaking into convulsive sobs. Aunt Jane rocked him, and his cries subsided.

"Well, your father should be tidied up by now. Do you want to see him?"

Andrew wiped his cheeks and nodded. Then he realized: Not only was his face wet....

"Oh no," he groaned.

"What's the matter, darling?"

Andrew pulled her face close to his and whispered in her ear: "I wet my pants."

"Andrew, don't worry. It's nothing to be upset about. It often happens when people faint. Let's go upstairs and you can change."

Andrew shook his head. His worst fear was that they would encounter Freddie enroute, who would never let him live down this humiliating episode.

"Please, bring me some clean clothes and I'll change here. I don't want anyone to know."

"All right." Aunt Jane kissed his cheek and got up.

"Close the door."

Andrew crouched as he waited for her to return, listening intently for any sounds of Freddie approaching. In a few minutes the door opened, and Aunt Jane handed him a clean change of clothes.

"I'll stand guard at the door while you get dressed," she told him.

He changed, bundled his soiled clothes into a ball, and tapped on the door.

"Is it clear?" he asked.

"Clear," Aunt Jane affirmed.

He cautiously opened the door. Seeing no one except Aunt Jane, he made a mad dash across the hall and up the stairs, in order to conceal the embarrassing evidence as best as he could. After stuffing the wet clothing under the rest of his clothes in his closet hamper, he returned down the stairs.

"All set?" Aunt Jane put her arm around Andrew and walked with him to the kitchen, where they stood in the doorway, unnoticed.

Andrew's father was seated on a high-backed stool; Aunt Gwen, assisted by Andrew's mother and Gram, was putting the finishing touches on a fresh bandage.

"Tape," Aunt Gwen pronounced. Gram peeled off a length from a roll and Andrew's mother snipped it off with a pair of scissors. Aunt Gwen grabbed it and applied it to the bandage. "Well, that should do it."

Andrew's father inspected her handiwork and smiled in approval. "And to think that I tried to talk you out of going into nursing, Gwen. First-rate."

"Now, put your shirt on," Gwen told him. "You keep flaunting your handsome physique like that and you'll send all the ladies into wild imaginings."

"*Wild imaginings*—now that's a thought," Andrew's mother laughed as she helped him into his shirt.

Aunt Gwen rolled her eyes; then she sternly eyed Andrew's parents. "Now, no cricket, soccer, rugger, and none of *that* either, you two," she ordered, as she watched Andrew's mother unbuttoning the buttons as soon as his father had fastened them. She groaned in exasperation. "Just go easy on him, Alice."

"I've never been too rough on you, have I, darling?" Andrew's mother teased.

"Have I ever complained?" he replied. They gazed at each other adoringly for a moment, then kissed.

Aunt Jane cleared her throat. Andrew's father turned quickly. "Andrew, come here." He rebuttoned his shirt and held out the cuffs to Andrew.

Andrew shuffled over to him and, without a word, fastened the cuffs.

"Thanks, old chap."

Andrew raised his eyes to him. His father nodded at Andrew's mother and Aunt Gwen, and they quickly departed with Aunt Jane and Gram. As soon as they were out of the room, Andrew collapsed into his father's arms.

"Andrew, it's all right. I'm so sorry I gave you such a scare." His father held him close and stroked his hair.

Andrew closed his eyes as he was assaulted with hideous images of carnage and destruction. He had always been so proud of his father, had always thrilled to imagine him soaring through a paradise far above the ordinary world, and had thought that the business of being a fighter pilot was ever so glamorous and noble. Now he realized that there was nothing glamorous at all about it: It was a bloody, savage, dangerous, brutal occupation. There was absolutely nothing noble about getting blown to smithereens miles above the earth. The sky was not a place of heavenly beauty and thrilling aerobatics and wondrous deeds. It was a place of terrible butchery and appallingly sudden death.

It was a slaughterhouse.

If only his father didn't have to go back! If only there were a way he could stay! Andrew groaned as he remembered how much he'd dreaded his father coming back minus an arm, a cripple. As awful as that was, at least it would have prevented any possibility of him returning to action. Better to go through life minus a limb or two than to—

His body shook convulsively and he pressed his face against his father's chest in a silent scream.

There are many who would hold an inquest in the House of Commons on the conduct of the Governments—and of Parliaments, for they are in it too—during the years which led up to this catastrophe. They seek to indict those who were responsible for the guidance of our affairs—

"We could start with you, Winnie," Freddie said.
"Hush," warned Gram.

...This also would be a foolish and pernicious process—

"On the contrary, I think it's an excellent idea," countered Freddie. Aunt Jane glared at him. Andrew's mother turned up the volume on the radio.

Of this I am quite sure, that if we open a quarrel between the past and the present, we shall find that we have lost the future....

"We'll lose it for certain, if we don't get rid of that warmongering sot—"
"Freddie, shut up," Aunt Gwen snapped.

...We abate nothing of our just demands; not one jot or tittle do we recede...Czechs, Poles, Norwegians, Dutch, Belgians, have joined their causes to our own....

"Why don't we throw in a batch of Pygmies, a horde of Untouchables, and a few cross-eyed Chinamen while we're at it—"

What General Weygand called the Battle of France is over. I expect that the Battle of Britain is about to begin. Upon this battle depends the survival of Christian civilization. Upon it depends our own British life, and the long continuity of our institutions and our Empire. The whole fury and might of the enemy must very soon be turned on us. Hitler knows that he will have to break us in this island or lose the war. If we can stand up to him, all Europe many be free and the life of the world may move forward into broad, sunlit uplands—

"Broad, sunlit uplands! What a load of rubbish!"
"Freddie—" Aunt Jane said.

"I think sunny, uplit broadlands sounds better—or what about upward, broadlit sunlands—"

"Stuff it!" Aunt Jane savagely cut him off.

But if we fail, then the whole world, including the United States, including all that we have known and cared for, will sink into the abyss of a new dark age made more sinister, and perhaps more protracted, by the lights of perverted science—

"*Perverted* science! Winnie must have been deep in his cups to have come up with that one!

Let us therefore brace ourselves to our duties, and so bear ourselves that, if the British Empire and its Commonwealth last for a thousand years, men will still say, "This was their finest hour."

Freddie let out an audible hiss of disgust. "God stone the crows! That is the most *appalling* barrage of drivel I have *ever* heard! I need a drink!" he exploded. He lurched to the liquor cabinet and pulled out a decanter of brandy, which he waved around for a few seconds in an unenthusiastic offer to share it. Seeing that no acceptances were forthcoming, he grabbed a glass from the bar, and sloshed it full of the amber liquor.

Holding his glass of brandy aloft, he pronounced: "A toast!" He cleared his throat. "A toast—to broad, sunlit uplands, and to finest hours, and to the destruction of perverted science and monstrous tyranny never surpassed in the dark, lamentable catalogue of human crime—oh, sorry, wrong speech—they *do* tend to all sound the same don't they? Well, after the Germans boot Winnie out and set up a proper, sensible government, we ought to at least keep him around for amusement, shouldn't we?"

"Well, it's happened—I guess it was just a matter of time," Thomas sadly observed. He held the newspaper at arm's length; whether it was to accommodate his far-sightedness or to put a greater distance between himself and the awful words glaring forth from the front page—*French Sign Armistice*—Andrew wasn't quite sure. Aunt Jane and Andrew's father had departed earlier to "take a walk," and Andrew knew that they would not be back for hours. His mother and Aunt Gwen were chatting in the drawing room; Aunt Gwen was giving last-minute instructions on the proper method of changing a dressing. She would be returning to London the next day, as Andrew had overheard her explaining to his mother: "Matron was so kind to let me take a week off to take care of Roger, but I really must be getting back. They've been so busy what with caring for the wounded from Dunkirk, and now we've got to be ready in case Hitler starts bombing London. We have to prepare for the worst."

Prepare for the worst. The words ran through Andrew's mind as he read, with Thomas, the terms of surrender the French had been forced to acquiesce to: the occupation of Paris, the setting up a German zone of control along the Channel and Atlantic coasts; the handing over to the Nazis all arms, munitions, military stores, and installations; the demobilization and disarming of the French army; the surrender of French warships into German or Italian control; the release of all German prisoners of war who were being held on French soil; payment by France for the cost of German occupation....

"Who could have ever imagined it would come to this?" Thomas shook his head.

"Are you having a LDV meeting tonight, dear?" Mrs. Tuttle asked.

"Yes, and we're not going to be named Local Defense Volunteers anymore. We're going to be called the Home Guard."

"Home Guard—that has a nice ring to it." Mrs. Tuttle clucked.

"Whatever they call us, we still can't do very much good, fighting with pitchforks and broomsticks."

Andrew wandered disconsolately down the stairs. It was well past his bedtime and the house was completely dark, except for a ribbon of light showing under the door to the library. It couldn't be Freddie within, for loud snores emanated from his bedroom. And if his mother were up late, reading, she would be in bed. Aunt Jane and Gram preferred to read in their rooms, too.

He opened the door a crack and peered in.

"Hullo, old chap." His father's face brightened. As Andrew shuffled over to him, his father picked up the leather bookmark from the table beside him, placed it in the book he was reading, and snapped it shut.

"The most useful and wonderful gift I've ever received," he said with a smile. "Now how many people have their own personal bookmark, lovingly made by the finest son any man could hope for?" He held his arms wide.

Andrew snuggled into his embrace.

"Couldn't sleep, old chap?"

Andrew nodded. His father rocked him gently and pressed him tight to his chest.

"I love you, Dad," Andrew whispered.

"I love you, too, Andrew."

His father looked into his eyes and spoke, almost inaudibly, the words, "March fourth."

"Why did you say my birthday?"

"Because it was the happiest day of my life."

"What about when you married Mum?"

"Oh, that was the happiest day of my life—until the day you were born."

"What did you say when I was born?"

His father smiled at him. "To tell the truth, I don't recall saying anything. I was quite speechless."

"Why?"

His father smiled even more broadly. "I'll tell you about it someday."

Andrew snuggled closer to him. "What did Mum say, I mean, what was the first thing she said to you?"

"Well, she was speechless, too, for awhile. She held you, and then she asked me what I wanted to name you."

"And you said Andrew, right?"

His father looked up for a second, then pursed his lips as if he were suppressing a laugh. "Well, I had wanted to name you Charles, after my brother."

"Charles!"

"Yes, but I can't imagine, now, calling you Charlie."

Andrew frowned. "It's not a bad name, but I don't think it matches me."

"Quite right, old chap. Andrew suits you perfectly."

"Because he was your best friend—Sparky was, I mean?"

"Well, that too. I just thought that Andrew was a very—" His father paused, as if searching around for the right word. "Good name."

"Why?"

His father chuckled. "I'll tell you about *that* some other time, too."

Andrew sighed and closed his eyes.

"What's the matter, old chap?"

Andrew debated whether he should tell what was burdening his heart and strangling his soul. His father shook him ever so tenderly. "Tell me, old chap." It was more a plea than a command.

Andrew opened his mouth; then a sob caught in his throat. He clamped his mouth shut and his body convulsed in a spasm of terror. "I don't—want you to—go—back," he sputtered, as the tears gushed forth.

His father held him close until his trembling subsided and his anguished cries turned to soft groans. Spent and limp with exhaustion, Andrew allowed himself to collapse completely into his father's tender embrace. He felt every last bit of strength draining from him; even breathing was a chore. Then he heard his father's voice, very soft and even.

"It would be foolish of me to try to give you a guarantee, Andrew. Even if there wasn't a war, I couldn't do that. Anything can happen, anytime. Freddie's father fell down the stairs, and broke his neck. And anything is possible, in spite of how bad things may seem. Dunkirk, for instance. We thought our army was lost—look what happened! Andrew, don't give in to despair!" He shook Andrew gently, then hugged him tight. "Look, you're fearing the worst right now—I know you've had a terrible scare. Remember what Churchill said: He said that if we opened a quarrel between the past and the present, we would lose the future. Well, the same thing goes for allowing fear and despair to control us—only we lose the present, as well as the future. It's all right to be...upset, sometimes. I certainly don't want you to keep things bottled up. There's a time to cry, and a time to hope. Now it's time to hope—let me tell you why." He repositioned Andrew on his lap, so that they were face to face, and gazed into Andrew's eyes. "The better you are at something, old chap, the better the chance will be that you will succeed at that particular endeavor. Take boxing, for instance. If I brought you to a boxing match, and you knew that one of the contestants had never boxed before, and the other one had years of experience, which one do you think would win?"

Andrew took a deep breath. "The one with more experience, I suppose."

"You suppose?"

Andrew nodded. His father smiled at him. "Well, you're right. You're right about supposing, too. You can't be absolutely certain, but you can be reasonably sure that the chap with more experience will win."

"The German pilots have a lot of experience—they fought in Spain years ago."

"Some of them did, yes. It gave them experience, and an opportunity to develop the most effective tactics, so they could train other pilots. But in France, they had to give away their secrets. One can learn from one's friends, but learning from one's opponents is even better. The Germans have some experienced pilots, but quite a few inexperienced ones, too. Now, I've been a pilot for eleven years. That's a long time, longer than you've been around, and look how much you've learned in your nine years. I've been a fighter pilot for two years, and I've been in France. That's given me the kind of experience that really counts, and I can train other pilots now."

"Freddie said that the Luftwaffe has better planes. He says the ME 109s and 110s, and the Stukas are superior to our planes."

His father smiled, but said nothing. Andrew pressed his query again. "Are they better?"

"Can't give away military secrets, old chap. I'll tell you, though, Freddie's not even half right. Next question."

"Do you think the Germans are going to win?"

His father's gray eyes at first registered mild surprise, then regarded him thoughtfully. "What do you mean by win?"

Andrew was perturbed at his father's request to define his terms. After all, *win* was a very obvious word. "Well, do you think they're going to invade England? And will we be able to defeat them in the end?"

"Aha—a two-part question. Well, no to the first one, and yes to the second. The first one will not be as easy as the Germans might think; the second will not be as easy as we might think."

"What do you mean?"

"I think that the fact that we are fighting for our own country now is a factor the Germans haven't considered. It's something that I had not realized until Dunkirk."

"That was in France."

"But it was our men. To me, Dunkirk was more English than England. Over two hundred thousand Englishmen in a few square miles—can't get any more British than that! For the first time, I felt cold, savage fury at the thought of the Luftwaffe trying to kill my fellow countrymen. Now anger can sometimes make you careless and defeat you, if you allow it to muddle your thinking. Or it can give you an edge, a significant edge, over your opponent. Now, as to how all this relates to your question about whether or not the Germans are going to invade—no, I don't think they are. The Luftwaffe has to gain air superiority first, and the fact that we are going to be defending our own country is going to make us a bit angry. I call it the 'fury factor'. What I experienced was cold-blooded rage, pure and simple, and it was a disconcerting, and sobering, experience for me to realize that I could feel that way. I wondered if, all along, this monster had been inside of me. Yet it reassured me immensely that the fury I felt provided me with the most intense concentration and heightened ability."

"But you still got shot."

"True. It was just a flesh wound, though—could have been worse. And it happened, not when I was angry, but when I was a bit cocky. We had finished our patrol and were returning home. I had just shot down a Stuka in full view of the men on the beach, and was feeling quite proud of myself. And I thought I was safe, too. In France, our flight commander gave us a lesson. He posed the question: What is the most dangerous time on patrol? He got every answer—take-off, sighting of enemy aircraft, engagement—all except the right one: *All the time* is the most dangerous time. As he said: 'It's not the ones I see that worry me, it's the ones I *don't* see.'"

"You didn't even *see* the plane that hit you?"

"I saw the tracer from his machine guns. I turned as quickly as I could, just as he opened up with his cannons. That's what's so great about the Hurricane: It's the most marvelous turning aeroplane! It can turn circles around a 109, and it can even make a tighter turn than a Spit. So if you get into trouble, all you have to do is turn out of it. I almost got away, but one of the shells hit the armor plating behind my seat. Fighter Command's pilots are well protected—the German fighter pilots don't have back armor. If they take a hit, that's usually the end of them."

"Then how did you get hurt?"

"Some shell fragments scattered around the cockpit, and one of them caught me in the shoulder. I didn't even realize it at first; I was just so startled by it all. I got a glimpse of the 109 heading back to France—probably low on fuel. That's the problem with the 109: It doesn't have much range, so it can't get very far from base for too long."

It still bothered Andrew that his father hadn't seen the 109 *before* he was hit.

"You ought to put a rear-view mirror in your Hurricane. So you can see if anyone's behind you."

His father winked at him. "Brilliant idea old chap! You ought to be on the design staff at Hawker's."

Andrew couldn't help but smile. How like his father to turn the most distressing conversation into a way to praise him! Andrew knew that his father had already thought of the idea himself, and that reassured him even more. He snuggled into his father's embrace again. His father was silent for a moment, then spoke.

"Well, I learned my lesson that day, old chap. Once you take to the air, you can't drop your guard, even for a second. The pilot who does may live to tell the tale—as I did—or he might not be so lucky. I won't make that mistake again; you can be sure of that. Even if there are no enemy fighters around, it's possible to make a fatal mistake. One of our best pilots killed himself buzzing his own airfield. For him, showing off was the most dangerous time—there wasn't a German plane within miles. So you see, even your old man can learn a thing or two."

"You're not old!" Andrew protested.

"I'm going to be thirty soon."

"Thirty's not old!"

"If you say so, old chap! I shall make a note of that: thirty's not old!"

"And when I turn thirty, *you* can remind *me*!"

"That's the spirit, old chap!"

Andrew laughed, and his father's deep chuckle provided an easeful counterpoint. Then he yawned, and his father whispered, "Time for bed, old chap."

Andrew threw his arms around his neck. "Please, please, can I sleep with you to-night—just once!"

His father considered his suggestion, and Andrew pleaded, "Just once, please!"

"All right. Let me write your mother a note. I'll tape it to the mirror in our room, so she won't think I've run off and joined the French Foreign Legion or something."

"Or gone to America and become a cowboy!"

"Have to learn to rope a steer first."

"And spit tobacco—just like all the rest of the Yanks!"

His father raised one eyebrow and evinced a worried frown.

Andrew laughed again. "Just joking!"

"About what? Me, or 'all the Yanks' spitting tobacco?"

"Both!"

"All right, then. Well, let's get to bed, shall we?"

Andrew hopped off his father's lap, stood in front of him, hands on hips, and re-minded him, "Note to Mum, first."

"Right." His father pulled open a drawer on the table next to him, extracted pen and paper, and dashed off a note to Andrew's mother. He placed the note in his pocket, and took Andrew by the hand. They climbed the stairs together and Andrew snuggled into bed and awaited his father, who appeared after a moment and slipped under the covers next to him. As Andrew snuggled against him, he heard the soft heartbeat and allowed himself to be lulled into a blissful limbo between dreams and consciousness, where he remained for a long time, until peaceful oblivion claimed him.

He awoke early. In the pale morning light that found its way around the edges of the blackout curtain, he surveyed his father's sleeping form. His hair was tousled. A lace of thick eyelashes lay against the smooth skin of his cheeks, his lips were slightly parted, and a wisp of white gauze peeked out from under the collar of his pajama top. He lay on his side; one arm was slung across Andrew's chest. Somehow he seemed more alive in sleep than he did awake, as if his true inner self were somehow revealed only in unconsciousness. It was all goodness, and gentleness, and love; qualities that were not obscured by any means when he was awake, but that somehow found full expression when he was deep in slumber.

Andrew lay very, very still, luxuriating in the nearness to his father, soothed by the sight of him, and calmed by his touch. If *now* could go on *forever*, he thought. Always, always to have him so near.

The corners of his father's mouth twitched.

Even if he's not dreaming about me, even if in his dreams he's not even aware of me, aware that I exist, even if he's dreaming that he's someone else entirely, not my father at all, I still feel that he is more my father like this, that the bond between us is even more sure and strong....

The twitch became a spasm, the lips pressed together worriedly, and a grimace replaced the peaceful expression. Soft moans accompanied distressed, jerky movements of his arms and agitated clenching of his fists.

"Dad—wake up! Wake up!" Andrew stroked his father's face with his fingers. "Please, wake up—"

His father's eyes fluttered open and he looked about, puzzled and perturbed.

"Dad, you were having a nightmare."

His father's eyes focused on him, then closed in remorse. "I'm so sorry—I woke you—"

"No you didn't—I was already awake. I was watching you sleep and then you got ever so upset. What was your dream—tell me!"

His father looked a little stricken by Andrew's request. He closed his eyes again and took a deep breath. Then he looked at Andrew again and forced a smile.

"It's nothing, old chap."

"What was it? Were you worried about the Nazis attacking us?"

"No, not exactly, just—well, it was more feelings than being afraid of anything specifically. You know, sometimes you have those dreams in which you've somehow forgotten to go to school all year, and now it's time for examinations, and you don't even know what they're about. Haven't you had them?"

"Yes, sort of. I dreamed once that I had an examination in Norwegian, and I didn't even know it, and Mr. Nugent was ever so upset."

His father smiled. "Sometimes I dream about flying, and I'm over a strange land, and I can't figure out where I am or where I'm supposed to go."

"Sometimes I dream I'm in school, and I've forgotten to get dressed. I'm stark naked and everyone is staring at me."

"Oh, yes, that's a classic! Or what about trying to run, and your legs won't move."

"Or trying to scream, and you can't make a sound," Andrew laughed. This presenting of their various nightmares for mutual inspection and evaluation was actually quite enjoyable. How like his father to turn even distressing topics into a delightful interchange of ideas! He snuzzled his face into the broad chest, and felt strong arms embrace him again.

"Can we stay here all day?" Andrew asked.

"All day?"

"Yes, we can talk, and then have breakfast—Lucia can serve us. Then we can talk some more, then have elevensies, then lunch, then we could take a nap, or rather you could take a nap and I could watch you again."

"Well, how about staying here for a long, long time? Then we can go for a walk later on." He got out of bed, walked over to the window, and pulled back the black-out curtain. "Look—there's a lovely golden haze on the meadow. It's a beautiful morning, and it's going to be a beautiful day! We could have a picnic with Charlie—what do you say, old chap?"

"Sounds smashing!

His father got back into bed.

"Dad, you forgot to tell me about the second part to my question last night."

"What question?"

"About whether or not we're going to win the war. You told me you thought the Germans wouldn't invade us, because it would be harder than they expected because everyone here would be so mad at them for trying to invade. And then you said we would win in the end, but that it would be harder than we expected. Why?"

"Well, old chap, because we'll be trying to invade Germany, and the Germans will be fighting for their homeland, and I expect that they'll be quite furious."

"Why don't they realize that Hitler is so bad?"

"Because they don't want to, for the most part, I think."

"Why don't they want to?"

"Because they wanted someone like him to lead them, to solve their country's terrible problems. They would like to believe that their problems are the fault of others, and they're right to some extent, but not entirely. We should have figured out how to order up the world a little better after the Great War, but the Treaty of Versailles, and the burden it imposed upon the German people, was a recipe for disaster. We won the war, but lost the peace. But some of the Germans' problems were of their own doing. They made the mistake of blaming the wrong people, like the Jews, for all that's gone wrong. All in all, I think they've gotten mixed up between the ends and the means."

"The what and the what?"

"The ends—what they desired: peace, prosperity, safety, happiness, pride in themselves. Those are good things. Hitler came along and promised them all that, mixed it in with some lies about what caused the terrible state their country was in: It was the fault of the Jews, the Communists, outsiders. He sprinkled a lot of half-truths and flattery around, and was able to convince a nation of people that they could attain their heart's desires by destroying others."

"Do you think it's going to take a long time to defeat them?"

"Longer than we think, yes. It's not going to be a piece of cake."

"How are we going to do it?"

"Make a beginning, somehow."

"What kind of beginning?"

"A reciprocal course. Make the end the beginning."

"You mean France?"

"It would seem the most logical place to start. But who knows? We might have a chance to make a beginning somewhere else, too. You should always consider every possibility. For now, though, defending Britain is the most important thing."

"How long do you think it will take before we win the war?

"That depends on how much help we have."

"Do you think America is going to help us?"

"I think so."

"Then how long do you think it will take?"

"Probably a few years, at least. Then again, anything is possible. Hitler might fall down the stairs and break his neck, like Freddie's father. I hope, for everyone's sake, that it's over sooner, rather than later. But in the end, you hope for the best and you plan for the worst." His father gazed at him for a moment. "Andrew, I hope you understand that, because of the war, we need to change your—" he cleared his throat, "itinerary for this summer."

"I suppose I won't be going to France with Aunt Jane."

His remark produced a wry smile from his father.

"Well, then I'll just stay here all summer, right? Except for going to Northumberland the week before school starts, though I wouldn't mind not—"

"Andrew, you're going to Northumberland in two weeks, when I go back to my squadron."

"*All summer?* I *hate* it there! Why do I have to go?"

"Well, this comes under the heading of preparing for the worst."

"What do you mean—do you think the Nazis are going to invade?"

"I hope, and I expect, that they won't. But we can't—" His father paused. He was very still, as if he were in a trance, then he continued. "We can't discount that possibility, not completely. And for my own peace of mind, I want you away from here."

"I'll be all right here, I promise!"

"I know you would try your best, but it really is better if you—"

"I *hate* it there!"

"Grandfather Howard is dead—you won't have to worry about him."

"But Greycliff reminds me of him. It's almost just as bad, remembering him, and Grandmother Howard—."

"Surely you aren't afraid of her."

"Not afraid, no, just...Well, she reminds me of him too. And even though she's not mean, she's not nice either. She never smiles or laughs. She talks so softly all the time. She's not at all like Gram."

"Well, I think she was just as intimidated by your Grandfather as you were. And she's had a difficult life. Your uncles were—"

"That's another thing. I don't like the painting in the front hall of Mum's brothers. It's scary. It's like their eyes are staring at me wherever I am. Even when I'm not in the hall I think that they're staring at me, their ghosts are staring at me, I mean, as if they hate me."

"Andrew, they died before you were born. How can they hate you?"

"Maybe their ghosts are at Greycliff, even though they were buried in France. Sometimes at night I think that they're looking through my window and they hate me for being alive and they're going to get me and—"

"They can't hate you, Andrew. And they're not ever going to get you. You don't think Charlie hates you, surely?"

"Charlie was a baby—he can't hate. But Mum's brothers—"

"They wouldn't hate you either. You're a part of them, just as you're a part of Charlie. They died before they had a chance to even begin living their lives, and I'd like to think that they're happy watching you grow up. They never had any children of their own, and I believe that they have a very special concern for you because you're all that's left, except for your mother, of the Howard family. I'd like to think that they're watching out for you, like guardian angels, and that every time you visit Greycliff, they're happy to see you, just as Charlie is happy when we visit him."

"I still don't like Greycliff—it's a horrid, spooky place. It's not like a home at all. It's more like a giant castle or musty old museum or something. It's too big."

"You know, as much as I felt uncomfortable around Grandfather Howard, I never thought of Greycliff as a horrid place. Do you know why?"

"Why?"

"Because three wonderful things happened there: Your mother was born there, you were born there, and I also met your mother there."

"You met Mum there?"

His father smiled.

"How did you meet, exactly? Did you get introduced?"

"It was at a party. I was invited by one of my flying students to be her escort, because her fiance was away at—oh, dear, I seem to recall it was a funeral. Friend of the family or something. Well, this woman whom I escorted, my pupil, was a good friend of your mother's."

"What sort of party was it? Was it someone's birthday or something special?"

His father cleared his throat and replied, "Oh, your grandfather always had parties, very lavish affairs, for all sorts of reasons." Something about the abruptness of his answer gave Andrew the impression that there was something about this particular party he did not wish to divulge. Andrew decided it would be best not to press the matter.

"Mum must have been the prettiest one there."

His father smiled again.

"Where did you meet? Was it in the hall, or the drawing room?"

"In the ballroom. It was being used for a dance, and your grandfather had hired an orchestra."

"What happened? Did you get introduced by Mum's friend?"

"Well, we saw each other across the room, and then Mum's friend introduced us."

"Then what happened?"

"Your mother asked me to dance."

"She did?"

"That's right."

"When did this happen?"

"After we were introduced."

"No, I mean, when was this party?"

"Oh, it was in the summer, two years before you were born, so it was 1929."

"So Mum was seventeen when you met. You were already at Oxford, weren't you?"

"Yes, but I was on summer holiday, giving flying lessons at an aerodrome in Northumberland."

"What did you talk about?"

"Oh, the usual things people tend to talk about when they're introduced—who they are, what they like doing, things like that."

"Suppose you didn't want to dance with her, for some reason, or suppose it was someone else who asked you to dance and you didn't like her, would you have to dance with her if she asked you?"

His father laughed. "Why are you worried about something like that, Andrew?"

"Suppose you didn't like her, or she was ugly—

"Ugly!"

"Well, you know—"

"I don't think you should judge people on appearances. There are many physically attractive people who are not so nice on the inside, and many people who may not appear attractive who are actually very good."

"Well, suppose you just didn't want to—would you have to dance with someone who asked you, just because they asked you?"

"'Have to'? No, you don't *have* to. But it's the decent thing to do, if someone asks you. Think of how you would feel, if you asked a girl to dance and she refused you, saying she didn't like you or she thought you were ugly or something like that. Wouldn't you be hurt?"

"I suppose."

His father smiled. "Do you know what, old chap? I think—" He brushed back a lock of Andrew's hair. "I think that someday, a girl will ask *you* to dance."

"*Crikey!*" Andrew exclaimed. "Can you read the future?"

His father picked up the glass snow-scene globe resting on Andrew's night table; it had a miniature Eiffel Tower within, and, when shaken, produced a snowstorm of white flecks. Peering into its depths, his father pronounced somberly, "I can see it, old chap— there's a girl asking you to dance. Don't you see?"

Andrew shook his head.

"You don't see it?"

Andrew shook his head again, then smiled at his father. "Will I accept?"

His father looked at him with a grave expression and said, "Of course you will."

"What if she's ugly and has a wart on her nose and a mustache and three legs?"

His father squinted at the globe. "I don't see her with a wart on her nose and a mustache—oh, she *does* have three legs, but you're managing quite well!"

"No!" Andrew chortled.

His father shook his head. "Sorry, old chap—things got a bit blurry. Not to worry, she only has two legs!"

"What if I refuse?"

"I don't see you refusing. Look—you're dancing with her!"

"I am?"

His father nodded.

Andrew peered into the globe.

"Will I marry her?"

His father's face puzzled; then he pursed his lips. "Sorry, old chap, can't tell. The crystal's gone dark."

Andrew eyed his father. "What if I don't want to dance with her?"

His father put his arm around him. "If someone offers you friendship, even if it's just for a dance, it's unkind to refuse. After all, it doesn't necessarily mean you have to get married to that person, though that's what happened with your mother and me. The point is, you should never throw away the possibility of friendship—with any-one, if they take that first step toward you. And you should always be open to taking that first step of friendship toward others. I don't think I would have ever asked your mother to dance, and if she hadn't asked me, you and I wouldn't be having this little chat right now."

"Crikey!"

"So you see, I consider Greycliff a special place. When you're there, think of your mother and me, meeting there, in the ballroom."

Andrew smiled and snuggled close to his father again. His mother and father, meet-ing there, falling in love, getting, married, then having him....

All of a sudden, he experienced a peculiar sort of vexation as he realized that his own existence hung on such slender threads of coincidence. If his mother had not asked his father to dance...If his father had not even been there—why was he there? Oh, right—he was escorting a pupil of his, whose fiance was at a funeral, friend of the family, or something...If that woman's fiance's friend hadn't died....

"What's the matter, old chap?"

"Um, what did the man die of?"

"What?"

"The man who was the friend of the family, whose funeral your student's fiance went to?"

"I can't recall. I don't know if I even knew the reason then."

"Oh."

His father gazed at him with a knowing sort of look, as if he realized, too, that their present happiness, not to mention Andrew's own existence, hinged on someone else's misfortune. Then he enfolded Andrew in his arms.

During the next two weeks Andrew tried to put away all thoughts of his father's return to his squadron, and of his own departure to Greycliff. Remembering his father's admonition that "fear can lose us the present, as well as the future," he resolved to live each day at a time, focusing on the joy of his father being with him, the specialness of each moment. It occurred to him that, even though his father getting hurt was something he wouldn't wish to happen, it had resulted in them being able to spend this time together. And that was a good thing, a very, very good thing. Why worry about tomorrow—anything might happen! Hitler might drop dead, and the Germans would forget all about this silly war, or somehow, some way, peace would be made, maybe even before his father would have to leave. Things had been rather quiet lately; everyone said it was the calm before the storm. Perhaps, Andrew thought, it is the calm *instead* of the storm.

All around him, though, England was bristling for invasion. The few times Andrew and his father had gone to town, they had seen street signs being removed (to foil invaders who presumably wouldn't know how to find their way around). The fields in the countryside were filled with obstacles to prevent airborne landings: trees felled and scattered around, nasty-looking bundles of poles with pointy ends, piles of rocks, and other malevolent impediments. "Dragon's teeth," anti-tank obstacles that looked like squat, miniature gravestones, dotted the landscape.

Anything is possible. That's what his father had said. Each day Andrew listened for encouraging news on the radio, scanned the newspaper, hoped to hear a sudden announcement that this stupid war had been called off. Maybe someone would shoot Hitler. *That* would solve things. *He* was the one who wanted a war, and without *him* all the other Nazis would forget about trying to conquer the world, surely! It would only take one person—*one person*—to realize what an evil man he was and do the deed.

He had a dream one night: He was in a large crowd of people, and everyone was yelling "He's coming, he's coming!" Andrew knew, of course, who *he* was. At the same time he realized, in his dream, that the crowd wouldn't be yelling in English, but in German, but he supposed he was a German boy in his dream and he would have to understand what everyone was saying, wouldn't he? The noise got louder, and now everyone was shouting "Sieg Heil," and making that funny sort of salute where they hit their chests and put their arms straight out. Andrew knew that it was up to him to *do it*, but he didn't have any sort of weapon or even an implement that he could use to do anyone any bodily harm. He ran frantically through the crowd, looking for something, *something*, that he could use, and cursed himself for not being prepared, cursed everyone around him for praising this evil man. What if everyone, all these thousands of people, had decided to put an end to this man? They could all do it, surely, with just their bare hands, if there were enough people against one man. Even one man, if he was very strong, if he knew just how to do it, could dispose of that evil man. But Andrew was just a boy, not very strong, and not very knowledgeable in the art of killing a grown person, or any person for that matter. He cursed himself again for his own powerlessness and lack of knowledge. What was the good in going to school, in learning all the things that were considered necessary to know—mathematics, French, Latin, geography—what was the bloody use in all those things if it didn't prepare you for this one crucial thing: putting an end to all the madness and evil in the world?

Andrew suddenly felt as if his legs were paralyzed; he had that awful feeling of wanting to run but not being able to, and he was terrified for he knew he had to find something quickly, very quickly, with which to kill Hitler. He tried to yell, hoping to get the crowd's attention, for maybe he could convince someone, *someone* to do the deed for him. But his voice only came out as a squeak, and the harder he tried, the softer his voice became, until he was trying with all his might to scream, and nothing came out, nothing at all. He woke up in a cold sweat, thinking that maybe he was really yelling but couldn't hear himself in his dream, and that the whole house could hear him and his father and mother would come running.

But no one came. He huddled down under his blankets, his heart pounding and his mouth dry, and lay petrified with fear and despair for a long, long time until sheer exhaustion overcame him and a restless sleep claimed him.

Chapter 5

"*A*ndrew! Sleepyhead—it's a beautiful morning! Let's have breakfast on the terrace and then we'll visit Charlie again—what do you say, old chap?" His father planted a gentle kiss on Andrew's forehead.

Andrew turned over and, his eyes still closed, extended his arms upwards. His father snuggled into them.

"What time is it?" Andrew murmured.

"Ten-thirty."

"Crikey—I really overslept!" Andrew's eyes popped open.

"Easy, old chap. Can't have a proper summer holiday without being able to occasionally indulge in the luxury of sleeping half the day away." His father brushed back a lock of Andrew's hair.

"Anything wrong, old chap?"

Andrew shook his head. He wanted to file the terrible dream away in some dark never-to-be disturbed corner of his mind—best not to dwell on it. If he didn't talk about it, it might be easier to forget. How many dreams had he had in his life, and how many could he remember?

Just don't think about it, don't talk about it, and this one will fade away, too. Don't need nightmares mucking things up—real life is perfectly capable of doing that well enough without any help. The full realization of his country's disastrous predicament hit him like a splash of cold water, banishing the peaceful, fuzzy half-cognizance left by departing slumber.

It seemed that with every passing day, this early morning blissful ignorance of the terrible current state of affairs was becoming increasingly short-lived. Andrew's vague pleadings with the Almighty for a sudden termination of hostilities, and his shaky faith that "all will come right," seemed nothing more than futile travail in the face of harsh reality, and his fears and feelings of doom piled higher and higher behind a dam of desperate hope. No miracle was forthcoming; Hitler seemed as hale and healthy and impervious to harm as God himself, and England was at a fever pitch of readiness for the inevitable onslaught of hostilities and atrocities that would no doubt be unleashed in a very short time. The war was an overwhelming, overshadowing, omniscient presence in Andrew's life that harrowed him more and more as his father's departure grew ever closer.

Andrew groaned as the realization hit him that his father would leave in just two days: only today and tomorrow to enjoy his presence. After that would come the morning when a farewell kiss would brush Andrew's cheek, words of love and encouragement would be whispered in his ear, and a fierce hug would bless him as they went their separate ways: Andrew, along with his mother, to safety in the North; his father to face the fury of Britain's attackers.

They wiped their shoes off on the mat by the kitchen door. Andrew's father preferred coming in through the kitchen, the better to catch a whiff of Mrs. Tuttle's wonderful cooking and, if his compliments were effusive enough, to receive a sampling of the forthcoming meal.

"Well, you two—have you worked up a proper appetite?" Mrs. Tuttle's eyes watered as she chopped a precious onion into bits.

"As always, Mrs. Tuttle. I fear we're about to collapse from starvation, and that delicious aroma is enough to drive one mad with anticipation of your usual wonderful culinary delights. You know, as much as I'd like to, I'm careful not to talk too freely to my squadron mates about your marvelous cooking. Some of them are filthy rich, and they would no doubt tempt you away with offers of vast fortunes if you were in their employ."

Mrs. Tuttle chuckled and pinched his cheek. "Just for that, you can have a taste. Wash up and sit yourselves down for a sample."

They were treated to corned beef stew, spicy and a little sweet, just as Andrew's father liked. Mrs. Tuttle poured them cups of steaming tea, and also let them have "just a titchy bit" of suet pudding.

Andrew's father finished the last of the pudding, noisily and meticulously scraping his bowl, which prompted Mrs. Tuttle to offer him, in a display of mock exasperation mixed with pride, a "titchy titchy more, and that's all!"

"And just a titchy titchy bit more for my little friend, too, and thank you ever so much, Mrs. Tuttle." Andrew's father winked at him, and Andrew tried to force a smile, but he couldn't get beyond a perfunctory turning up of the corners of his mouth. Andrew's father pushed himself away from the table, and held his arms wide for Andrew.

"You have to give me a hug for pleading to Mrs. Tuttle on your behalf."

Andrew slipped out of his chair and into his father's embrace.

"Now, old chap," his father said, "If you want to keep things to yourself, that's fine, but I'd be ever so happy if you'd tell me why you've been so quiet today. Did you have a bad dream last night?"

Andrew nodded.

"Tell me about it."

"Oh, it was silly."

"Silly? Then why are you so upset?"

Andrew bit his lip. "Because it's something that would never, never happen. I was silly to even dream it."

"People dream lots of silly things. There's nothing wrong with that."

Andrew sighed. "It was about *him*—about Hitler, I mean."

"Tell me, old chap."

"Well, I dreamt I was in this crowd, and Hitler was coming and everyone was yelling 'Sieg Heil', and I knew I was the only one to do it."

"Do what?"

"Kill him. Because if I could kill him then the war would stop."

His father's brow furrowed, then he exhaled a sharp breath and hugged Andrew.

The tears, which Andrew had thought he could keep in check, sprang from his eyes. He pressed his face to his father's chest and barely managed to stifle a sob. They clung to each other in silence, bathed in the long, golden shafts of light thrown through the tall kitchen windows by the setting sun.

After awhile his father spoke in a husky voice. "You want the war to go away—that's what your dream is telling you. And it's what I want, too, more than anything. You feel very, very afraid, and helpless too, don't you?"

Andrew nodded, not being able to get any words around the lump in his throat.

"You want to be able to do something to stop it, don't you? And you're very angry—angry with the world, and angry with yourself, that you can't." He stroked Andrew's hair. "Do you know what I believe?"

"What?" Andrew croaked.

"I believe that someday, somehow, you'll do something very special, something that will make the world a better place. I know that, right now, the world seems like a fearful and terrible place, but you will do something to set things right. I believe that very strongly."

"Why?"

"I just know you will, that's all."

"Do you mean you think I'll be Prime Minister or someone important and powerful?"

"Who knows? Anything is possible. But you don't have to be important or powerful to change the world. Even if you change a small part of it for the better, that's enough. And I do believe you'll do that, somehow, some way."

"How can I do that? I'm not anybody."

"Yes, you are. If you decide to make the world a better place, you're somebody. Do you know what Hitler is? He's a nobody. He's a vacuum that sucks everything away from people—their hopes, their goodness, their sense of right and wrong. You are going to do just the opposite—you will give goodness back to the world. It may be on a large scale—who knows, you might be Prime Minister someday! Or it may be on a small scale—and that, I think, is just as important. Most of the time it's simply a matter of choosing kindness over hatred. If you change a small corner of the world for the better, if you do a simple kindness for one person, it's a far greater thing than inciting millions to violence. There's a saying that it's better to build a chicken coop than to destroy a cathedral. As long as you decide to do what's right, you are doing something infinitely more powerful, and far better, than Hitler can do as the leader of a nation."

"Hitler's a pervert!" Andrew exploded.

His father's forehead furrowed into a deep cleft. "Do you know what a pervert is?" His words were measured and soft.

"It's—it's someone who's very hor—horrid," Andrew stammered. It's someone, who is—is evil, who's an awful person—or something that's ghastly and—and awful—like—like *perverted science*, that's what Mr. Churchill said, *perverted science.* Hitler's a pervert, all the Nazis are perverts, all the Germans are perverts—every one of them! They do terrible, horrible things. When they conquer a place, they roll this thing down the streets, it's like a big pole on wheels, with ropes hanging from it. They grab people off the streets and they hang them from it—men, women, anybody—and they roll this hideous contraption along and people are hanging from it and it's positively grisly. I saw it in a magazine that Freddie brought from American last fall—" Andrew choked into sputtery sobs.

His father's arms enfolded him again. As Andrew wiped his nose with his sleeve, his father leaned back and pulled a light blue handkerchief out of his pocket. He held it to Andrew's nose.

"Blow," he whispered. Andrew complied, honking noisily into the handkerchief. He took a few deep breaths, pulled it from his father's hands, and completed the necessary, but messy, business. Then he unwadded the handkerchief, noted the letters "RAF" embroidered in the corner, and held it out in front of him so that it filtered the sunlight into a bluish-grey haze.

"Can I keep this?" he asked.

His father nodded. Andrew folded the handkerchief into a neat rectangle and put it in his pocket.

"Roger! There you are!" Aunt Gwen stood in the kitchen doorway. She had just arrived from London the previous evening for a much needed break, after working for ten days straight. "There's news on the wireless about Oran!"

"What's Oran?" Andrew sat up straight.

"It's in North Africa," Aunt Gwen said. Then she addressed Andrew's father: "It's absolutely ghastly, Roger. Over a thousand French sailors killed, that's what they say now. Jane's positively distraught. Evelyne's oldest son is in the navy."

"What happened?" Andrew asked. "Did the Nazis kill them?" He knew Louis, Evelyne's son, and thought he was very nice. Louis liked to box, always had hysterically funny stories to tell about his adventures in the navy, and could play the saxophone. In fact, he had even given Andrew a few music lessons and, in return, Andrew taught him how to play chess.

"No, *we* did." Aunt Gwen answered.

"*We* did?" Andrew stammered. "Wh-*why?*"

"The chap on the BBC is reading Churchill's speech." Aunt Gwen rushed back down the hall. "Hurry now, you'll miss it."

Andrew was carried in his father's arms to the drawing room. "Why? *Why?*" he bleated.

"The French were going to surrender their warships to the Nazis, according to the terms of the armistice," Aunt Gwen explained. "We couldn't let them fall into the hands of the Germans. Our Navy signalled the French to either sail their ships to England or to America, or scuttle them, but they refused—"

...The action we have already taken should be, in itself sufficient to dispose once and for all of the lies and rumours which have been so industriously spread by German propaganda and Fifth Column activities that we have the slightest intention of entering into negotiations in any form and through any channel with the German and Italian Governments...

"Thank God Freddie's not around to hear *that!*" Aunt Gwen said.

...We shall on the contrary, prosecute the war with the utmost vigour by all the means that are open to us until the righteous purposes for which we entered upon it have been fulfilled.

Andrew's mother closed her eyes and slumped back against the sofa, Gram clenched her hands together and stared into space, and Aunt Jane sat, stunned and immobile. Andrew wriggled off of his father's lap and went over to his mother. He wrapped his arms around her and burrowed his face into her neck. She put her arms around him, and pressed her cheek against his.

They spent their last day together, Andrew and his parents, walking through the countryside: "ranging" his father liked to call it. They had no particular destination or itinerary, but an agenda they did have, and that was to reminisce about every event they could think of in Andrew's life.

"Remember when he took his first step?" his mother said.

"You were standing behind him." Andrew's father grinned. "And he was grabbing onto your fingers for support."

"And you said, 'Come to Daddy' and he yelled and tried to pull me forward but I wouldn't go with him. Then he yelled even louder and then I let go of his hands and he stood there, wobbled a bit, and took three—"

"Yes, it was three, that's right."

"—three steps to you, and he fell into your arms and just screamed and screamed for joy," Andrew's mother exclaimed. "And you covered him with kisses, and then we spent the next two hours passing him back and forth between us, moving a little bit farther apart every time."

"And within a week, he was positively running wild—thought he would break the four-minute mile before long!"

"Maybe someday he will! Remember his first complete sentence? It was 'Mum-mum fly plane.'"

"Came out sounding like 'Mum-mum fy pay,' his father chuckled. "Remember how he used to make this loud grumbling noise when you'd start the engine, then he would squeal with delight as we went down the runway, and then he would cheer and clap when you got us airborne?"

"Certainly the most enthusiastic passenger I've ever had the pleasure of transporting!"

As Andrew walked between his parents, holding his father's hand in his right, and his mother's hand in his left, a maelstrom of elation and anguish tore through him. If only he could set this day within the bonds of eternity: freeze it, like a motion picture frame, so that *now* would go on forever and ever. But time fell away from him like water hurtling over a precipice: one second, one minute, one hour closer to his father's departure.

The sun was setting, and they headed back towards Armus House.

It was still dark when he awoke. He grabbed the torch that he'd lately started keeping under his bed (better than turning on the lights and risking any crack of light escaping through the blackout curtains—never knew when there just might be a German bomber overhead). He shone it on the clock on his bedside table: It was four A.M. He collapsed back onto his pillow. Though his eyes ached with tiredness, he knew that sleep would elude him. He figured that his father would be up at five, so that he could catch the early train. He'd promised to awaken Andrew, so that they could enjoy their last breakfast together, but now Andrew feared that he would doze off just before his father came to wake him. His father would see that he looked so exhausted, and would let him sleep....

Andrew sprang out of bed, tore his blankets off and toted them, along with three pillows, down the hall to his parents doorway. He laid the bedding into a pallet of sorts, the three pillows lined up lengthwise to provide a cushion, and snuggled into his makeshift sleeping arrangements.

Count sheep—that's the trick, he thought. He tried to envision wooly white sheep jumping over a fence. The tenth sheep had a circle on its side, which distinctly formed itself into a R.A.F. roundel by the sixteenth sheep, the twentieth sheep sprouted wings, and the thirty-first sheep took on the undeniable shape of a Hurricane. Plane after plane soared skyward towards a blood-red horizon, disappearing in the distance, never to return.

"What do we have here?" A low voice whispered in his ear. Andrew felt a bristly cheek nuzzle his face. He sat bolt upright.

"I couldn't sleep—I didn't want you to leave—" The words stuck in Andrew's throat. "I mean, leave without waking me up for breakfast—"

His father scooped him up in his arms and started to carry him down the hall.

"Please, let me watch you shave. I'll make the lather for you."

"All right." His father turned into the main bathroom. "I'm going to take a shower first—you get the lather ready."

While steam filled the bathroom and the sound of humming emanated from behind the shower enclosure, Andrew put his father's shaving soap into the small ceramic mug and worked it into a froth with the shaving brush.

"Andrew, could you please hand me a towel?"

Andrew grabbed a towel from the stack piled on the table by the door and gave it to his father. His father stepped out of the shower with the towel wrapped around his waist and regarded the heap of lather approvingly.

"Thank you, old chap."

"Can I put it on you?"

"I was going to ask. Thank you ever so much."

His father sat on the small wooden stool in the corner by the sink, and Andrew proceeded to apply the lather to his chin and cheeks. He stepped back a bit to check his handiwork, saw a bare spot just in front of his father's left ear, and dabbed the last of the lather onto it. He nodded at his father, who stood up; Andrew took his place on the stool and watched his father slide the razor over his face. The gentle scraping noise, the soft murmuring sounds his father made as he checked his progress in the mirror, the sound of water splashing against his face—these innocuous sounds of the morning's ritual played as a counterpoint to the hammering of Andrew's heart. His father grabbed another towel and rubbed his face dry. He then twisted the towel and draped it ceremoniously around Andrew's neck.

"Presenting face for inspection, sir!" He knelt down to Andrew's level. Andrew ran his hands over his father's skin and nodded approvingly. His father then picked him up and Andrew pressed his face against his father's cheeks, now smooth and smelling wonderfully fragrant of shaving soap.

Mrs. Tuttle already had breakfast on the dining room table: Eggs Benedict, scones with strawberry jam, a bowl of fresh peaches and raspberries. Andrew's mother was seated in front of the window. She smiled wistfully as they entered; the sunlight played her hair into a goldeny halo, and her eyes shone with a thin film of tears. Andrew's father bent over and brushed a gentle kiss on her lips.

The soft clinking of silverware against china accompanied their hushed conversation. Mrs. Tuttle had certainly "outdone herself, as usual," his father observed, but the food tasted like wood shavings in Andrew's mouth. His parents talked about the wonderful time the past few weeks had been and planned future holidays: going to North Wales or the Lake District again; Scotland would be wonderful, too; perhaps even a trip to America someday. The war, an embarrassing, hideous aberration lurking in the shadows, was not mentioned.

Aunt Gwen, Aunt Jane, and Gram came in just as Mrs. Tuttle appeared with a second plate of scones. They seated themselves and joined in the conversation. Freddie— thank goodness for small blessings—was still away in London, and Gram told them that he was going away on a business trip to the United States the following week. "Just like Freddie to scuttle off to America at a time like this!" Aunt Gwen said.

"He's probably socking away his millions in some bank in Kansas someplace," Aunt Jane added.

"As much as he hates that 'bugger-all,' he's no doubt counting his blessings that it's there to protect his precious fortune." Aunt Gwen slapped a dab of jam on her scone.

"Freddie count his blessings?" Gram exclaimed. "Why, Hitler would sooner kiss Churchill!"

"And Churchill would sooner kiss Mussolini!" Aunt Gwen giggled.

"And pigs would sing!" Andrew's father pronounced, winking at Andrew.

Thomas poked his head in the doorway. "Car's ready, sir," he said softly to Andrew's father. The words seemed like a curse to Andrew, a announcement of awful doom, blotting out all joy and hope. His father carefully set his napkin down beside his plate and rose from his seat. He stood for a brief moment silhouetted in the sunlight; his features were blurred in darkness. Then he moved away from the table and slipped upstairs.

Andrew sat, paralyzed with dread. Aunt Jane whispered in his ear, "Come on." Taking his hand, she led him away from the table. Andrew trudged up the stairs to brush his teeth and comb his hair. Finished, he stood in the hall, awaiting his father, who appeared after a moment from the master bedroom, toting his kit-bag.

"Come on, old chap." He knelt down and put his arm around Andrew's shoulder. Andrew collapsed against him.

He's going, he's going, and there's nothing I can do....

"I love you, Andrew," his father whispered. Andrew tried to speak, but his words came out as a quavery moan. His father's arms tightened around him.

"Best be going, sir," Thomas said. "I can't guarantee that you'll make the train."

His father released him. "You'll ride with me to the station, won't you old chap?" Andrew nodded, the lump in his throat nearly strangling him.

Aunt Jane, Aunt Gwen, and Gram embraced Andrew's father while Andrew and his mother settled themselves in the car. His father waved Thomas to start the car while he got in the back seat next to Andrew.

Nestled between his parents, he couldn't bear to look outside as they drove to town, couldn't bear to watch the landscape rushing by, just as time itself was rushing inexorably into a bleak and fearful future. He laid his head on his father's lap and his fingers stroked the two rings around the cuff of his sleeve.

The car halted. Andrew stumbled out behind his father and stood, eyes closed, swaying slightly. He felt his father lifting him up and then he was clasped in his strong arms and carried through the station out to the platform. He was vaguely aware of his mother walking alongside and Thomas following behind, carrying his father's kit-bag. The sound of the approaching train screamed into his brain.

The train was slowing, slowing...now it was stopped. Andrew was gently set down; his father and his mother kissed, clung to each other, and kissed again. Then his father knelt down beside Andrew and embraced him. Andrew found, to his horror, that his arms wouldn't work; they hung limp at his side. There was a roaring in his ears, like the rushing sound he heard before he lost consciousness on the awful day in the drawing room....

"Andrew, don't give in to despair," his father whispered. "You're going to be safe, and that's what I want more than anything...Do you understand?"

His father paused, looked at him tenderly, and, seeing that Andrew was far past the point of coherent speech, hugged him again. "Andrew, don't give into despair—you're going to be all right. I know that you're going to be all right."

The train, the station, his father, his mother, and the sky above were swirling around him now. His breath came out in soft moans which became louder and louder as panic tore through him. Andrew's moans turned to shrieks and shrill words erupted from him. Hideous words they were, and even as Andrew heard them coming forth from him, he was sickened and distraught.

"I hate you! I hate you! You care more about your stupid war than you do about me! I hate you—hate you—hate—" His voice choked; he pushed his father away and staggered back. The rushing in his ears had stopped, the world had stopped spinning, and he stood, stunned and horrified. His breath came out in sputtery gasps and he closed his eyes.

"The train, sir," Thomas said ever so softly.

His father picked Andrew up again and whispered in his ear. "I know you're scared. I know you don't mean that. I love you." He kissed Andrew one last time, then passed his limp, dazed form to Andrew's mother, kissing her quickly as he did so. Andrew wanted to cry out that he loved him too, and of course he didn't mean those horrible things, but his voice came out as panicky bleats.

"I love you," his father whispered again. Andrew slumped against his mother as the station, the train, the sky, and a blue-grey shape blurred around him. He pressed his face into his mother's breast and closed his eyes.

He heard the train roar away, felt his mother's arms around him, and then there was silence.

Chapter 6

They took the train to Northumberland the next day. Of course, not *the* train, but two, plus the trip on the Underground, as usual. On the first leg of their journey, the Armus House to London trip, Andrew gazed outside the window at the barrage balloons floating high over London. They had always seemed so benign and friendly, their silvery, fanciful forms giving the city a carnival-like atmosphere—at least that's what Andrew used to think. Now they appeared as bloated harbingers of doom as they hovered ominously overhead, fastening cables against the sky to form a lethal net that would (it was hoped) disable the enemy planes that would be flung at England before very long: bombers to drop explosives and incendiaries, and fighters to shoot down the Hurricanes and Spitfires of the RAF, charged with protecting the only nation to stand against the might of Nazi Germany....

They arrived at Greycliff a little after nightfall. No lights blazed from the windows, but even if the place had been fully illuminated, it would have looked no less forbidding. Even in darkness, the two octagonal towers at the front corners loomed like malevolent sentinels, and the pretentious cascade of steps seemed intimidating, rather than inviting. Andrew always felt as if he were going to live in a museum every time he had to visit Greycliff. He hated "his" room, which had belonged to his long-dead uncles. There were still reminders of them in the cavernous chamber: the tin soldiers arranged on high shelves, the ancient books with crumbly bindings in the glass-enclosed bookcases, and the worn, glum teddy bears heaped on the window seat. The ghosts of the boys who had inhabited the room so many years ago seemed to be forever lurking about. Andrew always had the funny feeling that they were looking over his shoulder, waiting for him to drop his guard.

Grandmother Howard welcomed them in the vast front hall, if her perfunctory kiss and hushed, toneless greeting could be construed as a welcome. They were ushered in by Alfred, her chauffeur, who proceeded to carry their luggage upstairs. Andrew had resolved that he would not look at the enormous painting, prominently hung on the wall opposite the entrance and flanked by the two curved staircases, but his eyes almost against his will were drawn to the faces of his two uncles. They had been about Andrew's age when their likenesses were forever captured on the gigantic canvas, both of them sitting astride ponies. All four visages, the two human and the two equine, stared impassively into space. Sometimes Andrew imagined that not only were the human eyes following him wherever he stood, but that the ponies' baleful eyes were tracking him too. The ponies had been long dead, just as the boys had been dead all these years: both of Andrew's uncles, barely out of their teens, killed within hours of each other in France, twenty-four years ago in the Great War. Andrew's mother professed to have no recollection of them: "I was barely two years old when they went away—how could I remember?"

Maria, the maid, met them upstairs. She assured them that their rooms had been properly aired and that Mrs. Beaton, the cook, would have supper served soon. Andrew dashed into the nursery and shoved his suitcase into the closet by the bed. Unpacking would be left for the light of day tomorrow, as he didn't want to spend any unnecessary time, especially at night, sharing the spooky, enormous room with the ghosts of his dead uncles.

On his previous visits, at least he'd had brevity on his side to allay his discomfort at the prospect of his enforced presence at Greycliff: one week, and no more. For most of that time, he could count down the days on the fingers of one hand. Now the countdown would be in double digits for an interminable time: at least a full two months' worth of days and nights until he would return to school at the beginning of September...if there was no *trouble*, that is. With a stab of dismay and terror, Andrew recalled the conversation he had overheard the day before his father had left. He had not meant to eavesdrop, but the door to his parents' room was open a crack....

"If there's any prospect of trouble in the south—if it looks as if an invasion is still on—" His father had spoken softly, but earnestly, to Andrew's mother, "If we haven't beaten back the Luftwaffe by the time he's supposed to start school, keep him at your mother's. I don't think Hitler planned on having to fight us, and I expect that it'll take some time for the Germans to get things organized in order to attempt an invasion, so I think the push will come in late summer. It won't be until the end of September or early October that the Nazis would call off any plans for invasion, with fall weather setting in by that time—then you can be sure. Keep him in Northumberland until things are certain. I'd rather have him miss a month of school than have him mixed up with things in the south...."

As he followed his mother into her room, Andrew remembered the army of servants that had been at Greycliff the previous year: an upstairs maid, a downstairs maid, a "tween" maid who worked both floors, a laundress, a butler, a scullery maid, two gardeners, a groom for the horses. All these had been in addition to the three servants who now remained: Mrs. Beaton, who had been the family cook for thirty years; Alfred, who had been the chauffeur for twenty; and Maria, who had started out as the laundress four years ago and found herself promoted to tween maid, then to upstairs maid, then to the only maid, as all the other servants left to join the various armed forces. The women had joined the Auxiliary Territorial Services, the Women's Royal Naval Service, and the Women's Auxiliary Air Force. The men had enlisted in the Army, the Royal Navy, and the Royal Air Force. Maria, who like Lucia was of Italian origin, had taken on the responsibility for the entire household except for the culinary duties, which were Mrs. Beaton's domain.

"She's worth her weight in gold," Grandmother Howard murmured to Andrew's mother, after Maria had gone downstairs to set the table. Andrew stood stiffly by his mother's bed, hoping that his grandmother would depart also. The old woman gazed at him for a moment, neither smiling nor frowning. Andrew averted his eyes from her and made a show of inspecting the rose-patterned carpet. He then glanced briefly at the doorway, where she'd been standing and found, to his relief, that she was gone.

His mother turned and held out her arms to him. He shuffled over to her and collapsed into her embrace. Sighing, he turned his head to survey her room: It was a little smaller than the nursery, but no less gloomy. Dark tapestries were hung from the walls; heavy, ornate furniture lurked in the shadows. Her massive canopied bed could hold a family of six with room to spare. The frilly bed linens and curtains were stridently ostentatious, rather than inviting, and the high ceiling, like that in Andrew's room, gave the room the appearance of a canyon.

"Supper's ready, mum," whispered Maria, appearing in the doorway as quietly as Grandmother Howard had departed.

They walked in silence down one of the massive staircases and entered the dining room. Here again, all was forbiddingly formal. The table, which could seat forty, stretched out before them like a runway. They seated themselves at one end and were served a supper of Welsh Rarebit, potato soup, biscuits with jam, stewed apples, and Brussels sprouts. Andrew winced. He *hated* Brussels sprouts.

"Alfred has taken over the gardening, or at least attempted to control the weeds and grow a bit of a vegetable patch," Grandmother Howard said in her timid, whispery voice. "I told him not to worry about the shrubs and hedges quite so much, and forget about flowers, at least for this year. He's provided us with quite a harvest of potatoes, carrots, Brussels sprouts, leeks, cauliflower, and the like. Better to have food on the table than neatly trimmed shrubs, don't you think?"

Andrew's mother murmured an affirmative reply, and inquired about her mother's health, to which Grandmother Howard replied that it was very good, and that she was thankful for such soundness of body since young Dr. Blake had left to join the Royal Navy, leaving old Dr. Baxter to handle the practice alone: "One would have to be at death's door to expect a house call and, from what I hear, the wait at the surgery is hours long. Poor dear, he's doing his best, but I fear he'll work himself to an early grave with the extra load he's had to take on."

"He's always pushed himself so," Andrew's mother replied in a strained voice.

Grandmother Howard sighed, and finished her stewed apples. Laying down her spoon, she said, "I've had most of the downstairs closed off. I couldn't stand rattling around all these empty rooms. I moved the wireless from the drawing room to the morning room, a much cosier place—don't you think?"

Andrew's mother nodded, and turned her attention to finishing her meal. Grandmother Howard glanced tensely at Andrew; she seemed to be at a loss as to how to engage him in conversation. She finished her meal, and silence reigned until Maria came in to remove their empty plates—empty, that is, except for the pile of Brussels sprouts remaining on Andrew's plate. Mrs. Tuttle would *never* serve him something he detested.

Carrot cake—Mrs. Tuttle *had* served him carrot cake, just once, because it was his father's favorite and he was coming home for Andrew's birthday....

The tears rolled, unbidden and unchecked, down his cheeks. His mother looked at him tenderly.

"May I be excused?" he whispered.

His mother nodded, and he rose and hurried out of the room.

... Who can foresee what the course of other years can bring? Faith is given to us to help and comfort us when we stand in awe before the unfurling scroll of human destiny.

Andrew snorted. Perhaps the unscrolling furl of human destiny might sound better. Or undestined scroll of unfurling humanity—now that had a nice ring to it....

His mother glared at him. Andrew slumped in his chair.

...And now it has come to us to stand alone in the breach, and face the worst that the tyrant's might and enmity can do....

The Prime Minister's voice was drowned in static. Maria hopped up and adjusted the dial. Andrew rolled his eyes. He'd bloody rather listen to static than to another word of this appalling drivel.

We are fighting by ourselves alone; but we are not fighting for ourselves alone....

We're fighting, Winnie?

...here, girt about by the seas and oceans where the Navy reigns; shielded from above by the prowess and devotion of our airmen—we await undismayed the impending assault. Perhaps it will come tonight. Perhaps it will come next week. Perhaps it will never come....

God stone the crows! Why doesn't he just shut up?

...Let all strive without failing in faith or duty, and the dark curse of Hitler will be lifted from our age....

His father called at least once a week, sometimes twice; a letter came from him almost every day. Andrew found it harder and harder to connect the scrawls on the pieces of paper, and the scratchy voice on the telephone, with the living, breathing form of his father. He felt his throat tighten up every time he talked to his father, and was afraid that if he referred to their traumatic parting, even to apologize, the dam would burst and all of his anguish and terror would pour out in hysterical rantings again. He wanted so much to tell his father how much he loved him, but he couldn't do that, couldn't force the words out into an impersonal, mechanical device, couldn't bear to think of the words "I love you" traveling the cold, unfeeling wires strung over the miles between them. He had to feel his father's arms around him, hear his heart beating, see him, touch him, be anchored by his presence, before he'd be able pour out all of his terror and anguish and remorse without the threat of spinning out of control again.

Alfred chuckled and held the newspaper to Mrs. Beaton. They were not married to each other: Mrs. Beaton's husband had been one of the gardeners, and now he was serving on a corvette in the Royal Navy. Alfred had been widowed for some twenty years: His wife, along with his only child, a daughter, had died of influenza shortly after the Great War ended. As if four years of butchery had not been enough, a pandemic just after the Armistice was signed killed millions more. Alfred had never re-married.

"...this little nipper is not about to be evacuated to Canada without a fight—read this letter here, Mrs. Beaton." He pushed aside his bowl of turnip soup and displayed the open newspaper to her.

Mrs. Beaton set down the spinach and leek pie. Andrew, Alfred, and Maria were seated at the table tucked in a nook of the kitchen between the butler's pantry and the scullery. Mrs. Beaton dished herself a serving, sat down next to Alfred, and perused the item Alfred had pointed out, between mouthfuls of food.

Andrew had lately started having tea, and elevensies also, in the kitchen, for the atmosphere was by far much cozier than that of the dining room. As Andrew's mother did not protest his eating the two minor meals in the kitchen with the servants, he had settled into this, if not exactly pleasant, at least decidedly less unpleasant, routine. The main meals—breakfast, lunch, and supper—he still took in the dining room with his mother and grandmother, but at least the two snacks enjoyed in less formal surroundings buffered the unpleasantness of having to eat in the huge, gloomy room, and having to endure the strained conversation between his mother and grandmother. The servants' company he found more to his liking, though on the whole they were not quite as gregarious as the servants at Armus House. (Andrew had never really thought of Mrs. Tuttle, Thomas, and Lucia as servants, though; they were more like family friends.) Mrs. Beaton was not bubbly like Mrs. Tuttle; she was emphatically Scottish, and quintessentially taciturn. Nevertheless, her gruff company was preferred by Andrew to his grandmother's timorous demeanor. And Alfred, being the only male in the household, provided a needed balance to Andrew's life at this point. It wasn't just the numbers that gnawed at Andrew. Armus House was also disproportionately female, but not effeminate by any means: Aunt Jane's forthrightness and incisive intelligence, Aunt Gwen's cheeky sense of humor and no-nonsense way of ordering up things to her impeccably high standards, Gram's strength, cheeriness, and youthful outlook on life—Andrew had always found the atmosphere at Armus House infinitely more dynamic and stimulating than even that of his boarding school, let alone Greycliff. Grandmother Howard was exasperatingly unassertive and retiring to the point of spookiness; she flitted through the huge mansion like a wraith, as if she were an intruder in her own home.

"*...I would rather be bombed to fragments, than leave England,*" Mrs. Beaton read. "Aye, cheeky indeed—and with the heart of a lion. Only eleven, is he?"

"Quite right," Alfred said. "What do you say Andrew, how would *you* like to be evacuated to Canada or America? Whole boatloads of children being sent there now, there are. Wouldn't you like to take a nice, long voyage to the New World?"

"*Nice!*" Mrs. Beaton exclaimed. "And run the risk of being torpedoed by those beastly U-Boats? That steamship—what was its name? The *Arandora Star*, that's right. It was on its way to Canada and was sunk—hundreds and hundreds of people drowned. Positively ghastly!" She pursed her lips and looked worriedly at Andrew.

"My cousin was on that ship," Maria said. "He was born in Italy, so he was considered an enemy alien. They put him on that ship. He was *never* an enemy to England! He lived here all his life—he had a restaurant in London—" She looked down at her plate and said in a strained voice, "He was drowned."

Andrew folded his arms and glared at Alfred. "U-Boats or no U-Boats, I would rather be bombed into *atoms*, than leave England."

His father called the following day. As Andrew listened to the crackly voice sounding through the receiver, he tried hard to picture his father—his face, the kindness in his eyes, his easy grin—but he could not form in his mind's eye a vision of his father: living, breathing, talking to him, reassuring him that he knew, still knew, how upset Andrew had been at their parting. Andrew wanted to reassure him, too, that he hadn't meant those terrible things he had said, but his voice strangled in his throat and his stomach churned. He needed the complete picture in his mind, the totality of all that his father was, in order to be able to feel he could pour his feelings out, but that complete picture was denied him. If only he could be with him, touch him, feel his arms around him. How could he talk with this disembodied voice?

The "Battle of Britain", which had started with Luftwaffe attacks on shipping in the Channel and port cities in the south, soon devolved into what seemed to be a giant cricket match in the sky, if one could believe the scores published in the newspapers and announced daily on the radio: Luftwaffe losses: 13, RAF losses: 8; Luftwaffe 17, RAF 10; 12 for 2; 9 for 3; 39 for 9....

"*What do I do, if I hear the Germans are trying to land, or have landed?*"
Andrew was curled up in bed, trying to read in order to tire his eyes into sleep. He had grabbed the newspaper off the kitchen table just before going upstairs to bed.

"*I remember that this is the moment to act like a soldier. I do not get panicky. I stay put. I say to myself: Our chaps will deal with them! I do not say: 'I must get out of here.' I remember that fighting men must have clear roads. I do not go on to the road on bicycle, in car, or on foot. Whether I am at work or at home, I stay put!*"

A letter arrived from his father:

Dear Andrew,

I wish I could come visit you soon, but at the moment it's not all that easy to plan things ahead. Even though we can't be together, you are in my thoughts constantly, and I miss you so very much. I have your picture—the one of you holding the Hurricane aloft—tacked up over my bed. It's the first thing I see when I get up in the morning, and the last thing I see before I go to sleep.

There are a lot of new faces in our squadron. In fact, most of the pilots in my flight are new: There's Len, who joined the squadron just before I left for France—a strong, steady person, a little on the quiet side, but with all the necessary qualities to become a first-rate leader someday. Ginger, with red hair and a disposition to match, but he usually saves his ire for the Luftwaffe. Monty, the scholar—he read history at Cambridge, and we have long discussions late into the night. Doc—do you remember Doc? He's still keenly interested in science, and he was quite offended by the Prime Minister's reference to "perverted science". He believes that science has the power to save us, and to make the world a better place. Science and technology, in Doc's estimation, are tools, to be used for better or worse, depending on who wields them. "A scalpel can save a life, or take it," he says. He is convinced that this war will be won by the side that employs brainpower, as well as firepower, most effectively. He <u>does</u> agree with Mr. Churchill that this war will not be one horrible "prodigious slaughter" as the Great War was, but a "conflict of strategy, of organisation, of technical apparatus, of science, mechanics, and morale," to quote our PM. He also agrees with C. that the Germans sealed their doom in driving out their best minds, especially the Jews, and other intellectuals and scientists as well. Moving on to the other members in our "band of brothers" (that's what Ginger calls us), there's Barky and Roddy, high-spirited and possessing boundless energy. They are often roped into outrageous pranks by my wingman, Charlie, who thinks that the RAF has far too many silly rules, all the while trying to bend them as much as possible. He's a splendid chap, Charlie is—flies like a bird and is the sort of fellow one can trust implicitly.

Give a kiss to your mother, greet your grandmother too. I love you very much.

Dad

"What's that?" Mrs. Beaton glared at the large piece of paper in Alfred's hands. At the top, emblazoned in large letter, were the words: *A Last Appeal to Reason.*

"A tender missive from Hitler—the Luftwaffe dropped these over England the other day. Some were in the rubbish at the train station—"

"What were you doing, going through the rubbish at the train station?"

"I wasn't going through the rubbish. One of the chaps in the Home Guard works there, and he brought it to the meeting last night. Oh, by the way, we're to get rifles soon—from America."

"The Americans sent us rifles?"

"That they did—a half million of them. They're from the Great War, been packed in grease for over twenty years. The ladies in the Women's Volunteer Service are cleaning them up now."

"A half million rifles!" Mrs. Beaton exclaimed.

"And more! The Americans have also sent hundreds of field guns and thousands of machine guns—"

"Are they going to send us the destroyers Mr. Churchill asked for?"

"That's in the works, from what I hear. They're mothballed old things—President Roosevelt is trying to get them declared as scrap, so that he can 'unload' them on us."

Mrs. Beaton grunted, then leaned over Alfred's shoulder and perused the paper.

"Tender missive, indeed! 'Unending suffering and misery' that's what he's promised us?"

"*Mr. Churchill ought, perhaps, for once to believe me when I prophesy that a great empire will be destroyed,*" Alfred read, "*An empire which it was never my intention to destroy or even harm. I do, however, realize that this struggle, if it continues, can only end with the annihilation of one or the other of the two adversaries. Mr. Churchill thinks it will be Germany. I know it will be Britain.*"

Mrs. Beaton raised an eyebrow. "Cocky, isn't he?"

Alfred continued. "*In this hour I feel it to be my duty before my own conscience to appeal once more to reason and common sense in Great Britain, as much as elsewhere. I consider myself in a position to make this appeal, since I am not a vanquished foe begging favors, but the victor speaking in the name of reason. I can see no reason why this war must go on. I am grieved to think of the sacrifices it must claim. Mr. Churchill will once again brush aside this statement of mine by saying that it is merely born of fear and doubt of final victory. In this case I shall have relieved my conscience of things to come.'*"

"How frightfully decent of him." Mrs. Beaton squinted in disgust at the paper and, looking over Alfred's shoulder, read: "*It almost causes me pain to think that I should have been selected by Fate to deal the final blow to the structure which these men have already set tottering.*"

"Positively charming," Alfred observed.

Mrs. Beaton took the paper from his hands, folded it carefully, and filed it away in her stash of wrapping paper in a narrow cupboard by the sink.

"What are you saving that drivel for, Mrs. Beaton?" Alfred said. "Best to put it in the dustbin, where it belongs."

"Never know when there might be a shortage of toilet paper," huffed Mrs. Beaton.

He and his mother biked to town almost every day. It was a good idea, she said, to save on petrol when they did their shopping; their groceries could just as easily be transported by bike as by car. Besides, as she pointed out, it would give Alfred extra time to tend the garden, what with not having to be driving Mrs. Beaton to town all the time to do the marketing. Alfred had attached some extra wire baskets to their bikes, and three or four times a week they set out on their mission. They always had lunch at a restaurant after they arrived in town, which was a treat for Andrew—not so much that eating out was such a special occasion, but it was, at least, a welcome respite from having to consume a meal at Greycliff. Even in a commercial establishment, he felt more at home and relaxed than he did at his grandmother's house.

One day in early August they arrived in town a little after noon. After parking their bikes, as usual, outside the restaurant, they went in to eat. They were seated and Andrew's mother scanned the menu to see if there was "anything new under the sun," as she put it, though Andrew knew that the exercise would be a futile one. Rationing and shortages had taken their toll, and he would positively fall over in a dead faint if there turned out to be "anything new under the sun." The day's offerings were the same as they had been the day before, and the day before that: Potato crisp sandwiches, fish casserole, Lord Woolton Pie (a meatless concoction named in honor of the man who, as Minister of Foods, was responsible for the current dearth of culinary excellence: His unpalatable namesake was composed of potatoes, cauliflower, carrots, and onions, topped with a potato crust), Baked Cod with parsnip balls, and Soup of the Day.

"It's Mock Hare Soup today, mum," the waitress said as she took their order.

"A Mock Hare—now that's a creature I've never heard of." Andrew raised his eyebrows ever so high and glared at the waitress. "Is it really a field mouse in disguise, sent by Hitler to scatter nasty leaflets and spread vicious rumors? Stupid nit, now we're going to have him for lunch."

The waitress rolled her eyes. "It's potatoes, leeks, carrots, turnips, and celery."

"Potatoes, leeks, carrots, turnips, and celery—how exciting!"

Andrew said tonelessly. "Mummy—did you hear? Don't you think it's ever so marvelous? I'm positively thrilled to bits—"

"Andrew, that will be quite enough—please order your meal."

"I'll take the rump steak, extra mushrooms please—and they must be sauteed in *lots* and *lots* of butter, *piles* of butter, in fact, and not too brown, please, and for afters, truffles—"

"Andrew—" his mother warned.

"Potato crisp sandwich." He threw the menu down.

His mother folded her hands and looked sternly at Andrew; then her face broke into a smile. "Save your scathing wit for an occasion that really matters—don't tease the waitress so. It's not her fault, you know."

Andrew sighed. "I know."

"Everybody's getting tired of the food. Someday things will be better."

Andrew slumped back into his chair and gazed at the blotchy ceiling. "It would be so wonderful, to have things back to the way they were before."

"I know."

"Not just the food—everything, I mean."

His mother nodded.

"When can we go see him?"

His mother bit her lip. "I can't say."

"Will he be able to come to see us soon?"

"Not with how the way things are, right now. There's a war on, you know."

"But there's hardly anything happening! During the last three days, we've only shot down eight German planes, and haven't lost any at all of ours! That's a *war*?"

"Things can change. Besides, your father is busy training new pilots, you know that."

"Oh, Training Command is sending him pilots who don't know how to *fly*?"

"Andrew, don't be sarcastic. You know very well that merely flying a plane and being a fighter pilot are two very different things, and your father is very concerned that every pilot under his command—every pilot in his squadron, in fact—knows how to handle himself in a fight. It takes hours and hours of training and practice—"

"What harm would there be in getting away for just one day?"

"It would be more than one day. It's a full day's trip just to travel up here—you know that. Besides, he was on leave for a whole month, and now it's the turn of the other pilots in his squadron to have some time off. Some of them haven't had hardly any time away since Dunkirk, you know—"

"He was wounded! Do those clots in charge consider *that* a holiday?"

His mother sighed. The waitress appeared with their food and set it down for them. Andrew caught her eye and said gently, "Thank you very much." She blinked, and smiled tensely.

His mother nibbled at her Woolton Pie, and Andrew chomped on his potato crisp sandwich.

"...Right, I say—where *was* the bloody RAF?" The loud bellowing voice came from the man sitting at a table across from them.

"Just a bunch of glamour boys, that's all they are," agreed his companion.

Andrew slowly turned to the man. "What did you say?"

The man glared at him and took a sip of ale. "The bloody RAF, that's what I said. Where were they?"

"What do you mean, where *were* they?" Andrew's voice rose a half-octave in pitch.

Andrew's mother touched his sleeve. "Andrew, eat your food."

"Dunkirk!" the man barked.

"What about Dunkirk?"

"Andrew, *please*—" his mother pleaded.

The man wiped his mouth on his sleeve. "All this rot from Winnie about those fancy fighter pilots doing such a bloody marvelous job over Dunkirk! Called 'em Knights of the Round Table and Crusaders—what a load of drivel! I was there, I tell you, and I never saw no RAF, just Jerry planes bombing and strafing us, while the glamour boys did their stunts far away and never paid no mind to us poor blokes catching hell from the Huns. Glamour boys, that's what they are—"

A scream erupted from Andrew's throat and his hands were around the man's neck a split second later. "Don't you say that! My father was at Dunkirk—saving your stupid hide—he shot down a Stuka—"

"Andrew—" His mother was tugging at him as his hands tightened on the man's throat. They tumbled to the floor. The man's companion tried to pry Andrew's fingers away from the grimy neck as the victim himself flailed his arms and gasped, his beery breath reeking and his face contorted with shock and alarm.

"He was shot—he was almost *killed*—he was *there*! Don't you ever, *ever* talk about him like that, *you sodding bastard!*"

"Andrew!" His mother's shriek startled Andrew into loosening his grip. The man, now purple-faced, threw him off.

"Bastard—you! he yelled.

Andrew's mother pinned his arms behind him. "Andrew, let's go. Let's just take a walk, shall we—"

She gasped as Andrew spat in the man's face. The cook, who had been tugged over to the fracas by the horrified waitress, gazed helplessly at the wreckage before her: dishes smashed on the floor by the overturned table, one chair splintered, bits of food strewn everywhere.

"We'll pay for the damages, and your meal—" Andrew's mother said. She leaned over and hissed sharply in Andrew's ear. "Go outside, please."

Andrew stopped struggling against her. She released him, and warily watched his shuffling progress out the door.

Once outside, he leaned against the building and groaned. His mother appeared shortly. She stood before him, disapproval and dismay written on her face.

He looked away from her and tried to blink back the tears.

"Let's go home," she said softly.

Chapter 7

From Reichsmarschall Goering to all units of air fleets 2, 3, and 5. Operation Eagle. Within a short period you will wipe the British Air Force from the sky. Heil Hitler.

The daily scores rose alarmingly. 64 for 14; 138 for 27; 144 for 27; 180 for 34.... Andrew began to dread hearing the tallies on the radio. Back armor plating notwithstanding, Fighter Command's pilots were being shot down, and shot down in great numbers.

"Andrew, they're giving the Prime Minister's speech on the wireless," his mother called. "Come on downstairs—your father would want you to hear it."

Andrew, lying crosswise on his mother's bed, rolled over and glared at the ceiling. He had gotten into the habit of dividing his time between her room and the kitchen, preferring them to his own room and the morning room, which was now an "informal" drawing room, at least informal as far as Grandmother Howard was concerned. It was still a cold, uncozy place, even compared to the drawing room at Armus House. Though his mother's bedroom was just as forbiddingly formal, not to mention grotesquely ostentatious, Andrew felt more at ease there than in his own room, as he figured that his uncles' spirits wouldn't be lurking about in such decidedly feminine surroundings. As for the kitchen, it always had Mrs. Beaton bustling about, and her brisk and surly disposition was sure to set the ghouls scurrying. She wasn't surly, really, just a little sharp-tongued at times, dour for the most part. She worried so about her husband at sea....

"Andrew, your father is no doubt listening at this very moment. The speech is all about the pilots in Fighter Command, and I know your father would be so disappointed if you didn't hear it."

Andrew groaned, rolled over three times to the foot of the bed, shuffled through the hallway, and stomped down the massive stairs, as the voice of the BBC newsreader emanated from the morning room.

The whole Island bristles against invaders, from the sea or from the air....

God, he was getting tired of it all!

The gratitude of every home in our Island, in our Empire, and indeed throughout the world, except in the abodes of the guilty, goes out to the British airmen who, undaunted by odds, unwearied in their constant challenge and mortal danger, are turning the tide of war by their prowess and by their devotion. Never in the field of human conflict was so much owed by so many to so few....

Andrew's mother glanced at him, her face full of pride, anguish...and hope. Andrew snorted and glared at the floor. Right Winnie, all you can do is owe...You don't run the risk of getting shot to a bloody pulp or blown to bits. Hitler, twit that he was, was at least right about *one* thing (even Andrew's father had said that twits could be right on occasion, hadn't he?): that Churchill would not be among those who would suffer. What had the *Last Appeal to Reason* said? Andrew had grabbed it out of the cupboard after Mrs. Beaton had unceremoniously filed it there. His father had always said it was important to "know your opponent". That rule applied in boxing, chess, or any competitive endeavor; fighting a war, Andrew supposed, was no exception. Andrew recalled the words he had read on the crumpled missive: Churchill would not be among those who would suffer, it had said, for he "*no doubt will already be in Canada, where the money and the children of those principally interested in the war already have been sent.*" Like Freddie scuttling off to America!

...the Nazi tyranny is finally going to be broken. The right to guide the course of world history is the noblest prize of victory....

So that's what you want, you tin-plated despot! You won't be satisfied until you can shove everyone around!

I hope—indeed I pray, that we shall not be found unworthy of our victory if after toil and tribulation it is granted to us. For the rest we have to gain the victory. That is our task.

Our task? Andrew slumped down in his chair and squeezed his eyes shut. He tried not to listen—though he couldn't help it—to the irritating voice droning on about something about a "Destroyers for Bases" deal with the United States. The Prime Minister was working on an arrangement with President Roosevelt in which America would send fifty old destroyers to England. In return the United States would acquire several British naval and air bases in the Caribbean and the Western Atlantic. The sovereignty of the bases in the New World would not be transferred; instead, a 99 years' lease would be granted to America.

God stone the crows, Andrew thought. Yanks controlling British possessions—for almost a century? In exchange for a few mothballed old hulks? Freddie was right about them not missing a trick!

...Undoubtedly, this process means that these two great organisations of the English-speaking democracies, the British Empire and the United States, will

have to be somewhat mixed up together in some of their affairs for mutual and general advantage—

Mutual advantage? Let's not kid ourselves, Winnie!

...I do not view the process with any misgivings—

Of course you don't, you half-Yank, brandy-swilling, cigar-chomping megalomaniac! Why don't you give away half of India while you're at it!

I could not stop it if I wished; no one can stop it. Like the Mississippi, it just keeps rolling along....

Winnie must have been stewed to the gills to have said that!

Let it roll....

Full as a tick!

Let it roll on full blood, inexorable....

Lit to the guards!

...irresistible, benignant....

Pissed as a newt!

...to broader lands and better days....

Boiled, oiled, bottled, and corked!

Andrew exhaled loudly and stormed out of the morning room. Once in the front hall, he spun around and glared at the canvas of his uncles. *You think you can frighten me! You think that I can be so easily spooked...I'm not afraid of you, I'm not afraid of this house...It'll be mine someday—it's not yours, not yours at all anymore....*

As he inwardly ranted, he recalled Grandfather Howard's words, spoken to him a little over three years ago, almost on this very spot: *This will be yours someday.* The words, uttered in a gruff, toneless voice, conveyed neither pride nor gladness; they were just an observation, not a promise. His grandfather's face had been impassive as he pronounced this statement of fact, and Andrew had felt at the time that he was being "weighed in the balance and found wanting." He had also been surprised at what could be called an outburst, for it had been the only time, up to that point, that his grandfather had spoken a complete sentence to him. Six months later the second, and last, full sentence had been uttered by the dour old man: Andrew had decided one day to slide down the bannister of one of the curved stairways in the hall—the one on the left, he remembered. He had not reckoned on it having been freshly polished and, as he swung around the curve, his speed had picked up alarmingly. As the bannister curved slightly upwards at the bottom, he had been, in effect, catapulted off the end. He remembered flying backwards through space and crashing into a spindly table with a large (and not to mention priceless) Wedgewood vase on it. The vase had flown through the air, too, and had crashed into smithereens at the feet of Grandfather Howard, who had just happened to be standing there....

"I was just having fun," Andrew had protested to the stern figure.

Narrowed eyes, tightened lips, and the words, dripping with cold condemnation: "You were not put on this earth to enjoy yourself." The memory swirled around Andrew, so real and terrifying palpable that he had to force himself back to the present.

Damn him! Damn his spooky sons and his creepy old house! Damn the war, damn the Nazis, damn Hitler, damn Winnie...damn all the stupid sods who had gotten the world into such a mess! Why couldn't they have ordered up things a little better after the "War to End All Wars" was done, instead of mucking it all up so thoroughly! What was it his father had said? *They won the war but lost the peace.* His father, who had been a boy of eight when the last shot had been fired in that hideously devastating conflict, had now inherited the whirlwind born of the stupidity and shortsightedness at the settling of scores twenty-one years ago.

Armed with fury and bolstered with outrage, he strode across the hall to the library and flung open the door. The only way to banish the critical, sinister specters which haunted this odious estate was to declare, unafraid, his presence and his rightful place in it. It would be *his*, someday, no matter how much it had galled Grandfather Howard to admit it. It would be *his*, no matter how much he himself hated everything about it: its outsized dimensions, its calculatingly symmetrical design, its baleful gray exterior, its disgusting resplendence....

He surveyed the library, with its hundreds of ancient and priceless volumes carefully stowed behind dozens of glass cases. The books were for show, not for enlightenment, as Andrew had been enjoined from so much as touching them: "They're quite valuable, and very fragile," his mother had warned. How very different from Armus House where he was permitted, and positively encouraged by his father, and by Aunt Jane also, to read any and every book he wanted to! He glared at the large leather chairs, now draped with dust-sheets, then strode over to the corner study, an octagonal room which formed the base of one of the towers. A massive oak desk was enthroned in the center of the room and flanked by leather couches (sheet-covered, of course).

He whirled around and sauntered back across the library to the oval smoking room, a fusty chamber decked with Persian rugs and hunting prints, nestled between the library and the billiard room. He continued through to the billiard room, which wasn't used for billiards anymore; it had been converted to a bedroom for Grandfather Howard in his last months of life. Glaring at the morose maroon drapes and sulky furniture, Andrew reflected on how devoid of life and love this sprawling edifice was, not at all like Armus house, with its cheery, comfortable decor. Gram took such pride in making her home a place of beauty, serenity, and warmth. Andrew almost ached with homesickness for the walls papered in delightful floral designs, the plushy, chintz-covered furniture garnished by mountains of comfy pillows, the friendly botanical prints liberally hung in every room, and the clusters of photographs and mementoes displayed everywhere.

He wheeled out of the billiard room into the hall again, giving a perfunctory nod to the rooms at the other side of the house, which formed a mirror image to the ones he had just inspected: the large, formal drawing room in front, the octagonal flower room adjacent to it, the vast dining room behind, and the oval-shaped morning room nestled in the middle. He stomped into the ballroom at the back of the house, a room so huge that Armus House would almost fit inside of it. A piano sat forlornly in the far corner; marble planters, empty of flowers, lined the walls. Chairs and settees, all shrouded by the ubiquitous dust-sheets, were clumped at various intervals along the outside wall. The ballroom was flanked by the conservatory to the left and the kitchen to the right; Andrew debated for a moment as to which direction he should proceed next: to the kitchen to be subjected to Mrs. Beaton's sullen company, or to the conservatory. He felt that familiar tug: the conservatory—better there than anywhere else. By any stretch of the imagination it could not be said that Andrew *liked* the place; it would be more accurate to say that, out of all the rooms at Greycliff, it was the one he least detested. Perhaps there he might find escape from the shadows of the past and the gloom of the present.

He strode across the ballroom, his steps echoing through the capacious space, and flung open the double doors that opened into the conservatory. Like a runner making a sprint towards the finish line, he rushed at a cluster of sheet-covered lumps, tore back one of the dusty wrappings, and plopped down onto a gold velvet cushion.

How he missed the friendly, rambling, cozy rooms at Armus House! How he yearned for the light and laughter within its walls...its warm red brick exterior, garnished by the half-timbered second floor...its pleasant, inviting, and, above all, meant-to-be-lived-in rooms. It was a home above all, a place in which one's soul might find ease, comfort, and contentment...a place of joy and happiness and hope....

The tinkling sounds of the piano interrupted his reverie. His mother had lately taken to playing disconsolate Chopin melodies: sad preludes, waltzes in minor keys, wistful mazurkas, gloomy polonaises. He listened to the mournful waltz, his eyes wandering over the jumble of planters and pots which, unlike those in the ballroom, were bursting forth with greenery. His gaze at last settled on the portrait painted of his mother on her fourth birthday, and he felt that familiar double-edged stab of annoyance and delight at seeing his mother's younger self in this place. How like Grandfather Howard to display his sons in the front hall and relegate his daughter to a back room, and yet how fitting for her to abide in this sunlit space with its expanse of sky-dazzled windows and living things. Andrew felt the shackles of distress and dread loosen their hold as he allowed himself to be captivated and solaced by the little-girl likeness of the woman now grown. She still had the slightly chubby face of toddlerhood, but also the proud, erect stature of a young girl already aware of her status in the world. Her dress was a frenzied orchestration of lace and ruffles, and her hair rippled with an arpeggio of ribbons trying to tame her turbulent red curls into submission. Her lips were set in a prim, straight line, but one rather got the distinct impression that she was trying to force a serious expression at someone else's bidding, for her eyes twinkled with mirth.

He got up and shuffled over to the door to the ballroom. He stood there, watching his mother pour her soul out through her fingers onto the ivory keys, her face impassive and strained with concentration. Then he closed his eyes, and tried to imagine a stunningly beautiful young woman, smiling across the room at a dark haired young man....

It was no use—the image wouldn't come. Andrew scuffed across the vast room to the piano, just as his mother's fingers grazed over the keyboard in the ending notes of the haunting, pensive melody. She glanced at him, and dropped her hands into her lap.

"Piano's out of tune," she said, almost apologetically.

Andrew went to her side and sat down next to her on the bench. He leaned his head against her; her arms encircled him and she brushed a kiss across his forehead.

A letter arrived from his father:

Dear Andrew,

Things have been a bit busy lately, as you've no doubt heard. I'll try to write as often as I can, old chap, but I'm afraid my letters are going to be somewhat brief. Good news! Our squadron is due to be transferred to 13 Group—that's up north—in a few days. I hope to be able to get some time off once we're settled, so I'll definitely put Greycliff on the itinerary. Do you think you might be able to squeeze some time out of your busy schedule to spend with your old man?

Andrew almost screamed for joy. He read on.

Your mother has been writing me about your jaunts to town—sounds like you're getting lots of exercise and thriving in that country air.

Crikey, he thought. I hope she hasn't mentioned anything about that little incident the other week! He read on, hoping not to find any gentle admonishments or other indications to the effect that his father had been made aware of his horrid behavior.

My mouth is positively watering for a good home-cooked meal; the food here is ghastly, and the cook constantly reminding us that "there's a war on, you know" is cold comfort. His talents would best be put to use cooking for German prisoners of war!

Not that you're going to find it much better here, Andrew thought. Mrs. Beaton tries, though.

Give your mother a big hug. See you soon!

All my love always,

Dad

Andrew's spirit soared with joy. Everything was going to be all right!

Even the news broadcast on the BBC that evening was wonderfully optimistic: the destroyers were starting to arrive from America and over ten thousand Canadian troops had also reached England. British ships, carrying anti-aircraft guns and other stores, had sailed though the Straits of Gibraltar to the island of Malta, which had been under almost constant air attack from Italy. Fighter Command was daily "beating back the Luftwaffe," and further raids by Bomber Command on industrial targets in the Berlin area were "pulverizing Germany's war-making capacity." Andrew was in a such a joyous state of mind that Churchill's gloomy broadcast following the news did nothing to dispel his high spirits:

No one must suppose that the danger of invasion has passed....

That's all right, Winnie. Nothing better than an extended summer holiday, especially now with my father coming up north....

Every day, Andrew had perused the newspapers, listened to broadcasts on the radio, and, in general, kept his ears open whenever he and his mother went to town. Except for one abortive raid by German bombers on the Newcastle area on August 15, which was thwarted by the "gallant lads of Fighter Command," it was apparent that the Luftwaffe was concentrating all its energies on southern England. His father would be out of harm's way in just a few days....

"Andrew, your father's on the phone—why don't you get the extension in the study." His mother appeared in the kitchen doorway, breathless. Andrew was reading the newspaper at the servants' table and laughing at the latest *Addie and Hermy* misadventure.

He jumped up and dashed to the study, his heart pounding as he picked up the receiver.

"Dad—*Dad!* I got your letter! I can't wait for you to arrive! Will you be coming very soon, like you promised?"

There was a momentary silence at the other end, and for a brief, terrifying moment, Andrew feared that the call had been cut off. Then there was a sound of a throat clearing, followed by his father's even voice.

"Andrew—"

Andrew's heart sank. It was not only that his father had called him "Andrew," instead of cheerily addressing him as "old chap"; it was his tone of voice as well.

"Dad—you're coming up north, aren't you? You said you would!"

Another excruciating silence and then two horrible words: "I'm sorry—"

"Dad, you *said* you were—*you said you were*—" He was choked by hysteria, and it sounded as if his voice echoed faintly as he repeated his anguished assertion.

"Andrew, I'm needed here for a little while longer—"

"They *can't* make you stay, you can protest, refuse—you don't *have* to stay, they can't make you—"

"Andrew, I volunteered—"

"No! *No! NO! NO!*—"

"Andrew, please understand—"

"*No! NO! NoooOOO—!*You can't—you *can't*—"

"Andrew, please understand—this is important—"

"No it's not—*IT'S NOT!!!* It's a stupid, *stupid* war! You can't do this—I hate this stupid war—" There was an ominous click and the sound of soft static, just after Andrew screamed the word *hate*. His heart thudded into his stomach and his legs nearly buckled. "Dad—*DAD!*"

His voice rose to a shriek. "*Dad—can you hear me?*" He was answered by the soft crackly sound—the line had been horribly, dreadfully, appallingly disconnected! As the terror rose in him, he continued to scream into the receiver.

"Dad! I hate the war—did you hear me? I hate the *WAR!* Please say something—" a sob caught in his throat, and then the words came out, anguished and sputtery, "Dad—*DAD!* I love you! I love you—*LOVE YOU!*"

He sank to the floor. He heard the loud staccato of his mother's footsteps echoing across the marble tile of the hall—coming closer, closer now. He sensed her prying the receiver out of his hands, heard her call into it, "Roger—*Roger—!*", heard the final soft click as she set it down....

He felt his mother's arms around him, heard her whisper, "I'll try to get through to him...."

The sound of his heart hammering, the sound of the blood rushing in his ears, the sound of her trying to place the call, trying again...again...*again*....

He had completely lost his voice, yet his mouth remained open and his chest heaved with the effort of trying to force some sound, any sound, past his lips.

She wouldn't get through...He *knew* she wouldn't get through....

He found himself in his room, in bed. His first coherent thought was of wonderment, for he distinctly recalled that he had been in the study. What had he been doing in the study? How had he gotten upstairs? His second thought was the despairing, galling, horrifying remembrance of....

Wait a minute, it was dark outside...He must have cried himself into exhaustion and somehow...It must have been Alfred, yes, it must have been Alfred who had conveyed him upstairs to bed. Andrew's feet were bare and the covers were tucked around him. His mother must have settled his unconscious form into bed; he could almost feel the kiss on his forehead.

His third thought was the disconcerting awareness of what had roused him: church bells.

Church bells? They weren't supposed to ring church bells! That had been prohibited months ago, for church bells were only to be rung in the event of—

INVASION!

He threw back the covers and raced downstairs, his terror at hearing the announcement of invasion overlaying the distraught recollection of his last words to his father: *I hate*—That's all his father heard, that's all he heard was Andrew screaming those two words, but surely his father had filled in the blank...

Only that wasn't what I said, that wasn't what I said at all...I said I hated the stupid war, the WAR, not you, NOT YOU....

Hearing the sound of the radio, he staggered across the hall and down the narrow corridor which lead to the morning room. He leaned against the closed door for a moment, then heard his grandmother's voice:

"Well, if there's an invasion going on, they certainly aren't telling us anything, are they? Seems to be all hush-hush, isn't it? Why do you suppose they would keep it under wraps?"

"There are a lot of things they're keeping under wraps, mother," Andrew's mother replied, almost bitterly.

"Alfred was called away—he may have some news for us tomorrow, that's if they let him come home for a bit of rest," Grandmother said.

Andrew slowly opened the door. He saw his mother's stunned face, but whether she was in shock because of the announcement of invasion, or because of his sudden appearance, he was quite unable to discern. Gram stared blankly at him.

"Mum, what is it?" His voice was a desperate whisper as he stumbled over to her.

She jumped to her feet and hugged him. He collapsed into her arms, his chest heaved again, and a soundless cry of agony coursed out of his mouth.

"London's in flames, Folkestone and Eastbourne are in ruins, but the Jerries landing on the beach were roasted alive! There were pipelines laid out from all the beaches and our chaps pumped oil through them and ignited it when the Huns tried to get to shore. They say that hundreds of charred bodies are washing up on the French beaches right now, and the hospitals in France are clogged with burnt Jerries. Hitler went into a carpet-chewing frenzy!" Alfred wolfed down a scone, wiped his mouth, and continued. "And the Luftwaffe tried dropping paratroopers, dressed as nuns."

"*Nuns!*" Grandmother exclaimed. "How ghastly!"

"Our boys got them, though. British plunk and American rifles! Rounded up thousands of them!" Alfred gulped the last of his tea.

"Paratroopers dressed as nuns," Grandmother said in a horrified whisper. "Isn't anything *sacred* anymore?"

Andrew was not only exasperated with his grandmother's waily complaints, he was also quite distraught over his mother's unsuccessful attempts to place a call to his father. He had calmed down, a little, after yesterday afternoon's incident, affirming to himself that either his mother would eventually get through, or his father would call—he *would* call—*surely* he would!

"Mum—let's try again—please?"

His mother carefully set down her cup of tea. "All right," she said quietly.

He followed her into the study and sat gingerly on one of the sheet-covered couches as she made a few more disappointing attempts.

She replaced the receiver with a sad droop of her wrist after the fifth try.

"We'll try again right before elevensies, all right?"

Andrew nodded absently as he slowly let himself fall sideways on the couch. He tucked his knees to his chest and hugged them with his arms. His mother came over to him, sat down beside him, and stroked his hair. He wanted to hear her say that everything was going to be all right...all right...*all right*....

He sat up with a start. The sound of a door shutting had startled him out of his slumber. His mother was no longer next to him. He saw a flicker of movement outside the window—a flash of grey-blue....

He burst through the library, pounded down the hall, and exploded out the front door. There was a car, driving away, driving away very quickly now....

"Dad! *DAD!*" Even as he ran, his legs pumping furiously, he knew...*he knew*....

Someone was behind him, gaining on him. His screams turned to terrorized bleats, then to an anguished howl as he ran with all his strength to catch up with the car, even though the car contained, not his father, but the bearer of the message that his father had been—had been—

The footfalls were very near; he could hear the high-pitched, strained panting of his pursuer—his mother. He turned his head to look at her, saw her red-rimmed eyes and her face swollen with grief. He staggered, and gave one last anguished cry of horror and grief and despair. His mother caught him, and they tumbled to the ground together.

Chapter 8

*A*ndrew tried to claw his way out of his mother's grasp. He heard an unearthly howling—it was himself, he realized. His mother finally managed to encircle him with her arms, as he still continued to struggle and thrash. He was surprised at her strength; she held him in a vise-like grip, even as convulsive sobs racked her body.

His body went limp with despair and his voice changed to a keening wail. She continued to clasp him, relaxing her hold a bit; her kisses, distraught and tender, swept over his face like a whirlwind, and her tears mingled with his.

Spent, he closed his eyes, heard a muffled, rushing noise, felt himself caught in that swirling darkness, an absence not of sight alone, but of all sensation...almost. He seemed to hang suspended in space: He couldn't even feel the ground underneath him, though the grass prickled his face a bit. It wasn't a distinct perception; it was more like vaguely sensing a touch under the effect of a local anesthetic.

Now he was being upended, no...he was upright: His legs were hanging down and his head was resting against someone's shoulder and he was being carried, yes, he was being carried. As he dizzily snuzzled his face into the shoulder, he felt a scratchy fabric which smelled a little sweaty, which surprised him because his mother had been wearing a cotton dress and lilac cologne; he distinctly remembered the scent of her and the feel of the polished fabric against his face as they had struggled together.

"Do you want me to take him upstairs to his room, Miss Alice?" Alfred asked.

Andrew heard a muffled affirmation; a few moments later he heard footsteps against marble. Then he felt a rhythmic jostling, sensed they were going up, up...He heard his grandmother's distressed inquiries...wanted her to be quiet...be quiet...*be quiet*....

Then she was.

The smell of lilac; soft cotton against his face...Someone's arms were around him. He stirred and even before full consciousness came to him he realized he was crying.

A second later he realized why.

His mother's gentle kisses swept across his closed eyelids, down his cheek, back to his sweat-dampened hair. She clasped him to her breast and he burrowed his face against her. It was too much of an effort to utter a groan or a sigh, almost too much of an effort even to breathe. His chest hurt, his throat was tight and dry; even forcing his eyes open was an exertion.

He was in his bed now, and it was dark, mercifully dark. He didn't think he could endure the task of looking around and focusing his sight if it had been light. He saw a pale blotch; then the features of his mother's face came into focus as his eyes adjusted to the night. He touched her cheek. Speech was beyond him; it was the only way he could reach out to her, plead for comfort, pour out his grief, apologize....

His fingers were wet with her tears. She gasped, then broke into sobs. He twined his arms around her neck and the dam within him broke, as he screamed out his anguish and despair.

"Andrew, it's been three days. You ought to eat *something*." His mother strode into his room. Maria followed, bearing his lunch on a tray. Maria gently set the tray down on the table by his bed, nodded nervously, and swiftly departed.

He turned away and stared at the light streaming through the window.

How can the sun still rise and set as if nothing had happened?

"Andrew, listen to me! You need to eat, that's all there is to it. You're going to waste away, and what good is that going to do anyone?"

As he turned back to his mother the tears rolled down his cheeks. He didn't want her to think he was being defiant; he simply had no desire to eat. His stomach had been a rock inside of him for the past three days, his throat had tightened up every time he tried to speak. How could he possibly, *possibly* force food down—and keep it there? He had not even been out of bed, except to go to the bathroom, which was when he took a few sips of water; more to rinse out his mouth and to ease the tightness in his throat than to keep himself hydrated, though he sensed by the parched feeling all over his body that a few gulps of water a day wasn't enough.

No matter. One would die of thirst sooner than one would die of hunger....

"Andrew!" His mother cupped his chin in her hands and turned his face to meet her stern stare. Her expression softened. "Andrew, I know you're not trying to be difficult, but the fact of the matter is you need to eat or you'll become very, very ill. If you continue this way, we're going to have to call Dr. Baxter and have him put you in hospital. They will tie you down, stick a needle in your arm and drip sugar water through it. Then they will force your mouth open and pour cod liver oil down your throat so you get your vitamins. I don't want us to have to get to that point, do you? Because if you refuse to eat, you leave us no choice—do you understand?" She bent over and kissed him gently on the forehead; then she was all business and briskness again as she regarded his lunch tray. "Now, let's see—potato crisp sandwich—Mrs. Beaton knows how you like them—a little bit of beef barley soup, sorry, more barley than beef, but Mrs. B. does try so to stretch our meat ration...custard, applesauce, and trifle! Our diet should improve considerably since Alfred got us six chickens the other day. Mrs. B. was positively singing with joy, making custard this morning, what with all the eggs we're getting. We'll have fresh eggs for breakfast now—should give us extra protein now that cheese is rationed too. And a nice pot of steaming tea! What would you like to start with? Applesauce?" Andrew shook his head and turned away. "Custard? How about a sip of this delicious soup? Andrew!"

She set the soup spoon back down in the bowl, and turned his face back to look at her. She narrowed her eyes and lowered her voice. "Andrew, if you do not eat, I will go downstairs right now and ring Dr. Baxter. Do you want me to do that?" She glared at him. "Do you? Answer me!"

Andrew closed his eyes and managed to give a weak shake of his head. "All right, then," his mother said. "Let's start. How about a sip of tea?" Andrew opened his eyes and gave a slight nod. She proffered a tea cup to him; he tried to raise his hand to take it, but it fell back limply into his lap. He looked at her apologetically.

She smiled tenderly, then dipped the spoon into the cup and brought it to his lips. He sipped it; she smiled, and gave him another spoonful. After he had taken five more sips, she set the teacup down on the tray.

"Now, let's try the applesauce...."

It took the better part of an hour, but his mother managed to get most of the meal into him. She had to coax him along with an occasional taste of trifle. There was a bit of the dessert left when he had finished his main meal.

"If you'd like more trifle, I'll ring Maria—"

He shook his head. "Maybe for tea—" He was quite surprised that he managed to get the words out.

As she embraced him his arms went round her. "Please stay with me," he whispered.

He took a few deep breaths, tried to choke back the sob in his throat, heard his mother say, "It's all right—it's all right." His cries came out as deep, strangled groans.

He collapsed back onto the pillow, took a few deep breaths, gazed up at his mother.

"Is Dad going to be buried next to Baby Charlie?"

She took one of his hands in hers, squeezed it, and said gently, "We'll put a memorial stone...there." She swallowed, bit her lip, and blinked a few times.

"What do you mean, a memorial stone?"

She took a deep breath. "His plane went down in the Channel—nothing found, not a trace...he won't be...be there...." Her voice trailed off.

It was almost as if an unseen hand had yanked him upwards out of bed, so violent was his reaction to her statement. He plopped back onto the bed, scrambled up onto his knees, and grabbed his mother, his voice exploding out of him with outrage and amazement.

"He's missing—*he's missing!* They haven't found him—how can they say he's dead!"

"Andrew, his plane went down in the sea—"

"Did anybody see it? Did anyone see it go down?"

"No. He was hit...they saw his plane going out to sea...that's all."

Andrew's mouth dropped open in shock; then he hollered at the top of his voice: "He's missing. *MISSING!* They can't say he's dead if they haven't found his body. Even in court, they have to produce a body to prove someone's dead—don't they? If there's no body, there's no proof! *NO PROOF!* Don't you understand—he's not dead!" He's not—*he's not!*"

"Andrew, please understand—"

"HE'S NOT! HE'S NOT!"

"Alice—" Grandmother Howard slowly opened the door and took a tentative step forward. Andrew yelled at her, *"HE'S MISSING—MISSING—NOT DEAD—NOT DEAD—NOT DEAD—"*

"Mother—" Andrew's mother shook her head furiously and waved her hands in exasperation.

His grandmother stood there, rigid with shock; then her hands flew up to her mouth and she fled the room.

Andrew's mother grabbed his shoulders and shook him. "Andrew, he couldn't have survived. Nothing has been found—"

"He could have flown on to France, to Belgium—" Andrew wrestled out of her embrace, tried to collect his thoughts and work out a scenario: "If he got captured by the Germans—do you think they're going to ring us up right away with the news? We'll get a message—no! No! He wasn't captured—he was rescued—he's hiding someplace. He may not be able to get word to us, you see? It would be too dangerous! But he's all right!"

His mother closed her eyes in defeat. He stroked her face, realizing he'd probably startled her with his outburst. She was just stunned, that's all. He lowered his voice to a soft croon. "He's missing—*missing—MISSING!*...Please Mum, he's *not* dead...."

All right, he thought. No use getting into an argument—in time, she would see....

He heard the Prime Minister's voice coming from the radio in the morning room. His mother had not even informed him that Winnie was to be giving a speech that evening; usually she insisted that he listen to the Prime Minister's speeches on the BBC. Good old Winnie! Hearing Churchill was like a tonic—he certainly knew how to keep your spirits up! He was realistic, to be sure, but always had words of encouragement and hope....

> *The German effort to secure daylight mastery of the air over England is, of course, the crux of the whole war. So far, it has failed conspicuously, and has cost the Germans very dear. It has cost them very dear, and we have felt stronger, and actually are relatively a good deal stronger, than when the hard fighting began in July. There is no doubt that Herr Hitler is using up his fighter force at a very high rate, and that if he goes on for many more weeks he will wear down and ruin this vital part of his air force. That will give us a great advantage....*

No doubt about it, our RAF trounced the daylights out of the Luftwaffe! Dad said those Huns wouldn't beat us, didn't he?

> *...On the other hand, for him to try to invade this country without having secured mastery in the air would be a very hazardous undertaking. Nevertheless, all his preparations for invasion on a great scale are steadily going forward....*

Andrew sat down next to his mother and squeezed her hand. Don't worry, he wanted to say. Everything's going to be all right!

... We cannot tell when they will try to come; we cannot be sure that in fact they will try at all; but no one should blind himself to the fact that a heavy, full-scale invasion of this Island is being prepared with all the usual German thoroughness and method, and that it may be launched at any time now—upon England, upon Scotland, upon Ireland, or upon all three....

Let them come! We'll give it back to them!

Every man and every woman will therefore prepare himself to do his duty, whatever it may be, with special pride and care. The Royal Air Force is at the highest strength it has ever reached, conscious also of its proved superiority, not indeed in numbers, but in men and machines. Our shores are well fortified and strongly manned....

Good show, Winnie! We'll kick the Huns back to Hunland, easy as kiss your hand!

...It is a time for everyone to hold together and to stand firm, as they are doing....

Stand firm! That's what Dad would want me to do....

...behind the waiting forces are a people who will not flinch or weary of the struggle, hard and protracted though it will be, but that we shall rather draw from the heart of suffering itself the means of inspiration and survival, and of victory, won not only for ourselves, but for all; a victory won not only for our own time, but for the long and better days that are to come.

Andrew almost burst with joy. *Long and better days that are to come!* All day he had been wishing for a kind of...sign. Not proof, although a message that his father was all right would have sent him soaring with rapture....

He jumped up, whirled out the door and ran through the house, giddy with joy. He threw open every door to every room...It was his house—*his!* His father would come back, and Andrew would make sure that he never again would feel unwelcome or unworthy in this place. Never!

A memorial service was held for his father at the end of September. The night before, when Andrew's mother came to his room to tuck him into bed, she told him about it: It was to be held at a small chapel near his father's airfield. Even though his mother felt it was not quite safe for him to go back to school yet, she was sure there would be no problems if they were to go down the day before, stay overnight at Armus House, attend the service the next morning, then return straightaway to Northumberland. Her proposal was met with a look from Andrew that clearly conveyed his disbelief and contempt.

"Andrew, darling, I think it would be a good idea for you to go—"

"No!" Andrew turned from her.

"Andrew, you need to accept—"

"He's *missing!*"

"Andrew—"

"He's *MISSING!*"

"Aunt Jane and Aunt Gwen and Gram will be there. My mother is coming, also. You don't want to be left here all alone, with just the servants, do y—"

"*No!*" He pulled the covers up over his face and huddled down into the bed.

The next morning she awakened him. She was already dressed in a suit, ready for travel.

"You can still change your mind, darling."

He turned his head away. He had already resolved not to so much as acknowledge her departure, for even that would be a betrayal of his father.

"Wish me safe journey, Andrew." She gave him a soft kiss on the forehead.

He closed his eyes. After a moment he heard her footsteps, lonely staccatos against the parquet floor, fade into silence.

He decided to write a letter to the Prime Minister. For days his conscience had been nagging him about how terribly he had felt about Winnie and how beastly his attitude had been in general. Even though he had been worried about his father, it was still no excuse for his awful thoughts. He remembered the admonishments from the chapel services he was obligated to attend every day at boarding school (and twice on Sunday) about how God honors a "contrite heart" and about how important it was to "confess your sins." God was awfully busy, to be sure, but Andrew figured he at least stood a better chance of having his requests for his father's safekeeping honored (*hiding out, please God, not in some ghastly prison*) and his pleas for assurances as to his whereabouts answered speedily (*better yet, God, a personal appearance, if it wouldn't be too much trouble*) if he made amends with those he had wronged, even in his heart:

Dear Mr. Churchill,

I know you are a very busy man, and I don't expect an answer, but I wanted you to know how much I appreciate your encouraging speeches and all you are doing. I wanted you to know that I—

Andrew bit his pencil. *Used to have a very horrible attitude?...was quite beastly in what I thought of you?....said terribly nasty things in my mind about you when you were on the wireless?*

—used to get very upset when I heard you talking on the wireless, because I was very frightened because of the war. My father (Flight Lieutenant Roger Hadley-Trevelyan, RAF) always told me never to be angry at others because of fear or despair, and I confess that is what I did, and I was very wrong to do so, and I'm sorry.

There! His conscience was clear!

I want you to know that I admire you very much, and I think your speeches are absolutely smashing. I am always very encouraged by what you have to say, and I hope that you will continue to make such jolly good speeches. Even though things are very frightening now, it is good to hear you talk about the long and better days to come, and that we should stand firm. I believe as you do, that in the end, all will come right.

Andrew chomped on his pencil again. How should he close? *Your humble subject*—no, he wasn't writing to the King. *Your devoted servant*—no, too glaringly obeisant—Winnie would see right through it! He finally decided to sign it: *Your Fellow Countryman, Andrew Hadley-Trevelyan.* He addressed it to 10 Downing Street, London, and posted it the next time he and his mother went to town.

No one can predict, no one can even imagine, how this terrible war against Germans and Nazi aggression will run its course or how far it will spread or how long it will last. Long dark months of trials and tribulations lie before us....

Andrew dialed up the volume on the radio. It was now October and still his mother had not let him return to school. Even though he was on English soil, he felt as if he were abandoning his country by being safely tucked away in the North, far from the war's excitement. At least he could listen to the Prime Minister's speeches and bind the words into his heart. Good old Winnie—he knew how to say just the right thing to banish the demons of doubt and fear!

....We must be united, we must be undaunted, we must be inflexible. Our qualities and deeds must burn and glow through the gloom of Europe until they become the veritable beacon of its salvation....

*United, undaunted, inflexible....*Well, skip the united: Andrew knew he was alone in his conviction that his father would return. But undaunted and inflexible—Winnie *certainly* must have been thinking of him when he spoke those words: *Cheer up, Andrew—stand firm! Everything is going to turn out right!*

"What did Dr. Baxter say, Miss Alice?" Andrew had just come in from a walk and was tiptoeing through the dining room so as to surprise Mrs. Beaton. He was about to open the door to the kitchen when he heard her query, then his mother's voice in reply.

"He said not to worry. It's common for people to deny that someone they love is gone for good. He says Andrew's going through a phase. It's just his way of dealing with the shock of it all, and that sooner or later he'll be all right."

"What should we do in the meantime? He's always talking about his father coming back. Should we just tell him that he's not?"

"No—Dr. Baxter says not to argue with him, but not to agree either. Just listen to him. Mrs. Beaton, I do so appreciate the concern and the care you've shown him. He seems to be able to talk with you—"

"Oh, tch! No trouble at all. He's a bonny lad, he is—and I feel like he's one of my own, almost. After all, I saw him come into the world, and what a grand sight that was! I said to myself, I did, I said: 'This lad is going to be special—very special indeed!' He *was* special, I mean, and *is*, to us, that is, but I felt that he was meant for something wonderful, on a grander scale. He'll be all right, he will, Miss Alice."

Andrew heard a muffled sob, silence, then the sound of soft crying. Then, Mrs. Beaton's voice, gently solicitous:

"Miss Alice—don't you worry! He's going to be all right—he is, I *know* he is! Now, you'd best take care of yourself—you've been letting yourself get ever so thin. You still have your application in to be a ferry pilot, don't you? They might not take you looking as peeky as you do. Here, sit yourself down for some Woolton Pie. I used some stew drippings in it, and I think that it has a better flavor. Have you heard from that Air Transport Auxiliary?"

"Yes, my application is being considered, but it doesn't look promising. I don't have enough flying hours—"

"Tch—you have lots of hours, don't you?"

"Just a little over a hundred. The minimum is a hundred and fifty right now. I don't think they're going to be lowering the requirement in the near future."

"Well, not to worry. They'll be needing more pilots, what with the way things are going."

"Well, if I don't hear from them in a few weeks, I'm going to join the Auxiliary Territorial Services. I just feel that I need to be *doing* something!"

"Are you going to send Andrew back to school, then?"

"Yes, I've been in contact with his housemaster and he says that they haven't had any problems with bombings and such. They just have air raids a few nights a week, but no bombings in the immediate area. When they get an alert, they have to get the children into the shelters, you see, even though the possibility of them getting bombed is remote."

"Did you tell the housemaster about Andrew's problem?"

"Yes, I did. I just phoned him today, after I'd talked with Dr. Baxter. He needs to know how to deal with Andrew."

"So you say we're not to agree with him, or argue with him either?"

"That's about it."

"Sometimes he can be very emphatic, you know."

"Yes, I know."

"What should we do then?"

"Dr. Baxter says to say something like 'I know you loved your father very much.' He'll soon realize that his father is not going to come back and accept what's happened."

Andrew heaved a sigh. For some time, he'd had the feeling that everyone was humoring him—no, he *knew* everyone had been humoring him. They were treating him like some sort of deranged...*fool*. Worst of all, his mother was upset.

He walked quietly out to the hall. Best not to let on that he knew what everyone was up to. He was alone...alone in his belief that his father still lived. No matter, England was alone, too—the only nation in the world to stand against the Nazi tyranny. So even if he was the only one in the world who believed that his father was alive...well then, he was the only one!

Alone in the breach...that's what he was. Someday he would be able to say to his father *I never doubted—never!* (Well, he *had*, but just for those few awful days at first, and that was before he found out what had *really* happened.) Even if the whole world doubted, he would keep faith, and be able to look his father in the eye and speak his heart.

I never doubted that you were alive, that you would come back...I never gave up hope.

Chapter 9

*A*ndrew's mother took him back to school the following week. Classes had just been dismissed when Mr. Nugent met them at the dormitory. He greeted Andrew warmly, a little too warmly, Andrew thought, and didn't ask any questions about how his summer had been. Over tea he told them how the school year had gone so far: There usually were air raids a few times a week, so it was important to keep coats and warm clothing within easy access at night, preferably on the bed, and shoes nearby as well. Did he have any warm socks? Yes, Andrew answered, Mrs. Beaton had knitted him some. Good, murmured Mr. Nugent. He went on to say that Charles Provis and Simon Inskip had been sent to Canada, and there was a new boy in their class, Wilfred Smith. There were also two women teachers at the school now, Miss Fantle and Miss Baveystock; they taught the boys in the Infants' classes. They had replaced two of the men teachers, Mr. Heacham and Mr. Thackray, who had joined the RAF as intelligence officers.

"Darling, why don't you go upstairs and get your things put away?" Andrew's mother murmured tenderly. Notwithstanding her tone of voice, it was a command, not a request, and Andrew knew that he was about to become the topic of discussion. He shuffled up the stairs to his room and proceeded to unpack his clothes. His mother came up after a half hour, kissed him good-bye, and departed. Mr. Nugent then tapped gently on the door frame, even though the door was open. For a moment Andrew continued with his task of putting his woolen socks into the dresser by his bed. Then he looked up. Mr. Nugent walked in and sat on the chair by Andrew's bed.

"How have you been, Andrew?"

Andrew shrugged. "Fine," he mumbled. He turned away for a moment and collected his thoughts. He knew what he had to do. It was all his fault that his mother had gotten so thin—she had been *so* anxious about him. As much as Andrew wanted to convince her that his father was still alive, he knew that his adamant assertions had only distressed her. It wasn't *her* fault that she couldn't believe that his father still lived, and it was better to let her alone. No matter, he alone would carry the faith that his father was still alive. He didn't need to speak of it: It would be a secret that he would hide away in his heart. He would not tell anyone—*anyone*! Not his mother, not Gram, not even Aunt Jane. And he would certainly not tell his school chums—they would surely laugh at him behind his back: *He's nutters...he's daft as Lord Haw Haw...thinks his father is coming back!*

He closed the drawer and turned to Mr. Nugent. "My father was shot down."

"Yes, I know." Mr. Nugent's voice was almost a whisper.

"He might still be alive." This statement, spoken wistfully, was followed by a small sigh.

Mr. Nugent folded his hands together, brought them up to his chin, and gazed sympathetically at Andrew. Andrew bit his lip and looked down at the floor, trying to evince a look of doubt and sadness.

"What if he's not?" He looked up at Mr. Nugent and scrunched his face into a worried expression.

Mr. Nugent put his hand on Andrew's shoulder. "You and your father were very close, weren't you?"

Andrew nodded furiously, hopped up, and walked briskly out of the room.

There, he thought, it's done. Mr. Nugent probably thinks I've gone off to have a good cry, and now he'll be able to report to my mother that I'm "adjusting." I won't ever speak of my father again—not to him, not to my mother, not to anyone!

He had a dream that night: He was gazing out his bedroom window at Armus House and a spot of blue-grey appeared in the distance. Even in his dream, he could feel his heart pounding with elation. He flew out of his room and down the stairs. He expected that he would have to run a great distance to meet up with his father but, as he burst through the front doorway, he saw his father starting up the steps. One leap—and Andrew was in his arms.

"They told Mum you were missing. She doesn't believe you're coming back. I had to pretend,too...Mum was upset because I kept telling her you were alive—"

"I know." The words were whispered in his ear.

Andrew nuzzled his face against his father's neck. He felt gentle fingers stroking his hair, his cheeks, wiping his tears away. He closed his eyes and pressed his lips to his father's face, which smelled fresh and clean with shaving soap. A soft kiss grazed his forehead.

"I know you're alive—I know you'll come back—I know—*I know!*" Andrew moaned as the arms clasped him tightly. His low cry turned into a wail, which grew louder and louder until it seemed the sound of it would shatter them both. His father started shaking him, and Andrew was terrified to find that he couldn't stop the awful wail from coming out of his mouth. As his father continued to shake him, it seemed that everything around him got very jumbled up—the sky, the ground, Armus House, his father, all seemed to whirl around him.

"Andrew—*Andrew!*" His father's voice grew high pitched with distress.

"*ANDREW!*"

He awoke to find Gregory Thomas shaking him savagely. The blaring noise, like an up-and-down wail of despair, nearly drowned out everything else, but Andrew could see that the room was alive with commotion: Everyone was yelling, grabbing at coats and sweaters and socks and shoes, and scrambling out the door.

"Chop-chop!" Mr. Nugent's voice carried over the din.

Gregory flung Andrew's socks and shoes at him and dashed out.

"Andrew!" Mr. Nugent's call was sharp with agitation.

"Coming!" He pulled on his shoes, forgetting his socks. He jammed his arms though the sleeves of his coat and raced down the stairs. Mr. Nugent was counting heads as Andrew's classmates ran through the doorway.

"Quickly, quickly, Andrew—" Mr. Nugent pronounced "thirteen" as Andrew dashed out the front door to follow the dozen darkened forms of his classmates lumbering though the night ahead of him.

Thus, for Andrew, began "The Blitz."

A few days later, Andrew was walking with Colin Kirknewton to soccer practice.

"My father's missing," Colin said in a strained voice.

Andrew looked at him, wondering if he should dare reveal his secret conviction.

Colin bit his lip. "He wasn't evacuated at Dunkirk. We...we haven't heard anything..." His voice trailed off.

Andrew took a deep breath, looked around to see that no one else was around, and said in a low voice, "My father's missing, too."

"What happened?"

"He was shot down, on 7 September."

"That's when they had that terrible attack on London."

Andrew nodded. Colin went on. "My cousin lives in London, and he said it was awful. The whole East End was a gigantic inferno."

"We heard about it up in Northumberland. We also heard that Eastbourne and other towns on the coast were in ruins and that the Nazis were dropping paratroopers dressed as nuns. It was only later that we found out it wasn't true, except for London being in flames."

Colin bit his lip. "I think my father's still alive." He looked pleadingly at Andrew, as if asking him for reassurance.

Andrew swallowed and whispered, "I think my father is still alive, too."

Mrs. Bunch tried to make do with the more stringent food rationing and increasing shortages, but more and more sinister dishes started appearing at mealtimes: a horrid looking dish called "Poor Man's Goose," the ubiquitous Woolton Pie, and a ghastly green concoction with the ominous name of "Vitality Mold." They often had fish, which Andrew disliked, and what little meat to be had was usually mutton, kidney pie, liver, or creamed chipped beef on toast, all of which Andrew detested. His two least favorite vegetables, Brussels sprouts and spinach (cooked to a mushy pulp) were served with unpleasant regularity. Arthur Popham-Goode caused quite a stir among the boys in the Infants' classes when he avouched, straight-faced, that the ingredients in "Spotted Dick" were actually the cut up private parts of German prisoners of war. As this declaration was made after the dish in question had been consumed, it caused no small amount of distress amongst the very impressionable younger boys. After a night of dealing with hysterical wails at bedtime and nightmares all night, Miss Baveystock forced Arthur to publicly recant his statement in the dining hall the next morning.

Another dish also appeared: Boston Bake, composed of white beans, carrots, and bacon. Mrs. Bunch was enjoined from serving it more than once a week, and on the nights it was served Mr. Nugent prayed fervently at grace that "If it's possible, Most Gracious Lord, *please* let us not have any air raids tonight." Of course, God, being as busy as he was what with the war and all, was not always able to comply, and it was after consuming this particular dish that one of the more memorable—well, *infamous* would be more to the point—incidents of that year occurred.

The wail of the siren roused Andrew out of a deep slumber. He had long since gotten over the novelty of these nocturnal interruptions: the howl of the Alert; the shuffle in the dark for shoes, socks, and coats; the hustling down the stairs, out into the cold night, and down another set of stairs in the shelter dug near the playing field; the long, chilly wait, scrunched together on hard, *very* hard, wooden benches; the sound of bombs crumping in the distance; the feel of the earth trembling.

He found himself jammed between Colin Kirknewton and Nigel Willoughby-Ramsbotton and seated kneecap-to-kneecap opposite the new boy, Wilfred Smith. The distant thumps of bombs had abated, and they were waiting for the blast of the All-clear. Wilfred hissed at Andrew.

"Did you just spring a leak?" Andrew whispered savagely.

"Pull my finger." Wilfred held his pinky finger out to Andrew.

"What?"

"I said," Wilfred narrowed his eyes and his voice dropped to a threatening growl, "*Pull my finger.*"

Andrew narrowed his eyes back at Wilfred. "Why?"

"Because I said so," Wilfred hissed.

Andrew thought it best not to make an issue of things; Wilfred had proven himself to be quite pugnacious and Andrew had no desire to make an already unpleasant night any worse. Just humor the silly sod....

Andrew let out a small groan of exasperation and pulled Wilfred's finger. Wilfred's eyes bulged, and he let out a tremendous fart. "Andrew did it! Andrew did it!" he yelled in wounded wail.

"*Did not!*" Andrew yelled.

"Did too! Did *too!*" Wilfred shouted.

Andrew lunged at him and yanked him off the bench. They fell to the floor, Andrew bellowing his innocence, Wilfred snarling and kicking as Andrew clawed at his eyes. So furious was the commotion that Colin and Nigel fell on top of the struggling pair, and Andrew found himself turning his fury on Colin.

You told—you told everyone, you sodding bastard! It took all his strength to choke back the words; what actually came out of his mouth was a blood-curdling howl as he pummeled Colin. He should have never said a word about his father—Colin had blabbed it all over, surely he had, and now everyone was laughing at him behind his back: *He's nutters, he is—positively off his rocker! Thinks his father is coming back!*

"Andrew! Colin! Boys!" Mr. Nugent barked. "Be seated! Be seated at once, this instant!" He struggled through the maze of interlocked legs and proceeded to pry apart the combatants.

"Andrew, come with me," Mr. Nugent commanded. Andrew stumbled behind him, hooking his ankle on Harry Peel's leg and falling again. Harry laughed; Andrew pounced on him. Mr. Nugent disengaged Andrew's fingers from Harry's throat, hauled Andrew off and plopped him down on end of the bench, then sat next to him, effectively isolating him from the rest of the students.

"Andrew, what's bothering you?" Mr. Nugent's voice was gentle and sympathetic as he poured Andrew a cup of tea. "You can tell me. I want to help."

Andrew had already decided what he would tell Mr. Nugent. After they had returned to their beds following the All-clear, he had lain awake working out the explanation he would give. It would, he knew, be disseminated to the other boys (in private of course) and related to his mother as well.

Dad, even though I have to say this, it's not what I believe. I know that lying is wrong, but this really isn't lying. I just don't want Mum to worry. You're probably hiding out somewhere, pretending to be someone you're not, in order to escape being captured. You certainly can't let on that you're a British airman!

So I know you would understand that there are times when you have to be less than truthful.

Andrew blinked a few times, took a few deep, rapid breaths, and said in a quavery voice, "He's dead, isn't he?"

Besides, I said "he"—not "my father." I could be talking about anyone, you see. John's father, Colin's father, Grandfather Howard...anyone!

Mr. Nugent put his hand on Andrew's shoulder. "I'm very sorry," he whispered.

He sought out Colin Kirknewton. Thinking about it, after the fury within him had dissipated, Andrew realized that Colin probably had not told the other boys anything. Colin was a quiet person to begin with, and not given to blabbering other people's secrets. And even if he had, Andrew knew that he would not have been the butt of humor had the other boys known, anyway. Keith Vincent-Hill's father, a navigator in Bomber Command, had been shot down over Germany and declared "missing"; Keith made no secret of his belief that his father was alive and would come home one day. None of the other boys made derisive observations about Keith's convictions, either to his face or behind his back, and no wonder—nearly all of them had fathers, brothers, uncles, or cousins serving in the military, and they no doubt realized that someday they would have to face the prospect of someone they loved being declared "missing." For it was obvious that, even though the Battle of Britain had been won and that England no longer faced the immediate danger of invasion, Hitler would certainly make another attempt against Britain the following spring. In the meantime, the Luftwaffe was savaging London and other major cities, and "wolf-packs" of German U-Boats were mangling the shipping convoys bringing vital supplies from the New World. To effectively destroy the threat of tyranny, England eventually would have to invade the continent, and who knew how costly an endeavor that would be?

As Andrew followed Colin out of the classroom building after classes had been dismissed, any trace of anger he still harbored evaporated at the thought that he had not been singled out for ridicule the previous night. It had been pure coincidence, surely, that he had sat opposite Wilfred and thus had been the target of his silly prank.

Andrew caught up with Colin and nervously glanced at him. He felt horrible about what he had done and didn't want to lose Colin's friendship, besides. Even though he would pretend from now on that he believed his father was gone for good, he still felt a kinship with Colin and knew how hard it was to keep faith in spite of overwhelming odds. Most of all, he needed to keep his conscience clean, for he didn't want any unconfessed sin to tip the scales in his disfavor as he continued to entreat the Almighty for his father's safekeeping and eventual return.

"Sorry about last night," Andrew murmured.

Colin looked at him, bit his lip, and blurted, "That's all right."

"No, it isn't. I was upset about my father, but I shouldn't have been mean to you."

"I'm sorry about your father—I mean, you found out that he was killed, then?"

Andrew looked off into the distance for a moment, then turned to Colin.

"I hope your father comes back someday."

Andrew's mother arrived to pick him up for Christmas holidays. She was dressed in the uniform of the Auxiliary Territorial Services and, when questioned about her duties by Andrew's curious classmates, she replied that she worked on an anti-aircraft battery. This pronouncement was met with an awed hush and wide-eyed stares by most of the boys, except for Arthur, who was curious as to whether or not she was the only woman on the team.

"Oh no, I'm in a mixed battery. Some batteries are all male, some are composed of men and women together."

"Men and women together! Doesn't that cause problems?"

"Why should it?" Andrew's mother countered. "It's important for everyone on the team to do their job properly—if one person makes the slightest mistake, it ruins the work of everyone. We're all determined to do our best, for we don't want to let one another down. When we're working together, the only thing that matters is how well we do our jobs, and the men—at least all the men on *our* team—respect us for that. Most of them have worked before with women in factories and such, so it's not such a novel thing to be working with women on a mixed battery."

"Have you shot down many enemy planes?" Gregory Thomas asked.

"A few, but our objective is not solely to shoot down planes. If we can make the bombers take such evasive action so that they can't drop their bombs accurately, then we've succeeded in protecting the objectives that we are charged with defending— factories, military bases, airfields—"

"But the bombers are still going to drop their bombs," Keith Vincent-Hill pointed out. "They're going to do damage all the same. What if they drop their bombs on an important building or kill people? What if the bombs kill someone important—like the Prime Minister or the King?"

"We are only concerned about protecting our objective. If we can prevent the enemy planes from releasing their bombs accurately, then we've done our job. Other guns are sighted to defend other areas, and their batteries are concerned with protecting *their* objective. We worry about doing our job, not about other people doing theirs. That's how everyone works together."

On their way to London, she told Andrew that they would be celebrating Christmas a few days early because she would have to work on Christmas day. Furthermore, what with the war and all, she wasn't certain that they would be able to go up to Northumberland at the end of Yuletide holidays, which was their usual custom. She had requested a few days off after the New Year, but if anything came up she would have to work. This did not bother Andrew in the least, for he was hoping that her duties would prevent them from going up to Greycliff.

Please God, he breathed, that would be the best—*almost* the best—Christmas gift of all.

They changed to the Underground in London. It was late afternoon and, as they stopped at various stations along the way, Andrew was surprised and appalled to see mobs of people huddled on the platforms.

"People take shelter in the Underground at night," his mother explained.

They caught the train to Berkshire and were met at the station by Thomas.

"Andrew, you look like you need a bit of fattening up," Thomas said after they had gotten into the Bentley. "Haven't they been feeding you at school?"

"Mrs. Bunch has been serving up the ghastliest things," Andrew replied. "I'm sick of Woolton Pie and Boston Bake and Vitality Mold."

Thomas chuckled as he started the car. "Well, things have been quite stringent at Armus House, but my Vi does work wonders despite things, she does, and she'll no doubt proceed to stuff you like a Christmas pig. Speaking of which, Freddie managed to get us a ham—God knows where he got it from—so we'll at least have that for Christmas dinner."

"Freddie's back?" Andrew exclaimed in dismay.

"Got back two days ago," Thomas said. "Guess he'd rather endure the Blitz than a stay in America. By the way, Miss Alice, did you read today's newspaper? It has a copy of the speech President Roosevelt gave about that Lend-Lease thing he's trying to get passed into law."

"No, I haven't seen the paper yet," Andrew's mother said.

"What's Lend-Lease?" Andrew asked.

"If it gets passed, it'll mean salvation for us." Thomas pulled to the side of the road to let a despatch rider on a motorcycle pass. "America will lend us the equipment and supplies we need to fight the war and, after it's over, we'll return what we can or pay them back somehow. In his speech Mr. Roosevelt compared it to loaning a garden hose to a neighbor whose house is on fire. It'd be stupid to demand that the chap buy it, or refuse to sell it to him if he hasn't got the money, since the fire could spread to your own house and you'd lose everything, too. You help your neighbor to save his own house, and your own, and you get your garden hose back in the end. Wonderful way of putting it, isn't it? I do hope the American people see reason."

"I hope so, too, Thomas," Andrew's mother replied.

"I've heard that there are some American pilots in the RAF," Thomas said. "Most of them are in that Eagle Squadron—that's what they call it—that got formed up in September. There were even some American chaps who fought in the Battle of Britain."

Andrew's mother nodded absently and looked out the window. They rode along in silence for several minutes, then Thomas cleared his throat. "The news from North Africa is good—isn't it? We've got Mousso's army on the run and our army's taking so many prisoners that, instead of counting them, our boys are measuring them! One chap reported that he had 'five acres of officers and two hundred acres of other ranks!' And this one tank commander got stopped by hundreds of Italians with their hands up—he radioed back 'For heaven's sake, send in the bloody infantry!'" He chuckled. "Those Greeks are giving those Eye-ties a proper trouncing, too. That'll teach old Mousso to go messing about with his neighbors! Well, if that Lend-Lease thing gets passed and we can get the arms and equipment to whip the Jerries once and for all, and what with the thrashing we're giving those dirty ice-creamers, we might have peace by next Christmas—let's hope so, at least! Hullo, we're here."

Aunt Jane and Gram came running down the steps to greet them. Andrew was crushed in hugs and smothered with kisses, then conveyed inside, where Mrs. Tuttle awaited them with an offering of Apricot Upside Down Pudding.

"Gwen is working late tonight," Gram informed them as they seated themselves for tea. "She'll catch the early train out tomorrow morning. We'll set up the Christmas tree after she gets here—you know how she loves to decorate it. Then we'll celebrate Christmas the day afterward. She has to be back at work the next day—poor dear, she really misses Robert not being able to come home for the holidays. Give her lots of special attention, Andrew, won't you?"

Andrew nodded between mouthfuls of pudding. He had noticed the tinge of sadness in Gram's voice, as much as she tried to be cheerful. And Aunt Jane—the look in her eyes really frightened him: that vacant, stunned look; the same look she had when she had come home from France after Uncle Marc....

No, thought Andrew. Maybe she doesn't really know—or she's just not sure. Maybe, deep down inside, there's a faint hope, but not a firm conviction, and she doesn't think it would be right to divulge it right now. All the same, he decided not to press the matter with her.

It's not as if she has known everything about him, all the time. Just feelings sometimes, strong feelings. He might have been...knocked out, yes knocked out for awhile, after he crashed. It took him awhile to get his bearings, and now he's hiding out, careful not to reveal too much, pretending to be someone else.

What do I do, if my home is made uninhabitable by a bomb?

On the page opposite the article entitled *Your Best Friend is Your Gas Mask,* this woeful query was followed by the proper steps one should take upon being faced with this unfortunate predicament.

Andrew sighed and folded the page back, so as not to have any more reminders of this wretched war.

What do I do, if I hear the bloody war is over?

Andrew had always enjoyed Christmas, for, being the only child in an extended family of adults, he was the center of attention.

Every Christmas there had been piles and piles of presents under the tree for him; this year the amount of gifts was substantially reduced due to shortages, but the holiday still revolved around him all the same. Aunt Jane gave him a new chess set; Aunt Gwen gave him some Biggles books and a jigsaw puzzle of an anti-aircraft battery; Gram gave him a sweater she had knitted; from Freddie (who had consumed too much eggnog for breakfast and was already laid out to rest in the study) there was a book about sailing ships; from his mother, a wooden box about the size of a small travel case. It had brass hinges and lock, and the top was inlaid in a darker wood with the initials *A.H.* "For your treasures," his mother said. She handed him another present, one of two remaining.

"This one arrived at Greycliff. Your grandmother sent it here," his mother said.

Andrew withdrew a package wrapped in brown paper from a bright red box. He tore off the wrapping. It was a book: *My Early Life,* by Winston Churchill, and signed on the fly-leaf, *To Andrew Hadley-Trevelyan, from your fellow-countryman, Winston Churchill.* A letter fluttered down from the pages. The letter was typed, and signed at the bottom by the Prime Minister:

Dear Andrew,

Thank you so much for your kind letter, and for your encouraging words. I received your letter soon after the Destroyers for Bases transaction was concluded to the mutual satisfaction of our country and the United States. Wishing to impress upon President Roosevelt our continued resolve and determination in our struggle against tyranny, I arranged for your letter to be sent to him, so that he might know that even the youngest British citizens are undiscouraged and unshaken in their belief that we will ultimately prevail.

I have been informed by Fighter Command that your father was a superb officer and pilot, with a distinguished record and the esteem of his colleagues. He is one of "the few" to whom Britain owes its survival, and you have every reason to be very proud of him.

Winston Churchill

"My goodness, a letter from the Prime Minister!" Gram exclaimed. "What did you write him?"

Andrew shrugged. "Just a letter."

"Oh, Andrew, I think that's *splendid*!" Aunt Gwen said. "You ought to save this letter, put it in your treasure box. And he sent your message along to President Roosevelt, too!"

His mother handed him the final package. "It's from your father."

Andrew opened the present: a pair of boxing gloves. "He bought them just before he left," his mother said softly.

He lovingly stroked the gloves, closed his eyes, and tried to imagine that he was touching his father's hands.

Do you know, somehow, that I'm holding the present you got for me? I wish I could give you something....

He sat motionless, clutching the gloves, while the grown-ups opened their presents. Andrew had made packets of stationery for everyone; Mr. Nugent had obtained plain envelopes and paper and had set the boys in class to monogramming them and decorating them with colorful borders.

"Oh, Andrew, how clever! Positively smashing!" Aunt Gwen exclaimed. "I shall write you every week!" She gave him a fierce hug. Everyone else thanked him profusely as well, then they went into the dining room for elevensies.

Later that evening Andrew wandered into his parents' (he could not think of it as *just* his mother's) room. On his mother's dresser was his father's shaving mug and brush. He picked them up and sat on the bed, holding them in his hands.

His mother came in and sat down next to him. "I picked up some of your father's things at his squadron when I went down for the memorial service."

"May I keep these?" Andrew asked softly.

She nodded. "I know he would want you to have them." She put her arms around him and pressed her cheek against his.

I wish you could believe he's still alive. I don't want to distress you by insisting that he is, so I'll believe for both of us....

He placed the mug and brush in his treasure box, along with the letter and book he had received from the Prime Minister. He wrapped his father's letters in the RAF handkerchief, tied them with some leftover Christmas ribbon, and put them in the box also.

Aunt Gwen returned to London the next day; Andrew's mother the day after that, which was Christmas Eve.

"Darling, I wish I could be with you for Christmas, but the war doesn't allow for holidays," she murmured as she kissed him good-bye at the station. She then gave Gram and Aunt Jane a quick embrace. After the train had gone, they went to the home of one of Aunt Jane's friends in town, so that they could have tea before going to church for a performance by the choir of Handel's *Messiah*, which was their Christmas Eve tradition.

Sitting scrunched in the pew between Aunt Jane and Gram, Andrew could not help but reflect on how different this Christmas was from every Christmas past. Last year, everyone had been home for Christmas. Now there was only him, Aunt Jane, Gram, and Freddie. (Why couldn't *he* have stayed in America?) And Aunt Jane would be leaving the day after Christmas. She had recently joined the First Aid Nursing Yeomanry, or FANYs, and had to return to her duties. Andrew had inquired as to what sort of duties she performed, since she wasn't a nurse.

"We're also known as the Women's Transport Service," she had told him, "So we act as drivers, besides doing nursing."

Aunt Jane knew how to drive, which was quite uncommon for a woman to do at the time, so Andrew accepted her explanation, although he privately wondered why she had not chosen to do something that made better use of her talents—for instance, languages. Being fluent in French and German, as well as several other languages, should have certainly guaranteed her a more important job, such as translating or acting as a liaison between the British government and the French military personnel or other important people who were now in England. She knew German, too—what about translating German newspapers and documents and such? Besides her facility with languages, she was smart, too—surely she could have found something to do that made better use of her intelligence than simply driving a car!

The choir blasted out the usual *hallelujahs*, the performance ended, and Andrew made his way outside with Aunt Jane and Gram. Thomas had the car waiting for them.

Andrew rested his head against Aunt Jane's shoulder as Thomas drove them home. He closed his eyes for a few minutes and, when he opened them, he saw a large fire in one of the fields they passed. Several people were standing around, watching it.

"Why are they just looking at it?" he exclaimed. "Why don't they put it out?"

"Because it's a decoy fire," Thomas told him.

"A *decoy* fire?"

"It's to trick the German planes into thinking it's a target lit by incendiaries," Thomas explained. "So they drop their bombs in a field, not on an important factory or airfield."

After they arrived at Armus House they had a late supper of leftover ham. Gram had invited Thomas, Mrs. Tuttle, and Lucia to dine with them, a significant break with tradition. (Freddie would have been appalled at them "consorting" with the help, but he was by now well pickled, and past caring about such things.) Mrs. Tuttle had made the traditional Christmas trifle: a marvelous creation of ladyfingers layered with custard and different sorts of jams and marmalades. She had saved a month's ration of sugar to make the ladyfingers, and urged them to "Enjoy, enjoy—I can't promise one for next year. I've heard awful rumors that they're going to ration jam and marmalade."

"Jam and marmalade!" Gram exclaimed. "How ghastly!"

"I wish they would ration vegetables," Andrew grumbled. "I'm sick of them. I've eaten enough spinach and Brussels sprouts to last my whole life!"

Mrs. Tuttle pinched his waist. "Not enough, Master Andrew—you're looking quite peeked. Have yourself an extra helping of trifle. That'll put some fat on your bones." She dished him out a second portion.

Aunt Jane put him to bed and read to him from *A Christmas Carol*, which his mother and father used to do. His father would do the narrative and the voices of the male characters and his mother would do the female roles and the ghosts. Andrew's father could do voices so well: Scrooge had a sour, grumbly, voice; Bob Cratchitt had a gentle, quavery delivery; and Tiny Tim piped out every line with childlike wonder and excitement. Andrew tried to imagine his father's voice overlaying Aunt Jane's soothing, albeit somewhat flat, rendition, but to no avail.

I'll just close my eyes and pretend you're somehow with me, feeling what I'm feeling, hoping what I'm hoping—that we'll be together soon. If you can't have a happy Christmas, at least know that I'm thinking of you....

It was Sunday evening and Andrew, after having tea, had just curled up in bed to finish *Huckleberry Finn*. He had dropped off to sleep, and was awakened by a tap on his door.

"Andrew," his grandmother called. "Supper in a bit."

"Coming."

Andrew got out of bed, pulled on his sweater, and put on his socks and shoes. He turned off the reading light by his bed, and was about to leave the room when he decided to take a peek out his window. Whenever possible, he liked to look at the stars— even just a glance, trying to imagine his father looking up at the same sky....

Something was odd—*very* odd. Instead of the inky black night, there was a funny reddish glow. At first he thought it was a stunning sunset but then he realized: *It was to the east!*

"Gram!" he yelled.

"What is it, darling?" she called from downstairs

He stood mesmerized, staring out the window.

"What is it?" Gram entered the room and stood beside him.

"The sky—it's funny—look!"

He pulled back the blackout curtain. Gram's face at first registered a curious expression, then shock and horror.

"My God, it's London," she gasped.

Gram tried half the night, and all the next day, to get through to either Andrew's mother or Aunt Gwen, without success.

Thomas went to a Home Guard meeting and reported back that London was a frightful mess, but not completely incinerated.

"The City district and Southwark got the worst of it—all those warehouses and office buildings were set ablaze. St. Paul's is no doubt in ruins. There was fire all around it—impossible that it could have escaped being destroyed. But thank God for the filthy weather—a bloody great rainstorm moved in after the first raid, so the Jerries didn't come back and drop the high explosives. If they had, all of London would be in ruins."

Andrew spent another almost sleepless night, awakening around four-thirty in the morning on New Year's Eve day. He padded downstairs to make himself a cup of tea. He was in the kitchen, finishing his second cup, when Mrs. Tuttle shuffled in.

"You don't usually get up this early," Andrew said. It was a quarter past five.

She gave him a hug. "Couldn't sleep, either? Here, I'll make you some porridge."

"Do you think my mother's all right?"

"Oh, I'm sure she is." Mrs. Tuttle turned away and busied herself preparing the porridge, which she served to Andrew with a dab of jam, as he liked. He ate it at the table in the kitchen, sitting opposite Mrs. Tuttle. Thomas joined them after awhile—he couldn't sleep either, and Mrs. Tuttle served him the last of the porridge. Both of them had relatives living in London: Thomas's brother was a fireman, and Mrs. Tuttle had two sisters who cooked for families in Belgravia.

After having a third cup of tea to wash down his breakfast, Andrew wandered out to the drawing room. He curled up on the couch, pulled one of Gram's crazy quilts over him, and watched the tree until his eyelids grew heavy.

"Andrew!" The smell of smoke, and the familiar voice, startled him out of sleep.

"*Mum!*" He threw his arms around her. Her uniform was impregnated with an acrid, smoky stench and her eyes were red-rimmed. Something dreadful must have happened-

"Aunt Gwen!" he cried.

"She's all right." His mother kissed him gently, wearily, and plopped down on the floor.

"Why are you crying, Mum?"

"Oh, my eyes are just irritated from the smoke."

"You sound funny too."

"Smoke in the eyes, in the lungs, soot on my clothes—I need a bath—"

"Alice!" It was Gram in the doorway. "Oh dear, we've been so worried—we tried to phone—"

"Sorry, I couldn't get through, either."

"We're you able to contact Gwen?"

"Yes—she's fine. She's still working—" Andrew's mother stood, walked over to Gram, and gave her a hug.

Gram returned the embrace. "Poor dear—you look horribly exhausted yourself. How did you get here from the station?"

"Got a ride from a policeman—very nice chap. I shall always have a soft spot in my heart for officers of the law."

Gram smiled and gently stroked her cheek. "Why don't you get yourself to bed—"

Andrew's mother sighed, "Bath first—I feel absolutely grotty—"

Gram nodded and gave her another quick hug. As Andrew's mother was about to leave Gram piped, "Oh, did you hear about the speech Mr. Roosevelt gave? It was on the wireless yesterday morning."

Andrew's mother shook her head. Gram continued, "He told the American people that it was important that the United States send us the weapons and equipment and

137

supplies we need, so that we can keep fighting. He said something about the United States being the 'arsenal of democracy'".

Andrew's mother nodded wearily and trudged upstairs.

The terrible bombing of London had one redeeming aspect: Andrew did not have to go up to Northumberland to visit with Grandmother Howard. Several of his mother's coworkers on the anti-aircraft had been injured, so her leave was canceled. Aunt Jane and Aunt Gwen were similarly busy, and Gram, who was in the Women's Volunteer Services, could not spare the time either. She never knew when she might be called away to dispense tea to civil defense workers or people bombed out of their homes. Besides, travel by train was becoming a delay-ridden ordeal, made worse by having to suffer hideous overcrowding in fuggy compartments. His mother felt that they would be "doing their bit" by not adding to the crush of people already traveling.

Aunt Gwen was able to come home for three days during the first week in January; she spent about ninety percent of that time in bed, fast asleep. The rest of the time she was fussed over by Mrs. Tuttle, who bewailed her "emaciated" state.

"I've always been a bit on the pudgy side—never lost my baby fat, you know," she remarked to Mrs. Tuttle at tea one day.

"Well, you've more than lost it, dearie." Mrs. Tuttle served her up a second helping of plum pudding.

Mrs. Tuttle's sisters had turned up all right, but Thomas's brother was killed that awful night. St. Paul's had escaped the flames, but several other Wren churches were incinerated, as well as hundreds of other buildings damaged or destroyed. The raid that day brought the number of civilian deaths from enemy bombing in December to 3,793. As the year 1940 came to a close, the total number of civilians in Britain killed by enemy action reached nearly 24,000.

In America, the Lend Lease Bill was passed by the House of Representatives on February eighth. It still had to be approved by the Senate and signed into law by President Roosevelt (his signature was only a formality, of course, as he had proposed the idea in the first place), but this vote of confidence seemed to the people of Britain a promise that the much needed aid would finally come through. As Prime Minister Churchill stated in a radio broadcast the next day:

It now seems certain that the Government and people of the United States intend to supply us with all that is necessary for victory.

As Mr. Nugent gathered the class in his sitting room to listen to the broadcast, Andrew sat closest to the radio so that he might hear the Prime Minister's stirring words:

What is the answer that I shall give, in your name, to this great man, the thrice-

chosen head of a nation of a hundred and thirty millions? Here is the answer which I will give to President Roosevelt. Put your confidence in us. Give us your faith and your blessing and, under Providence, all will be well.

"Andrew!" The voice calling to him across the playing field was his mother's, but her uniform was—*blue*! He ran over to her.

"Mum—what happened to your uniform?"

She pointed to the embroidered gold wings over her left pocket, with the letters *ATA* enclosed in a circlet in the middle.

"Mum! *Mum!*" He threw his arms around her. "You got accepted! Why didn't you tell me!"

"I just got my uniform yesterday. And I didn't want to tell you that I was only on probation until I'd passed my training course—I didn't tell anybody, in fact."

"So they finally lowered the flying time requirement?"

"Yes, they're accepting pilots in order of ability now."

"Well, you've got over a hundred hours, don't you? And Dad said that you're a better pilot than most people with twice the flying time. Oh Mum—" he stepped back a few feet to admire her. "You look positively smashing! What do these mean?" He fingered the gold stripes on her shoulders: one on each side, with a dark blue background.

"Second Officer Hadley-Trevelyan, reporting for inspection, Sir!" She gave him a salute.

"Second Officer! Oh, *Mum*!" He gave her another hug, then released her. "Sorry, I've got your tie all messed up!" He smoothed the black necktie down against her light blue blouse, adjusted her cap, and stepped back again to make a more careful inspection of her uniform: It was navy blue, to be precise. The tunic had four large pockets; down the front were black buttons with a raised crown and the letters *ATA*. Around her waist was a matching fabric belt with a large brass buckle. The skirt hung to just below her knees.

"Oh, Mum, here—I want everybody to see you—" He pulled her across the playing field to his classmates, yelling, "My mother's in the Air Transport Auxiliary! Look! Look at her!"

Andrew's classmates came running over. Andrew's mother almost collapsed in laughter. "Andrew, I feel like a prize race horse being paraded around the ring!"

His friends stood, mouths agape, as Andrew announced, "My mother's a pilot in the ATA! My mother's a pilot in the ATA!"

"Crikey, a pilot! A *lady* pilot!" Arthur Popham-Goode breathed.

"And what's so outrageous about that, young man?" Andrew's mother chided.

Arthur reddened, and Duncan Paget inquired, "Are you going to be flying Hurricanes and Spitfires?"

"We're not flying operational aircraft—yet. Right now, we're ferrying Tiger Moths, Fox Moths, Proctors, Queen Bees, and Magisters, which are light single-engined planes. The more advanced pilots are flying Masters and Lysanders, and some are flying Oxfords and Ansons, which are light twin-engined planes. Pauline Gower, who heads the women's section of the ATA, is trying to get the wheels moving for us to be able to fly Hurricanes and Spitfires—things look promising so far."

"Hurricanes—*MUM*! Oh, won't—" Andrew was about to say, *Won't Dad be proud?*, but caught himself just in time. It had been ages since he had seen her this happy— the sparkle was back in her eyes, the lilt was in her voice again. He thought quickly and said, "Won't that be grand!"

Mr. Nugent came striding over to the playing field. Andrew ran to him, then tugged him along, all the while repeating, "My mother's in the ATA! My mother's in the ATA!"

Andrew's mother greeted Mr. Nugent with a broad grin, then asked if he wouldn't mind if she took Andrew home a little early for spring holidays. "I have a few days off before being posted to my ferry pool and Andrew's birthday is tomorrow," she told him, flashing a brilliant smile.

"I think that can be arranged." Mr. Nugent smiled at Andrew, then turned to Andrew's mother. "Why don't you come to my place for tea, and we'll get his school-work ready to take home with him. You can bring him back a day or two early next term so that he can take his examinations."

As Andrew walked beside his mother back to the dorm, his heart pounded with pride and excitement. *Dad, you should see her! She's positively smashing! Oh, Dad, I wish you could see her—you'd be so proud!*

Mr. and Mrs. Harris were going to town that evening and offered to give Andrew and his mother a ride to the train station. As they rode up to London, Andrew was filled with pride every time someone glanced at his mother's uniform.

It was dusk by the time they got into London to catch the Underground. After a few stops, they were halted in the middle of the tunnel for over twenty minutes. An announcement was made that passengers would have to disembark at the next station, as there were "equipment malfunctions." Busses would convey the passengers to stops farther down the line.

"Do you think the Germans have bombed any of the stations?" Andrew asked his mother.

She shook her head. "They only come at night. And it's been rather quiet for the last month."

The doors of the car opened and they were assaulted by a blast of fetid air. The noxious atmosphere reeked of misery and desolation, and was overlaid with the bitter stench of sweat, urine, vomit, and excrement. Andrew's tongue clung to the roof of his mouth as he viewed the scene: A sea of huddled bodies extended along the entire length of the platform; a row of triple bunks, all of them occupied, marched against the back wall. A white line was painted three feet from the edge of the platform so that passengers would have a clear walkway alongside the car. Beyond that, the crush of humanity was so great that only tiny scraps of concrete were visible between the bodies huddled on the slab. There were pallets and blankets laid out to give some sem-blance of comfort; at one end of the platform, a table, presided over by three WVS volunteers, was set up with a large urn of tea, piles of metal cups, and clumps of sand-wiches. Of the people sprawled on the platform, some were reading books or news-papers by the dim light, a few were already curled up in sleep (or perhaps they were only closing their eyes to the dismal scene around them), most stared impassively into space or talked with people around them. Babies wailed and fussed, children whim-pered or coughed. As the mob of people exiting the train had to move slowly, An-drew passed the time by listening to the conversation swirling about in this nightmarish purgatory. A woman, tears streaming down her face, slumped forward, moaning, "I can't bear it, can't bear it anymore...Me nerves are shot, shattered to pieces they are...If them sirens go off one more time, I'll die, I'll just *die*...." Her companion, a man with a wrinkled, grimy face, barked, "Shut up, just shut up—*for Chrissake, why don't you just shut up!*" Next to them, another woman recounted the bureaucratic nightmare she'd endured after her family had been bombed out of their home:

"We tried to find a rest center, but all the ones in our neighborhood had been bombed out, so we had to go to one two miles away. We lost everything, even our ration books and identity cards—had to trek to the Food Office to get new ones...then had to trek a mile in the other direction to a feeding center so we could get a meal. My sister was killed, so I had to get a death certificate at the Information Bureau...couldn't af-ford a private burial, so had to apply at the War Deaths Department to arrange for aid. Then there was the problem of getting clothing for the children—we only got out with just the clothes on our backs, so we went to an Assistance Board at some church. Then we had to contact a Billeting Officer to find out where we could stay...lost our gas masks too, so I had to go to get new ones at...."

A few bodies beyond, a tense encounter was underway. A small boy of about five years of age, his face tear-streaked, stood surrounded by several choleric importun-ers: young and middle-aged women who faced off on his behalf against a shelter warden. The issue at stake was the possession of a few spaces on the platform. Two elderly women stood next to the warden, who evidently had given them the places which the boy had been saving for his family. One of the boy's advocates, a huge woman with black hair, shouted at the warden:

"It's not fair—Dickie's been waiting in line since six o'clock this morning—*six o'clock!*"

Another angrily seconded the assertion: "He has that place every night—he has a right to save it for his family!"

A third added her testimony, in a bellicose howl: "It's wicked to take someone's place—all of us, standin' out in the perishin' cold all day to save places for our 'usbands and kids—it's 'onor and decency and fairness we're supposed to be fightin' for—" She glared at the warden. "You're as bad as old 'itler, you are!"

This accusation only infuriated the warden. He bellowed: "It's their place—I'm in charge here, and if I say it's their place, it's their place! The space wasn't taken, I say, and what's done is done! I'll hear no more of it!"

"Oh yes you will, you *evil* man, evil as old 'itler," the black-haired woman shouted.

"We're sorry—we didn't know—" one of the elderly women wailed.

"It's not your fault," the black-haired woman snapped. She yelled after the warden, who was making his way to the far end of the platform: "Don't you worry, Dickie, that *wicked* man shan't take your place again! I'll take off my clothes and lay them down to save your space! Even if I have to take off every last *stitch* of clothing and stand here stark naked—" Her voice rose in pitch and intensity—"*STARK NAKED* here on the platform, that's what I'll do to save you a space! Don't you worry!" She spun around and glared at the crowd of people, as if challenging the world to a duel. There were a few raised eyebrows, several sets of shoulders shrugged; then the woman imperiously sat down upon a pile of blankets as if it were a throne.

There was a long wait for the busses, so Andrew's mother decided to walk, even though it was nearly dark. "We need the exercise, anyway," she told him.

As they walked through the streets, Andrew saw the appalling damage wrought by the Luftwaffe: Hundreds of boarded-up windows and scores of bombed-out buildings greeted their progress. The untidy gaps in the rows of buildings stared out like missing teeth in a mouthful of decay. Some sites were completely clear; most others had dismembered buildings obscenely facing the open air. The wrecked structures exhibited various degrees of damage: from some buildings, only the front wall was missing, opening up the rooms behind to full view by the world and rather giving the appearance of a doll house, with furniture, rugs, and pictures on the wall to complete the scene. Other buildings had more extensive damage: charred walls, gutted rooms, floors sagging alarmingly or gone completely. From these blasted structures, the detritus of habitation—bricks, mortar, smashed woodwork, broken glass, furniture, and pieces of furniture—sprawled in ragged heaps; here and there the rubble vomited out onto the sidewalks. Andrew saw one building mostly blasted away, save for one wall still standing: a fireplace hung twenty feet up, knickknacks and pictures stood amazingly undisturbed on the mantle. A few feet away, half a staircase hung precariously in midair. The wall exuded flayed wallpaper which fluttered in the wind, like handkerchiefs waving farewell to the remains of the room—floor, ceiling, furniture, and the other three walls—now in a pile of rubble twenty feet below.

They passed a small park with sandbagged ack-ack emplacements and slit trenches; the flower beds were turfed up into vegetable allotments. Walking through a district of shops, they saw signs tacked to boarded-up windows: *We are carrying on—Hitler will not beat us!* and *More open than usual* and *They can smash our windows, but they can't beat our values!* Everyone, it seemed, was in uniform—men and women alike: from young despatch riders in their teens to elderly air raid wardens and WVS workers. Andrew's heart lurched every time he spied a RAF uniform—perhaps, he thought, his father might have just made it back and hadn't been able to contact them yet. How marvelous it would be to bump into him on a busy sidewalk!

"Alice! *Alice*!" A female voice hailed his mother from across the street. She turned around. A woman in an ATS uniform, who looked to be in her early twenties with bright red hair and a mass of freckles splattered across her face, dodged the traffic as she ran across the street to them.

"Audrey! Hullo—are you off duty tonight?" Andrew's mother called.

"Yes—I almost didn't recognize you! So you've got your wings!"

"Oh, Audrey, I was so nervous! But I passed out just fine!"

"See, I *told* you not to worry," Audrey laughed. "Who's your gentleman friend?"

"Oh, sorry, this is my son, Andrew. Andrew, this is Audrey Morris—we were in the same anti-aircraft battery."

"The famous Andrew!" Audrey exclaimed.

"Famous?" Andrew was puzzled. Then he remembered his manners and extended his hand, which Audrey clasped warmly. "Pleased to meet you."

"Pleased to meet *you*!" Audrey chirped. "Yes, famous! Your mother did nothing but talk about you—when she wasn't making life difficult for Luftwaffe, that is."

"She did?"

Andrew's mother giggled. "Oh, now, Audrey—"

"Yes she did," Audrey said. "She'd take aim and—*Good show!*—down would come a Heinkel, and then she'd say, 'Did you know what Andrew did in school?—then she'd turn round and get a Dornier in her sights and yell 'He got second prize in the school boxing tournament—'"

"Did you shoot down the German planes, Mum?"

"No, women can aim the gun, but we aren't allowed to fire it." Audrey squeezed Andrew's shoulder. "Well, my young man, it's good to meet you at last!"

"My birthday's tomorrow. I'm going to be ten," Andrew announced.

"Ten! Double digits! Good *show*!"

"We're trying to get to Paddington Station," Andrew's mother said. "I'm hoping that we can get home tonight so that Andrew can have his birthday celebration to-morrow."

"Oh, Alice—why don't you stay in London? We haven't seen each other in so long! We can celebrate—Andrew's birthday and my engagement!"

"*Finally?*" Andrew's mother squealed.

"Yes, and we've set the date for the eighth of April. Denis has arranged to get away for four days. Oh Alice, do try to come!"

"The eighth—that's my birthday!" Andrew's mother said.

"My mum's going to be twenty-nine," Andrew told Audrey.

"Oh, did she tell you that?" Audrey laughed.

"No, she really *is* going to be twenty-nine, aren't you Mum?"

"Come along." Andrew's mother put her arm around his shoulder and walked with him. Audrey matched her step as she walked on the other side of Andrew.

"Alice, it's getting dark—why don't we have supper and you can stay with me."

"Oh, Audrey, I don't want to impose on you."

"It is *not* an imposition," Audrey said firmly. "Besides, you invited me to Armus House last month. I'm just reciprocating! Oh, Alice, I've got so much to tell you! And you've got so much to tell *me*! Flown any Spitfires yet?"

"We're not flying operational aircraft yet. That's still in the works—someday soon, I hope. Right now we're ferrying only trainers and light twins. I'm a lowly sprog, so it's just Tiger Moths for me right now."

"A sprog?"

"Yes, that's what the old sweats call the newcomers."

"Well, when you get your first Spit, you'll have to come waggle your wings at us," Audrey said. "We promise not to shoot you down! Now, let's see—you'll be in a plane with the roundels, is it?"

Alice's mother rolled her eyes. "Right, and the Jerries are the ones with the crosses, remember?"

"Right, ours—crosses; theirs—roundels. I *must* get that straight!" Seeing Andrew's mother break into a broad smile, Audrey laughed. "You can help me get it right over dinner, all right? And if I still haven't gotten it down, you'll have to stay up with me into the wee hours of the morning, tutoring me. Come on." She took Andrew's arm in hers and marched him briskly along. "Andrew, help me with this—the Jerries are the ones with the...."

"Crosses!"

"Right! Now, just for being so helpful, I'm going to buy you dessert! I know a marvelous little restaurant. The cook is from Provence, and he is an absolute marvel! Come along!" She proceeded to walk even faster, taking very long strides, leaving Andrew's mother behind a bit. "Alice, if you see Denis, tell him it's off—I've found a *fascinating* young man and I don't think I want to settle down yet!"

"Oh, Mum—please! I'm ever so hungry!" He had been a mite peckish, but now that Audrey had mentioned supper, he was positively ravenous. Besides, he was delighted with this bubbly woman, and her company was by far a better alternative to a long trudge in the dark.

"Oh, all right, you two!" Andrew's mother laughed. "But your new beau has to be in bed before nine!"

"Or he'll turn into a pumpkin, right?"

"No, I'll turn into a piece of Woolton Pie, and you wouldn't like me very much!" Andrew was very pleased with his clever reply.

Audrey squealed with delight. "Sense of humor too—I *like* that in a man—shows character! He's not just another handsome face, is he? Well, here we are!" She ushered them into a small restaurant.

After being seated, they were presented with menus. Audrey pronounced the ratatouille very good, so they all chose that. "Wonderful bread, too," Audrey said.

Andrew positively gorged himself—it had been ages since he had eaten food so delicious!

"Now, birthday boy, for your cake...." Audrey hailed the waitress. "It's my friend's birthday, and we'd like to have a piece of cake to celebrate."

"Yes, madam, we have spice cake. Would you like three pieces?"

Audrey glanced at Andrew's mother, who shrugged and smiled. "Yes, three. And might you have a candle for us to light? I'd be ever so grateful!" She beamed at Andrew. "It's his birthday, a very special one—he's ten, and we'd like to celebrate."

"Happy Birthday!" The waitress smiled at Andrew, then addressed Audrey. "No candles, sorry, but we have some little flags—you can put one on top of the cake. Would that do?"

"A flag will be just perfect! We can sing *Hail Britannia!*"

The Alert howled in the distance. A chorus of groans swept through the restaurant. "Bloody hell, it's Moaning Minnie again!" one man groused.

Another man consulted his watch. "Right on time, too."

Andrew's mother tensed. "I think we'd better go...."

"Alice, been away for only a few weeks and getting twitchy already?" Audrey chided. She turned to Andrew. "Your mother was an absolute demon when the Jerry bombers came in—she'd get that look of fire in her eyes—"

Andrew's mother threw a worried glance at Andrew. "I really would feel better if we got into a shelter."

"Alice—they're only bombing the East End. Besides, the Underground isn't all that safe—you know that! Remember all those hundreds of people injured and killed at Balham Station last fall? And just this January, Bank took a direct hit—over a hundred people killed."

Andrew's mouth was watering at the thought of cake. "Mum—my cake! Please!"

Andrew's mother bit her lip. "All the same—"

"Mum, *please*—my cake!"

His mother scrunched her face in worry and fear. "Alice—don't *worry*!" Audrey assured her.

The waitress finally came with their cakes. Andrew pulled the flag out of his, pronounced, "Happy Birthday to me," and proceeded to devour his dessert. He had gotten only two mouthfuls in when they heard the drone of planes overhead.

Andrew's mother stood up. "Andrew, let's go—"

Andrew quickly shoveled another piece of cake in his mouth.

"Let's go!" His mother grabbed his hand and started to pull him towards the door.

"My flag! My flag!" He pulled himself away from her and dashed back to their table. As he snatched his flag, he heard a shrill scream, which intensified until it seemed his eardrums would burst. He stood frozen, chilled to the core.

So this is what it sounds like to die....

His distinct impression of the pandemonium around him as everyone rushed to the door, was that of a crowd of bathers in the sea, caught by a huge wave and slammed against the shore.

A deafening blast—intense light—tables, chairs, dishes, food, walls—and bodies—exploding out in a thousand different directions—the feel of the air around him crumpling....

Then darkness as he hurtled through space.

Chapter 10

It was a blustery afternoon in late fall, and Andrew was in his secret fortress in the attic at Armus House. The bare branches of the old oak tree scratched at the fan-shaped window at the top of the stairs, and the wind thumped on the roof. He had pulled wooden crates and old steamer trunks into a maze of sorts, and made a roof over the whole works out of ancient quilts. Large, old books were been pressed into service to secure the quilts on top of the "walls," but sometimes the quilts were a bit too heavy, and the piles of books holding them down weren't adequate enough for the job, so the "roof" caved in. And if he happened to be underneath it at the time, he would find himself trapped, which is exactly what had happened....

Only the quilt was ever so heavy, or perhaps the load of books had fallen right on top of him, because he couldn't move. Even if he were pinned by the books, he should still be able to budge them, at least a little bit. They were pressing on his chest so hard that he could barely breath. And the dust was awful! He coughed, trying not to make too much noise. He didn't want his mother to hear.

"Andrew! *Andrew!*" His mother's voice came from the bottom of the attic stairs.

Blast! She'd be ever so mad if she found such a mess!

He tried to stifle his cough, but the dust was even worse now—how could dust get worse, though? Must be those moldery old books....

"*Andrew!*" No, his mother's voice was coming from *above* him. How could *that* be? Perhaps he was disoriented—he was sure he was lying on his back, but perhaps he was really on his belly, so it sounded like his mother was above him when she was actually below.

Better keep quiet though. She'll go away sooner or later, and then he would somehow disengage himself from this ever more distressing entrapment, and sneak downstairs to his room. She would never know....

"*ANDREW!*"

She sounds *ever* so upset. Yes, keep quiet.

His mother had just finished reading him his bedtime story. She dimmed the light, then gave him a hug. He nuzzled his face in her hair, which had taken on a dark coppery glow in the faint light. Funny, the light bulb was sputtering and blinking. Must tell Lucia to change it tomorrow....

"I want to pat it," he mumbled. He ran his hands over her curly strands.

All of a sudden she was very still. He rubbed her scalp, but she didn't notice. She must have fallen asleep.

"Mum! *Mum!*" He poked her shoulder. "*MUM!*"

"Andrew!" The voice came from far away. But she was right next to him!
"ANDREW!"

"Mum—why aren't you moving?"

She didn't give a coherent reply. He had never heard her cry like that—a choking, screaming kind of wail.

"Mum! I'm—" He started to say, *I'm trapped under a pile of books*, but he wasn't. It was as if the whole attic had collapsed onto him. His mother was lying beside him— no, she wasn't! Her voice was very far away.

"Mum—where are you?"

"Andrew, are you all right?"

"I'm stuck! I can't move!"

"Are you hurt!"

Hurt? "No, I'm trapped!"

"I can hear them digging—they'll get us out soon. Keep calling to me!"

Digging! Now he was really in trouble! There must be a roomful of things on top of him! Everyone at Armus House must be trying to dig him out. He could hear voices. Some were calling, some were moaning, some were screaming....

"Andrew—keep calling to me!"

No, better to keep quiet.

"Don't worry, old chap—we'll get you out."

His father! He knew he shouldn't have been playing in the attic, but the sound of his father's voice was so warm and encouraging...He wouldn't be angry, not really. He would gently admonish Andrew, and then suggest they do something else together. Where was he, though? It was dark; Andrew couldn't see very much. It seemed as if he were nearby, though, from the sound of his voice. There were other noises, too: a sort of low, groaning sigh, scraping sounds, water trickling somewhere.

Then he heard his mother's voice in the distance. He couldn't make out what she was saying, but it sounded as if she were pleading with someone. A male voice now, insistent. His mother's voice again, rising in shrill dispute, then bursting into an outraged holler: "I will *not* go—*get your hands off me!*" There was the distinct sound of a scuffle.

"Mum! *MUM!*" He called to his father, "What's happening to Mum? Someone's hurting her!"

"I'll be buggered!" his father exclaimed. "It sounds as if your mother has just assaulted a policeman."

"Mum!" Even in the midst of his distress, Andrew was appalled that his father would say *I'll be buggered*. He had never, *ever*, said nasty words like that! And what was a *policeman* doing here anyway?

"Andrew—don't worry! I'm not leaving you!" his mother shouted.

"Andrew!" his father called. "Keep talking to me, old chap!"

"What—what do you want me to talk about?"

"Anything you want."

"Shall I tell you about Mr. Quinton? I don't like him very much. He makes me write with my right hand and he has bad breath."

"He sounds quite horrid, old chap. Who is he?"

"You know—he's my housemaster."

Grunts, muffled coughing. What was the matter with his father?

"Are you all right?" Andrew yelled.

Another grunt. His father's voice sounded closer now. "Keep talking, old chap. Tell me what you're learning in school."

"I'm learning my letters, and my sums. I like going to chapel."

"Oh, you do?"

"Yes—the vicar comes in from town every morning to give services."

"Do you like to listen to him?"

"Not exactly, but he's ever so funny. He blinks all the time he's talking, and he twitches his head, too—sort of snaps it back a little. When he gets excited about something he starts blinking and twitching like mad, and we all try not to laugh, but it's hysterically funny to watch. Arthur Popham-Goode says that he's going to have a full-blown fit someday, that he'll fall on the floor and start chewing the carpet!"

"Like old Hitler, eh?"

"Does Hitler have fits, too? I've never heard. He won't cause any more trouble, will he? I mean, now that he's got the Sudetenland."

"What?"

"You know, that place in Czechoslovakia. Hitler's got it now, hasn't he? So he's not going to start a war, right? Prime Minister Chamberlain said we have peace in our time."

More muffled grunts, and then that funny groaning noise again.

His father called, "Are you all right?"

"Yes, I'm fine. What do you think about Hitler?"

"What about him, old chap?"

"Do you think he'll start a war?"

His father cleared his throat and asked again, "Are you all right?"

"Yes, I'm fine."

There was a very loud scraping noise—like fingers against a blackboard. Andrew stirred. How long had he been out? The last thing he remembered was that horrific explosion; then he was scudding through space. He was trapped—someone was on top of him. A dim light filtered through, from somewhere...He could make out some red hair and a brown ATS uniform. It must be his mother. She was in the ATS—no, wait—she was in the ATA! Her uniform was navy blue—that's right! They had met a friend of hers after they had gotten into London yesterday. What was her name? She was so friendly and funny! She had bought cake for his birthday. His piece had a flag on it. He had run back to get it when the bomb had fallen—where was it? Still in his hand!

"I still have my flag," he announced, more to himself than to anybody in particular.

"What's that you say, old chap?"

DAD! How had he gotten back? How had he found him?

"Where are you?"

"Right here, old chap...almost right to you!"

There was that odd groaning noise again, then a loud crack. Bits of crumbled plaster rained down on him. He heard his mother screaming his name, over and over.

"Andrew, are you all right?" his father hollered.

"Yes, I'm fine."

"He's fine!" his father yelled. His cry was echoed by several other voices which progressively grew fainter. The last report was punctuated by his mother's call to *hang on—it's almost over!*

"Bloody hell!" His father must be ever so mad about something. He hardly ever said *bloody hell.*

"What's the matter?"

"Be right back, old chap."

Sounds of scraping and scuffing as his father made his way back to wherever he had come from. Talking now. Four or five different male voices, counterpointed by his mother's insistent pleas.

Now his father was making his way back to him. "Andrew, can you hear me?"

"Yes—I'm ti—" A yawn caught him, mid-syllable. "—tired. Would it be all right if I went to sleep?"

"That would be quite all right, old chap. Just close your eyes."

"Andrew?" His mother's worried voice filtered through the rubble.

"I'm tired, Mum."

"It's best if he sleeps, mum," his father said. "We'll have him out in no time at all."

"All right, Andrew," the deep Cockney voice said. "Put your arms round my shoulders, and I'll pull you out."

The voice roused Andrew out of his slumber. As he opened his eyes a blast of bright light hit him full in the face. He blinked a few times and saw a deeply lined face with a taut mouth, pouchy eyes, and a huge, bulbous nose. The rest of the features were encased in grime.

"Where's my father?"

"Your father?"

"He was just here!"

"No, old chap. I've been the only one 'ere. Come on, put your arms round me. Close your eyes, too. 'Ere—I'm going to wrap this scarf round your forehead. There's lots of loose plaster, don't want to get any in your eyes."

A scarf was wrapped around his head, covering his eyes. Strong arms grabbed him under his armpits, and he felt something slimy and gooey slip past him as he was hauled out of his prison. To be free! To be able to move his arms, wiggle his legs...He sneezed; the scarf slipped down and his eyes popped open. He snapped his head back to look at the space he had just occupied.

At first he thought his eyes were playing tricks on him. He recognized Audrey's face, but her eyes were open, glazed in death. A beam lay across her neck and shoulder. His view swept down to her waist—but she didn't have a waist, really, just a bloody, mucky mess of something horrid looking. A foot away from the mess there was another beam, and beyond that, a pair of legs....

He started screaming even as his mind put together what had happened. Audrey had been thrown on top of him, trapping him, and she herself had been trapped by the beams...and they had to cut her to get him out....

"Andrew, *ANDREW!*"

"It's all right, mum—he's just frightened. We've got him—we'll be out in just a minute." The man turned to Andrew. "It's all right, old chap—she was already dead. It was the only way to get you free, you understand? Now, up you go...."

Andrew heard another voice from a few feet away. It was a man's voice, but not so deep as his rescuer.

"Hand him to me, Jack. I can get him up to Archie and Hal."

Andrew, wailing softly, was passed to the other man, who conveyed him up to another pair of waiting arms. He shut his eyes and was passed along by several more pairs of hands until he felt his mother's arms around his neck and her kisses smothering him.

He coughed up a lungful of plaster dust in her face.

Bright light again. The vision came into focus, and a nurse in white stepped back from him.

"Andrew—" His mother's voice was quavery and choked. He turned his head and saw her lying in the bed next to his. She reached her hand across to him. His forearm was stiff and tingly—must have fallen asleep. He tried to reach out to her, but his arm flopped down uselessly.

"Mum—"

She slipped out of her bed, ignoring the nurse's admonishment that she "shouldn't be straining herself." She knelt by Andrew, caressed his face, gently kissed his cheeks, and enfolded him in an embrace.

"Now, miss, back to bed," the nurse ordered.

His mother kissed him again, then obeyed the nurse's command. After she had gotten back into bed, she turned to Andrew. Tears rolled down her cheeks.

"Oh, Andrew—I'm so sorry. I should have gotten us into a shelter—"

"It's all right, Mum. It wasn't your fault—" He found his voice breaking.

He rolled onto his back, gazed up at the chipped molding on the ceiling, then looked to his mother again. He caught something out of the corner of his eye—red, white, and blue. It was his flag, propped in a glass on his nightstand. He reached to it and picked it up.

"You were holding onto it when they brought you out," his mother said.

He twirled it in his fingers. "My birthday," he whispered.

After the shock of being bombed, the horror of seeing, up close, the grisly business of war, and the dismay he experienced as his father's gentle voice had changed into the gruff, Cockney accent of his rescuer, Andrew was seized with a strange feeling of sublime joy. The refrain ran over and over through his mind: *I've been bombed! I've been bombed!* He felt as if he were especially chosen by divine determination: to have escaped by a hairbreadth being blasted to smithereens—to *atoms*—and to have suffered no more than a concussion and the botheration of hacking up gooey chunks of phlegm for the next few days in the hospital.

He reflected on his experience during the next few weeks of his convalescence at Armus House. He had gotten a nasty thump, to be sure, but the realization dawned on him that his auditory mirage was more than just the reaction of his brain cells to being jostled around. He *had* heard his father. Somehow, some way, he was receiving the thoughts and feelings and hopes of his father. Andrew knew it was possible: It was just as it had been between his father and Aunt Jane. Perhaps that strange communication between his father and his aunt had changed frequencies, so to speak, and now Andrew was the recipient of his father's emotional communiques.

His father, Andrew was convinced, had suffered a jarring physical shock, too—being shot at, either bailing out or bringing his crippled plane in for a rough landing. He had probably been knocked out, also. Perhaps that had broken the "connection" between him and Aunt Jane, and after all these long months he had "found" Andrew! Perhaps it was all preordained that Andrew would suffer a similar traumatic experience, so that their minds would settle on the same wavelength, and the signals would start going back and forth. And his father *had* said that this birthday would be special, hadn't he? Although he couldn't have known it at the time, it was, in a way, a promise

Yes—a promise! Andrew smiled as he recalled his father's words: *It'll be a very special birthday, for sure. And you'll have a positively smashing time!* He was certainly right about the smashing time, Andrew thought.

And he promised that my birthday would be special, and it was, for he found me at last....

Should he tell Aunt Jane? It might ease her mind; then again, it might vex her. Not that she would be jealous. She probably wouldn't believe him, and she would no doubt tell his mother, as well.

No, better to keep it to himself, he decided.

The Lend-Lease Bill was signed into law by President Roosevelt on March 12th. It provided for seven billion dollars worth of equipment to be sent to Britain by the end of June in 1942. In effect, this amounted to half of America's economic and manufacturing assets to be given to the English people. That evening, Mr. Nugent gathered the class in his sitting room to listen to Prime Minister's speech on the BBC:

We shall not fail or falter; we shall not weaken or tire. Neither the sudden shock of battle, nor the longdrawn trials of vigilance and exertion will wear us down. Give us the tools, and we will finish the job.

Andrew went to bed that night, repeating over and over to himself: *We shall not fail or falter; we shall not weaken or tire.* That was all his father wanted of him, no matter how long the trial of vigilance might prove to be: to keep faith that he would return, and that all would be well.

April brought ill news from the Balkans: Germany invaded Yugoslavia, then Greece, where sixty thousand British and Commonwealth troops had just been sent from North Africa. The Yugoslavian government surrendered in less than two weeks. Greece signed an armistice with Germany a few days after that. Most of the Allied troops were evacuated to Crete, having left their heavy weapons, trucks, and aircraft in Greece. On May 20th Germany launched an airborne assault on Crete. In less than a week it was clear that Britain's battle for the island was lost, and the army was evacuated once more (prompting Freddie to remark, "Now we know what BEF means—Back Every Fortnight!")

The news of the appalling reversals in the Balkans and the Mediterranean stunned the British people. As Andrew heard the snippets of information about the miserable turn of events, he thought, *Crete's an island, too....*

Was this just a rehearsal for an assault against Britain? Andrew kept his deepest fears to himself. *Perhaps not...Maybe the Germans will be so tied up in the Balkans that they won't be able to do much damage anywhere else....*

The Luftwaffe renewed the bombing offensive against England during the first two weeks of May: Every night saw British cities, factories, and docks pounded by explosives and incendiaries. There was a devastating raid on London on May 10th, the largest one ever. The House of Commons was damaged and 1,436 civilians were killed, more than in any other single attack on Britain. It seemed certain that Hitler was getting an early start on softening up England for invasion. Surely the summer would bring another fearful onslaught of bombings.

On May 27th, President Roosevelt announced that "the delivery of needed supplies to Britain is imperative. This can be done. It must be done. It will be done." To this end, American naval ports were helping to ensure delivery and that "all additional measures" necessary to this endeavor were being taken. "The only thing we have to fear," the President added, "Is fear itself."

These were the very words Andrew used as his crowning argument to his mother's declaration to him, at the end of May, that he would be sent to Northumberland in June.

"Mum—the last German attack was over two *weeks* ago! They've given up! They're not going to invade! There's nothing to be afraid of—everything's going to be all right!"

Andrew looked earnestly at her, as if challenging her to provide an alternate explanation for the abrupt cessation of hostilities. For strangely, after that last terrible raid on London, all had been quiet. It was as if Goering had given his pilots the rest of the month off. The newspaper headlines queried: *What's He Up To?* The talk at Askew Court had been full of impassioned conjectures and speculation as to the reason for this baffling turn of events: *He's nuts—off his rocker*, Timothy Park declared; *He's just letting us get cocky*, John Gordon-Fairweather proposed; *He's sacked Old Fatty Hermy—can't fit in a plane, so he can't be head of the Luftwaffe!* Harry Peel laughed; *He's all tied up in the Balkans*, Andrew insisted.

"Even though the Luftwaffe has been quiet for the time being," his mother countered, "We still don't know what Hitler's up to. You're going to Greycliff until I can be sure that everything's all right."

"Mum—*please*! I spent most of last summer there! I don't want to go there *again*! President Roosevelt said—"

"You've already told me what President Roosevelt said, and I'm telling you, you're going to Greycliff. Now, be sure to have your things packed when I pick you up next Friday." She glanced at her watch. "I have to be getting back to my ferry pool. I wish I could spend more time with you, but I've arranged to take my two weeks' leave when I take you up to Northumberland. We'll have a nice time together. If the weather's nice, we can bike to town for lunch every day—would you like that?"

He couldn't say no, because then he'd run the risk of not getting away from that hated place for a few hours. And if he said yes, his mother would say "Fine, then it's settled." Which it was anyway, regardless of whatever he said. So he turned away and glared at the floor. His mother brushed a kiss on his cheek and departed.

Andrew sulked all the way up to Northumberland. His mother might be able to enforce his comings and goings, and to quash his protestations, but he was bloody well not going to be gracious about things. He glared out the window of the train and crossed his arms in silent defiance. His mother, after several unsuccessful attempts to engage him in conversation, sighed and opened the aviation texts she had toted along. Every so often, she would glance hopefully at him; meeting with his impassive stare, she would wordlessly return to her studies.

They arrived at Greycliff just before supper. Grandmother Howard, as usual, timidly greeted them. Andrew stood rigid as his grandmother give him a brief, awkward hug, then he scuffed into the dining room.

He viewed the meal set before them: mutton, potato and parsnip pie, watercress garnish, and Brussels sprouts.

Brussels sprouts! *Bloody hell!*

Mrs. Beaton's husband arrived at Greycliff a few days later, on a week's leave from his service on corvettes. Andrew vaguely remembered him from the summers years ago as a sturdy, vital man with a slight tendency to overweight. Now, Mr. Beaton looked markedly thinner than he'd been when he was a gardener on the estate. His

Royal Navy uniform hung from his gaunt frame like an oversized outfit on a scarecrow. Mrs. Beaton worried over him, plying him with extra helpings at mealtimes and foisting tidbits on him whenever possible.

In defiance of his unwanted exile to this hated place, Andrew had taken to eating all of his meals, except for supper, in the kitchen with the servants. Almost against his will, for he had determined to give no sign of acquiescing gracefully or happily to his enforced stay at Greycliff, he found himself being drawn to the brooding seaman. Mr. Beaton had always been rather soft-spoken; now he was positively a clam. His eyes held a haunted look, like a man who has seen things too awful to be spoken of aloud. He did not parade dourness, like most Scots; he seemed almost apologetic for his quietness. At first, it had upset Mrs. Beaton to find her husband helping Alfred in the garden, and she would admonish him, "Dear, it's supposed to be a time of rest for you!" Mr. Beaton's gentle reply was invariably, "This *is* rest." He would then give her a shy peck on the cheek, and return to working his hands into the soil.

Andrew, his mother, and Grandmother Howard had just sat down to breakfast when the phone rang. His mother lately had insisted that he take breakfast in the dining room: "It's unkind to your grandmother to be avoiding her all the time."

Maria answered the phone in the drawing room. She then came to the dining room and signaled to Andrew's grandmother.

As his grandmother brushed past him, Andrew continued to shovel porridge into his mouth. It was slightly better than the stuff he was served at school, but not half as good as Mrs. Tuttle's....

"Alice!" Grandmother Howard's voice was an octave higher than usual.

"Yes, mother?"

"Quick—turn on the wireless!"

"What is it...." His mother's voice trailed off as she dashed out of the dining room. Andrew thought he heard his grandmother say "Russia" but what could be so bloody exciting about Russia? He got up and trudged into the morning room.

His mother was fiddling with the dial on the radio. The reception wasn't very good but Andrew distinctly heard the words, "the German invasion of the Soviet Union." Then the voice was drowned by a high-pitched whine. His mother turned the dial a bit and caught a barrage of static.

"*What!*" Andrew exploded.

"Germany just declared war on Russia!" His mother sounded dazed.

Grandmother Howard appeared in the doorway. "Is it true? I just couldn't believe it...."

Andrew's mother shook her head in wonderment. "It's true—my God, it's true." She scooped Andrew up in her arms and whirled him around. He giggled with glee, then grinned at her.

"Does this mean that the Germans aren't going to invade us?"

"I would think not!" she laughed. "It seems that they're rather tied up at the moment!" Then she kissed him on the nose.

"Mum—*Mum!*"

"What, darling?"

He remembered that Grandmother Howard was in the room, so he pulled his mother's face close to his and whispered in her ear: "Does this mean I can go to Armus House?"

His mother smiled the most dazzling smile at him, and nodded her head.

Chapter 11

*I*f it was possible to consider any time during wartime as "positively glorious," then the year from the summer of 1941 to the summer of 1942 could be given that description, at least as far as Andrew was concerned. With Germany's attention, for the most part, turned east towards Russia, a reprieve of sorts was granted to England. There were a few medium scale bombing raids in the summer of 1941 on London, Birmingham, and Southampton. In the fall Manchester suffered a raid and a few coastal cities were attacked. Compared to the year before, though, when an average of two hundred bombers hit London nightly during the height of the Blitz, these raids were mere pin-pricks.

In the spring of 1942, the Luftwaffe launched attacks against the smaller, less well-defended cities of England; because many of these places were resort areas or of historical interest, they became known as the "Baedeker Raids," after the famous tourist guidebook of that name. The British people saw this respite as an end to the terror that had rained from the skies during the Blitz.

Unbeknownst to them, it was merely the eye of the storm.

With the stunning announcement of Germany's declaration of war against Russia, Andrew's summer holiday took a definite turn for the better. He tried to keep a serious face as he made the proper farewells to Grandmother Howard and the servants at Greycliff, but once the train pulled away from the station, he could no longer contain himself. He hopped on one foot, then on the other. As his mother and he were the only ones in the compartment, he was allowed to indulge in his ecstatic behavior. His high spirits were in no way dampened by the grim posters glaring down on them: *Careless talk costs lives* and *If danger seems imminent, lie on the floor.*

If danger seems imminent—*Ha!* Now the Russians would get a taste of terror and sudden death coming in an obscene shriek out of the sky. Let *them* suffer for a change!

Andrew and his mother arrived at Armus House on June 25th, three days after the German invasion of Russia. He ran up the front steps waving his arms like a conquering hero and was engulfed by Gram, Mrs. Tuttle, Thomas, and Lucia. Freddie had scuttled off to America just after the fall of Crete, and Andrew was delighted about that. He wondered if Freddie would be returning to England soon, now that there was no longer a threat of a German invasion. Over tea, he asked Gram about this possibility.

"He's going to be staying in America for several months," Gram told him. "Something having to do with his shipping business."

Andrew breathed a huge sigh of relief. Freddie gone for the summer, perhaps for the rest of the year!

Maybe my father will return before Freddie does!

Mrs. Tuttle proceeded to stuff Andrew with her culinary creations. With the ever-increasing shortages her skills were stretched to the limit, but she continued to "work wonders" as Thomas proudly proclaimed. Andrew put on a little weight, and the thin pinched look in his face was replaced by chubby cheeks and an ever-smiling countenance. He enjoyed long, golden days of "ranging" in the countryside, the lovely summer weather blessing his wanderings.

He visited Charlie's grave almost every day, for he knew it would ease his father's heart to know that Charlie was being looked after. His mother, Aunt Jane, and Aunt Gwen alternated with one another in brief visits to Armus House; sometimes two or even all three of them were there at once. Then Andrew would find himself the nexus of indulgence. His mother had one day off a week, as did Aunt Gwen. Aunt Gwen worked ten hours a day—officially, that is. By law, women were not to work more than sixty hours a week, but often Aunt Gwen worked double shifts, as the hospital was so short-staffed. Aunt Jane's days off were sporadic: usually she was home for only a day or two after several days away at work with the FANYs.

Andrew especially enjoyed his mother's visits, for she had all sorts of interesting stories to tell about her training and ferrying duties in the ATA. She was quite happy that the ATA used Puss Moths as "taxis," that is, to fly the ferry pilots to various places to pick up their planes and bring them back from their destinations. "At least I'm already familiar with it," she confided to Andrew. "Just like going on holiday with you and your father before the war—it's like being with an old friend again!" The ATA also had several Ansons, which were used for the bulk of the taxi work. The Anson seated about a dozen people; since it was a twin-engined plane his mother did not fly it, as she was only rated so far on light single-engined aircraft. The Puss Moth generally flew a single pilot for the odd aircraft in another direction, and Andrew's mother was often given the job of taxi pilot for it. In July she excitedly announced that the women ferry pilots were at last cleared to fly operational aircraft:

"The story going round is that Pauline Gower was talking at a party with Gerald D'Erlanger, who heads the ATA, and D'Erlanger remarked, 'I suppose there isn't any reason why women shouldn't fly Hurricanes, to which Pauline replied, 'Fine, when can they start?' But I imagine there had to have been wheels turning all along—for one thing, the Air Council would have had to agree to it, too. So they let four of most experienced women pilots do a circuit in a Hurricane. They were all from the "First Eight," who were the first batch of women to join the ATA back in early 1940. Now most of the women are ferrying Hurricanes, and I expect that before long, we'll be flying Spitfires!" Andrew was not quite so enthralled with the thought of his mother flying Spits as he was with the idea of her soaring about in Hurricanes.

Wouldn't Dad be thrilled?

Andrew made it a daily habit to fix his mind on the vision of his mother flying a Hurricane, knowing that it would give his father a sublime thrill when he "got the message." His joy knew no bounds when his mother announced that in August she was going to be posted to White Waltham for the Class 2 technical course; Class 2 being single-engined fighter aircraft, most notably Hurricanes and Spitfires. And, as White Waltham was not too far from Armus House, she had arranged to be "billeted" with Andrew! Andrew didn't mind rising early every morning to bid his mother good-bye; a car came round to pick her up, and he stood on the front steps waving happily until it disappeared from view. She generally arrived home about tea-time and it was the absolute high-point of Andrew's day to listen to her describe the day's activities. The school at White Waltham had Harvards and Hurricanes; before being allowed to fly them his mother had to do technical courses in class.

Besides having to learn a considerable amount of information about the planes they were flying, the ATA pilots also were required to be aware of a plethora of rules and regulations. The rules for non-operational flying in wartime were quite specific and to the point: Pilots were to *(a) avoid interference with or confusion amongst the active or passive defenses of the country, (b) avoid the risk of false air raid alarms, (c) avoid the risk of being shot down by their own defenses.*

Andrew's mother explained: "We must fly at all times within sight of the ground, in order to be recognized as friendly aircraft. We are to avoid coastal areas and other sensitive places: anti-aircraft batteries, artillery ranges, RAF flying schools, and the like."

There were all sorts of standing orders, restrictions, and protocols, such as the Emergency Winter Ferrying Scheme, Grades of Aircraft Priorities, and Bad Weather Flying Restrictions. The latter were quite comprehensive: Since many of the ferry pilots were not instrument rated, flying in or above cloud, mist or fog, and out of the sight of the ground was prohibited. Competition between pilots was strictly forbidden as well. His mother explained: "If two pilots are assigned to ferry planes to the same place, and one decides to turn back because of doubtful weather conditions or whatever, or even decides not to go at all, it's not allowed to reflect on that pilot's ability or judgement. You can't say that the one who got through is better than the one who chose not to proceed—we can't have the attitude that it's some sort of contest. We're always admonished: *Remember what happened to Amy Johnson.* She was one of the most famous pilots in the world, and one of the most experienced ferry pilots in the ATA, but she went out in bad weather. No one knows what happened— most likely she either got lost in cloud or couldn't put down because of fog. She was seen bailing out into the sea, but her body was never found."

His mother went on to tell of an experience of a friend of hers: "She was at a mixed pool—one with both men and women pilots, at a time when most of the women were in the two all-women's ferry pools at Hatfield and Hamble. Most of the men at this particular pool were young and a bit cocky. Many of them were Americans and they called themselves the "Dead-End Kids." They liked to brag that they could deliver their aircraft even when the birds were walking! They were very good pilots, mind you, very tough and self-reliant, and I don't think they realized that they could be a bit intimidating. Well, one day my friend and several other pilots at the pool were assigned to deliver some Spits. The weather was not very good—the taxi pilot, who was quite experienced, had to turn back twice. They finally got through to the factory in late afternoon and with the weather conditions such as they were, my friend and another woman pilot decided not to start, even though the men tried to convince them that it would be a 'piece of cake'. The other two women pilots in the pool let themselves be talked into having a go at it, and later one of them confessed that it had been the worst ferry trip she'd ever made. The visibility was quite poor with low clouds, and it started getting dark. Since she was new to the pool, she didn't know the landmarks very well. She was very lucky not to have gotten lost; she managed to get the Spit delivered safely, but learned a hard lesson about not letting oneself get talked into something against one's better judgement."

"Are the Americans really that bad?" Andrew asked.

His mother's reply was a vehement denial: "Darling, I didn't say they were *bad*—not at all! This particular group of pilots happened to be a little...lively, and they certainly didn't lack self-confidence, and those qualities are not undesirable. The ATA wants pilots who have the will and enthusiasm to do their jobs. Most of the men in the ATA are doing ferry work because they aren't able to fly operationally. Either they're too old, or have some sort of physical limitation that prevents them from being in regular service. Having been given this opportunity, they're determined to prove themselves. It's not always a swaggering, outwardly boastful kind of attitude. Most of the times it's simply doing the job, giving two hundred percent, no matter what." She smiled. "You could say that they have a lot in common with the women ATA pilots. We've been given a wonderful opportunity also, and we're as equally determined to prove ourselves."

"Still, it sounds as if the Americans can be...well, not very nice."

His mother furrowed her brow, then took his hand. "Just because people are different, it doesn't mean that they're not nice. It's true that most Americans tend to be a bit more confident and dynamic, almost boastful sometimes, but they're wonderfully friendly and gregarious too. And they're not all the same, either—there are some who are—" She took a deep breath and a funny sort of smile graced her lips. "A little more soft-spoken and quietly determined, and...dependable—the kind of person you can trust with your life." Her voice trailed off; she seemed to be deep in thought. Then she brightened. "Well, my friend, the one at the mixed pool—she's getting married to one of the Americans there!"

"The one who refused to fly after the men tried to tell her to? I should think that men wouldn't like that!"

"On the contrary, her husband-to-be positively admired the fact that she refused to allow herself to be pressured. He told her, 'I like a woman who can stand up for herself.' He also admitted that the trip in question had not turned out to be a 'piece of cake.'"

A dreamy smile spread across his mother's face. "Your father used to tell me to trust my instincts, and to never let myself be pressured into doing something that I didn't feel right about. In fact, when he was teaching me how to fly—"

"*Dad* taught you how to fly?" he exclaimed, astounded.

She seemed a little surprised that this was a revelation to him. "Didn't you know?"

Andrew shook his head. His mother said, "I thought you knew—well, I don't remember exactly telling you, I thought maybe your father had. Anyway, yes, your father was my flying instructor."

"He told me that he met you at Greycliff, at a party. He was escorting one of his pupils and you asked him to dance."

A look of rapture washed over her face—the same sort of look she used to have whenever she ran to greet his father after he'd been away....

"Yes, we met at Greycliff, and I *did* ask him to dance. He told me that he was a flying instructor and I asked him if he'd give me flying lessons."

"You did? Had you thought of learning to fly before?"

She rolled her eyes. "A little—my girlfriend had told me how wonderful it was and I thought it might be nice. But suddenly it became something I wanted to do very much."

"How suddenly?"

She laughed. "Before the dance was over!"

Andrew's heart lurched with excitement—it was almost the same sensation as that of a momentary fright, that feeling of the heart skipping a beat with terror, only this was a sort of ecstasy: *She still loves him...she still has that glow on her face, even thinking about him....*

Andrew threw himself into her arms. *She still loves him, she'll always love him...* As he nestled into her embrace, he wanted so much to be able to assure her that she would be with his father again.

Maybe she's beginning to hope again...soon she'll allow herself to believe it might be possible...she might be a little afraid to even wonder aloud.... Andrew had to check the urge to speak of his conviction that his father would return.

That might extinguish the spark that's beginning to burn...She might insist he's not coming back, for my sake...Don't want that....

He drew back from her, and looked into her eyes shining with love and joy...and hope.

She's starting to make the long journey back...Now it's just a wish...Soon she'll be able to believe it might be possible...Then she'll be more certain...After that, blessed assurance—she'll know—she'll know, just as I know....

She pushed back a lock of his hair.

...Dark brown, see? Just like his....

As her lips brushed his cheek, Andrew reached his hand to touch her face, her hair...Maybe his father could sense what was happening, could somehow feel her touch, across the miles, across the gap of time and space...

Do you know that she still loves you?...She wants to believe that you'll return....

Their unspoken memories wrapped around them as a cloak of happiness, and the silence seemed to bless their communion of hope.

...We're together again, the three of us, in a reality as certain as the air and sun-

light around us...and someday this promise will be fulfilled...He'll come home and we'll never be parted from one another again.

Andrew's mother showed him her Ferry Pilot's Notes: a bundle of 4 by 6 inch cards fastened together with rings, so that they could be carried in a pocket. Each card contained everything a ferry pilot needed to know in order to fly a particular type of plane. She also taught him the mnemonic used as a pre-takeoff drill: HTTMPPFGGFUST, which stood for: *hydraulics, trimmers, throttle friction, mixture, pitch, petrol, flaps, gills, gauges, fuel boosters, unlock controls, supercharger (for those planes equipped with one), tail-wheel lock.*

The absolute high point of that summer was his mother's promotion to First Officer after she had completed her Class 2 course: Now she sported *two* gold stripes on each shoulder! When she brought him to Askew Court at the beginning of September, Andrew proudly showed her off to his classmates.

Two stripes for a First Officer! Somehow it seemed so wonderfully auspicious—his father had his two rings for a Flight Lieutenant. It seemed to Andrew that it was a promise of sorts, an assurance that he would soon see an end to the waiting, an end to the separation and longing, an end to seeing his father only in his dreams. After that would come the beginning...the beginning of having his father home again, of seeing his parents reunited, of being a family once more.

Should I tell her that I know Dad's alive? Should I let her know that he's ever so pleased with her? He imagined that the hardest thing for his father now was being denied the joy of flying. He knew that when his father looked at the sky it was with an aching desire to soar through the heavens again—to be free!

The only joy he has right now is the realization that she's taken his place—she belongs to the sky now!

The school year following that sublimely wonderful summer saw terrible reversals for the Allies on nearly all fronts. The Germans advanced through Russia, laying siege to Leningrad and capturing Kiev. In a series of "pincer" actions, the German Army managed to capture two and a half million Russian soldiers. Despite aid from Britain, Russia's survival was considered to be a matter of weeks. Nevertheless, President Roosevelt approved one billion dollars of Lend-Lease aid for Russia, and the Lend-Lease Act was officially extended to cover the Soviet Union. The German Army continued to advance, though, and by December had moved to within the outskirts of Moscow.

On October 29th the American destroyer Reuben James, which was escorting a convoy eastbound from Halifax, was torpedoed by a German U-boat and sunk; 115 of her crew were drowned. This was the first sinking of a U.S. Navy vessel in "The Battle of the Atlantic": the name given to the endeavors by the New World to convey food and military supplies to a beleaguered Britain, and the efforts of the German Navy to prevent this massive rescue operation by sinking the ships carrying these vital materials.

Malta was besieged; on November 13th, the British aircraft carrier, the *Ark Royal*, was torpedoed by a German submarine and sunk near Gibraltar.

On December 7th, the Japanese bombed Pearl Harbor, bringing the United States into the war. At least the Yanks were no longer sitting on the sidelines! This stunning turn of events was followed by appalling news: the invasion by the Japanese of Thailand, the Gilbert Islands, Shanghai, Sumatra, Borneo, Java, Guam. One by one, British possessions fell: Hong Kong, Malaya, Singapore, Burma. These lands over which the Union Jack had flown, these far-spreading lands which had always been colored proud scarlet in Andrew's geography book, now turned into blood-soaked vestiges of a once great empire. The Philippines were also attacked; as 1941 drew to a close, Japanese forces occupied Manila. In April, twelve thousand U.S. troops surrendered at Bataan and were forced on what later became known as the "March of Death" sixty-five miles northward to prisoner of war camps. Six hundred Americans and five thousand Filipinos perished on the march. Over twenty thousand more died of starvation, brutality, and disease during the first few weeks after arrival at the camps. The remnant of American forces which had managed to escape to the island of Corregidor surrendered to the Japanese in May.

The brutal winter in Europe that year proved to be Russia's savior: The German forces were literally frozen to a standstill and in some places forced to withdraw several hundred miles.

The setbacks on the Eastern Front notwithstanding, the Nazi domination of the rest of Europe was nearly complete: From the Bay of Biscay to the Black Sea, from the Arctic Circle to the Mediterranean, over four hundred million people had fallen under Hitler's rule. To protect the northern shore of this "Fortress Europe" the Germans constructed a defense line of heavy artillery emplacements, machine-gun nests, beach obstacles, barbed wire entanglements, minefields, concrete bunkers, and observation posts. Three hundred thousand troops manned the strong points of this "Atlantic Wall." Hitler boasted it was impregnable, and the German Ministry of Propaganda declared: "This is why an enemy attack, even the most powerful and furious possible to imagine, is bound to fail."

England herself was spared the immediate danger of invasion that year, but her very existence hinged on not allowing the German navy control of the seas. This seemed to be nothing more than a desperate hope. In February, the German battle cruisers *Sharnhorst* and *Gneisenau*, and the heavy cruiser *Prinz Eugen*, sailed through the English channel to Norway; this 'Channel Dash' was a terrible blow to British morale.

The Battle of the Atlantic turned into a grim war of survival for Britain. The hunter-killer packs of U-Boats continued to decimate Allied shipping, threatening to strangle the lifeline of supplies from the "Arsenal of Democracy". This battle, fought over a front of millions of square miles, was one of the most savage and protracted of the war. The German navy sank over 15 million tons of Allied shipping, 3,478 boats in all, from 1939 to 1945. Half of the losses occurred in 1942: Nearly eight million tons were sunk that year, for a total of 1,664 ships. That amount alone was staggering, but what was truly frightening in terms of Britain's survival was the dreadful balance sheet comparing losses to production that year. Simply put, the U-Boats were sinking merchant ships at a faster rate than replacements could be built. In that year, too, eight thousand British seaman were killed. When the figures were tallied at the end of the war, some thirty-two thousand of Britain's merchant sailors had lost their lives. Considered as a ratio of the total number who served, the chance of a British merchant seaman being killed in this arena was about one in four. It was probably little consolation to the thousands who met their deaths by cold drowning or by incineration when their tankers were torpedoed that, in a grim reciprocal, a crewman of a German U-Boat stood about a one in four chance of *survival.*

At least Andrew and his schoolmates had a respite that year from the nearly constant raids they had endured during the Blitz. They could go to bed at night with the reasonable assurance that their sleep would not be interrupted by the wail of the Alert and the subsequent shuffling in the dark to the cold, damp shelters. Before the war, Andrew had never imagined that there would come a time when he would consider a full night's sleep to be a luxury. Strange, how war made one appreciate simple pleasures.

As a counterbalance to the bliss of uninterrupted sleep at nights, the food situation went from bad to worse. Appearing on the menu were items such as "Commando Casserole." Some of the older boys maintained that Mrs. Bunch used crow meat in this particular culinary creation: "Isn't it funny that there are a lot fewer birds around than there were before the war?" was the invariable query put to those who unwisely questioned this claim. Hideous-tasting powdered eggs from America appeared also. Mrs. Bunch tacked up posters of smiling chickens on the dining room walls: *Dried eggs are my eggs—my whole eggs, and nothing but my eggs* they proclaimed, but, smiling chickens notwithstanding, Andrew and his school chums refused to be taken in by such propaganda. Meat all but disappeared; once in awhile they had Pork and Leek Pie, or mealy-tasting sausages, or Spam. There was no dearth of vegetables, though: spinach, turnips, Brussels sprouts, leeks, parsnips, and the like continued to be served in appalling abundance. Sometimes they had "ice cream," a gag-in-the-throat concoction made without cream or sugar. Beans and lentils provided most of their protein; fish also: Cod Cakes, Sea Pie, and Sardine Fritters were often the main entrees. Mrs. Bunch made one abortive attempt at serving them whale meat; even the appellation "Sea Delight" did nothing to coax the boys into swallowing even a morsel of it.

When Andrew's mother came to pick him up for spring holiday, she took Mr. Nugent aside and told Andrew to "Pack your things, darling." When he replied that he already had his things packed, she smiled and murmured that he should "check to see that you haven't forgotten anything." Andrew climbed the stairs and, despite his mother's blithe demeanor, still worried that she might be concerned about him. Listening at the top of the stairs, he heard his mother laugh a few times. As he tiptoed back down the stairs, he heard her say, "Be sure that everyone gets outside, then."

Relieved as he was that his mother was not worried about him, Andrew still wondered what the topic of discussion had been. On their way to London, she told him, "I might be able to fly over your school sometime—if you see me, let Mr. Nugent know. I'll buzz the playing field to get your attention." So his mother was going to put on an air show for his schoolmates—how grand!

His mother wanted to spend the day in London shopping and walking around. "It's been ages since I've had a stroll in Hyde Park," she told Andrew. "Would you do me the honor of escorting me, young man?"

Andrew replied with a smile that he would be delighted.

They had a lunch of fish and chips and then set out for Hyde Park. After walking around the Serpentine, they made their way to Speaker's Corner.

"I wonder what will be on the agenda today?" his mother laughed. Andrew remembered how she and his father had always enjoyed the goings on at Speaker's Corner whenever they were in London: "It's more entertaining than listening to the wireless, and sometimes one learns a thing or two," his father used to say.

"I hope Lord Haw-Haw makes a personal appearance," Andrew said. "Then we could pelt him with eggs."

"Andrew!" his mother exclaimed, feigning a look of outrage. "One shouldn't waste rationed eggs on such a twit!"

"Then I'll smash a Woolton Pie in his face! And then fling chunks of whale meat at him!"

As they drew close to Speaker's Corner, they saw about a dozen men standing on wooden crates scattered throughout the crowd. Some of the men were practiced orators, discoursing at length with people in the crowd on various political and religious subjects. Some preached esoteric beliefs: One tried in vain to convince his listeners that the earth was flat; another expounded at length on the finer points of Druid theology. Some were purple-faced as they harangued the passers-by.

"...the trouble is that so many women insist on wanting to do jobs which they are quite incapable of doing! The menace is the woman who thinks that she ought to be flying a high-speed bomber when she really has not the intelligence to scrub a floor properly—"

Andrew threaded his way through the mob of people to the booming voice at far end of the crowd.

"These words, my friends, are not mine—they were written by the editor of *The Aeroplane*—" The man held out a tattered piece of paper to the crowd. "If it is the official position of such an esteemed publication to regard women pilots in such a manner, why does our government permit them then to fly aeorplanes—and get paid for it? It is an abomination of all that is good and decent, and an end to an orderly society and civilization as we know it. Will our government then order that men stay home with the children, while women head the families? Can you imagine the chaos that would bring? If we do not precisely define the roles and duties of the sexes and nip these contemptible perversions in the bud, then we will reap a whirlwind of judgement. If we let women be pilots now, then who knows what might happen? Give them an inch, and they'll take a mile—that's what will happen! Would you like to see a woman Prime Minister someday—"

There was a chorus of chuckles and derisive comments, to which the man replied, "You may scoff at it now, but I guarantee that such a thing would happen if we allow the roles of the sexes to be so blurred and perverted—"

"Don't you say that about my mother!" Andrew muscled his way through the press of bodies surrounding him. He stood, eyeball to belt-buckle against the man, who sputtered at Andrew's interruption. A few titters ran through the crowd.

"*Don't you say that!* My mother flies Hurricanes! She's a ferry pilot, and she's got more sense in her little finger than you've got in your entire body! She doesn't need to scrub any stupid floors either! She flies Spitfires, too, and you couldn't even fly a kite, you *stupid twit—*"

"Andrew!" His mother's sharp voice broke over Andrew's impassioned words. She came up behind him, standing tall and proud in her uniform. Even the wings on her tunic seemed to glare at the speaker. She put her hand on Andrew's shoulder and commanded him with her eyes to be silent. As much as Andrew wanted to blast the man further, he knew that her silence and proud bearing were more of a condemnation than anything he could have said. She then turned to the man, narrowed her eyes in contempt, and, without a word, drew Andrew away.

As they walked back towards the Serpentine, Andrew felt the eyes of the crowd following them, but he didn't dare turn around. His mother glared straight ahead. After they were out of earshot he said, "I'm sorry—I was just so angry at him. He shouldn't say things like that."

"People are allowed to say anything they believe," his mother said tersely.

"I don't think anyone there believed him, at least I think that most of them thought he was a stupid nit—"

"Andrew—" She turned to him, unsmiling. "Attacking people like that only lends credence to what they have to say. Civilized discourse is one thing; verbal brawling only damages your own position. I trust that I will never hear another outburst like that from you."

Andrew hung his head in dismay. "Yes, Mum."

Andrew's misconduct was soon forgotten in the excitement that followed: The next day Andrew's mother was notified that she would be transferred to White Waltham to take the Class 3 course: Light Twins. She would be able to fly the Anson now, as well as Oxfords and Dominies. She spoke excitedly about doing the Class 4 and the Class 4 "Plus" courses before long, which would qualify her to fly the heavy twin-engined aircraft: Wellingtons, Blenheims, Beaufighers, and Mosquitos, among others.

Sitting in his classroom, a week after he had returned to school, he heard the drone of a plane. Glancing outside, he saw a single-engined fighter swooping down over the playing field.

"It's my mother!" Andrew dashed to the window. "My mother flies Hurricanes!" As his classmates scrambled over to the window, he saw the plane soar skyward.

"Quickly, boys, outside! Chop chop!" Mr. Nugent called.

Andrew and his classmates scurried outside, clamoring wildly, while Mr. Nugent dashed from one classroom to another, calling, "Outside, everyone, outside!" All the other schoolchildren, from the Infants' classes on upwards, poured out of the classroom building and ran towards the playing field. The Hurricane circled them, waggling its wings. Then it flew off! Was his mother leaving so abruptly? Andrew watched as it banked into a 180-degree turn, then headed back to the playing field. It proceeded to dive towards the boys, all one hundred and ten of them, as they craned their necks skyward and cheered excitedly.

"What is this! I demand to know what's going on!" Mr. Harris came dashing out of the administration hall. He shook his fists at the Hurricane. "This is *outrageous*!" he bellowed. "Get his letters! Get his let—"

"My God!" Mr. Nugent yelled. "Over there! ME-110s—headed straight for us!" He grabbed Mr. Harris's arm and pulled him along to the shelters. The Hurricane bore down on the playing field and, like a sudden cloudburst on a summer day, a shower of candy pelted the hollering mob of children. The yells turned to squeals of joy as the boys scrambled down on their hands and knees to pick up pieces of jewel-colored hard candies wrapped in cellophane and brightly wrapped toffees.

Mr. Harris, who had flattened himself to the ground, now picked himself up and proceeded to yell himself hoarse.

"This is outrageous—*outrageous*! Children—back to your classes! Immediately!" His bellowings were to no avail, so he turned his fury on Mr. Nugent. "I demand that you do something about this!"

Mr. Nugent's voice carried sharply through the children's laughter and cries of delight: "Boys! Boys! I order you to clean up this mess—then back to your classes!" Wild cheering ensued, and in no time, the playing field was cleared of all offending evidence. The children then made their way back to the classroom building, shepherded by the other teachers, all of whom were trying to keep straight faces, Andrew noted—even Mr. Quinton!

"Did anyone get his letters?" Mr. Harris yelled. "This is monstrous—I shall make a report to the Air Ministry!"

"*Monstrous*?" countered Mr. Nugent. "Save that scathing denunciation for the bloody war! It's monstrous that children should have to huddle in bomb shelters and lose fathers and brothers and live in fear of invasion! This is positively the most civilized thing that has happened to them in the past two years, and you'll make no such report!" He turned to follow Andrew and the other boys back to the classroom building. Then he winked at Andrew and, out of earshot of Mr. Harris, said, "Splendid, positively splendid! Let's get rid of the evidence, shall we?"

"Oh, Mum, it was absolutely smashing! Mr. Nugent called for everyone to go outside, and when you dropped the sweets everybody just went bonkers! It was like

Christmas and Easter and everyone's birthday all rolled into one! One of the boys in the Infants' class was yelling, 'This is the best day of the whole war!' Where did you get the sweets, anyway?"

His mother smiled. "A friend of mine had it sent from America. Do you want to stop now for lunch?" They were strolling in Hyde Park, taking in a "bit of London holiday," as his mother called it, before going on to Armus House. His mother had a friend who had a flat in Chelsea. They would stay there for the night and then catch the train in the morning.

"Oh, yes, I'm getting a mite peckish. Tell her—your friend, I mean—tell her thank you very much from everyone! Do you think she'll be able to get any more?"

His mother looked as if she wanted to say something; then she blinked and turned away. "I'll ask," she murmured.

They walked out one of the south gates of the park, and his mother soon found a restaurant to her liking. As they were about to enter it, a man, coming out of the establishment, snapped his head in their direction and stared in astonishment at Andrew's mother.

"Alice!" he cried.

A stunned look crossed his mother's face and her eyes widened in surprise. Or was it alarm?

"Alice—I can't believe it's you! My God, you look as lovely as ever—" A group of people, exiting the restaurant, separated Andrew and his mother from this—this *stranger*. Who was he and *why* was he so delighted to see Andrew's mother?

"...I heard about Roger—so sorry, truly I am. I know that you were very happy together," the man said gently as the last member of the crowd went past. He stepped quickly into the gap and stood close—a little *too* close—to Andrew's mother as he murmured his sympathies and eyed her with a look that bespoke admiration and...intimacy. Then he glanced in Andrew's direction, seemed momentarily disconcerted, cleared his throat, and said quietly, "Your son?"

"Yes—um, yes—" Andrew's mother stammered.

Andrew stared at her, dumbfounded. He had seen his mother grief-stricken, hysterical, exhausted, angry—but never so completely flustered as she was at this moment.

"...Yes, um, my son, Andrew. Andrew, this is Viscount—"

"*Alice*! Let's not be so formal! After all you and I were once—" the man glanced at Andrew, seemed disconcerted himself for a moment, then cleared his throat and said, "Pleased to meet you, Andrew, my name is Hugh."

Andrew had the funny feeling that he was being—how could one put it? Not "weighed in the balance and found wanting," as he had felt with Grandfather Howard, but it was something like that...evaluated, yes—*evaluated*, as if this man had some future purpose in mind for him. The man proffered his hand in greeting. Andrew clenched his fists and stepped back. The hand was quickly withdrawn, and the glittering eyes regarded Andrew's mother once more. The man's face had a youthful charm, yet Andrew was quite sure that he was at least in his late forties. His hair was flecked with gray, and his figure, though not tending to overweight, had a settled, solid look to it. His crisp business suit, his manner, oozed success.

"Andrew and I were just going to have lunch—" his mother started to usher Andrew through the door.

"Alice—please, *please*—be my guest. Your son, too." Hugh put his hand on Andrew's shoulder.

I wish it wouldn't be considered impolite to fling your filthy arm away from me, Andrew thought. Better yet, chop it off, so you wouldn't be able to lay a hand on *her*, either. He backed away, slowly and evenly, until Hugh's arm was stretched to its limit.

The outstretched arm snapped back towards its owner, and the ringed fingers brushed aside a lock of her hair before settling on her shoulder.

"Lunch—that's all I ask," he murmured. "Nothing more—just your time. I just want to talk, that's all."

Right, and pigs might fly, Andrew thought savagely.

Andrew's mother bit her lip and glanced nervously at Andrew.

No, no, NO....

"All right," she said softly, looking back at Hugh.

As if those two words had given him a claim of ownership on Andrew's mother, this horrid man put his arm around her shoulder and ushered her through the door. Andrew followed, instinctively whirling around as he went through the door, as if he were a prisoner taking one last look at the free world before entering a dungeon of doom. The sun was shining, people were going about their business, and the world was oblivious to the calamity that was about to happen.

And Andrew was quite convinced that it would be a calamity for his mother to even look at, even *think* of looking at, another man. When he had vowed to keep to himself his belief that his father was still alive, he had never, *never*, considered the possibility that his mother, if she was not firmly convinced that his father was still alive, might yearn for...company. She might not have actively sought companionship but, as it was presently being made all too clear to Andrew, unsolicited attention was not to be discounted as an impossibility, either.

You're supposed to hope that he's coming back....

He felt as if he were entering through the portals of Hell as he shuffled behind his mother and her...friend.

What friend? Andrew knew that he had never met this...*Hugh*, had never even heard a word spoken of anyone with that name. Yet Hugh was obviously well acquainted with Andrew's mother. Andrew knew it would be considered bad form to tug his mother's sleeve and inquire, *Who is this man?*

He would have to find out, somehow. The opportunity came when, after ordering their food, Andrew's mother excused herself to "wash up a bit." She looked at Andrew, as if inquiring if it might not be a good idea for him to wash up too. Andrew turned away and made a show of intently inspecting the place settings on the table.

With Andrew's mother gone, Hugh's demeanor turned from smugness to nervousness. Andrew at first thought that he should be very cold and haughty as he tried to elicit from Hugh precisely what his relationship with his mother had been, but he decided against it. He feigned an amiable curiosity and asked, "How do you know my mother?"

Hugh, sipping a glass of water, seemed caught off guard. He gulped the last bit of water, set down his glass, and looked at Andrew.

"We were engaged once, your mother and I." Hugh smiled at Andrew. "Things didn't work out as I'd planned, however."

Andrew bit his lip. He instinctively knew that it was his mother who had decided the fate of their relationship, not Hugh. But what had happened? As if reading his mind, Hugh said, "They met at our engagement party."

Party! No wonder his father had been evasive when Andrew had queried him as to what kind of party they were attending when he and Andrew's mother had been introduced!

Now it was Andrew's turn to be uneasy. If this man considered himself to have a prior claim on Andrew's mother—if he viewed the marriage of Andrew's parents as an...aberration—well, then, he might be inclined to set things right....

Hugh evinced a tense smile. "It's in the past, and I know that your mother was very happy with him."

Him? Something in Hugh's tone of voice gave Andrew the distinct impression that his father had been labeled *that man*.

While he could not fault Hugh for being understandably hurt, it still chilled Andrew to think that he might want to pick up the pieces of the past.

"You know," Hugh said gently, "If things had turned out as I had planned, I'd be your father."

A shiver ran up Andrew's spine. He forced the terror down, down into the rock-hard pit of his stomach, and said evenly, "If you had married my mother, I wouldn't even exist."

The waitress set a plate of scones down on their table. Andrew stared at them, his heart hammering, and he knew that he had to take advantage of his present composure and ability to walk without his knees buckling with horror. But if he waited a moment more—

He stood, not even daring to look at Hugh's face. He wondered, though, as he walked briskly away, if he had left him amazed, hurt, or outraged.

No matter. He was now outside the restaurant. He felt his knees starting to weaken and he stepped quickly to the wall and leaned against it. Looking up at the sky, he tried to blink back the tears.

"Andrew." He saw Hugh standing next to him, looking apologetic and concerned. "Come back inside."

"*NO!*" Andrew felt the terror rising up again, choking him. "*NO!* He's not dead— he's missing! *MISSING! You stay away from her—*" He was vaguely aware of the passers-by giving him curious looks, and he felt the world spinning around him. As he stepped back, he tripped on a ridge in the pavement. He went sprawling, then crab-walked backwards as Hugh reached to give him a hand. His terror mixed with fury—

fury at himself for being so clumsy, fury at this man whom he had only known for a few minutes and who was responsible for his predicament.

"Andrew!" His mother's voice startled him as he was starting to get up, causing him to lose his balance again and fall back to the ground.

His voice choked in his throat. He was afraid if he tried to say anything at all he would break down completely. His fears turned to reality, as his mother stepped around Hugh. She grasped Andrew, pulling him up, and he collapsed against her and the sobs broke forth. He buried his face in her breast, knowing that he was creating a public scene but at the same time realizing he was incapable of composing himself.

"All right, there..." her voice crooned as her arms wrapped round him. He heard her say, "I don't think this is a very good idea...." At first Andrew thought that she was admonishing him, but then he realized that she was not speaking to him, but to Hugh. "Come on, let's get the train—would you like to go to Armus House today?" she asked him.

He nodded furiously, and she wiped his eyes with her handkerchief. As his sobs subsided to sputtery gasps, she put her arms around him and held him close until he calmed down enough to walk. She guided him to an Underground station, and the bustly atmosphere of the place had the odd effect of soothing him. By the time they got to Paddington Station, he was quite composed. The fact that his mother did not berate him for his behavior was comforting in itself. After all, it was quite obvious to him who was more important to her: himself or the man she had once intended to marry. The thought still nagged at him, as they rode through the countryside, that she might still consider a relationship, in some form or another, with her former fiance. Even a friendship would be dangerous....

The worse she could do would be to admonish me that her private life is none of my concern...but it is, *it is!*

"You aren't going to see him, are you?" He tried to force the panic from his voice, but was not very successful. The tears came again.

"I don't intend to," she answered gently.

Late spring and early summer of 1942 saw a mixed field of blessings and disasters: The Germans defeated the Russians at Kharkov, captured oilfields in the Caucasus, secured Sevastopol in the Crimea, and besieged Stalingrad.

April, however, saw the Doolittle Raid: Sixteen American B-25s, launched from the carrier *Hornet*, bombed oil and naval installations on the Japanese mainland. Though it did little real damage, it boosted morale for the Allies. At the end of May the British launched "Operation Millennium", the first thousand-bomber raid of the war, on the city of Cologne. "This is proof of the growing power of Britain's bomber force," Churchill announced. Lord Haw-Haw, broadcasting from Berlin, countered, "Give us more hell, as much as you can, and we shall repay hell with interest."

Also in May the U.S. Navy fought the Japanese at the Battle of the Coral Sea; though it was not a clear-cut victory for the U.S., it did serve to check the Japanese advance.

In June America won a decisive victory against the Japanese Navy in the Battle of Midway, ending the Allied retreat in the South Pacific.

The British, though, were driven back in North Africa. On June 21st, Rommel's forces captured Tobruk; thirty thousand English and Commonwealth soldiers surrendered. Two days later, the Allied cross-Channel raid on Dieppe, the first attempt at probing "Fortress Europe," resulted in disaster: One half of the raiding force of six thousand Canadian, British, American, and Free French soldiers were either killed or captured.

Late summer saw reversals for the Axis forces; In August, American Marines landed at Guadalcanal in the Solomon Islands and took control of the airfield there. General Montgomery took command of the British forces in Egypt and forced Rommel to withdraw his men from the ridge in front of El Alamien. On the Russian Front, Soviet forces attacked the Germans outside of Leningrad, and the Nazi advance in the Caucasus was slowed. Early September saw the beginning of the battle for Stalingrad, one of the most ferocious engagements of the war. It would eventually lead to the defeat of the German Army on the Eastern front.

That summer holiday, for the first time in two years, there was no mention of Andrew having to go to safety in Northumberland, which pleased him to no end. Since his mother did her Class 4 conversion at the end of August, the time which Andrew usually had to go to Greycliff, he was even spared the obligatory visit to Greycliff just before he had to go back to school, which was positively the icing on the cake. For this summer, at least, he would be not be a victim of the oppressive opulence and the strained atmosphere of that hated place. He would also be spared a particular disconsolation at the Howard estate: Mrs. Beaton had just received word that her husband's corvette had been torpedoed and sunk in the North Atlantic. Only a few survivors were plucked out from the unmerciful sea; Mr. Beaton was not among them. This sad news was related to Andrew by his mother as they rode the train up to London.

"Do write to her, darling, and extend your condolences to her," his mother urged him.

Andrew replied that he most assuredly would, though his condolences were already extended to the breaking point, as the war had cut a swath of grief and loss through his class at Askew Court. James Martin's and Nigel Willoughby-Ramsbottom's brothers, who had been rescued at Dunkirk, were killed in North Africa. Timothy Park's father was taken prisoner at Tobruk. At least Timothy's family had received word that he was safe; there had been no word as to the fate of Colin Kirknewton's father since the Battle for France. Duncan Paget's father was lost at sea. Keith Vincent-Hill's father was terribly injured when his Lancaster made a crash landing. He died a week later of burns. George Garton-Ward's sister, a nurse in Hong Kong, was killed during the Japanese invasion; Arthur Popham-Goode's aunt was interned on Sumatra; Wilfred Smith's mother was killed in a Baedeker raid. For most of the past year, muffled sobs from his roommates had been Andrew's lullaby as he snuggled beneath his covers at bedtime. Mr. Nugent usually made a late-night circuit through the bedrooms, soothing the ones newly grief-stricken, and comforting those who still ached with sadness long after they had lost loved ones. The distressed mourners were, by day, not so much ignored as left alone by their classmates, for all of them realized the need for one recently bereft to withdraw for a time and nurse the wounds of savage grief. There were no proddings to join in the games, no admonishments to finish a half-eaten meal. After awhile, the mourner would return to the fold, at first tentatively skirting the fringes of the group and avoiding eye contact and direct interaction. He would be subjected to a surreptitious and unspoken evaluation by the others as to whether the gashes of sorrow had healed into phlegmatic scars. After so many losses, Andrew and his classmates had developed a sixth sense as to when this was accomplished. In time, the mourner would be absorbed back into the group.

Andrew was sure that, for all of Mrs. Beaton's gruffness, her grief would not abate by summer's end, and he was glad that he would not have to endure it.

"I'll see about taking you up to Greycliff during the break between fall and winter terms," his mother told him as they rode the Underground to Paddington Station. "However, seeing as you can't visit your grandmother this summer, I would like you to write her a nice, long letter." This command, cloaked as a request as usual, was dutifully fulfilled by Andrew after he arrived at Askew Court. His missive was filled with tender regrets and poured forth his "longings" to visit Northumberland the following year.

"Laying it on a bit thick," his mother remarked wryly as she scanned Andrew's letter. She winked at him, and Andrew cocked his head and tried not to smile.

"Your grandmother misses you so very much," she said. "I don't think you realize how much you mean to her."

Andrew shrugged. "She was never very nice to Dad." He glanced at his mother, trying to ascertain how this first mention of his father in over a year had affected her.

She drew back, took a deep breath, and said quietly, "She was never unfriendly to him, Andrew. But while your grandfather was alive, she could not be overly cordial to him. She and your father got along, under the circumstances."

She turned away, and Andrew knew the "the circumstances" were to remain a private matter. He knew that Grandfather Howard had considered that his only surviving child had "married down," but his mother's reticence had given Andrew the distinct impression that there was more to it than that. He wanted to press the matter because he sensed somehow that it had something to do with himself, but he knew that even the mention of his father had unsettled her. They had not talked of him for so long....

Should I tell her? I've been so afraid to say what I believe, afraid that it would crush the spark of hope that I hope...I'm sure is within her.

Yet their encounter with Hugh still unsettled him. *She had said that she wouldn't see him again—hadn't she? But what if she changed her mind? What if there were others?*

A wave of horror washed over him. *What if, that day last summer, she were just reminiscing...nothing more? What if she's lonely? She probably meets lots of men all the time—other ferry pilots, RAF officers....*

"A penny for your thoughts," she said.

He took a deep breath, and tried to think of how he wanted to broach the subject without alarming her.

"Sometimes, I wonder—you know...I mean, if maybe he might sill be alive. I know that it's...unlikely, but, I think the fact that he hasn't been found means—might mean—there's still a chance. Sometimes I imagine that he would be very proud of you, right now. I think what it would be like for him to know that you're flying Hurricanes and Spitfires and twins. I think he'd be ever so happy, don't you?"

His mother nodded and enfolded him in an embrace. Andrew heard her sigh, wished that he could somehow impart to her his firm conviction that his father still lived, but he knew he shouldn't press the matter. It was enough to give her a vision of what might be, what could be....

The previous Christmas, Andrew had asked for, and had received, a book containing the famous speeches of Winston Churchill. He had made a thorough study of them and had been struck by how often the Prime Minister had encouraged his people through the darkest of times by giving them hope, and a vision of what the future could bring if they persevered. "Broad sunlit uplands" and "better days" were to be the reward of those who could see through the present distresses and reversals to the victory ahead. People could make their hopes reality, but it all started with the vision.

His mother looked at him a bit worriedly, so he reassured her: "I realize he probably won't be coming back, but all the same, I like to think that we shouldn't give up hope—completely. The war's not going to last forever, and someday we'll know for sure."

His mother nodded, a bit warily, Andrew noted. He said breezily, "I just like to pretend sometimes—you know. When I was being dug out after we were bombed, I thought I heard his voice. It was only the rescue worker, calling me 'old chap', like Dad used to do—and I did have a nasty bump on the head. But I wasn't afraid or upset, thinking that he was there with me. I was there for a long time, wasn't I?"

His mother closed her eyes and nodded.

"I also imagined that I was in the attic, hiding in a fort I'd built out of boxes and books, and that you were looking for me. I kept quiet because I thought you'd be upset—" His voice broke. "I didn't really know what happened—I'm sorry it made you even more distressed. It must have been awful for you." He buried his face in her shoulder and wiped his eyes in her uniform. "I'm sorry—" he whispered.

He heard her moan softly as she tightened her embrace around him.

"You know I'd never say anything...do anything to hurt you—you know that, don't you?" he said.

She looked at him through shining eyes, caressed his face lovingly, and wrapped her arms around him again.

His mother produced a delightful treat that summer: Cadbury bars.

"The ATA Medical Officer, Dr. Barbour, was quite concerned that we might be getting over-tired with a full day's ferrying and nothing to eat," his mother explained. "With butter, meat, and cheese all rationed, there's not much with which to make sandwiches, and often there isn't time to sit down to a meal anyway, as we often have to ferry another plane right away. Dr. Barbour managed to persuade the Ministry of Food to allocate the ATA a supply of two ounce Cadbury bars. All we have to do to get one is to present our ferry chit to the Pool Adjutant. He keeps the chocolate under lock and key—they're as valuable as the Crown Jewels!"

"But won't you get hungry?" Andrew was almost afraid to ask, what with chocolate bars being a delight beyond his wildest imaginings.

"Oh, I usually can get a roll and a cup of tea from the canteens at the maintenance units. And I know quite a few pilots at the RAF bases—even if the mess isn't open, they always have something stashed away and are quite willing to share."

Andrew looked at her intently, wondering if there was more to their generosity. His mother's blithe demeanor and the offhand way she'd mentioned it reassured him.

She wouldn't have spoken of it if she had anything to hide....

His summer holiday was slightly marred by the fact that Aunt Jane was "away" and probably wouldn't be able to come to Armus House before he had to return to school, and by Freddie's return, at the end of August, from his extended visit to America. Freddie had been away for over a year, and living in "Yankland" (being "exiled," as Freddie put it, although the exile had been self-imposed) had not improved his nature one whit. Andrew made sure he was around his mother every single minute while Freddie was in the house—even when she was in the bathroom he managed to "wander" up and down the hall. When she retired for the night, he called to her once or twice from his room to ask some sort of silly question or request a drink of water, knowing that she would be up until late and wouldn't mind. Fortunately, Freddie stayed at Armus House for only a few days; then he was off to London, much to Andrew's relief.

That night, Andrew went down to the library to find a book to read to help him get to sleep—after three nights of forcing himself to stay up late so as to thwart any lecherous intentions Freddie might still harbor (and he *did* still harbor them, for had Andrew noted the slight narrowing of Freddie's eyes whenever he looked at her), he found it hard to fall asleep. He perused the bookshelves, looking for something that would hold his interest, yet be dull enough to coax him to sleep. He settled on a study of naval tactics. The armchair looked cozy and inviting, so he decided curl up in it to read a chapter or two. If the book proved to be either entirely uninteresting or too exciting, he could exchange it for something else without having to make another trip downstairs.

The book proved to be suitably dull, and Andrew's head began to nod.

Just a few more minutes, and I'll go upstairs....

A sharp, mechanical noise jarred him out of slumber. In the vague haze of recently fled sleep, his eyes registered on the French doors leading outside to the small "reading" terrace. The handle was turning slowly, and the door was being pushed against its hinges by a tall figure standing outside. The outline of this nightly intruder was blurred by the gauzy curtains. Terror-stricken, Andrew pushed himself to a standing position on the chair. He stood on tip-toes and arched his back in fear, then lost his balance and tumbled backwards over the chair, just as the doors burst open.

Chapter 12

"**A**ndrew!"

"Aunt Jane!" Andrew scrambled to his feet and threw himself into his aunt's arms. "I was asleep—I was so frightened—I thought you were a—"

"Oh Andrew, I didn't see you! I'm sorry that you were startled." Aunt Jane carried him to the armchair and sat down with Andrew in her lap. "Dear me—I forgot my key and I thought I'd try the library door. It's a trick to work around the lock but I thought I could get in without disturbing anyone."

"Mum said that you weren't coming home this summer."

"Well, I didn't expect to get away, but things changed. I had an unexpected break. Actually a sprain—I sprained my ankle."

"Oh, you shouldn't have carried me."

"Not to worry—it's better now."

"How did you sprain it?"

"In the line of duty."

"How can you get a sprained ankle driving a car?"

Aunt Jane's response was to kiss him on the cheek. Andrew pressed the point: "How?"

"It wasn't while driving a car, my little interrogator. I was scampering around and took a tumble."

"What do you mean, scampering around?"

Aunt Jane ruffled his hair. "We FANYs have advanced degrees in scampering, in nosing into other people's business, and in being frightfully charming to all sorts of twits, nits, clots and imbeciles."

"Were you nosing into other people's business or being frightfully charming when you sprained your ankle?"

"I was scampering, didn't you hear? And I'm not allowed to divulge the reason unless you fill out a form in triplicate and file it with the proper authorities. Then you have to stand on your head and sing "God Save the King" and recite the Greek alphabet backwards. Everything has to be a secret nowadays, didn't you know?"

"Of course," Andrew agreed. "We're not supposed to know what's in Commando Casserole or MI-5 Pudding, and we're certainly not supposed to know that Sea Delight is really whale meat."

"That's my boy!" She tousled his hair. "Oh dear, I do hope you can get back to sleep after all this excitement."

"I haven't been sleeping well lately, anyway. Freddie was here for a few days and I was worried about him and—and—"

"And what?" Aunt Jane cocked her head quizzically, yet her eyes betrayed discernment.

Andrew shrugged and turned away. "Things," he mumbled.

She gently lifted his face towards hers and looked tenderly at him. "You're worried about your mother, aren't you?"

Andrew bit his lip and slumped against her.

"There, there," she whispered. "Don't worry, Freddie just likes to tease."

"I don't like it when he teases. I wish I could stop him altogether."

"It would be easier to teach a pig to sing," Aunt Jane laughed. "Freddie's all bluff and bluster anyway. Your mother knows how to take care of herself. Come on, we'd better get you upstairs. I think you're getting a bit too heavy to carry. You've obviously been hard at work eating Mrs. Tuttle's nourishing food, haven't you?"

Andrew snuzzled against her again. She held him close for a long time, then said softly, "Time for bed, my young man."

They stood up, and Aunt Jane hesitated for a minute. "Would you like to look outside at the stars for a minute? It's a lovely night."

Andrew smiled, and Aunt Jane led him by the hand outside to the terrace. As they gazed up at the millions of tiny pin-pricks of light fastened in the heavens he felt Aunt Jane's arms go around him.

"I'll be going away soon," she said. "Out of the country, I mean. I probably won't be back for quite some time."

"Where are you going?"

"Oh, different places—I really can't say. All very military and hush-hush."

"Will you write?"

"As often as I can, darling." As she looked up at the night sky her face was bathed in starlight. "But even if you don't hear from me for awhile—sorry to say, I'm going to be frightfully busy and might not be able to find the time or the opportunity—please know this: I will look at the stars every night and think of you. Will you promise to do the same for me?"

Andrew nodded.

"Promise?" she whispered.

"Promise," he replied.

Aunt Jane stayed for only a day. She went for a long walk with Andrew the next morning, lunched with his mother in the afternoon, had tea with Gram, then was off to London on the evening train to visit Aunt Gwen.

He returned to school and the autumn brought more optimistic news from various Allied fronts, most notably North Africa: General Montgomery's troops defeated the German and Italian armies at El Alamein. In Operation Torch, a combined Anglo-American force of over a hundred thousand men took control of thirteen hundred miles of northwest African coastline in less than four days. Rommel's army was now forced to fight a war on two fronts. As the Afrika Korps was being pushed out of Egypt, Winston Churchill declared: "Now is not the end. It is not even the beginning of the end, but it is, perhaps, the end of the beginning." On November 11th, British and Commonwealth forces entered Libya; two days later Tobruk was retaken. On November 15th, church bells were rung throughout England to celebrate the victory in North Africa.

On November 19th the Russians began their counter-offensive at Stalingrad, and three days later succeeded at a brilliant pincer move which trapped a quarter of a million German soldiers within what was left of the devastated city. Russia's savior, "General Winter," added its fury to the battle. The Luftwaffe was only able to supply one-sixth of the supplies needed by the encircled German troops. One hundred and fifty thousand German soldiers died of wounds, cold, disease—and starvation. The toll of Russian dead was far greater: More than a million Red Army soldiers died in a battle so ferocious that even the dogs fled the city. It would be known as *Rattenkrieg*, the War of the Rats.

The Battle of the Atlantic turned in favor of the Allies as the American, Canadian, and British navies improved in their defense of the vital shipping of supplies from the New World. Better aerial surveillance of shipping by long-range aircraft, improved radar, and the use of destroyers as convoy escorts contributed to Allied successes in battling the U-Boat threat. A new electronic detection device, high-frequency direction finder, or *Huff-Duff*, enabled ships to pinpoint U-Boat locations.

The siege of Malta was lifted when a convoy of merchant ships, sailing from Egypt under the protection of British aircraft, reached the harbor of Valetta. The news from the Pacific was encouraging, too: The Japanese were repulsed by U.S. and Australian forces in New Guinea and were losing ground on Guadalcanal.

Reciprocal course: The end of the beginning. It was happening, just as Andrew's father had said it would. Throughout the world, the Allied forces were turning the tide of two years of defeats and taking back what had been lost to the Axis powers. The victories, though, were not easy ones: The Japanese and Germans fought savagely for every town and every mile, retaking positions whenever they had an advantage, reinforcing wherever they could, and, even in the face of certain defeat, exacting a high price from their opponents as a payment for the victories won.

The ATA celebrated its third anniversary that September with a fanfare of publicity. Articles about the organization's activities appeared in newspapers and magazines, and there were radio broadcasts as well. Over one hundred thousand aircraft had been moved since the ATA's inception, and the number of planes ferried in the past year was almost equal to the total number ferried during the previous two years. Sometimes several hundred planes a day were shuttled about by the more than five hundred pilots now in the organization. The women of the ATA were now flying virtually every kind of military aircraft, from single-engined light trainers to four-engined bombers.

Andrew's mother sent him a newspaper clipping, illustrated by a photo of her climbing into a Spitfire. She flashed a brilliant smile and Andrew hoped that somehow, someway, his father would see the article too... *Wouldn't he be proud?* He tucked the clipping away in his treasure box during his next visit to Armus House.

Freddie scuttled off to America again and Andrew hoped that his stay would be prolonged. It gave Andrew no small measure of relief to have Freddie thousands of miles away, though he wondered why Freddie put up with being there, since a stay in "Yankland" always put him in an ill temper.

Aunt Jane wrote to him regularly; her letters were typewritten missives, as she explained to him in her first letter:

Since I'm required to spend long hours sitting at a desk, often having not much to do in the way of official duties (except for greeting twits, nits, clots, and imbeciles, and occasionally pecking out a memorandum or two), I thought I'd spend the time keeping up with correspondence (as well as brushing up on my typing skills!). At least it looks as if I'm busy; besides, you know that penmanship is not one of my strong points!

She always signed her letters with her distinctive signature: An ostentatious J with two big swirly loops, the remaining letters jumbled together.

Her letters were always sent via Andrew's mother: Aunt Jane, ever practical, said it was more expedient to mail her correspondence together, as she wrote to Andrew's mother also. Andrew's mother would then send Aunt Jane's letter to him along with a brief note of her own; as all the correspondence was enclosed together to save postage, he always delighted in receiving a "double letter" from the two of them.

In January 1943, President Roosevelt and Prime Minister Churchill met in Casablanca to coordinate the specific strategies of the Anglo-American joint war policy. Among the items agreed upon was the need for intensified bombing of Germany: complete, round the clock, all-out strategic bombing which would, it was hoped, bring about a speedy end to the war. The Americans would hit vital industrial and military targets by day; the British would bomb the cities at night. To this end, the RAF on January 16th carried out their first heavy raid upon Berlin in over fourteen months, and the Americans bombed Germany for the first time on January 27th.

In reprisal, Germany resumed its aerial bombardment of England, and the Ju-88s and Dorniers of the Luftwaffe returned in force for the first time in almost two years. In a single week 328 British civilians were killed, among them thirty-nine schoolchildren when their school in South London was hit.

However, this renewed offensive was nothing on the scale approaching the Blitz, and Andrew was awakened only twice that year by the wail of the Alert. These two times, however, were to have a more profound effect on his life than all the countless times he was roused during the Blitz.

The howl of the siren jolted Andrew out of slumber. At first he thought it was a fire engine or a police car, so unfamiliar was the sound. His roommates were equally disoriented too: Cries of "Whazit—whazit?" filled the air, and there was a mad scramble for coats, shoes, and socks.

"Chop, chop, boys!" Mr. Nugent called from downstairs. Andrew couldn't find his shoes, nor his socks, just his slippers. He couldn't find his coat, either, as he yelled frantically to Mr. Nugent.

"Just put on your robe," Mr. Nugent called. "I'll bring an extra jacket."

Andrew knew he was coming down with a cold, for his throat was scratchy and his nose was starting to run. Blast! Stupid, bloody Huns—now he was going to get bloody pneumonia!

He dashed down the stairs to Mr. Nugent's fretful implorings, grabbed the jacket, and ran to catch up with his classmates disappearing into the darkness and rain. Needless to say, he wasn't careful: He slipped and fell in a puddle, soaking himself to the skin. After hauling Andrew up and hustling him into the shelter, Mr. Nugent had him take off his wet clothes: "They'll just make it worse," he said, as he took off his own coat and wrapped it around Andrew's shivering form.

All these ministerings were in vain, for Andrew's cold went from bad to worse and he came down with a bad case of bronchitis. His mother was notified and she arranged to fetch him in a car that belonged to one of her friends in the ATA.

"We all get an extra petrol ration," she told him as she picked him up at school. She was accompanied by her friend, a tall brunette from Ulster named Winnie. "But it would be a waste to use it in the Bentley, considering the distance we have to travel to Armus House. Winnie's car gets better mileage."

Winnie's car was a battered old sedan with a noisy engine and Andrew was thus conveyed, if not in style, at least in some semblance of comfort, to Armus House. There was entertainment also. Winnie sang one song after another: *The White Cliffs of Dover*, *Knees Up, Mother Brown*, and *We'll Meet Again*, as well as several raucous ditties about the plight of lonely, love-starved servicemen with one thought on their minds—only Winnie hummed all the naughty parts! She also knew several American cowboy songs: "There are a lot of Yank pilots in the ATA, and I've learned a few cow tunes from them—imagine, singing songs about cattle!" The songs, though, were wonderfully melodious, in a strange sort of way, and Winnie could mimic a passable Texas accent that lent a soothing effect to her performance. Andrew, cosseted between two eiderdown quilts, was allowed to gorge himself on lemon drops (from America, his mother pronounced). There was a little excitement during the last part of their journey: too many lemon drops and the motion of the car took their toll on Andrew's sensitive stomach. Winnie had to pull over to the side of the road so that he could heave up partially digested chunks of bright yellow gunk. His retching caused him to gag up gobs of rust-colored phlegm from his lungs. The rest of the journey was a blur— he had a beastly headache, and felt ever so hot. There was a funny rattly sensation in his lungs every time he breathed; his teeth chattered and his whole body shook violently. His chest had begun to hurt horribly by the time they arrived home. He coughed as his mother got him out of the car, and it seemed his lungs would split from the pain. He collapsed into his mother's arms, and she and Winnie half-supported, half-carried him into the house. Their voices became very indistinct and the pain in his chest shot out to his arms and legs so that they ached and throbbed with every movement. He felt as if he were drowning; then he seemed to be floating up the stairs and down the hall to his room. His bed hit him full in the face, and the darkness closed in.

He opened his eyes to see his father sitting on a chair by his bed. His father leaned forward and stroked Andrew's cheek. Taking Andrew's hand, he asked in a voice barely above a whisper: "How are you, old chap?"

Andrew nodded and tried to speak, but his lips moved uselessly as he wheezed his reply, which came out as a quavery moan.

"Awful," he finally managed to say. "My chest hurts horribly. I ate too many sweets and got sick. Mum said they were from America."

"I got them for you—I'm sorry you got sick on them."

"No, that's all right—it was my fault. I shouldn't have eaten so many. How did you get here?"

"I painted a 109 to look like a Puss Moth and I flew across the Atlantic to America, and there some nice people invited me to supper. They had fourteen sons, and all of their names began with *J*. Then I flew back across the ocean to England."

Andrew saw that his father was dressed in a navy blue uniform, with two gold stripes on each shoulder. He reached out and touched them. "How did you get these?"

"I'm a First Officer. When you're first captured, you're made a Third Officer, and you aren't allowed to escape until you make First Officer."

"But you're supposed to be a Flight Lieutenant, aren't you? Where are the rings on your sleeve?" He grabbed at his father's wrist and stroked the cuff frantically. "There are supposed to be rings—where are your rings?"

His father gazed in consternation at his cuffs, then looked at Andrew again. He said, "I'll get the rings, I promise. Why don't you get some rest—I'll be back soon."

All of a sudden Andrew felt incredibly tired, as if a wave of drowsiness were washing over him. He fought to keep his eyes open but the darkness closed in, and he felt himself being sucked into a cold underworld of despair. He tried to fight his way back to consciousness, terrified that his father had left.

How to get back to the light—to his father? The darkness was all around, suffocating him and pressing him down, like a ton of rubble in a bomb-blasted building...and he was at the bottom. He tried to breathe but, even though he poured the last ounce of his strength into the effort, he couldn't get any air into his lungs. Completely, utterly exhausted, he felt his life draining away into the black void, and with it the assurance that his father been with him. It had all been an dream, just a dream, he realized. He was past caring if he lived or died. All life, all hope, was gone.

Then he had the strangest sensation that, even in this appalling darkness, his father was near. He knew he had to fight now, to make his way back, and this effort of will gave him strength. He vaguely sensed that he was somehow making progress back to the light. His mind sent commands to his arms and legs to move, but he wasn't sure if they were cooperating; he could neither see nor feel. He tried to call out, but heard nothing.

Then it happened, as suddenly as the blast of a bomb: All sight and sensation and consciousness returned to him. He heard himself yelling, felt himself clawing his way forward, then found himself in his father's arms.

His father looked startled, as if he were not expecting Andrew to awaken.

"Dad, you're back! You went away, and I got lost from you—I went to sleep...I'm sorry...I tried to get back and I thought I couldn't, but I did!"

His father's eyes widened with fright. Andrew was dismayed: *Why was he afraid?* He wrapped his arms around his father's neck and whispered, "Don't be frightened— you're back! I always knew you'd come back. They said you were missing, but I didn't believe you were dead." He realized that they were in a hospital room: There were two tall windows with bright sunlight pouring through them. His bed had a kind of tent around it, open at the top. There was a cylinder of gas at the end.

"What's that?" he asked his father.

His father swallowed, as if afraid to speak. "Oxygen tent," he replied, his voice a croak. His arms were around Andrew, but not in an embrace; he was simply holding onto him—and rather stiffly, at that. Andrew looked at the cuffs on his father's tunic. *Rings! Two rings!* Reaching down to touch them, he exclaimed, "You're a Flight Lieutenant again!" As he traced his fingers around the rings, he remembered when he had last touched them: on their way to the station that dreadful morning, two and a half years ago....

He hugged his father again. "You came back to me! You flew to America and got sweets for me—I got sick on the lemon drops when I was in the car. The Prime Minister drove me, and he sang *Knees Up, Mother Brown* and *We'll Meet Again*."

His father looked bewildered now. Andrew realized how ridiculous all of his blabberings were. Maybe it all *had* been a dream!

Andrew grabbed his father's hand and realized: *This was no dream!* He pressed his hand more tightly into his father's—this was as real as anything could ever be! A wondrous, heady feeling of euphoria and sublime peace swept over him. His breathing, which had been very rapid and labored, became deep and regular. It seemed he could swallow a roomful of air in a single breath—what a wonderful sensation! He squeezed his father's hand again and gazed into his eyes, which were a troubled dark gray. Andrew could always read his father's moods by the color of his eyes: They were a light, almost silvery gray when he was happy, but the color darkened when he was in a serious mood or upset about something. Perhaps he was worried because Andrew had been talking such nonsense!

"You got the sweets for me—you got them in America, didn't you?"

His father nodded, affirming Andrew's query, but he still appeared puzzled and tense. At that moment, Andrew's mother strode into the room. Her mouth dropped open in alarm.

What's going on here? Why isn't she happy to see him? Andrew saw that his father now had a look of distress on his face.

"Mum—he's *back*! I always *knew* he'd come back. Now you're together again!" He untangled his hand from his father's and grabbed at his mother, drawing her close.

Taking her hand, he pressed it into his father's hand and tried to work her fingers between his. She seemed a little reluctant and looked at his father with wide-eyed apprehension.

"You're supposed to be *together*!" Andrew pleaded.

It was then he realized: She was not wearing her wedding ring. She hadn't worn it since she'd come back from the memorial service for his father. Maybe she felt guilty that she'd believed he was dead! Andrew looked at his father's left hand; his ring finger was bare, too, and his hands were horribly scarred as well. He ran his fingers over the crumpled flesh; here and there it had little patches of different-colored skin, giving his hands an odd, crazy-quilt appearance. "Did your hands get burnt when you got shot down?"

His father's eyes widened again, and he looked at Andrew's mother, positively terrified. She appeared equally frightened.

"Mum, please don't be sad—it's all right! I know you had to believe what they told you—they didn't talk to me, so I didn't have to believe. But I believed for both of us!" Turning to his father, Andrew repeated, "I believed for both of us—please don't be upset with her! It's all right—I always believed you'd come back!"

His father's face became even more distressed.

Why isn't he happy that I've always believed he would come back?

With a sudden flush of shame, Andrew remembered words he'd said to his father at their last parting: *I hate you—you care more about your silly old war than you do about me....*

He pressed his lips to his father's ear. In a low voice, he said, "I'm sorry about what I said when you left—you know I didn't mean it." Then he uttered the words he'd been longing to say for so long: "I love you—I love you, Dad."

He tasted something salty, and realized his lips were wet with his father's tears. He had never known his father to cry; almost against his will, he drew back to confront the tear-streaked face.

Never had he seen his father so distraught, but it was not the sudden show of emotion that disconcerted Andrew. His father was never one to hold back feelings, but they had almost always been feelings of joy and happiness, of delight and surprise. Even when he had evidenced sadness or worry, there was a sense of hope and strength underneath it all.

This however was different: The sudden vulnerability shown by his father stunned Andrew, driving home to him all of the war's terrible cost. When it wasn't taking lives, it was inflicting a horrible suffering on the living. What dreadful things had his father endured? He must have burned his hands when he was shot down, but what ghastly things had happened to him afterwards?

He had always envisioned his father returning with that same jaunty smile, cheerily resuming life as if nothing had happened. At first Andrew was tempted to feel cheated by this less than blissful reunion, but as he nuzzled his face against his father's cheek, a feeling of sublime peace swept over him.

He was back! That was all that mattered! Maybe his father needed time to heal, to put back together the pieces of his life...Perhaps it wasn't meant for things to be exactly the same as they were before.

He always took care of me. He was always so strong and steady. Now it's my turn to take care of him....

He tried to kiss away the tears, as his father used to do for him, and felt the sandpapery feel of the stubbled cheek against his lips.

"I've got your shaving things at home. Mum let me have your mug and brush—I put them in my treasure box. She gave it to me for Christmas, and she gave me the boxing gloves you got for me, too. She knows where my box is—Mum?"

His mother was gone!

"Where's Mum?"

His father looked around, and Andrew saw again the fear in his eyes.

Andrew tried to reassure him. "Please don't be upset—you're back! I always knew you'd come back! I had to pretend that I thought you weren't—Mum was so upset—I heard her crying...I didn't want her to be worried—please don't cry!" He brushed the tears from his father's cheeks.

His father looked tenderly, fearfully at him, his eyes blinking back the tears. He said, his voice nearly breaking, "I just want you to get well."

Andrew noted the oxygen tent around his bed. It must have been quite serious for him to have landed in hospital, let alone to have been treated with such extreme measures.

But he wasn't ill anymore—he was *fine!* He took a deep breath, felt the strong rush of air into his lungs, and the unimpeded flow of expired air afterwards.

"See—I'm better! I am—I'm not sick anymore! I promise I'm going to be fine—*Mum!*"

His mother had come into the room, with a doctor and nurse in tow. The doctor stared at Andrew in amazement; then moved quickly to him. Andrew felt a cold stethoscope pressing against his back, then to his chest.

"Better, much better," the doctor murmured. "Let's get his temperature."

Strong arms were tugging him away from his father. Andrew's response was to cling more tightly. His arms wrapped in a vise-grip around his father's neck and his legs twined around his father's waist.

"Come on now, I've got to get your temperature." The nurse tried to disengage Andrew with her massive hands.

"No—NO! *NOOOO!*" He was shrieking now, and feeling very badly about creating such a scene, for his father's face was a mask of terror. Was he frightened of Andrew's distress, or upset because they were about to be parted?

"I'm sorry—please don't let them take me away—*NOOO!*" The nurse pulled at him again, and this time his voice came out in panicky gasps. "Please—please—no, don't take me away—No—NO—*NO...NO!*"

"Let's get this done, all right? The doctor needs to know your temperature. Be a good boy now. You've had your temperature taken before, haven't you?" Brute force having failed, the nurse now tried to appeal to reason.

He turned, saw the pleading smile framing crooked teeth, saw the starched white uniform with a gold pin in the shape of a cross over the left pocket, saw the look of worry in pale blue eyes behind thick, wire-rimmed glasses.

"I don't want you to take me away." Andrew pressed his cheek against his father's shoulder and tightened his grip again in preparation for another battle.

The thin lips pursed; then the blue eyes twinkled with a solution to the dilemma. "Well—let's work around that, shall we?"

Andrew looked at her warily, his arms still tight around his father. *Just in case....*

She addressed Andrew's father: "Why don't you get on the bed over there?" With a nod of her head, she indicated the bed across the room. "You can hold him while I take his temperature."

Andrew's father carried him to the bed and, still holding him, laid back against the pillows. Andrew settled against him, pressing his face into the RAF blue-grey fabric of his tunic. His nose touched one of the gold buttons. He grabbed at it; the thread securing it was frayed and the button came loose in his hand. His fingers closed around it.

"Andrew, give that back." His mother's voice was firm, with an edge of fear.

"I want to keep it!"

"Darling, you mustn't pull buttons off people's clothing. Give it to me please."

"NO!"

"Andrew—" As she tried to pry his hand open, her fingernails scratched his palm.

"*NO*—I want to keep it!"

His mother looked pleadingly at the nurse, who intervened. "You can't be allowed to have that. You might accidently put it in your mouth while you're asleep and choke on it."

"I won't—I promise!"

"Give it to me," the nurse ordered. "If you don't, we'll have to take you away again—you don't want that to happen, do you? Now, be a good boy."

He reluctantly opened his hand, and his mother took the button. He then felt the nurse pulling up his gown and proceeding with her task.

He looked at his father, wondering how he felt about this bizarre—and not to mention, horribly undignified—reunion. This was not at all how Andrew had envisaged things, what with his backside hanging out of this wretched hospital gown and a thermometer stuck in his bottom....

"I'm sorry," he whispered.

"What?" His father's voice was strained and husky with...It sounded like anguish. Was he still worried?

"I'm sorry that you had to meet me here—in hospital, I mean. I'm sorry I got ill. I'll get better—please don't be sad!"

He felt his father's arms go around him; then he sensed a kind of shuddering: his father was weeping again. Wriggling up so that his face was against his father's cheek, he whispered, "It's all right—I'm fine. Please don't be sad." He tasted the salt again, felt the stubbly face wet with new tears, heard the nurse say a number: *Ninety—some-*

thing. The doctor's voice: *Good, good—he'll be all right now* was the last thing he heard. He pressed his face to his father's cheek again, luxuriating in the sensation of the bristly skin against his lips. *He's back, he's back...I always knew he'd come back....*

The darkness was closing in on him again; he tried to hold onto his father, but he felt himself floating away....

He opened his eyes. The hospital room was the same: There was the vacant bed across the room, the two tall windows, lit with a golden afternoon glow...the nurse, standing above him. She had the same pale blue eyes, thick glasses—wire rimmed—and the gold cross over her left pocket. She smiled...crooked teeth, too.

"Andrew—" His mother was standing by his bed now.

"Mum—"

His mother's hand caressed his cheek. She looked relieved, but wary, too.

"Dad?" Even as he asked the question, the realization hit him: Real as it had seemed, he had only imagined everything.

His mother kissed him gently on the forehead, then drew back.

"You were delirious—you were asking for your father." She seemed almost apologetic, as if she herself had been responsible for his...ravings.

He slumped back against the pillow as she smoothed back his hair.

"It was so *real!*" He looked at his hand: There were scratches on his palm.

"See?" He held out his hand to her. "You scratched me, when you tried to take the button away."

She stroked her fingers over his palm.

"You were thrashing around, trying to get out of the oxygen tent. I'm sorry—I tried to get you back into bed. You were raving...You thought your father was here."

"It *happened!* It was real—he was crying—I wouldn't imagine him crying—he needed a shave—he had the rings around his cuff—his hands were scarred—then she took my temperature—" He threw a sharp glance at the nurse. "Didn't you?"

The nurse glanced nervously at Andrew's mother.

"She took your temperature," his mother affirmed. "You were delirious—we had to put you on the other bed because you were thrashing around." She put her arms around him. "Your fever finally broke a few hours ago. You're going to be all right—that's all that matters."

The crisis had passed but left a lingering after-effect: Blood tests indicated that he was anemic.

Quite anemic, the doctor said. This complication was a common result of pneumonia and was, no doubt, aggravated by poor nutrition. He ordered a blood transfusion. The thought of such a ghastly measure terrified Andrew, and he begged his mother to make that silly sod of a doctor see reason.

"Mum—*please!* I'm going to be all right. Please don't let them do this!"

"Andrew, don't be difficult. It'll help you to get better."

"I'll get better without it—*I promise!* This is going to make things worse! I hate needles and I hate blood!"

"Darling, it'll give you back your strength. All you'll feel is a tiny prick when the nurse puts the needle in. And if you don't like the sight of blood, you can keep your eyes closed and hold my hand. I'll be with you the whole time. Now, the doctor won't let you go home until you have the transfusion, so be a good boy, all right?"

Andrew knew it was useless to protest. He couldn't help but glance at the bottle of dark red liquid the nurse carried into his room. A wave of nausea swept over him and he buried his face against his mother's shoulder.

"There, there, darling—now hold your arm out. It'll be over in a second."

A stab of pain, soft murmurings from the nurse.

"There," his mother soothed. "The worst is over. Now just hold still."

"I *hate* it," he moaned.

"Andrew, it's helping you. Just think of all those millions and millions of blood cells as little boats, bringing oxygen to every corner of your body, like the ships from America bringing us supplies to help us fight the war."

"Is it your blood?"

"No, it isn't. I couldn't give you my blood—I'm the wrong blood type."

"Whose is it, then?"

"Oh...many people donate blood. It's from someone who cares, that I know. Oh darling, I can see the color coming back into your cheeks already. You're going to be fine, just fine!"

His mother had taken an emergency leave from the ATA, but now that Andrew was on the mend she needed to return to her duties. He was discharged from the hospital into Aunt Gwen's care. She arranged to take a few weeks off from work in order to nurse him at home. The doctor informed him that he would need to stay at home for at least another month in order to get completely well. Besides, what with the renewed aerial offensive by the Luftwaffe, the doctor said that he didn't want Andrew risking any more cold, draughty nights in a bomb shelter. Just before the Blitz, Thomas had put in an Anderson shelter, an arch of steel covered with earth. It never had been needed, but now was stocked with a supply of blankets and quilts, just in case.

Andrew spent the first two weeks of his convalescence almost entirely in bed, not being allowed to so much as lift a finger. Aunt Gwen fed him liquid and soft foods at first: milk, porridge, soups, beef broth, mashed fruit. As he recovered, his diet included as much protein as was possible under the circumstances: Thomas acquired some chickens and one of them was sacrificed to supply Andrew with chicken soup for a week. After that, Mrs. Tuttle discovered that a beaten egg, when sprinkled in simmering chicken stock, produced a kind of noodle that was nutritious and quite tasty as well. Since Andrew was under fifteen, he got the usual ration of seven pints of milk a week; this was supplemented by Aunt Gwen's trading their jam and tea ration for goat's milk from a neighboring estate.

"You need protein more than we need tea and sweets," she said. She also arranged for him to get a special allotment of orange juice. Normally this was reserved for children under five, but Aunt Gwen besieged the local Food Office with a barrage of documentation that his was a special needs case, and he was allowed to receive a two weeks' supply.

Mr. Nugent corresponded with Andrew almost daily to give him his assignments and tell him news of school. At first, Andrew was enjoined by Aunt Gwen from even holding a pencil to write. She tutored him by reading aloud from his textbooks and quizzing him briefly. The lessons were limited to half an hour; then he rested as she read to him awhile from *Great Expectations*, which Mr. Nugent had assigned for literature. Bedtime was *nine o'clock—no exceptions*, according to Aunt Gwen.

He had a daily bath too, in the morning. Even this ritual involved almost no effort on his part: Aunt Gwen undressed him in bed while the tub was filling; then, wrapped in a blanket, he was carried by Thomas to the bathroom, peeled out of the blanket, and deposited in the tub. Aunt Gwen scrubbed him thoroughly, shushing his bashful protestations with loud declarations on the importance of cleanliness. Back in bed, he was treated to a heavenly backrub by Aunt Gwen, then was dressed in a fresh "pneumonia jacket" of padded cotton. Aunt Gwen had obtained two for him, so that one could be washed and dried while the other was worn.

All of this cossetting would have been sheer bliss were it not for the dreadful daily enema which preceded his morning bath. ("Mustn't exert yourself!" was his aunt's stern admonition.) Andrew was rather inclined to think that this horrific procedure was invented for the express purpose of discouraging anyone from feigning illness in order to receive special pampering. Mercifully, these were discontinued after a week, when Aunt Gwen had determined he'd gained enough strength and could be spared this ghastly measure.

His enforced inactivity permitted him a lot of time in which to reflect about the fantastic experience he'd had while in hospital. Even though his mother had insisted he'd been delirious, he knew—he *knew* that being in his father's arms had been *no* hallucination. His father *had* come to him again, just as he'd visited him when he was being dug out of the rubble. Only this time, Andrew had not merely heard his voice; he had seen, felt, touched him—even *tasted* the tears on his stubbly cheeks! In the languid spaces of time between meals and ministrations and sleep, he mused on the various sensations of that wondrous encounter—feeling his father's arms around him, hearing the anguish and fear in his voice, touching the crumpled skin of his hands. Never—*Never* had it ever even occurred to Andrew that his father could have been disfigured like that and, even though it distressed him to see his father so injured, it was oddly reassuring, as well, for it attested to the absolute...*realness* of it all. Lying back against his pillows, in complete quietness of body and soul, Andrew would close his eyes and submerge himself in the rapturous memory of every detail: nuzzling his face into the fabric of his father's uniform, sensing the trembling sobs, pulling off the button and arguing against the protestations of his mother and the nurse, feeling his mother's fingernails scratch his palm...It had *not* been a delusion! His father somehow, across the miles, had known how ill he'd been—close to dying, even—and had come to him, had come to pull him away from the icy clutches of death itself.

As he recovered, Andrew was allowed more activity. He could sit up in bed for short periods of time to do written assignments. Aunt Gwen returned to work after a fortnight. Gram, who had been away nursing her brother with cancer, returned to Armus House to take care of Andrew.

He was permitted to bathe himself, and to eat lunch in the dining room: Aunt Gwen decided that a change of scenery would aid in his convalescence. He could sit at his desk for one hour a day, at first; that was extended to two, when he was considered by Aunt Gwen (after she'd made a brief visit home) to be much on the mend.

He enjoyed the increased activity, for he had become restless with his enforced dormancy. ("Good sign," Aunt Gwen had observed, "But you still must be very, *very*, careful. We don't want a relapse!"). In order to have something to pass the time after he was done with his schoolwork, he tried to teach Lucia to play chess. But she wasn't very good, even for a beginner. For the first time Andrew began to really miss his Aunt Jane. She often had been away during the last two years, but at least there had been the possibility of her coming to visit at anytime. Now she was "away."

She continued to write to him regularly: Her letters were usually brief and invariably vague about where she was and what she was doing. All that she revealed was that she worked at a desk, somewhere. She asked questions of Andrew and told little of herself. Evidently, his mother had informed her that he had been ill; her letters inquired as to his health and admonished him to take good care of himself.

Where is she? he wondered. No use asking—she had already told him that it was all very military and hush-hush. He considered the possibilities: The Far East, possibly? Or maybe Australia, or India. North Africa, perhaps?

North Africa! What with the turn of events there, someone who spoke French would be much in demand. He wrote to her, asking her if she spoke French on her job.

She replied with a teasing admonishment: *My little detective*, she called him. *Are you trying to pry military secrets out of me? All right, in answer to your query: I do speak French on occasion. No more questions!*

Why couldn't she have stayed in England—especially now, with him being home? As Andrew recuperated, he grew more and more restless. Gram went off to nurse her brother again, and the servants were usually too busy to entertain him much. Lucia soon lost interest in chess and made excuses not to play. No matter, she wasn't much of a challenge, anyway. Only Freddie, who had just returned from his "business trip" to America and was grousing about the "beastly" natives of Yankland, was around with any degree of regularity. Andrew definitely did not relish *his* company! He began to miss his friends at school and he longed for companionship and a break with routine. So when his mother phoned and informed him that she was bringing some ATA pilots to be billeted at Armus House, his joy knew no bounds.

"Oh, they're Americans. They'll be doing their Class 2 conversion course at White Waltham," she mentioned, almost as a casual aside before bidding him good-bye. "I trust that you will show them every courtesy, and do everything within your power to make their stay enjoyable."

Andrew assured her not to worry, that he would do exactly that, and that he would make certain their stay was a very delightful one indeed.

"All right, then. I'll be bringing them in three days."

As Andrew replaced the receiver, he nearly whooped with glee. No matter that they were Americans; they would at least provide a change of pace and, with any luck, a little excitement in his dull existence. Then again, the fact that they *were* Americans was a decided advantage.

Andrew smiled to himself. Yes, they ought to really liven things up at Armus House! *Americans*! What would Freddie think?

Chapter 13

*A*ndrew's mother ushered three women in ATA uniforms through the front door of Armus House.

"This is my son Andrew." She nodded at Andrew, who stood by the front stairs, eagerly clutching the bannister. He almost skipped over to them; then, remembering his manners, he extended his hand.

"Andrew, I'd like you to meet Marlys, Irene, and this is Frances—she likes to be called Kaz," his mother said, as she nodded to each one in turn. Andrew noticed that each of the women had a patch on her sleeve displaying the letters *U.S.A.*

"Pleased to meet you." He shook each of their hands, then stepped backwards to survey his new-found housemates. Marlys looked a little like Aunt Jane, with exotic looks that were even more pronounced: high cheekbones and delicate features that were framed with wavy hair of glossy black. Her violet-blue eyes were edged with long, dark lashes, and her figure was fashion-model slender, yet athletically fit. Irene, round-faced and a little more solidly built, had a wild, tously mane of blond hair, a generous smile, and laughing eyes of cornflower blue. Kaz was the tallest of the three, taller even than Andrew's mother. She was big-boned and sturdy, with plain (though not unattractive) features, no-nonsense straight brown hair, and matching brown eyes. She had a look of complete self-assurance and calm. Andrew got the distinct impression that, no matter what situation she might find herself in, she would be completely capable of meeting any challenge. Not that the other two seemed by any means incompetent or twittery; to the contrary, they looked to be quite able and self-reliant. It just seemed that Kaz possessed these traits to a greater degree. She was a lot like Aunt Jane, in spirit, Andrew decided, even though Marlys bore more of a physical resemblance to his aunt. Andrew was surprised that his first impressions of these women were so strong, and he wondered if he might have imagined some of the qualities that he was imparting to them. After all, they had only shaken his hand and murmured a few words of greeting.

He nervously bit his lip, then announced, "Mrs. Tuttle has tea ready. I helped set the table, and I helped to make the trifle, too. Mrs. Tuttle makes the best trifle, and we have potato soup and carrot flan—we have to eat that before the sweet, though—" he caught himself, embarrassed that he'd been babbling so.

Irene threw back her head and laughed. "They warned me that you English were very cold and inhospitable—what a pack of lies!" She looked around the front hall and winked at Andrew. "What a beautiful home, and what an enthusiastic welcoming committee!"

Andrew felt the blood rising to his face. His mother smiled broadly at him, and Kaz and Marlys looked at him with positive delight.

Mrs. Tuttle bustled out into the hall; Lucia followed two paces behind.

"This is Mrs. Tuttle, our cook, and this is Lucia, our maid," Andrew's mother said.

Mrs. Tuttle bobbed her head in greeting, and Lucia nodded excitedly.

"Your husband told us all about your marvelous cooking," Marlys said to Mrs. Tuttle.

Mrs. Tuttle chuckled, "Oh, he does go on, but I try, I try—"

"And every word of it is true!" Andrew affirmed. "Mrs. Tuttle is the best cook in the world, not like Mrs. Bunch at my school—she makes awful stuff called Commando Casserole, and she tried to make us eat whale meat once—she called it Sea Delight, but none of us were fooled! She makes us take cod liver oil, too!"

The three women grinned in unison; then they greeted Lucia, who ushered them into the dining room. After the women had seated themselves, Mrs. Tuttle and Lucia brought in the tea things.

"Where's Freddie?" Andrew's mother asked Mrs. Tuttle.

"Went to London yesterday, mum. He says he'll be back late this evening."

"Freddie—now is he the one you told us about?" Irene asked.

Andrew's mother nodded.

"Oh, Freddie's no trouble at all," Andrew said. "You just have to keep refilling his glass, and in no time at all he's completely potted!"

"*Andrew!*" his mother admonished.

Irene let out a peal of laughter. "Sounds like an uncle of mine. We called him Tight— he was, usually."

Mrs. Tuttle and Lucia brought out the soup and flan and rolls. "We have to use this unrefined flour now," Mrs. Tuttle apologized. "They say that milling white flour wastes too much of the grain. I know it doesn't look all that appetizing, but it's really quite good. I hope you don't mind."

Marlys took a bite of roll. "Oh, this is delicious!"

"Wonderful," Kaz agreed, tasting the carrot flan. "Alice, it really is so kind of you to arrange for us to stay here—"

"I assure you, it's my pleasure. Besides, we have the extra room, what with Jane away, and a guest room that's not being used. And Andrew has just been aching for company. I've had to warn him not to be—" She looked at Andrew, "too *tiresome*— isn't that right, Andrew?"

Andrew nodded. "Mum said that I shouldn't bother you too much because you might all be very tired at the end of the day, but if you're not too tired, may I help you to study? I helped Mum when she was at conversion school, and I know all about Masters and Hurricanes and Spitfires and—"

"Andrew—" his mother began.

"Oh, Alice, I think that's a wonderful idea!" Irene exclaimed. "You didn't tell us that this place came with an in-residence tutor!"

"If you're too tired, I don't want Andrew making a pest of himself—"

"I promise, Mum—I won't. I'll ask permission, and if they don't want to study with me, I won't pester them, I promise!"

Irene chortled. "What a jewel! Alice, I'd love to rent your son for a few months and send him out to Iowa to give lessons to my younger brothers. Now if you want to see tiresome, you ought to get a load of those monsters!"

"You're from Iowa?" Andrew asked. "Is that near Colorado? Mr. Nugent, my housemaster, went to Colorado."

"Iowa's about five hundred miles due east," Irene replied.

"*Crikey*! Five hundred *miles*! Oh, sorry, Mum says I shouldn't blurt out so—I mean, five hundred miles, that's quite a distance, I should say."

"Talk about distance," Marlys said. "I'm from California, and it's about seven hundred miles long from top to bottom."

"California!" Andrew exclaimed. "Have you ever seen any movie stars?"

Andrew's mother looked sternly at him. "Andrew darling, not everyone from California has seen—"

"As a matter of fact, I have," Marlys smiled. "My father is a doctor in Los Angeles—physician to the stars, he likes to call himself, so he manages to get himself invited to lots of parties. I used to tag along, and I've met a few famous faces. But after awhile, the parties are all the same and you find that there's really nothing new under the sun."

"What movie stars have you met?"

"Andrew, please don't pester—" his mother began.

"Oh, Alice, he's not pestering at all, just being a good conversationalist." Marlys turned to Andrew. "Have you seen *Gone with the Wind?*"

"Yes, my Aunt Gwen—she's a nurse—took me to see it last summer in London. I thought it was smashing! Especially the part when Atlanta was on fire, and I like the part when Scarlett shot that Yankee soldier. If any Nazi ever came in my house, I'd let him have it, right between the eyes! Mrs. Tuttle used to keep a claymore—it's this bloody huge sword that's double-edged—anyway, she kept it in the pantry, in case the Nazis invaded. She said that if any Huns meant to do her harm, she was bloody well going to take one of them with her—"

"Andrew!" his mother squealed. She lowered her voice. "I don't think that this is a pleasant topic of conversation for our guests—"

"Sorry, Mum." Andrew noticed, though, that Marlys and Irene were trying to stifle giggles, and Kaz grinning with delight. He turned back to Marlys. "Did you meet anyone who was in *Gone With the Wind?*"

"Uh-huh—Clark Gable, Vivian Leigh, Olivia deHavilland—"

"Clark Gable was the one who said, 'Frankly my dear, I don't give a damn', wasn't he?"

"Yes, he was."

"I heard that he had to pay a lot of money to be allowed to say *damn*."

"*He* didn't—it was the movie people who had to pay a lot of money."

"I think that's ridiculous! Now if he'd said, 'Stuff that for a game of soldiers, Scarlett—I don't care what the bloody hell—'"

A peal of laughter interrupted Andrew's declaration: Irene was slumped sideways in her chair, utterly convulsed by a paroxysm of mirth. Kaz and Marlys looked at each other and tried to suppress their laughter—not very successfully.

"Andrew, I do *not* want you using profanity!" his mother admonished.

"Sorry," Andrew said. Irene let out one last shriek, wiped her eyes, and beamed at Andrew.

"Andrew does have a tendency to get a bit high-spirited when he's excited." His mother raised her eyebrows in warning at Andrew.

"Oh Alice, I think you have a wonderful boy, and I think we're going to get along terrifically," Irene said. "Now, if you really want to see high-spirited, you ought a get a load of my brothers—for that matter, my sisters, too. Now the nine of us together just about set the world—"

"You have *eight* brothers and sisters?" Andrew exclaimed. "*Crikey!*"

His mother's eyes bulged in mortification. "Andrew, it's not nice to—"

Irene laughed again and tousled Andrew's hair. "Yes, my father used to say he had a baseball team, only we weren't as well-behaved! We all tried to outdo one another in being outrageous. My oldest brother was a barnstormer, and I was his wing-walker. Before I agreed to it though, I made him give me flying lessons."

"You were a wing walker?" Andrew said. "Oh, I think that's smashing!

"To tell the truth, I'd much rather be flying a plane than walking on one!"

Andrew's mother directed the conversation to Marlys, then to Kaz, eliciting from them how they came to be pilots. Marlys had taken flying lessons from a friend of her father's, who was a fighter pilot in the Great War. Kaz had worked for Piper Aircraft in Lock Haven, Pennsylvania. The owner of the company, "Papa" Piper, had offered flying lessons for $1.12 an hour to his workers. (Andrew gathered that that was quite a reasonable price.) As Kaz explained: "He figured that we would build better airplanes if we understood how important it was to have everything work right when the plane was airborne!" Kaz had gone on to become an instructor, giving lessons to the employees at the company, instead of building aircraft. "I'm so glad, though," she said, "that I had the hands-on experience of building planes. I think it has made me a better pilot, knowing exactly how every piece of an airplane fits together to work as a whole."

"How did you join the ATA?" Andrew asked.

"We were recruited by Jacqueline Cochran," Marlys replied. "She's a well known pilot in America. She set a number of records, and won the Bendix Race in 1938. She was the first person to fly it non-stop, from Los Angeles to Cleveland."

"She flew a P-35. It had extra fuel tanks built into the wings," Kaz added.

"Yeah," Irene said. "And the amazing part is that the plane was sabotaged and she still managed to win the race!"

"*Sabotaged?*" Andrew exclaimed.

"Now, that was never proven," Marlys countered.

"They found a wad of paper in one of the wing tanks and that doesn't constitute proof?" Irene raised her eyebrows in challenge.

"Jackie didn't believe it was sabotage."

"Oh, what was it, then, sloppy workmanship?" Irene turned to Kaz. "You worked in an aircraft factory. Did the workers usually stuff wads of paper in fuel tanks?"

Kaz shrugged non-commitally.

"What did she do, then?" Andrew asked.

"She didn't find out that something was wrong until she was over the Rockies," Irene said. "Her engine quit, and she tried switching fuel tanks to start it again, but no dice. She then tried rocking the wings, and the engine caught. She figured out that the right wing tank wasn't feeding fuel to the engine, so she had to elevate it every so often, to drain the gas out by gravity. After landing at Cleveland and winning the race, she went on to New Jersey, to set the women's cross country record."

"She was also the first person to fly through the Grand Canyon," Marlys added. "And she set the women's altitude record at 33,000 feet in 1939."

"She came to England in 1941, so that she could get an idea of what the women pilots in the ATA were doing," Kaz said. "She wanted to organize a ferry service of women pilots in America. So she arranged to ferry a Lockheed Hudson bomber across the Atlantic, with the idea of proving that women were capable of flying any kind of plane, any distance. Trouble was, there was a terrific fuss over it so she had let her co-pilot do the take-off and landing."

"Yeah, and on top of that, the plane was vandalized too!" Irene exclaimed.

"*Vandalized?*" Andrew blurted.

The other two women didn't protest Irene's assertion.

"Yeah," Irene said. "When she checked out the plane before take-off she found that the window in the pilot's cabin was smashed, the life raft was missing, and the wrench used to activate the oxygen system had been removed. She bought a wrench from a mechanic at the airfield while the window was being repaired."

"*Crikey!*"

"Once in England," Kaz went on, "She met with Pauline Gower, took a look-see at how the ATA was run, and returned to the States to try to start up a women's ferrying division. At the time, though, the powers-that-be didn't like the idea. So she set about recruiting American women for the ATA."

"How many American women are there in the ATA?" Andrew asked.

"There are twenty-five of us," Irene replied.

"They were chosen out of over seven hundred applicants," Andrew's mother pointed out.

Andrew's eyes widened. "It must have been awfully difficult to get in! Did you fly here—from America, I mean?"

"Nope—we took the cattle-boat special," Irene replied.

"Cattle-boat!"

"Come on Irene, it wasn't *that* bad," Kaz rejoined.

"I know cows, and I know the *smell* of cows, and *that* was a cattle-boat," countered Irene.

"How long did it take to get here?"

"Two weeks," Marlys said.

"Did you see any U-Boats?"

"Didn't see any, but they were probably around. Our convoy was accompanied by corvettes and destroyers and they were always shooting off their guns or dropping depth charges," Marlys replied. "Boy, was I ever glad to see England!"

"Did Jacqueline Cochran finally get to organize a women's ferry service in America?"

"Yes, she did," Irene said. "After she got all of us settled in England, she returned to the States and found that another woman pilot, Nancy Love, had organized the Women's Auxiliary Ferrying Squadron, or WAFS. It was an elite group: The women all had more than five hundred hours of flying time. Jackie was a little upset about all this happening behind her back while she was away in England, so she rattled some cages and got the go-ahead to start up another group of women pilots: the Women's Flying Training Detachment. The requirements to join were less stiff than those of the WAFS: Two hundred hours of flying time was the minimum. Jackie wanted to have an organization to train lots of ferry pilots, not just have a small group of highly-experienced ones."

As he listened to Irene and the other Americans, Andrew could not help but be enchanted by their distinctive speech and charming mannerisms. He had never met real, live Americans before and he was utterly captivated by these gregarious and lively women. Their speech was so different from the clipped, even, British canter: The words tumbled out of their mouths like horses going at full gallop. Their faces were so animated: They opened their mouths wide as they talked and they seemed to throw their whole bodies into the act of conversation, moving their hands and tossing their heads as they spoke. They looked like movie stars.

"Well, well—*Alice*! You didn't tell me you were bringing guests!" Freddie's voice boomed from the doorway.

"They're Americans, Freddie. You wouldn't like them." Andrew's mother snapped.

"Alice, you do me an injustice! When have I *ever* given you the impression that I would think ill of our—" Freddie smiled charmingly as his eyes ranged over the women, "Transatlantic cousins."

Andrew's mother rolled her eyes.

"Alice, aren't you going to introduce me to our guests?" Freddie importuned in a velvety voice.

"My late husband's cousin, Freddie Hadley-Trevelyan," Andrew's mother pronounced.

Andrew winced. Even though he knew his mother had accepted his father as being dead, it still disturbed him to hear her refer to his father as "late," as if their entire relationship had been negated by his...absence. He held the napkin up to his mouth to hide his sudden heavyheartedness.

Andrew's mother nodded at each of the women as she spoke their names. "Freddie, may I present Irene Bock, Marlys Walden, and Kaz—her real name is Frances, but she likes to be called Kaz, as her last name is—"

"Marlys, what a lovely name—well suited for an *especially* beautiful woman." Freddie crossed the room and sat in a vacant chair next to Marlys. He took her hand, brought it to his lips, and gently kissed it, his eyes smoldering with unconcealed lust.

Andrew's mother piped in a loud voice, "They're ATA pilots, and I've arranged for them to be billeted here while they do their Class 2 conversion course at White Waltham."

Freddie continued to gaze at Marlys. "How charming—and to think you've come all the way from America to aid us in our hour of need—"

Andrew's mother rolled her eyes again. "Freddie just got back from America a few weeks ago. He seems to find it less and less to his liking—"

"Alice!" Freddie evinced mock outrage as he glanced at Andrew's mother. His expression softened as he turned to Marlys. "Please disregard my dear cousin; I really don't know why she is so intent on misrepresenting me."

"I wouldn't dare *quote* what he had to say—now, Freddie, what was on the east coast and what was on the west coast and what was in the middle—"

"Alice!" Freddie managed a convincing expression of being tremendously wounded, then turned to Marlys again. "That damnable trans-Atlantic crossing, what with those beastly U-Boats, does tend to put me in a less than sanguine mood, so I fear Alice has seen me at my worst."

"Freddie, you've always *flown* to America and back—what have U-Boats got to do with—"

"To set the matter straight," Freddie said loudly to Marlys, "I happen to find your marvelous country very *much* to my liking. Your people have a wonderfully dynamic vigor, a spirited outlook on life, that is positively refreshing. I always feel vitalized, yes positively *vitalized*—" His eyes flickered with invitation as he lowered his voice to Marlys, "Whenever I set foot on American soil. I'll be returning to your lovely land this summer—if you could possibly arrange a leave from your flying duties, I would be ever so delighted to have your company. As they say, half the joy of visiting a foreign land is seeing it through the eyes of its people."

Andrew had never heard *that* one before, and he decided that Freddie must have made it up on the spur of the moment.

"I'm sorry, I've signed an eighteen month contract with the ATA, and it would be unthinkable to consider breaking it." Marlys smiled perfunctorily, then turned away from Freddie and glanced down at her plate.

"Well," Freddie turned to Irene and Kaz. "As I was saying, the more I visit America, the more I find it to my liking. There's a wonderful variety among your people, yet a common spirit and purpose. Quite frankly, I'm beginning to find England a bit unbearable, and to me a visit to America is an escape to blessed restfulness."

"Blessed *restfulness*?" Andrew's mother arched an eyebrow.

"Yes—England has gotten rather, shall we say?—disconcerting," Freddie replied.

"*Disconcerting*?" Andrew's mother echoed.

"Yes, haven't you noticed? London's a hotbed of wogs and malcontents—

"The *wogs* begin at *Calais*," Andrew's mother explained to the women.

Freddie narrowed his eyes at her, then proceeded with his execration: "London used to be quite a pleasant place—I'm distressed that our visitors must have seen it in its present repugnant state. It's positively gone to the dogs! It's ghastly with all those Bolshies blathering and everyone talking in their own jabberwocky—Frogs in their fancy uniforms, complaining about the food and Polacks—mind you, *Polacks*—strutting around in their RAF uniforms! Can you imagine, *Polacks*—flying *planes?*"

"Polacks flying planes?" Kaz seemed intrigued.

"Yes, dear girl—oh, I say, have you heard—" Freddie chuckled, then composed himself. "Oh, this is ever so funny—It seems there was this Polack chap, doing his first flight as co-pilot on a Lancaster. Well, they were coming back from their nightly bombing mission and one engine goes out. 'Not to fear,' says the pilot. 'I can get her home, just as easy on three engines; it'll just take a bit extra time. We'll be a few minutes late for breakfast, that's all.' The Polack chap nods; then another engine goes out. 'Blast,' says the pilot. 'Well, don't worry old chap, this Lanc is a good bus, and I'll be able to get us back on two engines. We won't make breakfast, but we'll be home in time for elevensies.' Then another engine goes out. 'Bloody hell!' yells the pilot. 'Well, you're lucky to be flying with one of the best pilots in the RAF, and if anyone can get a Lanc home on one engine, I can. I'm afraid that we'll miss elevensies, but we should make lunch. I just hope that our last engine doesn't quit on us; that would put us in a bit of a tight spot, wouldn't it?' 'Yes,' replies the Polack. ' *We'll be up here all day!*'" Freddie broke into that horrid wheezy laughter, so overcome by his own cleverness that he pitched forward in glee.

Andrew's mother rolled her eyes up at the ceiling in exasperation; Marlys and Irene looked at each other, uneasy and embarrassed; Kaz glared coldly at Freddie, who composed himself quickly, cleared his throat, and murmured, "Well, I see that perhaps our British humor is not to your liking, Miss, um—what did you say your name was?"

"*Kazmierski*, Frances Kazmierski," Kaz continued to regard Freddie with an icy stare. She lowered her voice slightly, and said in a measured voice, "But you can call me Kaz."

"Oh, that was positively smashing!" Andrew hopped on one foot, then another, as the women made their way down the upstairs hallway. He was not only absolutely enraptured with the way that Kaz had lured Freddie into committing such a gaffe, but he was thoroughly delighted by his mother's badgering of him as well: *Tell me Freddie, what's on the east coast, what's on the west coast, and what's in between?* He loved the way she had rolled her eyes at Freddie's sickening pretense of liking America or things American. Oh, it was rich—*rich!* Her manner towards Freddie had changed: She was much more assertive, almost adversarial, in her dealings with him. He recalled Aunt Jane's reassurance to him that his mother could take care of herself, and a glow of satisfaction swept through him as he realized she could—*she could!* He didn't have to worry about Freddie bothering her anymore! Unable to contain his exultation, he lugged one of Kaz's bags to the guest room despite his mother's protests that he shouldn't exert himself

"We have two rooms available," Andrew's mother told the women. "The guest room has two single beds, and a bath that also adjoins Jane's room. So two of you will have to share the guest room." She opened the door.

"Wow—this is beautiful!" Irene surveyed the lilac-papered room and the beds piled high with matching print coverlets. "Well, let's do this the fair way." She opened her purse and withdrew a deck of cards, which she shuffled. "High card gets the private room." She fanned the cards out.

As much as Andrew liked Irene and Marlys, he hoped that Kaz would get Aunt Jane's room. It just seemed right that someone who was so much like his aunt should inhabit her room. Marlys drew a four of hearts, Irene drew a seven of clubs, and Kaz—Kaz drew a Queen of diamonds! Andrew tried to hide his excitement because he didn't want to appear rude by conveying a preferential attitude towards Kaz in front of the others. He helped to carry Kaz's things into Aunt Jane's room, closed the door, and said to her in a low voice, "I'm so glad you got my Aunt Jane's room. You're so much like her, I think, and I'm sure that, if you knew her, you'd be very good friends."

Kaz smiled at him. "Thank you for the compliment, Andrew. Is that your Aunt Jane?" She indicated a framed photograph on the dresser.

"Yes, Andrew replied. "That was taken on her wedding day. She didn't get married in a dress; she wore a suit. That's her husband, Marc."

"He looks very nice, too. Is he away with your Aunt Jane?"

"No, he was killed a few years ago, in France."

"Oh dear, in the war?"

"No, before the war. They were in a car accident. He was killed, and Aunt Jane was hurt."

"So he was French?"

Andrew nodded. "I used to go to France for summer holiday. Aunt Jane spoke French like a native. She spoke several languages, in fact. I learned French in school and so we'd talk in French, pretending that we were natives. It was a lot of fun when we took the boat across the Channel or when we were in Paris, because we'd talk in French and pretend that we didn't understand the English tourists saying nasty things about the French people."

"That sounds like fun!"

"Oh, but it wasn't *half* as fun as seeing Freddie's face when you said your name was—what was it again?"

"Kazmierski," Kaz smiled.

"Kazmierski—I like that. I'm sorry about Freddie—he was ever so rude, wasn't he? I know that there was a Polish squadron during the Battle of Britain. My father wrote to me and said that there was and that they were very good—weren't they?"

"Not just very good—they were the best. They were the highest scoring squadron in the Battle of Britain."

"The *highest* scoring?"

Kaz nodded. "303 Squadron. They shot down more Germans than any other squadron. Most of them had been fighter pilots in the Polish Air Force when Germany attacked in 1939. Problem was, their planes were PZL Parasol fighters—no match for the 109s. Most of the Polish Air Force was destroyed in a few days. Many of the pilots who survived made their way to England after Poland fell. There are now eight Polish fighter squadrons in the RAF."

"They must be quite angry at what the Germans did to their country."

Kaz looked down at the floor. "I have cousins there. We haven't heard anything from them since the war started."

"I'm very sorry."

Kaz put her arm around him and her eyes rested on Aunt Jane's picture. "She looks like a very wonderful person."

"Oh, she is! She's ever so smart, too, and she knows how to put Freddie in his place, just like you did. When Freddie told her that she'd never find a husband because she was too intelligent, she told him, 'When I'm good and ready, I shall place an ad in the times: *Twits and imbeciles need not apply*."

"I *like* your Aunt Jane. I'd love to meet her someday!"

"She writes to me, and I write to her, too. I'll tell her all about you. What else do you like to do, besides fly and build planes, that is?"

"Oh—I like to sail, I like to travel. I love England. I'd like to take an extended vacation here when the war's over. I want to go to college, too, someday. I had to go to work when I got out of high school, though I have to admit that building airplanes and learning how to fly was wonderful, too. But I'd really love to go to college and study history."

"My father read history at Oxford. He also boxed and was in the flying club."

Kaz smiled. "I used to think that history was a very boring subject—you know, having to memorize names and dates and places and stuff. But when I got out of school, I started reading about the past and found it fascinating. When you get down to it, history is about *people:* how they lived, what they did, why they made their choices, what mistakes they made—and their successes, also, and how they coped with everything that life could throw at them. I really enjoyed stories about English history, especially about the Tudors and Queen Elizabeth—now she was an extraordinary person! If I could go back in time and meet one person, I think I'd like to meet her!"

"You would? I'm related to her."

"*Related?*"

"Yes—not descended from her, of course. She didn't have any children."

"Right—she never married. Even though everyone pressured her to get married and produce an heir, she did things her own way, and I think she was the best monarch England ever had." Kaz's eyes got a distant sort of look, as if she were reminiscing about an old friend. Then she looked at Andrew and smiled. "So you're related to her! Are you descended from Henry the Seventh?"

"No, my mother was a Howard, and Queen Elizabeth's grandmother, Anne Boleyn's mother—"

"Was a Howard, that's right!" Kaz beamed at him; then her expression changed, and she regarded him thoughtfully. "You have that look, too."

"What look?"

"There was a picture of Elizabeth, painted when she was about your age. How old are you?"

"I'm going to be twelve next month. March fourth."

"Yes, I believe she was twelve. It's a remarkable portrait. She looks very self-possessed, very wise, yet wary. She really doesn't look like a child at all, but like someone who has lived a lifetime and has no illusions, yet is prepared to face life head-on. Somehow—" she looked intently at Andrew, "I get the distinct impression that you're a lot like that. I think that, underneath that gregarious and fun-loving nature, there's a person who's very smart, very capable, and very strong."

Andrew blushed. He was extraordinarily pleased with Kaz's glowing assessment of himself, and wanted so much to believe that she was right—yet, he was afraid that she had overestimated him.

As if she had read his thoughts, Kaz said, "I don't think I'm wrong about you. There's a lot in here—" she gently laid her index finger on his chest, "That even *you* don't realize you possess."

As his mother kissed him good night, Andrew sighed fretfully.

"What's wrong, darling?"

He snuggled against her breast; she stroked his hair in a silent plea for him to speak. He moaned, and the words tumbled out.

"Do they ever do anything like that to you?"

"Who? And do they do *what* to me?"

"What they do in America."

"What do you mean?"

"The awful things they did to Jacqueline Cochran. Putting wads of paper in her fuel tanks, and smashing the window in her plane and stealing the wr—"

"Andrew—" She hugged him close. "Those were isolated incidents, and you shouldn't judge all Americans by the actions of a few. And no, nothing like that has ever happened to me, or to any of the other women ferry pilots. We're fighting a war, and everyone is doing their bit, and there's simply no place for ridiculous actions like that. We're doing an important job: moving vitally needed aircraft, and it would be stupid to sabotage planes just because women are ferrying them."

Andrew looked at her, fear and doubt in his eyes. "Andrew, believe me," she implored. She cocked her head, and smiled. "Oh, sometimes we have to put up with snide remarks—wisecracks, as the Americans call them. We just shrug them off. When the men see that we can do the job, they stop their teasing. And at some of the airfields, we have to put up with not being allowed in the mess—men only. So we wind up eating in the lavatories or storerooms. But those are only minor inconveniences, and they don't happen very often. Nothing more serious than that." She tousled his hair. "As a matter of fact, most of the men in the RAF are ever so nice, and they are quite appreciative of the work that we ferry pilots are doing."

Andrew pressed his face into her neck.

Instead of reassuring him, his mother's remarks had only distressed him even more.

"What are you doing?" Andrew peeked his head through the door to Kaz's room. It was open, so he didn't feel as if he were intruding. They had just finished supper, and the women had retired upstairs to "relax". He saw that the bed had been pushed against the wall, making a fairly good-sized space in the middle of the room. The women were sitting cross-legged on the floor, each holding a fan of playing cards in their hands. They each had a pile of colored, coin-sized circlets beside them; there was a larger heap of the discs in the center of the floor.

"Oh—come in, Andrew," Irene chirped.

"I'm not intruding, am I?" He suddenly remembered his mother's admonition not to be "tiresome".

"No, not at all," Kaz replied. "We didn't think you'd be interested in watching a couple of old ladies play cards."

"Cards? What kind of game are you playing?" Andrew ambled over to them.

"Poker," Marlys said.

"Poker? Oh, may I watch?"

"Sure—sit yourself down," Irene scooted back a bit to open up a space for him. "Do you know how to play?"

Andrew shook his head. "I've never heard of it. Can you teach me?"

"Well, that depends on if'n it's all right with your ma." Irene pursed her lips, and eyed Kaz. "I'll see your two, and raise you two more."

"Fold." Marlys threw down her cards.

"Call." Kaz tossed two white circlets down in the center pile, then presented her cards for inspection. "Full house."

"Shoot—you dirty dog! Howja know I was bluffing?"

"Someday I'll tell you." Kaz scooped the pile of chips towards herself.

"What—what happened?" Andrew asked.

"Kaz just cleaned us out," Marlys replied.

"How'd she do that?"

"Andrew—I warned you not to be tiresome." Andrew's mother stood in the doorway.

"Oh Alice—he's not being tiresome!" Irene put her arm around Andrew's shoulder. "In fact, we wanted to know if it's all right with you if we teach him how to play poker."

"*Poker?*"

"Oh Mum—please! *Please!* It looks like such fun!"

His mother smiled. "Well, all right." To the women she said, "If he starts to get a little too rambunctious, don't hesitate to pull in the reins!"

"Yes ma'am!" Marlys gave her a salute.

"I'll be good, Mum, I *promise!*"

"He promises, Mum." Kaz looked earnestly at Andrew's mother.

"Bedtime at nine." Andrew's mother eyed him sternly.

"Yes, Mum."

"Okay, let's start with the basics; then we'll progress to the finer points of the game." Irene collected the cards and spread the deck out face up. "The object of the game is to get the best hand, or, failing to accomplish that, to make everyone *think* you've got the best hand."

"What's a hand?" Andrew asked.

"A combination of cards. Right now we're playing five card draw, so we have five cards."

"Oh—is there more than one kind of poker?"

"Yeah. There's also five card stud, seven card stud—I'll show you the hands first. Now the lowest, is a pair—like this—" Irene pulled out two eights. Then there's two pair—" She pulled out two jacks and added them to the pair of eights. "Then there's three of a kind—" She hunted through the cards, and found another eight, discarded the Jacks, and displayed the cards to Andrew.

"What do you do if two people both have a pair?"

"Whoever has the highest cards wins." She grabbed the pair of jacks. "In this case, the person with the Jacks would win. Do you know the order of the face cards?"

"Yes, Aunt Jane and I used to play double solitaire sometimes—Jack, Queen, King, and Ace."

"Good. Now onto bigger and better things, after three of a kind, there's a straight— that's cards in sequence, like this." Irene pulled out a nine, ten, Jack, Queen, and King.

"They don't have to be the same suit, do they?"

"No, but if they are, that's called a straight flush—that's worth more."

"Oh."

Irene called out the hands in increasing order of value and displayed an example with cards pulled from the pile: "Full house—that's three of one kind, two of another. Flush, all the same suit. Four of a kind, then straight flush—remember that? Last, and the one that puts a smile on your face and a song in your heart: a royal flush. That's a straight flush, with ace high. Now, we also have wild cards—the jokers, here—" She pointed them out. "And whoever is dealing can decide what the other wild cards are going to be. We usually use aces for wild cards."

"What are wild cards?"

"You can use them for anything. Say if you have four clubs and an ace of hearts. You can use that for a club and call it a flush."

Andrew nodded. Irene went on. "Now, in five card draw, you deal five cards, face down. Everyone has a chance to discard any number of cards, and pick up different cards. Here—" She extended her arm to Andrew. "Sit on my lap, and we'll play a hand together. I'll do the betting."

"Betting?"

"This is where the fun starts. You bet that you have the best hand."

"What if you don't?"

"You can either fold, or bluff."

"Fold or bluff?"

"Fold—you quit, like Marlys did. Bluff, you raise the bets, pretend you have a good hand. But if someone calls you, you have to show your cards."

Andrew bit his lip in consternation. "It sounds very confusing."

"No, it's not," Marlys reassured him. "Why don't you watch a few games—you'll get the hang of it."

Andrew settled himself on Irene's lap. She told him in a low voice, "Keep a straight face. We don't want to give any hints to anyone, okay?"

"All right."

"Ante up," Marlys announced. "Five card draw, aces wild."Everyone threw in a white chip. "Oh, whites are one, reds are three, blues are five," Irene said.

"One, three, and five what?" Andrew asked.

"One hundred, two hundred, and five hundred dollars," Marlys said.

"I thought it was thousands," Kaz rejoined.

"Nah—it's millions!" Irene declared.

"*Millions!*"Andrew exclaimed. "Crikey!"

Marlys dealt the cards. Irene picked up the hand, and Andrew saw that she had three tens, a five, and a two. Kaz threw down one card, and Marlys dealt her one.

"Two." Irene took the five and the two and put them face down. Marlys dealt her two cards. Andrew saw that one of them was a joker; the other a nine.

"Dealer takes three." Marlys exchanged three of her cards for three more.

Kaz started the betting. "Three." She tossed in a red chip.

"See your three and raise you two." Irene threw a blue chip on the pile.

"Raise you one." Marlys put down a blue chip and a white chip.

Irene explained: "Kaz can match what Marlys has put in, which is six. She would have to add three more, or she can fold, or she can raise."

"Raise you two." Kaz tossed a blue chip on the pile.

Andrew lost track of the ensuing action. Everyone kept raising; finally Irene said to Andrew, "What do you say, my little friend. Why don't we shoot the wad?" Andrew shrugged and kept a straight face. Irene took the last of her chips—three red ones—and threw them down. "I'll see your three, and raise you six."

Marlys scrunched her face at her cards. "Fold."

"Call." Kaz pushed two red chips into the pile.

Irene spread her cards out for inspection. "Four of a kind—tens!"

"Damn—flush," Kaz said. "Andrew just glared at your cards the whole time. I didn't think you had a good hand."

"See, ma li'l poker face, we cleaned 'em out!" Irene hugged Andrew as she scooped in the chips. "Come to Momma, you darlin' li'l babies."

"Come to Momma, you darlin' li'l babies!" Andrew helped to pack their winnings into a neat pile. "I like this game! Can I play my own hand now?"

Andrew's daily routine settled into a delightful schedule, and the absolute high point of his day was the arrival of his "Transatlantic Cousins," as Kaz called their trio, derisively echoing Freddie's appellation. He arose early in the morning, so as to be able to breakfast with them. After they left, he spent the morning in bed, reading *Great Expectations* or studying his spelling or geography. After elevensies, he sat at his desk and worked on his mathematics assignments. Mrs. Tuttle called him down for lunch at one; he napped from two to four or five; upon awakening, he passed the time translating French or Latin assignments until the women arrived for tea a little after six. He quizzed them at teatime about their Class 2 work, using the Ferry Pilots Notes, as he had done with his mother. After tea, they helped him with his schoolwork: Kaz tutored him in mathematics; Marlys, since she had travelled extensively, helped him with geography; Irene gave him spelling tests. Supper was at eight and the conversation was generally about aviation topics or ATA gossip. Sometimes Andrew's mother made a delivery to White Waltham. If she couldn't get away to visit Armus House, she would give one of the women a special message for Andrew, sent along with some Cadbury bars. After supper, they usually played a few hands of poker; Andrew was now allowed to stay up until ten. Then, Irene read to him from *Great Expectations* until he started to nod off to sleep. The day ended with Irene's gentle kiss against his forehead, and her tender admonition: "Good night, sleep tight, see you in the morning light." With a few enjoyable rounds of poker to set his mind into a pleasant mood and Irene's gentle voice lulling him to sleep, Andrew found bedtime, which he had previously hated, a very pleasant experience.

He also enjoyed his evening lessons with the women, especially Irene's spelling "bees," a delightful and very effective routine she used to get Andrew to learn his words. He had twenty groups of twenty words he had to know: not only the spelling, but definitions also. He wrote the definitions in his copybook, using his father's dictionary, and also wrote a sentence using the word, as Mr. Nugent had directed. ("To be certain that you not only can recite the meaning, but know how to use it as well," Mr. Nugent would say.) Irene kept giving him the spelling tests over and over until he got every word right. If he misspelled a word once, she had him write it ten times as an assignment the next day. If he misspelled the word again, she made him write it twenty times. "The third time, it's thirty," she told him. "And then I'll really crack the whip if you miss it again—a hundred times!" Andrew had to write only a few words twenty times, and one—tenuous—thirty times.

"I keep forgetting either one "u" or the other!" he complained, for he had misspelled it the first time, *tenous*, the second time *tenuos*, the third *tenuouos*.

"Just remember *u-o-u*," Irene told him. "You-oh-you will get it right or you-oh-you will have to write it a hundred times tomorrow!"

And the next day, remembering her warning, he wrote it correctly. As a reward whenever he got all his words right, she gave him a wonderful treat: a bar of chocolate, sent from America. It was wrapped in brown paper emblazoned with silver lettering: *HERSHEY'S*. She also perused his copy-book to comment on his written definitions and the sentences he had written:

"Now for tenuous: I don't think the sentence really fits, Andrew. You wrote 'The ceiling of the bomb shelter was tenuous, and did not provide much protection.'"

"Well, the definition is 'having little substance or strength; flimsy.'"

"It refers more to something that holds two things together—a bond, or a link, or a relationship. Like—" She pursed her lips, and thought a moment. "'The alliance between Russia and Germany was a *tenuous* one—neither side really trusted the other.' Do you see what I mean? It can apply to nations, or to people as individuals. Say two people get married, and it's only because he has a lot of money—you could say that they had a *tenuous* relationship, because it was not based on love and respect, only on someone's bank account."

Andrew nodded. "I think I see what you mean." He crossed out his sentence and wrote: *All of Freddie's relationships with women have been rather tenuous because, deep down inside, he is a monumental twit.*

Irene narrowed her eyes as she watched Andrew write his sentence, then broke into a loud laugh. "I think you've got the idea!"

"Ante up, ante up, ante up-up-up," Irene called. "The game is seven card stud, one-eyed Jacks wild. The bet is a limit of two." Everyone tossed in a Hershey's kiss, Kaz's contribution to the fun: She had just gotten a package of wondrous confections from the "Arsenal of Democracy."

"I thought they stopped making Hershey's kisses last year," Marlys said to Kaz. "Shortage of tinfoil, wasn't it?"

"I have a friend who works in the plant in Hershey. She tried to convince me that working in a chocolate factory was heaven on earth, but I decided that making airplanes was more to my liking. Anyway, she knew that Hershey's was going to quit making kisses, so she bought up a ton of them and sells them. Plans to put herself through college with the proceeds. *And* she sends them to special friends."

"Crikey—I'd give *anything* to work in a chocolate factory!" Andrew exclaimed.

"You would?" asked Irene. "Do you think you'd get to eat chocolate all day?"

"Not *all* day," Andrew replied. "But an hour or two would be super!"

Kaz leaned over and tousled his hair. "My little chocolate monster!"

Andrew, over the past several weeks, had progressed from five card draw, to five card stud, to seven card stud. He liked seven card stud the best because he liked to see other people's cards; besides, there was a better chance of getting a good hand. The other players had a better chance at a good hand too, but that was what made it fun. He considered five card stud more of a challenge, and played it to keep his skills sharp. He enjoyed five card draw on occasion; after all, it was nice to get a second chance at a good hand, but he thought seven card stud was the most fun of all.

The cards were dealt: Marlys had a 2, 4, and a 6 of diamonds, and 3 of clubs; Kaz showed a King of hearts and a King of spades; and Irene, two eights. Andrew showed a Jack of hearts, and a 10, Jack, and Queen of Clubs. After peeking at the final, face-down card that Irene dealt him, he sat straight up and let his eyes range over the hands everyone had dealt.

"Three." Andrew tossed three kisses into the heap.

"It's not your turn, and the limit's two." Marlys said.

"Sorry." He took his candy back.

Kaz started the betting. "One." She tossed a foil-wrapped chocolate in the middle. Marlys tossed in one piece.

"See your one and raise two." Andrew threw in three pieces.

Irene tossed in four. "Raise you one."

Kaz threw down three kisses; Marlys four. "Raise another one," Marlys said.

Andrew tossed in four more. "Raise two."

Irene regarded her cards ruefully. "Well, stuff that for a game of soldiers, Scarlett." She threw down her cards. "Three of a kind, eights." She turned over a joker, a two, and a six.

Kaz tossed in four candies; Marlys started take up three more. She shook her head, and said, "Fold." She turned up a five of hearts and two nines. "Even if Andrew has a only a straight, he still has me beat."

"He doesn't have a straight." Kaz's eyes challenged Andrew.

Andrew glared back at her, and flung three chocolates on the growing heap. "Raise you two," he said evenly.

Kaz tossed in four. "Raise *you* two."

Andrew scooped up four more. "Two again."

"Looks like the kid is holding a royal flush," Irene warned.

"A flush for sure, at least," Marlys said.

"Nah—look at his face," said Kaz. "He always has that drop-dead stare when he's bluffing."

"He has the same drop-dead stare when he's got a good hand, too," Marlys rejoined. "That's the problem with these Brits! They all have these stiff upper lips and you can't tell what the hell is on their minds. Come on, Andrew." She grinned at Andrew. "Smile if you're bluffing."

Andrew threw her a icy glare. "He's got a flush, for sure," Marlys pronounced.

"Flush doesn't beat four of a kind," Kaz said tersely.

"Are you going to raise, call, or fold?" Andrew arched one eyebrow, and grabbed four more chocolates, indicating that he was ready to continue the betting.

Kaz narrowed her eyes at him. "He's bluffing. He doesn't have anything—right?"

"It'll cost you two more chocolates to find out." Andrew narrowed his eyes back at her.

"Shoot—fold." Kaz turned up her cards. She had a four of spades and two sevens. "Two pair—Kings over sevens," she said.

Andrew shrugged, and, still keeping a straight face, scooped the enormous heap of candy towards himself.

"Wait a minute!" Irene exclaimed. "Let's see what you've got."

"I don't have to show you," Andrew replied. "I won, fair and square. You all folded." He quickly grabbed his three down cards and sat on them.

Three pairs of eyes widened with outrage, three mouths dropped open in shock.

"I don't have to show you," Andrew insisted. "I won, that's all there is to it."

Irene and Marlys looked at Kaz. "You know what this means?" Kaz said in a low growl.

"No—*NO!* You can't make me—*Ahhh!*"

Irene grabbed his arms, Kaz pinned his legs, and Marlys proceeded to tickle his armpits. "*Ve haf vays uf makink you tok!*" she hissed at him.

"*Ahhhh—*" Andrew could not help but squirm, although he tried to keep his buttocks firmly pressed against the floor. "Get him in the ribs!" Irene yelled.

That did it. As Marlys wiggled her finger between two of his lower ribs, Andrew squealed and arched his back. Irene quickly reached under him and snatched the cards.

"Jeez Louise—look at *this*!" Irene cried. She displayed Andrew's cards: a three of spades, a five of clubs, and a two of hearts.

"He only had a pair! A lousy, stinking pair!" Marlys exclaimed.

"I won fair and square," Andrew protested. He looked somewhat undignified, with his face still red, his hair mussed, and his shirt hanging out. He gathered up his Hershey's kisses, stood up, and magnanimously tossed each one of the women three of the silvery wrapped delights. "For each of you—for being such good sports—*Ahhhh——*" The remaining chocolates flew in every direction as he was tackled once again—this time Kaz managed to grab him by the ankles and upend him.

"Does anyone want to buy a lyin', cheatin' varmint—cheap?" Irene hollered.

"I didn't lie and I didn't cheat. I bluffed, and that's fair—it's *fair!*" Andrew squealed.

"You have an unfair advantage, you Brit! You've had *years* of practicing that stiff upper lip!" Marlys said. "All right—put him down, we don't want to shake his brains out, do we?"

"We ought to at least get rid of some of his grey matter. It would even things up!" Irene laughed.

The next day Andrew's mother arrived at Armus House with the Americans. She had "hitched" a ride to White Waltham: "In a Stirling, flown by a Polish ferry pilot! He tried to teach me a little Polish." She turned to Kaz. "*Jak sie masz?*"

"*Dobrze,*" Kaz replied.

"What did you say?" Andrew asked.

"I said, 'How do you do?' and Kaz said, 'Fine, thank you.'" his mother said. "Oh, I've got a special treat. Let's sit down to tea first. This calls for a special presentation."

Andrew's mother got out the special china plate commemorating Queen Victoria's

Golden Jubilee in 1887 and set it carefully on the table. All eyes upon her now, she opened her bag and produced: *three oranges!*

"Oranges!" exclaimed Andrew. "Crikey! Where did you get them?"

"A friend of mine knows a American fighter pilot, and arranged a trade. I got them for you, Andrew, since you need your vitamins. Just let everyone have a slice today, and save the other two oranges for tomorrow and the day after. Oh—save a slice for Aunt Gwen when she comes home tomorrow."

After divvying up Orange Number One amongst everyone (including the servants, which left Lucia positively wide-eyed with delight), Andrew was left with a few slices, which he arranged ceremoniously on his plate, just for the pleasure of seeing them for a few moments before consuming them. They enthralled his tastebuds as he nibbled at them; he preferred to savor the exquisite taste of this most rare delicacy.

Marlys rolled her eyes back in bliss as she ate her portion, and sighed happily after swallowing it. "Sometimes I dream about the orange trees we have in our backyard in California. There's nothing like plucking an orange off a tree and stretching out on the grass to enjoy one. I can't *believe* how much I took that for granted! When I go back home, I'm going to sit out in the yard for a week, gorging myself on nothing but oranges!"

Mrs. Tuttle exclaimed, "Peelings—oh, I must scrape the peelings. I'll use them in the Norfolk Pudding tomorrow!"

"Oh dear, it'll be ever so hard for you to scrape these bits," Andrew's mother said. "We should have thought of that before we peeled it."

"Never you mind," Mrs. Tuttle soothed. "I can manage. But I'll take first dibs on the other one tomorrow. You'll remember, won't you Andrew?"

Andrew nodded, his mouth full of the last bite of orange. He slumped back in his chair, eyes closed in bliss, as the succulent morsel slid down his throat. He imagined having an orange tree, just outside his window, and being able to pluck a goldeny globe off a branch whenever he felt like it.

Someday, someway, I'm going to find a place with an orange tree, and I'm going to sit under it for a whole week and eat nothing but oranges!

Andrew celebrated his twelfth birthday with his new friends in attendance; his mother and Aunt Gwen were also there. Mrs. Bunch baked a Nutmeg Potato Cake which, despite having very little sugar or flour, and no eggs at all, was quite good.

Andrew's mother gave him small wooden models of various twin- engined planes: an Anson, a Beaufighter, and a Mosquito. Aunt Gwen gave him a backgammon board; Gram, still off nursing her brother, sent him some boiled sweets. Andrew's mother produced a gift from Aunt Jane: a book about King Arthur and the Knights of the Round Table. He also received a book from Kaz: short stories by O. Henry. Irene gave him some caramels and a book of crossword puzzles. Marlys produced a pair of flannel pajamas for him, a much valued gift indeed, what with the cloth rationing being so strict.

"Where on *earth* did you manage to get these?" Andrew's mother asked, amazed that Marlys should give something so precious.

"I packed several yards of flannel when I came to England," Marlys said. "I'd heard that cloth was very scarce, and I figured it might come in handy for something. I had a seamstress make them. It looks like they'll fit. I had to "guesstimate" Andrew's size—there's extra material in the hems so that they can be lengthened when he gets taller."

"Enjoy this year while you can, Mom," Irene laughed, after Andrew had blown out the candles on his cake. "You're going to have a teenager on your hands next year, and they can be a heap o'trouble, from what I've heard. Next thing you know, he'll be wantin' to drive the family car, wantin' to take out girls, sneakin' smokes behind the outhouse, and bein' thoroughly obnoxious, besides." She playfully elbowed Andrew in the ribs. "My mother always threatened to ship us off to someplace like Australia or Alaska or Outer Mongolia when we got to be too rowdy."

"Alaska—*Crikey!*" Andrew exclaimed. "Wouldn't you be afraid of the polar bears eating you?"

"My mother said that we'd be the ones to make life difficult for the polar bears!" Irene said. "As a matter of fact, one of my brothers *did* go to Alaska."

"Why on earth would anyone want to go to *Alaska?*" Andrew asked. "It's all ice and polar bears and dark all the time, isn't it?"

"In the winter it's dark almost all the time. In the summer it's light almost all day. My brother built himself a cabin, and lives off the land. He loves it there. He says after you've been to Alaska, everyplace else pales by comparison."

Andrew was astounded. "I can't imagine anyone wanting to live *there!*"

"Who knows? Maybe *you* might want to live there someday." Kaz smiled at him.

"Alaska? Cor, I don't think I'd *ever* want to live there!"

"Famous last words," Marlys laughed.

"Famous—what?" Andrew asked.

"Last words. What it means is that what you say might come back to haunt you," Marlys replied.

"Well, I don't know—" Kaz said. "The polar bears might have a hard time of it with this little guy around. Besides, it wouldn't be nice to unleash our intrepid poker player on an unsuspecting populace—might prove disastrous for international relations. I imagine even Outer Mongolians or Alaskans might not be able to handle this ball of fire!"

He wrote a long letter to Aunt Jane, telling her about his new friends. He tried to describe the women so that Aunt Jane would get a clear picture of them: Marlys' sophistication, intelligence, and warmth; Irene's sense of humor and friendliness, and Kaz's self-effacing confidence, cleverness, gentle wisdom, and tender concern for him. He recounted the joke Freddie had told, and tried to describe the look on Freddie's face when he found out that Kaz's name was short for Kazmierski: *You ought to have seen it, Aunt Jane—Freddie positively dropped a clanger!* He ended his letter by writing:

I miss you ever so much! I look outside at the stars every night and think of you, as I promised, and sometimes when I go to sleep I imagine that you're tucking me into bed and giving me a good-night hug. It's wonderful, though, having such terrific new friends. I wish you could meet them—I know you'd especially like Kaz. I think she's very much like you. She's quite smart and her brother used to warn her that she'd never find a husband. I told her what you had told Freddie: "When I'm good and ready, I shall place an advertisement in the Times: Twits and imbeciles need not apply." She thought that was wonderful! Remember when I asked you to marry Mr. Quinton, so that you could come and live at Askew Court?

Please write to me soon!

Love always,
Andrew

"Andrew! Lunch is ready!" Mrs. Tuttle called.

"All right—I just want to reread my letter to Aunt Jane. Mum's coming home tonight and I want to give it to her to mail."

He proofed his letter, and noticed that he had written "Mr. Quinton" instead of "Mr. Nugent". Silly of me to have made that mistake, Andrew thought—who'd want to marry Mr. Quinton, with his bad breath? He picked up his pencil to cross it out but just as he pressed the tip to the paper, the lead broke. Blast! He would have to sharpen the pencil in the study. He went downstairs, and put the pencil on Freddie's desk. He'd do it after lunch.

Mrs. Tuttle served him chicken broth soup with egg-drop noodles and a Spam sandwich. Mrs. Tuttle wanted to be sure he got enough protein: "You need to build up your strength, Master Andrew. Your mother's orders. Can't have you getting ill again!" Mrs. Tuttle kept the Cadbury bars Andrew's mother saved from her daily allowance, and used them to bribe Andrew to finish his meals: "Half a chocolate bar if you finish lunch, and you'll get the other half after supper!" Of course, Irene always shared with him the goodies in her packages from home: Hershey bars, caramels, and her mother's delicious homemade fudge. Andrew, along with many other children during the war, had developed an insatiable craving for sweets as a result of the strict rationing of sugar. Cough drops were considered a delicacy, and were used as barter in the various transactions common to boarding school. When Andrew's mother had dropped the load of candy on his schoolmates, she had earned the absolute adoration of a every boy in the school, and Andrew's popularity had skyrocketed. She made two other such deliveries in the following autumn, just after school started, and Andrew's esteem in the hearts of his schoolmates was assured. He had always been rather well-liked, but now he was the regarded as the school's hero, and he relished the role. Not that it went to his head; he liked, above all, to "fit in," but he privately delighted in the extra measure of admiration.

"Mrs. Tuttle—would you serve me lunch in the study?" Freddie's voice boomed from the hallway. It was a command, not a request.

"Sir, I didn't know you'd be getting in today," Mrs. Tuttle replied. "It'll be about fifteen minutes, is that all right?"

"Fine, fine. I've got a lot of work to do." Freddie was in a perfectly sour mood. Andrew looked over his shoulder and saw Freddie glowering in the doorway. Freddie said nothing to him; then he turned and disappeared down the hall. Andrew heard the door slam.

Well, I'll have to get my pencil another time, he thought. Mrs. Tuttle came into the dining room, and saw that he had only two more bites of Spam sandwich left. "I'll get your chocolate, Master Andrew, if you promise to make that sandwich disappear by the time I get back!"

"Promise!"

"Young man! Have you been cleaning your plate?"

"Mum!" Andrew bounded across the room and threw himself into his mother's outstretched arms. "I thought you weren't getting in until tonight!"

"I delivered a Spit to a maintenance unit this morning, and caught the Anson back to White Waltham," she said.

Mrs. Tuttle appeared with Andrew's chocolate on a saucer.

"How's our system of bribery working, Mrs. Tuttle?" Andrew's mother laughed.

"Oh, just marvelous! We're down to the last bar," Mrs. Tuttle told her.

"Don't worry, I've brought replenishments." Andrew's mother smiled and withdrew a stack of Cadbury bars from her purse.

"Oh Mum, can I have one now? Please?"

"All right, if you let me have a little bit."

"Would you like lunch, Miss Alice?" Mrs. Tuttle asked.

"Yes, thank you, Mrs. Tuttle. I'll go up and get changed. Can't wait to get into something comfortable. These ties drive me mad—I always feel like I'm being strangled!" She handed the chocolate bars to Mrs. Tuttle and loosened the knot on her tie, crossing her eyes as she did so.

Andrew marvelled that she could still look so beautiful, even with a comical expression on her face. "Oh Mum, I think you look smashing in a tie! Especially black— it looks so—" Andrew wondered how he could describe how wonderfully capable and important she looked. *Dad wore a black tie, too.* "Terrific," he pronounced. "Just terrific!"

She gave him a kiss. "Thank you, my little fashion critic. All the same, I'm going to slip into a comfortable pair of trousers and one of my old sweaters. Oh, just a minute—" She took one of the Cadbury bars from Mrs. Tuttle. "My young admirer and I are going to share this for afters." She handed it to Andrew. "I'll be right back down."

She went out to the hall; Andrew heard the door to the study open, heard a smooth "Hullo, Alice," murmured by Freddie. Andrew's mother replied with a crisp, "Hullo, Freddie," then sprinted up the stairs.

Tea was a delightful affair, what with Andrew's mother home and the Americans providing spirited company. Irene glowingly described Andrew's prowess at poker, and Kaz and Marlys reported that he was coming along very well with his schoolwork. Andrew replied that he helped them to study their coursework: "Just like we used to do together, remember Mum?"

Freddie took his tea and supper in the study, which suited Andrew perfectly. He left early the next morning, which delighted Andrew even more. If only he'd go back to America soon—what Andrew wouldn't do to have him out of the way entirely! As much as he was reassured by his mother's cool demeanor towards Freddie, he was still vexed by Freddie's presence.

His mother stayed the usual two days, then left for her duties. A week later he received a letter from her:

Dear Andrew,

I've had a very busy schedule these past few days ferrying, and just now had the time to sit down and write. The planes have been stacking up at the factories and maintenance units for the past few weeks because of stormy weather and, now that skies are clear, there's a push to get them moved. I ferried four different planes yesterday: a Spitfire, a Beaufighter, a Boston, and a Mosquito!

I forgot to tell you, darling, I saw your letter to Aunt Jane on your desk when I went upstairs just after I arrived home, and I put it in with my things so I could mail it with my letter to her—just sent it off yesterday.

I saw Irene yesterday. She tells me that you are doing very well with your spelling. See you in a few days!

Love,
Mum

Blast! Andrew thought. I forgot all about correcting the letter—it still has the mistake in it! Oh well, Aunt Jane will know that I really meant Mr. Nugent.

Andrew waited for a letter from his aunt, expecting that she would chide him about his error.

His mother came home a week later and produced a letter from Aunt Jane, which Andrew took it to his room and eagerly opened. He read:

Dear Andrew,

Have been frightfully busy—it does get tiresome being charming to so many twits! Your mother tells me that you are putting on weight—I've been ever so worried about your health after your bout with pneumonia. Do take care of yourself!

Your mother writes me that you are doing very well with your schoolwork. She says your "private tutors" are wonderful!

I remember you telling me that you wanted me to marry Mr. Quinton so I could come to live at Askew Court. You tease! You never liked Mr. Quinton—besides, you'll be starting your last year at Askew Court this coming autumn and what would I do? Leave him and follow you to Public School?

Much love,

Aunt Jane

Andrew stared, dumbfounded, at her letter. Why would she reply that she had remembered him asking her if she would marry Mr. Quinton? It wasn't just a mistake; she had also stated that she knew that Andrew had never liked him! She should have remembered that it was Mr. Nugent that they had talked about—surely! What was going on?

He tried to hide his anxiety at supper that night; he excused himself early. He hadn't even finished his food.

"Andrew—are you ill?" His mother jumped up and felt his forehead.

"No, Mum—I'm fine, really. I—I woke up very early this morning and couldn't get back to sleep. And I didn't fall asleep when I was supposed to take a nap. I guess I was excited about you coming home—that's all. Night."

She kissed his forehead. "Good night, darling. See you in the morning."

He trudged up the stairs. Once in his room, he plopped down on his bed. He grabbed the letter, which he had put on his bedside table, and reread it. No doubt about it: Something was definitely wrong.

By the next day, he had figured out what to do to either confirm his suspicions, or allay his fears. After breakfast, he excused himself to go to his room to "do a little schoolwork."

He sat down at his desk, chewed his pencil for a moment, then wrote:

Dear Aunt Jane,

I just got your letter from Mum. She's going back in two days, so I thought I would reply right away.

Everything is going well. I'm on my sixteenth spelling lesson. Marlys is helping me with South American geography. She lived for a few months in Brazil and says it's quite lovely there. Freddie is back in London again. He says he is going back to America this summer—hope it's sooner! Remember that night just before Dad went back to France, when came home for my ninth birthday? I said that Freddie didn't deserve to be liked, and we argued late into the night—remember? I said that we ought to ship Freddie off to Germany, to take over Lord Haw-Haw's job. I know you tried to convince me that I shouldn't be so harsh, but I still don't like him! I can't wait for him to go to America!

I wish you were here—I miss you so much! Please write soon!

Love,

Andrew

There, Andrew thought: two glaring errors. I said that we should drop Freddie from a bomber over Germany, *not* send him there to replace Lord Haw-Haw, and we *never* argued late into the night.

He gave the letter to his mother just before she left the following afternoon.

"Maurice!" Andrew heard Freddie's voice from the study as he was just about to walk past to the library. He had tried to settle himself down for a nap, but couldn't get to sleep, worried as he was about the letter to Aunt Jane he had just sent off with his mother. He'd decided to get a book out of the library; perhaps reading something would help take his mind off things. He stopped: the door was open a crack. Usually, he tried to avoid Freddie as much as possible, but the thought occurred to him that it wouldn't hurt to ascertain what Freddie might be up to. Andrew had noticed him pouring on the charm when Marlys was around, as well as being ever so friendly with Irene, and it irked him. Why did Freddie act as if he had the right to expect every woman to go to bed with him?

"...I thought you might like to know that you might get a chance to meet our resident lovelies sometime soon...."

God, what an insufferable twit!

"Yes, that's what I wanted to talk to you about. I overheard them talking about a holiday that they're going to have—several days off next week, and I thought it might be nice to propose a little visit to London, and that's where you come in Maurice. Are you game, old boy?"

That horribly annoying wheezy chuckle, and Freddie's voice boomed again.

"Well, you can take your pick—there's two of them, three actually, but unless you like a horse-faced Amazon with no tits and no sense of humor—"

A brief silence, followed by another blast of laughter. "Well, you never know, but the two others should prove to be absolutely delightful, so why take any chances? Let me tell you about them—sitting down, old boy?...Good—Well, I call them Mata Hari and the Farmer's Daughter. Mata Hari has wonderfully exotic looks—black hair, violet eyes, a face that would be put to better use prying military secrets out of willing subjects. She has a willowy figure, but with luscious curves all in the right places. You have to use your imagination when she's wearing that damnable uniform—why do the tailors have to hide all the good parts?...Wait—wait! You haven't heard about the Farmer's Daughter—she's a nice bit of work as well. A little more buxom, blond hair, blue eyes, reeking of innocence and trust, appallingly provincial—from *Iowa*, of all places, but, you know...What do you mean, she's not my type? Why can't a chap have a bit of variety. I think I fancy a change right now, and a little Iowa naivete might prove to be amusing—what do you think?"

There was a long silence, followed by that awful wheezy chuckle again. The chair creaked—

Careful, Freddie—don't lean too far back...Then again, maybe you'll fall back and break your neck, just like your father....

"What—*me* a dirty old man? Why Maurice, how can you think such a thing?...And I was going to let you have first choice this time!...Yes, yes. You can pick first this time, old boy...Mata Hari, then?...No, no, I usually *do* prefer the exotic types, but a change of pace right now would be—invigorating, yes—*invigorating*! A chap can't allow himself to get stale, you know, and I think I might like a roll in the hay with the Farmer's Daughter! What do you think, Maurice? Do you think the Luftwaffe might accommodate us and put on a good show while we're in London? It'd be just the ticket, to persuade our lovelies to seek sanctuary in my cozy little bomb shelter. God, how I miss the Blitz! Those were the days, weren't they, Maurice? Nothing like having a bomb shelter tucked away in the West End; a shame it's just sitting idle—" Freddie started crooning: "*I've got a nice little bomb shelter in the West End, that's deep and warm and dry...How'd you like to spend the night*—What's that old boy?"

Andrew heard a clink—glass against glass—a soft, ripply pouring noise; the sound of smacking lips; a light thunk as the glass was set down.

"No, old boy, I haven't given up on *her*—"

Her who?

"...Oh, she's been a tad standoffish lately, but not to worry, she'll come round. The boy was ill for awhile, and she was a little distracted, you know, and I do believe she *still* is grieving for dear departed Roger...No, no—she doesn't mope around, not anything like that. In fact, she's as cheery and bright as a day of sunshine; loves flying, but she's still a widow nonetheless, and you know, that's not necessarily a bad thing...Well, she's had a taste of it—she *knows* what she's missing, and sooner or later, she's going to get hungry for the delights of the flesh, and *I'll* be there to *comfort* her, never fear—"

Andrew's breath caught in his throat and a chill went up his spine.

"Oh, she's not so chaste as you might suppose, and she's certainly not one to stand on formality...Didn't you know? Roger took her for a tumble before they made it legal...How do I know? Well, old boy—It doesn't take a genius to figure *that* one out! The wedding was in September—big, lavish affair, she was the only daughter, you see, and her old man was positively breathing fire. I was there, you know. Well, the boy put in a appearance the following March. So you see, they *had* to get married. The way I figure it is, she did it once, she'll do it again...No, it wouldn't bother me in the least to make it legal, I'm an honorable man, you know—"

Andrew's knees nearly buckled and he grabbed the door frame to hold himself steady.

"No, no, no—I wouldn't send Charlotte packing. It'd suit me just perfectly to keep her in reserve—"

Andrew had met "Aunt" Charlotte several times, on Freddie's yacht and once at Armus House at a New Year's Eve party; she was at least ten years older than Freddie.

"Well, old boy, it's because older women are so *amusing*, you know. If one happens to suffer a dearth of companionship for one reason or another, it's quite useful to have one waiting in the wings. They provide quite a diversion, and one can use one's imagination in the dark—try it sometime! Of course it helps if one has had a few drinks—"

There was another clink of glass against glass, then an explosion of laughter.

Freddie's voice, shrill with glee, followed: "Right, old boy—it helps if *one* of us is a bit tight!" He cackled again, made an effort to control himself, snickered "The best part of it is, they're so *grateful*—"

Andrew's fingers gripped the door frame and he felt a sickening knot in his stomach.

"...Yes, quite right, having someone *so* appreciative is ever *so* delightful...Well, back to our American lovelies—"

Andrew shifted position, and fell against the door. It swung forward, and Andrew went sprawling onto the Oriental rug in front of the desk.

Freddie blanched, then his face reddened with fury.

"You little *eavesdropper*!" Freddie pointed the phone at Andrew.

A crackly voice emanated from the receiver. Freddie quickly put it to his mouth and said, "No, not you Maurice—call you back, old boy—bye."

Andrew scrambled back; Freddie moved quickly from behind the desk and blocked Andrew's escape. He shut the door, then grabbed Andrew by the collar and drew him up until Andrew's toes scraped the floor.

"*You sodding little bastard!* Didn't anyone ever teach you any manners?" Freddie dragged Andrew back towards the desk.

Andrew's voice came out as a terrified bleat. "You stay away from her—*you stay away from her—stay away from them, too!* I'll tell—*I'll tell* them what you're up to—"

"You'll do no such thing!" Freddie shook him savagely, and Andrew's body jerked like a marionette.

"Yes I will!" Even as he yelled, Andrew wondered to himself: *Why am I doing this? He's going to kill me!*

"No you won't—you'll keep your mouth shut if you know what's good for you—"

He's going to kill me anyway—I might as well go down fighting....

"I *will*—I'll tell them about your stupid old bomb shelter—they're my friends and when I tell them—and—" At that instant Andrew noticed the fountain pen on the desk. In one seamless motion, he snatched the pen and jabbed it into the back of Freddie's hand. Freddie's face contorted in pain as a spot of blood oozed from the site. He flung Andrew to the floor.

"And—you stay away from *her* too—*STAY AWAY FROM HER!*" Andrew felt rage mixed with sublime relief course through him.

Freddie narrowed his eyes, then his mouth grimaced into a triumphant leer.

"So that's it! Worried about *Mummy*, aren't we?"

Andrew's mouth dropped in stunned terror.

"We *are*, aren't we?" Freddie glared at him. Andrew closed his eyes and turned his head.

"Well, how *convenient!*" Freddie's voice had a smirky smoothness to it. "I think we might be able to come to an agreement, dear boy." Freddie narrowed his eyes. "*You* keep silent...and I'll leave *Mummy* alone. Does that sound like an acceptable exchange to you?" His voice lowered to a growl. "Does it?"

Andrew sputtered, "Y—yes. *Yes!*"

"Don't you even think of tattling to them! I'll know you've told. I'll *know*—don't even think that you could go blabbering and keep it a secret from me! If you tell, you'll only have yourself to blame for what happens to your mother. Do I make myself clear?"

Andrew nodded.

"Now get out of my sight, you little bastard!"

Andrew scrambled up, fumbled with the doorknob—much to Freddie's amusement—and at last managed to get himself out of the room. Freddie gave him one last, vicious glare, and pulled the door shut.

Alone in the hallway, Andrew allowed himself to slump against the wall.

"Andrew, are you all right?" Lucia came from the drawing room, a feather duster in her hand. She started to dust the pictures hanging on the wall.

"I—I'm fine. I was just—just going into the library."

Lucia nodded, and turned back to her duties.

Andrew stumbled down the hall to the library. Once inside, he closed the door and turned the key in the lock. He felt the tears coming, and he didn't want anyone walking in on him.

He curled up in the armchair, drawing his knees to his chest. He had never felt so desolate and wretched; pressing his face to his kneecaps, he broke into sobs. A wave of hatred swept through him. He had never hated anyone, not in his entire life, as much as he hated Freddie right now. He had seen the darkness of Freddie's true nature: He was vicious, cruel, and evil to the core. What was most disturbing was that he didn't use fear and intimidation just to achieve his purposes; he positively relished bullying and terrorizing others. Violence and victimization were not merely a means to an end; they were an end in themselves.

He hated Freddie, *hated*, *HATED* him, hated every man who had ever looked at his mother—Hugh, and anyone—no matter whether he knew them or not. He hated the war and the constant reminders of war: the posters on the walls and the newspaper stories and news broadcasts. He hated the wretched food, the rationing, the bomb shelters, the threadbare clothes—everything! Most of all, he hated himself for being so small and powerless. He wished he were ten feet tall, so he could smash in Freddie's sneering face and stomp his body to a bloody pulp. Bile rose in his throat as he remembered Freddie's snickering comment: "They *had* to get married...the boy put in an appearance six months later...."

Was it true? Was it really *true?* Freddie could lie through his teeth when it suited his purposes, but Andrew had the gnawing feeling that this sniggering assertion was not mere fabrication. How could he find out for sure?

The photo albums! By the door was a bookcase with dozens of volumes of snapshots. Aunt Gwen had been the family archivist, and the albums were filled with memorabilia and mementoes, as well as photos.

Andrew slithered out of the chair and, feeling as if he were about to open a Pandora's box of sorrows, walked to the bookcase and pulled out the album labeled *1930*.

September—Freddie had said September. He opened the book to the middle, figuring that would put him in the summer, and started to slowly turn the pages. A birthday party: Aunt Gwen's. Her birthday was August eighth. *Happy Birthday Gwen* was the message lettered on the cake, lavished by roses and hearts. Aunt Gwen smiled at the camera, looking at the same time both childish and grown-up. Andrew counted the candles: Seventeen. Aunt Gwen had been born in 1913.

He turned the page, and felt his heart fall into his stomach. There was a posed shot of a wedding party, and the happy couple was—

His parents!

No mistake about it—his mother wore a white and, even evident in the grainy photograph, outrageously expensive gown. Her wild curls were graced by a voluminous veil issuing from a diamond-studded tiara. (Andrew knew that her tiara would, of course, be set with diamonds—look at Grandfather Howard glaring at it!) Andrew's father wore a dark suit. Aunt Jane, gowned in some inscrutable pastel, stood beside Andrew's mother: the maid of honor. A man with a medium shade of hair (red, perhaps?) and a cheery grin (Sparky, of course!), stood next to Andrew's father.

The happy couple! Well, not exactly happy; their expressions were more amused than blissful, as if they were only going through this ostentatious formality for appearance's sake.

Maybe it was misfiled—it must have been in the spring, or early summer, surely!

He pulled the photograph from its corners and read the notation on the back: 7 September, 1930.

September seventh: The day his father...went missing. What an *awful* way to spend one's tenth wedding anniversary! Being shot down, having to ditch in the sea or forceland...Maybe he was injured, too.

September seventh: Six months, less three days, before the day Andrew was born.

Six months! It was true, horribly true! They *had* to get married, because of him! They had to put things right—no sense bringing a bastard (yes, a *bastard*, that's what Freddie had called him!) into the world. Andrew imagined that it must have pleased Freddie no end to spit that epithet in his face. *You sodding little bastard...Roger took her for a tumble before they made it legal...She did it once, she'll do it again....*

Andrew snapped the album shut, not even bothering to replace the photo properly. He jammed the book into the shelf and stumbled back to the chair. The tears came again; surprising that a body could have such a capacity for grief and anguish. He cried until his breath came out as hiccupy sobs, then burrowed his face against the arm of the chair and moaned out crooning wails of utter desolation.

Just when he thought that everything was all right...He had been so pleased with his mother's newfound assertiveness towards Freddie, so sure that she could take care of herself, so certain that Freddie was no longer a threat. He remembered his father's words: *All the time is the most dangerous time.* His father had said that he had been feeling safe—it was when he thought he could relax and drop his guard—when he had been shot.

I should have listened to him. I should never have thought that Freddie was no longer a threat. I shouldn't have been so smug in assuming she could take care of herself....

His tears spent, he draped himself sideways over the seat of the chair, stomach down, and hung his head over the arms. His gaze ranged over the shelves of books; he noted the different colors and varying widths of the spines of the volumes tucked neatly into place. He felt an awful heaviness of soul and knew what it was like to be utterly disconsolate and dispirited to the point of, if not death, then a horrible, paralyzing, life-draining despair. He perused the multicolored volumes again, trying to force his mind out of the rut of anguish and despondency, as if by inventorying the bookshelves he might stop this soul-destroying turmoil.

Something caught his eye: something sticking up from the pages of a slim, brown volume. He slid out of the chair, walked to the bookshelf, and withdrew the volume.

It was titled *Poetry Selections*. Andrew opened it to the flyleaf, and saw that it was signed with his father's signature. He opened the book to inspect the object sticking out from the pages.

It was the leather bookmark he had given his father over three years ago, on the day his father had gone back to France. It seemed like only yesterday; it seemed like a lifetime ago. Andrew traced the initials "R.H." and the roundel at the bottom.

Then he remembered: His father had been reading this book, sitting in the very chair that Andrew had just been miserably curled up in. Andrew closed his eyes and remembered: He had wandered into the room, distressed over discovering his father's bloodsoaked and terrifyingly still form in the drawing room earlier that day. His father had held him while he'd cried out his fear and terror, had tried to reassure and comfort him, had talked to him about the war, about flying, about his own skill and ability, about England's chances, about his predictions for the future: England would win, in the end, but it would not be an easy fight. What else had they talked about?

March fourth. That's what his father had said to him, as he had held Andrew close and tried to console him. *The happiest day of my life—the day you were born.*

An overwhelming, all-encompassing peace settled on him. The incident with Freddie seemed thousands of miles away, and his distress over his discovery of his untimely birth evaporated like mist in the sunshine.

He looked at the page the bookmark had reserved these past three years. There was an etching of a sunrise over a hillside on the left page; on the right side was a poem:

> *I've tried for many an hour and minute*
> *To think of this world without me in it.*
> *I can't imagine a newborn day*
> *Without me here...somehow...someway.*
> *I cannot think of the autumn's flare*
> *Without me here...alive...aware.*
> *I can't imagine a dawn in spring*
> *Without my heart awakening.*

Rapture soared through Andrew's soul as he read the words. It was a promise, a *promise*! It was as if his father were standing right beside him, telling him, *"Don't worry, old chap—I'm coming back. Life is too precious to be given up!"* Just like his father to know when he needed comfort and reassurance!

He reread the poem again: *I can't imagine a newborn day, without me here...somehow...someway.* He could almost hear his father telling him: *Even though we're far apart, I'm still with you! Don't give in to despair—even though you can't see me, even though I can't be with you, hold onto my promise! I'm alive—don't ever doubt that!*

Andrew hugged the book to his chest. His father had spoken to him, across the miles, across the gulf of time.

How could you know, when I would need you the most, you'd be there for me?

Chapter 14

"*W*ake up, Sleepyhead." Irene's gentle kiss brushed his cheek. "Andrew, it's tea-time. We don't want you to oversleep. You'll be up all night!"

Andrew stretched, rubbed his eyes.

"We have an exam tomorrow, and we're going to need your tutoring." Irene smoothed back a lock of his hair.

"I'll be downstairs in a minute."

"Okay. Oh, did you study your spelling words today? Maybe tonight you'll get all of them right—what's this?" She touched the volume of poetry Andrew clutched in his arms.

"Oh, just something I read to help me get to sleep." Andrew placed the book on his night table.

Irene read the title and smiled. "Poetry, how nice!"

"Hmmph—" Andrew rolled over and burrowed his face in his pillow. Irene rubbed his back.

"We'll wait for you downstairs. Hurry down!"

As soon as he heard the click of the door shutting, he flung himself face-up. His feelings of joy and assurance took second place to his vexation over the decision he'd made earlier: His mother's safety for his silence about Freddie's nefarious plans. At the time, he had not had a glimmer of doubt as to whose safety and well-being was more important to him; indeed, *paramount*—but now, the sound of Irene's voice accused him.

You're going to sacrifice them, like pawns in a chess game...You're going stand by and watch them go, like sheep to the slaughter, to keep Freddie from laying a hand on your mother....

He threw back the covers and hurled himself out of bed. He glared outside his window, then headed for the bathroom. He turned the shower on full force, icy cold. Gritting his teeth, he stood under the freezing water for a few seconds. The shock jolted him out of his melancholia, as he had hoped; he turned the water off, jumped out of the shower stall, and briskly toweled off. With a great effort of will, he pushed his feelings back and examined his decision on a purely rational level.

You had to make a choice, and you did. If you had chosen to protect your friends, you would have been responsible for whatever harm befell your mother.

"Andrew!" Marlys voice, clear and lilting, carried up the stairs. "We're sitting down to tea. Hurry up!"

"Coming!" He quickly dressed and clambered down the stairs.

"I just wanted to take a quick shower. I felt a bit grotty after such a long nap." He seated himself at the dining room table, noticed that Freddie was there too. Freddie generally didn't join the women for tea, preferring to work at his "accounts" and take tea in the study. He smiled at Andrew, and Andrew felt the color rising to his face.

Freddie turned his attention to Irene, asking her about Iowa and things Iowan. He waxed poetic about the beauty and grandeur of the American midwest and professed a yearning to visit again that "wondrous" land.

"Well, if you've ever gotten up at three A.M. to milk twenty- four cows, 'wondrous' sort of flies out the window," Irene laughed.

"You've milked a cow?" Freddie evinced a worshipful admiration that would have been more appropriate if she had claimed to have turned water into wine (or better, tea into Scotch).

Mrs. Tuttle set down another plate of scones and frowned at Andrew's uneaten meal. "Master Andrew, you're not getting ill again, are you?"

Freddie looked at Andrew, feigning concern. Then his eyes drilled into Andrew, warning him....

"No—No! I'm all right, really. I guess—I guess, I'm still a little sleepy. Um, I didn't sleep well last night. I think I'll go back to bed...try to sleep. I don't think I'll have supper tonight."

"Andrew, aren't you feeling well?" Freddie said.

"Um...um, yes, I'm all right...I'm just a little tired, that's all." Andrew stood up, a bit stiffly. "Good night."

"Night, Andrew," Kaz and Marlys said.

"Good night, Andrew," Freddie smiled. "Sleep well."

"Would you like me to read to you?" Irene offered.

"Uhh...no. That's all right—I'm just too tired to pay attention. I'll be fine in the morning."

Fighting back tears, Andrew strode out of the room. Then he dashed up the stairs, down the hall, and into his room. He peeled off his clothes as if they were contaminated and changed into his pajamas. As he snuggled under the covers of his bed, he grabbed his father's book as if it were a lifeline. He held it to his chest for a moment, trying to calm the hammering of his heart. Then he opened it to the page marked by the bookmark, and read: *I've tried for many an hour and minute....*

Freddie's sniggering declaration blasted through his mind: *They had to get married.*

He thrashed to one side, then to the other.

It just doesn't fit, it doesn't! They loved each other! They did!

It did *not* make sense: He could not help but remember being surrounded by love, feeling so utterly secure in his parents' delight in him and their devotion to one another....

If only Dad could come back right now, or just send word!

He pressed his face against his pillow, trying to stifle the groan of despair that rushed from his mouth. No sense tormenting himself with desperate longings.

He's hiding out, surely he is! That's why we hadn't heard anything. If he'd been in a prison camp, they would have gotten word of it—the Red Cross, someone would have notified us, surely! He might be in France—perhaps he's contacted Evelyne or one of Aunt Jane's friends. For some reason or other, he can't risk escaping, or even sending word....

As he clutched the book to his chest, he tried to console himself by remembering the wonderful encounters he'd already had with his father.

Somehow, someway, he came to me—twice! When I was being dug out of the rubble on my birthday, he was there with me: not in body, but in spirit, telling me that every-thing would be all right. It was the same when I was so ill. He was there, too! He was so real...I could touch him, feel his arms around me, feel the fabric of his uni-form and the rings around his cuffs, hear his whisper in my ear, taste the salt of his tears...He's with me right now, too...He knows, he knows, right at this very moment, what I've had to do, just as he knew that I had to pretend I believed he was dead. He knows that I've chosen to protect Mum from Freddie....

He was still in bed when he heard the knock on the door. He floated down the stairs: It was the same sort of funny sensation he had experienced when he'd been so ill with pneumonia and his mother and Winnie had conveyed him up the stairs to his room. Only now it was down the stairs...reciprocal course....

The front door opened, as if by magic, and his father stood in the doorway. An-drew noticed the stripes on his shoulder; there were no rings on his sleeves.

"You're a First Officer again. Weren't you were allowed to escape?" Andrew asked.

His father's arms went round him. "I can't stay," he murmured. "I have to go to America now, and get more sweets for you."

Andrew saw the worry in his eyes.

"I had to do it to protect Mum. I don't want Freddie to bother my friends either, but I had to promise not to say anything, so he wouldn't bother Mum. You understand, don't you?"

His father nodded, but his expression was still troubled.

Andrew told him, "She threw his key away, and when she met him at the restau-rant she told him that you were missing, not dead. So it's all right—*it's all right!* When you come home, you'll be together again—please don't worry! I found your book, and read your poem. I even memorized it. Would you like me to say it to you?"

His father picked him up. Andrew began: "I've tried for many an hour and minute to think of this world without me in it."

His father smiled joyously. Andrew took a deep breath and continued. "I can't imag-ine a newborn day, without me here, somehow, someway. I cannot think of the autumn's flare, without me here—without me here—" Shame coursed through him: He so much wanted to say it perfectly!

His father looked at him tenderly and spoke two words: "Alive...Aware!"

Andrew felt a wondrous, rapturous sensation of soaring freely through space and time: It seemed as if the war and everything else were a million miles away.

"*Alive...Aware,*" Andrew repeated. "You're alive, and you know about...about ev-erything, don't you?"

His father held him close. "I wish I could be with you."

"It's all right—it's all right!" Andrew's voice broke with longing and sorrow. If only they could be together—really together! For interlacing his joy at his father's presence was the realization that all this was not actually happening in time and space. This communion was not occurring in any physical dimension, but on a spiritual plane. There was no doubt in Andrew's mind that he and his father were really communicating with each other, but he knew that his own physical body was in his bed, alone, just as his father was—where? Andrew moaned. If only he could fly out of his dream and into his father's arms!

His father was looking intently at him now. Andrew racked his brain, trying to remember the last two lines of the poem, and he was about to apologize for forgetting them, when the words burst on his mind like a display of fireworks:

"I can't imagine a dawn in spring, without my heart awakening!"

His father's countenance was transformed: A look of sublime joy chased away the serious expression, and he threw back his head and laughed.

Suddenly, Andrew was awake in his bed, but he still heard laughter: Freddie's.

"Shhh-I think Andrew might be asleep." Irene's voice, tinged with concern. "He didn't look too well. I hope he's not coming down with something."

"Not to worry; the boy has the constitution of an ox. His mother does tend to fuss over him. It's understandable, I suppose, with all that's happened. She was positively distraught when he was taken to hospital with pneumonia. I tried to reassure her that everything was going to be all right—well, I suppose you can imagine what it must have been like for her. Terrible, really, what with poor Roger gone, and her having to raise a child by herself. Then there was that time when they were in London during the Blitz and the building they were in took a direct hit. They both had to be dug out of the rubble—"

"Oh my God, Alice never told me about that!" Irene's voice dropped to a horrified whisper.

"Well, it was positively ghastly. I wouldn't mention it to either of them. The b—I mean, Andrew was quite traumatized by it all—such an awful thing for a child to have to endure. And Alice was in a frenzy of terror through most of it. You see, the b— Andrew was knocked out when the bomb hit, and they both were trapped. Alice didn't know if he was dead or alive, until he came to and started calling—this was hours later. She was nearly beside herself with grief and despair by then. They got her out soon after that, and she got quite hysterical when they tried to take her to hospital. She attacked a policeman who tried to get her into an ambulance."

"Oh, no!"

"Oh, it was quite a scene! A photographer happened to be there and he snapped a picture of Alice in her glory—eyes blazing and teeth bared. It made the front pages of a few newspapers—not any respectable publications, but those tattly rags that the rabble are so fond of. There was quite a flap about it; she was in uniform, you see."

"Oh dear—how awful!"

"Well, they're both survivors, both made of strong stuff. Look at both of them, and you can understand what we English are like—stiff upper lip, carry on, never mind how bleak the outlook is. We got through the Battle of Britain, the Blitz, got through it all—"

How would you know Freddie? You skedaddled off to America and didn't come home until it was almost all over!

"...with pluck and fortitude. We were the only ones standing against the tyranny of Nazi Germany—"

We?

"...and we proved that all the fury of the enemy's might—"

What enemy? Didn't you say the Germans were ever so reasonable and only wanted to be friends with us?

"...could not, would not break us. We alone, stood against the Nazi menace—"

Since when have you considered them a menace, Freddie?

"...Standing by ourselves alone, but not for ourselves alone."

Irene's voice now, soft and awe-struck: "We used to listen to Edward Murrow's broadcasts on the radio. It used to send a chill up my spine to hear the sounds of the air raid sirens and the bombs dropping. What you all must have gone through—"

There was silence, then Freddie's voice, reeking of sham sincerity: "We never doubted for a moment that we would prevail, and that our friends would join us in our struggle."

Lay it on thicker, Freddie, and you could spread it over Thomas's vegetable garden!

"...and what is most wonderful is how Andrew—"

The boy, you mean!

"...has perked up since you've been here. It's positively heart-warming to see him on the mend, so full of life and vitality, and it's all been since you've come to stay with us at Armus House. He seems especially close to you, my dear."

"Oh, he's a terrific kid! I love flying, I love conversion school; it's a dream come true to be flying Spitfires, but the absolute high point of my day is coming here at the end of my day and sitting down to tea with him. He's a very bright boy, and he knows so much about airplanes. And he's a whiz at poker—I've never seen a kid his age with such talent! You ought to see him in action some time!"

"Well, as I said, I'm ever so grateful to you for what you've done. I've tried to be as much of a father to him as possible, for dear Roger's sake. There are no male relatives on his mother's side; Alice is an only child and has no cousins or other male relations. The only other man on our side of the family is Gwen's husband, but he's in the RAF and doesn't get home very often."

"I thought he was in the Fleet Air Arm. Gwen said that he had flown Swordfish."

"He was, but he was loaned out to Fighter Command during the Battle of Britain. They had a fearful shortage of pilots and things were looking quite bleak. At one point, so I've heard, Dowding had estimated that Fighter Command had only a few days to survive."

"I didn't know it was that close—how awful that must have been!"

"Yes—well, Robert decided he liked the RAF better than being in the Navy, so he managed to get a permanent transfer. Be that as it may, that leaves me to fill in the gap as far as Andrew having some sort of father figure in his life—a tragedy that a boy should lose his father at so young an age. Poor Roger, they never found him...."

Are you going to tell her how you tried to take advantage of poor Roger's absence by trying to seduce his wife?

The voices faded away, leaving Andrew sick with fury. It was bad enough to have to keep silent about Freddie's evil plans, but worse to have his own terrible experiences used as bait in luring the women to the slaughter.

If only he could dive back into the dreamscape of his father's presence, feel his arms around him again, be comforted and reassured...*You know that I had to do it to protect Mum....*

He clutched the book to his chest again, and repeated the poem to himself: *I've tried for many an hour and minute....*

"Oh, God, I think my back is done for," Irene groaned as she walked through the door.

"It's the neck that really gets it." Kaz lolled her head around in circles.

"My whole body's screaming in agony—I can't believe they expect us to do this tomorrow, too! Slave labor!" Marlys rasped.

"Isn't this war all about justice and decency?" Irene asked. "This is the most unjust, indecent—"

"Not unjust—even the top brass are having to do it too," Kaz said.

"What happened?" Andrew was waiting by the front door to great the women.

"They're torturing us to death, that's all. I think being racked might be a sight more pleasant—" Marlys arched her back and let out a hiss of agony.

"What?" Andrew was quite concerned now. It was clear that the women were not exaggerating their physical distress; at least, not much.

"I can't believe anyone would be so *stupid*!" Marlys said.

"Who?" Andrew asked.

"The assho—nitwits who put all that crap in the fertilizer!" Irene spat. "Crap besides crap, I mean!"

"What?" Andrew asked.

"Nails, can-openers, knives, forks—" Kaz began.

"Broken glass, too! Can you believe, *broken glass!*" Marlys howled.

"What fertilizer?" Andrew was truly bewildered now.

"The fertilizer they spread on the ground after they reseeded the airfield this spring," Kaz explained. "Evidently no one noticed it was spiked with this—this stuff—"

"Sabotage, that's what it was, sure as shootin'!" Irene exclaimed. "Some Nazi saboteur got into the fertilizer plant and spiked the mix with this stuff—"

"How'd he know that it was going to be spread at White Waltham, then?" Marlys said. "And how would he know that the idiots spreading it wouldn't notice all the junk in it?"

"Oh, they have ways," Irene muttered. "What other possible explanation is there?"

"So the Nazis put this stuff in the fertilizer?" Andrew asked.

"No—no, it was just some stupid *knucklehead!*" Kaz shot. "And no one noticed, and, what with the ground being so soft with the wet weather after it was spread, it all got pressed into the ground when the plane wheels went over the stuff. But then we had that nice stretch of sunny weather, and—"

"The ground dried out and now it's like concrete," Irene said. "Now all that crap is stuck in it—"

"Sticking out like spikes, puncturing tires—" Marlys added.

"So they closed the airfield—"

"Did away with all anti-slavery laws and—"

"Pressed all able bodies into service to pick the stuff out!" Irene shook her head in outrage.

"We no doubt looked like a bunch of field hands." Marlys said. "A line of us, making our way across the ground, carrying cardboard boxes and sacks and picking—"

"What's the matter?" Aunt Gwen came padding down the stairs, rubbing her eyes. She had a few days off from her job, and had just awakened from her afternoon nap.

"Tea first," Mrs. Tuttle announced from the dining room. She had evidently overheard the conversation, for she added, "You'll find that a cup of tea works wonders!"

"Dying and going to heaven would work wonders," Irene groaned.

"What happened?" Aunt Gwen pressed.

Mrs. Tuttle repeated her assertion that tea should be the first order of things, so, over cups of the steaming liquid and healthy helpings of Norfolk pudding, the tale of woe was repeated for Aunt Gwen's benefit.

"Poor dears," she murmured. Then she brightened. "I have it!"

"What—a transfer to the Bahamas?" Marlys asked.

"No, I'll give you each a backrub! It's my specialty!"

"Oh Gwen, you're supposed to be resting!" Marlys protested.

"Oh, I'd love to! It'd be no trouble at all, really!"

"But there's three of us," Irene pointed out. "We don't want to wear you out!"

"I'm used to doing more patients than that every night! Twenty minutes each should do it. It'd take only an hour to have the three of you on the road to recovery! You decide amongst yourselves who'll be first—I know! I'll teach Andrew how to give shoulder rubs; that way, the ones who have to wait will have a little relief!"

The women looked at one another, grateful at such a considerate offer, but still a little unsure whether or not to accept. It was, after all, such a generous thing to do.

"Please!" Andrew said. He hated seeing the women in such distress and relished the idea to be able to alleviate some of their discomfort. He also was anxious to do something—*anything*—to ameliorate his own terrible guilt at his having betrayed them by agreeing to Freddie's demand for his silence. "Aunt Gwen gives the most marvelous backrubs. When she took care of me after I got out of hospital, she gave me one every day, before my bedtime, and it was ever so wonderful! That's why I got better so quickly!"

The doubtful faces showed definite signs of being allowed to be persuaded. "I know!" Andrew exclaimed. "You can draw cards—highest one gets the first backrub, next highest gets the first shoulder rub from me!"

Smiles broke out on all faces. Andrew leaped up from the table and ran upstairs. He got the cards from Irene's room, clambered down the stairs, and dashed into the dining room. After shuffling the deck, he fanned the cards out, face down, for the women to choose. Marlys drew an ace, Kaz a seven, and Irene a two.

Aunt Gwen gave him a quick lesson on the fine art of giving shoulder rubs: "Squeeze them, like this—it's like kneading bread." She demonstrated her technique on Kaz, who sighed with relief as the kinks were massaged into oblivion. Then she ushered Marlys upstairs.

Andrew proceeded to knead Kaz's shoulders according to Aunt Gwen's instruction and was rewarded by groans of relief.

"Hullo, what's this?" Freddie's solicitous voice startled Andrew.

Irene explained the reason for Andrew's ministrations, adding, "Marlys got first dibs on the backrub, Kaz on the neckrub, so I have to wait my turn."

"Poor dear, maybe I can be of assistance." Freddie stood behind Irene and gently rubbed her shoulders. "I just want to help—just relax. I assure you, I won't take any indecent liberties—just want to help—" His voice lowered to a tender croon of concern as his fingers kneaded languorous circles on her shoulders and up the back of her neck. "Lean forward a bit—relax—close your eyes—good." He eyed Kaz, who was sitting next to Irene; he and Andrew were standing side by side. Kaz's eyes were closed too, and she was slumped forward. Freddie then gave a sideways glare to Andrew, his face a savage warning: *Remember—your silence in exchange for your mother's safekeeping.*

"Paranoid," Irene said.

Andrew wrote: "P-A-R-A-N-O-I-D."

"Good—did you get the meaning?"

"It means afraid, doesn't it?" Andrew had not looked up the definition yet; he had heard the word used before and took a guess.

"Not exactly." Irene took the dictionary and flipped through the pages. "Here it is— *Paranoid: characterized by suspiciousness or delusions of persecution.* Now, use it in a sentence."

"Some people are paranoid of getting bombed."

"I think that the fear of getting bombed is a justified fear. But if you think that no matter what you do you're going to get killed by a bomb, and you worry all the time about it, then that's being paranoid. Do you understand?"

Andrew shrugged.

"Let's try another one." Irene scanned the list. "Acquiescence."

Andrew wrote: "A-C-Q-U-E-I-S-C-E-N-C-E."

"I before E," Irene corrected.

"Sorry," Andrew mumbled.

"That's okay—it's the only one you missed. Not bad for a first spelling test. Ten times by tomorrow!"

Andrew nodded.

"Did you get all your sentences written?"

"Uh-huh." Andrew showed her his copybook. Irene read, "*If there could be acquiescence between people, we wouldn't have any more wars.*" She pursed her lips. "What do you mean by that?"

Andrew shrugged. "Acquiescence means agreement. If people would agree with each other we wouldn't have to fight any wars—right?"

"Well, not exactly; I mean, acquiescence doesn't mean agreement—"

"That's what the dictionary said." Andrew slumped back in his chair, folded his arms, and scowled.

Irene put her arm around him. "It does, sort of, but it has a little different meaning."

"What?" It was not question, but a challenge.

Irene looked at him, concerned. "Acquiescence implies a kind of giving in to an opposing side, not because you agree to what they want, but because there's the threat of force if you don't comply. It usually occurs when one side is bigger and stronger than the other. For instance, Austria had to acquiesce to being annexed by Germany. Do you understand?"

Andrew nodded.

"Silence is acquiescence." He heard Marlys' voice behind him.

"Wh—what?" he stammered.

"Silence is acquiescence," Marlys repeated. "If you keep silent when you know someone is doing something wrong, then you're allowing that person to commit a crime. Even though you may not approve of it, not speaking out against it is the same as giving your approval."

"Nobody likes a tattler," Andrew pointed out.

"It depends on what your motive is. Are you telling just to get someone in trouble, or to prevent wrong from being done?" Marlys countered. "Think of an air raid siren: It's designed to "tattle," isn't it? It's purpose is to warn people that danger is coming, so they can protect themselves."

Andrew threw down his pencil. "I think I'll go to bed now."

"Andrew, aren't you going to have supper?"

"I'm not hungry."

"You didn't have supper last night. Are you coming down with something?"

"I'm fine—I really am—I'm just tired. I—I didn't sleep very much during my nap."

"Ready for supper, everyone?" Kaz stood in the doorway.

"Um, Andrew is going to turn in," Marlys said.

"Andrew, are you all right?" Kaz asked.

"I'm fine—I am!"

"What's the matter?" Aunt Gwen sidled past Kaz into the room.

"Andrew says he doesn't want to have supper tonight," Irene told her.

"Andrew! You're not getting ill again?" Aunt Gwen furrowed her brow in distress.

"No—I'm fine, really I'm fine!" Blast, Andrew thought—maybe I should put a notice in the *Times*: *I'm fine, I'm really fine—just tired—*

Aunt Gwen pressed her hand to his forehead. "You don't feel feverish, but perhaps I should take your temperature—"

"No—*NO! NOT THAT!* I mean, I'm really all right...Please, could you just give me a backrub—just a short one? It might help me get to sleep." Andrew was feeling quite tense after all the interrogation. A backrub might soothe his distress, as well as deflect any further inquiries about his health.

"Boy, that backrub sure did the trick, Gwen; these old bones are as good as new," Irene said. Kaz and Marlys murmured in agreement.

"You go on and start without me. I'll be down in a few minutes," Aunt Gwen told them.

Kaz, Marlys, and Irene departed, and Aunt Gwen had Andrew take off his shirt and lie face-down in bed. She proceeded to knead his back, starting down near his waist and working upwards in soothing, circular motions.

"What do you remember about Dad?" Andrew asked her.

She paused in her circuit up his spine and sighed softly. "I remember walking between him and Jane, going to visit Charlie's grave. We used to take sweets to leave for him. We'd spread out a blanket in front of his grave, and play jacks. Your father would pretend to be Charlie, and he would babble and fumble around trying to pick up the jacks while the ball bounced and rolled away. It was ever so funny—"

"When was this?"

"Oh, the summer after Charlie died."

"I wish Charlie had lived—he'd be twenty—" Andrew quickly calculated. "Twenty-four now, right?"

"Yes, that's right. I wish he'd lived, too. Sometimes I imagine what he'd be like. I see lots of young men in hospital, about the age he would have been, and I try to think of what he'd be doing, what sort of person he'd be."

"I think he'd probably be in the RAF, like Dad."

"I think so, too." She kneaded his shoulders, feathered her fingers down his back, and started again on an upwards course.

Andrew took deep breaths and tried to focus his thoughts on his father...and Charlie. He imagined what it would be like to have an uncle who would care for him until his father returned, who could protect him, help him—someone to whom he could turn right now....

He pictured his father and Charlie shuffling a soccer ball between them, sparring in a boxing match, soaring through the sky in Hurricanes, doing aerobatics in a marvelous dance far above the earth, their contrails lacing a wonderful design in the heavens....

He felt himself transported to a dreamland where he was floating through time and space, and the feel of his father's arms around him was as real as the caressing strokes Aunt Gwen smoothed upon his back, and he heard his father's voice: *Alive...Aware....*

"Irene, I don't think the brass appreciated your entertainment," Marlys said, as the women filed through the front door.

"What entertainment?" Andrew walked down the stairs.

The women looked up at him, then turned to one another and laughed. They looked a little perkier than they'd appeared the day before.

"Didn't you have to clean the airfield today?"

"Naah—no chance of that!" Irene laughed. "I think the brass have found a new calling: being *massahs!* You know I think they really get a charge out of seeing us picking our way across the landing ground, like field hands. I'll bet they just settle back with their mint juleps and talk about whether they should declare war on the damn Yankees."

"Still, I don't think your singing *Them Old Cotton Fields Back Home* went over very well," Marlys remarked.

"Everybody *else* loved it," Irene countered as they walked into the dining room. "The way I figure it is, if they're gonna *treat* me like a field hand, I'm gonna *act* like one!

"Hullo, would you lovely ladies care for a bit of refreshment?" Freddie, wreathed in smiles, strode into the room, carrying a tray with a decanter and four glasses.

Irene lifted her head a bit and said, "You'll have to pour. My body has just fled North to freedom—oh, thank you very much." She giggled as Freddie handed her a glass.

"Not at all," Freddie murmured. He filled two more glasses, and offered drinks to Marlys and Kaz, along with smiles: a broad, leering one for Marlys, a polite, conciliatory one for Kaz. They both accepted Freddie's offering; perhaps it was Andrew's imagination, but he was sure he detected a flicker of mistrust in Kaz's eyes, even though she returned his smile.

Freddie filled his own glass and downed his brandy slowly (for him), while the women sipped theirs.

"Boy oh boy, that puts the fire back in the old bones!" Irene set down her glass, which Freddie refilled instantly.

"Here, perhaps I can get the knots out." He slipped behind her and began to gently massage her shoulders.

"Here's a proper feast for my weary little chicks." Mrs. Tuttle bustled into the room, carrying a tray laden with their tea things: potato pie, sausages, and pear flan. Lucia followed with the teapot and a plate of scones.

"Ooh, Mrs. Tuttle—you've outdone yourself!" Marlys exclaimed.

"I know it's a bit out of form for tea, but I happen to have a bottle of some exquisite white Bordeaux," Freddie said. "I think it would go down very well with the delights Mrs. Tuttle has set out for us." Without waiting for assent or protest, he sauntered out of the room and returned with a bottle and four wine glasses. As he poured the wine, he smiled at Marlys and launched into a glowing appraisal of California and things Californian: "Such a marvelous climate, sun-kissed and benign; architecture that surpasses the cathedrals of Europe; the place scented with the fragrance of orange blossoms; the most delightful beaches; a true oasis of culture, peace, and beauty in this war-torn world...."

Mrs. Tuttle came in to refill the teapot and said to Freddie, "Aren't you going to take tea in the study, as usual, Sir?"

"No, Mrs. Tuttle; I've gotten my accounts sorted out—" He turned to the women. "You see, I'm heavily invested in quite a number of ship-building concerns and other related businesses in your fair land, and it's quite an effort to keep on top of things—

"Liberty ships, you mean?" Marlys asked.

"That, and other things as well; I find the business climate in the States much more to my liking. As close as the ties are between our two countries, I see a fundamental difference in the way Americans approach the task of getting things done, and our British way, or what has lately *become* the British way, of doing things. As much as I hate to disparage my own country, I've come to the conclusion that the American way is the best way. The British leaders take the position that one must kill the Goose that Lays the Golden Egg. Did you know that we have a hundred percent tax on corporate profits?"

"A *hundred* percent!" Irene exclaimed. "Boy, that's enough to kill off any enterprising ideas people might have!"

"Well, sadly, you're right, my dear, though there are a few of us who have put the duty of serving King and country above personal profit. For instance, I assisted in the Dunkirk evacuation. How could one think of a balance sheet, knowing the terrible plight the BEF was in? Were it not for the miracle of Dunkirk, we would not have had an army—"

"You were at Dunkirk?" Irene asked.

"No, not precisely; however it was up to me to organize the fleet I had at my disposal, no small feat—"

Andrew glared at Freddie: *All you did was tell Maurice to handle the details; no doubt that was an extraordinary undertaking while you were plotting to debauch my mother—*

"...However, I feel that I'm serving my country in a better way by being a small part of the production effort in America. After all, that's the key to winning a war—supply. Pluck and fortitude are the foundation, and we British have that in abundance, but without the tools, any effort is ultimately doomed. That's why our Anglo-American partnership is so effective: It's a beacon to the world of brotherhood and cooperation, a shining example of how differences can enhance the individual efforts of both sides. And the way you Americans approach getting things done is, as I've said, and have *always* believed, could teach the British leaders a thing or two. Far from killing the Goose that Lays the Golden Egg, your government quite sensibly, gives it every persuasion to lay more: bonuses for getting the jobs done quickly, tax breaks, exemptions from anti-trust laws, other incentives as well, with the resulting production of war material on a scale that the world has not seen before, and which will win the war."

Freddie refilled Irene's wine glass, and his own. Noting that Marlys's glass was almost empty, he topped hers off as well.

"Well, that's the long and short of things—as I see them. My business takes me frequently to your wonderful nation, as it's rather difficult to manage things from a distance. Be that as it may, I've at last gotten affairs sorted out from this end, though working in the study through tea-time has been the reason for it. I must apologize for not having been an attentive host during your stay so far, and I promise that I shall make amends. More wine?"

"No thanks, I'm about ready to float away," Irene smiled. Freddie pointed the wine bottle at Marlys and Kaz; they declined as well.

Freddie sipped his wine, set the glass down, and addressed Marlys. "As I've said, my business often takes me to California, and I so look forward to my visit this coming summer. In fact, I've promised to give my associate, Maurice, a well-deserved holiday in your fair state. He's what you would call my right-hand man—handles the affairs for me here while I'm abroad. Indispensable, really, and a clever, hard-working chap—couldn't do without him. I took him with me on a business trip to the United States several years ago. We motored up the California coast, from San Francisco up to the Redwoods, and he so longs to see them again. Fascinating—perhaps our paths might have crossed—"

"The Redwoods are over six hundred miles from Los Angeles," Andrew piped. "Hardly a chance of your paths crossing."

Freddie glanced at Andrew, his expression sanguine, his smile benign, but behind the placid eyes the warning was clear: *You're skating on very thin ice....*

Andrew bit his lip and turned to Marlys. "I've heard the Redwoods are very beautiful. Have you ever visited them?"

"As a matter of fact, I have," Marlys answered. "And they *are* wonderfully majestic. I've seen cathedrals in Europe, palaces all over the world, but nothing compares with being in a forest of Redwoods. Before I saw them, I used to think they were just tall trees. I wish everyone could know what it's like to walk in the Redwoods. They have a primeval grandeur that is beyond anything else in this world."

"Oh, I must tell Maurice—he'd be ever so pleased." Freddie beamed at Marlys, and threw a benevolent glance at Andrew. "He positively waxes poetic about our visit there, and I know he'd so love to talk with someone who shares his appreciation for that beautiful region. Perhaps I can arrange a meeting between you and him sometime. I've told him that you all have been staying with us, and he's been quite eager to make your acquaintance. He so misses America; I think he fancies settling down there someday and, what with my business affairs in the States getting a little to complicated for me to handle alone, I'm considering setting him up there to manage things for me. What do you say? I know!" Freddie slapped the table, as if an extraordinarily brilliant idea had just smacked him over the head. "You're all going on holiday next week, aren't you? If you haven't made plans—I mean, if you might be able to spare some time out of the schedule you've undoubtedly set out for yourselves, might you consider a little visit to London? Say, perhaps, for a day or two?" He gazed at Marlys, then at Irene. Then, as if suddenly recollecting that he had excluded Kaz from his invitation, he looked at her and said politely, but without a trace of eagerness: "And you, my dear, the invitation includes you as well."

Kaz said evenly, "Thank you, I'll think about it." Her response produced a flicker of unease in Freddie's eyes. He turned back to Marlys and Irene. "Please consider it. It would give me so much pleasure to show you around London—why, there are so many things to see and do—"

And at the top of the list is your bomb shelter....

Marlys looked at Irene and smiled with a bit of uncertainty. "Well, I don't know—we'd like to see London, but it's so hard finding a place to stay. We thought we might go in for a day and look around."

"Oh, don't worry yourself about a place to stay. I can arrange accommodations for you. It'd be no trouble—"

"Oh no, we couldn't impose—"

"Imposition—not at *all!* What I meant was, I can see to hotel accommodations for you, the very best!"

Marlys glanced at Irene again. "Well, I'm afraid that on our salaries—"

"My *dear!* It would be my pleasure to see that everything is taken care of. After all, it's the *least* I can do, considering that you've come all this way to render us assistance in the struggle. And I've been so often the recipient of the *wonderful* hospitality your country has to offer that I would consider it a privilege to return the kindness that has been shown to me. Well, I don't want to pressure you, but I'd be ever so grateful if you'd accept."

The women glanced at each other. "We'll think about it, thank you," Marlys said.

Freddie's gaze lingered on her, then on Irene. Then, lifting his wine glass, he said, "I know it's customary to offer a toast at the beginning of a meal, and I'm not at all sure that it has ever been done at tea-time, but I'd like to take this opportunity to break with precedent." He lifted the glass an inch higher, "To friendship, to the alliance between our two countries, to our shared common heritage, and to the delightful differences that enrich our partnership: Hands across the sea, and may the world always remember the union of our two peoples, forged by war, but ensured by the peace we carry within our hearts."

The next day he received a letter from his mother. She had been extremely busy lately, what with all the aircraft that needed moving. She also enclosed a letter from Aunt Jane:

Dear Andrew,

Your mother tells me that you are much on the mend—Good show! She has reports from your new friends that you are turning out to be quite a clever card player—I never learned how to play poker, but it sounds fascinating! It must be ever so much fun to try to make everyone believe you have a good hand, and to win by pretending that you've got better cards that the other players!

Your friend Kaz sounds ever so friendly—I'm glad, too, that she's in my room. Your other friends seem very nice too—it must be exciting having a house full of pilots! I wish I could have seen the look on Freddie's face after he told that horrible joke and found out that Kaz was of Polish ancestry!

Speaking of Freddie, I do remember the night we stayed up late and discussed the subject of Freddie not deserving to be liked (and of sending him to Germany to replace Lord Haw-Haw!). Andrew, while it's true that Freddie can be ever so tiresome, don't let yourself get so worked up over him. Enough to know he's a twit and turn your attention to more important things, just as your father would do! I don't know if I've ever said this to you, Andrew, but you are turning out to be quite a special person. It gives me no small joy to see (as much as I can "see" you through your letters and what your mother writes to me of you) how very much like your father you are now, and how you are growing more and more like him every day. I know he would be so proud of you, too. How I wish I could be with you!

Much love,
Aunt Jane

Andrew stared at the letter, stunned and distraught. It was *true*—something was terribly, *terribly* wrong! If she had only mentioned the bit about sending Freddie to Germany to replace Lord Haw-Haw, he might have chalked it up to a faulty memory; after all, it was only a little thing, even though his aunt had a photographic memory. She could remember addresses and phone numbers of acquaintances from years back, conversations, birthdays, all manner of things. But she would have *certainly* remembered that night before Andrew's father had left: She had seen through Andrew's ploy to attempt to stay up late and had *not* fallen for it. In fact, as indulgent as she had always been with Andrew, she had never, *ever*, acquiesced to his appeals to stay up past his bedtime: *Bedtime is bedtime—it can wait until morning!* She had always said that! Always! *Always!*

He flung the letter onto his bedside table. If only he knew what was going on! It wasn't like Aunt Jane to commit such glaring errors. It wasn't like her at all!

The sight of the letter, neatly typed, with his aunt's scrawly signature at the bottom, tormented him. Disdaining even to touch it, he took one of his books and used it to scrape the letter along so that it fell behind the table onto the floor and was hidden from view. Even his room seemed to be a place of fearful turmoil and menace. He grabbed his sweater and dashed out, down the hall, down the stairs, and through the front door.

Once outside, he tried to escape the vexing fear by running, running as fast as his legs would carry him.

It isn't her! It isn't Aunt Jane writing those letters! What's happened to her?

He covered ground as if pursued, and soon found himself at Charlie's grave. He walked slowly towards it, then reached out his hands to trace the inscription carved in stone: A name, two dates, and a farewell benediction.

He slumped against the headstone and slid to the ground. Pressing his face against the cold granite, he tried to transport himself back to that occasion, just after his father had returned from France when the two of them had picnicked on this very spot. If only it were possible to order up an event from the past, as one would order a meal in a restaurant, and enjoy a living experience of sweet remembrance. He imagined his father and himself, lounging on the blanket and enjoying peaches and chocolate and the halcyon day. His mind somehow filtered out the fear and apprehension he had felt at that time; all he remembered was the joy of his father's presence.

If only you could be with me again....

It was getting cold, and he huddled against the stone and closed his eyes....

Voices awakened him: Aunt Gwen's, Aunt Jane's, his father's, and someone else's—male, though not as deep as his father's voice. He opened his eyes, and at first saw a blur of light and color; the scene came into focus and he saw that his father, his aunts, and someone else in an RAF uniform were seated in a circle in front of him. His father was dressed in uniform also, with rings around his cuffs; Aunt Jane was wearing her FANY attire, and Aunt Gwen, a nurse's dress and cap. They were playing jacks, and did not appear to notice him. His father was facing him, Aunt Gwen and Aunt Jane were on either side, and the figure in the RAF uniform was seated opposite, so that the man's back was to Andrew. Andrew was afraid to say anything at all, afraid that even his breath would shatter the scene and he would be left alone. But then his father looked up and saw him, and his face burst into that rapturous smile. "Andrew—old chap!" His voice had that happy inflection, that way of saying Andrew's name so that it sounded like a song.

"Andrew!" Both his aunts looked up from the game, and the man turned to him. He looked very worried. "How are you?" he asked.

Somehow Andrew had the disconcerting feeling that the face, though he could not ever recall seeing it, was familiar. The voice he knew also—but from where? Sparky—no, it wasn't Sparky. He recalled the faces of his father's squadron mates, the ones he had met; it wasn't one of them, either. A flying student, perhaps? Andrew's father used to invite his students to supper at Armus House. Or maybe it was one of his father's friends from Oxford.

No, not any of these: Andrew had the distinct feeling that the man was not someone he had met a long time ago. It was someone he had met recently; of that, he was very sure. He just couldn't quite place him.

Still, that was no reason to be impolite. Andrew answered, "I'm fine, thank you."

The man looked at him intently, as if doubting his words, then said in a voice laced with anxiety, "I just want you to get well."

"I'm fine—I really am!"

Who *was* this man? And why was he so worried about Andrew's health?

His befuddlement must have been evident, for his father said, "Don't you know Charlie?"

"It can't be him—he died when he was a baby!" Andrew replied. Then, to emphasize his point, he turned to indicate the words on the headstone.

But the stone was smooth: Not a thing was written on it.

"He didn't die," his father said. "I made sure that he was all right, didn't I?" He looked at Charlie, who nodded.

"Is it really Charlie?" He turned to Aunt Jane.

"Yes it is, Andrew...*Andrew...ANDREW!*"

The scene vanished; now Kaz was standing over him, shaking him and calling his name. Hours had passed—it was almost dark.

"*Andrew—ANDREW!* Wake up!"

Suddenly he was very cold; his teeth started chattering and he clutched himself for warmth.

"Good grief, Andrew! What are you doing here? We've been looking all over for you!"

"We?"

"Me and Marlys and Irene; Thomas, Lucia, Mrs. Tuttle, and Freddie, too."

"*Freddie!*" Andrew's body jerked with a spasm of dread.

"Yes—we've all been so worried! When we got home, Mrs. Tuttle thought you were upstairs taking a nap. Irene went to wake you for tea and you were nowhere to be found. We just about tore the house apart and then set off to find you. Marlys and I went with Thomas in the car. He dropped us off at places along the way where he thought you'd be, since he can't go very far on foot—"

Andrew tried to stand and found his legs wouldn't work very well; he stumbled at the first step he tried to take. Kaz caught him.

"Andrew, you're freezing! You could have *died* out here of hypothermia!"

"Hypo what?"

"Hypothermia—low body temperature. Here, put my jacket on. I'll carry you."

Kaz carried him with no trouble at all; his arms clung tight around her neck and his legs wrapped around her waist. He was quite surprised at how strong she was. She kept up a steady, brisk pace until they got to the road. There she set Andrew down and whistled loudly; she was answered by a distant shout from Marlys. Presently Marlys appeared over the top of a hillock on the other side of the road. Kaz waved to her, and Marlys dashed to them.

"*Andrew!* What have you been *doing?* We've been looking *everywhere* for you!"

Andrew had been working on an explanation while he was being toted by Kaz.

"I just wanted to go outside—it was such a nice day and I wanted to go for a walk. I got tired, and stopped to rest. I guess I fell asleep, that's all. I'm ever so sorry for all the trouble I've caused...."

"Here, let me carry him, Kaz. Gosh Andrew, you're *freezing!* Gawdalmighty, hope you don't get pneumonia again!"

"Here comes Thomas," Kaz said.

The Bentley slowed to a halt just beside them; Andrew was loaded into the backseat and sandwiched between Kaz and Marlys. Thomas had brought along one of Gram's crazy quilts; Kaz wrapped it tightly around Andrew.

He must have dozed again for the next thing he knew, the car was stopped in front of Armus House and Thomas was blaring the horn.

"I told them that would be the signal that we found him," he explained to the women. "Lucia and Vi should hear it. I'll drive on to find Freddie and Irene. They went the other way from us, towards the old mill."

"Marlys, run upstairs and start the bath," Kaz said. "That should thaw him out a bit."

Marlys dashed inside; Kaz followed, carrying Andrew. The sound of rushing water and a halo of steam emanating from the open bathroom door greeted their arrival at the top of the stairs.

"We're only allowed to fill the tub five inches," Andrew reminded Kaz.

"To hell with five inches. Come on, in the tub—almost full, Marlys?"

Marlys nodded. Kaz set Andrew down and started to peel off his shirt. "I can get myself undressed," he protested.

"Okay, I'll wait outside until you're in the tub. Pull the curtain around and call me— I'll come in and sit with you."

"I can take a bath by myself."

"One of the classic symptoms of hypothermia is delirium. I don't want you slipping into unconsciousness and drowning yourself—not after all the trouble we've gone through to find you! Call me when you're ready," she said firmly.

Andrew found himself blubbering: "I'm sorry—I didn't mean to—I'm sorry— *Sorry!*"

Kaz hugged him tenderly. "It's all right. I didn't mean to make you feel bad. We were so worried about you. Please, please, don't ever do anything like that again, all right?"

Andrew sniffled and nodded furiously. Kaz grabbed a hand towel from the stack on the table and pressed it to his nose.

"Blow," she ordered.

Andrew complied; Kaz took another towel and blotted his cheeks. "Oops, think we're going to overflow the tub—" She jumped up and shut the water off.

"Okay, now—get undressed. I'll get your spelling words and sit on the chair by the tub. We'll have a spelling test; shake the cold off of those brain cells and get them working again, okay?"

She went to get the spelling words while Andrew stripped and got in the tub. He heard a knock. "Ready?" Kaz called.

"I've got to pull the curtain—wait a minute." That accomplished, he called, "Ready."

As he sank down into the warm waters, he heard the door open, then Kaz's voice: "I've got your copy-book, so let's start."

The blessed warmth was starting to infuse through his body, soothing the convulsive shivers and the disquiet he felt within. He took a few deep breaths. Kaz asked, "How are you?"

The question perturbed him, until he remembered: It was what Charlie had asked him in his dream. Funny, he couldn't remember what Charlie had looked like, but the feeling still persisted that Andrew had seen him somewhere—somewhere recently—but *where*?

"Andrew, are you all right?"

"Um, yes—I'm fine."

"C-H-I-M-E-R-A"

"Great. Did you look up the definition? It isn't written here."

"Yes, it's some kind of monster with a lion's head and a goat's body and a something else. I forget."

"A serpent's tail. That's the original meaning, though. What it refers to in present usage is something, either a creature or thing, that's composed of incongruous parts."

"Oh."

"*Acquiescence.*"

The word stabbed him like a dagger.

"Andrew?"

"What?"

"*Acqui—*"

"I know—*I know!*" I don't know. Could you go on to the next word?"

"Silly boy," Freddie chided. "We were looking all over for you! Thomas had to waste precious petrol chasing after your stupid hide. Aren't you ashamed of yourself?"

Andrew was tucked in bed. Kaz, Irene, and Marlys had already bid him good-night; then Freddie had come in and had said he wanted to have a "few words" with Andrew. Kaz had started to protest that Andrew already felt rotten enough about what had happened, to which Freddie had replied solicitously that he was concerned for Andrew: Perhaps having a "little chat" would allay "the boy's" distress. The women had filed out, leaving Andrew alone with Freddie.

"...You might have frozen to death out there—it's quite cold and damp and we would have had no way of finding you. And to wander off to a graveyard, of all places! Never would have thought to look for you there!"

Andrew glared at Freddie. *Dad and I always used to go there together—you know that! It would have suited you just fine to have sent everyone on a wild goose chase— at least Thomas knew that I'd be there!*

Freddie narrowed his eyes. "You very well could have frozen to death out there, and I'd have to be the one to comfort your poor dear mother. Now, we wouldn't have wanted that to happen, would we?"

He awoke and noted the time on his alarm clock: Ten-thirty. He needed a drink of water; after Freddie had left he had cried himself to sleep. Now his throat was tight and dry.

He padded down the hall to the bathroom and drank a glassful of water. On the way back to his room, he noticed a band of light under Kaz's door. It seemed to him like the light of the beacons he used to see on the occasional Channel crossing by night: welcome and reassuring, defining a sure course in the inky darkness.

He gently tapped on the door. The rustle of bedclothes, soft footfalls, the door swinging back....

Kaz's eyes opened wide in surprise and she drew him in.

"Andrew, what's wrong?"

Andrew pursed his lips, as if that could hold back the tears; which was a futile gesture, for they spilled down his cheeks like water over a millwheel. Kaz's arms went round him.

"Andrew, sweetheart, what's the matter?"

His body convulsed with silent sobs; he dared not make a sound, fearing that the others might hear him. He felt completely, utterly overwhelmed and distressed to the point of panic. His guilt about his acquiescing to Freddie's demands for his silence; his discovery of his own untimely birth; his fears for his mother, and for Marlys and Irene (he even felt guilty that Freddie had taken advantage of his flight to go searching with Irene—in the wrong direction, no less!); his anguish over Aunt Jane. Last, but not least, Freddie's recent warning: All these tormented him and strangled his soul so completely that he could not even imagine what it would be like to be at ease and free from care, let alone happy. It was all too clear to him that it would serve more than one purpose for Freddie if he himself were "out of the way," and this recent insight into Freddie's appalling malevolence was enough to scare the life out of him. During the Blitz, there were times when, dispirited into irrationality by fatigue, Andrew had been convinced that somewhere a bomb had *his* name on it, and no matter what kind of precautions he took, no matter how hard he tried to hide, *it* would find him, somehow, some way. Now that horrific imagining had been given life, and form, and a name: *Freddie*. Even the dream vexed him. The odd feeling of having seen Charlie somewhere before only added to his anguish: like having a toothache and drowning at the same time.

Kaz held him close until he slumped against her in exhaustion.

Finally, she asked quietly, "I know that something has been bothering you. Do you want to talk about it?"

Andrew had expected an inquiry along those lines, and knew that it would be churlish to request comfort from someone and then to refuse to divulge a reason. He had been sworn to silence about Freddie's plot, but there was still Aunt Jane....

He took a deep breath and whispered, "I got a letter today from Aunt Jane—" His voice broke as the fear rose up within him: fear, and the horror of not even knowing exactly what it was he was afraid of, like a gnawing sense of malice and evil, a monster without form or definition....

"Is something wrong?"

He was about to say: *I don't know*, and then an even greater fear wrapped its icy tentacles around his pounding heart, and this time it was a terror that was clearly defined, that screamed a warning at him: *Whatever you tell Kaz will be relayed to your mother, and it will only cause her worry and distress. Bad enough to do that anyway, worse for her to be distracted if she's flying planes....*

"Did your aunt write to you about anything that upset you?"

"Um...um, she, um...she wrote about my father. She said that...um, that I'm very much like him—like he was, I mean, and that he would be proud of me. I miss him so much—I wish he were here—" His voice choked again; then a sob rose up in his throat and broke forth into a sputtery howl: He cried for his father, and for having to conceal the other reasons for his distress: the deep sense of shame he felt in having to betray his friends; his overwhelming feelings of inadequacy in being so small and powerless; the soul-crushing responsibility that he carried; his anguish for Aunt Jane.

Kaz slipped her arm under his knees and effortlessly picked him up. Cradling him like a baby, she carried him to the armchair in the corner and sat down with him in her lap. He cried softly again, hoping for exhaustion to overtake him once more. However, as his sobs turned to moans and his body hung limp with fatigue, his distress was not abated. The distressing terrors seemed to take advantage of his utter prostration to torment him anew. "I'm sorry, I'm sorry...sorry for all the trouble I've caused...." His voice broke again.

He felt a gentle kiss on his forehead, heard a whispered "It's okay...don't worry about it." He pressed his face into the shelter of her neck and was cradled by her strong arms. After a long, long while, sleep released him from the waking nightmare that had grafted itself onto his soul.

Even as he felt the shadows of sleep mercifully closing in, he was aware of a terrifying transformation taking place: He was no longer just himself, but a monstrous chimera composed of himself and his awful fears merged into a single, abominable entity that awaited his coming to consciousness again.

The house was quiet, but, even before he opened his eyes, he sensed that the day was late. He was back in his bed again; Kaz must have carried him back to his room after he'd fallen asleep. There was something on the nightstand by his bed: a piece of paper folded like a boat, with another piece of paper folded into a small package and a small heart drawn on in, tucked inside. He picked it up and opened it.

Dear Andrew,

I thought about waking you this morning, but you seemed to be so deep in sleep that I didn't want to disturb you. I figured you needed your rest more than anything—sometimes things are better after a good night's sleep...and sometimes they aren't. Please know that I care—I want so much to be able to do something to chase away all the sadness you feel about your father. Maybe, though, your feelings need to come out and, as distressing as it all is to you, it's a part of what you need to go through. It's a lot of hard work to push all the bad feelings away. Maybe that's what you've been doing and it's all caught up with you, finally. I'm glad that you came to me.

If you still want to talk, my door is always open. I'm no expert on solving problems, but I'll try to help in whatever way I can, even if it's just listening.

Kaz

He refolded the letter and put it in the drawer of his nightstand. As he stared at the ceiling, the vestiges of the disturbing dreams he had experienced the night before swirled around him. They weren't really dreams; they were more like disjointed images, spooky and disconcerting. He was at school: The other boys were laughing at him because he had a pig's snout in place of his nose. Then he was at Charlie's grave and he realized that he had also sprouted blue wings and a yellow snake for a tail. The snout was still there, too. The scene shifted again, and he was at the restaurant with his father. His father held a small red box in his hands and proffered it to Andrew, but as Andrew tried to take it slipped from his grasp. He saw that, in place of his hands, he had goat's hooves. He looked at his father, pleading for...what? Forgiveness—that's what he wanted. He felt so very ashamed of what he had become, what with that hideous snout and tail and the wings now protruding from the sides of his head where his ears should have been. His father tried to pretend that everything was all right, but there was a look of unmistakable dismay in his eyes....

Mrs. Tuttle greeted him in the dining room. "Feeling better, Andrew? My, you gave us quite a scare." She gave him a hug and went back to the kitchen to get his breakfast.

"I've just baked scones. Would you like some?" she called.

"Yes, please."

"Feeling better, Andrew?" Freddie stood in the doorway.

Andrew's head snapped round. He swallowed, and his voice came out as a squeak. "Yes, better."

"Good." There was an imperceptible pause before Freddie's response, a brief silence that inaugurated malice into this unwanted encounter. Freddie's eyes bored into him. He walked slowly to the table, and sat down. His expression changed abruptly to one of amiability. "Thank you, Mrs. Tuttle, I think I'll have a bite to eat, too."

Andrew turned round as Mrs. Tuttle set a plate of scones on the table. "I'll get more tea, sir—would you like more scones, too?"

"That will do nicely, Mrs. Tuttle." Freddie watched her retreat to the kitchen, drummed his fingers on the table, slapped his hand down. "Music! How would you like some music, Andrew? Helps the digestion." His eyes, gleaming with enmity, bored into Andrew.

Andrew felt the skin prickle on the back of his neck. Without waiting for a reply, Freddie got up and put a record on the gramophone. It blared forth a loud, jazzy song. Freddie cocked his head in the direction of the music. "Like it? Chap named Glenn Miller. All the Yanks are mad on him. Mind you, I don't usually find this sort of music to my liking—such a cacophonous racket, isn't it? But once in a while, it suits me."

Andrew took a sip of tea, forcing it past the tightening in his throat. Mrs. Tuttle came in with a plate of scones and a fresh pot of tea.

"Thank you very much, Mrs. Tuttle," Freddie said evenly. He dismissed her with a glance. As she walked past the gramophone, she said, "Would you like me to turn this down, sir?"

"No thank you, Mrs. Tuttle. I didn't sleep well last night, and some loud music would do the trick in waking up the brain cells." He turned to Andrew, and asked, "How about you, Andrew—did you sleep well last night?"

Andrew set down his cup, trying to control the trembling of his hands. The cup clattered against the saucer.

"I slept quite well, thank you," he said crisply.

Freddie's face puzzled into a frown. "So then you don't remember?" His voice was solicitous, but his eyes were steely pools of malevolence.

"Remember what?" To Andrew's consternation, his voice quavered.

"Dear me, you must have been sleepwalking again last night."

"I don't sleepwalk—I never have," Andrew blurted. His mind was racing along a million different tracks, trying to ascertain the goal of this unpleasant conversation, and his first reaction was to get defensive. Too late, he realized he'd said the wrong thing.

Freddie's eyes glittered alarmingly. "Yes you do. Quite often, in fact. I mentioned to the women that you've done it quite frequently, and once in awhile, I've even had to stop you from opening the front door and wandering off into the night with nothing but your pajamas on. Last night, though, I saw you knock on the door to Jane's room, where what's-her-name—the Polish one—is staying. So I rather doubted that you were sleepwalking last night. Your actions seemed quite purposeful, not at all like someone going off silly-arsed in a trance. Was there, hmmm—something you wanted to discuss with her?"

Andrew swallowed. "I just wanted to tell her how sorry I was for causing so much trouble."

Freddie glared hard at him. "*And?*"

Andrew's heart beat time to the clattery music. He took a deep breath and said, "I told her that I was upset because I missed my father."

Freddie smiled, but the eyes remained cold. "That's what she told me. I mentioned it at breakfast—I was *ever* so concerned about you. I told the women that you're prone to sleepwalking and going off silly-buggers, like you did yesterday. Would you like more tea, Andrew?" He raised an eyebrow, waiting for Andrew's reply. Andrew's neck twitched; Freddie evidently interpreted it as an affirmative reply, and refilled his cup. "You like your tea with milk and sugar, don't you, Andrew?"

Andrew set his face firmly ahead, trying to steel himself against further bodily betrayals. Freddie ministered to his tea, stirring it a little longer than was strictly necessary, all the while regarding Andrew worriedly.

"You know, Andrew, I'm ever so concerned for your safety and welfare. You've had more than your share of close scrapes for someone your age. There was that time you were nearly blown to bits in London—that must have been absolutely terrifying! The woman with you was killed, wasn't she? They had to cut her in half to get you out."

Freddie shook his head. "Ghastly, positively ghastly. Then you nearly *died* of pneumonia; your dear mother was quite distraught! She was by your side almost the whole time—the doctor didn't give you much hope for a chance of recovery. Your poor mother has been through so much, hasn't she?"

Andrew wasn't quite sure where this conversation was going, but he was certain it was not to a happy destination. Freddie poured himself a cup of tea, added milk and sugar, leaned back and sipped it thoughtfully, as if he were evaluating a fine wine. Setting the cup down, he furrowed his brow in consternation and said in a low voice, "I've been hearing some disturbing talk. All very hush-hush—you see, the authorities don't want word getting out of the, ahhh...*progress* the Germans have been making in developing certain weapons. Could cause a panic, you know, so it wouldn't do to go blabbering about it to anyone and everyone. You *can* keep a secret, can't you Andrew?"

Andrew was too afraid to even look at Freddie, let alone reply. The blaring music seemed to mock him.

"I *know* you can, Andrew. That's why I'm entrusting you with what I know. You see, I have it on very good authority that the Germans have their top scientists working on a few remarkable inventions, devices that could change the whole course of the war. Everyone here is so confident it's only a matter of time before Germany's defeated, and they're absolutely quivering with excitement at the thought of trouncing the Huns once and for all. But you know what they say about pride going before a fall. Hitler has a few aces up his sleeve, and once these inventions are perfected...well, they'll make the Blitz look like a garden party. Terrible things they are: a special kind of radio beam that can destroy a plane in mid-air. Now that would certainly put a damper on Bomber Command's nightly forays, not to mention the Yank Air Force's plucky endeavors, wouldn't it? Pilotless planes, too—can you imagine hundreds, even thousands of them over the skies of England? The mind positively boggles at the thought! And the ghastliest thing of all: a bomb that could destroy an entire city! Can you imagine that? One bomb, and London—or any other city, for that matter—obliterated!"

Andrew blurted, "That's ridiculous!"

Freddie smiled and added more tea to his cup. "A hundred years ago people used to think that the idea of flying machines was ridiculous, too. Look what scientific progress has achieved! What an amazing time we live in—anything is possible, isn't it?" He waited a moment for a reply. Andrew continued to stare at his tea, mouth clenched. His hands, hidden under the table, bunched into fists.

"Anything is possible," Freddie repeated softly. "Knowing about these things, and knowing how concerned your mother is for your safety, well, I'd thought of keeping quiet about them—not telling a soul. They were told to me in strictest confidence, you see. And yet—" He cast a penetrating look at Andrew. "I feel that it's wrong for me to keep such information to myself. If I failed to inform you, and your mother, of what I knew, and if something terrible were to happen to you because I kept silent...well, I'd never be able to forgive myself. In fact, I've taken it upon myself to see to your welfare, for your dear father's sake." He leaned back, withdrew a piece of paper from his breast pocket, and set it down before Andrew. "I've been making inquiries among my friends in America. Go on, open it—" he waved his index finger at it.

Andrew picked it up, unfolded it, and glared at the listings on the page.

"It's a list of boarding schools—the very best, I can assure you. They also offer all sorts of interesting things for a young boy to enjoy: horseback riding, hiking, archery, fencing...this one here—" Freddie's finger jabbed at one near the bottom of the list, "This one offers *skiing*. Can you imagine, Andrew? How would you like to learn to ski? Your father had always wanted to take you to Austria or Switzerland and teach you to ski. Imagine how happy he'd be to know you were learning to schuss down the slopes in America! He was ever so eager to take you on holiday to the United States, wasn't he? And I'm sure, that if he were alive and knew about the terrible dangers facing Britain, he'd want to make sure you were safely out of the country—hmmm?" Freddie heaved a sigh and shook his head dolefully.

"Your *poor* mother—she's been so weighed down by her cares for you. I'd like to be able to help shoulder that burden for her; after all, we're family, and we do need to look out for one another. She should be informed about these things, so that she could see to your safety, don't you think?" He examined the plate of scones, picked out one to his liking, sliced and buttered it. He offered one half to Andrew, holding it in mid-air, waiting for an acceptance. Andrew stared straight ahead. After a few seconds, Freddie set it gently on Andrew's plate.

"You should really eat more, you know. You're looking rather peaky. Or perhaps it is because you haven't been getting much rest—hmmm? Come, come now, you shouldn't feel ashamed to admit you've occasionally had a sleepless night. Happens to everyone, at one time or another. Sometimes all one needs is a good night's sleep to set things right again, put back the sparkle in the eye and the spring in the step. There are times when my concerns over my shipping business drive me to distraction, and I toss and turn, fretting about things." He bit into a scone, munched it, and waved his fingers at the uneaten scone on Andrew's plate. "Andrew, have a bite to eat! What are you trying to do—waste yourself away?"

Andrew tore of a bit of scone and nibbled listlessly at it, feeling like a condemned prisoner eating his last meal. It slid down his throat like a stone. Meanwhile, Freddie devoured his. "My, Mrs. Tuttle has certainly *outdone* herself, hasn't she?" He brushed his fingertips together when he'd finished and noted that Andrew's scone was largely untouched. "Dear boy, are you bound and determined to starve yourself to death?" He stabbed Andrew's scone with his fork and plopped it on his own plate. "Can't let good food go to waste, can we? Now, where were we? That's right—you haven't been sleeping well—that's it, isn't it? Well, as I was saying, everyone has that problem at one time or another. I don't think your poor mother caught a wink of sleep the whole time you were in hospital, until it was clear you were on the mend."

Freddie finished the last of his scone and pushed his plate away. He ruefully regarded Andrew's empty plate, picked it up, and slowly conveyed it to the far end of the table. He glared at it for a moment, as if analyzing its position amongst the new surroundings, then turned to Andrew. "There are those who eschew any kind of medical intervention, and in my opinion, that's just plain silly. If the offerings of medical science make life a little more bearable, then it's not unwise to avail ourselves of them. A mild sedative is sometimes all that's needed to induce a restful sleep, and I keep a liberal supply on hand, just in case. You never know when it might come in handy. For instance, one of my acquaintances in London became somewhat agitated during an air raid. Even though we were safe in my bomb shelter, she still was quite fretful and anxious. Luckily, I happened to have a dose of sleeping powders with me, and just a pinch, mixed in with a glass of brandy, was enough to induce a relaxed state in my distressed little friend. After consuming said beverage, she spent the remainder of the night...*unperturbed*, one might say."

Freddie gave a slight shake of his head and said in a low voice, "If you ever have trouble sleeping again, please come to me and I'll see to it that you have a bit to help you get a good night's sleep. Mind you, someone your size shouldn't take an adult dose—that could prove extremely dangerous. Might induce coma, irreversible coma, perhaps, or something even worse. Wouldn't want that to happen, would we?"

Andrew quickly turned away from him. "No, of course not," Freddie murmured. "Your poor mother would be ever so upset." Freddie laid his arm across Andrew's shoulders. "And with all she's gone through already—look at me, Andrew." His hand slid upward, along Andrew's neck to his face. Exerting a slight pressure, he coaxed Andrew's head back around to face him; then he stroked his hair with his other hand. His voice dropped to a barely audible croon. "Sometimes, even waiting the few minutes for a sleeping powder to work is a little too much to bear. For those instances, something more efficacious is called for." He reached into his breast pocket and pulled out a silver cigarette case. He opened it, and Andrew saw that it contained not cigarettes, but a small hypodermic.

"Damn!" Freddie bellowed. He snapped the case shut. "Out of cigarettes—be a good lad, Andrew, and fetch me one. They're in a rosewood box on my desk." He sat back and smiled benignly at Andrew.

For a brief, horror-filled moment, Andrew was afraid his legs would fail him. His brain barked the command to his legs; he quickly stood up and clumped his feet across the room, aware that Freddie was watching every step.

He got a cigarette from the box and retraced his steps to the dining room. Wordlessly, he handed the cigarette to Freddie and turned to leave the room.

"Andrew!" Freddie barked. "I'm not quite finished with you yet. Sit down." Pulling Andrew's chair back, he indicated to Andrew to be seated. Andrew glared at him, and plopped down in the chair at the far end of the table, where his plate lay. He expected Freddie to be irked, but instead Freddie heaved a sigh of concern, stood up, and moved to the chair next to Andrew's. Seating himself purposefully, he lit the cigarette and gazed for a moment at the smoke curling upwards.

He took a drag on the cigarette, then crushed it out on Andrew's plate. Evincing another look of worried concern again, he placed his finger on the corner of Andrew's eye and said, "You've got such dark circles under your eyes, Andrew. Getting to bed early might do the trick. Yes...I'll see to it that Mrs. Tuttle gives you a proper meal at tea. Then you won't have to wait up until supper. Rest—lots of rest; that's what you're here for, aren't you? Might be better to send you back to school, what with the late hours you've been keeping lately. Playing poker till all hours of the night—not good for the constitution, is it? I think I might have a talk with your mother about that. Well, run along."

The record on the gramophone played out just as Andrew stood up, and the rhythmic click of the needle against the silence accompanied his brisk footsteps out of the room.

"Things are coming along just swimmingly, Maurice. I popped the question to Mata Hari and the Farmer's Daughter, and they seem quite intrigued...Mata Hari, the one from California, remember? Now, do you remember anything about our trip up the California coast?"

Andrew was in the library, and Freddie's voice came loud and clear through the open door to the reading terrace. The study also opened onto the terrace; Freddie must have opened a window to air out the study. The level of cigarette smoke occasionally even got to *him*....

"What do you mean—all you can remember is a redhead in a tatty little hotel in Yahooville! First off, the name of the place was Eureka, and you were with the blond— *I* had the redhead...Yes, I'm quite sure of it. I seem to recall that you were ever so eager to ascertain as to whether or not she was a nat—"

The chair squeaked, and a blast of laughter split the air.

Just lean back a little farther...Maybe you'll fall back and break your neck, just like your father...He fell down the stairs, didn't he? He was probably drunk, just like you always are...Like to get you *to the top of the stairs when* you've *had a snootful, then give you a gentle nudge in the right direction....*

"Do you mean to tell me you don't *remember?* Really, Maurice...Now, can you recall anything else? About our drive up the coast, I mean. I told Mata Hari...Of, course, I had a bloody hangover too, but *someone* had to drive!...So all you can recall is spewing on some tree?"

Freddie howled in derision. "First off, Maurice, it wasn't just a tree, it was a bloody great tree, and it was red, remember? Why the hell do you think they call them Redwoods?...No, not the whole bloody tree, you clot, just the bottom part—"

Andrew turned a page in his book: If Freddie happened to discover him in here, it would not appear that he was obviously eavesdropping.

"...Well, you're going to have to remember more than *that!* Mata Hari was ever so thrilled with the bloody great trees, and you're going to have to convince her that you were, too. So remember: *majestic, cathedral-like*, and—oh yes, *primeval! Primeval—* yes—that should do it! Can you remember...Maurice, you are such an expert at dealing with bureaucrats and the brass, why do you always get so tongue-tied when you're with a member of the weaker sex? The same principle applies whether you're dealing with snotty paper-pushers in the Navy or whether you want to have a crack at a popsy that needs a little persuading: Just baffle them with bullshit, that's all there is to it—"

The blood rose to Andrew's head, and he clenched the book in his hands until his knuckles turned white.

"...*Really*, Maurice, you're going to have to strike out on your own sometime. You can't always expect *me* to arrange your trysts—"

Andrew tried to silence the thudding of his heart; it seemed to fill the room. He was sure that Freddie could hear it....

"Oh, we might have to accommodate the Amazon...Well, I *had* to ask her; it would have appeared churlish otherwise...No, no, I don't think she'll accept, but just in case, you might arrange something with that dotty old uncle of yours—the one who still thinks we're fighting the Boers."

Freddie's voice lowered slightly, and Andrew had to strain to make out what he was saying.

"...Well, if all goes according to plan, by this time next week, you'll be getting a crack at Mata Hari, and I'll be finding out if the Farmer's daughter is a natural blond—"

What was Freddie saying? He seemed to be talking through clenched teeth.

"...It'll be cracking great fun, Maurice, but consider it also as doing our bit for King and Country—"

Andrew held his breath.

"...Well, after what the Yanks have been doing to *our* women, I think it's time we evened the score!"

He heard the car pull up. The last thing he felt like doing was going downstairs to tea, but he knew if he did not put in an appearance, and Kaz came upstairs looking for him, Freddie might get suspicious. He had made it clear that he expected Andrew to come to tea....

He snapped his mathematics book shut, and walked out of his room and downstairs to tea. The purposefulness of his step belied his heavyheartedness. He forced a smile as he entered the dining room. Freddie sauntered in, carrying a tray with glasses and a full decanter of brandy. Irene and Marlys were seated at the table.

"Where's Kaz?" Andrew asked.

"She went out to the kitchen," Marlys replied, as she accepted a glass of brandy.

Andrew wondered whether to go looking for her; he was afraid that anything he did might be misinterpreted by Freddie as a prelude to spilling the beans. His dilemma was solved by Kaz's appearance through the door to the kitchen. She carried a tea-pot, and smiled at Andrew. "Andrew! Are you feeling all right?"

"Yes—I'm fine." He turned away from her, and addressed Marlys and Irene.

"Did you still have to pick all that stuff out of the ground today?"

"Nope," Irene laughed. "They finally freed the slaves and got these giant magnets to do the dirty work."

"Giant magnets!" Freddie exclaimed.

"They're towed behind a tractor," Irene said. "The brass finally put together the few dozen brain cells they have between them, and got the brilliant idea that magnets could pick the stuff out of the ground better than underpaid field hands."

"Not so brilliant," Marlys countered. "Magnets don't pick up glass—"

"Shhhh," Irene hissed. "They might hear you!"

Freddie chuckled and proffered a glass of brandy to Kaz. She declined. Mrs. Tuttle came in with their tea things, and the meal proceeded. Freddie was ever so charming; Irene and Marlys were friendly in return (or perhaps they were being polite?); Kaz was close-mouthed. Over the second pot of tea, Freddie again broached the subject of Irene and Marlys spending some time in London: "I talked with Maurice today; I hope I wasn't being premature in telling him all about you. He is ever so eager to make your acquaintance—" He focused his attention on Marlys. "He positively extolled the California scenery—I must give him a holiday there soon. He remembers our visit there as being one of the most enjoyable times he's ever known. I must see to it that he has another holiday there soon. More tea?" Marlys nodded, and Freddie filled her cup. He raised the teapot in query to Irene, and she accepted also.

"Well, I don't want to press, but please consider it. Maurice has been working ever so hard lately, and I feel a little guilty about the business concerns that I've heaped upon him. I do owe him a holiday, and he does so want to make your acquaintance."

Kaz stood up and said, "Andrew, we need to get cracking on your math homework. Come on."

Andrew followed her to his room. Once inside, she shut the door and sat on his bed. She folded her hands, and her expression grew very serious. "Andrew, is something wrong?"

Andrew took a quick breath and answered, "I...I'm still upset about my father, that's all. And about what happened yesterday."

"Freddie said that you've done this sort of thing before, and that you sleepwalk too. Is that true?"

Andrew shrugged. "I guess."

Kaz lifted one eyebrow, half-quizzically, half-disbelieving. "I talked with Mrs. Tuttle; she said you've *never* done anything like this before, and that you don't sleepwalk either." She waited for Andrew's reply. Seeing that none was forthcoming, she went on. "She also said that Freddie had a little chat with you this morning. He put on some music, turned it up loud, which she thought was somewhat unusual. She got the distinct impression that it was not a very—" She paused, then said softly, "Friendly conversation. What's going on, Andrew?"

"Nothing!" Afraid that his intense reaction might have fueled Kaz's concerns, Andrew added softly, "Nothing—I mean...well, he was just a little upset about me going off yesterday, that's all."

"Mrs. Tuttle didn't think Freddie was upset at all. In fact, she thinks that he's—" Kaz took a deep breath, as if searching for the right words. "He's trying to scare you...threatening you, maybe?" She reached for Andrew's hand, and squeezed it. "Is he?"

Andrew nodded furiously. "No—*NO!*" He racked his brain trying to think of an explanation. "He was just worried. He doesn't act all upset when he's worried. I mean, you might be sometimes worried about things when you're flying, I mean if something goes wrong, but you don't get upset, right?"

The probing look Kaz gave him indicated that she agreed with Andrew's answer, but was not entirely convinced of the truth of his denials. She squeezed his hand again and said, "Well, if you ever want to talk, let me know, okay? Now, let's look at your math assignment."

"...Well, I think it would be fun. I think Freddie's being very kind and sincere...."

Andrew was heading down the hall to the bathroom and the women's voices filtered through the closed door. Not that he was intending to eavesdrop, but....

"...So he stuck his foot in his mouth at first! Happens to the best of us. I think that deep down inside, he's a very caring person—"

"Sure Irene—he cares about one thing!" Kaz's voice was heavy with sarcasm.

"No, really! When we were looking for Andrew, he was very troubled and concerned."

"Freddie told me that he was only eight when his own father died," Marlys added. "He knows what it's like growing up without a father, and I think he feels responsible for Andrew, in a way. Gosh, it must be hard on Andrew, what with all he's been through."

Andrew heard footfalls on the stairs and beat a hasty retreat to his room. Freddie's voice sounded at the end of the hall. "Ladies—supper is ready. I have an exquisite St. Emilion that has just reached its peak—"

"Coming!" Irene and Marlys shouted in unison.

Andrew heard a knock on his door. "Come in," he said.

Irene entered. She was wearing a shirtwaist dress, white with tiny pink rosebuds on it, which she often wore when she changed into something more comfortable after teatime. It accentuated her coloring beautifully, and it gave Andrew a stab to know Freddie would think so, too.

"Coming to supper, Andrew?"

"No...I didn't get much sleep last night. I think I'll turn in now."

She crossed the room to Andrew's desk, where Andrew was seated, and, putting her arms around him, gently brushed a kiss on his cheek. "Well, get a good night's sleep, okay? The poker games just aren't the same without you."

"All right." He turned around to give her a hug. "Goodnight."

"Goodnight—see you in the morning light," she whispered. She left, and Andrew heard Kaz's voice: "Isn't he coming to supper?"

"No, he says he's going to go to bed; he's still pretty tired..." Irene's voice faded on the stairs. In the distance, Freddie voiced some sort of solicitous query.

Andrew shoved the chair back from his desk, grabbed his geography book, and settled down on his bed. Perhaps trying to memorize South American capitals would settle his mind.

He had just opened the book when there was a knock on the door.

"Come in."

Kaz entered. "Are you sure you don't want to have supper?"

He nodded. "I didn't get much of a nap. I was trying to catch up on my school-work."

"Well then, I'll say goodnight, in case you drop off before we finish supper." She walked to the bed, leaned over, and gave Andrew a hug.

He returned her embrace; then, to his dismay, a lone tear leaked out of his eye. He nuzzled his face against her shoulder, hoping she wouldn't notice.

But she had. "Andrew, honey, what's wrong?"

He blinked, trying to hold back the tears, but only succeeded in bringing on a veritable waterworks. The tears splashed down his cheeks; he moaned, and buried his face against her shoulder.

"I'm tired...I'm just tired, that's all...please don't tell anyone else—please...It's just...I haven't thought about him in such a long time, and I tried to forget what happened, that's all...."

Kaz held him close as he shuddered and gasped. Then she stroked his hair. "It all makes me feel so—" she sighed deeply, "so terrible, in a way. I was just thrilled at the chance to join the ATA, but it makes me feel guilty, you know, that it took a war for women to be allowed to do the jobs that men did. It's only because there aren't enough men pilots to do the work that we have the opportunities we have. Up until now, it was all abstract to me. I just focused on my flying, and I was so thrilled that I was chosen to be a ferry pilot. When it hits home that the only reason that I have this chance is because of a stupid war that's taking the lives of so many men—men like your father, it doesn't seem right. I wish you could have your father back, somehow."

Andrew squeezed her. "I wish he could see Mum—he'd be ever so proud. If he were here to have a say about things, he'd let women do anything they wanted. He and Mum used to take turns flying the Puss Moth we had, and he was happy that she was a pilot too, because then he didn't have to fly it all the time."

"It sounds like he was—" Kaz smiled. "As we would say, quite a guy."

Andrew nodded, and reached over to his treasure box. "I want to show you something." He got the key out of the top drawer of his nightstand and opened the box. "These are my special things." He took out the shaving brush and mug. "These belong to my father. Mum let me have them. This is his handkerchief, and his letters. Here's my flag; I got it on my tenth birthday. Here's a newspaper clipping with Mum's picture and here's a book from Mr. Churchill, and a letter, too. I wrote to him and he wrote back."

Kaz smiled. "What about the other book?"

Andrew took the volume of poetry selections, and opened it to the page with the bookmark. "It's my father's." He showed Kaz the bookmark. "I made this for him, when he went back to France, just after my birthday. Those are his initials, and I carved the roundel at the bottom." He creased the page of the book open, and gave it to Kaz. She gazed at the poem, then read it aloud. Her voice was deep, with an almost masculine resonance, and imbued the words with a sort of...promise, as if it were his father speaking to him. When she reached the last line: *I can't imagine a dawn in spring, without my heart awakening,* her voice dropped to a hush, as if she were saying a prayer.

She replaced the bookmark, and gently closed the book. "That's very beautiful."

A strange sort of peace washed over Andrew; not exactly freedom from fear, but a sense of safety, at least for the moment. He knew that he would have to face all the distressing realities sooner or later. But for the moment, an oasis of calm surrounded him, and he drifted off to sleep in Kaz's arms.

He awoke in darkness, and noted the time on the clock: two-thirty. He heard the squeak of a floorboard in the hallway, and his blood froze.

What if Freddie's coming to get me?

The distant sound of water running allayed his fears somewhat: Somebody had to pay a late night call to the W.C., that's all.

What if he tries to do something? I could scream—scream bloody murder. That's assuming I'm awake, though, and able to scream....

What if he tiptoes in here, puts his hand over my mouth while I'm asleep, jabs me in the backside with a needle, then drags me out....

He flung back the bedclothes, his heart hammering.

A warning—if only I had a warning he was coming....

He cautiously opened his door and, seeing no one, crept down the hall and stole down the backstairs.

There were a few high stools in the storeroom next to the kitchen, he knew. Also some old crockery, and a few old carving knives, as well.

He took the stool up to his room in the first trip. Returning to the storeroom, he fetched an old chipped teapot and a nasty-looking knife. He placed the stool against his door and set the teapot on top of it, near the edge.

That should make a great bloody crash if someone tries to open the door.

Andrew regarded his alarm system for a moment. The floor was hardwood, and the teapot should break if it were knocked over; then again, it seemed fairly sturdy. If only he could be sure, but the only way to test it would be to destroy it. What to do?

Then he remembered: He had a box of marbles on the top shelf of his closet. He had considered himself to have outgrown such childish amusements, which was why they'd been put away. Good thing he hadn't seen fit to part with them—they could certainly be put to good use now....

He carried his desk chair over to the closet and retrieved the box from the top shelf. He got the teapot, sat cross-legged on the rug by his bed, and carefully placed the marbles within. He then set the teapot on the stool again.

When those marbles go clattering across the floor, it ought to wake up the whole house!

He decided to put the knife under his pillow. Before tucking it away, he inspected it critically. It was huge—ought to do a lot of damage. He gently ran his finger along the edge of the blade...sharp, too...He imagined himself, slashing away while Freddie went skidding on the marbles....

What if he somehow manages to grab the knife away from me? He's more than twice my size...Even if he's flailing around, he still might be able to take it away from me...If only I could even things up a bit....

After removing the stool and teapot to the corner of his room, he retraced his route to the storeroom and cast his eyes over the shelves, not exactly sure what he was looking for. Then he saw the jugs of cleaning solutions on one of the top shelves.

Bleach! He remembered once, when he was bored and restless, following Lucia around as she did her chores. He had looked too closely as she'd cleaned the bathroom, and a drop of bleach had splashed into his eye. Lucia then had to hold his face under running water for several minutes to take the sting away. What to put it in, though; that whole jug wouldn't do....

There were some jam jars with latched lids in a box on the floor. He picked one up, flipped open the metal latch, poured some bleach into the jar, and replaced the lid.

He carried the jar up to his room and placed it on the floor, underneath his bed but within easy reach. Then he set the stool and teapot back by his door and put the knife under his pillow.

There!

He had drawn blood once on Freddie.

It would be easy to do it again.

"Andrew, what say we play a few hands of poker tonight? We're getting awfully stale." Marlys passed the Ginger Cream to Andrew.

Andrew glanced at Freddie, noting the mouth drawn into a flat line. Completely in the dark as to Freddie's feelings about the matter, he shrugged.

"Come on, ma li'l poker playin' fiend." Irene winked at him. To prevaricate at this point would cause suspicion, he realized. He really wanted to play, but then again....

"Well, let him finish dessert, first," Kaz said. "How about it, Andrew, just a few rounds, okay?"

Andrew felt as if he were staggering under the burden of having to weigh every single thing he did, of having to be so concerned as to how Freddie might interpret things. It was as if his life were jumping from one awful decision-making ordeal to another: when, and where, to have breakfast, lunch (he had taken that in the kitchen too, having decided that Mrs. Tuttle's worried glaces were more tolerable than the thought of another confrontation with Freddie), supper...and now, whether or not to enjoy a friendly game of poker. And how long should he play? To play only a game or two would make the women concerned; to play longer might arouse Freddie's suspicions.

Damned if you do, and damned if you don't....

He shoveled the last spoonful of Ginger Cream into his mouth.

Wish Freddie would disappear in a puff of smoke....

"Come on, Andrew," Irene urged. "Just a few games."

If only Dad were here!

Marlys grabbed his hand and pulled him upstairs to Kaz's room. Irene and Kaz followed.

Best not to protest...Freddie might get suspicious....

Okay, it's five card draw, aces wild." Irene sat on the floor, shuffled the cards, and dealt.

"Well, what have you two made up your minds to do for vacation?" Kaz sat down beside her.

Marlys picked up her cards and squinted at them. "Oh, we've decided to accept Freddie's invitation. It's only for two days."

"Two days with Freddie? I wouldn't trust him for two minutes," Kaz tossed down a card. "I'll take one."

"Oh, he can be a bit pushy," Marlys said. "But I can take care of myself. I'd just like to see the sights in London, and Freddie knows his way around."

"I'll bet he does!" retorted Kaz.

Marlys put down three of her cards, picked up the three Irene dealt her, and pursed her lips as she added them to the cards she'd kept. She always pursed her lips when she had a bad hand. "I don't think he'll be any trouble."

"Andrew?" Irene asked.

"What?"

"How many cards do you want?"

"Um...none—I mean one. Two!"

"Do I hear three?" Marlys laughed. Kaz raised an eyebrow.

"Two." He bit his lip.

"He invited you too, Kaz," Irene said.

Kaz glared at her cards. "He's bluffing."

"Why don't you take him up on it, then?" Marlys pressed.

"What, call his bluff?" Kaz shrugged. "It might be fun to see him squirm."

"You mean you'll go?" Marlys asked.

"No...just pretend I like the idea. Maybe I should drag it out a bit. Keep him guessing. The thought of him tossing and turning, wondering if he's really going to be stuck with me for a couple of days..." She scrunched her face at her cards. "Might prove to be a jolly good show."

"Come on Kaz, it sounds like it'll be a great time!" Irene urged.

Andrew held his breath. The only hope he had for the situation was if Kaz went along. Her presence might be enough to deter Freddie. She would surely look out for the others...unless Freddie sent her off with Maurice's dotty uncle.

"Naah."

"What do you think, Andrew?"

"Huh?"

"About Freddie—do you think we can trust him?" Marlys laughed.

His heart started pounding. If only they hadn't asked him!

Fear knifed through him. Freddie had meant to scare him with his threats about sleeping powders, but he suddenly realized: *What if he's planning on using something like that on them?* He remembered Freddie's sniggering recounting of how he had calmed his "distressed little friend" during an air raid. Freddie had seemed so sure of things too, when he'd talked with Maurice: There was no question whatsoever of the women refusing...A hideous image assaulted him: Irene and Marlys, their unconscious forms slumped on the floor, Freddie standing over them, triumphant. A sob welled up within him. He tried to hold it back, but it broke, like a torrent tearing a dam to bits. He collapsed against Kaz.

"Andrew, what's the matter?" Kaz's arms went around him.

If only his body hadn't betrayed him...betrayed his mother! "Andrew, honey, what's the matter?" Irene asked.

Andrew was horrified by the words that came out of his mouth; it seemed as if a demon inside of him were doing the talking: "Please don't tell him that I told you!"

"Tell who, what?" Irene asked.

All of a sudden, Andrew experienced the same sort of out-of control feeling of seeing his world fly apart that he'd had when he'd been bombed. He took a deep breath and said, "Freddie. I heard him talking about how he was going to, well, you know... He wanted to get you into his bomb shelter and then he could, he could, I mean, if you were frightened and upset...I heard him talking about using some—something—he puts it in a drink, and then it—it would be easy to...to—" He looked at Irene and begged, "Please don't go!"

Irene's mouth dropped open in shock. "A mickey?"

Marlys hissed, "That *bastard!*"

Andrew went on. "He told his friend Maurice that he could take Marlys even though he—Freddie, I mean—usually likes the exotic types but that he preferred Irene because he thought it would be a nice change to see how it would be with someone who was, well, he said—he said something about Iowa naivete being amusing—" The words gurgled out him like water out of a fountain. "...And pro—provincial, he said."

Irene was livid. "*Provincial!* Why that low-down, *scum-sucking*— He wants to see *provincial*, I'll give him a little *provincial* knee in the b—"

"*Don't!*" Andrew shouted. He lowered his voice. "If he knows that I warned you he'll, he'll—"

"He'll what?" Kaz asked.

Andrew lowered his eyes. It was already awful enough that he'd told of Freddie's plot, but to tell *everything*! Something stayed him from telling the worst of Freddie's threats: It was so vaguely hinted at, so muddled and mixed up, that Andrew was afraid that if he pulled all the tangled threads together, his thoughts alone would bring doom upon himself. An even greater fear ravaged him: *They wouldn't believe it...They wouldn't believe me! As smarmy as Freddie is, they would never believe that he would be capable of such a thing...*He forced that to the periphery of his mental whirlwind and said evenly, "He'll bother my mother again. He promised not to bother my mother anymore if I kept quiet about what he was planning to do with—with Irene and Marlys."

"What do you mean, *bother* your mother?" Kaz asked.

He had forced Freddie's threats against himself deep down to the depths of cold rationality, but the terror bubbled up and interfused itself with his anxiety for his mother. He now felt a sense of utter panic at the thought of Freddie wanting her, as if that were a threat against his own life. The words poured out again. "He keeps trying to get her to—to—but she *won't* but he keeps pressuring her. I heard him say that she's lonely and misses my father and that sooner or later, he—*he'll*—" he choked, and burst out: "He was even bothering her before my father went missing. When my father got called back to his squadron because of Dunkirk, Freddie tried to get her to stay in London with him. He dropped a key in her pocket but she threw it away!"

"That *creep*!" Marlys was livid. She turned to Kaz. "Well, I wonder what his plans were for you? Divide you in two or auction you off to the highest bidder?"

Kaz snorted. "I'm not his type. Too tall and flat-chested, I think!"

"No sense of humor either," Andrew blurted out. The words were tumbling out so fast he couldn't help it. He looked at Kaz, sorry for his outburst; she arched an eyebrow at him.

Irene announced, "Well, I'm going to march *right* down and tell Freddie that he can take his hidey-hole and his mickey and stuff it right up his—"

"No, *NO!* If he realizes you're on to him, he'll know I told you about him!" Andrew said. "Then he'll start bothering my mother! I just want him to leave her alone!" The terror for his own safety had now merged fully into the fear he had for his mother, so that any menace to her was a threat to his own existence. As the horror of it all savaged him, he slumped forward and closed his eyes, felt the darkness close in. Kaz's voice, steady and crisp, brought him back from the edge of the abyss.

"Andrew's right. I don't think that the frontal attack is the way to deal with this."

"Well, what should we do?" Irene asked.

Kaz seemed deep in thought. All eyes were upon her. She finally spoke.

"I think we should give Freddie a taste of his own medicine."

"How are we going to do that?" Marlys said.

Kaz looked at Marlys and Irene, and then at Andrew. A smile slowly spread across her face. She lowered her voice and said, "I have a plan."

Chapter 15

The next morning, Andrew awoke, excited—no,thrilled! Kaz's plan was perfect, absolutely *perfect!* He couldn't wait for the women to return that evening, and rehearsed over and over in his mind what was supposed to happen and what he was supposed to do. He hoped Freddie would stick to his usual routine.

He went downstairs and joined Kaz, Marlys, Irene, and Freddie for breakfast. The women chatted about the different types of American and British fighter planes, comparing the P-47 to the Hurricane and Spitfire. The discussion centered for the most part on the advantages and disadvantages of inline vs. radial engines.

"An inline engine is more streamlined," Irene said.

"But you don't need coolant with a radial engine. One less thing to worry about," countered Kaz.

"But with that radial engine, a P-47 can be easily mistaken for a Folke-Wulf 190," Irene rejoined. I sure hope some trigger-happy American gunner doesn't shoot down one of our own planes by mistake!"

"Well, having an inline engine doesn't guarantee that a twitchy gunner isn't going to make that mistake anyway. You can just as easily mistake a Spit or a Hurricane for a 109." Marlys said.

"Yeah, but still, the P-47's isn't as good as the Spit," Kaz threw a casual glance at Freddie as she spoke.

"So you think the British have better airplanes than the Americans?" Freddie asked Kaz.

"As far as the fighters are concerned, right now they do," Kaz replied.

"I don't think I'd be happy flying P-47's if I'd been used to flying Spits." Irene reached for a scone. "I've heard that the pilots in the Eagle Squadrons are not exactly thrilled with them,"

"Well, they're a piece of cake compared to flying P-39s," Kaz said.

"P-39s!" Irene sputtered. "You can't be serious!"

"A P-39, now is that like a P-40?" asked Freddie.

"No," Marlys replied. "P-40s—they're also called Tomahawks or Kittyhawks, depending on the model—were the fighters used by the Flying Tigers in China. Pretty good against the Japanese fighters."

"But not so good against a Me-109." Kaz looked directly at Freddie. "Compared to German fighters, P-40s are underpowered. They're better suited to ground attacks." Usually Kaz evidenced a mild disdain for Freddie whenever he was around and never attempted to include him in conversation, but this morning she was actually being sociable with him. Not overly so—that would arouse suspicion—but just friendly enough to give the impression that she was willing to forget past slights. Freddie didn't seem wary of her change in behavior; in fact, he was equally nice and polite to her in return, and joined in the conversation.

"Now, the P-39 has an engine that's mounted behind the cockpit," Kaz explained to Freddie. "So the center of gravity is farther back, which makes the plane very unstable. It tumbles easily—"

"And your ass is grass if you get into a spin," Irene said.

Andrew knew enough about aerodynamics to know that mounting the engine behind the cockpit made for very different flying characteristics, and that there might be trouble if a pilot was not familiar with the form. He tried to recall if his mother had ever mentioned flying any P-39s. She, though, usually referred to planes by their names, as the British did; the Americans called their planes by the letter and number designation.

"What's the name of the P-39?" he asked.

"The Airacobra," Marlys replied.

Airacobra? The name didn't sound familiar, either, but then....

"Does my mother have to fly Airacobras?" he asked.

Marlys shook her head. "No, I don't think she does. At least she hasn't mentioned that she's flown one."

"Yeah, that Alice is a real type-catcher," Irene said.

"Type-catcher?" Andrew asked.

"She likes to fly as many different types of planes as she can," Marlys told him. "We're not allowed to pick and choose what types of planes we fly—we fly whatever we're given—but some pilots prefer to get the familiar, and others like the challenge of flying different kinds of planes."

"So what about this Airacobra?" Freddie asked.

"The Americans couldn't even *give* them away to the British in Lend Lease," Kaz said. "They finally gave some of them to the Russians and, as for the rest, someone got the brilliant idea that they would be very useful in North Africa, so some American pilots had to fly about sixteen of them across Spain and Portugal. About half of them were forced down because of engine failure, mechanical problems, what-have-you."

"Shoot, P-39s, P-47s." Irene rolled her eyes. "Boy, I don't think that I'd want to fly with the Americans right now. I bet Jake is glad he's still with the RAF!"

"Who's Jake?" Andrew asked.

Irene bit her lip and looked quickly at Kaz and Marlys. *Uh-oh*, her eyes seemed to say. There was a momentary silence; then Kaz said quickly, "Oh, he's a friend of ours. An American. He's a fighter pilot in the RAF."

"I thought all of the Yanks were with the Eagle Squadrons. Weren't they transferred over to the American Air Force last summer?" Freddie asked.

"Not all of the pilots in the Eagle Squadrons transferred to over to the AAF," Kaz replied. And there are some Americans in the regular RAF squadrons who never even joined the Eagles. A few of them joined the RAF before the Eagle Squadrons were formed, and even fought in the Battle of Britain." She then went on to tell some funny stories about the exploits and mishaps of American pilots. Freddie listened intently and laughed at all the funny parts.

Good, thought Andrew. *Very good.*

After breakfast, Irene followed Freddie into the study and Andrew heard them talking and laughing. She came out after a few minutes and met Andrew, Kaz, and Marlys in the front hallway. "Dinner at eight!" she whispered excitedly. "Freddie's going to have Mrs. Tuttle serve us in the study."

Kaz and Marlys smiled.

The car arrived, and the women hurried out the front door. Andrew waved to them as the car pulled away. Irene answered him with a V-for-Victory sign. Now, to find a way to make the day go by quickly, he thought. He worked on mathematics for about an hour, then translated a few passages in his Latin book. Mrs. Tuttle called him downstairs for lunch at noon; afterwards he went upstairs and curled up in bed and read more of *Great Expectations*.

"Great Expectations!" Andrew thought, as he mind turned again to the plan already set in motion for the evening. It would be the first step in realizing his own great expectations: for Freddie to stop bullying him and for his mother to be safe from Freddie's lecherous attentions. Maybe his father would return before long! He went over to the window and looked out on the driveway, remembering the last time his father had come home. He imagined what it would be like to see his father coming up the front steps again, to see him wave and smile and open his arms wide....

The afternoon hours passed by very slowly. A little after six, he heard the sound of a car in the driveway. He looked out the window and, as expected, he saw only Kaz and Marlys get out of the car. Irene was nowhere to be seen, but Andrew knew that she was curled up on the floor of the car. He ran downstairs to greet Kaz and Marlys. They were chattering about what a busy day it had been for them. Freddie, who had been working in the study, came into the hallway and, not seeing Irene with them, inquired of them as to where she was.

"Oh, she got stuck out," Marlys said. "She won't be back until tomorrow."

"Stuck out?" Freddie queried.

"She had to ferry a plane to a maintenance unit and couldn't get a ride back tonight," Kaz explained.

Freddie evidenced a mild disappointment. Marlys flashed him a brilliant smile. "Boy, what a day! I could use a drink!"

"Scotch?" Freddie asked.

"Lots of it!" Marlys told him. "You pour!"

"I'd be delighted," Freddie murmured. He put his arm around Marlys's shoulder and they walked together into the drawing room.

The door closed behind them and Andrew ran into the study. Freddie's reading glasses, where were they? There, on the desk! Andrew grabbed them and stuffed them under his shirt. He ran down the hall into the kitchen and out to the back door. Kaz was waiting for him. "All clear, Andrew?"

Andrew nodded. "They're in the drawing room."

Kaz opened the door and waved at the garage. A few seconds later, Irene made a dash for the house. She took the porch steps two at a time. "Everything in place?" she asked, breathless.

"They're in the drawing room," Kaz said. "I expect that Marlys has finagled an invitation to dinner by now."

Irene smiled and ran up the back stairs. After a few minutes, Andrew and Kaz heard Freddie and Marlys come out into the hallway.

"Let's make it eight-thirty," Marlys said. "I'm beat, and a hot bath and a good nap would really put me in a better mood."

"Eight-thirty, then," Freddie replied.

"Oh, would you be a dear and come upstairs and tap on my door a little after eight? I'm a very sound sleeper, and I wouldn't want to be late."

"Glad to oblige." Freddie sounded very pleased with the change of plans for the evening.

They heard Marlys walk up the stairs and Freddie walk back into the study. Andrew sauntered down the hall to the drawing room and put Freddie's glasses on the mantle. He left the room just as Kaz entered. She winked at him.

"Time to reel him in," she muttered.

Andrew grinned.

As he walked into the hallway and past the study, he heard Freddie grumbling. Peeking in, Andrew asked, "May I read the evening paper?"

"After I'm finished," Freddie snapped. "I can't read it until I find my glasses!" He looked under a stack of papers and swore.

"I think I saw them in the drawing room," Andrew said.

Freddie grunted and strode out of the study and into the drawing room.

Andrew tiptoed back into the hallway. The door to the drawing room was opened a bit. He positioned himself behind the door and observed the scene through the crack between the hinges.

Kaz was on the floor on her hands and knees, tears in her eyes. "Where could it be?" she fretted. "It must be in here. It's the only place it could possibly be!"

"Lost something?" Freddie inquired.

Kaz nodded. "My mother's locket. It's very special. It's the only thing I have to remember her by." She looked up at Freddie, despair in her eyes. "She died when I was ten."

"I'm very sorry," Freddie said gently. "It must have been rough for you—growing up, I mean."

"It wasn't easy, most of the time. My father was too busy running his business to have time for me, so I was on my own. The happiest times I can remember were a few sailing vacations we took in New England."

"You like boating, then?"

"Oh, yes! When this war is over I'd like to get my own sailboat, live near the ocean somewhere, and take to the sea whenever I get the urge!"

"What a splendid idea! I keep a yacht in London, but I don't get much chance to get away. The war has rather taken a bite out of my free time. When it's over I hope to cruise up and down the Thames whenever I please!"

"Let's hope it's over very soon!"

"Hear, hear!"

They both laughed and Kaz said, "I'm really sorry we got off to a bad start. It was my fault—I wasn't on my best behavior."

"No, it was *my* fault entirely!" protested Freddie. "I apologize." He sat down next to her.

She gently laid her fingers on his arm. "No, it was mine. I wasn't in a very good mood that day, and I took it out on you."

"Well, this nasty weather of ours is enough to spoil anyone's humor."

No, no. It wasn't that. It was—" Kaz's voice caught in her throat. "It was something personal."

"Anything you'd care to talk about?"

Kaz was silent for a moment; then tears rolled down her cheeks. "I'd just gotten a letter from my fiance. He wanted to break things off."

Freddie's hand was on her shoulder. "I'm sorry."

Kaz sniffled and wiped her eyes. "Well, you see, we were engaged to be married, but we already had—" She sniffled again. "I mean, we were—" she paused, and lowered her voice. "Together."

"I see," Freddie sympathized.

Marlys tiptoed to Andrew's side and peered through the crack. Andrew whispered, "She's terrific! How does she do that?"

"She did some acting before she got interested in flying. Summer stock and some off-Broadway stuff. She's amazing! She can even cry on cue. You should see her when she *really* turns the faucets on!"

Andrew turned around and saw Irene just around the corner at the top of the stairs, waiting for their signal. He also noticed Mrs. Tuttle, Lucia, and Thomas at the far end of the hall.

"I let them in on the secret," Marlys explained. "They want to see the fireworks too."

Mrs. Tuttle and Thomas crept silently into the dining room, where they could hear things better through the door that adjoined onto the drawing room. Lucia worked her way down the hall, dusting pictures very meticulously.

By now Kaz's voice was quavering. "It's just so difficult, being alone again. When you're used to being with someone like that, it's—it's the worst thing in the world to know that it's over, and that there will never be any hope of—" She turned away from Freddie.

Marlys nodded at Irene, who tiptoed down the stairs to join them. She bent down and peeked through the crack.

"...There, there." Freddie put his arms around Kaz's shoulders and held her close. He glanced at his watch.

"I'm sorry." Kaz made an effort to compose herself. "I shouldn't be laying my troubles on your shoulders."

"They're big enough to hold them," Freddie murmured tenderly.

"Now?" whispered Andrew.

"Marlys shook her head. "No, wait."

Kaz's face brightened. "There it is! Under the cabinet!"

She got up and walked over to massive, ornate cabinet Freddie's father had brought back from India. She bent over and peered underneath it. "It's all the way towards the back."

"Here, I'll move it for you," Freddie said.

"Oh, I don't think there's any need. It's just high enough off the floor for me to squeeze under it. See?" She laid down on the floor, on her stomach, and inched her way underneath. "I've got it!" she exclaimed. "Uh-oh. It's one thing to get in, but I can't seem to get out! Oh dear, I feel like such an idiot!"

"Here, let me help," said Freddie. He grabbed her legs and started to pull her out.

"No wait, my knees—my knees—don't pull at them. Just reach under and grab me by the waist."

Freddie cooperated, and soon Kaz was free. At once she turned over onto her back and, as she did, she hooked her foot around Freddie's leg and pulled him down on top of her.

"Oh, I'm sorry, I'm sorry! How clumsy of me!" she cried.

Freddie lifted up and bit and rested his weight on his right arm. "I didn't hurt you, did I?" he asked.

"No, I'm fine, really, I'm all right." She looked into his eyes. "Are you all right?"

Freddie's response was to brush back a strand of her hair that had fallen across her face. She closed her eyes, and Freddie ran his finger gently along her lips. Then he bent his head down and kissed her.

Kaz responded with a passionate, open-mouthed, lingering kiss that lasted—well, longer than was absolutely necessary.

"Shoot!" Irene whispered. "I thought she was just going to *kiss* him, not knock his *socks off!*"

Marlys, her mouth agape, was staring at the scene. Irene seemed momentarily mesmerized, too, then she elbowed Marlys.

"Go—*GO!*" she hissed.

Marlys launched herself into the room.

"Freddie, on second thought, let's make that nine—" Marlys gasped at the sight of Freddie and Kaz intertwined with each other on the floor. "Oh, my *God!* What, so Kaz is the appetizer and I'm the main course? You cad! You *creep!*"

Irene winked at Andrew, then burst into the room as Kaz and Freddie were struggling to get up off the floor. "Freddie, I thought I wouldn't be able to make it but—" Her expression froze and she lashed out, "Why you two-timing—"

"Make that three-timing," Marlys interrupted.

"Weasly, slimy, low-down, bag of scum-infested, no good—"

"Bastard!" finished Marlys.

Appearing appropriately flustered and apologetic, Kaz made a great show of getting up off the floor. "I'm sorry!" she pleaded with Marlys and Irene. "Please don't be angry—I didn't know!"

"We're not mad at *you*," Marlys huffed. "Mr. Man-About-Town apparently thinks it would be amusing to see how many women he can put the moves on in the shortest period of time! Well, Freddie, hope we didn't spoil your average! Better luck next time!"

Freddie, speechless with distress, lurched towards Irene. He clutched at her arm, beseeching her for understanding.

"Get your paws off me, buster, or your *ass* is *grass!*" She flung his hand back.

Marlys and Irene stormed out of the room. Kaz followed them, looking back at Freddie with regret and sympathy. "I'm sorry," she whispered in a choked voice.

Andrew scurried down the hallway to the kitchen. He heard the door to the study slam shut. A few seconds later, Mrs. Tuttle, Lucia, and Thomas joined him. Mrs. Tuttle was laughing so hard that tears rolled down her cheeks.

"Now I can die with a smile on my face! It does these poor old bones good to see that bounder finally get the tables turned on him!"

Andrew ran up the backstairs and into Kaz's room, where the women had gathered.

"Shhh, keep it down," warned Kaz. They made a supreme effort to lower their voices as they laughed, and they took turns recalling the look on Freddie's face when Marlys and Irene had burst into the room.

"You were wonderful!" Andrew threw his arms around Kaz. "I'm just so glad that everything is going to be all right and that Irene and Marlys aren't going off with Freddie and that he won't be angry with me and bother my mother again!"

Kaz hugged him back. "It was wrong of Freddie to put that on you, to make you feel responsible for protecting your mother.

"Just the same, I'm so happy that everything is going to be all right."

"Sure, everything is going to be all right," Irene agreed. "Don't you worry about your mother! She's not the *least* bit interested in Freddie right now."

Kaz shot her a look of warning, and Andrew wondered briefly what she was so concerned about. She looked back at Andrew and said, "If it will make you feel any better, I'll have a talk with her the next time I see her, and tell her what Freddie was up to. You don't have anything to worry about!"

"Thanks," he exclaimed. "Thanks, all of you for helping!"

"A pleasure!" Marlys squeezed his arm. "What are friends for? Beside, it was terrific fun!"

"This calls for a celebration!" Irene announced. "I got a package from home today. A month's supply of Hershey bars!" She started to get up and then said, "Shoot! I left them on base! Well, we can have a celebration tomorrow!"

"Hershey bars!" Andrew's mouth watered at the thought.

Speaking of eating, we'll have to go downstairs and eat dinner pretty soon," Kaz reminded them. "It's important to keep a straight face in case Freddie is there."

"You're asking the impossible," Irene told her. "It'll be a effort to keep from rolling on the floor in hysterics!"

"I know!" Marlys said. "Let's have dinner up here. We could tell the servants to tell Freddie, in case he asks, that we're all too upset to sit down to dinner."

Mrs. Tuttle happily accommodated their request to take supper upstairs, and they all carried the dishes and food up the backstairs to Kaz's room. Irene threw an old sheet onto the floor, and they ate picnic-style. As they talked into the late hours of the night, Andrew's head began to nod. Irene tucked him into bed.

"Sleep tight," she whispered. "See you in the morning light." She gave him a kiss on the forehead.

Andrew was awakened the next morning by the sound of a car pulling into the driveway. He jumped out of bed and looked outside the window. Kaz, Marlys, and Irene were getting into their car. He had overslept!

He opened the window and called, "Irene!"

She turned around and waved to him.

"Don't forget the chocolate!" he reminded her.

"Don't worry, I won't!" she called.

Andrew went downstairs. Freddie was nowhere to be found.

"He left for London early this morning," Mrs. Tuttle chuckled. "Didn't say goodbye to anybody—I wonder why?"

For Andrew, it was the best day he'd had in a long time. The burden of protecting his mother and keeping silent about Freddie's nefarious plans was off his shoulders and, best of all, Freddie was gone. He finished reading *Great Expectations*, went down to lunch, then in the afternoon did three French lessons and studied a new list of spelling words. Lucia came into his room to dust. As she worked, she chuckled to herself and said over and over: "Get your hands off me, buster, or your ass is grass."

He was leafing through his geography book when he heard the sound of the women's car pulling up to the house. He had almost forgotten! *Hershey bars!* He ran downstairs as Kaz and Marlys came in through the front door.

"Where's Irene?" he asked. "Did she really get stuck out tonight?"

Marlys burst into tears and ran up the stairs. Andrew noticed that Kaz's eyes were red-rimmed.

"What happened?" Andrew asked. He felt his heart skip a beat. "Where's Irene?"

Kaz took a deep breath and said, "She was flying a Hurricane. She went out in clear weather, but she got caught in fog and crashed into a hill...." She put her arms around Andrew and her voice broke. "She was killed instantly."

The funeral for Irene was held two days later. Gram and the servants attended; Andrew's mother also. Aunt Gwen came home with a bad case of bronchitis and was promptly put to bed. Mrs. Tuttle fussed over her. "Miss Gwen, you've got to take better care of yourself. You're so thin and you should be getting more rest!"

"That's hard to do; it's been so busy at the hospital lately. I can't remember the last time I got a full night's sleep."

Andrew's mother was going to take him back to school after the funeral. "I wish that we could have been ill at the same time, at least," he said to Aunt Gwen.

"Well, it's my turn to be down for the count," she replied. "See you in the summer!"

Andrew noted the dark circles under her eyes, realized that she was also very, very thin. "Take care of yourself." He squeezed her hand.

"Mrs. Tuttle will see to that!" she smiled.

At first, Andrew's mother had suggested that it would be better for him to stay home, but he protested.

"She was my friend! I want to say goodbye to her!" So he was allowed to accompany his mother to the funeral.

Services were held at a small church near White Waltham. Andrew sat between his mother and Kaz in the front row of the sanctuary. He saw that the coffin was closed, and wondered why. He remembered attending the funeral of Grandfather Howard five years ago, remembered seeing the open casket with the grim, waxy figure in it: His grandfather had been as intimidating and severe in death as he had been in life.

Why couldn't he be allowed to see Irene one last time? It must have to do with military regulations, Andrew decided. He turned around and saw the sea of ATA uniforms, saw the stunned, anguished faces of the pilots who wore them, men and women alike. Andrew realized they were not simply mourning the loss of a friend and colleague; their grief was interlaced with the realization that it could just as easily have been any one of them. Just because they did not fly in combat did not mean that they were immune from danger: They risked their lives every time they took to the skies.

Andrew looked at his mother.

It could just as easily have been her....

The service over, the mourners filed past the coffin and walked out of the church. They stood outside in clumps of blue and grey and black, then slowly dispersed into cars and busses. Andrew excused himself to go to the lavatory.

He was washing his hands at the sink when two of the pallbearers entered. They took no notice of him.

"I'm new at this," one of them said. "I was surprised that the coffin was so heavy. I heard that the plane exploded in mid-air and there wasn't much left in the way of remains."

"That's right," the other one answered. "The wreckage and what was left of the pilot were strewn over a square mile."

"So what was in the coffin?" the first one asked.

"Mostly sandbags," was the reply.

Andrew went into one of the stalls, hunched over the toilet, and was violently sick.

Chapter 16

A few days after Irene's funeral, Andrew was taken by his mother back to Askew Court, as the doctor had determined that his health was completely restored. The Luftwaffe now was primarily attacking coastal areas in "tip-and-run" raids, and Andrew's mother figured that the chances of Askew Court suffering an air raid were nil. Besides, even if one should occur, what with the warm spring weather there was little chance of him suffering the terrible exposure that had led to his illness previously. Even so, he was sternly instructed by his mother to always, *always*, have his coat, shoes and socks close at hand when he went to bed.

It was strange to be back in school after being away so long. Mr. Nugent gave Andrew some tests and seemed surprised with the excellent scores he got. When Mr. Nugent remarked that it looked as if Andrew had had special tutoring while he was away, Andrew told him about the Americans: "They all tutored me: Kaz helped me with math, Marlys with geography, because she's travelled so much. Irene tutored me in spelling." As he showed Mr. Nugent the tests he had taken, Andrew looked over the papers. He saw Irene's neat handwriting correcting his misspelled words, and the tears began to roll down his cheeks.

"Anything you want to talk about?'" Mr. Nugent asked gently.

Andrew swallowed. "She was killed."

"I'm sorry."

Andrew took the papers and tucked them into his notebook. "I want to keep these."

"All right."

Andrew gazed out the window. "We had a lot of fun, too. They taught me how to play poker. We had some, um, interesting adventures." He thought of the trick that they had played on Freddie, and smiled. "They took care of me."

"It's good to have friends like that. Friendship is a gift that blesses the giver as well as the recipient. I believe they were enriched by knowing you too, Andrew."

Andrew nodded.

Mr. Nugent laid his hand on Andrew's shoulder. "Death ends the physical life, but it does not destroy the bonds of love we carry in our hearts."

All of his roommates were asleep; their soft, even breathing and the occasional grunts and muffled snores assured Andrew that he was the only one still awake.

He turned over for the hundredth time, it seemed, and tried to quell the tornado of thoughts and feelings ravaging through him. The last several days had brought a maelstrom of terror, anguish, despair, guilt, hope, relief, exhilaration, joy...and shattering grief.

How could she be dead? How could she be smiling, laughing, so incredibly alive one day, and dead the next?

It had been so appallingly sudden; surely she hadn't felt a thing...wasn't even aware of it at all...flying a plane one second, blown to atoms the next....

He turned, and squeezed his eyes shut. The darkness could not chase the vision from his mind: Irene, dressed in her rosebud-print dress, leaning over him and writing out the words he'd missed, laughing gleefully at his prowess in a poker game, giving him a goodnight kiss....

Why don't you take the people who are half-dead anyway, those who don't deserve to live...those who grumble and squabble and hate and hurt others? Why take someone who is so full of life and love and has everything to live for?

His long suppressed memory of Audrey assaulted him again: Every night he'd had nightmares of seeing Audrey's body cut in two. He tried to remember her before that awful episode: She had red hair, she was about to be married, she was so friendly and bubbly and funny...like Irene.

Audrey was only torn in two—Irene was blown into a million pieces....

His mother had asked him to write a letter to Irene's family: "It doesn't have to be anything eloquent or profound, just tell them how much she meant to you. Tell them of the simple, everyday things you did together, and of how much you miss her."

This Andrew had done, with a cold, paralyzing heaviness of heart. The words he'd put to paper seemed disembodied scrawls thrown against the blankness around them: *This isn't her! How can people end up being nothing more than bits of flesh and words on a piece of paper?*

It seemed that every thought of Irene scudded him into a bottomless pit of anguish, into a free-fall of grief and despair. Even his coherent thoughts seemed alien from him; it was as if his real self were trying to grab onto a phantasm of rationality. It was with a great effort of will that he forced his mind to remember what had happened just after Irene's funeral:

They had been standing outside the church, waiting for Thomas to bring the car around. Andrew's mother had been talking in low tones with Marlys, and Andrew had been next to them, holding Kaz's hand. Kaz had been staring off into space with a stunned sort of glare into which Freddie had stumbled. Andrew knew that her mind had been a million miles away, lost in a limbo of sorrow and anguish, but the expression on her face could have been easily mistaken for anger...and it was, evidently, by Freddie.

Andrew noted the flicker of alarm in Freddie's eyes as he realized he was in her field of vision, her stony glare fixing him like a spotlight. A wash of panic ever so momentarily crossed his face. Andrew noted, too, that Kaz remained impassively oblivious to Freddie's presence.

But Freddie thought that she was mad at him....

Andrew, discerning all this, faced Freddie squarely and, ever so slightly tilting his head in Kaz's direction, fastened him with a hard stare: *She knows....She knows ev-*

erything you've said, everything you've threatened...Everything you've done...If anything happens to me, your ass is grass, buster.

Freddie blanched and turned abruptly away. Andrew experienced a momentary exhilaration at seeing Freddie so vulnerable, without even a word being said. At that moment, he felt he could tell Kaz the worst of Freddie's threats. Later though, at the cemetery, as he saw Irene's coffin being lowered into the ground, he knew that he had to bury this most secret fear, too. He was safe—of this he was certain—and he knew that Freddie would not dare call his bluff.

Even in death, she protected me....

As they had walked away from the grave, Andrew had felt a strange feeling of power, not only in being able to control his fate, but in seeing Freddie for what he really was: nothing more than a conniving, bullying, pathetic shell of a person who knew nothing beyond the perverse delight that came from victimizing others, and whose threats were nothing more than hollow ragings.

His newfound feeling of security had exacted a price, though. While it gave him some measure of satisfaction to realize that he could turn the tables on Freddie and play the game of fear and intimidation just as well, the whole experience had dealt him a sobering blow.

Is this what life is all about? Is it nothing more than constantly trying to prevent oneself from being victimized by others, of always having to figure out a way to keep from being squashed by the ambition and hatred of someone stronger?

The world around him didn't offer much in the way of rebuttal, and Andrew realized that it would be pointless to discuss his fears with any adults.

What are they going to tell me, anyway? They're fighting this damned bloody war over that very issue...Even though we're winning, that doesn't prove anything except 'might makes right'...There's nothing noble about war! It's nothing more than a doing it to the other chap before he does it to you....

There was a stretch of warm sunny weather in April, and one Saturday afternoon Mr. Nugent announced that they were all going on an outing to town. They would go to the cinema and afterwards have a picnic in the park. It was a three mile walk to town, and the fresh air and exercise would be good for them, according to Mr. Nugent. Organizing all the classes into "squadrons", he appointed a "Squadron Leader" to head each one. Andrew was chosen Squadron Leader for his class.

"Squadron Leaders, appoint two Flight Commanders," Mr. Nugent called. "Everyone in the squadron is to pair up; each pilot has a wingman. Divide yourselves up into "A Flight" and "B Flight"; chose a name for your squadron. Flight Commanders, see that everyone in your flight is present and accounted for and report to your squadron leaders. Squadron leaders, report to me. All right, order up!"

There was a flurry of activity and excited chattering as everyone got organized. Andrew chose Gregory Thomas and John Gordon-Fairweather to be his Flight Commanders. They decided to call themselves "Hurricane Squadron". Mr. Nugent called for a report, from youngest to oldest.

"Spitfire Squadron, present!"

"Lancaster Squadron, present!"

"Beaufighter Squadron, present!"

"Stirling Squadron, present!"

"Hurricane Squadron, present!"

"Mosquito Squadron, present!"

"Tally-ho!" Mr Nugent gave the order and they marched down the road to town. Andrew's class brought up the rear of the procession, and they chatted excitedly about going to the cinema and the fun they planned to have at the picnic.

"Watch out for the Yanks!" Arthur Popham-Goode warned.

"What, Yanks?" Andrew asked.

"American GI's," Keith Vincent-Hill explained.

"Oh, Americans," Andrew replied. "There were some American women living at my Gram's house while I was ill. They were ever so nice."

"*Nice*?" Duncan Paget snorted. "Yanks are anything but *nice*!"

"My uncle says that one Yank makes more noise than thirty Englishmen, or ten Australians," Keith said.

"Overpaid, overfed, and over here!" Nigel Willoughby-Ramsbottom proclaimed. "That's what my father says!"

"Overpaid, *oversexed*, and over here!" James Martin corrected.

"Oversexed?" Andrew was curious.

"Right!" said John Gordon-Fairweather. "My granddad says that Yanks all have their brains in their Willies!"

"Cor, they must have awfully big Willies!" Colin Kirknewton exclaimed.

"No, they have awfully tiny brains!" Gregory Thomas declared.

"A Yank got our cook's niece pregnant, and they had to get married," Harry Peal said. "Cook cried all day, wouldn't even attend the wedding, because of the shame of her niece having to marry a Yank."

"Marry a Yank!" Nigel exclaimed in disgust. "If my sister ever even *looked* at a Yank, my father said she could pack her bags and leave! He told her, 'No daughter of mine is going to be a Yank-basher!'"

"My cousin taught me a song about Yanks," Timothy Park said. "Would you like to hear it?" He noted with satisfaction the eager looks, lowered his voice a bit so that Mr. Nugent wouldn't hear, and proceeded to sing:

Dear old England's not the same,
The dread invasion, well it came.
But no, it's not the beastly Hun,
The Goddammed Yankee Army's come.

They moan about our lukewarm beer—
Think beer's like water over here,
And after drinking three or four
We find them lying on the floor.

They swarm in every train and bus,
There isn't room for both of us.
We walk to let them have our seats,
Then get run over by their jeeps!

Yanks say they've come to shoot and fight,
It's true they fight, yes—when they're tight.
I must admit their shooting's fine.
They shoot a damn good Yankee line!

"I know another one!" Harry cried. Without waiting for any sort of prompting, he launched into a verse:

Alas, they haven't fought the Hun
No glorious battles have they won
That pretty ribbon just denotes
They've crossed the sea—
Brave men in boats!

"I say, did you hear the one about the two Yanks who went to a war film? One fainted and the other got a medal for carrying him out!" Nigel laughed.

"What has the I.Q. of a hundred?" Arthur asked.

"What?" Harry said.

"Ten Yanks!"

"What do you call twenty Yanks at the bottom of the North Sea?" George Garton-Ward asked.

"What?" said Timothy.

"A start!"

When they got to town, Andrew found that his friends had not been exaggerating in their descriptions of the dreaded "Yanks." The streets were full of hordes of the loud, obnoxious creatures. Dressed in olive drab, they littered the streets like clumps of muddy leaves. Yanks didn't talk; they bellowed. They didn't laugh; they guffawed. They didn't queue up at the bus stops; they pushed and shoved each other; they whistled and hooted at the women on the streets. There were dozens of them reeling from intoxication, even at this early hour of the morning; Andrew counted no less than six altercations, including one out-and-out fistfight, on their way to the cinema.

Behind Andrew and his classmates walked a few Yanks, talking loudly.

"Say, what happened to Roscoe?"

"He got stuck on K.P. again."

"Poor bastard! That new C.O. is a real hard-ass. If chickenshit were gold, he'd be Fort Knox."

"No shit."

"Yeah, he's always lookin' for an excuse to chew Roscoe's ass."

"Somfabitch ninety-day wonder—"

"Yeah, them ninety-day wonders is all a bunch of shit-heads—"

"Nothin' worse than bein' stuck on K.P. on the day the Eagle shits!"

"Yeah, poor Roscoe—he gets the shit detail, and we're getting shit-faced—"

"Shit-faced, what's that mean?" Andrew asked Timothy.

"It means drunk," Timothy replied.

"The Day the Eagle Shits means payday," Nigel volunteered.

"Why do they call it that?" Andrew was astounded that so much profanity could be employed in such a short period of time.

James shrugged. "What do you expect? They're Yanks. They can't say anything without swearing. They're all like that."

As if to prove his point, the Yanks then proceeded to sing a song in which practically every other word was the "f" word.

There were Yanks in the cinema, too, and during the newsreels they howled and whistled whenever a woman was shown. Andrew got very annoyed when they started yelling lewd remarks at a clip of a female ATA pilot.

"Hey darlin', I'll climb in your cockpit anytime!" a voice in a loud Texan accent drawled.

"Sweetheart, wanna join the Mile High Club?" another voice in a Brooklyn accent hollered. Mr. Nugent stood up and addressed them.

"Please, be civilized! There are women and children present!"

An American officer stood up and threatened to revoke the leave of any serviceman who made another remark, and the theater was silent.

Andrew sat, deep in thought. His formerly positive perception of Americans was changing. He found it hard to believe that Kaz, Marlys, and Irene could in any way be associated with this repugnant, foul-mouthed crowd. Well, they were women; maybe American women were just better behaved. Andrew knew that the requirements to join the ATA were stiff; that would naturally serve to weed out the vast majority of those with coarse manners and crude behavior. After all, only twenty-five out of seven hundred had been chosen—seven hundred *pilots*, that is. They certainly must have been better educated and better behaved than most. The women *must* be different from the rest of the obnoxious mass that populated that uncivilized land. *Yanks!*

The movie started: *The Wizard of Oz.* Andrew had seen it before, but now he paid particular attention to the dusty, dreary Kansas landscape. How alien and barren that land was! When Dorothy landed in Oz and the film went into color, Andrew thought that England was very much like Oz: so green and colorful and lovely. In spite of the bombings, in spite of the destruction, Andrew was proud of the fact that England still retained much of its beauty and order. Look at America! Americans didn't have to live with air raids, and with bombs blowing their world to pieces, and one would think that they could create a more pleasant landscape in their part of the world. Look at how ugly and grimy and desolate it was! How could Dorothy ever want to return to a place like *that*! Andrew turned around and looked at the foreigners.

I hope they don't decide to stay here. When this war is over, I hope that every last one of them goes back to where he belongs.

He received a letter from Aunt Jane. He was almost afraid to read it; for weeks now, his anxiety about Aunt Jane had been pushed back behind his other concerns and worries. He hadn't even looked at the sky since he'd gotten that last letter from her. Now, the sight of this latest missive vexed him, for he couldn't even define, let alone deal with, the disturbing emotions he had about the whole matter.

He finally tore open the letter and read it:

Dear Andrew,

Your mother wrote to me about Irene's terrible accident. Even though I didn't know her, I felt as if I'd lost a dear friend. I can only imagine what you must be feeling now, and I wish I could be with you. Your mother told me that she wrote to Irene's family, and that you did, too. It was good that you told them of your friendship with her—don't ever think that your remembrances of her are not treasured by them, despite their grief. Rarely is anyone ever beyond comfort, and your assurance to Irene's family that you will always carry the memory of her is the greatest thing you can do for them at this time.

I expect that this letter will find you back at school, as your mother also wrote that the doctor pronounced you hale and whole at last! Do take care of yourself—remember to keep your coat on your bed at night, and your socks and shoes nearby.

Cheer up—the war's not going to last forever! It's heartening to realize that, after all these years, it looks as if we'll have peace before long!

Much love,
Aunt Jane

He crumpled the letter and tossed it into his wastebasket. If he only knew what was going on!

Irene's death had come so quickly on the heels of the resolution of his terrible dilemma over protecting his mother from Freddie's attentions, but, even with that particular piece of business having been taken care of, Andrew still found himself worrying about her.

She might be safe from Freddie. Kaz had promised to talk to her and certainly would have told her of the dangers of even accepting so much as a drink from him, so Freddie was not a problem anymore.

But what if there were others? After the incident with Hugh, Andrew had never quite been able to shake the fear that his mother might attract, not only admiring glances, but interested attention as well. He recalled the glitter in Hugh's eyes: Of course, he'd once been engaged to her, and evidently still harbored strong feelings, but something told Andrew that it was not all just sweet remembrance that had accounted for his interest. He had clearly shown every indication of wanting to renew their relationship. Andrew shuddered as he recalled the look Hugh had given him: the *What do we do about the boy* glance. And his mother's indecision upon meeting this former flame vexed him even more.

She wasn't sure—then again, she wasn't certain that she *didn't* want to accept his invitation. It didn't take too much urging to get her to accept...Andrew tried to fight back the chilling fear: *If I hadn't been there....*

She *had* promised that she wouldn't see Hugh...No, not promised...She said she didn't *intend* to see him.

What if she changed her mind? What if there were *other* men who found her attractive? What if she really didn't carry a flicker of hope that his father might still be alive, just sweet memories....

And if she didn't believe his father was alive, then she might want...companionship—and more! He remembered Freddie's snickering assertion: *She's had a taste of it...She knows what she's missing....*

Who knows? he thought. Maybe she *is* really lonely...Perhaps flying is not enough for her...And if she believes that Dad is gone for good....

He had resolved to be quiet about his belief that his father was still alive, in order not to distress her. But now, it was clear that keeping things to himself might result in *disaster*.

She has to believe he's coming back!

Maybe, Andrew thought, if I can plant a little seed of doubt in her mind...If she realized she can't be absolutely certain that he's dead, then she can begin to believe he's alive....

Silence is acquiescence...Knowing now the danger of keeping quiet, if I were to continue to keep things to myself, I'd be responsible for the consequences....

His mother came to visit him a few weeks later, and she took him to a restaurant in town for lunch. Was it his imagination, or was there was something different about her? She seemed somewhat preoccupied, yet happy. Andrew sipped his tea, trying to ascertain if he was being...*paranoid*.

"There's been a change of plans for summer holidays this year," she announced, after they'd placed their order. "I'll pick you up on the last day of school and take you up to Northumberland first,"

"*What!*" Distress split his voice, and dismay churned through him. He had so wanted to get this encounter off to a good start! He thunked his cup into its saucer, took a deep breath, and said: "Why? The Nazis are hardly bombing us at all!"

"It would just work out better, that's all."

Andrew sensed that there was something else going on that she obviously had no intention of communicating to him at this time. He tried another tack.

"I could go home with Gregory Thomas. He lives only a few miles from Armus House and his mother could see that I get there, and then you could meet me and we could both go to Northumberland."

"It would be a shorter trip if we went to Northumberland directly from school."

"We always used to go to Armus House first. Why can't we do that this year too?"

"Well, things change."

Andrew hated it when his mother dismissed his arguments with a platitude. His thoughts were interrupted by a booming voice from the table next to them.

"Open it, darlin'!" Andrew cringed at the American accent.

"Ooh, luv, you didn't have to!" a woman with a London accent tittered as she eagerly unwrapped a package. She finally got the strings untied and pulled out a pair of nylons. She gasped. "Ooh, luvy!"

The man grinned. "Stick with me, darlin', and you'll be fartin' through silk!"

The woman pursed her lips and glared at him, clearly indicating that she was scandalized with his remark.

The man laughed. "Come on, darlin', you can't say that you haven't heard *that* one before!"

Her expression softened, and a smile played at the corners of her mouth. She broke into a giggle. "No, I can't say that I haven't." She lovingly fingered the nylons.

The waitress came and inquired of Andrew's mother if they would like dessert.

"Would you like some ice cream, Andrew?" his mother asked.

Andrew hoped that it would be real ice cream, not the paste-like substance that had been foisted upon him at school. "Yes, please," he said.

"Two dishes of ice cream," his mother told the waitress.

A loud crash issued from the pub, which adjoined the restaurant. There was the sound of a scuffle, more crashes, cursing (in American accents, of course); then the bartender unceremoniously escorted the guilty culprits outside.

The waitress brought Andrew and his mother their ice cream.

"What was that all about?" Andrew asked the waitress.

The waitress tossed back her head in disgust. "Two Yanks—they got into an argument over which of them had the prettiest wife."

"And they started fighting about *that?*" Andrew was amazed that two people could come to blows over something, well, so ridiculous. Not that considering one's wife attractive was ridiculous; it was just stupid to get into a fight about it.

"Not exactly," the waitress said. "They tried to settle the argument by showing each other pictures of their wives."

"Beauty being in the eye of the beholder, I wouldn't think that would solve anything," Andrew's mother observed.

"Oh, it was easy to see that both of their wives were equally beautiful," the waitress said.

"Equally?" Andrew asked.

"Yes, equally," the waitress replied. "They were both married to the same woman!"

"*What!*" Andrew exclaimed.

"They call them Allotment Annies," the waitress explained. "These women in America, you see, they get themselves married to a Yank that's about to ship out. They get an allotment check from the government, for being the wife of a serviceman. Well, if they're married to two servicemen, they get two checks. If they're married to three, they get...."

"We get the picture, thank you very much," Andrew's mother said firmly.

"...There was one Annie I heard about, she was married to *seven* Yanks!" the waitress proclaimed.

After the waitress had departed, Andrew said, "Stupid Yanks, serves them right for being married to the same woman!"

"Andrew, I don't think the woman in question bothered to enlighten them as to her, um, other matrimonial commitments," his mother rejoined.

"Well, they should have known! It just shows Yanks are bloody stupid about things."

"Andrew, I will *not* have you swearing. Nor is it fair to judge all Americans by the behavior of a few. Marlys and Kaz are Americans," she reminded him.

"They're not like the Yanks—the soldiers, I mean. You haven't heard swearing until you've heard Yanks. They use the "s-h" word and the "f" word all the time, all of them do! And by Yanks, I mean the men. The women aren't a problem, it's the men who are. I can't wait until they all go back to their own country. Back to Yankland!"

"Andrew, I don't want you using that word. The Americans are here to help us fight the Nazis."

"The only fighting they're doing is with each other, that's all I can see!"

"You may not be able to see it, but there are Americans fighting and dying in the skies over Europe, probably even right now, as we speak. There are American sailors and merchantmen risking their lives in the Atlantic, to bring needed supplies to our country. There have been Americans helping us since the beginning of the war, during the Battle of Britain."

Andrew stabbed his dessert with his spoon. He hated to be lectured. He took a bite of ice cream and gagged: It was the same pasty stuff he'd been served at school. He slammed his spoon down contemptuously.

"Why can't we have real ice cream, just for once? I mean, is that too much to ask?"

His mother sighed. "The war isn't going to last forever, Andrew. Someday we'll have regular ice cream again—just be patient."

"I'm sick and tired of being patient! All I want is a dish of real ice cream, just once. Is that too much to ask?"

His mother pursed her lips. Andrew went on. "We pray all the time in chapel for the war to end. I'm not going to pray anymore for that. I figure that it's just too much for God to handle. Besides, everyone is praying for it anyway, so why should I pray for it too? I figure that if God can't give me one dish of ice cream before—" Andrew thought that it would be a good idea to lock God into a time frame, "Before the year is out, then he's not worth praying to. That's all I want, a dish of ice cream—is that too bloody much to ask?"

His mother did not reprimand him for swearing. In fact, she did not say anything at all. Andrew continued. "That, and for Dad to come back—soon."

He hadn't expected to blurt it out like that, but there—it was done!

His outburst caught his mother with her spoonful of ice cream midway between the dish and her mouth. The spoon hung, motionless and suspended, and was carefully replaced in the dish. His mother folded her hands at the edge of the table, gave him a wary look, took a deep breath, and said, "Andrew, your father is—"

"He's *missing*, you said. That doesn't prove anything. I want to believe he's coming back. There's nothing wrong with that, is there?"

"It may not be wrong, but it's not the best thing."

"Mum, he's missing! *Missing!* That doesn't prove *anything!* The longer we go without hearing anything, then...then that's all the more reason to believe that he's alive." He grabbed her hand, laced his fingers in hers and squeezed tight, as if he could impart his faith to her.

"I know he's alive Mum, I *know* it! When we were bombed in London, while I was trapped, I heard his voice! I know it was *him* really talking to me! Even though he wasn't there, he knew I was in trouble and he was trying to reach me. It's a sign that he's alive—Mum, he's *alive*! It's like it was between him and Aunt Jane. I could hear him calling to me, telling me to be brave, telling me to hang on—and I did! How do you explain *that?*"

"Andrew, you were delirious. You heard the rescue worker calling to you and you wanted to believe it was your father."

"It was *not* my imagination!" Andrew yelled. Several people in the restaurant looked in his direction. He lowered his voice. "I *didn't* make it up. I wasn't even *thinking* about him, and I heard his voice. And then when I had pneumonia he was there with me—he was holding me! I could feel his arms around me—he was crying—I could even taste the tears—and his face was bristly—he needed a shave. I felt the rings around his sleeve—there were two—and the button on his uniform—I pulled it off and you got upset, and then you took it away from me. He held me when I got my temperature taken—*Mum! It was real!* I know he wasn't really there, but he was sending me some sort of message—he's coming back! *He's not dead!*"

His mother seemed almost paralyzed with shock—or was it fear? He realized that his voice had risen to an agitated pitch again. He swallowed, then, trying to keep calm, said in a low voice, "I *know* he's alive, Mum. He might be a prisoner. He could be trapped behind enemy lines—hiding out somewhere. Please Mum, please! *Please* believe that he's still alive!"

His mother gulped; her eyes searched around, as if she were trying to locate an answer to his plea on a molecule of air.

All right, time to trundle out the big guns....

"Mum, do you believe in Mr. Churchill?"

"Well, yes, of course I do," she replied, a little baffled. "He's our Prime Minister."

"Well, then, don't you believe what he says? He says," Andrew took a deep breath. "He says we ought to hold together and stand firm, and not flinch or weary of the struggle and that we should draw from the heart of suffering the means of inspiration and survival, and we must—must—*must* not flag or fail, and not weaken or tire, and we must never, *never*, surrender, and—and—we must stand firm, and we must be undaunted and we must be inflexible, and we should go on to the end, because in the end all will come right—he *said* that, Mum! Our *Prime Minister* said that! Everything's going to come right! Can't you believe that?"

He had never seen that look on his mother's face, that look of stunned horror, as if he had just proclaimed that Adolph Hitler were God's chosen messenger.

A crash issued from the pub.

Yanks!" the waitress groaned.

It seemed that the noise of the scuffle, and the yells and the oaths screamed in a drunken rage, unleashed the terrible anguish he was struggling to contain within him.

She doesn't believe—she never did....

He slumped forward onto the table and shoved the dish of ice cream, or whatever awful stuff it was, onto the floor. A sob convulsed him; then he felt his mother's hands gently stroking his hair. He lifted his face up to her.

"Please—please, just consider it," he begged. "If you can't believe he's alive, then believe he might not be dead—he might not be—that's all! He hasn't been found— that means there's still hope! Please!"

"All right," she said gently.

She closed her eyes and turned away.

Two weeks later, the wail of the air raid sirens awakened everyone at Askew Court in the middle of the night. As they sat huddled in the shelter, the sound of the bombs seemed unusually close. There was a moment of silence, then a deafening blast that seemed to split the air apart, followed by two more explosions. Everyone, even the older ones, cried out in a shriek of terror at the sound; there was a series of distant thumps and then all was still. It seemed that everybody was afraid that even the slightest movement would trigger another round of violent assaults on their ears. Finally they heard the All-clear and filed out, eager to ascertain the visible results of the night's bombing.

The dining hall and kitchen were completely destroyed, and the classroom building was badly damaged. Mr. Harris instructed the housemasters to take everyone back to the dorms and to wait until the classrooms were inspected to see which rooms were still usable.

The terror of the previous night was forgotten as the children contemplated the fortuitous turn of events. No school today, at least! Even their pangs of hunger as breakfast was delayed did not dampen their spirits. Mrs. Harris managed to scrounge up enough oatmeal to feed them all and cooked it in her own kitchen. They ate their porridge, sitting down on the floor in the dormitory. Mr. Harris started contacting parents to come and pick their children up as soon as possible.

The Red Cross brought some food for them later that afternoon and, after a supper of sandwiches and carrots, they went to bed. The next day, Mr. Harris spoke with Andrew.

"I've tried contacting your mother, but her ferry pool commander says she's on leave and can't be located. I called your grandmother's house, and the maid says that your grandmother and aunt are away but that they're expected back tomorrow afternoon. You live near Gregory Thomas, don't you?"

"Yes, I could go home with them."

"I'll speak to Mrs. Thomas; I think that would be a good plan."

Andrew went to bed that night, excited by the happy change of plans. No more school! And he would be going to Armus house first after all!

He lay awake in bed that night, planning on how he might surprise Gram and Aunt Gwen when they arrived. He could hide in the dining room and have Lucia announce that there was a visitor for tea. Maybe he would hide underneath his bed and pop out and surprise them. He hoped that Kaz and Marlys were still there; Kaz would certainly be able to think of a clever plan. Maybe Kaz and Marlys could pretend that they were having an important guest for dinner, and Andrew could get Thomas to drive him up to the front porch, like a visiting dignitary. Things were turning out just splendidly, and Andrew was delighted just thinking about the surprise he was planning for Gram and Aunt Gwen and the look of astonishment that would be on their faces as he made his appearance.

He had no way of knowing that his clever little scheme was *nothing* compared to the surprise that lay in store for him.

Chapter 17

$\mathcal{M}$rs. Thomas dropped Andrew off at Armus House a little after noon. Andrew met Lucia in the front hall.

"Are Kaz and Marlys coming home tonight?"

"No, they were transferred a few weeks ago. They left you some letters and a package."

He was disappointed that he wouldn't be seeing Kaz and Marlys. Well, he would have to think up a plan to surprise Aunt Gwen and Gram by himself. He went up to his room and found the package and letters on his dresser. Opening the package, he found a half dozen Hershey bars. From Irene, he thought, and suddenly he didn't have any appetite for them. He read the letter from Kaz.

> Dear Andrew,
>
> I wish that I could have said good-bye to you under better circumstances. I have been posted to Hamble, which is an all-women's ferry pool. (They say all the glamour girls go to Hamble. Marlys won't have any trouble fitting in, but as for Yours Truly—I hope they don't mind a little character around the place!) It was great knowing you—let's keep in touch! You can write me c/o the ATA, Ferry Pool 15, while I'm here. My address in America is on the back of this letter.
>
> Study hard, be good, and write!
>
> > Much love,
> > Kaz

Andrew turned over the letter and peered at the address: someplace in Pennsylvania. There was a letter from Marlys, too. She gave her address in Los Angeles, California. She also left him the deck of cards they'd played with. He went down to lunch.

"Where's Gram and Aunt Gwen?" he asked Mrs. Tuttle.

"Your grandmother's brother died last week, so she's got to see to settling his estate. She'll be back this afternoon. Aunt Gwen is off on holiday with your Uncle Robert. He got three days leave and they went off to the seaside."

"Is Aunt Gwen doing better, then?"

"The doctor doesn't want her back at work for another month. She's still so thin and pale. Your Uncle Robert thought that a holiday and sea air would perk her up. They're coming home later today."

"So Uncle Robert will be coming back too?"

"Yes, they're due to arrive this afternoon, around tea-time. Your Grandmother called and told me to set two extra places at tea—she's expecting some visitors."

"Really? Did she say who was coming?"

"Oh, no, not to me. I'm just to prepare dinner for six, that's all."

"Well, make that seven. Oh, and don't tell them that I'm here. I want to surprise them."

"Right, Master Andrew. How would you like a bit of trifle for afters? I'm going to make it now. Your grandmother told me she wanted something special for tonight."

"Trifle! Oh, that would be super! Can I watch?"

"Certainly." Mrs. Tuttle served Andrew a lunch of lentil soup; then she proceeded to make a custard, all the while lamenting the shortage of sugar and milk: "Not nearly enough, and can't make a proper custard, either, with these beastly powdered eggs. The chickens haven't been laying, what with the latest bombing raids." She looked through the cupboards for some fruit preserves for the filling. "Here's some tinned plums—could chop them up, I suppose. And here's a few dabs of strawberry jam." She held up a jar that was almost empty.

Andrew pointed out some jars with bright orange filling. "What about using that?"

"Carrot marmalade! Saints preserve us, having to use carrot marmalade to make trifle!" She cut up some sponge cake into cubes, and layered the cubes with the marmalade, jam, and custard.

"You could always put lots of sherry in it," Andrew suggested. "Then everyone won't notice the carrot marmalade and how little custard it has."

"Good idea! Thanks to Freddie, that's one thing we aren't short on!"

Mrs. Tuttle trundled into the drawing room and opened the liquor cabinet. Andrew was astonished at the sight of the bulging shelves.

"Crikey, that's enough to keep Freddie shit-faced till Christmas!"

"Master Andrew, such language! Don't you dare get caught using words like that in front of your gram! Where did you pick up such language?"

"The Yanks talk like that all the time! They can't say anything without swearing! They all talk like that—all of them do, all the time!"

"Well, that may be true, but that doesn't mean that you should go around sounding like them. Your poor mother would be shocked to see you turning out like a Yank!"

"I'm sorry," Andrew said. Mrs. Tuttle's assessment of the odious trans-Atlantic invaders gave Andrew pause. She had been delighted with the American women; yet she found the "Yanks" repulsive, as he did. It seemed so incongruous that Kaz and Marlys and Irene were of the same nationality as these uncouth barbarians. He wondered what Mrs. Tuttle thought about this discrepancy.

"Do you think the Yanks are all that bad, too?" he asked her. "I mean, Kaz and Marlys and Irene were so—so...*decent!* It's sometimes hard to believe that they were Americans. Sometimes Irene was...well, her language was a bit colorful, but she was never crude—not like Yanks—the men, I mean."

"Well, that's the men for you!" Mrs. Tuttle pronounced. "Sometimes there's a world of difference. Look at Lucia. Italian women are so well-mannered and industrious, but Italian *men!* Even Lucia says they're lazy, lecherous beasts! Just look under any haystack and you'll find an Italian prisoner of war with a Women's Land Army Girl!

It can be the opposite too. From what I've heard, the Russian men are ever so friendly and cheerful, but the women—surliest females on the face of the earth! My nephew is a merchant seaman. He usually does the Murmansk run and he says Russian women are the meanest you'll ever find, just as soon bite your head off as give you the time of day!"

Andrew nodded. So there *was* an explanation for it all. He watched as Mrs. Tuttle peered at the various bottles of intoxicating beverages. "Freddie has enough to open up his own pub!"

"Oh, that's not even half of it! More under the bar."

Mrs. Tuttle opened door after door, revealing huge stores of spirits hidden within. "Where did Freddie get all that?" Andrew asked.

"From the Yanks."

"Yanks! I thought Freddie didn't like Yanks!"

"Like them as people, no. Like them when they grease his palm, yes. As he says, sometimes you have to dance with the Devil to get what you want—ah, here's some sherry. Let's pour it over the works!"

Mrs. Tuttle scooped out a serving for Andrew before she liberally dosed the trifle with the alcoholic garnish: "Don't want you meeting your gram all squiffy, Master Andrew!"

Andrew wolfed down his dessert, then went back upstairs. He thought he might pass the time studying the assignments that Mr. Nugent had given him to do over the summer. He tried to get interested in studying his history lesson, but his mind kept wandering. Then he tried reading some of O. Henry's stories, but he was too excited to concentrate on them, either. He went downstairs to tell Mrs. Tuttle of his plan to surprise Gram: He thought he would wait in the dining room and have Mrs. Tuttle announce that there was an important visitor for tea. As he was talking, he heard the front door open. He peeked through the kitchen door to the hallway.

It was Gram!

"Never mind, I'll run up the backstairs and hide in my room. Just don't tell her I'm here!"

Mrs. Tuttle nodded, and Andrew scurried up the backstairs to his room. A few minutes later he heard Gram walk up the stairs and down the hallway. He opened his door and announced, "I see you have a spare room here. Would you mind terribly if I moved in for awhile?"

Gram turned sharply around, her eyes wide with shock. Her mouth dropped open in—Andrew wanted to think it was surprise, but it looked more like...alarm.

"We were sent home from school early. Askew Court got bombed. I came home with Gregory Thomas. Mum told me that I had to go to Northumberland first, and I was so disappointed. But here I am! Isn't it grand?"

Andrew expected Gram's face to break into a smile of welcome, and he was disconcerted by the look of dismay she gave him. He realized that perhaps he had startled her.

"I'm sorry, I didn't mean to scare you," he said.

Gram seemed more agitated than ever. "Oh dear, oh dear, this is awful, they'll be here any minute...." her voice trembled and she fluttered her hands.

"Who? Who's going to be here?" Andrew asked. "Is it someone impor—"

The sound of a car door slamming interrupted him. He ran back into his room and looked out the window. He saw a car parked in the driveway; then his heart lurched as saw a figure in the familiar blue RAF uniform walking around it. Andrew couldn't see the man's face, for his back was to Andrew. The man opened the car door, and Andrew's mother got out. They kissed, and Andrew's soul exploded in joy.

"Dad!" he shrieked. He dashed out of his room, tore down the stairs, and burst out the front door.

"Dad! Dad! You've come back! I knew you would! *I knew you*—"

The figure in the uniform turned and, in a split second, Andrew's mind registered the look of shock and horror on his mother's face as he nearly threw himself into the arms of a complete stranger.

Chapter 18

*A*ndrew recoiled at the last instant. Too stunned to move or even speak, he stood paralyzed for a moment—a moment which seemed like an eternity. The stranger stared back at him; he too seemed frozen in shock. Then Andrew's mother moved close to the man and grasped his arm. He looked at her, apprehensive. It was then that Andrew saw it: the wedding ring on his mother's hand. The realization hit him like a bomb.

"No!" he screamed. "No! *NO! He's not dead! How can you do this when he's not even dead!*"

He was vaguely aware of Gram's distraught explanation as she dashed down the front steps.

"I'm sorry! I'm so terribly sorry! He came home from school unexpectedly—I just found out—"

Andrew felt his whole body convulse in shock and horror. He turned and lurched back up the steps. His mind was reeling as he bolted up the stairs and threw himself down the hall, into his room, and onto the bed.

How could she do this? How could she turn her back on his father, give up hope, betray him like this?

As the sobs racked his body, he felt himself spiraling into a pit of despair and anguish. Then, a hand was on his shoulder. It was his mother's.

"Oh Andrew, I didn't mean for you to find out like this. I was going to tell you—I was hoping to spend some time with you next week, up at Greycliff. What a terrible shock for you to find out like this. I'm so sor—"

Andrew flung himself away from her. "He's not dead, he's *missing!* How can you give up hope? He could come back *anytime!*"

She took a deep breath and said gently, "Andrew, your father is *not* coming back. You're going to have to accept that."

"No! *No!* He *is* coming back! *You* don't want to believe that but *I* know he's alive. I *know!*"

"Andrew—" She grasped both of his hands, and looked at him, imploring, sad. The silence betrayed the gigantic gulf that was now between them. Then she spoke, her voice barely above a whisper. "Andrew, his name is Jake. He—"

"No." The word was spoken softly, but firmly, by the stranger, standing in the doorway now. His eyes held Andrew's mother, urged her to be silent; then he motioned with his hand for her to come to him. He was of medium build, a little shorter than Andrew's father, with dark brown hair, taut mouth, and a look of quiet determination. He seemed wary, yet self-possessed, and gave the impression of a man who was somewhat unsure of others, but completely at ease with himself. His dark gray eyes betrayed a look of terrible maturity that seemed out of place with his otherwise boyish features.

Andrew's mother looked back at him, her face a question and a plea. He shook his head, once, and his eyes continued to compel her to come to him. The unspoken communication between them disturbed Andrew even more: It not only excluded him but made him acutely aware that there was a bond between them that he was powerless to deal with. Andrew's mother turned to Andrew; she squeezed his hands and then released them. "I'm sorry," she whispered, and then she was gone.

Just like that!

Andrew was flabbergasted that a complete stranger could order his mother around like that. With one word, and a flick of his hand! He slumped back into his bed as waves of nausea and horror engulfed him. It was awful, horrifying, terrifying, that life could be so monstrous and cruel! It was hard enough not knowing where his father was or when he would be coming back, but the belief that he was alive was something that Andrew clung to with every ounce of strength within him. He thought that he could count on his mother to believe that too—now she had betrayed him, betrayed his father!

He heard the sound of another car pulling up to the house. Who could it be now? He went over to the window to investigate, and saw Aunt Gwen and Uncle Robert walking up the front steps. Did they know about this too? Of course, they did! Mrs. Tuttle had said six for dinner tonight: *Someone special is coming.*

They were *all* in on this! He crept out of his room, down the hall, and looked down on the front hallway. Gram was talking to Aunt Gwen and Uncle Robert, but Andrew couldn't hear what she was saying. Then she opened the door to the drawing room and they all disappeared inside. The door was shut and Andrew could hear the low murmur of conversation, then the stranger's voice, adamant, insistent about something. Though Andrew couldn't make out what he was saying, he sensed it was something important and, despite his distress, curiosity got the best of him.

He started down the stairs, intending to investigate, when Lucia appeared in the hallway. Of course she would choose to dust right now! She swiftly worked her way down the hallway, and started to dust the molding around the door to the drawing room. She cocked her head, and the rhythm of the feather duster slowed to a complete halt. All of a sudden, she jumped back; the door swung open and everyone filed out. The front door opened at almost the same instant, and Freddie strode through. There was a brief introduction; Freddie shook hands with the stranger abruptly and without any enthusiasm. Uncle Robert shook the stranger's hand a little more warmly, and Aunt Gwen and Gram gave him a hug. The whole scene sickened Andrew even more. How could they welcome this man, accept the fact that he had taken the place of Andrew's father, give him their affection and best wishes?

I thought this was what the war was all about! Decency and loyalty and all that rot. Well, there's decency and loyalty for you.

"...Yes, yes some other time," Andrew's mother was saying. She and the stranger walked out the front door. Andrew scurried back to his room to see what would happen next. Looking out the window, he saw them standing by the car, talking. His mother's back was to Andrew, so he could see only the stranger's face. The man was obviously listening to something Andrew's mother was saying. Then Andrew saw his lips form the word "No". Andrew's mother reached her hand to his face and touched his cheek, and this time his expression was grim and determined. *No, no, no.* It was clear enough to Andrew what he was saying. He looked away for an instant, then back at Andrew's mother. He spoke again; this time the words seem to tumble out and Andrew did not have a clue as to what he was saying.

No about what? What was it that the stranger was so insistent about? *No, it's all over? No, I'm leaving now, forever*—what?

Andrew held his breath and hoped that the stranger would make it clear that he intended to end everything right then and there, and to go away, for good. *Forever.*

It's a good thing I was here, Andrew thought. Now he'll leave, leave forever....

But now Andrew's mother and the stranger were embracing, then kissing. Andrew's mind flashed back to the times he had seen his parents together like that. How could his mother *be* like that with another man? He remembered how sickened and scared he had been at the thought of Freddie, and Hugh...this was even worse! All the time he had been worrying about them! As his father had said: *It's not the ones you see; it's the ones you don't see.* Right!

The stranger had already gotten in the car and was driving away. Andrew's mother stood in the driveway until the car was out of sight. Then she turned and, as she was walking back to the house, she glanced up and saw Andrew looking down at her. He froze his expression into a stony glare.

He turned towards the door and waited for her. He heard her footsteps in the hall, then a gentle tap on the door. He said nothing. Another soft knock and then her voice, "Andrew, may I come in?"

He did not answer her.

The door opened slowly. She stood in the doorway, like a schoolgirl about to have an unpleasant encounter with the headmistress. Her words were measured and soft.

"Andrew, I know this is an awful shock for you. I didn't mean for you to find out this way—" Her voice broke. "I know that you still want to believe your father is alive—"

"You want to believe he's *dead!*" Andrew's voice was savage.

"Andrew, he's not coming back."

"How do you know? How do you know for sure? He's missing, *missing*, not dead! He could be anywhere! He could be in a prison camp, or behind enemy lines, trying to make his way back! Just because you haven't heard from him doesn't mean he's dead!"

"His plane was shot down."

"Lots of planes are shot down. Did anybody see him crash? Did they find the wreckage? Did they find the body?"

"It was over the sea. Nobody saw it."

"How do you know he crashed into the sea? How do you know he crashed at all? How do you know for sure?"

"I know. Someday you'll understand."

"All I understand is that you want to be with *him!*" Andrew couldn't bring himself to speak the stranger's name. "You gave up hope because you don't care! You *never* did!"

"Andrew, that's not true."

"Yes it is! Go away! I don't even want to talk about it anymore! You want to believe he's dead, then believe it! *Don't tell me what to think!*" Andrew spun around and glared out the window. He heard her walk over to him, felt her put her hand on his shoulder. He kept his back to her, kept silent.

The silence lasted for just a few seconds but it seemed like an eternity. Then she spoke.

"Don't unpack your things. We're leaving for Northumberland tomorrow." Then she was gone.

Andrew threw himself down on the bed. The tears came again, and he was glad to be alone. It was getting late, and he watched the light fade from the sky and darkness take its place. It hurt too much to even think, to even try to make sense out of everything that had happened. The thoughts and fears and horrible feelings were beginning to overwhelm him, and he felt himself spinning out of control in a horrible vortex of desolation and terror. He knew he had to go outside, to get away from his room, this place which still reeked of misery and betrayal. He decided to walk down the backstairs so as not to attract attention, and was just at the bottom of the stairs and about to open the door to the kitchen when he heard Freddie's voice.

"Well, I'll be buggered! A Yank! *A bloody Yank!* Can you believe that Alice would take up with one of *them!*"

"He seems like a very nice chap." It was Uncle Robert speaking now.

"He's a Yank, isn't he? They're all alike—a bunch of uncivilized, ill-bred, uncouth, ignorant, vulgar, boorish, swaggering oafs. They spit in the streets and chew gum. Damned colonials could never rule themselves; now they're over here, trying to order us around!

"They're here to help us fight the war, Freddie. We need them."

"Fight? They can't fight worth a damn! Their so-called army is the most undisciplined, spineless, slovenly bunch of misfits and malcontents to ever presume to be a fighting force. I've seen British soldiers on pub-crawls in better marching form than your blessed Yanks! The only thing Yanks are good at is boasting, but at the first sight of battle, they fall apart. Look at that fiasco at Kasserine Pass—a bloody shambles if ever there was one! They were properly routed in the Philippines and caught napping at Pearl Harbor. No doubt the chap who was supposed to be minding things was off wanking somewhere! They didn't help us in the last war until it was all but won and as for needing them now, we need them like we need a fox in the henhouse! Overpaid, oversexed, and over here!"

"But he's RAF."

"Well, he may not be overpaid, but it's still two out of three in my book! Bloody lecherous beasts, why can't they fornicate with their own kind and leave our women alone!"

"He's not like that—you're wrong, Freddie. Anyway, I'm glad for Alice. In spite of everything that's happened, you can tell they're happy together. That's all that matters."

"What matters is that he's a Yank! Just scratch the surface and you'll find that he's just like the rest of them. Damn, what's this family coming to! A Yank, a bloody Yank! You're fortunate that you're leaving tomorrow, Robert. You won't have to deal with it!"

Andrew crept back upstairs and stumbled down the hall to his room. Once within, he closed the door behind him, leaned against it, and slid down to the floor.

Just when he thought things couldn't be worse! *A Yank!* It was bad enough to see his father replaced by another man, but a *Yank!* He knew that Freddie spoke out of jealousy, but that didn't mean he was wrong. He remembered the Yanks in the movie theater, whistling and shouting lewd remarks, and it sickened him to think that his mother let herself be the object of this man's attention. What was his name—Jake? Typical Yank name—he should have known! But where had he heard that before? Right, Irene and Kaz had spoken of him the morning that they had plotted revenge on Freddie. A Yank in the RAF, who didn't want to join up with the Americans.

What's the matter, Yank? Think that you're too good for them? You're just like the rest of them: uncouth, uncivilized, spineless, overpaid, oversexed, and over here!

And everyone, *everyone* except Freddie, was taken in by him! He never thought that he would be on Freddie's side about anything. Freddie was right—what *was* this family coming to?

Freddie need not have worried about what the family was coming to.

Andrew and his mother left for Northumberland the next morning. A week later, during a night raid by the Luftwaffe over southern England, a Dornier, crippled by anti-aircraft fire, broke off from the main formation and headed back to France. In an effort to maintain altitude, it jettisoned its bombs at random over the English countryside. One of them fell directly on Armus House, instantly killing Gram, Aunt Gwen, and Freddie as they slept.

Chapter 19

*A*ndrew's mother was just about to leave Northumberland and return to duty with the ATA when they got word of what had happened. Andrew received the news from his mother and took it with an icy silence. It was not that he didn't feel grief for Gram and Aunt Gwen.

He walked calmly up to his room, then broke down in sobs.

As Andrew and his mother travelled to London, he stared stonily out the train window during the entire ride. He didn't say a word to his mother.

He kept silent on the journey from London to the church in Berkshire at which services were held. Thomas, Mrs. Tuttle, and Lucia were at the funeral, Thomas and Mrs. Tuttle having been spared, since their quarters were over the garage, as was Lucia, who had been given a few days off and was in London with friends who were about to leave for America. Lucia was particularly distressed; were it not for Gram's kindness, she would certainly have met with the same awful fate.

Freddie was literally pulverized, as the bomb had fallen directly onto his room. From the whispered conversation around him, Andrew gathered that the scraps of flesh picked out of the rubble were not quite adequate to make a positive identification. ("Looks like it's sandbags in the coffin for our dear departed Master Freddie," Thomas muttered under his breath.) Aunt Gwen's room was next to Freddie's; what could be identified as her remains were scattered over several square feet, but at least some recognizable pieces could be buried. Gram's room was down the hall from theirs; it too had been completely destroyed, along with the rest of Armus House. Her coffin was closed also; Thomas had helped the firemen sort through the rubble and he did not reveal to anyone what he had seen. "Best to remember her as she was," was all he said.

Andrew grieved deeply for Gram and Aunt Gwen; he felt as if his soul would break in two, though he fought back the anguish so as not to elicit any sympathetic outpourings from his mother.

I don't want her comfort, her assurances, her love, anything! She's made her choice—let her live with it!

As for Freddie, Andrew was a little more philosophical, though not a little astonished, that he had come to such a fitting demise:

I wished for him to disappear in a puff of smoke...and he did!

Aunt Jane wasn't able to come for services, Andrew's mother explained:

"She's doing some very important work right now, and can't be reached. I sent word to her—she probably won't hear about it for awhile."

Kaz and Marlys also attended the funeral; Andrew at first felt a stab of bitterness at seeing them, as distressed as he was with finding out that they had known all along about his mother and Jake. However, looking upon Kaz's tear-streaked face, all rancor within him vanished and he threw himself into her arms, sobbing inconsolably.

If my mother had enjoined them to silence, then it was right for them not to betray a confidence. Besides, it's not their fault....

Mercifully, *he* was not there.

Gram was buried next to Grandfather Hadley-Trevelyan, and Aunt Gwen was buried next to Charlie's playground. Brother and sister, side by side, Andrew thought, and he wondered how his father would feel upon hearing the news, if somehow the news were able to reach him. Gram and Aunt Gwen, gone...Aunt Jane—where was she? With a shock, Andrew realized that, if his father returned now, he himself would be the only family member left to greet him.

Andrew's mother arranged for Thomas and Mrs. Tuttle to live in their quarters over the garage for as long as they so desired, and saw to it that they were given a pension out of the Hadley-Trevelyan family trust, as well. Lucia professed a desire to follow her friends to America; she had a second cousin there and wanted to start a new life in a place called Connecticut. Andrew's mother made sure that she received a tidy sum from the trust, enough to pay for passage and have a small nest egg with which to start her new life.

Although he treated his mother with brusqueness or icy indifference, Andrew carefully observed all that she said and did. *Know your opponent.* That's what his father had taught him. Any tidbits of information she dropped about this Yank she'd taken up with might come in useful. *That's the key to defeating someone: knowing his weaknesses and turning them to your advantage....*

His mother, though, said nothing about *him*. She did, though, leave Andrew with Thomas and Mrs. Tuttle the day after the funeral, saying that she had to go up to London to meet with the family solicitor concerning the disposition of the Hadley-Trevelyan family trust. She would be back the following day.

Right, Andrew thought. It's going to take her a day and a night to meet with the solicitor....

And pigs might fly!

His mother returned, as promised. She said nothing about *him*, though she did mention something (Andrew overheard her hushed conversation with Thomas and Mrs. Tuttle) that came as a surprise to Andrew: Freddie had a *sister*!

Half-sister, to be precise. All that Andrew could ascertain was that her name was Daphne, that she was several years younger than Freddie, and that she and Freddie had the same mother, as both her parents had been killed in the Blitz. She was heir to Freddie's personal fortune, which was somehow tied to the Hadley-Trevelyan family trust. At this point, Andrew's mother lowered her voice to Thomas and Mrs. Tuttle, and Andrew couldn't catch what she was saying.

Andrew's relief at Freddie's fortuitous demise was somewhat marred by this revelation. A sister! The sodding bastard—why did he have to leave a female counterpart behind? *He* was bad enough, but the thought of a feminine version of him left to walk the face of the earth was truly frightening! Andrew imagined Freddie's leering face, framed with long curly hair and topping a buxomy figure, and shuddered.

She'll be trouble for sure...If there's any justice in the world, she'd be locked up in a loony bin or a home for incorrigibles.

Andrew and his mother returned to Greycliff. The journey up to Northumberland passed in the same icy silence as their two previous trips during the past several days had transpired.

Andrew was, for once, glad for Greycliff's immense size, as it afforded him plenty of opportunities to avoid his mother. He sometimes wandered through the house; as soon as his mother came into the room he happened to be in, he would wordlessly saunter out and find another room that was more to his liking. For the most part, he stayed in his room; when his mother knocked on the door, he would slip out through the nanny's alcove adjoining his room and sneak down the backstairs to the kitchen. When he was forced to sit with his mother at mealtimes, he ate in silence.

His mother came into his room. She was dressed in uniform.

"Andrew, I have to leave in a few minutes. I might be flying some planes up to Scotland. If I pass over Greycliff, I'll circle around to get your attention, perhaps drop some sweets, all right?"

He didn't answer her.

"Andrew, I have to go now. I'll try to get another leave soon."

She waited for an answer. Andrew kept silent.

"I can wait a few minutes. Would you like to write a short note to Aunt Jane so that I can send it along to her?"

He turned from her.

"Goodbye," she said. "I love you."

Right, thought Andrew. You don't love me, you love what's-his-name. Go back to *him!* Go back to your loverboy Yank!

A few minutes later he heard the sound of the car pulling away.

"Andrew! Andrew!" Grandmother Howard was calling him. "It's your mother!"

It had been two weeks since his mother had left. Andrew heard the drone of the Spitfire's engine and, through his window, saw the plane circling over the front lawn. He stayed in his room.

Grandmother Howard was standing in his doorway now. "Andrew, your mother wants you to come outside and greet her!"

"I'm busy."

"What?"

"I have a lot of schoolwork to catch up on. I'm in the middle of studying geography. I don't want to be behind when I go back to school next year."

"Just a few minutes to greet your mother is not going to put you behind, surely!"

Andrew glared at her for a moment, and then bent his head over his geography book. What could she do about it, drag him outside?

She was a small woman; Andrew was nearly as tall as she was and weighed almost as much, besides.

"Andrew!" It was more of a plea than a command. When Andrew did not respond, she turned away, defeated, and left him alone. The plane continued to circle and, after a few minutes, dropped a shower of candy on the lawn. Then it flew off.

An hour later, he went outside to collect the brightly colored leavings scattered in the grass. He walked into the morning room, where Grandmother Howard sat reading, and wordlessly dumped his mother's offerings into the waste basket. His grandmother looked at him, startled and fearful. He glared back at her, challenging her to report to his mother his rejection of her favors.

It was now the middle of July. A month had gone by and he had not seen his mother fly over Greycliff. She had called several times, though. Andrew was careful not to answer the phone; let Maria do that—that's what maids were for, anyway. It had developed into a familiar routine: Maria would answer the phone and call for Andrew. After Andrew would refuse to take the call, Maria would say, "He can't come to the phone right now, would you like to talk to Mrs. Howard?" Grandmother would chat a bit and then call for Andrew again. Andrew had decided that it would be best not to be too antagonistic all the time. Even though he was not especially close to his grandmother, he knew it wouldn't be wise to further alienate her, so he would take the receiver, say "Yes?" very curtly, listen to whatever his mother had to say, grunt whenever necessary, and hand the phone back to his grandmother.

He was sitting outside under an oak tree in the garden when he heard the sound of a Spitfire in the distance. He saw the plane heading for the house; it was too late to make a run for it. Besides, Grandmother Howard was walking towards him, signaling with her hands that his mother's plane was overhead.

What does she think I am, blind and deaf? Andrew thought. It would look like too much of a scene if he ran inside; better to make his mother think he just didn't care. He stood up, put his hands in his pockets and looked at the ground.

"Andrew, come out from under the tree so your mother can see you!"

Andrew walked towards his grandmother, slowly, very slowly, and stood next to her, his hands still in his pockets and his head bent down. He occasionally glanced up at the sky, just looking with his eyes, not lifting his head.

The Spit flew several hundred feet above them, then soared upwards to about two thousand feet. At the apex of its trajectory it made a quarter-turn. Andrew expected it to continue turning until it was facing them, which would put it in a good position to come over them. Instead, the plane continued on its course, heading away from them at a right angle. Andrew saw a puff of white vapor coming from the side; then he heard the engine sputter and die. He held his breath, waiting for it to restart, but the ominous silence was unbroken. The Spit drifted away from them; like a leaf, silent—terribly, terribly silent.

The plane disappeared into the distance, losing altitude, as Andrew and his grand-mother watched, horrified. Andrew felt his body go into a spasm and the momentum propelled him into a run back towards the house. He heard himself screaming, *"It's my mother—she's going to crash! She's going to crash!"*

Alfred ran out from the garage. "What happened?" he asked.

The words tumbled out of Andrew, half of them in a croak, half of them in a scream. *"The engine quit—she's gliding—off to west—towards town."*

Grandmother Howard caught up with them. "Get the car, quickly!"

Alfred disappeared into the garage and, in a few seconds, drove the car up to them.

"Andrew, stay here!" his grandmother warned. "Alfred, hurry!" she cried as she got into the car.

"I'm coming too!" Andrew hollered. He threw himself into the front seat of the car and slammed the door.

"Andrew, you mustn't—"

"I said I was coming!" To Alfred he screamed, *"GO!"*

Alfred hit the accelerator and veered down the drive. He took the corner at the road a little too fast and the car swerved across the road, then recovered and sped towards town.

Andrew was in a cold sweat. He bit his lip to keep it from trembling. He would have given anything to be able to take back the last five minutes—better yet, the last several weeks—and he couldn't get out of his mind the damning realization that the last thing his mother had seen of him was a sullen, sulky boy who wouldn't even look up at her, who wouldn't even acknowledge that she existed. The last words he'd spoken to her were in anger: *Go away!*

What if her last memory of him was that of the bitter, petulant child who had made his feelings of hatred and contempt for her all too clear...and those last words, uttered in rage....

He moaned and closed his eyes for a second, then forced them open again. He needed to look for the plane—or rather, for the wreckage of the plane. He suddenly remembered Irene's funeral, and the words of the pallbearers: "The wreckage and what was left of the pilot were strewn over a square mile...."

Sandbags in the coffin.

He fought waves of nausea and panic as he imagined, or rather tried *not* to imag-ine, what they would find when they came to the site of the crash. But there was no turning back now.

They were almost into town. "...She couldn't have gone more than a few miles," Grandmother Howard was saying. "Where could she have landed? It's so rough and hilly here!"

Alfred's face exploded in realization. "I know *just* where she would go!"

He turned onto the south road, which led out into the country again.

"Nicholson's Pasture!" Grandmother Howard breathed.

"She'd try to make it there!" Alfred affirmed.

The road was very bumpy and curvy now and Alfred had to slow down. They turned at the sign that read: "Nicholson's Stables and Riding School". The road rose to a hillcrest and, as they reached the top, they saw it: the Spitfire, lying in a field below, tilted to one side with one wing pointing skyward and the other wing caught against a moss-covered stump. A crowd of people had gathered round. Alfred pulled to the side of the road and Andrew opened the door and hit the ground running before the car stopped.

He saw that the canopy was open and the plane was empty. He clambered up onto the wing and looked inside. On the floor was a canvas sack. He picked it up and poured out the contents: candy and chocolates.

"Where's the pilot?" he asked the onlookers.

A little boy spoke up. "I saw it! I saw it all! The plane came down and went along all right and then it spun round and round like a top!" He demonstrated to his audience, putting one hand on the ground and pivoting around on it while pointing the other arm towards the sky.

"The pilot! Where's the pilot?" Andrew was frantic.

"It was a woman pilot! A *woman!*" one man exclaimed.

"Where is she?" Andrew cried.

A woman spoke. "The ambulance just came and took her away." She pointed towards town.

The little boy chimed in. "She's dead! I could tell she was dead! Her eyes were closed and she wasn't moving!"

Chapter 20

*A*ndrew felt his knees turn to jelly, then was aware of Alfred's hand on his shoulder. "Andrew, she might have been just knocked out. They took her to hospital—let's go back to town and find out for sure."

Andrew half stumbled, half ran, back to the car. Once inside, with the car underway at a good clip, he allowed himself the luxury of closing his eyes.

Please, please God...Please let her be alive! I'm sorry, I'm sorry, I'll take everything back that I thought about her. I'll never speak crossly to her again. I'll even—

He shuddered, and felt as if an invisible hand were reaching into his heart, into his soul, taking hold of the one thing that he struggled to hold back in his bargaining with the Almighty.

I'll even accept...him, if that's what you want me to do...if you'll give me back my mother...please!

His eyes still closed, he was conscious of the car making a series of turns. They must be in town now. The car slowed, then stopped. Andrew opened his eyes. They were at the hospital.

He dashed up the steps to the front entrance, Grandmother and Alfred following him. They walked into the front lobby, where a formidable figure in a frumpy grey dress sat behind a desk. She eyed them suspiciously. "May I help you?"

Andrew's grandmother spoke. "We were looking for a woman pilot—my daughter. She was flying a Spitfire and crashed in Nicholson's Pasture. Is she here?"

The receptionist nodded. "She was just brought in. The doctor is attending to her right now."

"Is she all right?" Andrew asked.

"The doctor will discuss that with you," the receptionist said curtly. To Andrew's grandmother she said, "I need to fill out some forms. Please sit down." She pointed to some chairs next to her desk. Andrew noticed his mother's Flight Authorization card on the blotter.

"Let's see...." The receptionist peered at the card. "Your daughter's name is Alice Givens?" She pronounced it *Jivens*.

"It's pronounced Givens," Grandmother Howard corrected, saying the name with a hard *G*.

"Maiden Name?"

"Howard."

"Date of Birth?"

"April 8, 1912."

"Husband's name?"

295

"Jacob Givens."

"Where can her husband be contacted?"

"He's a reconnaissance pilot in the RAF. I don't know what squadron he's in. You might contact the ATA. I'm sure that there would be some information about him in her records."

"Home address?"

"His? Or ours?"

"Both, preferably."

"We live at Greycliff." Grandmother Howard indicated that "we" meant herself and Andrew. "This is her son, Andrew."

The woman glanced at Andrew, then resumed her paperwork.

Grandmother Howard continued. "Her husband is American. I know that he's from a place called Scotch Plains, New Jersey. I'm sorry, I don't know the full address."

"Does she have any medical conditions that we should be made aware of? Illnesses, drug allergies, that sort of thing?"

"No."

The receptionist wrote down the information on the admission papers. Andrew stared ruefully at the pen issuing squiggles across the form. He was torn between relief and dismay. Relief, since the receptionist was asking questions about his mother's medical history, so she must be all right. Dismay, because the whole line of questioning had made him uneasy. Her husband this, her husband that—this stranger, whom Andrew had only seen for a few minutes was an especially significant person right now. For that matter, he was the *only* significant person right now, at least as far as the authorities were concerned.

He wandered over to a window in the far corner of the lobby. The sun was still shining. People were going about their business: Women hurried along, clutching bundles of groceries; children scampered down the sidewalk. It seemed as if he were watching a movie—unreal, unconnected with shattering events that had just taken place. He heard a man's voice behind him.

"We're still working on her." Andrew turned around and saw that a doctor was talking to Grandmother. "As far as we can tell so far, she has a broken arm and a nasty bump on the head. She's unconscious. We'll let you know as soon as she's out of treatment." Then he was gone.

Andrew walked over to his grandmother. Tears were etching their way down her crinkled cheeks. He put his arms around her, and held her close.

After what seemed like an eternity, the doctor returned.

"She's in a room now. You may go in and see her."

They followed him down a long corridor and through a maze of shorter passageways to a plain, sunlit room with two beds. Lying on the bed closest to the door was his mother's still figure.

"She hasn't regained consciousness," the doctor said. Andrew noticed that her right arm was in a cast and that she appeared to be in a very deep sleep. He went to her and touched her hand.

"Mum," he whispered.

She did not stir. He looked to the doctor. "Is she—I mean, when is she going to wake up?"

The doctor glanced down for a moment, then looked back at Andrew. It was a few seconds before he spoke.

"There's really no way to tell, right now. Maybe in a few hours, maybe in a day or two...."

"Is she going to *wake up?*" Andrew's voice was frantic.

The doctor looked at Grandmother Howard. "Very often people do wake up, and recover quite nicely. Don't assume the worst right now."

"Is there anything we can do?" she asked.

The doctor exhaled sharply. After a moment he spoke.

"Well, it may not be considered standard medical practice; that is, it's not something that's taught in medical school. However, I've noticed that, many times, people who have been in a coma or in some sort of state of unconsciousness, upon awakening, report that during that time they've heard or felt things that have happened. On some level, they have been aware of what has been going on around them. I believe that if you talk to her, touch her gently, try to make her aware of your presence, it might bring her back...sooner. It's no guarantee, but I think it's worth trying. I'll arrange for you to stay in her room for a few days. If she regains consciousness, the best thing would be to have familiar faces near her."

"Thank you, doctor," Andrew's grandmother said. Her face took on a worried look. "Is there—when she regains consciousness—is there a possibility that there could be some memory loss? Amnesia, I mean? I know that it can happen. One of my cousins fell off a horse and was knocked out. When he came to, he couldn't remember the last five years of his life. He had just gotten married, and he didn't even know his wife! I've heard that sometimes people can have a complete loss of memory: They don't remember anything at all, not even their own name!"

"Well, it's a possibility, but I wouldn't worry about it right now. Often people have no recollection of the trauma that they have experienced, mercifully. Sometimes the last few weeks or months are a bit fuzzy. Total amnesia is, well, quite rare, considering the number of head injuries that do occur."

"Thank you very much," Grandmother said. "We really do appreciate everything you've done." She looked at Andrew. "I'll tell Alfred that we'll be staying here, and send him home to get some of our things." She disappeared down the hall.

The doctor put his hand on Andrew's shoulder. "Don't worry," he said. He looked as if he wanted to say something else, but what else was there to say? Then he, too, was gone.

Andrew, now alone with his mother, knelt by the bed and patted her hand.

"Please, Mum, wake up! Remember, Mum, you had an accident. You were flying over Greycliff and the engine quit. You were just about to drop some candy for me.

I'm sorry I didn't wave to you— I'm sorry that I've been so cross. Please come back! Please, Mum—I love you!"

His mother remained as still and unresponsive as she had been when he first entered the room.

Andrew and his grandmother spent the rest of the day in his mother's room. Andrew sat beside his mother the whole time, holding her hand and saying over and over, "I'm sorry, Mum—I'm sorry. Please come back!"

The nurse brought in a tray of food for supper. "She has a ration book, so she gets the meal, and I thought you two would like a bite to eat," she explained. Andrew and his grandmother took a few nibbles, but sent most of it back; neither of them felt much like eating. Later, the night nurse brought a cot into the room, which Andrew slept on; he insisted that his grandmother take the vacant bed on the other side of the room. His grandmother took the first watch that night, letting Andrew get some sleep. He tossed and turned and woke up several times before he finally got a full four hours worth of sleep, awakening at three in the morning. His grandmother was snoozing in the chair by his mother's bed. Patting her hand, he whispered, "Go to bed, I'll stay with her now."

Andrew held his grandmother's arm as she shuffled across the room to her bed. He returned to his mother's side and sat down in the chair. His eyes adjusted to the dark, and he looked at his mother's face. She could just be sleeping, he thought.

His thoughts wandered back to the matters his grandmother had discussed with the doctor. What if she woke up and didn't remember anything? No, the doctor said that complete amnesia was rare. What if she woke up and couldn't remember... couldn't remember, say, the last few months, the last year or two? Grandmother's cousin couldn't remember his wife, but could remember everything up until a few years before his accident. What if...what if she couldn't remember Jake, but could remember everything that had happened before a year or two ago? Even several years wouldn't matter. It was unlikely, he thought, that the last twelve years would be a blank. Certainly she would remember her own son!

And if she remembered me, she would remember Dad too....

The first few shafts of daylight broke through the gaps around the edges of the blackout curtain. Andrew got up and pulled it back. Dawn was streaking across the sky, chasing the dark away. *The darkest hour is just before dawn.* He couldn't remember where he had heard that, but hope and relief slowly rose within him.

Maybe everything is going to turn out all right after all. If she wakes up and doesn't remember Jake...Perhaps this all happened to put everything back to the way it should be.

Andrew's grandmother slept until seven o'clock, when the day nurse came in and chased them out.

"I have to tidy her up a bit. The doctor's going to look at her. I can get you a breakfast tray and you can eat in the solarium or, if you'd prefer some *real* food, there's a nice restaurant across the street. We'll come get you if we need you."

"That sounds like a good idea," Grandmother replied. "Come along, Andrew."

Andrew reluctantly left the room and followed her down the hall. Just before they passed the nurses' station, they heard an angry bellow from one of the rooms.

"What do you *mean*, I don't get breakfast because I don't have a ration book?" Andrew noted that the voice had an American accent, with a distinct Southern drawl. "I came over here to fight for your country, *your* country, and you're going to let me starve to death because I don't have the necessary paperwork! You Brits are all alike— you need a form for everything! You could win the war by just giving all your stupid paperwork and bureaucratic bullshit to the Nazis. What else do I need—written permission to fart?"

"What's that all about?" Grandmother asked the nurse at the desk.

"He's an American soldier, got hit by a car last night. He looked to the left instead of to the right when he was crossing the street. He has a sprained ankle and a bump on the head. He's going to be released to an American hospital—soon, I hope."

"You can't expect one to be in a good temper when one is hungry and denied food because of not having the proper paperwork. My daughter is still unconscious, and we're going out for breakfast. Why don't you use her ration book for him?"

"How kind of you. Yes, I'll arrange for that. Thank you very much!"

Andrew and his grandmother had a breakfast of scones and tea at the restaurant. When they returned to the hospital, the nurse met them as they were walking down the hall.

"The American soldier was very grateful for your generosity and he wants to thank you personally. I don't know if you're up to paying a social call—"

"It would be no trouble at all," Grandmother told her.

The nurse ushered them into the soldier's room and introduced them to him, saying, "These are the people who lent you the ration book."

The young man, lying in bed with his left ankle in a splint, extended his hand to Andrew, and nodded to Grandmother. Andrew noticed that he was young, in his early twenties perhaps, with brown hair, a friendly face, and an easy grin.

"I'd just like to thank y'all for being so kind and hospitable," the young man said. "I wish there was some way I could return the favor."

"Don't worry about that," Grandmother told him. "We have no need of it right now. My daughter is still unconscious, and it seemed like a perfectly sensible thing to do. We, that is, Andrew and I, went out for breakfast."

"The nurse told me that she's a ferry pilot and that she had to make a forced landing. I sure hope she wasn't hurt too bad."

Andrew hung his head, and the soldier reached for his hand and squeezed it. "Hey, your ma's gonna be okay," he said gently. His face brightened. "Look at me. I got knocked out for a minute, and I'm right as rain now. Pleased to meet you, Andrew. Oh, the nurse forgot to introduce me to you—name's Napoleon Bonaparte, but you can call me Frenchy for short!" He winked at Andrew.

Andrew smiled; he couldn't help himself. Even though the young man was a Yank, he seemed like a perfectly nice fellow, and Andrew found his breezy manner and affable nature appealing. Maybe there were some Yanks who weren't so bad, after all.

"Hey, I'm just joshing you. As a matter of fact, my nickname's really Frenchy, but my real name is Gerry Versailles." He pronounced it *Ver-sails*.

"Ver-sails," said Grandmother. That doesn't sound French."

"It's spelled V-E-R-S-A-I-L-L-E-S, just like the Treaty, but my family has been in America so long that people don't bother with the French pronunciation anymore."

"What part of America are you from?" Grandmother asked.

"Lexington, Kentucky."

"My daughter's husband is an American. He's a pilot, and is from a place called Scotch Plains, New Jersey."

"New Jersey's in the northeast, near New York City. My sister is a nurse in New York, and her fiance is from New Jersey. He's in the Pacific right now, but she visits his parents. Your son-in-law is with the US Army Air Force, right?"

"No, actually he's with the RAF. He used to be a fighter pilot, but now he's in photo-reconnaissance. He and my daughter were married a few months ago."

Gerry looked at Andrew and cocked his head slightly. An expression of sympathy filled his eyes.

Andrew spoke softly. "My father was shot down. Three years ago. He was in the RAF."

"Like your stepdad?"

Andrew looked away. He didn't want to acknowledge any relationship with Jake, or affirm that Jake and his father shared any kind of similarity.

"I'm sorry." Gerry said. "I lost my pa when I was about your age. It's rough, I know."

"The doctor would like to speak with you." The nurse stood in the doorway and motioned to Andrew's grandmother.

"Excuse me, it was very nice meeting you, Gerry." Grandmother started to leave.

"The pleasure's mine, Mrs. Howard. Oh, I um...I'd like to apologize for—well, I guess you heard me carrying on about the rules and regulations and the British way of doing things and I... well, I didn't mean it!"

"Of course you didn't," Grandmother said cheerily. "Hunger does horrible things to a person!"

Gerry smiled with relief. "Thanks again for the ration book."

"Not at all," Grandmother replied.

"Bye Andrew." Gerry said.

"Bye." Andrew followed his grandmother back to his mother's room. The doctor was waiting in the doorway.

"Her vital signs, her reflexes and reactions look good. I can't promise you anything, but it does look hopeful."

"Thank you," Grandmother said.

After the doctor left, Andrew went over to his mother's bed, put his arms around her, and hugged her close. "Come on, Mum. You're going to be all right!"

Andrew remained by his mother's side for the rest of the day. She did not awaken, but tossed and wriggled every so often, like someone caught in a dream. Every time she moved, Andrew grabbed her hand and stroked her face and spoke softly to her.

A little after noon, Grandmother excused herself to go out to the restaurant. "I'll nip on over for a bit; then you can go out to get a bite to eat."

Andrew nodded. After she left, he sat by his mother's side, took her hand and squeezed it. Now that he was alone with her, he could tell his mother again what still lay as a burden upon his heart.

"I'm sorry, Mum. I'm sorry I was mean to you. Please wake up! I promise I won't ever be cross with you again. It's all right, your being married again, and all—I just want you back! Please!"

Andrew suddenly had a funny feeling that he was not alone. He looked over his shoulder, and there, standing at the foot of the bed, was Jake. He was staring at Andrew's mother, his face stunned and fearful. He glanced at Andrew, then stepped to the right side of the bed, opposite Andrew, and sat down on the bed right next to Andrew's mother. He reached his hand to her face and stroked her cheek. Andrew immediately noticed the glint of the wedding ring on his finger, then saw that Jake's hands were terribly scarred. They looked like a kind of bizarre patchwork of different-ent colored bits of skin appliqued to the scorched and disfigured flesh beneath. Jake brushed his fingers across her lips and whispered, "Alice".

Her eyes suddenly opened. She stared at Jake. Her expression looked bewildered at first; then her eyes seem to glaze over.

"Alice?" Jake said, startled and worried.

She continued to regard him with an uncomprehending, puzzled stare. Andrew's heart seem to skip a beat.

She doesn't recognize him! She doesn't even know him!

He tried not to show his elation. Forcing himself to be very calm, he squeezed his mother's hand gently.

"Mum," he said softly, confidently.

She turned to look at him. Andrew expected her face to break into a look of awareness and recognition. Instead, she fixed him with the same vacant, unknowing gaze.

"Mum—?"

There was not even a flicker of comprehension in her eyes. He stared at her, stunned, and the silence roared in his ears. The room seemed to swirl around him and he felt himself dropping into an abyss of terror.

She doesn't know me either!

Chapter 21

*H*is mother's eyes closed again, and Andrew felt a paralyzing horror descend on him. His breath came out in spasms, and he blurted out, "She doesn't remember...She doesn't recognize us!"

He felt a hand on his shoulder: Jake's. At that moment all his animosity and hatred disintegrated; Jake's touch felt like a rescuing clasp. A scene flashed through Andrew's mind, one of his earliest memories. He had fallen into the goldfish pond at Armus House and had almost drowned. At the time he was only about three or four years old and couldn't swim. It was Freddie who had pulled him out: Freddie, whom he had always disliked; Freddie, who then had proceeded to shake him savagely and call him a silly blighter. Yet, at that moment, Andrew had never in his whole life been more grateful for the touch of another human hand...until now. Jake's gesture was more than an expression of comfort; it also spoke the anguish and anxiety that he shared with Andrew. Their eyes met, and Andrew felt as if he were being carried away by a force over which he had no control; he had, by no volition of his own, formed a bond of fear and hope with this interloper, who was now a partner in this terrifying experience.

Jake spoke to Andrew's mother again. "Alice, we're here. It's us, Andrew and me. Come on, Alice, wake up!" He stroked her face insistently. Andrew noticed that his hands were trembling. Her eyes fluttered open again; she looked first at Jake, then at Andrew. Andrew desperately tried to ascertain if she recognized them, but her expression was inscrutable: It was impossible to tell if it was confusion, or concern, in her eyes.

Then Andrew felt her hand move in his; she was attempting to pry his fingers from hers. His hand went limp, and she held it gently, as if weighing it; then she grasped it and placed it on top of Jake's hand, the one which rested on her injured arm. As if exhausted by the effort, she closed her eyes again, but her hand firmly held Andrew's hand on Jake's.

Andrew's voice came out as a whispery croak. "Mum?"

She opened her eyes again, and in them Andrew read clearly what was on her mind and in her heart: A plea.

By nightfall, Andrew's mother was sitting up in bed and chattering happily. Andrew and Jake both spent the night in her room; Jake on the cot and Andrew in the spare bed. At first, Grandmother had insisted that Andrew come home with her and let his mother and Jake have some time alone together, but Jake had intervened and said that it would be better for Andrew to remain so that either one of them would be awake at all times, just in case. He added that he had been up all night and all day, and would no doubt sleep much too soundly to be aware if something happened. Furthermore, he insisted that he would be quite comfortable on the cot; it wasn't any worse than many of his previous sleeping arrangements. "There were lots of times when I slept in the cockpit of my plane or underneath it," he added. He took the first watch, sitting in the chair by the bed, and Andrew immediately fell asleep. Just before dawn he woke up and he saw that Jake was still awake. Andrew went to him, nodded that he could take over. Jake staggered across the room and collapsed onto the cot.

Around eight o'clock his mother awakened. Andrew motioned to her to be quiet and whispered, "Jake was up almost all night." She smiled, and it looked as if she were about to say something when the nurse walked in.

"Well now, aren't we feeling much better now? We had a nasty bump on the head, didn't we?"

Andrew's mother grinned and said, "We're very hungry too, and horribly grotty as well, and we would be absolutely delighted with a nice hot bath right now!"

Jake stirred, and the nurse announced, "Rise and shine, sleepyhead!" To both Andrew and Jake she said, "Both of you, out of here in ten minutes! We've got to get tidied up. The doctor will be here soon."

Jake sat up and rubbed his eyes. He was still in his uniform, which was now wrinkled and disheveled. "I brought some spare clothes, so I just need to find a place to change," he said groggily.

"Change in here. I won't mind," Andrew's mother suggested. Then she added playfully, "I promise to behave myself!"

Jake crossed the floor and kissed her on the forehead. "Have I ever complained?" he asked.

Jake's words suddenly hit Andrew like a thunderbolt. Instinctively he shuddered; for some reason what Jake had said seemed like a deja-vu.

Where had he heard those words before?

"Hey, hey, look's like someone is up and at 'em and raring to go!" Gerry was standing in the doorway, balancing himself on crutches. To Andrew he said, "See, I told you everything was gonna be okay! You just got to believe a good ole boy when he tells you something!"

Andrew introduced him. "Mum, this is Gerry Versailles. He used your ration book yesterday. They weren't going to feed him because he didn't have one."

Andrew's mother extended her hand. "Alice Givens. Delighted."

And this is my husband, Jake."

Jake and Gerry shook hands. "You're from America, too, aren't you?" Gerry asked him.

Jake nodded. Andrew's mother said, "Andrew and Jake were just going out for breakfast."

"Well, hey, I'm going to be discharged soon and I was going to go out to eat, too.

If you two wouldn't mind, I'd love to treat you. I'd like to be able to return the favor, since you were responsible for keeping me from starving to death yesterday!"

Andrew's mother glanced at Andrew, then at Jake. Hope was in her eyes. Jake and Andrew both shrugged, and she chirped, "Oh, that's so kind of you! Of course!"

"Great! I'll charm this pretty little nurse into getting my discharge papers signed toute suite." Gerry winked at the nurse, who was well over twice his age and outweighed him by half again.

In a few minutes they were ready to go. Gerry tramped down the hall, crutches swinging in accompaniment as he eagerly propelled himself ahead. Jake and Andrew helped him down the hospital steps; Andrew held his crutches as Jake steadied him. That obstacle negotiated, they continued on their way.

"Just make sure I look the right way when we cross the street!" Gerry laughed.

"After awhile you'll get used to it," Jake reassured him.

"You been here awhile?" Gerry asked him.

"Over three years."

They crossed the street and arrived at the restaurant. They were seated, and noted the daily fare scribbled on a blackboard.

"Well, Andrew," Gerry said. "You've been here before—any suggestions?"

"The scones are very good—the porridge is lumpy, though."

"Scones it is—Jake?"

"Fine with me."

Gerry placed their order, and conversation resumed.

"Andrew told me that you're a fighter pilot," Gerry said to Jake. "Were you in the Battle of Britain?"

Jake nodded.

"You flew Spitfires, then?"

"Not then; there weren't enough to go around. I flew Hurricanes."

"Hurricanes? I've heard of them. So, some of the fighters in the Battle of Britain were Hurricanes?"

"*Most* of the fighters in the Battle of Britain were Hurricanes. In fact, there were about twice as many of them as there were Spitfires. Spitfires just got the publicity."

"Wow, I didn't know that! You always hear about the Spitfires and how they won the Battle."

"Actually, the Hurricanes shot down more German planes than all other defenses combined, both on the ground and in the air, Spits included. They accounted for about eighty percent of all enemy aircraft destroyed. In fact, if we'd had only Spitfires during the Battle of Britain, we probably would have lost to the Luftwaffe."

Gerry whistled. "You don't say! I always thought that the Spitfire was the better airplane."

"Well, to be honest, it is," Jake replied. "The Spit is more maneuverable and much faster, and climbs better. If I had my choice, I would have preferred flying Spits then, and my squadron was eventually equipped with them. But the Hurricane had one important advantage: Its turnaround time was much shorter than that of the Spitfire's.

It took only nine minutes to get it re-armed and refueled. The Spit took almost half an hour, and during the Battle of Britain it could only be serviced at a few bases that were equipped to handle them. The Hurri's short turnaround time was a crucial factor in our being able to hit the Nazis in the air, before they got a chance to hit us on the ground. The Hurricane also had a longer range than the Spit, so it could stay airborne longer."

"But from what I've heard, the Hurricane was no match for the ME-109," Gerry said.

"For the most part, it wasn't. The 109 could outclimb it, outdive it, and was faster. The Hurricane could turn circles around a 109, though, and if you knew how to use that advantage, you could inflict a lot of damage. For the most part, though, the Hurricanes took on the bombers, and the Spits, which were faster and climbed better, went after the fighters. You could say that they complemented each other very well."

"Were there any other differences between flying Hurricanes and Spitfires?"

"Spits were good in the air, but a tricky piece of business on the ground. The undercarriage retracted outward, not inward like the Hurricane's, and that put the wheels closer together on the ground. So it wasn't as quite as stable on take-off and landings as the Hurris were. Hurris were better suited to carrier operations; the Spits tended to skitter around the deck too much. The Spit didn't have great forward vision on the ground, either. Your view was blocked because the plane stuck so far out in front, and you had to weave it around to see where you were going."

Their food was served and, between mouthfuls, Jake talked more of the relative merits of Spitfires and Hurricanes: "During run-ups, the Spit had a tendency to tip forward, so you had to get someone to sit on the tail. If you hear any wild stories about a pilot taking off with his rigger or somebody on his tail, they're probably true. Sometimes if the ground was rough, one of the ground crew sat on the tail while the pilot taxied out. If they didn't get off fast enough, they got a wild ride!"

Gerry laughed. "I *have* heard a tale or two—heard one about a guy who took off with a WAAF on his tail!"

Jake reddened and cleared his throat nervously. Gerry's eyes bulged. "*Not you—*"

Jake cleared his throat again. "Well, there might have been more than one—"

Gerry howled and slapped his leg. "Well I'll be a son of a gun—here I am, talking with the culprit! When did you realize you had a passenger?"

Jake chuckled. "After I'd taken off, I couldn't get the plane leveled out. I radioed to my wingman that I was having trouble, and he flew in close to see what was wrong. Then he yelled *Bloody hell, Jake—you've got a WAAF on your tail!* I was as nervous as hell coming in for a landing."

"Was she okay?"

"Oh, after we'd peeled her off the tailplane, she was all right, sort of. I gave her a bottle of whisky and persuaded her commanding officer to give her a week off. She returned to duty, not a bit worse for wear, but she never volunteered to tail-sit my plane again!"

Gerry laughed heartily. "Well, I could see where she might be a bit gun-shy. What other differences were there? Between Spits and Hurris, I mean."

"The Hurricane had four sets of controls to the elevators and rudders," Jake replied. "That was an advantage if you got shot up on one side. It was an incredibly rugged airplane, and a great gun platform. It was a stable, steady kite; steadiness was not the Spitfire's strong suit. Anyone who's ever flown a cannon-firing Spit could appreciate that." Jake paused, and drank his tea. After swallowing a few mounthfuls of food, he continued.

"The Spit, though, had the advantage against the German fighters, and the Hurricanes were largely withdrawn from fighter operations in England after the Battle of Britain. They were put to good use in North Africa, though."

"Why didn't they have so many Spitfires at the time?" Gerry asked. "I mean, if it was better against the 109, you'd think they would have had more of them."

"Hawker had gotten the Hurricane into production a whole year ahead of the Spitfire, and they were cranking them out pretty fast. Supermarine had a lot of early production problems with the Spit, since it was a radically new design for a fighter. It was originally designed as a racing seaplane. Once in the air, though, the Spit was in a class of its own. It was a joy to fly—" Jake smiled and gazed into space.

"I've seen that smile before," Gerry said.

"What?" Jake shook himself out of his trance.

"A Spitfire smile," Gerry said. "One of the pilots at our base trained on Spitfires, and he'd get that funny smile on his face too, whenever he talked about Spits."

Jake laughed. "Well, they used to say, the Hurricane's like a good friend; the Spitfire is like someone you fall in love with." He sipped his tea, glanced at Andrew a bit nervously, seemingly at a loss as to what to say to include him. He turned to Gerry again.

"It's funny, the whole thing of Spits versus Hurris extended to the Germans as well. They had a certain amount of 'Spitfire Snobbery', too. One of the guys in our squadron went to visit a German fighter pilot that he'd shot down; this was early in the summer of '40, before things heated up. The German was in the hospital, and our pilot brought him some cigarettes and stuff. The Jerry refused to believe that he'd been shot down by a Hurricane, kept on insisting that he was hit by a Spitfire!"

"Boy, that's a good one! Gosh, I can't believe I'm sitting here, talking to a pilot who was in the Battle of Britain! You must have seen quite a lot, huh?"

Jake was suddenly silent. He looked into his cup of tea. "Yeah," he said softly. After a moment, he cleared his throat and said to Gerry, "So, you're with the US Army Air Force?"

"I'm an armorer, in a fighter squadron. Eighth Air Force."

"P-47's, then?"

"Yeah, Jugs," Gerry smiled. "I like what I do, but I know it's nothing compared to your job."

"Well, don't underestimate your importance. We pilots depend on the guys on the ground. I had the best ground crew anyone could want. They were tops, really knew their stuff and put a thousand percent into what they did. Quick thinking, too. For instance, one time I had just landed my Hurri and was waiting for it to get turned around. I was talking with my fitter, then I looked up and noticed that my armorer was peeing on the wing!"

"*What?*"

"That was my reaction," Jake said. "So I yelled, 'Banger— what the hell are you doing to my plane?'" and he says, 'Sir, there's an incendiary jammed in the gun— it's split, and it's smoking, sir. Just putting out the fire!'"

Gerry laughed. "That's what you call thinking on your feet! Hope they gave the guy a medal!"

Jake rolled his eyes. "The adjutant wanted to bring him up on charges—indecent exposure, because there were WAAFs around. Even the WAAFS thought it was ridiculous, and our squadron leader persuaded the adj to drop it."

"How'd he make the guy see reason?"

"He promised that, if he proceeded, everyone in the squadron would drop their drawers the next time we had an inspection by the Wing Commander."

Gerry shook his head and chuckled. "I'll remember that one; who knows, I might have to utilize unauthorized equipment to save one of Uncle Sam's airplanes!"

Jake grinned, then asked, "What part of the South are you from, Gerry?"

"Lexington, Kentucky."

"Bluegrass Country—real pretty out there."

"Sure is. Have you ever been there?"

"I've flown over it. I was a commercial pilot in the States, off and on, before I joined the RAF."

"What did you do when you weren't flying?"

"Went to college."

Gerry whistled. "Good for you! I mean, being a pilot and also wanting to get that sheepskin. What did you major in?"

Jake downed his tea and said tersely, "Pharmacy."

"Pharmacy! Uh, I mean, that's an interesting combination. Didja ever get called the "Flying Pharmacist"?

Jake shook his head. "No." There was a brief silence; the waitress refilled their tea, and Jake continued. "Actually, I didn't finish up my degree. And I didn't tell too many people about it, besides."

"Oh," Gerry said. "What made you interested in a career in pharmacy?"

Jake grunted, and sipped his tea again. "I wasn't."

"Oh."

Jake evinced a tense smile and said, "Well, going to college wasn't my idea, either."

"Oh."

They continued eating; then Gerry said to Jake, "You're from New Jersey, aren't you?"

"Yeah, a town called Scotch Plains."

"My sister's fiance is from New Jersey. A place called Dunellen. Ever heard of it?"

"Yeah, it's just a few miles from Scotch Plains."

"Funny, you don't sound like you're from New Jersey. If I hadn't known, I would have thought you were from the Midwest."

Jake smiled. "You have a good ear. Actually, I spent a lot of time in Nebraska when I was growing up. Every summer, and also my last two years of high school."

"Didn't care too much for New Jersey, huh?"

Jake stared at his tea. "Something like that."

It bothered Andrew that Jake could be quite chatty when he was talking "shop," but when the conversation turned to personal matters, he became quite reticent. What was he trying to hide?

The conversation turned to technical matters again.

"I heard," Gerry said, "That early on in the Battle of Britain, the guns on the British fighters were harmonized at four hundred yards."

"Yeah," Jake replied. "The idea was to be out of range of the German guns but, shoot, you couldn't hit the broad side of a barn at four hundred yards. All that guaranteed was that a pilot who was a mediocre shot would get a few hits; the good shot was penalized. If you got in close, you wound up scattering gunfire all over the place, so most of us had our guns reharmonized to two-fifty, even before the big guys sent word officially. I set mine to fifty yards."

"*Fifty?*" Gerry whistled in amazement. "Boy, you liked to get in close, didn't you?"

Jake answered, simply, "Yeah." He glanced at Andrew again, then turned to Gerry.

"Are you planning on going back to Bluegrass country when the war's over, Gerry?"

"Oh, I'm not sure. I think I'd like to wander around the country for awhile, then probably settle back East. My sister plans on settling down in New Jersey after the war's over. Her name's Mary Jo. Right now, she's a nurse in New York City, at Bellevue Hospital."

"Bellevue." Jake grinned. "That's where all the nuts go, right?"

"Yeah," Gerry laughed. "Well, you hafta be nuts to like New York, but she likes it. She's my twin sister."

"My father has a twin sister!" Andrew exclaimed.

"Is that so?" Gerry asked.

Andrew suddenly felt embarrassed talking about his father in the presence of the man who had taken his place; it seemed almost sacrilegious to his father's memory. Then a thought crystallized in his mind. His feelings about Jake were a maelstrom of conflicting emotions: The anxiety and relief which had bound them together the day before still affected him, holding the hostile passions in abeyance. The dislike was still there, but it expressed itself more objectively as an attitude, rather than an emotion.

It might not be a bad idea to talk about my father in front of Jake, Andrew decided. What could be the harm in letting him see that the man he so blithely replaced was someone very special and wonderful, not just a faceless entity?

"My father's sister was my Aunt Jane. My father's name is Roger." Andrew paused, leaving a space of silence around his father's name.

He had a name, didn't you know that, Yank?

Jake pressed his palms together. His eyes glared ahead, yet seemed distant. Andrew went on. "They were very close. They knew what the other was thinking or feeling, even when they were miles apart."

"Really?" Gerry was astonished.

Andrew noted Jake's reaction: He continued to stare into space, silent. His jaw twitched slightly.

"Yes," Andrew said. "They knew if the other was in trouble if they were apart, and when they were together they could tell what the other was thinking, without saying a word—" Andrew's voice choked in his throat as he suddenly felt overcome with a terrible longing to see his father again. Sitting here with the man who had replaced him only made things worse: *If only he were here to make things right again.* Even talking about Aunt Jane had unnerved him too: *Where is she? And what's happened to her?*

"Excuse me." Jake jumped up and, without another word, left Andrew and Gerry alone to finish their meal. Andrew noted the tense look on his face and the flash of what looked like guilt in his eyes.

Good... Very good.

Gerry looked at Andrew. "Mary Jo knows me better than I know myself, and I could tell what she was feeling, with her not having to say anything a 'tall. It's not as fantastic as knowing what the other was thinking or feeling miles away, like what you just told me about your father and your aunt, but oftentimes I used to get this funny feeling that something was wrong even if we were away from each other, and I was usually right. I never told any of the other guys about it; they woulda thought it was something weird. To them, a sister is someone you pester or tease, not someone you feel close to. It's good to know that someone else has had the same experience."

Jake returned. Gerry looked at his watch. "Whoa, I'd better be getting back. My ride's due any minute."

After Gerry paid the bill, they returned to the hospital. Gerry went to the nurse's station to collect his things. Jake and Andrew started down the hall but the nurse called them back.

"The doctor is seeing her now. Why don't you wait here until he's finished." They walked back to the nurses' station and found Gerry reading a message.

"Looks like another snafu," he muttered.

"What's a snafu?" Andrew asked.

"Situation Normal, All F—Fouled Up. US Army standard procedure. My ride won't arrive until tomorrow. Looks like I'll be hanging around." He turned to the nurse. "Know where I can find a room for the night? Close by?"

Andrew had an inspiration. "Why don't you stay with us? I'm sure it would be all right with my grandmother."

"Gosh, I don't want to impose. It's really kind of you to offer."

"No, it would be no trouble at all! We have a huge house, with lots of spare rooms. I'll give my grandmother a call."

Andrew had the nurse ring Greycliff, talked with his grandmother, then announced to Gerry that it would be all right for him to stay: "Alfred is going to bring my grandmother here in a little while, so that she can spend some time with my mother. Then we'll all go back to Greycliff together."

"Alfred—is he a friend of your grandmother's?"

"No, he's the chauffeur."

"Wow, I never thought that I'd be riding around with a chauffeur! Nothing like going in style!"

The doctor approached the nurses' station. He nodded to Jake and drew him away. After spending a few moments in conversation with him, the doctor returned to Andrew and Gerry.

"Your mother is going to be just fine," the doctor told Andrew. "She'll probably be able to go home in a day or two. You may go in and see her now."

Andrew excused himself. Gerry said that he would be waiting in the solarium.

Entering his mother's room, Andrew saw that she was sitting up in bed, drinking a cup of tea. She set the cup on the table, and Andrew ran to her and gave her a gentle hug.

"It looks like I'm going to be spending several weeks on the mend." She squeezed him with her uninjured arm. "Perfect that it happened during summer holiday! Now we can spend some time together."

Andrew smiled at her, then snuggled his head against her breast. It was all behind them now: the estrangement, the bitter words, the angry silences. He vowed never again to speak to her crossly, never again to berate her for the choices she had made, never again to fling at her his belief that his father would someday return. He would keep his faith in his father's return as a secret thing, tucked away in the depths of his soul, and believe for both of them.

Chapter 22

*G*erry accompanied Andrew and Grandmother Howard back to Greycliff that afternoon. He was as wide-eyed as a child in London for the first time, and delighted in being chauffeured "in style", as he put it. When they arrived at Greycliff, his mouth hung open in astonishment.

"Golly, I've seen pictures of places like this, but I never thought that I'd be seeing one up close, let alone spending the night in one!" Andrew got the impression that Gerry came from a background of, to put it kindly, modest circumstances.

Alfred helped Gerry up the steps; Maria opened the front door for them. Grandmother introduced her: "This is Maria, our maid. She'll show you to your room. I thought you might not want to trouble with going up and down the stairs, so I've arranged for you to stay in the billiard room; it's on the ground floor. Actually, it's not really a billiard room now; my late husband was an incapacitated by a stroke just before he died, and couldn't climb stairs, so I had the room converted to a bedroom. It's remained that way; I don't have any reason to change it back. I hope it will be adequate."

"Gosh, adequate's not the word," Gerry replied. Alfred came in, carrying Gerry's duffle bag. Gerry rummaged through it. "Oh, great! It's okay—my camera. Good thing I packed it in the middle of all my clothes. When I got hit by the car, it went flying. I hope you wouldn't mind if I took a few pictures."

"Not at all," Grandmother replied.

Andrew carried Gerry's duffle bag, following Maria and Gerry down the hall. Gerry's eyes opened wide when he saw his room, with its paneled walls and ornate furniture. "A four poster bed!" he exclaimed. He hobbled over to the window and looked out at the garden. "Boy, I can't believe this! I feel like the Lord of the Manor!"

Grandmother appeared at the doorway. "Oh, I forgot to mention, we'll be having high tea at four. Do come!"

"High tea! I don't have anything really nice to wear—"

"Oh, it's nothing formal; just tea with cucumber sandwiches and a bit of smoked salmon, and some biscuits for afters. Supper is at eight. I'm afraid with the rationing, it's not going to be fancy, but it should tide you through the night."

"Oh, I'm sure it'll be just dandy. See you at four!"

Andrew remained in the room while Gerry unpacked his things.

"Gosh, what's it like to grow up in a place like this?" Gerry asked.

"Oh, I didn't grow up here," Andrew replied. "I usually spent just a week in the summer. I lived at boarding school most of the time, and when I wasn't at school, I used to live at Armus House, in Berkshire. That was my father's home, or rather his family's home."

311

"So you're here for just two weeks?"

"No, I'm here for the whole summer." Andrew looked away for a moment. "The Germans bombed Armus House two months ago, and my aunt and my other grand-mother were killed."

"And your dad was killed, too—that's rough."

"He's not dead—he's missing!" Andrew blurted out.

Gerry looked at Andrew. "So you think he's still alive?"

Andrew took a deep breath. He didn't know what had brought about his outburst; after all, he had vowed to keep silent about his belief that his father was still alive. Looking at Gerry, he said quietly, "I know he has to be alive. They never found him, so how can they say he's dead?"

Gerry shook his head. "Gosh, kid, I don't know. That's a tough one." He was silent for a moment, and then said, "In a way, it was easier for me. My pa died when I was eleven. I saw him being put in the ground, and it was something awful, but there was no doubt about it. The bad part was, my ma got married again to a guy who drank, and well, he had a temper, too. My ma took in laundry, squirreled away pennies, so my sister could go away to school." He pulled out his wallet and took out a snapshot. "That's Mary Jo, when she graduated from nursing school. I used to call her Jary Mo. My full name is Gerald Beauregard, so she called me Gerry Bo."

Andrew studied the picture. "She's very pretty," he said.

"And smart as the dickens! She's smart enough to be a doctor, but there's no chance for something like that. She's happy, though, being a nurse. She works in the deliv-ery room at Bellevue—that's the big city hospital in New York. She says that some-times they get so busy with women having babies, there's not enough doctors to go around and she's had to deliver more than a few babies herself—she calls it 'catch-ing babies.' I saw her just before I shipped out, a few months ago. Gosh, I miss her." He pulled out another photo. "Here's my ma."

Andrew studied the photo. "She looks like a very nice person."

Gerry nodded. "She was. She died last year." He cleared his throat and looked at his watch. "Well, it's about an hour until—what do you call it—high tea? It's such a beautiful day! I'd love to just sit outside for awhile. What do you say?"

They spent the rest of the afternoon sitting outside on the lawn and talking. An-drew told Gerry about how his father had been in France and at Dunkirk, how he loved to fly, how he liked to go for walks, how good he was at boxing...how he loved to look at the stars. He talked about his mother, too: all the kinds of planes she flew, and how she used to drop candy on his boarding school.

Gerry smiled. "Sounds like you're mighty proud of your ma."

Andrew nodded.

Gerry then talked about his job: "It's up to me to load the ammunition. It has to be done just so, or the guns jam. I clean and maintain the guns, too, but I also like to help out with doing other things on the plane. There are three of us who work on it: the Crew Chief and the Assistant Crew Chief, who are responsible for the engine and the airframe, and me. I usually do the little odd jobs when I've taken care of the guns, like polishing the canopy. It's real important that it's clean as a whistle—no smudges or specks—so that my pilot can see clearly. Don't want him mistaking a speck of dust for a German fighter, or vice versa. I also paint the swastikas on the side when my pilot bags a Jerry. My name is painted on the plane, under the Crew Chief's and Assistant Crew Chief's. My pilot's name is at the top, in bigger letters 'cause he's the pilot, y'see? I feel like, when that plane goes out on a mission, part of me goes, too. And I want that part of me to come back."

He stared up at the sky. "Every time my pilot takes off on a mission, I sorta give him a blessing. I touch the tail of the plane with my thumb, then say to him, 'Sir, you come back, y'hear?' I say it exactly like that—don't change a word of it, like it's some kind of prayer you have to say word for word. And he says, 'I will, Gerry—don't want to let a good ole boy down.' He's from Tennessee. We say that to each other every time, it's sorta like a kind of ceremony, you know?" He picked a blade of grass and examined it, then put it down. "I really think he's gonna make it. There's a saying: 'Do five, stay alive.' Means that if a pilot does five missions, he's got what it takes to keep on top of things, and he's also picked up a few tricks. Ain't no squarehead gonna get the better of him." He sighed. "I hope so. I mean, I know he's gonna come back, but all the same, when he makes it in, I'm mighty relieved."

"What's your pilot like?" Andrew asked. He found Gerry's use of the possessive in referring to "his" pilot rather touching.

"He's tops! I mean, everyone looks up to fighter pilots, but my pilot's really special. He doesn't swagger around, but he's the kind of guy you know you can trust. He's sorta quiet. He does get a little crazy when he's drunk, though. That's always after missions, mind you. Nevermind what you hear, ain't no pilots I know of who'd go out on a mission shit-fa—I mean drunk. Want the plane tanked up, not the pilot. Afterwards, though, they like to unwind—helluva way to make a living, when you get right down to it. Anyway, he's got what it takes, I think. He's something, that's for sure, and I'm not saying it just 'cause he's my pilot."

Maria came out to tell them that tea was ready. They made their way to the dining room. Grandmother chatted with Gerry, asking him questions about America. "You must be quite homesick, being so far away from home," she said.

"Well, sometimes. But it's also exciting being here. I've always wanted to travel, to see new places. I was real happy when I found out I was gonna be sent to England. I always wanted to visit London and Scotland, and all them castles and moors and everything. I was on my way up to Scotland when I had my accident. At first I was really upset, 'cause I thought I'd be spending the rest of my leave in a hospital room, but, gee, this is really something! You folks are just so kind to take me in and—"

"Well, we're delighted to have you as our guest," Grandmother replied.

They talked some more, and presently Maria came in and told them that supper would be served soon.

"It looks as if we'll be enjoying a long, extended meal," Grandmother said. "And I'm happy to say that we have a treat for supper. I didn't want to make any promises, even though Alfred is a good shot—"

"Pheasant!" cried Andrew, his mouth already watering.

"Pheasant?" Gerry's mouth hung open in astonishment. "Gosh, I never thought that I'd ever be eating pheasant!"

"Oh, it's absolutely delicious!" Andrew exclaimed. Gerry didn't need any more encouragement, for at that moment Mrs. Beaton came in bearing a platter of roasted fowl, with an aroma so sweet it sent Andrew to salivating even more. Mrs. Beaton carved off a few pieces and served them. Gerry tasted his portion, and his face broke into a glow of delight.

"Not many foods can put a smile on your face," he said. "Wait till the other guys get a load of this. Pheasant!"

"Let's take a picture," Andrew suggested.

"Great! I guess there's still enough light." Gerry said.

Andrew ran to get Gerry's camera. He took a picture of Gerry, holding fork in left hand and knife in right, posed in front on the bird in question, a broad smile on his face.

The moment put to permanent record to quash any doubts that Gerry's friends might have about his amazing meal, they fell upon their delectable entree. Mrs. Beaton removed the platter to the kitchen, so that she, Alfred, and Maria could also enjoy the succulent treat.

They talked late into the night. When Gerry noticed Grandmother nodding, he excused himself. "I don't want to keep you folks up so late, especially Andrew. I'm sure he's excited about seeing his mother tomorrow."

The next morning, Gerry appeared at breakfast, smiling and shaking his head. "What a delightful surprise to be waked up by that pretty little lady and served a cup of tea before getting out of bed! I don't think the guys on the base are going to believe that!"

"Well, let's take another picture," Andrew said. "Then no one could say that you were lying!"

"Great idea!" Gerry exclaimed, and so they arranged for a replay of the incident, with Gerry back in bed and Maria serving him tea while Andrew snapped the picture.

"I'd like to get some more photos before I have to leave," Gerry said. They spent the rest of the morning taking pictures: Gerry standing on the front steps, Andrew and his grandmother in the garden, then Alfred took a picture of all three of them on the front lawn with Greycliff in the background.

Andrew and Gerry remained outside for the rest of the morning. They sat on the lawn and talked some more about Andrew's father. Presently Gerry asked, "How do you feel about Jake?"

Andrew shrugged. "My mother's married to him—that's her business. He doesn't have anything to do with me."

Gerry looked at Andrew and furrowed his brow. "I think he's got a lot do with you, whether you want to admit it or not. You can't pretend he doesn't exist." He looked away. "I never really accepted my stepfather, but that was 'cause he drank, and when he was drunk, he was pretty mean. I just wanted to get away from him. In fact, I did, for a while. Jumped on a train and rode the rails. At first it was kinda fun, and there was lots of other kids doing it too, 'cause times was hard. But sleeping in boxcars and scrounging for food out of garbage cans gets old after awhile. Then I heard about the CCC, the Civilian Conservation Corps, and I joined up, 'cause for an honest day's work you got three square meals and a place to sleep and thirty dollars a month. We had to send twenty-five dollars home. Some guys griped about that, but I thought it was just great. You see, when my stepdad used to come home drunk after getting paid, my ma had to go through his pockets, after he was passed out that is, to get enough money to pay the rent and buy groceries. Yeah, being able to send something home to my ma, that was the best part of being with the CCC. Another great thing about it was that we took classes in the evenings. I got my high school diploma that way. It was also swell working outdoors, cutting trails and building lodges and shelters and fire lookouts. I was in Oregon, mostly, and some of them places in the mountains are about as close to heaven as you can get on God's earth. There was this one place, Green Lakes—so beautiful it almost made your eyes hurt. I think about that place whenever I get to feeling down. Someday, I'd like to go back there, just spend the whole summer drinking in the peace and beauty. Hey, I've been getting off the subject here." Gerry gave Andrew a playful punch on the shoulder. "Point is, I think I could have gotten along with my stepfather if he'd been a halfway decent guy, even though I missed my dad, still miss him, even now." He looked into Andrew's eyes, with a kind of tender concern, which reminded Andrew of the way his father would look at him and say, Everything all right, old chap?

"What I'm saying, Andrew, is I think you should give Jake a chance. He seems like a nice person. It has nothing to do with what you believe about your dad. I hope that someday he does come back. Well, look at it this way: From what I've seen of Jake, and from what you've told me about your dad, I think they would have, well...I think that they would have understood each other. I mean, they were both fighter pilots. That says a lot."

"That doesn't mean anything," Andrew said.

"From what I've seen of fighter pilots, I know that what they say is true: That there are two kinds of people in the world: fighter pilots and everybody else. Those of us on the ground, we do our job. I load ammunition; the engineering crew sees to it that the plane is serviced. We know that we're going to be alive at the end of the day. The pilot—well, when you get right down to it, he may or may not come back. He knows that. Every time he goes out, he knows that it might be his last time, no matter how good he is, no matter how good we do our jobs. A fighter pilot is completely on his own up there: He's pilot, radio operator, navigator, gunner, sometimes even bombardier, if he's doing low-level attacks. It takes a unique kind of person to fill a tall order like that, to be an expert at all those jobs that would get divvied up among a bunch of people on a bomber crew. A fighter pilot has to be on top of things all the time. There's no room for mistakes. I remember one time, there was this pilot from our squadron who had some, well, girl troubles. He went out one day; it was on a long distance mission and they were using drop tanks. He forgot to switch to external fuel after taking off and, when they were over Germany, they got into a dogfight and he had to jettison his tank. He didn't have enough fuel to make it back, and he went down. We haven't heard from him since. He might be in a POW camp but he was probably killed. Just being careless, just worrying about his problems when he should have been paying attention to what he was doing, cost him his life. It takes a special kind of person to keep a cool head up there, and also to live with the knowledge that even if you do everything right, it still may not be enough. That's why I think that your father and Jake would understand each other. I think that they're very much alike."

Andrew looked away. "They're not alike at all," he mumbled.

Gerry was silent; then he sighed. "Okay, I won't say no more about it. Come on, help me up. I think I'd best be getting back to town. My ride's due to arrive soon."

As they walked back to the house, Gerry stopped to pick some wildflowers. "For your ma." He winked at Andrew.

Once in the house, Gerry hobbled to his room, where he proceeded to root through his dufflebag.

"Everything got sorta shuffled around here—bet it's on the bottom—" He withdrew a small book, and thumbed through it.

"They gave us these when we got here. They figgered we was all a bunch of ignoramuses 'bout England, and they was prob'ly right. They wanted us to read this so we'd know a little more about things here—" He thumbed through the booklet, then nodded with satisfaction and tore out a page.

"Here—read this." Gerry handed him the page.

Andrew read:

British women have proven themselves in this war. They have stuck to their posts near burning ammunition dumps, delivered messages afoot after their motor-cycles have been blasted from under them. They have pulled aviators from burning planes. They have died at their gun-posts, and as they fell another girl has stepped directly into the position and 'carried on'. There is not a single record in this war of any British woman in uniformed service quitting her post, or failing in her duty under fire... When you see a girl in khaki or air-force blue with a bit of ribbon on her tunic, remember she didn't get it for knitting more socks than anyone else in Ipswich.

Andrew handed the paper back to Gerry, who folded it in half and set it down on his bed next to the bunch of flowers he'd picked.

"Can I see that?" Andrew asked.

"Sure." Gerry handed him the booklet.

Andrew glanced through the pages, noting the curious admonishments: *Don't make fun of British speech or accents. You sound just as funny to them but they will be too polite to show it...You are higher paid than the British "Tommy." Don't rub it in...Don't show off or brag or bluster...Don't try to tell the British that America won the last war...NEVER criticize the King or Queen...The British are often more reserved in conduct than we. On a small crowded island where forty-five million people live, each man learns to guard his privacy carefully—and is equally careful not to invade another man's privacy. So if Britons sit in trains or buses without striking up conversa-*

tion with you, it doesn't mean they are being haughty and unfriendly. Probably they are paying more attention to you than you think...Don't be misled by the British tendency to be soft-spoken and polite. If they need to be, they can be plenty tough...You are coming to Britain from a country where your home is still safe, food is still plentiful, and lights are still burning. So it is doubly important for you to remember that the British soldiers and civilians have been living under a trememdous strain. The British have been bombed, night after night and month after month. Thousands of them have lost their houses, their possessions, their families...In "getting along" the first important thing to remember is that the British are like the Americans in many ways—but not in all ways...They are not given to back-slapping and they are shy about showing their affections. But once they get to like you they make the best friends in the world....

Andrew found it quite odd to think that the English people would be made the subject of such explanatory notes, as if they were some sort of exotic tribe with strange customs, but he still couldn't help but be amused.

Why do Yanks find us so strange? They're the ones who are different!

And yet, looking at Gerry, he couldn't help but think that, for all their differences, they had a lot in common, too. And even the differences made their interaction so...special. It was the discovering: the finding out about their dissimilarities, as well as the ways in which they were alike, that made it all so wonderful.

As they were getting into the car, Gerry asked Andrew to take one last picture of Alfred holding the door for him as he entered the car. "Just so my buddies will believe me!"

When they arrived at the hospital, they saw a US Army Jeep parked at the curb.

"I think that's my ride," Gerry said. Alfred pulled over, hopped out, and opened the door for Gerry. The driver of the Jeep stared in amazement as Gerry got out. Alfred acted very deferential and respectful as he escorted Gerry to his ride. When Gerry was settled in the Jeep, Alfred tipped his hat at him and said, "Have a nice ride, guv'nor!"

Gerry shook hands with Andrew. "I guess this is good-bye. Take it easy, kiddo. Oh, they wanted these back." He handed the crutches to Andrew. "Could you please take them to the nurses' station? And give this to your ma." He handed Andrew the flowers and the page from his book, then laid his hand on Andrew's shoulder. "I'm really glad I met you. Thanks for everything."

Andrew smiled. "I'm glad I met you, too."

Andrew waved as the Jeep drove off, then went into the hospital. After dropping off the crutches at the nurses' station, he walked down the hall.

As Andrew approached his mother's room, he heard his mother and Jake talking.

"All of a sudden my oil temperature soared and I saw I was leaking coolant," Andrew's mother said. "Either the line was damaged and suddenly broke, or it might have been a fitting—anyway, I tried to throttle back, but it was too late. The engine seized."

"You should have bailed out. Your were high enough."

"I couldn't take the chance that it would crash on a house or kill someone."

"You could have headed east. The plane probably would have reached the sea."

"What if it didn't? I just couldn't take that risk. I figured that if I could reach Nicholson's Pasture, landing would be no problem. I did it wheels up, of course, but a few seconds after I put down the plane lurched to the right and then spun round. I must have caught a wingtip on a rock or a mound. That's all I remember. I hope I didn't do any serious damage. No one got hurt, did they?"

"No, just you."

Andrew peeked into the room and saw Jake sitting on the bed. "Next time, don't be a bloody fool—just ditch the kite," he said softly to Andrew's mother.

Andrew expected his mother to bristle at Jake's words—imagine, him calling her a bloody fool! Instead, her face softened, and she smiled a tender, bittersweet smile. In her eyes was a curious look of pain, love, and understanding, as if those words had stirred a compelling memory for both of them.

No, Andrew thought, it's not that. She's just probably touched that Jake was so concerned about her.

That's all it is.

But he couldn't shake the feeling there was more to it than that.

"You've been so worried and preoccupied lately," Jake was saying. "I know it's been difficult for you. I wish we could see each other more often, but then again, sometimes I feel like I'm the cause of all your worries."

"It's not your fault," Andrew's mother told him, her voice breaking. "He just misses his father. He's not really angry at you."

Jake was silent.

"Jake, it's not your fault," Andrew's mother repeated. "Please don't blame yourself. Look, everything's going to be all right. Don't *you* go worrying now."

A shiver went down Andrew's spine. He jerked his head away from the door.

It's all my fault, he thought. Gerry's words about the pilot in his squadron haunted him: *Just worrying about his problems, when he should have been paying attention to what he was doing, cost him his life....*

He stumbled away from the doorway, closed his eyes, and slumped against the wall.

My mother's been upset all this time because I've been acting so horribly. If I hadn't said all those mean things to her, if I'd acted as if I had accepted the fact that my father was dead and had not been angry with her for marrying Jake...When she woke up from the coma, the first thing on her mind was her concern that I get along with Jake.

Maybe it was the last thing on her mind before she crashed.

He remembered his fervent entreaties to the Almighty when he was so afraid that his mother might have been killed. *Please let her be all right—I'll do anything, even....*

This was God's way of teaching him a lesson. *I never really considered that my actions could affect someone like that. She might have been killed, and it would have been all my fault...From now on, I'm not going to give her any cause for worry. I'll pretend that everything's all right...I'll be friendly to Jake...I'll never talk about my father again.*

He walked back up the corridor to the nurses' station, turned around and ran back down the hall so that it would appear that he had just dashed in. He bounded in to her room, breathless, and exclaimed, "Mum, it's so good to see you again! You look positively smashing!" He smiled at Jake. "It looks as if you've been taking good care of her!" He was proud of himself for managing to sound sincerely grateful and friendly.

Jake smiled a cautious, timid smile, and Andrew's mother squeezed his hand and looked at him reassuringly. *See*, her eyes told him, *I told you that everything was going to be all right.*

Andrew went over to his mother and kissed her on the cheek. Then he presented her with Gerry's gift. She read the page from the booklet, and smiled.

"What a nice young man! How was your day with him?"

"Just super! Gerry's so nice, and we had a smashing time. He loves it here and seems to be ever so fascinated by everything. I used to think that America was not really like a foreign country because they speak English too, but I guess it really is different." He looked at Jake. "Was it difficult for you to get used to being here?"

Jake seem startled that Andrew had asked him a direct question. He hesitated, then said timidly, "A little."

"What were some of the things that you found that were different?"

Jake bit his lip and said, "Oh, the accent, some of the expressions." He smiled. "When I came over here, I thought that everyone talked funny. After awhile, I realized, it wasn't them—*I* was the one with the strange accent."

"What else is different?" Andrew feigned a curiosity that he didn't feel.

Jake thought for a moment, and said, "Everything here is so organized and neat. It's very beautiful here, too, very green and colorful, especially in the summer." He looked at Andrew's mother, as if for reassurance. She smiled broadly, then looked at Andrew.

"Well, the doctor says I can go home tomorrow! I'm going to need some help, though. With my good arm out of commission, I can't even do simple things like cut my food or write or even wash my other hand for meals! Would you mind helping your poor old crippled mother for the rest of the summer?"

"Oh, Mum—" Andrew threw his arms around her neck.

"I'd apply for the job, but I have to leave tomorrow." Jake grinned. "I'm glad you're going to be in such good hands!"

"Oh, good news," Andrew's mother said. "The doctor said I could have a bit of leave this evening—'*spring this joint*', as you Americans would say." She winked at Jake. "So I thought that it would be nice if we all went out for supper. I'm getting tired of this ghastly hospital food!"

"Super!" Andrew exclaimed.

Jake nodded. "Sounds great."

"Well, it's settled!" Andrew's mother said. "And with two nice young men to escort me, I'm going to be the envy of everyone!"

There was a tap at the door. The nurse came in, carrying a parcel. "The chauffeur brought these in for you," she said.

"Oh, my clothes! Can't go out to a nice fancy dinner with my backside hanging out." Andrew's mother looked with disdain at her hospital gown. "You two, scoot!" she commanded, and Jake and Andrew withdrew while the nurse stayed to help her get dressed.

While they were waiting in the hall Andrew said to Jake, "I'm so happy that she's going to be all right. It was all so scary."

"Yeah," Jake said. He glanced at Andrew, and Andrew saw in his face a look that was an odd mixture of sadness, pain, and...recognition? It occurred to Andrew that Jake must have suddenly realized that he, Andrew, bore a certain likeness to his mother. Even though everyone said that he looked more like his father, Andrew was aware that his resemblance to his mother, though not as pronounced, was there nonetheless. His eyes were the same color as hers—not quite hazel, not quite blue, and he had a light sprinkle of freckles across his nose, just like her. It gave Andrew a certain amount of satisfaction that Jake seemed to feel uncomfortable about it.

What did you expect? I'm her son—I always will be, and you can't change that.

He almost wished he had red hair, just to make the resemblance more striking. As much as he would have liked to rub it in, Andrew realized that the most important thing in the world to him was his mother's well-being and peace of mind, and that hinged on her not worrying about Jake. She would be aware if Jake felt uncomfortable or uneasy, so it would be not only pointless, but counterproductive—perhaps *dangerously* counterproductive—to alienate Jake at this point.

In an effort to be conciliatory, Andrew said, "I was ever so worried."

Jake nodded, not speaking. Andrew noticed the look of apprehension and guilt in his eyes.

It was my fault for being so mean to her, but it was your fault for marrying her in the first place....

It took a great effort to push his emotions down, deep down, and say, without a trace of hypocrisy, "I'm glad she's going to be all right. I don't want her to be worried about us anymore—about you and me, I mean. She loves you very much and she's happy with you—that's all that matters. I'm not angry anymore. I really wanted to believe that my father was still alive, that's all, and I just had to accept the fact that he wasn't coming back. It has nothing to do with you."

Instead of evidencing relief, Jake now looked as if he were paralyzed with fear. Andrew tried hard to hide his exasperation: *I'm trying to make him feel better, and he acts as if I'm accusing him of committing the unpardonable sin.*

Maybe Jake didn't understand.

"My mother," Andrew said. "I don't want her to worry."

"What—?" Jake looked at Andrew, as if Andrew's words had nothing to do with whatever was really bothering him. Andrew was annoyed.

He's not following this conversation at all—It's as if his mind were on something else altogether.

They stood in silence until Andrew's mother walked out into the hallway. "It's so wonderful to look civilized, don't you think?" she laughed. Jake took her arm, and they all went out to eat.

Andrew had Alfred drive him to the hospital early the next morning. So excited was he that his mother was going to be released, he ran down the hall to surprise her. Jake's voice, insistent and a little louder that usual, made him halt before he reached the door.

"I don't want him to know!"

"But you've seen how he's changed! I told you that everything was going to be all right!" Andrew's mother's voice, pleading and reassuring.

"That's why I don't want to tell him. How do you think he would feel if he found out?"

"I know he would understand."

"I can't take the chance that he won't."

"Jake...."

"Alice, promise me that you won't tell him. I don't want to be worrying about it. I want to be the one to decide when, or if, he should be told. He's your son, I know, but this concerns me, too. Please...."

"All right. I won't say anything."

Say anything about what? What deep, dark secret does he have to hide?

Andrew remembered the nagging feeling he'd had at breakfast with Jake and Gerry. It had seemed to him that Jake had felt uncomfortable talking about himself; in fact, he had revealed very little in the way of personal information. It wasn't mere shyness; Andrew had suspected something at the time, and now his suspicions were confirmed: Jake *was* hiding something.

What?

Chapter 23

*A*ndrew soon forgot all about Jake and the mysterious secret he was so intent on keeping. It was, after all, the best summer he'd ever had. His mother was with him and she belonged to him—*exclusively*. He tried not to think too far into the future, as she eventually would have to return to her duties in the ATA and he would be going back to school in September. So each day, Andrew delighted in the many different ways in which he could assist his mother. He insisted on bringing her a cup of tea in the morning himself; he buttered her toast and cut her food; he helped her to put on her socks and shoes and tied the laces for her. Maria took care of assisting her in bathing and dressing and undressing, but it was up to Andrew to take care of her the rest of the day, and he relished the responsibility. It was one way that he could make up to her for all of the terrible things he had said; he also delighted in being able to be with her. It had been so long since he had known a time of uninterrupted and unrestricted contact with her. Even when she had been at Armus House while doing her conversion courses at White Waltham she still had been gone most of the day. Now she was at home all the time!

Grandmother provided pleasant company but did not intrude. At first Andrew was worried that she felt left out. He brought up the subject one day and she reassured him, saying, "She was my little girl for eighteen years; it's your turn now."

His mother received occasional phone calls from Jake, and letters too, but this limited contact did not bother Andrew very much. After all, Jake was far away and he himself was here. There was a lot to be said for a "home ground" advantage. Once in awhile, Andrew mentioned Jake briefly in conversation, just to reassure his mother that he had accepted Jake as a part of her life now. After one such instance, she grasped Andrew's hand and said, "I'm so glad you're not upset anymore—I know it was a terrible shock for you to find out about us like that." To which Andrew reassured her that it wasn't her fault, that he was glad she was happy, and that he thought Jake was very nice. Her response was to enfold him in an embrace.

"He's ever so kind, and he cares for you very much, Andrew," she told him. It seemed to Andrew that she wanted to add something; instead, she sighed, and hugged him again.

Once, she broached the subject of his father, but Andrew reassured her on that score: He realized his father was not coming back, and she didn't need to worry about *that* anymore. They would have gotten word, would have heard something by now, surely. Andrew told her that, even though he missed his father, he wanted to get on with life and not dwell on the past. And so the subject was closed.

For the most part, they talked about pleasant and untroublesome things: Andrew talked about school, his friends, and the things he had done with Kaz, Marlys, and Irene. His mother laughed when he told her how he had bluffed them with a pair of Jacks. He knew that Kaz had told her about the trick they had played on Freddie (since Kaz had promised to talk to her about it), but he decided against bringing it up, as it involved the worries he'd had about Freddie bothering her. It was all a moot point anyway since Freddie was dead. Besides, it was obvious now in retrospect that there had been no danger of her becoming involved with Freddie, since she had been seeing Jake at the time.

His mother talked at length about being in the ATA. Andrew already was quite familiar with much of her routine, but it was still fascinating to hear her talk of it.

"On a clear day, we'd be off bright and early. Other times we would have to wait around for weather to clear, so we'd pass the time reading, playing cards, writing letters; that's when I'd get most of my letters written to you. Then, if the weather got better, we were told to report to the operations room for our chits. We mostly flew aircraft from the factories to the maintenance units, where they would be fitted with radios and other equipment, and then from the maintenance units to the squadrons. Or we'd fly the unserviceable planes from the airfields to the repair facilities and, after they were repaired, back to the squadrons. Since I have a Class 4 Plus rating, I get to fly Hudsons, Mosquitos, Beaufighters, and other advanced twin-engined aircraft. I'd like to get my four-engine rating so that I can fly the heavy bombers, such as Lancasters, Stirlings, Fortresses, and Liberators. A few of the women in the ATA have their Class 5 rating—that's on four engines."

"After briefing, we'd go to the Met for the weather information, and then to the Maps and Signals Office to find out the positions of barrage balloons and get news of airfield serviceability. It's *very* important to know if the barrage balloons have been moved. They don't distinguish between friend and foe, and flying into a barrage cable is nasty business. We usually avoid flying near large towns because of the risk of drawing fire from the anti-aircraft guns. Some of the gunners are too keen about shooting down anything that flies; they'd shoot first and try to figure out if it was friend or foe later. They'd shoot at a Hurricane, thinking it was a ME-109." She smiled. "Well, I know what it's like for them; one is apt to be so anxious that no enemy planes get through that one can be a little too twitchy."

"The Hurricanes and the 109s look a little alike from some angles," Andrew said. "The canopy is similar."

"The Hurricane's tail is more rounded, as are the wingtips. The dead giveaway is the radiator: The Hurricane has a big one, located under the fuselage; the 109 has two small ones, one under each wing."

"If we got a plane that we had not flown before we'd go to the library for a book of maker's handling notes, which would tell us all we needed to know about flying that type of aircraft. We have our Ferry Pilots' Notes to refer to, as well. Some of us are "type catchers": We love to get our hands on some of the rarer types of aircraft and want to be able to say that we've flown every kind of plane in the RAF."

"Marlys said you were a type catcher," Andrew laughed.

"Well, I like a challenge. I've flown Typhoons, Bostons, and even a few Skuas. We'd get all our information and then pile into the Anson. One of us would be assigned the duty of taxi pilot: ferrying us to our starting points and collecting us at the end of the day."

"All, in all, we've proved ourselves: We've shown everyone that women can do the job just as well as the men. Our safety record is better than that of the men's; we get our planes to the destinations, on time, we don't panic in emergencies—"

"I know that," Andrew said proudly. "I don't see how you could not be terrified when that engine cut out on you—"

"Well, there wasn't time. I was too busy concentrating on what I needed to do. Actually, having an engine quit isn't all that scary if you know how to handle the situation. One of the other women had a truly frightening experience. She was flying a Typhoon and the bottom of the fuselage fell off in the air. There was nothing beneath her feet! She managed to land it and the watch office clerk scolded her for bringing in only half a plane!"

She noticed Andrew's look of alarm and soothed him: "Don't worry—those kinds of things rarely happen. And the pilot was able to land safely."

She continued. "It's so wonderful to be able to do what I love most—flying, and to know that I'm doing something worthwhile, that makes a difference. Imagine getting paid for having fun! And now we're even getting paid as much as the men!"

Andrew was astounded. "You mean the men got paid more than you did?"

His mother nodded. "Our pay was twenty percent less than that of the men doing the same job. It wasn't until this past June that it was decided that we would receive the same rate of pay as the men."

"That's ridiculous! How could they get away with that? I mean, just because you're women—"

His mother sighed, "It's just that. In the beginning, there was a lot of opposition to women being able to fly at all. So to placate the critics, the Treasury set our pay lower than the men's, which was the usual practice for women anyway."

"That's not fair! You should have protested, gone on strike or something!"

His mother smiled. "There's a war on, you know. We're needed. The best way that we could plead our case was to do our jobs well and prove we were every bit as good as the men. It was a giant step even being allowed to fly at all, and the first women ferry pilots were only allowed to ferry light trainers. They then progressed to fighters, then to twins, and now that there are women flying four-engined planes, no one can say that we're inferior in any way to the men."

A few weeks after his mother had come home from the hospital, a package arrived. "I went to Armus House on one of my days off," Andrew's mother told him. "Thomas was sifting through the rubble, trying to find anything that could be salvaged. This was the only thing that wasn't blown to bits." She opened the package. "I had it at my billet, and asked one of my friends to mail it to me. It's the only thing that survived the blast. Everything else—pictures, everything—is gone. I knew you would want it." She pulled out Andrew's treasure box. There were a few nicks on it but it was otherwise undamaged. It was locked, but Andrew remembered that he had thrown the key in with the few things he had brought up to Greycliff.

He carried the box up to his room and tried the key. The lock opened with a satisfying click. Lifting the lid, he noted the contents: his birthday flag, the newspaper clipping of his mother, the letter and book from the Prime Minister, his father's shaving mug and brush and the letters from him wrapped in his RAF handkerchief, and his father's book of poems. The bookmark was still in place; Andrew opened the book to the page it marked and read the poem that he had already memorized by heart.

...I can't imagine a newborn day,

Without me here...somehow...someway.

Andrew's spirit soared. It was his father's promise to him that he would return and, even though he had never doubted it, the fact that this book remained, out of everything else at Armus House that had been destroyed, was immensely reassuring to him. It confirmed his belief that his father was still alive, somewhere. Somehow, someway he had managed to hang onto life, in spite of everything. Andrew hoped that his father would understand why he had to convince everyone else that he had accepted the fact that he wasn't coming back. After all, it wouldn't do to have his mother upset, he thought with a shudder. His father *would* come home, and Andrew would see to it that no harm came to her until he did. He tried to push away Freddie's snickering remark, "They *had* to get married!", and instead remembered how much his parents had loved each other. They *had* loved each other, *still* loved each other— Andrew was sure of that. Maybe his mother was lonely and hurting; she'd probably had the opportunity to meet lots of men and it was to be expected, sooner or later, that someone would take advantage of her. It wasn't her fault; if she needed someone right now to ease the pain, that was all right. Living in a war zone had taught Andrew that nothing was permanent, least of all relationships that formed in a crucible of fear, loss, and uncertainty. The war would not last forever, and neither would his mother's relationship with Jake.

One day, out of nothing more than idle curiosity, he asked his mother what had happened to Jake's hands.

"He went down in flames during the Battle of Britain," she told him. "He managed to bail out, but his clothes were on fire. He was able to extinguish the flames with his hands but, as his parachute opened, the shrouds caught fire, so he had to climb up the shroud lines before they burned through. He was over the sea and because the parachute wasn't completely deployed he hit the water quite hard and broke his ankle. It was a good thing he wasn't over land; he would have been killed. His other leg was badly shot up, too. Otherwise, he was more or less intact, except for shrapnel wounds and burns on his chest and arms. His clothing had protected him for the most part, but his hands were terribly scorched. He spent months in convalescence; he was a "guinea pig" in the work being done on burn victims. There were many other pilots burned then too, some of them hideously. The doctors grafted skin from his thighs onto his hands. He joked about the saying *getting a strip torn out of your hide.* He said that he was a living demonstration that the military could sometimes carry things to extremes."

Her face turned serious. "Better not mention anything about it to him. He wouldn't tell me what had happened to him, except to say that he burned his hands when he bailed out. I learned about it from his flight commander. It was a terrifying experience, and his recovery was a painful ordeal. I admire him for going back up there again, after what happened."

One day Andrew was washing his mother's left hand before supper.

"I never realized the things you couldn't do with one arm out of commission," she laughed. "Oh, there's a bit of soap under my ring. Could you please take it off and rinse it?"

As Andrew gently pulled the ring off her finger he remembered the rings she had worn before: a wide, gold wedding band, etched with a lacy, intricate design, and a matching engagement ring with a big, sparkly diamond. He looked with disdain at the plain, thin circlet of gold. It weighed almost nothing in his hands. He briefly toyed with the idea of "accidentally" dropping it down the drain, then decided against it. It wouldn't do any good, anyway. Even though Andrew had relegated his mother's marriage to Jake to the category of "matters that need not be taken seriously," it still annoyed him that Jake had evidently decided to be so cheap about things.

She deserved better.

A package came for Andrew at the beginning of August. The return address bore the name: Sgt. Gerald Versailles. Andrew eagerly tore the wrappings and opened the box. Inside were some candy bars, some photos, and a letter from Gerry. As Andrew munched on a Clark Bar, he read the letter:

Hi Andrew!

I got your address from your grandma. I just wanted to thank you and her for the swell time I had. (And your mother, too for keeping me from starving to death!)

My ankle healed up O.K., and I'm back at work. I told my buddies about my stay with you at Greycliff, and they thought I was telling tales until I showed them the pictures. I had some copies made for you.

I hope things are going well for you. How's your ma? I'd like to keep in touch. If you want to write back, use my APO on this package. Say hello to everyone for me!

> Your friend,
> Gerry

Andrew showed his mother the snapshots.

"It looks as if you two had a wonderful time," she said. "Are you going to write back to him?"

Andrew nodded. "I'd like to keep in touch. He seemed like a good friend from the moment we met. He understood—well, we just had a lot in common. I almost forgot he was a Y—" He didn't realize what he was saying, until the words were nearly out of his mouth. He expected his mother to be offended and upset. Instead she smiled.

"That's what true friendship is all about. It doesn't matter what's on the surface, but what's inside."

As the end of August approached, Andrew wondered when his mother would start making plans for him to return to school. He hesitated to mention it, for it would be a signal that the summer, and the special time that he and his mother had shared, would be over. He had enjoyed being with her all the time and he did not look forward to being away from her.

He consoled himself with the thought that Jake would not be seeing very much of her either.

When he turned the calendar page over to September, he remarked with a sigh, "I just hate the thought of having to go back to school. I wish we could have a few more weeks together, somehow."

His mother looked a bit relieved and said, "Well, sometimes wishes do come true, you know."

"What do you mean?"

"It looks as if we're going to have a few more weeks together."

"Oh, is school starting late? Do you mean they haven't gotten things fixed up yet?"

"Not exactly."

"What do you mean?" Something in his mother's tone of voice made Andrew feel a little uneasy.

His mother smiled at him. "I didn't want to mention it until I was sure, and I just found out yesterday that things are all set." She paused, then continued. "You're going to America. Jake and I will take you there by ship in a few weeks. I had planned to put you in boarding school there but Jake's mother would like for you to stay with her, that is, with her and Jake's father. Well, she has this idea that boarding school is something horribly barbaric. We'll be staying with them for several days, and you can decide what you want to do. If you would rather live away at school, that would be all right."

Andrew was flabbergasted. *America!* It was absolutely the *worst* thing that could happen! He wouldn't even see his mother at all! He would be miles away, across the ocean, and Jake would be....

"What...what if I don't *want* to go to America? I mean, why now? Things aren't so bad! It's not like it was during the Blitz. I know that my school got bombed and Armus House too, but that doesn't mean that the Nazis are winning. The war's going to be over soon!"

"I think that things are going to get worse before they get better."

"Mum, everything's going to be *fine*! I can take care of myself—I promise that nothing is going to happen! I don't want to go! Please let me stay here!"

"Andrew, I want what's best for you. Look at you! You're so small and thin. Being ill this past winter, the rationing, the shortages, everything else—I worry about you so. It would put my mind at ease to know you were safe, well-fed, and taken care of in America."

That did it. Andrew was prepared to protest the idea with every ounce of strength and resolve within him but the fact that it all boiled down to his mother not being worried about him blew the wind out of his sails.

He got up from the table and trudged upstairs to his room. He threw himself down on the bed and groaned. *America!* What had he done to deserve this! A thought flashed across his mind; where had he heard it? *Pride goeth before a fall.* Maybe God was punishing him for being so smug about having the home ground advantage while Jake was away. Thinking about it, Andrew got quite annoyed with God.

It was all right for Him to teach me a lesson. After all, I guess that's His job, to teach people lessons. But how could He do something that would benefit Jake in the process? I thought that God was supposed to be for decency and loyalty and that sort of thing. How could He do this? Maybe with the war on, He's been so busy with other things and He probably slipped up on this one. He meant to teach me a lesson, but didn't realize that it would have harmful repercussions. That's it! Perhaps He'll realize His error, and set things right. After all, we're not supposed to leave for a few weeks.

Every morning, Andrew awoke with the hope, which became more and more and more desperate with each passing day, that somehow, someway, this wretched America business would fall by the wayside. Maybe the war would suddenly end. Maybe his father would return. Maybe his mother would decide to break up with Jake and forget the whole idea. Well, if his mother broke up with Jake, he wouldn't have to worry about things. Still, it would be better if he didn't go to America anyway: He could prevent her from getting involved with anyone else.

Maybe everything will turn out right. Sometimes the darkest hour is before dawn...like with Mum's accident. He tried to keep from worrying but, as the end of September drew near, there were no assurances to the contrary.

Maybe God will take care of things at the very last minute.

But more and more, fear gnawed at him.

Perhaps He's just gotten so overworked with all that's happening.

To be sure, God had been working overtime, for the Allies had seen victories in every corner of the globe that spring and summer. In May the Allies had defeated the Axis forces in North Africa, and 250,000 German and Italian soldiers were taken prisoner. The Battle of the Atlantic was going well for the Allies: It was the now the U-Boats that were being hunted to extinction.

The massive tank battle at Kursk on the Eastern Front broke the back of the German army. British bombers were also pounding the German homeland; in what became known as the Battle of the Ruhr, fifteen thousand bombs were dropped in twenty nights.

The Allies invaded Sicily on July 9th; on September 3rd, they crossed the Strait of

Messina and landed on the Italian mainland. Mussolini was overthrown, and the Italian government negotiated an armistice with the Allies.

Andrew's fears heightened when his mother announced one day at breakfast: "Jake is coming tomorrow. We're going up to Scotland the day after that to board the ship. Perfect timing too—I'm so glad that I'm not going to be a helpless cripple on the voyage." She had just gotten her cast off the day before.

The next day, Andrew watched with dismay as his mother got in the car and Alfred drove her to town to meet Jake.

Maybe there'll be a train wreck or something—Please, God!

An hour later, while he was in the dining room having lunch, he heard the car pull up to the house. Leaving his meal unfinished, he ran upstairs to his room. He just wasn't ready to meet Jake yet. He heard the sounds of laughter in the hallway, then some excited conversation. Andrew couldn't quite make out what was being said, then he heard Jake ask: "Where's Andrew?"

"He's having lunch in the dining room," Grandmother replied.

Evidently Andrew's mother went to the dining room to check, for there was a brief pause, and then her voice in reply: "He's not there; I'll check to see if he's in his room."

As Andrew heard her climb the stairs and walk down the hall to his room, he felt like a condemned prisoner hearing the sounds of the executioner approaching.

"Andrew, Jake wants to see you! He has something special for you."

Andrew forced himself to smile. "Oh, I must have been daydreaming—I didn't hear you." He followed her down the stairs, walked up to Jake, and nodded politely. "Hullo," he said, trying to sound friendly and untroubled.

"Hi," Jake replied. He took a breath, and smiled. "Here's something for you. I hope you like it." He handed Andrew a rather lumpy brown paper package, wrapped in string. Andrew untied the string and folded back the wrapping to reveal a model plane, made of wood. Recognizing it as a Spitfire, he feigned delight.

"Oh, a Spitfire! It's super—thank you! You fly Spitfires, right? I remember when we had breakfast with Gerry and you talked about the differences between Spitfires and Hurricanes."

Jake nodded, then looked briefly at Andrew's mother, as if seeking reassurance. She smiled and slipped her hand in his. Grandmother said to Jake, "You must be hungry after that long journey. Lunch will be ready shortly. Alfred, will you take Jake's things upstairs?"

Alfred, who had been standing by the door, moved to pick up Jake's suitcase, but Jake said, "Oh, no need. I'm headed in that direction, anyway." He picked up his suitcase and followed Andrew's mother up the stairs.

Andrew watched them with a sinking feeling in his chest that was close to panic, knowing that Jake would be sharing his mother's room. Up until this time he had considered their marriage more of a legal technicality than anything else. Even when Jake had spent the night at the hospital, alone with Andrew's mother—well, that was another thing. After all, it was more or less a public place, with nurses and orderlies coming and going. This was...*different*.

"Andrew, why don't you get washed up for lunch?" his mother called.

"Um, I already ate. I think I'll go outside for a walk." Andrew turned, and walked out the front door. Once outside, he walked quickly, fearfully, as if trying to escape the demons that were threatening to shatter his now shaky belief that somehow things would work themselves out. He had no idea where he was going. Finding himself at the top of the hill behind Greycliff, he looked out to the sea in the distance.

He realized that he was still holding the model Spitfire in his hand. I came up here to escape Jake, Andrew thought, and I managed somehow to bring a reminder of him along, anyway. He regarded the plane ruefully for a moment, then idly spun the propeller with his finger. He thought of the model Hurricane his father had given him, more than three years ago. It seemed like a lifetime had passed since then; a lifetime in which the pleasant, secure, peaceful existence he had known had been shattered forever, just like the wooden Hurricane he had left at Armus House. Andrew cursed himself for leaving it behind when they came up to Greycliff.

I should have taken it with me, he thought. He cursed Jake for causing him to forget about it.

If I hadn't been so upset about finding out about my mother and him—it's all his fault!

He stretched out his arm, holding the plane in his hand and for a brief instant he thought of flinging it at the sky in anger. If only he had the strength, he could hurl it away, far away, far enough to reach the gray, forbidding, lifeless sea in the distance.

The next morning his mother gently shook him awake just as the first light of dawn broke across the sky. Andrew ate his breakfast in silence, hoping that everyone would interpret his lack of conversation as a sign of sleepiness, not despair. His mother chattered excitedly about the voyage. "We'll be going on the *Queen Mary*—it's an *enormous* ship, over a thousand feet long! I've heard it's like a floating city! You'll have your own cabin, Andrew— won't that be fun!"

After breakfast, he went up to his room and perfunctorily packed his belongings into his suitcase. He placed his treasure box in first, then packed his clothes around it. As much as he wanted to leave behind the wretched model plane Jake had given him, he knew his mother would be upset if he forgot it, so he packed it in as well. As he was cleaning out his drawers he came across the letter and the snapshots from Gerry. He'd planned to write to Gerry, too, but the distressing news about his being sent to America had pushed that task to the background. I should write to him when I get to America, Andrew thought, though he really didn't feel much like communicating with anybody right now, even through written correspondence. He looked at the pictures and remembered that happy day not so long ago: It seemed as if an eternity had passed since then. He unlocked his treasure box and placed the photos and the letter inside. After snapping the lid shut, he turned the key in the lock. He packed a sweater on top of the box and slammed down the lid of the suitcase.

He went downstairs and wandered into the dining room. No one was in there. Spying a small, green booklet on the table, he went over and inspected it. It was embossed with a gold eagle and the words: *PASSPORT, United States of America*. Idly, he opened it. He didn't expect to find anything interesting and he figured that any personal information about Jake he might uncover was not going to change things. Still, he was curious. His eyes scanned the words printed next to Jake's photo: *Surname: Givens; Given names: Jacob Jay; Place of Birth: New Jersey, U.S.A.* Suddenly Andrew's eyes opened wide with horror and his mouth dropped open in shock.

So *this* was Jake's terrible secret!

Chapter 24

*A*ndrew stared in disbelief at the entry: *Date of Birth: August 14, 1918.* 1918! That made Jake six years younger than Andrew's mother. *Six years!* How could his mother *do* such a thing! He remembered Freddie's sniggering remark: "Older women are so amusing—they're so grateful!" It sickened Andrew to think that his mother had let a younger man take advantage of her like that—didn't she realize that she was making herself the target of ridicule and disdain? He remembered how charming and polite Freddie had been to Aunt Charlotte when he was around her, and how he'd smirked about their relationship behind her back. It infuriated Andrew to think that Jake was probably doing the same thing, laughing about her with his friends, congratulating himself for being so clever in having an older woman for a companion—after all, it was quite amusing, as Freddie had observed, to have someone so appreciative!

"Alice, have you seen my passport?" Jake's voice came from the hall.

"I think you might have left it in the dining room," Andrew's mother called from upstairs.

Andrew jumped away from the table just as Jake entered the room. As their eyes met, Andrew hoped that Jake didn't notice the look of shock and mortification on his face. Jake spied his passport and tucked it into his jacket pocket. Smiling at Andrew, he asked, "Almost ready?" Nodding dumbly, Andrew averted his eyes; he couldn't bear even to look at Jake. He stumbled out of the room and up the stairs.

"All set?" his mother queried as she passed him on the stairs. Alfred came in from the kitchen and climbed the stairs after Andrew. He got Andrew's suitcase and carried it downstairs. Andrew looked through his dresser again and decided to take a few more items of clothing. He carried them downstairs and gave them to his mother.

"I don't think you'll need all of these," she said, sorting through his sweaters and shirts. "Most of them are summer things and you'll no doubt outgrow them by next year, surely, with all the nourishing food you'll be getting. Once we're in America, we'll go shopping for some new clothes for you. Imagine—clothing isn't rationed there! Jake's mother wrote me that boys your age wear long trousers! Isn't that ever so wonderful—oh, darling—" She gave him a swift hug. "You'll look so grown up! Won't that be exciting?" She picked out a few shirts and one sweater: Andrew's favorite of blue-gray. "We'll take these—I have a bit of room left in my bag." Noting Andrew's dejected gaze, she hugged him. "It's going to be wonderful—you'll see! I know it's a bit frightening going to a new place, but just wait—you'll find all sorts of new and exciting things to see and do. Remember how it was when your father first took you to Askew Court? You were frightened then, but look how things turned out!

Oh, darling, you'll have a marvelous time! You'll make new friends, and Jake's mother seems ever so nice!"

There was a tearful goodbye with Grandmother; Andrew's sadness at having to leave her was mixed in with the distress he felt about his mother and Jake. Mrs. Beaton gave him a hug and murmured "Safe journey, Andrew."

"Safe journey," Maria echoed softly.

The car ride to the train station was a blur, as was the trip up to Scotland. As they were about to board the ship they were informed that they would all have to share a cabin. It was a troop ship, and there were many new arrivals: American servicemen going home on leave, some of them wounded, so space was at a premium. Andrew accepted the news with a cynical resignation. After all, if God were going to abandon him, He might as well do it up good and proper. It was just a crowning touch to everything else that had happened. He vaguely recalled a case of Irish whiskey changing hands; he knew that his mother had acquired it on a ferry flight to Northern Ireland and wondered why she had brought it along. The purser said, "I can get you into a larger stateroom, but you're still going to have to share."

As Andrew walked up the gangplank, he looked at the massive ship, painted a dismal gray, and topped with three huge funnels and two towering masts. It seemed to him that he was entering the bowels of hell. What *else* could possibly go wrong?

As if the Almighty were getting in one last dig, Andrew spent the next two days being seasick—not just a little queasy, but horribly, wretchedly, wrenchingly seasick. He couldn't believe that the human body could take that much punishment; every time he had another heaving attack, he thought it would surely kill him—he almost wished that it would! Dying would be a definitely preferable alternative; after all, he had nothing left to live for. He wished he had the strength to crawl out of bed and throw himself overboard, but he was denied even that escape: He had barely enough energy to stagger across the cabin to the bathroom and drape himself over the toilet.

Suddenly, mid-heave, the words from the poem broke through his despair: *I've tried for many an hour and minute, to think of this world without me in it.* It seemed as if his father were speaking to him, urging him not to give up.

He felt as if he were dangling over a canyon of despair, hanging by his fingertips onto a precipice—but that his father was somehow, someway, holding him fast, supporting him in this hour of darkness. Andrew realized that he had to hang on—even if all else in his world was lost, his father would come back. That was the one bright, shining light in the black desolate center of his being. He crawled back to his bed and collapsed, mumbling: *I've tried...I've tried....*

He had vague recollections of Jake and his mother coming and going. They went out for meals, and his mother would bring back some bits of food and some crackers. Andrew tried to take a few bites but everything came back up anyway, and he lost all appetite for food. His first night passed fitfully: He woke up several times, feeling as if his stomach were doing somersaults. Once the sound of moaning awakened him. At first Andrew thought he was hearing his own voice in a dream, but then he realized it was Jake's. The moans turned into words. Andrew listened to Jake's distraught, disjointed ravings: *Heinkels, two o'clock low—roger, got them—I'll attack from below...Bandits above! Bandits above!...109s coming down...Break!...Break!....* Jake's voice had risen to a shriek and Andrew's mother, awakened now, tried to soothe him. Andrew heard her whisper, "It's all right, it's all right...." Her entreaties were drowned out by the sound of Jake thrashing around under the sheets and his groans as he came to consciousness. "You had another nightmare," Andrew's mother told Jake, her voice barely audible. "Darling, it's all right...I wish I could chase away all the terrible feelings you have about...."

"Shhh—" Jake whispered furiously.

"I know, I know," Andrew's mother soothed. "Would you like a backrub? It would help you to get to sleep. Come on." She patted Jake gently, and he rolled over onto his stomach. Andrew watched as she kneaded her fingers against his back, first firmly and quickly, then more gently and comfortingly. He heard Jake's slow, even breathing, the rustle of the sheets as his mother snuggled under the covers, then silence.

When Andrew awoke the next morning he saw he was alone in the cabin. His mother and Jake must have gone out for breakfast. He felt a little better and his more lucid frame of mind permitted him some thought. The more he considered the situation, the more upset he became. He had intended to spend the voyage being aloof and cool with Jake—not exactly churlish, just a little distant, and things were not working out as planned. It was hard for one to be cool and aloof when one was spewing one's brains out.

A wave of dizziness and nausea suddenly overcame him, and he rolled out of bed and crawled to the bathroom. It seemed his stomach was engaged in an exercise in futility: There was nothing down there to bring up, so why keep trying? As if to protest, his contrariness, his stomach did a violent flip-flop. He slumped over the toilet and gagged.

He was dimly aware of the sound of water running in the sink and turned his head for a second. Andrew couldn't lift his eyes above knee-level but he recognized that it was Jake standing next to him. Another violent heave overtook him and he lowered his head into the toilet and retched; he was so limp with exhaustion that he almost fell head first into the bowl. Then he felt an arm go round his chest, supporting him, and something wonderfully cold and damp press against his forehead. He realized that Jake was kneeling down behind him, holding him and squeezing a cool washcloth to his face. Andrew was so startled that he couldn't even protest, and so weak he wasn't able to move a muscle, anyway. Even speaking would have been too much of an effort; besides, the cold compress was so marvelously soothing. He took a few deep breaths, and for a moment he thought that he was going to be all right. But then he choked and gasped and started gagging again. As he squeezed his eyes shut, tears of humiliation coursed down his cheeks. Jake blotted Andrew's face gently with the washcloth and said, "Okay...okay...it's something awful, I know. Everybody gets it at one time or another. Take it easy, just take slow, even breaths. That's fine...." He pressed the washcloth against the back of Andrew's neck and stood up. Andrew heard the sound of water running again, then felt Jake squeeze another cool compress to his forehead. He took slow, shallow breaths and felt the nausea pass.

"Are you all right?" Jake asked.

Andrew nodded weakly and pushed himself away from the toilet. He knew he didn't have enough strength to stand; he was even more exhausted now than he had been before. He wriggled out of Jake's arms and started to crawl back to his bed.

"Do you want me to help you?" Jake followed him.

Andrew didn't even have the strength to shake his head. Besides, he was afraid that even that little bit of movement would bring on the nausea again. Realizing he'd over-estimated his energy level, he stopped for a moment. All of a sudden his arms collapsed under him and he crumpled to the floor. In the next instant he felt Jake's arms go around him and lift him up. As Jake carried him to his bed, Andrew remembered the last time he had felt his father's arms around him, and recalled with shame and anguish the last words he had said to him: *You care more about your stupid war more than you do about me! I hate you! I hate you!* Closing his eyes, he wished desperately that it were his father's arms around him, instead of Jake's. He wanted to see his father again, touch him, tell him that he was sorry for the terrible things he'd said, throw his arms around him and be filled with the joy of being with him once again. His mind flooded with the memory of the vision he'd had of his father when he'd been in the hospital.

It wasn't just a vision! I could feel him...feel him crying, touch his face and the fabric of his uniform and the buttons on his tunic...taste the salt of his tears....

He was dimly aware of Jake tucking him into his bunk. Then he heard the door open and his mother's voice: "Oh dear, is everything all right?"

Andrew moaned.

"Maybe we'd better call the doctor," she said.

"No...no...." Andrew groaned. "I'll be all right...I promise." His mother's threat of medical intervention was the last straw. He could live with his present wretched condition but he could not bear a fate worse than death, namely, the thought of his person being assaulted by all sorts of nasty, pointy objects and having assorted malevolent-looking devices poked into various bodily orifices. If he were going to die, so be it; but he was determined not to let himself be assaulted or tampered with.

His mother regarded him anxiously. "I don't want you to get too ill. I'm afraid you're starting to get a bit dehydrated. Let's see if you can keep some water down."

"I'll get some," Jake said. He went into the bathroom and brought back a cup of water. "It's lukewarm. That might sit better in his stomach." He gave the cup to Andrew's mother and she coaxed Andrew to a semi-sitting position. Jake took some pillows from their bed and stuffed them under Andrew's head and shoulders.

"Sip it slowly, darling." Andrew's mother held the cup to his lips. Andrew tasted the water on his lips and let it drizzle into his mouth. As he sloshed the liquid around in his mouth it washed away the sour, dry sensation that had been there before. He felt it trickle down his throat and ease the dull ache produced by the constant gagging and retching.

"All right, we'll see if you can keep that down for a bit," his mother said. "I brought some crackers, so we'll try those in awhile." Jake brought over another damp washcloth and she pressed it against Andrew's forehead. She stroked his face and smoothed his hair back. In a few minutes, he was asleep.

Andrew awoke feeling much better. He didn't know how long he had been asleep. His mother was still beside him, but Jake was gone. He munched on the crackers and managed to keep them down. His mother was pleased.

"It looks as if you've turned the corner, darling. I'm so sorry it had to start out like this, but you'll be just as good as new in no time!"

Andrew nodded feebly. Relieved as he was that the awful sickness had passed, he was still distressed by the general turn of events. The fact that he had been the object of Jake's ministrations upset him even further. He felt as if he were betraying his father by letting Jake take care of him like that. He had meant to keep Jake at arm's length, avoiding any form of familial interactions and certainly not permitting him to exercise any of the prerogatives of parenthood. Andrew hoped that his father would understand that it was not his intention that things happened the way they did. He resolved that, in the future, he would be more standoffish with Jake. Not rude or hostile, of course—that would upset his mother. Just a little aloof and distant. Andrew knew that, if he kept his actions and demeanor understated and low-key, his mother would naturally interpret his behavior as typical British reserve.

"I think I'll go up to lunch," Andrew's mother said. "I'll bring you back something to eat." Just then Jake walked in. He smiled at Andrew. "Feeling better?"

Andrew turned his face into the pillow.

"He looks better," Jake said.

Andrew felt his mother give him a kiss on the back of the head. "We'll be back shortly," she murmured. "Why don't you try a few more sips of water?"

Andrew moaned a vaguely affirmative reply. His mother and Jake went out to eat.

His mother brought some food back to the cabin and, after a lunch of sandwiches and applesauce, Andrew was feeling almost completely recovered. His mother spent most of the afternoon in the cabin with him, chatting happily about the journey, and exclaiming over how impressive the *Queen Mary* was.

"It's like a floating city! It was originally intended to carry about two thousand passengers but, since it's been converted to a troop ship, there are lots more than that on board now—over ten thousand! The dining room is grand—there's even a theater! As soon as you're up and feeling better, we'll give you a tour."

She talked about how exciting it was to be going to America: "We'll sail right into New York Harbor and you'll be able to see the Statue of Liberty! Jake has told me so much about America—I've always thought that it was somewhat similar to England, since everyone speaks English and it was originally a colony, but it sounds as if it's very different. Huge open spaces, beautiful scenery, friendly, gregarious people. What's even more wonderful is that we'll be staying with Jake's family, instead of being tourists who see the sights but don't get to know the people. I'm sure you'll like his parents. His mother has written me a few letters and she sounds so warm and friendly. She grew up on a farm in Nebraska—that's a state in the Midwest. His father is a chemist. They're called "pharmacists" in America. They live in a town called Scotch Plains. It has a nice ring to it, don't you think? A town with such a pleasant name has to be lovely, I'm sure."

His mother continued: "The rationing is not so severe there as it is in England. Imagine being able to have lots of butter and milk and eggs again! And meat! Jake says his mother is a terrific cook—she makes all sorts of wonderful cakes and pies. It'll be so good for you to have such nourishing food again! You'll grow like a weed and fill out marvelously!" She looked away for a minute, then back to Andrew. Her voice was low and pained as she spoke. "You were *so* frightfully thin and peeked after your bout with pneumonia—you looked like a starving refugee." She brushed a kiss across his cheek. "And so pale, too. I was so worried about you—"

"I was just a little tired, Mum—I really wasn't all that—"

"Darling, you *were*. The doctor told me that he'd never seen anyone with such a severe case of anemia as yours. And now that you and Jake are getting on so well, I want to tell you something."

"What?"

She smiled tenderly at him. "It was Jake's blood that you got for your transfusion."

"*Jake's?*" Revulsion bubbled up within him. He took a few quick gulps of air, trying to banish the grimace he knew was on his face. Afraid that his effort had not been all that successful, he burrowed his face in his mother's neck. To his relief she interpreted his gesture as stunned gratefulness: "Oh darling—he does so care for you! There was a fearful shortage of blood at the time and Jake knew that his blood was the same type as yours, so he offered to donate—for you. For you to be well again."

Andrew tried to force the horror of it all down, deep down. He felt violated. If only he had known at the time, he would have taken that sodding bottle of blood and smashed it on the floor rather than let one drop of Jake's wretched blood taint him. But of course, he had not known, had not even known of Jake then.

He heard the door open. "Been doing some more exploring, darling?" Andrew's mother asked.

Jake!

Andrew could not even bear to look at him, so he kept his face pressed to his mother and sighed, as if suddenly overcome by an attack of drowsiness.

"It's just nice to walk around," Jake said. "I'd almost forgotten what it was like to just be able to go for a hike and enjoy the scenery. Ready for dinner?"

"You go on, Mum," Andrew murmured. "I think I'll rest for a bit."

"All right darling. I'll bring you back some sandwiches." Then she breezed out with Jake.

After his mother and Jake had departed, Andrew got up and walked around the cabin. He hoped the effort would take his mind of his distress, and it did, a little.

It wasn't my fault that I got defiled by Jake's evil blood...And I know my father would understand, would even try to assure me that everything would be all right, despite all the awful things that happened...Yes, he'd put everything right....

He felt a lot stronger, but he was still a little stiff. Maybe a short walk up and down the corridor would get the kinks out.

He changed his clothes and went outside. He walked slowly up and down the corridor a few times, then decided to turn the corner at the end and explore the next passageway. Just as he reached the corner, he almost collided with a small boy running from the other direction.

"Sorry—" Andrew started to say.

"Come on, come on!" the boy cried excitedly. "You're going to miss the show!"

"What show?" Andrew asked.

"The Spike Jones show!" the boy exclaimed. He grabbed Andrew's hand and pulled him down the corridor. Andrew was so startled by the boy's insistence, and intrigued besides, that he let himself be dragged along. Even though the boy was a head shorter than Andrew and a few years younger, he was a dynamo of energy and enthusiasm. Andrew felt as if he were being carried along by a whirlwind. They veered left around a corner, then right, then left again, then burst through a set of double doors and raced up a flight of stairs.

"What's a Spike Jones show?" Andrew puffed.

"You haven't heard of Spike Jones?" the boy asked, incredulous. "He's marvelous! The band, I mean. They do a show that's hysterically funny! They throw a duck up in the air and then they shoot it!"

"Shoot it? Not a live duck, surely!"

"Oh no, it's not live!"

"But why do they shoot it?"

"Because they sing a song about a duck and then they shoot it!" the boy responded, with perfect logic.

Andrew accepted this explanation with a certain amount of amusement; after all, it made absolute sense to the boy. He realized that they had already climbed more than one flight of stairs—he lost count of exactly how many—and that he had no idea of how to get back to his cabin. He hadn't even thought to note the number of his cabin, so he was hopelessly lost already and completely dependent on this small boy to guide him. They burst through another set of double doors and ran down a short corridor. Andrew could hear the sound of a band playing.

"Hurry! They're starting!" the boy yelled. They ran into a large room, like a theater with rows of seats. The boy scurried up the aisle and sat on the floor in front of the first row of seats. Andrew followed close behind and sat down next to him.

The band members, all wildly dressed in garish suits of checks and plaids, played a kind of loud, jazzy music. They were, as the boy had promised, hysterically funny. First, one of the trombone players put on a gorilla mask; then two of the other band members put on masks of Hitler and Mussolini and they sang a very uncomplimentary song to the Axis leaders. They played another song and took turns dancing with a mop; then the base fiddle player stopped playing. There was a sort of knocking coming from within the instrument; the fiddle player spun the fiddle round and opened the back, and a midget reeled out and staggered across the stage!

Besides the trombones, there were trumpets, clarinets, a tuba, a saxophone, and drums. There were also several unconventional musical instruments: a washboard, some cowbells, several whistles and horns, some toy cannons, and something the boy called a kazoo. After every song the boy clapped excitedly and cheered while everyone else in the room applauded politely and indifferently. The band began to play a song, and then stopped; it looked as if the tuba player was having problems. He blew and blew, his face contorted with effort, but only pathetic squeaky noises issued from his tuba. "Oh, this is wonderful—this is positively smashing! Watch what happens!" Peter exclaimed.

A look of realization suddenly spread over the tuba player's face. He looked into his instrument and pulled out—a *skunk!* The boy shrieked with glee, and told Andrew, "They let me pet the skunk—it doesn't smell."

The band started to play another song and the boy bounced up and down in a frenzy of excitement. "Here's the song about the duck!" he exclaimed. The band members made duck noises during the song and, at the end, one of them tossed a fake duck into the air and another one pulled out a revolver and shot at it. The boy applauded enthusiastically and was completely unrestrained in expressing his exhilaration and delight at the amazing performance. "That was super, absolutely super!" he cheered. Andrew was quite impressed and fascinated by it all. He had to admit they were *very* funny. So he clapped vigorously too. The boy grinned at him and said, "My name's Peter. What's your name?"

"Andrew."

"My mother's going to meet me outside." The boy took Andrew's hand and pulled him along.

Outside, Peter spied his mother. "Mummy, Mummy! I have a friend! His name is Andrew!"

"Pleased to meet you." Peter's mother smiled at him.

"Mrs.—" Andrew began. He had not forgotten his manners.

"Barrett," she said. "Liz Barrett. Can we walk you back to your cabin?"

"Uh, I don't know where it is. I don't even remember what number it is." He felt ashamed at his ridiculous predicament. "I've been seasick for the past two days and haven't been outside my cabin until this evening. I was feeling better and went out in the corridor to take a walk and Peter came along and—"

"You got swept away by our resident typhoon!" Peter's mother laughed. She turned to Peter. "Do you remember where you found your friend?"

Peter's eyes searched back and forth for the answer; then he looked apologetically at his mother and shrugged.

"Was he on the same deck as our cabin, then?"

Peter repeated his routine of eye movements and shoulder motions.

"Peter!" Liz mussed his hair in amused exasperation. "You'd forget your head if it wasn't secured to your neck. Well, not to worry," she said to Andrew. "We'll find a purser and get you delivered to your destination." They walked along and presently encountered an official-looking man carrying a clipboard. Liz explained the predicament.

"What's your name?" the man asked Andrew.

"Andrew Hadley-Trevelyan. But the cabin might be registered under Givens. That's my mother's husband."

"Did you say Hadley-Trevelyan?" Liz asked. "Are you any relation to Alice Hadley-Trevelyan?"

"Yes," Andrew replied. "She's my mother. Do you know her?"

"She's in the ATA, isn't she?"

"Yes—are you a ferry pilot too?"

Peter announced proudly, "My mother flies Spitfires and Lancasters and Halifaxes and Stirlings and—"

"You have a Class 5 rating?" Andrew asked.

"Why, yes!" Liz seemed pleased with Andrew's knowledge. The purser, who had been flipping through papers in the clipboard, nodded at Liz and pointed to an entry on one of the pages.

"We've found you—you're just a few cabins down from us!" Liz smiled. "Come along—oh, Gib—" she waved at a man who had just turned a corner and was approaching them. "This is my husband, Gibson," she said to Andrew. "Gib, this is Andrew Hadley-Trevelyan. Peter snagged him on his way to the show tonight."

"Pleased to meet you, Andrew," Gib said. He had an American accent. Andrew guessed him to be in his late thirties.

"My daddy's in the ATA too!" Peter proclaimed.

They went back down the stairs. Peter talked excitedly about the show and Gib chatted with him, laughing at his descriptions of the band and asking him questions about the performance. As they entered the corridor, Andrew saw his mother and Jake coming from the other direction.

"Mum!" He ran ahead to greet her.

"Andrew, have you been out for a walk?." His mother's eyes widened at Liz. "Liz! What a surprise—how good to see you!"

"It seems as if Andrew got dragged along to a performance tonight," Liz told her. "He and Peter watched the Spike Jones show. I hope you weren't concerned."

"We were just coming back from supper. We didn't even know he was gone." Andrew's mother looked at him, pleased. "It looks as if you've had a good bit of cheering up. Was it fun, darling?"

"Oh, yes, it was marvelous! They danced with a mop, and sang a song about a duck and shot it—it wasn't real—and a man in a gorilla mask played the trumpet."

"And they pulled a skunk out of a tuba and they put on masks of Hitler and Mussolini, too, and sang a nasty song!" Peter added.

Andrew's mother laughed. "Sounds lovely! Oh, I'm sorry, I've forgotten my manners. Liz, this is my husband, Jake Givens. Jake, this is Liz Johnson. She's in the ATA too. We were based together last year."

"It's Liz Barrett, now." Liz slipped her hand into Gib's. "We were married this spring."

"Wonderful!" Andrew's mother exclaimed. "I had a feeling about you two! Jake and I were married this spring, too. He was in Fighter Command, but now he's in a photo-recon unit."

Jake shook hands with Gib. "So you're in the ATA too? I heard that there are quite a few Americans in the organization."

Gib grinned. "In my case, ATA stands for Ancient and Tattered Airmen. I was considered too old for regular RAF service."

"And a good thing he was, too." Liz beamed at Gib. "We met in an Anson! Got married in one, too! Not airborne, of course. We found a minister who had a zest for the unusual and who liked to perform wedding ceremonies in odd places. Never had done one in an Anson before, so he was quite happy to oblige!"

"Would you like to come in and chat?" Andrew's mother asked Liz and Gib. "It's been so long since we've seen one another!"

They all entered the cabin. "Oh, Andrew, I brought a few bits of food for you." Andrew's mother gave him some sandwiches. He settled on his bunk and started to eat.

"Where's your room?" Peter asked him.

"Right here," Andrew answered. "We're all sharing the cabin."

"You mean you don't have your own room?" Peter exclaimed, incredulous.

Gib chuckled. "Peter, you're probably the only person on the entire ship who has a cabin all to himself!"

Liz explained: "Some of Peter's cousins were going to come along but they canceled at the last minute. So he's all by himself."

"Mummy, I know!" Peter cried. "Andrew can stay in *my* cabin! Then I won't be by myself!"

"That sounds like a lovely idea, Peter, but it's up to Andrew's parents to decide."

Andrew thought it would be bad form to correct Liz's use of the plural in using the term *parents* in this instance, since Jake could not be considered his father. It only annoyed him momentarily, since he was more interested in Peter's suggestion. The possibility of not having to share close quarters with Jake had a definite appeal.

"Please Mum—it would be so much better! And I'm feeling just fine now!"

Andrew's mother shrugged and smiled at Jake. She turned to Liz and Gib. "It's all right with us, but we wouldn't want to impose—"

"Oh, no trouble at all!" Liz replied. "After all, there are three extra bunks in Peter's cabin and it would be so nice to know he's not alone."

"It's settled, then!" Peter proclaimed.

Andrew was quite amazed and delighted with the turn of events, and he had to admit he really liked Peter. He'd already shown himself to be a wonderfully boisterous and fun-loving companion. Though Peter was younger, he seemed to be leader in their newly-formed relationship, and his exuberance and sheer energy more than compensated for his smaller stature. And, oddly enough, Andrew did not really mind.

He had found a friend.

The grownups talked about flying, and Liz and Andrew's mother reminisced about their experiences in the ATA and talked about the latest happenings. Gib talked with Jake about flying Mosquitos and asked him about photo-recon work. Andrew noticed again that Jake was willing to talk about planes and technical details and such, but didn't volunteer much in the way of personal information. They talked about the United States and about places they had been to.

"I'm going to Eaglebrook!" Peter announced. "That's in Massachusetts, and it's where my daddy went!" He smiled at Gib.

Andrew wondered why Peter could so naturally and affectionately call a man not his father "Daddy."

Liz was saying, "Well, we'd better be going. These boys have had an exciting evening and it's time for them to get tucked into bed."

Andrew's mother got his suitcase and handed it to Jake. They all walked back to Peter's cabin, which adjoined the one Liz and Gib shared.

"Oh, this is just super! Thank you very much!" Andrew said to Liz and Gib.

"Don't let Peter keep you awake with his chattering. Lights out and no talking in fifteen minutes!" Liz said firmly.

After they had washed up and were settled in their bunks Andrew said to Peter, "Gib seems quite nice. He's not your real father, though."

"He's my daddy now. My real daddy was killed two years ago. He was in the RAF, in Coastal Command."

"Was he a pilot, then?"

"No, he was a gunner."

"So he was shot down?"

"Yes."

"Where?"

"I don't know. Over the sea someplace."

"Did they, you know, find him?"

"No. His plane and everyone, they never found anything. That's what my mother told me."

"So he's missing?"

"Yes, I suppose you could say that, but he's dead too."

"How do you know?"

"They told us. If they had found him, they would have told us, surely."

Andrew wondered how Peter could so glibly accept the fact that his father was dead without any real evidence, relying only on what "they" had said. He somehow sensed that it would be useless to argue the point. Instead he asked, "Do you remember your father?"

"Not really. He was tall, I know. I don't remember what he looked like."

"Do you miss him?"

"I don't really remember him, so how could I miss him? He went away when I was four. That was over three years ago."

Andrew was silent. How awful, he thought, not to even remember your own father! Not to be able to even recall what he looked like! Then again, Peter was so much younger, and it was not his fault that he did not remember. He evidently had seen no reason to doubt what "they" had said, either. After all, how could you miss someone you didn't even know? Yet, Peter seemed perfectly content to have Gib take his father's place. He even called him "Daddy"!

I guess if you're sure your father isn't coming back, it's probably a sensible thing to do, Andrew thought.

After all, Gib is the only father that Peter has ever known. Well, Gib seems really nice, too. It's probably perfectly natural for Peter to accept him as his father.

Andrew decided not to pursue the subject further. After all, Peter seemed perfectly happy with the situation, and it would be to no purpose to question his beliefs and the choices he had made.

As he heard the soft sound of Peter snoring, Andrew lay awake for awhile, thinking. Things weren't as bleak as they had seemed before, at least for the time being. He still wasn't happy about going to America, but at least his existence—immediate existence, that is—had taken a turn for the better. He was definitely in a happier frame of mind and at least the voyage itself, if not the ultimate destination, might prove to be a rather pleasant prospect. Andrew's thoughts then turned to his father, and he remembered the happy times they'd had together. Even though Gib was only Peter's stepfather, their relationship reminded Andrew of what it had been like with his own father: how he had always listened intently to whatever Andrew had to say, how he had smiled if it was something amusing, how he had asked questions or commented eagerly about whatever Andrew had been talking about. He said his father's poem to himself and it seemed to him a benediction to a day that had turned out quite happily after all.

He knew that I was distressed and he came to me, in a way. He provided a friend and companion for me, even made sure that I saw the show...Just like him to be so clever in finding a way to take my mind off my troubles....

He could almost imagine his father saying: *Not to worry, old chap, everything's going to be all right!*

Andrew smiled as he remembered all the hysterically funny songs and skits in the Spike Jones Show. He imagined taking his father to the show someday, imagined how his father would be so delighted by the antics of the band and how they would laugh together.

He quietly slid out of his bunk and went over to his suitcase, which was standing in the corner. After opening it, he felt around for his father's book. He had no trouble locating it, and he carried it back to bed with him. It was too dark to read but he slipped his hand between the pages marked by the leather bookmark, and hugged the book tightly to his chest as he fell asleep.

Chapter 25

*A*ndrew was awakened by a knock at the door. "Boys—breakfast in half and hour!" Gib announced. "Andrew, your parents will be coming soon. We're all going to have breakfast together."

"Okay, Daddy!" Peter called.

As Andrew was washing up, he heard his mother's voice in the cabin. "Did you have a good night, darling?"

"Oh yes. I fell asleep right away and didn't wake up until Gib knocked on the door."

Just as Andrew came out of the bathroom, Liz and Gib came in from their cabin. "All set?" Liz asked.

They walked down the corridor; Andrew's mother knocked at her cabin and Jake joined them. They continued on to the stairway and descended one flight to a large foyer, then proceeded through a set of double doors to the restaurant. Andrew was amazed at the incredible number of people milling about and going in various directions: mostly American servicemen, some women, and a few small children and babies. He did not see anyone close to his own age, except for a few teenaged girls.

As they entered the restaurant, Andrew was astonished: It was a vast space, larger than the ballroom at Greycliff. They were seated, and breakfast was served. Andrew, ravenously hungry, started to wolf down his food.

"Take it easy," Jake cautioned. "You don't want to put too much strain on your stomach yet."

Andrew ate a little more slowly, trying to hide his irritation. Who was Jake to tell him what to do?

The grownups chatted about planes, of course. Liz talked about the various four-engined planes she had flown: The Lancaster was as "easy as an Anson," she pronounced. "If you can fly twins, you can fly Lancs." The Stirling was a bit more of a challenge:

"It has a giant undercart, so you sit about twenty feet above the ground. It's tricky to land, because it requires a large change of attitude, but it is quite maneuverable and a real joy to fly. Liberators are pigs, heavy and sluggish on the controls. Give me a Fort any day—they're almost as easy to fly as a Lanc, but positively loaded with gadgetry. You Yanks aren't satisfied unless you can complicate things to no end!" she teased Gib.

"Ah, we Yanks know how to make life interesting—what's so bad about that?" Gib teased back. "I've never heard you complain before."

Liz giggled, and Andrew noticed that his mother smiled at Jake, as if they shared a special secret.

"Alice was telling me that you were on convoy patrol," Liz said to Jake. "Were you in the Western Approaches?"

"No, on the Murmansk run."

"Were you on the Jeep carriers, then?" Gib asked.

"No, on CAM ships."

"You flew Hurricats?" Gib was incredulous.

Jake nodded.

Liz laughed. "I heard that duty was only for crazy Polacks and batty Brits."

"Well, they do allow the occasional deranged Yank to sign on," Jake smiled.

"What's a Hurricat?" Peter asked.

"It's a Hurricane that's catapulted off a converted merchant ship, called a Catapult Aircraft Merchant ship, or CAM ship," Gib told him. "The Nazis have this four-engined, long-range aircraft, the Focke-Wulf Condor, that would spot a convoy and bomb the ships. It would also radio the position of the convoy to the U-Boats. These Condors could be spotted on radar and when they were, the Hurricats would be launched to seek out and destroy them before they could locate the convoy."

"Did you land the plane back on the boat?" Peter asked Jake.

"Nope. It was a one-way ride."

"That's wasting planes," Peter said.

"Better than getting a whole convoy of ships destroyed," Gib rejoined. He turned to Jake. "Did you ditch the plane, then?"

Jake shook his head. "Nope—had to bail out. The Hurri was great for catapult operations, since it was so ruggedly built, but it had one disadvantage: It was about the fastest sinking airplane ever designed. That big air scoop would plow into the sea and the aircraft would be hurled onto its back and go down like a rock. We tried to bail out close to the CAM ship, instead. We had a dinghy attached to our parachute, and we'd ride it until the rescue boat from the ship picked us up. Piece of cake," he grinned, then he glanced at Andrew's mother. A look of guilt washed over his face, and he shrugged apologetically. "Unless your dinghy overturns."

Andrew's mother narrowed her eyes, capturing Jake in a stern gaze. It was obvious that she did not regard Jake's assessment of things so lightly. Then her expression softened; she reached for his hand and clasped it. Jake winked at her and squeezed her fingers, as if in reassurance.

"Oh, that sounds like cracking great fun!" Peter exclaimed. "I'd love to parachute out of an airplane and go for a swim!"

"No, you wouldn't," Gib said. "The waters on the Murmansk run are horribly cold—three minutes in the drink and you're dead."

"Oh." Peter was solemnly silent for a moment. Then he asked Jake, "Why didn't you use Spitfires?"

"Hurricanes were more sturdily built and could be fitted with catapult spools. They were cheaper to use, besides; most of them were old Battle of Britain rejects. If you're going to dispose of an airplane, you want it to be one you can afford to lose. Spitfires were more valuable, so we didn't want to use them."

"You should have used Spitfires," Peter told him.

"Why do you say that?" Liz asked.

"Because—" Peter made sure all eyes were upon him, "Then you could call them *Spitcats*!" He laughed, nearly falling sideways into Gib.

"All right, now, finish your breakfast." Gib tried to be firm but his face broke into a smile, which made Peter laugh all the more. Peter finally settled down and proceeded to consume the rest of his meal in short order.

After they returned to their cabins, Peter announced that he wanted to explore the ship. "Be back by one o'clock for lunch," Liz told him.

"Come on!" Peter grabbed Andrew's hand and pulled him along the corridor.

"Where are we going?"

"I know some American soldiers—"

"You do?"

"Yes—there's Sarge, and Cowboy—he's from Texas and he's a real cowboy, and Mikey—he can wiggle his ears and turn his eyelids inside out. And there's Ray—he's a cook and has comic books that he lets me read—"

"Comic books?"

"Yes—they're ever so much fun!" Peter dodged around people as he slung Andrew behind him. "He has these Superman comic books—"

"*Superman*—who's that?"

"He's positively smashing! He has X-ray vision and he's ever so strong and he flies—"

"What kind of plane does he fly?"

"He doesn't fly in a *plane*—he flies all by *himself!*"

"*What!* How can he fly all by himself?"

"He's from the Planet Krypton—"

"From *where?*"

"Krypton," Peter said, matter-of-factly. "And he fights for truth, justice, and the American way!"

Andrew broke free from Peter and slowed. American way indeed! The American way was to sit back and let the other chap do the fighting, then take the credit for yourself!

"...then there's Batman—" Peter grabbed Andrew's hand again.

"Oh, my father had a batman when he was in the RAF," Andrew said. "He used to bring my father tea in the morning—"

"No, this Batman dresses up like a bat and drives a Batmobile!"

"A *what*-mobile?"

"A Batmobile. And the GIs let me watch them play cards—" Peter veered around a corner.

"What kind of card games do they play?" Andrew was intrigued.

"Poker!" Peter turned another corner and snapped Andrew around like a skater on the end of crack-the-whip.

"*Poker?*"

"Yes. They're teaching me how to play. Would you like to learn too?"

"Poker! That sounds like fun! How do you play?"

"Well, you try to get a good hand. "But if you don't you can pretend you do—it's called bluffing. Then you bet. You can use money or chips or things like that. We use cigarettes. Sarge—he's in charge of the game—he says he doesn't want anybody getting off the ship flat broke, so that's why they don't use money, but most of the other soldiers do...."

They flew down a wide flight of stairs. Andrew followed Peter through a doorway which led to a another set of stairs, more narrow. They thundered down the steps to the next level down. All the while, Peter explained the various hands:

"A pair is the lowest, then two pair, three of a kind, straight—that's five cards in a row...."

They burst out into a narrow corridor, made even narrower by lines of bunks, placed along the walls. Peter quickly negotiated a series of turns: *right—left—right—left—right* (or was it *left—right—left—right—left?*) and dashed down a short, even narrower corridor, upon which several doors opened. Andrew could hear sounds of some sort of fearful commotion in progress:

"Go, you bastard, *GO!*"

"Move your ass, Spanky. What the hell's the matter with you!"

"Go—Go—*GO!*"

"What are they doing?" Andrew asked, alarmed.

"They're having roach races!" Peter yelled over the din.

"*What* kind of races?"

A chorus of unintelligible shouts rose to a crescendo of hysterical hollers, then peaked with gleeful shrieks. Dismayed groans provided an dissonant harmony.

Peter sauntered into the room. "Give us some gum, chum!"

"Give us a chew, Lou!" one of the soldiers answered. He was quite young, probably not much older than seventeen, if he was even that. He had blond hair, a lopsided smile, and a face that in Andrew's estimation had never seen a razor. He took a pack of gum from his shirt pocket and proffered it to Peter.

"Hey, only if you've got a sister, mister," another of the soldiers, swarthy and solidly built, bellowed in a New York accent.

"I've told you, I've got a sister, but I haven't met her yet." Peter told him. "She's in America. Her name is Diane and she's sixteen."

"Has she ever been kissed?" the soldier asked.

"I don't know, I'll ask her."

"You do that, kiddo," the soldier chuckled.

Peter withdrew a stick of gum and handed the pack to Andrew. Never having chewed gum before in his life, Andrew cautiously pulled out a stick. He followed Peter's motions of unwrapping it and stuffed it into his mouth. It had a pleasant minty taste, but he wondered how one disposed of it when one was "done." He decided to keep a watchful eye on Peter to find out.

"Hiya, Pete!" the other soldiers called.

"Hiya guys!" Peter answered. He turned to Andrew. "Yanks say 'Hiya!'" He nudged Andrew. "Say it," he whispered.

"Hiya," Andrew said nervously.

"Hey—Pete!"

"Hey, El!" Peter laughed. He explained to Andrew. "El's from the South—they all say 'Hey!'"

This all was a little...strange. "Hey," Andrew said politely.

"Hey, kiddo!" El grinned. He was slightly built, with kind eyes and an earnest expression. "What's your name?"

"This is Andrew. He wants to watch," Peter told him.

Andrew noticed a chalk circle drawn on the floor. A horrid looking insect skittered victoriously around the perimeter; two others stooged aimlessly within.

"Did Buckwheat win again?" Peter asked.

"Yep, he's really moving," El answered.

"What's Buckwheat?" Andrew whispered to Peter.

"He's the one that won—there!" Peter pointed to the bug outside the circle.

"What is he?" Andrew asked.

"He's a cockroach," Peter replied. "This one—" He indicated one of the roaches in the circle, "Is Alfalfa—see? He's long and skinny. The other one, the fat one, is Spanky. They're racing roaches."

"*Racing roaches?*"

"Yeah—only Spanky's gonna be put out to pasture if he doesn't start hauling ass!" The soldier with the New York accent bent his head down to the short, fat roach and bellowed, "Hear that, Spank—get the lead out!"

"Maybe he needs to lose weight," Peter suggested.

"Yeah, Spanky." The soldier scooped the roaches into a small glass bottle. He screwed a lid, which was punched with tiny holes, onto the top. Holding the bottle up to eye level, he fixed a stern gaze at the entrapped inhabitants. "No more lasagna, y'hear? Bread and water for you, pal!" He tucked the bottle in his shirt pocket.

Andrew surveyed the cabin. It was smaller—*much* smaller—than the one that he and Peter shared, and had no bath, besides: Instead of a pair of double bunks, there were two sets of bunks, each four tiers high. There was enough vertical space above each bed for an adult to lie down on, with an inch or two to spare.

Peter then introduced the other soldiers to Andrew. "This is Sarge." He indicated a stocky, grinning soldier who was chomping on a cigar. He pointed out the one who had given them the gum. "That's Mikey, and that's Ray—" He nodded at the soldier with the New York accent, "And over there, that's Cowboy."

"Howdy, Andy," Cowboy grinned. He was tall and lanky, with youthful features set in a sun-leathered face.

"They say *howdy* in Texas," Peter explained.

"Howdy," Andrew said.

The soldiers smiled at Andrew.

"Hey," Ray exclaimed. "Why don't we bet on him?"

"Great idea!" Sarge replied.

"Oh boy!" Peter hollered.

"What, *bet?*" Andrew was a little apprehensive. What in the world did that mean? He wondered if he was about to be auctioned off to the highest bidder.

Peter reassured him: "They try to guess things about you, and they bet to see who's right. They did it with me and it was ever so much fun!"

Andrew looked to Ray, who had his knuckles pressed to his mouth, as if in thought. "Let's see," he said after a moment. "How many letters in his last name?"

"But—" Peter started.

Ray clapped his hand over Peter's mouth. "No hints," he said, winking at Peter. Peter's eyes glowed with excitement.

Ray then scrutinized Andrew carefully, as if he could ascertain by visual inspection the correct answer. "Ten," he pronounced. He threw a cigarette down.

Andrew was subject to similar inquiring looks by the other soldiers.

"Five," Mikey said.

"Eight," El pronounced.

"Nine," Cowboy grunted.

Sarge smiled at him. "Twelve," he declared.

As each number was pronounced, a cigarette was tossed into a pile by each of the bettors.

Peter, almost bursting with excitement, nudged Andrew. "Tell them what your last name is."

Andrew looked around at the eager faces. "Hadley-Trevelyan," he said.

Four mouths dropped in dismay. "Hadley-Trevelyan!" Sarge hollered triumphantly. "How do you spell that, anyway?"

"H-A-D-L-E-Y-T-R-E-V-E-L-Y-A-N." Andrew replied.

"Fifteen!" Sarge chortled, slapping his thigh. He scooped the cigarettes towards himself. "Hey, Pete—why don't you pick the next one?"

"Oh boy!" Peter exclaimed. "How about what day of the week he was born on!"

Everyone picked a different day of the week while Andrew wondered how they were going to ascertain the correct answer. Even *he* didn't know what day of the week he'd been born on. And it seemed unlikely in these cramped quarters that there would be calendars for the past dozen years.

After the bets were all in, El reached into his shirt pocket and pulled out a tattered piece of paper.

"What's that?" Andrew asked.

"It's a perpetual calendar," El replied. He turned the paper to Andrew. "See—it's got fourteen different calendars, and a list of about two hundred years up in the corner." He jabbed at the page with his finger. "You look up the year you want, and see what number calendar you use. When's your birthday?"

"March 4, 1931," Andrew replied.

"1931!" Ray exclaimed. "You're *twelve?*"

Andrew nodded.

"Twelve!" Cowboy laughed. "Shoot, I got a kid brother who's half your age and twice your size!"

"Hey, you guys," Sarge said. "These kids have been living in a war zone, and if you think the food you had to eat was lousy, these kids got worse, and not enough of that, besides." He winked at Andrew. "When you get stateside, you chow down y'hear?"

"Yeah," Mikey laughed. "Have a hamburger for me!"

"And apple pie!" El added.

"Veal scallopini!" Ray smiled.

"A T-Bone steak!" Cowboy declared. "Medium rare, smothered with onions."

"Fried chicken—crispy and golden on the outside—" El sighed.

"Eggplant Parmigiana—"

"French Fries—"

"Hey guys," Sarge said, "Let's get back to business—what are we supposed to be betting on?"

"Day of the week Andrew here was born on," El said, squinting at his perpetual calendar. "Now, March 4, 1931—let's see...Wednesday! You were born on a Wednesday—no one picked Wednesday!"

"So the pot goes to the next round," Sarge said.

"Wednesday—" El smiled at Andrew. "*Wednesday's child is full of woe*—are you full of woe, Andrew?"

Andrew was taken aback by El's directness. "I—I—don't think so," he stammered.

"I was born on a Tuesday!" Peter piped. "May 28, 1935—If you're born on a Tuesday, you're full of grace!"

"You're full of beans, you little turkey!" Sarge laughed. "Okay, you pick the next one!"

Peter, face flushed and hair rumpled beyond recognition, sat up and pronounced: "Number of letters in his middle name!"

Various numbers were put forth; Sarge's guess at eleven was the highest. When Andrew revealed his middle name—Roger Leslie—everyone howled with outrage, except for Sarge, who roared with triumph. "Roger Leslie—exactly eleven letters!"

They then bet on how many letters were in his mother's first name, what day of the week she was born on, and what letter her maiden name began with (the closest one won.) Then Peter piped up that he wanted to play poker, and informed everyone that Andrew was eager to learn how to play. Peter then reiterated the order of the winning hands as Andrew feigned intense concentration.

Sarge shuffled the deck and dealt the cards. Andrew noted that the cards had various military planes, both friend and foe, pictured on them. Peter explained: "The Army gives these special cards to all the soldiers, so they can practice aircraft identification." The soldiers started to play five card draw.

"In this game, you can get rid of cards you don't like, and get new ones," Peter told him.

Andrew nodded. He and Peter watched a few games and then Sarge asked, "Wanna play seven card stud, Pete?"

"Oh boy!" Peter exclaimed. He wedged himself between Mikey and Ray. "Kings wild!" he chirped.

"Okay, Kings wild," Sarge agreed. He gave Peter a handful of cigarettes and dealt the cards. Andrew watched the game with interest. He pretended to be very intent on trying to understand how the betting went, but he really was studying the players, trying to figure out each one's style of betting and whether or not they were bluffing. El won the first game, bluffing with what turned out to be two pair. Andrew noticed that he narrowed his eyes when he bluffed. Sarge won the next game with a flush. He kept a completely deadpan expression during the entire game. As more games were played, Andrew took note of everyone's various idiosyncrasies: Ray hummed *Lili Marlene* when he bluffed; Mikey cleared his throat; Cowboy scratched his ears. Sarge was a bit harder to figure: the only indication he gave as to what kind of hand he held was that, though his expression remained unchanged, his eyes sort of twinkled when he got a good hand. Peter tried to bluff, but his face was an open book. Andrew could almost guess his hand exactly by the degree of consternation or elation he exhibited. In one game, he got very excited about getting a full house but, because the game was called, he lost: Sarge had a flush. It didn't seem to matter to Peter, though; he was just ecstatic having the second-best hand. Sarge gave him half of his winnings. "Next time you win a game, you give me half of your loot—deal?"

"Deal!" Peter laughed.

"Let's let Andrew play now." Sarge moved back a bit to open up a space for Andrew.

Mikey and Cowboy decided to sit the next game out. They slouched back on one of the bunks and watched. Another soldier scuffed into the room. "This is J.D." Peter said to Andrew. To J.D. he asked, "Where are you from again?"

"Atlanta, Georgia," J.D. answered. He pronounced it "Et-lay-na, Jaw-ja". He was tall and thin, with sandy hair, a crooked smile, and a splash of freckles across his face.

"Oh, is that where Sherman marched through and burned it down?" Andrew asked. "I saw *Gone With the Wind.*"

J.D.'s faced tensed and he lowered his eyes.

"We don't talk about that in front of J.D." Sarge said. "He's kinda touchy about it."

"Only happened eighty years ago," El said. "Sherman marched through North Carolina, too."

"Really?" said Mikey. "They didn't show that part in *Gone with the Wind.*"

"Movie was too damn long anyway," Ray laughed. He ducked as J.D. threw a dufflebag at him.

"Yep," said El, ignoring the ruckus. "After Sherman blazed through Georgia, he turned left at Savannah and decided to do a repeat performance up through the Carolinas. Woulda pleased the man no end to have torched the entire South."

"Somfabitch woulda burned Richmond too, but he runned outa matches," J.D. muttered.

"J.D., sit down and play." Sarge said. "You too, Andy. Seven card stud. Kings wild."
Sarge gave the cards to Peter. "You deal."

Peter's face glowed with excitement as he dealt the cards. If he'd been chosen to
be knighted by the King, he could not have been more honored. Andrew received two
queens, a two, and a Jack of Spades, face up. Nothing useful face down, but then,
that's what the game was all about. It looked as if J.D. had the makings of a flush:
three clubs and a joker. Ray had a pair of nines; no one else showed anything promising. Sarge dropped out before the hand was dealt; Peter ran out of cigarettes. "Know
when to fold them, Peter," Sarge chided. "You threw them all away on hands you didn't
have a chance on winning."

The betting was furious; Andrew kept on raising. He displayed eagerness and confidence, and finally Ray and J.D. folded. J.D. had a flush. Andrew threw down his
cards. He said, "Why did you keep betting? I had three of a kind. Three of a kind
beats a flush doesn't it?"

Mikey howled with laughter. "You guys thought he had four of a kind! He wasn't
bluffing at all! He thought he already had you beat!"

Sarge and J.D. exchanged exasperated looks. "Okay kid," Sarge said, "Let's go over
it again. A pair, two pair, three of a kind, straight, full house, flush, four of a kind,
straight flush, royal flush. Got it?"

Andrew nodded as Sarge stated each hand, as if he were trying to carefully commit things to memory.

In the next game he folded before the cards were dealt, even though he had a pair
of Jacks. "Whyja do that kid?" Sarge said. "You might have gotten a good hand. You
coulda bluffed! I once won with a pair of Jacks over a flush, just by bluffing!"

"Sorry," Andrew said.

"Let's try it again." Sarge shuffled the cards and gave them to Peter.

Andrew watched as Peter dealt the cards. He didn't bear the soldiers any malice;
in fact, he rather liked them. They were friendly and easy-going, and Andrew found
their company quite enjoyable. He was amazed at how his attitude towards Yanks had
changed so much in the past few months; there was a time when he would have crossed
to the other side of the street rather than face them—and now, he was sitting down
with them, enjoying a friendly game of cards! He hoped they wouldn't mind being
duped. After all, it was going to be a long voyage, with not much else to entertain a
twelve year old boy. Why not have some fun?

His inexperience established, it was time, as Kaz would say, to reel them in.

Forty-five minutes later, Andrew was the delighted owner of an enormous pile of
cigarettes. He feigned astonishment at his incredibly good fortune.

"One more game," Ray said.

"I'll sit this one out," Sarge said. He got up and sat down outside the circle, behind
J.D., facing Andrew. He reached across and handed the deck of cards to Andrew. "Why
don't you deal?" he suggested.

"Thank you," Andrew said politely.

"You get to chose the game when you deal."

"Oh, um, right. Five card—what is it when you can get different cards before you start betting?"

"Draw." Sarge answered dryly.

"Right, draw. Um, can I pick whatever cards are wild?"

"Sure."

"All right, um, threes and fours wild."

Sarge rocked back on his heels and eyed Andrew as he dealt the cards. As Andrew dealt a card to J.D., he glanced at Sarge. Sarge winked at him.

Andrew won the game with four of a kind, using two fours, a King, and a three. J.D. and Ray had to fold anyway—they were out of cigarettes. El suggested that Andrew trade the cigarettes in for candy. Everyone had enough to barter with; the soldiers received back enough cigarettes to keep them in nicotine heaven, and Andrew got a sizeable heap of Mars Bars and Baby Ruths in return.

"Don't get started with those filthy things, anyway," El advised Andrew. "It's a nasty habit, and hard to break."

"Yeah, preacher," Cowboy scoffed. "What else are we gonna do for fun on this tub?"

"No booze, no broads," J.D. agreed. "Smokin' just might be the only pleasure left."

"Whaddayamean, no broads?" Mikey rejoined. "There's broads on this boat!"

"They're for officers only, lamebrain," J.D. countered. "If Uncle Sam can figger out how to pack ten thousand horny guys on this tub, why the *hale* cain't he figger on providing a few dames for the enlisted men?"

"Don't listen to them," El said to Andrew and Peter.

"Why?" Peter asked.

"Because they've only got one thing on their minds."

"What's that?"

"Um, ask your father," El told him. "No, wait a minute, don't ask your father."

"Why?"

"Um, well...Sarge, why don't you explain it to him."

"Me?" Sarge bellowed. "Who do you think I am, a doctor or something? You were the one who brought it up—*you* explain."

"You're the oldest—you'd be better at it," El replied.

"Thanks a lot, pal."

"I'll explain it to him," Andrew said.

"You will?" Peter exclaimed. "Oh, thanks awfully!"

"You know about this kinda...stuff, Andy?" Sarge asked.

"Um...yes, I know."

"Your dad already had a man-to-man talk with you, huh?"

Andrew looked away for a moment, then turned to Sarge and shrugged. "I just know, that's all." The truth was, he had been fortunate to have shared a room with Arthur Popham-Goode, who was quite knowledgeable about the subject, having a mother who was half-French (he bragged). Arthur therefore took it upon himself to make sure that those less enlightened about these delicate matters benefitted from his excellent tutelage. Arthur also kept a few "etchings" that he had pinched from one of his cousins and, for a small fee, let his eager pupils see the acts, which he so vividly described, displayed in marvelously illustrated detail. Andrew, having a steady supply of Cadbury bars, was treated to several exclusive private showings of the aforementioned material and as a result considered himself to be quite well informed on the subject. He may not have had an exhaustive understanding of all of the details, but he at least possessed a thorough grasp of the basics, and could very well figure out the rest for himself.

"Know about what?" Peter asked.

"I'll explain it to you after lunch, all right?"

"All right." Peter's eyes glowed with anticipation.

Andrew considered that, given Peter's age and level of understanding, a few drawings should suffice to give him a basic understanding of the subject under discussion. After all, Andrew thought, that was how *he* had learned.

"Well, it's a quarter to one." Mikey looked at his watch. "How about lunch, you guys?"

"Cor, we have to get back to the cabin to meet my parents!"

Peter exclaimed. "Bye!"

"I want to stretch my legs a little. I'll walk with you," Sarge followed Andrew and Peter out the door.

As they were walking down the corridor, Andrew said to Sarge, "That was a terrific game. Thanks for letting me play."

"Sure kiddo, anytime!" Sarge said. "Howzabout coming back after lunch for another couple of games?"

Andrew was a little bewildered, but pleased. He suspected that Sarge was on to him, but he found it intriguing that he was inviting him back.

"Fine," Andrew replied. "I had a lot of fun!"

"Bet you did, kid," Sarge said with a wink.

Andrew and Peter agreed not to mention anything to their parents about their extra-curricular activity. Since Andrew was carrying the candy bars, Peter went ahead to their cabin to check to see if the coast was clear. Andrew waited around the corner and heard Peter call, "Come on, come on, they're not here yet!" Andrew scurried into their cabin and hid the candy in a drawer.

"Boys! Lunch!" It was Liz.

"Crikey, that was close!" Peter breathed.

They walked outside, trying to act nonchalant.

"What did you two do this morning?" Liz asked.

"Oh, we just looked around," Peter said.

They met Andrew's mother and Jake.

"Did you have a nice morning, darling?" Andrew's mother asked.

"Oh yes—super!" Andrew replied. "Peter and I went exploring. I can't believe how huge this ship is!"

"You're looking so much better, but take it easy," she said. We don't want you to have too much excitement!"

"Oh no, Mum, I'll be careful," he promised.

After lunch, Peter skipped excitedly alongside Andrew as they walked to their cabin. Once within, Andrew got out some writing paper from one of the drawers and proceeded to make a few sketches. He tried to remember the details of the drawings that had been surreptitiously circulated at his boarding school. Peter stared, dumbfounded, at the sketches. Andrew tried to explain the physiology of the topic under discussion, but his exposition was received by Peter with an astonished gape.

"Grownups don't *really* do *that*...do they?"

"Of course they do—where do you think *you* came from?"

"Mummy went to hospital, that's what she told me."

"Well, the doctor helps to get the baby out, but this is how it gets made in the first place."

"Well, how does—does doing that—that—" Peter bobbed his head nervously at the drawings. "I mean, doing that—that thing get a baby started?"

"I don't know, it just does."

"How does the baby get out, then?"

"I don't know that, either—that's what doctors are for. They know how to figure it out."

"Oh!" Peter stared intently at the drawings for a long moment. Then he threw Andrew a troubled, disbelieving look, as if to say, *This is all a joke, right?*

Andrew nodded gravely at Peter, and said, "I know it sounds rather strange, but this is what—what grown-ups do, really."

"*Crikey!*" breathed Peter.

"Well, let's go play poker," Andrew suggested. Peter seemed quite overwhelmed by this extraordinary revelation, and Andrew thought that a diversion would allay his anxiety.

They proceeded to the poker game. Peter at first clumped lackadaisically; upon descending the second set of steps, his pace quickened. Once through the door, he was positively scampering through the labyrinth of corridors leading to the soldiers' cabin.

Andrew settled down between Mikey and El. Sarge handed him a fistful of cigarettes. Ray and J.D. were playing also. Cowboy was lying on one of the bunks, reading a paperback western.

"Seven card stud, aces wild," Sarge said, and dealt the cards.

Andrew didn't receive very good hands in the first two games. Then he got three spades and a joker, face up. He bluffed, and won. Then he got a straight, and won when the game was called.

"Boy, this kid is having the most incredible run of beginner's luck!" Mikey exclaimed.

As they played a few more rounds, Andrew learned a little more about the soldiers. They were going home "on rotation," the Army's policy of releasing one percent of the men in any one "outfit" to go "stateside": "The way it works out," Ray explained, "Is that if'n you're one of the lucky bastards, like yours truly, you get to go back to the good old U.S. of A. right away. But if'n you ain't so lucky and hafta go to the end of the line, you gotta wait something like seventeen years to get to see the old stomping grounds again."

"Seventeen years!" Mikey exclaimed. "If I had to wait that long, I'd be—I'd be, um...." He squinted and bit his lip.

"Trying to figure out how old y'are, kiddo?" Ray teased.

"Lay off," Sarge said gently.

"Thirty-*six*!" Mikey exclaimed. "That's as good as dead!"

"Seventeen years," El mused. "That'd make it 1960. Wonder what the world would be like in 1960."

"It might not be a half bad place to live if'n the assholes runnin' things could figger out a way to stop the fuckin' wars," J.D. grumbled. "Shit, I don't want my kids having t'ship off t'some hellhole and have their asses blown off. Seen nuff of that for my lifetime and theirs too."

There was spirited talk as to how things should be ordered up so as to prevent a repeat of the devastating conflict which had enmeshed most of the world. Then the conversation rambled on to what everyone had been doing "back home." Mikey was from Pennsylvania and wanted to be an auto mechanic: He could take a Jeep apart and put it back together again. (Blindfolded, and with one hand tied behind his back, he affirmed.) Ray was from New York—New York *state*—he emphasized. He was a cook at an Army Air Force Base and planned on having a restaurant when the war was over.

"I ought to get in on one of them high stakes poker games going on. I heard that some guy with the Eighth Air Force won five thousand dollars yesterday! He's going to buy hisself a house when the war's over. Yessir, five thousand dollars would be enough to set me up in a really nice location, get all the equipment—"

"Just think of all the guys who are buying that house!" Sarge said. "They're not going to have two nickels to rub together when they get to New York—helluva way to start leave."

"Yeah, gotta save some money for the gyp joints," J.D. muttered. "Those damn New Yorkers—all a bunch of swindlers. Soon as swipe the shirt off your back as shake your hand. If'n they do, you better count your fingers afterwards."

They played a game of five card stud, and the other soldiers talked about their plans for the future: J.D. wanted to travel around the world, to *see if'n there's anybody with a lick of sense anywhere*; Cowboy wanted to have a ranch of his own: "Riding the rodeo is all right, but it gets old after awhile. Like to have my own place, maybe in Montana or Eastern Oregon. Real nice mountains in Oregon. Blue Mountains is real pretty, Ochocos too." El wanted to go to college. "Maybe I'll be a teacher, or a writer," he said. Mikey wanted to be an auto mechanic and have his own "filling station and garage". Sarge smiled as everyone talked, but did not say anything about his plans.

"Shit, this kid is having all the luck!" Mikey threw down his cards. "He's already won the last three games!"

"Mikey, you're too young to swear," Ray said.

"Am not!"

"Are too!"

"Okay you guys, cut the crap," Sarge told them.

"Looks like we're going to be trading some more candy bars," Ray said. "I've got a half-pound Cadbury bar. How about trading it for forty cigs, Andrew?"

"Twenty," Andrew countered.

"Thirty-five."

"Twenty-one."

"Thirty."

"Twenty-two."

"Twenty-five."

"Twenty-three."

"Chiseler," muttered Ray. "Boy, this kid knows how to drive a hard bargain."

"That's not all he knows," Sarge said.

"What do you mean?" Mikey asked.

"Tell us, Andrew. What else do you know?" Sarge looked straight at Andrew. "You know how to play poker, don't you?"

"Of course he knows how to play poker!" Mikey said.

"I mean, he *knows* how to play poker." Sarge smiled. "Don't you, Andy?"

"Um, I don't know what you mean," Andrew said.

"What's going on?" Cowboy looked up from his paperback.

Well, Andrew thought, it really wouldn't be fair to carry this too far. He allowed a slow smile to spread across his face. "I just thought I'd have a little fun—I hope you didn't mind."

Five pairs of eyes bulged with disbelief.

"I was wondering when you guys were going to catch on!" Sarge hollered. "The kid's a pro!"

"Here, you can have your cigarettes back," Andrew said.

"No, you won 'em fair and square," J.D. laughed.

Sarge was chortling with glee and, after the shock had worn off, everyone else joined him. Ray slapped him on the back.

"Nice going, kiddo!"

It was, for Andrew, a very curious revelation into the American psyche. If he had pulled a stunt like that with a group of British soldiers, they would have been quite annoyed at being taken advantage of, though they would have pretended not to be. The Yanks, on the other hand, were positively delighted by his chicanery. To them it was all in fun, even if the fun was at their own expense. They were less concerned with their own egos and more focused on just enjoying the game and having a good time. Andrew remembered how he had viewed Americans not too long ago: uncivilized, uncouth, boorish oafs—damned colonials who couldn't even rule themselves.

Maybe on the surface, the British appeared to be more refined and civilized, but digging deeper, there was something wonderfully refreshing and unaffected about Americans. They were a little rough around the edges, true, but then again, they didn't take themselves so seriously, either. Yanks, Andrew decided, could teach Brits a thing or two.

"Okay, okay," Sarge was saying. "Not a word about thing goes outside this room! I want to have a little fun with this. Let's see if Big Wheeler would like to have a friendly little game of poker tomorrow."

"Who's Big Wheeler?" Andrew asked.

"Eddie Wheeler. He fancies himself to be a pretty hot poker player. I'd just love to see him taken down a peg or two!" Sarge said. "Wheeler's a lot of bluff and bluster, but he can take a joke."

Andrew looked at Peter. Peter was bobbing his head up and down excitedly, "Oh, that ought to be such fun, Andrew!"

Andrew shrugged and smiled. "All right, tomorrow then."

Sarge said, "Just wander in here, kinda ignorant like, and ask if you could play a game or two. I'll tell Wheeler that we just taught you how to play yesterday. Then show him your stuff, like you did today."

"Oh boy, I just can't wait to see the look on Wheeler's face!" Mikey exclaimed.

"Mikey, you make yourself scarce tomorrow!" Sarge told him. "You'll give it away for sure—you couldn't keep a straight face at your own funeral!"

"Aw Sarge—"

"Hey," Ray said, "I've got something that'll keep Mikey's mind off of the game." He winked at Mikey. "No charge, either." Mikey's eyes opened wide; it was evidently something of great importance to him.

"Nah, he's too young," Sarge said. "Maybe in another coupla' years."

"I'm *not* too young!" Mikey protested.

"Shoot, this is the guy who didn't know what a short arm inspection was!" Ray laughed.

Mikey turned a distinct shade of pink. "Shut up," he warned.

J.D. was not to be deterred. "'Sir—" He imitated Mikey's quavery voice. "Sir, I don't think I need a short arm inspection. Both my arms are the same length!" J.D. crumpled to the floor in hysterics. Peter laughed too, and Andrew, so as not to be considered ignorant, chuckled as well. He would have to find out what it was they were talking about.

"....Okay, J.D.," Sarge was saying. "There was probably a time when *you* didn't know what a short arm inspection was."

"Sure, when I was four years old!" J.D. cackled. At this Mikey threw himself on top of J.D.

"Can it, you guys," Sarge yelled, pulling Mikey off of J.D. To Mikey he said, "All right, you can read Ray's book if it'll keep you from spilling the beans. And the rest of you, keep your traps shut!"

"Um...." Andrew thought it would be a good time to bring up his concern. "If you happen to see me with my mother please don't mention it to her. I don't know if she would, well, understand. She knows I know how to play poker, but I don't want her to know, um, well, you know—that I'm being a card shark."

"Mum's the word, then." Sarge winked at Andrew.

Andrew realized that his stomach was grumbling. "I think I'd better be getting back—it's tea time, I mean, dinner. See you all tomorrow." He counted out twenty-three cigarettes and gave them to Ray. Ray got the Cadbury bar out of his duffle bag and gave it to Andrew. "Why don't you save the rest of the cigarettes I won for to-morrow?" Andrew suggested.

Sarge gathered them up and put them in a cigar box. "Okay, kiddo. See you tomor-row!"

On the way back, Andrew tried to be casual in querying Peter as to what this "short-arm inspection" was.

"Do soldiers get this short arm inspection often?"

"Oh yes, all the time, J.D. says."

"Um, how exactly do they do it? I mean, um, I know about short arm inspections, how they do them in the RAF, I mean. But how do they do them in the American Army?"

"Well, they make them drop their drawers and then they inspect their Willies."

"Their *Willies?*" Andrew was so shocked by this revelation that he forget to feign knowledgeableness of the subject.

"Yes," Peter said excitedly. "They have to get them inspected."

"Why?"

Peter seemed a little unsure. "Well...they're mad on inspections in the Army. They inspect just about anything. That's what J.D. says. He says that the Army is nothing but inspections and chickenshit rules and regulations, that's what J.D. says. He says they grab your balls and make you cough." He imitated J.D.'s drawl: *They 'spect yo' insides, outsides, backsides, frontways, sideways, every which way from Sundays!* So I suppose someone decided that it would be a good idea to inspect Willies."

"What do they inspect them for?"

"Something having to do with the veedee."

"*Veedee*—what's that?"

Peter shrugged. "I don't know, but it's something very important. They even have a movie about it—it's called the *Veedee Special.* And then the chaplain gives a talk and tells you not to do it, and the doctor tells you what to do if you get it, and the C.O. tells you what the army will do to you if you get it."

"What happens if you get this veedee?"

"They give you a shot in the *bee*-hind, with a needle a foot long. J.D. told me all about it."

"A foot long!"

"Uh-huh, and it's *square* and it's got Beagle burrs on the end." Peter's eyes were round with horror.

"Beagle burrs! What are they?"

"I don't know, but they must be bloody awful. He says that you can't even sit down for a month after getting it!"

Crikey, Andrew thought. What an appallingly humiliating ordeal to have to endure—having one's private parts the subject of a summary inspection! And to what purpose? To get a nasty jab in one's posterior if one failed? No wonder Yanks could be a bit churlish at times—that would be enough to put anyone in a bad temper!

"...and then J.D. said, 'When lightnin' strikes, remember to act like it's rainin', boys, and wear your rubbers!'" Peter exclaimed.

"What?"

"That's what else J.D. said when I heard them talking about short arm inspections."

"*Act like it's raining and wear your rubbers?* What does *that* mean?"

"I don't know. It must mean something different in America." Peter scrunched his face. "One time, just after my mummy and daddy got married, we were all having breakfast, and I asked my mummy if I could have a rubber, because I needed to rub out a mistake I'd made in my copybook. My daddy spit out his tea and Mummy said, 'Dear, it doesn't mean the same thing over here.'"

They turned the corner to the corridor that led to their cabin and found Andrew's mother waiting for them.

"Where did you get the chocolate bar?" she asked.

Andrew realized that he was still holding the Cadbury bar in his hand. "Oh, one of the American soldiers gave it to me," he replied, then he added, "Let's all have it for a snack tonight. There's enough for all of us."

"How nice," his mother said. "So, you're meeting new people and making friends?"

"Oh yes, Mum. The Americans are really nice."

"What sort of things do you do?"

Andrew glanced at Peter. "Oh, they bet on us," Peter piped. "They try to guess things about us, like how many letters in our last names and what day of the week we were born on—things like that."

"They also bet on things about you, Mum," Andrew said. "Like what letter your maiden name started with and how many letters were in your first name."

Andrew's mother laughed. "Sounds like fun!"

Gib and Jake were walking down the corridor towards them.

"Daddy!" Peter ran to Gib and threw his arms wide.

"How'd you like a ride, Sport?" Gib knelt down and Peter climbed up on his back and put his arms around his neck. Gib locked his arms around Peter's legs and stood up.

"My daddy gives me horsey rides!" Peter announced as Gib carried him to the dining room.

After dinner they all went to the Spike Jones show, and Peter displayed as much excitement and enthusiasm as he had the shown the previous evening, clapping wildly and cheering at the end of each number.

They all had chocolate and tea in the stateroom which Andrew's mother and Jake shared, since it was the biggest. Peter pretty much monopolized the conversation, talking over and over again about his favorite parts of the Spike Jones show. Then his head began to nod, and Gib picked him up and carried him, piggy-back style, back to his cabin. Andrew followed.

"See that he washes up and brushes his teeth," Gib told Andrew.

"All right," Andrew replied.

After washing up, they dressed in their pajamas and settled down in their bunks.

"I hope I didn't keep you awake last night," Peter told Andrew. "Mummy says I snore."

"No, I could hardly hear you," Andrew said. "I slept quite well. It's nothing compared to sharing a cabin with my mother and Jake. Jake woke me up. He was having some kind of nightmare, and he was yelling in his sleep."

"What was he yelling?"

"Oh, fighter pilot talk. Bandits and 109s and Heinkels and saying stuff like "roger wilco"—that sort of thing. Then he started screaming "Break, break!" and then my mother woke up too and she shook him out of it."

"Who was he talking to?"

"I suppose another fighter pilot."

"Do you think he's talking about someone who got killed?"

"How would I know?"

"Why don't you ask him?"

"Because...well, because we don't talk, really." Andrew tried to figure out a way to explain things to Peter. "Look, it's not like it is between you and Gib. Jake is someone who married my mother. That's all. That doesn't mean I have to like him. My mother got married to him because she was lonely." Andrew didn't want to tell Peter that he believed his father was still alive. For one thing, he didn't want to plant any doubt in Peter's mind that *his* father might be alive—if Peter had accepted his death, and perhaps there was good reason for him to believe that he was gone for good, then that was what was best. After all, Peter didn't even remember his father, and he was quite happy to regard Gib as his father.

"But why don't you like him?" Peter was determined to press the issue.

"Because...." Andrew searched for an explanation. "Well, because he's younger than my mum. Six years younger, in fact. Men who want to be with women who are older than them...well, they do it because they think it's amusing, not because they really like them."

"They *do*?"

"Yes, of course they do."

"Jake seems like he really likes your mother. Like my mummy and daddy. He's thirty-eight, ten years older than her."

"But it's all right for a man to be older than a woman. Not the other way around."

"Why?"

"Because that's the way it is."

"Why is it that way?"

"How should I know? Because!" Andrew was exasperated with Peter's questioning. Why did he need an explanation for everything? Peter was silent, and Andrew was afraid he had hurt his feelings. "Listen, I'm sorry. I didn't mean to be cross with you. I don't know the reason for everything, either, but things are the way they are because—" Andrew realized he was tying himself up into philosophical knots, "—that's the way they are."

"Oh," said Peter.

"Don't mention anything about it to Jake or my mother, or even to your parents. I know that Jake doesn't want me to know. He wants to keep it a secret from me."

"How do you know?"

"Because I heard him telling my mother not to tell me. He made her promise. He didn't know I was listening."

"Oh."

"Besides," Andrew went on. "If Jake is six years younger than my mother, that would make him only thirteen years older than me. That's not old enough to be a father, or even a stepfather. Gib is older than your mother, so it's all right for him to be your father. But it's not all right for Jake to try to be my father."

"Do you think that it will ever be all right?"

"Never."

Peter was quiet, and Andrew thought that the conversation might have been too disturbing for him. Andrew tried to think of something reassuring to say to him, but then he heard the sound of Peter's soft, even snores.

Andrew lay awake a for a long time. His conversation with Peter had brought a lot of things to the surface and he was disquieted by his feelings of resentment towards Jake. Why shouldn't I be upset with him? Andrew thought. After all, he took advantage of my mother, he's younger than her, and he wants to keep that a secret from me.

But, even though Andrew tried to count the ways in which Jake was deserving of contempt, his mind was barraged by recollections of the many ways in which Jake shown truly decent human qualities: the time in the hospital when they had shared that terrifying experience and how Jake had tried to comfort him; the joy they had both known when Andrew's mother recovered; the way Jake had taken care of him during his miserable bout of seasickness. It was all so disconcerting: It was as if someone else were intruding on his consciousness, trying to fill his mind with thoughts that he didn't want to acknowledge. Andrew grabbed his father's book, which was tucked away beneath his pillow. Maybe the way to get Jake out of my mind is to concentrate on my father, he thought. He slipped his hand into the place marked by the bookmark and said the poem to himself. Then he drifted off to sleep.

That night Andrew dreamt that he was in his room at Armus House. He saw his father walking up the front steps and ran down the stairs to greet him but, when he opened the front door, no one was there.

Chapter 26

*W*hen Andrew awoke the next morning, he felt a dreadful uneasiness that bordered on panic. At first, caught in the limbo between sleep and consciousness, he couldn't figure out why he was so disquieted. Then, as his thoughts began to form a coherent pattern, he remembered the dream he'd had the night before. He shuddered as he recalled his terror at finding his father gone.

It must mean something, Andrew thought. Why did my father disappear? He remembered that, just before he'd fallen asleep, he had been thinking about Jake and his redeeming qualities. Maybe that was it!

To allow Jake to have a place in my life at all is as good as betraying my father. Maybe my father, wherever he is, can sense that someone else is trying to take his place. Perhaps he knows I'm going away. He might think he'll never see me again....

Andrew took a few deep breaths. It was all very clear now. He knew what he had to do. He could not give any quarter to Jake at all, at least not in his heart. For his mother's sake, of course, he had to pretend to accept Jake. But his inner self, his true self, had to deny Jake any part in his life. He could not allow anything, or anyone, to interfere with the remembrance of his father.

"You're a little quiet today," Andrew's mother said to him as breakfast was being served. "Are you feeling all right?"

"Oh yes, Mum, I'm fine." Andrew attacked his food with a gusto he didn't really feel. "May I have some more juice?"

"I'll get some." Jake grabbed Andrew's glass and got up.

Peter was aquiver with excitement. As he wolfed down his food, he kept glancing at Andrew; it was obvious that he was anticipating the upcoming game. Liz and Gib warned him repeatedly to slow down. "If you get an upset tummy, you won't be able to watch the Spike Jones show tonight," Liz admonished him.

"I'll take him for a walk after breakfast," Gib said. "The exercise should settle him down."

Andrew shot Peter a look of irritation: Now you've done it!

Jake returned with a full glass of juice for Andrew. The grownups had another cup of tea. When they were finished, Gib said to Peter, "Come on, Sport—time to get our morning constitutional."

"Why don't you and Andrew go along?" Andrew's mother said to Jake. "Liz and I are going to catch up on some letter-writing."

"Sounds like a good idea," Jake said.

They walked up several flights of stairs to the open-air promenade. Peter skipped excitedly ahead as Gib talked with Jake. Andrew brought up the rear, silent and brooding. They walked to the front of the ship and leaned against the railing overlooking the foredeck. Looking down, they saw several dozen men strolling around, all of them dressed in grey coveralls with the letters *PW* on the back. Jake's face paled; he turned and walked away. Gib, watching the men on the foredeck, did not notice. One of the men was smiling up at them—a wistful, almost apologetic smile.

"Hullo!" Peter called.

The man did not answer, but raised his hand as if in greeting and continued to smile all the while.

"Why doesn't he answer us?" Peter asked Gib.

Gib did not look at Peter, but continued to gaze at the man, with an odd look of pity and sadness on his face. Finally he said, "Well, he's one of the lucky ones. Going to spend the rest of the war in a prison camp."

"Prison camp!" Peter was shocked. "What's he done wrong?"

"He's a German prisoner," Gib told him. "They all are." He indicated the rest of the men walking about. "They're going to POW camps in Canada or America."

"A *German*!" Peter exclaimed. "He doesn't look like a German!"

"Well, what did you expect to see? Someone frothing at the mouth or wearing horns?"

"But they did all those terrible things! How could they be so hateful?"

"Hate is the product of fear and despair. People who are without hope are easy to control: They will believe anything, do anything, follow anyone, if they think that it will be a way out of their despair. After losing the Great War, Germany was in a fearful shape, and the German people suffered terribly. They were ready for someone to come along and promise to solve their problems. It's not wrong to be afraid, or to face despair, but when people give in to hate, thinking that it's a way out of their problems, then evil triumphs. It can happen to anyone, even us."

"We're *not* like the Nazis!" Peter sputtered indignantly.

"Look at that man," Gib said. "He's not that much different than you."

"You're defending him!" Andrew declared angrily.

"I'm not trying to excuse what the Nazis have done," Gib said. "But it's important to realize that we all have the same capacity for evil within ourselves. Don't think it couldn't happen to you. Remember that despair is a dangerous thing. When you are without hope you are vulnerable to anyone who wishes to control you. Don't ever let anyone, or anything, take advantage of your despair." He put one hand on Peter's shoulder; the other on Andrew's. "And remember, never turn your fear into hate." He turned around. "Where's Jake?"

"He walked off. He was quite upset when he saw the Germans," Peter said.

Gib sighed. "It's one thing to be keen on winning a war. It's another thing not to be able to put things behind you. I hope that Jake...." his voice trailed off and he looked at Andrew, concern on his face.

Andrew was annoyed. What do you expect me to do? he wanted to say. Jake isn't anything to me—he married my mother, that's all. What he can or can't put behind him is none of my concern.

He glared back at Gib.

They walked in silence back to the cabin.

Peter and Andrew got to the poker game a little later than they'd planned, but it wasn't a problem. The poker game was well underway, and "Big Wheeler" was clearly on a roll. He was a big, burly man with a booming voice. A pile of cigarettes lay on the floor. The GIs were playing five card draw; Wheeler threw down a full house and chortled, then scooped the cigarettes towards himself.

"Can we watch?" Andrew feigned timidly as he approached the circle of players.

"Yeah, yeah kid. Just don't get in the way!" Sarge growled, not even glancing at them. Cowboy, El, Ray, and J.D. didn't even look up from their cards.

Mikey, lying in one of the bunks, was deeply engrossed in a paperback book entitled *The Physiology of Sex*. Andrew huddled behind Cowboy, who was dealing. They watched a few games and then, when Wheeler was distracted by winning another round, Sarge winked at Andrew.

"Can I play, please?" Andrew pleaded. "Seven card stud?"

"Kid watched us playing yesterday," Sarge said in an amused voice. "Okay, kid." He turned to Andrew. "A coupla games, all right? Face cards with facial hair are wild. Then amscray!"

"Oh boy!" Andrew wedged himself between Ray and El.

Andrew was glad that his first hand wasn't very good. He folded early. Wheeler won, throwing down his cards with a flourish and proclaiming loudly, "I'll make that a flush, with a pair a queens on the side!"

In the next game Andrew was dealt a Joker, a Queen of Clubs, a ten of hearts, and an eight of diamonds, face up. Wheeler's eyes narrowed. He was showing two aces, a five, and a seven, all of different suits. Cowboy had a pair of nines. Sarge and Ray had nothing; they folded early. Andrew kept raising, nervously biting his lip, and repeatedly checking the three cards he had face down. Cowboy threw his cards down, and Wheeler called. He had a full house.

Andrew turned over his cards and acted dismayed. "Three of a kind!" he grumbled, pointing to a Queen of Diamonds. Then his eyes widened. "No, four of a kind, four of a kind!" he cried excitedly as he pointed to a Jack of Spades. "He has a mustache!"

Sarge rolled his eyes. "Wanna quit while you're ahead, kid?"

"Oh no, please one more game!" Andrew begged him. "This is fun!"

Cowboy dealt again. This time Andrew showed a Joker, and a three, five, and a seven of hearts. He looked at his face-down cards and bit his lip. Then he took a deep breath and lowered his eyes. A smile flirted with his mouth as he kept raising. Wheeler had a pair of tens; Sarge had a King of Diamonds and two threes. Andrew kept raising, and they all folded.

"Let's see that flush, kid," Sarge said. He turned over Andrew's cards and revealed— nothing! Andrew shrugged.

Wheeler's eyes widened.

"Beginner's luck!" Sarge said, then he added, "Deal him in again, Cowboy."

Andrew didn't have a very good hand in the next game, so he folded and pretended to pout. Wheeler won with four of a kind. In the game after that, Andrew got a pair of Kings, but it looked as if Sarge was working on a flush, so he folded again. "One more game," he asked Sarge.

"Let's make it five card stud," Wheeler said.

"Five card stud—how many cards are face up in that?" Andrew asked.

"Two," Cowboy replied. "Still wanna play?"

"Oh, yes, that sounds like fun!" Andrew said.

An hour later, Wheeler was eyeing Andrew's huge pile of cigarettes and scratching his head. "Kid sure has a knack for the game," he said. "With a little practice, he might be pretty good!"

Mikey exploded in laughter.

"Did I say something funny?" Wheeler asked.

Sarge started chuckling, and the rest of the soldiers joined in. "Something's going on here," Wheeler said, suspicious.

"Meet our secret weapon," Sarge said. "And I do mean *secret!*"

Andrew looked Wheeler straight in the eye, and smiled. Wheeler did a double-take, then threw back his head and howled.

"Like I said," Sarge told him, "Let's keep it top secret. There's a few more people I'd like to con before this tub makes port."

Wheeler pounded Andrew on the back so hard his teeth nearly shook loose.

"Can I play one game, please?" Peter pleaded.

"Sure, one game." Sarge replied. "What'll it be?"

"Five card draw!"

"Five card draw it is," Sarge announced.

"Face cards with facial hair wild!" Peter hollered.

Andrew decided to sit the game out. Mikey took his place. Ray dealt, and when Peter's turn came to discard, he piped, "Five!"

"Hey Pete, don't throw them all away," Sarge admonished.

"I don't have anything good!" Peter complained.

Sarge threw his hand down. "I'll sit this one out." He looked at Peter's hand. "Take a look at this, Pete." He withdrew one card. Peter, astonished, exclaimed, "Cor, I didn't see that I almost had a fl—"

"Shh," Sarge warned. "One please," he said to Ray. Ray slipped him one card, which Sarge placed in Peter's hand. Peter's eyes popped wide open with excitement and his face broke into an ear-splitting grin. "I bid three!" He threw in three cigarettes.

"It's not your turn," Ray snapped. Wheeler started the bidding with one cigarette. Peter raised it by three.

"Kid's holding a flush," Sarge told Cowboy, whose turn was next.

"A flush don't beat a straight flush," Cowboy said. "I'll raise two."

"You're bluffing," J.D. said.

"Am not!"

"Are too! Y'always scratch your ears when ya bluff."

"Do not!"

"Do too!"

Mikey folded. So did J.D. Ray raised two more cigarettes. Wheeler folded, Peter raised three more. Cowboy considered his hand, and folded. Ray threw down his cards.

"Okay, kid, let's see that flush!"

Peter threw down four clubs and a Queen of Diamonds: "See! She has a mustache—there's a little smudge under her lip! It's a flush!"

Five pairs of eyes peered at the card, and five mouths hung open in disbelief. Peter chortled, "It's a flush—it really is—"

"Why you dirty dog!" J.D. hollered.

Ray grabbed Peter by the ankles and dangled him, head down. Peter shrieked with glee. "Noogies for sale!" Ray announced. J.D. and Mikey proceeded to rub Peter's scalp vigorously, while Peter, red faced, screamed with laughter.

"Geez, that makes two of 'em!" J.D. exclaimed. "We ought to notify the Immigration Service that there are two very dangerous individuals about to disembark on the shores of our fair land—lyin', cheatin' varmints, they are, disguised as sweet-talkin' angel-faced schoolboys!"

"Bluffing isn't cheating," Andrew pointed out.

"All right—make that bluffin', lyin' varmints!" J.D. laughed.

Ray lowered Peter onto the floor. Mikey proceeded to tickle him under the ribs and Peter wriggled with rapture.

"Okay, let's give it a rest," Sarge said. "I think these kids have had enough excitement for now. Let's meet back here at two."

"Okay," Andrew said. Peter, still giggling, picked himself off the floor and followed Andrew out. They walked up to the restaurant level. Mikey, Ray, and Sarge walked behind them. As they came out into the foyer, Andrew saw his mother and Jake coming out from main stairway. The soldiers proceeded past them, to the main stairway.

"Aren't you going to have lunch in the restaurant?" Peter called.

"Nah—that's officer country," Ray replied. "Low-lifes not allowed. We're going up to the promenade."

"Where do you eat?" Peter asked.

"They got this special greasy spoon joint for the enlisted slobs," Ray laughed.

Andrew waved at them, then ran to greet his mother.

"Those are some of your friends?" she asked.

Andrew nodded.

"I'm positively famished!" Peter exclaimed.

"Come along," Andrew's mother said to him. "I promised your parents I'd round you up and take you to lunch."

They found Liz and Gib reserving a table for them in the restaurant.

"Don't act too excited and don't wolf down your food," Andrew whispered to Peter as they sat down.

"Well, what did you boys do all morning?" Gib asked.

"Oh, just looked around," Andrew replied. Peter sputtered, and started coughing.

"Well, I'm glad you two found each other," Liz said. "I was afraid that Peter would be bored and lonely when I found out his cousins weren't coming along. After all a troop ship is probably not the most exciting place in the world for a young boy."

"Oh, it's um...." Andrew search for the right word, "Interesting!"

"Yes, interesting," agreed Peter.

"Holy Mackerel! I don't think this kid has cracked a smile in the last two hours!" Wheeler hollered. "Talk about a poker face!"

"Are you going to raise?" Andrew said, his voice dripping with irritation. Only he, Wheeler, and Sarge were left in the game.

"Hmm, I'll see your two, and...." Wheeler contemplated his cards, "...Call!"

"Four of a kind!" Andrew threw down his cards.

Wheeler and Sarge groaned, and Andrew scooped up the last of the cigarettes. He traded twenty for a Superman comic book from Ray, and the rest for candy bars and chewing gum from Wheeler.

"Chow down kid," Wheeler laughed. "You look like you could stand to put on a few pounds. Are your folks sending you to the States to get fattened up?"

Andrew was disturbed by Wheeler's crack about his slight stature, because it seemed to confirm the reasons that Andrew's mother had given him as to why he was being sent to America. I'm *not* thin, he thought.

"You ought to see Andrew's parents!" Mikey said. "They don't look anywheres near old enough to have a kid his age!'

"How old were they when they had you?" Fourteen?" Ray asked.

"He's not my real father." Andrew unwrapped a package of gum and carefully withdrew a piece. "My mother married him a few months ago. My mother was nineteen when I was born."

"Could have fooled me. She doesn't look a day over twenty-one," said Ray. "Neither does he."

Peter looked at Andrew, expecting him to answer. Andrew stared back at him and slowly handed him the pack of gum, as if to seal an unspoken agreement to keep silent about the matter. Peter took out a piece and unwrapped it. He stuffed it in his mouth and chomped a few times, then said, "I've got a stepfather, too. My real daddy was killed two years ago. He was a gunner in Coastal Command."

"Sorry to hear that, kiddo," Sarge said.

Peter chomped a few more times. "My daddy now is really nice. He's a ferry pilot, just like my mother and Andrew's mother."

"Your mothers are *pilots?*" Mikey was incredulous.

"Yes, they fly Spitfires and Typhoons and Tomahawks and Mosquitos," Peter told him.

"Hurricanes and Beaufighters too," Andrew added.

"Wow!" exclaimed Mikey. "I didn't know women flew planes for the RAF."

"Both our mothers got married to Americans," Peter said. "Andrew's daddy now is a fighter pilot."

"He *was* a fighter pilot," Andrew said. "Now he does photo reconnaissance." He considered correcting Peter on his usage of "Andrew's daddy now" in referring to Jake, but thought better of it.

"So he's with the Army Air Forces?" El said.

"No, he's in the RAF," Peter replied. "Andrew's real daddy was a fighter pilot in the RAF, too."

"What's a Yank doing in the RAF?" Mikey asked. "I thought all the Eagle Squadron pilots joined with the US forces."

Andrew shrugged. "I don't know. Anyway, it's none of my concern."

The soldiers all looked at him. Feeling uncomfortable with the unwanted attention, he picked up the deck of cards and pretended to examine the drawings of the various planes. He finally grunted and threw down the cards. "Well, we'd better be going."

"Hey, kid," Sarge said. "Coming back tomorrow?"

"Sure." Andrew smiled, just to break the tension, then gathered up his winnings. "See you all tomorrow."

"Wear your poker face. I'll round up a few new faces." Sarge jumped up and followed Andrew and Peter down the corridor. As they walked along, he put one arm across Andrew's shoulder, and the other across Peter's. They continued in silence up to the sun deck, where they parted ways. "Take it easy, kiddo," Sarge said to Andrew. "You too." He winked at Peter.

Andrew and Peter wandered up to the railing overlooking the foredeck. Andrew noticed that there was a guard, standing off to one side and looking down on the prisoners. He had a gun. The prisoners were filing out through a door. The deck was empty for a few minutes; then a new group of prisoners filed onto the deck.

"There he is!" Peter whispered. "The one we saw this morning."

The prisoner cocked his head and caught sight of Peter and Andrew. He walked over and smiled up at them.

Looking back on the incident later, Andrew had no idea what possessed him to do what he did. He glanced at the guard and saw that he was distracted. As if he were obeying an impulse of which he had no understanding, Andrew took one of his Hershey bars and held it in one hand, over the railing. The man moved quietly until he was standing right under Andrew. Andrew let the bar drop and the man caught it in his hand and swiftly hid it in his sleeve. He winked at Andrew, and nodded his head.

All of a sudden Andrew was seized with a gut-wrenching fear. He turned and bolted. He had a horrible feeling that he had done something abominably wrong, that he was guilty of a terrible betrayal...Perhaps, by running himself into sheer exhaustion, he would be able to exorcise the awful impulses which had prompted him to commit such an traitorous act. Giving a gift to a *Nazi!*

He flew down the stairs, wheeling down, down, bursting into a corridor. It was crowded with soldiers and he had to dodge around in order to get through. Running blindly, he slammed through several sets of doors, then flew down another set of steps.

He dashed out into another passageway, very narrow and unfamiliar. He careered through a maze of narrow corridors; then exhaustion overcame him. Slumping against the wall, he collapsed onto the floor.

He had no awareness of time passing. He wished desperately that he could undo what he had done, or that he could grab hold of the part of him which had caused him to commit such a terrible thing and tear it away, so that it would never tempt him again. He was overcome with self-loathing, and the hatred he directed at himself boiled over until he felt a contempt for everyone and everything.

He felt a hand on his shoulder. "Are you okay?" It was Jake. "We've been looking for you."

Andrew looked up. It was as if the Devil himself were standing in front of him. Jake was a living symbol of all that was evil: He personified the lack of decency and loyalty in Andrew's world, and epitomized all that had gone wrong in his life. Especially now. Andrew saw clearly now what had happened: At the moment that he had dropped the candy into the prisoner's hand, he had chosen to block out everything except the fact that he was giving something to another person. It was as if, at that instant, something had blinded him to the awfulness of what he was doing.

"Andrew?" It was the first time that he heard Jake speak his name to him. As he looked at Jake, Andrew felt contaminated by his association with him. Jake had also chosen to block out the context in which he had made his choices, and that was why he had violated all that was decent and good.

He took advantage of my mother at a time when she was vulnerable and despairing. He doesn't care that he's caused her to betray her husband; he's not one bit concerned about the man he so blithely replaced. If he had his way, he'd be happy if no one remembered my father at all!

Andrew was in no mood to have anything to do with anybody that evening. After following Jake at a comfortable distance to the dining room, he ate his supper in silence. His mother fussed over him. "Are you all right, darling? Not seasick again?"

"No Mum, I'm fine. May I be excused? I'm just tired."

"All right, darling. Are you sure that's all?"

"Yes, I think I'll lie down for awhile." He got up and walked back to his cabin. Once there, he threw himself down on his bunk.

The door opened a few minutes later, and Peter entered.

"You dropped the candy when you ran away. I picked it up and saved it for you." He opened the drawer that held their stash.

"You can have it. I really don't care for Hershey bars."

"You don't? What about the gum?"

Andrew shrugged. "You can have it if you want."

Peter regarded Andrew with concern. "What's wrong?"

"I don't know. I felt scared after I gave the candy to that prisoner. I know that it was the wrong thing to do."

Peter was silent for a moment; then he said softly, "I wish that it weren't—wrong, I mean."

"I do too."

"Do you want to go to the Spike Jones show?"

"No, not tonight."

Peter's disappointment was clear. Andrew tried to cheer him up. "Tomorrow, I promise. Have a good time."

"All right."

Peter left and Andrew was alone with his demons. The day's events played like a newsreel in his mind: seeing the prisoner that morning, and Gib's words, "Don't let anyone, or anything, take advantage of your despair."

That was what Jake did to my mother! Damn him, damn him, damn him! He saw that she was lonely, that she was weak, that she was vulnerable, and he moved right in!

Andrew groaned. If only he could stop thinking about it all! It seemed as if everything that he'd believed to be true and good and honorable had been shattered. If only he could feel his father's arms around him again! In spite of what he had learned about his own untimely birth, Andrew still wanted to believe that his parents *had* loved each other, had loved *him*, but the despair he felt was threatening to extinguish even that hope.

Sleep finally overcame him, but the nightmare that had tormented him the night before returned with an even more terrifying twist: He dreamt that he again saw his father walk up the front steps of Armus House, and that he ran downstairs to the front door. He tried to call out to his father, but his voice would not come. Then he heard his own voice, as if shouted over a loudspeaker, yelling, *I hate you! I hate you!* He wanted it to stop, but it just got louder and louder and, when he opened the front door, his father wasn't there. He woke up in a cold sweat and lay in the darkness, his heart pounding.

Gib's words played over and over in his mind: *Don't ever turn your fear into hate.* Andrew knew that he had not hated his father. He had just been afraid, horribly afraid, that his father would go away and not come back. If only he could tell him that!

"Andrew! Time for breakfast!" Gib called. "*Andrew!*"

"I'm awake. I'll be ready in a few minutes."

"We'll save you a seat. Hurry up!"

He tumbled out of bed and hunted around for some clean clothes; he had fallen asleep without getting undressed the night before. He had no more clean shirts, and had to settle for one that he had worn two days before. Then he remembered that he'd packed some of his things in his mother's bag. After dressing, he made his way up to the dining room.

"Andrew, are you all right?" his mother asked.

"I tried to wake you, but you wouldn't open your eyes," Peter said.

Andrew gulped down a glass of juice. "I'm all right. I woke up during the night and couldn't get back to sleep for a long time."

"Is anything bothering you?" his mother said.

"No Mum, I'm fine. I guess all the excitement and everything finally caught up with me." He forced a smile.

Everybody else had finished breakfast. "Come on Sport, time to wear you out!" Gib said to Peter.

"I'll come along," Liz said. She followed Peter and Gib out of the dining room.

Jake finished drinking his tea. He stared into the empty cup for a moment, then glanced at Andrew's mother. She smiled at him, and he set down his cup, reached over, and squeezed her hand. "See you later," he whispered. He got up, and left.

Andrew stared at his meal and idly stirred his porridge. He didn't want to look at his mother. He felt her hand stroke his face, felt the hot tears splashing down his cheeks. He bit his lip to keep it from trembling.

"What's wrong, darling?"

"Nothing!" He shook his head furiously.

She took a deep breath and said, "I know it's hard for you, going away to a strange place. And after all that's happened, too. It hasn't been an easy year for you, I know."

Andrew nodded.

"Anything you want to talk about?"

Andrew shook his head.

"We're not going to see one another for awhile," she said. "If there's anything you want to say, anything that's on your mind, we should talk about it. Hmm?"

Andrew shrugged. He wished that he could ask her if she really loved his father, but that would just stir up all the unpleasant memories of the bitter things he had said to her after that disastrous first meeting with Jake. As if reading his mind, she said, "You know, Jake was terrified of meeting you. He doesn't want you to think that he's trying to take your father's place.

Andrew nodded. His throat tightened horribly and he clenched his jaw.

His mother reached for his hand. "I know you still miss your father."

He closed his eyes and looked away.

"It's all right, you know," she whispered.

Do you miss him? he wondered. He couldn't bear to look at her.

Again, as if aware of his thoughts, she said, "I still miss him, too."

He opened his eyes, and looked at her. Her eyes were full of sadness and understanding, and a flood of relief swept through him. Maybe she had given up hope that his father was still alive, but she had not stopped loving him. *I still miss him, too.* That was enough. He squeezed her hand back. Leaning over him, she put her arms around his shoulders. Neither of them spoke for awhile, and Andrew was suddenly aware that the room was empty. He saw the sun streaming in through the windows and, in the distance, the sea, silvery blue and glistening. He heard the low hum of the ship's engines, the muffled sounds of conversation and laughter from the corridor outside the room. But in this oasis of peace and remembrance, all was still. It was enough for now to know that his mother still carried the memory of his father in her heart. Some-day, somehow, he would return, and neither Andrew nor his mother would ever feel the pain of longing again. Everything would be set right: They would be a family again, and they would be together, always, as it should have been all along. His mother ca-ressed his face and looked into his eyes. "You are so much like him," she whispered, and she embraced him again.

The silence and stillness was broken by the clattering of crockery and the soft screeching of chairs being pulled across the floor as the cleaning staff cleared the tables and tidied the room. Andrew and his mother rose and, still holding hands, walked slowly out of the room. They climbed the stairs up to the open promenade, and walked along, hand in hand, sharing the silence as the gentle sea breeze swept over them. After awhile, as if by mutual agreement, they stopped and looked out towards the sea. Andrew gazed at the rhythmic bobbing of the waves and the playful lap of the water against the side of the ship; for how long, he did not know. It had a mesmerizing, tran-quilizing effect on him and he felt the tension in him begin to subside. He looked at his mother. She was staring out at the distance, where the sky met the sea. Her face was set in a controlled stare, but a tear trickled down her cheek.

He was last seen going out to sea....

Andrew gently reached his hand to her face and wiped the tear away. She turned to him, her eyes full of sorrow and longing. He put his arms around her and she buried her face in his shoulder. Suddenly he felt very grown-up, holding her close like that. He realized that, in some ways, he was no longer a child, and that the boundaries that defined them as parent and son were becoming blurred. After awhile she sniffled, took a few deep breaths, and pulled away from him.

"I'm sorry, darling. I didn't mean to—"

"No Mum, it's all right. It's—" Andrew didn't know how to express how immensely reassuring her tears were to him. She, too, had been trying to put up a brave front and had been pushing the emotions of love and grief and loss far, far down so that she could make it from one day to the next. Andrew felt a tender sympathy for her, looking for some sort of love and comfort in the face of overwhelming despair and sadness. He realized that he could not begrudge her some respite from the terrible loneliness and longing she felt. But when his father returned, there would be no need for her to seek comfort in Jake's arms, and his effect on her would wear off, like a drug.

Nothing personal, Andrew decided. At that moment, he did not feel any real emo-tion of hate towards Jake, only an unfeeling, almost cold analysis of the role that Jake now played. He was a temporary relief, nothing more. When Andrew's father returned, all would be restored and Jake, well, Jake would quietly fade away, like a dream.

He smiled at his mother and hugged her again. "It's all right, Mum. I know, I know."

She wiped her eyes. "I meant to try to help you and here you are, comforting me."

They continued walking, hand in hand, as Andrew basked in the feelings of joy and mutual sympathy he felt with his mother. It had been such a long time since he had felt so hopeful about the future, and ages since he'd felt so happy at the present state

of things. It didn't matter about his mother and Jake: The only thing that was important was what was in her heart. The grief that he and his mother shared, though painful, excluded Jake, who could not even begin to comprehend the sorrow that bound
them together. His mother's relationship with Jake was a tenuous link, *having no substance or strength*, as Andrew remembered the definition Irene had made him copy
in his spelling notes.

"It looks like it's getting close to lunchtime." Andrew's mother looked at her watch.
"I promised Jake that we'd meet him in the dining room at noon. He said he was going to take a walk."

Andrew realized that he needed fresh clothes. "I'm all out of clean shirts. Some of
my things are packed away in your bag. Can you get them for me so I can change
before we eat?"

His mother reached into her pocket, pulled out the key to her room, and gave it to
him. "Here, why don't you go on your own? I'll save us a seat."

Andrew walked briskly to the cabin, feeling so glad and lighthearted it felt as if he
were walking on air. He turned the key in the lock and let himself in. His mother's
bag was near the bed, which was piled high with crumpled linens. He opened the bag
and rummaged through it; his clothes were near the bottom. He withdrew his mother's
things and piled them on the bed. One of her sweaters slipped off the opposite side,
and Andrew leaned over the bed to retrieve it. All of a sudden, he was knocked over
by a tremendous force and pinned, face down, on the bed. He tried to call for help,
but his face was pressed against the mattress and his cries came out as muffled moans.
He was trapped: Someone held him fast—someone strong and determined. Andrew
couldn't see, since the blanket was over his head, and he thrashed and kicked in the
darkness. Whoever was holding him down was incredibly strong and determined, and
Andrew wrestled and grappled with his unseen opponent. He felt a hand on his neck;
the hand then slid around to the side of Andrew's face and Andrew, with a burst of
strength that sprang from fright, turned his head, and bit the hand as hard as he could.
A scream of pain issued from his unseen assailant, and Andrew was aware of a violent eruption of thrashing and clawing by his attacker. He tried to wriggle free and,
as he was struggling to escape from his opponent, it finally occurred to him that he
could cry out for help. That he did: an ear-piercing shriek that even surprised himself. His attacker yelled, more of a cry of agony and terror. The bed linens exploded,
and Andrew broke free and saw who his assailant was.

Chapter 27

*J*ake!
He was still thrashing around, battling the sheets. His eyes were closed and he was moaning, as if in pain, and his wails of "Fire, fire, *fire*...." sent chills up Andrew's spine. Andrew was horrified at the spectacle. He tried calling out to put a stop to Jake's nightmarish ravings, but he was so frightened that his cries came out as unintelligible bleats, which did not achieve the goal of waking Jake, but seemed to agitate him even more. Andrew didn't dare go near him, either. He grabbed his mother's bag and threw it at Jake, but that didn't work: Jake grabbed at the bag and started beating it, his screams of distress and terror increasing. At his wit's end, Andrew picked up a pitcher of water on the dresser and splashed the water at Jake. Jake sputtered and gasped; his eyes popped open as he sat straight up and stared, flabbergasted, at Andrew. Andrew stared back, then stammered, "I...I came in to get some of my things and I didn't know you were here and I put some of Mum's stuff on the bed and her sweater fell off and I tried to get it and you...you attacked me...."

Jake, soaking wet, gaped at the water pitcher in Andrew's hand.

"Thanks," he said weakly. "I guess I needed that."

"Not at all." It seemed like the only appropriate thing to say in the face of this rather bizarre incident.

Jake groaned and covered his eyes with his hand. Then, wiping his face, he looked back at Andrew and asked, "Are you all right?"

Andrew nodded dumbly. Jake closed his eyes and let out a loud breath. He was naked from the waist up, and Andrew noticed that his chest was badly scarred, though not quite as disfigured as his hands were. The flesh was mottled and puckered with scar tissue and pocked with a few deep, crater-like gouges.

"I'll...I'll get my things...." Andrew started to collect his clothes.

"I'm sorry," Jake apologized again. "I didn't mean to frighten you...."

"Of course you didn't. You were having a nightmare." Andrew didn't intend to reassure Jake; he was just trying to be civil and attempting to put a veneer of normalcy on this absurd situation.

Jake nodded and moaned as he fell back onto the pillows.

"Well, I'll be going, "Andrew spoke as if he were a dinner guest bidding a polite farewell to his host. He knelt down and gathered his clothes from his mother's bag. Then, more to fill the awkward silence than to comfort Jake, he said, "It's all right, really."

But of course it wasn't. Not only had his high spirits been dashed; his hopes about the future had also been unsettled by this unpleasant experience. That morning, it had been so comforting to finally get everything sorted out, to have the reassurance that his mother still missed his father, still wanted him back. Her relationship with Jake had been pushed into the background, and Jake's presence in Andrew's life became just a minor inconvenience.

The last few minutes had changed all that. Their struggle was upsetting to Andrew not just for its frightening suddenness, but because it seemed to symbolize a fearful new aspect in his dealings with Jake. Even though neither of them had been aware that they were battling one another, and as much as Andrew wanted to deny any kind of link with Jake, it now seemed that their lives were bound together in a disturbing nexus of fear and pain.

At lunch, neither Jake nor Andrew brought up the incident, but Andrew was conscious of a charged atmosphere. It was almost as if the rules had been changed. On the surface, they were polite to one another, as before, but Andrew sensed that Jake was somehow fearful of him. It wasn't mere embarrassment and shame; it was more like...guilt. Furthermore, Andrew had the funny feeling that it had nothing to do with his mother, or with Jake's relationship with her. It seemed as if Jake's nightmare had unlocked some terrifying memories for him, not just of physical harm, but of something else.

He was terrified of meeting you. That was what Andrew's mother had said of Jake. Why? Was it only because Jake had married her? Or was there something else? Andrew stole glances at Jake as often as possible. Though he didn't expect Jake to reveal any secrets, he was still curious. Jake was more subdued than usual; Andrew wondered if his mother noticed. She was not very talkative either, and Andrew sensed a certain distance between her and Jake. Not exactly an estrangement, but a drawing away from each other into a private contemplation of their respective memories.

He was terrified of meeting you. To Andrew, it was strange to think back on the time just before he'd met Jake, to realize that a complete stranger was living in fear of him. Andrew recalled when his mother had taken him to lunch after he had returned to school, how he had tried to get her to believe that his father was coming back...and her dismay. He should have suspected something then. Andrew shuddered at the thought of her giving lip service to his request that she ought to consider the possibility that his father was still alive, while all the while planning (she *was* planning it at the time, surely!) on becoming Jake's wife. He wondered if his father could somehow sense what was happening—that he was being replaced by another.

His father. Andrew's memory of his father was the one shining, unspoiled, unsullied thing that Andrew could hold onto, free from Jake's contaminating influence. That, and the bond he and his mother shared—a bond forged of sadness and longing, but a bond none the less. As much as Andrew hated to see his mother unhappy, it heartened him that she was, he knew, focusing her thoughts on the remembrance of his father, instead of on Jake. If only she could believe that he was still alive!

Then a thought occurred to him: Just as he'd been completely oblivious to Jake's existence, but Jake had been aware of him, so...Even though Andrew's mother did not believe that his father was alive, that did not alter the fact that he *was*. He lived, and was thinking about her, even though she was not aware of him. Her denial of his existence did not change anything at all. As much as Andrew wanted to plant the seed of hope in her mind that his father would someday come back, he was afraid that to do so would be too upsetting to her, at least now. It might even drive a wedge between them. He didn't want to see a replay of the recriminations and accusations that had estranged them before. It was enough that she was thinking about his father, feeling the pain of loss, treasuring the memory of him in her heart...Someday she would have the strength to believe that he would return.

His mother picked at her food, a look of pensiveness on her face. Jake ate in silence, too, remote and troubled. Perhaps the disturbing experience earlier had produced a favorable result, after all, Andrew thought. Jake, lost in the throes of his private demons, had no thought to spare for her. He could not even *begin* to comprehend her feelings and private pain. Whereas Andrew...He reached his hand under the table and squeezed her hand. She squeezed his hand back and looked at him, gratefulness in her eyes and a wistful, sad smile on her lips.

He smiled reassuringly back at her. It's all right, he wanted to say. *I know.* She laced her fingers into his, and Andrew was flooded with a wonderful feeling of peace and relief.

Everything's going to be all right....

"...So Augie wakes up the next morning with one hell of a hangover, and he's assigned to fly a Spit back down to England...." Gib, chatty and amiable, was smoothing over the silence with a hilarious story from his extensive store of amusing anecdotes. The quintessential life of the party, he loved to talk and enjoyed entertaining others with his tales and witty conversation. And yet, he managed to be chatty without sounding jabbery. His stories were always interesting and funny, and he always tried to draw other people into the conversation. If he happened to be the only bright shining light of wit in the face of taciturn company, instead of being discouraged, he turned on the charm even more.

"...So he turns on the oxygen to clear his head and he's up to twenty five thousand feet over Scotland. The oh-two, as usual, gets rid of the hangover and Augie's feeling good, so good, in fact that he just dozes off. The next thing he knows, he's flying at two thousand feet, *inverted!*" Gib laughed and smacked the table. Liz giggled, Peter roared, and Andrew's mother smiled. Andrew grinned too; then he noticed that Jake was the only one not paying attention. He was holding his teacup, staring at the contents. He looked up, and his jaw muscles tensed. Then he smiled wanly at Andrew's mother, and said, "I think I'll go out for a walk."

Andrew's mother watched him as he shuffled across the floor, hands thrust in his pockets. Andrew was momentarily annoyed at her concern, but then he reasoned: *Well, I can't expect her to ignore him entirely.* At least he was alone with her. He squeezed her hand again. She turned to him, gratefulness in her eyes. Suddenly, Andrew saw the key to winning her away from Jake. If Jake was going to be a source of worry and concern to her, it might just vex her enough to turn her away from him.

And if I'm the one that she could turn to for reassurance and support, maybe she won't need him anymore!

"Would you like to go for another walk?" He spoke tenderly, solicitously to her.

He saw Peter's look of disappointment. As Andrew and his mother got up to leave, Peter said, "Come on, Andrew, I want to show you something! Just for a minute!" He grabbed Andrew's hand and pulled him away, across the floor and out the door.

"Don't you want to play poker? The guys were asking about you," Peter asked. "Where were you?"

"I was talking with my mother," Andrew replied. "I promise I'll come in a little while. I just want to spend some time with her now."

"Is there anything wrong?"

Andrew shrugged. "No, not really. I'm not going to be seeing her for a long time, and there's some things we need to talk about, that's all."

"Oh."

Andrew put his hand on Peter's shoulder. "I'll be there, promise."

"Okay. Sarge invited a few new guys for the game this afternoon. He said to tell you, same routine as before, you know?"

Andrew nodded. At that moment, his mother and Liz walked through the door.

"How about our walk, Mum?" Andrew asked.

She smiled and took his hand. They climbed the stairs to the open air promenade, and walked along in silence, looking out at the sparkling sea. Andrew's mother sighed.

He knew what she was thinking. "I wish Dad could be here."

She nodded. Andrew went on. "He always wanted to go to America, he said. Remember?" He wanted to add that he believed that his father would realize his wish someday.

His mother was silent. Andrew decided not to pursue the matter further. Let her be alone with her thoughts. He had planted the seed of remembrance; her memories would nourish it. They turned around and walked along, towards the front of the ship.

Peter came running towards them.

"Andrew! Come along—I've got to show you something!" He took Andrew's hand. Andrew turned around, and waved to his mother.

"All right, darling. Be back in your cabin at five."

Peter scurried along, Andrew in tow, descending down the many flights of stairs and negotiating the maze of turns to the soldiers' cabin. J.D., Sarge, and Ray, along with two new faces, were starting a game of five card draw. Andrew seated himself in the corner.

"Now, what is it again?" he asked Cowboy, who was lying on one of the bunks. "I remember a pair, two pair, three of a kind...um, a straight?" Cowboy nodded. "Four of a kind, flush, full house...."

"No, you got it backwards. It's full house, flush, four of a kind," Cowboy corrected, as he winked at Andrew.

"Hey kid, wanna play a hand?" Sarge asked.

"Oh, boy!" Andrew squeezed himself between J.D. and Ray.

The two newcomers smiled indulgently. Andrew grinned back at them.

Two hours later, they were scratching their heads at Andrew's enormous mound of cigarettes. A few more soldiers had drifted in during the meantime, intrigued. Andrew was in high spirits, but still managed to keep a straight face. It was such jolly good fun! He enjoyed being the center of attention, and was finding, more and more, that he really *liked* being with...Yanks. He was also reeling with happiness over the time he'd had with his mother.

Everything's going to be all right....

"Hey kid, do you want to raise or call?" Sarge chomped on his cigar.

"Um, um, I'll raise...two." Andrew hesitated before tossing down two cigarettes. Ray raised one, and the betting went another three rounds before Ray decided to call. He waited until everyone had shown their cards: Ray had a full house, Sarge had a straight, J.D. had three of a kind, and the two newcomers each had two pair. All eyes were on Andrew. He waited a few seconds, furrowing his brow in consternation as he examined his cards. Then he threw down a straight flush as his face broke into an ecstatic grin of triumph. Sarge roared with delight, and all the others laughed and shook their heads.

Andrew was in such high spirits that he didn't notice that one of the onlookers, standing in the corner, held up a camera and took his picture.

"...And what's even more fun is you can say all sorts of naughty words, and the Yanks don't even know you're swearing!"

"What?" Andrew led the way through the zig-zagging passageways to the soldiers' cabin.

"We don't have the same swear words as they do," Peter explained. "Well, some are the same, but a lot of them are different. You can say bloody and bugger all and get stuffed, and they don't even know you're saying anything nasty. It's cracking great fun!"

"Really?"

"Yes—do you want to try it?"

There was a roach race in progress; Andrew could tell by the shouts and moans and shrieks that Buckwheat had left Alfalfa and Spanky in the dust again.

"Give us some gum, chum!" Andrew sang as they entered the cabin.

"Give us a chew, Lou," Mikey grinned. He proffered a pack to Andrew.

"Hey Andrew," El exclaimed.

"Hey El!" Andrew called.

"Howdy Andy!" Cowboy nodded his head.

"Howdy!" Andrew replied.

"You deal, kiddo!" Sarge tossed the deck of cards to him. There were three new faces present: Sarge introduced them as Grover (from New *Ham-Sha*, Grover announced in a nasally twang) and Woody (from *Orrygone*, Sarge said; he was corrected by Woody, who pronounced it *Ora-gun*). The third newcomer was called "Pops," though he looked to be only in his mid-thirties.

Andrew sat, cross-legged, on the floor. "Five card stud," he announced. "Threes and fours wild."

"Anyway," Wheeler said, "I *know* a guy who *knows* a guy who *seen* a guy put salt-peter in a pot of soup—swear to God! Anyway, you can't deny the effects of eating Army chow—they gotta be putting something in it, that's for sure!"

"It's all in your head, pal," J.D. countered. "Why the hell would the army go to the expense of puttin' it in all the tons of chow they feed to everyone, when they can get the same result by makin' you *think* they've put it in?" He tapped his skull. "Me, I ain't never paid no mind to them rumors, and I ain't never had the *least* bit trouble in that department, not the least bit of trouble a'*tall!*"

Wheeler called, and won the first game with a flush.

"*Buggeration*!" Peter threw his cards down. Andrew's eyes popped wide; he looked to see what the reaction was to Peter's outburst. Sarge grinned, the others merely threw Peter amused glances. Peter smiled at Andrew, as if to say, *See—it's all right!*

Andrew threw his hand down. "*Bloody hell!*" he yelled.

"Hey, Andrew, watch your language!" El admonished him.

Peter leaned forward and whispered, "Bloody's all right, but hell is still a swear word in America."

As Andrew digested this information, Peter hollered, "*Balls up!*" This too, received only agreeable glances

"*Gor blimey!*" Andrew exclaimed.

Peter raised an eyebrow at him: *You can do better than that!*

"*Sod all!*" Peter piped.

"*Stuff that for a game of soldiers!*"

"You kids in for another round?" Sarge asked.

Though Andrew knew that the voyage would soon come to an end, he tried to push that prospect to the back of his mind. After all, it wouldn't do him any good to dwell on it, and he might as well enjoy the last bit of time of his carefree existence. So the remaining days of the voyage settled into a pleasant, predictable pattern of walks with his mother in the mornings, roach races and poker games with the Americans in the afternoons, and Spike Jones shows in the evenings. He only saw Jake at mealtimes and, since Jake remained distant and uncommunicative, Andrew was able to have his mother's attention to himself.

Two days before they were to arrive in New York, Andrew's mother came to collect Andrew and Peter for breakfast.

"Run along," she said to Peter. "I need to talk with Andrew."

Her tone of voice indicated that it was not going to be a friendly chat. Peter threw Andrew a worried glance as he exited.

His mother waited, glaring at Andrew, arms crossed, until the door was shut. She exhaled sharply and said, "Gib overheard a very interesting remark made by one of the American servicemen yesterday. The words were, and I quote, 'Don't let anybody con you into playing poker with that English kid. He's a regular shark.'" She continued to regard Andrew with a penetrating look. "As you and Peter seem to be the only two English boys on the ship, I thought that you might have some idea of whom they were speaking."

Andrew tried to block the flash of guilt that crossed his face, but it was no use. Funny, he had no trouble keeping a poker face in a room full of grown men (even when Mikey turned his eyelids inside out and wiggled his ears), but with his mother it was another matter.

His mother narrowed her eyes and her voice was tight with displeasure. "You've been *gambling?* Playing poker for *money?*"

"Oh no, Mum, not money! Sarge doesn't want us playing for money. We use cigarettes, and then I trade them in for sweets and comic books, see?" He pulled open the drawer that held his winnings. It was now crammed full of comic books, candy bars, and packages of chewing gum and Lifesavers.

His mother's eyes widened at this store of ill-gotten gain. She gasped in astonishment, then burst into wild laughter.

"Well, seeing as you haven't been fleecing some poor, unsuspecting soldier out of his life savings, I guess I can't be too upset with you. Just keep it friendly!"

"Yes Mum, I will!" he promised.

While he was walking on the promenade with his mother after breakfast, they passed Sarge, El, J.D., and Cowboy, who were looking out over the railing.

"Hullo," he nodded to them.

"Hiya, Andy!" Sarge said. The others murmured greetings. Their eyes were riveted on Andrew's mother; one would think they had never seen a woman in their lives before.

"So these are your American friends, darling?" Andrew's mother said pleasantly.

"Yes, we are. We, um...well...." Cowboy was floundering. Andy and Pete like to hang around us because they, um...."

"They like to wheedle candy out of us," Sarge salvaged the explanation. "Yeah, Andy's a great kid. He sure is!"

Andrew's mother raised an eyebrow, "Yes, I've witnessed the results of his 'wheedling'. Quite impressive, I must say."

The soldiers looked at Andrew, tight-lipped and wary. He glanced at his mother and said to the soldiers, "She knows."

Andrew's mother laughed. "I hope that my son has not been too ruthless in despoiling you of your store of provisions."

The GIs all smiled in relief and Sarge chuckled, "Well, we would have been happy to share it with him anyway, and he provided a helluva—I mean, a lot of entertainment in the meantime!"

"Yeah," J.D. agreed. "That boy is really somethin' else! A real sight to see!"

"He's a swell kid, all right," Sarge affirmed.

"A swell kid." Cowboy bobbed his head. "You ought to be proud of him."

"I am." Andrew's mother looked affectionately at Andrew.

"He's mighty proud of you, too," J.D. told her. "'He always tells us: My mother flies Hurricanes.' Bet you're as capable as you are pretty!"

"Well, thank you," she replied. "Though I must say, not all men are as gracious as you in their appraisal of women pilots. Once I was getting ready to take off in a Beaufort—it was the first time I'd ever flown one—and a Wing Commander in a hurry to get to London hopped in at the last minute. As I taxied down the runway I turned around to greet him and he just about fell over in shock. 'My God! It's a *woman*!' he blurted out. I didn't intend to frighten him, but I guess I nearly gave him a heart attack when, after I'd taken off, I pulled out my Ferry Pilot's Notes and told him that I needed to consult them because I'd never flown a Beaufort before. He went white as a sheet, but I got him to our destination without incident. I guess he thought he was paying me a compliment when, after I'd landed, he shook his head in disbelief and muttered, 'Amazing, truly amazing!'"

The soldiers laughed, clearly enchanted with her, and J.D. assured her, "Well, it sounded like he was mighty impressed, ma'am. Don't you worry, there's a lot of us who think it's a swell idea, that's for sure!"

"Yeah, just swell," Cowboy echoed.

She smiled, and then her eyes caught a figure in the distance, striding towards them. "Jake!" She waved at him.

"It seems that our boy is the notorious card shark Gib spoke of," she said as Jake approached them. "Here are some of his victims: Sarge, El, Cowboy, and J.D." She linked her arm in Jake's and smiled at the GIs. "And this is my husband Jake."

Jake shook hands with the soldiers. Andrew knew that his mother's use of the term *our boy* was a British expression, and that she was not necessarily implying that Jake had a claim on him, but he was annoyed, just the same. I *don't* belong to Jake, he thought.

"Got the cobwebs cleared out, darling?" She spoke solicitously to Jake. Jake glanced at her and grunted and unintelligible reply. He smiled apologetically at the soldiers, said, "Nice meeting you," then turned and walked away. Andrew's mother watched him, concerned. She turned to Andrew. "Why don't you take a walk with your friends, darling?" Without waiting for a reply, she walked briskly away, catching up with Jake.

Andrew watched her, his lips pursed in dismay. The soldiers gazed at her departure also; Cowboy and J.D. grunted. They shuffled off in the other direction, whistling aimlessly, their hands thrust in their pockets.

He felt a hand slap his shoulder. "Hey kid, how about a game of five card stud?" Sarge asked.

Andrew sat, trying to concentrate on the game of five card stud he was playing with Sarge, J.D., Mikey, and El, but it was no use. Peter was there, watching the proceedings with a few of the other Americans they'd met: Davy from South Dakota, Murph from *Baahston*, Jackson from *Tenn-see*, and Clint from the *Great State o' Maine*. Andrew had lately become quite a sensation aboard the ship; as word spread about the "English boy who plays one helluva mean game of poker," each day more and more soldiers drifted in to the cabin to watch Andrew until sometimes it was standing room only. Most of the onlookers had already "lost their shirts" in high-stakes poker games but, since cigarettes were still in abundance, they were delighted to be included in the games whenever one of the "regulars" sat back to take a breather. Andrew got to know each of them as always "somebody" from "someplace." Americans set great store by their home states, much more so than the English by their counties.

"Where are you kids headed to?" Sarge asked.

"I'm going to Massachusetts," Peter replied. "Andrew is going to New Jersey."

"New *Joisey*," Jackson laughed.

"Is that how they pronounce it?" Peter asked.

"Yeh, dey aw tawk like dat," Mikey said.

"Jake doesn't talk like that." Peter looked at Andrew for an explanation.

Andrew shrugged. "He spent a lot of time in Nebraska, he said. He has relatives there."

"Nebraska, just next-door to South Dakota," Davy said. "Guess anyone would want to be from Nebraska instead of New Jersey. Armpit of America!"

"Is it very bad?" Andrew asked.

"Ugly as sin, and that's the God's honest truth!" J.D. agreed. "Factories, refineries—the place smells like one big fart! I was once in New York City and went over to New Jersey to visit a friend of mine who'd moved there. Felt as if I were goin' down into hell—that place would do the devil himself proud! Even New York City was better. You couldn't *pay* me enough to ever *think* of movin' to New *Jersey!* Too bad, kid. Your mother shoulda' married a Georgia boy—now that's a fine place!"

"You applying for the job, J.D.?" Sarge said.

"Well, havin' met Andrew's mother, I wouldn't have no complaints about that. Mind you, I respect the fact that she's spoken for." He smiled at Andrew. "All the same, that husband of hers is one lucky man!"

Ray and Murph nodded in agreement, which surprised Andrew. They appeared to be in their early twenties, as was J.D. and most of the other Americans present, except Sarge, who was probably a few years older, and Mikey, of course, who didn't look a day over sixteen. No doubt they were aware of the fact that they were several years younger than her; still, Andrew felt compelled to point this out to them.

"You're too young for her—she's thirty-one!"

"Can't say as I'd find that to be a problem." J.D. furrowed his brow as he looked at his cards.

"Well, as a matter of fact, her husband *is* six years younger than her."

Peter cocked his head, obviously startled that Andrew would reveal this terrible secret. Andrew smiled a brief, tense smile. As he figured it, the voyage would soon be over, and they would all go their separate ways. If the Americans considered the age discrepancy between his mother and Jake to be a shocking thing, it really wouldn't matter at this point, as Andrew probably would never see any of them again. Besides, he was interested in seeing if they would show any kind of aversion to the state of affairs that existed between his mother and Jake.

"Hmm, zat so," J.D. said absently, without so much as raising an eyebrow. He peered at the last card as it was dealt to him. "Shoot."

J.D. always said *Shoot* when he had a good hand. "*Waaal*, I'll bid one." He threw down a cigarette. "Your turn, Andrew."

"Fold," Andrew said. Ordinarily, he would have tried to bluff on this one (he was showing two jacks). Sarge raised an eyebrow, but said nothing. J.D. smiled and said, "Don't see that that makes a difference, kid, if'n they're happy with each other. And I sure wouldn't mind changin' places with him, not at all!"

Andrew looked closely at his face, trying to discern if he was disguising any kind of disdain about the situation, and decided that J.D. was being entirely truthful about his feelings. He looked at Mikey and Ray, and they seemed not to be perturbed at all by Andrew's disclosure. In fact, Ray agreed. "Me neither."

Andrew knew them well enough to know that they weren't bluffing or trying to conceal any kind of revulsion about the situation. On one hand, it alleviated his anxiety to know that his mother was not the object of ridicule and aversion that he had imagined her to be; on the other hand, it bothered him that the soldiers did not find Jake's role in all of this to be not the least bit outrageous.

He stared at his cards, trying not to betray his feelings about the situation. He looked up and noticed that Sarge was looking at him.

"Feel like calling it quits, kid?"

Andrew nodded.

"Count me out, too." Sarge said. He pushed himself back from the circle.

Davy and Clint took their places. "Five card draw, aces wild," Ray said, dealing the cards.

Cowboy wandered in, reeking of some sort of peculiar overpowering essence.

"*Whoeee!*" J.D. hooted. "Gawdalmighty, where you been, Cowboy? You smell like a whorehouse!"

Cowboy reddened, then mumbled, "Better'n smelling like you been rolling in cowshit." He plopped himself onto one of the bunks, pulled a harmonica out of his duffle bag and blew a few puffs into it.

"Why do you play the harmonica?" Peter inquired.

"'Cause it's easier to carry around in your back pocket than a guitar," answered Cowboy. He pronounced it *"GIT-tar."* He blew a few more blasts, then launched into a lilting tune.

As Andrew looked at the faces of his new-found friends, he saw that they were full of longing, remembrance, weariness, and hope. He realized that they had all been too long in a strange land, and he felt their aching for familiar surroundings as an almost tangible thing. Their happiness and relief at the prospect of returning to their homes and loved ones settled on his heart and gave him a strange sense of shared joy. Even though Andrew was starting to feel the pangs of homesickness and the stabs of anxiety at the realization that he was the one who was going to a strange new place, he did not begrudge his friends their good fortune at returning to their native land. He was happy for them, and he wished them well. After all, there had been a time when they, too, had faced the prospect of being strangers in a strange land.

He remembered the time that he had been in the cinema, just after his distressing first introduction to the obnoxious Yanks, when he had wished savagely: *I hope that every last one of them goes back to where he belongs.* It struck Andrew that he was able to hope for the very same thing now, but in a completely different spirit.

I hope that you all go back to where you belong....

Everyone was silent for a few moments after the song was over. Finally Sarge cleared his throat and said, "Well, Andrew, let's trade in that pile of loot for something edible. I put out the word that there was cigarettes to be had for candy, so there's a sizeable pile here if you'd care to deal." He produced a dozen candy bars out of his duffle bag. "My offer is twenty cigarettes per bar. Taking your winnings today and yesterday, that should come out about right."

He obviously expected Andrew to haggle, as usual, because he was surprised when Andrew said simply, "All right."

The exchange made, Andrew stood up and said, "Well, I'd better be getting back." He then realized that they would be arriving in New York the next morning and that he probably wouldn't get a chance to bid his friends farewell, what with all the bustling about and last minute packing that was bound to ensue. He nodded his head and said, "I guess this is good-bye. It—it was very nice meeting all of—" He found his voice catching in his throat.

Ray clapped him on the back and said, "Same here, kiddo—take care of yourself!" His pronouncement was echoed by the rest of the soldiers. A few of them produced small, diary-like books, with *My Life in Service* inscribed on the front, and Andrew and Peter signed the autograph pages towards the back. Andrew was glad for this bit of busywork in the face of the inevitable parting of ways. Goodbyes were always so distressing. He wished them all safe journey; they replied with a plethora of benedictions: *Take it easy, kiddo; have a great time; don't take any wooden nickels; see ya round.* Andrew nodded his head once more, and said, "Bye." He turned to leave.

"Bye," Peter echoed. He scooped up Andrew's winnings.

"I'd like to stretch my legs," Sarge said. "I'll walk with you."

As they were going up the stairs, Sarge laid a hand on Andrew's shoulder and said, "Don't pay J.D. no mind about what he said about New Jersey. It's a nice place, really. Some of it's ugly, but most of it's nice. I spent a summer there with some cousins who lived near the Delaware River, and it's mighty pretty country there. You staying with your stepdad's family?"

"For awhile," Andrew replied. "I'll probably go away to school."

"He can come up to Massachusetts and go to my boarding school," Peter said. "I mean, Deerfield—that's for the older boys, but it's next to Eaglebrook, where I'm going. We can still be friends with each other."

Andrew nodded. "I'd have to talk with my mother about it, since she plans on having me stay with Jake's family. She said I could change my mind if I wanted to, though. I don't think it would be a good idea to live with them."

"They don't want you?"

"Oh, no, it's not that. They want me to stay with them. At least that's what my mother said. I just think it would be better for me not to be with them."

"You and your stepdad don't get along?"

Andrew shrugged. "We don't have much to do with each other, that's all."

"It sounds as if your stepfather is as much in need of some tender loving care as you are," Sarge said gently.

"I'm just fine!"

"You're not too happy about going to America, I can tell."

Andrew turned away. He didn't want Sarge to see the emotion his face betrayed.

"Hey, it's all right, Andy. Geez, you're just a kid, going away from your home. It's scary, I know. I grew up as an Army brat, and I remember the achy feeling I used to get in the pit of my stomach whenever we had to move from one place to another, even though I was going with my family. I tried not to show it, but it was there, just the same."

Andrew swallowed and tried to force the tears back.

"Hey—" Sarge squeezed Andrew's shoulder. "Don't try to be a hero."

"I'm not trying to be a hero," Andrew whispered fiercely.

"Oh yes you are. Anything you want to talk about?"

Andrew shook his head. Sarge said, "Well, if you don't want to talk with me, you ought to at least talk with your mom. That's what moms are there for, you know."

"No I can't!" Andrew blurted out the words savagely, before he realized what he was saying. Seeing Sarge's shocked look, he added in a low voice, "You don't understand."

Sarge regarded Andrew, compassion in his eyes. "You think that because she's so busy flying planes that she can't be bothered with your problems?"

"Something like that," Andrew muttered. He took a deep breath. "I rather not talk about it."

They turned into the corridor and walked along in silence. Peter was a few steps ahead, skipping and turning circles as he joyfully contemplated the load of candy bars in his hands. When they arrived at their cabin, Andrew said to Sarge, "Well, I guess this is goodbye."

"Wait," Sarge said. "Listen, if you'd like to keep in touch, I'll write down my APO for you." He took a Hershey bar from Peter, unwrapped it and handed the candy back to him. He then pulled a stubby pencil out of his shirt pocket and wrote on the back side of the wrapper. He folded the wrapper in half, then in half again, and thrust it at Andrew.

Andrew grunted in acknowledgement, and put the wrapper in his pocket. "Safe journey," he said.

Sarge smiled. "Safe journey to you too, kiddo." He turned around and walked back down the corridor. Just as he was about to turn the corner, Andrew's mother and Jake came from the opposite direction. Jake almost bumped into Sarge.

"Sorry," Sarge said.

"No, my fault," Jake assured him.

"Escorting our boy back with his winnings?" Andrew's mother inquired cheerfully.

"Yes, m'am," Sarge nodded.

"Well, now that the voyage is almost over, he won't be able to do too much more damage."

"Hey, we didn't mind a bit. He certainly has made the trip an enjoyable one. You ought to think of renting him out for entertainment at parties! We're all going to miss him."

"I'm sure he's going to miss all of you, too. I'm glad that the voyage has turned out to be fun for him as well."

Sarge remained at the corner, watching as Jake and Andrew's mother walked up the corridor to meet Andrew.

"Darling, did you have a nice time?" his mother said.

"Oh yes, super!" Peter called from inside the room, acting as spokesman for both of them. Andrew managed a smile; he hoped his mother didn't notice how troubled he was.

But she had. "Is there something bothering you, darling?" she asked.

"Oh no, nothing. Nothing at all. I'm just hungry." Andrew spoke emphatically and cheerily. "In fact, I'm positively famished! Let's eat before I collapse from hunger on the spot!"

Andrew's mother smiled, but her face betrayed her concern, as well as disbelief that Andrew had been entirely truthful. And Andrew, looking past her, noticed that Sarge was still standing at the corner, regarding the whole exchange with a look of consternation on his face.

Liz, dressed in a stunning red evening dress, gave Peter a goodnight kiss. "Now boys, lights out in half an hour. We need to get an early start tomorrow, since we'll be arriving in New York."

"Mummy, please, can't I just see the dance for a minute?"

"No, Peter, you need your rest. Besides, this dance is not for children."

Andrew's mother breezed in. She was dressed in a wispy creation of pale green with a daringly low-cut bodice.

She would never wear something like that if Dad were around...She wouldn't need to! No doubt she's trying to shake Jake out of his gloom....

"Night, darling. Pleasant dreams."

"Night, Mum." He forced a smile as she gave him a kiss on the forehead.

After she and Liz had departed, Peter lay in bed for awhile, glaring at the ceiling. Andrew finished up his Batman comic book.

"I say, why don't we go up and say goodnight to our daddies?" Peter winked at him.

"Your mother said—"

But Peter was already up and changing back into his day clothes.

"Well, aren't you coming?"

The thought of his mother dancing in Jake's arms was enough to convince Andrew that he could do worse than put in an appearance at this frolicky affair. Maybe his mother would choose to cut the evening short....

He followed Peter up three flights of stairs and down a short corridor. The loud, pumping sounds of the band pounded around them. Peter tentatively opened a door, releasing a fresh blast of noise. He peered within.

"I see them! Come on!"

Andrew followed Peter through the maze of tables and chairs which fringed the dance floor. The room was a sea of brown uniforms, interspersed by a sprinkling of colorful finery—the men outnumbered the women by about twenty to one, and nearly all the women were partnered on the dance floor. Andrew glared at the couples dancing frenetically to the blaring, jazzy music.

"Andrew—over here!" Peter called. He was clambering towards a table, around which were seated Gib and Jake and several American officers. Andrew's mother and Liz were nowhere to be seen.

"...so the guy takes off in his Spitfire, but he snags some telephone wire on his tail wheel." Gib was relishing his role as raconteur. Everyone at the table listened attentively, except for Jake, who seemed somewhat listless and preoccupied.

"...and his wingman calls out over the R.T., 'You've got some wire on your tail wheel!' Only the R.T. isn't working right, and all the pilot hears is *on your tail*. So he goes into a series of violent aerobatics, thinking that he's got a German on his tail. By the time he gets back to base, he's figured out what's going on, and he slaps his wingman on the back and says, 'I wondered why you sat back and watched while I took on the whole Luftwaffe single-handedly!'"

The officers roared with laughter; Jake smiled. Peter approached Gib from behind and tapped him on the shoulder.

"Hey Sport! You're supposed to be in bed!" Gib exclaimed.

"We just wanted to watch. Just a minute!"

"Just a minute then," Gib said, with parental authority.

"Pull up a chair." Jake smiled at Andrew. He grabbed an empty chair from an adjacent table and placed it next to his.

Andrew sat down while Peter settled himself on Gib's lap.

"Well, what have we here?" Liz appeared at the table, along with Andrew's mother, both of them fresh from the dance floor. They were with two American officers. "Two boys who should be in bed!"

"Oh, Mummy—*please!*" Peter's face fell.

Liz's expression softened. "Well, just for a little while, then it's off to bed with you!"

"Well, I think I'll sit this one out," Andrew's mother said. "Oh dear, there's no empty seats. Well, just have to make do." She smiled at Jake, seated herself sideways on his lap, and put her arm around his shoulders.

"Are you worn out yet?" Jake was solicitous, but did not appear to be very worried.

"Getting there," she replied. "You'll have to carry me back to the cabin tonight. I'll have danced my legs to stumps!"

She whispered something in Jake's ear, then pulled back to see his reaction. He reddened, and she shrieked with glee. The music started up again and she grabbed Jake's ginger ale and took a sip.

Although he tried not to show it, Andrew was disconcerted by her behavior. It was one thing to accept in his mind the idea that it was all right for her to find companionship and comfort until his father returned. As long as it remained an abstract concept, he didn't feel threatened. Seeing her sitting on Jake's lap, drinking from his glass, whispering in his ear, laughing over a private joke—well, that was different. It wouldn't do for her to get too attached to Jake, he thought.

It wouldn't do at all.

"I think I'll sit this one out, too." Liz plucked Peter off Gib's lap, set him on the table, and sat down in his place. Peter turned and held his arms wide to one of the Americans; he was rewarded with a welcoming nod. He climbed into the vacant lap and grinned.

Andrew's mother turned to the officers and announced, "May I present my son, the card shark! He's been entertaining the troops with his poker wizardry, and I daresay he's won his weight in sweets!" She turned back to Andrew and said, "Well, my little poker-playing fiend, I want you to scoot off to bed shortly. You need to get a good night's sleep, since we'll be arriving tomorrow." The band started playing another tune, and she and Liz got up.

"Marvelous band!" Liz exclaimed. "Sure beats anything ENSA can trot out!"

"ENSA—what's that?" one of the officers asked.

"It's an organization the British government set up to give shows and concerts in camps and factories—sort of like your USO," Liz explained. "ENSA stands for Entertainments National Service Association."

"I thought it stood for Every Night Something Awful," Andrew's mother laughed.

"That too!" Liz giggled. "Well, whose turn is it now?"

Two of the officers at the table stood, then escorted the women to the dance floor. Andrew watched his mother as she danced with ease and grace. Her partner was clearly enchanted with her....

"Would you like a Coca-Cola?" Jake asked.

Andrew looked sharply at Jake, and nodded without enthusiasm.

"Peter? Coca-Cola for you, too?" Jake inquired.

"Oh yes, please!"

Jake left, and returned with two glasses of some sort of brown liquid, topped with a tan froth. He set them down in front of Andrew and Peter.

"Jake, will you dance with me? Just once, darling?" It was Andrew's mother, back from the dance floor. Jake evidenced obvious reluctance with the idea, shaking his head and murmuring politely, "No, why don't you go on—"

"Darling, it's a slow dance. Please?"

"Come on Jake," Gib encouraged. He rose and said to Liz, who had just returned: "May I have the pleasure of this dance, my dear?" Taking her hand, he glanced at Jake and said, "We don't want our wives to feel neglected."

Jake smiled. "I don't think there's much of a chance of that," Andrew's mother looked at Jake pleadingly. He took a deep breath and stood up. "You don't know what you're getting yourself into," he said, trying to hide his nervousness.

"Well, you know that I rush in where angels fear to tread."

"Tread is a very appropriate word for what you're about to expose yourself to."

"I'm perfectly capable of taking care of myself, darling," Andrew's mother laughed.

"Yes, I'm sure you are," Jake said with a smile.

Jake's words unsettled Andrew. He couldn't quite place where he had heard them before, but they struck a disturbing chord in him. Suddenly he remembered. Right! Just what Freddie had said to his mother when he had tried to get her to stay with him in London!

"Peter, why don't you entertain our guests?" Gib suggested.

Peter's face glowed with delight. He proceeded to throw himself into the role of host with enthusiasm. "Have you seen the Spike Jones Show? It's positively smashing! They throw a duck up into the air and they shoot it! And they sing a nasty song about Hitler...."

Andrew's mother was leading Jake onto the dance floor. She turned, and put her arms around him. He stood stiffly, holding her as if she were made of glass. She moved his hands to a more relaxed position, and started to dance with him. His motions were listless and lumbering; it was obvious that she was leading.

Andrew remembered what a terrific dancer his father was: On rainy afternoons at Armus House, his parents used to put some Gershwin music on the gramophone and dance through the conservatory. Andrew was always enthralled at the sight of them: It seemed as if they were one entity, their movements in perfect sync with one another. Andrew looked in disgust at Jake: He was stumbling around like a three-legged ox! Andrew resolved to comment on the comparison when his mother and Jake were finished. He turned over in his mind what he might say. *Remember what a great dancer Dad was?* He would mention it casually, nonchalantly, but it would at least serve to remind his mother of the man who should be dancing with her now....

Andrew's mother winced as Jake stepped on her toes. His expression was chagrined, bordering on panic. She smiled and kissed him swiftly and playfully. Then her expression became serious, intense, and she gazed into his eyes. Their movements slowed, and she closed her eyes and kissed him again, her lips lingering on his, her hands brushing down from his face and stroking the back of his neck. His arms tightened around her, and they stood together, swaying slightly, locked in an embrace. It seemed as if they were welded together. The other couples swirled around them, the crowd became thicker, and soon they were lost from sight.

Andrew felt a knot in his stomach. What did she see in him? He was clumsy, cheap, lacking in social graces, even prone to fits of madness...How many times had his mother been awakened in the night by his nightmares? Had she ever witnessed the kind of appalling behavior that Andrew had seen that afternoon in their cabin? He sipped the sweet, fizzy beverage that Jake had brought him, and contemplated how wonderful it would be to discomfit Jake by loudly comparing him to the man he had replaced.

"Come on Sport—bedtime!" Gib had returned to the table, with Liz on his arm.

"Daddy, please!" Peter pleaded.

"Bedtime," Liz repeated firmly.

"Hop aboard, Sport," Gib knelt down on the floor, and Peter climbed onto his back. "You come along too, Andrew."

"I'll wait for my mother. I want to say goodnight to her."

Liz and Gib exchanged embarrassed glances. Liz smiled, and said, "Your mother and Jake, um, stepped out for a breath of fresh air. She asked us to make sure you got to bed."

Andrew glared at her. Breath of fresh air indeed!

"I'll do the honors, dear," Gib said. "I already have ferry duty, anyway. Besides, it looks as if your dance card is going to fill up pretty quickly now that Alice has called it a night."

Liz threw him a sharp glance and Gib cleared his throat, discomposed that he had inadvertently divulged the reason why Andrew's mother and Jake had left. One of the officers cocked his head towards Jake's empty place and muttered, "Lucky man!"

His words seared into Andrew's brain. A white hot rage boiled up inside him as he thought of his mother...and Jake.

"Come on, Andrew." Gib was marching out of the room, Peter clinging to his back. Andrew tromped morosely behind.

"Faster, faster," Peter cried, and Gib picked up the pace once they were out of the room. Gib jogged down the corridor and Peter called, "I want to be a ferry pilot now!"

"What do you want to fly, Sport?"

"A Spitfire!"

Gib made a high-pitched whirr as he weaved and dodged along the corridor.

"Now a Lancaster!" Gib obliged by slowing down and lowering his voice to a powerful thrum. They came to the stairway.

"Descending to fifteen thousand feet. Throttling back—adjusting elevator trim tab for descent—" Gib said. "Uh-oh, we're losing our little friend. That's what the bomber pilots call the fighter pilots. Come on, Andrew!"

Andrew sullenly picked up his pace. His mind was a whirlwind of distressing imaginings and his heart was a leaden weight within him. They arrived at the cabin and Gib helped Peter gather his things to get ready for bed. They walked into the bathroom, Peter holding Gib's hand and jabbering excitedly.

"I think it would be jolly good fun to ride on top of a Spitfire! Of course, I'd make sure that I had a parachute...."

Andrew tried to shut out Peter's chattering as he brushed his teeth. Peter's high spirits only accentuated his own turmoil.

"You've got to do a better job than that brushing your teeth," Gib admonished Peter, observing the slapdash job he did. "Here, spit. Now, open...." He carefully and methodically scrubbed Peter's teeth. "They're going to rot and fall out before you're twelve." He filled a cup of water and gave it to Peter. "Rinse—slosh it around a bit. Now spit."

After wiping his mouth, Peter reached his arms to Gib. Gib picked him up and carried him to bed.

"Come on sleepyhead," Gib said. He carried Peter to bed, and snuggled him under the covers.

"Night, Daddy," Peter mumbled.

"Night, Sport." The words were barely on Gib's lips before Peter's deep, heavy breathing indicated that the evening's excitement had finally caught up with him. Gib pushed a lock of hair out of Peter's eyes. After a moment, he stood and walked over to Andrew's bunk, then sat down. He looked uncomfortable, almost apologetic. He took a deep breath and said, "Andrew, just because your mother left with Jake doesn't mean she doesn't care about you. You mean the world to her—"

"No, I don't!" Andrew snapped.

"I know she cares very much about you—"

"She cares about *him!*"

"Andrew, love doesn't give of itself at the expense of someone else. Just because your mother loves Jake doesn't mean that she loves you any less. Don't think that she doesn't care—"

"Don't tell me what to think!"

"Andrew, remember what I said about not turning your fear into hate. I think you're making that mistake right now."

"I am *not!*" Andrew sat bolt upright as rage coursed through him. "I am *NOT* afraid! I'm not afraid of anything at all!"

"I think you are," Gib said gently. "Would you like to talk about it?"

"I don't want to talk about anything! I'm not afraid!" Andrew yanked the covers up over his head. After a minute, he heard Gib get up and leave.

Andrew lay, curled up in a ball and sick with despair. Suddenly he realized that Gib would certainly tell Liz what he had said and Liz would tell...Andrew groaned. All of his efforts to try to put on a brave face and give his mother no cause for worry were going to go up in smoke. She would know, and she would be upset. Now on top of his despair, panic beset him.

Chapter 28

At first, when Andrew awoke the next morning, he had no recollection of the conversation he'd had with Gib the night before. Still half asleep, he half sat up in bed, trying to clear the cobwebs of slumber away from him. Then harsh reality hit him and he fell back onto his pillow and groaned.

"Hmm...." Peter stirred, then sat bolt upright. "America! We're going to arrive in America today!" He jumped out of bed and hurriedly gathered up his clothes. "Come on, come on!" He tugged at Andrew. "You don't want to miss it!"

"What's there to miss?" Andrew grumbled. He saw no point in Peter's eagerness to get moving, as if America were going to somehow disappear if they weren't on time to see it. If only!

"The Statue of Liberty!" Peter exclaimed. "Daddy says it's the most wonderful sight!"

"You go on," Andrew told him. "I'll be along soon."

Peter almost fell flat on his face as he tried to get his pants on and walk at the same time. He put on his sweater inside out, forgot to tie his shoes, and was out the door before Andrew lumbered out of bed.

As he dressed, Andrew tried to figure out a way to repair the damage his outburst surely would have caused. If only he hadn't said anything! Wait—Gib certainly wouldn't have disturbed Andrew's mother last night. If he could get to her before Gib did....

He leapt out of bed and in a few seconds was dressed and racing down the corridor to his mother's cabin. Maybe she hadn't left for breakfast yet!

He knocked on the door.

Jake answered, "Come in."

Andrew noticed that Jake, if not exactly cheerful, was in a much more relaxed and upbeat mood than he had been for days. Little wonder! He smiled shyly at Andrew. Andrew nodded, perfunctorily; then it occurred to him that he ought to begin with his dissimulation. He injected an amicable tone into his voice. "I'm sure you'll be happy to be home at last."

"Andrew? I thought you were going up to the dining room with Liz and Gib." His mother's voice came from the bathroom.

"I thought I'd stop here first. I, um...." He looked down at his feet and realized he was wearing the socks he'd worn yesterday. "I'm out of clean socks. I thought you might have some of my things still packed in your bag."

His mother appeared from the bathroom, brushing her hair. She nodded toward her bag in the corner. "Take a look in there."

Andrew pretended to search diligently as his mother returned to the bathroom. He looked at Jake, who was busy packing his clothes in his suitcase, and said, "You'll be glad to see your family again, won't you? How long has it been since you've been home?"

Jake suddenly looked uncomfortable, as if Andrew had touched a nerve. "Uh...almost four years," he said tersely. He turned quickly away and resumed packing.

Andrew sensed that Jake was not exactly thrilled at the prospect of seeing his home again. It wouldn't do to have him troubled like that. Damn him! Andrew tried another tack.

"Scotch Plains—that's a very nice name. I'm sure it's a lovely town. Is it like Scotland—I mean, is that why it's called Scotch Plains?"

Jake shrugged, and managed a wan, almost apologetic, smile. "I think it was named after a guy named Scott. It's...nice, I guess."

There was an awkward silence as Andrew tried to think of something to say in response. Jake was as chatty as a pile of stones! Damn him again!

Mercifully, Andrew's mother appeared again. "Darling, could you get this back button on my dress?" she asked Jake. She stood in front of him, her back nestled against his chest, and lifted her hair. Jake fastened the button at the back of her neck. Andrew got a sinking feeling in the pit of his stomach as he watched his mother and Jake in this ordinary, yet intimate, domestic ritual.

Dad should be the one doing that....

Andrew's mother turned around to face Jake and smiled warmly at him, her face conveying appreciation—well, it was *more* than appreciation, Andrew realized. The glowing expression on her face spoke a pleasant shared secret, a quiet joy, and it was clear that her happiness was not the result of Jake merely helping her to get dressed. Jake reddened, and Andrew's mother gently traced her finger down his cheek as she gazed lovingly into his eyes. Andrew felt completely forgotten—he might as well have been a piece of furniture!

That look! And the *way* she looked! She was beautiful, *always* was beautiful, even without a stitch of make-up and her hair in disarray, but Andrew noted that today she had taken special pains with her appearance.

All tarted up, Andrew thought. For *him.* To meet *his* family. "Andrew, did you get enough sleep last night?" She smiled affectionately at Andrew, but it was not the same intimate smile she had bestowed upon Jake.

"Yes, I...I fell asleep as soon as my head hit the pillow," Andrew stammered; then an idea occurred to him. If Gib did happen to mention the incident last night....

"In fact, I don't even remember *anything* after I got washed up and ready for bed. I was probably sleepwalking—I don't remember a thing about getting into bed at all. I suppose Gib must have made sure that I got to bed all right."

There. If Gib or Liz did mention Andrew's outburst, his mother wouldn't be concerned if he had already professed to have no recollection of anything having happened. And if he could continue on with being cheerful and friendly towards Jake,

394

his mother would discount Gib's report of what Andrew had said as being perhaps the babblings of someone half asleep. Or maybe she would even question the accuracy of Gib's account. *Whatever.*

"Ready?" Andrew's mother said cheerily. "Oh, did you find any clean socks, Andrew?"

"No, I'll look through my things again after breakfast."

"I have an extra pair of clean socks," Jake said. "Here." He tossed Andrew a pair of socks from his suitcase. "They're a little large for you, but they'll do until my mother can do your laundry."

"Have you been pumping Jake for information about New Jersey?" Andrew's mother smiled brilliantly at him.

"Um, yes." Andrew hoped his mother didn't take his attempt to make conversation as an indication that he intended to remain with Jake's parents.

"Well, I'm sure you'll like it very much." She walked over to the porthole and looked through it. "What a storm!" she exclaimed. "I hope it isn't pouring like that when we get off the ship." She turned to Andrew. "Well, as soon as you're ready...."

Andrew realized she was expecting him to change into Jake's socks. He sat down on the bunk, took off his shoes and socks, and put Jake's clean socks on. He felt strange wearing Jake's clothing, as if he were committing an awful betrayal. He might as well have been putting on a Nazi uniform.

As they walked to breakfast Andrew was glad that his mother was chattering happily about their upcoming arrival. All of his dissembling had been a strain, he realized, and he really didn't feel like talking. He noticed Jake was rather quiet too.

"Is London much like New York?" Andrew's mother asked Jake.

Jake seemed to be contemplating an answer, and Andrew expected a detailed reply. Finally Jake shrugged and said, simply, "No." He smiled apologetically at Andrew's mother, as if it were his fault that the two cities were dissimilar. She took his hand and squeezed it.

"I know," she whispered.

Andrew got the distinct impression that his mother's reassuring words to Jake had nothing to do with New York at all.

They found Liz, Gib, and Peter saving seats for them in the dining room. Peter was almost bursting with excitement as he anticipated seeing the Statue of Liberty.

"I don't know if they're going to allow anyone on deck today, what with this terrific storm outside," Gib told him.

"But they can't not let us see it!" Peter protested.

Liz and Gib exchanged amused glances. "Come on Sport, eat your breakfast," Gib coaxed. Peter shoveled in a few mouthfuls of cereal; then his face lit up. "The Spike Jones Band!" he exclaimed. "Their cabin is on the other side of the ship and they have a porthole! I helped carry their things back to their cabin one night."

"Well then, your dilemma seems to be solved," Gib chuckled. "But you need to get your clothes packed before you go sightseeing!"

This admonition prompted Peter to a veritable feeding frenzy as he tried to make short work of the remainder of his meal.

Turning to Jake, Liz said, "You must be excited about going home after all this time. What's New Jersey like?"

"New Jersey smells like one big *fart!*" Peter announced. "That's what J.D. says!"

Liz's eyes bulged with horror. Then she sat up very, very straight and pursed her lips in a firm, disapproving line. She stood, as regal as the Queen, and said in a low, measured voice, "Come with me, Peter."

"No! Please, *no!*" Peter wailed. "I'm sorry—*I'm sorry!*"

"Come with me," Liz repeated.

Peter looked pleadingly at Andrew. "J.D. said it—didn't he? That's what he said, didn't he? Tell them—tell them!"

Andrew tried to suppress his smile. How could he deny what J.D. had said about New Jersey? He saw his mother's warning look, cleared his throat and shrugged.

"He did! *He did!* Please Mummy, I don't want to have a *chat!*"

Jake looked decidedly uncomfortable. "Liz, it's all right. Please don't—"

"We are going to have a little chat about what *does* and *does not* constitute civilized behavior. Come along, Peter."

Peter threw one last beseeching look at his father. "No, *No!*" he implored Gib. "Please Daddy, *please*—tell her I'm sorry!"

"Go with your mother, Peter," Gib said gently.

Liz turned and walked out of the room, not even checking to see if Peter was following. Peter looked for all the world like a condemned man about to mount the scaffold as he shuffled after her.

They were gone a few minutes. Andrew silently ate his toast. Peter's outburst had provided a moment's distraction; now, his heavyheartedness returned. That awful feeling of time slipping away from him was vexing and terrifying.

Liz returned; she bent close to Jake and murmured, "Please try to keep a straight face." Then she signaled to Peter, who was standing in the doorway.

Peter took long, slow, strides. Arriving at Jake's side, he tugged on his sleeve and stood on tiptoe to reach up to Jake's ear. Jake bent down a little; his expression was serious and his lips were set in a firm line, but Andrew could see he was trying to suppress a grin. Peter whispered something in his ear, then drew back, looking sincerely remorseful. Jake nodded, and smiled; Peter then clambered up onto his lap and sat down. Draping Jake's arms over his shoulders, he nestled himself against him and grinned with triumph.

The grownups, except for Jake, finished drinking their tea.

"You'd better get back to your cabin and finish packing," Liz said to Peter.

Peter slithered down from Jake's lap and was off and running. Andrew decided to remain at the table. If he left, Gib might take advantage of his absence to tell of his outburst the night before. He ate slowly, and was relieved when Liz and Gib excused themselves to do some last minute packing. After a few minutes his mother and Jake rose to leave. Andrew accompanied them back to their cabin, just in case. As they arrived, Peter came running from the opposite direction and grabbed Andrew's hand and pulled him along.

"Come on—we don't want to miss it!"

Andrew's mother waved happily as he was again swept up in the whirlwind of Peter's enthusiasm. He followed Peter as he whizzed up the stairs, down a corridor, and burst through several sets of double doors. They veered into a narrow passageway which ended in two doors, one on either side. Peter knocked on the one to the left.

"It's our fan club!" One of the trumpet players opened the door.

"Come in!" called the trombone player. "I know you'd like to hear us give one last performance, but sorry we can't oblige—our instruments are all packed."

"No, that's all right," Peter said. "We were wondering if we could look out your porthole to see the Statue of Liberty when we get to New York. They're not allowing anyone to go on deck because of the storm."

"Why of course! Anything for our fan club!" one of the clarinet players said.

The trombone player was looking out of an open porthole. "Looks like you arrived just in time. We're sailing into New York Harbor now." He lifted Peter up to the porthole and held him by the legs as Peter thrust his head outside.

"I can't see anything—it's all foggy!" Peter whined. Then his body suddenly stiffened with excitement and his legs shot straight backwards. "*I see it!*" he cried. "*I see it!* Cor, it's *wonderful!*"

"It's quite a beautiful sight, that's for sure," the trombone player said softly as he peered out.

Peter arched his back. The trombone player held onto him, and after a few moments said, "Well, let's let Andy have a turn. Come on, down you go."

"Andrew, it's absolutely smashing!" Peter exclaimed.

Andrew thought it impolite to refuse, and didn't want to disappoint Peter, besides. He let himself be lifted up to the porthole, and looked out at the towering, sickly green statue. It seemed to hover in the mist, like a ghostly apparition. A shudder ran down Andrew's spine. It was almost as if this inanimate edifice were a real person, embodying a strange, terrifying power that was present in this new land. She seemed to be saying to him: *You have come to this land. You are an American now!* He felt dwarfed and mocked. He was to be cast upon the shores of this foreign land, like a sailor shipwrecked and beyond hope of rescue. There he would remain until the war was over, and there was no telling how long that would be.

He pushed himself back into the cabin. "Quite a sight, isn't it?" the trumpet player asked. Andrew nodded dumbly. He hoped that none of the band members, or Peter, ascertained how distraught he felt at this moment.

"Kid's just speechless," the tuba player said.

"Well, sometimes it takes your breath away to see it, no matter how many times," the trombone player said, gazing out of the porthole.

Andrew felt sick with despair. He was going to be swallowed up in this fearful place, was going to be chewed up and spit out, an unrecognizable pulp from the Andrew everyone had known. From the Andrew his father had known.

His father!

His father was no doubt facing the same fate—at this very minute. Whether he was a prisoner, or a fugitive in an enemy land, he was probably trying to hang onto his sense of self, fighting fear and despair, striving to keep his spirit and soul intact in the face of evil and oppression. As Andrew thought of the struggles his father was surely facing, he was infused with a sense of hope, and a purpose: He knew he had to fight, to hang on, to somehow resist being changed, so that he would still be his father's son. When the war was over and they were reunited, he and his father could pick up the threads of their lives. Things would be different, of course: They would both be a little older, a little wiser, and Andrew hoped, perhaps better people for having undergone their respective experiences. But they would be together!

And where was his father now? If he only knew! Was he in a prisoner of war camp? Or hiding out, behind enemy lines? He would now be thirty-two, almost thirty three. With a start, Andrew realized that his father's birthday was only a few days away. He vowed that he would spend that day, all day, doing nothing but thinking about him.

"You kids had better be going. It's not as if we want to kick you guys out, but your parents will be looking for you," the tuba player said.

Peter and Andrew shook hands with all the band members, then returned to their cabin.

Andrew's mother and Jake came to his cabin just as he was closing up his suitcase. Peter was jabbering happily about seeing the Statue of Liberty.

"Everything packed?" Jake asked. Andrew nodded, and Jake picked up his suitcase.

"The sweets! Wait, the sweets!" Peter ran over to the drawer and pulled it open.

"You take whatever you want. Take the comic books too," Andrew told him.

"Really! Oh, thanks awfully!" Peter quickly sorted through the candy bars, and took about half.

"Take the Hershey Bars," Andrew said. "I really don't need them."

Goodbyes were said; Peter wanted to exchange addresses with Andrew. Jake wrote down his parents' address and gave it to Peter. Andrew was about to say that he wouldn't be staying with them permanently, but decided against it. This was not the time, nor the place, to discuss the matter.

Andrew followed his mother and Jake as they disembarked in the driving rain. They were jostled on all sides by the mob of people pouring out of the ship.

"Andy, take it easy kiddo!" There was J.D., with Cowboy, Sarge, Mikey, Ray, Wheeler, and El.

"See ya in the funny papers!" Wheeler hollered.

"Be sure to write!" Sarge called.

"Hey, don't take any wooden nickels!" Mikey yelled.

"Yeah, watch out for the guy with the ace up his sleeve!" Ray shouted.

Andrew gave a wave and tried to smile; then his friends were lost in the crowd.

They were herded into a large building where they were subjected to some sort of official proceeding; Andrew kept his face pressed to his mother's side most of the time. Then they were disgorged into the pelting downpour.

Jake hailed a cab and the next thing Andrew knew, they were hurtling through the streets of Manhattan. It was, Andrew realized with dismay, nothing at all like London; indeed, like nothing he had ever seen before. London and New York were both large cities, but the similarity ended there. London was a pleasant place, like a collection of small villages adjoining one another; lovely to look at with its parks and flower gardens and wonderfully ancient buildings. The architecture was pleasing to the eye, suffused with history, and the buildings themselves seemed to sing of the events and people of the past. Though London was a bustling, busy city, it was not overwhelming: It was gentle on the eyes, gentle on the ears, friendly and full of life and hope. It was clean and tidy and orderly, like a scrubbed, well-dressed, well-behaved child. New York, by contrast, was outsized and threatening. It was cacophonous, confusing, frightening. The streets were like canyons, flanked by towering, ugly skyscrapers, and littered with trash. All in all, New York was a heartless, unruly, filthy place—like a dirty, ill-behaved street urchin. The ride in the taxi was truly terrifying; Andrew was sure that he had never travelled so fast before, not even in a train. The driver weaved and swore his way through the streets, swerving around corners, and finally screeched to a halt in front of a large edifice. As they carried their bags into the building, Andrew realized it was a train station. Jake bought tickets and said to Andrew's mother, "The train leaves in half an hour. I'll give my mother a call and tell her we're coming."

Andrew waited by the ticket counter while his mother followed Jake to a pay phone. Jake talked briefly on the phone, then handed the receiver to Andrew's mother, who chatted for a few minutes as she smiled at Jake. She then looked over to Andrew and waved at him to come over.

"Jake's mother wants to talk with you, darling." She thrust the receiver at him. A jolly voice crackled through the wire.

"Andrew! Hello! How was your trip?"

Andrew, caught off guard by the friendly voice, stammered, "Um...It was very nice."

"I'm looking forward to meeting you. Has Jake told you much about New Jersey?"

"Um...Some." Not sure of what to say next, he added, "I'm looking forward to meeting you, too." He really didn't mean it, of course, it just seemed like the proper thing to say in order to end this uncomfortable conversation. He handed the receiver back to his mother, who spoke a few more words. Then she handed it back to Jake, who said good-bye and hung up.

"Come on, Andrew, stay close!" his mother admonished him as they proceeded to the platform.

They entered the train by one door at the front of the car, much like a bus; not by a separate outside door for each compartment, as in England. The interior of the car was completely open, with seats in a row, one behind another; not divided into compartments with seats facing each other, as on British trains. Jake escorted Andrew's mother to a seat and indicated to Andrew that he take the seat across the aisle from them.

As soon as Andrew had settled himself in his seat, the train began to move. He closed his eyes. There was not much more that he needed to see at this point. He had never, even in his most furious protests against being sent to America, imagined that it could be *this* bad. He felt lost, forsaken, torn away from everything familiar, abandoned to an unknown fate. They might just as well have tossed him off the ship as it sailed past the dock!

In the excitement of their arrival, the hurry of packing, and Andrew's frantic efforts to prevent his mother from finding out about his outburst the night before, he had pushed his feelings of hatred towards Jake deep down, but now they surfaced again, though in a curiously transformed cast. Whereas before he had been consumed by fury, he now felt completely drained of emotion. His anger now manifested itself as a calm, icy attitude of contempt towards Jake. Andrew experienced no small degree of satisfaction as he felt this change within him. His feelings were no less intense, but his anger was now a kind of serene moral outrage instead of the flustery wild ire he'd felt before. How very British he was, after all! The link to his mother country had grown ever more tenuous the deeper he got into alien territory. Now, however, he felt a renewed sense of hope as he contemplated how his transformed feelings had solidified his bond with the country and people he had left behind. The English people had proven, after three years of war, that all the powers of evil could not undo them. They had faced the Blitz and the threat of invasion, with calm, controlled stoicism; angry and outraged, yes, but never unsettled or provoked to displays of frenzy and fear. Whether they dug bodies out of the rubble, tended the wounded, rebuilt shattered cities, built weapons, carried arms, flew planes—every person did his or her "bit." Andrew's father had chosen to be a fighter pilot, Andrew's mother a ferry pilot, both of them doing their jobs with professionalism and a sense of purpose.

Just as the British people would ultimately win the war by channelling their outrage into a concerted effort to defeat the Nazis, so Andrew knew that he could defeat Jake by the same cool, calm, purposeful course of action. It did not yet occur to him specifically what he could do, but that would come later; in fact he relished the thought of plotting his retaliation. He would have to be careful, though—nothing obvious to worry his mother....

"We're in New Jersey now," Jake said.

Andrew opened his eyes to survey this marvelous New Jersey of which his mother had spoken so glowingly. Peering through the filth-encrusted window, he saw an ugly sprawl of factories, refineries, and grimy warehouses—just as J.D. had said! Wondering if what else J.D. had said about New Jersey was also true, he stood and opened the window a crack. A sulfurous stench assaulted his nostrils. Right! J.D. was right about that, too! The place *did* smell like one big fart!

"Close the window, darling," his mother said.

He snapped the window shut and plopped back into his seat, satisfied. He was glad that his mother had gotten a whiff of the noxious odor—maybe she wouldn't think so highly of Jake anymore, seeing as he came from such a smelly place! She might even have second thoughts about leaving Andrew in this awful country!

Andrew folded his arms across his chest, narrowed his eyes, and fixed Jake with a cold stare of disdain. He expected Jake to be uncomfortable, maybe even a little embarrassed; he did not at all expect the expression on Jake's face: *fear.*

Andrew turned quickly away to hide his surprise. Why fear? He looked out the window, but the monotonous, blighted landscape did not offer any answers, or at least not any pleasant explanations. His momentary astonishment at Jake's reaction gave way to black despair over his mother's plans for him: He was to be discarded, abandoned, immured in this hideous desolation, and she didn't care one bit. Not one bit!

He closed his eyes again; better not to see anything at all than to view this soul-destroying ugliness, contemplate his appalling destiny.

Andrew had no recollection of dozing off, but apparently must have done just that, because the next thing he was aware of was his mother's voice: "Wake up, Andrew. We're almost there."

Opening his eyes, Andrew found that the repulsive industrial sprawl had been replaced by rather pleasant tree-lined streets and attractive houses which were constructed, for the most part, of wood—not of stone or brick, as in England. The train slowed, then braked to a halt. Andrew followed his mother and Jake out to the platform.

Jake stood stiffly for a moment and looked cautiously to his left; a cry came from the other direction, and he turned quickly to his right. A woman in a flowery print dress was running towards him, her arms outstretched and her face bursting with joy. She looked to be in her late forties, with light brown hair streaked with gray. Though she was somewhat chubby, she was surprisingly agile and swift. With her round face, rosy cheeks, twinkling eyes, and wide smile she reminded Andrew of Irene. She threw her arms around Jake, half-laughing, half-crying, as Andrew and his mother stood back and witnessed the emotional reunion.

There was another witness to the scene: a dark haired, stockily-built man, with a solemn face and taut mouth, who walked slowly towards them. He stopped and stood awkwardly, unsmiling, his hands clenched at his sides as he regarded the fervent welcoming embrace before him. His eyes were distant and skeptical, with a trace of sadness in them. His expression was one of resignation, laced with bitterness; like the look of a man holding a bad hand in a game of poker who is too dismayed to bluff.

"Mom..." Jake groaned, as his arms went round her. She pulled back a little from him and looked at him, her face perturbed. She stroked his cheek; then his hand came up to brush a tear from her eyes. She caught his hand and a spasm of pain crossed her face as she saw the scarred flesh.

"It's okay, Mom...really." Then Jake's eyes met those of the man standing a few feet away. The man nodded his head curtly. "Dad—" Jake said quickly, his voice betraying the tension that was almost a tangible presence.

Jake's father pursed his lips, gave another abrupt nod and said, tersely, "Son." He took a step back, and looked down. There was an awkward silence; then Jake turned and reached towards Andrew's mother. "Mom, Dad, this is Alice. Alice—my mom, Lois; my father, Gene."

Andrew's mother flashed a brilliant smile, and put her hand on Andrew's arm. "My son, Andrew," she said. She was at once enveloped in an embrace by Lois, who laughed warmly and heartily. Lois then moved to Andrew and put her arms around him in greeting. She laughed again and released him. "I'm sorry if I got carried away, Andrew. I know boys your age aren't supposed to like being hugged."

Andrew's mother chuckled, "It's fortunate that boys do eventually outgrow that sort of thing!" She then moved to Jake's father and gave him a swift kiss on the cheek. "It's so wonderful to meet you." She nodded at Andrew and he took the cue.

"Glad to meet you." He extended his hand to Mr. Givens. Mr. Givens grabbed it for an instant, then gave a quick nod and said in a flat voice, "Andrew."

"I hope you brought your appetite," Lois said. "Alida is cooking the fatted calf for us."

Jake's father grabbed one of the suitcases and walked ahead. Andrew's mother skipped to him and linked her arm with his while Jake and his mother walked together, arm in arm. Andrew brought up the rear.

At the car, Mr. Givens loaded the baggage into the trunk.

"Oh, I'd like to sit up front," Andrew's mother chirped. She nodded at Jake and his mother. "That way, you two can visit and I can enjoy the view."

They seated themselves in the car, Andrew sitting in the back seat next to Lois, who sat in the middle, with Jake on the other side. Andrew's mother chatted with Jake's father about the voyage and about how delighted she was to be in America: "If only for a visit, but maybe someday for a more extended stay. I've always wanted to see the United States and it's like a dream come true to finally be here."

Lois turned to Andrew. "It's so good to meet you at last! I hope you'll like staying with us. When I found out that your mother wanted you to come to the States, I thought how wonderful it would be for you to live with us, instead of away at school. After all, we're family now." She put her arm around Andrew's shoulder.

Andrew nodded and tried to smile politely. "Thank you, Mrs. Givens." He knew that it would not be a good idea to bring up the fact that he did not expect to remain with them, and that he would rather live at a boarding school. There would be time to deal with that later. As nice as she was, she was *not* family!

"Oh Andrew, call me Lois—no need to be so formal."

Andrew grunted in reply, acknowledging her request, but not at all sure if he should comply with it. It seemed strange to think of being on a first name basis with Jake's mother.

"Don't be shy, now." Lois gave him a hug, then turned to Jake.

"Well, you never told me how you two met, except to say that Alice was a ferry pilot, so I naturally assumed that it was somewhere in the line of duty. Now I want to hear all the juicy details."

Andrew's mother turned her head and glanced ever so briefly at Jake, but the enigmatic, questioning look she gave him was discernable, at least to Andrew. Jake returned her glance with a cautious, tense expression, as if warning her, and pursed his lips. There was an uncomfortable silence; then Jake mumbled, "Well, that's about it. Alice ferried Spits to my squadron." He shrugged and forced a smile.

"Jake was one of the few men that I knew who didn't make snide remarks about women pilots," Andrew's mother said brightly. "One time I ferried a Spitfire to a fighter squadron and one of the pilots rolled his eyes when he saw me getting out of the plane. He turned to another pilot and cracked, 'Women flying Spits! We might as well give them up, old boy. What will it be next—monkeys flying Lancasters?'"

"How awful!" Jake's mother exclaimed. "I would have thought that they would appreciate having women help out in the war effort. After all, you women are doing a very important job—one that requires a lot of skill and dedication."

"Well, we do it because we know we're needed, not because we expect to be appreciated. And I'm just happy to be able to fly, to do something I love. It doesn't really matter what anyone else thinks."

"Alice has a Class 4 rating, Mom," Jake said. "She flies twin-engined aircraft, like Beaufighters, Mitchells, and Mosquitos."

"What type of plane do you like the most?" Lois asked.

"Oh, the Spitfire is wonderful!" Andrew's mother said. "Powerful, yet turns on a dime, as you Americans would say."

The car slowed, and Mr. Givens pulled up into a driveway that led to a modest (as far as Andrew was concerned), two storey wooden house. It was painted light blue, with white shutters and trim. A dark-haired woman in a grey dress opened the front door and skipped down the steps. She threw her arms around Jake as he got out of the car.

"Well, the prodigal returns! A happily married man, to boot!"

Jake returned her hug, then introduced Andrew's mother. Andrew found it outrageous that a cook should be so familiar with her employers.

Lois asked her, "Well, how are we coming along with dinner?"

We?

Alida answered, "The roast beef is just about done. I was just about to mash the potatoes."

"I'll do the potatoes. Why don't you do the gravy?" Lois suggested. She turned to Andrew's mother. "Alida makes the *best* gravy."

Andrew was prepared to accept that America was a much different place from England, but he couldn't imagine that Lois was going to help the cook prepare dinner. What were servants for, anyway?

"I'd like to help, too," Andrew's mother said.

"Oh dear, you've had such a long journey," Lois told her. "Besides, everything is just about ready. It was so nice of Alida to offer to help."

So nice of the cook to *offer* to help? And now Andrew's mother was being contaminated by these strange American ways. Imagine, she was offering to *help out* in the kitchen! Look what Jake had dragged her down to!

"Oh dear, my phone's ringing," Alida said. "I'll be right back." She ran into the house next door, which was a little larger and fancier than the Givens's residence. Andrew shook his head as he realized...Alida was not their cook! She was their next-door neighbor!

They went into the house. Jake and Mr. Givens carried the suitcases upstairs. Andrew's mother set her bag down behind the sofa in the *living room*, as it was called, and started to follow Lois to the kitchen, which was located through a door past the stairs.

"Oh no, dear," Lois admonished her. "Why don't you let Jake show you to your room. Andrew too. I just need to take care of a few last-minute things."

"Well, call me if you'd like me to help," Andrew's mother offered. She climbed the steps. "Come along, Andrew," she called.

Andrew tromped up the stairs. Halfway up there was a landing; the steps continued in the opposite direction to a hallway at the top which ran front to back. There were two large bedrooms to the right, at the front of the house: the master bedroom, Andrew guessed, which was across the hall from the stairs and which contained a large bed and a dresser with photographs on it, and a second bedroom with a single bed. The bed was covered with a blue corduroy bedspread; at the foot was a folded patchwork quilt. Mr. Givens indicated to Andrew that this was to be his room. "Used to be Jake's," he grunted.

Andrew surveyed what was to be his quarters for the next several days. It was not an unpleasant place, at least to an objective eye: The walls were painted white and there were two windows, one in front and one on the side, framed by curtains of the same blue material as the bedspread. The other furniture consisted of a blue-painted chest of drawers by the bed and a similarly painted desk under the front window.

"The bathroom is down the hall," Mr. Givens said to Andrew. Andrew shuffled down the hall, passing by the guest room which his mother and Jake were to share. It was behind the master bedroom, opposite the stairs. It had rose-patterned wallpaper and a four-poster bed with a matching spread. Andrew continued along the hallway to the two rooms at the back: a tiny room to the right, next to the guest room, containing a few chests of drawers, a narrow bed, and an ironing board; and a bathroom to the left, next to the stairs. The hallway ended at a glass-paned door, which led to a balcony of sorts that looked over the backyard.

"Sleeping porch," Mr. Givens explained. "We have a canvas bed that we put out there in the summer."

"Why don't you wash up, Andrew?" his mother called. "Lois says dinner's almost ready."

Andrew, feeling unbearably filthy from the ride on the train, was only too happy to comply with her request. After washing and changing, he descended the stairs.

Just as he reached the bottom of the stairs, Jake and his mother came out of their room and walked briskly down the steps.

"I'm back—sorry!" The front door opened and Alida walked in. "Rhoda Wagner— she wants the scoop on Jake's wife and kid. She saw you coming down the street."

"She who sees and hears all," Lois called from the kitchen. "Well Jake, some things change and some things remain the same, and nosy neighbors are still a fact of life around here. Do you know any cloak and dagger outfits in England that need a spy? Rhoda's talents are just being wasted over here!"

"She wanted to know all about Alice—I told her she's a pilot and she was quite impressed. She said, 'Such a pretty girl, flying planes!' As if you needed to pass an ugliness exam in order to be a pilot!"

A loud meow and the sound of scratching came from the other side of the front door. "Cat wants in." Alida opened the door, and a gray and white striped cat slipped in. It dashed across the living room to Jake and rubbed its head against his ankle.

"Lindy, how are you boy? Do you remember me?" Jake reached down and stroked its head.

"How could he forget you, Jake? You're his hero!" Lois was standing in the kitchen doorway, drying her hands on a towel. "You saved him from certain death, you know."

"Jake, you never *told* me," Andrew's mother said, her face aglow with delight.

Lindy meowed; Jake sat down on the sofa and the cat hopped up onto his lap. He sat, facing Jake, his eyes closed in blissful adoration. Jake scratched him behind the ears. "It's just a cat," he said bashfully.

Lindy opened one eye and gave a sharp meow, as if to admonish him. Lois explained: "Jake found him in a hanger when he was flying one summer between semesters at Rutgers. Lindy must have been only a day or two old. His eyes weren't even open yet and he was half starved. Jake carried him home in his pocket and fed him milk from an eye dropper. Lindy's a silver tabby, not very common."

"Jake, what a wonderful thing to do!" Andrew's mother stroked Lindy's head. The cat cocked its head towards Andrew's mother and purred. "Oh, he likes me," she giggled. Lindy then rolled over on his back and wriggled. Jake rubbed his belly and said, "Hey there, boy, did you miss me?"

"Andrew, you've never had a pet," his mother said. "Oh, I know you're going to *love* it here."

Andrew bit his lip and looked away. He would have to deal with this matter, sooner or later. Maybe tomorrow....

"Chowtime, people!" Lois called.

"Sorry, Lindy." Jake gently put the cat on the floor.

They walked to the dining room, which was behind the living room at the far end so that the two rooms made an *L*. A door at the back of the dining room led to a short passageway which ran back to the kitchen. A small breakfast room was just behind the dining room. Lois came through the door, carrying a large platter that held an immense slab of roast beef. She set it down on the table. Andrew gaped at the sight. That piece of meat would have fed twenty people, easily! Andrew surveyed the rest of the bounty on the table: a huge bowl of mashed potatoes, a large casserole filled to the brim with sweet corn, another casserole of green beans, a basket piled high with rolls, and a saucer containing a chunk of butter the size of a hen's egg. Andrew's mouth watered. He wondered if the butter was their entire week's ration, just set out for show.

"Help yourself, Andrew." Lois passed the basket of rolls and the butter to him. Andrew took a roll and cut off a small piece of butter, about half the size of a small marble, which was the usual serving at school.

"Don't you care for butter, Andrew?" Lois asked.

Andrew bit his lip. Despite his feelings about Jake, he didn't want to make a bad impression, for his mother's sake. Since he didn't want to appear gluttonous, he thought it better to err on the side of caution. He was flustered that he had already offended.

"That's about all one gets in England, because of the rationing," his mother explained. "Andrew's gotten so used to it, I'm afraid."

"Well here, don't be shy." Lois passed the plate back to him. Andrew hesitated. How much was the usual portion in the United States? Sensing his discomfort, Lois briskly cut off a large piece, almost the size of a walnut. "Help yourself." She handed him the bowl of potatoes. Mr. Givens carved the roast beef and offered Andrew a thick slice. It was enough to feed half of Andrew's class at school, *if* they were lucky enough to even get beef at all!

"Alida, be sure to take some of that gravy home with you!" Lois called.

"Okay," Alida called back. She appeared in the doorway. "Good to see you again, Jake. Alice, Andrew—nice meeting you."

"A pleasure meeting you, Alida," Andrew's mother replied.

"I'll put the coffee on before I go." Alida disappeared back into the kitchen.

"Thanks," Lois called.

"Boy, it sure is good to see Alida again," Jake said. "Sure is good to be home, too." He looked around the room, then smiled wistfully as his eyes focused on his mother.

"It's good to have you home, Jake," Lois said softly.

They ate their meal, Andrew's mother and Lois doing most of the talking. Lois asked Andrew's mother about what it was like to be a ferry pilot, what kinds of planes she flew, how the system worked, and how the ATA was established.

"The ATA was formed just after England declared war on Germany in 1939," Andrew's mother said. "There were many male pilots who weren't eligible for the Royal Air Force for reasons of age or fitness, so it was decided to make use of their talents for transport duties—delivering despatches, mail, VIPs, and medical supplies. Later, as more and more pilots were needed for operational duties in the RAF, the ATA was given the task of ferrying aircraft from the factories and maintenance units to the squadrons. In December, 1939, Pauline Gower was appointed to form a women's ferry pool at Hatfield. She had been a commissioner in the Civil Air Guard and was a commercial pilot, too, with over two thousand hours of flying time. The standards for the first recruits—they were called the "First Eight"—were very high. They had to have at least six hundred hours of flying time. At first they were only allowed to ferry trainers, and during the winter of 1940 they flew open-cockpit Tiger Moths and Miles Magisters to Scotland and the North of England. It was a bitter cold winter and the pilots flew through snow, gales, and freezing rain. Later the required flying time was lowered and more women joined. In between ferrying duties, we take conversion courses to qualify for piloting different types of aircraft. We aren't allowed to go on to a Class 6 rating, to fly the flying boats, though—on moral grounds."

"Moral grounds?" Lois asked.

"Well, there was concern about what would happen if the plane had to make a forced landing, and a woman was 'stuck out' at sea with a male crew."

"I would think that *that* would be the last thing those guys would be thinking about," Jake laughed.

Andrew's mother went on: "Some of the women have flown Otters and Walruses—they're single-engined amphibians and can be used on either water or land. But women are not allowed to land them on water. I'd like to get one in my logbook, but no joy so far."

First helpings had already been consumed, and Lois inquired around, "Seconds, anyone?"

"Please Mom, everything." Jake stabbed another slice of roast beef. "More, sweetheart?" he asked Andrew's mother.

"Yes, lovely," she replied. Lois passed her the casserole of sweet corn and Jake plopped another slice of roast beef onto her plate.

"Andrew, don't be shy," Lois admonished him.

Jake speared another slice of meat and put it on Andrew's plate. Lois dished out a huge mound of potatoes and a generous portion of gravy. Though Andrew had already consumed more food in one sitting than he usually ate in a day, he had no problem making short work of the second round of food.

"Well, Andrew, I hope you'll like it here." Lois passed the basket of rolls along. "I realize it might take some getting used to, but I promise to keep a full cookie jar for you—how's that?"

Andrew nodded. "Thank you."

"Oh, and speaking of goodies, let's get dessert underway." Lois stood up and started collecting the finished plates.

"I'll help," Andrew's mother said. She took Andrew's plate. Jake, without a word, gathered up the serving bowls. The three of them took the dishes to the kitchen, leaving Andrew and Mr. Givens at the table alone. Mr. Givens pursed his lips, then sighed as he pushed himself back from the table. He regarded Andrew with an uneasy look, as if trying to ascertain if Andrew were friend or foe. Lois's voice carried from the kitchen.

"Alice, can you get the tray of coffee cups? Jake, why don't you carry the saucers and forks?"

Andrew's mother came in with the cups, set them down, and returned to the kitchen. She appeared again, carrying a pot of coffee, which she set on the table. Jake followed with the saucers and forks.

Jake poured a cup of coffee for her, then one for himself. He added cream and sugar, took a sip, and smiled. "Boy...real coffee. I'd almost forgotten what the stuff tastes like. Is it still rationed?"

"Nope, hasn't been since July," Lois called from the kitchen. "You came at a good time. Everything was scarce last year because of the German attacks on shipping. Now things are much better. The Navy has practically gotten rid of the U-Boats, so everything is more abundant—sugar, cocoa, coffee, everything, just about."

"Do you need any more help?" Andrew's mother called. Andrew couldn't believe it: His mother acting as if she were a maid! Imagine! Carting dishes from the kitchen and helping to clear the table!

"No fine, thanks—you all stay put. I'm just about to bring out dessert."

Lois appeared, carrying a huge chocolate cake ablaze with candles. "Happy Birthday, Jake!" she sang.

Jake blushed. "Mom, that was two months ago!"

"So we didn't get a chance to celebrate it then! Better late than never! In fact, we've missed your last four birthdays, so you'll just have to eat four pieces of cake to make up for it!"

"No problem with that," Jake said. Lois put the cake in front of him.

"Make a wish," she said.

Andrew's mother looked at Jake, and Andrew sensed that a special message passed in the loving gaze she gave him. Jake smiled briefly, then blew out the candles.

"Well, which one is this?" Mr. Givens asked. "Your twenty-fourth?"

"Twenty-fifth, Dad," Jake said. He seemed a little embarrassed at having to correct his father, but didn't seem at all flustered.

Andrew was stunned. Jake's deep, dark secret out—just like that! He didn't even seem to be upset, not in the least! What was going on here? Jake had practically implored Andrew's mother not to reveal his secret and now he had blurted it out without so much as batting an eyelash! It didn't make sense!

Andrew looked quickly to his mother, but she, too, seemed nonplussed by the revelation. "You old man," she teased.

"Oh, before you cut the cake, why don't you open your present?" Lois disappeared into the pantry, then returned, carrying a huge box wrapped in white paper. She set it in front of Jake.

"It's really for both of you—something for when you two have a place of your own together."

A place of your own together. Those six words sickened Andrew. How could his mother even consider settling down with Jake when the war was over! His father would come back—he *had* to come back!

"...Well, open it!" Lois was saying.

Jake tore off the wrapping and lifted the lid. "Oh Mom, it's beautiful," he said softly.

Andrew's mother was looking at the gift, which was still hidden from Andrew by the top of the box. Her eyes opened wide with wonder, and she cried, "It's lovely!" She pulled out a white spread, appliqued with a design of colorful, delicate circular outlines, like hoops, interlaced with each other.

"It's a wedding ring quilt," Lois said.

"Oh, where did you get such a beautiful thing?" Andrew's mother asked.

"She made it," Jake said with a smile.

"*Made* it?" Andrew's mother exclaimed. "Oh, it's gorgeous! Thank you so much!"

Lois beamed. Jake regarded her with an expression of tenderness. "Thanks Mom," he whispered.

"Thank you *so* much," Andrew's mother gushed. "We'll treasure it, always."

Always. The word flung itself, like a rock through a picture window, at the core of Andrew's deepest longings. It can't be *always* with Jake—not when my father comes back, he thought. She can't even consider staying with Jake once....

"...Okay, let's make short work of that cake," Lois was saying.

Jake cut the cake into slices and passed out a serving to everyone. He gave Andrew an extra large portion.

Andrew watched as everyone started to eat. Jake took a bite of cake and closed his eyes in bliss as he savored the first mouthful. "Oh, Mom—it's been ages since I've tasted anything this good. Absence makes the heart grow fonder, but I think this is even better than I remember!"

Lois smiled broadly. "Well, I had to make a few adjustments, what with the rationing and all, and I do think it's an improvement on the basic recipe. Instead of eggs and oil, I use mayonnaise, and I substitute honey for part of the sugar."

"This is positively delicious," Andrew's mother said. "Andrew, try it," she urged, seeing as how Andrew had not even touched his cake.

Andrew took a bite. It was good, *incredibly* good, but he was irked that his first taste of something so scrumptious (he couldn't even *remember* the last time he'd had chocolate cake!) was marred by the feeling of foreboding within him.

Always. That's what his mother said. He would have to do something to put that idea out of her mind. But what?

"...Alice sent us some pictures from your wedding, Jake." Lois jumped up and went to the buffet. She opened a drawer and pulled out some photographs. After leafing through them, she handed one to Mr. Givens.

"Remember this one, Gene? Isn't that a beautiful cake!" She turned to Andrew's mother. "It must have been delicious!"

Andrew's mother and Jake exchanged an amused glance.

"What's so funny?" Lois pressed.

Andrew's mother opened her mouth, as if starting to speak, but giggled instead. Jake grinned at her. Finally she composed herself and said, "It *was* beautiful, but quite inedible—it was made of wood!"

"Wood!" Lois exclaimed.

"It was a fake cake, Mom," Jake said.

"*A fake cake!* Why?"

"Sugar is so strictly rationed in England," Andrew's mother explained. "It's usually impossible to get together enough ingredients for a proper cake so they have cakes made out of wood, decorated like the real thing. You just rent one and use it for show." She pointed to the photograph. "There's a little drawer in the bottom layer to put a bit of fruitcake or something in, for the happy couple." She beamed at Jake. "I get a Cadbury bar whenever I make a ferry trip, so I put two in—Jake was ever so surprised!" Jake raised his eyebrows in a playful, inviting glance at her; she responded with a wink. They kissed briefly, playfully. Lois regarded them with obvious delight.

Everyone returned to devouring the scrumptious dessert. Andrew, though, found that it tasted like stale bread in his mouth. He took a few gulps of milk to wash it down. Lois refilled his glass.

"Another piece, Andrew?" Jake cut another slice of cake.

"No, thank you," Andrew replied politely. Jake plopped the piece of cake onto his own plate. "Alice?" he asked.

"No, darling—I'm positively stuffed!"

"Suit yourself." Jake started to devour his second helping. Andrew's mother eyed his plate, then quickly nabbed a piece with her fork. "Just a bite," she said playfully. Jake raised his eyebrow in amusement, as if daring her to try again. She accepted his challenge, stabbing another piece with her fork and smiling in triumph as she consumed it. The third time she attempted to steal a bite, Jake was ready for her. He took a piece of cake on his fork and held it up to her mouth. She smiled, opened her mouth a little, and Jake fed her the morsel. As she savored it, her eyes locked on Jake with a look of pure delight.

Andrew felt his heart drop into his stomach. That look! In a flash, he remembered the look on his mother's face when she had helped Aunt Gwen to bandage his father's injured shoulder. That look of adoration, of bliss, of complete devotion—that was a look meant for his father alone! Not for anyone else, not ever!

"Delicious, Mom—thanks." Jake scraped the last of the icing off his plate.

"So Jake, when are you going to join the Army Air Forces?" Mr. Givens pushed his chair a bit back from the table and folded his arms across his chest.

There was an uncomfortable silence. Lois looked apologetically at Jake; Andrew's mother looked concerned. Jake stared at his empty plate for awhile. Finally he sighed, cleared his throat, and said, "It seems like a good idea to wait, at least for awhile."

"Wait? What are you waiting for? The Eagle Squadron pilots joined the AAF over a year ago!"

Jake and Andrew's mother exchanged a glance, unspoken, but as effective as any voiced communication. Jake's look was tremulous, yet overlaid with a veneer of defiance; Andrew's mother evinced an empathy that startled Andrew. It was a look that testified of a shared distress: an understanding on the deepest level of Jake's alienation from his father.

She never looked at Dad like that!

He recalled how withdrawn and tense Jake had seemed during the latter part of the voyage; without knowing the cause, Andrew had hoped that Jake's moodiness would drive his mother away. Now that the cause of Jake's anxiousness had been made clear, the vexing truth was that it seemed to have cemented their relationship, rather than weakened it. His mother, he knew, had also defied her own father. Even though it was by involving herself with Andrew's father, it still galled Andrew that it provided this sort of commiseration between her and Jake.

Jake glared at his father.

"I was never in any of the Eagle Squadrons."

"You're still an American."

"I've been with the RAF for over three years. You get used to things, the equipment, tactics. If you've been used to doing things one way, it can be hard to switch. Flying British aircraft is second nature to me now—I'm good at it—and I don't see the point of changing."

"You'd get paid more, for one thing."

Jake laid his fork down. "More money is not going to do me much good if I'm not around to enjoy it. And I have a better chance of staying alive in a Spitfire than in a P-47."

"Do you mean to say that the American planes aren't any good? I've heard that the Thunderbolt is a damned good plane."

"It's more commonly referred to as the Repulsive Scatterbolt. It can't climb, can't turn—"

"If it's so damned awful, then why are the Americans using them at all?"

"It dives real well," Jake said caustically. "If all you had to worry about was diving, then I guess the P-47 would be a good plane to be in. Now, if I could fly P-51s—once they get the bugs worked out of them—I would consider it."

"Consider it!" Mr. Givens's voice was curt with outrage.

"Oh, the P-51 is just a marvelous fighter—probably the best one there is!" Andrew's mother chirped. "It's a fine example of Yankee ingenuity. The RAF said daylight bombing of Germany couldn't be done on a mass scale because of the problem of fighter escort. Trust the Americans to think of a solution!"

"What's so wonderful about the P-51?" Lois asked.

"Range, for one thing," Andrew's mother replied. "With its specially designed wings and drop tanks, it will be able to escort the bombers all the way to their targets in Germany. It's faster and more maneuverable than the German fighters, has a Rolls Royce Merlin engine—"

"The engine is a credit to English inventiveness," Jake said. "The P-51 was originally fitted with Allison engine, so it had poor high-altitude performance. The Americans almost scrapped it. But the British thought it was a superbly designed fighter and some English engineers tinkered around with it in their spare time and refitted it with a Merlin engine. That completely transformed it into a first-class fighter—probably the finest one ever designed. It's going to win the war for us."

"A perfect example of Anglo-American cooperation, then," Lois said.

"And German ingenuity—it was designed by a German who immigrated to America," Andrew's mother added.

"Wow—is that so!" Lois exclaimed. She turned to Jake. "So you're still flying Spitfires?"

"Spits and Mosquitos," Jake replied. "I'm not doing fighter escort right now—I'm in photo-reconnaissance. Since I have a twin-engine rating, I fly Mosquitos a lot."

"Mosquito—what kind of a plane is that?" Lois asked.

"It's a high speed, high altitude plane," Andrew's mother replied. "It's made of wood—"

"Wood!" Lois exclaimed. "Is that safe?"

"Oh, they're incredibly sturdy," Jake said. "What's more, since they're made of wood they don't show up very well on radar. Drives the Germans nuts. We're in and out before they know about it."

"The plane was originally designed because we faced a shortage of metal alloys," Andrew's mother said. "It's actually made of a plywood-balsa-plywood sandwich construction, and it turned out to be one of the most outstanding British aircraft in the war—it's called the 'Wooden Wonder.' Besides being used for photo-recon, it's used for precision bombing, night fighting, mine-laying, torpedo bombing—"

"Target marking with the Pathfinders, too," Jake added. "It's also used as a light transport, a long-range intruder and fighter, a dual-control trainer, and a fighter-bomber. It's the fastest plane in the RAF—over four hundred miles an hour. And it has a range of 2500 miles."

"I must say, though," Andrew's mother said, "The cockpit layout leaves much to be desired!"

"What's wrong with the cockpit?" Jake teasingly challenged "So cramped! And climbing up that flimsy ladder to get in through that tiny hatch in the side, or worse, through the floor—"

"The floor?" Lois asked.

"Yes, in the bomber version," Andrew's mother continued. "It has two seats and since they're staggered, there's not much room for a control pedestal. So all the controls are crammed on the dashboard. The throttle levers are too short to operate with the palm, so you have to use your fingers. You have to be a concert pianist to enjoy them! Now the Beaufighter—"

Jake rolled his eyes. "You and your Beaufighters!" He grinned at her, half-proud, half-amused.

"The Beaufighter has a *superbly* designed cockpit," Andrew's mother countered, a mischievous grin on her face. "It's *wonderfully* roomy, the seat is placed perfectly, *right* in the center, the trimmers and throttle levers are solid and rugged—"

"And you need to be a hunchbacked acrobat to get into it!" Jake retorted. He turned to Lois. "No kidding, ma—there's these handrails on the roof, and you have to *swing* your legs over the *back* of the seat—"

"It's quite simple, once you get used to it, a piece of cake—

"*Piece of cake?* Then why does it take a whole *page* of handling notes to give directions on getting in and out of the blasted thing! You have to roll backwards—"

"It's not difficult for those of us who are agile." Andrew's mother winked at him. He smiled, and reddened slightly.

The conversation turned to other planes and to the war in general, with Lois and Andrew's mother doing most of the talking. Lois was very attentive and eager to hear about the experiences Andrew's mother had in being a ferry pilot; she asked a lot of questions and laughed at the funny incidents Andrew's mother described. Clearly, she was enchanted with her new daughter-in-law. Andrew, despite his feelings about Jake, felt a surge of pride that his mother had made such a good impression. Jake talked less, usually adding a comment or explanation to the conversation, avoiding any eye contact with his father. Mr. Givens regarded the exchange ruefully, much like a spectator at a soccer match whose favorite team has lost control of the ball.

Lois had told Andrew that he needn't worry about filling the bathtub only a few inches full when he took a bath that night: *Use as much as you want and take a nice, hot soak,* she had told him.

So Andrew thought he might as well enjoy the luxury of being fully immersed in the wonderfully warm water. He slid down in the tub until his head was completely under the water—what *decadence!* He knew he wouldn't enjoy such coddling if he went away to boarding school, so he might as well enjoy it while he could.

He had been prepared to dislike Jake's parents on sight, just because they were, well, Jake's parents. Having met them, his feelings had changed, much to his surprise. He really liked Lois: She was so friendly and jolly and eager to please. Mr. Givens was a complete opposite, but Andrew sensed that he was a man who was deeply disappointed in his son, and more hurt than angry. The estrangement between Jake and his father gave Andrew a perverse sort of satisfaction. If Jake had failed in a relationship with his father, it stood to reason that he might fail at other relationships as well.

Andrew stood, soaped up, then lay down again to rinse off. He then got out of the tub, grabbed a big, fluffy towel, and proceeded to dry off. After dressing himself, he walked down the hall to his bedroom. The guest room door opened a crack. Lindy was ushered out by Jake's foot gently prodding him through the door.

"Sorry Lindy, you can't sleep with me anymore."

The door was shut and Lindy meowed a soft, plaintive howl of protest and regarded the closed door with a look of disgust. Andrew heard his mother's voice: "Maybe he just wants to take notes."

"It wouldn't do him any good," Jake replied. "He's neutered."

"Poor thing!"

"What do you mean poor thing? I didn't want him responsible for bringing any more strays into the world. Besides, neutered cats make better pets. They're less trouble—they don't roam, don't spray, don't howl at the moon—"

There was a low, amused murmur from Andrew's mother; Andrew couldn't quite make out what she was saying. Then she emitted a peal of laughter that was all too audible.

Cats aren't the only creatures that are a lot less trouble if they're neutered, Andrew thought savagely. He wanted to kick open the door and put a stop to the gaiety and domestic bliss that was proceeding under the newly-made quilt that symbolized his worst fear.

Always!

Andrew shuffled down the hall to his—or rather, Jake's—room. He looked through his suitcase for some clean underwear, but there wasn't any. Then, remembering that his mother had left her bag downstairs behind the sofa, he went down to the living room to get it. He thought it would be polite to bid Jake's parents good night; he had noticed that the door to their bedroom was open and that it was vacant. They might be in the dining room. They weren't, but Andrew heard their voices coming from the breakfast room. The door was closed. Andrew lifted his hand to knock, but his hand stayed as he heard Mr. Givens's voice, seething with anger.

"He doesn't have any intention of ever joining up with the Americans, Lois. He hasn't changed a bit. He's going to do whatever he damn well pleases and to hell with serving his country!"

"The British are on our side, Gene," Lois said. "We're all in this together."

"Well, then, what's so awful about joining the Americans, then?"

"He's used to flying with the RAF. He has his rank—"

"He'd still get to keep his rank if he joined the Army Air Force—"

"If he's good at flying the British planes, why change to something that's unfamiliar?"

"Because he just wants to have his own way, that's why."

"Gene—"

"Hell, Lois, he's always been like that. If I had known that he was out barnstorming when he was living in Nebraska I—"

"You would have what? Kept him here? It was best for everyone for him to live with my brother's family during his last two years of high school. Besides, the high school here was on half-sessions. He got a better education in Nebras—"

"Half the time he was out barnstorming anyway—"

"He just missed a few weeks in September and part of May and June. Wanda made sure he studied his lessons. Didn't he graduate eleventh in his class?"

"Out of a class of twenty-three? That's not saying much!"

"He tried to please you. Didn't he go to Rutgers—"

"No, he didn't do that to please me. We had an agreement. He went to flight school for a year, first, before he went to Rutgers."

"That was so he could earn money in the summers and pay for college. He never took a cent from you—not for flight school, not for Rutgers—"

"And he didn't live up to his end of the agreement either. He quit halfway through his junior year—"

"There was a war on—"

"Not here, there wasn't. That was two whole years before Pearl Harbor. If he'd stayed, he would have gotten his degree in pharmacy by now."

"Gene, Jake never has been, and never will be, cut out to be a pharmacist. Flying is what he loves. Can't you accept that?"

"I'm not saying he shouldn't fly. He just should have finished college first."

"He thought it was important. If it hadn't been for the British holding off the Nazis back then, we'd probably be surrendering to Hitler right now—"

"There wasn't any fighting when he went over—"

"Britain and Germany were at war—"

"It was a damned phony war at the time—"

"Jake wanted to—"

"He was just looking for an excuse, any excuse, to go off half-cocked. He never even considered the consequences, either. What he did was against the law in those days—he could have lost his citizenship, been thrown in prison—"

"Gene—"

"*Two years in prison*, Lois! That's what the punishment was back then for violating the Neutrality Act—"

"Gene, can't you just accept what he's done? Be proud of what he is? Look at all those medals and commendations he's gotten! I know it would mean a lot for him to hear you say—"

"He doesn't give a damn what I say, or think—"

"You're wrong. You know that Jake—"

"That's the whole damn thing, Lois, I don't know him. I don't know my own son!"

There was a long silence, then Lois's voice, subdued: "She's wonderful, isn't she?"

"Yeah. She'll be good for him. Maybe straighten him out."

There was another pause; then Mr. Givens said, "Well, I'm going to turn in."

Andrew crept away from the breakfast room and stole up the stairs. Once in his room, he reflected on the conversation he'd just heard. He was proud that Jake's parents thought so highly of his mother, though it annoyed him a little that they considered her in terms of how good she was for their son, as if she were a vitamin pill or a spoonful of cod-liver oil.

Well, not exactly. They genuinely liked her, and Jake's mother was ever so delighted by her abilities and accomplishments. Not so Mr. Givens's attitude towards his son: The rift between them was a veritable chasm. Andrew closed his eyes and remembered the wonderfully close relationship he and his father had shared—still shared.

I'd never think of doing anything to hurt him—ever!

Even though Jake's estrangement with his father had provided a shared experience between him and Andrew's mother, Andrew realized there was a flip side to it as well: It was a definite indication that Jake had...problems. Mr. Givens didn't seem to be a bad sort. He wasn't exactly charming, but Andrew sensed that he was basically a decent chap. Clearly he had been hurt by Jake's behavior. Even without seeing his face, Andrew had been aware of the pain in Mr. Givens's voice when he spoke of the alienation between him and his only son.

He doesn't give a damn what I say, or think...I don't even know my own son!

If Jake could hurt his own father like that, then there was no telling what he was capable of! Andrew wished that his mother could see Jake for what he really was: churlish, belligerent, and hateful to the core.

If only she could see!

Andrew closed the door to his room and sat down upon the bed. He would not be staying in this hated land, of that he was certain. The awful feeling of doom he had experienced upon seeing the Statue of Liberty had convinced him that America was *no* place for him (though he would somehow have to figure out a way to make his mother realize it too). For the time being, though, he could at least effect some convincing demonstrations of Jake's shortcomings. He looked up at the ceiling and smiled.

Right—what Jake needed was a taste of his own medicine!

Just need to stir things up a bit, that's all.

Chapter 29

S hafts of golden sunlight streaming through the windows awakened Andrew the next morning. Lindy was lying at his feet, curled up in a furry spiral. Something was missing, Andrew sensed; then he realized he had gotten so used to the faint hum of the *Queen Mary's* engines and the gentle motion of the ship that being on dry land was a strange sensation. He heard faint clanking sounds from downstairs. Someone was already up. He looked at the clock on the dresser: seven-thirty. He slipped out of bed, being careful not to disturb Lindy, got dressed, and padded downstairs.

Mr. Givens was standing by the stove, pouring a cup of coffee. He was dressed for work in a businessman's suit and tie.

"Good morning," Andrew said softly.

"Morning." Mr. Givens poured some cream into his coffee. "Did you sleep well?"

"Yes, very. Do you always go to work this early?"

Mr. Givens grunted. "Got some things to catch up on at work before I open the store."

"Oh, that's right—my mum said that you were—I'm sorry, I forget what the word is here. It's what we call a chemist in England."

"Pharmacist."

"Right, pharmacist." Andrew said the word very slowly, then smiled at Mr. Givens. "My aunt Gwen was a nurse. She was very good at taking care of people. She took care of me when I was ill with pneumonia."

Mr. Givens sipped his coffee. Though he was looking at Andrew, his eyes held a distant, hard gaze. It was obvious he was thinking about something else. Andrew went on. "Anyway, I thought it was terrific how she knew how to take care of people. I've always been fascinated by that sort of thing—you know, medicine."

Lois came into the kitchen from the breakfast room. "Well, up so early Andrew? I thought you'd want to sleep in."

"I guess I'm excited about being here. It's all so new and different. I just wanted to thank you for letting me stay with you. I mean, it's very kind of you to do this."

The expression on Mr. Givens's face softened. "Um...glad to have you here, Andrew."

Lois beamed. "Well, Andrew, how about pancakes and sausages for breakfast?"

"Yes, please." Even though Andrew wasn't crazy about sausages, since he had to eat so many of the mealy things for a main course at tea or supper, he supposed that pancakes would make for a hearty enough breakfast.

"Well, I'd better be going." Mr. Givens gulped the last of his coffee, gave Lois a quick peck on the cheek, and was out the door. Lois lit the burner on the stove and started mixing up the pancake batter. Soon the pancakes and sausages were sizzling and giving off a delightful aroma.

"Did you sleep well?" Lois asked Andrew.

"Oh yes. Mmm, that smells good."

"Well, if you want seconds, just holler." Lois scooped the pancakes and sausage onto a plate. "Would you like some real maple syrup? Gene's brother lives in Maine and brings us a batch whenever he comes to visit."

"Yes, that sounds delicious."

Lois poured a dollop of syrup on the pancakes and handed Andrew the plate. "Why don't you take that to the breakfast room. There's a pitcher of orange juice on the table—pour yourself a glass. I'll grab another cup of coffee and sit with you. Would you like milk, too?"

"Yes please."

Andrew carried his plate down the corridor to the breakfast room: a cheery, sunny place papered in yellow gingham wallpaper. Lois followed, beverages in hand. She indicated Andrew's place at the table, already set with a placemat, silverware, and a glass.

Andrew poured himself a glass of orange juice. As he sipped the delicious liquid, he considered that he might as well enjoy the pleasures of such delicacies during the brief time he was to spend in this unpleasant land. The food was good, at least! He took a bite of pancake and the taste of the maple syrup, sweet and savory, melted in his mouth. He cut a piece of sausage, popped it in his mouth, and was pleasantly surprised by the hearty taste.

"These sausages are terrific! May I have some more, please?"

"Sure," Lois replied cheerily. She went out into the kitchen and before long the delightful smell of the sizzling meat wafted into the breakfast room. She returned with another glass of milk.

"I thought you might like a refill," she said.

"Oh, I don't want to use up your milk ration," he protested.

"Milk ration!"

"Yes, I'm only allowed a pint a day in England."

"This isn't England," she smiled. "You can have as much as you want!" She set the glass beside his plate.

"Thank you so much." Andrew took a gulp of milk. "It's been so long since I've tasted anything so good."

"Well, eat your fill and don't be shy about asking for seconds. I think the sausages are just about done." Lois got up and went out into the kitchen. After a few minutes she returned with a plate of sausages which she set at Andrew's place.

"I hope you're settling in all right, Andrew. I know it must be strange, coming to a foreign country. Jake wrote me about how strange everything seemed to him when he first got to England. I never thought of England as a foreign country, since we speak the same language. Anyway, I thought it would be a good idea for you to stay at home for the rest of the week just to get used to things. On Monday you can start school."

Andrew knew it would be bad form to mention that it would be pointless for him to put in an appearance at school, since he would not be staying in America. So he asked, "What day is today? One loses all track of time aboard ship."

"It's Thursday, the seventh."

The seventh. Three more days until his father's birthday. Andrew wondered if his mother was aware of it.

"Well, early bird! Did you get a good night's sleep?" Andrew's mother was standing in the doorway, dressed in slacks and a sweater.

"Yes, Mum."

"I'll start breakfast for you and Jake," Lois said to Andrew's mother. "Is he up yet?"

"Yes, he'll be right down." Andrew's mother seated herself next to Andrew as Lois bustled out to the kitchen. "Are you enjoying the food, darling?"

"Yes Mum, it's very good."

"See, I told you the food was marvelous here. You'll be getting lots more of it, too. Soon you'll wonder how you ever lived with the shortages in England."

Better not to broach the subject of his returning to England—at least not now, Andrew thought. As he munched on his food, he considered that the element of surprise might give him a definite tactical advantage when he approached his mother on the subject of his returning to England with her. If he grumbled now, it might make her counter-attack with protestations that he should stay. Let her think, for now, that he was "adjusting." Then, when he caught her off guard with vehement pleadings to be allowed to leave this hated land, she would *have* to acquiesce—surely!

His mother's eyes widened at the pitcher of orange juice.

"Do you have orange juice all the time here, or is that just for special occasions?" she called to Lois.

"Oh, we have it all the time."

"Isn't that *wonderful,* Andrew!" His mother beamed at him. "Imagine—having orange juice every day!" She poured herself a glass, took a sip, and smiled blissfully. "It's been positively *years* since I've had orange juice! Oh Andrew, you're going to *love* it here! Imagine, having all the orange juice you want! You'll have to write to your friends in school about this—won't they be *green* with envy!"

"Morning, Andrew." Jake appeared in the doorway.

Andrew's mouth was full of sausage, so he grunted as he chewed his food.

Jake sat down at the table. Lois's voice rang out from the kitchen. "Jake, would you and Alice like some coffee?"

"Yes Mom, thanks."

Lois brought two cups of coffee and set them on the table, then returned to the kitchen. Andrew's mother and Jake sipped their coffee in silence for a few moments; then Andrew's mother reached for Jake's hand and squeezed it. He set his cup down and smiled at her. She smiled back.

There it was again! That *look!* Andrew looked at his mother, then quickly turned away, trying to hide his consternation.

"I'll see if Mom has any plans for tonight. There's a place I'd like to take you for dinner," Jake said to Andrew's mother.

Lois appeared, carrying two plates of food which she set down on the table.

"Oh my, what a treat!" Andrew's mother said. "Thank you ever so much!"

"Mom, I was thinking of taking Alice out for dinner tonight. Would that interfere with any plans you might have?" Jake asked.

"No, that's fine. I figured you two would probably want to get away on your own while you were here. Your father should be home about six, so you can take the car."

"Thanks Mom."

"Remember, right side of the road!"

"Yes Mom."

"Where do you plan on going?"

"I was thinking of the George Washington Inn."

"George Washington!" Andrew's mother exclaimed. "Not that horrible rebel leader!" Her eyes twinkled.

"The same," Jake grinned.

"Don't ever tell my mother that I visited such a place. One of her ancestors fought in that war, you know,"

"What a coincidence," Jake laughed. "So did one of mine."

There was a knock at the back door. Lois went to answer it. A moment later she reappeared with a short, plump black woman who was dressed in a light grey dress and a white apron.

Jake stood up and extended his arms. "Sarah!"

The woman emitted a peal of throaty laughter and embraced him. "My, my! It sure is good to see you—look how you grown!"

"I'm just as tall as I was four years ago, Sarah."

"I mean, you grown on the inside, I can tell," Sarah said soberly. Then she smiled. "You a family man, now."

Jake smiled bashfully, then introduced Andrew's mother, who in turn introduced Andrew.

"I gonna sit me down and have a nice cup o' coffee," Sarah announced. She plopped down into an empty chair.

"Jake, would you get a cup for Sarah?" Lois asked.

"Now don't go to any trouble on my account." Sarah leveled Jake with a look that was both imperious and cheeky, indicating that that was precisely what she expected him to do.

"No trouble Sarah, no trouble at all." Jake hopped up and went to the kitchen. Returning with a coffee cup, he pronounced, "Black and sweet, right?"

"Jus' like old Sarah!" She took a few gulps of coffee and, holding the cup in both hands, regarded Jake with a gleam in her eye. "Now, I got to hear how this one—" She cocked her head at Andrew's mother, "finally lassoed you."

Andrew's mother giggled; Jake blushed and cleared his throat. "Well, Alice is a ferry pilot. She delivered a Spitfire to my base one day, and, um, that's how we met." He shrugged, and looked at Andrew's mother.

"I fell for the accent," Andrew's mother told Sarah. "It's rather exotic, don't you think?"

"What accent?" Sarah threw back her head and chortled. "So Jake, you finally find a woman that don't mind you flying off into the wild blue yonder!"

"How could I complain?" Andrew's mother said.

"Right, what's good for the goose is good for the gander! So how long you been flying?"

"Oh, I learned before Andrew was born. I've been with the ATA for two and a half years, since the spring of 1941."

"Zat so?" Sarah said. "What kind of planes you fly?"

Andrew's mother ticked off the many different types of aircraft she had flown, adding that at first women were only allowed to fly light trainers.

"We finally were allowed to fly Hurricanes and Spitfires in the summer of 1941. I took my conversion course in August."

"Conversion course?" Sarah asked.

"Yes, in order to advance to each new class of aircraft— operational single-engined, light twins, heavy twins, those with tricycle undercarriages and such, we need to go to school."

The discussion then turned to exactly what ferrying entailed: flying unfamiliar aircraft at a moment's notice, avoiding barrage balloons and anti-aircraft positions, landing in makeshift airfields. Cup after cup of coffee was consumed; there was a lot of laughter as Jake and Andrew's mother recounted various amusing incidents.

"How about lunch?" Lois finally said.

"Seeing as we already sitting here round the table, that sounds like a fine idea," Sarah boomed. Lois got up and clattered around the kitchen for a few minutes, then returned with a plate of sandwiches, which everyone demolished in short order.

Andrew tried to hide his bewilderment at this whole scene. It was obvious from her uniform that Sarah was the maid, and yet she had seated herself at the table like one of the family, had in fact spent the *entire morning* there without doing a stitch of work! It would have been unthinkable for Lucia or Maria to even consider doing such a thing, *and* to be on such familiar terms with one's employer, *and* to presume to eat at the same table with the mistress of the house. *America!*

Let's polish off the rest of Jake's birthday cake." Lois jumped up and scurried to the kitchen.

"Chocolate, I 'spect?" laughed Sarah.

"How'd you guess?" Jake asked.

Lois brought out the remainder of the cake. "I'll get some saucers," Jake said. He went to get them as Lois put on another pot of coffee.

"Let's see, this you twenty-sixth, right?" Sarah called to Jake.

"No, twenty-fifth." Jake said.

"Sorry 'bout that."

"You're not the only one who got it wrong." Jake set the saucers on the table.

"Gene thought it was his twenty-fourth," Lois said.

Sarah grunted. "So how you father treating you?" she asked Jake.

Jake shrugged. "You know Dad."

"He's been on the grumpy side for the past two weeks." Lois served up the cake. "On account of all the chicken and meatless meals I've been serving, so as to have enough red stamps for some good cuts of meat for Jake and his family. I also wanted to have a good supply of bacon, sausage, and butter. You know Gene—he's like a grizzly bear if he doesn't get a good hunk of meat often enough. And there's only so many ways you can cook chicken. Give him a few days with a good steak or roast for dinner and he'll be just fine. Why just this morning, he had a good breakfast of sausage and pancakes—I swear he was almost smiling!"

Sarah snorted. "*Almos'* smiling, you say?"

"You know Dad." Jake shoveled a piece of cake into his mouth.

"Well, he was worried about you, too, Jake," Lois said. "Especially after, you know, what happened."

The phone rang and Lois jumped up to answer it. She called from the living room, "It's for you, Jake."

Jake jumped up to take the call. It was obvious that the caller was an old friend, from the tone of delight and surprise in his voice. He settled on the sofa, feet resting on the coffee table as he chatted on the phone. Lois regarded him with a look that was half joy, half troubled remembrance.

As if reading her mind, Sarah squeezed her shoulder and said, "See, I *tole* you he gonna be all right!" She turned to Andrew's mother. "She just beside herself when she hear 'bout Jake's accident, thought they might cut his hands off or something—"

"Well, I've heard of that happening—" Lois began.

"That's years ago! Doctors now, they can do all kinds of things. I *tole* you not to worry! See? What all that worrying done you, girl?"

"I know it must have been horribly upsetting for you, hearing about Jake's accident," Andrew's mother said softly to Lois. "But I visited him as often as I could when he was in hospital."

"We didn't hear too much from the hospital about his condition," Lois said. "From what little they communicated to us just after it happened, I got the impression that it was...Well, they said the burns on his hands were severe. And his other injuries, his legs shot up, too—"

"It was quite serious for awhile," Andrew's mother told her. "They treated the burns with tannic acid, with the idea that it would form a protective crust. Well, so little was known about the treatment of burns in those days and the pilots and victims of incendiary bombs were—" She stared into her empty coffee cup. "Well, some of the treatments were new. What happened with Jake was that the crust sloughed off and he got a bad case of septicemia. I was with him for three days, until he battled it off...." Andrew's mother was silent for a moment, then took a deep breath and continued. "Then they gave him hot wax treatments, then electric current therapy to stretch his tendons, which had gotten contracted. Then, when he was transferred to East Grinstead, they wrapped his hands in saline dressings. The worse part for him was being so incapacitated and helpless. With his hands bandaged, he couldn't even brush his teeth or scratch his nose. He was completely dependent on other people to take care of him. For some people that wouldn't be much of a problem. For Jake, though, it was a—" She paused, and smiled. "Well, you know Jake."

Lois smiled wanly, but didn't say anything. Andrew's mother went on. "And then he had a broken ankle and his other leg shot up, which complicated things even more. Because his hands were burnt he couldn't even get up and around with crutches, and that was extremely frustrating for him."

Lois reached over and squeezed her hand. "I'm so glad he had you to look after him."

Sarah stared at the two of them, skeptical and baffled, as if contemplating a jigsaw puzzle with a piece that didn't quite fit.

Jake came into the kitchen as Andrew's mother was helping Lois with the dishes. Andrew had been roped into doing the drying.

"Who was that who called?" Andrew's mother asked Jake.

"Oh, a friend of mine from school, Al Ledford. He was wounded at Guadalcanal so he's home permanently. He'd like to get together some evening—I mean, he and his wife. They invited us for dinner. Would you mind?"

"Sounds super!"

Jake smiled. "It'll give me a chance to show you off."

"Honestly darling, I'm not all that...."

"Yes you are." Jake put his arm around her and kissed her on the lips. "Well, is Sunday evening okay?"

"Sunday would be fine, darling."

Andrew stared disconsolately through the kitchen window. *Sunday. October tenth.* She had forgotten, after all.

After lunch, Sarah started in on the household chores, with Lois helping. Andrew figured, since it was a special occasion what with Jake being back and all, that Lois was being magnanimous in assisting Sarah in the housekeeping duties. It was odd, though, that Sarah seemed quite comfortable with this arrangement.

Andrew's mother and Jake decided to go for a walk, as it was a lovely day. They urged Andrew to come along but he told them he would really rather rest up. He spent the rest of the afternoon in his room, lying in bed, his heart heavy and his stomach churning with anger.

She had forgotten! How could she not remember his father's birthday? How could he believe that she missed him if she could just blithely accept a dinner invitation on the day when she should be remembering him, thinking of him...Maybe it was all just empty words, what she had said that morning: *I miss him too.*

Andrew punched his pillow. It was all lies, all a bunch of empty babble!

"Andrew?" Lois's query was accompanied by a light tap on his door. "Andrew, would you like to have some cookies and milk?"

"Come in," Andrew moaned.

The door opened and Lois walked in carrying a glass of milk, which she set down on the dresser. She went back to the hallway and returned with a plate of cookies.

"Just out of the oven." She extended the plate to him. "Oatmeal raisin."

Andrew took a cookie and nibbled on it. He tried to smile, to say something in appreciation for this small kindness, but his voice stuck in his throat. He grabbed the glass of milk, and sipped it slowly, hoping that Lois wouldn't notice the tears that splashed down his cheek and onto the sheets.

But she had. She took the dishtowel that was draped over her shoulder, and blotted his face.

"I'm—I'm just tired," Andrew sputtered. "I guess I'm a little worn out from everything."

"Why don't you take a nap, Andrew? I won't wake you for supper. Just come downstairs whenever you want and I'll fix you something to eat."

Andrew nodded. Lois pulled the shades and tiptoed out.

It was dark when Andrew awakened. At first he thought that he had slept all night, but it was dark outside and the clock on the dresser showed the time to be nine-thirty. He lay in bed for a few minutes, waves of despair washing over him.

She forgot all about it. She doesn't really care. If she still loved him she would have remembered....

Andrew groaned and heaved himself out of bed. Maybe getting up, having a bite to eat, would take his mind off the wretched refrain that played through his head like a broken record.

She didn't even remember...She doesn't care at all...She doesn't miss him one bit....

He padded down the stairs. Mr. Givens was reading the newspaper in the living room. *US Naval Guns Smash Japs on Wake Island; Nazis Attack 8th Army*, the headline read. He glanced up.

"Hello, Andrew. Feeling better?"

"Andrew?" Lois stood in the doorway to the kitchen, wiping her hands on a dishtowel. "Would you like some supper?"

Andrew nodded.

"What would you rather have? Leftover roast beef or some meat loaf?"

"Roast beef, I guess."

"Well sit yourself down in the breakfast room. It'll be ready in a few minutes."

Andrew shuffled out to the breakfast room. Presently Lois brought in a plate of roast beef, potatoes, and sweet corn.

"How are you feeling, Andrew?"

"Better, I guess. I was surprised I slept so long. I only meant to take a short nap."

"Well, what with everything, I imagine it's all very overwhelming—your trip, coming here, everything so different."

Andrew nodded weakly, then began to eat his food.

They heard the sound of the front door opening and Jake's voice in the living room. A muttered reply from Mr. Givens, soothing, cheery words from Andrew's mother, and then Jake appeared in the breakfast room.

"Hi Mom." He gave Lois a kiss on the cheek.

"How was dinner?" Lois asked.

"Terrific."

"Which room did you eat in?"

"The Delaware Crossing Room."

Andrew's mother exchanged a few more pleasant words with Mr. Givens. Her buoyant laugh preceded her entrance into the breakfast room. As she slipped her hand into Jake's, she smiled at Andrew.

"Darling, did you have a nice nap?"

Andrew nodded. His mother went on. "When we got home from our walk, you were asleep. I guess all the excitement finally got to you. Are you feeling better?"

"Yes, Mum."

She pressed her hand to his forehead and evinced a worried frown.

"I'm fine, Mum," he insisted, a little irritated.

His mother turned to Lois.

"He was *ever* so ill with pneumonia this past winter. Had to be put in *hospital!*"

"Yes, you wrote to me about that," Lois said.

"Please see that he gets lots of rest and that he doesn't overexert himself. He tires easily and mustn't be allowed to get exhausted. Or chilled." She turned to Andrew. "Bundle up properly when it's cold, darling."

"Yes, Mum."

"Be careful *not* to get your feet wet."

"Yes, Mum."

"You *did* bring your flannel pajamas and sweater, didn't you?"

"Yes, Mum."

"We'll go clothes shopping in Plainfield on Saturday and get him a whole new wardrobe!" Lois said.

"Lovely!" Andrew's mother exclaimed.

"Did you two have a nice time at dinner?" Lois asked.

"Marvelous! We had a table right under a gigantic painting of Washington crossing the Delaware." She winked at Jake.

Jake laughed. "Alice gave the waitress a hard time about that. She laid the English accent on very thick and said haughtily,'I say, I think it was very unsporting of you colonists to attack on Christmas Eve.'"

Lois laughed. "What did the waitress say to that?"

Andrew's mother grinned. "She said that it just goes to show that a handful of Englishmen, no matter how ill-equipped and out-numbered, could beat a bunch of Germans anytime!"

"Germans!" Andrew blurted out.

"Hessian mercenaries," Jake explained. "The British hired German soldiers to do a lot of the fighting during the Revolutionary War."

Andrew stabbed the last piece of roast beef on his plate, popped it in his mouth, chewed it in short order. He stood, and asked Lois, "Is it all right if I take a bath now?"

"Sure, anytime. You don't have to ask permission."

Andrew took a deep breath, then glanced at his mother. "Good night, Mum. You don't have to wait up for me. I'll see you in the morning." He hesitated a moment, then kissed her quickly on the cheek.

"Good night, darling," she murmured.

Andrew walked briskly out of the room, climbed the stairs, and got his things together to take a bath. He thought a long, hot soak would relax him, but he was just as tense after half an hour in the tub as he'd been before. As he was toweling off, he heard his mother and Jake climbing the stairs, their voices animated and carefree. He waited until he heard them enter their room, then threw on his clothes and slipped down the hall. As he passed by the guest room, he heard the sound of soft laughter from behind the closed door.

He awoke late the next morning and found Lindy asleep at his feet again—he must have slipped in during the night. Andrew reached over and stroked the striped fur. Lindy responded with a throaty purr.

There was a tap on the door.

"Andrew?" It was his mother. She slowly opened the door.

"Sorry, Mum—I must have overslept. What time is—"

"Ten-thirty, and no, you don't have to worry about getting up early. I just thought that if you slept too late, you would have trouble getting to sleep tonight. But you can stay in bed all day if you like." She smiled as she sat down on the bed; then her face took on a serious, disturbed cast.

"Mum, is everything all right?" Andrew tried to inject a note of concern into his voice as he secretly rejoiced.

Maybe she had a disagreement with Jake. Or perhaps she's worrying about something having to do with him....

She took a deep breath and closed her eyes.

"Mum—?"

"Oh, Andrew, I'm so sorry. I forgot, I completely forgot, and there's no excuse for it!" Her words spilled out in a torrent of guilt and self-recrimination. "Your father's birthday. Oh darling, I can't believe I didn't remember—"

"Mum, I understand. What with all the excitement, coming here, everything so different, and Jake—" Andrew paused. "Well, I know that Jake and his father don't get along, and I know you're concerned—"

"Oh Andrew!" His mother threw her arms around him and squeezed him tight. "You're so wonderfully understanding—" Her voice broke, then she released him, drew back a little, and gazed at him. She stroked his cheek and whispered, "You're so much like him, in every way...."

Andrew put his arms around her. He wanted to say something comforting to her, but his voice caught in his throat. It was enough to share the silence with her, to feel the peaceful communion of their hearts bound together by words that need not be spoken.

After a long, long time she said brightly, "Well, I thought it would be nice if we could spend Sunday together, just the two of us, doing something special. Does that sound like a good idea?"

Andrew nodded. "I'd like that very much."

"Well, then, let's go downstairs and have some breakfast. Jake's mother has biscuits, eggs, and bacon ready. We can do our planning on a full stomach—how does that sound?"

"All right."

"Then get yourself dressed and come downstairs. Oh, Jake's mother did your laundry yesterday. I'll get it." She departed, then returned with a wicker basket of his clean clothes, all neatly folded. His treasure box and the model Spitfire that Jake had given him rested on top. "They were packed in your suitcase," she said. "Would you like me to put them on top of your dresser?"

Andrew nodded. She set the basket on the floor and put the plane and the box on the dresser, then gave him a swift kiss on the cheek before departing.

"Here's my book of red stamps and a list of what we need—flank steak, hamburger meat, bacon, and sausage. Are you sure you don't mind doing this, Jake?" Lois asked.

"Not at all. I was going to go for a walk anyway, so I might as well have a mission. Besides, I'd like to see Mr. Kozac again."

"So you have to use these stamps when you go shopping?" Andrew's mother peered at the book of stamps.

"We get red and blue stamps. Red stamps are for meat and dairy products, blue stamps are for canned goods," Lois told her. "Every month the points change, depending on the supply of certain items. This month flank steak is eleven points a pound, hamburger meat is six points a pound, sausage is five."

"Oh, my, it seems very complicated."

"You have rationing in England, too."

"Well, we have a ration book to allot certain things, like meat, eggs, cheese, sugar, and tea. I usually lived in a billet and handed my ration book over to the people I lived with. When I was home this summer after my accident, the cook took care of the shopping."

"Jake wrote to me about your accident. That must have been frightening."

"Oh, I didn't have time to be scared; it was nothing serious, really. I just got a broken arm and a nasty bump on the head. What upset me more than anything was the fact that I'd pranged the kite."

Andrew was perturbed that his mother seemed to take the incident so lightly—this, the most terrifying experience of his life! His stomach knotted up as he remembered the sound of the Spitfire's engine cutting out, and the sight of his mother in the hospital, still and silent as in death....

"...I'd *never* had an accident before and was proud of my record. Pauline Gower was very stern about that, that we get our deliveries in without mishap. It was understandable, considering the attitude of many of the men towards women pilots. Pauline wanted us to have a spotless record, or at least a blameless one, so that no one could point a finger at us and say that we couldn't do the job properly. In the first year of the war, she'd fought a tough battle with the Air Ministry to get women pilots recognized as competent to fly operational aircraft. Any mishaps or delays were taken very seriously. She insisted that she didn't want us to so much as bend a blade of grass when we took off or landed. The investigation of my accident put the blame solely on mechanical failure, and my ferry pool commander wrote me that it was fortunate I was familiar with the area and knew where I could land safely. But I was still upset."

"I still think you should have ditched the plane." Jake kissed her gently on the lips. "Well, it's over, and it wasn't your fault. "Besides, everyone is entitled to at least one prang. Look at my record. Prangs and wizard prangs galore."

"*Prangs* and *wizard prangs?*" Lois asked, bewildered

Andrew's mother explained: "A prang is when you do a bit of damage. A wizard prang is when the plane is...how do you Americans say it? Oh, right, when it's *a complete write-off.*" She looked at Jake and furrowed her brow. "Well, flying Hurricats off of CAM-ships can give you quite a respectable score of wizard prangs." She kissed Jake firmly, as if chastising him. "Thank God you didn't do that for long."

"What's this about Hurricats?" Lois asked.

Andrew's mother glanced at her, surprised, then back at Jake, perturbed. The unspoken words conveyed the accusation: *Do you mean you haven't told her?*

Jake cleared his throat. "Well, I'd better get to the butcher's. He grabbed Lois's ration book. "I'll buy."

"No you won't," Lois said, but Jake was already out the front door.

Lois turned to Andrew's mother and said, "Now, what's this about Hurricats?"

Andrew's mother bit her lip and looked away for a second, like a child called to account for the misdeeds of playmates. She looked back at Lois and said, "Why don't you put on another pot of coffee and we'll sit down and talk about it."

Andrew watched in consternation as the minute hand on the kitchen clock slowly swept from three to nine. His mother had suggested that he go upstairs and "tidy up" so that she could be alone with Lois for "just a few minutes."

Even when Jake's not around, he can still manage to ruin things!

The voices in the breakfast room suddenly became more audible and distinct as the door was opened and the women walked down the passageway to the kitchen.

"...Getting pneumonia probably saved his life," Andrew's mother was saying. "After he recovered they had mostly switched to Jeep carriers, so no more one-way rides. Jake then went back to his own fighter squadron."

"So Jake flew Hurricats after he was at Training Command?" Lois asked. "He wrote to me that he had been assigned to Training Command after he had recovered from his accident. I was relieved because it sounded like something that was, well, less risky."

"He *was* assigned to Training Command but he didn't want to go, so he arranged a transfer to Hurricats."

"He didn't tell me *that.* So, he wasn't assigned to the Hurricats, then?"

"No, it was strictly volunteers only. He made only three trips—the last one was the one when he was in the water for almost five minutes. If he had been in the Western Approaches or on the Malta Run it wouldn't have been so bad, but this was on the run to Murmansk and the water was much colder...."

Lois took a deep breath and looked away. Andrew's mother laid her hand on Lois's arm. "Well, now that he's flying Mosquitos he's as safe as someone flying a desk in London. They haven't lost a photo-recon Mossie yet. They're up at forty thousand feet and by the time the Germans know they're there, which isn't often, the Mossies are halfway back to England before the Luftwaffe can get its fighters up to that altitude."

"So when did he start flying Mosquitos?"

"Just before we got married," Andrew's mother smiled. Lois squeezed her hand.

Andrew leaned back against the sink, folded his arms, and glared at the floor. His mother put her arms around him.

"Well, what would you like to do today?"

Andrew shrugged.

"I'm going outside to pick some corn." Lois started down the passageway to the back door. "Today's my neighborhood shopping day. I trade corn and peaches for things from the neighbors: raspberries from Alida—she has a greenhouse—mushrooms from Rhoda Wagner, walnuts from Mrs. Swift, and green peppers from Mrs. Schaeffer. We'll all go together. Everyone's looking forward to meeting you two."

"Darling, let's help out." Andrew's mother gave him a gentle nudge out the back door.

There were some bushel baskets piled on the back porch. Lois grabbed two and handed one apiece to Andrew and his mother. "I'll pick, and you two can tote."

Andrew had not even seen the back yard yet. The only window facing the back was in the breakfast room, and the view was blocked by large bushes up against it. He was surprised to find that the yard was quite large. From the street, the houses seemed very close together and the front lawns quite small, so Andrew had assumed that the back yards were like the postage stamp-sized back gardens found in the towns in England. He surveyed Lois's domain: One side of the yard was given over to sweet corn, the stalks bunched together in several square-shaped patches. A path went down the middle of the yard; to the other side was a vegetable garden. Beyond that, at the very back of the property, was a small orchard of several peach trees.

"...this lot is double-deep," Lois was saying, "So the back yard extends all the way to the street behind. We bought both lots when we had the house built because I wanted room to grow corn and have a vegetable garden and a few fruit trees. The peaches I can in the summer—there's enough to last all year. I also make up a big batch of corn relish in the fall and put that up too...."

Lois picked a few dozen ears of sweet corn and put them in the baskets which Andrew and his mother carried. That task finished, they returned to the house. Lois picked up another bushel basket on the back porch and went into the pantry, which was located between the kitchen and the breakfast room. Andrew followed her. To his surprise, the pantry was quite large, with shelves running down both sides and a small window at the end. The top two shelves on the right side held nothing but pint-sized Mason jars of peaches, gleaming like golden jewels.

"This is just ready stock," Lois said. "I've got a whole storeroom full of canned peaches and corn relish in the basement." She took three jars of peaches off the top shelf and put them in one of the baskets.

"Well, let's get going," Lois said. "All the neighbors have been dying to meet both of you."

The last thing Andrew wanted was to be paraded around the neighborhood like a prized pig.

"I think I'll lie down for awhile, Mum. I'm still feeling a bit tired."

"Oh, dear, you aren't coming down with something, are you?"

"No, I'm just tired, that's all." He gave his mother a quick kiss and fled up the stairs.

Hearing his mother's voice from the front walk, Andrew descended the stairs. He found Jake sitting on the sofa, his feet up on the coffee table as he read the newspaper. Andrew glanced at the headline on the front page: *Yank Landing on Wake Island Hinted; Japs Quit Vila Airbase*. Smaller letters heralded another story: *3 Key Nazi Cities Hit After London Attack*.

No doubt about what news had priority here—as far as the Americans were concerned, Europe was just a sideshow!

Jake lowered the newspaper and looked up. "Hi, Andrew."

Lois and Andrew's mother burst in through the front door. They were laughing and chattering.

"Well, how was your expedition to the butcher's?" Lois asked Jake.

"I put everything in the refrigerator. Mr. Kozak gave me a canvas bag to carry everything in."

"Oh gosh, I forgot to give you my shopping bag."

"No problem, he said you could return it sometime next week. Well, what's for snack?"

"The bottomless pit returns," Lois laughed.

"I'm still full from that apple cobbler," Andrew's mother groaned.

"Apple cobbler? I didn't see any apple cobbler," Jake said.

"You have to go to Rhoda Wagner's to get it," Lois told him.

"Oh-oh, I'm not sure I'm up to the inquisition that's sure to accompany it."

"Don't worry, we told her all your dirty little secrets."

"All?"

"No, not all," Andrew's mother said.

"Your stint on Hurricats, for one." Lois looked accusingly, but not too harshly, at Jake. Jake went over and put his arms around her. "You told me you had been assigned to Training Command," Lois said.

"I was."

"Jake—"

"Listen, I didn't want you to worry. Besides, I wasn't on the CAM-ships very long."

"So I'm told."

Jake hugged her. "I don't want to talk about it now. How about if I take you out to dinner—say, Sunday night? We can talk about it then, okay?"

"Okay."

"And um....It wouldn't do Dad any good to know about this, I mean...uhhh...No need to throw more fuel on the fire, know what I mean?"

"Loose lips sink ships." Pressing her finger to Jake's lips, Lois whispered, "Mum's the word."

"What the hell is a Hurricat?" Mr. Givens lowered his newspaper and glared at Andrew.

"Oh, I thought he told you," Andrew said.

Mr. Givens stared balefully at Andrew.

"Oh, I'm sorry; I guess he didn't want you to know." With Lois loudly clattering around in the kitchen, and his mother and Jake upstairs in their room "chatting," Andrew thought that this would be an opportune time to make Mr. Givens aware of Jake's misadventures.

Mr. Givens continued to glare at Andrew.

"Please don't tell him that I told you. He might get angry at me," Andrew pleaded. "I mean, it's all right if you want to talk to him about it, just don't mention that I told you."

Mr. Givens grunted. Andrew went on. "I just know he was on the Murmansk run."

"Murmansk!"

"Yes, you see the Hurricat was catapulted off of a CAM-ship—that's short for Catapult Aircraft Merchant ship. The Hurricat couldn't land on the ship afterwards, so the pilot bailed out into the sea and was picked up. They said that it was a duty only for crazy Polacks."

"Crazy Polacks?"

"Crazy Polacks and, um, who else?" Andrew bit his lip and furrowed his brow. "Oh, right, hot shots! That's right—crazy Polacks and hot shots!"

Mr. Givens snapped his newspaper open and glared at it. Andrew retreated to the kitchen.

"So, I heard you were on Hurricats and CAM-ships," Mr. Givens said tersely.

Jake abruptly stopped chewing his food and looked at his father, fear and alarm in his eyes. He finished chewing his food, swallowed, and said simply, "That's right." He stabbed another piece of steak.

"More mushrooms, anyone?" Lois's eyes searched back and forth as if trying to discern how Mr. Givens had been made aware of this interesting bit of information. Andrew, his face impassive with concentration, methodically cut his steak into small pieces.

"Thanks Mom, yes." Jake passed his plate to her and Lois ladled out a spoonful of sauteed mushrooms.

"Peas?" Lois asked.

"Thanks—oh, just one spoonful."

"You know, you can mix your peas and mushrooms together," Lois chirped. "They're quite tasty that way. I didn't want to do it in the serving bowl because I figured that some people would rather eat them separately. Sometimes people like to put mushrooms on their steak, instead—"

"So you were on these catapulted—" Mr. Givens said.

"Catapulted Aircraft Merchant ships, Dad."

Mr. Givens grunted. "And what was the whole purpose of this?"

"It was to protect the Lend-Lease convoys. The Germans had these long-ranged, four engined planes, Focke-Wulf Condors, that would find the convoys and radio their position to the U-Boats. We'd get the Condors on radar and launch the Hurricats to shoot them down before they found the convoy."

"So this is where you fit in?"

"Yeah."

"And these Lend-Lease convoys were headed to—"

"Murmansk, Dad."

"Murmansk!" Mr. Givens snorted. "Roosevelt's biggest mistake was giving those Commies all that loot without even extracting any kind of guarantee that they'd pay us back—"

"They've been fighting the Nazis for over two years, Dad. They tied up over three mill.un German soldiers on the Eastern Front. They broke the back of the German army at Kursk—"

"Kursk—where the hell is that?"

"Kursk was the biggest tank battle in history, Dad. This past July—"

"That's besides the point. All I'm saying is that the Russians are nothing but a bunch of chiselers. They want something for nothing—"

"They've been doing most of the dying in this war, Dad. If Hitler hadn't decided to attack Russia in 1941—I don't know what would have happened to England. Maybe we might have held out, maybe not—"

"We!"

"The Allies, I mean." Jake threw his napkin down on his plate. "The Russians wore the Germans down. We couldn't have defeated the Germans in North Africa, we couldn't have gone into Italy if it hadn't been for the Russians doing the fighting and dying first. I'd say that's enough compensation for all the equipment we've sent them—"

"Well, I guess you can afford to be generous with other people's money, seeing as you're not an American taxpayer."

Jake's jaw twitched.

"How about some nice peach-raspberry pie?" Lois inquired cheerily. "Alice helped me crack the walnuts for the crust, and it has that delicious cream filling that you like so much, Gene—"

"Thanks Lois, I'll take a piece," Mr. Givens said.

"Jake?" Lois looked at Jake and touched his arm.

"No thanks Mom, I'm not hungry." Jake got up. "I think I'll go upstairs and, um, try to make some sense of my savings account. I don't see any deposits for this past May in my passbook."

"You didn't send any money that month. That was when you got married, remember? I figured you used your money for—

"Oh, right. Well, I still want to...um, look at things. Save a piece for me—I'll be down later." Jake walked briskly out of the dining room. Andrew heard his steps, double-time, on the stairs.

"Oh, this is *lovely*—I can't wait to see their faces!" Lois exclaimed.

Andrew watched in consternation as Rhoda and Alida set up a tier of little white pillars around the edge of a large round cake iced in white and garnished with lavender roses. Rhoda set a second layer on top.

"The top layer's chocolate, right?" Lois asked.

"Yes, I used your recipe," Rhoda said.

"They're going to be so delighted, don't you think, Andrew?" Lois smiled happily at Andrew, and Andrew, in order to be polite, returned her smile. "I can't get over their having a fake cake at their wedding. Tonight they get the real thing!"

"Did Alice have a nice time shopping today?" Alida asked Lois.

"My word, she was like a kid in a candy store! She bought dresses, blouses, slacks, nighties—a few nice hot little numbers, ought to really curl Jake's toes. Then we got Andrew completely outfitted in new school clothes. He looks so nice in long pants, doesn't he?" Lois beamed at Andrew. "Alice told me that it's illegal in England to make long pants for boys under twelve because of the shortage of cloth. Can you imagine!"

Rhoda and Alida shook their heads in amazement. A few of the neighbors started to filter in. Lois introduced Andrew to a middle-aged couple, Mr. and Mrs. Casini. They were the parents of Jake's best friend, Danny, who was a Seabee in the South Pacific.

"How's Danny doing?" Lois asked Mrs. Casini, who, to Andrew's surprise, spoke with a thick Irish brogue. "Building more airstrips?"

"Building airstrips and everything else," Mrs. Casini replied. "They built a hospital last week, and showers for the nurses. Danny offered to 'launch' the showers by being the first one to use them, and he invited all the Seabees and nurses to watch the ceremony!"

"Watch him take a shower?"

"Oh, he had his trunks on! But at least he could brag that he's been in the shower with a bunch of nurses!"

"He always was a silver-tongued devil!" Lois laughed. "I'm sorry Shannon couldn't be here."

"He'll be in New York for another week. Bonnie's father has been sick for so long, and it was no surprise that he finally passed on, but it would have been nice if Shannon could have seen Jake. Collie said she'll be able to come, though. She has a guitar lesson just after supper, but she'll be able to make it in time."

The phone rang and Lois went into the living room to answer it. After a moment, she returned.

"That was Helen," she told Mrs. Casini. "She says they'll be leaving in a few minutes. Jake and Alice think that they're just coming over here for dessert." She went to the stairs and called for Mr. Givens, who clumped down the stairs and proceeded to mumble around a few gruff welcomes.

A crowd of people was now milling about the house: all the neighbors, and friends of Jake's from school. Lois introduced them all to Andrew, who was presented in turn as "Jake's boy," much to his annoyance, though he tried to hide his feelings. He greeted everyone politely, but coolly. Let them think it was typical English reserve!

He thought that there might be a chance to slip upstairs but he was backed into a corner by Rhoda, who wanted to know all about how Jake and his mother had met, how often they saw each other, if they planned on having a family, and, if so, how many children, where they planned on settling down....

There was a crunch of gravel in the driveway and Lois called to everyone to get into the dining room. She closed the double doors, and she and Andrew and Mr. Givens sat in the living room. Jake and Andrew's mother walked through the entrance, followed by a woman who was obviously pregnant and a man who had hooks for hands. Pleasantries were exchanged; then Lois suggested that they all go into the dining room to have coffee and cake.

"Chocolate, I hope?" Jake laughed.

"See for yourself!" she chirped.

Jake opened the doors to the dining room and was greeted with a tumultuous blast: *Surprise!* Jake stood stunned for a moment, then a wide smile split his face; Andrew's mother, startled at first, dissolved in a fit of giggles and shrieks of delight as they were enveloped by the crowd. Lois happily flitted around the fringes while Mr. Givens chatted, glum-faced, with Mr. Casini.

With everyone so preoccupied, Andrew at last got the chance to slip, unnoticed, up to his room.

Andrew was putting his dirty clothes into the hamper in the spare room when he heard his mother's voice from the guest room, as clear and audible as if she were standing next to him. He examined the adjoining wall and found that it was a partition wall; evidently the guest room and the spare room had at one time been a single room and had subsequently divided in two.

"...I was just thrilled! It just the most wonderful thing—I can't get over how kind and friendly everyone is here—"

"Well, we Yanks aren't all a bunch of obnoxious barbarians, despite what you Brits think," Jake said.

A high pitched giggle and a soft smack preceded Andrew's mother's response: "I didn't mean it that way—you know that! Your mother seemed so nice, and I could tell from her letters that we would get along famously, but she's even more wonderful than I could have ever imagined!" There was a brief pause; then she spoke again, but this time in a voice that was subdued and dead serious.

"Are you going to tell her?"

"No."

"There's no good reason to keep it from her."

"There's no good reason to tell her, either."

A pause; then Andrew's mother spoke again. "I know she'd understand."

"That's not the point. I don't think it's right to burden her with it and expect her to keep it from him—"

"I know she wouldn't tell him if you asked her—"

"Listen, when I decided to join the RAF I didn't tell my father—you know that—but I didn't tell my mother either. I didn't want to put her in the position of having to keep a secret from my father. She has a heart of gold, but she doesn't dissemble very well. I'm afraid he might suspect—"

"He's going to have to find out sometime. You can't keep it from him forever."

"If I have to, I will."

"Jake—"

A feeling of triumph rose within Andrew. This was better than anything he could have hoped for. It had all the makings of a first-class row! He had never, *ever*, heard a cross word between his parents—not even the faintest *hint* of a disagreement—*real* disagreement, that is. Andrew had hoped to sow discord between Jake and his father, but now to have conflict between his mother and Jake—absolutely super! He bit his lip in excitement.

"Alice, please. All right, maybe not forever, but not now. Okay? I don't think he'd understand."

There was a pause, then whispering from Andrew's mother. Andrew couldn't quite make out what she was saying. Then silence. No sounds of gently-spoken endearments, soft laughter, or love-making. He waited a few more minutes....

Nothing but silence.

Good.

Andrew tiptoed out and walked softly down the hall to his room. Flushed with triumph, he threw himself down on his bed and folded his arms behind his head. He looked up at the ceiling and smiled. Lindy, who had been sleeping on the rug, hopped up onto the bed and approached Andrew. Andrew stroked his back, and Lindy arched his body and purred. Then he settled down next to Andrew.

Andrew caressed Lindy's ears, which he seemed to adore; he purred louder and closed his eyes in bliss. Andrew wondered what horrible secret it was that Jake wished to keep from his father. It would be nice to know what it was, so that he could mention it sometime to Mr. Givens. No matter—whatever it was, Jake was upset enough already about it, and tension in the house was high. Andrew remembered Jake's words: *There's no good reason to burden her with it and expect her to keep it from him. I don't think he'd understand.*

It never occurred to Andrew that Jake was *not* talking about his father.

Chapter 30

"Andrew, wake up—it's our special day." Andrew heard his mother's voice, felt her gently shaking him. He rolled over, opened his eyes and grunted.

"We'll go to church this morning, then spend the rest of the day together, all right, darling?"

"What?" he mumbled.

"It's your father's birthday, remember? Why don't you get dressed and come down right away. Lois is making a special breakfast for us this morning."

Andrew nodded and his mother withdrew. His father's birthday! He did a quick mental calculation: His father would be thirty-three today.

Where is he? France, Germany, Belgium, Holland...If only I knew! Is he hiding out in the country, in a city, or is he in a prison camp...If only, somehow, some way, he could contact me again—like he did when I was bombed, and then again when I was so ill. If only I could hear his voice, feel his arms around me, even if it isn't really happening, just a promise that he's with me in spirit, at least....

He threw his clothes on and hurried downstairs. Wonderful smells, as usual, were coming from the kitchen.

"Have a seat in the dining room, Andrew," Lois called.

Only Mr. Givens was seated at the table. He was drinking coffee and reading the Sunday morning paper. Andrew heard Lois and his mother bustling about in the kitchen.

"...yes, and then you pour it over everything," Andrew's mother was saying. In a few minutes, Lois appeared, carrying a plate in each hand. She set one plate in front of Mr. Givens and one in front of Andrew. Andrew's eyes widened.

"Eggs Benedict!"

Lois smiled. "It was your mother's idea. I hope it's just as good as what you're used to."

Andrew's mother came in through the doorway with another two plates. "I thought it would be a nice way to celebrate your father's birthday. Remember how mad he was on Eggs Benedict?"

"I've almost forgotten what if tastes like, but it looks super!" It *did* look wonderful, but Andrew was more delighted by the fact that his mother had thought to remember his father this way.

"Well, dig in, you two!" Lois urged.

Mr. Givens put his paper down and proceeded to eat.

"Mmph, good," he said between mouthfuls.

Andrew took a bite. "It's delicious," he agreed.

Jake came into the dining room.

"Sit down and stuff yourself," Lois told him. "I'll fix you a plate."

Jake smiled a quick, terse smile. "Gosh, it looks great, but I think I'll pass, Mom. I'm, uh—" Jake looked as if he were thinking up an excuse, "I'm afraid I might go to sleep in church on such a heavy breakfast. I'll fix myself some toast." He disappeared into the kitchen.

Just as Mr. Givens was finishing, Jake came into the dining room with a plate of toast.

"Would you like some more coffee, Gene?" Lois proffered the coffee pot to her husband.

"I'll take it in the sunroom." Mr. Givens stood, held out his cup to Lois, which she filled. He then took his newspaper and shuffled out to the sunroom.

Andrew's mother turned to Jake. "Darling, just try a bite. It's ever so delicious." She cut a piece and offered it to Jake on her fork. He opened his mouth, and she fed him the morsel.

"Good," he said. "Well, I'll have it some other time, okay?"

"I'll make it again before you leave next Monday," Lois promised.

Monday! Dismay knifed through Andrew's cheerful mood. Just a little more than a week to persuade his mother that he should leave with her....

He felt an awful lurch in his stomach. What if he couldn't persuade her to let him leave? What if, despite all his protestations and arguments, he found himself stranded in this terrible place, while his mother went back to England...with Jake? Their duties would keep them apart for most of the time, but still, they would manage to see one another. And the fact that Andrew's mother would not have to divide her free time between the two of them meant that she would certainly be spending almost all of her time off with Jake. Not to mention the ferry deliveries to his base....

His mother had said that Jake was just as safe flying Mosquitos as he would be sitting behind a desk in London.

Too bad. If only Jake were doing something a little risky. In the event that Andrew *was* forced to remain in this place (*surely* his mother wouldn't force him, but just in case) it would be nice if Jake were in a more dangerous line of work.

But there was really nothing he could do about the flying duties Jake had chosen. He stabbed the last piece of Eggs Benedict with his fork, popped it in his mouth, and chewed it thoughtfully.

On the other hand, perhaps there *was* something he could do.

"Please turn to Hebrews, Chapter 11, for this morning's Scripture reading."

The fluttering of pages being turned sounded like dry leaves blowing across a courtyard. Andrew's mother pulled out a Bible from the hymnal rack in front of them and shared it with Andrew and Jake, who was sitting on the opposite side of her, to her right. Andrew sat between his mother and Lois, and Mr. Givens sat to Lois's left. The noise died down as everyone found the passage the minister had indicated. He cleared his throat and read aloud:

Now faith is the substance of things hoped for, the evidence of things not seen.

The words exploded on Andrew's sorrow-strained soul like a grenade. *The substance of things hoped for...the evidence of things not seen.* He had not seen his father for over three years. How he longed to just see him, somehow, someway, just once! Or to get a picture, or a letter—*something!* It seemed to Andrew that his faith that his father was still alive was sometimes stretched to the breaking point. How easy it would be to go on believing if he had some indication, anything at all—even a word spoken by an escaped prisoner! Just some tangible proof that his father still lived! Andrew looked at the words again. It was as if God Himself were telling him to have faith, not to give up hope, and, despite the absence of proof, to believe with all his heart in his father's return.

Women received their dead raised back to life....

The rest of the Scripture reading, and the sermon that followed, were a blur of words to Andrew. The whirlwind revelation he had just experienced blocked all else out. *Women received their dead raised back to life.* He looked at his mother, who was sitting erect and still, her eyes focused on the minister at the pulpit, her hand in Jake's. Andrew wanted to grab her, make her see: *If you believe that Dad will come back, it will happen!*

Andrew's enforced silence during the rest of the sermon caused him to rethink his impulse. No, that wouldn't be wise. It would just upset her and she would start worrying again. Besides, the Bible didn't mention anything about needing more than one person to believe in something. It would be enough that Andrew, alone, kept faith in his father's return.

"Please turn to hymn number thirty-three."

Thirty-three! Today was his father's thirty-third birthday!

It's a sign, a sign that God is pleased with my faith! My father will return!

The hymn wasn't a song Andrew knew; indeed, all of the hymns here were new and strange, except for the Doxology sung at the beginning of the service. No matter, it was the fact that it was number thirty-three that was important. What clever ways God had of giving people special messages!

Andrew looked outside his window at the beautiful blue sky and the vivid autumn foliage: riotous splashes of yellow, orange, and red.

I can not think of the autumn's flare, Without me here...alive...aware....

His father *was* alive, and aware. The poem that he'd marked was a promise. The fact that the book had survived intact, when Armus House and everything in it was blown to smithereens, was an added assurance that he lived, and someday would return. Andrew had never felt more convinced of it. He hoped that his father was at this very moment enjoying a beautiful autumn's day, feeling the sunshine on his face, seeing a tree bright with autumn's colors.

Please God, please not in a cell, cooped up. Even if he is in a prison camp, at least let him be allowed to go for walks outdoors. Better yet, free somewhere, though still living in hiding and unable to get back across enemy lines...maybe on a farm in the country, or in the mountains. I understand that he can't get word to me. Just please keep him safe.

Andrew opened his treasure box and took out his father's book. He sat on the bed and read the poem once, and then again. He closed the book and repeated it to himself one more time, then looked out the window at the bright blue sky, at the flare of colors in the trees.

"Happy Birthday, Dad," he whispered.

"Whatever happened to the Puss Moth?" Andrew asked his mother. They were enjoying the picnic lunch Lois had packed, and basking in the golden autumn sunshine at a pleasantly serene park. They had spread out one of Lois's old quilts, and now sat on it as they gazed at the nearby lake that reflected the surrounding trees like a mirror. A few ducks glided across the water, momentarily marring the surface.

"We sold it the year before the war started. Probably a good thing we did too, since the government requisitioned civil airplanes early in the war."

"I loved it when you'd fly and Dad and I would sit in the back seat. I thought it was great the way you and he took turns at the controls. When you'd fly, he'd tell me all about what you were doing. I liked sitting next to you too, but I really liked watching you fly the plane."

His mother lay back on the blanket and smiled blissfully. "Your father was a good flying partner, and a good teacher. He had such a gift for instructing: He was a perfectionist, but very patient. Whenever he was teaching me a new maneuver or giving a bit of instruction, he never did it condescendingly, or with a critical attitude. He corrected, but gently, so that I didn't feel tense about it the next time."

Andrew closed his eyes, envisioned himself and his father sitting together in the back seat of the Puss Moth, while his mother flew the plane.

We'll do it again, the three of us, someday....

His mother gazed at the sky, then looked at him. "Why don't we take a walk around the lake? Jake said he'd pick us up at four, so we have enough time to go for a walk before he comes."

"Super."

They packed the dishes back in the picnic basket and put the litter in the trash can. Andrew's mother took his hand as they walked around the lake.

"Jake said he'd make reservations for us at the George Washington Inn. Oh, I hope you don't mind—he wanted to take his mother out to dinner too, so we're all going to go together in the car, but once there, we'll be in separate rooms. The Inn is a huge place and has several dining rooms, some large, some small. They have petrol rationing here too, not as strict as in England, but it would still be a good idea to go out together, instead of separately, so as to save on fuel. I asked Jake to get us a table near a large stone fireplace in one of the larger rooms. He and his mother are going to eat in one of the smaller rooms that Lois likes because it has a nice view. I hope it's all right with you."

"Fine." He squeezed his mother's hand to let her know that it was really all right.

As they walked along they reminisced about times before the war: the holidays spent in Scotland; visits to Eastbourne where they had "tromped up the downs" and had stood at the top of Beachy Head, looking out over the Channel; hikes they had done in the Lake District and in the mountains of North Wales. Andrew's mother talked freely about those days, but, as if by mutual agreement, they did not touch on anything that had happened after his father had joined the RAF, or anything having to do with the war at all. That was all too painful. It was enough that his mother could talk about the happy times before his father became a fighter pilot, the times that were to her now sweet memories.

If only they were more than memories! If only she could believe that he's still alive...that we'll do all those things together, again!

"There's Jake!" They were halfway around the lake, and Andrew's mother was pointing at a figure standing by their picnic basket.

"It's not four o'clock, is it?"

Andrew's mother looked at her watch. "It's three-thirty. He said he might get here a bit early and go for a walk by himself." She waved to Jake and he lifted his hand in acknowledgement. He stood in place for a minute, and then proceeded to amble slowly around the lake, his hands thrust in his pockets, his eyes downcast. It was obvious that he was not trying to catch up with them.

Andrew's mother watched him for a moment. She bit her lip, concern on her face.

Jake must still be in a funk over that spat he and his father had the other night, Andrew thought. While he had decided that Jake's estrangement with his father was a good thing, he was still vexed about his mother's concern for Jake.

She should be thinking about Dad, not about Jake!

"Well, let's order dessert, shall we?" With a glance from his mother, the waitress came to their table. Andrew's mother asked for the dessert menus, which were delivered forthwith.

Andrew scanned the list of choices. He had positively stuffed himself on Yankee Pot Roast, but he hoped that the restaurant had what he was looking for. There, near the bottom!

He closed the menu. The waitress looked at him, waiting for his order. "I'll take the carrot cake, please."

"Andrew, you hate carrot cake!"

Andrew shrugged. "It's Dad's birthday."

"You still hate it, and it's silly to force yourself to eat something you detest just on principle."

"I really don't hate it that much."

"Yes, you do. I have an idea." She looked at the waitress. "I'll take the carrot cake. And please bring an order of...." she pointed to the menu and showed the waitress her choice. Then she turned to Andrew. "You may have a bite of my carrot cake. Your father would understand that you didn't want to eat the entire thing."

Andrew smiled. "All right." As they waited for their desserts, he sat back and viewed the room. It was decorated in the "Colonial" style, as his mother had pointed out, with a large painting of the Surrender at Yorktown hanging on the wall opposite them. British troops in scarlet uniforms marched in retreat as the Americans, in blue uniforms and various ragtag outfits, rejoiced at their departure.

"One order of carrot cake and one...." The waitress set a large dish in front of Andrew, "Cherry delight."

Andrew stared, astonished, at his dessert: Two scoops of vanilla ice cream topped with cherries in sauce.

"I thought you would appreciate it," his mother said.

The creamy, sweet taste of real ice cream delighted Andrew's taste buds. "It's very good. I'd almost forgotten what real ice cream tastes like."

His mother chuckled. "Remember this past spring when you said you were going to pray to God to give you some real ice cream? See, sometimes your prayers do get answered, after all!"

The ice cream stuck in Andrew's throat, and he had to swallow extra hard to force it down.

He *had* gotten what he had prayed for! But he had never *imagined* God would send him to America in order to answer his prayer. If only he had thought to qualify his request at the time! He should have prayed that God would not send him *three thousand miles away* in order to provide a dish of ice cream; He should have provided the ice cream *right here in England.* But how could he have known, have even *imagined*, that this would happen? After the wonderful revelation in church that morning, Andrew was beginning to think of God as a pretty decent chap, someone who would cheerfully obtain anything you wanted, sort of like a friendly shopkeeper who got whatever you asked for off a shelf and gave it to you with a smile. A regular chum. The idea that God sometimes had *other ideas* gave Andrew a deep sense of foreboding.

Sometimes God could have a pretty perverse sense of humor.

He was not amused.

"Aaagh—Jake! Right side of the road!"

"Sorry." Jake had made a left turn into the lane closest to them. Luckily, there was no oncoming traffic. He veered across the center line to the right side of the road.

"You're going to have a terrible time getting used to things again when you get back to England," Lois said.

"I don't plan to do any driving for awhile. We're going to take the train to Northumberland, stay there overnight, and then go by train again back to our bases. Then it's back to the wild blue yonder—no need to worry about what side you're supposed to be on."

"Now keep to the same lane when you turn here," Lois said. "Right turns, same lane."

"Right," Jake said.

The rest of the ride proceeded without incident. When they arrived home, they found Mr. Givens seated in his easy chair, reading the paper as usual.

"Did you have a nice time?" he asked.

"Wonderful!" Lois said. "Hope you weren't too lonely."

"Uh, no. Fact is, time passed so quickly, I didn't realize it was getting late. Special section here in the Sunday paper about the island hopping in the Pacific. Guadalcanal, Russel Island, New Georgia, Rendova, Vella Lavella—looks like the next stop is Bougainville, then on to Rabaul." He put the newspaper down. "After Pearl, it's good to know that our boys are giving the Japs a beating."

"Well, we'd better be turning in." Jake looked at Andrew's mother.

"Yes, Andrew starts school tomorrow, so we ought to get a good night's sleep," she agreed. She turned to Mr. Givens. "Andrew has to be at school at eight-thirty. Why don't you knock me up at a quarter to seven. That way, we'll have enough time to get ready."

Mr. Givens blanched. Lois's jaw dropped; she looked like a dead carp. There was total silence for a few moments.

"What she means, Dad," Jake said, his face a shade of deep claret, "is that she would like you to *wake* her up."

"Well, that's what I said, didn't I? I was saying that if he knocked me up—"

"Alice—" Jake tried to make frantic shushing noises, but he was so flustered he hissed like a deranged snake.

"Jake, what's the matter? Did I say something wrong? Oh dear, I don't know what it is, but I'm sorry—I didn't mean to offend." She looked at Jake's parents, chagrined, then back at Jake, her eyes pleading for an explanation.

"I'll tell you later," Jake told her.

"No, please tell me now—I want to apologize for whatever it was I was supposed to have said!"

Jake reddened even more and drew her a few feet away. He whispered into her ear. She listened intently at first, then her mouth dropped open in horror and she shrieked in dismay.

"Oh, *No!* Oh my God—" She looked at Jake, her eyes wide with shock. Then her expression became distressed and embarrassed. She shrieked again, then collapsed in laughter against Jake. He held her up, just barely, because he was now convulsed in laughter as well. Mr. Givens continued to stare at them, but a smile started to twitch the corners of his mouth. He looked at Lois, who was already overcome by a fit of giggles, and a broad grin spread across his face.

It was the first time that Andrew had ever seen him smile.

Chapter 31

What if I can't convince her that I shouldn't stay here?

After catching a few snatches of fitful sleep, interspersed with prolonged periods of wide-eyed, heart-thudding anxiety, Andrew awoke at four-thirty, too jittery to get back to sleep. It wasn't just the thought of being marooned in this wretched land that vexed him; it was the appalling prospect of starting school the next day. At church the day before Lois had introduced him to several boys "his own age." They were big, shambling, sullen-faced youths who glared at him suspiciously, then snickered behind his back.

Lindy lay at his feet, sleeping peacefully. At that moment Andrew would have given anything to be able to exchange his unpleasant human predicament for a serene feline existence. To have nothing more worrisome that finding just the right sunbeam to lie in; to eat, sleep, play, and have one's belly rubbed! He gently stroked Lindy with his foot; the cat responded by stretching in pleasure and uttering a soft meow.

"Lindy, come here, boy," Andrew whispered.

Lindy opened one eye, stretched again, and yawned widely. He then crept up the length of Andrew's body, padding so softly he seemed almost weightless. Arriving at Andrew's chest, he fixed Andrew with a critical glare, like that of a country squire evaluating a tradesman who has proposed to do some work on the estate. He executed a few counter-clockwise turns, then settled down and positioned himself, Sphinx-like, his face to Andrew. Andrew scratched Lindy's ears and stroked the side of his neck. Lindy blissfully lolled his head from side to side and purred.

At six-thirty he heard sounds of stirring from the rest of the house: talking in the bedrooms, steps in the hallway, the sound of water running. Groaning, he got out of bed, put on his robe, and stepped outside his door. He met Mr. Givens in the hall.

"Big day, huh, Andrew?"

Andrew nodded.

"I'll drive you there on my way to work."

"Thank you," Andrew said weakly.

"Well, see you downstairs."

After getting washed and dressed, Andrew shuffled down the stairs.

"Morning," Lois called. "Have a seat in the breakfast room. Do you want one egg or two?"

"One's fine."

Lois seemed more cheerful than usual, humming softly to herself as she bustled about the kitchen.

Mr. Givens was already seated at the breakfast table. There was a glass of milk at

Andrew's place, along with a smaller empty juice glass, which Andrew filled with orange juice from the pitcher. Lois came in with a plate of scrambled eggs, bacon, and toast for him.

"More toast, dear?" she asked Mr. Givens.

"Yes, please." Mr. Givens glanced at Lois, his face suffused with color. A smile darted across his lips. Lois moved behind him, leaned over, and whispered something in his ear. His smile grew broader; he cleared his throat and took another sip of coffee. Lois winked at him and took his plate, then returned with the toast.

As Mr. Givens munched his toast in distracted silence, Andrew ate the last of his meal, though he wasn't all that hungry. Eating seemed more an automatic motion than a pleasurable experience. A month ago, bacon would have been considered a rare treat, to be savored and enjoyed. Today, however, he might as well have been eating strips of tree bark.

Mr. Givens grunted, stood, and went into the kitchen. After a few minutes, Andrew did the same.

He found Mr. Givens drinking a cup of coffee by the stove. Lois was packing lunches. There were footfalls on the stairs. Andrew's mother came into the kitchen.

"Do you want a quick breakfast?," Lois asked her. "Gene's going to leave in a few minutes, but I can fix some toast."

"No, we're going out to breakfast after we get Andrew settled in school. Jake says there's a restaurant not too far away. We'll walk home afterwards—it's a beautiful day."

"Isn't it!" Lois agreed cheerfully.

Jake appeared in the doorway. The stove was located right next to the door, and he hesitated a bit, seeing his father standing there. Mr. Givens nodded at him.

"Coffee?" he asked.

Jake blinked and his eyes darted to Lois, then back to his father. "Uh...yeah. Thanks," he croaked.

Mr. Givens took a cup down from one of the hooks hanging behind the stove and poured Jake a cup.

"Cream and sugar, right?"

Jake nodded.

Mr. Givens put a heaping teaspoonful of sugar into the coffee, added a dollop of cream, stirred it, and handed it to Jake.

"Thanks." Jake's voice croaked again. He took the cup and sipped his coffee.

Mr. Givens grunted, and resumed drinking from his cup. His back was to Lois, who was next to the sink, so he did not see her standing there, stock still and mouth agape. Neither did he see Andrew's mother, who was leaning against the refrigerator. Her face glowed with rapture.

If Andrew had just witnessed Churchill sitting down to tea with Hitler, he would not have been more surprised.

Or dismayed. He watched Jake and his father, standing not more than two feet from one another, peacefully drinking from their cups. His mind frantically worked to make some sense out of it all. Just a temporary setback, he finally realized.

Just because you've lost the battle, doesn't mean you've lost the war.

"Here it is," Jake said. "Thanks, Dad."

Mr. Givens grunted. Andrew, his mother, and Jake got out of the car and stood before the school.

This was a *school?*

The building before them was a huge, hulking edifice of dark brick, two storeys tall, and overwhelmingly ugly. It was if it had been expressly designed to make people feel insignificant and demoralized. Looking more like a prison than a school, all it needed were bars on the windows to complete the effect.

They walked to the main entrance. There were already a few dozen children waiting outside.

"This is a high school and junior high. They have grades seven through twelve," Jake remarked, more to Andrew's mother than to Andrew. "I thought it might be a good idea to get here a little early." He held the door open for Andrew's mother. "They probably want us to fill out some forms first."

"The inevitable forms," Andrew's mother laughed. "We English left our mark on the colonies, after all."

They walked up a flight of stairs to a hallway; Jake ushered them into the office. There was a tall counter running the length of the room, separating it into a reception area in front and a workspace in back for two secretaries. To one side was a door with the word *Principal* stenciled on it, and a chair beside it. One of the secretaries rose from her desk and approached them. She was young, probably in her early twenties, with black hair and dark brown eyes.

"May I help you?"

"I'd like to enroll my son in school," Andrew's mother said. "We just arrived last week."

"I'll get you some forms to fill out." The secretary opened a drawer and took out a few printed pieces of paper. "The one on top is an information card. Why don't you fill that out now. You can take the rest home and return them tomorrow. Here's a pen."

Andrew's mother and Jake exchanged smiles; then Andrew's mother started filling in the card: *Name (last): Hadley-Trevelyan. Name (first): Andrew. Name (middle): Roger Leslie.*

"There's hardly enough room to fit it all in," Andrew's mother said. She wrote in small print, but still had barely enough room to scrunch everything in.

Date of Birth: March 4, 1931. Mother's name: Alice Givens. Father's name:

Andrew's mother paused, and signaled the secretary.

"His father was killed three years ago. This is his stepfather." She indicated Jake.

The girl bit her lip, picked up the form, and took it to the other secretary, an older woman, who was seated at the other desk. The younger secretary murmured to her, and the older one answered something in a low voice.

The young secretary returned and said, "Cross out the word father, put the name of his stepfather down, and write "stepfather" next to it. Andrew's mother did that, writing in the space: *Jacob Givens (stepfather)*

Just like that, Andrew thought, as he glared at the line drawn through the word "father." My father doesn't even get a mention at all. As far as they're concerned, he doesn't even exist.

Andrew's mother completed the form, indicating as guardians Jake's parents and putting down their address and phone number. The girl took it over to the older woman, who perused the form. The woman's jaw dropped and she turned to Jake. She lowered her reading glasses down onto her tip of her nose and peered over them.

"Jacob Givens!" she exclaimed.

"Mrs. O'Neal," he said shyly.

"My, what a welcome! Do you remember all the students so well?" Andrew's mother asked the woman.

"Just the ones who've made a lasting impression," Mrs. O'Neal replied.

"A good one, I hope," Andrew's mother said.

Mrs. O'Neal's silence was sufficient enough to deny that possibility. Jake smiled nervously.

"I see. You weren't jesting when you told me you were a naughty boy," Andrew's mother teased.

"Oh, not really naughty," Mrs. O'Neal laughed. "Just a little misguided. Behold...." She pointed to the chair next to the principal's door. "The Jacob Givens Memorial Chair!"

"Mr. Fisk isn't still here, is he?" Jake asked.

"No, he retired four years ago, with quite a few gray hairs, too."

"I hope he's forgotten that incident with the shaving cream," said Jake.

"He'll *never* forget that, Jake," Mrs. O'Neal answered gravely.

"*Shaving cream?*" Andrew's mother asked. Jake smiled enigmatically.

"Why don't you visit around after school's out, Jake?" Mrs. O'Neal suggested. "Some of your old teachers are still here: Mrs. Larsen, Miss Lashua, Mrs. Herbst...Oh, Eleanor!" Mrs. O'Neal hailed a middle aged woman who came into the office. "Three guesses as to who our distinguished visitor is!"

"The woman squinted at Jake, shook her head. "They all change so much—I haven't a clue."

"Jake Givens, Mrs. Larsen, come to pay my respects," Jake grinned.

"Jake Givens!" Mrs. Larsen exclaimed. "Well, it's about time—you never did pay this place any respect while you were here! What have you been doing with yourself? Keeping out of trouble, I hope."

"Only making trouble for the Luftwaffe, fortunately," Andrew's mother laughed. "Jake is a pilot in the Royal Air Force."

Mrs. Larsen arched her eyebrows and smiled at Andrew's mother. Andrew had never seen anyone hide astonishment so well. Jake introduced Andrew's mother, then Andrew, to Mrs. Larsen.

"The Royal Air Force, is it?" Mrs. Larsen chuckled. "The Americans already knew of your reputation as a troublemaker, then?"

Jake smiled. "I've been trying to stay out of trouble."

"For the most part, he's been a very good boy," Andrew's mother looked slyly at Jake. "Except for that prank you played on Bomber Command."

"Prank on Bomber Command?" Mrs. Larsen exclaimed. "I'd like to hear about that one!"

A bell rang. Mrs. Larsen said, "Oh dear, I'd better be getting to my class. Jake, why don't you stop by at lunchtime? I'd love to hear about your adventures and I'm sure the other teachers would want to meet you again."

Jake looked a little nervous. "Oh, I don't think so."

"Jake, please—I'm sure everyone else would *love* to see you," Mrs. Larsen pleaded.

Andrew's mother squeezed Jake's hand. "Darling, I think it sounds like a wonderful idea."

Jake took a deep breath, still uneasy.

"Jake, I'd love to!" Andrew's mother winked at him, then turned to Mrs. Larsen. "We'll be there."

Mrs. Larsen laughed. "You know where to find the faculty room, don't you Jake?"

Jake gave another enigmatic smile.

"It's down the hall from the cafeteria," Mrs. Larsen reminded him. "Of course, you can't follow your nose to find it anymore; we finally got the smell out." She winked at Jake. "*And* we found a good home for the skunk."

"*Skunk?*" Andrew's mother raised her eyebrows.

"I'm sure Jake would be happy to relate the details of *that* particular incident to you," Mrs. Larsen said as she departed.

"See you at lunch," Andrew's mother called.

"I'll be there, too," Mrs. O'Neal said. "Well, let's see about getting Andrew settled." She turned to the young secretary. "Consetta, we'll put Andrew in the seventh grade. Whose class has the least students right now?"

"Mrs. Tercek's—she had two students leave last week."

"Good," Mrs. O'Neal said. She turned to Andrew's mother. "We'll take care of everything. You can go."

Andrew's mother looked at Andrew. "Well, darling, we'll see you after school. Would you like us to come and meet you—"

"No, Mum, no." Andrew was adamant. "I can find my way home."

"If you get lost, you know the phone num—"

"Yes, Mum, I know."

"All right." She took a step toward him. Andrew stepped back. *Please don't*—

Jake took her arm. "Let's go."

"All right," she said softly.

As Andrew watched them walk out he wanted more than anything to be able to go with them. Maybe Dad feels like this, he thought. Trapped, far from home and familiar surroundings. This place did not have the intimate, homelike atmosphere he had known at Askew Court. It was more like an institution...a prison....

"This is your first time in an American school?" Mrs. O'Neal asked.

"Yes," Andrew mumbled.

"I'll show you to your class, then. Here's your schedule, and a map of the school." She walked out of the office into the hallway; Andrew followed. The interior of this horrid institution was just as repugnant as the exterior. The hallway was lined with metal lockers and tile; the floor was of appallingly ugly linoleum. He felt a stab of longing for the polished parquet floors and the wood paneled walls, burnished by time, of Askew Court.

"...Everyone in your homeroom goes to the same classes: Math, Science, English, Reading, History, Phys. Ed. and Health. Art class on Monday and Music on Wednesday. Study Hall on Tuesday, Thursday, and Friday. The room numbers are printed next to the class. Here's your homeroom." She indicated to Andrew to wait outside the door; he heard the sound of voices in unison reciting the words:

...indivisible, with liberty, and justice for all.

The sounds of scuffling feet and scraping of chairs followed. Mrs. O'Neal signaled Andrew to follow her into the classroom. The thing that Andrew noticed immediately was that the class was large, about twice the size of his class at Askew Court. He guessed there were about twenty-five or thirty pupils. And there were girls—*girls*! How could you learn with *girls* in class? And his teacher was a woman too! On top of that, everyone was dressed differently—no uniforms here!

"Mrs. Tercek, you have a new student." Mrs. O'Neal looked at the information card. "Andrew Hadley-Trevelyan."

Andrew noticed a few raised eyebrows and smirks.

"Hello, Andrew," Mrs. Tercek said. She was young, of medium build, with brown curly hair and prominent front teeth. "Where are you from?"

Andrew hesitated for a moment. He couldn't properly say that he was from Berkshire, since Armus House had been destroyed. He cleared his throat and replied, "Northumberland, England." There were a few titters and snickers from the class. Mrs. Tercek glowered at the culprits. Turning to Andrew, she said, "There's an empty seat in the back. Please be seated. We'll reorganize the seating next week, get everyone alphabetical."

As he took his seat, Andrew felt as if he were the two-headed boy on display in a circus sideshow. He looked down at the desk, knowing that all eyes in the room were upon him.

"Announcements, class," Mrs. Tercek said. "Mrs. Bischoff will be here on Wednesday to sell War Stamps, so remember to bring your money. And in case any of you have forgotten, tomorrow is Columbus Day, so there will be no school." This last announcement was greeted by cheers.

"Quiet, please." Mrs. Tercek glanced at the clock. "We have a few minutes before you have to go to your first class." She looked at Andrew. "Andrew, did you just arrive in America?"

Andrew felt the blood rush to his head. "Yes, last week."

Snickers and titters again.

"And how did you find America?"

"Turn left at Newfoundland," a voice from the back of room hollered. The class erupted in guffaws and giggles.

"Class, class!" Mrs. Tercek rapped her desk. The laughter subsided.

If you really want to know, Andrew thought, I find America to be the most obnoxious, repugnant, uncivilized, uncouth—

There was a buzzer, then the sound of commotion in the hallway. "Class dismissed," Mrs. Tercek called.

As he followed the other students out of the room, Andrew had another shock: Everyone in his class—*everyone*—was taller than him! *Even the girls!*

Out in the corridor, he had another shock. Everyone in the whole *school* was taller than him! Most of the students were as tall as grown-ups: They towered over him and there seemed to be hundreds and *hundreds* of them pushing through the halls. It was like rush hour at Paddington Station, only not as orderly! He found his first class: Reading, with Mrs. Larsen. She greeted Andrew warmly. Andrew nodded at her. By this time he had figured out that the less he opened his mouth, the better. Mrs. Larsen told him to take an empty seat near the back of the room. The day's lesson began, which was all about a book called *The Last of the Mohicans*. After class, Mrs. Larsen told Andrew to come up to her desk. She gave Andrew a copy of the book and told him to read as much as possible by Wednesday.

"We're halfway through the book." She handed him a sheet of questions about the story. "Please have these questions answered by the end of the week. Perhaps Jake can help you. He wasn't a very attentive student, but I do remember that he liked this story."

Andrew nodded. Not that I intend to ask for Jake's assistance, he thought to himself.

"Your next class is Math with Mrs. Malandreatos," Mrs. Larsen said. "It's just across the hall."

Andrew looked at his schedule: Period 2, Mathematics, Mrs. Malandreatos. As he walked across the hall he expected to find a short, dark woman with a heavy Greek accent, wearing a frumpy black dress, no doubt. He thought he was in the wrong room when he met with a tall, slim young woman with strawberry blond hair and a splash of freckles across her nose. He stood in the doorway and looked at his schedule again.

"Mathematics, Mrs. Malandreatos," the woman said. "And you are—"

Andrew walked up to her desk and said, as softly as he could, "Andrew Hadley-Trevelyan."

"Take a seat, Andrew." Mrs. Malandreatos went over to a bookcase under the window, pulled out a book, and gave it to Andrew.

The class was studying geometry: calculating circumferences, perimeters, and areas of various figures, which Andrew had already learned.

After Math class, there was Science with Miss Van de Veer; the subject under study was reptiles. Miss Van de Veer showed the class a garter snake, an iguana, and a blue-tailed lizard. Then, lunch. Andrew was already feeling hungry and he welcomed the respite from academics. Carrying the lunch Lois had packed for him, he followed his classmates to the cafeteria and sat down at one of the tables. He was heartily sick of this American school, American people, and America in general, and all he wanted to do was eat his lunch in peace.

Andrew's classmates, however, had other things in mind.

"Blimey, it's a Limey!" The taunt came from a youth with a bulky build and bulging forehead.

"It's a Slimey Limey!" another boy, with a pinched face and piggy eyes, snickered.

Andrew took a bite of his sandwich. The filling was some ghastly brownish substance that gagged in his throat; Andrew remembered that Lois had called it *peanut butter*. He put the sandwich down and munched on an oatmeal raisin cookie. He kept quiet; he knew very well that to open his mouth would invite ridicule.

"Oy say, this Limey's deaf an' dumb, 'e 'is!" the first boy taunted him in a travesty of a Cockney accent.

Andrew fumed, but kept his tongue. It was bad enough to have his speech made fun of, but to be mocked in a vulgar Cockney accent was galling. These stupid clots wouldn't know the King's English if it bit them on the arse!

"Why don't you twerps just shut up!" A girl from the next table spoke. Andrew did not recognize her as being in his class.

"Miriam, why don't you just stick it up your nose?" the Cockney-mouthed boy retorted.

"Her Jew-nose," the other boy tittered. The rest of the boys laughed.

"Quiet, please!" One of lunchroom monitors stood at the head of the table. "If you boys can't behave yourselves, then the entire table will have to eat in silence. Keep it up, and there'll be no recess either!"

"Now look what you've done!" Cockney-mouth snapped savagely at Andrew.

"Yeah, Limey," his sidekick added.

Andrew ate the rest of his cookie, then everyone was dismissed for recess. He shuffled outside, leaned against the building, hands in his pockets, and glared at the ground.

"Hello."

He looked up. It was Miriam.

"Hello," he said.

"My name's Miriam Kantor. What's yours?"

"Andrew Hadley-Trevelyan." Andrew's voice croaked a bit. He tried to hide his nervousness, for he had never, not in his entire life, spoken to a girl his own age.

"You're from England, then?"

Andrew nodded.

"Did you just get here?"

"Yes."

"You came by boat, then?"

Andrew nodded again.

"Were the U-Boats any problem?"

Andrew shrugged. "I never saw any."

"Was it a big ship?"

"The *Queen Mary*. It was converted to a troop ship."

"That must have been interesting! Did you meet any of the American soldiers?"

Andrew nodded. "Um, a few." He looked down, embarrassed. It was all so disconcerting, talking to a girl like this...and it all had happened so suddenly! When he was in England, the thought had occasionally crossed his mind that after he finished public school, perhaps when he was at the university (Oxford, of course), it would be expected that he would, well, socialize. At the time, the idea of that had seemed in the far distant future; certainly nothing to worry about at the present. He rather expected that his father would, when the time came, explain to him all that would be required of him on such an occasion, in order that he would be well-prepared in the social graces so as not to make a fool of himself: how to conduct himself, proper topics of conversation, and so forth.

This was not at all how he had envisioned things—all of a sudden, out of the blue, with no warning or preparation, having to hold a conversation with a gir—

"My cousin spent a few weeks in England. She said it was very nice."

This statement yanked Andrew back to the here and now, away from the what should have been.

"Oh." Andrew pursed his lips. "Did she visit England from America?"

"No, she came from Germany." Miriam looked away for a moment, then continued. "She stayed in England a few weeks before sailing to America."

A bell rang, and everyone filed into the building. Miriam was lost in the crowd.

By the end of the school day, after Art with Miss Lashua, Phys. Ed. with Mr. Scurlock, English with Miss Fittipaldi (She told Andrew to call her *Miss Fitt*) and History (American!) with Mrs. Henschell, Andrew was quite convinced that an extended stay in hell would be preferable to spending one more minute in this dreadful country. Moreover, it would be in everyone's best interest for him to return to England forthwith.

All he had to do was convince his mother of that.

As he shuffled home he plotted his strategy. Arriving at the house, he quietly opened the front door. He heard sounds of laughter and conversation in the dining room, and paused in the vestibule.

"...and even Jake's old principal dropped by," Andrew's mother was saying. "He was quite eager to find out how Jake had turned out and I believe he was quite pleased. He thoroughly enjoyed hearing the story about the mischief Jake unleashed on Bomber Command."

"Oh, I never heard about that," Lois said.

"Something else Jake didn't write home about," Andrew's mother laughed. "It happened in early summer, 1940. Jake's squadron was at a pub one night and a squadron of pilots from Bomber Command walked in. Well, a lively discussion developed as to the merits of each of their respective roles. The controversy was not resolved to anyone's satisfaction, so—"

"Bomber Command started it," Jake said. "They buzzed our base and dropped toilet paper."

"And some very uncomplimentary leaflets, too," Andrew's mother added. "Well, Jake decided that the honor of Fighter Command had been impugned and that the culprits had to be brought to justice."

"Oh dear," Lois said.

"Jake formed—now what did you call it, darling—a pass—"

"Posse." Jake said.

"Right, a *posse.*"

"Oh God," Lois groaned. "I don't even want to know—"

"Oh nothing all that horrible," Andrew's mother assured her. "Tell her, Jake."

There was a brief silence; then Jake said, "We drove to the bomber base, kidnapped the Wing Commander, took him back to our base and made him pick up the mess."

Lois roared with laughter. Andrew's mother said, "Mr. Fisk nearly split his sides laughing about that one! Oh, and then he really got a fit of giggles—started talking about shaving cream—what was that all about, Jake?"

"Oh, I remember getting called in for *that* one," Lois said. "Jake slid an envelope of shaving cream under Mr. Fisk's door—not all the way, just the open end. Then when Mr. Fisk grabbed at it, Jake stomped on the envelope and Mr. Fisk got a blast of shaving cream. And then there was the skunk—"

"Andrew!" His mother noticed Andrew standing in the vestibule. "How was school, darling?"

Andrew shuffled into the dining room. He wanted to blurt out everything to his mother, tell her how positively ghastly school had been, how much he hated it here, how much he wanted to go back to England. But he very well couldn't talk about all that with Lois and Jake sitting there. Better to talk with her privately later on. He shrugged and sat down.

"Would you like some peach pie, Andrew?" Lois asked.

Andrew nodded. Lois got up and bustled out to the kitchen, returning in a short time with a large slice of peach pie, still warm from the oven, and a glass of milk which she set down before Andrew. He took a bite of the pie and noticed his mother and Jake regarding him with concern.

Jake cleared his throat. "What classes are you taking, Andrew?"

Andrew pulled out his schedule from his pocket and, without a word, handed it to Jake, who perused it. "Miss Lashua—I had her for Art—she's terrific," Jake said. "Miss Van de Veer—" He turned to Lois. "That's Starr Van de Veer, remember? She used to live around the corner from us. She had a pet snake and she'd let it loose in the lunchroom. Now she can bring her snakes to school as part of her job." Turning back to Andrew, he said, "And you have Mrs. Larsen for Reading—good. She was one of my favorite teachers. What are you reading?"

Andrew fished out his copy of *The Last of the Mohicans* from the pile of books he was carrying and passed it to Jake.

"Hey, if you have any assignments or reports to do, I'd be glad to help while I'm here," Jake said.

Andrew took another bite of peach pie, then pushed it away. "I think I'll rest up a bit before dinner," he said.

He trudged up the stairs. Once in his room (Jake's room, he reminded himself) he threw himself down on the bed. A flood of memories washed over him. He thought about Armus House, where he had spent the happiest times of his childhood: his father and mother with him, Gram and Aunt Gwen and Aunt Jane, too, before she got married to Jean-Marc and moved to France. He remembered all the wonderful holidays he'd taken with his family to Scotland and London and Eastborne, and flying with his parents in the Puss Moth, looking down upon the English countryside spread out below, green and friendly like a large, lovely garden.

"Andrew?" His mother's voice interrupted his reverie. "Andrew, may I come in?"

He sat up in bed. "Yes, Mum."

She came in and sat on the bed next to him. "Darling, how was school? Is everything all right?"

All right—since you've asked, let's have it out.

"No," he said flatly. "It was awful." He swallowed. "They made fun of me because of the way I talked. It's a horrible place. Everyone was mean." He looked away. He had thought that he would have to work at putting on a convincing performance when the time came to speak to his mother about his returning to England, but he found, to his surprise, that he didn't need to force a show of emotion at all. Those were real tears rolling down his cheeks.

"I hate it! I don't want to stay here! I want to go back to England with you—"

His mother leaned toward him and stroked his cheek. "That's not possible, Andrew." Though her touch was gentle, her voice was firm.

"*Why?*" he shouted. Then he lowered his voice. "Why can't I? I can just get back on the boat with you, and go back to England."

His mother took a deep breath. "We've discussed that before. It's better for you to be here. Look at all the wonderful food you're getting—lots of meat, milk, ice cream, real eggs, and orange juice! You've no doubt put on five pounds in the few days you've been here—"

"Mum, I promise that if I go back, I'll eat much better! It's just that the food was so bad at school that I didn't have much of an appetite. I promise, if I go back I'll eat everything on my plate—even spinach! You can even ask Mr. Nugent to make sure—"

"Andrew, it's also a matter of your being in a safe place. I don't have to worry about bombs falling on you here."

"Mum, it's not so bad now! Compared to The Blitz, it's *nothing!* If you were so worried about the bombs, why didn't you send me to America during the Blitz?" Andrew folded his arms and glared at his mother intently. *There*, try to explain that!

She sighed. "You were probably safer in England than on a ship going across the Atlantic then."

"Well, England's safer now, too!"

"It seems that way, at least for now. You never know—"

"Mum, nothing's going to happen! It's all over—I mean, we're bombing Germany into smithereens right now! What can they do—"

"Until the white flag goes up over Berlin, there's no telling what can happen—"

"Mum, I told you, *nothing's* going to happen! Germany's done for! They're not going to bother us any more!

"Oh, are you going to arrange this personally with Goering?"

"Mum, please—"

"Andrew, it's better for you to be here. You're *not* going back to England." The tone of her voice indicated to Andrew that she wasn't going to budge. He turned away.

"Darling, I know it's hard for you to understand, but you need to stay here. I don't want anything to happen to you."

"Nothing's going to happen!"

"If I were absolutely sure of that, you could come back with us. Nothing is certain now."

Andrew snorted with disgust.

She's just paranoid. She's overreacting.

"Just because one silly little bomb falls on my school—"

"Andrew, please trust me. I know it's difficult for you now. You're in a new place, new school, new friends—"

"What friends!" Andrew spat.

"Give it a chance, Andrew. If you make up your mind that things are going to be terrible, then they probably will—"

"I didn't decide for everybody to be mean to me!"

"All right, if you still don't like it after a month or two, I'll arrange for you to go to boarding school here, all right? Perhaps up in Massachusetts with Peter—"

"I don't *want* to go to boarding school here!" Andrew hollered. The way he figured it, if American kids were so mean, it would be far worse to be stuck with them for twenty-four hours a day, instead of for only eight. And going to boarding school in America wouldn't change the fact that he would still be three thousand miles away from his mother—and Jake. He lowered his voice and pleaded, "I just want to go home—please!"

"Andrew, *No.*" The last word was spoken with sad finality.

The silence hung in the air between them. There was nothing more to say.

Lois invited them to her Red Cross Meeting that night.

"We meet every Monday. It's mostly rolling bandages. Sometimes we have a speaker give a talk about the war and the work of the Red Cross, nothing near as exciting as what you've been doing, Alice. I've told the other women there about you, and they'd love to meet you."

Andrew's mother smiled at Jake. "Would you mind, darling?"

"Of course not," Jake answered. He seemed to be, if not exactly buoyant, at least more relaxed and cheerful than he had been ever since their arrival. As usual, Lois and Andrew's mother had done most of the talking at dinner, but Jake and his father had exchanged a few words with each other, on non-controversial topics such as the weather and the inconveniences of rationing, without setting each other off.

"Jake, would you mind driving Alice and me to the meeting?" Lois asked.

"Sure," Jake replied.

"It would be wonderful if you came in and met with everyone for awhile."

"Oh Mom, I'm not very good at small talk."

"Just for a minute or two, Jake, please! I've been so excited about you coming home, and everyone wants to meet you."

"Okay, just a for a minute."

"Good. We can get a ride home with Rosemary Schaeffer—no need to fetch us."

Andrew thought for a moment. If he accompanied them to the meeting, returning with Jake, alone....

"Mum, can I go with you? I mean, just to see things. I'll come home with Jake."

Andrew's mother seemed surprised by his enthusiasm; her eyebrows arched ever so high and her lips formed a tight line. She glanced at Jake. He shrugged and smiled. "Fine by me."

"Meeting starts at seven-thirty," Lois said. "We'd better get ready. I'll get the dishes soaking in the sink."

"I'll finish them up, Mom," Jake said.

By now, Andrew's mother seemed accustomed to the business of assisting Lois with clearing the table and cleaning up after supper. With Jake helping, the dining room was put in order and the dishes set to soaking in no time at all. Lois then went upstairs to change into her Red Cross uniform. She proudly displayed the ribbons she had earned for her many hours of service.

At the meeting, which was held at Lois's church, everyone crowded around Jake and Andrew's mother, chattering and asking questions. As it turned out, the speaker for the evening had been called away, and Andrew's mother was prevailed upon to give a talk about the ATA. Jake wanted to stay and listen, so he and Andrew and Lois sat together in the back row. Andrew's mother briefly talked about how the ATA came into existence and how the first women ferry pilots—the "First Eight"—ferried trainers to Scotland in the bitter winter cold in 1940:

"The return journey to Hatfield had to be made by train and, what with one thing or another, the trip might take three or four days. After arriving back at base, a pilot would often be sent off once more without a proper night's sleep in her own bed. These First Eight carried a heavy responsibility: They couldn't be too cautious and not move enough aircraft, because then they would be accused of not being able to handle the job. On the other hand, they had to have an impeccable safety record: One accident caused by pilot fatigue would discredit all women pilots. Happily, these first women pilots proved that they could do the job no matter what demands were placed upon them, and they did not have one accident that first winter. Since then, the safety record of the women of the ATA has been better than that of the men. Eighteen more women pilots were allowed to join in 1940 and there are now over a hundred women pilots in the ATA, not only from England and the Commonwealth but from many other countries. We have twenty-five American women in our organization, three women from Poland, one from Holland, one from Ireland, and one from Chile. In fact, the ATA has pilots from thirty countries! We have pilots from many European nations, such as France, Czechoslovakia, Spain, Belgium, Austria, and Norway. Other aviators in our organization hail from India, Ethiopia, Siam, Cuba, and China. In this respect, the ATA is truly a unique organization, the likes of which will probably never be seen again, for it has literally gathered pilots from the four corners of the earth."

She spoke of Pauline Gower's leadership and insistence on excellence, and exactly what ferrying entailed: flying the planes from the factories to the maintenance units and at the same time checking them out for defects; taking the planes from the maintenance units to the airfields; flying out damaged planes to be repaired; and flying the repaired planes back to the squadrons. She explained how the conversion courses worked, the use of the Ferry Pilots' notes, and the hazards and trials that Ferry Pilots had to contend with: barrage balloons, anti-aircraft fire, mechanical failure, the weather—and for the women, the attitude of some men. She mentioned the incident in Hyde Park and everyone laughed when she cited Andrew's words: "My mother flies Hurricanes—you couldn't fly a kite!" He felt a little flustered when everyone turned around to look at him, but a little delighted too; he had always thought that his mother was angry at him for his outburst.

She went on to say that ferry pilots flew without radios, and without any navigational equipment other than a compass and gyro. Often they had to land at primitive and makeshift airfields, which were sometimes pastures or fields with fencing removed or gaps cut in bordering hedges, and were often quite small. When she mentioned that ATA pilots were expected to do three-point landings, Jake waved his hand and asked her to explain what a three-point landing was.

She smiled and answered that most planes had two main wheels in the undercarriage and a tail wheel. If there was sufficient runway, pilots could land on the main wheels first, then set the tail wheel down just after that. To make a three-point landing, one had to set all three wheels down simultaneously, which called for no small amount of skill, for in such a maneuver a stall could easily occur and result in damage to both plane and pilot.

She concluded her talk by telling of Jacqueline Cochran's role in recruiting American women pilots for ATA duty, and how she had then set up the American counterpart of the ATA women's division: the Women's Airforce Service Pilots, or WASPs, which in August had merged the Women's Auxiliary Ferrying Squadron, the elite organization founded by Nancy Love, and the Women's Flying Training Detachment. The WASPs, too, had earned the respect of men who had previously scoffed at the idea of women flying planes for wartime duty. In fact, Andrew's mother noted, one man had said that he preferred to have women for ferrying duty because, as he explained, "They're more reliable than the men because they don't fly around with an address book!"

Afterwards, Andrew's mother made her way to Andrew and Jake. Lois was chatting with some other women about how delighted she was that Jake and his "new family" were home for a visit, and she told them that Andrew would be remaining in America for the duration of the war.

Andrew listened ruefully to Lois, then turned to his mother. "I always thought you were upset with me that time we were at Speaker's Corner."

She put her arm around his shoulder. "I was angry, but not at you. I'm sorry if I lost my temper, though. The whole thing made me so upset, but it also made me more determined to do a good job, just to prove that twits like that were wrong."

One of the women announced that it was time to start to work rolling bandages, so Andrew and Jake departed. Although he was not in the mood for conversation, Andrew knew he had to take advantage of the opportunity he had of being alone with Jake. How to work it into the conversation, though....

"Your mother's really something," Jake said with a smile as they rode home.

Andrew grunted.

Jake went on. "She once told me it was a shame that British women weren't allowed to fly in combat. She'd heard that Russian women were flying on bombing missions and strafing attacks on the Eastern Front, as well as being fighter pilots. She said that men just blathered about women being the 'weaker sex' because they were afraid that the women would prove themselves to be just as good as, or even better than, the men. She's probably right; I wouldn't want to be the Jerry with your mother after me if she were flying in combat." He chuckled. "One time she was delivering a Spit to my base. I was up with a new pilot, training him on maneuvers. Your mother recognized my letters and flew along beside me and waggled her wings. I sent my trainee down and your mother signaled to me that she wanted to challenge me to a mock dogfight. We chased each other across the sky and boy, she was pretty good in those tight turns! With a little training, she'd make a great fighter pilot." His mood turned serious. "All the same, I'd be worried sick about her if she were...."

Andrew saw his chance. "Why aren't you flying in combat any more?"

"I'm doing photo-recon work."

"Do you have any guns on your plane?"

"Nope, no guns. No unnecessary weight at all. Just me, a navigator, and a couple of cameras. We want to get in and out fast, get the pictures, not tangle with the Jerries."

"What's so important about pictures? If you're going to fly over enemy territory, why not drop some bombs or shoot someone?"

"Knowing what to hit is just as important. You just can't blind drop bombs all over the place. And, after the bombing raid, you have to know if the target's been destroyed. That's why photo-recon is important."

"So if you saw an enemy aircraft, you wouldn't fight him."

"Couldn't. No guns."

"You could ram him."

"Not in a wooden plane. The whole idea is to go in high and fast without being detected. Mossies are good for that. They're faster than anything the Germans have and aren't picked up on radar, either. Well, not to worry—I've never had any Jerries bother me when I've been on photo-recon missions."

Too bad, Andrew thought.

They turned into the driveway. Jake turned off the ignition. Andrew glared at him and said icily, "Everyone knows that reconnaissance duty is for pilots who are too afraid to fight. I would think that you'd want to be killing Germans instead of making film stars out of them."

The following morning, even before he opened his eyes, Andrew had the feeling that he'd overslept. It occurred to him that he should be getting ready for school. When he opened his eyes and looked at the alarm clock, his intuition was confirmed: nine o'clock. He had remembered setting the alarm the night before; why hadn't it rung? He leaned across to the dresser and checked it.

It had been shut off.

What was going on here? His mind, still a little foggy with sleep, puzzled over the situation and then the reason—the *wonderful* reason—burst on his consciousness. The reason why he didn't have to go to school was that his mother had decided to let him go back to England! That was it—that *had* to be it! She had thought about it and had decided that it would be best for him to return with her!

He bounded out of bed, threw on his robe, and flew down the stairs.

"Good morning, Sleepyhead!" Lois was at the stove, as usual. "How about cottage potatoes and ham? I turned your alarm off after you went to sleep last night, thought I'd let you sleep in, seeing as there's no school today."

Andrew's mouth hung open in dismay. "*No school?*" he croaked.

Lois looked at him, surprised, and then burst into laughter. "My, are you *that* disappointed that it's a holiday?"

"*Holiday?*" Andrew said weakly.

"Columbus Day—you'll have to get used to a whole different bunch of holidays here!" She ladled some fried potatoes and a slice of ham onto a plate and proffered it to Andrew. "Here you go—take this into the breakfast room. Your mother and Jake are having coffee."

Andrew took a deep breath. He tried to keep his voice from trembling. "No, thank you," he said softly. "I'm not hungry." He turned away and climbed the stairs.

Once in his room, he threw himself onto the bed.

A holiday! A damned bloody holiday!

"Andrew?" His mother's voice was solicitous and gentle. She opened the door a crack. "Andrew, are you all right?" Andrew turned from her as she stepped into the room. "Lois told us that you were upset because there wasn't any school today." She sat down on the bed and put her arm around him. "I thought you said you didn't like school—"

"I thought you didn't get me up for school this morning because you'd decided to let me go back to England with you!" Andrew was chagrined to feel the tears coursing down his cheeks

"Oh, so *that's* it," his mother said. She took a deep breath and said, "Andrew, I know it's difficult for you to understand, but it's much better for you to be here in America. Please trust that I'm doing what is best for you."

Andrew bit his lip to keep it from trembling and turned away.

"Andrew, if your father were still alive, don't you think that he would want you to be safe?"

"I'd be just as safe back in England!"

"Perhaps," she sighed. "Perhaps not. Andrew, look at me." She touched his cheek. "Andrew, nothing is more important to me than your safety. *Nothing.*"

What about what's important to me? Andrew thought savagely. You're going back with *him* and leaving me here....

"Andrew, someday you'll understand—"

"I'll *never* understand!"

"Do you believe that I love you?" she said softly.

Andrew looked at her, into her eyes—tender, loving, and pained. What could he say?

"Yes." His voice broke. His mother gathered him into her arms and hugged him fiercely.

"All right, that's all that matters." She held him close for what seemed like an eternity, and Andrew felt as if he were in an oasis of time and space, far removed from the concerns of the world. He could almost believe he was back in England and that in the next moment he would hear his father's voice: *Everything all right, old chap?*

A soft, insistent meow and the sensation of a small furry body trying to nudge its way between his mother and him brought Andrew back to October 12, 1943 and Scotch Plains, New Jersey.

"Lindy! You always like to get in the middle of things, don't you?" Andrew's mother laughed. She released Andrew and Lindy meowed as he wedged himself into the narrow space between them. Lindy began to purr and Andrew's mother stroked his back.

"He likes you, Andrew. See, you already have a friend."

Andrew grunted as he scratched Lindy's ears.

"Why don't you come down for breakfast in a few minutes? I'll ask Lois to reheat your food." She kissed him on the forehead and added, "We're going to go on a picnic today, to a place in the mountains called Washington Rock. Jake's father left us the car, and Lois is going to pack all sorts of delightful things to eat. Come on, it'll be a wonderful day."

At breakfast, Lois didn't chide him over his disappointment in not having to go to school, and Jake looked at him with undisguised sympathy. Andrew concluded that his mother must have told them of his real reason for being upset. He really didn't mind Lois knowing, but he was perturbed that Jake was aware of his feelings about the situation, especially after his scathing denunciation of Jake's present choice of a career. Andrew felt as if he were a cornered fox, baring its teeth at a pack of snarling dogs closed for the kill—all his fierceness could not change his inevitable doom. Jake could afford to be compassionate because he was not the one at a disadvantage. Damn him!

Later, upstairs in his room, Andrew sat on his bed and absentmindedly stroked Lindy. There was a knock at the door.

"Andrew?" It was Jake. "Can I come in?"

Andrew groaned. Why couldn't Jake just leave him *alone?*

"Andrew?"

"Yes," Andrew said coldly.

The door opened a crack. Jake slipped into the room. He handed two pieces of paper to Andrew. "Mom found these when she was going through your pockets before she washed your clothes. Here." He offered them to Andrew. Andrew mechanically took them and examined them. One had Peter's name and address on it, the other— Andrew squinted as he read the name: *Sgt. Kevin Ferguson.* Who in the world was that? He turned the paper over and saw that it was a Hershey bar wrapper. It took a few seconds for the mystery to unravel: Sarge! It never occurred to Andrew that Sarge had a real name. He tossed the papers onto his dresser. Right now, he was not in the mood to correspond with anybody.

Jake stood in front of Andrew for a moment, then took a deep breath and spoke.

"Andrew, I know that it must be very hard for you, being in a new place. I wish there was something I could do to make it easier for you."

You could disappear in a puff of smoke.

"I'd like to help. Is there anything you'd like to talk about?"

How about the subject of your going back to being a fighter pilot?

Jake stood up. "Well, let me know if there's anything I can do to help. Okay?"

Andrew narrowed his eyes in savage condemnation. He was not even going to dignify this one-sided conversation with a response. There was nothing to say. As he continued to glare at Jake, an idea suddenly occurred to him:

Maybe there *is* something Jake can do.

Chapter 32

*O*f course, Andrew knew that he would have to wait until he and Jake were alone. *It wouldn't do for anyone else to overhear what I plan on saying to Jake.*

He looked at Jake again; then, without a word, he stood and walked to the front window, keeping his back to Jake. After a bit, he heard Jake get up and leave the room, softly closing the door behind him.

Andrew walked back to the dresser. He took the two pieces of paper with Peter's and Sarge's addresses on them and shoved them into the bottom drawer of the dresser, behind his sweaters. The model Spitfire Jake had given him lay on top of the dresser; perhaps he would leave it here—"forget" to pack it—when he sailed back to England next week. Andrew smiled. Sometimes, as Freddie used to say, *You have to dance with the Devil to get what you want.*

They spent the day at Washington Rock, an overlook in the Watchung Mountains so called because George Washington had viewed the British troops from this point during the Revolutionary War. By now, Andrew was heartily sick of all of the reminders of that particular "spot of bother" which had taken place in this area a century and a half ago: It was Washington this, or George Washington that—George Washington Bridge, George Washington Inn, George Washington slept here, George Washington slept there—no wonder the man never had any proper heirs, what with him sleeping around in all sorts of strange places! Wonder how *Mrs.* Washington felt about that!

While Lois set up the picnic blanket, Andrew wandered over to a large stone monument, and read its inscription:

From this rock
General George Washington
Watched the movements of
the British forces
During the anxious months
of May and June 1777

And at the bottom, the words: *Lest we Forget*
No, you people aren't *ever* going forget your stupid little scrap, Andrew thought.
"Would you like a sandwich, Andrew?" Lois asked.
His appetite was in high gear from his feverish plotting on just how exactly to ap-

proach Jake. Trying to hide his excitement that he might—no, he would, he certainly *would*—be sailing back to England next week, Andrew nodded unenthusiastically.

"My, what an appetite you have, Andrew," Lois chuckled. To Andrew's mother she said, "Jake was such a picky eater until he was about twelve; then, my goodness, almost overnight, he was eating me out of house and home! Boys get that way right about this age. I had five brothers, and it sure was a good thing we lived on a farm! Of course, there was a lot of hard work to be done, and a person could really work up an appetite in no time at all."

"You're from Nebraska, right?" Andrew's mother asked her.

"Uh-huh."

"How did you wind up in New Jersey?"

Lois smiled. "I had an aunt who lived in New Brunswick. She was my mother's older sister, and had already married when my mother's family moved out west, just after the Civil War, so she stayed in New Jersey. My mother was the baby of the family; she was born after her family had settled in Nebraska. My grandfather had been in the Union Army, and after the war was over, he wanted to move to the Midwest and farm. I went to visit my aunt one summer, when I was sixteen. She was in poor health, so I took care of her, and I used to go down to the corner pharmacy to pick up her prescription once a week." She blushed.

"Well, there was this incredibly handsome, very nice—but oh, *very* shy young pharmacist working there. He was just out of school and was filling in for the owner, who was away on vacation for the summer. Well, I managed to get down there almost every day—Gene must have thought I was incredibly scatter-brained at first! Needing soap one day, out of talcum powder the next, fresh out of rubbing alcohol the day after that...." She laughed, self-consciously and joyously. "I found out that he was living in a boarding house. He was trying to save enough money to buy his own business. It was a real flea-bag place, and the food was awful. He mostly ate sandwiches at the store when he had a free minute. He couldn't even leave the place to go out for lunch, and didn't want to spend the money anyway. So I started fixing lunch, for two of course, and I'd bring it to the store. Then I invited him to my aunt's home for dinner, and convinced my aunt to let one of the rooms in her house to him for the summer. She had a huge place and lived alone. She needed some repairs done around the place anyway, and Gene traded off rent for fixing the place up. I was on cloud nine for the rest of the summer—fixing breakfast for him in the morning, bringing him lunch at the store, dinners together. My aunt took her meals in bed, so it was just the two of us."

"How romantic!"

"Even so, I had to ask Gene to marry me. He was so incredibly shy, I was afraid he would never pop the question!"

"What did he say? I mean, well, he agreed, obviously. Was he surprised?"

"I'll say! We had just finished eating breakfast and we were carrying the dishes out to the kitchen. I suppose I could have picked a better time to ask, but I was leaving the next day and we were talking about...what was it? Oh, I remember! He told me that he was going to miss my 'wonderful cooking', as he said, and the great company, and then he was very quiet. I kept waiting for him to say something, but he just blushed, and didn't say a word. So I said, 'Well, why don't we get married? Then, you won't *have* to miss my cooking!' That's when he dropped the dishes!"

"Oh my!"

"So I said, 'Do I take that as a yes?' He just stood there, with his mouth open, and finally nodded his head and said 'Yes.' That's when *I* dropped the dishes I was carrying, threw my arms around him, and well, there we were, standing with pieces of broken crockery strewn around our feet! Gene wanted me to finish high school first, so we were married a year later."

Jake, who had wandered off while Lois was recounting her courtship with his father, stood off in front of the monument, his hands thrust in his pockets. He looked out toward the distant New York skyline.

"He's just like his father," Lois whispered fiercely, her face suddenly very serious. "Oh Alice, he won't admit it, but he's just like him!"

Andrew's mother nodded. "Very, very much so," she agreed.

The rest of the week went along much as Andrew had expected: school was a trial of taunts and sniggering looks every time he opened his mouth. No matter—if all went according to plan, he would be bidding good riddance to the whole sodding lot of them by Friday afternoon.

Mrs. Tercek insisted that he learn the Pledge of Allegiance, which irked him, since he was *not* an American (this he asserted quite vehemently to her) and had absolutely *no* intention whatsoever of remaining in this despicable place (this, not wishing to tempt fate, he kept to himself). Mrs. Tercek then countered with the argument that one's citizenship had nothing to do with it: He was in America, in an American school, and he *would* say the Pledge of Allegiance, just like everyone else.

"Gina and Bronia and Antoinette aren't American citizens either, but they say it, and you will, too. It has nothing to do with nationality. You are in this country, and you will obey its laws and customs."

Andrew wanted to protest that, speaking of laws, the Geneva Convention prohibited forcing someone to swear allegiance to an enemy country, or something to that effect. America wasn't technically an enemy country, but it wasn't *his* country, and he couldn't very well swear allegiance to two different nations, could he? However, he saw no point in getting into a dispute over the matter, since he wouldn't be staying, anyway. Besides, he was heartily sick of the snickers and giggles that ensued every time he said anything. Better to keep one's mouth shut as much as possible.

Only Miriam was friendly to him. There seemed to be an unwritten rule that boys and girls sat separately at lunch, but during recess she sought him out and talked with him. She was eager to know what England was like and how the war was going, as if he had more information about the progress of the war because he'd been closer to it. Most of all, she wanted to know if the stories, or rather rumors, about the Nazi atrocities against the Jews in Europe could possibly be true.

"I really don't know," Andrew had replied. "I hope not, although with Nazis, you never know. I mean, they bombed civilians, not just military targets—cities, homes, schools. My school was bombed last spring. So was my grandmother's house."

"It's one thing to drop bombs all over the place. They just wanted England to surrender, and they thought that by bombing they would demoralize the British people."

"That was a big mistake. They only succeeded in making us angry and more determined than ever not to surrender."

"But this whole thing about the Nazis killing Jews is different from dropping bombs on a enemy country. I mean, if these stories are true, the Germans are murdering people—men, women, and children—just for the purpose of exterminating them from the face of the earth, not just to win a war."

"Well, they're just stories. I know the Nazis are bad, but they just might be rumors, you know, things blown out of proportion. I don't think it's quite as bad as these stories make it out to be. People just don't do things like that."

Miriam looked at him, doubt and apprehension in her eyes. "I hope you're right."

Andrew was beginning to despair that he would never find himself alone with Jake; but Saturday morning Lois announced that she was going grocery shopping, and Andrew's mother wanted to accompany her. Lois offered to take Andrew along too, but he said he'd rather stay home and do some reading.

"Jake, would you like to come with us?" Lois asked.

Jake, who was sitting on the sofa reading a newspaper, said cheerily, "No thanks, Mom. I think I'll catch up on the news. Can you believe it—Italy just declared war on the Nazis!" He displayed the headline on the newspaper: *Italy at War With Germany*.

"That news is a few days old, Jake," Lois said. "Here's yesterday's paper." She tossed him Friday's edition of the *Courier News*.

"Well, it's something, isn't it!" Jake shook his head and smiled. "Nothing worse than being on the wrong side of a mad Italian! Remember when I put the firecrackers under Mr. Casini's porch?"

Lois rolled her eyes. "Don't remind me! Well, is there anything special you'd like me to get for you at the store?"

Jake smiled.

"Chocolate, right?" Lois teased.

"How'd you guess?"

"See that smile?" Lois said to Andrew's mother. "That's a chocolate cake smile!"

After Andrew's mother and Lois had departed, Andrew went out into the kitchen and grabbed a few cookies from the cookie jar. He returned to the living room and sat on the sofa next to Jake, then picked up a section of the paper Jake had discarded on the floor, and pretended to peruse it. Jake glanced at him and smiled uneasily.

"Would you like a cookie?" Andrew asked him.

Jake, thoroughly surprised, sputtered, "Uh, yeah...Yeah, thanks."

Andrew proffered an oatmeal raisin cookie to him. "Your mother makes super cookies."

"Yeah, she sure does," Jake smiled.

Andrew leaned towards Jake and looked at the newspaper he was reading. "That's really something, isn't it? Italy declaring war on Germany, I mean."

"Yep, sure is. Germany's done for, no question about it."

Perfect! Andrew tried to hide his eagerness, so he purposely lowered his voice and forced himself to speak slowly and deliberately. "That's what I think, too. Mum, though—" He chose his words carefully, "She seems to be, um...overreacting. I mean, if Germany's just about done for, it doesn't make any sense to suddenly start worrying about things and thinking that the Germans are going to invade England or start blitzing us again. I mean, there's no way that could possibly happen now! They bombed us a little this past year, but that was nothing compared to the Blitz! I should know, I was in London and Mum and I were in a restaurant when it got bombed and we were almost killed—"

"I know about—I mean, your mother told me." Jake put the newspaper down and his face grew serious. "Andrew, I know it must have been a terrifying experience for you, but she was not only scared out of her wits, but torn apart by guilt about the whole thing. She blamed herself for not getting you into a shelter as soon as the Alert sounded. It's the only time I've ever seen her completely distraught. Even when—" He checked himself, took a deep breath, and continued. "She only wants you to be safe."

"Well, why didn't she send me away during the Blitz?"

"Across the Atlantic in 1940? It was bad enough in England, but ten times worse in the Atlantic. You would have had a snowball's chance in hell of getting across safely."

"So why bring me here now? I mean, I know it's safer now, but completely unnecessary since Germany's just about beaten!"

"Don't you like it here?"

"I like your mother, and your father's very nice, too, but I don't belong here!" Realizing that Jake was trying to sidetrack him, he tried another tack. "You didn't like it in New Jersey either, so you went out to Nebraska. How would you have felt if you were told: 'No, you can't go to Nebraska; you have to stay in New Jersey.'?"

"That's different. Nobody was dropping bombs on Nebraska."

"Well, nobody's dropping bombs on England, either. I mean, not hardly!"

"Well, we can't be certain of anything, not until the white flag goes up over Berlin. I'd give that at least another year."

"The war's over—I mean, it's just as good as being over! All we have to do is invade France, and that should be a piece of cake what with the pounding we've been giving Germany."

Jake said tersely, "War is never a piece of cake." He lifted the newspaper to his face and glared at it. Conversation over.

Andrew, enraged, pulled the newspaper out of Jake's hands. He wanted to scream at Jake, throttle him if need be, but the cool, clear voice of reason prevailed. He had to salvage this conversation—Jake was his only hope. He lowered his eyes. "Nothing's going to happen." His voice was barely above a whisper. He looked at Jake and tried to soften his expression. "I know my mother worries about me, and you worry about her—" He forced a smile. "I want it all to work out between us...It can, you know." He paused, watching for Jake's reaction.

Jake eyed him warily. Andrew continued. "I know things got started badly...between us, I mean. I'm sorry for the things I've said. I think it would be better for all of us, especially for Mum, if we got along. I think that Mum, well, with all the tension she's been under, you know, about us...I think it just got to her finally. Sometimes when you're really upset you make things out to be worse than they really are. I mean, why would she suddenly get scared about me being in England?"

Jake cleared his throat. "I know that she wants you be safe, Andrew."

"But she's overreacting. She's *paranoid*."

Jake smiled indulgently. "She's your mother. It's her job to be paranoid."

Andrew tried to hide the agitation in his voice. He didn't like the way Jake was so skillfully deflecting the thrust of his argument. Trying for a counter-attack, he said, "Well, sometimes she overreacts for nothing. Remember back at the end of the Blitz, when the Germans stopped bombing us for a few weeks? I wanted to go to Armus House, since it was clear the Germans had given up. My mother made me go to Greycliff instead, even though there was no reason for it. I mean, the Germans weren't bombing us anymore! I told her that everything was going to be all right if I went to Armus House, but she wouldn't listen. It turned out she was wrong—the Germans attacked Russia instead. So all her worry was for nothing!"

"Well, no one knew at the time what the Germans were planning on doing. In light of the circumstances at the time, I think she made a very prudent decision. You can't fault her for being cautious."

"But she overreacted—that's the point!"

"So she overreacted! That's not committing the unpardonable sin. As they say, hindsight is an exact science. What if the Germans hadn't attacked Russia, and had decided to try to finish off England? No one can predict the future, so you hope for the best and prepare for the worst."

"But she's *paranoid!*"

Jake smiled at Andrew. "Well, just indulge her, then."

Aha! Andrew thought. "So you think she's blowing everything out of proportion, then? You don't think there's any danger, do you?"

Jake's face grew serious again, but he kept silent. Andrew's heart soared. Deep down inside, Jake *did* believe she was overreacting!

"She won't listen to me, but she'll listen to you. I'd be ever so grateful if you would talk with her, convince her to let me go back to England." Andrew looked pleadingly at Jake, and laid his hand on Jake's arm. "I'd be ever so grateful...always."

Jake stared at him; he had a distant, uneasy sort of expression on his face. Andrew tightened his grip on his arm.

"Please!"

Jake looked as if he were in a trance. He's probably so stunned by this offer of reconciliation that he doesn't know what to say, Andrew thought. He smiled, and the smile came easily now, because he knew that he'd finally connected with Jake. He remembered his mother's words: *He was terrified of meeting you.*

Andrew was now holding out the hand of friendship to Jake, and he felt a strange surge of power that Jake should be so intimidated by him; that Jake could be so easily swayed to do his will. He tried hard not to appear to gloat, and kept his smile even, his eyes warm and sympathetic. Suddenly, as if the spell were shattered, Jake's head snapped back, and he shuddered.

"Andrew...." His voice was a strangled whisper. He closed his eyes. "All I want—" He broke off, corrected himself. "All *we* want is for you—"

Andrew's mouth dropped open in horror. Jake's slip had betrayed him! *He* was behind it all! It was *he* who wanted Andrew away!

Andrew's soul exploded in fury. He sprang back from Jake.

"I know what *you* want! *You* want me away from my mother! You want her all to yourself!"

Jake, his face white and his jaw slack with dismay and shock, shook his head numbly. "No...I want—"

"You want to get rid of me!" Andrew shrieked. "It's not enough that my father's gone—you want to get rid of *me* too!"

"Andrew, no —"

"You don't care about anyone except yourself, you stinking Yank! All you wanted was to get at my mother! If my father were still around, you'd stab him in the back, wouldn't you! *You'd stab him in the back just to get at her*—" Andrew felt himself spinning out of control with white-hot rage, and this feeling was as frightening to him as his discovery of Jake's role in his exile. Gib was right! Fear and hatred went hand-in-hand! Jake had been afraid of him, and he had turned his fear into hatred: What was a more despicable thing than to separate a mother and her son? Some of the rumors Andrew had heard about Nazi atrocities were that they separated families: Mothers were separated from their children, husbands and wives were separated, brothers and sisters too. Andrew had previously discounted such tales: How could anyone be so inhumane and cruel? It came as a jolt to Andrew that he knew someone in the flesh who could be capable of such a thing. He now saw Nazi Germany as a nation full of people like Jake, and anything—even the unspeakable, the *unthinkable*—was possible. People who had no regard for human life, for the love of family—people like that were capable of anything! He glared at Jake, and then, his mind no longer able to bear his feelings of revulsion at Jake's appearance before him, he turned, stumbled away, and flung himself up the stairs.

Once in his room—*Jake's room*, he reminded himself—he caught sight of the model Spitfire lying on the dresser. He picked it up and, with all his strength, hurled it against the wall. The plane crumpled; the wings flew off and the propeller snapped off and bounced across the floor. There was a nick in the wall where the plane had hit; Andrew walked over and ran his finger along the mark. His heart was still pounding, but a strange sense of calm settled on him. The only way he would defeat Jake would be to refuse to take things lying down: His having lived through the Blitz had taught him that. The British people had gotten angry, but they had gotten even, and Germany was now paying the price for having dared to attack England. Andrew knew he had lost the battle: He would spend the duration of the war here, three thousand miles from his mother. But he had not lost the war.

Whatever it took, he would get even with Jake.

Andrew spent the rest of the morning in his room, his mind a whirlwind of plans, plots, and seething rage. The only outside intrusion into his fevered designs and emotions was the ringing of the telephone around noon. Andrew listened, thinking that Jake would eventually answer it. The phone rang about a dozen times, then was silent: Obviously Jake was not at home.

His mother and Lois returned a little after one. Andrew heard Lois calling to Jake, then heard footsteps on the stairs. A knock on his door preceded his mother's voice: "Andrew?"

He quickly kicked the pieces of the shattered plane under his bed and opened the door. He tried to fix his expression into an unperturbed gaze. "Mum...I guess I fell asleep...."

"Darling, do you know where Jake went?"

"He was reading the newspaper in the living room."

"He didn't tell you if he was going out anywhere?"

"No."

His mother's face puzzled into a frown. "Come on down for lunch, then." She turned, and quickly descended the stairs. Andrew heard her talking with Lois, then Lois's voice: "Maybe he left a note somewhere. Why don't you check your room, and I'll look down here."

Footsteps on the stairs again. Andrew's mother slipped into the room she shared with Jake. She emerged after a minute, her face traced with anxiety. "Nothing in here. Did you find anything?" she called to Lois.

"No, nothing down here, either."

His mother descended the stairs again, without so much as giving Andrew a glance. He stood in the doorway for a moment, irked by his mother's excessive concern for Jake. *I wonder if you would be so concerned about me if I disappeared,* he thought. He composed himself before going downstairs. It wouldn't do for his mother or Lois to detect any anger or agitation on his part. It suddenly occurred to him that Jake could return at any moment, and tell all.

If I act calm and nonchalant now, it will certainly cast doubt on anything Jake might say!

He found his mother and Lois in the kitchen, putting the groceries away. Both of them were speculating about where Jake had disappeared to. They obviously were trying to act unperturbed; however, Andrew detected a definite undercurrent of unease. They sat down to lunch in the breakfast room, and the theorizing continued.

"He seemed to be in such a good mood when we left. Maybe he just went for a walk." Lois suggested.

Andrew's mother nodded.

"He didn't say anything to you, Andrew?" Lois asked him.

"No."

"Did anyone come to the door?"

"No—" Suddenly Andrew had an inspiration. "I heard the phone ring when I was upstairs. Maybe someone called him."

"Did you hear him mention anyone's name, or say anything?"

"No, I really wasn't listening. May I have some cookies for dessert?"

"Sure, help yourself." Lois started to gather up the dishes, and Andrew's mother got up to help her.

After following them out into the kitchen, Andrew took a few cookies out of the cookie jar, then brought them back to the breakfast room. He heard his mother and Lois start with the washing up; then, Lois said that she would make a some phone calls. She had a few ideas as to where Jake might have gone: "Maybe he dropped by to see Al Ledford, or perhaps he's at the Casinis's. Shannon isn't back from New York yet, but Collie, his sister, is a music teacher in grade school. Jake might be visiting with her."

Andrew finished his cookies and went out to the living room. He decided he would remain downstairs until Jake returned from wherever he had gone. Better to stop him in his tracks right away if he started making hateful accusations. He half relished, half dreaded Jake's return. He thought that it would be best to act very bewildered, very hurt, when Jake would begin to recount the morning's episode.

Just completely deny everything, he reminded himself. Jake would then be perceived as the troublemaker, the mean-spirited one who wanted discord and strife. Maybe Andrew's mother would turn on him, seeing him for the vengeful, hateful one and—

Andrew smiled.

Perhaps all was not lost, after all.

Jake did not return for supper that night, nor before Andrew went to bed. Mr. Givens accepted Lois's explanation that Jake had "gone out" for the day, and did not press for any particulars.

It was about ten-thirty when Andrew heard a car pull up in the driveway. He looked out his window and saw that it was a taxicab. The driver got out, opened the rear door, and hauled out a torpid, reeling figure: Jake! The driver led, or rather dragged, Jake up the front steps, and tapped lightly on the front door.

"Hit's okay...hit's okay...hit's openeded," Jake stuttered.

Andrew heard his mother's and Lois's voices, laced with shock and relief.

"Don't worry about the fare—the bartender paid it," the cabdriver said. "Well, put this guy to bed and have lots of coffee ready in the morning. He's going to have one hell of a hangover."

Andrew couldn't believe his good fortune. This was even better than anything he could have ever concocted! He dashed down the stairs to the landing and his eyes feasted on the scene: Jake, supported on one side by Lois, on the other side by Andrew's mother, staggering and lurching across the room. The trio made their way to the foot of the stairs, where Jake's eyes, bleary with inebriation, focused on Andrew. His jaw sagged, and he moaned softly as large tears coursed down his cheeks. Andrew stared back at him, his face conveying shocked bewilderment and a trace of condemnation. Andrew's mother whispered something into Jake's ear, and Jake's body slumped, almost dragging Lois and Andrew's mother down with him. Andrew's mother glanced sharply at Andrew. "Go to your room, Andrew," she hissed.

Andrew turned and ran up the stairs, his heart pounding with elation. It took a great deal of effort to keep his expression a puzzled mask until he got into his room and shut the door. Once within, his tight-lipped countenance was replaced by a wide grin, and his heart soared with glee.

What luck! Jake completely stewed to the gills, swacked to the eyeballs, rat-assed, stinking, shit-faced drunk! If ever Andrew needed reassurance that there was a God in heaven, here was proof positive that He was still ordering things about!

"...He's never, *ever* been like this." Andrew heard his mother's low voice outside his door.

"Do you need any help getting him into bed?" Lois whispered.

"Just help me get him into the room—I'll get him settled."

Andrew heard shuffling noises, his mother's low, soothing voice, the sound of Jake's inert body thudding onto the bed, and tortured groans that faded into quiet sobs. Whatever Jake might say to Andrew's mother would most likely, Andrew hoped, be dismissed as the babblings of a drunk. *A drunk!* Suddenly, he remembered Jake's agitation about some deep, dark secret.

A secret that he didn't want me—or his father—to know about. I thought it was that Jake was so much younger than Mum, but that wasn't it. Jake wasn't upset at all when Lois announced his age at his birthday celebration. It all fits together! Jake has a drinking problem!

Andrew's face broke into a triumphant smile, and he had to check himself from laughing aloud. This would be the wedge he could use to drive his mother and Jake apart, as well as the instrument he could employ to sow even more discord between Jake and Mr. Givens.

Best of all was that, if he played his cards right, his mother might see fit to take him back to England after all, if she severed ties with Jake.

Chapter 33

"*D*oes your husband know?"

"No, he was fast asleep when I went to bed after we got Jake settled. He woke up early this morning and didn't mention anything to me about hearing things last night, either. Thank God for that, at least!"

"Yes, with Jake and his father finally on speaking terms, this would destroy everything!"

Andrew was standing in the kitchen, having tiptoed down the stairs to grab some cookies before breakfast. It was early, a few minutes after seven. He had not expected anyone to be awake at this hour on a Sunday morning, and the sound of voices coming from the breakfast room had startled him so much that he nearly dropped the cookie jar lid on the floor.

"Well, I told Gene that Jake got in very late last night and isn't feeling well," Lois said. That's the truth, at least. Is he in very much pain?"

"Yes, terribly." Andrew's mother spoke in a soft, strangled voice, as if she herself were the one in agony. "He has a beastly hangover, but that isn't the worst of it. He just lies there, not moving, not saying a word, with tears pouring down his face—" She broke off, then resumed, her voice now emphatic, almost angry: "It's so *unlike* him! He's never, *ever*, done anything like this, not even when—" Sudden silence again, then she repeated herself: "It's just not like him! He never fit in with the pub-crawling crowd—in fact, he used to get teased by the other pilots in his squadron for being such a straight arrow. He'd occasionally take his ground crew out and buy them a round, but it was more to be sociable with them, not to get sloshed. I've never known him to be even a bit squiffy!"

"Something must have happened!" Lois spoke vehemently. "Maybe someone called him and told him that one of his friends had been killed. I haven't written to him about anybody he knew who was killed. I figured, what good would it do for him to know when he's got to keep his wits about him when he's flying? Maybe I should have—"

"No, you did the right thing."

"All the same, Jake never wrote me about...specifics, but I've heard that things were pretty bad during that first summer that Jake was in the RAF. Have you ever known him to go off the deep end when someone he knew was killed?"

Andrew's mother stammered, "He—well, he often keeps things to himself."

There was something about her tone of voice that made Andrew suspect that, though his mother was thoroughly baffled by Jake's behavior, there was something she was concealing from Lois.

His thoughts were interrupted by a loud clumping down the stairs and Mr. Givens's voice: "Lois?"

Not wanting to risk being found out as an eavesdropper, Andrew quickly sauntered into the breakfast room as though he had just descended the stairs.

"Mum?" His voice echoed Mr. Givens calling again, "Lois?"

"In here," Lois said. "You two, you caught me before I had a chance to get breakfast ready."

"Ah, I thought I'd do some paperwork before church." Mr. Givens gave Lois a quick kiss.

"Gene, it's Sunday. Day of Rest, remember? Why don't you sit in the sunroom and read the paper. I'll get you a cup of coffee."

Mr. Givens shuffled off to the sunroom and Lois got up and went into the kitchen. Andrew sat down next to his mother. He was going to ask how Jake was feeling, but then thought better of it. He didn't want to be warned not to mention anything to Mr. Givens. Instead, he asked, "Can we have Eggs Benedict for breakfast?"

"Oh, darling, that's a little too much for Lois to whip up on short notice. Tell you what, I'll ask Lois to fix some for you on Tuesday, after we leave."

Andrew had to bite his tongue from saying: *No point in that—I'm not going to be staying here, anyway.*

"Whadyamean, he came in drunk last night?" Mr. Givens glared at Andrew. They were both in the car, alone, Mr. Givens having dropped Lois and Andrew's mother off in front of the church before he parked the car. Andrew had stayed in the car as he had just "noticed" that his zipper was open and he had to fix it before going into church. He then had casually mentioned to Mr. Givens that it was too bad that Jake couldn't come to church and that he hoped that Jake's hangover wasn't too serious. This had prompted an echoing query from Mr. Givens: *Hangover?* So Andrew, of course, had been duty-bound to inform Mr. Givens about Jake's lapse the previous night.

"I'm sorry, I thought you knew about it," Andrew mumbled.

Mr. Givens's mouth set into a grim line. Without saying another word, he got out of the car and stalked up the church steps. Andrew scurried behind him. Nodding perfunctorily at the greetings murmured to him as he moved through the vestibule, Mr. Givens's eyes all the while searched the crowd until they rested on Lois. Then the eyes blazed with fury as he caught Lois's attention. Lois smiled an apology to the person with whom she was chatting, and threaded her way through the web of parishioners.

Figuring that it would be a good idea to melt into the background, Andrew ducked into the crowd and found his way to his mother's side. The chords of the piano and organ resounded and they were swept by the mob into the sanctuary.

"We'll save a place for Jake's parents," his mother said as they sat down in one of the pews.

Lois and Mr. Givens did not appear beside them—not after the first hymn was sung, announcements were made, and latecomers straggled in; not after long prayers were said; not after the Scripture reading. The doors in the back of the church were shut and the sermon began.

Andrew glanced at his mother. She stared straight ahead, but her eyes were clouded and troubled. He took her hand and looked comfortingly at her. She glanced at him, evinced a tense smile, and stared ahead again. Andrew squeezed her hand.

No matter what happens, Andrew wanted to say, *you'll always have me*.

As they were filing out of church he felt a hand on his shoulder. He turned and saw Lois standing beside him. Her face bore a strained expression.

"Um, Andrew, the young people are meeting at the pastor's house for the afternoon, and you've been invited."

"*Young* people?"

"They're high school students, a little older than you, but we thought you'd enjoy spending the afternoon with them."

What I'd really enjoy, Andrew thought, is to see Jake and his father have it out—

"They're having lunch, then I suppose they'll play some games or something," Lois continued. "Come on, I'll introduce you to some of them." She took his hand and pulled him over to a cluster of teenagers. Andrew's mother followed.

Lois then introduced him to the *high-schoolers*, as they were called: Bob, the pastor's son, gregarious and chatty, with red hair and a sprinkle of freckles on his face; Susie, his sister, a miniature version of her brother but with longer hair and a toothy grin; Lynette, a rather shy, bookish-looking girl who regarded Andrew with undisguised curiosity; and Lars, a lanky, blond, soft-spoken youth who towered over everyone. Lois told Andrew that she would return later that afternoon to fetch him. His mother gave him a swift quick kiss on his cheek, much to his humiliation.

"So, Andrew," Bob said as they walked across the parking lot to the pastor's house, "How do you like America so far?"

"It's all right," Andrew replied abruptly.

"What kind of ship did you come over on?" Lynette queried.

"A big one," Andrew snapped.

They arrived at the pastor's house. There were about a dozen more high-schoolers and Andrew was peppered with questions which he answered as briefly as possible, often in monosyllables or grunts: *What's England like? You people drive on the wrong side of the road, don't you? Are the Germans bombing England very much?*

"Were you ever in a building that got bombed?" Lynette asked.

Her question startled Andrew and he stammered a reply: "Um, once."

"What was it like?"

The image of Audrey's torn body assaulted him, like a beast let out of a cage. He had tried not to ever think of it but now it crowded out all else: the lively chatter around him, his imaginings of the scene sure to be occurring between Jake and Mr. Givens (*Damn*—and he was missing it!), his plan for convincing his mother to let him return to England.

Lynette was looking intently at him. Andrew suddenly found himself unable to say a word. Mercifully, the pastor's wife announced that lunch was ready. Andrew jumped up and joined the press of people filing into the dining room.

There was a stupendous amount of food set out for the group, enough to feed five times that many people in England. Andrew piled his plate high with sandwiches, sliced apples, and cookies. Might as well help himself to everything while he could!

A girl, all chattery and giggly, breezed in and was introduced to Andrew (the English boy, as he was now called).

"What part of England are you from?" she tittered.

"Northumberland."

"Is that near London?"

"No."

To know one in particular she exclaimed, "Don't you just *love* his accent? Isn't he the *cutest* thing?"

Why don't you just tie a bow around my neck and stick me in a shop window? Andrew thought.

The interrogation continued: *They don't have very much food in England, do they? What was it like being in a bomb shelter? You're probably glad to be away from all that, aren't you?*

Would you like to know how many times I pee every day? Andrew wondered.

That gave him an idea. He got up, put his plate down on his chair and went over to Bob, who was bringing out another plate of fruit from the kitchen.

"Where's the W.C.?" Andrew inquired.

"The what?" Bob asked.

Bugger it! Couldn't these imbeciles understand English?

"The *bathroom*," Andrew hissed.

"Oh, through the kitchen, just before the door outside to the porch."

Andrew walked through the kitchen, slipped out the back door, and made his way across the parking lot. After cutting across a small field to a side street, he began walking purposefully, quickly. He had no idea where he was going; he only knew that he wanted to get away from the curious eyes and prying questions.

All I want is not to be different, to be in a place where I'm not gawked at, fawned over, made fun of...All I want is to go back home, where everyone talks like me, acts like me, thinks like me...where I fit in, where I belong....

He tried to plan what he would say to his mother. He hoped that he would be able to have some time alone with her and that she would not be so utterly absorbed in her worries about Jake that she wouldn't listen to what he had to say. Well, it would do for her to be a little upset about Jake, but not too much....

Suddenly Andrew realized he was in very unfamiliar territory. He tried to recollect the route he'd taken from the church but it was no use: He'd been so intent on getting away he hadn't given a single thought as to how to find his way back.

He found himself across the street from a school with a playground. He crossed over to it and settled himself on one of the swings. After listlessly swaying from side to side and back and forth, he leaned back and gazed at the sky: a shimmering blue canopy with a few benign, puffy clouds. Was his father looking up at the sky, right at this very moment? It would be late evening in Europe right now. The sun would be setting and the stars would soon be coming out. Did his father still look at the stars?

Could he still look at the stars, or was he locked up in some dark cell, some hole...and what about Aunt Jane? Could she still see the stars too?

The tears blurred his view, so that the white clouds dissolved into the blue sky. Hearing the excited chattering of children approaching from behind, he got up and walked around to the side of the school building. He leaned against the wall, then slowly slid down until he was sitting, or rather, was hunched over, in the dirt.

"...he sure is one strange little kid, isn't he?"

"Yeah, I don't think he spoke more than ten words the entire time he was there. Well, he's a Brit, so that explains it. They're all like that." Older voices now, male: one with a croaky voice in the throes of pubertal change; the other, deeper and bolder.

"What do you mean?" The quavery voice plummeted an octave on the last word.

"Oh, Brits are all a bunch of cold fish—arrogant bastards, pardon my French. I mean, the kid didn't tell anyone where he was going, just walked right out—probably thinks we're a bunch of low-lifes and he doesn't want to be contaminated by hanging around with people who don't stick their noses up in the air at everyone."

Andrew kept very still. The voices were just around the corner from him. Luckily, the wall by which the boys were standing extended outward by a few feet from where it met the wall behind Andrew, so he was hidden in a small alcove—the boys would have to make a concerted effort to find him.

The bold voice continued: "My brother's stationed over there. He came home on leave this past spring and, boy, was he ever glad to get away from that place! Said it was a crying shame that we're enemies with Germany, not England. The English are as nasty as the weather, that's what he said—all a bunch of sour pusses: tight-lipped, pompous, and surly. Not a one would ever give you the time of day. He said he never met a Brit that didn't deserve a swift kick in the ass."

"The kid's mother seemed real nice. She's a pilot, isn't she?"

"Well, there's some Brits that ain't so bad. But most of them are really snotty. They call our boys overpaid, over-sexed, and over here. Well, you know what Brits are? Underpaid, under-sexed, and under Eisenhower! Their army's a joke—none of them can fight worth a damn! They surrendered at Tobruk, they got their asses kicked in Malaya and Burma, and they ran away at Dunkirk. One time, my brother seen this Brit soldier running down the street and he yells to the guy, 'Hey—didja run like that at Dunkirk?' My brother said he never seen such a bunch of yellow-bellies in his whole life! Now, if the Nazis had tried to bomb New York or Washington, the American people wouldna stood for it, not for a minute! We woulda bombed them Krauts back into the Stone Age. The Brits, they just took it—bombs falling all over the place, and they just ducked for cover. It wasn't until *we* showed up that the Heinies got their heinies kicked. Stupid Brits—we had to save their butts in the last war and then they went and screwed things up again. They never even paid us back the debt from that war, so why the hell are we helping them now?"

"Gosh, I didn't know that—"

"Well, you'd think those Brits would be grateful for that, and for all the help we gave them to fight *this* war—all that Lend-Lease stuff and Bundles for Britain and all that—"

"The British appreciate everything, don't they? I mean, that's what the papers say—"

"The Brits are nothing but a bunch of snotty, sneaky bastards. They'd like to take over the whole world. They took over half of it, anyway, and most of the people they conquered are no better off than the people under German rule are. Don't forget, we had to fight a war to get rid of them! And what about India? Do you think the Brits are ever going to give it up? Why we should send American boys to die to protect their damned Empire is beyond me!"

"But Germany's our enemy too—"

"It wasn't the Germans who bombed Pearl Harbor! I think we should concentrate on licking the Japs and leave the Brits to fight their own battles, just like they left France to the Krauts when they skedaddled at Dunkirk. Besides, they don't even want us anyway!"

"What do you mean?"

"My brother says that they act like they know it all, and they resent the help we're giving them."

"Really?"

"Yeah, he says that one time he got to talking with some Brits in a pub and he was telling them how much better the Americans were doing in bombing Germany—I mean, the Brits were doing night-bombing, and that wasn't even making a dent, just blind dropping a bunch of bombs all over the place! That's no way to fight a war. Well, these Brits acted all so hoity-toity and said, 'We've been fighting the Nazis longer than you Yanks; we don't need you to tell us how to do things.' Well, if they're so much better why haven't they beat the Krauts yet? You tell me! It wasn't until we went over there that the Nazis saw the business end of a well-placed bomb. And the Brits don't even appreciate how we're helping them!"

"Golly, I didn't know it was as bad as that—are they all like that?"

"Well, not *all*—the broads are all right, my brother says."

"The women?"

"Yeah, they can be pretty accommodating, if you know what I mean. All you have to do is wave some candy bars or a pair of nylons at them. My brother, he says he once shacked up with this broad for a whole weekend for—*get this*—three oranges!"

"Oranges?"

"Yeah, she wanted them for her kid!"

"She had a kid—was she married?"

"Yeah, but her old man was off in North Africa. As they say, when the cat's away...."

As the voices were fading, Andrew heard another one: female. He recognized it as Lynette's: "Have you seen him?"

"Nah, he's not around here. I hope someone pounds his pompous little British ass for all the trouble he's caused...."

"Randy!"

"Sorry Lynette, didn't realize there was a lady around...."

All was silent except for the sound of the children playing. Andrew decided to wait until he thought that Lynette would be up the street, then unobtrusively follow her back to church. After he thought was a safe interval, he stepped out from behind the alcove and bumped smack into Lynette, who was just about to turn the corner.

"Andrew!" she shrieked. "We've been looking all over for you! Your mother's really worried."

"My mother?" Andrew said with dismay.

"She and Lois came to pick you up and we couldn't find you anywhere. Everybody's been looking for you. Come on!" She grabbed his hand and started to pull him along. Andrew yanked his arm back and clumped a few paces behind her.

"Andrew, is anything wrong?"

Andrew glared at her.

She stopped, looked at him, and sighed. "I guess you were a little upset with all of our questions. I'm sorry, we didn't mean to be rude. We were just curious. I guess you think Americans are really nosy and blabbery. We, I mean *I*, didn't mean to pry."

Her sympathetic candor caught him off guard.

"No—I mean, I'm not upset."

"Yes, you are." She put her arm across his shoulder. "Come on." They walked for a minute, silent; then she spoke. "I guess sometimes I'm too curious for my own good. I'd like to be a writer someday and I want to find out everything I can—about people, about places, about things that have happened."

Her eyes had a curious, faraway look; she seemed to be talking more to herself than to Andrew. He noticed that her speech was different from typical "Jersey" accent. It didn't have the harsh edge and guttural intonation; it was more of a gentle drawl with a pleasant lilt, though he couldn't quite place it as being distinctly southern like Gerry's or J.D.'s or El's, or western like Cowboy's. As if suddenly realizing that she was not alone, she focused back on him. "I guess you were kinda overwhelmed by all the attention. You probably felt like you were a freak or something. Everyone was just eager to find out more about you, that's all."

"I'll bet they're just as eager to see my pompous little British ass get a pounding," Andrew replied sullenly.

"Oh no, you didn't hear that pinhead, did you?"

Andrew glared at her.

"Well, if brains were lint, Randy wouldn't have enough to fill his own belly button."

Andrew burst out laughing. Lynette smiled and squeezed his shoulder. "He's got a bad case of what you could call "foot-in-mouth disease. I hope that you don't judge all Americans by people like him."

Andrew couldn't help but like Lynette's friendly manner and unique way of describing things, which belied his initial impression of her as being shy and withdrawn.

He said, "No, I've met some very nice Americans. In fact, some of my best friends are Americans."

"Oh, really?" Lynette chuckled.

Andrew turned away. After a moment he said, "I'm sorry if I caused everyone a lot of trouble. I just wanted to get away."

"Hey, it's all right. It was good for everyone to get off their butts for a change. To tell the truth, I was glad to get out of there. I hate crowds and all the meaningless chitter-chatter you have to put up with. I'd really rather be with someone I can have a real conversation with—" She winked at Andrew, "Someone like you."

They turned a corner and Andrew saw the church across the street. His mother was standing on the front lawn, her face a mask of distress. Lois stood beside her, her arm reassuringly around her shoulder. Lynette hailed them. His mother's knees nearly buckled with relief; she recovered and dashed across the street to embrace him.

"Andrew, darling, oh my God, I was so worried...." She squeezed him in a deathgrip.

Andrew squirmed with embarrassment. "I just went for a walk."

His mother released him and looked gratefully at Lynette. "Thank you ever so much."

"Oh, it was no trouble. Beautiful day to get out and go for a walk—" Lynette laughed. "And we had a nice time talking on the way back."

"Thank you again. We do appreciate how kind you all have been." Andrew's mother steered him across the street to Lois.

"Andrew, why didn't you tell anyone where you were going?" Lois admonished him.

Andrew shrugged in reply.

"Well, come on, get in the car," Lois said.

Andrew wordlessly obeyed, seating himself in the back seat of the car. His mother got in beside him.

He was vaguely familiar with the route they had taken to church and noticed that Lois was driving through a series of unfamiliar streets. "Where are we going?" he asked.

"I thought it would be nice for us to go to a restaurant for supper, just the two of us," his mother replied. "Don't you think that's a wonderful idea?"

As much as he wanted to see the fresh evidence of the massacre certain to have taken place at the Givens domicile (a lot of blood on the floor, perhaps, and, with any luck, Jake's body decoratively laid out, beaten to a gory pulp) Andrew was glad he would have some time alone with his mother. He started planning what form his argument would take, what evidence would be most useful in convincing her to whisk him back to England, how best to approach her. He had to make her realize that Jake was behind it all, that he was acting out of hatred and jealousy. How had he gotten to her? Perhaps he had frightened her with stories of secret weapons the Nazis had, just as Freddie had tried to do!

Just like Freddie, Jake wants me out of the way! Andrew nearly exploded with outrage.

I've got to make her see that!

"I'll be by in about an hour to pick you up," Lois said as she dropped them off outside a restaurant.

After being seated, they ordered their meals. Andrew's mother smiled at Andrew but her expression was somewhat strained, as if they were two strangers and she were trying to think of how to break the ice.

Andrew decided to get right to the point. "How's Jake?" he said, trying to sound as if it were an unimportant concern of his, that he was just making small talk.

The smile was abruptly replaced by a taut stare. "He's doing better," his mother said softly.

Andrew snorted.

"Darling, I know how upsetting it must have been for you, but everything is going to be all right."

"No it's not," he snapped.

His mother bit her lip; she seemed at a loss for words. Andrew decided to press on. "Mum, I didn't want to say anything about it before, but I think there's something seriously wrong with Jake. He's unbalanced. When we were on the ship, that time I went to my cabin to get some of my clothes out of your bag, Jake attacked me. I didn't know he was there—he was underneath the blankets. I leaned over the bed to get something and he grabbed me and started screaming and—"

"Darling—" his mother did not seem as shocked as he thought she would be. "Oh darling, Jake told me what happened. He was horribly upset about it; he was afraid he'd frightened you. He'd been having a dreadful nightmare. I was going to talk to you about it but the next time I saw you, you were in such a cheerful mood—I thought that you had forgotten all about it. I didn't want to bring it up—maybe I should have. I just thought that you weren't concerned about it. Jake said that you were very understanding and kind...."

Kindness and understanding had nothing to do with it, Andrew thought.

"...He was so grateful for what you did." The tension was gone from her face, and she beamed at him. "I wish I could have seen it: You with a pitcher of water in your hand, Jake drenched and sputtering!"

It wouldn't do for her to be amused about things! Andrew kept his face serious and tried to convey the gravity of the situation. "Mum, it wasn't that I was frightened...I mean, I was a little startled, but—" He took a deep breath. "Mum, I'm worried about you. I know Jake has nightmares and he gets, well, wild. The first night on the boat, when we were all sharing the cabin, I heard him—he was yelling stuff and you had to calm him down."

His mother's expression went tense again. "What did you hear?"

He wondered why his mother was so concerned about *that*. What *had* Jake said? "Um, fighter pilot stuff," Andrew replied. "I don't quite remember exactly. I just remember that he was yelling and thrashing around. I'm afraid that he might really get out of control someday...that he might hurt you. What if things get so bad that you had to leave him? I know that it would be very upsetting for you, but if I were in

England, if you would let me go back, I mean, I would be there to help you." He lowered his voice. "If I were...so far away...here...and you were in England...*away from me*...I couldn't help you. It's not *right* for me to be here!"

"What's right is for you to be safe—"

"It isn't *right!*"

"Darling, I know you're a little frightened about being in a strange country but this is what's best. Andrew, I want you to be safe. I don't want to worry about another bomb dropping on you or you getting so horribly ill again—"

"But there *aren't* any bombs dropping on England now—I mean, not hardly! And I'm not going to get ill again—I won't even catch a cold, I promise!"

"I know you have high hopes and good intentions, and though we can hope for the best, we have to plan for the worst."

Andrew always hated it when his mother counter-attacked with platitudes. If she couldn't see that Jake meant to do *him* harm, maybe a flanking attack—arousing her suspicions that Jake might do *her* harm, might prove effectual.

"Maybe you have to plan for the worst, too. Maybe Jake's not ready to be married, yet. He's six years younger than you, isn't he?" He eyed his mother, to see how she would react to his statement.

She took a deep breath and fixed Andrew with a dead-serious glare. "Andrew, his being younger than me is not important."

"But he's still too young! And he's...deranged, sometimes. What if you have to leave him?"

The waitress served them their meal. Andrew's mother carefully unfolded her napkin in her lap and said softly, "Andrew, Jake is *not* too young. When I was his age, you were six years old. He's *not* deranged, either, and I'm *not* going to leave him, so don't worry about it."

Andrew exploded. "Dad wasn't like that! He would never do anything like that! Ranting and raving and coming in drunk!" Several diners, as well as the waitress, looked sharply in their direction. Andrew lowered his voice. "Dad wasn't like that at all! He was strong and good and dependable—you could count on him."

His mother folded her hands and looked down at the table for a long, long time. Finally she said, "Darling, I know you miss your father very—"

"What did Jake say to you to make you want to send me here? Did he scare you with stories that the Nazis have some kind of secret weapon or something? Pilotless planes? Some kind of bomb that could destroy an entire city?"

It was as if he had slapped her. She recoiled, and there was a stunned, terrified look in her eyes. So Jake *had* gotten to her with some crazy story! God, what a bastard! What a clever, sneaky, sodding bastard!

"Andrew—" His mother's voice was crisp and severe, although she spoke in a whisper. "Andrew, you are *not* to be spreading rumors about secret weapons or what you think the Nazis might be up to. Do I make myself clear?"

Andrew stared at her, dumbfounded. She had never, *ever*, been so abrupt with him.

"Do I make myself clear?" she repeated.

Andrew nodded.

"Eat your food. It's getting cold," she said sternly. She sawed viciously at the meat on her plate.

"Eat your food," she hissed.

More out of fear than anything else, Andrew mechanically started to consume his dinner. Halfway through, his mother laid her utensils down and her expression softened.

"Andrew, I want you to realize how serious it is—starting or repeating rumors. Hitler is always bragging about having some kind of secret weapon that will annihilate us or destroy our armed forces, something against which we have no hope. There's a crazy story going around that the Nazis have some kind of special radio beam that can destroy a plane in midair. Even though that sort of thing is utter nonsense, repeated often enough it's enough to scare and demoralize people. And that's what the Nazis want: for us to lose hope. If you start a rumor or repeat frightening stories like that, you've done just as much damage to your country as an enemy bomb. Do you understand?"

Andrew nodded. "Mum, I wasn't going to start any rumors."

She looked at him tenderly. "All right."

They finished their meal in silence. The waitress came over and asked them if they wanted dessert.

"Would you like some ice cream, darling?" his mother asked.

Andrew shrugged. His mother ordered two dishes of vanilla ice cream, which the waitress brought to them.

Andrew scraped his spoon around the frozen lump and consumed it half-heartedly. This conversation was not going as he had planned, and he had the sinking feeling that he had lost his chance to leave this hated land. Jake had gotten to her, had terrified her with crazy stories...and she didn't even realize it! He had taken advantage of her fear and guilt—

Guilt!

He laid his spoon down on the table and fixed his mother with an icy stare.

"It's not fair! It's not fair at all! I made one little mistake—I couldn't find my coat and socks and I slipped and fell in a puddle and caught a cold and you have to punish me—"

"Andrew, you're not being punished—"

"Yes, I *am!* You brought me here because I caught a little cold—"

"It was not a *little* cold, Andrew. You nearly died of pneumonia."

"No, I didn't!"

"Yes, you *did! You* don't remember it, but *I* do, Andrew! You were unconscious and you were gasping for breath and turning blue and—" Her voice choked.

Andrew couldn't bear to see her upset like this. "All right, I *was* very ill," he conceded. "But that's no reason to punish me for what happened—"

"You're not being pun—"

"Please—*PLEASE!* Please give me another chance! I promise that I'll keep my coat and socks—"

"Andrew, that's not the point—"

"How would you feel if you made one little mistake and you weren't given another chance? When you had your accident, how would you have felt if you were told you couldn't fly again because of what happened?"

"Andrew, that's not the same thing—"

"Yes it is! *You* were given another chance—why can't you give *me* one?"

"Andrew, my accident was caused by mechanical failure. It wasn't my fault—"

"Well, my getting sick wasn't my fault either! It wasn't my fault that we had an air raid, and that it was cold and wet, and that I couldn't find my coat. This stupid *war* isn't my fault, either, and you're punishing me for it—"

"Andrew—"

"I *hate* it here! I *don't* want to be here! If you leave me here, I'll figure out a way to get back to England—I'll run away, I'll stowaway on a ship, hide in a plane or something. I'll get back! You can't make me stay here!"

His mother stared at him, dumbfounded; her mouth trembled and huge tears welled up in her eyes and trickled down her cheeks.

"Would you like anything else, ma'am?" The waitress stood over them, check in hand. Andrew's mother put her hand up to her face, shielding her eyes. The waitress laid the check on the table and turned away. All of a sudden Andrew was filled with remorse and cold, savage fear. How could he have been so insensitive and stupid? He had bungled everything! The thing he was more afraid of than anything else, even being left in America, was that something would happen to his mother. After her accident, he had vowed to himself never to cause her another moment's anxiety. The accident had been all his fault: She had been so upset by his behavior after that disastrous first meeting with Jake, had been so worried and preoccupied about everything...The same terrified feeling that Andrew had experienced when he had seen his mother's plane fall out of the sky hit him again. Oh God, what a bloody fool he was....

He took both her hands and laced his fingers tightly in hers. "Mum I'm sorry. I didn't mean it...really I didn't. I won't do anything like that—I promise! Mum—please! Please don't worry!"

His mother disengaged one of her hands and wiped her eyes. She looked drained and overwhelmed. It suddenly occurred to Andrew what a tremendous strain she had been under, what with Jake's recent behavior.

Not to mention the pressure he had undoubtedly put on her to get her to send me to America, Andrew thought. Scaring her with stories of Nazi secret weapons! No wonder she was close to cracking!

And now I've made things worse, first by wandering off and causing her such worry, then by threatening to run away.

Guilt splashed over him and fear settled on him like a thick, suffocating fog. What if she went back to England, worrying about him?

What if she had another accident?

"Mum, please, *please* don't worry. I promise, I *promise* I won't do anything like that. Please don't be upset!"

His mother emitted something that sounded like a strangled, sputtery sigh. Her shoulders convulsed and she tried desperately to compose herself. Andrew was afraid that, if he said anything else, she might break down completely. He didn't even want to look at her, so he lowered his eyes and squeezed her one hand that was still entwined in his. As he regarded their interlaced fingers, he caught sight of the thin, pitiful circlet of gold on her ring finger. Fury welled up in him.

Jake! It was all *his* fault! Andrew might have acted impulsively in wandering off, and had been impetuous in threatening his mother. However, he *had* felt remorse for what he'd done. But what Jake had done was unconscionable, absolutely abominable. He had cold-heartedly and calculatingly played upon her fear and guilt, terrorizing her into doing his bidding. The ring caught the light and gleamed, almost with a sadistic triumph, Andrew thought. The fact that Jake had not shown the least bit of concern for *her* safety galled him. Couldn't she see through *that?*

The words tumbled out of him. "Mum, why don't you stay here too?" He lowered his voice. "If something is going to happen—if you think it's unsafe for me to be in England, then it's unsafe for you, too!" There, that should tip her off as to Jake's *real* motive! It hadn't been in Andrew's initial plans to convince his mother to remain in America, and he had spoken rather impulsively. But even as he voiced his plea, he realized that his staying in America—as long as his mother stayed too—would not be such a bad idea. She would be away from Jake: *That* was the important thing.

His mother managed a tremulous smile, and what she said next stunned Andrew completely. "You sound just like Jake."

"Wh—what do you mean?" Andrew sputtered.

"He wanted me to stay here, too." She was somewhat more composed, as if focusing on Jake's concern for her had chased the demons away. "He should have known better than to try to convince me to do that!"

"*Wh-why*! I mean why wouldn't you want to stay here, where it's safe?" Andrew was just as bewildered by his mother's choosing to return to what she had been made to believe was certain danger as he was by Jake's efforts to prevent her from doing so. What was going on here?

"Andrew, I'm not going to run away from my responsibilities!"

"What do you mean?"

"Andrew, I was accepted into the ATA over hundreds of other applicants. I was given a trust, don't you see? I'm not going to betray that trust. I was chosen, I was trained. My country has invested in me, and I won't walk away from that."

"Mum, you're just a ferry pilot! I mean it's not like you were a fighter pilot or flying bombers or—"

Her eyes blazed at him as she cut him short. "Don't *ever* think that what I'm doing is not important! I may not be a fighter pilot or a bomber pilot, and God knows they have the most dangerous, fearful jobs of all, and they deserve every bit of recognition and glory. But what I'm doing is needed too. We ferry pilots may not get the attention, and we're not in this job for the recognition. But we're doing our bit and even though it's behind the scenes, it's necessary to the total effort of winning this war. If every ferry pilot decided to call it quits, to wait out the war in some safe place far away, it would deplete the ranks of the pilots in Fighter Command, in Bomber Command, in Coastal Command, to do *our* jobs. And who knows how much that might tip the balance in favor of our enemies?"

Her tirade startled him: He knew she was proud, independent, determined, *spirited* (as his father used to say, smiling with unfeigned admiration). But looking at her like this, her face flushed, her eyes fiery with indignation, Andrew felt ashamed that he had belittled her role. "I—I'm sorry, Mum," he stammered.

She brushed her hand on his cheek. "Apology accepted. Now I'll quit lecturing you." She folded her hands and spoke softly. "Andrew, I just want you to be safe. You need to be in a place where you're not constantly having to scuttle off to air raid shelters, where there's plenty of food, where you're protected and cared for. I'm needed in England, but you need to be here."

Andrew nodded, overwhelmed almost to the point of tears by his mother's fear and concern for him, wanting so much not to cause her anxiety and worry. All the same, he felt the black, cold hand of despair tightening its grip on his soul. And then, in a flash, he realized why Jake had suggested to her that she stay in America.

*I've lost, I've lost—I'm going to be stuck here, and Jake—*hatred rose like bile in his throat*—Jake's won! He's gotten to her—scared her senseless, manipulated her, all for his own evil purposes. Clever, clever man! He even pretended to be concerned for her safety, and obviously made a half-hearted attempt to persuade her to stay in America, knowing full well that she would refuse to do anything of the sort. It would suit his purposes to throw the scent off of his real motive!*

His mother's eyes suddenly flickered in recognition. Andrew looked over his shoulder and saw Lois standing by the cash register. Andrew's mother got up and went over to her. Andrew watched as Lois excitedly chattered something to his mother, then saw his mother's mouth form into a stunned *o* of surprise. Her face, though, was not alarmed. On the contrary, it seemed as if she had received news of some incredibly good fortune that she couldn't quite believe. She walked quickly back to the table and, without so much as a glance at Andrew, picked up the check, dropped a few coins for a "tip," and paid their bill at the register. Andrew, unsummoned, followed her and Lois out of the restaurant.

A car was waiting for them by the door; Alida was in the driver's seat. Andrew and his mother got into the backseat and Lois settled herself in front. The two older women chattered about inconsequential matters: recipes, ration points, and what-not. Andrew's mother was silent; Andrew could have been a million miles away for all the attention she was paying to him now! He wondered why Alida was picking them up, but decided it would be best not to ask.

Alida pulled the car into her driveway; Lois thanked her and got out. Andrew noticed that the Givens's family car was not parked in the drive. Perhaps Mr. Givens had departed in a fury (after having done grievous bodily harm to Jake, surely!). Andrew tried not to appear too eager as he climbed the front steps. He may have missed being a witness to the jolly good show that was sure to have taken place that afternoon, but he hoped to feast his eyes on the after-effects: perhaps overturned furniture, holes in the walls, shattered dishes and knick-knacks littering the scene, blood on the floor—please God!

But the scene that greeted him was undisturbed and peaceful: no sign of any kind of row. The house was eerily quiet as well. Lois dashed up the stairs. Andrew's mother followed her. Andrew made a quick walk-through of the first floor: not a sign of disorder anywhere, and no sign of Jake, nor of Mr. Givens. He climbed the stairs and noticed that the door to the master bedroom was closed. His mother and Lois were talking in low voices within. He looked in the guest room: No one in there, either.

He walked down the hall and, having ascertained that the bathroom and spare room were likewise vacant, went into his room and shut the door. He pressed his ear up against the wall that adjoined the master bedroom, but could not discern what his mother and Lois were saying.

Rats! If only they had gone into the guest room! The wall between it and the spare room was thin enough for him hear what was being said on the other side. Andrew flopped back onto the bed.

Bloody hell! What was going on?

He must have dozed, for the next thing he was aware of was his mother gently shaking him. "Darling, why don't you take a bath and come downstairs for a snack?"

He rubbed his eyes and stumbled down the hall to the bathroom. After a long hot soak, he padded down the stairs and was served a piece of chocolate cake in the breakfast room. His mother sat beside him, sipping a cup of cocoa. Lois went into the kitchen and proceeded to wash up the day's dishes.

His mother set her cup down on the table.

"Andrew, I know it's going to be hard for you at first but things will get better. After awhile, you'll even wonder how you lived with the air raids, the shortages, the war always so fearfully close. You're with people who are going to take good care of you, and I shouldn't have to tell you that I expect you to behave yourself and also to be considerate and respectful of them." She paused for a moment, then went on. "When I put on my uniform, I'm not just me—I represent every pilot in the ATA. You're my son and you represent me, and I expect you to act accordingly and to show Jake's parents every courtesy, regardless of how you feel about being here." She waited for Andrew to acknowledge her request. He nodded and she continued. "I don't know when we'll be able to see each other again, but remember that I'll be thinking of you every day."

Andrew glumly finished his cake. He was afraid to say anything, afraid that the words would stick in his throat, afraid that his eyes would fill with tears if he so much as looked at her. He scraped his plate, focusing on getting every last bit of icing off. His mother reached into her pocket and pulled out a dollar bill. Laying it before Andrew she said, "I've set up an account for you here so that Lois can buy clothes and things for you, and so you can have some pocket money every week. I figured that one dollar would be about right for you. That's about five shillings, quite a bit of money for someone your age, but I'd like for you to have enough to spend on sweets and special things for yourself."

Andrew regarded this bribe ruefully; surely Jake was behind this too!

As if I could be so easily bought off!

He wanted to fling the odious currency in his mother's face but that would be pointless. He was doomed anyway.

He looked at the undersized, drab dollar bill. It didn't even *look* real; it looked more like play money you'd get in a game. He picked it up and put it into his pocket. Without a word, he stood, then plodded out of the room and up the stairs. He dressed in his pajamas, got in bed, and pulled the covers over his head. Presently he heard a tap on the door, but made no response. He heard the door creak open, felt his mother sit down on the bed next to him. She gently pulled the covers down and started to stroke his hair. He responded by turning onto his stomach and burying his face into the pillow. Her hand moved down his back and she rubbed his spine and shoulder blades. He expected her to say something, to plead with him, admonish him, explain, cajole, defend her decision one last time, but she was silent. She kissed him on the back of the neck and quietly slipped out.

Andrew turned over and stared at the ceiling, feeling completely drained of life and hope. He felt dead, utterly dead, and had an almost physical sensation of blackness and coldness enclosing his soul.

He heard a car pull up and the thought occurred to him that it might be Mr. Givens, or perhaps Jake being shepherded home again in an intoxicated state. He got out of bed and went to the front window to investigate. It was a car pulling up to the house next door, on the opposite side from Alida's. Andrew slumped down to the floor. He didn't even have the energy or the willpower to make it back to bed. He might as well spend the night in vigil, waiting for either Jake or Mr. Givens to come home, though he was far past the point of feeling capable of any kind of satisfaction at seeing Jake staggering in inebriated or Mr. Givens coming home in a huff. It was more with a detached, dull stupor that he surveyed the quiet night scene, much like a battle-weary sentry who no longer cares whether the morrow brings defeat or victory, deliverance or death.

It was morning, and Andrew awoke to find himself in bed. He didn't remember climbing back into bed the night before; surely he would have been aware of his mother or Lois helping him back.

Pushing his puzzlement aside, he went downstairs. Lois, as usual, was in the kitchen, preparing breakfast. What was unusual was that she was humming!

"Here, Andrew—pancakes are ready." She flipped two onto a plate for him and added three links of sausage and a spoonful of scrambled eggs.

"Good morning!" Andrew's mother appeared behind him.

"Morning!" Lois chirped. Andrew noticed that his mother had a relieved, almost buoyant expression on her face.

"Here Alice, you take these and I'll put on another batch." Lois got another plate and piled it with pancakes, sausages, and eggs.

"Thanks awfully!" Andrew's mother took the plate. "You're spoiling me terribly with all this wonderful food! I know I'm going to wail and moan about the meager fare when I get back to England."

"Well, enjoy it while you can."

"I certainly will!"

"Lucky Andrew, he doesn't have to give it up." It was Mr. Givens. He moseyed into the kitchen and watched as Lois ladled the pancake batter into the skillet. He laid his hand on Andrew's shoulder and smiled, actually *smiled*, at him!

Lois humming, Mr. Givens smiling, Andrew's mother as cheery as a maid given an unexpected day off—*what* was going on?

Thoroughly bewildered, Andrew carried his plate into the breakfast room. As he sat down, his mind started exploring the possibilities. Maybe Jake had spent the night elsewhere and everyone was relieved that the bloody awful scene was over. But it was more than relief that he sensed. Not a sigh of thankfulness that it could have been much worse, but a light-hearted spirit of exuberance and joy—but *why?* What had happened? If Mr. Givens had vented his anger at Jake, he might be expected to be pleased about it, but Lois and Andrew's mother were in a state of cheerfulness as well. Andrew took a few bites of pancake. Realizing he didn't have any milk, he went back into the kitchen to pour himself a glass.

"Morning, Dad...Mom." Jake bounded down the stairs.

"Morning, Jake," Mr. Givens replied, his voice easy and calm.

"Pancakes are almost done, you two," Lois smiled.

"Coffee?" Mr. Givens took down a cup from over the stove.

"Yeah, thanks," Jake replied.

Mr. Givens filled the cup with coffee, stirred in two spoonfuls of sugar, added a splash of cream, and handed it to Jake. Jake took a few sips, then looked at Andrew with a benevolent expression.

He's probably gloating over me being stuck here. He's finally got my mother all to himself.

Andrew stomped back into the breakfast room, feeling even more despondent than he'd felt the night before. The bizarre behavior evidenced by everyone had only added gall to his bitterness. What the bloody hell was going on?

Jake and his father entered the room, each with plate in hand, and proceeded to devour their food. Lois appeared with a coffee pot and filled everyone's cups, chattering all the while about the nice weather, what a perfect day it was for travelling, and so forth. Andrew got up and scuffed across the living room and up the stairs, leaving the chummy crowd to themselves.

Once in his room, he noted the time: seven-thirty. In less than an hour he would endure the final parting from his mother; then he would be dumped off at that hideous school to endure another wretched day of being taunted and teased, one of many, no doubt, stretching into a bleak and hostile future. He dressed, and was about to go to the bathroom to brush his teeth when there was a tap on the door. He opened the door and his mother entered, carrying two gaily wrapped packages, one large and one small.

"Here's a few going-away presents, darling. Even though you're not the one going away, I thought they might be appropriate."

Andrew took the larger parcel, sat down on the bed, and undid the wrapping. There were four framed prints of airplanes: a Hurricane, a Spitfire, a Beaufighter, and a Mosquito.

"I brought the prints over from England, but had them framed here." She held up the picture of the Hurricane. "I hope they'll remind you to think of me every now and then. Jake's father said that he'd hang them for you."

Andrew stared at the Hurricane, as if by focusing on it he might keep the feelings of despair and panic from overwhelming him. His mother sat down beside him and put her arm around his shoulder.

"Open the other one, darling."

He unwrapped the smaller package, thinking it might be a book. Instead, it was a framed photograph of his mother getting into a Spitfire, the same picture as the one of her in the newspaper clipping.

"The newspaper gave me a print. I brought it here and had it framed too, so that you'd have a picture of me after I'm gone.

"Andrew clenched his jaw, trying to check the tears welling up in his eyes. One trickled down his cheek; his mother wiped it away with her finger.

Andrew, I know it's a bit upsetting for you now but, believe me, this is what's best for you. I know we've been over this before, but please, please believe that all I want for you is to be safe and well."

Andrew tried to keep the lump in his throat from bursting forth into sobs. He swallowed once, swallowed hard again and slumped against her. Her arms encircled him and she hugged him tightly.

"Do I have to wait until the war is completely over?" he asked.

"That would probably be best."

"What about when we invade France? There shouldn't be any danger then!"

His mother was silent.

"Mum—*please!* Everything should be all right once we're in France. *Please!*"

"We'll see."

"Jake? Alice? We'd better get moving." Lois called from the bottom of the stairs.

"All right," Andrew's mother replied. She turned to Andrew again. "Darling, I know that you're a little frightened, but everything is going to turn out fine! You're going to have a wonderful time here—right now you only see the bad side of it. I think—" she looked at Andrew with sympathy and pride, "I think that you're going to have such a good time here that you won't want to leave when it's time for you to return to England."

Andrew snorted. "And I'll eat Hitler's underwear, too."

She sighed and smiled wistfully. "Well, perhaps you'll have mixed feelings about leaving. I know you'll be glad to return to England, but you'll be a little sad to leave America, as well." She brushed a kiss against his cheek. "Oh darling, things are going to turn out so much better than you expect them to!"

"Jake and I will take care of the luggage and the tickets—why don't you two go out and wait for the train?" Mr. Givens said.

As he walked out to the platform, Andrew sensed a faint rumble, saw a pinpoint of light in the distance, and waited wordlessly as the train bore down upon them.

His mother hugged him. He wanted to rage at her; perhaps it would shock her into staying, at least for awhile.

No, it wouldn't, he thought, and we would both part, distraught and guilt-ridden. The remembrance of the last time he had seen his father forced itself into his already anguished thoughts, despite his attempts to push it away: the angry words, the accusations, the distressed look on his father's face. *No*. No last minute hysterics here: That bitter experience had taught Andrew well. Of course, he would see his father again, and he would be able to properly apologize for the hurt he had caused him. He would make it all up to him and never, *ever* again say or do anything mean. Until then, he had to live with the guilt that he had caused his father such pain, that his father's last memory of him had been the hurtful words spoken in anger and fear. Andrew had learned his lesson, a bitter one, to be sure.

A sudden wave of panic hit him. Maybe it had happened to teach him how important parting words were. He would see his father again, surely, but—the horrible thought savaged him:

Maybe this is the last time I'll see her!

He nearly crumpled as he clung to her.

"Please, please Mum! Be careful, *please!* Don't fly unless it's absolutely clear weather...Double-check the barrage balloon locations—"

"Andrew, don't worry. Please don't worry, darling." She hugged him tightly but her embrace failed to console him. He knew it. *He knew it!* This would be the last time he would see her....

The train screamed into the station, echoing the shrieking despair in Andrew's soul. If only he were big and strong enough to hold her back, to keep her from boarding the train and being conveyed to certain doom. If he were a grown-up he would be able to convince her not to go. He felt so small and powerless: He was just one little boy who couldn't change a thing and the war was a giant, all-powerful malevolent entity which demanded, simply, that people die. Gram, Aunt Gwen, Mr. Beaton, Irene, Audrey...the war had pointed its cruel finger at them and had stolen their lives. No pleas, no bargaining, no reprieves, no mercy....

His mother gave him a farewell kiss.

"I love you. Be a good boy." She then hugged Lois and Mr. Givens and, in a few horrible seconds, disappeared into the train with Jake. The train immediately pulled away, and Andrew did not even have the chance to see her face through the window one last time. He watched in anguish as the train receded into the distance until it was a tiny smudge far, far away; then it disappeared completely.

Lois put her arm around his shoulder. "Come on, you'll be late for school," she said gently.

He trudged back to the car, got into the backseat, and slumped against the door. Lois got in next to him.

"Well, on the other hand, it looks like a good day to play hookey—what do you think?" She winked at him. Andrew nodded weakly and closed his eyes.

Mr. Givens brought them back home and departed for work.

"Why don't you rest up today, just get back into your pajamas and pretend you're horribly ill," Lois suggested. I'll bring lunch upstairs for you later on."

Nodding dumbly, Andrew trudged upstairs to his room. After changing back into his pajamas, he got into bed. Lois entered the room, carrying a plate of cookies and a glass of milk.

Andrew had been so engrossed in his own misery that he hadn't realized that he had been acting rather churlish. He hadn't meant to, but that was how his behavior would naturally have been perceived. He apologized to Lois:

"I'm sorry if I'm acting impolite. I know that all this has nothing to do with you—I mean, it's not your decision. You're being very kind."

"Don't you worry. I know it's not easy for you." She gave him a kiss on the forehead, then departed.

He tried to eat, but even the freshly-baked cookies gagged him. He took a gulp of milk, then choked on it as a sob exploded in his throat.

Why had he been singled out to be sent to a place that he didn't want to be in? Through his tears, he realized: The whole *world* was full of people who were in places they didn't want to be in! British servicemen in North Africa, in Burma, in P.O.W. camps in Germany; Yanks in England grousing about the "surly, snotty Brits"; the French there too, whining about the food; Jews (it was said) in concentration camps; children exiled to faraway places. He knew, also, that he wasn't the only "Bundle from Britain" to be cast upon American shores, but that was no consolation.

Did his father now feel this kind of despondency, this despair? Andrew opened his box and took out his father's book. He was hoping that the words of the poem would reassure him, drive out this horrible blackness of spirit that was choking the life out of him.

But as he read the poem, it seemed to be nothing more than words strung together. So someone didn't want to die! *Lots* of people didn't want to die, and did! He remembered how happy Irene had been that morning after they had gotten even with Freddie. Aunt Gwen and Gram, always so cheerful; Audrey, too, who had bought him a piece of cake to celebrate his birthday. Did she expect to end up being sawn in half a few hours later?

Maybe his father had never even looked at that poem, or had glanced at it briefly and had forgotten it. He may have absentmindedly stuck the bookmark at a random spot between the pages.

He might not even be alive....

Sick to his stomach at the thought of even allowing such a thought to enter his mind, Andrew stumbled down the hall. He went into the bathroom and ran the water in the tub, then got in and lay on his back, staring at the ceiling. He turned over and plunged his head under the water, holding his breath for a long, long time, long enough to feel his lungs nearly burst. He tried to keep his head under long enough to feel blessed unconsciousness take over, but just as the swirling, sparkly darkness seemed about to explode into nothingness, he instinctively convulsed, reared up, and swallowed a gulp of air. He turned over on his back again, his mind reeling with the horror of what he had just attempted. It wasn't that he had a clear purpose in his mind to end it all— he knew, deep down inside, that it was wrong. It was oddly tantalizing, though, to stand on the margin of being and not being.

Maybe it's the only kind of power I have. I can't go back to England, I can't stop people being mean to me, I can't bring my father back, I can't stop the war....

Then a horrifying image burst on him: His mother, sobbing in Jake's arms because....

They found me, drowned in the bathtub....

And Jake, pretending to comfort her, but his face leering with triumph.

A white-hot rage tore through Andrew.

You bastard! I'm not going to let you win!

Chapter 34

"*I* don't feel right saying anything to you while they was here, Lois, and I don't know if I doing the right thing by telling you, but things jus' don't add up."

"What do you mean, Sarah?"

Andrew stopped at the foot of the stairs. His stomach was telling him it was time for elevensies and, even though he realized that this particular institution was not part of the form in Yankland, he thought that one of Lois's oatmeal raisin cookies and a cup of tea might hit the spot. It was his third day home from school; he'd caught a nasty cold on top of his distress over his mother's departure. Never before in his life had the prospect of illness been so welcome: He *might* even come down with a touch of bronchitis or maybe, with a bit of luck, pneumonia. His bout with pneumonia had not been all *that* bad, despite what his mother had said.

He tiptoed through the kitchen, leaving the cookie jar undisturbed.

"...Mind you, I think she the sweetest thing ever walked the face of the earth. If God Almighty decided to sit Hisself down and make the perfect wife for Jake, he couldna done no better job." Sarah's voice took on that oratorical tone that was reserved for the things about which she felt particularly passionate; it was just slightly more emphatic than her usual speech, which was always booming and assertive, whether she was conversing with someone or merely talking to herself as she did the chores.

She could give lessons to Churchill, Andrew thought, as he crept by the pantry.

"She's a godsend, that's for sure," Lois agreed. "As much as I'd hoped that Jake would find someone really special, I never thought he would pick somebody so wonderful—"

"I get the feeling *he* not the one what did the picking."

"What?"

"See the way she look at him?"

"Well, she's in love with him, that's obvious. And have you ever seen Jake so happy?"

"Tell the truth, I don't see much o' Jake, not for the past nine years. But no, I can't *never* recollect him being so happy as he is now. But *he* not the one what started things, if you get my drift."

"What do you mean—that *she* started it?"

Andrew halted by the doorway to the dining room, held his breath.

"Why not? Been known to happen!" Sarah punctuated her declaration with a blast of laughter which was counterpointed by Lois's hearty chuckle.

"Well, as they say, like father, like son!" Andrew could almost hear Lois wink her eye. There was silence, save for the soft clunking sounds of Lois picking up and re-placing the knickknacks as Sarah polished the sideboard underneath. It was apparent that Lois's helping Sarah with the chores was a regular, accepted routine. *America!*

"What were you saying about things not adding up?" Lois's voice took on a seri-ous tone.

A loud grunt from Sarah, then her voice, low, but insistent. "Well, they jus' don't add up. She say she visit him in that hospital when he got hisself all burnt."

"It was so good of her to do that, Jake being so far from home and all—"

"But he say they meet when she fly a Spitfire to his base."

"So? They met before he was shot down, then."

"He got shot down in one them Hurricanes, not no Spitfire. She don't even join that there Air Transport Auxiliary 'til March o' 41, *and* she say she don't fly them fighter planes 'til summer o' 41.

"So?"

"When was Jake's accident?"

"End of September."

"End of September *when*?"

There was a pause, then Lois's voice, hushed with realization.

"*1940!*"

"So how she be visiting him almos' a whole year before they meet?"

Andrew lay in bed, trying to concentrate on *Last of the Mohicans*, but the point of the story eluded him. It had to be just about the most boring thing he'd ever read.

But it was not just the ponderous prose and the unexciting account of life in the buggerall of the American wilderness that accounted for his mental wanderings.

Why would he lie? Why would Jake say he'd met my mother when she'd ferried a Spitfire to his squadron?

Andrew had rejected several possibilities for Jake's dissimulation. Did Jake not want his mother to know that anyone was visiting him in the hospital? No, that didn't make sense. Why wouldn't he want her to know someone was looking after him? Could Jake have gotten a nasty thump on the head when he'd had his accident and thought they'd met someplace else? Jake might be many things, but he certainly wasn't that dotty.

What was Jake hiding?

Lois brought him up a lunch of chicken pot pie and peach cobbler. While he ate, Andrew flipped through his history book.

Bloody hell! They've had more presidents in a century and a half as we've had kings and queens in almost a thousand years! No wonder Yanks can't seem to get organized, what with changing their leader every few years! Everyone seems to think that Franklin Roosevelt being President for eleven years is so bloody amazing—that's nothing! Look at Queen Victoria—she ruled England for more than half a century!

"Andrew? Why don't you take a nap for the afternoon?" Lois came in to take his tray downstairs. Sarah stood behind her, polishing the mirror in the hallway.

"Um, that sounds like a good idea. All this reading has made me a bit sleepy."

Lois beamed at him as she took the tray from the dresser. "Oh, Sarah and I are going over to Alida's for the afternoon."

"Oh?" Andrew didn't mean to pry, but his reply came out as an interrogation.

"Yes—um, Sarah is going to—going to—"

"Do some things." Sarah glared directly at Andrew, her voice emphatic, almost bossy.

"Yes—yes—" Lois looked at Sarah, and smiled nervously. "Do some things—and Alida and I are going to—to—"

"Visit," Sarah intoned.

"Yes, we're going to visit." Lois bobbed her head and, as if for emphasis, repeated, "Yes, visit, we're going to visit. Oh, I'll leave Alida's number by the phone in our bedroom, in case you want to get in touch with me. I'll be back around five."

"All right."

"Help yourself to the cookie jar."

"Thank you."

"My, my, Lois—ought to take this boy to meet the President, what with all them fine manners he got!" Sarah said. "Heard more pleases and thank yous in one morning than in all my born days!"

Andrew accepted Sarah's compliment with a smile. Sarah's being on a first-name basis with Lois was another disconcerting thing. Lucia or Maria always bobbed their heads respectfully to their mistresses, saying, "Yes, mum" or "Right away, mum", and they would *never* have dreamed of speaking so familiarly with their employers. Even Mrs. Tuttle, for all her bubbliness, and Mrs. Beaton, for all her surliness, were appropriately submissive when speaking with Andrew's grandmothers. It was all right for them, though, to be affectionate with Andrew, and for Mrs. Tuttle to be motherly with Andrew's father, but the familiarity, though amiable, was still polite and deferential. Likewise, Mrs. Beaton treated Andrew's mother as a daughter, but in a gently courteous sort of way, without upsetting the bounds of their respective stations in life. Still, Andrew knew that his mother got more in the way of comfort and lovingkindness from Mrs. Beaton than she did from Grandmother Howard.

He sighed and closed his eyes, remembering his summer at Greycliff. Hard to believe that it was just last month; it seemed like a lifetime ago.

A lifetime—and half a world away.

Even with his curiosity piqued as to Lois and Sarah's mysterious dissembling as to what they were going to be doing at Alida's, and his puzzlement over the inconsistencies in the accounts of precisely when his mother and Jake had met, he could not chase away the wave of longing that swept over him.

Funny, he had always hated Greycliff.

Now he would sell his soul to be there again.

"Andrew? Are you up to having company?" Lois's voice sang from the bottom of the stairs.

"What?"

"There's someone here to see you."

Who in the world could possibly want to see me?

"Uh, what? I mean, who?"

"It's me, Lynette."

It took a moment for the name to register.

Lynette, that's right! The girl who'd found him last Sunday!

He heard quick footfalls on the stairs; then Lynette was standing in his doorway.

"I brought your assignments from school. I talked with Miss Van de Veer today and she said you'd been out all week. Thought you'd like to get caught up with your school-work, that is, if you're up to it."

"Um, thank you." Remembering his manners, Andrew smiled in welcome. "Please, have a seat." He indicated the chair at the desk. Lynette pulled the chair over to the bed and sat down.

"How are things going?"

"Oh—all right, I suppose."

"Not great, huh?"

Her directness startled him.

"It...I mean, I'm fine, thank you."

"No, you aren't. Don't try to pretend that coming to a strange place, being made fun of for the way you talk, is such a terrific thing."

She smiled sympathetically at him. "Miss Van de Veer told me about it, hey—" She grabbed Andrew's hand as he looked away. "It's not something that *you* should be ashamed about. Those jerks—" Her voice seemed to catch in her throat. "I know how you feel."

Andrew had to check himself from blurting out *How could you know how I feel?*

"I was ten," Lynette went on, "But I still remember, like it was yesterday, how everyone made fun of what I was, what I looked like, how I talked."

"You?" Andrew had noticed a subtle difference in the way Lynette spoke, but it was not obvious enough to be the object of derision—at least, that's what he thought. Lois, for instance, was still possessed of what Andrew recognized as the American Mid-western accent: There was the slight lengthening of the vowels, the almost impercep-tibly slower cadence to her speech; still, nothing that was glaringly different. Then he realized he'd been rude. "Sorry, I didn't mean to be impolite." He felt the color rise to his face.

"Here's your tea, and a plate of cookies." Lois came into the room, carrying a tray laden with tea things and a plateful of "snickerdoodles," scrumptious cinnamony treats. She set the tray down on the dresser. "Holler if you want any more cookies."

"Thanks," Lynette smiled.

After Lois had departed, Andrew said, "You're not from New Jersey, are you?"

"I'm from West Virginia. When I first came here, I got called 'Stupid Hillbilly' and 'Dumb Hick' so much I just about forgot my own name."

"You?" He suddenly recalled Freddie's derisive appellation—*Inbred, Imbecilic Hillbillies*. Feeling his face flush again, he stammered, "Sorry, I didn't mean—it's just that you don't seem—I mean, you seem so—so intelligent, and you talk very nicely, I mean, not like people in New Jersey. They all sound like gangsters, don't they?"

Lynette chuckled. "Well, now that you mention it, they do." She sipped her tea. "Well, I don't think my accent is quite as obvious as it was when I first came here. All the name-calling got to me, so I figured if I kept my mouth shut, I wouldn't get teased so much. Then the teachers gave me bad grades. They thought I was stupid because I didn't talk in class"

"Why did your family move here?"

Lynette's expression turned serious; then she spoke softly, as if she were apologizing. "I moved here by myself. My father died when I was ten, of the Black Lung Disease. He was a coal miner. So I came to New Jersey to live with my sister."

"I'm sorry," Andrew said.

Lynette squeezed his hand, and a flash of guilt and sadness swept across her face. "Oh, gosh, I came to cheer you up, and you're comforting me."

"It's all right—I don't mind, not at all."

Lynette glanced at the picture on the dresser.

"That's your mother, isn't it?"

"Yes, it is."

"I think that's terrific—her being a pilot and all, I mean." She gazed at the picture, a pensive expression on her face. Andrew wanted to ask her about her mother: Why had Lynette not stayed in West Virginia with her?

Suddenly, Lynette brightened.

"Howabout we make a deal!"

"A deal?"

"A trade: You tell me about England, because I'd like to write a story about an English boy who comes to America. In return, I'll teach you how to speak New Jerseyese."

"New Jerseyese?"

"Yeah, after I got teased so much for the way I talked, I figured that if I learned to talk New Jerseyese, I wouldn't get razzed so much."

"Razzed?"

"Made fun of."

"Oh."

"I'll give you some pointers, so if you'd like to try them out, you won't sound so different. Though I really like how you talk—please don't change permanently. Deal?"

"Deal!"

"Okay, lesson one. What are we doing now?"

"Visiting—"

Lynette made circular motions with the palms of her hands, as if trying to draw the answer out of Andrew.

"Drinking tea—chatting—" The hand movements became rapid and frenzied. "Talking—"

"Right, but not quite."

"Talking?"

"*Tawking.*"

"Tawking?"

"Yeah, New Jerseyites don't talk, they *tawk.*"

"*Tawk.*"

"Very good!"

"Now, what's a hot beverage that you usually drink in the morning, or when you get together with friends to *tawk*?"

"Tea, of course."

Lynette shook her head.

"Cocoa—coffee—"

"It's *cawfee.*"

"Cawfee?"

"Right—*cawfee*!"

"*Cawfee.*"

"Now, tell me the name of the place at which the ocean meets the land. People go there to play in the surf and get sunburned to a crisp."

"The seaside—the coast—the seashore—"

"Close."

"Seashore?"

"The *shaw.*"

"Yeah, the *shaw*. Now, I'll make up a saying for you, so that you can practice. My sister's—that is my *sistuh's*—name is Margaret, only everyone here calls her Mawgrut."

"*Mawgrut.*"

"And she loves to talk, and drink coffee, and go to the shore. Only here you'd say, My *sistuh Mawgrut*, likes to *tawk*, drink *cawfee*, and go to the *shaw*. Go ahead, say it."

"My sistuh Mawgrut, likes to tawk, drink cawfee, and go to the shaw."

"Very good!"

"Crikey, I sound like a gangster!" Andrew laughed.

Lynette smiled. "Come to think of it, you do!"

Lynette visited the next day, and recorded in her notebook everything that Andrew told her about England. He constantly found himself qualifying things: "This is what it's like now, because of the war—of course it wasn't always like this." However, Lynette seemed to guide the conversation to Andrew's recollections of the war's impact on his country. He found himself talking of the endless nights in the bomb shelter, the horrid food, the shortages, the rationing, the destruction he'd seen, the invasion of his country by Yanks—he politely said *Americans*. He remembered the trivial incidents that had been impressed so strongly in his memory: his blessedly brief encounter with the evacuees at Greycliff; his recollections of the bombed-out buildings in London; the sight of the mass of humanity huddled in the Underground; the little boy who was so upset about his places being taken by the shelter marshall. Andrew could recall exactly what the boy had looked like, with his tear-streaked face and shabby clothes. He even recollected the conversation that had taken place between the women and the shelter marshall: *Evil man, evil as old 'itler...Don't you worry, Dickie...Even if I have to take off every last stitch of clothing and stand here, stark naked on the platform...That evil man shan't take your place again.*

Dickie...his name was Dickie. Funny that he should remember the name of a boy he'd only seen for a few seconds....

Lynette asked if he remembered anything about the Battle of Britain, and he told of listening to the scores on the radio, of biking to town to do the shopping, of being so angered by the soldiers in the restaurant who had denigrated the RAF. At first, he wasn't going to tell Lynette of his brawl with the inebriated detractor, but when she asked, "What did you do, then?" he felt somehow obliged to reveal what had happened, as if holding back would be a lie of omission. Far from being shocked, she seemed positively delighted by his account of the subsequent brawl, and pressed him with more questions: *What did the man do? What did your mother do?* And in the telling, Andrew experience a strange sense of peace and satisfaction and even delight about the whole thing—it must have looked incredibly hilarious! It seemed as if his remembrances—even the distressing, unspoken ones—were being blessed by her presence, and the secret things of his heart were gently dealt with. He could not speak of the most awful memories: seeing Audrey's torn body, hearing of Irene's tragic accident, learning about the deaths of Gram and Aunt Gwen, finding out that his father had been shot down and believing, during those first terrible days, that he was gone forever. The feeling was strong within him, though, that Lynette somehow sensed that he was holding back some of his most dreadful remembrances and, mercifully, she did not pry.

After Lynette's departure, he felt happier than he had been for days, and he proceeded immediately to write to his mother before his mood evaporated, as he knew it would upon his returning to school. He had to reassure her that he was "settling in," for he didn't want her to worry about him: worry when she should be concentrating on flying, remembering the barrage balloon locations, dealing confidently with any emergencies that might arise, keeping her wits about her at all times—not distracted by concerns for him. Even though their parting had not been acrimonious, it had not been amicable either, and he had to dispel any concerns she might have about him.

So he wrote to her of all the wonderful food he was getting, of Lois's tender care (he mentioned that he'd caught a bit of a cold, but was on the mend and would be returning to school before long), of Lynette's visit and her "New Jerseyese" lessons, of Lindy's constant entreaties for affection. Even as he wrote, Lindy was stretched out alongside Andrew's legs, blissfully purring as he nuzzled his nose into Andrew's thigh.

After supper that night, Lois stood him up against the wall in the kitchen, just next to the entryway to the living room, on the opposite side from the stove. She wanted to measure him, and keep track of his "growing" while he was in America. Andrew noted the penciled marks next to where he stood and the heights and dates written above them; obviously Lois had tracked Jake's progress, too: Next to *8/14/22* (the bottom mark) was written *39 1/2" 37 lbs* Andrew glanced at some of the other notations: *2/14/26 47" 50 lbs; 11/14/28 53" 63 lbs*, and the last one: *8/14/36 69" 140 lbs*.

"Since your birthday is March 4, I'll measure you again on December 4, and every three months after that—quarter-year intervals, just like I did with Jake," Lois said. When your mother comes back, she can see just how you've grown."

Not that I expect to be here all that long, Andrew thought ruefully. Everyone says we're going to invade France by early spring, and it should take only a few weeks to send the Germans fleeing back to Germany, the same way they came...I ought to be back in England by the beginning of June....

"...Hmm, 58 inches," Lois said.

Andrew was dismayed to see that Jake, at the same age, had been two inches taller.

At his weighing in on the bathroom scale, he was further distressed to discover that Jake, at the age of twelve and three-quarter years, had outweighed him by twenty-three pounds.

"Hmm—seventy pounds," Lois murmured. Then she put her arm across his shoulder. "Time to start chowing down—how about a piece of peach pie?"

He returned to school on Monday and, despite Lynette's cheery greeting in the hall whenever she saw him between classes, he found the experience to be odious and de-grading. When Miss Van de Veer asked him about his voyage to America, he replied that the ship had to go "tiddly-bits" (that is, zig-zag course, to avoid the few U-Boats that might still be lurking about). The class roared with derisive laughter; thereafter, he was called "Tiddlybits," which was worse than being called "Slimy Limey."

He misspelled a crucial word in a "spelling bee" in Mrs. Larsen's class— *Honourable*. Andrew spelled it correctly: H-O-N-O-U-R-A-B-L-E. Groans from his team and cheers from the other side bewildered him; "It's H-O-N-O-R-A-B-L-E," Cockney Mouth sneered. Andrew argued that it *was* spelled with a *U*, and Mrs. Larsen had agreed that he *had* used the correct English spelling and that she would accept it as being correct. The students on the other side protested so loudly—*No fair! If one of us had spelled it that way, we would have been wrong*—that Mrs. Larsen had to relent. Andrew thus lost the competition for his side; he refused to be mollified by Mrs. Larsen's apologies and reassuring words after class.

The "State Capital Bee" that Mrs. Henschell had every Friday was just as detest-able. He could bloody care less what all the silly capitals of all their silly states were! The class was studying local history and Andrew could bloody care less, either, about all the stupid people who had settled in Scotch Plains in the 1600s, fleeing Scotland to avoid religious persecution (from the Church of England, Mrs. Henschell pointed out, and everyone glared at Andrew as if he had personally burned heretics at the stake). Nor was he the least bit interested in all the silly battles George Washington had fought, nor could he give a hoot about the stupid Lenni Lenape Indians.

Math class was no better: They were now calculating word problems having to do with money (bloody *American* money, that is): *If John gets a quarter for mowing Mr. Green's lawn every week from April through November, and a dime for raking the leaves in Mrs. Brown's yard every other day in September and October, how much will he earn in a year?* Stupid bloody Yanks, Andrew thought, why don't they have gardeners, like everybody else?

Though Miss Fitt said that his writing skills were excellent, she pointed out that he wrote his dates backwards: "It should be 10-18-43, not 18-10-43." Andrew thought it would be an exercise in futility to point out that writing the day first, then the month, then the year, was the sensible, logical, *right* way to do it, but after all, Yanks were not known for being sensible or logical!

Art Class with Miss Lashua was all right, in spite of the fact that Andrew wasn't very good at drawing. Miss Lashua was nice, though, and quietly whispered pointers to him as he hunched over his sketches. Study hall, which was held in the lunchroom, wasn't so bad either: He wasn't forced to interact, and could concentrate on getting some homework done. Several classes shared the room for the period, Miriam's class included, and she sat next to him. Strict silence was enforced, but Miriam began passing notes to him. She would fold her missive into one of her textbooks and set the book off to the side, in front of Andrew; when the monitor wasn't looking, he would take the book, read her note, and reply. Usually they communicated about their classes, but she would sometimes get a little personal, asking him about his life in England and if he'd gotten a letter from his mother, or things to that effect.

Music class was terrible, though, what with him having to endure listening to Dvorak's *New World Symphony*, or being forced to sing stupid, stupid songs about *Wagon Wheels Rolling Westward O'er the Prairie.*

Phys. Ed. class was the worst: Being so small, he couldn't run as fast as the other boys; besides, all the games were different—basketball, for instance, which he hated with a passion. Tossing a silly ball through a silly hoop was just the sort of bloody stupid game Yanks would think of!

In homeroom, Mrs. Tercek rearranged the seating so that he was alphabetically integrated into the class: He found himself seated between Leszek Barzinski (whom everyone call Les) and Patrick O'Malley (whom everyone called Pat), behind Sarina Ferrara (whom everyone called Sara), and in front of Wannetta Hatfield (whom everyone called Wannie). As soon as he got settled into his seat, he was prodded from behind by Wannie, who announced ever so haughtily that she was related to the Hatfields of "them Hatfields and McCoys what had that big feud. Related on my pa's side and my ma's side—distantly, that is." When Andrew glared balefully at her, she repeated her query: "You heard about them Hatfields and McCoys—dincha?"

Andrew raised one eyebrow and said, his voice dripping with disdain, "Should I have?"

Wannetta's response was a snort of contempt. Andrew turned around and a pang of self-pity tightened around him like a noose.

He could almost hear Freddie sniggering at him from beyond the grave: *How do you like Yankland, boy? Look at you—surrounded by Micks, Dagos, Polacks, and Inbred, Imbecilic Hillbillies!*

Mrs. Malandreatos signaled to Andrew after she had read the messages the office helper had presented to her.

"Andrew, you forgot your lunch. Mrs. Givens brought it for you and it's in the office. You may leave to get it."

Snickers and giggles accompanied his footsteps out of the room.

He scuffed down the hall and into the office. Mrs. O'Neal greeted him, then filed through the sacks on the counter. "Let's see—Andrew Hadley-Trevelyan—here it is." She pulled out a sack with Andrew's name printed neatly on it and handed it to him.

"Andrew—you're Jake's kid, aren't you?" Andrew turned, and was startled by the man's resemblance to his father—the same dark hair, even features, about the same height and build. The eyes were brown, though. Andrew tried not to show his annoyance with the oft-heard and much-hated possessive label that seemed to hang around his neck like a nametag on an evacuee: *Jake's kid, Jake's new kid, Jake's stepkid, Jake's stepson, Jake's boy....*

"Hi, I'm Shannon Casini. Pleased to meet you, Andrew. My brother Danny and Jake were pals."

"Oh, how do you do?" Andrew's greeting was automatic. He tried to hide the surprise in his voice; he rather expected that Mr. and Mrs. Casini's offspring would talk in a sort of bizarre hybrid Italian brogue. He was taken aback by Shannon's breezy American accent that had just a trace of Jersey inflection.

"I'm sorry I didn't get a chance to meet Jake when he was here—I was in New York for two weeks and got back the day after he left for England. How's he doing?"

Andrew shrugged. "Fine, I suppose."

Wish I could tell you that he just got shot down. Silly man, flying in a plane with no guns.

"Great, just great. Boy, I would have liked to have seen Jake. I'll always remember him as a little boy, always tagging along, dreaming up some kind of mischief. Well, how are you doing, Andrew? How do you find America?"

"Turn left at Newfoundland." Andrew was in no mood to be chatty; the words were out of his mouth before he could stop them. He cringed inwardly, thinking that he was about to be sternly admonished for his churlishness.

The brown eyes crinkled with mirth glee and a hearty laugh prefaced the observation: "Are you sure you're not just Jake's *step*son? You sound like a chip off the old block!"

He was taken aback by Shannon's frankness, but found himself being drawn to unabashed warmth of the man.

After all, he doesn't have any idea of all that's happened. No reason to get shirty over things.

"Are you settling in okay, Andrew? It must be quite a change from what you're used to."

As much as he liked Shannon (funny, he had only known him for a few minutes), Andrew didn't see any point in relating his woes.

"It's all right."

It was obvious from the single raised eyebrow that Shannon didn't quite believe him. He said nothing, though.

The buzzer went off and, within seconds, the hall was a seething mass of yelling, bellowing, shrieking humanity. Four students burst through the door and, interposing themselves between Shannon and Andrew, proceeded to sort through the lunch sacks.

Andrew grabbed his lunch and slipped out the door.

He found the Givens home to be an oasis of affirmation in a desert of intolerance, ridicule, and humiliation.

Not a complete desert, Andrew thought, for were it not for Lynette's occasional greetings and Miriam's friendliness, he would have certainly felt a complete pariah. He only saw Lynette, though, for the briefest moments in the hallway between classes, and Miriam only shared his study hall three times a week.

He and Miriam walked together part of the way from school, going their separate ways as Andrew turned in at the Givens's street. Once within the benevolent blue enclave Lois would greet him with some sort of mouth-watering treat from the oven and make him drink a big glass of milk. He'd go upstairs to finish his homework, then return downstairs at four-thirty to listen to *Sergeant Preston of the Yukon* on the radio. The show was broadcast from a New York station, so on occasion the reception wasn't very good. Most of the times, though, it came in loud and clear, and it gave Andrew a feeling of being in—well, not exactly in England. But at least Canada was part of the Britain's dominion, so he felt that the program provided a kind of connection with those who owed allegiance to the King. Sprawled on the sofa with Lindy curled up on his chest, Andrew would listen to the stirring exploits of Sergeant Preston, his noble horse, Rex, and his wonder dog, King. That over, Andrew would dial to the local station and catch a quartet of programs: *Terry and the Pirates* at five; *Dick Tracy* at five-fifteen; *Jack Armstrong* at half-past, and *Superman* at a quarter to six. The news came on at six, and Andrew listened to that, too, even though he had long since figured out that the war in the Pacific warranted (for whatever inane reason) twice the amount of coverage as the war in Europe. Still, he managed to catch some crumbs of information about how things were progressing in his country.

After dinner was the *Lone Ranger*, followed by a bedtime snack. On Sunday afternoons, he'd listen to *The Shadow*, which was broadcast from New York. Andrew always felt a shudder of delight and fear creep up his spine when he heard the intro-duction: *Who knows what evil lurks in the hearts of men? Only the shadow knows....*

But so do I, Andrew would think.

It's not just the Nazis and Japs who are the evil ones! Some of the worst people around are wearing RAF uniforms!

He was plagued by nightmares. In one dream, he was on the beach at Eastbourne and he saw the Queen Mary steaming through the Channel. He tried to swim out to reach it, but the water was so cold, and the ship was sailing away so fast, that he ex-hausted himself and started drowning in the icy, murky darkness. Then Freddie pulled him out and called him a "silly blighter," and told him if he didn't stop playing "silly buggers" he was going wind up sharing a grave with "dear, departed Roger."

In another dream he was at Askew Court and Mrs. Bunch was up on the roof of the dining room, shooting down crows to make Commando Casserole. In another recur-ring nightmare, he would find himself on the front lawn at Greycliff as his mother flew overhead in a Spitfire. A puff of white smoke issued from her plane, and the plane hurtled into a tailspin, twirling round and round, faster and faster, like an ice skater in a spin. He never did see the plane crash, but he always heard a deafening roar. Then people would run past him to the site of the calamity, and a small boy would try to drag Andrew to see the sight, saying, "It's a bloody great crash, it is—absolutely smashing! Come on—you're going to miss it! What's left of the plane and the pilot is scattered over a square mile!"

The worst dream of all was one in which he was being dug out from under some rubble. As he was pulled free, he saw his mother lying on the ground. She was cut in two, and the blood soaked through her uniform until she nothing but a crimson mess. Then Andrew would awaken in a cold sweat, heart pounding, mouth dry, to await the coming of the dawn.

Chapter 35

"*A*ndrew—you hit the jackpot today! There's a letter from your mother, and V-Mail from somebody else," Lois called from the kitchen. "I just took a batch of snickerdoodles out of the oven. Why don't you sit yourself down and have some while you read your letters?"

Andrew set his schoolbooks on the table by the front door. He grabbed his mother's letter, which lay on top of the stack of mail, and ran his fingers over the neat handwriting, as if he could somehow commune with his mother by touching the letters she had penned. He picked up the piece of V-Mail and noted the sender: Sgt. G. Versailles. As he glanced at the pile of mail beneath, an envelope caught his eye. It was addressed to Mr. Gene Givens, and it was from Jake!

Jake—writing to his *father?*

Moreover, the envelope fairly bulged with what felt like several sheets of paper within. If it had been a thin piece of mail, Andrew might have been able to figure it as a curt missive from Jake to his father, but this fat communique reeked of intimacy and affection.

He tore open his two letters as he shuffled to the dining room. Lois set down a plate of cookies for him. He decided to read his mother's letter first.

Dear Andrew,

   I'm so glad you're settling in so well. Lynette seems like such a nice girl. I'm glad you have a friend! I just got a letter from Lois—she says you're back in school. Please take care of yourself and remember to bundle up properly when it gets cold! I don't want you getting ill again!

She'll still be worrying about me when I'm a grandfather, Andrew thought wryly. He read on: His mother still hoped to get into the Class 5 conversion course but doubted that she would, as there were so many other women pilots ahead of her in seniority. His mother urged him to write to his grandmother, and also to Aunt Jane:

   It's been months since you've written to her, and I know she misses you terribly. Do send her a letter, darling. I know she'd love to hear all about your journey and everything you're doing in America!

Andrew scanned the rest of her letter—nothing about Jake.
Good. Maybe things aren't going well between them. Maybe that's what Jake wrote

to Mr. Givens about, either telling him the "bad" news, or asking for fatherly advice.

That's it—that *has* to be it!

For weeks, Andrew had been carefully planning just how to sow the seeds of discord between Jake and Mr. Givens, though his distress over the awful time he'd been having in school had pushed his schemes somewhat into the background. Better not to start bad-mouthing Jake right away, though, he thought; Mr. Givens might get suspicious. Better to cultivate an amiable relationship with the man, first.

Then, upon a foundation of mutual respect and trust, I can mount an offensive against Jake.

As for writing to Aunt Jane, Andrew knew that he would put the task off for awhile. He had to create a fiction of his happiness and well-being when he wrote back to his mother, but creating a fiction and writing to a fictitious person (for he knew beyond a shadow of a doubt that something dreadful had happened to his aunt, though he had no idea what) made for doubly difficult duty.

He read the letter from Gerry:

Hi Andrew!

I sent a letter to you at Greycliff, and your grandma wrote me a real nice letter back and told me that you'd gone to America. How about that!

Yes, how about that, Andrew thought.

Still, no need to get shirty; Gerry no doubt would want to trade places with him in an instant.

I'd give anything to trade places with you, kiddo, but c'est la guerre, you know. And I got this funny feeling that you probably would like to trade places with me! Sometimes I get to thinking about all the things I found so different when I came here, and I try to imagine what it would be like for you, getting a taste of America for the first time. Hope things are going O.K. for you. Your grandma wrote me that you're staying with Jake's folks. You're probably real busy with school and all, but if you find a few minutes to spare, drop me a line.

Your friend,
Gerry

P.S. Oh, I wrote to Mary Jo, and told her all about you, and also that you're staying in New Jersey now. She goes to Dunellen every month or so to visit with her fiance's family, and I thought you two could meet each other sometime, seeing as Dunellen is not too far from Scotch Plains. How about it?

"Who's the letter from?" Lois asked.

"An American serviceman that I met when my mother was in hospital. His name is Gerry Versailles and he's an armorer with the Eighth Air Force."

"Oh yes, Jake mentioned him. Said he took you two out to breakfast. Sounds like a very nice man."

Andrew nodded as he munched a snickerdoodle. After washing it down with some tea, he said, "Gerry has a sister who's a nurse. She works in New York. She comes to New Jersey sometimes to visit her fiance's family in Dunellen, and I was wondering if I could meet with her."

"Sure, why don't you invite her here for supper?"

"Oh, I don't want you to go to any trouble. I could just visit—"

"No trouble at all, Andrew. I'd love to meet her!"

"Are you sure? I don't want to impose—"

"Imposition—never!" Lois mussed his hair.

"What did Jake say, dear?"

Mr. Givens sliced the roasted chicken and proffered a piece to Andrew. Lois served up a lot of chicken, not only for lunches, but for suppers as well, since chicken was unrationed. Still, they dined on beef fairly often, at least a lot more than Andrew had been used to in England.

"Gene?"

"What?"

"What did Jake say? Must be important—in all these years I never got a letter half as thick as the one you got from him!"

"Oh—talk to you later about that."

"Is anything wrong?"

"Uh—nothing wrong, really. Talk to you later, okay?"

"Okay."

Mr. Givens didn't talk to Lois about Jake's letter while Andrew sprawled on the living room floor after supper and listened to the *Lone Ranger*. Andrew tarried downstairs after the program was over, saying that he'd finished all his homework. But Mr. Givens didn't mention anything then either, nor did he mention anything over a bedtime snack of peach cobbler. Andrew finally said good night and went upstairs. After brushing his teeth, he went into the spare room.

If he couldn't be with Jake's parents to hear what Jake had to say, at least he could *overhear* things.

Maybe my mother has finally given Jake the heave-ho; perhaps they've had a fearful row and he's decided to call it quits. No matter who's done the quitting, as long as it's over!

He shut the door and lay down on the rug next to the heat register in the floor. After grabbing an old atlas off of the shelf under the window (in case he was caught eavesdropping, he could always say he was looking up something for his history assignment), he settled himself next to the grate and listened to the faint conversation issuing up from the breakfast room. Wonderful things, heating ducts! They went to all *sorts* of interesting places!

As he flipped through the atlas, a piece of paper fell out. Andrew saw that it was a handbill for a barnstorming company: *Casey's Flying Circus* was printed in big letters at the top. Below was a photo of biplane, with four people standing in front of it: three men and a woman. One of the men looked very young, not much more than a boy, Andrew thought. Andrew noted the names of the barnstormers: *Casey, famous ace of the Great War—Wanda, the wacky wingwalker—Nate and Jake, the fabulous flying duo!*

Jake!

Andrew peered at the picture of the boy with the shy smile on his face. It *was* Jake!

"...so he transferred to a fighter squadron." Mr. Given's soft voice wafted up through the grate.

"Fighter squadron! Oh, no!" Lois cried in dismay.

Fighter squadron! This was even better that a spat! People might squabble, and then patch things up, but Jake in a *fighter* squadron....

"...He wants to be in on the invasion—"

"Oh, Gene—" Lois moaned.

"Lois, he's a good pilot—he's had lots of experience. He'll be all right. He says that going over France now is a piece of cake compared to what the Battle of Britain was like. The Germans are putting up kids with hardly any training or experience. Most of their best fighter pilots have already bought it. The Luftwaffe doesn't rotate its pilots out of operational duty, like the RAF and AAF do; they just keep them flying until they're shot down and injured or killed."

"But a *fighter pilot*—"

"He's not the crazy kid he was, Lois. Doing a crazy stunt is how he got hurt—"

"Crazy stunt?"

"He rammed a German bomber—two, in fact. He went in between them and tore off his wings in the process. Both of them exploded in midair and caught Jake's plane on fire."

"He *told* you this?"

"Lois, honey, he's not going to do anything stupid. And he wants in on the invasion—it's important to him, after Dunkirk and all."

"He wasn't even *at* Dunkirk. He was still in training then—"

"Well, it's important. Being in the RAF, he's around guys who were over Dunkirk, and it's a big thing with them—with the British pilots, I mean—to be able to see...well, Jake calls it the 'reciprocal course. Going in to the continent again, after the British had to retreat back in 1940."

"First getting burned, then almost drowning, then getting so sick with pneumonia—" Lois's voice dropped to a whisper of anguish.

"Well, Jake used to be a thrill seeker. That's why he flew the Hurricats. Said he got bored with the circuses and rhubarbs over France—"

"Circuses and rhubarbs?"

"Oh, they'd send over a bunch of bombers and fighters over France to try to scare up the German fighters, same thing the Luftwaffe did over the Channel in the Battle of Britain. The Germans bombed the ships to get the RAF to send up the fighters, so they could shoot them down; that was the real objective. Anyway, Jake wasn't too excited about going on what he called 'duck shoots' over France, so that's why he volunteered for the Hurricats."

"He almost *died*, Gene!"

"Well, he's not a wild and crazy kid anymore, Lois—he's changed. He really *has!*"

There was a long silence, and Andrew feared that Jake's parents had left the room and were about to come upstairs, when Lois' voice, almost inaudible, wafted up from the darkness.

"...Never thought I'd live to see the day when you'd be defending him, Gene." Andrew couldn't tell if it was wonder or anguish in her voice.

"Well, things change, Lois."

"What did you two talk about that night? I thought after you'd found out about Jake coming in drunk the night before, you'd never want to see him again—"

"He told me some things in confidence. I told him that I wouldn't tell you, wouldn't tell anybody...I'm sorry—"

"No need to apologize for having a heart-to-heart talk with your son. Just tell the nosey mom to jump in a lake!"

"No, I'm going to tell the nosey mom to...." Mr. Givens's voice faded, and Andrew could hear Lois's faint giggles at the bottom of the stairs.

He slipped out of the spare room and went into the bathroom. There, he flushed the toilet and ran the water and made all sorts of noises, pretending to be in the throes of his pre-bedtime routine.

Jake—a fighter pilot again!

And all it had taken was just a few choice words on Andrew's part: *I would think that you'd rather be shooting down Germans instead of making film stars out of them!*

With any luck, Jake just might do something...crazy.

With any luck, the bastard might be gone for good.

As Andrew walked to school, his mind was a whirlwind of plans and possibilities.

Jake is bound to buy it sooner or later, surely! Still, can't afford to get smug about things: Fortune doesn't favor the complacent. Every time I've breathed a sigh of relief that things were going well, disaster has struck. First, I was relieved that Freddie wouldn't be a problem, and then Jake came along! Then, I was so happy to have the summer with my mother, gloated about having the home ground advantage—and I got packed off to America! And I was delighted at the estrangement between Jake and his father, and now it's all been ruined—this chumminess between Jake and his father has got to stop! What's gotten into Mr. Givens, anyway? He's not supposed to be defending Jake!

Got to put a stop to all this...Can't start bad-mouthing Jake right away, though. Got to get on the good terms with his father, first, establish a kind of rapport. Then I'll just drop a few tidbits of interesting information...Mr. Givens ought to be disabused of the notion that Jake is a such a terrific chap! Wish I could disabuse my mother of the notion, too, but she's so arse over tip in love with the man!

His mother! Andrew knew that he would have to continue to reassure her that all was well, even as he turned the corner and saw the wretched building in which he would be imprisoned for the better part of the day.

Wish it were three o'clock! Wish the place would go up in a puff of smoke! Like to see a Stuka scream out of the sky and blow the whole sodding building to bits! Still, can't let Mum know how I feel—can't risk having her worry—

God Stone the Crows!

That's it!

That's it!

Andrew had to check himself from skipping with glee.

If Mum had her accident because she was so upset about me, about the way I acted when I found out about Jake...What if Jake and his father had a falling-out? I'll bet Jake's as cocky as a bartender with a cellar full of Scotch, now that he and his father are getting along. But if he were upset because he and his father were at each other's throats again, albeit long distance...If he were distracted enough to make a stupid mistake when he should be paying attention....

He walked into the front entrance, but the depressing interior could not dispel his elation.

Got to make bloody sure that happens.

Andrew adjusted the height of the striking bag and gave it a swift jab. He had fallen into the habit of spending half an hour in the Givens's basement after having "tea" when he got home from school. Jake had installed a miniature gym there complete with weights, chin-up bar, sit-up board, punching bag, and striking bag. The physical activity in itself was a tonic; furthermore, Andrew found that trying to punch the stuffings out of the striking bag was a blessed release after enduring his daily miserable exodus through the American public school system. Not only was it horrid and demeaning, it was pointless as well. What he was getting could not, by any stretch of the imagination, be called an education: learning a bunch of silly state capitals and a currency system that must have been designed by imbeciles, besides having to spell words incorrectly and write dates backwards.

He pummelled the striking bag until it hummed like an engine going full bore. He imagined it was Jake's face, being shredded to a bloody pulp. The punching bag was Jake's body, and every blow Andrew threw to it was smashing a vital organ to bits.

Got to bring him down, literally bring the sodding bastard down....

Even when Andrew chatted with Mr. Givens or asked him for help with his science homework, he imagined every friendly word spoken to Mr. Givens was a nail in Jake's coffin. He exulted that Jake's father seemed to be warming to him.

He'll have to believe what I tell him about Jake. He'll have to!

His one attempt at reaching out to others was met with a hostile rebuff:

He caught up with Antoinette one morning after homeroom, and asked her, in French, what she thought of America. She turned to him, eyes blazing with fury.

Ainglais! You have no right to speak in my language! You are all cowards, all of you! You left us and ran away—at the first sight of battle, you all ran away, like scared rabbits, and left us to the Boche! Cowards—you are all a nation of cowards!

This scathing denunciation was delivered in French, and though Andrew was quite sure that the knot of spectators viewing Antoinette's impassioned tirade didn't have any idea what was being said (French was only taught in the upper grades), he had no doubt that everyone was aware he was getting a strip torn out of his hide. Antoinette shot him one last, withering glare before flouncing down the hall, the titters and snickers of the other students applauding her progress.

He wrote to Gerry. At first, he thought it would be bad form to complain about America to an American, but somehow Gerry seem to sense that Andrew's exile was not all bliss. Perhaps that special "twin" sensitivity extended to others as well; it certainly seemed to be the case with his father. Andrew was able to dissemble with his mother and convince her that all was well when it wasn't, but he never could get anything past his father. Somehow he always seemed to know when Andrew was troubled and the gentle question, "Anything wrong, old chap?" always drew out the knots of trouble and worry to be lovingly untangled.

He penned his letter in study hall, the day after Antoinette's vituperate tirade.

Dear Gerry,

I got your letter the other day. Thank you for writing. I wish I could tell you that things are going well, but, in all honesty, they're not. I guess New Jersey is probably worse than most other places in the United States; I met some GIs on the Queen Mary, and they certainly seemed to think so. Everyone here is so mean—most everyone that is. They tease me about the way I talk. If they don't tease they look at me as if I've got two heads, or something, and ask me stupid questions about England. Even some of the teachers are mean. Jake's parents are nice, though, and two of the girls in my school are friendly, but it really doesn't make up for all the rest of the meanness. I want to be back in England so badly, it's almost like a stomachache.

Is the war going to be over soon? In England, people say that, what with the pounding we're giving Germany, we might not need to invade, that Germany will just be bombed into submission and surrender, just like that. Since you're in the Eighth Air Force, I thought you might know something, if it isn't a military secret to give it away. I want to go home more than anything, even if the food isn't all that good and even if we do get bombed a bit. I lived through the Blitz, and what the Germans are doing now is nothing compared to that.

Well, I hope things are going well for you.

Your friend,
Andrew

The nightmares still continued, no matter how much Andrew tried to concentrate on not having any bad dreams before closing his eyes for the night. He put all thoughts of malice against Jake away upon retiring, for, as much as he knew his hatred against Jake was justified, he knew that negative emotions might set his mind on a fearful course to distressing destinations in dreamland. After looking up at the sky and trying to push his worries about his Aunt Jane out of his mind, he would snuggle under the covers and faithfully recite his father's poem, hoping that he would have a dream about his father instead of the vexing or terrifying nightmares that invariably churned through his nocturnal imaginings. But every night he dreamt of Mrs. Bunch's unorthodox manner of procuring food, or of the *Queen Mary* sailing past him as he vainly tried to swim out to reach it, or of his mother's plane hurtling to earth as he helplessly watched.

Andrew had no sooner gotten the ball, when it was whisked away from him by a small boy, one called "Shorty." He was actually shorter than Andrew, so Andrew was not technically the smallest one in school, but the appellation "Shorty" was not derogatory, for the boy was lightning fast and could sink baskets from anywhere on the court. Shorty was invariably picked first when teams were chosen; Andrew was invariably chosen last, for he had been quickly sized up as being of no account in this silly game.

"Come on, Andrew, you're hardly trying!" Mr. Scurlock yelled as Andrew clumped apathetically across the gym.

What was the use in trying, in wearing himself out chasing a stupid, sodding ball back and forth across the court? He hardly ever got possession of it anyway, and never, *never* was able to get the silly thing through that stupid net.

"Come on, Andrew, you're hardly trying!" Cockney Mouth and his sidekick hooted at him from the sidelines. Laughter from the other boys echoed through the gym; thereafter, Andrew was called "Hardly Trying," which was even worse that "Tiddlybits".

Miss Fitt assigned everyone in English class to write about their experiences of the war:

"Someday people will want to know what your lives were like at this time. Perhaps your children will want to know, or perhaps your grandchildren might someday ask you what life was like during the war. So think of all the little details of your lives: You might perhaps explain what it's like to live with rationing. Believe it or not, someday we'll be able to go grocery shopping without using red stamps or blue stamps, and we'll be able to have as much meat as we want! Perhaps you could tell what you were doing when you heard Pearl Harbor was attacked, and how you felt at the time. If any of you have fathers or brothers or sisters in the service, you might tell something of them, and of what they're doing. This will constitute half your grade for the marking period, so put a lot of thought into it."

The assignment gave Andrew an idea; besides being necessary for his grade, he could also accomplish another objective. After class, Andrew went to Miss Fitt and asked if she might accommodate him on the matter:

"I have to write to my Aunt Jane and, as I haven't written to her for quite some time, there's a lot that I need to tell her." The truth was, Andrew had put off the dreaded task because he didn't know what he could say to someone he wasn't sure even existed. Corresponding with someone involved an emotional interaction on some level, and all he felt was a sense of uneasiness about the whole matter. The idea of it being an assignment would, he knew, spur him to discharge his responsibility: All he had to do was write "Dear Aunt Jane" at the top.

"That's a wonderful idea, Andrew!" Miss Fitt exclaimed. "I think it would be interesting for you to tell her about the things you find so different in America and what were your first impressions of the United States. Attach a note to your letter reminding me not to write on it; I'll list my corrections and comments on a separate page."

He started his letter in study hall and found it surprisingly easy to write of his experiences of the past three months. He breezed over the traumatic experiences, as if his mother had already informed his aunt of them; no need to go into gory detail, and no need to stir up distressing memories. He didn't want to write of how unhappy he was in America, either, in case his mother happened to glance at his letter. So he wrote:

Dear Aunt Jane,

    I'm sorry it's been so long since I've written. No doubt Mum has already told you about Gram, Aunt Gwen, and Freddie. It was such a terrible thing, and I didn't feel like writing, or doing much of anything, for awhile.

He chewed his pen—this would be the most difficult thing to write about.

    You probably know about Mum and Jake, and about Mum's accident, too. It was a very frightening time, because she was in a coma for awhile, but she came out of it all right—just chatters more than ever now!

There! He went on to write about his voyage on the *Queen Mary*, mentioning the Spike Jones shows and the roach races the GIs had; he didn't say anything about the poker games, though. He wrote of seeing New York for the first time and of meeting Jake's parents:

    They are very nice, and the food here is better, too. They have rationing here in America, but it's not so strict as in England. I drink four glasses of milk a day and orange juice every morning, and have beef a few times a week. Lois, Jake's mother, also grows sweet corn in the backyard, but they don't call it sweet corn here, just corn....

It occurred to Andrew that translating some of the American words into English would be an almost effortless project, and take up valuable space, besides.

Even though Americans are supposed to speak English, they really don't. They use so many different words for things. For instance, Americans call a wireless a "radio"; a lorry is a "truck"; and petrol is "gas." Americans say "Hi" and "Howya doin'?", instead of "Hullo" or "Good day." They don't say "Cheerio"; they say "Take it easy." Instead of "all right" they say "O.K." or "okey-dokey." A tart is a "pie," a scone is a "biscuit," a biscuit is a "cookie," sweets are called "candy," a crisp is a "chip," and a chip is a "French fry."

Once on the subject of food, it was easy to churn out reams of stuff. Then he went on to tell of the funny American customs, and the peculiar accents. He recounted Lynette's "New Jerseyese" lesson and imagined, as Miss Fitt had mentioned, that he was writing for posterity: Someday he would tell his children all about his experiences in America, and they would marvel at how bizarre things were in this peculiar country.

I hope that there won't be another war coming down the road in another twenty or thirty years! I want my children to grow up in a peaceful world, in that same world I knew before the war mucked up everything. God forbid that they should have to be packed off to America too!

The sound of the buzzer interrupted his reverie. Miriam smiled at him; he put the letter in his file (which was called a *binder* in America) and gathered up his things. He walked out into the brisk autumn air, Miriam at his side. Once down the street, he turned round to gaze at the school.

What a ghastly sight! Perhaps he might bring his children for a visit here someday, just so they could see how ugly things were in America! The houses, for instance, looked like flimsy shacks—why didn't Yanks build proper homes out of brick and stone!

Yes, he would bring his children here someday, just so they would be able to appreciate how wonderful their country was!

"This is marvelous, Andrew." Miss Fitt handed him back the twenty pages he'd already written. "You know, there's really not much I can teach you in the way of writing skills. I'm afraid you find diagramming sentences and learning, or rather, relearning the rules of grammar and punctuation a little boring, don't you?"

Andrew shrugged. He didn't want to insult her by agreeing.

She grinned at him. "This is very, very good, and far more than I expected from someone your age. If you'd like extra time to work on it, you may be excused from class and go to study hall to work on it instead. Would you like to do that?"

Andrew's ecstatic smile was his answer.

It was a wonderful arrangement, for he now could spend most of the afternoon being left to himself to work on his assignment, and the two study halls (with the exception of the days he had music and art) buffered the unpleasantness of Phys. Ed. class, which he found to be the most hateful subject of all.

Funny, he had always liked games at Askew Court. Though he wasn't the best at cricket or soccer or rugby, he was reasonably good and "fit in" well with any team that might be organized. And he excelled at boxing; Mr. Nugent always put him in practice with someone whose skills needed polishing.

But Americans didn't play cricket or soccer or rugby, and though they did have boxing in the United States, it wasn't a part of Mr. Scurlock's Physical Education curriculum.

If only I could be allowed to do my Phys. Ed. in the Givens's basement, instead of being made to endure this wretched class!

Even Mr. Scurlock called him "Hardly Trying," and a wave of laughter would sweep through the class whenever he upbraided Andrew for his shortcomings.

Someday I'm going to mash his stupid, sodding face in! Like to see how he likes being made fun of....

"...Hardly Trying—you're in!"

Andrew shuffled over to the clump of boys dancing ridiculously around the stupid bloody bouncing ball. His teammates scowled at him, and he knew full well that it would be pointless to even pretend any interest in this silly game.

He turned in his assignment to Miss Fitt, who nodded approvingly as she scanned the thirty-eight pages he'd written.

"Quite a tome, Andrew. I'll read this over tonight, and return it to you tomorrow." She pursed her lips for a moment, then looked to Andrew, as if for approval of some sort. "Would you mind making a copy? You can do it in study hall. It would mean being out of class for a little while longer—is that okay with you?"

"Delighted!"

He came home from school the following Thursday to find Lois and Sarah having a "coffee break" in the breakfast room. Sarah was puzzling over a booklet.

"This here Q stand for A, and T-H-E is M-B-P and I figgered out all these words here—see, *that* and *are* and *these*. What you s'pose this here word is—*T*-blank-blank-*E-S*.

Andrew peered over Sarah's shoulder, noted that the booklet she held was titled *Cryptikquotes.* "These are the—" He glanced at the rest of the enciphered quotation. "These are the times that try men's souls," he pronounced.

Sarah's jaw dropped in amazement. "How you get that so fast?"

Andrew shrugged. "It's a quote by Thomas Paine—we learned about in History class last week."

Just one of the many useless bits of information I'm being force-fed, he thought. The man was nothing but a rabble-rouser! Who bloody cares what he said?

"*These are the taaahms that traah maaan's sooouls,*" Sarah intoned. She seemed to take extraordinary pleasure in reciting it, enunciating every word and speaking in a rolling cadence.

She could outdo the orators on Speaker's Corner, Andrew thought.

Sarah shook her heard, then let out a snort of contempt. "Sumpin' a *man* would say. How come he don't say nothing 'bout times that try women's souls?"

Lois grinned. "Goes without saying, Sarah, because that's *all* the time!"

Sarah threw her head back squealed with laughter. "Ain't that the *truth!*" She slapped Andrew on the back. "Men! If they ain't got nothing to trouble theyselves already, they bound to go looking for it!"

Lois laughed. "Andrew's not a troublemaker, Sarah."

"Well, if they ain't troublemakers, they *trouble-lookers*!"

Andrew smiled, not for the hilarity of Sarah's observation, but for the idea that had just occurred to him. He had not sent off his letter to "Aunt Jane" yet, as he wanted to write his mother a short note to enclose along with it. The night before, he had lain awake for quite some time, wondering about his aunt. If only there was some way he could find out what was going on! It had occurred to him that he might be over-re-acting; that Aunt Jane was really all right and that there was a simple, reasonable ex-planation for the distressing lapses he'd noted in her letters. But he couldn't flat-out *ask* if everything was fine.

Or could he?

God Stone the Crows!

Why hadn't he thought of it before?

Chapter 36

*O*f course, it was all Jake's fault.

Andrew lay on his bed and glared at the ceiling.

If I hadn't been so upset over Jake and my mother, he thought, *and* so distressed about being exiled to America (all *his* fault, too!) *and* so distraught because things are so awful here (and I'll bet he's just chortling with glee because I'm so miserable here, the sod!), I would have been able to think clearly about things.

Well, it wasn't *all* Jake's fault, Andrew conceded, but it was *mostly* his fault. I started worrying about Aunt Jane before I found out about Jake, and then there was all the trouble with Freddie, and Irene's death, and Gram and Aunt Gwen getting killed, and Mum's accident. Still, I was mostly upset about Jake and all the horrible things he did, so that's why my mind has been so muddled lately! If it hadn't been for Jake, I would have been able to figure out right away, or at least sooner or later, how to find out for sure if there was really something wrong with Aunt Jane.

Maybe she was just tired, or distracted, when she wrote. Perhaps she simply forgot things altogether.

But there's something she would *not* forget!

It was Aunt Jane who had taught him all about ciphers and secret codes. There were many ways to disguise what one wanted to communicate, so that only the intended recipient of the message would know what was really being said. A nonsensical sentence would have a secret meaning: *The vicar's cat drinks Scotch*, for instance, might mean *Pick up supplies at the usual location*. This worked if there weren't too many messages to be memorized, and if everything that might need to be communicated were already put into code. If it was not feasible to have everything prearranged in a secret code, one might encode the individual letters of the message: For instance, *A* might stand for *T, B* might stand for *H, C* might stand for *E,* or something like that. The trouble was, those types of codes could be easily broken by someone who could look at the frequency in which certain letters appeared, and by the way the letters were arranged. A way to make a code more difficult to break would be to keep changing the letters in encoding. Thus, A might stand for T one time, for L another time. But this kind of code would be difficult to use.

"If you had some kind of machine that automatically did this, and your contact had the same kind of machine, you could send messages to each other and it would be almost impossible for someone else to figure them out," Aunt Jane had told him. "But it may not be possible to carry around a machine. And if the machine fell into enemy hands, they would be able to use your code."

So she had taught him a very special kind of code, one that could be employed very easily with a pen and a piece of paper and the knowledge of the "secret word". When she went away to France and corresponded with him, she would write him a few sentences at the end of the letter in cipher, and he would do the same when he wrote to her. When she returned to England after Uncle Marc's death they didn't correspond so frequently, because they were able to see each other more often, so their use of the cipher fell by the wayside.

It was best if each person has his own "secret word," according to Aunt Jane. Aunt Jane's secret word was *JANE* and Andrew's was *ANDREW*. As Aunt Jane had told him, "One may forget many things, but one would not forget one's own name!"

The code worked like this: One wrote the letters of the alphabet in a grid of five letters across and five letters down, putting Y and Z in the last spot together. (Z was not used very often, and when it was, it would be easy to tell from the sense of the message whether the letter was Y or Z.) But first, one wrote the secret word, and the rest of the alphabet after that, skipping over the letters in the secret word. Andrew's grid looked like this:

$$
\begin{array}{ccccc}
A & N & D & R & E \\
W & B & C & F & G \\
H & I & J & K & L \\
M & O & P & Q & S \\
T & U & V & X & YZ \\
\end{array}
$$

To encode a message to Aunt Jane, Andrew first would break down his message into pairs of letters: HO WA RE YO U. Then he would take his grid, and circle (in pencil, lightly) the H and the O. They formed the corners of a "box", with I and M the opposite corners. He would then use the opposite corner letter in the same line of the real letter to substitute: H became I and M became O. If the letters were on the same line, or in the same column, the letters to the right were substituted. If the letters were in the last column, the first letters in the row were used. When a single letter was left over at the end, a "null", or random, letter would be chosen to complete the pair, and the recipient would discard it from the sense of the message. Thus, the message HO WA RE YO U would look like this: IM BN EA US XO. The beauty of this system was there were many different substitutes for each letter, making any message almost impossible to decipher. Yet it was quite simple to encode and decode, as long as one knew the secret word. Finally, the letters were written in groups of five; null letters were added at the end if the last group contained less than five letters. So the message would appear thus: IMBNE AUSXO.

A last, secret signal was incorporated into the code, to be used if all was well, for that was what real spies did when they were sending messages. If the signal was omitted, it was an alarm that the sender had been captured and was being forced to send and decipher messages against his will. It might be a special word included in the message, or it might be a certain protocol, such as making a particular error. For example, if the signal was to make a mistake on the fifth letter of every message, *How are you* might become *How aqe you*? It was a good idea for each person to have a different signal, for extra security. Andrew chose his code to be a mistake on the seventh letter of every message, and Aunt Jane chose hers to be an error on the tenth letter.

Andrew had not gotten his assignment back from Miss Fitt yet, but he decided to work on his cipher, so that he could add it to the last page of the letter. He got a piece of scratch paper and wrote out his alphabet grid. At the bottom of the page, he wrote *Are you all right*. He then broke the letters into pairs, and put an error on the seventh letter: AR EY OU OL LR IG HT.

After a few minutes, he had it enciphered: NEATP VSIKE LBIUX. He folded the paper, and put it in his treasure box.

Miss Fitt returned his assignment to him the following day, when he stopped at her classroom at the end of the day.

"I stayed up late to read it, Andrew. Very, very good! I don't see writing this good, even in my twelfth-grade English class."

As soon as he got home, Andrew added the cipher to the last page, as a postscript. He wrote a short note to his mother, assuring her that all was well, and asked Lois for an envelope. Andrew put his letters into it, addressed it to his mother, and asked Lois if she would mail it the next time she went by the post office.

Andrew grunted as he hauled himself up for his twentieth chin-up, then released his grip on the bar. He smiled as his feet slapped the floor. Twenty! He would try for thirty next week. Although he was still quite small, Andrew was pleased that his body was losing some of its distressing thinness and starting to fill in quite nicely. He had been noting his progress on the bathroom scale, and had already gained five pounds!

Lindy, perched on one of the shelves Jake had installed to hold his weight equipment, gazed impassively at Andrew. As Andrew walked over to him, he rolled over onto his back and displayed his belly for Andrew to rub. Andrew stroked Lindy's silky underside, and Lindy responded by purring and writhing with pleasure.

I wonder if cats worry about other cats liking them, Andrew thought. Do they shun other cats because they meow differently or have another color of fur? All Lindy has to do is rub against someone's ankle, and he's accepted—why do people have to be so complicated?

In the past few weeks, Andrew had made every effort to "fit in" to his new surroundings. He tried to tone down his accent, to speak a bit more slowly, and to affect a slight Jersey pronunciation of various sounds. He also attempted to make his inflection less "clipped," and his tone a bit flatter. But the whole charade made him feel uneasy: He felt as if he were betraying who he really was. It was hard not to feel that the way he'd spoken all his life *was* the proper way. Still, every time he opened his mouth at school there were the invariable snickers and smirking remarks.

It was galling to be made to feel like an outsider, but he knew he wasn't alone in his isolation. Funny, he had never imagined that his best friend would be a girl. It surprised him to find he had a lot in common with Miriam, but then, she was a sort of outsider too. Andrew noted that she did not travel in "cliques" with the other girls. He also observed that, although girls were not so loud and obvious about it, they could be just as cruel in their own way to those who didn't "fit in." There were the eyes slightly narrowed in scorn; the smug, mocking smiles; the quick half-twirl of disdain as backs were turned to the object of contempt.

He continued stroking Lindy's fur, delighting in the sheer bliss Lindy exhibited at being ministered to. Despite the continuing daily trial of attending school and being subjected to almost universal ostracism, despite the ever-present distressing realization of his predicament in being stranded in Yankland, Andrew felt happier than he'd been in weeks. Ever since he'd mailed his letter off to "Aunt Jane," he had felt a wonderful sense of release and purpose and had experienced a marvelous clarity of mind, as if a weight had been lifted from him. It was the *not knowing* that was worse than anything else—that, and the feeling of helplessness he'd felt in his anguish over his aunt. It was all that, and not knowing what to do, besides, that had so distressed him and muddled his thinking.

Now, he felt so wonderfully serene, for he'd figured out a way to find out for sure what was wrong—if, indeed, there *was* anything wrong. He felt as if he had dealt once and for all with this particular bogey and, even though it would be awhile before he found out the truth, he was not going to be vexed anymore by it. Having been freed of this one worry, he found his mind fixing with eager anticipation on another project: that of establishing a more solid rapport with Jake's father. Although Mr. Givens was just as reserved as Lois was outgoing, Andrew believed that to be a plus, for he sensed that his own British demeanor was something that pleased Jake's father, rather than repelled him. But so far, they had talked about Andrew's science homework and not much else. Andrew knew that he had to establish a deeper bond with Mr. Givens, sort of a father-son relationship, for he needed to have a deeper connection with the man in order to bring Jake down.

If Jake presumed he can take my father's place, then I'll just take his place, here, with his father. The bastard is probably smirking, too, over having the home ground advantage with my mother. Well, I have the home ground advantage here, and Jake is in for a nasty surprise when he finds out that his father doesn't think so highly of him anymore.

For weeks Andrew had been wondering how to approach Mr. Givens; then an idea occurred to him. It was something that had been puzzling him for some time, anyway, ever since he'd been on the *Queen Mary*. The GIs, for the most part, had been up-front and direct about most things, but there was a minor bit of lore that Andrew still found baffling. Jake's father would certainly be able to give him a satisfactory explanation.

He started coming down with a cold after church on Sunday and spent the next few days in bed. Lois fussed over him, tucking extra blankets on top of him and bringing him cup after cup of steaming hot lemonade. He tried to put on a glum face in spite of the glee he felt at being granted a respite from school. Sarah came by on Tuesday, since Thursday was "Thanksgiving": a holiday, Lois explained. There was the customary "pitching in" by Lois in the duties that should have been done by her domestic help.

What's the use of having a maid if Lois is doing most of the work anyway? Andrew wondered, as the opening notes of Beethoven's *Emperor Concerto* blasted from the gramophone, or *record player* as it was called in America. Lois positively *loved* Beethoven; she maintained that putting on one of the great composer's symphonies or concertos got her into a "housecleaning mood."

When the women came upstairs, Sarah's musical tastes took preference and she sang the "blues" at the top of her voice. Andrew tried to concentrate on his math homework as Sarah's throaty voice wafted in from the spare room, where she was doing the ironing.

Not quite the same as Lucia softly humming some Italian aria, but pleasant all the same, Andrew thought. Lindy, who'd been sleeping by Andrew's side all day, stretched and lazily rolled over so that his belly was to Andrew's thigh. Andrew scratched the back of Lindy's neck, and Lindy responded by purring loudly.

It's been so easy to get Jake's cat to like me—I'll bet if Lindy had to choose between Jake and me, he'd choose me. It shouldn't be too difficult to produce the same result on Jake's father, either. Just a few kind words, friendly conversation, appreciativeness for the kindness and hospitality he's shown me...Then I'll bring Jake down!

Chapter 37

*L*ois spent the next day in a frenzy of baking: Breads, pies, cakes, and cookies issued forth from the kitchen in torrential abundance from daybreak until dusk. Mr. Givens's brother and his family would be arriving that evening from "upstate" New York, and Lois wanted to make sure there would be enough to eat.

Andrew didn't know just how many Givens relatives would be descending upon them, but as long as the number was below a hundred, there probably would be enough food to last a week, at least.

Though his cold was almost gone, Lois thought it would be best if Andrew stayed home for the day. She didn't want to risk him getting exposed to the cold weather just as he was on the mend. With Thursday and Friday as holidays, and the weekend following that, Andrew faced the welcome prospect of an extended respite from school. He didn't know what this Thanksgiving holiday was all about, but he was thankful, at least, that he would not have to face school for several days!

Mr. Givens's brother, Lee, and his family arrived about suppertime. Lee was a taller, thinner version of Mr. Givens. He was an apple farmer, and had packed about fifty pounds of apples into every nook and cranny of the battered jalopy that had conveyed the family to Scotch Plains. Lee's gregarious and chatty wife, Velma, had brought along ten quarts of her special homemade applesauce, a few bottles of apple brandy, and some apple chutney; the cornucopia of foodstuffs was swapped for a few dozen jars of Lois's canned peaches and corn relish.

Their daughter, Lee MacKenzie, or Mac, as she was called, also came, along with her three daughters and a dozen jars of honey. Mac was a beekeeper and she boasted that her bees had brought the family to Scotch Plains:

"I traded honey for gasoline to get us here!"

Mac's two older girls, Lisa and Leona, seven and six respectively, were shy and giggly, but the youngest, Lee-Ann, who was four, made no secret of her adoration of Andrew. "I like how him talks," she explained to Lois after insisting that she be seated next to Andrew at suppertime. "Him talks like that Lassie-boy."

"Lassie-boy?" Lois queried.

"That boy that says 'Lassie, my Lassie come home!' Lassie knowed she belonged to him, and she swimmed a river and comed home." She smiled at Andrew and gazed at him adoringly.

"Oh, *Lassie!*" Lois said. "So you saw that movie? I never got a chance to see it, but I heard it was very good."

"Lee-Ann saw it ten times!" Leona announced.

"Ten times!"

"Yes," Mac said. "It opened in town just before Lee-Ann's birthday and when I asked her what she wanted for her birthday, she said that she wanted to see *Lassie Come Home* a hundred times! We compromised at ten times, though."

"Him talks like that Lassie boy," Lee-Ann repeated, smiling at Andrew.

"Roddy McDowell," Mac explained to Andrew. "The English boy who was in the movie."

Lee-Ann continued to gaze ardently at Andrew. Every time he asked someone to pass the butter or the rolls, she smiled the most blissful smile at him. When they sat down in the living room after supper, she made a bee-line for the space next to him on the sofa. It was a confounding experience for Andrew to find himself so adored, and to encounter someone, albeit a child, who found his accent so enrapturing. Velma asked him about England, and he tried to be diplomatic about the differences between England and America, emphasizing the things he found to his liking in the United States, such as the abundance of food and the absence of bombing raids. He felt a bit uncomfortable, though, being the focal point of conversation. Not wanting to offend, either, he shrugged politely when Lee asked if there was anything he *didn't* like about America.

"I miss my mother," he said after awhile. He let the silence linger; then Mr. Givens spoke.

"Well, Lee, how does Hank like being a ninety-day wonder?"

This was the first time Andrew had ever heard that particular term unpreceded by an expletive. Curious to find out exactly what a ninety-day wonder was, and why they were so despised, he asked, "What's a ninety day wonder? I mean, I've heard about them, but I don't know what they are."

"The Army and Navy needed to train a lot of officers very quickly," Mac explained. "The usual route for officers is through West Point or Annapolis, or going in with a college degree. There just wasn't the time for that, so there was a special program set up for those men that the military deemed suitable as officer material. My husband had been a construction foreman for several years, so he was accepted for officer's training. He's in the Army, with the combat engineers."

"He was in Sicily," Lee added. "The engineers really did wonders there."

"Sicily's very mountainous country," Mac said, "And the Germans made good use of the terrain in withdrawing. They blew just about every bridge they crossed, mined the bypasses around the bridges, and the beaches and orchards where they expected our troops would bivouac. It was the engineers' job to dispose of the mines, as well as build bridges and repair roads."

"Ernie Pyle wrote a column all about the engineers in Sicily," Velma said.

"I read it," Lois said. "He said that Sicily was an engineer's war."

"It sure was," Mac affirmed. "Especially when they had to build that bridge at Point Calava. The road is built into a sheer rock wall that goes straight down to the sea, and the Germans blasted a hundred and fifty feet out of the road, leaving just the rock juttings. One infantry battalion got across the gap, and another one went over the ridge, to pursue the Germans. So the engineers had to build a bridge across the gap, fast, to get supplies and support to them. It was the kind of job that Hank said would have taken weeks under normal circumstances—the bridge got built in a night and half a day. Hank said it was the gawdawfulest-looking bridge he'd ever seen in his life, but it was *our* bridge, he said, and it could hold anything the US Army wanted to send across it."

"When it was done, they were going to send a test jeep across, seeing as it was a two-hundred foot fall into the sea if the bridge didn't hold," Velma added. "But General Truscott, who commanded the Third Division, got in that first jeep and went across. Hank wrote that it was the most wonderful thing he'd ever seen. It's one thing for a general to say he believes his men can do the job; it's another thing for him to put his money where his mouth is."

Mr. Givens then talked of Jake, and Lois beamed as he recounted some of Jake's adventures and misadventures. Andrew noted that Lee seemed surprised by Mr. Givens's enthusiastic report of Jake's activities.

"He was just promoted to Squadron Leader, which is equivalent to a Major," Jake's father reported proudly.

Lee-Ann began to rub her eyes, and Mac announced that it was bedtime for the "little ones." Lisa and Leona protested that they wanted to stay up late since it wasn't a school night, and Lee-Ann insisted that Andrew read a story to her.

Andrew was glad to oblige; Lee-Ann wrapped her arms around his neck and begged to be carried up the stairs. Transporting his tiny adoring fan, he tromped up the stairs, following Lee and the older girls. Lee and Velma shared the guest room; Mac and her daughters were billeted in the spare room, where Mr. Givens had set up the canvas bed, which was a sort of an oversized cot, and some pallets on the floor. Lee-Ann directed Andrew to the spare room, where she retrieved a battered book. Then they went to Andrew's room. Andrew settled Lee-Ann onto his bed and sat beside her; Lindy hopped up and snuggled next to Andrew, on the other side from Lee-Ann.

Andrew began to read: "*By The Shores of Silver Lake*, by Laura Ingalls Wilder." He pointed at the words on the cover, for he remembered that his father used to do that for him.

"Here's where we was." Lee-Ann opened the book to a place marked by a cloth bookmark. Andrew began to read:

Chapter 15: The Last Man Out. Next morning the sun shone but the wind was colder and there was a feeling of storm in the air. Pa had come from doing the chores and was warming his hands by the stove, while Ma and Laura put breakfast on the table, when they heard a wagon rattling....

As he read on, he was able to figure out that the central characters of the story were members of a family named Ingalls. They had lived on the prairie long ago, at least before there were automobiles; people got around in horse-drawn wagons. The father's name was Charles, the mother's name was Caroline, and they had four daughters: Mary, Laura, Carrie, and Grace. People on the prairie lived far apart from one another; the passage that Andrew read concerned the efforts of "Pa" to aid a man ill with consumption who would not survive the winter in a claim shanty, fifteen miles from the nearest neighbor.

Wolves, big "buffalo wolves," were also a problem in this desolate land; Pa had to make sure the stable was solid from attack.

But there were happy times, too, in this barren country. Pa played the fiddle, and the girls sang and danced to the music in the evenings:

Faster and faster he played, and faster they danced, with higher and higher steps, back and forth and whirling back again till they were breathless and hot with dancing and laughing.

"Now then," said Pa, "try a bit of a waltz," and the music flowed smoothly in gliding long waves. "Just float on the music, glide smoothly and turn."

Laura and Carrie waltzed across the room and back, and around and around the room, while Grace sat up in Ma's lap and watched them with round eyes and Mary listened quietly to the music and the dancing feet....

Andrew felt Lee-Ann slump against him, so he laid the book down and eased her into a reclined position. With Lindy dozing on his other side, he felt enveloped in a cocoon of affection and peace.

Snug as a bug in a rug, he thought, and that strange feeling of *deja-vu* descended upon him. Why was it all so familiar?

Then he remembered: the night he and his parents had lain out under the starry spring night, with him nestled in the middle, three and a half years ago. The night before his father was called away....

The door opened a crack, then wider. "Andrew..." Mac's face broke into a tender smile as she regarded her sleeping daughter. "Thank you so much for reading her a story," she whispered as she picked Lee-Ann up.

"Not at all," Andrew smiled. "It was a very nice story."

Mac glanced at Lindy as she carried her daughter to the door. "Does Lindy sleep with you?"

"He usually sleeps in the spare room, but since you're in it, I guess he'll sleep with me." He stroked Lindy's back, and Lindy responded by wriggling closer to Andrew and purring loudly.

"Lucky Lindy." Mac grinned. "Well, pleasant dreams, Andrew."

"Pleasant dreams," Andrew replied.

Andrew switched off the light by his bed and snuggled under the covers, Lindy's throaty purr lulling him to sleep.

He was in a cabin with rough wooden walls, and he heard the sound of a fiddle playing. He pushed open the door to the next room, and came upon a scene: a man, whose back was to Andrew, playing the fiddle as two girls danced together before him. The girls were about Andrew's age, dressed in long dresses of bright calico; the man was dressed in canvas trousers and a shirt of black and red plaid. To one side of the man sat two women whose backs were also to Andrew; they too, were dressed in colorful calico finery. The man played a lively waltz and the girls whirled around, faster and faster, until they both were squealing with delight and exhaustion. The two women clapped to the music; then they turned around and looked at Andrew. He was astounded to see that one of them was his mother and that she was holding a baby girl on her lap.

"Andrew!" his mother called. "Isn't it wonderful? Here, come sit next to us." The other woman smiled at him, and he had the funny feeling that she was somehow familiar, though he was quite sure he had never seen her before. The baby looked at Andrew and giggled, and he had the strangest feeling that he should know her, too. Now the dancing girls noticed him; they waved to him as they continued their jubilant waltz. The man playing the fiddle slowly turned, and Andrew saw that he was—

His father!

Without missing a beat, his father smiled the most blissful smile at him. Andrew tried to call out to him, but his voice wouldn't come. The dream jumbled all around him, and he found himself hurtling through a calico whirlwind, then falling into darkness....

He awoke, the notes of the waltz still playing in his mind.

I've seen him! I've seen my father!

It was a bizarre vision, to be sure. Imagine, his father playing a fiddle and dressed in a lumberjack's kit, and his mother wearing a calico dress! And there were the four girls— why did they all look so familiar? They weren't Mac's daughters, of that Andrew was sure: The dancing girls were older than Lisa and Leona, and the baby was younger than Lee-Ann. But where had he seen them?

No matter. He had seen his father, and euphoria swept over him as he replayed the scene again and again in his mind. His father had smiled at him, that same wonderful smile that was for Andrew alone. His eyes, too, had twinkled with mirth and joy, and Andrew sensed that his father's rapture was not only a response to Andrew's presence, but was brought about also by the laughter and happiness of the four girls.

The girls are probably the girls from the book I read to Lee-Ann, and I got the story muddled up in my dream...Maybe that's why they seemed so familiar....

He almost couldn't contain the joy within him; if it were possible for him to fly, he would be soaring through the air in a dance of rapture!

It's a promise—a promise that everything is going to be all right, that we're all going to be together again!

"Lee-Ann, no! Andrew's still sleeping!"

Mac's frantic whisper having awakened him, he rolled over to see Lee-Ann skipping towards him. She threw herself at him; then, her arms twined around his neck, gleefully pronounced, "Him's awake already." Tightening her embrace, she pleaded, "Read story?"

"I'm so sorry," Mac told him. "I turned my back for a second, and she was already halfway down the hall." To Lee-Ann, she said firmly, "Don't pester, sweetheart. Andrew hasn't even had breakfast yet, and he probably has other things to do."

"That's all right. I really don't have anything to do today," Andrew said. "I wouldn't mind reading to her all day, if that's what she wants."

Lee-Ann's face broke into a rapturous smile; she squeezed Andrew so tightly he almost turned purple.

"All right, dear." Mac untangled her daughter from Andrew. "Andrew can't read to you if you choke him to death!"

Lee-Ann grabbed the book off the dresser, where Andrew had left it the night before. She opened it to the page marked by the bookmark, then snuggled against Andrew.

"We'll read just a few pages before breakfast, all right?" he said. "Then, we'll read the rest of the day, if you'd like."

Lee-Ann bobbed her head excitedly, and Andrew began to read aloud to her.

He read a few pages into the next chapter; then Lois called to announce that breakfast was ready. He carried Lee-Ann down the stairs, and was surprised to see Mr. Givens seated with everyone else at the dining room table.

"You're not going to work today?"

"Even pharmacists take Thanksgiving off!" Lois laughed.

Thanksgiving! It must be a very important holiday for Mr. Givens to stay at home!

"Dig in, everyone!" Lois spread her arms wide over the array of abundance on the table: piles of apple pancakes, heaps of scrambled eggs, sausages galore. There was a gigantic bowl of fruit salad, composed of peaches, apples, grapes, and scattered with a few bits of some yellowish-looking fruit Andrew had never seen before. After dishing up a serving for himself, he tried a bite.

"This is delicious—what is it?" He pointed to one of the pieces in his bowl.

"Pineapple—haven't you ever had it before?" Lois asked.

"No, never," he replied.

"Never had pineapple!" Velma exclaimed.

"Well, it's hard enough to get here," Lois said. "It's probably scarcer than hen's teeth in England. Alice was amazed that we had orange juice every morning. She said that in England, only children under five got a ration of orange juice."

"Once my mother brought home three oranges," Andrew said. "She said a friend of hers got them from an American fighter pilot. We practically had a celebration, because it had been so long since we'd had oranges!"

Lois laughed. "Jake wrote me about that. He got them by some creative bargaining with a pilot in the Eighth Air Force, guy he went to flight school with. His friend had always wanted to fly a Spitfire, so Jake let him take up his Spitfire in exchange for the oranges."

"*Jake* got the oranges?" Andrew failed to check the dismay in his voice; no matter, Lois didn't seem to notice.

"Uh-huh, didn't your mother tell you?"

Andrew quickly stabbed another piece of pineapple and proceeded to chew it vigorously, all the while struggling to maintain an air of composure. After swallowing it, he mumbled, "No—no, she didn't. It was before I met Jake. I...I wouldn't have known who he was, anyway—then, I mean." He savagely sliced his sausages.

Damn him, *damn him*! Even the memory of that delightful occasion was now marred by the knowledge that the oranges had been procured by Jake.

There's nothing—nothing in my life that Jake hasn't managed to ruin!
He chomped on his sausage as he tried to calm himself.
Except for the memory of my father.

Andrew's agitation evaporated as soon as breakfast was over and Lee-Ann took his hand and drew him away from the table. As she led him up the stairs she chattered happily about the "House on the Prairie Peoples"; evidently, there was a whole series of books which told of the Ingalls family's adventures in the American Midwest. Andrew spent the rest of the morning snuggled up with her, reading aloud the story of these people who had lived long ago, in a world so completely different from anything he could ever have imagined. A few months ago he would not have been the least bit interested in a story about people living in the "bugger-all" of the American wilderness, but now he read as if some strange force compelled him to discover more about these people and their lives. He felt as if his life were somehow bound up with the story now unfolding before him. He realized it was partly because of the dream he'd had the night before with the vision of his parents together again, but it was something else, too: a wonderful feeling of love and belonging and peace that the story stirred within him.

Lois called them down about noon for a light lunch, as dinner was to be served around five. As Andrew descended the stairs, the aroma of roasted turkey nearly drove him mad with anticipation. Lunch was grilled cheese sandwiches, sliced apples, and "crispies," which were leftover piecrust scraps served hot from the oven and spread with melted butter and cinnamon sugar. They were wonderfully flaky and tender; Andrew had never tasted anything so scrumptious. Velma was the official pie-baker for the feast that was to be served that evening, and it was her own tradition to make seven different kinds of pie on this special day: pumpkin, apple, peach, blueberry, cherry, mincemeat, and lemon meringue. She had been up since 5 A.M., as the pies needed to be baked before the turkey went in the oven at ten o'clock.

After lunch Andrew read some more to Lee-Ann. They were almost at the end of the book and something dreadful had happened: The Ingalls family had just moved into their claim shanty, and little Grace had wandered off and disappeared. Ma and Pa, Laura and Carrie fanned out to begin the desperate search, for the prairie was so vast and desolate that a child might be lost forever. Finally, Laura found her in a tiny valley, sitting in the midst of a circle of violets:

> *Laura sank down and took Grace in her arms. She held Grace carefully and panted for breath. Grace leaned over her arm to reach more violets. They were surrounded by masses of violets blossoming above low-spreading leaves. Violets covered the flat bottom of a large, round hollow. All around this lake of violets, grassy banks rose almost straight up to the prairie-level. There in the round, low place the wind hardly disturbed the fragrance of the violets. The sun was warm there, the sky was overhead, the green walls of grass curved all around, and butterflies fluttered over the crowding violet-faces.*

Laura stood up and lifted Grace to her feet. She took the violets that Grace gave her, and clasped her hand. "Come Grace," she said. "We must go home."

A soft click startled Andrew; he looked up from the book to see Mr. Givens standing at the foot of the bed, camera in hand. Mr. Givens smiled, and said, "You two just looked like a picture together."

"More picture!" Lee-Ann exclaimed, and Mr. Givens obliged her by taking a few more snapshots of the two of them. Lee-Ann was a ham: She grinned impishly, then threw her arms around Andrew and planted a sloppy kiss on his cheek.

"I'll get copies made to send your mother," Mr. Givens told Andrew. "I know she'll love these."

His remark gave Andrew an idea: What better way to reassure his mother that all was well, that he was happy and thriving, than to give her a photographic record of just how wonderful things were? He had written several letters to her so far, all of them blithe and chatty and pouring forth his praises of the land he'd been exiled to, but snapshots ought to convince her once and for all that there was no need for her to worry anymore about him.

At dinner he asked Mr. Givens to take a picture of him presiding gleefully over the gigantic roasted fowl; he held a knife in one hand and a fork in the other, as if he were to consume the entire bird himself.

The dining room table seem to groan with the bounty that was set upon it. Besides the turkey, there were bowls heaped with mashed potatoes, sweet potatoes, stuffing, carrots, and sweet corn. There was a platter piled high with all the different breads Lois had baked the day before. There were lashings of cranberry sauce and huge slabs of butter and enough gravy to drown a cat. Speaking of which, the Thanksgiving festivities had turned Lindy into one disgruntled feline, as he had been confined to quarters in the sunroom: Lois said he was not to be trusted anywhere near a roasted turkey, for a few years before he had demolished one that had been left unguarded for a few minutes. Lindy pressed his nose to the glass-paned French doors, and Andrew found his baleful glare ever so comical.

Lee said grace, his "Amen" echoed loudly by everyone. Within seconds, it seemed, bowls and plates were flitting over the table and animated conversation emanated as if a radio had suddenly been switched on. As everyone was having seconds, Lisa piped, "Let's do the thank yous."

"Thank yous?" Andrew asked.

"Every year we say what we're thankful for," Mac explained. "From youngest to oldest. Lee-Ann goes first."

Lee-Ann broke into an ecstatic grin. "I thankful Andrew read me story all day! And I thankful Lassie comed home."

"That's only a movie!" Lisa mocked. "You can't be thankful for something that's only *pretend!*"

"Lassie comed home, that Lassie-boy said, 'My Lassie come home.' So I thankful Lassie comed home."

"That's stupid!" Leona scoffed.

"Leona, don't ridicule your sister," Mac admonished.

Lisa was thankful there was no school that day, and Leona was thankful for the seven kinds of pies and all the good food they had because, as she pointed out, "Lots of people don't have hardly anything to eat because of the war."

"Andrew?" Lois smiled at him.

The memory of the dream he'd had the night before suddenly burst upon him, but how could he say that he was thankful that his parents would be together again some-day? All eyes were upon him, and he found himself at a loss for words. He so much wanted to share his happiness with these people but, as they were Jake's family, he knew that wouldn't be fitting. Finally he said, "I'm thankful for being able to remember."

The grownups mostly professed thankfulness that, this year at least, they could look forward to the end of the war—soon, it was hoped.

"There were times last year when things looked pretty bleak," Velma said. "Remember hearing about the Philippines?"

"I didn't think anything could be worse after what happened at Pearl Harbor," Lois added. "But Bataan—it was just awful, hearing about those poor men going on that death march. Thousands dying, so many more enduring God knows what."

"Oak still hasn't heard anything about his son." Lee spoke softly, but directly, to Mr. Givens.

Mr. Givens regarded his brother with a blank stare, but his eyes betrayed a look that an odd mixture of indignation and pain. He was completely still for an interminable moment; the ticking of the clock punctuated the silence. Lee nervously cleared his throat. Mr. Givens turned to Velma and said, "Still seven kinds of pie this year, Velma?"

"As always, Gene."

Mr. Givens pushed himself back from the table a bit and nodded at Velma. "I think I'll start off with a piece of your wonderful apple pie."

Lois and Velma hopped up and proceeded to convey the pies to the dining room.

"I know!" Andrew exclaimed. "Why don't you take a picture of me with all the pies. My mother would be ever so delighted!"

"Good idea," Mr. Givens smiled. He got the camera, and, with Andrew presiding with glorious anticipation over the wonderful array of pastries, snapped a picture. Lee-Ann wanted to be in a picture with Andrew and the pies, so Mr. Givens took another one.

After dinner, Lee-Ann wanted "more story," so Andrew took her upstairs again. She ran to her room to get *By the Shores of Silver Lake*, then got into his bed and snuggled next to him. Lindy, who knew the form by now, slithered into the room, hopped up on the bed, and settled himself next to them.

"Who's that?" Lee-Ann asked, pointing to the picture on the dresser.

"That's my mother," Andrew said.

"Where her is?" Lee-Ann asked.

"She's in England."

"Why her not here with you?"

"Because she went back to England."

"Why her put you here?"

"Well, that's what she wanted."

"Why?"

"I suppose she thought it would be better for me to be in America."

"Where your daddy?"

Her question took Andrew by surprise; he had to think a moment about what to say.

"My father got shot down. He was a fighter pilot."

Mercifully, Lee-Ann did not voice any more queries about his father. "Why you living with Aunt Lois?" she asked.

"Well, my mother got married to Jake and, when she wanted to send me to America, Lois said I could stay here."

"You stay here forever?"

"No, when the war's over, I'll go back to England."

"Why?"

"Because that's my home. That's where I belong."

Lee-Ann was very still for a moment, then she threw herself against him and moaned, "I not want you go back!"

Andrew didn't know what to say. Lee-Ann looked up at him and pleaded, "Please stay here! Please!"

He put his arms around her. "I'll probably be here for awhile. But—" An idea occurred to him. "Remember Lassie? She was away from her home, and she knew she had to get back to where she belonged. Well, I have to go back to where I belong. Someday, when the war's over."

Lee-Ann looked up at him, her face streaked with tears. "I wish you belonged here!"

All he could do was hug her, overwhelmed by this expression of ardor and anguish. He took a corner of the sheet and wiped her cheeks. "Now, don't cry. I probably won't be going for awhile."

"I not want the war be over!"

"You mustn't say that. War's a terrible thing. People get hurt and killed, and the sooner the war's over, the sooner the killing and the hurting will stop. Your daddy's going to come home when the war's over—don't you want that?"

Lee-Ann nodded, then threw herself into Andrew's arms again. "I want get married to you!"

"*Married!* Getting married is for grown-ups, and you're not a grown-up, Lee-Ann, and neither am I."

"I get married to you when I grown-up!"

"Well, you don't decide that sort of thing when you're little. You wait until you're grown up, and then you decide whom you want to marry. Tell you what—" He smiled at her. "Let's decide to be friends. We already are, but let's promise that we will always and always be friends—how about that?"

Lee-Ann's blissful smile was confirmation of her acceptance; she nestled into his embrace and, within a few minutes, was fast asleep.

"Oh, I'm so sorry—I tried not to wake you up," a voice whispered.

Andrew opened his eyes to see Mac lifting her daughter from the bed. "You two sleepyheads—for some reason a big turkey dinner sends people straight off to dreamland. My mother and Aunt Lois have already turned in for the night; of course, they've been up since early morning preparing the Thanksgiving feast. You go back to sleep now. Pleasant dreams, Andrew."

"Pleasant dreams," Andrew murmured.

Mac softly closed the door, and Andrew turned out the light. Lindy repositioned himself into the curve between Andrew's arm and chest and went back to sleep.

As he stroked Lindy's sleeping form, Andrew was suddenly overcome with—well, not exactly hunger, but an urge to have just a taste of that delicious pumpkin pie. He'd never had pumpkin pie before, and found it positively delicious.

He got up and crept down the stairs. Padding into the kitchen, he heard voices coming from the breakfast room: Mr. Givens's and Lee's.

"...and what's past is past. You ought to at least write to Oak. I think hearing from you would do him a world of good," Lee was saying.

"There's nothing I have to say to him. I didn't have anything to say to him four years ago, and I don't have anything to say to him now," Mr. Givens said.

"What are you going to do—carry a grudge to your grave? Oak was wrong, but that's no reason for you not to take the first step."

"I'm sorry about what happened to Eric. He was a good kid, and I hope he's okay. But I have nothing to say to Oak about it. How he's dealing with it is his business, not mine, just as how I dealt with what happened with Jake was my business, not his."

"You and Oak are more alike than you realize. You both have only one son and you both know what it's like to fear the worst. Last time I saw Oak, he told me, 'If I knew either way about Eric, even the worst, it would be something I could deal with. But not knowing is a living nightmare.' Gene, I know how bad it was for you when you heard about Jake's accident. You're not one to show things, but I knew. Just as I knew how it tore you apart about what Dad—"

"Let's not talk about *him*—"

"It's been over thirty years, Gene. It's time to make peace—"

"Dad made things pretty clear the last time we spoke. I'm not going to cross him—"

"You know he only spoke out of fear. He thought that he could scare you into—"

"What he intended doesn't matter. I made my choice, and I chose to live with the consequences. Dad was the one who delivered the ultimatum, not me. And he's never let me know that he's changed his mind."

"You know he's just as proud as you are. The only reason he threatened you was because he thought you despised him."

"I didn't despise him. I just wanted to choose the kind of life I wanted to have."

"Why don't you tell him that, then?"

"No reason to."

"There's every reason to, Gene."

"What does he want—for me to say I'm sorry? Because I'm not—"

"This isn't about apologizing or deciding who's wrong about things, Gene. It's just time to make peace—"

"I'm not going to go stirring things up, Lee. I've never looked back after what happened, and I'm proud of what I did. I've made a life for myself, the kind of life I wanted, and I've buried the past. No regrets."

There was a long silence; then Mr. Givens spoke again, this time in a soft, strained voice. "I really appreciate your friendship, Lee, yours and Reed's, all these years."

"Well, what are brothers for, Gene? Dad has never asked me where I spend my Thanksgivings, but he knows. And he's never let it come between us. That's why I think—"

"Lee, I know you want us all to be one big happy family. But you know, we never were, especially after Mom died, and there's really not much reason to try now."

"You and Jake were at odds with one another since the day he was born, and look at how things are now. Things *can* change. I don't know what happened between the two of you, but it had to have been something really special." There was a pause, and Lee spoke a little more softly. "Lois couldn't stop bragging on Jake's wife. Did she have something to do with things?"

There was a long pause, then Mr. Givens said, "It's private."

"Okay, I understand. I'm just glad for you—both of you."

There was another long silence, then Mr. Givens's voice, almost inaudible: "Thanks."

Lee spoke. "Well, I guess I'll turn in." Andrew heard the breakfast room door open. He knew he would be detected if he tried to run up the stairs, so he strode boldly into the passageway.

"Sorry." He almost bumped into Lee. "I wanted to get a bite to eat. Do you know where the pumpkin pie is? It's ever so delicious."

"In the refrigerator." Lee walked into the kitchen, opened the refrigerator door, and sorted through the shelves crammed with leftovers. He pulled out a pie plate which contained a slice of pumpkin pie and a few slices of lemon meringue.

"Oh, perhaps I shouldn't take the last piece—"

"No, go ahead. We've got enough pies to last us for another week. Gene, would you like a slice of lemon meringue?"

"Sure."

Lee served up the slices of pie; he and Andrew carried the plates back into the breakfast room.

"Perfect end to a perfect day," Lee pronounced, as he scraped the last bit of meringue off his plate.

"I hope you had a nice day, Andrew. With all the excitement, I was afraid you'd get lost in the shuffle," Mr. Givens said.

"Oh, no—I had a smashing time. I really liked reading to Lee-Ann."

Lee grinned. "My friends say they feel sorry for me because I've got just a daughter and granddaughters, but I wouldn't trade a one of them for all the boys in the world. They're all jewels, but Lee-Ann's the apple of my eye." He winked at Mr. Givens. "You'll be looking forward to having a few grandkids of your own pretty soon, Gene."

Mr. Givens smiled politely. Andrew's heart skipped a beat.

She can't have any more children—she would have had more after me, surely....She must have told Jake, and he's told his father. It's not the sort of topic for polite conversation, certainly not something one would discuss with someone who has no business knowing....

Mr. Givens laid his fork down. "Guess I'll turn in." Without saying another word, he walked out of the room and climbed the stairs.

"Let's not leave the womenfolk more dirty dishes." Lee smiled at Andrew. "They've been working hard all day. Tell you what—I'll wash, you dry."

"All right," Andrew replied. They carried the dishes out to the kitchen and made short work of getting them washed, dried, and put away. Lee wiped down the counters and inspected the spotless kitchen.

"Looks good," he said. "Well, pleasant dreams, Andrew."

"Pleasant dreams to you, too."

Andrew didn't have any pleasant dreams that night, but at least he didn't have any unpleasant ones, either. He awoke a little after nine, well-rested after an undisturbed night's sleep.

It's not as if I should expect to have a dream about my father every night, he thought. The dream I had the night before should do me for a long, long time. Maybe it was the trying so hard that sabotaged things—best not to chase after things so desperately.

An idea occurred to him, though, and when Lois announced at breakfast that they were going to go to Plainfield to do some shopping, he asked if he might come along.

"Sure, we'll all squeeze in somehow."

After breakfast he went upstairs to his room and opened his box, in which he had stashed his weekly allowance. He had not spent a cent of it yet. He counted out five of the drab, undersized dollar bills; he didn't think that would be enough money for what he planned to buy, so he asked Lois if he could borrow a few dollars. She gave him ten dollars, and told him that his mother had arranged for him to have that much for extra spending money before Christmas.

Mr. Givens had already gone to work, but had left the car for them; Lee would be staying home to "put up" some shelves in the basement. So the seven of them—Lois, Velma, Mac, Andrew, and the girls—piled into the car.

Crikey, Andrew thought. *I've never been surrounded by so many females in my life!*

They drove to Plainfield, with Lee-Ann chattering excitedly all the way. As Lois was driving down a side street looking for a place to park, Andrew spotted a book and china shop.

"Would it be all right if I went in there while you go shopping?" he asked.

"Sure," Lois replied. "We're just going to get some clothes for the girls. We'll come get you when we're done."

There was a parking spot just up the street from the shop; Lois pulled into it and everyone was disgorged from the car and went their separate ways.

A bell jangled as Andrew opened the door to the book and china shop. A slight, grey-haired woman smiled at him from behind the register.

"May I help you?" she asked.

"Yes, um, I'm looking for some books by Laura Ingalls Wilder."

"Oh, the Little House series."

"Yes, uh...it's for a gift."

A gift for myself, he thought to himself as the woman led him to the back of the shop.

"Good thing you're getting your Christmas shopping done now," she smiled. "These sell like hotcakes just before Christmas. Which ones did you want?"

"Um, all of them."

The woman smiled even more broadly and selected one of each book in the series. "Looks like you're getting my last copy of *On the Banks of Plum Creek*—must remember to order more." She thumbed through the books. "Let's see, *Little House in the Big Woods, Little House on the Prairie, By the Shores of Silver Lake, The Long Winter, Little Town on the Prairie, These Happy Golden Years*, and *Farmer Boy*."

After he'd paid for the books at the front counter, he noticed a collection of china figures displayed in the front window and his eyes widened with delight at one of them.

"Oh—it's lovely! May I buy it?"

"Of course—they're for sale. Which one do you want?"

Andrew pointed to the figure of a collie.

"Oh, what a wonderful choice!" the woman said. "It looks just like Lassie, doesn't it?"

"Yes, it does. I have a little friend who would be ever so enchanted with it."

"Would you like it wrapped?"

"Yes, please." While the woman was wrapping the china collie, Andrew selected two different Shirley Temple paper doll books for Lisa and Leona. Lois came in just as he was paying for them.

"You've got to see Lee-Ann!" she told him. "She picked out this dark green velvet dress, and she's just about to explode with excitement—she wants to show it to you."

"Super—I'll just stash these in the car."

"She looks like Scarlett O'Hara wearing the drapes of Tara," Lois laughed as they walked up the street. They put the package in the trunk and went into the clothing store. Lee-Ann skipped up to Andrew and twirled around, the skirt of her dress billowing out in an orbit of deep green.

You look positively smashing!" he exclaimed.

"Is smashing good?"

"Yes, it means ever so wonderful. You're as pretty as a princess!"

"You got princesses in England?"

"Why yes, we have two. Their names are Elizabeth and Margaret."

"They in America too?"

"No, they're in England."

"Why their mommy not send them to America?"

"Because...." Even as Andrew racked his brain for an answer to Lee-Ann's query, a flash of anger smacked him. Even the *Queen* hadn't sent *her* children away from England! He should have brought up that particular point to his mother, but of course his thinking had been so frantic and muddled. And it was too late now to present this particular argument.

It was all Jake's fault!

If I hadn't been so enraged by Jake's deviousness in getting me exiled to America, I would have been able to think more clearly.

Damn him!

Lucky, lucky princesses! They don't have Jake to push them around! And even if they did, being princesses, they could have him charged with treason and have his head chopped off! Or have him hanged, drawn and quartered....

He felt a tug on his trousers.

"Why their mommy not send them to America?"

"Oh, well...I suppose she thought it would be better for them to remain in England. Sometimes different mommies decide different things for their children." He forced a smile and extended his arm to her. "Come on, m'lady—I shall escort you to your coach!"

After they'd returned home, Andrew presented his gifts to the girls. Lisa and Leona were delighted with their paper dolls, and excitedly set to work cutting out Shirley's finery. Lee-Ann was positively enthralled with her "Lassie Come Home." She sat for a few moments, reverently holding the china collie in her hands, then gently placed Lassie back in the box and threw her arms around Andrew.

"It's my own Lassie Come Home!" she exclaimed.

"Hey, let's make Lassie Come Home a home," Lois said. She went into the sunroom and got a small wooden box that looked like a miniature log cabin. The roof hinged open to reveal a hollow within. Lois lined it with some velvet, and Lee offered his handkerchief as a blanket.

"There, she's as snug as a bug in a rug," Velma laughed as Lee-Ann placed the handkerchief-wrapped collie into her new "home."

The older girls spent the rest of the afternoon playing with their paper dolls; Lee-Ann sat with Andrew and recounted the entire plot of *Lassie Come Home*. He hadn't seen it, but had heard about it, and he listened intently to Lee-Ann's narration.

After Mr. Givens arrived home they ate a supper of turkey pot pie. Lisa asked Andrew if they had turkey pot pie in England.

"I've never had turkey pot pie, but we have Shepherd's Pie and Woolten Pie and Stargazey Pie, and other kinds of pies, too."

"What's Stargazey Pie?" Leona asked.

"Mrs. Tuttle, our cook, used to make it for us. It's a pie, made from some sort of little fish, and the fish heads are poking up through the crust. They look as if they're gazing up at the stars, which is why it's called Stargazey Pie."

"Eeech!" Lisa gagged. "*Fish heads?* Sticking out of a *pie?* Oh God, I'd die if I ever saw that!" She shuddered with horror.

"Lisa, that wasn't very nice," Mac said. Apologize to Andrew, please."

"I'm sorry, but I still think that fish heads sticking out of a pie is *disgusting!*"

"Lisa, that's enough!" Mac's voice was firm.

"Lisa isn't very fond of fish," Velma explained to Andrew. "Big ones, little ones, live ones, dead ones—Lee can't even open a can of sardines without Lisa clearing out of the house."

"They're *horrible*—they're all slimy and their eyes are scary," Lisa said.

"Did you like that Stargazey Pie?" Lee-Ann asked Andrew.

"Oh, it was rather fun. My father used to pretend the fish were having a party, and he'd make voices, as if they were talking to one another." Andrew smiled at the remembrance. Somehow, it seemed perfectly natural to talk about his father in the company of Jake's relatives. He knew they wouldn't think he was being churlish—which he wasn't—or begrudge the memories he had of his father, and the love and longing he felt in his heart. He knew the girls missed their father, too, although he was not missing. Still, he was far away and in the thick of things. From what the news reports seemed to indicate, the "soft underbelly" of Europe was proving to be not so yielding as had been supposed, and things were sure to get worse when winter came. Although Andrew had never met Mac's husband, he breathed a silent prayer that he would come home safe and sound.

He will, surely he will, just as my father will come home....

That night, he dreamt that he was sitting in a circle of violets, with the sun shining down on him and butterflies fluttering all around. He was alone, but he wasn't afraid, for he knew that his father would come to get him.

And sure enough, there he was, standing at the crest of the ridge from which the little valley angled down. He waved; then a second later, it seemed, he was holding Andrew in his arms. The scent of violets, the feel of his father's uniform brushing against his face, the gentle breeze playing around them—all these Andrew sensed as vividly as if he'd been awake.

"Come on, old chap," his father said. "We must go home."

Andrew snuggled his face into his father's shoulder, and felt himself being carried, carried home.

Chapter 38

*A*fter the departure of their guests the next morning, the house seemed eerily quiet. Andrew was reminded of Greycliff, with its vast tract of rooms devoid of life and happiness. Lois spent the day tidying the upstairs. Lindy, after wandering disconsolately through the house, curled up on the triangular table in the corner of the breakfast room and cat-napped his loneliness away. Even the house itself seemed to grieve with desolation, as if the very walls longed for the lively pattering and chattering of children.

Like Greycliff, in being bereft of life and laughter, Andrew thought, but like Armus House, in a way, for it was meant to be lived in, to be a place of joy and love and happy times.

He could almost sense a kind of pain exuding from the place, as if this barrenness were an old wound. After trudging up the stairs to his room, he stretched out on his bed. Though Lee-Ann had not been gone more than an hour, Andrew already ached to have her by his side. He recalled how she had thrown her arms around him and sobbed at the last minute, begging him not to go back to England until she could come for another visit the following Thanksgiving. Loath to make any rash promises (for he would *surely* be back in England by next Thanksgiving), he'd taken her upstairs to his room and had shown her the books he'd bought.

"I got them because of the wonderful times we had reading them together. Also, I've been having bad dreams every night ever since I came to America, but after reading to you, I had good dreams."

When Lee-Ann asked him what his good dreams were about, he told her they were about his father. Then she threw her arms around him again and laughed with joy, as if she were making his dreams her own.

Looking up at the ceiling, a wave of longing swept over him.

If I had a sister, she would be like that...happy and bright and devoted to me....
What if?

What if my parents had had more children after me? And why didn't they? Surely they wanted to have more—but couldn't.

He had always rejoiced at the fact that he was an only child, for he had enjoyed his parents' undivided attention and affection. Now, however, he regarded his lack of siblings as a curse, not a blessing. Perhaps with a brother or sister to support him, he might have been able to prevent his mother from remarrying. Or, that failing, he would at least have had a companion in his exile, and, after the war was over, a fellow-in-arms to aid him in his struggle to wrest his mother from Jake.

The wresting, he knew, would be considerable, for with every passing day the bond between his mother and Jake would grow stronger. They couldn't be together all the time, but they could be together far more often, and with much less distraction, than if Andrew were in England. Perhaps they were together at this very moment! What with the time difference it would be evening, close to nightfall. Perhaps Jake was whispering sweet nothings in her ear right now! Maybe they were snuggling up under the sheets, Jake ever so craftily alleging all sorts of Beastly Weapons the Nazis had up their sleeves, and affirming what a Good Thing it was that Andrew was out of harm's way in America. And she would be looking back at him with cow-eyes, ever so grateful that Jake had made her aware of such Dreadful Dangers, and ever so appreciative that he'd arranged for Andrew's dispatch to America. That Jake had done the arranging, Andrew did not doubt for a moment, for motive was the proof of guilt. And what could suit Jake's purposes better than to have Andrew out of the way?

The liar! He lied to my mother about all those weapons the Nazis are supposed to have, and he lied to his mother, too! Mum said she took care of him when he was in hospital with burns, but he said they met when she ferried a Spit to his base!

Andrew knew that Jake's dissimulation did not disillusion Lois in the least. Even taking Lois's essentially sanguine nature into account, Andrew knew that she couldn't be happier that things had turned out so well, what with Jake having made such a fine choice in a wife, not to mention that Jake and his father were on such good terms. She was not about to let herself be confused by the facts! Andrew was positive, furthermore, that Lois had not made Mr. Givens aware of this particular spot of bother, for what with Jake and his father being on such friendly footing, Lois no doubt considered that it would be to no one's benefit to expose Jake's nefariousness.

Almost no one's benefit, Andrew thought.

He awoke the next morning and found that his voice was so hoarse it sounded as if he had a full-blown case of laryngitis. He didn't feel unwell at all, and knew he had only strained his vocal cords from doing so much talking during the past few days. Still, when Lois furrowed her brow in concern, pressing her palm against his forehead and murmuring worrisome commentaries about the state of his health and might it not be a good idea for him to stay home from church and, if he wasn't feeling any better by bedtime, to stay home from school Monday, Andrew cleared his throat and coughed and blinked his eyes and agreed that yes, that sounded like a very sensible thing to do.

Coffee pot in hand, Lois shuffled out to the dining room. Andrew heard low, muffled conversation, sensed the concern in Mr. Givens's voice, and knew this would be a good time to make his move. Not that he planned on blurting out the evidence of Jake's dishonesty right away—best to smooth his way to discrediting Jake with amiable conversation and a request, of sorts, for assistance that Mr. Givens would certainly be able to give.

Actually, *enlightenment* would be a more accurate term: enlightenment on that particular subject about which Andrew had been wondering for the past several weeks. Since Mr. Givens was a medical-type person, he was logically the person to approach with this matter. Also, since Jake had rejected an education, career, and, in short, anything to do with the medical field, it would be a smart tactical move to approach Mr. Givens with a medical-type question and to profess appreciation for any subsequent illumination he might provide.

So, after breakfast, while Lois was in the kitchen doing dishes, Andrew lingered at the breakfast table while Mr. Givens had a second cup of coffee. Andrew had refused Lois's offer of breakfast in bed, saying that he didn't want to put her to any trouble. Lois fixed him a steaming hot cup of honey lemonade which he sipped as Mr. Givens drank his coffee, copying his motions exactly. As Mr. Givens perused the Sunday paper, he occasionally grunted; it was hard to ascertain whether it was with interest, satisfaction, or consternation.

"What is it?" Andrew tilted his head as Mr. Givens let out a groan and cleared his throat loudly.

"Tarawa." Mr. Givens shook his head in stunned dismay.

"What's Tarawa?"

"In the Gilbert Islands."

Andrew pursed his lips and cast his eyes from side to side, trying to place this mysterious name. Mr. Givens noted his bewilderment.

"In the Pacific."

"Oh." Andrew nodded. "Is that near the Solomon Islands?" He recalled Mr. Givens mentioning them.

"No, the Gilbert Islands are farther north."

"Oh." Andrew didn't want to parade his ignorance any further. He had, on occasion, glanced at maps of the scores of nondescript tiny islands sprinkled across the vast Pacific and found them to be quite unworthy of his interest. As far as he was concerned, it did not matter one whit whether it took the United States two months or two years or two centuries to hop across those inconsequential bits of land; the hop across the twenty-odd mile gap between Britain and the European mainland by Allied forces was the only thing that was important. The Nazis needed to be driven out of France, back to Germany: Only when that happened would his exile in this wretched land come to an end.

Reciprocal course—send the Huns back to Hunland. Then Andrew would be able to return to England and thus have the opportunity to deal with Jake at close range. For now though....

Mr. Givens shook his head again and let out a slow breath, dropping the newspaper onto the table as if he were laying a shroud over a body. Andrew glanced at the photo glaring out from the sea of newsprint: the corpses of American soldiers, sprawled on a beach, their limbs grotesquely splayed against the sky.

"...a thousand killed, just on that tiny island. Christ, if we ever make it to the Japanese mainland, it'll be a goddamed meat-grinder, for sure."

"Dear?" Lois stood in the doorway.

Mr. Givens cleared his throat nervously as guilt washed across his face.

Lois gave him a swift kiss him on the lips, then drew back and looked at him with tenderness. "It's not nice to take the Lord's name in vain, *especially* on Sunday."

"Sorry." Mr. Givens smiled sheepishly as he refolded the paper, hiding the photo within the pages.

Lois kissed him again. Turning to Andrew, she inquired, "Would you like some more hot lemonade?"

"Um...no, thank you." As much as he would like to accept Lois's offer, for his throat was starting to tighten with nervousness, he didn't want Lois interrupting the conversation he was planning on having with her husband.

Lois smiled at him, then returned to the kitchen. Mr. Givens flipped through the pages and settled on another news item. "*Allies Attack Across Sangro River in Italy*," he grunted approvingly.

"Hmm." Andrew feigned an interest he didn't feel. He could not care less about Italy, either.

Mr. Givens sipped his coffee. The loud ticking of the grandfather clock reminded Andrew that he'd better not wait any longer. He looked directly at Mr. Givens.

"May I ask you something?"

"Um...yeah, sure."

Andrew took a deep breath, then bit his lip. Mr. Givens glanced at him and took another sip of coffee.

Andrew cleared his throat, and asked, "Do you know anything about short arm inspections?"

His query caught Mr. Givens in mid-gulp; he made a funny choking sound and sprayed a mouthful of coffee halfway across the table. He gagged, coughed loudly, and stared at Andrew, mouth agape. The expression in his eyes alarmed Andrew.

Fear.

Make that terror.

Lois appeared in the doorway. "Dear, are you all right?"

Mr. Givens croaked, "Fine—I'm f-fine."

"Are you sure? You aren't coming down with a cold too, are you?"

"No—no, I'm fine. Not a cold—I'm—I'm fine." Andrew got the distinct impression that Mr. Givens considered a cold to be a much preferred alternative.

"Do you want me to get you anything?" Lois asked, concern still in her eyes.

"No. No thanks."

Lois raised one eyebrow. "Okay." She returned to the kitchen.

Perhaps this was not a very good idea after all.

"I'm sorry." Andrew started to get up. "I didn't mean to upset you. Never mind."

"No, no, wait. Um...don't go." Mr. Givens gave Andrew a funny sort of look; the terror was replaced by a kind of unease that was overlaid with resolve, the look of someone who has a duty to perform in spite of fearful prospects. "S-s-sit down."

Andrew sat back into his chair and waited for Mr. Givens to speak.

"Where did you hear about this...uh, short arm inspection."

"I heard some soldiers on the ship talking about it. I know what it is but I don't know why they do it."

"You know what it is, then? Did the soldiers tell you?"

"No, Peter did."

"Peter?"

"He was a boy I shared a cabin with."

Mr. Givens nodded rather absently. It seemed he was buying time while working on what to say. Andrew went on. "Peter said that they—the soldiers, I mean—have to get their Willies inspected...by some sort of medical person."

"This Peter, he's about your age?" Mr. Givens took another sip of coffee.

"No, he's eight."

Another spray of coffee issued from Mr. Givens's mouth.

"An eight-year-old kid told you about short arm inspections?"

"Um...um, yes, sort of. But Peter didn't know why; he said the Army was mad on inspections, that's all."

"What else did he tell you?"

"Not much, actually. I don't think he really knew. It has to do with the veedee."

"The *veedee*," Mr. Givens echoed. It was not exactly phrased as a question; it was more a pronouncement of doom. He took another sip of coffee.

Trying to be helpful, Andrew added, "He said—I mean Peter—he said, or rather, he said that J.D. said, 'When lightnin' strikes, boys, act like it's rainin' and wear your rubbers.'"

Another spray of coffee greeted Andrew's pronouncement; Lois appeared in the doorway again.

"Gene, are you all right?" Her voice was heavy with doubt.

"I'm fine—*fine*!" Mr. Givens looked at her. She furrowed her brow and retreated to the kitchen.

Mr. Givens turned to Andrew, cleared his throat *very* loudly, was silent for a moment, then spoke.

"Did your—uh—father ever have a...talk with you?"

"Oh yes, we talked all the time about all sorts of things," Andrew chirped. He smiled, hoping this would allay Mr. Givens's nervousness.

"Did he—ahhh—ever talk to you about the facts of life?"

Andrew was throughly baffled. "What sort of facts?"

Beads of sweat broke out on Mr. Givens's forehead; he withdrew a handkerchief from his trouser pocket and mopped his face.

Andrew, though perturbed that this conversation was not turning out at all as he'd intended it to, was oddly mesmerized by the exchange.

Mr. Givens looked at him for a moment, then said softly, "Do you know where babies come from?"

"Oh, I know *that*."

"You do?"

"Yes, Arthur Popham-Goode—he was in my dormitory—he had these etchings. They showed people, um, without their clothes on, doing...um, things. Arthur told us that's where babies came from. He let me look at the pictures for a long time, by myself, in exchange for half a Cadbury bar. You see, we didn't get sweets very often, and Arthur was mad on Cadbury bars, and—"

"Did this...Arthur...explain—" Mr. Givens grimaced, then tugged at his collar, "Ex—explain how, um, uh...uh, how babies get made from doing this...uh...thing?"

Andrew shook his head.

Mr. Givens remopped his face.

"Dear, you'd better start getting ready for church." Lois's voice rang from the kitchen.

"Yes, dear." Mr. Givens cleared his throat again before turning to Andrew. "Ahhh—I'll get you some stuff to read. While we're at church, I mean. Then when I get home, we'll have a talk. Okay?"

"All right."

Mr. Givens grimaced again, then started to down the last of his coffee.

Andrew took a deep breath. "Um, could I um, ask one more question?"

Mr. Givens held his free hand out in a "halt" gesture, swallowed his coffee, and set his cup down. Folding his hands, he regarded Andrew intently, and said, "Okay."

Andrew pursed his lips, then blurted. "Do you know what Beagle burrs are?"

"Beagle burrs?" A look of bafflement washed across Mr. Givens's face. Then he shook he head. "Never heard of them. Where did you hear about these, um, Beagle burrs."

"They're at the end of the foot-long needle."

Mr. Givens's eyebrows shot up. "Foot-long needle?" Andrew had the feeling he was being teased.

"Um, the one that's square, the one you get in your bottom when you fail the short arm inspection."

To Andrew's astonishment, Mr. Givens smiled. "Foot-long square needle."

"With the Beagle burrs," Andrew reminded him.

"Beagle burrs," Mr. Givens repeated, his face serious again. "I'm really sorry, I've never heard of Beagle burrs. Who told you about these...Beagle burrs?"

"Peter did."

Raised eyebrows again. "Your eight-year-old friend?"

Andrew nodded. "Well, actually J.D. told him."

"J.D.?"

"His real name is Jefferson Davis. He's from Atlanta, Georgia."

"Atlanta, Georgia." Mr. Givens nodded. "Beagle burrs...Beagle burrs." Suddenly his face lit with realization; then he burst out laughing. "Biggole burrs—*big ole burrs*! *Big old burrs!*" He shook his head, and fairly chortled with amazement. Laying his hand on Andrew's shoulder, he said, "There's no such thing as a foot-long square needle—more like an inch long. And it usually *doesn't* have big old burrs on the end!"

Lying in bed, Andrew puzzled over two gigantic books he had been given. They had been retrieved from the bookcase in the spare room by Jake's father just before he went to church and, judging by the stiffness of the spines, had been unopened for quite some time. Andrew noted the scrawled signatures on the inside front covers: Jake's. Although if Andrew hadn't known that the books were Jake's texts from college, he would never have been able to decipher the almost illegible scrawl: a *J*, over-laid with what appeared to be a *G*, followed by a bumpy scribble that degenerated into a line. It was as if the owner wanted to make it clear that he did not care for these books, nor for their contents.

Andrew opened one of the tomes, a black one entitled *Human Physiology*, to the page marked by Mr. Givens with a strip of scrap paper and found that he was presented with a chapter entitled *The Reproductive System*. He scanned the chapter; it presented him with some bewildering information about this particular aspect of the human anatomy. As near as he could figure it, the female body had a rather curious internal morphol-ogy: Some tunnely-like structures that had a long name beginning with an *F* served as a link between two lump-like things called *ovaries* that contained *ovum*, and another structure that was either called a *uterus* or a *womb*. And somehow, the *ovum*, when it got *fertilized*, grew into a baby in the *womb*. Andrew knew all about fertilizer, which was what Thomas and Alfred spread on the gardens to make vegetables grow.

Only this was not exactly what was meant by fertilization, at least in this case. As Andrew read on, he got onto more familiar ground: a sub-section entitled *The Male Reproductive System*. At least the drawings looked familiar! But the text revealed some even more astounding information in regards to the function of what Andrew had here-tofore believed to be the quite simple duty of the male apparatus. The inner workings of the whole system were taken up with the production of curious little creatures that looked like fish with long tails, and had a long name that began with an *S*. They were so tiny they could only be seen under a microscope! Two bizarre processes, both of which started with an *E*, effected the journey of these peculiar creatures to their union with the *ovum*.

Andrew slammed the book shut and opened the other text, a red one entitled *Basic Microbiology*, to the page Mr. Givens had marked: *Venereal Diseases*. Andrew scanned the text; the information presented turned out to be even more baffling, and the pictures were not quite so interesting. There were these tiny *microorganisms*, one of which looked like a corkscrew, the other like a pair of kidney beans nestled together. They were so small, also, that they could only be seen through a microscope. As to how these things related to his query as to what a short arm inspection was, Andrew didn't have a clue. He snapped the book shut and retreated downstairs to read the Sunday comics.

When Jake's parents returned from church, Andrew noticed a distinct light-hearted mood in their manner. Lois was always in a good mood anyway, but now she seemed positively blissful; Mr. Givens had a funny glow on his face. Andrew, sprawled on the floor in the midst of the scatterings of the Sunday paper, was treated to a special measure of attention by them. Lois crouched on the floor beside him and gave him a kiss on the forehead; Mr. Givens dropped to one knee and rested his hand on Andrew's shoulder. Andrew, feeling quite relieved that Jake's father wasn't upset and nervous anymore, returned their greetings with a smile of welcome. He was glad that his plans were back on track.

I'll bet Mr. Givens never felt like this about Jake!

The conversation at lunch was light and exuberant. After scraping the last bit of Canadian War Cake off his plate, Mr. Givens sat in silence for a moment, but it was not a somber silence; more a pause to contemplate...something. Andrew somehow sensed that Jake's father didn't seem to be reminiscing as much as reflecting. Lois laid her hand on his arm; he smiled at her, then cleared his throat. He stood and nodded at Andrew.

Andrew didn't need any verbal instruction as to what was expected of him. He rose, and followed Mr. Givens up the stairs.

They went into Andrew's room. Mr. Givens sat on the bed; Andrew sat beside him. Folding his hands in his lap, Mr. Givens regarded Andrew intently for a moment, then took a quick, deep breath.

"Forgot something," he mumbled.

He stood, then left. Having been given no signal that he was expected to follow, Andrew remained seated on the bed, wondering if he was doing the right thing by staying put.

Mr. Givens returned, carrying a small brown bag, which he set on the dresser by Andrew's bed.

"Got this at the store on the way back," he said, as if an explanation were in order. Andrew wasn't sure if he was expected to take it, so he glanced at it, and smiled. Maybe it contained candy, or some sort of treat; he didn't want to appear too eager or greedy by grabbing it.

"Thank you very much," he said.

Mr. Givens nodded, then fixed Andrew with a very, *very* serious look.

"You read the stuff in the books?" he asked.

Andrew nodded.

"Did you...um, understand it?"

Andrew started to nod his head; then he bit his lip and shrugged. "Sort of," he said.

"Sort of," Mr. Givens echoed. He looked away from Andrew; his eyes had a funny, faraway gaze. He turned back to Andrew. "What don't you understand?"

Andrew couldn't quite explain what he didn't understand, so he shrugged again. "It's not quite that I don't understand it. It just seems all a bit...strange."

"Strange," Mr. Given's repeated. He rocked rhythmically back and forth, like a child on a hobby horse. He did it for only a few seconds, but it seemed like a lot longer to Andrew. The rocking slowed and was replaced by a few nods of his head. Then Mr. Givens bit his lip and looked at Andrew again.

"Do you understand how this...these...those things you saw in those pictures, the ones that your friend showed you. Do you understand how...how that starts a baby?" The last five words were spoken so quickly that they could have been one long word.

"Yes, um, I mean I think so." Mr. Givens didn't say anything, so Andrew went on. "The woman has this thing called an ovum, and the man has these things...those fishy-looking things. Sorry, I forgot. They're a long word that starts with an 's'".

"Spermatozoa."

"Right—spermatozoa." Andrew said the word slowly and carefully; he wanted to let Jake's father know that he was paying close attention.

"You can call them sperm for short."

Andrew nodded. "All right."

"You understand how they get together to start a baby?"

"Umm—I think so—yes." Andrew opened the black book to the page that was marked. "The ovum goes from here to here to here, right?" Andrew traced the course in the illustration.

"Right." Mr. Givens said.

"And then the...the spe...spe...I'm sorry, I forgot the name again."

"Sperm."

"Right, sperm. It gets put in here," Andrew jabbed his finger at the structure at the bottom at the diagram. "And that makes the ovum grow, right?"

"Right," Mr. Givens smiled at him, then glanced away, again nodding his head a few times.

Andrew looked at the book again. He had originally intended the primary purpose of this conversation to be a means of getting closer to Mr. Givens; gathering information had only been secondary. Now however, he realized that he might be able to elicit certain information about a matter that had been vexing him.

"This doesn't happen all the time, does it? I mean, a baby doesn't get started every time people do this thing?"

"No, there's only a few days out of the month that a woman can get pregnant. The ovum has to be at the right place at the right time, you understand?"

Andrew nodded. Perhaps that was the reason why his parents had not had any more children: timing. Or perhaps there was another reason.

"Is it possible that a woman can't have children—I mean, no matter whenever she does this thing?"

Mr. Givens pursed his lips, then said, "Yes, it's possible. Something might be wrong with the...ahhh...plumbing. You know, like if something's blocked somewhere. And when women get older, they can't have any more children, either."

Andrew's eyebrows shot up. "You mean, if a woman is, say, over thirty—she won't have any more children, then?"

"Oh no, thirty's too young. Say more like fifty."

"Oh."

Andrew bit his lip. "Is it possible that a woman might have a child...once—or—or maybe a few children, and then something happens that she won't have any more children after that? You know, something goes wrong with the, um, plumbing."

Mr. Givens nodded. "It's possible."

Andrew heaved a silent sigh of relief.

Mr. Givens reached for the bag. "Sometimes people can, uh, prevent the woman from getting pregnant, even when, um, things are in the right place at the right time."

"They can?"

Mr. Givens reached into the bag. Instead of pulling out a handful of candy or something good, he withdrew a small, flat package. "This."

"What?"

"This does."

"This does what?"

"Keeps a woman from having a baby."

"*That* does?" Andrew was completely baffled as to how this nondescript item could be employed to the purpose Mr. Givens had indicated.

"What's inside, I mean."

"Inside?"

"Uh-huh." Mr. Givens folded his hands; clearly he expected Andrew to open this mysterious thing.

Andrew tore at one end of the package and withdrew an object that looked like a narrow balloon. His face puzzled in consternation as he regarded this curious item.

"The man uses this." Mr. Givens said.

Suddenly Andrew realized: "*Oohhh....*" His eyes bulged in astonishment; then he glanced nervously at Mr. Givens: Did Jake's father expect him to try it on?

"It's used to prevent V.D., too," Mr. Givens told him.

"The veedee? What's that?"

"Venereal disease—didn't you read the other book?"

"Oh, right—about the things that look like corkscrews or kidney beans? They're a disease?"

"They're infections that spread when people do this thing."

"You mean people get this every time they do it?"

"No, only if one of them has it. Then it can spread to the other person. Like getting a cold from someone, only you get that if someone sneezes or coughs on you. People get syphilis and gonorrhea by sexual contact—doing what we just talked about. Unless they use protection." He waved his finger at the object dangling from Andrew's hand. "That's why guys have to get short arm inspections."

"How do short arm inspections keep people from getting V.D.?"

"Well, a doctor, or medical person, can tell if somebody's infected. Then they can give them some medicine to cure it."

"Oh, the shot with the Beagle burrs—I mean, big old burrs?"

Mr. Givens smiled. "Well, the needle shouldn't have any big old burrs on it. They give penicillin, and it stops the infection. But it's better not to get V.D. in the first place."

"By using this...this thing?"

"It's called a condom, but in England they call it a French letter. People here some-times call it a rubber."

"Like 'When lightning strikes, wear your rubbers'?"

Mr. Givens hesitated for a second. "Yeah." It was sort of a pronouncement, but one without conviction.

"You mean it doesn't always work—this thing—this rubber, thing?"

Mr. Givens drew a breath. "It's not that it doesn't work—most of the times it does. But there's a better way."

"There is?"

Mr. Givens nodded.

"What?"

Mr. Givens laid his hand on Andrew's shoulder. "Well, how do think you could keep yourself from catching a cold?"

Andrew shrugged. "Not go near anyone who has a cold, I suppose."

"Right." Mr. Givens smiled at Andrew, then withdrew his hand. He placed his hands on his thighs, and his face returned to a serious expression as he continued to regard Andrew.

For the second time, Andrew was bombarded with a stunning revelation. "So if people don't do this thing, they won't get those diseases, right?"

"Well, if they don't do it with someone who's infected."

"Oh." Andrew bit his lip. "So you just don't do it with someone who has this disease, right?"

"Yeah—the only problem is, it's sometimes not possible to tell if someone has it. Well, with a man, it's usually easy to find out—that's what short-arm inspections are for. If the woman has it, it's not so easy—in fact, it's usually impossible for a guy to tell. Only a doctor can tell."

"Oh."

Mr. Givens folded his hands together, then unfolded them and laid them against his thighs again. He was silent for a long, long time. Then he spoke, softly.

"The best way is to only, uh, do this with one other person. These venereal diseases get spread when lots of people have this kind of contact with lots of other people, understand?"

Andrew nodded. "I understand."

Mr. Givens went though a hand folding and unfolding routine again, and his eyes took on a funny faraway look. "It's not just that—getting V.D., I mean. There's also the possibility of the woman getting pregnant, even with using protection. It's only right to bring a child into the world if two people are committed to each other—for the child to have a family, I mean. It doesn't always happen that way. I mean, people can decide to have a baby, and the guy can get killed. There's a war on...or things just don't work out...." His voice faded.

Andrew kept silent; he sensed Mr. Givens was wrestling with some inner demon. After clearing his throat, Jake's father continued. "But it isn't...good...when two people don't intend to stay together, and bring a child into the world. Do you understand?"

"Um...yes. I think I see what you mean."

Mr. Givens acknowledged Andrew's assent, then spoke again. "Besides the V.D., and besides having a baby, it's..special. I mean, it's a special way for two people to be together, and it's best if they're together like that only with each other, and they plan on being together, always." The hands folded together again. "Well, I guess it's not easy to tell that to people nowadays, what with the war and all. If a guy isn't sure he's going to be around to settle down, after the war's over, I mean, then he probably figures, what's he got to lose? Things are different now from when I was young. It seems the war has made people kinda crazy. I guess you can't fight a war without it changing everything else." He put his hand on Andrew's shoulder again. "I want for you to know what's best, to make the right choices, no matter what happens. Wait until you meet that special person. Do you understand?"

Andrew nodded.

Mr. Givens smiled at him, then took a deep breath. His voice, a voice unlike anything Andrew had ever heard from the man, seemed to rush out in a torrent of emotion.

"There's nothing more wonderful than finding that special person, in deciding to be together, in being closer to that one person than to anyone else. I mean, not everyone decides to get married, not to say it's wrong not to...get married, I mean. Lots of people get married, too, when they shouldn't, and things can turn out to be not so good. But if you find that one special person, it's...wonderful. And it's wonderful to be a family, to look forward to having children—" his voice broke off, and the glow abruptly vanished from his face. Andrew noticed that his jaw muscles twitched as he stood up. He turned from Andrew and strode out of the room, shutting the door behind him.

Baffled by his behavior, Andrew decided not to follow him. It was all very curious: Jake's father had seemed somewhat flustered, at first. But then, he had overcome his nervousness and Andrew had been very reassured by the concern and...tenderness Mr. Givens had shown for him. But just when he'd seemed most at ease, he'd suddenly been overcome with a kind of anguish and sorrow that drove out all else.

Maybe he was just upset, remembering that things weren't always so wonderful between him and Jake. Andrew imagined all the arguments and angry silences that must have filled the Givens home, what with father and son at odds with each other for all those years.

He absently flipped through the black book, seeing, but not really seeing, pictures of babies growing from a nothing-looking bunch of cells to things that looked like fish, then to more baby-looking creatures that were crunched up in what looked like impossible contortions.

He got ever so upset when he mentioned children...But he doesn't have "children," really, just one son: Jake.

Andrew closed the book.

One mystery cleared up—another to take its place.

Chapter 39

*A*llied Invasion of Europe Expected by Mid-March

Andrew almost shrieked with joy at the sight of the headline on one of the newspapers Mr. Givens had brought home. Scanning through the accompanying text, he discovered that this pronouncement was derived from certain matters discussed at the conference attended by Churchill, Roosevelt, and Stalin in Tehran in late November.

Mum promised I could come home as soon as we invaded Europe. That means that I'll only have to spend another three months in this wretched place! And if it took the German army less than two weeks to drive from the French border to the Channel, we ought to be able to push the Huns back to Hunland by the end of March, to Berlin by the end of April, surely! And when Germany's trounced once and for all, my father will be able to return—what a glorious summer we'll have!

Mr. Givens took a few more photos of Andrew and sent those off, along with the Thanksgiving pictures, to Andrew's mother. One snapshot was of Andrew being measured by Lois on December fourth, his twelve and three-quarters birthday, showing his height at fifty-seven inches. Andrew held up a printed card displaying his weight: eighty-two pounds. "A twelve pound gain in less than two months," Lois noted with satisfaction. She pinched his biceps. "And it's not blubber, either! Look's like all that exercise equipment of Jake's is good for another generation!"

Lois's references to Jake were not so annoying now. Previously, whenever Jake had been mentioned, Andrew had felt a gut-wrenching knot of anger. Now the sound of his name and the reminders of him around the house—his service portrait, recently taken upon his promotion to Squadron Leader, and the various school pictures scattered about—did not pique Andrew's animosity any more than the mention of Nazi Germany trigger his ire. His outrage at Jake had again settled into a simmering umbrage, for he knew he would defeat Jake in the end, just as the Allies would be victorious before long. Germany's days were numbered, and so were Jake's.

Just another few months and the war will be over. I'll be back home, and Jake won't be so smug over his bloody home ground advantage. My father will be home, too, and he'll see to it that Jake is sent packing!

Andrew rubbed Lindy's silky underside as the contented feline lay in a triangle of sunlight on the living room floor. It seemed odd to Andrew that he enjoyed the company of Jake's cat so much, but then, he was living in Jake's home, sleeping in his bed, using his exercise equipment, and being cared for by his parents.

Jake's parents: Andrew's feelings towards them were taking a quite unexpected turn. Despite all his resolve not to let himself be tainted by his sojourn in this wretched land, he couldn't help but like Jake's mother and father, and he knew the feeling was mutual. Of course he'd planned on cultivating a friendly relationship with them, so as to discomfit Jake; however, he now found himself being drawn into their lives and caring about them on a much deeper level than he'd ever intended.

And that was the thorn.

Andrew's tete-a-tete with Mr. Givens about the "facts of life," far from being a prelude to an attack on Jake, had instead instilled grave reservations within him over his plans to sow discord between father and son. For one thing, the talk of "waiting" had taken away Andrew's lust for blood by touching upon a sore spot of his own: his nagging doubt about his legitimacy. His parents hadn't waited, had they? Freddie's sniggering declaration "They *had* to get married!" savaged him again, like a taunting demon, stirring within him the familiar vicious skirmish between fear and faith.

Even though they had to get married because of me, they really loved each other— surely they did!

The vision of his mother's red hair, streaming out behind her as she ran to embrace his father, had become an emblem of sorts for Andrew: a symbol of his hope that his parents did not see their relationship with each other as only a duty. Closing his eyes, he tried to recall that blissful expression on his mother's face, that look of complete adoration and sublime passion and utter joy, that look that was only, *only* for—

The image of Jake blotted out all else, like the shadow of an eclipse throwing its darkness across the sun. All Andrew could see was his mother and Jake together: She, gleefully swiping a piece of cake from his plate, happily sipping from his glass, giving him that silly-arsed infatuated smile in the ballroom as he stomped all over her feet. He, with that tiresome reticence and infuriatingly secretive demeanor. Even though Jake's drinking problem had come to light, something still nagged at Andrew.

You're hiding something, Yank!

As Andrew stroked Lindy's ears, he mulled over the main reason why he'd lost all stomach for waging a vendetta against Jake.

After that talk with Mr. Givens, Andrew had sat on his bed for a long time, digesting all of that astounding information and contemplating what had passed between them— something that was more than mere dissemination of biological facts and advice. Mr. Givens's fumbling explanations and exhortations had touched on an intensely private matter; Andrew knew that beneath the gruff exterior there was a soul as vulnerable as a child's, and to activate animosities might shatter that tender spirit beyond repair. He could not tear father and son apart without hurting both of them, and the crux of the matter was that he couldn't bear to cause Jake's father any more pain.

Andrew sensed it was not just the estrangement from Jake all those years that had aggrieved Mr. Givens—there was something else, too. When Jake's father had mentioned "children," it had triggered something in Andrew, confirming the strange disquietude he'd felt at the departure of Lee's family. Jake may have caused more than his share of anguish to his father, but he wasn't the only one who'd brought pain into this home.

There were others.

The announcement of the expected invasion of the continent had thus relieved Andrew of his self-imposed obligation to provoke a conflict between Mr. Givens and Jake. With only three months (four at the most, surely!) left for him to remain in exile, he did not see any reason to try to bring Jake down, at least not soon. Given such a short time frame it would be unlikely that any serious breach could be effected; better to wait until he was back in England and then mount an offensive against Jake from close range.

Perhaps when the war's over the silly sod will decide he doesn't like England after all—of course, my mother wouldn't go traipsing off after him! She'll see him for the flighty, shallow person he is and choose to stay where she belongs.

As Christmas approached he was faced with a dilemma: He'd spent all of his Christmas money on books for himself and had only a few dollars saved from his weekly allowance to buy Christmas presents for Jake's parents. He was ashamed to admit to Lois that his finances were in such a dismal state, and considered that asking her for a loan to buy her own Christmas present would be bad form and certainly not in keeping with the holiday spirit.

Friday, thank God! As he opened the front door, he felt a wonderful ease. Two whole days home from school!

"Andrew, hello!" Lois called from the kitchen. "V-Mail from Gerry for you! Oh, I got a letter from your mother, too. She also sent along a letter from your aunt. The letters are on the dining room table."

Andrew felt his stomach do a flip-flop.

Aunt Jane!

His heart skipped a beat at the sight of the envelope bearing his name, type-written as usual.

What if she doesn't answer my question? That means for sure that something has hap—

He whisked the letter off the table and dashed up the stairs to his room. His heart thudding, he ripped the flap open and tore out the letter. His eyes shot to the bottom of the page. There, beneath the scrawly signature were five blocks of five letters:

KJLGL JNXCO NQBXI ZZLSS MJFVG

Quickly sketching the alphabet grid with JANE as the secret word, Andrew deciphered the message:

I AM FINE WHI ARE YOU WORRIED

Andrew's soul soared with rapture. Even a mistake on the tenth letter!

She was all right!

She was all right!

"Good news?" Lois dished him up a serving of peach cobbler.

"Oh, yes, wizard great smashing news!" The words were out of his mouth before he realized he would have to explain exactly what the *wizard great smashing news* was.

"Oh, my aunt's just fine—she's doing just fine!"

Lois smiled. Andrew took another bite of peach cobbler and opened Gerry's letter.

Dear Andrew,

Got your letter, and I'm glad you feel that you can "talk" to me. I wish there was something I could do to make things easier for you. I was hoping that your experience of America would be better than it's turning out to be. You can't expect everyone to like you, but as long as you have a good friend or two, it makes everything else bearable. Are things going O.K. with you being with Jake's family?

I'm going to get another 48 for Christmas, which I'm really looking forward to. Your grandma invited me up to Greycliff for Christmas and she said I could bring a few of my buddies too. It sure is nice of her to be so hospitable. She said your mom is going to be there also. Hope things get better for you. Merry Christmas!

Your friend,

Gerry

Andrew clenched the letter so tightly the edges tore.

"Andrew, is everything okay?" Lois furrowed her brow in consternation.

"Uh...everything's fine."

"Gerry's okay, isn't he?"

"Yes, he's fine."

"I was afraid you'd gotten some bad news."

Andrew furiously shook his head. "No, no, everything's just fine." Andrew folded the letter and set it aside.

Bloody hell! Bloody, bloody hell! I should have never told Gerry about things! Now he'll tell my mother!

"Why don't you read your letter from your mother, Andrew?"

"Um...yes." Opening his mother's note, he scanned the page. Nothing earth-shattering: Filthy weather, little flying, etc., etc., etc. Then, at the bottom:

I'll be going up to Greycliff for Christmas. Your grandmother invited Gerry and some of his friends to come for the holidays. I'm so looking forward to seeing him again—he was such a nice young man! Kaz and I have plans to go on a "turkey run" to Ireland, so I'll be able to bring a Christmas bird for the festivities. Neither Kaz nor Marlys will get Christmas off, but they won't lack for companionship for the holidays—Marlys is seeing a Wing Commander who is talking very seriously in terms of future plans and Kaz is dating a very nice Norwegian chap (I'm not sure what he does—some sort of liaison work, I think). Anyway, he seems quite taken with her.

Happy Christmas to you, my darling!

553

All my love always,
Mum

Bloody, damned, bloody hell!

"Don't you want to finish your peach cobbler, Andrew?"

"Um, no...I'll save it for later, sorry."

As he clumped up the stairs, letters in hand, Andrew considered his dilemma. It was only eight more days until Christmas—not nearly enough time to get a letter to Gerry before he left for Northumberland. Gerry would most certainly mention Andrew's unhappiness.

I never thought he would see my mother! If only I'd told him not to say anything to my mother if he happened to meet her! If only I hadn't told him anything at all! Now she'll know, and she'll be upset...damn!

Miss Fitt caught up with him in the hall.

"Andrew, would you please stop by my classroom before you leave today?"

"I'm almost finished with making that extra copy for you—just a few more—"

But Miss Fitt was already dashing off to her class.

In study hall the minute hand of the clock seemed to crawl at a snail's pace; finally, the class was dismissed. Miriam walked with Andrew to Miss Fitt's room and waited outside for him.

Miss Fitt looked up from her desk and smiled.

"Your writing assignment was very good, and I took the liberty of showing it to a friend of mine from college. She's a writer."

"Oh."

"I hoped you wouldn't mind."

"No—no, I don't mind at all."

"Good. She's putting together a book of interviews and letters and accounts from children who, in one way or another, have been affected by the war."

"Um—oh, really?"

"Yes, she was quite delighted with your letter and wants to use it in her book. She's paying ten dollars for each submission, and will keep the identities of her contributors confidential. She'll only use first names in the book. Are you interested?"

"Uhhh—yes. Yes, that sounds like a...a nice idea."

On the way home from school, he discussed the matter with Miriam, and she thought it was "terrific."

"You'll be a published author!" she exclaimed. "Will you autograph a copy of your book for me?"

"I'm only contributing—there are others who are writing or being interviewed for the book."

"Even if it's just a line, it makes you an author—who knows, maybe you'll write a book of your own someday!"

Andrew didn't want to affirm her prophecy, as that would be conceited, nor did he want to protest it, for that would be churlish. So he smiled.

Lois thought it was a "fantastic, wonderful idea"; Mr. Givens shrugged at being asked his opinion. "Okay by me," he said.

A few days later, Andrew was handed a check for the vast sum of ten dollars. Mr. Givens cashed it at his store and gave Andrew ten one-dollar bills. The following Saturday, Lois took him to Plainfield and he bought Christmas presents: a brown tweed sweater for Mr. Givens and a bright red housecoat for Lois. Even though he knew Miriam didn't celebrate Christmas he bought her a gift too: a blown-glass bluebird, which he wrapped in white tissue paper.

He gave Miriam her present as they were walking home on the last day of school.

"Happy holidays," he said shyly. He thought she would wait until later to open it, but she pulled him along to a path that cut between the back property lines on his block and ended at a grape arbor in Alida's backyard. She sat on a bench in the arbor and tore back the wrapping, opened the box, and exclaimed in delight at the exquisite glass creation.

"It's beautiful—thank you very much," she murmured.

"Um—I'm glad you like it."

"It's the nicest thing anyone's ever given me."

"Well, see you next year."

"Next year," she whispered. A light snow was beginning to fall, and a few fluffy white flakes dusted her hair and coat.

"Well, bye," he said. "I hope you have a nice time over the holidays."

"You too—bye," she whispered.

"Andrew, can you set up another row of chairs?" Lois set down another plate of cookies on the dining room table.

Andrew unfolded another wooden chair, borrowed from church, and placed it behind and a bit to the left of the end chair in the previous row. Crikey—they were going to have a housefull! He didn't mind the work—at least it kept him from thinking about his dilemma...almost.

Actually, it only pushed his mental turmoil a bit beneath the surface, so that his anxiety was only an undertow instead of a crashing wave of distress.

As he set the last chair in place, there was a knock at the door.

"Can you get that please, Andrew? That's probably the Casinis—they like to get everything set up ahead of time."

Opening the door, Andrew saw that Lois was correct. Mr. and Mrs. Casini stood in the doorway. Mrs. Casini held a plate of iced cookies in her hands, and Mr. Casini carried two oddly shaped cases. Shannon stood behind them, flanked by two women with dark hair. Three children—two girls and a little boy—were sandwiched between Shannon and his parents.

"Merry Christmas!" Three generations of voices greeted Andrew.

"Um, Happy Christmas—won't you please come in?" Andrew stepped back and saw that Shannon and one of the women carried oddly shaped cases also, only larger than the one Mr. Casini had.

"Your first Christmas in America, Andrew!" Mrs. Casini exclaimed in her sing-songy Irish brogue. "Are you enjoying all the festivities?"

"Um, yes, it's been very nice, thank you."

"Andrew, I'd like you to meet my wife, Bonnie, and my sister, Colleen, but everyone calls her Collie," Shannon said. "And these are my daughters, Mary and Carla, and my son, Patrick."

The women greeted Andrew with brilliant smiles; the two girls, both school-aged, curtsied. The boy, whom Andrew guessed to be about three, stared at Andrew with huge brown eyes.

"Carlo, Fiona—have a sample of the Christmas goodies before the mob gets here!" Lois called from the dining room. "Bring the younguns too!"

"It's so good to finally meet you, Andrew," Collie said as they walked to the dining room. "Shannon's told me about you."

"Pleased to meet you, too," Andrew murmured. "So you and your father and Shannon are going to be giving a concert?"

"Yes, it's a family tradition. We give it here, because our living room is so small. My father plays the mandolin, Shannon plays guitar, and I play both."

The sound of a stringed instrument being plucked interrupted their conversation. "I'd better get in on the final tune-up," Collie smiled. "Nice meeting you, Andrew."

Andrew felt a tug on his sweater.

"You sit next to me?" Patrick asked him.

"Um, yes I'd be glad to," Andrew replied. He was rewarded by a shy smile and a twinkle in the dark round eyes.

Hearing the sounds of people filtering in, Andrew went out to the living room and saw Lynette standing next to a woman who was hugely pregnant. He went over to them and was introduced by Lynette to her sister, Margaret. Margaret had three children, reciprocals of Shannon and Bonnie's offspring: two older boys and a little girl. The boys were introduced as Matthew and Mark; the girl as Luke, though she was called "Lukey."

"Front row, front row!" Patrick pulled Andrew towards the first row of chairs.

Shannon, Collie, and Mr. Casini were seated in three chairs in front of the sunroom doors, facing the audience. Shannon and Collie held guitars; Mr. Casini held a mandolin. The murmur of conversation died down. Mr. Casini cleared his throat.

"Our gracious hostess gets to choose the first song."

Lois beamed; obviously this was a familiar tradition. "*Joy to the World,*" she pronounced.

"Excellent choice," Mr. Casini smiled. He laid his mandolin down. Collie and Shannon nodded to each other, then began to play. It was the strangest rendition of *Joy to the World* that Andrew had ever heard. It wasn't blasted out as a shrill, sustained peal; rather, it was played as a lilting ballad with a slightly syncopated beat. Andrew was taken by surprise by this unconventional rendering of a carol he had heard so many times before. He sat on the edge of his seat, trying to capture every nuance of the melody that seemed to touch his very soul.

Collie and Shannon then played *Good Christian Men Rejoice* in three-quarter time, so that it became a gentle tune that waltzed its way through the room. *Deck the Halls* was played, not stridently and ostentatiously as it usually was, but with a kind of quiet joy, as Collie plucked a high descant to Shannon's melody.

Oh, Dad—I wish you could hear this!

Closing his eyes, Andrew imagined that the music was dancing through his soul and being amplified out to his father's waiting heart.

I've heard his voice, seen him, touched him—surely he'd be able to hear all this, if I try hard enough to send it to him!

Mr. Casini joined them on the mandolin, and the three of them played *Hark the Herald Angels Sing* as tenderly as a whispered cradlesong, slipping now and then into a haunting minor key. Shannon strummed a soft rhythm as Collie played a solo melody first; she and Mr. Casini then alternated on the melody and accentuated one another in a lovely counterpoint. *O Come All Ye Faithful* was played in the same lullaby style, with Collie again playing the melody on guitar for the first verse; Mr. Casini then soloed on the mandolin; then the two of them alternated in harmonizing for the third verse. Watching them, Andrew imagined that father, daughter, and son made a beautiful tableau, with Shannon's face so serene as he provided the anchoring background rhythm, Collie's gaze of intense concentration as her fingers danced over the strings of the guitar, and Mr. Casini's rapturous glow as he brought forth such heavenly sounds from a simple instrument made of metal and wood.

Collie then switched to the mandolin and they played more carols: *Away in a Manger, Angels We Have Heard on High, O Little Town of Bethlehem, Noel,* and *What Child is This.* As Shannon strummed the guitar, Collie and Mr. Casini wove wondrous harmonies on their mandolins, as one, then the other, soared and trilled, a glorious interlacing of song-threads into an exquisite tapestry of sound. Mr. Casini then took a seat in the front row, and Collie and Shannon nodded to each other, smiled, and launched into the quirkiest arrangement of *God Rest Ye Merry Gentleman* Andrew had ever heard: Instead of the doleful, dirge-like tune, it was played in a wonderfully exuberant style with a jazzy beat.

Everything ceased to exist for Andrew, save the music and his sublime communion with his father. He felt the music coursing through him and radiating out to seek his father's waiting heart.

Oh Dad—isn't this the most wonderful thing you've ever experienced! I know you can't really hear all this; you can only sense how lovely it is. But someday you'll be able to listen fully, hear the beauty of every note, be soothed and uplifted as I am!

He sought out Collie after the concert was over and discovered that she gave guitar lessons. To his joy, she agreed to take him on as a pupil. She said he didn't need to get a guitar right away:

"Wait a few months, then I'll help you pick one out. In the meantime, you can borrow one of mine."

Shannon clapped him on the back.

"You've been bitten by the music bug, Andrew!"

Andrew gave him a smile. He wasn't quite sure if he'd been "bitten"; all he wanted was to give something to his father.

As he lay in bed that night, he imagined his father being soothed and encouraged by the music sent to him across the miles, across the awful chasm of war.

He always gave to me. The times he's come to me in these past few years, in dreams or in imaginings, he's always given to me, always comforted and reassured me. This is something I can give to him.

"Merry Christmas, Andrew!" Lois's voice rang from the kitchen. "Come on down and open your presents!"

"Coming!" Andrew pulled on his bathrobe and headed down the stairs. He already felt rather ambivalent about this Christmas; even the greeting of "Merry Christmas" seemed alien.

It should be "Happy Christmas." If I were with my mother, we'd be wishing each other a Happy Christmas and having some plum pudding and tea.

A dull sense of fatalism had replaced his nagging fear.

Gerry has probably already told her!

Forcing a smile, he entered the kitchen and said, "Happy—I mean, Merry Christmas."

"I like the sound of 'Happy Christmas,' Andrew, and a Happy Christmas to you, too!" Lois beamed. "Would you like some hot chocolate to fortify you for your gift opening?"

"Yes, thank you." He picked up the mug of cocoa from the counter and sipped the hot, hearty beverage.

"I've got kuchen in the oven; it's our Christmas morning tradition. It'll be done by the time we've opened our presents." Lois poured two cups of coffee and carried them out to the living room. Andrew followed, toting his cocoa.

The Christmas tree, which they had set up the day before, stood in splendor in the front corner nearest the sunroom. Lindy was already eyeing some red birds made out of feathers with beads for eyes.

"Lindy—no!" Lois called.

Mr. Givens, dressed in his red plaid robe, was already seated on the sofa. Lois handed him a cup of coffee and sat down beside him. Andrew settled himself, cross-legged, in front of the Christmas tree and waited for a signal as to what he should do. As he wasn't sure of the form for the gift opening, he didn't want to offend by presuming anything. This was the first Christmas he'd ever spent away from Armus House and he couldn't help but reflect on the wild course the war had set him upon. Imagine, celebrating Christmas in New Jersey, America, with people he had not met, or even known about, until a few short months ago!

"I almost forgot we had a child in the house again for Christmas—no impatient knocking on the door at 7 A.M. like Jake used to do." Lois grinned at him. "Time to open your presents!"

Andrew reached for a medium-sized package (he knew it was poor form to go for the big ones first) and saw that it was from Mr. Givens. He tore back the candy-cane wrapping to reveal a photo album with the first several pages mounted with the snapshots taken at Thanksgiving and in the days following. Andrew couldn't help but smile as he gazed at the pictures of himself presiding over the feast and snuggled with Lee-Ann and Lindy. There was even the photo of himself being measured.

"I got copies made," Mr. Givens said. "Thought you might like to have something to remember your stay here. It has room for lots more pictures, too."

The album was quite thick, and Andrew considered that Mr. Givens would have to do an incredible amount of picture-taking in the next few months in order to have the pages filled before summer. Surely he would be back in England by then!

He smiled at Jake's father. "Thank you very much."

"Gene, why don't you get your camera and take some pictures of Andrew opening his presents," Lois suggested.

"Great idea." Mr. Givens got his camera from the sideboard in the dining room and took a few snapshots of Andrew opening more of his gifts.

Andrew received lots of clothes from his mother, which Lois had bought out of the money Andrew's mother had set aside for the holidays. Opening the smallest box, he found the best present of all: a certificate good for twenty guitar lessons.

"I didn't buy as much clothing as your mother put aside for. I think you're starting on a growth spurt and you'd just outgrow things in a few months, anyway." Lois said. "I figured she would think music lessons would be a nice idea."

"Oh, smashing—yes, wonderful idea!" Andrew agreed. He'd planned on using his allowance to pay for his lessons, and now he would have the money free for other things.

He turned around and grabbed another present. Peering at the tag, he saw that it was from Jake. He forced the grimace from his face, tore back the wrapping to reveal Jake's gift to him: a pair of boxing gloves.

"I wrote to Jake that you're using his gym for your boxing practice," Lois said. "His gloves are so old, and he thought it would be nice for you to have new ones, so he asked me to take some money from his account to buy some."

Andrew nodded, hoping the bobbing motion of his head would allay the rage churning within him.

The stinking sod! He probably figured I was using the punching bag as a substitute for him! No doubt he's hoping that, if I wear the gloves he's given me, I'll be too distracted to make each punch count!

"They're very nice." He set the gloves aside and reached for another package: this one a joint present from Lois and Mr. Givens. It was rectangular, about the size of a good-sized dictionary, and made a soft rattly sound as he shook it. Pulling off the reindeer-adorned paper, he withdrew a huge box of chocolates.

"Oh, thank you—thank you ever so much!" He proffered the box to Jake's parents and they each selected a piece. After reading the legend on the inside of the lid which indicated what the various swirls on the top of each piece stood for (just as his father had said!), he selected a raspberry cream.

"Your mother told me how much you loved sweets and how thrilled you and all your friends were when she flew over your school and dropped the candy I'd sent to Jake," Lois said.

"J—Jake gave my mother the *sweets?*" Realizing his eyes were wide with dismay, Andrew blinked a few times, turned his head, and pretended to inspect a Christmas ornament.

"Gene gets candy wholesale, and I mailed some to Jake," Lois explained. "He wrote me that candy was in such short supply in England and that kids were even eating cough drops as sweets. He asked if I'd send him a few pounds of candy so your mother could make a special delivery to you and your friends. I sent candy off a couple of times, in fact."

"Oh." Andrew forced his lips into an upward curve, took a deep breath, and selected another piece of chocolate—vanilla nougat. He chomped on it until it was a mushy wad.

The fucking bastard! He just used this to get to my mother, thinking that she would be so thrilled with his generosity. He wanted her to believe he was such a wonderful person, getting sweets from America to give to me. Damn him!

"Gene, why don't you take a picture of Andrew holding the boxing gloves, so you can send it to Jake," Lois said.

"Okay." Jake's father focused the camera while Andrew held a frozen grin on his face. Of course, his mother would see the picture too and he wanted her to have no doubts that he was happy with Jake's present.

"You've been saving the biggest one until last" Lois laughed. "Bet you were told not to open the biggest present first!"

Andrew shrugged, smiled, then tilted his head to one side.

"Go ahead, admit it," Lois said. "You've been dying to find out what's inside, haven't you?"

"Well, actually I was."

Lois threw back her head and chortled. "Honesty—I like that in a person! Well, dig in!"

Andrew checked the tag on the present. "*Happy Christmas, Andrew! Hope this present gives you nice thoughts of home. Love, Lois.*" He smiled. "A nice British Christmas greeting."

As Andrew peeled back the paper, he saw various scraps of fabric joined together. As he unfolded it, he saw that it was a quilt appliqued with scenes of England. The white cliffs of Dover marched across the middle section of the panorama; the top and bottom sections of the quilt were divided into three blocks each, displaying an RAF roundel, the Union Jack, a Spitfire, Big Ben, a red double-decker bus, and London Bridge.

"It's lovely," he whispered. "Thank you."

He handed Lois the present he'd bought for her and she eagerly unwrapped it.

"Andrew, my goodness, how *beautiful!*" Lois stood up, wrapped herself in the crimson robe and slowly, regally turned around.

Jake's father opened his present and smiled with delight at the sweater. "It's very nice," he said softly, looking at Andrew with eyes shining forth with....

Gratefulness, Andrew thought. *I'll bet Jake never gave him a present, not freely or ungrudging, at least! Bet Christmas with Jake around was a trial to everyone!*

"...the best Christmas we've had in years, isn't it, Gene?" Lois's face looked about ready to split with rapture, and she gazed at Andrew as if he had invented Christmas single-handedly.

"Sure is," Mr. Givens agreed.

"Well," Lois said. "I think the kuchen is about ready to come out of the oven." She walked towards the kitchen, stopped for a moment, turned and smiled again at Andrew.

A wonderfully cinnamony, nutty aroma blasted into the living room and sent Andrew's taste buds into a salivating frenzy.

"Well, let's rendezvous with Lois's marvelous creation in the dining room, Andrew." Mr. Givens made his way into the dining room, Andrew following. A rustle of paper accompanied their progress; Lindy was already engaged in a ferocious battle with the swatches of discarded wrappings.

Lois set down a pan filled with a marvelous expanse of the most delicious looking pastry Andrew had ever seen. Buttery mounds were adorned with heaps of raisins and nuts, and beribboned with swaths of melted brown sugar laced with cinnamon. Lois got two brandy snifters from the china closet and set them on the table. She then got out a bottle of Lee's apple brandy from the sideboard.

"Oh—that's right, we have a youngun in the house again!" Lois beamed at him.

She's been beaming at me so much the power company ought to start charging her, Andrew thought.

Lois dashed to the kitchen and returned, carrying a bottle of apple juice. She filled another brandy snifter with the juice and placed it before Andrew. Mr. Givens poured the brandy into the other snifters.

"*Happy* Christmas," Mr. Givens said, lifting his glass.

"*Happy* Christmas," Andrew and Lois echoed in unison.

Lois looked at her husband, then at Andrew.

"End of the war in '44," she said softly.

Chapter 40

"*W*hat you figgered happened 'tween Jake and his father, then?"

Lately, Andrew had started coming in through the back door when he got home from school, as he and Miriam usually cut through Alida's grape arbor. It afforded them a bit of privacy, and they would linger for awhile under the bare branches and talk about things a bit more personal.

He stood inside the back entrance; evidently, neither Lois nor Sarah were aware that he'd come in. From the soft thunking noises coming from the dining room, it was evident that Sarah was helping Lois with the dusting.

"...I know Jake told Gene something when they went out together, after that night Jake came home drunk. I was all prepared for one hell of a scene when Gene stomped up the stairs to Jake's room when we got home from church. They were in there for the longest time. I wasn't exactly listening at the door, and neither was Alice, but the only way we knew that one of them hadn't killed the other was because we heard both of them talking."

"'Bout what?" Sarah asked.

"I wasn't really listening, so I don't know. Then Alice and I had to go get Andrew, and then there was that whole mess when Andrew wandered off. Alice was almost a basket case, what with her worrying about Jake, and then Andrew disappearing like that. Well, after we'd found Andrew, I dropped him and Alice off at a restaurant for supper and went home. I found Gene and Jake sitting together at the dining room table, drinking coffee as if nothing had happened, as if the past twenty-five years hadn't happened either! Not that they were all smiles. Jake had obviously been crying—crying! I've never, ever, seen him cry, not since he was three! And Gene was—well, I don't know how to describe it. It was as if all the pain and anger had just drained out of him, and the look on his face was like the look he had when he held Jake in his arms for the first time and saw those newborn eyes looking up at him. Twenty-five years of battling and strife, just washed away, and now they were father and son. They didn't tell me what they'd been talking about, they didn't say anything at all, at first. There was this silence, this peaceful silence—so different from all the angry silences they'd had, and they finished up their coffee, and Gene asks me, 'Okay if we use the car for the rest of the day?' And I say, 'Sure, I'll get Alida to pick up Andrew and Alice.' Jake nods his head, as if he wanted to say thanks, but it looked as if he would burst into tears if he tried to talk. Then they walked out to the car together, Gene's arm across Jake's shoulder, and drove off. They got back late that night; I woke up when I heard them across the hall in Andrew's room. I got up to see what was going on, and found Gene and Jake tucking Andrew into bed. They told me they found him asleep on the floor in front of the window. Gene wouldn't tell me, though, where he and Jake had been or what they'd talked about, except to say that everything was okay."

"What you 'spose they talk about?"

"I have no idea, but whatever it was, it was enough to bring them together—Thank God for that. Oh, Andrew should be home soon—I'll put on the kettle for tea."

Andrew rattled the doorknob, and called out, "Hullo, I'm home!"

"Hi Andrew!" Lois exclaimed. "I made some chocolate-chip cookies today. Sit yourself down, okay?"

"Right!"

Andrew lay in bed, trying to get to sleep, but it was no use. He had not one, not two, but three things to vex him.

He wondered, first of all, what it was that Jake and his father had talked about that day. It must have been something positively astounding for it to end the estrangement between them—but *what?*

The bastard—he probably lied through his teeth about something! If I only knew what it was, then I could deal with it! I wish I could ask Mr. Givens what it was, but then, he didn't even tell his wife, didn't even tell his own brother what it was! And he'll probably think badly of me, sticking my nose into something that's not my business!

As he tried to push that perturbation aside, he was tormented by an even more pressing worry:

Gerry has already told Mum how miserable I am here, and now she's fretting about me. I'll probably get a letter any day from her and she'll tell me how upset she is about things....

Another wave of anxiety crashed over him.

What's the matter with Lynette?

For the past three days, she'd walked by Andrew in the school hallway without giving him so much as a passing glance. She usually greeted him with at least a friendly smile and often with a cheery *Hey, Andrew!* Now, however, she stared straight ahead, unsmiling and unspeaking.

There must be something horribly wrong for her to be like this!

"What do you mean, you don't go home from school? Where do you go, then?"

Miriam shrugged. "I stay with Eva, until suppertime."

"Your cousin?"

"Uh-huh."

"I thought Eva lived with you."

"She does, but she babysits for some kids."

"*Babysits!*" The word exploded out of him.

Miriam seemed puzzled by his outburst. "What's wrong with that?"

"She *sits* on babies?"

"What?"

"You said she babysits. Why in the world would anyone want to *sit* on babies?"

Miriam started laughing, then tried to compose herself as she realized Andrew's bewilderment.

"She watches some little girls at their home because their mother works in a defense plant. The two oldest go to school and the youngest one is home all day. I help Eva out with the kids so she can get supper ready; then we go home about six, after their mother gets off work. I can't believe you've never heard of babysitting before! What do people do in England when they need someone to watch their children?"

"That's what nannies are for."

Miriam giggled.

"What's so funny?" he asked.

"You," she replied.

He was disconcerted by the look of amusement on her face.

"Well, what if you don't have a nanny, what do you do, then?"

"There's always servants. Mrs. Tuttle minded me when my mother or grandmother or aunts weren't around."

"What if you don't have servants?"

"Well, I guess you'd have a someone be a child-minder, then."

"A *child-minder?*"

"Uh-hum."

"Well, that's the same thing as a babysitter."

"If you say so. It's a more sensible term, anyway. You *mind* a child, you don't *sit* on it!"

Miriam squealed with laughter.

"Did I say something funny?"

Miriam's reply was a joyous smile; the look on her face was like the look his mother gave him whenever he'd done something marvelously pleasing. He was both disconcerted and captivated.

They walked along in silence for awhile; then he asked, "So your mother doesn't mind you not coming home right away?"

The happy expression on her face was rapidly replaced by a wistful gaze into the distance. After a moment, she sighed.

"She's usually...resting. I'd rather not disturb her." She quickly turned to him. "How are your guitar lessons coming along?"

"Oh, quite nicely. Collie taught me some chords, and different kinds of strumming patterns, to sort of get the knack of playing. I'm also learning to play the notes separately. This week I'm working on scales."

"Sounds like fun."

"It is, actually. It's...."

"What?"

He searched for the right word.

"Soothing. It's something I can do that's, um, comforting."

She smiled shyly at him.

They were at the grape arbor now. "See you tomorrow," he said. "Have fun *babysitting.*"

Her smile widened. "I'll be careful not to squash the little ones!"

Arriving home, he found a letter from his mother on the table by the front door. It was paired with V-Mail from Gerry again. Andrew didn't know which one to open first.

Gerry surely wouldn't let me know if he told Mum about things. And Mum certainly wouldn't mention Gerry talking to her—she'll just worry, that's all.

As he picked up the two letters, he noticed his mother's letter was thicker than usual. He shuffled to the kitchen.

"Andrew, how about some apple crumble-up? Just took some out of the oven," Lois called from the kitchen.

"Yes—thank you."

He sat down at the breakfast table and stared at the two pieces of mail.

Well, which to open first?

"What does your mother say?" Lois called.

"Uh—I haven't read her letter yet." The matter decided, he stuck his finger into the flap of the envelope and tore it open.

He scanned his mother's letter: Christmas had been absolutely "marvelous": She'd gotten a bird on her "turkey-run" to Ireland and brought it to the festivities. Gerry and four of his friends had shown up with "all sorts of <u>wonderful</u> treats." She wrote that the American Army gave servicemen going to visit with British families a packet of special rations for each day's stay:

...tins of evaporated milk and tomato juice, also bacon, sugar, coffee, shortening, butter, and rice. One of Gerry's friends, Seamus, a cook, even brought a ham! Needless to say, Mrs. Tuttle was thrilled to bits with all this bounty! One of the other chaps, Razz (short for Razzle-Dazzle, which he <u>swears</u> is his real name!) used to play the piano in a nightclub. He treated us to a concert of Christmas carols, done in Ragtime! I played a few songs too, but I'm afraid I sounded like a plodding beginner next to Razz! (I'd love to introduce him to Kaz—then they'd be Razz and Kaz—Kaz, however, is still involved with her mysterious Norwegian.) I've never seen your grandmother so happy, and everyone had a smashing time! Alfred sang at the top of his voice, and Maria got on <u>very</u> well with another of Gerry's friends, Vern, who's a crew chief....

Andrew's eyes flew down the rest of the letter: Jake couldn't get away for Christmas. (Good, Andrew thought—hope he spent Christmas freezing his arse off over enemy territory someplace.) Nothing to indicate that his mother was aware of things; then again, she might not have wanted *him* to worry about *her*, and figured there was not much she could do about things at this distance, anyway.

But she's probably still worrying about me....

"How are things?" Lois asked.

"Oh, fine. Mum had a very nice Christmas, she says. Gerry came with some of his friends—here." He pushed the letter over to Lois, and took a bite of apple crumble-up to fortify himself before opening Gerry's letter.

The first few paragraphs reiterated the "terrific Christmas" he and his friends had enjoyed at Greycliff. Then, at the end:

> Your ma showed around all the pictures of you in New Jersey. Her face was lit up like Times Square when she talked all about the "smashing" time you're having in America. She was real happy to know you're growing so well and she really liked that picture of you smiling over all those pies! Well, it sure doesn't sound like the Andrew I know, or maybe you just had a bad day when you wrote. Anyway, I didn't want to say anything to her. If you had a bad day, and everything's O.K. now, wouldn't be no point in saying anything, right? And if you're still upset, I figured you didn't want her to know, else you would have told her. I figured you didn't want her to worry about you, even though that's what mothers are for, you know. Anyway, if you don't want her to know, you can "unload" on me, anytime!
>
> Well, Happy New Year. End of the War in '44, kiddo!
>
> Your pal,
Gerry

"Good news?" Lois asked

"Oh, yes, smashing good news!"

"What's up?"

"Oh—uh—" How could he tell Lois that he was glad his mother didn't know how miserable he was in America?

"Uh, Gerry had a very, a very...nice Christmas." He bobbed his head and smiled. "May I have some more apple crumble-up?"

With that one dilemma out of the way, he was now emboldened to do something about another of his worries.

I can just ask Lynette what's the matter! Maybe I can help her, though, just as Gerry's helping me.

He knew where Lynette lived, for he'd once gone with Lois to deliver some things from the pharmacy to Margaret. He decided to go there after school and phone Lois from there.

After saying good-bye to Miriam, he went to Margaret's house. His knock on the door was answered by Lukey.

"Mamahadababyjohnalaska," she babbled.

"What?"

"Our mom had a baby and his name is John Alaska," Matthew translated. "His middle name's Alaska, because our dad's in Alaska, in the Army Air Forces. Come on in. Lynette's in the kitchen."

"Andrew?" Lynette walked into the living room. "What a surprise! I'll put some tea on." She had a smile on her face and looked positively exuberant.

Andrew followed her into the kitchen.

"Well, what brings you here, Andrew?" She set the kettle on the stove. "Not that I mind! I'm about to go buggy here, anyway—it's good to have another adult to talk with!"

"Um, well, I was worried about you. I thought something was wrong. You seemed terribly unhappy and I haven't been able to find you after school—"

"Oh gosh, was I that obvious? I'm sorry; I was worried about Margaret."

"Your sister?"

Lynette nodded as she took two mugs from a cupboard and set them on the stove.

"Why were you worried about your sister?"

Lynette turned from him. After a moment, the teakettle started whistling. She poured the hot water into the mugs, then sat down at the kitchen table.

"She was going to have a baby."

"You were worried about *that?*

Lynette gazed out the kitchen window.

"My mother." Her voice dropped to a strangled hush. "My mother...she died having a baby. When I was nine."

"I'm sorry."

"The midwife couldn't make it—she was tied up with another delivery. My aunt came and tried to do what she could for my mother, but...Oh, God, she was hollering, and crying, and then she was screaming—" Lynette closed her eyes again, as if the darkness could somehow shut out the vision of that horrible memory. "Then she was dead. The baby too." The final seven words were spoken in an angry, abrupt finale.

She opened her eyes, shook her head again, this time in a kind of furious resolve.

"I'm never, *ever* going to have children—I'm never even going to get married, either! Who needs it! Who *needs* it! All that pain and agony of having babies and then a lifetime of doing scutwork and wiping snotty noses and never having a moment to yourself."

Andrew didn't know what to say.

She seemed suddenly aware of his presence again, and a look of remorse flooded her face.

"Oh Andrew, I'm sorry—"

"No—I mean, don't be. Don't be sorry, I mean."

She smiled. "Thanks."

"Not at all." He tried to smile, but he was afraid his mouth looked like a crumpled line. "What are friends for?" he said softly.

She squeezed his hand, then got up and went to the stove. "Milk and sugar, right?"

"Right," he said.

She brought their tea to the table, then sat down and took a sip. After staring pensively at her beverage, she spoke, this time softly, almost wistfully.

"I really love the boys and Lukey, I mean. I don't mind taking care of them—in a way, they're like my own. I came here when Matthew was a baby, just before Mark was born. I've watched them, and Lukey too, grow from little babies to toddlers to walking, talking pint-sized people. It's been really wonderful—maybe I can enjoy them because I don't have the burden of parenthood and I can work out all my motherly instincts on them. Since their father's away, I try to help Margaret out as much as I can. Not many people get to try out parenthood without having to take on a lifetime responsibility, so it's a good experience for me. I don't mind doing it; Margaret's kids are the only children I'm ever going to have, in a way, and they're really special...." Her voice trailed off.

"You shouldn't decide something just because you're afraid," Andrew said. "I mean, you say you don't want to have any children, but that's because you're afraid that what happened to your mother will happen to you. You don't need to have lots of children, you know. You can have just one. I mean, my parents only had me."

"Well, it's not just fear—"

"Or because you think you'd have to throw your mind away to be a parent. My mother's a pilot, and I can always remember her flying. Having me didn't stop her from flying or being intelligent."

Lynette sipped the last of her tea, then spoke again. "I know I just need to write—I *need* to, I *want* to, more than anything else. I know I couldn't do that, couldn't give my best, if I had a family to worry about."

"Maybe you can. Have you ever thought about that?"

"Lots of times. It wouldn't work, I know. What with being here alone with the kids these past few days, I can scarcely get my homework done. I have to rush home after school to be here when the boys get home, then pick up Lukey at the babysitter's, then do the housework and make supper, then clean up and put the kids to bed. It's all right for awhile, but not for years and years. I'd go nuts—I really would."

Andrew glared at his tea, then felt Lynette's hand on his.

"Hey, I know you care. But I know I'll be happy doing what I want to do—isn't that the most important thing?"

"I suppose."

Lynette squeezed his fingers.

"Thanks," she said.

"For what?"

"For caring. You'd be surprised how little of that is around."

Andrew didn't know what to say to that.

"Hey," Lynette said, "I already *know* what I want out of life. And I'm going to have it. Isn't that the best of all possible worlds?"

"But you *need* someone—*everybody* needs someone!" Andrew blurted. "Isn't it better to share your life with someone else? I don't want you to be lonely."

Lynette gave him an impish grin. "Hey, I won't rule out having a torrid affair or two— or more! A writer has to know about love and passion and all that stuff, so the experience will come in handy."

"That's not funny!" The words exploded out of him before he realized what he'd said. Lynette withdrew her hand from his.

He felt the color flooding his cheeks, wished the floor would open up and swallow him. "I'm sorry," he mumbled. "I didn't mean to yell at you...." He swallowed, and the lump in his throat felt like a boulder. "It's just that—that, well, being with someone is—it—it's supposed to be...forever, and always...." His voice trailed off into nothingness.

"Andrew, I'm sorry. I didn't know you felt that way about things."

He bit his lip.

"Hey," she said. "Would it be okay with you if I had just *one* passionate love affair? I mean, I think a person can only fall in love once, right? Everything else is measured by the one time you lose your heart completely, and it can't ever be that way again, not with anyone else." She held her index finger up before him and grinned again. "One—okay? Just don't tell the pastor about my plans. He'd give me a talking to, for sure."

"Hmmph." He didn't know if it would be right to condone her premeditated misbehavior.

"Oh, all right." He felt a gentle squeeze on his shoulder. "You know—" She gazed at him with an odd look of amusement mixed with admiration. "Someday, you're going to make a terrific husband for some lucky woman!"

He caught another cold—thank God!

He spent five glorious days in bed, happily working on his assignments, which Miriam brought to him every afternoon. He would bathe after lunch—the steamy air really cleared his sinuses. Then he would dress in a pair of jeans and a sweater and settle himself on the sofa to await her arrival. She would sit in the wing chair facing him, and tell him about the school day. Even though they weren't in the same class, they still had the same teachers, so Andrew got pretty much the same information from her that he would have gotten had he actually been in school—without all the snide remarks and sniggering looks, of course.

On the first two days, Monday and Tuesday, Miriam was cheerful and chatty. But on Wednesday, she seemed restrained and tense—she didn't even smile once. After relating her history notes, she stared ahead into space.

Andrew took a sheet of paper, drew a question mark on it, folded it, and handed it to her without a word.

Her eyes softened, and she gazed gratefully at him.

"What's wrong?" he asked.

She hung her head, sighed deeply.

"It's Eva."

"Your cousin?"

She nodded. "She talked with some friends last night. They just got here from England and...." She shook her head furiously. "It's happening—nobody wants to believe it, but it's happening! Eva's friends say the Nazis are killing Jews by the thousands, by hundreds of thousands. They're shooting them, starving them, putting them into these sealed rooms and pumping some kind of poison gas in—then burning all the bodies afterwards. The people the Nazis aren't killing, they're using them for medical experiments and other awful things—men, women, even children...."

"What—are you sure? I mean, are *they* sure—Eva's friends?"

Miriam slowly nodded her head.

"There have been all kinds of things in the papers already about it. Last year the *New York Times* had a bunch of articles about it. There was stuff about it in some British newspapers two years ago, and even Edward Murrow reported on it. He said the Jews are being systematically exterminated—he said that exactly!"

Andrew took her hand. What could he say? That he was sorry? That he wished all of it wasn't happening?

She squeezed his hand and tried to blink back her tears.

On his way home from his first day back to school, he tried to chat Miriam out of her melancholy, but it was no use. She answered his questions and commented on his observations, but only after a fashion. Her voice was flat and lifeless; her gaze, distant and troubled. They parted ways at the grape arbor and he scuffed through the back yard to the house.

He heard the sounds of Lois clanking in the kitchen as he came through the back door. Odd, she didn't call to him.

As he walked into the kitchen, he saw Lois bending over the sink. Her eyes were red-rimmed.

His heart skipped a beat.

Maybe everything's going to turn out all right, after all!

Lois turned to him and burst into tears. Now he was sure:

Something's happened to Jake!

Chapter 41

*A*ndrew forced his face into a puzzled frown, even as his heart soared with rapture.

"Lois—what's the matter?"

She hiccupped, choked on a sob, then blurted out:

"It's Mac's husband—I got a letter from Velma. Hank was killed in Italy."

"Lee-Ann's father? Oh, no...."

Lois nodded. Andrew instinctively put his arms around her. All of a sudden he felt horribly ashamed.

If Lois could be so distraught over the death of her nephew-in-law, she would be positively shattered if Jake....

"I haven't even called Gene yet." Lois wiped her eyes on her apron. "I don't know if I should—I don't know if it would be a good idea to tell him while he's at work...." She shook her head. "No, no—I'll wait until he gets home tonight. Yes, that would be best." She looked thankfully at Andrew, as if she'd just consulted him and he'd given her the correct guidance.

Andrew gave her another hug. "Why don't you go upstairs and lie down? I'll finish with the washing up and make us some tea."

"Tea—oh, no, I forgot—oh, no I'm sorry, Andrew—"

"Don't fret about forgetting to make tea. I'll take care of it. You go lie down now."

She gave him a swift kiss on the cheek and went upstairs.

While the kettle was heating up, Andrew did the last of the dishes. Then he wiped the counters and swept the floor as the tea was steeping. As he was getting some milk out of the refrigerator, he noticed some leftover roast beef on a plate and got an idea.

He carried the tea things upstairs on a tray and set it on the nightstand. Lois sat up and took a sip of tea.

"There's some roast beef in the refrigerator," Andrew said. "I can heat it up for supper, and I'll boil some noodles and we can have corn relish, too. Why don't you just rest up—I'll take care of everything, all right?"

"Oh, Andrew—I don't expect—"

"You don't expect anything from anybody—you do everything around here," He squeezed her hand. "I'll take care of things—you just rest up—okay?" He said *okay* with an emphatic American accent, and Lois gave him a weak smile.

"Okay," she said quietly.

Andrew gave the bad news to Mr. Givens when he got home. Lois had fallen asleep, and Andrew figured it was best to let her rest. She came downstairs while they were eating. Mr. Givens got up and gave her a hug. "Andrew told me," he said gently.

Lois hugged him back, then gave him Velma's letter. Mr. Givens read it with a look of consternation on his face. Suddenly he exploded.

"Jesus Christ! Using engineers as infantry! What the hell is going on over there?"

Lois didn't admonish him for his language.

The phone rang. Lois got up to answer it. Andrew overheard her voice in the living room.

"...Yes, yes—I got the letter today...What?"

Andrew craned his neck so he could see around the doorway. Lois had a look of unmistakable alarm on her face.

"Lee-Ann? Oh, no!"

Andrew felt his heart thud into his stomach. He got up, stumbled over to Lois, and sank down onto the sofa.

Oh, God—something's happened to Lee-Ann!

Lois seemed oblivious to his presence; she nodded and stared into space as she talked.

"Yes...yes—yes that's fine—just call me and let me know...yes—all right...Bye." She dropped the receiver on the cradle and continued staring ahead. Andrew cleared his throat, not from a desire to get her attention, but from the awful strangling sensation he felt.

She turned to him, startled.

"Lee-Ann?" His voice was almost a croak.

"Oh, Andrew—I should have asked you but—"

"What?

The words tumbled out. "Lee-Ann—she's just...just...When she heard about her father, she went into this state. Mac is just distraught over her. Lee-Ann doesn't eat, doesn't do anything, just stares ahead. She didn't say a word for three days and just a little while ago she said 'See Andrew'—that's all she said, 'See Andrew.' She keeps saying it, over and over. That's why Mac called."

"Lee-Ann wants to see me—*why?*"

"I don't know—but she's very insistent about it. I told Mac, sure, bring her down. I'm sorry, I should have asked you, but I just couldn't—"

"No, don't worry—I mean, that's fine with me, but I don't know how I'll be able to help—"

"She just wants to see you—don't worry about having to do anything...I guess we'll somehow figure things out when she comes."

Andrew watched the stiff, tiny figure step from the train onto the platform. Lee-Ann stared blankly ahead and walked, robot-like, towards Andrew. Mac followed behind her, her face etched with sorrow and strain.

He'd had experience with another's grief before, but this was different. At Askew Court, whenever one of his classmates had lost a parent or sibling, the other students had dealt with the situation by ignoring the grieving boy. It wasn't out of coldheartedness, but from the realization that there wasn't much one could do to remedy the situation. Furthermore, to draw attention to another's sorrows really wasn't a good thing, either. Best to let the mourner sort things out for himself.

Andrew knew, though, that Lee-Ann did not make the journey all the way from upstate New York so that he could ignore her.

He knelt down on one knee and Lee-Ann fell against him. His arms went round her and he lifted her up. She burrowed her face into his shoulder.

"Oh, Lee-Ann," he whispered.

What could he do?

What did she want of him?

He would have given his soul to put everything right for her, but he had no idea what she expected from him.

Why had she come to see him?

In the car, Andrew sat in the backseat, holding Lee-Ann. She wrapped herself so tightly around him that he felt as if they were joined at the hip. Mac sat next to them, her hand resting gently on Lee-Ann's back. He remembered what he had felt like when he'd first heard about his father: that reeling, sickening spiral into black despair and nothingness. He knew he shouldn't tell her that he knew what she was feeling, for his anguish had been relieved by the discovery that his father was only missing, not dead. Lee-Ann's father was to be buried in Italy, so there was no question, no question at all about the cold, hard fact that he was gone for good.

The car pulled up to the house and Andrew maneuvered himself out of the car, with Lee-Ann still twined around him. He carried her up the front steps. Once in the house he felt as if she were asking him to take her upstairs to his room, even though she didn't say a word or even look at him.

He carried her to his room and sat down on the bed with her. He felt that awful sense of uncertainty and inadequacy churn through him again.

What should he say?

What should he do?

He sensed that her breathing was becoming spasmodic, and he felt a fresh panic at his inability to deal with the situation.She drew back, and fixed him with a glazed stare.

"My daddy got killed." Her voice was flat, mechanical.

"I know." He knew it was an inane reply, but he had to say something.

She lowered her eyes, as if thinking hard about something, then spoke again.

"I said I didn't want the war to be over."

He started to agree with her, not knowing what else to do.

Instantly it was all very clear.

"Are you afraid your daddy got killed because you said you didn't want the war to be over?"

She nodded; then the tears rolled down her cheeks. She pressed her face against his shoulder again, and started to choke and wail in awful, keening sobs.

He held her tightly as she flailed against him.

"Lee-Ann, it's not your fault—please, please don't think it is! It *isn't!* Your father got killed by the war—it wasn't anything you said or did!"

Her body now got very rigid; she shut her eyes tightly, as if she didn't want to hear him.

"Lee-Ann, you said you didn't want the war to be over because you wanted me to stay. If I could stay here after the war was over, then you'd want the war to be over, right?"

She opened her eyes, nodded.

"See? That proves it! It's not your fault! Please, please believe that!"

She looked away from him, eyes wary.

"Will you believe it for me?"

She looked back at him; her eyes seemed to beg permission of him.

"You *can* believe it, Lee-Ann! You *have* to believe it! If you don't, then...then, it's just the same as saying that I'm wrong—that I'm lying to you! Please, please, for me, believe it isn't your fault—it *isn't!*"

She crumpled her lips together.

He brushed a strand of hair from her face. "Say you believe me—please. Here, I want you to repeat after me. Say *It's not my fault.*"

Her eyes took on that horrid glazed look again.

"All right, one word at a time. Say *It's.*" He smiled at her, placed his fingers gently against her lips.

"It's." The word was barely more that a soft rush of air.

"Good! Now say *not.*"

"Not." A little louder.

"Smashing! I knew you could do it! Now say *my.*"

"My."

"*Fault!*" He said the word in a deep, oratorical voice, giving her a silly-serious look.

"Fault." The word was more of a moan.

"Now, all together now: *It's not my fault.*"

She was silent.

"Bet I can say it faster than you—*Itsnotmyfault.*" He narrowed his eyes at her in challenge.

She bit her lip and turned away.

"All right, you can say it some other time." He put his arms around her and held her close. "You don't even have to say it to me; you can say it to yourself, if you'd like, all right?"

"I hungry."

The whispered declaration startled Andrew out of slumber. Lee-Ann stood beside his bed. She didn't have a bathrobe on, just her flannel nightie. She was shivering.

"Mommy's sleeping."

"Yes, well...here, let me get you something to put on." He pulled on his bathrobe, then got up and rummaged through his drawers.

"Here—" He pulled out one of his sweaters. "Put your arms up so I can get it on— that's good."

Not the height of fashion, Andrew thought, as he regarded the gray tweedy sweater with the pale pink flannel billowing out from underneath. Still, it should be warm enough.

He held her hand as they tiptoed down the stairs. Good thing, for she stumbled with fright at the sight of two eyes glowing in the darkness.

"Don't worry, it's only Lindy—I think he wants a bite to eat, too," Andrew whispered.

A reconnaissance of the refrigerator's contents revealed a bowl of macaroni and cheese, a chicken drumstick, and some tapioca pudding. Andrew put the macaroni and cheese in a pot and set it on a burner. While that was heating up he cut the meat off the drumstick for Lindy, who butted his head against Andrew's ankle and meowed.

"Shh, Lindy—you'll wake up the whole house," Andrew whispered. He gave Lee-Ann a few scraps of chicken. She giggled as Lindy gobbled them out of her hand. Andrew set down the rest of the chicken on a saucer and Lindy proceeded to make short work of that, too. Once done, he began to wash himself; one would think he'd gotten his whole body filthy from the way he meticulously licked every bit of fur on his person.

"Well, Lindy's washing up. Maybe you'd better do the same," Andrew said. He held Lee-Ann up to the sink so she could wash her hands.

The macaroni and cheese was sizzling. Andrew dished it out onto a plate and poured a glass of milk, then took them into the breakfast room.

"I'll get the rest of your food. Why don't you start eating?"

Lee-Ann set to demolishing the works as Andrew brought in two bowls of tapioca pudding. He wasn't hungry enough for a meal, but a bit of pudding would tide him over for the night.

"Lee-Ann?" Mac stood in the doorway.

Lee-Ann grinned at her. "Andrew fixed me food."

Andrew noted the astonishment and relief on Mac's face. She smiled at her daughter, then at Andrew.

After gobbling up the tapioca pudding, Lee-Ann's head began to droop. Mac gathered her up and carried her up the stairs. Andrew followed them into the guest room. Mac tucked her daughter into bed, then turned and put her arms around Andrew.

"Thank you so much," she whispered.

"Where we going?" Lee-Ann's head swivelled back and forth as Lois drove them to Plainfield.

"I told you, it's a surprise," Andrew replied.

Mac smiled. Lois pulled up to a movie theater. Lee-Ann's eyes indifferently scanned the posters on the front of the building. Suddenly a look of rapture burst across her face.

"Lassie! They have the *Lassie Come Home* movie here!"

"Yes, that's what we're going to see," Andrew smiled. He got out of the car, held the door open for Lee-Ann, and escorted her to the ticket booth.

"Meet you here at four-thirty," Lois called.

"My mommy and Aunt Lois not see Lassie, too?" Lee-Ann asked.

"They're going to do some shopping—it's just you and me," Andrew said.

Lee-Ann smiled the most dazzling smile at him, then waved excitedly at her mother. Andrew paid for the tickets, then held out his hand to her and said in a very low and formal, "Will you do me the honor of accompanying me to the theater?"

Lee-Ann giggled something unintelligible and Andrew said, "You're supposed to say 'Delighted.'"

"Delighted!" Lee-Ann giggled.

After getting some popcorn, they walked into the theater to look for seats.

"Andrew! Here—sit by us!"

"Miriam!"

"You know that girl?" Lee-Ann asked.

"She's a friend of mine from school. It looks like she has some friends with her. Would you like to sit with them?"

Lee-Ann nodded and Andrew sat down with her in a pair of seats by Miriam. He put Lee-Ann in the seat closest to Miriam, and sat himself in the aisle seat.

"Andrew, this is my cousin Eva." Miriam indicated a young woman seated four seats down from her; between her and Miriam were three little girls. Miriam introduced them as Ann, Lorna, and Georgina. "Eva and I are babysitting them today," she said.

Andrew nodded. He still found the term "babysitting" a bit ridiculous, but then, Americans could be so decidedly unsensible about things!

He introduced Lee-Ann and told Miriam she was visiting from New York; he thought it best not to say why.

"Is this the first time you've seen *Lassie Come Home?*" Miriam asked Lee-Ann.

"No, I seed it hundreds and hundreds times!" Lee-Ann declared.

Miriam smiled. Lee-Ann put her mouth to Andrew's ear and whispered, "Have to go potty."

"Oh, no," he said.

"She take me," Lee-Ann pointed to Miriam.

"Uh—she needs to—" Andrew began.

"No problem," Miriam laughed. "I think I'd better take everyone to get freshened up." As she stood up, Eva stood also. "No, no—I can take care of everyone," Miriam assured her. She herded her charges, along with Lee-Ann, towards the back.

Andrew nodded at Eva across the gap of empty seats.

She smiled shyly. "Hello," she said. "Miriam has told me much about you. You are from England?"

"Yes, I came here last autumn."

Eva nodded. "England is such a lovely place. You must miss it very much."

"I do, yes, very much."

Eva's face brightened. "I was in England for a few weeks, after I left Germany. We— that is, my friend that I came from Germany with, and my friend's parents and I—we stayed in London. You have been to London, no?"

"Oh, yes, many times."

"It is the loveliest city I have ever seen, and it has so many wonderful things. I loved the Speaker's Corner—have you been to it?"

"Yes, my father used to take me there. It's quite an interesting place."

"It is wonderful, so *wonderful*, to listen to people who are free to talk about anything they want to say. It is so different from the way things are in Germany. In England, anyone can say what they want to, without fear." She looked off into the distance. "Almost every day I was in London, I walked in your Hyde Park and spent most of my time at the Speaker's Corner. I said to myself as I listened, 'This is the sound of freedom.' You cannot imagine how marvelous that is."

Andrew nodded. He didn't know how to reply to Eva's impassioned declarations.

She focused her gaze on him. "England stood alone against the Nazis—for over a year. We Jews will not forget that."

"All right—everybody get settled—" Miriam shepherded the quartet of girls into their seats as Andrew stood to let them by. Lee-Ann settled into her seat and munched on her popcorn.

The lights dimmed, then darkened. A newsreel about the fighting in Italy was shown. Andrew glanced at Lee-Ann; she didn't seem distressed, or even interested in the news from that corner of the globe. A *March of Time* clip about juvenile delinquency was next, followed by a few trailers for coming attractions. A moment's silence; Lee-Ann stiffened. *Lassie Come Home* blazed across the screen, and Lee-Ann was transported. Andrew thought she would gaze reverently, silently, at the film, but that was not to be the case. As Andrew had not seen it, she insisted on divulging every detail of the plot to him, much to the annoyance of the people around them (Miriam and Eva and the girls not included, of course).

"That Lassie, she waits for that Lassie boy every day," Lee-Ann whispered to Andrew. Loud shushes echoed around them.

She lowered her voice a little. "That rich man buys Lassie, but Lassie gets out and runs home." The shushes increased in volume and intensity.

"Here, sit on my lap," Andrew suggested. "You can whisper very softly in my ear, all right?"

This she did, and Andrew was treated to a running commentary on the action. He could usually anticipate a crucial scene, for Lee-Ann's body would tense, and she would whisper, "That Libbets Taylor, she lets Lassie get away," or "Those men don't shoot Lassie—they know she's good." When Lassie swam the river and collapsed in exhaustion, Lee-Ann grabbed his hand and assured him that "some very nice olden people" would take care of Lassie and send her on her way.

Lee-Ann got particularly agitated when a kindly peddler who had befriended Lassie was attacked by robbers; the man had a little dog who, with Lassie, defended her master. Sadly, the little dog was killed. Lee-Ann slumped back against Andrew and sniffled. He gave her his handkerchief. She dried her eyes and clutched his hand as Lassie, after leaping from a second-story window to evade some dog catchers, limped home to her master.

"She waits for that Lassie-boy and he runs to her and says 'My Lassie come home,'"

Lee-Ann predicted, and it was so. Miriam smiled at her, then at Andrew. The lights went on and the theater became alive with chattering, shrieking voices. Americans did not queue up to leave a theater, Andrew noted; evidently they considered that the mob approach was best. He decided it would be wise to remain seated until the crowd thinned out. Miriam and Eva, along with their charges, remained seated also as Lee-Ann chattered on about the movie. As the last of the mob exited the theater, Eva consulted her watch.

"We have to get to the bus stop—let's go, girls."

"Yes, we'd better be going," Miriam said.

They walked out of the theater into the sunshine. Lois and Mac were waiting for them. Lee-Ann ran up to the car and excitedly announced to her mother that she had seen the movie with "lots and lots" of Andrew's friends.

Lois, recognizing Miriam, invited them to ride home. "Just all squoosh in—save your bus fare for a rainy day!"

Once home, Lois invited them all in for juice and cookies. Afterwards, Lee-Ann and Georgina played with some Deanna Durbin paper dolls, which Mac had bought for Lee-Ann. When the girls had to depart, Lee-Ann wanted Georgina to come back again. Eva said she would ask Georgina's mother if that would be all right.

At bedtime, Lee-Ann snuggled next to Andrew.

"What are those things?" She pointed at the pictures on his England quilt.

"These are special things about England." He pointed at the various emblems. "There's an RAF roundel, that's Big Ben, that's a double-decker bus—"

"What are those mountains?" She pointed to the middle panel.

"Those are the white cliffs of Dover."

"Do you live near them?"

"They weren't very far from my home in Berkshire."

"Does Lassie live near you in England?"

"She lives in Yorkshire, which is south of Northumberland. That's where I lived with my Grandmother Howard after my home in Berkshire was bombed."

"What about that place that Lassie got home from?"

"Scotland? That's north of Northumberland."

"So Lassie goes through North-lumber-land to go to her home?"

"Yes, I suppose she did."

"Did you see her?"

"Um—no, I didn't."

"Maybe she walked by your house."

"Perhaps she did."

"Her paws got all bloody when she walked on the rocks."

"They did, yes."

Suddenly she was in his arms, sobbing.

"I don't want that little dog to die."

"That was very sad, wasn't it?"

She nodded furiously and wiped her eyes on the sheets. "She 'tected that man."

"She protected him, yes."

Lee-Ann's face was swollen with grief. Andrew knew she was not crying for just the little dog.

Lee-Ann insisted on staying with Andrew "for ever and ever," but Mac had to return home. A compromise was reached, whereby Lee-Ann would remain in New Jersey for three more weeks. Lois would then bring her back to New York. Georgina's mother, who was one of Mr. Givens's customers, happily agreed to have Georgina spend days with Lee-Ann. Georgina didn't have any friends her own age in her neighborhood and, as her older sisters were in school most of the day, she was often lonely for companionship. So she and Lee-Ann hit it off "famously." Lee-Ann was in seventh heaven with her new-found playmate, and Andrew to spend the afternoons and evenings with her.

It was the closest Andrew had ever been to actually enjoying his stay in America. Miriam would walk home with him so that she could pick up Georgina and bring her back to her home, where Eva watched Georgina's sisters while their mother was at work. Not right away though: Miriam would linger awhile after arriving with Andrew, for they would all be treated to an afternoon snack of some sort of delicious treat from the oven. Then Andrew would practice on his guitar: After doing his scales and the various exercises Collie had given him, he would play different sets of chord progressions. He let Lee-Ann or Georgina strum the strings while he fingered the chords. They all listened to the radio from five to six, then Miriam would take Georgina home. At bedtime, Andrew read to Lee-Ann from *The Little House in the Big Woods*.

To help pass the time during the day, Lois decided to teach the girls to crochet. It was Lee-Ann's idea to make a granny afghan for her mother, as she explained: "My mommy's sad too about my daddy."

As the afghan took shape, Andrew was fascinated by how bits of different colored yarn could be transformed into something so exquisitely beautiful. It almost looked like a cathedral window, with blocks of brilliantly colored roundels of yarn that were edged in black and sewn together. Andrew was fascinated too, by how Lois and Lee-Ann and Georgina so nimbly worked the yarn; their fingers seemed to dance over their creation as they laughed and chattered and tried to keep Lindy away from the skiens of yarn by their sides. Lois tried to teach Andrew to crochet, but he couldn't even get the hang of a chain stitch, let alone execute the complicated maneuvers necessary to perform a double crochet. After some coaching by Lois, he could sew the blocks of yarn together without too much trouble, so that was his contribution to the project.

One night after supper, Lee-Ann got out her crayons and a bundle of papers and started drawing. Her picture appeared to be some sort of webbed structure; Andrew watched as it took form.

"Is that a bridge?" he asked.

Lee-Ann nodded. "My daddy builded a bridge." She drew what looked like a Jeep with some very important person driving it: The man had large yellow stars on his shoulders.

"Is that the general who went across the bridge your father built?"

"Yes, it's that General Truscott. He drove the Jeep across that bridge my daddy builded."

She took a stubby piece of blue crayon and rubbed it sideways near the top of the paper, creating a blue sky over the scene.

"Why don't you draw some more pictures of your father?" Andrew suggested.

Lee-Ann tilted her head and stared at her drawing.

"You can draw pictures of the happy times you had together, before he went away," Andrew said.

Lee-Ann said nothing. Her head continued to bob forward and back, whether from acknowledging his suggestion or merely keeping time to some inner rhythm, Andrew didn't know. He gave her a kiss on the forehead and went upstairs.

The next day, when he arrived home from school with Miriam, Lee-Ann presented him with a stack of drawings, showing all sorts of happy times with her father: a trip to Niagara Falls, a visit to the Bronx Zoo, Christmases and picnics and birthdays.

On the day of Lee-Ann's departure, Mr. Givens drove them all to the train station. Lee-Ann locked herself around Andrew in a farewell embrace, and only Lois's entreaties that the train was about to leave *now* convinced her to release him and get on the train. She waved at him through the window, and he waved back until the train was out of sight.

He took Lee-Ann's drawings to a bookbinder in Plainfield, to be made into an album. He also requested some blank pages of heavy black paper be inserted at the back, for snapshots and mementos. A service photo of Lee-Ann's father, contributed by Lois, was mounted on the front of the book and his name, *Henry Keller LeClaire*, was embossed above it. Andrew kept the book for a few days before mailing it; alone in his room, he would stare intently at the snapshot of the man with the winsome smile. The eyes of this person whom he would never know seemed to be looking at him, watching him, like the eyes of his dead uncles...but not like them. These eyes were kind, imbued with a gentleness and joy, and Andrew felt as if they were bestowing upon him a kind of benediction.

He mailed the book to Lee-Ann on the day before his birthday. He considered that, even though it was something he was giving away, it was a gift that had enriched him as much as anything he had ever received.

His thirteenth birthday was celebrated with much fanfare; evidently Americans took very seriously one's becoming a "teenager." Lois measured him and happily noted how much he'd grown: He was now 58 inches tall and weighed 90 pounds.

"Bet you'll break a hundred before the year is out!" she proclaimed.

Before the year is out, I'll be back in England, Andrew thought, but I'll certainly write to her and let her know.

His mother arranged for him to have fifty dollars with which to buy a guitar. Collie went with him to a music store in Plainfield and helped him pick one out.

As mid-March approached, Andrew grew fitful with anticipation. He would usually awaken several times during the night, sure that his disquietude was a premonition that the invasion was on. Then he would creep down the stairs and turn the radio on very low. He would press his ear close to the amplifier so that he might hear the wonderful news that the Allies had landed in northern France (the Pas-de-Calais, of course—why *wouldn't* the Allies pick the shortest route across the Channel and the quickest way to Germany?)

As March drew to a close, his annoyance that his nightly forays were proving to be unproductive excursions to listen to late-night music, or static, was turning into outrage.

Bloody hell! What's holding things up? If they don't get on with the invasion, I might have to spend all summer here!

April brought, not invasion, but an invitation.

Andrew squinted as he tried to make out the scrawly handwriting on the page before him.

Dear Andrew,

So sorry I didn't write sooner but Eaglebrook is absolutely smashing! I am learning how to ski it is cracking great fun so is horseback riding, archery, etc. I have a sister her name is Diane she is very nice she goes to college and plays poker too. I will be staying this summer with Grandmother and Grandfather Barrett in Holyoake so is Diane they say I can have a friend spend the summer with me would you like to?

Your friend,
Peter

Andrew folded the letter and set it aside. That night at supper he casually mentioned the invitation to Lois. She said it sounded like a nice idea, but she would check with his mother first. When she asked him if he intended to spend all summer in Massachusetts, he shrugged and said, "We'll see."

Lois appeared puzzled by his lack of enthusiasm, and asked, "What do you mean?"

"Well, if the war's going to be over soon, which it will be, as soon as we invade, that is, then I'll want to go back to England right away, so I can—" He caught himself at the last moment—thank *God* he didn't say, *So I can see my father again.*

Lois raised her eyebrows.

"So I can see my mother again, right away, I mean—" He thought quickly. "Surely, there will be mobs of people wanting to come to America when the war's over, soldiers going home and all that, you know, and it will probably be quite difficult for her to get transport here. It would be the sensible thing for me to go there." He tried to inject a lilt into his voice, as if his planned scenario was, of course, the best way to go about things.

Lois consulted her husband with a silent glance.

"Okay by me," he shrugged.

Turning back to Andrew, she said, "Well, go ahead and make your plans—who knows? You might have all summer to spend here, so might as well plan on having a nice vacation. You can travel by train. I'll take you to New York and put you on the train to Massachusetts."

Andrew nodded, mentally calculating that, even if the invasion didn't occur until May, he would surely only have a few weeks of summer to spend in America. Besides, it wouldn't take *that* long to hop on a train to New York and set sail for England forthwith.

He received a package from Mac. Within was a drawing by Lee-Ann, showing what appeared to be a little log cabin perched on a white cliff. Standing next to the cabin was a boy with a brown and white dog: "Lassie and Andrew and the Little House on the White Cliffs of Dover," wrote Mac.

She also enclosed a letter from her husband, which she wanted Andrew to read and then return to her, as she was saving all of her husband's letters. Most of them she had already put in the book Andrew had sent.

Andrew sat in the quiet of his room and read the neatly penned missive of a man who now lay dead a half a world away:

Dear Mac,

Got your letter yesterday with the pictures of your Thanksgiving in New Jersey. It was like a ray of sunshine in this place (funny, I always used to hear "Sunny Italy"—let me tell you, whoever wrote that line never saw Italy in December!) I passed around the pictures to all the guys and they got a kick out of them too. You got a few marriage proposals, but I told your eager suitors you were already spoken for! Anyway, you can't imagine how wonderful it was to see my beautiful girls, all of them! It looks as if Lee-Ann has found a true friend in Andrew— that snap of them reading together made me want to be right in the picture with them. I also liked the one of the two of them looking over the Thanksgiving feast. Hope I get a chance to meet Andrew someday. Until then, it's nice to know that my Lee-Ann has found a friend indeed!

Love, love, always,
Hank

Mary Jo Versailles came to visit him in April. Her fiance's parents had just gotten back from Florida so, while she was staying with them in Dunellen, she "paid" Andrew "a call."

She was just as tall as Gerry and had the same blue eyes, brown hair, and gentle drawl.

"Everyone still teases me that I have to wear shoes up North," she laughed, as they sat around the table for Sunday dinner.

She loved being a nurse, loved New York City, and talked of how there was always something to see and do in that exciting place.

She told Andrew she had just gotten a letter from Gerry and that he somehow had found a way to insert the number *nine* more than a dozen times in the letter:

"Like, 'remember when we was nine years old' or 'remember our house at 9999

Georgetown Street'—We never lived at 9999 Georgetown Street. So I figured he was telling me he's in the Ninth Air Force now, which is the one that's all involved with the invasion, whenever that's supposed to happen."

Before she left she gave Andrew a photo of herself and Gerry, taken on one of Gerry's visits to New York. He had a wry smile on his face, as if he thought New York City were a colossal joke.

"He never liked New York very much," Mary Jo laughed. "Always couldn't wait to get back to Bluegrass Country!"

Lois measured him on June 4. He had grown an inch and a half since his thirteenth birthday and weighed ninety-six pounds.

"Looks like you're going to hit a hundred before long," Lois laughed.

Though he was not upset to be growing so rapidly, Lois's words still rankled. He had expected to "hit a hundred" in England, *not* in America.

Bloody hell! Aren't they ever going to get on with the invasion!

"Andrew—wake up!" Sleep fled as he felt Lois shaking him awake. It was light outside, but still early, he sensed. Why was Lois waking him at this ungodly hour?

"The invasion—it's happened!"

Andrew threw on his robe and dashed downstairs. Lois gave him a cup of cocoa as he curled up near the radio and listened to the stunning news:

Under the command of General Eisenhower, Allied naval forces, supported by strong air forces, began landing Allied armies this morning on the northern coast of France.

And then the word: Normandy.

Normandy!

He shook his head in disbelief.

"Normandy! I can't believe they wouldn't pick the Pas-de-Calais. It must be some kind of feint."

"What do you mean?" Lois asked.

"Well, the Pas-de-Calais is the shortest way across the Channel, and the quickest route to Germany—everyone knows that. Normandy's so far away; besides, it's all hedgerow country—not an easy place to fight a war. Bet you this Normandy landing is only a diversion. The Allies will probably land at the Pas-de-Calais once the Germans move their forces to Normandy."

"Do you think so?"

"Bet you they do."

Lois let him stay home from school that day. As she told him: "The days are few and far between that you can learn more by staying home than by going to school, but I think this is one of those days. Your assignment is to set yourself by that radio and listen!"

"Yes, ma'am!" He gave her a mock salute.

He piled the sofa cushions on the floor and listened to the crackly reports emanating from the huge, glowing box. There was, from all reports, a mind-boggling number of men landed on those hostile shores: a hundred and fifty-five thousand. Still, there were hundreds of thousands of more soldiers still in England. Surely they were being held back for the real assault.

They'll probably get the Jerries all tangled up in the hedgerows, then POW! A quick jab across the Pas-de-Calais, then straight left to Germany.

Piece of cake.

He returned to school the next day. The talk in the hallways was euphoric and jubilant: *End of the war in '44!*

It was all very exciting, and Andrew allowed himself to be caught up in, though not completely bowled over by, the excitement over Normandy.

After all, it *was* only a feint.

Still, it was at least a very hopeful, very promising event. Andrew was encouraged and even made a little light-hearted by the wonderful goings-on in that special corner of the globe.

The exuberance continued into the next day. There was another reason for all the excitement: It was only a half-day of school. There was some sort of teachers' meeting; evidently, notices about the shortened school day had been given out on the day Andrew had stayed home from school, so it came as a surprise to him. This was just the icing on the cake for him: The unexpected fewer hours of school was like getting to go on an surprise holiday.

After bidding good-bye to Miriam in the grape arbor, he decided to sneak in quietly. Lois always loved surprises.

As he opened the back door, he heard a blast of laughter from Sarah. He remembered it was her day to "clean."

"A straight flush, if you please, and come home to momma, you darling little babies!"

"Shoot, I got four of a kind—first decent hand I've had all afternoon." Andrew recognized Alida's voice. "You have to go *ruin* it by getting a straight flush!"

"I'm just on a roll, girl," Sarah chuckled. "You in for another game?"

"Shoot, why not?" Alida said. "Might as well throw good money after bad. What about you, Lois?"

"Sure, deal me in," Lois said. "I have a feeling my luck is about to change."

Suddenly everything made sense.

No *wonder* Sarah always needed help from Lois in getting the housework done— she spent afternoons playing poker! That was why she and Lois always went to Alida's to "do some things" whenever Andrew happened to be at home.

Another thought occurred to him: Would his mother have made Lois aware of his...talents? His mother could be very forthright and spirited and chatty but then, would she go bragging to her new mother-in-law about her son's poker-playing abilities?

He doubted it.

He ambled into the breakfast room and evinced a look of puzzlement and naivete as he regarded the cards on the table. A pile of steel pennies lay in the center, and a straight flush was spread triumphantly in front of Sarah. Three pairs of eyes startled, then looked at him warily.

"Hullo," he said, "What sort of card game are you playing?"

Chapter 42

*L*ois glanced back and forth from Sarah to Alida, then stared at Andrew, guilt and trepidation in her eyes. She looked as if she'd been caught with her hand in the cookie jar.

"Uh—card game?"

Andrew tilted his head.

"Poker," Sarah said evenly.

"Poker?" He raised his eyebrows. "I've heard of poker. How do you play?"

Lois grimaced. Alida peered at him, as if evaluating whether or not his feeble mind might be able to grasp the complexities of the game. Sarah snorted.

"You know what a pair is?" Sarah asked him.

"Oh, you mean something like two hearts or two clubs?"

"No, not the same suit. The same number."

"Like fours or sevens or aces, that sort of thing?"

"Uh-huh."

Lois shook her head and looked doubtful.

"I don't know if his mother would like him learning to play poker."

Alida squinted and shrugged.

"Well, I don't think it will do him any permanent damage."

"Hmmm...I don't know...." Lois's voice trailed off.

Andrew evinced a longing, hopeful expression. "Oh, *please*, I'd be ever so grateful if you'd teach me! And I don't think my mother would mind."

Lois pursed her lips, then smiled. "All right, sit down."

Andrew quickly pulled back a chair and sat down. He opened his eyes very wide and feigned an expression of eager concentration.

"Okay." Alida gathered up the cards. She looked through them and picked out two sixes. "This is a pair."

Andrew stared with rapt attention at the various hands Alida displayed for him. He nodded his head a lot and repeated each term twice, sometimes three times, as if trying hard to commit things to memory.

"Okay, let's play," Alida said after explaining to him what a royal flush was.

"Ladies wild, remember?" Sarah prompted.

"What?" Andrew asked.

"Oh, we use queens as wild cards," Alida said.

"*Wild* cards?" Andrew raised his eyebrows very high. "What are wild cards?"

"A wild card you can use for anything," Lois explained. "Jokers are also wild."

"Crikey—that's *super*! Oh, I can't *wait* to play!"

"We'll teach you five card draw first," Alida said. "There's also five card stud and seven card stud."

"There are *different* ways to play poker?"

"Uh-huh," Sarah said.

"Now, in five card draw," Alida said, "You can discard cards that you don't want, and get others."

"Really?" Andrew chirped. "Oh, that sounds marvelous!"

Sarah dealt the cards. Andrew was glad his first hand wasn't very good. Lois discarded two cards; Alida discarded one. When Andrew's turn came, he chewed his lip as he regarded his cards. Finally, he said, "Five."

"Now, you can't go switching all them cards," Sarah admonished him.

"Well, I don't have any of those hands Alida told me about," Andrew complained.

"See what you got close to and try for something."

"Like what?" He showed Sarah his hand.

"You're not supposed to show others what you've got," Alida said. "Even if you don't have anything, you can still bluff."

"Bluff?"

"Pretend you've got a good hand, even when you don't. Or fold, whatever you want to do."

"Fold?"

"You quit betting. Oh, we'd better get you started here. Sarah? You've got most of the loot. Care to make a contribution?"

Sarah grunted and gave Andrew a handful of pennies. Lois and Alida added a few from their small clutches of coins.

"Wait a minute—I've got some money of my own," Andrew said. "I'll pay for the pennies." He bounded up the stairs and returned with a quarter and two dimes. He gave Sarah the quarter and Lois and Alida the dimes, then sat down again.

"Well, I think I'll fold this game, but I'll watch to see how you bet, all right?"

Lois folded early and Alida won the game with a flush, which beat Sarah's full house.

Sarah dealt another round. This time Andrew didn't have a good hand, but after the betting had gone round a few times he furrowed his brow and studied his cards and asked, "If you have two wild cards and two of another kind, is that two pair or four of a kind?"

Sarah glared at him; Lois looked astounded.

Sarah threw her cards down.

Lois and Alida seemed disconcerted for a minute, then said in unison, "Fold."

"What?" Andrew said.

"You won—four of a kind," Sarah said.

"But I don't *have* four of a kind!"

"What?" Alida blurted.

Andrew shrugged. "I was just asking." He showed his hand: a pair of threes.

Sarah rolled her eyes and silently dealt the next hand. As Andrew sorted through his cards, he happened to glance over at the corner table, behind Lois, and saw Lindy sitting on it, in his favorite looking-out-at-the-world position. Only Lindy was not exactly looking out at the world; he was staring intently at Andrew.

Andrew was momentarily unnerved.

He could *swear* that cat knew what he was up to.

In the next round he got a straight and bet furiously, not really caring whether he won or not. As it turned out, he beat out Sarah's three tens; Lois and Alida folded.

The next round he let go to Lois; he only had a pair of tens. The round after that saw some furious betting by Sarah and Alida; Andrew kept raising and, when there was a sizeable pile of pennies in the center of the table, he chewed his lip again, stared at his cards, and asked, "The queens are wild, right?"

"Uh-huh," Sarah said.

"Jokers too?"

"Uh-huh."

"Hmmm...." He cocked his head and studied his cards for a moment. "What happens if you have four wild cards?"

Sarah's eyes bulged; Alida's jaw dropped. They consulted one another, silently, then threw down their cards.

"Why did you quit?" Andrew feigned astonishment.

"Four wild cards makes it a straight flush," Lois explained.

"Four wild cards? But I don't *have* four wild cards, just two pair." He showed them his cards.

Sarah and Alida both blanched; Lois's mouth hung open.

"Let's play another round," Sarah said.

Andrew thought it best to throw the next few games. He did a lot of frowning at his cards and lip chewing before folding. Then he received three Jacks and the Queen of Hearts. There was furious betting again and Andrew went along, but he pursed his lips a lot and tried to appear very uneasy about things. Sarah called. Alida had a full house, Sarah had a flush, and Lois had four tens. Andrew pretended to be very upset before he set down his cards.

"I only have three of a kind." He displayed his cards to the women, and there was a moment's silence. Andrew acted very bewildered, then looked at this cards again.

"*Crikey!* I *forgot!* Queens are wild, aren't they? So, I have four of a kind!" He opened his mouth very wide and shook his head slowly, as if thoroughly flabbergasted.

Sarah pushed the pile of pennies towards him, then silently dealt the next round.

Andrew looked at his cards in consternation, didn't ask for any new cards, and let the betting proceed. Once the pile had grown to sizeable proportions again he furrowed his brow and asked, "Now what is it called when you have cards all in a row and all the same kind—a flush straight?"

Sarah rolled her eyes, folded. So did Lois and Alida.

"Why did you fold?" he asked.

"It's called a straight flush," Sarah said evenly.

"Oh—well, that's very interesting. So *if* I managed to get all the cards in a row, and *if* they were all the same kind, I'd have a flush straight."

"Straight flush." Sarah corrected.

"Right."

"Wait a minute," Alida said. "You mean you *don't* have a straight flush?"

"No," he said, showing his hand. "Just a pair of fives."

Forty-five minutes later Andrew had, in the American parlance, "cleaned up." He regarded his humongous pile of pennies with amazed delight.

"Best run of beginner's luck I've ever seen," Alida breathed.

Lois nodded. "Sure is."

Sarah was silent. Lindy glared at him.

"I don't think so," Sarah said finally.

"What?" Lois asked.

"I said, *I don't think so.*" Sarah narrowed her eyes at Andrew.

"Wh—what's wrong?" Andrew sputtered.

"I *don't* think it's beginner's luck. You get my drift, Andrew?"

Andrew felt a smile playing at the corner of his mouth. He coughed to prevent it from cracking across his face, but it was a futile gesture. His cough came out as a laugh. He covered his hand over his mouth and leaned over. Sarah reached over, pulled his hand away to reveal an ear-splitting grin. Her eyes bulged.

She threw back her head and roared with laughter.

"What—what's going on?" Lois cried.

Great heaving chortles shook Sarah's frame. She squealed and whooped, and finally settled into giggles of delight.

"That boy's a shark with the biggest, whitest teeth I ever seen! Tried to make out like he was a guppy!"

Andrew smiled shyly. "I was just having a little fun." He pushed his pile of pennies towards Sarah.

"Here, you called my bluff."

Sarah laughed wildly as she scooped the pennies into her lap.

"Smartest white boy I ever seen!"

The women jumped at the sound of a car pulling in to the drive.

"Oh, dear—it's Gene!" Lois said.

Instantly, there was a flurry of activity. Alida gathered up the cards and put them into the top drawer of the corner table. Sarah deposited her pennies into her crocheted tote bag, grabbed a cloth from out of the broom closet next to the pantry, and proceeded to polish the windows in the breakfast room. Lois and Alida scurried into the kitchen. Lois busied herself with peeling potatoes; Alida started putting away the dishes in the drainboard.

Lois whispered to Andrew. "Gene doesn't know—I don't think he'd be too pleased to find out that Sarah is getting paid for playing poker."

Andrew winked at her, opened the refrigerator, and took out a bottle of milk. He got a glass from the cupboard and poured himself a half-cup.

"Lois?" Mr. Givens called from the front porch. He opened the door, walked in. "Lois,

I tried to call, but the line was busy. I just need to get some papers—have to get right back to work."

He walked into the kitchen.

"The line was busy?" Lois said. "I wasn't on the phone at all today."

Mr. Givens nodded at her, said, "Maybe the upstairs phone is off the hook." He climbed the stairs and returned a few minutes later with a stack of papers. "That's what it was—receiver was off the hook."

"Sorry, I must—I mean, Sarah must have knocked it off when she was dusting."

Mr. Givens grunted.

"Why don't you have a cup of tea, dear," Lois said. "The kettle's on, and I baked some molasses-oatmeal bread this morning."

Mr. Givens grunted again. "Sure, just for a minute." He ambled into the breakfast room. Andrew followed.

Sarah, languidly polishing the window, turned and nodded at Mr. Givens.

"Afternoon, Mr. G.," she said. It sounded like a command.

"Afternoon, Sarah," Mr. Givens replied. He gave her a brief smile, then sat down. Andrew sat down next to him.

"How's school, Andrew?" Mr. Givens asked him.

"Oh, it's all right."

"Well, school year's just about over. You still want to go visit your friend in Massachusetts?"

Andrew shrugged. "I guess so."

Mr. Givens nodded at him. Lois brought in their tea and bread. They munched in silence, Sarah's soft humming providing an easeful ambience.

Mr. Givens consulted his watch. "Gotta go. Bye, Andrew." He stood up, and departed.

Sarah continued humming and polishing. Lois and Alida came into the room. Alida stroked her brow in mock relief.

"Close call—thanks for going along, Andrew."

"No problem," Andrew smiled.

He was invited to join the bi-weekly poker sessions with Lois, Alida, and Sarah: on Thursday afternoons in the Givens home, and on Tuesdays at Alida's. And so the end of the school year turned out to be quite a happy time for Andrew, what with getting to polish his poker skills twice a week and happily anticipating his return to England before long.

Any day now, the Allies are going to deliver a knock-out blow across the Pas-de-Calais. We'll drive the Huns back to Hunland in a few weeks, and then I'll get to go back home!

However, it was beginning to look as if an invasion across the Pas-de-Calais might never happen. More and more, it was looking as if the punch at Normandy was the real blow, not a feint. Even though it had taken the Allied forces barely half a day to ram through Hitler's much touted Atlantic Wall, and only a week to establish a bridgehead forty-two miles long, the American army proceeded to get bogged down in the hedgerow country. Far from ensnaring the Germans, the U.S. Army was itself being chewed apart in the tangling maze of sunken roads and ancient hedges planted hundreds of years before. It was a land ideally suited to the Nazi defenders.

Andrew had written to his mother the day after the Normandy Invasion, hoping that the flush of euphoria following this auspicious event might prompt her to let him return to England forthwith.

This was not to be so: Even before her letter arrived denying his request, the news of a frightening new weapon, the V-1, reached him.

"It's like the Blitz all over again," one British woman was quoted as saying, and this *Vergeltungswaffen*, or revenge weapon, though on the whole ineffective for tactical or strategic purposes, brought a new kind of terror to the British people—that of anonymous, mechanized death raining from the skies.

As his mother wrote:

> It's positively <u>ghastly</u>, darling. Everyone calls them doodlebugs, which sounds so pleasantly innocuous, but they are <u>beastly</u> things—pilotless, jet-propelled flying craft that are launched from France. When their engines cut out they spiral in and explode on impact. Jake's squadron has been busily "chasing" them, as he calls it. They either shoot them down or get close enough to flip them over with their wings, which upsets the gyros of these horrid devices and they go tumbling down.
>
> Be that as it may, England is <u>no</u> place for you to be right now, Andrew. Though the RAF is doing a superb job of getting to most of these buzz bombs, our pilots can't get every single one of these awful things, and the danger won't be over until the launching sites in France are captured. So until then, you must remain in America. Lois wrote me that your friend Peter has invited you up to New England for the summer. Do go, darling—I think you'll have a <u>marvelous</u> time!

And so, Andrew's summer itinerary was decided by these wretched doodlebugs. Lois went with him on the train to New England.

The Barrett home in Holyoake was larger and more rambling than the Givens home. It had a huge front lawn and backed up against a golf course. Gib's parents were both like Lois: warm and gregarious. They delighted in Peter's company and were happy that he had a friend to spend the summer with. Gib's daughter, Diane, who was home from college, also enjoyed the company of her spirited stepbrother. Andrew wondered what had occurred to cause Gib not to be married to Diane's mother, but didn't ask. Had she died, or had things not worked out between them?

Part of the answer to the mystery was provided the next day, when Diane announced she was taking Peter and Andrew to her mother's place so that they could go swimming. She drove them in a "roadster," which her stepfather had gotten her for a graduation present.

Diane's mother, who was called "Aunt Amelia" by Peter, had obviously married into the wealthier class, judging by the size of her estate. The sunken swimming pool in the backyard was flanked by a tennis court and a miniature putting green. The house, or rather, mansion, was almost as big as Greycliff, and built in the "colonial" style.

Diane's mother didn't seemed the least bit perturbed by Peter's presence, though Andrew wondered how she could accept the child of her former husband's new wife. Peter chattered happily with her about having Andrew to visit with him all summer, and she pleasantly questioned Andrew about how he liked being in America. She had two daughters by her second marriage, Sandra and Anita, who were about Peter's age. They were delighted to see Peter and, giggling wildly, proceeded to drag him off to the pool. Aunt Amelia's husband, whom Peter called "Uncle Grant," arrived home from work at dinnertime and joined everyone in the pool for a game of tag.

The next day, Diane decided to take her grandparents' collie, Madison, for a walk. Madison looked *exactly* like Lassie, and was a delightful hiking companion to boot. She took it upon herself to make sure they all stayed together, running circles around them as they ambled up Mount Tom. Every so often she would pick up a stick in her mouth and carry it to Peter, who threw it for her. As the stick sailed off into the distance, she would dash furiously to keep pace with it and fling herself up in the air to catch it. She never tired of this activity and Andrew, whose only experience of dogs up to that point had been some unfriendly hunting hounds at Greycliff, was charmed by this amiable canine.

At the end of July they heard news of the breakout by the Americans near St. Lo. Andrew thought of Sarge and Mikey and J.D. and Cowboy and Ray and El and the others. Where the war went, they, no doubt, were not far away.

Had they been at the murderous beaches of Normandy, or in the deadly bocage country, or, even now, tearing their way across France?

Andrew breathed a silent prayer that they were all right.

On his train ride south to New Jersey at the end of August, ecstatic talk swirled around him about the recent triumphant Allied entry into Paris.

End of the war in '44!

On September 7, the British government announced that the V-1 threat was over. Andrew wrote to his mother again, quoting from the news clipping of the announcement (which he also enclosed, just in case there was any doubt as to his claim) and pointing out that now that these horrid doodlebugs were a thing of the past, there was really no reason why he should stay in America:

Not that I'm unhappy here, Mum, but I do miss you ever so much. Please let me come home! Everyone's saying that the war will be over by Christmas. Germany's done for, and there's absolutely no reason for me to remain in America—I'd be so much happier in England with you!

Lois pressed Andrew into service helping out with the harvesting of her back garden. He plucked peaches and tomatoes, pulled carrots and radishes, and shucked peas and corn. He had already put in several days of field work before he realized that, in England, someone of his station in life would never get his hands soiled doing such menial, manual labor. And oddly enough, he wasn't even perturbed. He enjoyed the long sunny days outdoors, and looked with pride at the basement shelves bursting with the fruits (and vegetables) of his and Lois's labors.

Returning to school, he had two rather pleasant surprises: Miriam was in his class, and his English teacher was Shannon Casini. Even though he liked Miss Fitt, he thought that having Shannon for a teacher would be even better. Of course Shannon would let him sit in study hall during class, but it would still be nice to "touch bases" with him about his assignments. Surely someone who had been published would not be required to sit in a silly old eighth grade English class! He decided, though, to wait a week or two before approaching Shannon about being excused from class.

He still had Miss Van de Veer for science and Mrs. Malandreatos for math and Mrs. Henschell for history. He also had a class called "shop," which seemed, much to Andrew's annoyance, very much like a training ground for tradesmen. He certainly did not relish the idea of being forced to saw and hammer and construct things out of wood. An education, he believed, was supposed to ensure that one wouldn't have to get one's hands all splintery in the performance of menial tasks. Wasn't that what servants and tradesmen were for?

Still, since he didn't expect to be in America for more than a few weeks at most, Andrew didn't allow himself to get too peeved over his enforced training in carpentry. Mr. O'Reilly, his shop teacher, was actually quite nice, though rather on the quiet side.

He rejoined the bi-weekly poker sessions and began to discover more about Alida and Sarah.

Alida's husband was a colonel in the Army, and based in England. Sarah's son, Marshall, was also in the Army. He had just been promoted to sergeant, and Sarah bragged on his newly-won rank by invoking his full name and title whenever possible. She boasted of his career in guard duty at the ammunition dumps in France:

"These Germans, sometimes they think they real smart 'bout things. They get some Germans boys dressed up in American uniforms and they go through the American lines, talking English good as any American, calling out baseball scores and talking 'bout movie stars, then they blow up the ammo dumps. So some army-man gets the smart idea of using colored boys for guard duty at the ammo dumps, since them Nazis ain't got no colored folk. So any white boy tries to get close, he got to get past Sergeant Marshall Pershing LaRose and his friends first! Marshall say it's the most fun he have in this whole war!"

A letter arrived from his mother:

Dearest Andrew,

It sounds as if you had a <u>wonderful</u> summer! Lois wrote me that you came back tan, tall, and sturdy—all that hiking and swimming must have toned you up quite nicely! Our summer was quite busy too, what with the male ferry pilots making runs to France. The women pilots have not been allowed to ferry to the continent—yet. The lack of "facilities" for women there seems to be the snag, though the lack of "facilities" for women at the many places we've had to ferry to and from in Britain was never considered a problem! As you can imagine, we are all very disappointed about being fettered to our island perch while the men soar off to the continent!

For the time being, though, I've been assigned to Prestwick. It's my first experience in a "mixed pool," that is, with men and women together. It's quite a change from being in an all-female pool, but I like it very much. There are a few other female pilots here, most of them "ab initios"—they had no flying experience at all before joining the ATA, and were trained to fly after joining! Can you imagine that! Four years ago, my paltry hundred hours wasn't enough, and now they're <u>training</u> women to fly! I am rather looked on as an "old sweat" by the other women, as I have been in the ATA longer than any of them. We ferry a lot of Swordfish and Barracudas and, as I am the only woman pilot here with a Class 4 rating, I get to fly many of the twins that come this way. Prestwick is a very busy place; just about every type of aircraft you can imagine comes in and out of here. There are quite a few Class 6 pilots posted here (all men—<u>drat</u>!) who fly the Sunderland and Catalina flying boats. In addition, Prestwick receives the large aircraft ferried over from North America; the ATA pilots here ferry them farther afield. I've been all over Scotland, and have made several trips up to Lossiemouth. The Ferry Pool Commander there is an American chap and ever so nice. Did you know, Andrew, that there were many American men who joined the ATA before America even entered the war? They sailed across the Atlantic, braving those ghastly U-Boats in those perilous days; some of them never even made it to England.

After thinking it over, darling, I think it's best that you remain in America for the time being. It just amazes me how much you've grown and filled out, and a few more months of Lois's cooking is bound to put you at the peak of health. Why, you'll be as tall as me before long! You know that what I want for you is best.

All my love,
Mum

Bloody hell!
What was the matter with her!
Andrew had closely monitored all the news reports and tidbits of information from Britain, and there was nothing, *nothing* that even remotely smacked of danger there. No raids, no doodlebugs—*nothing!* In fact, the last bit of information he'd heard from his country were reports of some gas main explosions. The war must *really* be grinding down if the only exciting thing to report on were some silly old gas explosions!

He crumpled the letter into a ball and threw it against the wall.

To add insult to injury, Shannon told him that it would not be permitted for him to "skip" class and do his classwork in study hall.

"I thought you were my friend," Andrew snapped at Shannon.

"That still doesn't mean I can let you skip class," Shannon replied.

"Miss Fitt let me go to study hall and do my work there. I wrote an assignment that got published in a book. Besides, I looked through your grammar book, and I already know everything already. I'd just be bored silly having to study it all over again."

"I plan to do more than just teach grammar, and it's important that you participate in class. You can't do that if you're off in study hall."

"Why should I participate in class? Everybody hates me, anyway."

"That's not true—I don't hate you."

"You're the teacher. It's your job to like people."

Shannon was silent for a moment. Then he spoke. "I really think it's best for you to be in class, Andrew. If you have any problems with the other students, you can come to me, okay?"

Despite regular letters from Gerry, who sympathized with his plight and offered encouragement, and visits from Mary Jo every other weekend, Andrew could not shake his despondency. He felt as is he were the victim of some supreme practical joke, and the image of Jake smirking over his plight tormented him day and night. Even cheery letters from Aunt Jane did not dispel his melancholy.

The only thing he found solace in was his nightly recital of his father's poem as he looked up at the sky. And, of course, his music.

"That's terrific, Andrew," Collie said. "Now do a C-minor, diminished."

Andrew stretched his fingers over the frets and played each string separately, then strummed the chord.

"Very good, Andrew—oh, hello! Have a seat and listen up—you'll be playing as good as Andrew some day, Antoinette."

Andrew's head snapped around, and his eyes met Antoinette's. She reddened, then sat down.

"This is Antoinette's first lesson, Andrew. Why don't you play *Red River Valley* for her?"

It took all of Andrew's concentration not to fumble the song he'd played so many times. When he had finished, he placed his hand against the strings and stared straight ahead.

"That was very nice," the soft voice behind him said.

The phone jangled. "Sorry—" Collie got up to answer it. "Andrew, play something else—I'll just be a minute," she called from the kitchen.

He felt a hand on his shoulder. "You play very well," Antoinette said.

"Thank you." He instinctively turned, met her gaze.

There was an uncomfortable silence.

"So you're going to be taking guitar lessons?" Andrew asked. Immediately he realized what an inane question it was.

Antoinette nodded. "I heard Collie play at our church last week, and I knew I wanted to play like that. It is so—" She started mumbling something in French; Andrew only caught snatches but he realized what she meant.

"Comforting," he said.

"Yes, comforting," she affirmed quietly. Something terribly troubling clouded the honey-brown eyes.

"What part of France are you from?" he asked, trying to draw her from her reverie.

"I am from Oradour, Oradour-sur-Glane. It is a small village southeast of Poitiers."

Andrew shook his head. "Sorry, I've never been farther south than Paris."

"You have been to Paris?"

"I used to spend my summers in France, before the war. My aunt lived there—"

"Sorry that took a little longer than I'd expected." Collie breezed back into the room. "Well, Andrew, I want you to practice all of your minor chords this week, and go over your scales, too. And—oh, I almost forgot! I got that sheet music in for *The White Cliffs of Dover*." She sorted through the stack of music books and papers on the table by the front door. "Here—" She handed the sheet music to Andrew. "Work on this, too. See you next Monday!"

"Next Monday." Andrew nodded at Collie, at Antoinette, too. Antoinette gave him a strange Mona Lisa smile: a gentle curve of the mouth, eyes in a solemn gaze.

When he arrived home on Thursday afternoon Lois, Sarah, and Alida were sitting around the breakfast table, reading magazines. They usually waited for him before starting the poker session and passed the time reading or chatting until he arrived.

There was a stack of old *Life* magazines in the center of the table; Sarah often got leftover periodicals from a lady she cleaned for on Mondays. The women greeted him; then Lois got up to get him a snack. Sarah and Alida asked about his day while absently flipping pages in their magazines. Suddenly Sarah's eyes bulged. She did a double take at Andrew; her eyes switched from his face to the issue of *Life*, and back to him again.

"You ever play poker on that ship you was on?"

"Why yes, with some American G.I.s. I pulled the same routine on them that I did on you."

"You did? You ever pull a straight flush on them?"

"Um, yes—why do you ask?"

Sarah stared at the magazine and shook her head slowly, as if she couldn't believe her eyes. Then she thrust the magazine at him and pointed to a picture in the middle of the page.

Andrew's jaw dropped in astonishment. There, in the pages of *Life*, was a photo of him with a grin of triumph on his face as he displayed a straight flush. Sarge and J.D. were on either side of him, laughing; Cowboy was looking on, his eyes wide in amazement. The caption to the photo read: *A British schoolboy, on his way to the United States aboard a troop ship, enjoys a friendly game of poker with American GIs.*

596

"My God, that's *me!*"

Lois came in with a plate of cookies, and Sarah pointed to the picture of Andrew.

"This boy so good at poker, he got his picture in *Life* magazine!"

Lois was so startled she dropped the plate of cookies on the table; the loud clattering sent Lindy scurrying from his perch on the corner table. Alida eyed the photo article.

"*Children of War*, that's what it's called." Her eyes narrowed as she scanned the other pictures: a young British toddler staring glumly at the camera as his father, in army uniform, planted a good-bye kiss on his cheek; legless Russian children recuperating in a hospital; Italian boys, no older than Andrew, toting guns; a Polish girl, grieving over the body of her sister, who had been strafed by Nazi warplanes.

As Andrew's eyes ranged over the grim images of war, he wondered why he, gleeful and seemingly carefree, had been included in this disturbing montage. After all, if the intent of the article was to show what a terrible thing war was for children, why show a picture of a boy having a cracking great time while the world went to hell in a handbasket?

He turned the page and, seeing only more distressing images, felt a little guilty at being the only child with a smiling face. If only somehow, some way, the more terrible things of his past four years had been included in this collage of devastation and death!

"Okay Hardly-Trying, you're up!"

Andrew trudged onto the court. The other players gave him withering looks. He had lately started hating the sight of a rainy day, for the inclement weather meant that Phys. Ed. class would be held in the gym, and that meant basketball. On fair days, Mr. Scurlock would have the boys run laps outside, which was less disagreeable to Andrew. Running he could do fairly well—just put one foot in front of the other and go. All the many years of "ranging" through the English countryside with his father had given Andrew a pair of sturdy legs which wartime shortages had not taken their toll upon. Lois's nourishing food and his daily work-out sessions in the gym downstairs had only increased his strength and stamina. Besides, he was fast catching up to his classmates in stature and more and more in these running sessions found himself outdistancing the majority of the boys in the class.

He enjoyed running because it was a completely individual activity; he didn't have to worry about what anybody else was doing. Anything he did (or didn't do) had absolutely no effect on anyone else: It didn't lose the game, nor did it bring about an attack of savage looks. At times he would look at the landscape beyond the school and wish that he could break free from the pack and run into the distance, alone, with only the wind as his companion.

Shorty, in possession of the ball, quickly veered left, then right; he passed the ball to Cockney-Mouth, who proceeded to dribble it up the court. However, one of the bounces got away from him and the ball, as if it had a mind of its own, bobbled straight to Andrew. Andrew, startled, smacked the ball with his left hand, turned quickly, and was about to dribble it down to his team's basket when the shrill blast of Mr. Scurlock's whistle split the air.

Mr. Scurlock signalled that Andrew's offense was the mortal sin of "travelling."

He knew he'd been falsely accused: The bewildered glances of the other boys confirmed his conviction.

Andrew held onto the ball as if it were made of gold. He had gotten it, fair and square, and his hands were clean of any wrongdoing.

Mr. Scurlock glared at him, silently commanding him to give up possession of his only triumph in this wretched silly game.

Andrew glared back.

"Andrew!" Mr. Scurlock barked.

"No," Andrew said. "I wasn't travelling. I *wasn't!*"

"You *were!*" Mr. Scurlock took a menacing step towards him.

"Was *not!*"

"Andrew—"

"You're *lying*—"

"*Andrew!*"

Mr. Scurlock took another step, and it was then that it happened.

The ball, which had for the last few seconds been Andrew's dearest possession, now transformed itself into a foul symbol of all that he hated about this horrid land.

"You *twit!*" The ball shot from Andrew's hands like a shell from a cannon and smacked squarely against Mr. Scurlock's groin. Mr. Scurlock doubled over, then looked up, his face contorted with shock and rage.

Andrew's heart skipped a beat; there was a collective gasp from the mob, then a silence so heavy it seemed to suck the soul from his body.

He lurched back a step and, as if recoiling, bolted across the gym and out the door.

Once in the hallway, it took him a split-second for him to regroup and plan his escape: Outside, *outside*, away from this hated place. He'd run all the way to New York—he felt as if his legs would be able to carry him that far. Then he'd jump on the first ship headed east. Something was churning up from his very core, something that turned his heart into a jackhammer and his legs into pistons...he would run and run until he ground his limbs to bloody pulps.

He flew out the front door, looked quickly over his shoulder, and ran smack into Shannon Casini.

They bounced off one another, like two billiard balls cracking apart.

"Andrew—" Shannon broke his fall and grabbed at Andrew. Andrew twisted and fell on top of him.

"Sorry—" Andrew disentangled himself from Shannon's flailing arms and scrambled to his feet. He helped Shannon up.

"Andrew!" Mr. Scurlock stormed out the door. Behind him billowed the entire Phys. Ed. class, a gigantic cape of drooling disaster seekers.

Andrew moved quickly behind Shannon.

"What's going on?" Shannon asked.

Mr. Wachtel, the principal, darted out of the building. After herding the other boys back inside, he addressed Mr. Scurlock.

"What's the problem?"

"He assaulted me—he also used profanity!"

"Profanity?" Andrew was bewildered. Was *twit* some sort of ghastly swear word in America?

"He used the *S-H* word!" Mr. Scurlock hollered at Shannon.

"The *S-H* word—*What!*" Andrew cried. "I *didn't!*"

"You *did!*"

"Did *not!*" Andrew turned to Mr. Wachtel. "I called him a *twit!*"

Shannon made a funny, muffled snort; he grimaced, put his hand over his mouth. Mr. Scurlock glared at him.

"Let's go inside and sort this out," Mr. Wachtel urged.

"I want him suspended! Better yet, *expelled!*" Mr. Scurlock yelled.

"Earl, calm down," Shannon said.

"You keep out of this, Shannon!" Mr. Scurlock snapped.

"Let's all go inside, shall we?" Mr. Wachtel pleaded.

Shannon put his arm around Andrew's shoulder and escorted him back into the building. Mr. Scurlock and Mr. Wachtel followed them.

Andrew sat in the outer office with Shannon while Mr. Scurlock ranted and raved in Mr. Wachtel's office. Mrs. O'Neal and Consetta ceased activity at their typewriters, inclined their heads slightly, and listened to the goings-on within.

After a few minutes, Mr. Scurlock huffed out. He didn't so much as look at Andrew, or at Shannon.

"Andrew." Mr. Wachtel stood at the door.

Andrew looked at Shannon, and it was then that he felt the tears stinging his eyes. Shannon put his hand on Andrew's shoulder.

"Let's talk things over, okay?"

It was decided that Andrew should be suspended for the rest of the week, effective immediately. Mr. Wachtel seemed a bit reluctant to sentence Andrew to this sort of banishment; Andrew took the news with an impassive glare, all the while silently rejoicing.

Consetta got his books and things. Shannon offered to drive him home; before leaving, he called Lois and explained what had happened.

On the way home, Shannon tried to soft-pedal Andrew's punishment.

"You know, you really can't expect to slam a teacher in the nuts with a basketball and get away with it. Mr. Wachtel just wanted to send a message to the other boys that that kind of thing isn't acceptable. Nothing personal." He grinned. "He doesn't want anybody else to get the idea that you've set a precedent for student-teacher relations."

Lois met them at the door, a look of consternation on her face. Shannon discussed with her what the plan should be for Andrew's exile.

"I'll stop in after school and bring his assignments, also catch him up on what we've been doing in English class."

"He was absent from school so much last year, he has the routine down pretty well,"

Lois said. "He was really good about getting his work done, and all of his absences didn't seem to hurt his grades very much—not at all, in fact." She smiled at Andrew. "Straight A's in everything, except Phys Ed."

After Shannon left, Andrew silently chomped on some freshly baked chocolate chip cookies. Lois sat across the table from him; every now and then he heard the soft clink of china, and knew she was sipping her tea. Finally, he looked up at her.

She gazed at him, a wistful, enigmatic look on her face.

He knew what it was.

Remembrance.

Andrew didn't let on to Lois how much he delighted in his exile. He settled into the same routine of home study that he'd enjoyed all the times he was ill the previous year. The only difference was, since he didn't need to rest, he could use the gym. After doing his schoolwork in the morning, he had a short workout before elevenses. He finished his studies in the afternoon, then did another work-out session downstairs.

Returning to school the following Monday, Andrew spent his morning classes in an agony of worry over having to re-enter Phys. Ed., which was his fourth period class. He trudged from his third period mathematics class to the boy's locker room and was just about to open the door when he felt a hand clasp his shoulder.

"Andrew."

He turned around and saw Shannon behind him, dressed in shorts and a short-sleeved shirt.

"I just talked with Mr. Wachtel—he's agreed to let you be excused from Phys. Ed., but you need some sort of alternative physical activity. Get changed and meet me at the front office."

Shannon didn't give any explanation and Andrew was too flabbergasted to ask what he had in mind. After changing into his gym clothes, he dashed to the office, where he found Shannon chatting with Mrs. O'Neal. Shannon smiled at him, then walked outside. Andrew followed.

"What—what are we going to do?"

"Stretch first." Shannon proceeded to do some leg stretches. Andrew copied him.

"Come on, let's go!" Shannon did a slow trot down the front walk, then picked up speed as he turned the corner. Andrew tagged along behind.

"Where are we going?"

"Away."

"What?"

"Away—" Shannon glanced over his shoulder. "Isn't that what you want?"

"Well—yes," Andrew huffed. "But where?"

"There are some nice open fields south of here. Best places in the world to clear out the cobwebs."

"Don't you have to teach?"

"This is my lunch period—I'd rather run than eat. Well, I usually grab a quick sandwich just before the next class."

They ran in silence for a few minutes, then Shannon said, "I talked with some of your classmates about what happened last week. They told me about what's been going on in Phys. Ed. class."

"What?"

"They say that Mr. Scurlock has been giving you a hard time, and that he was wrong on that call last week."

"Who says?"

"Some of the boys I talked with. I made it a point to talk with several of them—alone, that is. Kids are more apt to be forthright about things when there's no peer pressure involved."

They turned a corner and Andrew switched to the other side of Shannon.

"Whom did you talk with?"

Shannon didn't answer.

Andrew ran in front of him, twisted sideways, and repeated, "Whom did you talk with?"

Shannon's head snapped in Andrew's direction. "Did you say something? I can't hear out of this ear." He pointed to his left ear.

"Sorry?"

"I'm deaf in this ear—got a bad cold when I was a kid. It went into an ear infection that destroyed the hearing in my left ear."

"Oh, sorry."

"What did you say?"

"Whom did you talk with? About Mr. Scurlock, I mean."

Shannon grinned. "I don't divulge my sources. Suffice to say, not everyone in the class hates you, Andrew."

Andrew frowned just as Shannon glanced at him. He was momentarily taken aback by the look on Shannon's face—the same *Anything wrong, old chap?* look his father used to give him. They turned another corner. The blocks of tightly packed houses gave way to open fields.

"You okay, Andrew?" Shannon asked.

Andrew couldn't help but smile.

"I'm fine."

Andrew wondered if Lois would write to his mother about what had happened. Though he could usually predict what Lois would do in any given situation, he wasn't quite sure whether or not she would make his mother aware of things. On the one hand, Lois was not one to dissemble or keep things from people. On the other hand, Andrew suspected that she wouldn't want to trouble his mother over his misbehavior. He also suspected that it was not so much that Lois didn't want his mother to worry, but that any hint of trouble might be used as a pretext for bringing him back to England.

The next few letters from his mother verified the latter assumption. His mother made no mention of the incident. If she had been informed of it, she *surely* would have written something appropriately admonishing. Instead, her letter gushed forth with happy exclamations over Lois's glowing reports of his progress:

She wrote that you're growing like a cornstalk, Andrew! See—it really is better that you remain in America. You know I only want what's best for you, darling, so keep "chowing down" and remember to bundle up, now that winter's coming. Let's hope that you don't have so many nasty colds this year.

He wrote his mother yet another letter, pleading to be allowed to return to England by Christmas holidays:

Even though I had a very nice Christmas here last year, I would so love to spend Christmas at Greycliff. I can't bear the thought of spending another Christmas away from England. Collie has taught me to play Christmas carols, and I could bring my guitar with me when I come back to England, and we could both give a Christmas concert—you on the piano and me on the guitar. Wouldn't that be smashing! I'm sure Grandmother Howard would be ever so pleased. Although it's all very nice here in America, I miss England, and it would be so wonderful for us to spend Christmas together!

The very day he posted his letter, an announcement on the evening news chilled him to the core.

The reported "gas main explosions" in his country were not gas explosions at all, but a horrific new weapon, the V-2. Unlike the V-1s, which cruised along like airplanes and could be shot down or nudged to their doom, the V-2s were rockets, flung from launching sites in Germany. After blasting up into a trajectory sixty miles above the earth, they screamed down at five times the speed of sound and exploded their fury upon the enemies of the Third Reich.

A letter arrived from his mother several days later:

So you see, darling, it was all for the best that you didn't return to England. Who knows what might have happened? These rockets are the ghastliest things of all—there's absolutely no warning, no way to detect their presence until they crash down. With the buzz-bombs, at least, they made a funny whirring noise as they passed overhead, and as long as the noise didn't stop, you were safe. And we could deal with them—at the end, before the launch sites were captured, only one in six of the V-1s managed to get through our defenses. With these beastly rockets, there's no defense at all, save defeating Germany once and for all. And until the white flag goes up over Berlin, you are to stay in America.

I've said this before, but you must believe me—all I want is what's best for you, darling. Keep eating Lois's wonderful food, stay well, and pray for the war to be over soon.

When Lee's family came for Thanksgiving, Lee-Ann rushed into Andrew's waiting arms. After she exclaimed over how much he'd grown, he exclaimed over how tall she was getting, which she was.

"You talk like a grown-up, too," she giggled.

She'd lost some of her baby fat, though none of her little-girl charm. She brought along her "Daddy's book" and Andrew looked at it with her and asked her more about the "happiest times" that were set down within its pages.

His quarterly height check and weighing in on December 4 revealed that he was now sixty three inches tall and weighed 114 pounds: a two-inch, ten-pound gain from September.

With the coming of December, Andrew hoped that some sort of last minute dash by the Allies might expedite his return to England before the holidays. The British and American armies were already advancing upon German soil, and Allied planes were bombing Berlin at will. Gerry wrote that it was rumored General Eisenhower had a standing bet with Montgomery that the war would be over by Christmas.

End of the war in '44 was on everyone's lips.

Before Christmas, please God! Andrew prayed every night after looking up at the dark sky and thinking of his father and Aunt Jane.

After all, Christmas was supposed to be a time of miracles.

He walked down the stairs, rubbing the sleep from his eyes. The radio crackled with some sort of war news; every so often Andrew caught the word *Ardennes.*

"What's going on in the Ardennes?"

Lois shook her head in dismay.

"Just when we thought everything was going so well—"

"*What?*" Andrew's voice split with panic. Lois threw him a worried glance, then continued. "The Germans launched an offensive in the Ardennes—sounds like this is an all-out assault...." She shook her head again.

Andrew stumbled into the dining room and sank onto a chair.

God stone the crows! I won't be able to leave this place until hell freezes over!

Even the flurry of Christmas cards that descended upon him failed to check his melancholy. He received holiday greetings from his mother, Grandmother Howard, Aunt Jane, Gerry, Mary Jo, Kaz, Marlys, Mr. Nugent, and Peter, who also enclosed an invitation:

The golf course behind our house is all covered with snow it is cracking great fun to ski on and Grandfather and Grandmother Barrett say you can spend Christmas holiday with me I can teach you to ski would you like to come?

As further distressing news of what was now being called "The Battle of the Bulge" made its way back to Andrew, he decided that he might as well spend his Christmas holidays in Holyoake, since God wasn't being very cooperative about returning him to England. Lois said that she would take him to New York the day after Christmas and put him on the train to Massachusetts.

Shannon came down with the flu just before the annual Casini Christmas concert. Andrew was pressed into service in his stead by Collie, who offered him a month's free guitar lessons in exchange for his being the third member of the Casini trio.

As he strummed an accompaniment to the mandolin duet by Collie and Mr. Casini for *O Little Town of Bethlehem*, Andrew felt a quiet joy and assurance deep within his soul that the beautiful music he was helping to create was making its way to his father's waiting heart.

When he's back, I'll be able to play for him, and he'll hear and see and feel it all at once!

Next Christmas—please God!

He awoke late the day after Christmas, which was the day Lois was to take him to New York. Descending the stairs, he expected to be greeted by the usual sounds and smells of breakfast cooking.

But the house was deathly silent as he tiptoed down the stairs.

"Andrew?" Lois's muffled voice wafted down the stairs. Andrew took the steps, two at a time, up to the second floor. Lois called again from the master bedroom, and Andrew cautiously opened the door.

"Lois?"

"Oh, Andrew—I'm sorry, I've got a whopping case of some kind of indigestion or bug or something. There's some strudel left over from yesterday—it's in a pan on the top of the refrigerator. Would you mind dishing out your own breakfast? I think I might be okay by lunchtime—"

"Are you sure it's nothing serious?" Andrew was alarmed by the whiteness of her face, the taut grimace of her lips.

"Sure, sure, it's nothing. I'll be able to take you into New York tomorrow, okay? I'll call the Barretts and let them know."

"Is there anything I can do for you? Would you like a cup of tea?"

"No...no tea...could you—" Lois's face was suddenly contorted by what Andrew could only imagine was excruciating pain. She reached under the covers and produced a hot water bottle. "Could you please fill this again with hot water? It really seems to help."

"Of course." Andrew took the water bottle, refilled it, and tiptoed into Lois's room. Lois, her eyes squeezed shut in agony, was arching her back and biting her lip.

"Lois? Are you all right?" he asked.

"Fine—I'm fine, really, just fine...just a little gas, I think, that's all...."

Andrew handed her the hot water bottle. "I'll call your husband if you think there's something wro—"

"No, nothing's wrong—I'm fine, really. Don't bother him." She forced a smile that looked more like a gash of pain.

Andrew nodded, turned and left the room.

He tried to interest himself in eating breakfast, but even the delicious pastry stuck to the roof of his mouth. He washed it down with a gulp of milk. Lindy furiously rubbed his head against Andrew's leg and wailed plaintively.

"Something wrong, Lindy?" Andrew reached down and rubbed Lindy's ear. Lindy looked up and gave a loud meow, like a cry of distress.

Andrew pondered his dilemma. On the one hand, Lois had assured him that she just had a bad case of indigestion, or a bug—nothing to worry about. And she *had* asked Andrew not to bother her husband.

On the other hand, what if something *was* wrong?

Even as he picked up the receiver and dialed the number for the pharmacy, he felt as if he were doing something horribly wrong. He tried to keep the panic out of his voice, but he feared he wasn't very successful. Mr. Givens arrived within minutes, flew up the stairs, then called for him after only a few heartbeats, or so it seemed to Andrew. Andrew clambered up the stairs and found Mr. Givens, ashen-faced, in the hallway with Lois slumped against him.

"Help me get her down the stairs, Andrew."

With Andrew supporting her on one side and Mr. Givens half-carrying her on the other, Lois was conveyed down the stairs and out to the car, where she collapsed on the backseat.

Andrew sat on the front seat, next to Mr. Givens, who far exceeded the prescribed victory speed limit as his hands clutched the steering wheel. Andrew wanted to ask him if Lois was going to be all right, but he knew that he shouldn't. They sped to the hospital as Lois's moans turned into shrieking gasps of pain.

"Appendicitis—it was a good thing you got her here right away, before it ruptured," the surgeon said.

"Can we see her?" Mr. Givens asked.

"She's still very groggy, so don't be upset if she doesn't recognize you."

"We won't be." Mr. Givens looked at Andrew. "Just as long as she's all right."

"She'll be fine." The surgeon turned, and walked back down the corridor. Mr. Givens and Andrew followed him.

Lois looked like a frightened child against the stark white hospital linen. She tried to talk, but her words came out as soft, garbled moans.

"Don't try to talk," Mr. Givens whispered, giving her a gentle kiss on the forehead. Her hand thrust out, grabbed Andrew's arm. He put his hand on top of hers and she gave him a look that was a mixture of apology and thankfulness.

"I'm just glad you're all right." Andrew squeezed her hand in reply.

Mr. Givens took Andrew back to the pharmacy, for, family emergency or no family emergency, there were prescriptions to be filled. There was a stack of boxes in the back of the store.

"Our weekly order came in today," Maybelle, Mr. Givens's cashier, explained between customers. "I just haven't been able to get it put up—it's been so busy."

"I'll take you home in a minute, Andrew," Mr. Givens called from his cubicle. "Just have a few orders to fill."

"I don't mind staying," Andrew replied. He looked at the tower of boxes, at the crush of customers, and knew he didn't want to spend the rest of the day in a quiet, empty house.

He walked to the back of the store and pulled down the top box.

"Where does the toothpaste go?" he called to Maybelle.

"Andrew, you don't have to do that," Mr. Givens protested.

"I don't mind. I'd rather keep busy, actually."

Maybelle showed him where everything went, and he put away a week's worth of toothpaste, soap, shampoo, and other sundry items.

As he was organizing the magazine rack, a teenaged boy sauntered into the store.

"Delivery for Mrs. Yerganian, Alex," Mr. Givens said.

The boy insolently put his hands on his hips.

"Charge, right?" he said.

"Yes, charge, Alex," Mr. Givens sighed. He handed a package to the boy.

"Here's your tip, Alex," Maybelle said. She fished a nickel out of the cash register and handed it to him as he walked out.

Andrew walked over to Maybelle.

"What was that all about?"

Maybelle glanced over her shoulder at Mr. Givens.

"Means they pay when and if they can. He's too soft-hearted for this business, figures no one should go without medicine they need just because they can't pay for it. He carried dozens of families during the Depression." She scooped a dime out of the till and gave it to Andrew. "Here, why don't you get yourself a cup of cocoa? There's a diner two doors down."

Mr. Givens took him out to the diner for supper. They ordered the blue-plate special: ham, cabbage, and boiled potatoes. Andrew stared out the window until they were served. As he started to cut his ham, he felt an awful lump in his throat. He put his utensils down.

"What's the matter, Andrew?"

The words started to choke in his throat.

"I was just so worried—I'm sorry she was really ill, but I would have felt terribly if...if it had turned out to be nothing—I just didn't know...."

Mr. Givens laid his hand on Andrew's arm.

"Even if it had turned out to be nothing more than a bad case of gas, you did the right thing. When it comes to the safety and well-being of someone you love, it's always right to err on the side of caution."

"But she said she was all right—I didn't want to—to—"

"She'd be at death's door insisting she was fine. She never thinks of herself—" Mr. Givens quickly looked down, blinked. Andrew gazed out the window. After a minute, he heard Mr. Givens clear his throat, then say softly, "I'm glad you were there, Andrew."

Andrew swallowed, looked back down at his plate.

Mr. Givens cleared his throat again. "Well, you'll have to fill in for her at the poker game this Thursday. Or are you already a regular?"

"What?" Andrew's head snapped up.

Mr. Givens smiled. "I've known for years."

"You—you mean you don't mind Sarah not—not—"

"Sarah's a very special person, and I'm glad she's Lois's friend. I'd pay her just to show up—wouldn't care if she played poker all day and ate us out of house and home, but she has her pride, you know. And—" Mr. Givens's smile broadened. "Half the fun of it is that they think they're getting away with something. You won't spill the beans about this, will you?"

"Spill the what?"

"You'll keep it a secret that I know, all right?"

"All right." Andrew smiled, and took a bite of ham.

Suddenly, a thought hit him.

"How did you know about me? That I play poker, I mean?"

"Oh, Jake told me."

"*Jake?*"

"Yeah, he said you creamed a bunch of GIs aboard the *Queen Mary* by pretending you didn't know the game."

"He *did?*"

"Yeah—he thought it was just terrific. Well, eat your supper. You want some apple pie for dessert?"

After supper they visited Lois again. She was a bit more lucid, though quite upset over not being able to take Andrew to New York. Mr. Givens suggested that Mary Jo might be able to meet Andrew at the train station and put him on the right train for Massachusetts.

When Mr. Givens called Mary Jo the following morning, she was more than happy to help out. She had the next few days off and offered not only to meet Andrew, but to have him spend the day in New York with her, if he could come right away. She and her roommates were going to the theater to see *Oklahoma* that evening and had an extra ticket because a friend had canceled. Andrew could go out to dinner with them, see the show, and stay overnight at their place. Mary Jo would put him on the train to New England the next morning.

Although Andrew was certain he wouldn't be interested in a stage show about the *bugger-all* of the American West, he thought it would be churlish to refuse.

And so it was arranged. Mary Jo met him at the station, and led him through the maze of shrieking streets to a bus stop, from where they caught a bus to her flat, which in America was called an "apartment."

It was a "fourth-floor walk-up" and walk up four flights they did. In the corridor, they met with a young woman with a nasally New England twang and an older woman with a thick German accent. They were grappling a mattress towards Mary Jo's apartment.

Mary Jo introduced them as Betty, her roommate, who was from Maine, and Mrs. Stumpff, their neighbor, who was loaning them the mattress.

"So you are my girls' little friend from *En-ge-land*!" Mrs. Stumpff asked Andrew.

"Um...Yes." Andrew felt as if he were being interrogated.

"Goot."

Mary Jo grabbed the middle of the mattress. "In the front bedroom," Betty directed Mrs. Stumpff, who was at the leading end.

"We're putting you in Marsha's room—back there." Mary Jo indicated a room just next to the bathroom, near the hall entrance. Marsha's going to bunk with us."

The women got the mattress wrestled into the front room and threw it on the floor between two twin beds.

"Time for a coffee break!" Betty plopped on the sofa.

"Did someone say *cawfee* break?" A voice in a broad New York accent cracked across the room.

"Marsha! What are you doing home so soon?" Mary Jo asked.

"Delivery room's as quiet as a convent, so I took the rest of the day off."

"What sort of delivering do you do?" Andrew asked.

"Human *beans*, kiddo!" Marsha mussed his hair. "Creatures like you, only smaller. Not as well behaved, either." She looked around, mock bewilderment on her face. "Someone said *cawfee*. Where's the *cawfee?*"

"I get you coffee—kuchen, too," Mrs. Stumpff said. She waddled out, and returned in a few minutes with a pot of coffee and a platter of the delicious pastry.

They sat down to eat. Andrew felt a little disconcerted, listening to Mrs. Stumpff's heavily accented German and answering her questions as to the whys and wherefores of how he happened to be in America. When she said something about "that hoodlum guttersnipe Hitler," he was positively flabbergasted. He thought it would be poor form, though, to discuss politics with her and inquire as to her reasons for her views.

Later, he broached the subject with Mary Jo, who told him that Mrs. Stumpff had left Germany just after Hitler came to power because she suspected he was "up to no goot." Later, her sister was shot for sheltering Jews.

"Both her sons are in the US Army in Europe," Mary Jo said. "They interrogate captured Germans." She also said that Mrs. Stumpff always looked out for "her girls": One time when Betty was working night shift, a drunk had started harassing her as she walked to the bus stop.

"Mrs. Stumpff flew outside, armed with a cast-iron frying pan, and gave the guy whatfor," Mary Jo chuckled.

They decided to go out and have crepes for dinner. As they walked along the city streets, Marsha and Mary Jo linked arms with Andrew and smiled at the passers-by, as if they were dating a movie star.

At the restaurant Andrew ordered their meals in French, which so impressed the waiter that he brought the chef out to meet them. The chef beamed and nodded as Andrew praised his cooking, then brought them out some samples of a special dessert he'd made.

There was a low murmur of conversation from a table nearby and Andrew saw, out of the corner of his eye, that the grumblers were four sailors, who were eyeing Andrew jealously. He tried to suppress a smile as he ate his dessert, thinking how odd it must look for a boy his age to be out on a date with three women in a city where the men seemed to outnumber the women by ten to one.

Crikey! If Dad could see me now!

After they were shown to their seats at the theater, Andrew eyed the program indifferently.

Oklahoma! Ought to be as boring as a newsreel about Alaska or Antarctica!

To his astonishment, the show was a marvelous riot of color and motion and wonder and passion and pride and hysterically funny songs. A man sang of the wonders of the Kansas City, a magical place with telephones, central heating, and indoor plumbing. Another song, *The Farmer and the Cowman Should Be Friends,* had each side throwing accusations against the other: Farmers were stingy, unfriendly, and guilty of the unpardonable sin of fencing in the rangelands. Cowmen were lecherous drunkards and not to be trusted. The song started out as a dance, but ended up in a hilarious brawl.

It was the song, *Out of My Dreams,* that touched him most deeply, for it was his own heart's cry for his father to step out of the shadows of nightly imaginings and take Andrew in his arms again.

The show ended with a jubilant tune, *Oklahoma,* sung with whoops and hollers. It reminded Andrew of his countrymen singing "There'll Always Be An England" in stodgy reserve; the two songs, so different, were both expressions of solidarity and pride. As Andrew joined in the applause, Mary Jo turned to him and said, "Look's like you enjoyed it, Andrew."

"Oh, it was smashing!"

"Great, wasn't it?" a sailor seated next to Andrew said.

"Yes, super!"

"What brings you to New York, kiddo?" the sailor asked.

"I'm going to New England tomorrow and I'm staying overnight here with my friends."

"How did you happen to wind up in America?" another sailor, in the next seat, asked. "I mean, if you don't mind me asking?"

Andrew shrugged. "The war."

The first man laughed. "Yeah, it sure has a way of getting people to see new places, don't it?" He stuck out his hand. "My name's Wally, and this is my pal, Marty. What's your name?"

"Andrew."

"Pleased to meet you, Andrew."

Andrew nodded. Marsha, seated on the other side of Mary Jo, called across, "Hey, Andrew—wanna get something to eat before heading home?"

"Super!" Andrew said.

"I heard nothing beat's Lindy's cheesecake, Andrew," Wally laughed. "Try and hold out for that. Hey—better yet, me and Marty was just talking about going out for some.

Why don't you come along with us—our treat. And—" He winked at Marsha, "If you could persuade your friends to come along, they'd get treated to Lindy's cheesecake, too—now don't that sound like a fine way to end up an evening?"

Marsha smiled shyly. "Well, I really don—"

"Hey, we wouldn't ask for anything more than your company—no phone numbers, no pestering, no following you home—just an hour. We just got in yesterday, just want to talk our fool heads off, don't we Marty?" He nudged his companion, who stuttered something unintelligible. "Marty's from Maine—he don't talk much."

"Really?" Betty leaned across Marcia. "I'm from Maine too."

"Howzaboutthat!" Wally exclaimed. "Two people from the Great State o' Maine, meeting in the Big Apple. This calls for a celebration!"

Marsha looked at Betty, who looked at Mary Jo, who shrugged.

"Well...."

"Great, it's settled!"

And before he could say *Bob's your uncle*, Andrew found himself wedged in with the women and the two seamen around a tiny table in a noisy restaurant and enjoying a delicious piece of cheesecake. Wally and Marty were actually merchant seamen, as Wally explained: "If you're in the US Navy and you get a screw-up for a captain, there ain't much you can do about it. If you're in the Merchant Marines, you can tell the captain to go to Hell, then you can find yourself a better boss!"

Andrew was more or less paired with Mary Jo, whose diamond-garnished ring finger spoke for itself. Betty and Marty seemed to gravitate towards one another, though they actually said very little, for Wally dominated the conversation with his stories of the sea. His tales were intended as entertainment for everyone, though he seemed to smile an awful lot at Marsha. Andrew knew that in England this particular pre-courtship activity was called "chatting up." He wondered what it was called in America.

"...now you never know what cold is 'til you been on the Murmansk run, so cold it'd freeze the ass off a polar b—I mean, uh, freeze the nose off your pretty little face." Wally grinned at Marcia, then took another bite of cheesecake and washed it down with a gulp of coffee.

"Well, this was back in '42, and we was on this CAM ship—that's Catapult Aircraft Merchant ship. See, the Krauts had these planes called Folke-Wulf Condors, long-range aircraft that would get a fix on the convoys and radio the U-boats to home in. So when we'd get the Condor on radar, we'd launch a fighter plane called a Hurricat off the CAM ship. The pilot would shoot down the Condor and while he was doing that, we'd put out a rescue boat, 'cause the Hurricat couldn't land on the ship, see? It was a helluva one way ride—the pilot would try to bail out near the rescue boat, then ride his dinghy and get picked up. That is, if all went well. If something went wrong and he went in the drink, he'd freeze to death quicker than he could spit. Jeez, I can't figure why anyone would want to do that for a living, but thank God there was nutcases who did, 'cause they were the only thing between us and them fuckin' Condors. Hurricat duty was volunteers only—a lot of guys were fighter pilots from the Battle of Britain who wanted some excitement, I guess."

"Remember that guy who almost bought it?" Marty said. "Guy we had to form a bucket brigade for, remember?"

"Yeah—" Wally leaned forward, talked a little louder. "We was heading back from Murmansk and we pick up a Condor out of Norway, so this Hurricat pilot zings off into the wild blue yonder and shoots the bastard down. We put the rescue boat out all right, but it was a real rough sea and the guy's dinghy flips over. By the time we get to him, he was froze solid as a block of ice."

"He was American," Marty added.

"Howja know that?" Wally asked.

"I heard him talking once."

"What do you mean you heard him talking—the guy was a clam!"

"He was talking to Doc—they knew each other from college."

"Doc?" Marcia queried. "You had a doctor on board?"

"Not a real doctor, just a Medical Officer," Wally said. "Doc—" he turned to Marty. "He was a pharmacist, wasn't he?"

"Pharmacy student. He never graduated. He went to Rutgers—you know, that college in New Jersey. I got to talking to him once and the reason I remember it was because one of my cousins went to Rutgers—"

Andrew froze.

"Shoot, an American—howzabout that!" Wally exclaimed. "Well, we get this guy back to the ship, and I thought he was a goner for sure. Doc gets all crazy and starts slapping the guy and screaming at him—like hitting a statue, I thought. So then Doc yells at us to get one of them big packing crates, and we set it up in the corridor outside the galley and line it with some tarps. Meanwhile Doc is tearing the guy's clothes off. Then we get him into the crate and we form a bucket brigade from the sink to the crate. We was slinging buckets of warm water down the line as fast as a cat streaking cross a hot sidewalk, and Doc was hollering and shaking and smacking him—"

"Was he all right?" Betty asked.

"Well, he came to, after awhile. Started thrashing and retching and screaming at Doc, like he was mad at him for saving him. He was hollering fighter pilot stuff, you know like, 'bandits above' and 'roger' and 'break, break!' And he was screaming 'Whyja do it?' over and over again. You'd think a guy who got half near froze to death wouldn't have much strength, but the guy was swinging like a prizefighter. Took three of us to hold him down. I thought he was gonna be all right, but then he came down with pneumonia, real bad. The last I saw of him was when they took him off the ship on a stretcher when we made port. His face had that awful dusky blue look—he was out like a light. Maybe he came through all right, I don't know." Wally glanced at Marty, then looked back at Marsha. "Hope he made it—he saved our hides."

"Yeah," Marty whispered.

No one spoke, and the silence seemed to accuse Andrew.

It wasn't him—there were probably other American pilots on Hurricats....

Marty cleared his throat.

He went to Rutgers....

"Yeah," Wally said. "I'd like to think he made it."

Why the bloody hell should I care...So what if they don't know if he made it or not?

"Andrew, is anything wrong?" Mary Jo asked him.

"Um—I'm fine." He scraped the last bit of cheesecake off his plate. "May I have another piece, please?"

As it turned out, Wally and Marty escorted them home and were invited up for coffee. Andrew excused himself and went into Marsha's room. Mary Jo sat with him for awhile and showed him pictures Gerry had sent her from France. Andrew smiled at a snapshot of Gerry wearing a beret, standing in front of the Eiffel Tower, with a comical expression on his face.

The next morning Mrs. Stumpff knocked on the door and presented them with a pan of freshly baked kuchen. When it was time for Andrew to leave, she fussed over what she considered was an unacceptable dearth of warm clothing. She went back to her apartment and returned with a sweater that had belonged to one of her sons, plus a hat and scarf, too. She also packed Andrew a lunch of two cheese sandwiches, some dried apples, and a hefty chunk of kuchen.

He rode to Massachusetts on the same route he'd taken the previous summer, but through a different countryside altogether. Once out of the city, the glistening whiteness of the winter landscape enchanted and soothed him. There was something about new-fallen snow that promised that all would come right, somehow, some way.

No sooner had he arrived in Holyoake than Peter was urging him outside for his first skiing lesson. Grandmother Barrett bundled Andrew up in Gib's old ski clothes and Peter loaned him the brand new steel-edged skis he'd gotten for Christmas.

"I'll use my old wooden ones, since I already know how to ski. You ought to have the steel-edged ones to learn on—skiing on them is as easy as kiss your hand!"

They tromped across the snow covered golf course, and Peter proceeded to give Andrew his first ski lesson.

However, steel-edged skis notwithstanding, Andrew found that this new endeavor *wasn't* as easy as "kiss your hand," though the sight of Peter whizzing down a small hillock certainly made it look so.

"Just point the skis in a *V* and press down on your inner edges. Whatever way the edge points, is the way you'll go. Look now—" Peter made a few turns back and forth. "See—piece of cake! Now, to stop, press both skis down, like this!" Peter came to a clean halt.

Andrew tried, but, before he could say *Bob's your uncle*, found himself face down in the snow.

"Don't worry, you'll get the hang of it! Try it again!" Peter snaked along, making it all look so incredibly easy.

Andrew tried again but met with a similar fate; this time, the snow got up his nose and into his ears.

"Here, I'll go right alongside you—" Peter skied from the top of a small rise back to Andrew's side. "Now go, then press your inner edges in to stop."

Andrew lurched behind Peter, tried to dig in the wretched skis. He jerked to a halt and fell face down again.

"Bloody hell!"

"No, that was positively smashing!" Peter exclaimed. "You stopped *before* you fell down!"

With the snow stinging his teeth, Andrew found it hard to believe that he did the right thing, but he was urged up by Peter and made to try again.

And again....

By the time dusk threw long shadows across the snowscape, Andrew had not only managed to go and stop without falling down, he'd also made a few respectable turns.

"Hey Wingnut! Hot chocolate for you and your friend!" Diane's voice cracked across the frozen white.

Over steaming cups of cocoa, Andrew's amazing progress with the tricky new sport was chronicled: Peter could hardly contain himself as he exclaimed over how quickly Andrew had learned.

"These new steel-edged skis are smashing!" Peter affirmed. "You can turn on a dime and they give you change!"

"Yeah, smashing is what you'll be if you don't take it easy," Diane admonished. She turned to Andrew. "I drove to Eaglebrook to pick Peter up for Christmas vacation. His class was just finishing up their ski lesson on the hill behind the school, so I thought I'd walk over to check things out. I expected to see a lot of falling down and trudging around. Well, here comes Wingnut on his steel-edged skis, zinging down the mountain, like a bat out of hell going to a fire!" She tousled Peter's hair.

When Peter went outside to throw snowballs for Madison, Diane chatted with Andrew over more cups of cocoa.

"That Pete's a pistol, isn't he? The first time we met, he shook my hand very politely, then asked, 'Have you ever been kissed?'" She laughed. "Liz was just mortified, but Peter was very insistent about needing to know. He said he'd told some GIs on the Queen Mary about me, and they had asked him to find out!"

She stirred her cocoa. "In a way, I've got the best of both worlds—two sets of loving parents. I met Liz last fall and really liked her right away. She and my dad are perfect for each other."

"Your mother seems very nice, too," Andrew said. He wanted to ask "What happened?" but thought Diane would be offended by such nosiness.

Diane smiled pensively, as if understanding his unspoken question. "My parents split when I was five. They were so young when they got married, but I think things would have worked out if it hadn't been for my Grandmother Pruitt—my mom's mother. She thought my mom married down, and still calls my father 'That man.' Well, my mom got married to Grant soon after that, and I was sorta mad about things. Grant, though, was really kind and patient, and neither he nor my mom ever said anything against my father, or ever made me feel like I was being disloyal by loving him." She gazed outside at Peter, who was flinging snowballs at Madison and hollering with glee as the exuberant canine caught them in her mouth.

Andrew polished his skiing skills over the next few days, getting to know every knoll and valley on the golf course behind the Barrett home. On the sixth of January Grandfather Barrett put him on the train to New York. Mr. Givens, who had taken the morning off from work, met him there; then they both took the train to New Jersey.

"Andrew!" Lois, lying on the sofa, held her arms wide for him. "Did you have a nice time?"

"Oh, yes, smashing!" Andrew gave her a hug. "I didn't expect you'd be home so soon."

"I *can't* stand hospitals," Lois said. "I finally convinced the doctor I could get better ten times faster in my own home. People from church have been bringing over casseroles for dinner, and Gene's gotten to be a gourmet chef in the breakfast department." She winked at her husband.

Mr. Givens leaned over and gave her a kiss. "Well, I'd better get back to work."

After he'd left, Lois said, "Well, there's a whole stack of mail for you on the front table. One of the letters has an APO return address on it, so I knew it had to be from Gerry."

Andrew walked over, saw the letter sitting on top of the pile.

His heart sank.

He picked it up and carried it into the living room, then froze, holding the letter in his hand. He couldn't bear to open it.

"What's the matter?" Lois asked.

"It's not from him; it's from someone else in his outfit." Andrew said. He stared at the unfamiliar handwriting, at the name *Sgt. Ryan Binde* in the left upper corner.

The room seemed to spin for a moment; the ticking of the grandfather clock sounded like hammer strokes. Lindy slept, oblivious to all sorrow and pain, in a triangle of sunlight.

The letter slipped through his fingers and fluttered to the floor.

Chapter 43

ois looked sharply at him, then at the letter lying on the floor.

Andrew was afraid to so much as touch the ghastly missive, as if leaving it on the floor indefinitely would somehow nullify the terrible news he knew it contained.

Lois slowly got up from the sofa and picked the letter off the carpet.

"Do you want me to read it?" she asked.

He hung his head. He couldn't even nod.

The sound of paper tearing, like an obscene shriek, then a soft moan from Lois....

She looked up at Andrew, and her eyes, brimming with tears, told him the worst.

"He's dead, isn't he?"

She nodded, wiped her eyes.

He shuffled over to her, and took the letter from her hands. He sank to his knees, and read the neatly penned lines.

Dear Andrew,

I'm an armorer in Gerry's squadron, and his friend, too. I didn't know if anyone would contact you, seeing as you're not related to Gerry, but I know he would have wanted me to tell you what happened.

On New Year's Day, the German Air Force launched an offensive against our airfields. Gerry was walking with his pilot to his plane when our base was attacked. As they ran to shelter, they were strafed. Gerry's pilot was shot up pretty badly, but survived, because Gerry threw himself on top of him. I wish I could say that Gerry made it too, but he didn't.

I still can't believe he's gone. I can't begin to tell you what a terrific guy he was, but I think you know that already. He was the best armorer in the whole squadron, and everyone's friend, too. He always had a smile on his face, and was always ready to lend a hand, or show a new guy the ropes. He was always tickled to get a letter from you, and he told me what a wonderful time he had at your grandma's place, after his accident. I went with him to Greycliff last Christmas along with some other guys from our outfit, and we sure had a swell time.

Andrew, I wish I could be writing you under better circumstances. All of us here are taking his death pretty hard. I'm always thinking I ought to be able to turn around and see him standing there with that goofy grin on his face, and it hurts like hell to know that he's gone for good.

If you want to write to me, you can, otherwise, I know how you feel.

Sincerely,
Ryan Binde

615

Andrew crumpled the letter and threw it against the wall.

"God, I wish I'd never met him!" His voice choked into a sob. "If only I'd never been friends with him...."

In the next second, Lois's arms were around him.

"Never think that turning your back on people is the way to solve things. It's worse than hate, Andrew."

He gulped, then slumped against her. It was more than he could bear. In his mind's eye, he saw all the dead bodies tumbling into a black void of despair...Audrey, Irene, Mrs. Beaton's husband, Aunt Gwen, Gram...all of them, gone forever and ever, Amen.

Lois hugged him tightly as the grief and rage sputtered out of him. Then she led him to the kitchen and pressed a cool wet washcloth against his swollen face. She tried to phone Mary Jo, and found out from Marsha that Mary Jo had already left for Kentucky, to attend a memorial service for Gerry. He had been buried temporarily in Europe; after the war was over his body would be sent home. Mary Jo wanted him buried in the Lexington cemetery, next to their mother.

"Betty went with her—I couldn't get off work," Marsha said. She told Lois the name of the church where the memorial service was to be held. Lois arranged to send some flowers there, which Andrew insisted on paying for.

The next day, Lois gave him the sad news that Sarah's son and Alida's husband had also been killed in the hostilities. Marshall had volunteered for combat during the Battle of the Bulge, and had to accept a demotion to Private for doing so. Alida's husband was killed, along with over five hundred others, when a V-2 hit a cinema in Antwerp.

When he returned to school, he found Cockney-Mouth in especially belligerent form. Andrew didn't know if he'd done something to provoke him, or if his tormenter was still angry over that mishap in gym class when the wayward basketball had bounced straight to Andrew, or if the boy sensed Andrew's grieving and vulnerability.

Perhaps all three. In any case, at recess Andrew found himself the target of shrill taunts and fists waving around his face in challenge. Miriam started to pull Andrew away, but this only whetted the boy's appetite for a row.

"Hey Slimey-Limey—need a girl to protect you?"

Andrew turned sharply around, ignoring Miriam's entreaties to turn his back on trouble.

"Whooee—Hardly-Trying wants to fight!" As the wagging fists came near him, Andrew instinctively clenched his hands and brought them up in a boxer's guard position, shielding his face. At the same time, he slid his left foot forward.

"Looky here everybody—Tiddlybits thinks he's Joe Lewis!"

A mob of students flowed to Andrew and his challenger, like iron filings drawn by a magnet.

"Hardly-Trying thinks he's a man!" Cockney-Mouth began to dance around, wagging his fists and taunting him in a quavery falsetto. Then he threw a jab, which Andrew easily blocked with his left forearm.

Cockney Mouth backed off a bit, glared hard at Andrew. His voice dropped to a gravelly rasp.

"I'll teach you a lesson, you little Limey shit."

It all happened so fast, Andrew wasn't quite sure what he did, or why; it was as instinctive and involuntary as a sudden sneeze. The boy lunged at Andrew, swinging his right fist in a wild over-hand punch, which would have knocked Andrew flat had he not quickly sidestepped to the right. As his tormentor lurched forward, Andrew then delivered a swift counterpunch: a solid left-hook to the boy's nose. There was a loud, squishy smack and Cockney-Mouth reeled back, shrieking like a tea kettle and covering his face with his hands. At first, Andrew thought he was only pretending to be injured; then he saw the blood spurting out from between claw-like fingers.

The sight of that crimson fountain caused something deep within Andrew to snap; he lowered his head and charged, connecting squarely with his adversary's mid-section. He heard a loud thud, then the sound of his own screaming as the two of them crashed down together. Then he was sitting on the boy's chest; his hands closed round the thick, fleshy neck. He was vaguely aware of Miriam attempting to pry his fingers loose.

Someone very strong was tugging him from behind. He thrashed wildly to shake away the interference. Miriam at last succeeded in disengaging his fingers from the boy's throat and he was pulled backwards. He turned, and found himself in Lynette's arms.

Shannon appeared, his face etched with shock. Cockney-Mouth lay in a heap: Every so often, soft wails emitted from behind his bloody fingers. Shannon looked from Andrew to the sodden mess on the ground, and back to Andrew again.

Lynette got up, and interposed herself between Andrew and his vanquished badgerer. Mr. Wachtel ran to the scene and bent over the moaning boy in an attempt to ascertain the extent of the damage, while Shannon pulled Andrew to his feet and silently urged him away from the scene.

As he was being conducted to the front office, Andrew had the same funny, floaty feeling he'd experienced when he'd come down with pneumonia.

When Mum took me upstairs to my room...then later when Dad came to see me....

Shannon sat him down in a chair by the door, then sat down beside him. Every so often he glanced at Andrew, but did not say anything.

Mr. Wachtel appeared. He raked his fingers through his thinning hair as he stared blankly at Andrew. Then he turned to Shannon.

"I have a meeting with the superintendent in ten minutes. Can you deal with this, Shannon?"

"Sure." Shannon stood, and motioned Andrew to Mr. Wachtel's office. Andrew clumped inside. Shannon shut the door, indicated to Andrew to sit in one of the two chairs by the principal's desk. Andrew paused a moment, then plopped down into the seat. Shannon sat down beside him, pressed his hands together and brought them up to his mouth, as if contemplating how to proceed. He cleared his throat.

"Andrew, I know how you feel—"

"You have no *idea* how I feel!" Andrew snapped.

"Lois told me about your friend," Shannon said gently.

Andrew turned away, then felt Shannon's hand on his shoulder.

"I'm sorry. I wish I could somehow make everything all right for you."

There's only one person who can make everything all right....

"I have a feeling that there's more to this than just the death of your friend. No matter what's happened, you're not going to solve anything by slamming other people around."

"I'm *not?* What the bloody hell do you think we're doing to Germany and Japan! We're bashing them into smithereens, so that we can have peace—."

"It's not the same, Andrew—"

"It's *not?* The only difference is, I just used my fists, and the people out there are using bullets and bombs—"

"Andrew, no matter what's happening out in the world, no matter how crazy things are out there—" Shannon waved his hand towards the window, "You have to make your own choices, and those are choices you'll have to live with for the rest of your life, war or no war." He was silent for a moment, gazed out the window as if contemplating something, then spoke.

"When I was about your age, I used to help my father out in his shoe repair shop after school. He not only worked all day in his store, he had a job as a night watchman too, so that he could make enough money to send me to college. He'd come home from the store around six, grab a few hours sleep, and then go off to his other job at midnight."

"Well, one afternoon I went to his store, as usual. I looked through the window and saw that he was sprawled in a chair behind the counter, asleep. I opened the door carefully, so as not to jangle the bell and wake him, and I started to work in the back. My father slept on, but then this guy burst through the door. He pounded his fist on the counter and bellowed, 'Casini, you lazy wop, gimme some service!'"

"I don't know what came over me. All of a sudden, my hands were around the guy's throat and I was bashing his head against the wall. Then my father's hands were on mine, and he pulled me away. He apologized all over the place to the man, which just infuriated me even more. The man stormed out, then my father turned to me." Shannon's face reddened.

"My father was really upset with me, because the guy could have made a lot of trouble for him, could have even sued him. My father would have lost his business, all that he'd worked for all his life, just because I lost my temper. I might have gotten into a lot of trouble, too. If the guy had gone to the police, I probably would have been charged with assault. If that had happened, I wouldn't be sitting here right now with you."

He put his hand on Andrew's shoulder.

"Andrew, everything you decide to do or say, or even think, is a choice about what kind of person you want to be. I know that you've seen more than your share of terrible things, and you've known more grief and pain and fear than most people endure in an entire lifetime. But you can't let that destroy the goodness that's deep down inside."

Andrew turned away; Shannon's words reminded him of another time, long ago, when his father had told him about the markings on chocolates and had talked about choices, too.

Shannon cleared his throat.

"I have to decide some sort of disciplinary action for this—nothing personal, but I can't let this go, you understand?"

Andrew nodded.

"Okay...." Shannon bowed his head for a moment, then looked at Andrew. "A week's suspension. I'll stop by every day and catch you up on the work in English class and bring you your assignments." He raised an eyebrow, as if asking Andrew's opinion.

Andrew glared back at him.

"I'm positively crushed."

Shannon smiled. "I'm sure you are."

The more Andrew thought things over, the madder he got.

Jake! It's all his fault that I'm stuck in this bloody place!

He plopped back on his bed and stared at the ceiling. If his exile had lasted for only a few months, it would have been bearable, but one thing after another had pushed his day of redemption farther into the future. Last December he had fully expected to be back in England in only a few months, but the invasion didn't go off in March as predicted, then when it did go in June the stupid Yanks had to get tangled up playing silly-buggers in the hedgerows. Then there were the bloody buzz-bombs, then the bloody rockets, then that bloody, bloody Battle of the Bulge. It had taken weeks for the Allies to regain the ground they had lost in that offensive and get back to where they had been at the middle of December. And, from all indications, it looked as if the final push into Germany was going to be the hardest thing of all.

I'll probably be here next Christmas, too!

Last year, he'd put aside his plans to sow discord between Jake and Mr. Givens, since he had not thought he would be around very long for his efforts to have any effect. But now....

The bastard is no doubt laughing up his sleeve that I've been stuck here so long. It wouldn't bother him one bit if this bloody war lasted forever!

Lindy nosed through the door and hopped up onto Andrew's belly. Andrew absently scratched the silky ears.

Best to finish what I started!

Andrew cleared away the supper things while Mr. Givens helped Lois up the stairs. After feeding Lindy and putting the dishes in the sink to soak, Andrew went out to the dining room with some hot chocolate and cookies.

"Thanks, Andrew." Mr. Givens looked up from the newspaper and smiled, then turned back to the paper. "Well, the Germans are in full retreat on the Eastern front, and Hungary just signed an armistice with the Allies."

"Hmmm...." Andrew forced a smile, sipped his cocoa. He glanced at the comics, then spoke, trying to sound as if he were making idle conversation.

"Is Jake going to join up with the Americans?"

Mr. Givens shrugged. "No point in that now—the war's just about over."

"Well, it's probably best for Jake to stay in the RAF. The Americans are very strict about certain things, like drinking, you know." He tried to sound casual as his eyes scanned the page; he didn't dare look at Mr. Givens.

"The RAF pilots go on pub crawls all the time, that's what my mother says. And Jake told me that he goes out drinking all the time with his fitter and rigger. When we went on board the *Queen Mary*, I saw him carrying a case of Irish whisky. The ship was run by the Americans, so it was dry, you know." He stood. "Well, I've got to finish up some homework—see you tomorrow."

The next day, Andrew received a letter from, of all people, Jake!

Dear Andrew,

My father wrote me about what happened to my mother. He was so glad that you were there, and that you called for help. I just wanted to let you know I'm very grateful for what you did.

I hope that things are going all right for you. I know it must be hard being so far away from England, but it looks as if the war here will be over soon. I know how much you want to see your mother again.

Best wishes,
Jake

Best wishes indeed!
I'll bet the bastard knows how much I want to see my mother!
Andrew tore the letter into bits, and flushed the hypocritical confetti down the toilet.

At breakfast the following morning, Andrew looked over his history book while Mr. Givens read a magazine.

Mr. Givens gave a *hmmm* of interest.

"What is it?" Andrew asked.

"Oh, this article here about another American who was in the Battle of Britain. Guy by the name of Art Donahue. He was burned too."

Andrew craned his neck to inspect the article.

Mr. Givens smiled at him. "It sure was great that your mother was able to look in on Jake when he was hurt."

Andrew cocked his head slightly, and evinced an expression of puzzlement.

"That's what I don't understand."

"What?"

"About my mother visiting Jake back in the fall of 1940, when he had his accident. Jake says he met my mother when she ferried a Spit to his base, but she didn't even *join* the ATA until March of 1941. It doesn't add up."

Mr. Givens glanced at him, startled, then a look of consternation clouded his face.

Good! Now Mr Givens knows his son is not only a drunkard, but a liar as well!

Andrew quickly got up.

"Well, I'll do the washing up. Would you like another cup of coffee?"

Andrew turned the dial on the radio to *Terry and the Pirates*. He'd gotten all his schoolwork done by two o'clock; Shannon had just been by with his assignments, and the rest of the day was his to enjoy. He might do a little studying at bedtime, if he felt like it, that is.

There was a knock on the door. Strange...Alida always walked right in, and Miriam usually called out his name. He got up to answer it.

A young woman with light brown hair stood on the front porch. She was tall, and dressed in slacks and a casual jacket. She eyed him quizzically, then asked, "Are you Andrew Hadley-Trevelyan?"

"Uhh...yes."

Who *was* this woman and *what* did she want with him?

"Andrew, who is it?" Lois stood in the kitchen doorway, drying her hands on a dishtowel.

"Hello," the woman said. "My name is Barbara Levand. I'm a reporter with *Life* magazine."

"*L—Life* maga-magazine?" Andrew sputtered.

Bloody hell! Is there not enough excitement in the war that correspondents are reporting on schoolyard scraps?

"May I come in?"

"Yes, certainly." Lois walked over and extended her hand to Barbara. "I'm Lois Givens. My son is married to Andrew's mother." Though Lois was friendly, she could not conceal her bewilderment.

Barbara shook hands with her, then fished into her shoulder bag and withdrew a small piece of paper. She handed it to Andrew.

He saw that it was the snapshot of himself on the *Queen Mary*.

"Is this you?" Barbara asked.

"Yes, it's me." He handed it back to her.

She smiled.

"So I've found you!"

"Found *me?*"

"Yes," Barbara said. "You have no idea what a challenge it was to find out your whereabouts. People have been asking about you."

"About *me?*"

"Yes, your picture was in an photo-article I did called *Children of War*."

"Yes, I know."

"You've seen it?"

Lois nodded. "Yes, we did."

Barbara smiled. "Well, we got a deluge of mail on that article, and Andrew's picture elicited the greatest response. A lot of people are wanting to know about 'the boy on the boat.' Here—" She withdrew a stack of letters from her bag. "You can read these, if you like. And they're only the tip of the iceberg. There are thousands more like them at my office."

"Would you like to sit down and have some coffee?" Lois asked.

"Yes, thank you." Barbara handed the pile of letters to Andrew. "I'd like to talk with you about something, but why don't you read some of these letters first?"

She walked with him the dining room. After seating himself, Andrew withdrew a letter from the stack and began to read:

Dear Sirs,

   Your article, "Children of War," has made me more aware of the awfulness of war than anything else I've ever read. We need to do something after this war is over, so that children will not ever again know the horrors of war, but I know that keeping the peace is going to be a lot harder than winning the war. That picture of the English boy playing poker with the American soldiers somehow gives me hope that we might be able to begin, somehow. Even though there may be differences between people, we can somehow work things out and be able to get along, maybe even be friends. We don't need to let the differences divide us. That's what I think this picture is all about.

   I'd like to know if you could write more about that boy. I hope that he is doing okay. It must have been hard for him, being sent so far away from home, but it looks as if he is making the best of things.

Andrew looked up at Barbara.

"All of the letters here are along the same lines," she said. "I'll leave them with you, so that you can read them, okay?"

Lois brought in coffee and peach pie, and Andrew handed the letter to her. She sat down and read it as Barbara went on. "Almost everyone who has written about 'the boy on the boat' has asked us how he's doing. We were a little stunned by the response, and it took some doing to find you. The soldier who sold that picture to us didn't even know your name, only that your mother was a ferry pilot and your stepfather was an American in the RAF. I got hold of the passenger list of the *Queen Mary* for that voyage, and proceeded to do some sleuthing; I have some sources in England, too. The fact that the soldier was pretty sure your stepfather was still in the RAF was a big help. Most of the Americans joined the US Army Air Forces two years ago."

"That's my son, Jake." Lois got Jake's picture from the living room and proudly showed it to Barbara, then nodded at the photo on the sideboard. "And that's Andrew's mother and Jake at their wedding."

Barbara gazed at the wedding picture a moment, then turned back to Andrew.

"I'd like to know if you'd be willing to have a story about you appear in our magazine. I'd be writing it, but it would be your story. Whatever you want to tell about yourself is up to you. You don't have to even be identified. We can give you a pseudonym, and not reveal where you're living, if you'd rather keep your privacy. People just want to know about you and what's happened to you. Will you consider it?"

Andrew was a little taken aback. All his life, decisions had been made for him without his having any say-so whatsoever; now someone was asking him to decide if he wanted his life to be an open book to millions of people. He looked at Lois.

"You don't have to decide now," Barbara said. "I want you to think about it, but I also want you to know that I believe a story about you will do a lot of good."

"Why?"

Barbara leaned back in her chair and gave him an odd look, as if she were evaluating him somehow, and as if she were pleased with what she saw.

"I believe that you represent something special. The constant theme of all the letters we got about you is that you have given people hope. With all the hatred and fighting and violence that there is in the world, people need that. They also need to believe that there is a way for people of different nationalities, different cultures, to put aside their differences and get along—even if it's just to sit down for a friendly game of cards."

Andrew looked at Lois, who was positively beaming.

"I think it's a *wonderful* idea! We probably should contact your mother, though, but I'm sure she would agree." Lois turned to Barbara. "She's still in England, so it might be awhile to get word to her."

Barbara smiled at her. "Certainly. I'll arrange for you to send a cable to her, at our expense of course. I'll leave the letters with you, and get in touch next week. Here's my card, in case you'd like to contact me." She put a card on the table, then stood.

"Thank you very much," she said.

"Not at all," Lois replied. She showed Barbara to the door. Returning to the dining room, she sat down next to Andrew.

"I think it's a wonderful idea, Andrew."

Andrew shrugged. The idea that everyone seemed to think he epitomized harmonious relations between differing peoples both amused and troubled him.

Should I tell Barbara how I really feel about America?

Mr. Givens didn't think it was a wonderful idea, though.

"Damn reporters, like a bunch of vultures. Always wanting to dig up blood and gore or something sensational."

"I don't think she's like that, Gene." Lois scooped out him another serving of mushroom and lentil casserole for him.

"They're all like that. If there's a gory angle to it, she'll find it."

"She said it would be Andrew's story—"

"What about what's good for him?"

Andrew's head followed the exchange back and forth, as if he were watching a tennis match. Lois and Mr. Givens seemed oblivious to his presence.

"It would be good for him, Gene—"

"All that publicity, like being in some kinda goldfish bowl. It would be too disruptive, and it wouldn't do him any good, might even do a whole lot of harm."

"Barbara said Andrew wouldn't even be identified, if he didn't want that. They would give him a different name, not even say where he lived, even."

"He'd still be on display. I just don't want him to get hurt, Lois. You never know what might come out of this."

She said this would be my story. She said I wouldn't be identified—but there are people who will know it's me.

He lay in bed, holding his father's book of poems to his chest.

Yes, there's someone who will know it's me....

He told Barbara he wanted to go by the name *Roger*. She didn't ask why he'd chosen that particular name. She just smiled.

"Where would you like to start?"

He was a bit taken aback.

"I thought you were supposed to know where to start. I mean, don't you usually ask questions or something?"

"This isn't an interrogation, Andrew. You tell me what you want me to write."

"I don't know where to start."

Should I tell her that I want my father to know I'm all right...that I think of him all the time?

No, Mum will read the story and then she'll worry....

If only, somehow, some way, I could let him know!

"Well, why not start at the beginning?" She leaned forward, and smiled.

"Beginning?"

"Yes, why don't you tell me about England?"

He told her all about England, about the bombing raids, the food shortages, about how the war had ravaged his country. He told her about his mother and all the different kinds of planes she flew, and about how she had dropped the load of candy on his school. He didn't mention her accident, though.

He told her about his voyage on the *Queen Mary*, about Peter and Sarge and Ray and Mikey and El and J.D. and Cowboy and the others, about the poker games and roach races and the Spike Jones shows. He told her about Lois and Mr. Givens and Lee-Ann and Lynette and Shannon and Collie.

He didn't tell her about Miriam, fearing that (what with their being the same age and all) things might be misinterpreted. Nor did he talk about how miserable he'd been in America.

He didn't say a word about Jake.

He talked about Kaz and Irene and Marlys, but didn't mention that Irene had been killed. He told her of the time he was bombed, but not about Audrey, only to say that a friend of his mother's had been killed in the blast.

"So you were bombed, and then dug out of the rubble?"

Andrew nodded. "I went back to get my flag. I'd gotten it to put on my birthday cake, since they didn't have any candles—"

"What kind of flag?"

Why was she giving him the third degree about a silly old flag?

"A Union Jack—wait, I'll show you. I was holding it when I got carried out, and I saved it and put it in my treasure box."

He ran upstairs to get it. It had somehow gotten to the bottom of his treasure box, and he had to take everything out to get it.

And then he realized how he could tell his father how much he loved him...how he longed for his return....

He set the flag on top of his father's book of poems, and carried them downstairs to Barbara.

"See—this is the flag I got—"

Barbara took it from him and inspected it carefully, as if it contained some sort of secret message.

"Were you hurt?"

"No, I was put in hospital, but that was because I got a concussion and breathed in some plaster dust, that's all—"

"What were you wearing when you got dug out?"

"My school uniform."

"What did it look like?"

"Um, a gray blazer and short trousers, a white shirt, and a red tie. The blazer had an *A* on the pocket, for Askew Court."

Barbara suddenly looked stunned.

What had he done to upset her?

"Is anything wrong?" he asked.

She glanced at the flag, then stared at him, a strange look of wonder on her face.

"No, nothing's wrong." She smiled. "What kind of book is that?"

"It's very special. It belongs—belonged to my father." He opened it. "I made this for him." He handed the leather bookmark to Barbara. "It marked this poem, here. I found the book after he...was shot down."

He handed the open book to Barbara, and she read aloud:

> *I've tried for many an hour and minute.*
> *To think of this world without me in it.*
> *I can't imagine a newborn day*
> *Without me here...somehow...some way.*
> *I can not think of the autumn's flare*
> *Without me here...alive..aware.*
> *I can't imagine a dawn in spring*
> *Without my heart awakening.*

She slowly closed the book.

"That's very beautiful, Andrew."

"Could you please put it in the story? I'd be ever so grateful if you would. It means a lot to me."

Barbara looked at him and Andrew had the funny feeling she was seeing someone else.

"Would you be able to? Please?"

She nodded. "Of course."

When Barbara greeted him the next afternoon, she presented a large brown envelope to him.

"I had this sent by courier last night."

"What is it?"

"Open it."

He opened the envelope and pulled out a large photograph. His heart skipped a beat. "It's *me!*"

He remembered the feel, and the sound, and the smell of being carried out of the rubble when he had been bombed, but he did not remember the sight of that awful time, for his eyes had been shut tight.

His school uniform was spattered with something dark—blood? And there was his mother leaning over him, her face contorted with horror and relief.

"Where did you get this?"

"We collected hundreds of pictures for the *Children of War* article. I had to sort through all of them, and only a few made the story. I almost picked this one, but then I came across the one of you on the *Queen Mary*. I had to make a choice between the two photos. Even though the picture of you playing poker with the GIs didn't really seem to fit with the other pictures; after all, it shows a kid with a smile on his face having a great time. Still, something inside me wanted that smiling boy in the center of the page."

She shook her head in wonder. "Incredible, that both those pictures were of you!"

She pointed to the photo. "I'd like to use this one in the story too. I was going to use the snap of you on the *Queen Mary* to begin the article, but I think this other picture should be in it also. I think it would be important to point out that you weren't always smiling and happily playing poker." She tilted her head, as if to ask him what he thought.

He shrugged. "Fine."

She put the photo back in the envelope, then looked at him.

"How do you *really* feel about being in America, Andrew?"

He turned away quickly, then composed himself.

"It's all right, I guess."

"You guess?"

"It's fine." He tried to sound sure of himself.

"Was it all that easy, coming to a strange land, being so far from your home?"

"Well...it's just the war. Lots of people have to go to different places."

"Yes." She laid her hand on his arm. "They do." She was silent for a long time, then said, "Would you like to go outside for a walk?"

"All right."

After getting their jackets, they walked outside into the sunlight. Barbara gazed up at the sky for a moment, then looked at Andrew.

"What do you want most of all, Andrew?"

"I want this stupid war to be over—doesn't everyone?"

No, not everyone....

"Of course everyone wants it to be over, Andrew. Why do *you* want it to be over?"

He was suddenly very angry with her.

"So I can go back to England! So I can see my father ag—"

He turned from her.

Then she spoke, in words that were measured and soft.

"So you think your father might still be alive?"

He stared up at the sky, then turned back to her.

"Just forget I said anything, all right?"

"Why?"

"I don't—" He swallowed to keep his voice from quavering. "I don't want my mother to worry—"

"That's what mother's are for, you know," she said gently.

He shook his head furiously.

"No—*NO!* I don't want her...her—"

Her arm went around his shoulder.

"Please don't write about it—please!" he whispered.

"I won't, if you don't want me to."

They walked on in silence.

"Do you think your father is alive?" she asked.

He didn't answer her.

"Andrew—" She stepped in front of him, and put her hands on his shoulders. "Andrew, I won't write anything that you don't want me to. But if you're going to clam up, I won't be able to write anything at all. Please don't shut me out—"

He closed his eyes, shook his head.

"Andrew, I can understand your not wanting your mother to worry. You want her to think that you're doing fine, don't you? And—" She tilted her head, as if she suddenly realized something. "That poem—you wanted me to put it in the article, because it would be a way that you could let your father know that you want him to come back, right?"

"Something like that," he mumbled.

She smiled at him. "Roger—that's your father's name, isn't it?"

He nodded, turned away from her. She squeezed his shoulder.

"Andrew, let's take the rest of the day off, all right? What I mean is, I'll quit being a reporter for the day. Nothing that you say for the rest of today will be used in the article. You can talk about anything you want. If you're absolutely miserable being here, if you hate everyone and everything, that's all right. Anything you say will be forgotten tomorrow. How about that?"

He stared ahead.

"Andrew, you can trust me!"

He shrugged.

"Okay, let's go home," she said quietly.

They walked back to the house in silence, then sat down on the sofa together. Barbara took the photo out of the envelope and looked at it again. Suddenly, her eyes narrowed. She pointed at his blood-spattered uniform.

"You said you weren't hurt—what's this?"

Something awful was churning up inside of him, a sick-making, desolate feeling of horror. He took a deep breath to force it down, but his gasp met with the anguish screaming out of him and produced a strangled cry. Barbara's arms went around him and he slumped against her.

"Andrew?"

He had to say it, even though it would tear his soul apart to even think of it. His words were half-screamed, half-whispered.

"They had to cut her to get me out...."

It seemed like hours...maybe it was. The ticking of the grandfather clock and the muffled sounds of Lois bustling about the kitchen were the only things he heard; Barbara's arms around him, the only thing he felt.

The tears came, and came in torrents; they coursed down his cheeks, silent, insistent, unceasing.

He must have slept, for he suddenly was aware that the shadows were longer, the room dimmer, and his face was dry.

He sat up, but didn't dare look at her. Lindy hopped up on his lap, so for awhile he stroked the furry back arched in demand for affection.

Without looking at Barbara, he said, "Levand—is that a French name?"

She didn't answer him right away, and he thought that she might be a little insulted. What an inane question!

"No, it's not. It's not even my real name, in fact."

"What?" He turned to her.

She looked at him, as if asking for...understanding.

"My real name is Levandauskas. It's Lithuanian. I changed it to Levand because—" She gave him a look that begged *please understand.*

"Well, I'd gotten out of college, and wanted to get a job as a journalist. It wasn't easy— this was during the Depression. I was told that if I didn't have such a 'foreign-sounding' name I'd have a better chance. So I changed it to Levand, and I got a job right away." She turned away from Andrew, spoke even more softly.

"I was always teased in school. Even though I was born in the U.S., I was always tagged as a foreigner. Even when I graduated from high school, the principal didn't even say my name when he handed me my diploma, just called me 'Barbara L.' I guess I just got tired of being different." She gave a soft snort of laughter. Something about the look on her face seemed to touch something deep within him, and he found himself pouring out all that he'd held back.

He talked of how distressed he was at coming to America, his problems in school, how he longed to be back in England. He told her that he'd been suspended from school, twice, for fighting. He told her about Gerry, too.

Lois invited Barbara to stay for supper. Because it was snowing and Lois worried about her getting back to her hotel in Plainfield, she insisted that Barbara stay the night also.

At supper, Mr. Givens was cordial, but not overly friendly. Barbara asked him about his business; she seemed to know quite a lot about biology and medicine.

Then she turned to Andrew.

"I need to have some pictures of you, so a photographer is coming out from New York tomorrow. Do you happen to have a picture of your mother?"

"Yes, I do. She's climbing out of a Spitfire. The picture was in a newspaper article."

"Oh, really? I'll have to see about getting permission from the paper to use the picture. Do you know what newspaper it was?"

"I have the article—I'll show it to you."

"Perfect!"

"This photographer," Andrew said. "What sort of pictures will he want?"

"It's a *she*, and her name is Amy. She'll probably want candid, natural shots—just showing what your life's like now."

After supper, Andrew stayed up late into the night with Barbara in the rose-papered guest room. He talked first of Irene's death, then about his mother's accident and about how afraid he was for her. He told her of Gram and Aunt Gwen, and also of Aunt Jane: how worried he'd been over her, and how relieved he was when he found out all was well with her:

"I wrote to her and asked her why she'd made the mistakes. She said she was so busy and tired, what with her duties and everything, that she just forgot about things. She used to be ever so good at remembering things, but what with the war and all—" He shrugged. "It bothered me a bit that she forgot, but I was still ever so glad that she was all right."

Amy arrived the next morning. She was a dynamo of energy, very gregarious and friendly. After chatting with Andrew, she let him take some pictures with her camera. Then she took a few photos of him: lying on the floor, listening to the radio with Lindy settled on his chest; helping Lois in the kitchen; practicing his guitar. Mr. Givens came home for lunch, and Amy took some pictures of him and Andrew, talking and munching sandwiches. Mr. Givens showed her the photos of Andrew's first Thanksgiving and all the pictures of his quarterly measurements, and Amy was quite excited over them.

"Could we use these in the article? We'll pay you for them."

"No charge," Mr. Givens smiled.

After lunch, Barbara suggested that they go for a walk in the new-fallen snow. They happened upon Lynette, who was taking her nephews and Lukey out for a cure of "cabin fever." Andrew introduced Barbara and Amy to her. When he mentioned that Barbara was a correspondent for *Life* magazine, Lynette's eyes widened.

"She's doing a story about me," Andrew said, a little embarrassed; then he explained how it all had come about.

Lynette turned to Barbara.

"So you're a writer! That's what I want to be, more than anything! How did you get to be a correspondent with *Life*?

"Well, having a college education under your belt is a big help. And, in the meantime, if you want to be a writer, write—about anything and everything."

"Oh, I do—all the time!"

Barbara smiled. "And read. Don't limit yourself to what's considered 'literature.' I'm interested in medicine too, and I took a lot of biology courses in college. I was assigned to England during the first few years of the war and got some interesting assignments because I knew more that the average reporter about medical things. I once did a story about pilots who'd been burned during the Battle of Britain. It was the hardest story I ever had to do, though. Seeing, and writing about, the painful ordeal these guys had to face every day as they recovered from burns and then got their faces and hands reconstructed by plastic surgery...." She shook her head. "Well, the word *courage* doesn't even come close. I still think about those guys, dream about them, even. Dr. McIndoe, the plastic surgeon who worked on them, used to send them out to walk around London, just so they could get used to being stared at. Once I went out with a group of them and it made me so furious to see the looks of revulsion on peoples' faces. These guys saved England—they didn't deserve to be treated like sideshow freaks!" She smiled, embarrassed, at Lynette. "I'm sorry, I'm getting up on my soapbox."

"Oh, no, not at all! I want to know all that you've seen and done and written about!"

"Well, that might take awhile, but I'll try to hit the highlights."

Andrew slipped away and started tossing snowballs to the boys and Lukey. Matthew found a piece of wood about the size of a baseball bat, and Andrew acted as a "pitcher," throwing snowballs at the youngsters, who took turns at "bat." Amy skipped around them, shooting one picture after another.

Lukey started complaining she was cold, so Andrew picked her up and snuggled her against him for warmth, then walked over to Barbara and Lynette.

"...the important thing is not so much *what* you're writing, but *why* you're writing it," Barbara was saying. "If you're just writing to entertain, or think that people only want to read about something sensational, then you haven't accomplished much. Maybe you want to make people aware of something they didn't know. Maybe you want to shake them out of their complacency, make them think, change what they believe. You have to have a goal in everything you write."

Lynette's face was aglow with—well, it wasn't the cold, Andrew decided. Lukey squirmed out of his arms and ran to Lynette.

"Sorry, I'd better be getting these little ones in." Lynette picked Lukey up and gave her a hug. "It was so nice talking with you—thank you for—for talking about things. I'll be looking for your story."

They arrived home to the wonderful smell of strudel and hot chocolate. Lois had certainly outdone herself.

Andrew went upstairs to get the picture of his mother. His sweater had gotten a bit damp, so he took it off and threw it over his bedstead. As he sorted through his drawers for another sweater, his hand brushed against a scrap of paper. He withdrew it, and saw that it was a Hershey wrapper with the name *Kevin Ferguson* and an APO written on it.

Sarge!

He'd forgotten all about Sarge's offer to write and now, holding the slip of paper in his hand, he knew he needed to get in touch with him.

Gerry's gone—I should have been writing to Sarge all along, too....

As he put the paper into his treasure box, he noticed the snapshots Gerry had sent him. He grabbed them and brought them downstairs, along with the framed picture of his mother. Amy exclaimed over the photos, saying they were "just perfect" for the article. She also thought it would be nice to have a few "formal" shots of Andrew, so she arranged for him to go to New York with Lois the following Saturday.

Barbara and Amy left that night. The following Friday afternoon, Lois took Andrew on the train to New York. They had dinner and checked into a very nice hotel, courtesy of *Life* magazine. Amy wanted to have the photo shoot at the studio the next morning, then go out in the city in the afternoon.

Andrew was a little nervous about the photo shoot. The studio was cavernous and intimidating: dark in the corners, bright gashes of light angling in all different directions. The make-up session was horrid—he hated getting that gooey stuff slopped all over his face. ("Just to take the shine off," Amy soothed.) He'd brought along a few changes of clothes, as Amy had asked him to, and she settled on a gray tee-shirt, which was a little too small for him, and a pair of blue jeans, which were a bit too tight; Lois had bought them at the beginning of the school year and he'd almost outgrown them.

"Perfect!" Amy pronounced.

She had him stand against a mottled blue backdrop.

"Now, fold your arms—not so tight—here—" She pulled a small table behind him. "Lean back against this and cross one leg in front of the other—big smile now!"

He smiled tensely as she took the first shot.

"Loosen up Andrew—really smile. Think about your first kiss!"

"What!" he blurted. Amy took the next shot.

"That's a throwaway, Andrew, but you've got the idea!"

He wanted to protest that he'd never been kissed, but instead, blushed furiously. Amy snapped another picture.

"Hey Andrew!" Lois called. "When you have a pair and two wild cards, is that two pair or four of a kind?

As Andrew laughed, he heard the click of the camera.

"Perfect!" Amy exclaimed. "Now say 'Frankly my dear, I don't give a damn!'"

Andrew grinned. "If *I* were Rhett Butler, I'd say, 'Stuff that for a game of soldiers, Scarlett!"

He heard more clicks as he spoke, then Amy told him one joke after another as she took several more shots.

It was close to noon and Barbara thought it would be a good idea to break for lunch. Lois gave Mary Jo a call, to see if she might be able to meet them for lunch. As it turned out, Marsha and Betty were also off for the day. Mary Jo suggested meeting at a tea-room called *Zoya's* that she'd recently discovered. Barbara and Amy thought that sounded like a great idea.

"We can get some more shots of you around the city this afternoon," Amy said.

Arriving at the restaurant, Andrew greeted Mary Jo with a swift, fervent hug. She seemed even more precious to him now that Gerry was gone, and he sensed that she felt the same about him.

As they sat around a large round table, feasting on all sorts of delicious sandwiches, Andrew was aware of the murmur of disgruntled voices, all emanating from unattached sailors and soldiers at neighboring tables.

Crikey—I'm having lunch with six women! If only Dad could see me now!

Zoya, the proprietress of the tea house, was a tiny Russian woman with sparkling eyes and a hearty laugh. She was overjoyed to find out that Andrew was English.

"The English—they give it to those Germans, first and best!" She brought him some incredible layered dessert ("No charge for English!" she proclaimed) and Amy took a snapshot of Andrew presiding over the grand creation, fork poised and eyebrows raised in delight, with Zoya beside him glowing with pride.

After lunch, as they were strolling along to see the sights of New York, Marsha and Mary Jo walked along either side of Andrew, linked arms with him, and flashed wide smiles for Amy's camera.

Marsha invited them all to her mother's home on Staten Island for Sunday dinner the next day. As they rode the Staten Island ferry the next morning, Amy got a few shots of Andrew standing against the railing, with the Statue of Liberty in the background.

Dinner with Marsha's family was a lavish, noisy affair. There were scores of sisters and aunts, and dozens of cousins. Marsha's grandfather, a soft-spoken man who'd fought in the Great War ("with the English," he smiled), chatted with Andrew while the women clanged and hollered in the kitchen and produced all sorts of wonderful things with bizarre names: lasagna, mannicotti, calzoni, and cannelloni.

After he'd returned to Scotch Plains, Andrew wrote to Sarge, telling him about the last year and a half (the highlights, of course), and about the article:

We had a cracking great time in New York; somehow it seemed so different from what I remembered from my arrival here. Barbara said the article should appear sometime next month, so watch for it!

I apologize for not having written sooner; I'm afraid I misplaced your address. It was a little rough for me here at first, but things are better now. I hope you're doing well. Please write if you can, even if it's just a few lines.

Waiting to hear from you—

Andrew

A letter arrived from his mother, containing distressing news: She was ferrying planes to the continent:

Oh Andrew, you can't imagine how <u>wonderful</u> it was to fly over the Channel and touch down in France! I felt your father's spirit with me, seeing the reciprocal course, knowing that we are so close to realizing the end of this awful war. Almost five years since the Germans tore through France and tossed our army into the sea, though it seems a lifetime ago that the world was at peace....

Andrew groaned.

Bloody hell! Why does she have to go silly buggers all over Europe—there's still a lot of shooting going on!

If only she'd stay in England!

Barbara was waiting for him when he got home from school the next day. She presented him with a large box, which she said was "part of the surprise."

He opened it to find two thick photo albums.

"Amy made these up—" She handed one to Lois. "For you and your husband, and one for you, Andrew. They have all the pictures she took. She sent one to your mother, too."

Andrew flipped through the leather-bound album. There were literally hundreds of snapshots, more than had been taken of him in his entire life up to that time.

What a wonderful thing to be able to give to my father when he comes back...It'll make up—a little bit, anyway—for the years we've been apart....

He noticed a flat brown envelope, *Life*-sized, lying on the sofa next to Barbara.

"Is that the article?" he asked.

Barbara smiled as she handed the package to him.

"It just came out—it's hitting the newsstands just about now."

Andrew opened it, withdrew the spanking new issue of *Life*, and gasped.

"Crikey! I'm on the *cover!"*

He gazed at his picture, one of the studio shots: He'd been caught, mid-laugh, slouching back against the table, his arms crossed in front of him in a carefree way, as if he were having all the fun in the world. The shot was to mid-thigh, which surprised him, as he thought that it would be a rather formal portrait from the chest up. At the top right hand corner was the picture of him on the ship; below it was the photo of him being carried out of the rubble on his tenth birthday. The headline read: *The Story Behind the Boy on the Boat.*

Andrew was dumbfounded, and not a little perturbed.

"I shouldn't have worn that tee-shirt. And those jeans, they're a bit too tight...."

"As Amy would say—'Perfect'!" Barbara grinned. "My editor saw those studio shots of you and wanted you to be on the cover."

"But why me? I mean, isn't the war more important?"

"You're important too, Andrew." Barbara said, suddenly solemn. She took the magazine from Andrew, opened it to the story, and gave it back to him. He glanced through the pictures first: There was a very nice one of him and Mr. Givens: Mr. Givens had a smile on his face as Andrew chatted with him...another shot of him playing in the snow with Matthew and Mark...of him practicing his guitar...lying on the floor with Lindy on his chest. There were shots taken in New York of him walking down the sidewalk with Mary Jo and Marsha...on the Staten Island ferry...at Marsha's for Sunday dinner. There was also the picture of his mother, and the snapshot of himself and Gerry in England, and the photo Mr. Givens took of him at his first Thanksgiving.

Then he began to read:

I knocked on the door, expecting to see the same little-boy face that smiled over a straight flush on a troop ship as astounded GIs looked on. Instead, a young man, tall and solemn, politely greeted me....

He read on, as his story unfolded:

He would like to be called 'Roger,' after his father, who was a fighter pilot in the RAF and shot down in the Battle of Britain....

He saw, to his joy, his father's poem, and smiled at Barbara. As he read through the story, he was a little amazed by how Barbara wove the events of his life through a larger tapestry, not just of the war, but of the reasons and wherefores of how misunderstandings and prejudices take root. He read his own words:

When I was in England, we sort of looked on the Yanks as invaders. We weren't very happy about these strange creatures taking over our country. They were so different from us, so barbaric and loud and uncouth, at least by our standards. I remember my schoolmates saying nasty things about Yanks and I couldn't disagree with them, but then I got to know some Americans and found out that they really weren't so bad after all...I can't say that I was very happy about having to come to the United States, though. I found America to be a frighteningly strange country, and it took a lot of getting used to...It was difficult at first, and especially hard as I was teased because I was different, in the beginning, that is...There were very nice people, though, who befriended me, and that has made all the difference...I think I have more friends here than I ever had in England....

I know Mum would like to read that, Andrew thought. It's true, though....

I think that's the key, getting to know people as individuals, not looking on any group of people as a faceless mob. When I played poker with the GIs on the ship, we had a great time...I pretended, at first, that I didn't know how to play. When they found out that I was "taking them for a ride," they were just delighted, which quite surprised me....

The story ended with Barbara's question to him, and his reply:

I asked him what he wanted most of all.
He gazed into the distance for a moment, then said quietly, "I just want the war to be over."

He looked questioningly, gratefully at Barbara.

"Just a little dramatic license," she smiled. "Or rather, a little *un*-dramatic license. It still means the same, no matter whether you yell it or whisper it, doesn't it?"

Andrew nodded, then closed the magazine.

"Do you have another copy? I'd like to send this to my mother."

"Oh, I've already arranged that. In fact, it's winging it's way to her right now."

Andrew looked at the cover again, and pointed to the picture of himself with the GIs.

"I didn't realize how much I missed them. "This one—Sarge—" he pointed to Sarge. "He gave me his address. I wasn't very happy about things when I arrived here, and I just threw it in a drawer. I found it while you were here doing the story, and I wrote to him. I've been waiting for a reply—I hope he isn't upset that I didn't write to him all this time."

Barbara gazed at Sarge's face. "I don't think he will be. He looks like a very nice person."

"He is—all of them were, but especially Sarge. He sort of looked out for everyone, and he knew that I was a little upset about going to America. He tried to talk with me, but I was rather rude...." Andrew looked again at Sarge's wide grin. "I just want to hear from him. I hope he sees the story. He'll be so pleased, I think."

Mr. Givens stamped in, brushing clumps of snow off his coat.

"The weatherman said there would be a chance of light snow flurries. Boy, that's the understatement of the year!"

Lois sat him down in his easy chair and gave him a cup of cocoa. Andrew showed him the article. Mr. Givens was quite impressed with the photos, and the story; he even phoned Lee to tell him about it. Andrew talked with Lee-Ann, and she was ecstatic when Andrew mentioned that she was pictured in the article.

The snowstorm was showing no signs of letting up, and Lois wouldn't hear of Barbara staying at a hotel. She insisted that Barbara spend the night in the guestroom. As it was a Friday, they stayed up late and Barbara talked about the various places she'd been to and assignments she'd worked on. The next morning, Lois, Andrew, and Barbara breakfasted late and, while they were enjoying a second cup of tea, Andrew heard the clink of the mail slot.

"I'll get it—" He got up, walked to the front door, and gathered up the letters scattered in the entryway.

Strange....there was the letter he'd written to Sarge. Why had it been returned?

Then he saw it—stamped in red across Sarge's APO:

Deceased: Return to Sender.

Chapter 44

"*A*ndrew?"

Barbara stood before him. Without a word, he handed the letter to her.

"Sarge." His voice was barely above a whisper.

"Oh, no, Andrew—I'm so sorry...." Barbara put her arms around him. He heard Lois's voice, heard Barbara explaining what had happened, felt himself being led to the sofa.

Lois sat on one side of him; Barbara on the other. Neither of them spoke for awhile, then Andrew felt the words pouring out of him.

"I should have written to him sooner—now it's too late—I should have—" The words caught in his throat and he leaned forward, pressing his face into his knees as the tears soaked through his jeans.

He sensed Barbara's face very close to his, then heard her whispered voice.

"You can't undo the past Andrew, but you can do something."

"What?" he moaned.

Barbara was silent for a moment, then spoke.

"My brother was a tail gunner on a B-17, with the 8th Air Force. One day, his plane came back from a mission, all shot up. It burst into flames just after it landed. There were no survivors."

Andrew looked up at Barbara. There were tears in her eyes.

"A few weeks after Richard was killed, my parents got some letters from a family in England. My brother had been friends with this family, and had spent his leaves with them. There were two boys, about your age, and Richard taught them how to play baseball and brought them candy and comic books whenever he visited them. Their father had been either killed or captured at Dieppe; they never found out what happened. The boys and their mother wrote letters to us, telling about all the wonderful times they had with my brother, and about how much they missed him. Andrew, those letters mean more to us than all the medals and official commendations we got from the government. Richard is gone for good, but these people gave us something very special of him. Andrew—" She put her arm around him. "Nothing can bring Sarge back, but you can give something of him to his family. Find out who they are, and write to them."

"How would I do that?"

"Write to his commanding officer. Use the APO address if you don't know his unit."

Andrew shook his head. "I don't know—they may not want to hear from me. I mean, it might upset them to be reminded about him—"

"Andrew, it *won't* upset them to hear from you, I promise. Your memories of him will be more precious to his family than you could ever possibly imagine."

Taking Barbara's advice, he wrote a query addressed to "Anyone in Sgt. Kevin Ferguson's unit who knew him." Barbara gave a copy of the *Life* issue with his story, and he cut it out and enclosed it with the letter, which he mailed to Sarge's APO.

Barbara phoned to report that the issue with his story was doing very, *very* well: Newsstand sales were more than triple the usual trade.

"My sources inform me that most of the purchasers are teenaged girls," Barbara said. "My editor is *very* delighted, as you can imagine."

A few days later, he arrived home from school to find a note from Lois, saying she was over at Alida's. He went up to his room to study. After forty minutes of swotting up the Civil War he was a bit hungry, so he decided to go down to the kitchen to grab some cookies. As he started down the stairs the phone rang. Arriving on the landing, he saw Lois pick it up in the living room. She must have come in without him hearing her.

"Well, hello!...Yes...Yes...It's a wonderful story about Andrew, yes it is, and— What?...His *father?*"

Andrew froze.

"WHAT?—HERE?...He's coming *HERE?"* Lois shrieked.

Andrew closed his eyes.

Oh God, oh God, oh God...He saw the story and he's coming for me!

"Yes, I'll tell him..." Lois was standing now, her face a mask of stunned shock. "Yes, I'm sure he'll be surprised. Well, goodbye."

Andrew clung to the railing as he walked down the last seven steps to the living room. Lois looked at him in wonder.

Don't worry...Even though I'll be leaving you, we can still see each other from time to time...I'll tell my father how kind you were to me—

"That was Lee," Lois said.

"Wha-*who?"*

"You know, Gene's brother."

It took a second Andrew to figure out that Lois was talking about Lee-Ann's grandfather. What did he have to do with this?

Lois shook her head slowly. "He called to say his father wants to come here!"

Andrew regrouped his shattered emotions and focused on the issue at hand. He didn't want to divulge that he knew about the estrangement between Mr. Givens and his father.

"Your husband's father? Why, I mean, what happened?"

"Gene hasn't seen, hasn't even spoken to his father for over thirty-five years."

"Why?"

"Gene's father expected all his sons to be farmers, and he wouldn't hear of any of them wanting anything different—don't know why, except that I'll venture to guess he's very stubborn, just like his son and—" Lois rolled her eyes. "His grandson. Well, Gene wanted to go to college and his father said that if he chose to do that, he would never speak to Gene again. So Gene left. And they haven't spoken a word to each other all these years."

"But now he wants to see him—why?"

"Lee gave him a copy of that issue of *Life* about you, and showed him that picture of you and Gene. His father read the story, then told Lee he wants to come here to see you...and Gene! Tomorrow! Oh dear, I don't know how I'm going to break this to Gene—"

"You'll think of something," Andrew assured her.

She gave him a hug.

"I can't *believe* it! My God, after all these years! And it's all because of you, Andrew—" She squeezed him even tighter. "Gene had his doubts about the article. He said, 'You never know what might come out of this.'" She shook her head in amazement.

When Mr. Givens arrived home, Andrew busied himself setting the table while Lois settled Mr. Givens on the sofa and gave him a glass of apple brandy.

"Special occasion?" Mr. Givens smiled.

"Drink your brandy and then I'll tell you."

Andrew heard Lois's low murmur, followed by a holler from Mr. Givens.

"*WHAT!* He's coming *HERE? TOMORROW?*"

Lois's soothing voice, then her husband's sputtery interjections.

"The st-story about Andrew—he's coming because of that? Wh—what if h-he—what if comes here and things turn out to be even worse—"

"You haven't spoken to him since you were eighteen—what could be worse than that?"

Silence, then Lois's voice, soothing and low.

"Everything's going to be fine, Gene. Lee is driving him here. They'll arrive around suppertime. I'll cook up a roast, okay?"

A low, pained grunt from Mr. Givens.

"Well, Gene, like father, like son. I think you two will hit it off pretty well...sooner or later."

Mr. Givens arrived home the next day at precisely seven minutes after six.

"Maybelle's closing up the store. At least I didn't get any last minute prescriptions."

Lois, dressed in her best housedress and apron, basted the roast for the twentieth time, then gave her husband a kiss as Andrew tore the salad greens. Mr. Givens nodded absently at him.

"Relax, Gene," Lois urged. "Everything's going to be fine—"

A crunch of gravel in the driveway.

Mr. Givens froze. Lois gave him a nudge.

"Go out and greet them—"

Mr. Givens clumped through the living room and out the front door. Lois and Andrew followed a few paces behind.

Lee was already at the foot of the steps, with an ancient, stooped figure hanging onto his arm.

Mr. Givens walked quickly down the steps, took his father's free arm; then he and

Lee gently guided him up to the front door. At the threshold, the old man turned to Mr. Givens and said in a soft, strained voice:

"Well, we have some catching up to do."

Lois stepped to her father-in-law and enfolded him in a warm embrace.

"Dad, I'd like you to meet my wife, Lois," Mr. Givens said. He then motioned to Andrew, who stepped forward and shook the old man's hand.

"I'm Andrew, pleased to meet you, sir."

"You two must be famished after that long trip. I'll get supper on the table in a minute." Lois flew to the kitchen while Mr. Givens and Lee ushered their father to the dining room and seated him near the window, facing the sideboard. The old man's eyes fixed on the picture of Jake and Andrew's mother at their wedding. Mr. Givens brought the picture to his father.

"Jake and his wife, Andrew's mother," Mr. Givens said.

The old man silently regarded the photo until Lois brought in the roast. Andrew, remembering his manners, helped her to bring in the rest of the supper things. Before seating herself, Lois got out a bottle of Lee's apple brandy and poured everyone a dash (except Andrew—apple juice again for him), then nodded to Lee, who raised his glass and pronounced a toast.

"Dad and Gene, all the best in the future."

Andrew made it a point to tell the old man, privately of course, about how Mr. Givens had carried so many customers during the Depression, and of how kind he and Lois had been to him. He showed him the album of the photos Amy had shot, and all the pictures of himself that Jake's father had taken.

When the old man asked him about Jake, though, Andrew was torn between wanting to tell him how evil Jake really was, and wanting to do what was right by Mr. Givens. So he said that Jake was a pilot and a bit on the quiet side, and that he really didn't know him very well because he hadn't spent all that much time with him.

"Because of the war, you know."

"The war...." The old man nodded, seemed to be deep in thought. Then he spoke, more to himself than to Andrew.

"War—goddamnedest business if ever there was one. Nobody wins, except the profiteers. My father made his fortune in the Civil War, selling rifles, moldy blankets, rotten beef and anything else to the Union Army. I was a kid at the time, so I didn't know about that, only knew that we were living high off the hog while one-legged veterans begged in the streets. I found out, though, when I was old enough to know better. Turned my back on him, on his dirty money and his smart ways. He wanted me to go to college, get an education so I could follow in his footsteps. I took a small inheritance from my mother and bought me a farm. Never looked back. I'm proud of what I did, do it again without a second thought."

Listening between the lines, Andrew knew what the old man was really saying.

"You can be proud of your son, too," Andrew told him. "He works hard, six days a

639

week, ten hours a day. He's good and honest and kind. He's always done what's fair, and more than fair, sometimes."

The old man regarded Andrew thoughtfully, nodded once, then smiled.

"I guess I'll have to take your word on that." He seemed to retreat into his thoughts for a moment, then said, "That grandson of mine turned his back on a college education, didn't he?"

"Well, actually, he *did* go to college—"

"But he left, didn't he?" There was a twinkle in his eye.

"Well, um, yes...but that was to fight in the war. He joined the RAF, you know."

The old man grunted. "Never said I didn't have any respect for someone who chose to fight, or had to fight, in a war. If it's on the side of right, I mean. You Brits stood up to that bully Hitler, and I'm proud that my grandson took part in that. It's the ones who take advantage of war and the sufferings of others, to further their own ends—they're the ones who ought to burn in hell."

Lee and Grandfather Givens, which is what Andrew started calling him, stayed for three days, then returned to New York. As Lois, Mr. Givens, and Andrew stood in the front yard waving them off, the phone rang. Lois ran to get it.

Andrew and Mr. Givens walked into the house and heard Lois's distressed voice.

"Oh dear, it does sound as if you're all in a fix...I'll try, but I have to see if it's all right with Gene...Yes, Andrew is still here—I'm not sure—Well, I'll ask...Bye...."

"What's up?" Mr. Givens asked.

Lois blew a slow blast of air through lips slack with consternation, then spoke.

"That was Rose—you know, my sister-in-law in Nebraska. They've had three new babies in the past week. One of my nieces had twin girls this past Monday, and my nephew's wife had a baby boy two days ago. They're going crazy with all the work and need an extra warm body to pitch in, so Rose called and asked if I'd be able to come out for a week or two. I'd like to, but I really don't want to leave you and Andrew alone, though...."

Mr. Givens gave her a hug.

"Andrew and I can take care of ourselves, can't we, Andrew?" He winked at Andrew. "We did all right when you were in the hospital—"

"You ate out every night—"

"No problem—we'll do it again."

"Gene—"

"Hey, I can manage anyway, even if we don't go out to eat. What do you think I did before I met you?"

"You lived in a crummy boarding house and ate lousy food."

Mr. Givens grinned, then gave her a kiss. "We'll manage, don't you worry. You go. You haven't seen your family in years."

Lois pursed her lips together for a moment, as if that would help her to plan things out.

"Sarah can cook you supper on Thursday...and I'll make up some casseroles. All you need to do is take them out of the icebox and pop them in the oven. Andrew can do that...I'll see if Alida can't have you over a few times...and Rhoda Wagner—I'm sure she'd *love* to have you and Andrew come to supper."

Mr. Givens smiled at her as he put his arm around Andrew's shoulder. "We'll take care of ourselves. Now, pack your things and don't worry about us."

Mr. Givens took Lois to the train station the next morning, which was Saturday. Andrew went along to see Lois off. As he stood on the platform waving at the departing train, he decided he would rather spend the morning at the pharmacy. After all, he could do worse than spend the morning keeping busy, and he knew there were shelves to be stocked and racks to be organized. Mr. Givens protested a bit when Andrew started in to work, but Maybelle hushed him and gave Andrew a wink. He even made a few deliveries on foot to some customers who lived nearby, easing the pressure on Stan, Mr. Given's other delivery boy, who went by bike to deliver the orders farther away.

Mr. Givens took him out for lunch. Over root beer floats and grilled cheese sandwiches, Mr. Givens reminisced about the early years of his marriage:

"Lois's aunt died just before we were married, and left her house on Mine Street in New Brunswick to Lois. We turned it into a boarding house for Rutgers students. Lois cooked and cleaned, and I worked two jobs. Jake was born then; I wasn't able to be home much, but he didn't lack for company, what with a dozen boys living with us, and about as many more taking meals. Lois's reputation as a first-class cook got around and we had a waiting list of students who wanted to live with us, or at least be able to enjoy her cooking. We did pretty well and were able to save enough in a few years to buy the business and the house here."

"Jake was four when we moved to Scotch Plains, and he wasn't very happy about things." Mr. Givens smiled. "I remember him pestering us to move back to New Brunswick so he could be with 'the boys.'"

After lunch, as Andrew was restocking the candy bins, he heard a familiar voice.

"I was wondering if you could tell me who this is on the cover of *Life* magazine, sir?"

"Miriam!" He blushed at the sight of her holding up the issue with his smiling face on the cover. She was with Eva, who had Ann, Lorna, and Georgina in tow.

"We're taking the girls to the Saturday matinee, as usual," Miriam said.

Mr. Givens came out from his cubical and greeted the girls, then turned to Andrew.

"Why don't you take the afternoon off?" Without waiting for Andrew to reply, he fished some change out of his pocket and handed the coins to Andrew. Then he filled a bag with Tootsie Rolls from one of the candy bins, and handed it to Eva.

"No charge," he smiled.

Eva proceeded to sort through her purse and gave Mr. Givens some change.

"Eva, he said *no charge*," Miriam told her.

"No charge—we have to pay now, no?"

"No, it's free," Miriam explained.

Eva's eyes widened. "Free?" She said something unintelligible to Miriam, who replied in the same strange guttural tongue—Yiddish? Eva bit her lip, then smiled at Mr. Givens.

"Thank you very much."

Mr. Givens waved Andrew off.

"Have a nice time!"

They took the bus to Plainfield and, as the movie didn't start for another half an hour, Eve decided look around in one of the "five and dime" stores. Miriam whispered to Andrew that this was one of Eva's favorite activities:

"She doesn't usually buy much; she just loves being able to walk into a store. She says that when she was in Germany, Jews weren't allowed to go into the stores or even walk on the sidewalks."

Eva bought some lace and thread. As they were waiting in line to check out, Andrew heard some excited whispering. Out of the corner of his eye, he saw three teenaged girls giggling over a copy of *Life* and stealing glances at him.

"It's *him!* It's *got* to be!" one of them whispered.

As he walked out of the store with Miriam and Eva, he realized he was being followed. The whispers and giggles trailed them to the movie theater. Miriam noted it too; she grinned, and put her arm in his as they walked along. By the time they got to the theater, seven more teenaged girls had joined with the original three. As Andrew waited in line with Miriam and Eva for tickets, the girls pressed a little closer, making small talk with him about the movie. After all the teasing he'd gotten about his accent over the past year and a half, he was surprised that the girls seemed to be entranced by the way he talked. They gazed at him as if he were a movie star and smiled ear-splitting grins whenever he opened his mouth to speak.

Crikey! Wouldn't Dad be amazed to see me now!

Andrew let himself into the house, pausing to pick up the mail scattered in the entryway. There was a letter, with Sarge's APO as the return address. Above it was the name: *Sgt. E.J. Price.*

He tore open the envelope and read:

Hey Andrew,

It's me, your old buddy El. Your letter found its way to me, and so I'm writing to you.

First about Sarge: He was killed at Normandy. We were both at Omaha Beach, and you probably have read about how bad it was there. He died quickly, which if you're going to die is about the best way to do it, I guess. He had a daughter, Debbie, who was four then....

Andrew shook his head in amazement. *Sarge had a daughter! Why had he never mentioned it?* He read on:

...Sarge's wife died when Debbie was born, and Debbie lives with his mother now, in Kansas. Sarge didn't talk much about his wife or his daughter. I was the only one he told, and he was a little drunk at the time. I guess that's the kind of thing you keep to yourself, for the most part....

El went on to give the name of Sarge's mother—Ethel Ferguson—and her address in Kansas. He concluded by writing:

I'm sure she'd like to hear from you, Andrew. Sarge told me that he told her all about you. I sure liked that story in Life about you, and that picture of you with Sarge and Cowboy and J.D. sure brings back a lot of happy memories. I'm glad you're doing O.K.

Your friend,
El

Andrew remembered Sarge talking about having brothers, and about his father being in the Army, so the fact the he had a mother came as no surprise to Andrew.
But a daughter!
Andrew wondered if she might have any memory of her father. She would have been two or three years old in the fall of 1943, which would have been the last time she'd seen him.
Andrew shook his head. *He* could barely remember anything before his fourth birthday. He was reminded of Peter, who blithely professed to have no recollection of his own father. At the time, Andrew had felt a little sorry for his young friend, who had been denied this link with his heritage, but had not considered the tragedy from the other side of death's veil.
It's not only that the fathers have been lost to their children, but the children have been lost to their fathers as well.
This is something I can give to Sarge: the remembrance of him in the heart of his child.

It was a good thing Lois was away, for she always checked to make sure Andrew always got to sleep at a decent hour. Mr. Givens, however, took him at his word that he had a bit of studying to do, otherwise Andrew would not have been permitted to stay up until the ungodly hour of two A.M., and on a school night, no less.
His lengthy epistle to Debbie was not exactly organized; it alternated between detailed accounts of various events Andrew remembered of Sarge, and his own impressions of, and feelings for, his late friend:

What I remember most vividly about your father, Debbie, is how he cared so much about everyone: He was the one who organized the fun, welcomed the newcomers, soothed the animosities, broke up the fights, gave words of advice and encouragement and cheer, showed kindness to everyone....

He enclosed with the letter the picture Barbara had given him of him and Sarge on the *Queen Mary*. He also enclosed a copy of the story as well. When he gave the thick missive to Mr. Givens and asked him to mail it, Mr. Givens arched his eyebrow in query, but said nothing.

Lois returned from Nebraska, chattering happily about the *wonderful* time she'd had.

"The place is just busting with babies and children!" She told Andrew. "All of my brother's children and grandchildren under one roof! Oh, I brought along the photo album and a few copies of *Life*, and everyone *loved* the story about you! They'd be delighted to meet you; perhaps if you're still here in the summer, we can both make the trip there. You've never been farther west than Washington Rock, and I think it would be good for you to see the rest of the country before you go back to England."

Andrew smiled at her, but inwardly seethed.

God stone the crows! If I have to stay here until summer, I'll go bloody mad!

Andrew's fourteenth birthday was celebrated with a giant chocolate cake and the usual ceremony of his height check and weighing-in. There were now seven pencil slashes on the kitchen wall marking his progress, and the freshly-made one was dead even with Jake's height at the same age: sixty-five inches. Andrew noted with satisfaction that, at 120 pounds, he outweighed Jake by four pounds at the same age, as well.

Lois squeezed his biceps. "All that muscle—you're not doing weights that are too heavy, are you?"

"I'm only doing seven pounds; just a lot of repetitions."

"All that running with Shannon has given you a nice set of leg muscles, too. Aren't you going out for track? I think you'd really like it—running with the other boys, that is."

Andrew shrugged. "I'd rather run on my own, or with Shannon. I'm really not all that interested in racing."

Lois smiled at him. "If you say so."

It turned out to be a good thing that Andrew did not commit himself to any after-school activities, for Alex, who delivered for Mr. Givens on Monday, Wednesday, and Friday, decided to join the Marines.

Mr. Givens was quite upset, and not just because he was losing an employee.

"Damn! Alex has only three more months before he graduates, but just because he turned eighteen he's got ants in his pants to see some action—afraid the war's going to pass him by. Gawdalmighty, after that bloodbath on Iwo Jima, you'd think he'd have second thoughts...."

Andrew volunteered to fill Alex's position. At first Mr. Givens was reluctant to hire him:

"Don't want your mother to think that I'm treating you like a hired hand or something."

Andrew assured him that he was more than delighted to do the job; besides, it would be good exercise.

"I'll write to Mum and tell her it was my idea, all right?"

He got into the habit of carrying a pocketful of lollipops on his rounds and giving some to any children who happened to be in the homes he delivered to (with their mother's permission, of course). He loved to see the smiles of delight when he produced this unexpected treat.

One day while Andrew was restocking the candy bins, Mr. Givens got a call:

"...Yes...Yes, we do...Yes, he is very nice...Yes, have your doctor give me a call, and I'll get it to you right away...Thank you very much—bye." He called to Andrew.

"That's the sixth new customer you've brought in this week, Andrew. You're going to make me a millionaire with that charming accent of yours!"

"Hey, are you complaining, Gene?" Maybelle called.

"Not at all!" Mr. Givens laughed.

Collie offered to reschedule his guitar lessons to Tuesday nights at seven. This worked out quite well, for he often got in more than an hour of lesson time, as there were no students following him. He and Collie played duets, usually ballads and Celtic melodies, after the formal lesson was over. They alternated with each other playing melody and accompaniment, and Collie was very pleased that Andrew was developing into quite an accomplished classical guitarist.

One day he asked about Antoinette, for she had left just before Christmas to go back to France.

Collie's usual cheerful demeanor was replaced with a grim expression.

"It was just horrible, Andrew. She found out the Nazis slaughtered almost everyone in her entire town—men, women, and children. It happened just after D-Day. There were only two survivors out of over six hundred people—all of Antoinette's family were killed. She wrote me a rambling, hysterical, almost incoherent letter. I wrote back to her, but she hasn't replied. Her mother's friend, Nicole, whom Antoinette stayed with here, just went to France to try to find her. Oh, Andrew, I'm so worried about her! I just hope she's all right...."

He arrived home to hear Lois talking on the phone.

"...he's doing fine—wait a minute, he just walked in. Do you want to talk with him?...I'm sure he'd like—what?...No?...You don't?...But I'm sure he'd like—"

"Does someone want to talk with me?" he asked Lois.

Lois gave him an enigmatic look: half-puzzled, half-knowing, but did not hand the receiver to him.

"...well, uh, all right...Are you sure?...Okay, give me back to your father...."

Andrew waited as Lois chatted a few more minutes. She said good-bye, and hung up.

"That was my family in Nebraska. Everything's going relatively smoothly, considering there are three babies squalling at all hours of the night."

"Who wanted to talk with me?"

Lois smiled at him, a funny sort of smile he had never seen before. She put her arm around his shoulder.

"I hope things work out for you to be able to go to Nebraska this summer. I think you'll have a *wonderful* time."

A package arrived from Barbara, containing several dozen letters for him.

"One of the secretaries here has already read through them," Barbara wrote. "Sometimes we get crank letters and hate mail, no matter whom or what we do a story about. We don't want to pass along anything that might be upsetting, though none of the letters for you were in that category. The letter that's at the top of the bundle is quite interesting—it seems as if the writer knows you."

Andrew withdrew the letter and read:

Dear Roger,

I read this story in <u>Life</u> and I think I know you. I am German POW and was on Queen Mary in Fall 1943, as story says you were on ship then too. You drop Hershey bar to me, no? You were with little friend, at time I think is your brother but is no mention of him in story. I remember you run away, and I worry that I cause trouble for you. I share your gift with other POWs and it make us very much gladness. We all think is fine gift and are not so afraid to go to USA.

I am in camp in Illinois and work farm. It is hard work but I enjoy and we are treated well. I am carpenter before war and last week I build a barn for people that barn burn down last month. I think to build is better than to go to war, no?

I am happy you are well, and I hope war is over soon. I always remember your kindness to me.

Sincerely,
Erich Bonhoeffer

"Who is it from?" Lois asked.

"From a German POW—I dropped a Hershey bar to him when I was on the *Queen Mary*." He handed the letter to her.

She read it and shook her head in wonder.

"That's *wonderful!* But why did you run away?"

"I was afraid I'd done something wrong—you know, giving something to a German."

Lois smiled at him. "That's about the rightest thing anyone could do! Tell you what—why don't you write him. I'll ask Gene to get us a whole carton of Hershey bars, and we'll mail it off to him."

Andrew smiled. "All right."

Lois poked through the rest of the letters. There's enough here to keep you busy until next Christmas. I'll make you a cup of tea and you can start in on them, all right?"

While Lois was in the kitchen, Andrew scanned through several more letters. There were a few from adults, who expressed their enjoyment of the story and wished him the best. One of them was from a teacher in Texas, who wrote:

I have made your article required reading in my English class. Living in this part of the country, we are very much isolated from the effects of the war and I wanted my students to read, first-hand, how children their own age have been affected by war. I also think it's important from them to see that there is something beyond the fighting and destruction; after all, we are going to have to rebuild some kind of peace from the ruins of this conflict. I think your story has conveyed how it is possible to put aside our differences, and to come together in peace and friendship with others of different backgrounds and nationalities. It starts—it has to start—on a personal level, and your story is a wonderful example of what can be achieved.

Most of the letters were from girls about his own age, many of whom had enclosed photographs of themselves. One letter in particular left him quite bewildered. He showed it to Lois:

"She wrote some numbers down—I think it's a phone number. See? 39-24-35. I think she wants to go on holiday with me. She says she wants to take me 'around the world.'"

Lois's eyes bulged as she read the letter; she cleared her throat *very* loudly, folded the letter, and put it in her pocket.

"You *do* seem to have an effect on the ladies, Andrew. I think *I'd* better censor the rest of these. That secretary may have weeded out the crackpots and hatemongers, but these sweet young things aren't going to get past *me!*"

His mother wrote and said that she was very, *very* pleased with the article:

It's absolutely <u>marvelous</u> darling! I showed it to all the pilots in my pool and I carry it with me all the time, in the event I have occasion to show it off (which is quite often!). Jake liked it very much, also. We met last week when I ferried a Typhoon to his base in Germany. He managed to get two days' leave, and we caught an Anson back to England....

Bloody hell—she's flying to Germany! Doesn't she know the war's still going on over there?

Barbara called him again.

"Andrew, did you ever write a letter to Winston Churchill?"

"Yes, I did, actually, but that was quite a long time ago—"

"In 1940?"

"Um, yes. Why do you ask?"

"One of the researchers here was going through some old newspapers and found your letter; it had been forwarded to President Roosevelt, and he gave it to the news services. At the time, he was trying to persuade the American public to help England. A lot of people in the United States believed that England would be defeated by Germany and it wouldn't be wise for us to get involved. Your letter was introduced by a comment from the President. He said that the people of England would stand firm against Germany, and even the youngest British subjects believed that there was nothing to fear."

"The President said that about my letter? *Crikey!*"

"That's not all, Andrew. One of our reporters is assigned to follow Eleanor Roosevelt—the First Lady does get around, you know. Well, Mrs. Roosevelt asked about you. She wants to invite you to the White House sometime."

"*Me?*"

"And Jake's parents, and me, too. We won't disclose your name to her unless it's all right with you."

"Yes—I mean, no—I mean, that's fine with me."

"All right. I'll pass that along to Mrs. Roosevelt."

Shannon had been trying to persuade Andrew to run in an open invitational track meet.

"It's more of a cross-country race, a four-mile run to be exact. You don't need to be on the team."

Andrew shook his head as they ran through a small pasture south of town.

"Come on, Andrew, I think you'd be terrific."

"I'd rather not."

"Your times are really good—I've been keeping track. You can do four miles, easy. Besides, I would think that you'd get a real charge out of beating some Americans."

Andrew's head snapped around; Shannon winked.

"Do I take that as a yes?"

He was still working his way through the pile of mail when a letter arrived from Sarge's mother. She was quite overwhelmed by Andrew's letter about her son; over and over she expressed her appreciation for his "wonderful kindness":

> ...Debbie wanted me to put the picture on the table by her bed, so she can see her daddy every night before she goes to sleep. I read her the letter every night, and she has just about got it memorized. I can't begin to tell you how much it means to us to have your thoughts and memories of Kevin. He talked about you a lot when he was here two years ago, and I am so thankful that you wrote us this letter. We will treasure it always.
>
> God bless you,
Ethel Ferguson

Enclosed with the letter was a snapshot of Debbie and her grandmother. They were standing on the front porch of a rather dilapidated house: The screen door was torn and the paint was peeling. Debbie was wearing a frayed, though obviously cleaned and pressed, gingham dress.

As he was reading the letter again, the phone rang. Lois answered it; her eyes widened, and she said, "Why don't you talk with him about it?" She handed the phone to Andrew. "It's Barbara."

"Andrew?" Barbara sounded excited. "I'm sending some more letters to you, but I wanted to call you about one of them. This man wants to set up a trust fund for you. It's all above board: He's a wealthy financier, and is very insistent about doing this. I don't know how you feel about it and, of course, your mother would have to agree to it. I sent her a cable, and I'm waiting to hear from her."

Andrew, caught a little off guard by all this, was not quite sure how to reply. He thanked Barbara and said goodbye.

That night as he lay in bed, he considered his situation. He knew that, what with Grandfather Howard's immense wealth, not to mention the Hadley-Trevelyan Family Trust, he would never lack for anything.

But there was someone who would.

He phoned Barbara the next day, and explained the situation.

"So you see, I really don't need any more money. I would be happier if this man would give it to Debbie. She's the one who really needs it."

"Are you sure, Andrew?"

"Positive. Can you ask this man about it? I hope he'll agree to it, because I want this more than anything."

"Okay, why don't you write to him to and explain why you want to do it. Send the letter to me, and I'll send it to him. Oh, we told Mrs. Roosevelt your name and address, so you'll probably get an invitation to the White House sometime soon."

Andrew excitedly told Lois and Mr. Givens about the forthcoming invitation, and the reasons for it. They were both flabbergasted.

"My goodness, Andrew—this is something you'll be able to tell your grandchildren!" Lois laughed.

Andrew asked Mr. Givens if he would take the snapshot of Debbie and her grandmother to a photography shop to get a print made. From the issue of *Life* he cut out the picture of himself and the GIs on the *Queen Mary* and drew a circle around Sarge. He enclosed both pictures in the letter he wrote to his would-be benefactor. He also wrote to his mother, explaining his plan.

A week later, an invitation from the White House arrived. Andrew, Lois, Mr. Givens, and Barbara were invited to meet with President and Mrs. Roosevelt for fifteen minutes on April 26, 1945. Mrs. Roosevelt enclosed a brief note for Andrew:

...My husband was very delighted with your letter to Prime Minister Churchill. As you know, America was neutral then and my husband was trying to get the Lend-Lease Bill passed. He needed to convince the American people that England would not go down, and that any aid sent to Britain would not fall into Nazi hands. Your letter was one way of getting the word out to the American people that the English people would not let themselves be defeated....

He showed the note to Lois, and she shook her head in wonder. "You've been published twice, Andrew—first in the newspapers, then in the book. Three times, if you consider the article in *Life*—after all, you gave the story to Barbara."

Andrew put the invitation and the note in his treasure box, along with the copy of the newspaper clipping of his letter.

Andrew tensed; he tried quell the butterflies in his stomach, but this was, after all, his first real race. Of course, he had competed in races at Askew Court, but that was long ago, or so it seemed. And the games were only with his classmates.

This was different.

There were runners from all the neighboring towns, and some from as far away as New Brunswick and Sommerville. Most of the them were older than him. Shannon, Lois, Miriam, and Lynette had come to see him run. He could see their heads bobbing in the crowd of spectators.

"On your marks—set—"

The crack of the starter pistol split the air. The mob of runners surged forward like a giant, multi-headed creature, then scraggled apart as the faster runners broke ahead and the slower ones trailed behind.

Andrew found himself in a space between the van of the fastest runners and the main pack. He lengthened his stride, got a good breathing rhythm, and moved in on the leaders.

He passed the one mile mark and started to get his second wind; he could tell that some of the runners in front were starting to lag. He would not spend himself—yet. Best to keep his strength for the final stretch.

He passed one, two, three runners. Even though he didn't feel any strain, he took quicker, deeper breaths. He passed a few more runners, then found himself in fourth place.

Runner number three was having problems; he grimaced in pain, staggered a bit, lost his place to Andrew.

Andrew caught up with runner number two, ran beside him for awhile, then moved out ahead.

He trailed runner number one for a long time. The boy's sturdy legs pumped at an even, strong pace. The finish line was in sight; Andrew threw himself forward in a pent-up blast of power and flew ahead of his competitor. Even as he saw his only challenger disappear behind him, Andrew couldn't quite believe what had happened. The crowd cheered and screamed as he approached the finish line, but how far ahead was he? A yard, three yards, seven yards—should he keep up this lung-bursting pace or ease up?

Just take a peek—

He turned his head a bit, saw that he was at least ten feet ahead—

His left foot jerked into a hole, and his body slammed to the ground. A blur of legs went by as his ankle exploded in pain.

He felt Shannon's arms around him.

"Don't try to move, Andrew. Hopefully, it's just a sprain."

A small mob gathered around him. All he wanted was for the ground to swallow him up.

He felt Miriam beside him, heard Lynette and Lois murmuring condolences. The crowd thinned away from him, and Shannon helped him to his feet.

"Don't put any weight on it, Andrew. Lynette, give me a hand."

Supported by Shannon and Lynette, Andrew was conveyed to Lois's car. He closed his eyes and bit his lip as the pain began to savage him. Lois sped to the hospital and Shannon patted his hand.

After an interminable wait at the hospital, a few X-rays, some pain pills, and murmured commentaries by the on-duty physician, Andrew's fate and sentence were pronounced: a bad sprain, keep off the affected limb for at least three days.

Shannon helped Lois get Andrew up the stairs to his room. He positioned pillows under Andrew's ankle, then offered a perspective on things.

"You did really well—you were way out ahead."

Andrew snorted, turned away.

"Okay, you made a mistake. Remember—never look back. Next time you'll know not to do that."

Andrew fixed Shannon with a glare of defiance.

"There won't *be* a next time!"

His enforced convalescence gave him enough free time to read through the pile of mail from Barbara. The letters urged him away from his anguish: Being adored was a wonderful tonic. He was finally able to put things into perspective.

It was a silly old race, anyway!

The news of the death of President Roosevelt stunned the nation, and came as a personal blow to Andrew.

Only two more weeks, and I would have met him!

Andrew had never before witnessed an outpouring of grief on such a mass scale—even young children were disconsolate. There was a special prayer service at Lois's church; Andrew didn't go, preferring to mourn alone. Miriam was stunned.

"He's the only president I've ever known. I can't imagine anyone else. What now?"

His mother wrote to him, expressing her sorrow over the death of this great man:

He was our friend from the beginning, Andrew. I shudder to think of what might have happened to our country if anyone else had been in the White House....

She went on to tell of her frequent trips to the continent, which only added distress to Andrew's melancholy.

If only she'd quit this silly business!

"Andrew!" Lois's voice greeted him as he arrived home a few days later, Thursday afternoon—poker day. "Someone's here to see you."

A tall thin figure approached him. He looked vaguely familiar, though Andrew couldn't quite place him.

"Hey, Andrew!"

"*El!* What are you doing here?"

"I was sorta passing though—figgered you'd be getting out of school about this time."

Andrew noticed that El was wearing civilian clothes. His face was pallid and gaunt.

"You've been discharged, El?"

"Got me my million dollar wound—half my ass blown off, thank you very much."

El walked stiffly towards him. Before Andrew knew it, his arms were around his old friend.

"It's really good to see you, El."

"Good to see you too, kiddo! Great ballsafire, you've sure grown! You were knee-high to a grasshopper and scrawnier than a starved alleycat last time I saw you. Sorry I didn't call—I just decided on the spur of the moment to hightail it out of than damned hospital and see the world. 'Sides, I didn't know your phone number, just your address. Your grandma here—" He winked at Lois, "Has been feeding me all kinds of lip-smacking delights whiles I been here waiting for you."

Sarah called from the dining room. "You ain't been protesting too much!"

El grinned. "And *that* nice lady has been making off with my life savings! We played ourselves a few hands of poker, and she's mighty good!"

Sarah let out a blast of laughter. "You not too bad fo' a white boy! Not half as good as Andrew, though!"

"Yeah, he's something else," El chuckled. He turned to Andrew. "They told me about you pulling your routine on them—nice going, kiddo!"

"Sarah was the one who caught on to him," Lois told El. "Well, would you two like to sit down and play another couple of hands?"

Andrew smiled at her. "It's such a beautiful afternoon—I'd really like to go to the park."

"Well, I'm sure you two have got a lot of catching up to do," Lois said. "I'll pack a picnic lunch—you can take the bus. I'll call Gene and ask him to pick you up when he gets off work, okay?"

"Super!" Andrew replied.

El toted the picnic basket on the bus, and Andrew carried one of Lois's old quilts. They arrived at the park and spread out their picnic things near the lake. As they munched on sandwiches, they made small talk, then fed the ducks. After awhile, Andrew spoke.

"I wrote to Sarge's mother—well, I wrote to Debbie, actually, and told her about her father. Mrs. Ferguson sent me a very nice letter back."

El looked off into the distance, cleared his throat.

"What happened at Normandy, El?" Andrew asked.

El shook his head slowly, gazed up at the sky.

"It was one big fuck-up, Andrew."

"What? I listened to the wireless reports all day, and it sounded as if things went rather well."

"Well, a lot of times they don't tell all, Andrew." El glanced at Andrew, then snorted and looked off into the distance again. After awhile, he spoke in a hollow voice.

"I heard it wasn't too bad at the other beaches, but Omaha was a fuckin' slaughter-house. Everything that could go wrong—did. Our bombers were supposed to take out the big guns and the pillboxes, but they dropped their bombs too far inland. The naval bombardment was off too, and the engineers and demolition guys got slaughtered before they could get the beach obstacles out of the way. We were told we were going up against old men and boys—a cinch, they said. We caught hell on the beaches, and went up against a crack infantry division. Sarge—" He cleared his throat.

"We were in the landing craft, and the coxswain wanted to let us off faraways from shore. Sarge pointed his rifle at the guy and told him to bring us in. We were so loaded down with equipment we'd have drowned in even five feet of water. Lotsa guys did—never even hit the beach. We got in to shore, and as soon as the door of the landing craft let down, we got hammered by machine-gun fire. Sarge was hit even before he stepped out. Bullet through the head. He fell into the water and I tripped over him; that's probably what saved my life. Our outfit took over eighty percent casualties. Grover, Murph, Clint—they were killed...'Scuse me—"

He walked over to the lavatory, stayed within for a few minutes, then ambled out. He sat, cleared his throat very loudly, stared at the grass.

"What about the others?" Andrew asked.

"Others?" El seemed somewhat distracted.

"Cowboy and J.D. and Mikey and Ray."

"Oh, yeah. Well, don't know about Mikey and Ray—they weren't in our outfit. Ray was a cook, wasn't he?"

"Yes, and Mikey was a mechanic."

El nodded absently. "Right." He closed his eyes, took a few deep breaths, then muttered, "Fuckin' bocage country."

"Sorry?"

"Those fuckin' hedgerows—fuckinist place to fight a war...can't imagine hell being any worse. Those fuckin' Krauts fuckin' near chewed us to pieces and that God-Almonty-Montgomery was farting around near Caen for over a month while we caught hell—sorry." El reddened. "I didn't mean anything against you Brits, I mean you guys were in it from the beginning...." He blinked several times, as if trying to collect his thoughts.

"Ray and Mikey, I don't know 'bout them," he finally said.

"You said that."

"Yeah...yeah. Uhh...."

"Cowboy and J.D?"

"Yeah, right...J.D...we were in those hedgerows. Fuckin' hedgerows...can't imagine hell being any worse. J.D...right...Well, we were inching along one of those sunken lanes, and we hear something. J.D. reaches into his back pocket for a grenade, and...and—"

"And what?"

El rocked rhythmically back and forth.

"He pulled the fuckin' pin out—just the *fuckin' pin!* He looks at this fuckin' pin, says

'Aw, shit,' and backs up against a bank. God, it was just a few seconds that it happened...it seemed like forever...waiting for him to get blown apart—'scuse me—be right back, okay?"

Without waiting for Andrew's acknowledgement, El plodded to the lavatory again. He was gone a little longer. On his way back to Andrew, he stumbled a few times.

"Sorry—got my ass half near shot off, you know...can't walk so straight sometimes...yeah, fuckin' bocage country, can't imagine hell being any worse. We finally broke out, near St. Lo. Shit, we bombed up St. Lo so bad—sure liberated the hell out of that place, that's for sure. Never want to see another place like it, like the far side of the moon. Can't imagine hell being any worse. We were breaking out and our bombers were going to go in and get the Krauts, but there was some fuck-up and they bombed us instead. Cowboy got killed—after weeks of fighting in those fuckin' hedgerows, he gets killed by American planes! Wheeler got killed, too. Remember Wheeler?"

"Um, yes, I do."

"Yeah, Cowboy and Wheeler both of 'em—'scuse me."

This time El staggered off to the lavatory. Andrew had a sinking feeling in the pit of his stomach. Something was wrong—really wrong. El was never one to swear—well, not much, at least. But wasn't just the barrage of profanity that bothered Andrew. There was something else wrong with El, and it wasn't just his war wound. El was gone a long, long while. Andrew thought he should go in and check on him, but then El reeled out, lurched over to Andrew, and plopped down on the blanket.

"Then there was that fuckin' Battle of the Bulge. Shit, I thought nothing could be worse than Normandy, but this was fuckin' worse...If the Krauts didn't get you the cold would...Lotsa guys just froze to death...They sent us all these fuckin' replacements—kids, seventeen, eighteen years old, never even got to know their names, and they were gone...Davy—you remember Davy? He was killed in the Malmedy Massacre—Krauts captured a bunch of G.I.s and machine gunned 'em—Fuckin' Krauts—I killed so many of them, I lost track...I was so fuckin' drunk most of the time, anyway...In Normandy they got this terrific stuff—Calvados—some kind of rot-gut made from apples, terrific stuff...Then was this time in Germany we broke into this warehouse full of cognac, we all got so shit-faced we wouldna been able to remember which side we was on or what the hell the fighting was all about. I got three commendations for bravery—don't know what the fuck I got them for...Yeah—I was so fuckin' drunk I couldn't find my ass with both hands most the times...I killed so many fuckin' Krauts—there was one...*there was one....*"

El looked at Andrew, as if seeing him for the first time. He drew his knees up against his chest and was silent for a long, long while; when he spoke, his voice was low and strained.

"It was while we were chasing the Krauts back across France. We captured one of them—a bunch of them, in fact, but this one—I got assigned to escort him back to a holding area. They just told me to take him back...he was walking right in front of me...I never saw his face, and...and—" El's head lolled a bit, and he looked at Andrew, as if asking forgiveness for some terrible sin.

"What?" Andrew whispered.

"I shot him—I just shot him—" El's voice choked, and huge tears rolled down his cheeks. "I shot him in the back as he was just walking along, his hands over his head—I never saw his face, until I turned him over." El buried his face against his knees. "He was just a kid, a fuckin' kid, no older than you, Andrew. Fuckin' Krauts, they threw in a bunch of kids to cover their retreat—" He looked skyward for a moment, then sniffled and blew his nose on his sleeve.

"'Scuse me."

Andrew watched, horrified, as El careered to the lavatory. He waited a minute—it seemed more like an eternity—then tentatively walked over to the building.

He peered into the men's room and saw El's inert figure sprawled, face-down, on the floor. His head lay in a pool of vomit and a hip flask lay inches from his outstretched hand. Andrew picked up the flask and sniffed at it. It was empty, but smelled of something strongly inebriating. He flung it into a corner. Then he bent over El, turned his head a bit, and pulled him away from the fetid muck. He out went to get a napkin. After returning to the lavatory, he moistened the napkin with some water from the sink and wiped El's face.

El groaned.

"It's all right, El. Can you walk back to the quilt?"

El hiccupped, whimpered, turned his head and vomited again. Andrew cradled his head above the cement floor until he was spent, then wiped his lips with a clean corner of the napkin. El closed his eyes and his body went limp.

Andrew grabbed him under the armpits and managed to drag him outside. He had to stop a few times to catch his breath. After a year and a half of lifting weights and exercising, Andrew was not exactly a weakling; still, he had never quite appreciated how heavy a torpid figure could be.

As he maneuvered El onto the quilt, El seemed to awaken a bit, then lapsed into incoherence.

"...Fuckin' hedgerows...fuckin' mud...fuckin' 88s...."

Andrew looked—there wasn't a pay phone in sight.

"...Fuckin' cold...fuckin' snow...fuckin' Krauts...fuckin' ninety-day wonders...fuckin' M.O.s—sending us back over and over again...."

He shouldn't leave El alone, not even for a moment—what if he managed to get up and stagger around? He still might even crawl or roll around. Bloody hell—what if he fell into the lake?

He noticed two young girls throwing bread to the ducks. He could walk over to them and still keep an eye on El....

"Hullo—I was wondering if you might be able to help me."

The girls glared at him. "Our mother says we shouldn't talk to strangers," the taller girl said.

"She says perverts try to get little girls to help them, then they kidnap them and do nasty things to them," the smaller girl affirmed.

"Well, I'm...um, not a pervert, I promise," Andrew said. "I just need you to make a phone call for me. Wait a minute—" He ran back to El and searched through his pockets.

Thank God! At least he had a scrap of paper and a pencil on him—also a pocketful of change. He took out a few coins, then walked back over to the girls and held out a quarter to the older girl.

"Could you please make a phone call for me? I don't want to leave my friend alone—he's sick."

The older girl walked warily over to El. She bent over, sniffed, then stood up.

"He's not sick—he's *drunk*," she announced.

No shit, you wretched little twerp....

She gave El a look of contempt, then walked back to Andrew.

"Well, uh, yes he is, actually, but...but it's the war, you know."

The girl rolled her eyes and snorted.

Andrew wrote Lois's phone number on the paper and handed it to the girl.

"Please call this number and say that Andrew needs to be picked up right now. It's an emergency. Here—" He showed her the handful of change. "I'll lay this right down on the ground near us. When we leave, you can have it, all right?"

Andrew watched as the girls walked off. He then turned to El, who was moaning softly. El started mumbling something about Hershey bars, then started yelling, "In my footlocker—get them—get all of them. *Now!*" He then said something in sort of a German-English pidgin: "Sitten down—eat! *Eaten!*"

The two girls returned to the lake and, keeping their distance, ruefully regarded El. Every so often, the younger one would squint at the pile of change, as if trying to determine its value from a distance. They said nothing.

The Givens's car pulled up. As Lois and Sarah rushed out, the two girls swooped down upon the coins like pigeons diving on breadcrumbs.

"Oh my *Lord!*" Sarah breathed as she bent over El.

"I'm sorry—he—he—" Andrew was at a loss as to how to explain how all this had come about.

"Come on." Sarah kneeled down and pulled El's head up onto her lap. Mr. Givens arrived at the scene, draped one of El's arms over his shoulder and, with Sarah's help, pulled him to a semi-kneeling position.

"I'll carry him under the arms," Mr. Givens said. "Andrew, Lois, get his legs."

It took a while to get their moves coordinated, but they finally managed to get El to the car. They spread him out on the backseat as Sarah gathered up the picnic things.

"I'll take you home first, Sarah," Mr. Givens said. "Thanks for your help."

"Not at all," Sarah said.

Andrew sat in back, wedged between El and the door; Sarah sat up front, next to Lois.

They dropped Sarah off at her place, a tiny, ramshackle house in Plainfield; then Mr. Givens suggested that Andrew sit up front.

"I'd rather stay with El," Andrew told him.

If he tosses his biscuits again, I don't want him to choke to death....

They arrived at the house and managed, using the same system they had employed at the park, to get El inside.

They laid him for a moment at the foot of the stairs. Lois looked at El, sighed in sympathy.

"Well, let's try to get him up to the guest room."

Andrew shook his head. "We'd better not. He might get up and wander around—maybe fall down the stairs and hurt himself. Let's put him in the sunroom. I'll lay the sofa cushions out and cover them with some old blankets."

He quickly saw to arranging El's quarters; then they maneuvered El onto the makeshift bed. All the while El muttered about Hershey bars and babbled in fractured German.

Mr. Givens mopped his brow. "Will you two be all right?"

"We'll be fine." Lois gave him a kiss. "You'd better get back to work."

Andrew went to El and arranged the blankets over him. Then he sat next to him, holding his hand, until Mr. Givens arrived home for supper.

As Andrew's bedtime approached, he felt more and more uneasy about leaving El alone downstairs.

"I'm afraid he might wake up and leave," he told Lois. "I'd rather sleep outside the door so that if he wakes up, I could make sure he stays until he's all right."

"You have school tomorrow, though," Lois said. "What if he woke up in the middle of the night? You wouldn't get much sleep."

"I'll be fine. Besides, it wouldn't be the first time I had to get up in the middle of the night, then go to school the next day. During the Blitz I did it all the time."

"Well, okay. Let's get the mattress out of the spare room, so at least you'll be comfortable. And I'll set out the coffee pot on the stove; all you have to do is light the burner. He'll probably need a few quarts of coffee when he wakes up."

Lois and Mr. Givens said good night to Andrew as he settled himself next to the sunroom door. Lindy curled up beside him, and El's snores lulled him to sleep.

A groan, muffled grunts, a soft cough.

As his grogginess faded, Andrew puzzled out why he was lying outside the sunroom door.

"El? Are you all right?"

"*Oh, God....*"

Andrew got up and slowly opened the sunroom door.

El glanced briefly at Andrew, then looked away. His face was contorted with pain and mortification.

"It's all right, El," Andrew said. Stay there—I'll make you some coffee."

Lindy padded in and sniffed around El's arms, then stepped up and settled himself into a sphinx-like position El's chest.

"Good Lindy." Andrew stroked Lindy's ears. "You keep an eye on him until I get back."

He got the coffee going, and made himself a cup of tea. He carried the steaming beverages into the sunroom.

"The coffee's black—I'll get cream and sugar if you'd like—"

"Black's fine," El whispered. He gently lifted Lindy off his chest and gingerly maneuvered himself to a sitting position. He took a few sips of coffee, gazed into the cup as if it were an oracle, then looked at Andrew.

"I'm really sorry—"

"El, it's all right. I'm just glad I was around to help you."

El closed his eyes.

"Good morning!" Lois, standing in the doorway, spoke softly. "I see Andrew got you your morning coffee." She handed a towel and washcloth to El. "I thought you might like to freshen up. There's a bathroom next to the back door—I'll get breakfast while you take a shower, okay?"

El smiled wanly. "Okay."

"I have to get ready for school," Andrew said. "See you in a bit."

At breakfast, Lois chattered with El as if nothing had happened. Mr. Givens talked politely about the weather, medical matters, and other benign topics.

After breakfast, El took Mr. Givens aside and whispered something to him. Mr. Givens went upstairs, then returned carrying a package of gauze, some adhesive tape, and a bottle of iodine. He motioned El into the sunroom. It was obviously some sort of private matter, so Andrew helped Lois clear the table and do the dishes.

After a few minutes, Mr. Givens came into the kitchen.

"I dressed the wound on his backside, but he really should see a doctor. I'll take him to Dr. Schulte on my way to work."

Andrew wandered into the sunroom. El was stuffing his things into a dufflebag. Lindy peered into the dark recess of the olive-drab sack.

"Hey Lindy—here's a trinket for you." El took out a Purple Heart, dangled it at Lindy.

"El, that's special," Andrew protested.

"Aw, I don't need it." El tossed the medal onto the floor. Lindy batted it across the tiles.

"El—" Andrew laid his hand on El's arm. "El, you can't go on like this. You weren't like this when we were on the *Queen Mary*."

El glared at the floor. Lindy swatted at the Purple Heart and it scudded the length of the sunroom; the sound of metal scraping tile seemed to satisfy El, though he didn't smile.

"That was a long time ago, Andrew."

"You've got to stop drinking, El. It'll kill you."

"The war's already done that."

"No it hasn't! You still have your whole life ahead of you!"

"My life's behind me. All I want to do is forget everything."

"You shouldn't try to do that. Remembering is all we have left."

El shook his head slowly.

"No."

Andrew grabbed him by the shoulders.

"El, when Barbara did that story about me, I found myself remembering a lot of things that I didn't want to even think about. But it came out all right in the end. If you try to keep things bottled up, it'll destroy you. You said you wanted to be a writer. Well then, write about all that happened. You need to tell it, and people need to know."

El pulled away.

"El, the war's almost over—"

"It'll never be over, Andrew. Oh, we're all gonna kiss and make up. Bring down the curtain on this war. But it's not gonna be over. They'll just take it on the road and open it in the next town. Sure as hell there'll be another war ten, twenty years from now— maybe sooner. Maybe you'll get *your* ass shot off someday, too—" He swallowed, then whispered, "Sorry—I didn't mean to snap at you."

"That's all right." Andrew touched El's sleeve, then realized: What right do I have to think he needs to apologize?

And then Andrew felt the words tumble out of him, like spring water gushing from the side of a mountain: How this sacrifice of American lives counted for something, this sacrifice freely given, not owed, not one breath of it owed. The Americans had paid for mistakes not of their making, had suffered and died for European arrogance and greed. He grasped El's hands, and told him: It was *we* who presumed ours was the right to run things to our own satisfaction, then expect you Americans to clean up after our mess. And it was only right that our empire be dismantled. It had been given in trust, and now it was time for it to be set free. By grace the sacrifice was—would be—a worthy one, for the world, with America's help, has been freed from a terrible tyranny.

Andrew thought, but didn't tell El: At least we went out with a bang, not a whimper. We lost all, but we gained everything. And perhaps the good, what little good we left, might sprout, grow, endure; and the bad blow away like chaff.

His desire to shed his country, *himself*, of this uncomfortable, undeserved Empire was an immediate, almost physical sensation, as a man enduring a tedious dinner party might wish to tear free a tight necktie, strip off a starched shirt, and go for a solitary walk in the forest.

Britain would decline, America would rise, and Andrew felt somehow caught up in this transatlantic tangle, as if he were straddling both a thoroughbred stallion and an aging, tired drayhorse.

And would the Yanks make the same mistakes? Would they be overcome with the desire to dominate and possess, to gain at the expense of another's loss? It was all right in the conduct of war, but not a wise course in the establishment of peace.

Andrew felt as if their roles were reversed: he the ancient sage, El the callow youth. And he tried to convey all that was in his heart, as a father, regretfully looking back on his own past life of folly and sloth, might urge his son not to repeat the same mistakes.

Andrew remembered (where?) something he'd heard a British soldier say, which was as close to a compliment as a GI could expect from a Tommie: The Yanks make a lot of mistakes, at first, but they learn fast.

The Yanks with their easy, breezy freedom and open hearts were not incapable of bungling things, but they might make a better go of it than we did, Andrew thought. Please God, they can't do worse.

El was looking at him, his expression composed of equal parts of confusion and dullness, like that of a dimwitted old man staring at a wife he no longer recognizes. Andrew realized it had all been too much for him, at least in his pain and alcoholic haze.

"El, last night you were mumbling something about Hershey bars, and saying something in German. What was that all about?"

El blinked, took a deep breath.

"It was after we crossed the Rhine. We were in some forest someplace, and I was scouting out the area. I heard something, then these bunch of kids come up. 'Bout twenty of them, all of them with their hands over their heads. They looked to be mostly eleven, twelve years old. The oldest—he couldn't have been more than fifteen. They were all saying to me: 'Kamerad, Kamerad,' over and over. The oldest one was the only one whose voice had changed. I felt like I'd walked slap into a playground full of grammar school kids. I took them back to my outfit, sat them down. They looked half-starved. I had some Hershey bars in with my stuff, so I told one of my buddies to get them, and gave them to those kids. While they were eating, I walked away, unloaded my rifle, then walked back and pretended like I was guarding them. I wouldn't let anyone else guard them. If you can't trust yourself, who can you trust?"

Andrew grasped El's hand. "That's wonderful, El."

"It doesn't make up for what I did."

"No it doesn't. You can't undo the past. No one can. But you *can* trust yourself, you know."

"I'm not so sure about that."

"You *can*—but you've got to stop drinking."

El sighed.

"That's easier said than done, kiddo."

"You've *got* to do it, El, even if it's the hardest thing you ever do. Sit down and write, instead. You'll be creating something, instead of destroying yourself. Promise me you'll try—please! If not for your sake, then for mine. I can't bear to see you like this."

El grunted, then grimaced. "I'll try—okay? Don't want to make any promises."

"Good—that's a start."

"Andrew—it's time for you to get to school." Mr. Givens stood in the doorway. "I'll drive you, and then take El to Dr. Schulte's."

"Aw, now," El said. "That's real nice of you, but I don't need—"

"I don't want you to get blood poisoning from that wound," Mr. Givens said firmly. He smiled, then turned and walked away.

"Guess I shouldn't argue with your old man." El cracked a weak grin, then finished packing his things.

Mr. Givens dropped Andrew off at school. After getting out of the car, Andrew reached into the window and shook El's hand.

"Take care of yourself, El—I mean it."

"I will."

"Write to me, all right?"

"Okay, I will. The best to you, Andrew."

As the car pulled away, Lynette ran up to Andrew.

"Andrew—guess what!"

"What?"

"I got a job at *Life* magazine! I've been writing to Barbara, and she arranged it all. It's just for the summer, working as a receptionist-typist and general all-round office girl, but it's the chance of a lifetime!"

"That's smashing!"

"And it's all because of you!"

"Well, you're so talented, you wouldn't have had any trouble getting it anyway—"

"Don't sell yourself short, Andrew. You got me my dream job, my first step towards being a writer. Someday, I'll dedicate one of my books to you!"

Lynette's exuberance washed over him like a refreshing spring shower, momentarily banishing the unease he felt about El. He walked with her into the building. It wasn't until he was in his first period English class with Shannon that the worries about El began to torment him again.

Oh God, I hope he never touches another drop....

His mother's letters, which had been coming as frequently as two, even three times a week, suddenly stopped.

Maybe she's just been a little busy...Perhaps the mail's just been held up....

One week, two weeks went by, and still no word.

Adolph Hitler committed suicide on April 30th; Berlin surrendered to Soviet forces the next day.

As much as he hated to do it, Andrew asked Lois if Jake had written lately.

"No, he's not much for writing. Gene got a letter from him last week. Jake was so excited about the US and Russian armies meeting at the Elbe. Jake said he trained Russian pilots on Hurricanes when he was up in Murmansk."

Germany surrendered on May seventh; May eighth was proclaimed V-E Day, and America went berserk with joy.

Andrew listened to the radio reports of the celebrations in London. He found it hard to rejoice with his countrymen, even at the end of almost six years of war, for he was heartsick with fear.

Something's happened to her!

His stomach churned with dread as he walked up the front steps. He knew he would sort through the pile of mail on the table by the door, knew there wouldn't be a letter from his mother. It had been more than three weeks since he'd heard a word from her. He let himself in, looked at the letters scattered on the table by the door: bills, a letter to Mr. Givens from Lee, another package of "fan mail" from Barbara—he would open it later.

He walked to the front window and gazed out at the lovely spring day, trying to calm the terror raging within him.

Maybe I got a letter, and Lois has already put it by the tea things in the breakfast room....

"Lois—did I get any mail from my mother today?"

"Sorry, no," Lois called from the kitchen. "You got another package from Barbara, though."

He gazed out the window again.

Oh God, please let her be all right....

"Sorry no mail, but would you mind a personal appearance, young man?"

Chapter 45

*A*ll Andrew knew was that one second he was staring disconsolately out the window; the next second he was in his mother's arms. She was laughing and crying as she ran her fingers through his hair and smothered him with kisses. He was too overcome to speak. Funny, she seemed smaller....

"Let me look at you, darling." She pushed him away a bit, gazed over him, shook her head slowly in disbelief.

"I knew you'd grown...all those pictures I'd gotten of you—Oh, Andrew—I can't believe—it's been so long—" She threw herself at him again. "Oh, Andrew, you're so like him—" she whispered as she embraced him once more.

To be with her again, to hear her speak of him—he felt as if he would burst with joy....

"Well, you two, how about catching up on each other over a nice piece of apple cobbler?" Lois laughed.

"Sounds smashing!" Andrew's mother exclaimed. She drew him into the kitchen. Leaning against the sink was Jake.

Back like the bloody plague, Andrew thought.

Jake blinked, nodded at Andrew, swallowed.

"Oh Jake, look how much he's grown! Can you believe it!" Andrew was presented by his mother for Jake's inspection. "Your mother has certainly taken good care of him!"

Andrew gently disengaged himself from his mother, then took her hand and led out of the kitchen and upstairs to his room.

"I just want to show you something."

"What?"

What? He had no bloody idea what—all he wanted was to get her away from Jake....

His eyes searched his room, then settled on the giant box of letters under the window.

"Look, Mum—" He brought the box to her. "All these letters—people wrote to me about the story."

Her eyes widened. "My goodness, Andrew—you're quite a celebrity! How could you possibly answer them all?"

"I've answered a few. It would be so nice to have some kind of special machine to do the same letter over, just change the name and a few things. But I really don't mind all the work. It's rather fun to get so much mail."

She poked through the letters.

"All of that pretty stationery! You seem to have a quite a few female correspondents."

"Oh...they're from people of all different ages. A lot of mothers and teachers have written."

Her eyes searched the room, then focused on the drawing Lee-Ann had given him.

"That's from Lee-Ann, Mr. Givens's great-niece," Andrew told her. "It's Lassie and me and the Little House on the Prairie on the White Cliffs of Dover."

His mother laughed. "Yes, Lois wrote me about your little friend. It was so good of you to comfort her after her father was killed." She hugged him again, gazed lovingly at him once more.

She didn't have to say it—her eyes said it all:

You're so like him!

Her embrace seemed to force the words from him:

"I was so worried about you—I hadn't heard from you for weeks and weeks. I was afraid something had happened—"

"Darling, I've been writing all along. Haven't you gotten any of my letters?"

He shook his head. "Not for almost a month. I was so afraid for you, when you said you were flying to Germany—" He cleared his throat, trying to suppress the catch in his voice. The effort only brought tears to his eyes.

"Oh *darling!*" She hugged him even more tightly.

He burrowed his face in her shoulder. It was all in the past now—the war, the fear, the anguish of being apart. The sight of her, the sound of her, the feel of her arms around him—it was almost enough to shatter him with joy.

The only thing I need is for Dad to come home!

"...Well, we thought it would take weeks to get transport to America." Andrew's mother handed the basket of rolls to Lois. "There was a mad rush westward after V-E Day, but Jake bumped into a B-17 pilot he'd once done a favor for—tell them, Jake."

Jake shook his head, "It was nothing, part of the job—"

"You're *so* modest, darling!" Andrew's mother chirped. "Well, last year Jake was escorting a B-17 back across the Channel after it had gotten badly shot up on a raid over Germany. It had no radio, was flying on only two engines, and had no choice but to land at an emergency airstrip. As they approached the airstrip, Jake noticed another Fortress coming in for a landing from the other direction, so he made a mad dash towards the oncoming plane, waggled his wings and buzzed round and round it. The pilot pulled up just in time. Well, this pilot sought out Jake and said if he ever needed a favor to give him a call. Wouldn't you know, Jake ran into him in London yesterday, found out he was flying back to the States, and before you could say 'Bob's your uncle,' Jake and I found ourselves on a B-17, headed westward. Sorry, there wasn't time to cable you that we were coming."

"Oh, no problem," Lois laughed. "I almost dropped the phone when you called this morning. Andrew had just left for school. You missed him by about ten minutes."

"Mum—can't I stay home from school tomorrow?" Andrew asked. "We can go out together for a picnic—just the two of us. There's so much I want to tell you!"

"Well, we'll see."

"He's doing just fine in school, Alice," Lois said. "I don't think missing a day will hurt him."

"Is that all right with you, Jake? You don't have any plans, do you?" Andrew's mother asked.

Bloody hell! Why does she have to ask his permission? He won't be satisfied until she's a simpering, subservient ninny! It was never like this with Dad—

"Fine by me," Jake smiled.

"We can have a picnic by the lake," Andrew suggested. "We could take the bus. If you'd like, I'll even take you to Plainfield to go shopping." He thought he'd better plan things out so that they wouldn't need to be driven anywhere; it wouldn't do to have Jake chauffeuring them around.

"Sounds lovely," his mother said.

They had a marvelous time at the lake. Andrew got a little hoarse recounting all that had happened (all the good things, that is) during the past year and a half. He brought along the book in which his letter to Aunt Jane had been published. His mother shook her head in delighted amazement as she read it.

"Oh darling—I'm so proud of you! How did it all come about?"

"It was an assignment for English class. We had to write about the war and our experiences and all. So I thought I'd write a letter to Aunt Jane and use it as my assignment, too. My teacher, Miss Fitt—"

"You have a teacher named *Misfit?*" his mother squealed.

"No, not really. I mean, her name is Miss Fittipaldi, but she told us to call her Miss Fitt, for short. Well, she had a friend who was writing a book about children and the war, and Miss Fitt showed her my letter and she wanted to use it."

"That's just marvelous, darling! Isn't it fabulous how many wonderful things have happened because you came to America?"

Andrew nodded, grabbed a cheese sandwich, and took a bite. He wanted to bring up the subject of how soon they'd be going back to England, but thought it might put a damper on his mother's rapture over how well he had "settled in" in America. So he asked, "When is Aunt Jane coming home?"

His mother shrugged. "Probably not for a few more months. Wars may be over in a day, but it takes a long time to get things all organized, or rather, unorganized, when the shooting's over."

"Where is she right now? She would never tell me where she was. I figured she went to North Africa, since she knows French. Did she get to go to France?"

"Yes, she did."

"I can't wait to see her again! It's been so long, even longer than I've been away from you. She won't even recognize me!"

His mother smiled, poked through the tin of cookies Lois had packed, and pulled out a snickerdoodle. Between bites, she talked about her ferrying duties.

"1944 was the busiest year for the ATA. Aircraft production was at its peak just before the Normandy Invasion and any bad weather resulted in an appalling backlog. And the *planes!* I remember being so thrilled flying my first Hurricane four years ago; last year I flew Typhoons, Tempests, Corsairs, Hellcats, and Mustangs. I transferred to

Hamble just before the invasion, and saw the build-up of all sorts of ships and landing craft in the Channel."

"The date and destination of the Invasion were, of course, top secret. I knew something was up when I ferried a Spitfire to a maintenance unit at the beginning of June and found that the station was abuzz with a bizarre activity: Black and white stripes were being painted on the planes. I found out later that these were the special 'Invasion Stripes,' so that Allied planes would be clearly recognized."

"No one expected the Invasion to go when it did. The weather just before it was the ghastliest ever—horrendous rain and gales. Eisenhower took a gamble that the weather would clear, and it did. At Hamble we were aware of what had happened when, that morning, we found that all the ships and landing craft had gone."

"As I wrote you, the ATA began ferrying to the continent in the fall—just the male pilots, what with the appalling lack of loos for the ladies! Finally, at the end of December, we women were allowed to go, too. Besides ferrying planes, the ATA ran a sort of transport-ambulance service, carrying supplies in the Ansons to the forward bases and returning to England with wounded and war orphans."

"Have you seen Marlys or Kaz lately?" Andrew asked. "They used to write to me every week or so, but I haven't heard from them for the past few months."

"Oh, their contracts were already up and they left for America in March. Marlys was going to start up a charter service in Los Angeles. I don't know what Kaz planned on doing. She called things off with her Norwegian chap, and Marlys decided she didn't want to marry her Wing Commander. Well, that's the way of it with wartime romances sometimes." She pursed her lips, looked as if she wanted to say something, but grabbed a chocolate chip cookie and munched it in silence.

Andrew's heart skipped a beat:

That's the way of it with these wartime romances sometimes....

Better not ask her when they would be going back to England, at least not today, he decided. If she were brooding about Jake, let her brood. Also, he didn't want to give her the impression that he was too eager to return home, fearing she might think he'd been dreadfully unhappy.

Best for her to look to me for comfort, not to worry about how I'm doing.

I'll just wait a day or two, then casually mention it. After all, she's only just arrived— better give her time to relax and think about things....

Perhaps by this time next week, I'll be in England!

His mother came to his room after supper. He had gone upstairs to practice his guitar, banking on the premise that his mother would choose his company over Jake's, which she did.

He played *All Quiet on the Potomac* for her. It was a gentle, bittersweet song, sure to stir up memories of happier times.

She seemed lost in thought as he played the final chord. Then she touched his arm.

"I thought of telling you about this while we were at our picnic today, but we were having such a lovely time; I didn't want to ruin things. Not that I don't want to ruin

things right now—" She sighed. "I guess there's never a good time for bad news...."
She gazed at Lee-Ann's drawing.

"What, Mum?" He squeezed her hand.

If it's all over with Jake, never fear...I'll be here to comfort you, and when Dad comes home—

"Andrew, I know I should have written to you about this but—" She bit her lip. "I just didn't want to break this to you from a distance." She took a deep breath, then spoke.

"Thomas and Mrs. Tuttle—there was a V-1 attack last August. They were killed...."

"*Killed?*" he croaked.

She nodded. "At least it was over very quickly...." She blinked, and a tear slid down her cheek.

He put his arms around her, and realized he was crying too.

Andrew hated returning to school the next day; his grief over Thomas and Mrs. Tuttle was aggravated by the thought of his mother being in Jake's company all day.

Bet he's trying to comfort her....

As soon as he got home from school, he urged her to come to his room, where he played gentle ballads on his guitar until supper. It seemed to soothe her; she suggested that he play for everyone that evening.

"Jake's parents hear me practicing all the time. I don't want to bore them," he told her. "Tell you what—why don't you come upstairs after supper and I'll give you another private concert."

So that night she curled up on his bed as he played lullabies, folk songs, and even a few Christmas carols. It was quite late when she kissed him good-night. As he lay in bed and thought of her snuggling up to Jake, he knew he should approach her about returning to England.

Jake won't be very happy about going to England, surely! All the more reason to get things arranged as soon as possible.

The next morning at breakfast Andrew's mother seemed to have recovered from her melancholy. She chattered excitedly about Jake's role in the Normandy Invasion.

"Jake flew low cover over the Invasion armada. He said it was the most incredible sight, wasn't it darling?"

"The Channel was so thick with ships and landing craft it looked as if you could get from England to France just by hopping from one boat to another," Jake said.

"The Allies had complete air superiority, isn't that right, Jake?" Andrew's mother gazed adoringly at Jake, as if he had won the war single-handedly.

"The Luftwaffe only put up two fighter planes. It was about the closest thing to a piece of cake the RAF has ever seen. We just went wherever we wanted, shooting up anything that didn't have a white star or a roundel on it. It was a duck shoot, really. It seemed as if the war was over for us. The guys on the beaches, though—it was just beginning for them."

Andrew couldn't get a word in edgewise.

I'll wait until I'm home from school, get her away from Jake, then pop the question.

All day in school he mentally rehearsed what he should say. When he arrived home his mother greeted him with a warm embrace.

"Darling—I have *wonderful* news for you!"

We're going back to England!

"You're going to *love* this!"

Right away!

"How would you like to get out of school a few days early?"

All right, in a few weeks, then....

"I'd love to, Mum."

"Oh darling, this is the most *marvelous* thing, and Jake has arranged it all! We're going to ferry some planes out to California!"

California!

"...We're picking up a Stinson Reliant in Pennsylvania, then flying down to Georgia to get another plane, a Skyfarer. They both need to be in California by the second week of July. We decided to give ourselves a few weeks, so that we can sightsee various places and visit with Jake's relatives in Nebraska. When we get to California we can take a few more weeks to tour around. Wouldn't you just *love* being able to pick oranges off a tree? We could see Hollywood, San Francisco, the Redwoods, maybe even go up to Oregon! Jake used to go on holiday in the mountains in Oregon—he says they're ever so lovely! Then we could motor back to New Jersey, stop off along the way and visit different places. We'll just take the whole summer off and see America—just the three of us! Oh darling, doesn't that sound *wonderful?*"

Enfolding him in another embrace, she didn't see the dismay that swept over him. Then she pulled him into the kitchen. Jake was sipping a cup of coffee by the stove.

"Oh Jake, I told Andrew all about it!" Andrew's mother gushed. "Have you called your relatives in Nebraska?"

"Yeah, they're looking forward to meeting you—and Andrew." Jake smiled at Andrew. "They really liked that story in *Life* about you. Don't be surprised if they roll out the red carpet for you!"

"Well, um—I've got some homework to do. I'd better start in on it."

"Don't you want some chocolate chip cookies, Andrew?" Lois asked. "Fresh out of the oven!"

"Um, no thanks...later, all right?"

He took the steps, double time. Once within his room, he flung himself onto the bed.

Bloody, bloody hell! That bastard had to go and ruin everything!

"I'll be sorry to lose you, Andrew." Mr. Givens passed a platter of ham to Andrew's mother and smiled at her. "Your son has brought in more new customers in the past two months than I've gotten in the past two years. Everyone thinks he's the nicest kid—and they just love that English accent."

Andrew's mother beamed as she transferred a slice of ham to her plate. "That's wonderful, Andrew!"

"Like to find someone as nice as him for a replacement," Mr. Givens said. "I'll put an ad in the paper. I'd appreciate it if you'd interview some candidates, Andrew."

"Be glad to," Andrew replied.

There was a knock at the front door.

"I'll get it," Andrew said.

He opened the door to find Shannon standing on the front porch. Shannon put his finger up to his lips, then walked to the dining room and waved at Jake.

"Hiya, Charlie!"

"Shannon!" Jake jumped up, threw his arm around Shannon's shoulder and pounded him on the back.

"Tail-End Charlie—good to see you!" Shannon noted the puzzled expression on Andrew's mother's face, and explained:

"My brother Danny used to tag after me, and Jake would tag after Danny. That's why I called him Tail-End Charlie, or Charlie, for short."

"We're just about to have dessert—peach pie," Lois smiled. "Your favorite, Shannon."

"Excuse me," Andrew said. "I've got to finish up my homework."

"Hey Andrew, stay awhile," Shannon urged.

"I'd better not. I've got to get ahead on all my schoolwork because I'm leaving school a few days early."

"You are—why?"

"Jake and Alice are going to ferry some planes to California, and Andrew is going along," Lois said.

"California, no kidding!" Shannon exclaimed. "You'll really get to see the country, Andrew. What an opportunity!"

"Yes, um—well, see you tomorrow," Andrew said.

The excited conversation nagged at him as plodded up the stairs.

Buggeration!

I thought Shannon was my friend! Jake won't be satisfied until he's ruined everything for me. Even Lindy is schmoozing up to him!

Andrew's mother presided over his quarterly measurement check on June fourth.

"Sixty-seven inches—you're almost as tall as me!" she chirped.

He weighed in at a hundred and thirty four pounds, and his mother was ever so pleased with that too.

"We ought to keep you in America for good," she laughed. "At this rate, you'll tower over *me* before long."

Not funny, Andrew thought.

"Well, um, why do you want this job?" Andrew asked.

"'Cause you ain't gonna find anybody faster 'n me!" Applicant Number 11 smirked.

"Well, I have your phone number. I'll get in touch with you if Mr. Givens decides to hire you for the position," Andrew said. "Next!"

Applicant Number 12 shuffled forward, clutching his cap in his hands. He was at least a head shorter than all the other boys who'd applied for the job. Andrew glanced at the application: Harry Nigel Crossley had indicated his age as being fourteen.

And pigs might fly, Andrew thought.

"Did you see that kid's bike?" Applicant Number 11 cocked his head at Applicant Number 12. "What a *wreck!*"

"Um, thank you very much," Andrew said.

Harry Nigel Crossley bit his lip, swallowed.

"You're fourteen?" Andrew asked.

"Yes, sir, fourteen—I'm sorry I don't ha' me docs. We lost everything in the Blitz, all our docs, everything, but I *am* fourteen, I am." The boy's Cockney accent was so strong he might have been born with the Bow Bells ringing over his head. "I'm in the sixth grade because I missed so much school during the Blitz and then we moved away from London because of the doodlebugs, so I missed school then, too."

"All right, fourteen it is," Andrew said.

Harry chewed his lip.

Strange, Andrew thought. If I were in England, I would have turned away at the sound of a Cockney accent—now it sounds like music.

"You're from London, then, Harry?"

"Yes, London, yes sir."

Andrew smiled. "You can call me Andrew."

"Yes—um, thank you."

"When did you come to America, Harry?"

"Six months ago. Me sister got married to a Ya—sorry, an American GI, and we, that is Gert, me, and me brother Bob—he's me younger brother, he's eleven—we came to America."

"Are your parents still in England, then?"

"Um—no, well, me mum is, in a way. She was killed in the Blitz, in May of '40 she was, and me dad was killed in North Africa. That's why me and Bob came to America with Gert."

"Sorry to hear that. Well, what kind of experience do you have, Harry?"

"None, sir—I mean, uh, Andrew, but I'm fast on me bike. It's old, but I'll buy a new one as soon's I can, and I'll work 'ard for you and do me best, no fear about that, I promise."

"Why do you want this job?"

"I like to work, I do, and I'd like to get a job so I can get a new bike, which I'll get right away, I promise, and some, um, things for me and me brother and I'll save too, I promise."

Andrew noted Harry's tight-fitting, threadbare clothes.

"Andrew, delivery for Mrs. Federico," Mr. Givens called.

"Why don't you come with me?" Andrew said. "Meet me at the back of the store."

He picked up the package from Mr. Givens and waited at the back for Harry. A chorus of squeaks and crunches preceded Harry's progress; he rode up to Andrew on a battered, ancient contraption.

"Follow me," Andrew said.

The chain on Harry's bike kept slipping. Harry kept assuring Andrew: "Sorry, sorry—I'll get a new bike as soon's I can. This one belonged to Russ, Gert's 'usband."

At Mrs. Federico's, Andrew handed the package to Harry.

"Here's some lollipops, too. I give them to any children at the house; first I find out if it's all right. Mrs. Federico has two little boys."

Harry knocked on the door. Mrs. Federico answered.

"Good day to you, mum," Harry said. "Delivery from Givens Pharmacy."

Mrs. Federico smiled, paid Harry for the order, and gave him a nickel tip.

"Thank you very much, mum, and here's some treats for your boys." Little eager hands reached for the lollipops.

"Thank you," said Mrs. Federico. "A new delivery boy, Andrew? Is Stan leaving too?"

"No, I am," Andrew replied. "My mother arrived here from England last week."

"Oh, Andrew! So you're going back to England then? Sorry to see you leave. You take care of yourself."

On the way back, Harry kept apologizing for the slow progress of his bicycle.

"Don't worry about that," Andrew assured him. "This bike comes with the job. If Mr. Givens decides to hire you, you can use it."

After arriving back at the pharmacy, Andrew introduced Harry to Mr. Givens. Harry seemed very nervous at first; then Mr. Givens asked, "When can you start?"

"Right now, I mean, tomorrow—would that be all right?"

"Can you be here by three-thirty?"

"Yes, sir."

Mr. Givens looked at Harry's application. "Are you sure? You live all the way in Plainfield—"

"Oh, I can, sir, I can! I'll come straightaway after school, no fear about that."

"Well, then, be here tomorrow, about three-forty-five would be fine." Mr. Givens turned back to his work.

"I got the job?" Harry whispered to Andrew.

Andrew nodded and smiled.

"Oh, Gene, can you imagine those poor boys losing both parents? It must have been terribly frightening for them to come to America alone. At least Andrew had his mother and Jake." Lois set out another bowl of scrambled eggs on the breakfast table.

"They didn't come alone; they came with their sister and they're all living with her mother-in-law."

"Let's invite them all to supper sometime, okay?"

"Are you going to try to fatten them up with your delicious home cooking?"

"Well, Harry's so thin, even more so than Andrew was. He really should have a bite to eat when he gets in."

"I tell him to grab a candy bar and give him money for some hot cocoa when he comes to work."

"Well, I'll pack a nutritious after-school snack for him. You can bring it with your lunch."

Mr. Givens gave her a hug. "You'd mother the whole world if you had half the chance."

It was while his mother was taking him clothes shopping that Andrew got the idea.

When he got home, he went to the spare room and got the huge box containing all his outgrown clothes.

"See Mum? I don't need them anymore. I'm sure they'll fit Harry, and the smaller ones should fit Bob."

"That's a marvelous idea, darling. We can take them with us when we pick up Bob and Gert for supper tomorrow. Lois is going to stop by the store just before closing time and pick up Harry so he can show us the way."

Andrew went with Lois and Harry to Plainfield the next day. Harry and Bob lived in a small upstairs apartment with their sister and her mother-in-law. The boys shared a tiny room and slept on pallets on the floor. As it turned out, Gert couldn't come; she was pregnant, and the doctor had just ordered her to stay off her feet.

Andrew was disconcerted at the sight of Gert: She couldn't have been more than a year or two older that he was.

When the war started, she was probably playing with dolls. Before it's over, she'll have a real baby of her own.

"Gert—look at all these clothes!" Bob exclaimed. He rooted through the box and pulled out Andrew's first pair of jeans. "These'll fit me—don't they look grand?"

Gert was propped up on the sofa with pillows under her legs. "Thank you so much," she said to Andrew. "It's so kind of you to give all these nice clothes to my brothers."

"Not at all," Andrew told her. "I've outgrown them, so it's just the sensible thing to let someone else have them."

To Andrew's delight, Jake would not be home for supper; he'd decided to go out to dinner with Shannon. Lois put out a fantastic spread for the boys: roast beef, scalloped potatoes, baked sweet corn, lots of biscuits.

"So you boys were in London during the Blitz?" she asked.

"Yes mum, we were," Harry answered. "We got 'vacuated the year before and got sent to the country."

"We had to ride the train for a long, long time," Bob added. "When we got to the place where we 'ad to stay, they put everybody in the town square and then people came and picked out who they wanted. We was left over at the end, so they put us in a truck and drove us through town, and called out if anyone wanted to take us. It was 'orrible."

"This lady took us, but she was mean," Harry went on. "She used to lock us in the larder—"

"And 'er 'usband did nasty things to Gert," Bob said.

Harry glared at his brother. Bob bit his lip, then said, "Our mum came to get us, right before Christmas, and said we was never going to be 'vacuated no more."

"So when the Blitz started, we sheltered in the tubes," Harry said.

"Dickie was the youngest. He wasn't in school yet, so he waited outside the tube all day to save our spaces."

"Dickie?" Lois asked.

"Our brother," Harry said.

"Remember when that shelter warden took Dickie's places?" Bob looked at Harry. "And Mrs. Makepeace said that next time, she'd take off all 'er clothes and lay them down to save our spaces—"

Dickie!

"Was this Mrs. Makepeace a large, black-haired woman?" Andrew asked.

"Why yes, she was," Harry replied. "Did you know 'er?"

"I saw her—I'm sure it was her! What Underground station were you sheltering at?"

Harry shook his head. "I don't remember. It was near where me mum worked, near 'yde Park."

Andrew turned to his mother. "What station were we at when we had to get off the train? Remember, right before my birthday, when we got bombed."

"I don't remember, darling. We were on our way to Paddington Station."

"Could it have been near Hyde Park?"

"Yes, I believe it was."

Andrew turned back to Harry. "Did this happen in March—March third, to be exact?"

Harry nodded his head. "Yes, I think it was. I remember, because Dickie died a week after that, on March tenth, me dad's birthday."

"He *died?*"

"He got pneumonia," Bob said. "He was waiting outside all day and Mrs. Makepeace said he was coughing, but he told 'er he was all right and he 'ad to save our spaces. When they let everyone in at four o'clock in the afternoon, Dickie laid down on his space and Mrs. Makepeace thought he was asleep. But then she 'eard 'im breathing funny, and she turned 'im over and 'is lips was blue. She ran and carried 'im to 'ospital, but he died. We went to get our mum, but she didn't get there in time. Dickie was already dead. After that, our mum said we weren't never going to go in the tubes no more."

Andrew stared at the ceiling.

Dead! Of pneumonia!

Because he had to wait out in the cold all day to save a few square feet of safety for his family!

It was a good thing tomorrow was Saturday, for he surely would not get to sleep very soon. Dickie's tearstreaked face tormented him every time he tried to focus his thoughts on something else.

When sleep did come, it brought with it a dreadful nightmare:

He was waiting outside the Underground, and his chest started to hurt horribly and he couldn't breathe. The pain shot out to his fingers and toes and his breath rattled in his lungs. All he wanted to do was curl up in a nice warm bed, but he couldn't leave— he had to save a place for his mother and father....

He awoke in a cold sweat; after a long, long time, he fell into a fitful sleep. His mother awakened him at noon.

He walked home with Miriam, as usual. He didn't tell her his thoughts.
The only consolation of the whole thing is that I'll get to see you again....
"When will you be coming back here?"
"Sometime in August, I suppose."
"Then you'll be going back to England, won't you?"
"Probably."
She gazed off into the distance. She'd been doing that a lot lately, and long before he'd told her he was leaving for California. The horrific images of the concentration camps had stunned everyone. Miriam had not seemed so surprised by it all; her anguish went deeper than that, to a place beyond Andrew's reach.
"Have you heard from Eva yet?"
Miriam shook her head. "I hope she's all right. I worry about her, wandering around Europe, trying to find her family. She told me she would never rest until she finds them, or finds out what happened to them."

"Andrew, another load of mail," Lois chirped.
"My goodness!" Andrew's mother gaped at the package from Barbara.
"You also got a letter from your German POW," Lois said.
"*German POW?*" Andrew's mother asked.
Andrew's mind frantically searched for some way to explain how it was that he was corresponding with a former soldier of the Third Reich, but Lois was already telling the tale to Andrew's mother.
"...and so he dropped the Hershey bar to him, didn't you Andrew?"
"Well, um, I didn't mean to—it was sort of an accident. I was holding it and it slipped...." Andrew saw the upturned corners of his mother's mouth.
"...And then this man recognized Andrew in the *Life* article," Lois went on, "And wrote him the nicest letter thanking him, so Andrew wrote back to him and we sent him a package of Hershey bars—what does he say Andrew?"
Andrew tore open the envelope and scanned the letter, trying to make sense of the fractured English. Erich thanked him profusely for the chocolate bars, said he was doing well and was glad the war was over, and worried about his family still in Germany. At the end he wrote:

I must stay here for while. We see films about concentration camps in Germany, and it is very much shock. I am very much regret the terrible things of my country, not only to Jews but to all others. I hope such things never happen no more forever.

"Oh darling, you've got two Irvine jackets too!" Andrew's mother laughed at Jake.

"Well, let's bring all four of them," Jake said. "Never know when an extra one might come in handy."

"Here, Andrew, try this extra one of mine on." His mother held out the jacket for him. "It should fit you just fine—see?"

Andrew fastened the jacket, then inspected himself in the mirror in the guest room. *Just like Dad....*

"Don't you look *smashing*, darling!" his mother squealed. "Oh, I've got something else for you." She reached into one of her drawers and gave him a pair of sunglasses. "You'll be sitting up front with me in the Reliant and I don't want the glare to hurt your eyes. Now, have you got all your things packed?"

"Yes, Mum."

"Good, we'll be leaving very early tomorrow. We'll take the train to Philadelphia and pick up the Reliant, then we'll fly down to Georgia to pick up the Skyfarer. Oh, Andrew, this is so *marvelous!*

No point in trying to reason with her, Andrew thought. Besides, she doesn't care about me anyway. She only cares about *him*, only wants to do what *he* wants to do....

"We'll get to see the United States from the air, darling! Not even many Americans have that opportunity! Aren't you thrilled?"

Andrew nodded absently. "Well, I'd better get to bed. See you in the morning. Night." He gave her a kiss on the cheek.

Jake kept pointing out various features of the eastern seaboard on the way down to Georgia. Andrew, sitting in the backseat of the Reliant, glanced out ever so briefly when his mother exclaimed over something, then turned back to reading one of the books he'd toted along. He could care less about Washington D.C., Kitty Hawk, Fort Sumter, or any of the other sights Jake pointed out.

The Skyfarer was at an airfield outside of Savannah. They landed there just after seven o'clock. Jake went to the hangar to take a look at the Skyfarer while Andrew and his mother tied down the Reliant.

Jake came back, shaking his head.

"What's the matter, darling?" Andrew's mother asked.

Jake motioned her to follow, then turned and walked back to the hangar. She skipped along after him. Andrew followed; as far as was possible, he was bloody well going to make sure she didn't spend any unnecessary time alone with Jake.

"Now I know why we're getting paid so well for this job." Jake went into the hangar and pointed to a small plane.

"The Skyfarer?" she asked. She walked towards it. Like the Reliant, the Skyfarer was a single-engined craft, only smaller.

"Look's like a sturdy enough kite to me," she pronounced.

Jake raked his fingers through his hair. "I should have checked things out—"

"What's the problem?"

"The problem is, it's only got sixty-five horsepower."

Andrew's mother stared at him. "You've *got* to be bloody joking."

Jake let out a slow breath.

"Oh, dear," Andrew's mother said. "Well, it's a good thing we allowed ourselves a bit of extra time. What do you think it'll do—ninety miles an hour?"

"With a tail wind, maybe. It's not the speed that bothers me, Alice. It's how we're going to get this thing over the mountains."

"Perhaps I should fly it. I'm a bit lighter than you, so—"

No, NO—I don't want to be alone with Jake....

"No, Alice. You'd better take the Reliant. The Skyfarer is a little tricky. It was built for a paraplegic, so it has all hand controls."

"Darling, I've flown more kinds of planes than you have—"

"It would be better for you to be in the Reliant, with Andrew. We already decided that, remember?"

"But—"

"No buts—you and Andrew go in the Reliant. You two will just have to fly circles round me all the way out to California."

They got an early start the next morning; if at all possible, Jake wanted to make it to Nebraska in two days. The day was already unbearably hot and humid by the time they got to the airfield. Jake took off first to get a head start. Andrew helped his mother do the pre-flight checklist, then called out her airspeed as she sped down the runway, just like he used to do when they all flew together in the Puss Moth.

They flew over the cotton fields of the South. As the Skyfarer was so much slower, Andrew's mother flew circles, arcs, and ornate curlicues in the Reliant, weaving a fanciful counterpoint to Jake's slow progress. They refueled and had lunch at noon, then continued on their way. Andrew would have liked to have stopped for tea in the afternoon, but Jake had already decided to go straight on as far as possible.

"We need to take advantage of the daylight and good weather as much as we can," he told Andrew's mother. "I've already called my folks in Nebraska to tell them we'll be a little late."

They arrived outside the small town of Daniel in the late afternoon. Jake didn't want to chance going to another airfield farther away, fearing that it might get dark before they got there. The mosquitos buzzed about them as they tied down their planes, and the sultry heat wrapped around them like a soggy blanket.

Why the bloody hell did the Yanks ever fight their stupid Civil War to keep this Godforsaken place?

They took a taxi to the only hotel in town, a dilapidated structure with cockroaches skittering along the floors.

"They's a place t'eat down th' street, 'cross from th' *PO-leece* station." The girl at the desk waved her hand in the general direction.

"This will be my first taste of southern cooking," Andrew's mother chirped as they walked along the main street of town. (It appeared to be the *only* street in town.)

"Don't get your hopes up," Jake said.

Andrew's mother skipped ahead a bit, her head swivelling around to look at the sights.

She acts as if she's in Wonderland, Andrew thought. He tried not to show his disdain for this wretched place, knowing that Jake would exploit any spot of bother.

His mother slowed as she approached the restaurant; she turned in consternation to Jake and pointed at the sign posted on the door:

Whites Only.

Jake's eyes narrowed as he regarded the cardboard missive.

"Why don't we just buy some groceries and eat at the hotel?" Andrew's mother suggested.

They walked back down the street. Jake looked clearly perturbed; Andrew's mother seemed deep in thought.

Good! I don't care what rains on their parade—just as long as it gets rained on!

Andrew's mother slipped her hand into Jake's.

"I never realized before now that this is what it all boils down to, darling. Please don't think I'm judging your country—it's only that I see mine for the first time." She gazed around; her eyes flashed at a *Whites Only* drinking fountain.

"We British don't need to post signs. Everyone is expected to know his or her place. It was a part of my upbringing that I never questioned, or even realized was there, until now." She shook her head. "What a waste—what a stupid, bloody, waste!"

Jake put his arm around her shoulder. They came to a grocery store. The only sign affixed to it read: *Effie Mae's General Store, Established 1914. All Welcome.*

"Well, this looks like the place," Andrew's mother smiled.

Inside, a tiny gray-haired woman greeted them.

"I'm Effie Mae. What can I do for you?" she asked in a soft drawl.

"Alice Givens, pleased to meet you. We just got into town and would like a bite to eat," Andrew's mother said. "Perhaps a loaf of bread and some sort of sandwich filling—cheese or something like that."

"I've got a case of cold cuts," Effie May said. "I can make you some sandwiches—see that there sign?" She cocked her head to the sign over the deli case. "Potato salad or coleslaw on the side, Coke or lemonade or iced tea to drink. You can sit out on that screened-in porch over there—it catches a nice breeze."

"Sounds lovely." Andrew's mother beamed at Jake. "Um, let's see—turkey and Swiss cheese sounds good to me. What about you, Jake?"

"Fine with me."

"Andrew?"

Andrew scanned the sign. "I'll take the chicken salad."

Effie Mae went behind the counter and started putting the sandwiches together.

"So, you folks just get into town? Where y'all from?"

"My son and I are from England," Andrew's mother said. "My husband Jake is from New Jersey, but he spent the last five years in England, in the RAF."

"England! My, that's a pretty country, all those castles and palaces. I've never been there, but I read all the time. What brings you to this neck of the woods?"

"We're ferrying some planes out to California."

"California! My, y'all are going to get to see the country, aren't you! Would you like potato salad or coleslaw?"

Andrew's mother inspected the salad bins in the deli case.

"Decisions, decisions—they both look so good!"

"I'll give y'all a scoop of each. Coleslaw's my mother's special recipe, used to take first place in the county fair nearly every year. Would you like some iced tea? It's fresh made."

"Marvelous—thank you very much!" Andrew's mother said.

Effie Mae handed them their plates and they went out to the screened-in porch.

"You just set yourselves down. I'll bring a pitcher of tea and some glasses."

"Thank you ever so much," Andrew's mother said.

Effie Mae brought in the iced tea. "Would you mind if I set with you for awhile?"

"Not at all!" Andrew's mother moved to make room for her.

"It's just that we don't get visitors here very much. I always like to talk with people from other places. I've hardly been out of Daniel for the past thirty years. Running a store doesn't give a body much free time to roam the world. I went to Mobile three years ago, to visit my sister. Did you folks fly all the way down from New Jersey?"

"Pennsylvania, actually," Andrew's mother replied. "That's where we picked up one of our planes. We got the other plane near Savannah. We're hoping to get to Nebraska tomorrow. My husband has relatives there."

"My, that's halfway cross the country! I've never been west of the Mississippi. I've got a picture book of the Rocky Mountains. Some of those places out there look like the far side of paradise." She smiled at Andrew. "And you're going to get to see it all— what a lucky boy you are!"

Andrew, chomping on his sandwich, nodded perfunctorily.

"These boys, just about this age they like to eat you out of house and home. Would you like another sandwich, Andrew?"

"Um, yes please."

"Oh, if y'all would like dessert, I've got some pecan pie. In fact, you can have the whole pie in exchange for a favor for me, if you don't mind." Without waiting for acknowledgement, she launched into her request: "Would you mind sending me some postcards whenever you stop someplace? I'll give you a roll of stamps. Just address the cards to me, Effie Mae Lancaster—I'll give you my address. I'd so like to have post-cards from all the places you see."

"We'd be glad too," Andrew's mother replied with a smile.

The blast of an engine split the air.

Effie Mae narrowed her eyes. "I wish he would get that muffler fixed."

Through the screen Andrew could see a dark blue pickup, splotched with rust primer, pull up to the store. Four men got out and sauntered in.

"Effie Mae!" A tall jowly man yelled. "You seen Ellis?"

Effie Mae stood up, her shoulders squared and her eyes defiant. She walked up to the man.

"No, I haven't, Clay."

"Now, Effie Mae," one of the other men said, "We know his momma does your laundry. You know she won't tell us where he is, but this is all for his own good, *y'unnerstand?*"

"Why don't you leave that boy alone, Robey?" Effie Mae said. "He hasn't done anything wrong."

"He's been gettin' out of hand, steppin' on the wrong toes, if you get my drift," Robey said.

"Maybe those toes need to get stepped on," Effie Mae said. Her pronouncement was greeted with indignant silence.

"Well, we'll find him, don't you worry," Clay said. "If you happen to see him in the meantime, you'd best tell him to mind his ways—maybe we'll go easy on him. Can't let these niggers get too uppity, you know that." He arched an eyebrow, then turned and grabbed a Coke out of the cooler.

"Thank you kindly, Effie Mae." He strutted out of the store, his minions in tow.

Effie Mae stood still for a moment, then turned and walked out to the porch. She looked apologetically at Andrew's mother.

"What's going on?" Andrew's mother asked.

Effie Mae sighed. "Some people—never happy unless they got someone to bully around. That boy hasn't done anything wrong, 'cept come out square against their hateful ways." She shook her head.

Andrew's mother bit her lip, looked worriedly at Jake. He reached for her hand, but said nothing.

Good! At least she sees that this wretched country is not so bloody marvelous after all!

"I wish there was something we could do," Andrew's mother said.

"It'll take a whole lot of doing to change things 'round here." Effie Mae cleared their dishes, then brought in the pecan pie and served them each a slice.

"This is marvelous!" Andrew's mother tasted a piece. She glanced at Jake, who was eating his portion—in silence.

"Just take the rest with you," Effie Mae said. "You can return the pie pan to me when you leave."

"Well, we're leaving very early tomorrow morning."

"Are you staying at the hotel?"

"Yes, we are."

"You can leave it there. I'll pick it up."

"Oh thank you! This will make a delicious breakfast."

Before they left, Effie Mae gave them her address and some stamps. Andrew's mother purchased some food for the next day and a thermos.

"We brought one thermos along, but since we're flying two planes, it would be nice to have one for each of us."

Effie Mae filled the thermos with coffee for the next morning.

"Y'all have yourselves a nice trip, and thank you so much for your kindness in agreeing to send me those postcards. Now, you don't have to send a whole bunch, just a few from special places—especially California." She patted Andrew's shoulder as he left. "You lucky, lucky boy—getting to see the country!"

On their way back to the hotel, Jake looked nervously at Andrew's mother.

"I'm sorry about all that, Alice—"

"Jake! It's not your fault!"

Jake looked off into the distance. "I wanted you to see the country, have a wonderful time. I just feel awful that you got to see the ugly side of things—"

"Jake—it doesn't for one minute change what I feel—" She looked into Jake's eyes, and spoke in a low voice. "What I feel towards this land, and for you. You experienced, first-hand, bigotry and intolerance in my country, and you looked past the bad and saw the good, didn't you?"

Jake nodded and put his arm around her waist. He said nothing more as they walked to the hotel.

They arose before dawn and ate a quick breakfast of pecan pie and coffee (orange juice for Andrew), then Jake called the taxi to take them to the airfield.

It was barely light as Andrew's mother and Jake did the preflight checks on their planes. Andrew helped his mother, glad that he would have her company to himself for the rest of the day. They settled into the cockpit and watched as the Skyfarer trundled down the runway and lifted off.

Good—he's gone! Now it's just my mother and me.

Andrew's mother pushed the starter button, and the Lycoming radial engine roared to life. The Reliant proceeded along at a stately pace, like a debutante parading her finery at her coming-out ball. As the plane arrived at the end of the taxi strip, Andrew's mother turned it onto the access path, inching it slowly forward so that the nose was almost flush with the runway.

"All right, co-pilot, let's do the pre-takeoff checks."

Andrew nodded. His mother locked the brakes, set the mixture to full rich, revved the engine, and turned the magneto switch from *both* to *left*. Andrew eyed the RPM gauge and noted the slight drop in revolutions. She switched the knob back to *both*, and RPMs increased.

"Check," he said.

She switched to the right magneto, then back to both; the RPMs dipped and rose again.

"Check." Andrew knew his mother was watching the gauge too, but he still felt important.

She pulled the pitch control back, and the RPMs dropped much further this time.

"Check."

She pulled the throttle out to the idle setting, reset the pitch control to take-off position, then cranked the trim tab, located on the ceiling of the fuselage, to the take-off setting. She turned to Andrew and smiled.

"What next, copilot?"

"Check controls."

She pushed on the left rudder pedal, then on the right, making sure there was full freedom of movement. She turned the wheel left, then right, then moved the control column in and out.

"Next?"

"Check manifold pressure."

She pushed the throttle all the way in. Andrew noted the increase in manifold pressure.

"Check."

His mother reset the throttle to idle, then she looked skyward, first to the left and then to the right. Andrew's gaze followed hers. It was the pilot's responsibility to check for incoming planes; all the same, he liked to keep an eye on things. He glanced back at his mother. She smiled at him.

"Safety belt?"

"Check."

Staring straight ahead, she began to taxi the plane out onto the runway. Andrew glanced out his window and what he saw stunned him so much his voice came out as a shriek.

"*Mum!*"

"Wh—" She looked out, following his gaze, then her jaw dropped in horror.

"Oh, my *God!*"

Chapter 46

A black teen-aged youth, his face a mask of terror and exhaustion, was running down the taxi strip. Several hundred yards back, the dark blue primer-splotched pickup was in hot pursuit. It had just entered the far end of the taxi strip; the boy was about two-thirds of the way to the Reliant. The pickup slowed, revved its engine. The unmuffled blast roared in almost animal-like ferocity.

"Open the door—" Andrew's mother screamed. In the next breath she urged the boy in a panicked shriek.

"Quick—inside!"

Andrew quickly unlatched his safety belt, turned around, and threw open the passenger door. An instant later, the boy flung himself into the backseat.

"Fasten your safety belt!" Andrew's mother snapped her head back and barked the order. The boy complied, fumbling with the catch.

Andrew's mother glanced skyward, back and forth, then lined the Reliant up with the center of the runway. The pickup, acting like a confused beast, lurched forward, then back, turned one way, veered, jerked the other way, then did a U-turn and proceeded back down the taxi strip away from them. The roar of its motor was overlaid with yells and curses. Andrew's mother scrunched her face in puzzlement at the sight.

As the truck turned onto the access path at the far end of the strip, her eyes bulged in outrage.

"Bloody hell—those bastards are trying to block the runway!"

Andrew had never heard his mother swear so, nor had he ever seen the madly determined look now sweeping across her face. Her lips were drawn in a tight line and her eyes blazed with fury.

"Hang onto your seats—we're going to be in for a wild ride! Andrew, call out the speed—as loud as you can!"

"Right!" he yelled. By now, the pickup had turned onto the runway. Andrew's mother pressed hard down on the brakes and pushed the throttle in until the engine screamed in protest. The truck, aiming at them, swerved a bit as it picked up speed. There were perhaps half a dozen men in the back, all wagging their arms triumphantly. A rope with a noose tied on the end swirled out from one of the outstretched hands.

God stone the crows! She's not going to charge them!

He watched, mesmerized, as she quickly released the brakes. The plane sprang forward.

"Airspeed!" she screamed.

"Uh—forty...forty-five—"

The plane sped down the runway.

Christ on crutches—she's bloody daft!

It was all he could do to keep his eyes on the airspeed indicator.

"Fifty...fifty-five—"

Get out of the way, you bastards, or we'll all end up in a tangle of broken parts and bloody bits!

"Sixty...Sixty-fi—"

She yanked the flap lever to the one-half setting. The plane popped skyward, like a piece of toast shooting out of a toaster. Andrew felt his heart plummet into his stomach. His mother whooped as the plane soared upwards. She pushed the wheel forward, dropping the nose to gain airspeed, then adjusted the throttle and pitch control to the climb setting. After milking up the flaps, she banked the plane into a wide turn so that they could view the scene below.

The pickup veered to and fro like a drunkard, then slewed off the runway. The men in the back flung themselves out and stumbled away from the vehicle as it fell sideways into a ditch. The driver tried to wriggle his chubby body through the window; even from a distance it was obvious he had overestimated the size of the opening through which he was trying to extract his portly form. He glared up at the Reliant, and his mouth formed into a gash of rage.

"Bloody rotters!" Andrew's mother hollered. She waggled the Reliant's wings, then flew onward.

Andrew's jaw dropped. His mother glanced at him, then grinned mischievously.

"Your father taught me that little maneuver. It certainly came in handy when I had to dodge an ME-110 that came in to strafe the airfield as I was taking off in a Spit!"

"*Dad* taught you that?"

She nodded, then tilted her head towards the backseat. The young man sitting behind them seemed frozen in a state of stupefied amazement: His mouth hung open and his eyes were wide with astonishment.

Andrew's mother smiled at him, then reached back her hand in greeting. "Alice Givens, at your service, and this is my son, Andrew."

The boy raised his hand; she grasped it.

"Uh-uh—'Lis Olney," the boy mumbled.

"Ellis?" Andrew's mother queried.

"Uh, L.S. Just the letters," the boy replied softly, as if embarrassed by his name.

"Oh, what does L.S. stand for?"

"Just L.S." He looked uneasy. "Thank you very much...." He swallowed. "Thank you."

"Not at all," Andrew's mother said cheerily. She nodded at Andrew, bidding him to be polite in this bizarre situation.

Andrew, following her lead, extended his hand. "Andrew Hadley-Trevelyan, pleased to meet you." He said his last name a little louder than his first.

The boy took his hand. "Pleased to meet you, too." Andrew noticed the dark eyes flicker with curiosity.

"Well, my young man—" Andrew's mother addressed L.S. as if he were a young viscount, "Where to from here?"

"Um, just away, thank you kindly." He lowered his voice to a whisper and said fiercely, "Just away."

"Away it is!" Andrew's mother proclaimed.

She set her face ahead again; to Andrew she looked like a sculpture of a goddess on the prow of a ship. She adjusted the throttle and pitch control to cruise, then cranked the trim tab for level flight.

Andrew looked out ahead and saw the little Skyfarer plodding along.

"There's Jake," he said.

"My husband," Andrew's mother explained to L.S.

The dark eyes puzzled again.

"We're ferrying these planes out to California," Andrew's mother said.

L.S. nodded. He continued staring at Andrew's mother.

"Are you all right?" she asked. "I hope you're not too shaken up from our short field take-off. It's quite a simple maneuver, really."

"Uh...I've just never met a lady pilot before." L.S. smiled weakly. "Fact is, the only lady pilot I ever heard about was Amelia Earhart."

"Oh, there are quite a few of us around. I was a ferry pilot in the Air Transport Auxiliary in England. There were over a hundred women pilots, and we flew everything from light trainers to four-engined bombers."

L.S.'s eyebrows shot up in surprise. "How did you learn to fly?"

"My late husband, Andrew's father, taught me."

As L.S. glanced at Andrew, his eyes narrowed in what seemed to Andrew to be a kind of understanding.

Andrew's mother pulled up alongside Jake, who noticed their passenger. He pointed at L.S. and put his hands in a palms-up "What's going on?" gesture.

Andrew's mother flashed him a brilliant smile and answered him with her left hand in a V-for-Victory sign. Jake's face registered realization of the identity of their passenger. He grinned, and gave her a thumbs-up.

They landed to refuel and grab a bit to eat. Andrew's mother gleefully related to Jake what had happened and introduced L.S. to him. Jake laughed as he shook L.S.'s hand, and said he hoped L.S. wasn't too shaken up by the unorthodox takeoff.

"I've never even been in a plane before," L.S. told him. "I'd probably have been shaken up by *any* kind of takeoff."

Because of a strong headwind they were already quite a bit behind schedule. Jake doubted that they would make it to Nebraska by nightfall so he called his relatives and told them to expect their arrival the following day. L.S. wanted to call Effie Mae to ask her to give a message to his mother that he was all right.

"We should be at my folks' place in Nebraska by early afternoon tomorrow," Jake told him. "Why don't you ask your mother to be at the store about dinnertime, and give her a call then?"

They landed at an airfield in Iowa a little after five o'clock.

"We can sleep in a bit tomorrow, since we won't be having to chase the daylight," Jake said.

Andrew's mother wanted to do a bit of shopping. She bought some postcards (one to send to Effie Mae, of course), a coffee cup with a pig painted on the side, and a few personal items for L.S.: toothbrush, toothpaste, underwear, socks, sunglasses. They had supper at a diner; L.S. looked around warily as they walked in, as if expecting trouble. There were a few curious glances as they walked to a table, nothing more.

Andrew found himself sharing a room with L.S. at the hotel. As he was unpacking his things, there was a knock on the door.

Andrew answered it, expecting to see his mother, but the door swung back to reveal Jake. He was carrying a stack of clothes.

"L.S., I thought you might be able to fit into my things. When we get to Nebraska tomorrow, we can gather up some more clothes. I have two cousins who are about your size."

"Thanks," L.S. said softly.

Jake cleared his throat. "Listen, Alice and I were talking things over. You're welcome to stay with us as long as you want. If you'd like to go anywhere, we'll get you there somehow. How old are you, anyway?"

"Seventeen."

"Have you graduated from high school yet?"

"No."

"You ought to finish out your schooling. Do you have relatives or friends you can stay with someplace?"

L.S. shook his head. "My whole family's in Daniel, and I—" he looked apologetically at Jake. "I can't go back there."

"Don't worry about it. You can come with us. I think things will fall into place for you, somehow. You can even come back with us to New Jersey, if you'd like."

L.S. smiled. "Thank you very much."

"Well, you two—" Jake grinned at Andrew. "Get a good night's sleep. My folks are quite a lively bunch, and they might wear you out with all their welcoming. Good night."

"Night," L.S. said.

The door softly shut. L.S looked at Andrew. "He's very nice," he said.

Andrew grunted as he finished unpacking his things. There was an uncomfortable silence. Andrew didn't want L.S. to think he was being snobbish, so he smiled at him.

"I guess you never expected to be in Iowa," he said.

L.S. shook his head, grinned. "Not in my wildest dreams."

"Well, to tell the truth, I never expected to be in Iowa, either. I thought I'd be back in England by now."

"How long have you been here—in the U.S., I mean?"

"Almost two years."

"That's a long time to be away from home."

Andrew nodded. "It is." He took a deep breath, wondered what to say next. He found his new roommate a little intriguing: For one thing, L.S. didn't speak with that peculiar patois Sarah used. At first Andrew had been irked by Sarah's mangling of the English language, but after awhile he came to enjoy listening to her. Her dialect was orderly, as orderly as Latin, in its own way. L.S., though, spoke in unadulterated American English graced with only a soft drawl. And though L.S. did not seem to be exactly secretive, Andrew got the distinct impression he was holding back something. He recalled the look L.S. had given him when he'd realized that Andrew's father was "out of the picture."

As if he knew what that was like....

After three days of rising before dawn, it was nice to lie in bed for awhile. Andrew awoke to the distant shrilling of roosters, then turned over and dozed some more. His mother tapped on the door at seven.

"Boys—breakfast in a bit."

L.S. stretched and groaned, then got up, showered, and dressed himself in Jake's clothes. Andrew had just finished washing up when his mother knocked on the door.

"Ready in a minute," he called.

After a breakfast of ham and eggs they went out to the airfield. Jake showed L.S. the preflight check on the Skyfarer: Start at the front of the plane and inspect the propeller for nicks, shake it a bit to check for looseness; open the cowling and check the oil, look for any loose wires or leaks or anything out of order; walk around the plane and inspect the wings for tears, make sure the pitot tube to the airspeed indicator isn't blocked, jiggle the control surfaces, check the tires, inspect the elevator and rudder. As he already knew the form, Andrew did the preflight check on the Reliant, with his mother supervising, of course.

"Why don't you let L.S. sit up front this time, darling," his mother suggested. "I know this was to be our special time together, but it would be nice for him to have a good look at things too. You two can take turns at being co-pilot, all right?"

"Good idea," Andrew said with a smile. He really didn't mind sharing his mother with someone else, just as long as that someone else wasn't Jake.

Jake and L.S. walked over to them. "I figure we should make it to my uncle's farm about noon," Jake said. He spread out his map; Andrew's mother opened hers and marked the route Jake indicated. "I'll go in low and buzz the place. Then we can land at the airstrip. It's only about five miles away—here." He jabbed his finger at the map.

Andrew's mother nodded, smiled at Jake, then gave him a quick kiss on the lips.

After Jake took off, Andrew's mother showed L.S. the pre-takeoff check. As they sped down the runway, a look of ecstasy spread across his face; he laughed with glee as the wheels left the ground.

"Getting used to it?" Andrew's mother grinned.

"Used to it isn't the word!" L.S. exclaimed. He gazed out the window. "I've never known anything so wonderful—it's all so beautiful from up here."

Andrew looked out—it was scenic, in a way, but not so marvelous as England. The landscape here was so plain and stark: an orderly, unexciting gridwork of squares and rectangles in various hues of green and brown. This plain checkerboard could not begin to compare to stunningly beautiful, almost magical crazy-quilt English countryside. In his mind's eye he saw England, *his* England, spread out below him like a friendly garden, dotted with castles and villages and laced with meandering streams.

The Skyfarer banked into a turn, circled lower, went into a dive down to a T-shaped blue farmhouse, then soared upward. Andrew's mother followed, playing tag with, then overtaking the Skyfarer. As Jake went in for another pass, Andrew saw a girl in a yellow dress run outside and twirl around, her arms waving skyward. Andrew's mother made another swoop also, and this time Andrew could make out long brown hair framing the girl's face. She stood still now, her head thrown back and her arms held upwards, embracing the sky.

Jake led the way to the airstrip; they landed and tied down their planes.

"They ought to be here pretty soon," Jake said.

Presently, a puff of dust appeared on the horizon. As the puff grew larger, Andrew saw that it was preceded by a battered red pickup. The truck screeched to a halt and two teenaged boys spilled out and careered to Jake. Their mad dash was accompanied by a wild yowling; one of the boys grabbed Jake by the armpits, the other yanked his feet off the ground. As Jake went down, the two boys piled on top of him, their mad hollering drowning out Jake's chortles. The tangle of flailing arms and legs looked like some bizarre, twelve-legged beast writhing in the dust.

Andrew's mother watched in amused bewilderment. She arched an eyebrow, smiled at Andrew.

"Must be some sort of peculiar American greeting ritual."

An older man, thirty or so, strode over. He was about six foot tall and lean; his face was deeply tanned and creased with a smile. He stood for a moment, hands on his hips, shaking his head slowly.

"These boys...." He grabbed Jake's hand, pulled him out of the fracas.

"Quit your brawling, Jake, and introduce me to your family."

"*My* brawling—they started it!" Jake laughed.

"Yeah, heard that one a million times." The man slapped Jake on the back. "You're just as wild as you always were—" He grinned at Andrew's mother. "Just what did you see in this crazy kid?" He extended his hand to her. "Wayne Jay—I'm Jake's cousin. Pleased to meet you."

"Alice Givens." Andrew's mother gave him a brilliant smile as she shook his hand. "This is my son, Andrew." She put her arm around Andrew's shoulder and presented him to Wayne. Andrew reached out his hand and Wayne grabbed it in a crushing grip, then slapped Andrew on the shoulder.

"Oh, and these are Wayne's younger twin brothers—one of them is Boyd," Jake said, waving his arm at his identical attackers. "The other is Blaine—never could tell them apart."

The two boys, lanky and even taller than Wayne, smiled and shook Andrew's hand, then his mother's. They both had sunbleached hair and easy grins. One, wearing a red plaid shirt and jeans, said "Boyd"; the other, in a white tee-shirt and brown trousers, said, "Blaine."

"Well, let's get a move-on, " Wayne said. "The women are cooking up the fatted calf and a whole herd of chickens. Phyl and Mel can't wait to see you."

"My goodness, more brothers?" Andrew's mother said.

"Sisters," Wayne chuckled. "Phyl for Phyllis and Mel for Melinda. Sorry you're going to have to ride in the truck. The old chariot had a flat—Phyl's fixing it right now."

"Oh, we also brought along a guest. I told your father." Jake looked around. "Where's L.S.?"

Andrew saw L.S. sitting in the Reliant. Jake followed Andrew's gaze, walked over to the plane. Andrew stood for a moment, then, hearing the low buzz of earnest conversation, went over to see what the problem was.

"...I already told them you were coming, L.S., and they want you to come to dinner," Jake said.

"I don't want to be any trouble. I really don't mind staying here."

"L.S., you're *not* trouble. My folks really want to meet you—come on."

Wayne sauntered over to the Reliant.

"Hey, L.S." Wayne put his hand on L.S.'s shoulder. "Those womenfolk have already cooked up enough food to feed half the state and we're going need all the help we can get eating it. Come on—" He gently pulled L.S. from the plane, put his arm around his shoulder as he led him over to the truck.

"Hey guys, meet L.S.!" Wayne called to his brothers. Boyd and Blaine dashed over to meet L.S., shook his hand, then slapped him on the shoulder.

"Sorry, you younguns are going to have to sit in the back," Wayne said.

Boyd and Blaine hopped into the back of the truck and together pulled Andrew and L.S. in.

Wayne started the engine, and the pickup bounced and churned down the dirt road. Andrew braced himself against L.S. and closed his eyes to keep the dust out. The roar of the engine was too loud for conversation. After awhile, he sensed the truck slowing and making a few right-angle turns. It stopped and Andrew opened his eyes.

They were at the blue farmhouse. The girl in the yellow dress came running down the steps as Jake got out of the cab. She threw herself into his arms, laughing and crying his name. She then embraced Andrew's mother. Andrew hopped out of the truck; no sooner had his feet hit the ground than he found himself standing face to face with this alarmingly attractive girl. She was barely five feet tall; Andrew guessed her to be about his own age, perhaps a little younger. Her long hair, a light goldeny brown like the color of autumn leaves, framed a face with enchantingly high cheekbones and large brown eyes. Her lips formed into an alluring smile as her eyes fixed on him.

"You must be Andrew," she said.

"Uh, yes—I'm—um—"

"I'm Jereen, Wayne's daughter—pleased to meet you. Did you have a nice trip?"

"Um, yes, very nice, thank you."

Jereen smiled at L.S. "Jake told us to expect another guest—you're L.S.?"

"Uh—yes. L.S. Olney, pleased to meet you."

Andrew heard a high-pitched commotion, saw a mob of women dressed in floral print dresses descend the steps like a flower-bedecked parade float going downhill. His mother and Jake were enveloped by this bright garden of welcomers as several small children buzzed excitedly at the fringes.

"We'd better get inside before the crowd does," Jereen said to L.S. and Andrew. Taking each of them by the hand, she sidestepped the throng and led them into the house.

They entered a front foyer with a staircase leading up to the second floor. That's the parlor over there—" Jereen nodded at the room on the right as she led them into the room to the left, a living room of sorts occupied by at least a half dozen babies: babies toddling, babies creeping, tinies lying on their backs and wriggling their arms and legs, all of them clamoring above the din. As the mob of people surged through the front door, Andrew saw his mother's red hair bobbing in the midst, heard her lilting laugh.

"Let's get ourselves seated." Jereen ushered Andrew and L.S. into a large dining room. There was a long rectangular table down the center and a small, low, round table in one corner. Three high chairs stood in another corner with a sheet of oilcloth beneath them.

She pulled out a chair at the long table, indicated to Andrew to be seated, pulled out another chair two chairs down for L.S., then seated herself between them. The crowd streamed into the room; the children seated themselves at the round table and the toddlers were settled in the high chairs. The women then went into the kitchen and returned bearing platters and bowls of all sorts of meats and side dishes. There was a huge slab of roast beef, a platter of sliced ham, a gigantic bowl of fried chicken, as well as offerings of sweet corn, green beans, peas, potatoes, and rolls. As accustomed as he was to the bounty in America, Andrew was astounded by the enormous amount of food.

Andrew's mother and Jake talked with an older man, whom Jereen pointed out as "Grandpa John," her father's father. With the table by now laden with enough food to feed all of Askew Court twice over, the adults then seated themselves around it. Andrew's mother and Jake sat opposite Andrew. Grandpa John seated himself at the head of the table. A young woman, sturdily built, sat next to Andrew.

"Hiya Andrew—I'm Phyl, Wayne's sister," she said over the din. "That's my younger sister over there, next to your friend."

"Hi, I'm Mel." A girl who looked to be not much older than her twin brothers, leaned forward and smiled at Andrew.

"Phyl and Mel are living here because their husbands are in the Navy," Jereen explained. "Those are Phyl's boys over there—" Jereen pointed to the round table, "The ones wearing blue overalls—Cash, Cary, and Lex. Her littlest, Marky, and Ann-Marie, the only girl, are in the highchairs. And Mel's got the two little twin girls in the playpen."

Grandpa John stood, cleared his throat, and the noise of the crowd abated.

Uh-oh, Andrew thought, remembering the interminable pre-meal benedictions at his boarding school. *Time to impress the Almighty with a lengthy discourse on how unworthy we are of all this....*

Uncle John took a deep breath. "Lord, thank you for bringing Jake and his family and L.S. safely to us, protect them on their way, keep Cash and Shep safe too and bring them home, bring a speedy end to this war, and thank you for this food, Amen."

Andrew's eyes were still closed when he heard the clamor of conversation and dishes being passed.

Jereen smiled at him. "My grandpa says if you can't say please and thank you to God in one breath, then you're just boring Him and everyone else. And he says, be careful what you pray for—you just might get it!" Between mouthfuls of food, she introduced the rest of her family. "That's Grandma Rose, and my mom—everyone calls her Wannie—and over there at the table with Phyl's kids are my sisters Jolene—she's nine, and Jenna—she just turned four. I've got two baby brothers, too—that's Johnnie, in the highchair, the one with the carrots all over his face. Jimmie is in the playpen with Mel's twins. They're all four months old. Jimmie was born just two days after the twins; that's when Aunt Lois came to help us out. At the other end of the table is my great-aunt Euelene. She's Grandma Rose's older sister—she came out to Nebraska in a covered wagon."

"Do you all live here?" he asked.

Jereen nodded. "There's five bedrooms upstairs in the main house. My grandparents, Blaine, Boyd, and Mel and Phyl and their kids all live up there. Great-aunt Euelene has a room off the kitchen. You probably saw the addition on the back when you were flying overhead—that's where my family lives. You'll be staying in my room—you and L.S., that is. It has a trundle bed for when I have friends sleep over. When we heard L.S. was coming, we just pulled out the lower bed. Would you like some more corn?"

"Yes, please," Andrew said. He looked around the room as Jereen served him. He couldn't get over the size of this extended family, all living under one roof in a place no larger than Armus House. He mentally calculated: twenty-one people. *Crikey!*

Jereen passed the bowl of sweet corn to L.S., who passed it to Mel.

"L.S., don't be shy," Jereen chided. "There's plenty of food to go around twice—here, have a roll." She placed a roll on his plate.

L.S. smiled. "Thank you."

Andrew looked across at his mother, who was happily engaged in conversation with Mel and Phyl. She was definitely the center of attention—she...and Jake. Everyone was beaming at the honored couple, and the sight of his mother and Jake being feted by these adoring strangers gnawed at Andrew.

It's as if she's not even my mother anymore. All they care about is her and Jake. I'm nothing but an afterthought.

Jereen touched his arm; he noticed a faint pink blush sweeping across her cheeks.

"I was really looking forward to meeting you. Aunt Lois told me all about you. I was so glad when I heard you were coming out here." She looked away for a moment, then back at Andrew. Her cheeks were scarlet now.

Andrew felt a tug at his sleeve.

"Would you like to see my baby kitties?" Jenna stood at his side, imploringly him with big blue eyes.

"I'd like that very much," Andrew said.

Jenna giggled, then skipped around Andrew as he got up.

"Jereen, go with your sister," Wannie said.

"Yes, Mom."

L.S. stood also.

"You see my baby kitties too?" Jenna squealed.

L.S. nodded.

"There's some ham scraps in the refrigerator," Wannie said. "Take some for Shelly."

"Shelly's the mommy kitty," Jenna explained. She hopped up and down as Jereen got the saucer of ham, then dashed outside to the barn.

"Jenna, not so fast," Jereen called. Jenna ran back to them and skipped circles in front of them all the way to the barn.

Jereen pushed open the massive barn door. It took awhile for Andrew's eyes to adjust to the dimness. He stepped into a shaft of light at the center of the barn, sensed Jereen walking just behind him, now standing close—very close to him.

He turned, and his eyes met hers again. The bright light bathed her skin with a luminous glow and lit her hair to the color of wheat. She looked like a goddess, yet not like a goddess, for the look in those dark eyes was all too mortal. He felt mesmerized by her gaze, knew he should look away or he would be more terribly, wonderfully bound to her with every passing second. Even in the warmth of the light, he felt goosebumps prickle his skin.

The strident mewing of tiny felines broke his trance.

"Jereen—Shelly's *hungry!*" Jenna called.

Jereen blinked, then hurried to Jenna and L.S. in the back corner of the barn. They were crouched over a cardboard box. Andrew ambled over, saw a tortoise-shell cat contentedly nursing several squirming mounds of calico and striped fur.

"Here—" Jereen put a few bits of ham into L.S.'s hand. "Shelly loves any hand that feeds her."

L.S. laughed as Shelly gobbled the tidbits from his palm. Andrew knelt next to L.S. and stroked the side of Shelly's face. The cat responded by nuzzling into his caress.

"She likes you, Andrew," Jereen said.

"She's a nice cat," Andrew smiled.

"You have a cat, don't you?" she asked.

"Yes, Lindy—he's a silver tabby." He continued stroking Shelly as L.S. fed her more scraps.

"Once you stop nursing your kitties, Shelly, no more kitchen scraps for you," Jereen laughed. "You have to get back to mousing, and teach your little ones too."

"Shelly's a *mouser*—catches lots of mouses!" Jenna proclaimed.

"Jereen!" Wannie's voice carried into the barn. "Time to wash up!"

"I have to go," Jereen said. "Would you please watch Jenna?"

"Be glad to," Andrew said.

Jereen smiled at him, then got up and left. Once she was out of the barn, L.S. arched his eyebrows at Andrew.

"What?" Andrew said.

"*You* know what," L.S. replied. He tilted his head at the barn door.

"She's just being nice, that's all."

"She's being nice, but that's *not* all," L.S. smiled. "When girls get that look in their eyes, it means just one thing—"

"Stop it!"

L.S. looked away.

"Sorry, I didn't mean to snap at you," Andrew said. He felt the color rise to his cheeks.

"Nothing wrong with being liked," L.S. soothed.

Andrew grunted.

There was everything wrong with being liked, if the one doing the liking was Jake's cousin.

Andrew and L.S. brought Jenna back to the house. Dessert was being served and they were queried as to their preferences.

"We've got strawberry-rhubarb pie, Apple Brown Betty, and carrot cake." Phyl pointed out the offerings in the center of the table.

Andrew looked across at his mother, who was oblivious to his stare. She was positively basking in all the attention from her newly acquired relatives; from time to time she gazed adoringly at Jake.

Andrew fumed.

Just because he's got this bloody huge family doesn't mean he's so wonderful...Rats and roaches have huge families too!

"Andrew, what would you like?" Phyl asked him.

"Carrot cake," Andrew said crisply. He glared at his mother.

"Carrot cake's my favorite—it always has been." He spoke evenly, keeping his eyes locked on her the whole time.

The smile faded from his mother's face and she looked at him in consternation.

Jake touched her sleeve.

"Alice?"

She glanced at Jake, forced a smile, then looked back to Andrew. He took a bite of carrot cake, looked intently at her as he chewed it.

Jake withdrew his hand from her arm.

Good!

Not wanting to unsettle his mother completely, Andrew turned to L.S. and talked to him about the sights they'd seen on their trip. Jereen came in from the kitchen, carrying a pot of coffee in on hand and a teapot in the other.

"I thought that you would like some tea with your dessert, Andrew," she said.

He nodded, smiled at her. Best to let his mother know she needn't have any fear of him being churlish with Jake's relatives, or even with Jake.

All that's needful for her is to remember....

"Remember laying the foundation for the addition, Jake?" Wayne asked as they walked through the kitchen. "We turned the pantry into a hallway, see?"

Andrew followed his mother and Jake into "Wayne's Annex," as the new addition was called. The short corridor opened onto a small kitchen.

"We all usually eat together in the big house. It's more efficient to cook for one big mob instead of two small ones." Wayne continued talking to Jake. "Here's the living room—it closes off to a guest room. The sofabed pulls out. You and Alice can bunk in there. There's a bath right down the hall." He led the way up a narrow flight of stairs. "The girls are up here, two rooms and a bath—thought it would be nice to have an extra bath for the girls. You know how they can be, remember, Jake? Andrew, L.S., you'll be in Jereen's room."

Andrew set his suitcase down in the daisy-papered room and studied his disconcertingly feminine quarters. The curtains were of white organdy; the bedspread was of some frilly yellow fabric. The trundle bed was pulled out and covered with a patchwork quilt. There were pictures of Clark Gable and Gary Cooper tacked up on the walls; the dresser was adorned with a flouncy crocheted doily and a white jewelry box.

"Why don't you rest up a bit, boys. We got the dance to go to tonight," Wayne said.

"Dance?" Andrew asked.

"Sorry, guess we forgot to tell you. We have square dancing every Friday night—you're both welcome to come."

"Oh, uh, I don't have any clothes to wear to a dance."

"Just wear your jeans. We have some shirts that my brothers outgrew. You'll fit into them just fine."

Andrew whispered desperately to his mother as she sorted through the shirts Wayne had given her.

"Mum—I don't even *know* how to dance! I never learned—"

"It's *square* dancing, darling. You just follow the commands—piece of cake. Here, let's see how this one looks on you." She selected a black shirt with pearly buttons.

Andrew put on the horrid garment.

"Oh, darling, you look so *dashing* in black—"

"Mum, I don't *want* to go—"

"Andrew, don't be churlish—"

"L.S. isn't going—"

"That's because he said he didn't want to—"

"I don't want to go either! Why are you letting him—"

"Because he's our guest, darling, and it's not right to force a guest—"

"But it's all right to force *me* because I'm only your son—"

"*Andrew!*"

He saw the look of dismay and hurt on her face, hung his head.

"Mum, I'm sorry—" He put his arms around her.

"Oh, Andrew—" She hugged him back. "You'll have a *marvelous* time! Remember how you felt about coming to America? It didn't turn out to be so bad after all, did it? Why, all of the letters I got from you were positively brimming with delight at the wonderful time you were having in the United States. That's one of the reasons I decided not to take you back to England right away—I thought you would want to stay in America a bit longer."

Andrew grunted. He turned and glowered at himself in the mirror. Being hoisted by one's own petards was *so* unpleasant.

His mother, standing behind him, draped her arms around his shoulders and smiled at his sullen reflection

"Andrew, Alice! We're almost ready!" Jake's voice drifted up the stairs. "Alice, Wannie has some dresses for you to try on."

"Come on, darling." She gave Andrew a kiss on the forehead. "You're going to have a positively smashing time!"

He found himself wedged in between Jereen and Phyl in the backseat of Wayne's "chariot," a graciously-sized automobile that had seen better days. Andrew's mother and Jake sat up front with Wayne and Wannie; Mel, Grandma Rose, and Grandpa John sat in the backseat on the other side of Jereen. All the adults chattered excitedly, Jereen was very quiet, and Andrew didn't say a word.

"...so the last time you were here was the summer of '40, wasn't it Jake?" Grandpa John asked.

"No, it was the summer of '39," Jake replied. "I went to England in early 1940."

"You went through Canada, didn't you?" Wayne asked.

"Yeah. Well, that's how just about everyone from the U.S. who wanted to join up with Great Britain went in those days, when America was still neutral."

"How's it feel coming back to a whole passel of younguns, Jake?" Wannie asked.

Jake laughed. "I feel like Rip Van Winkle waking up in a nursery! When I was last here, you and Wayne only had Jereen and Jolene, and Phyl and Cash just had Cash Junior. He was starting to walk, and Phyl had just found out she was expecting again. I thought she was kidding around when she said she'd name it Cary if it was a boy."

Phyl let out a loud chortle. "*Me* kid around, Jake?"

"How are Shep and Cash doing?" Jake asked.

"Still in the Navy," Grandpa John replied. "They're both on supply ships, so at least they're not in the thick of things."

"We just hope and pray the war's over soon so they can come home." Grandma Rose said. "People just went nuts on V-E day, but the war's not over yet, not until Japan runs up the white flag. That's probably not going to be for a whole 'nother year, at least."

Wayne shook his head. "It's been a bloody enough business island hopping—look at Iwo Jima. And Okinawa. Godawlmighty, over twelve thousand Americans killed there. The invasion of Japan is sure to be a hundred times worse. They're estimating at least a million, maybe two million American casualties."

"Well, maybe the Japanese will just see reason when they're completely cut off, and we won't have to invade," Wannie said.

"That didn't happen with Germany," Grandpa John pointed out. "Those Nazis fought for every last inch of Berlin. Used boys and old men, didn't they Jake?"

Grandma Rose patted him on the thigh. "Now John, let's have a nice evening without talking about the war. Jake and his family are here. Let's just have ourselves a nice time."

Jereen glanced at Andrew. She was so close to him that she was practically sitting on his lap. Her pale blue crinolined skirt flounced up over his thighs and a vague scent of lavender traced around him. The neckline of her white blouse scooped low over her shoulders, grazed the tops of her breasts, and cinched tightly around her midriff.

Andrew realized he was starting to sweat.

This damned bloody heat—it's like a furnace! How can people stand it here!

He would have given anything to be at the house with L.S. and Great-aunt Euelene, even if it meant "babysitting" a whole "passel of younguns." L.S. had said he would much rather rest up after all the excitement, and no one had pressured or *ordered* him to go. Andrew was vexed by the image of the tranquil domestic scene he'd left at the house: L.S. and Great-aunt Euelene sitting on the sofa, surrounded by a sea of little ones.

The car slowed to a halt in front of a large clapboard building. There were clumps of crinolined women milling about; a few middle-aged men and several teenaged boys were scattered throughout the knots of dazzling finery.

"Looks like the boys beat us here—even with them having to pick up all their friends," Wayne said.

Jereen's fingers brushed against Andrew's elbow as they walked up to the building. The crickets were starting to chirp, and from within the building came the crooning of fiddles being tuned. As their party entered the building there were cries of wonder and welcome as several dozen people thronged around Jake and Andrew's mother.

"The prodigal returns," Grandma Rose smiled.

Andrew ruefully watched the mob of people exclaim over his mother. She was wearing one of Wannie's dancing dresses, a voluminously flouncy creation of dark green that set off her red hair most exquisitely. Jake was showing her off as if she were some prized pig; what was worse was that she seemed to relish the attention. She was grinning like the village idiot, and her head was bobbling and swiveling so much it was a wonder it didn't completely disconnect itself from her body.

The music started up: It was serious now. A bass viol thumped a loud beat; three fiddles and a two banjos played a loud, lively tune. The musicians were all women, except for the bass player, an ancient man who was barely as tall as his fiddle. A man called out for everyone to form into "squares." Andrew's mother and Jake moseyed towards the sidelines as the serious dancers ordered themselves up in the center of the room.

"Jake—dance with me!" Jereen grabbed Jake's hand and pulled him towards a half-formed square. Jake grinned in farewell at Andrew's mother; she waved a mock good-bye and laughed.

"Come on, little sister—I'll be your fellah!" Phyl grabbed Mel's hand and pulled her to the remaining gap in the square, across from Jake and Jereen.

The dance started up in earnest. The caller yelled out various commands, and the dancers swirled to and fro, skipping and circling and turning this way and that.

Andrew's mother gazed at Jake, who was in the process of doing something called a "do-se-do" with Jereen. Andrew had to admit that Jake, clod that he was, acquitted himself rather well in this peculiar activity.

It really can't be considered dancing, though—it's nothing but following a bunch of silly directions. Bet if that caller yelled for everyone to do push ups or run in place, they'd do it!

Jereen's skirt twirled around her thighs as she did some sort of complicated maneuver around Jake; her face shone with rapture as she danced several other steps with him.

The music pounded to a crescendo; the dancers were ordered to "honor your partners," which they did, like mindless sheep.

Andrew glanced at his mother. Her attention was completely absorbed at the sight of Jake, laughing with delight at this wretched activity. Andrew looked in the other direction and noticed a side door cracked open a bit.

I could just slip out—go for a walk until this whole stupid thing is over....

"Andrew!" Jereen's fingers pressed against his arm. "They're having the Beginner's Dance next—dance with me, please? You'll love it!" She pulled him across the floor.

His head snapped involuntarily around, and he saw his mother—*smiling!*

Smiling at me being dragged across the floor—

He looked at Jereen, and she gazed at him, fervent, imploring, adoring...and then it hit him.

Someday a girl will ask you to dance....

He felt a hot blush creep up his cheeks and hoped that Jereen didn't notice. Now Jake was urging Andrew's mother across the floor, and she didn't act as if she were protesting very much. Jereen stopped next to Phyl and Mel.

"*Hot diggity dog*—Jereen's snagged herself a fellah!" Phyl chortled. "And here comes Jake and Alice—where are those boys!" She squinted, scanned the crowd. Spotting the twins surrounded by a cluster of adoring young females, she stuck two of her fingers in her mouth and blew an ear-piercing whistle.

Mel took up the cry, blowing a loud blast in chorus. Boyd and Blaine waved off their admirers and threaded their way between the squares already formed up. Boyd grabbed Phyl and twirled her around, flaring her skirts around her hips; Blaine did the same with Mel. They positioned themselves at either side of Andrew and Jereen, leaving Jake and Andrew's mother to stand opposite.

The caller announced that this was a beginner's dance and that he would teach them a few simple steps first.

Simple's not the word for it, Andrew thought, as he obliged and followed the instructions for *honor your partner, swing your partner, promenade,* and *do-se-do,* which was nothing more than crossing one's arms and walking around one's partner. *Allemande left and right* involved the imbecilic act of walking around in one direction or the other and sort of shaking hands with everyone else's partner, which anyone with more than one leg and less than three could do without a bit of trouble.

The music started up and they were commanded to "honor your partners." A few other simple commands followed: circling in one direction, then the other, swinging partners, then corners, then the couples opposite. Andrew then found himself traded off to his mother; they did a few do-se-dos and promenades.

Boyd and Blaine, however, took these simple maneuvers to new heights. The bowed with outrageous panache, gazing ardently at their partners (their sisters, no less!) as if

696

madly in love with them. They swung Mel and Phyl with a graceful flourish, they promenaded most elegantly, and they snapped their hips in the do-se-dos. Phyl almost collapsed with laughter at their antics; Mel giggled with delight.

Andrew was then traded off to Phyl, whose thick-muscled arms nearly whipped him off the floor when she swung him, then to Mel, who smiled sweetly at him as they promenaded.

Crikey! I've danced with a girl, my mother, and two married women!

As he looked at his mother being promenaded by an adoring Blaine as she chortled with glee, he realized that somehow, some way, somewhere along the line, everything had changed for him. No longer did the music irk him: it seemed to course through him, become part of him, send his soul soaring to a joy he'd never known before. No longer did the dance seem like a series of silly steps; it was now, for him, a kind of organized exuberance, and he was a part of it all. It was so different from the kind of dancing he had seen aboard the *Queen Mary* in which every couple, independent of and oblivious to all the other couples, twirled across the floor like bits of thread scattering in the wind. This square dancing was, by contrast, a wonderful tapestry of color and motion with every person linked to the whole. Every move he made was reflected a hundred-fold by the others who were also a part of the marvelous plan of movement and rhythm and rapture.

He was traded back to Jereen just as the music ended; her radiant face greeted him as he took her hand and they promenaded back home. The band thumped out a jubilant finale and the crowd cheered and clapped. Phyl, Mel, Blaine, and Boyd whistled loudly in enthusiastic accompaniment.

Jereen smiled at him. "Dogs bark, pigs squeal, and Jays whistle."

He realized he was breathing a little rapidly. Jereen put her hand around his waist.

"Would you like something to drink?'

He nodded, not wanting his speech to betray his breathlessness. She led him to the refreshment table and offered him a cup of punch which he eagerly took, for his throat was now dry and tight.

"Would you like to go outside for some fresh air?"

Her query caught him mid-gulp. As he swallowed his head bobbed a bit; evidently, she interpreted it as an affirmative reply. She took his empty cup, set it on the table, and pulled him outside.

It was dark now; he glanced up at the night sky dazzled with stars, and thought of Aunt Jane, of his father.

Oh Dad, do you know what's happening to me now?

He walked a little ahead of her, towards a cluster of pickup trucks. The music started up again.

"Did you like it?" Jereen asked.

"What?"

"The dance."

"Oh...yes, it was quite nice."

He leaned back against the hood of a battered green truck, jammed his hands into his front pockets, and looked up at the sky again. She stood beside him, gazed up at the sky also, then at him.

Should I "chat her up?" What should I say? Should I look at her, or look away?

Her soft, solicitous voice sliced through his reverie.

"Were you excited about flying across the country?"

"Uh, well...It came as a bit of a surprise."

He felt her hand on his shoulder.

"You really would rather be in England, wouldn't you?"

He bit his lip, looked at her. The large dark eyes beheld him, enjoined him to be honest. He gazed up at the sky, saw all the constellations his father had taught him, knew that this was not a time for dissembling or glibness.

"It's been such a long time...so long. Sometimes I'm afraid that I've been away too long and I...." He shook his head.

Just what *was* he afraid of?

"Do you think you'll lose yourself, lose who you are, if you can't get back to where you belong?"

Her directness nearly took his breath away. He closed his eyes, nodded.

How did this stranger know my deepest fear?

Soft fingers touched his cheek.

"I wish you could see that you haven't lost yourself, Andrew. You're thousands of miles from your home and your life hasn't turned out the way you expected it to, but that doesn't mean that it's turned out wrong. Somehow, some way, I think that everything has come right for you."

He realized the music had stopped and that Jereen had moved closer, alarmingly closer to him. He stood still, very still, as the laughter and cheering resonated on the night air.

What should I do? Move away, stay here, touch her—where? Should say something to her? What?

Her fingers slid down his neck, traced along his shoulder, back across his chest. She gently pressed one of the pearly buttons, looked intently at him.

If only she weren't Jake's cousin!

The distant clamor dwindled to soft sounds of conversation that rippled through the darkness. No dancing now, but a sort of intermission, evidently. Andrew saw two of the banjo players step outside and light up cigarettes.

The sweet cry of a single fiddle seared through the muted chatter, playing a haunting melody that tore though Andrew's soul. It seemed to be more a cry of the heart than a musical composition, a sweet, desperate yearning for...something. *What?* Now a guitar joined in, its gentle, rolling chords attending to the soaring melody.

"What song is that?" he asked.

"It's a Civil War song. I can't remember the name. Something about a farewell."

A farewell...a farewell in wartime.

Closing his eyes, Andrew felt the music slide through him, touch the secret places of his heart, pour out all the longing and pain and desperate hope for everything to be right once more. He hadn't realized how deep were the scars of war he carried within him until this plaintive melody knifed though the defenses he'd built around his battered spirit. All he wanted—*all he wanted*—was for things to be right once more—for the war, and its aftermath, to end with the ravaging of his life.

That's what I want—Peace!

"That's what I want," he whispered, more to himself than to this girl by his side.

"You want everything to be all right again," she said gently.

He tried to say yes, but his reply came out as a soft moan. He pursed his lips and swallowed, trying to quell the sob rising up within him. That would be the last straw: crying in front of this terrifyingly lovely girl, in front of....

Jake's cousin....

He walked back towards the building—not so quickly, though, as to give the impression he was fleeing her.

"I just want to hear it a little better." He tried to make it sound like an plea.

She walked beside him, her crinolines softly rustling, like the sound of birds fluttering skyward. The music soared, then plummeted in a wistful denouement, the strains of the violin carrying on the night air, then fading into silence.

The caller cried out for the dancers to form into squares. Andrew ambled inside and watched as the dance came alive in a wondrous pattern. He caught a glimpse of Jake, dancing with Mel, then with Phyl. Looking beyond the sea of dancers, he saw his mother happily chatting with Grandma Rose and some other women. His mother caught sight of him, tilted her head a bit and smiled as if to say *I told you so.*

The dance ended and, as the neat squares swirled into streams of people weaving their separate ways, it was then that Andrew noticed Jake staring at him. His eyebrows were raised in—Andrew was not quite sure whether it was in query or surprise or alarm.

Perhaps all three.

On the way home he found himself again jammed between Jereen and Phyl. His mother exclaimed over how *marvelous* the dance had been, and though Jake grinned at her all the way home, Andrew got the distinct impression his mind was elsewhere.

Bloody hell! I hope he doesn't think I have designs on his cousin!

He tried to distance himself from Jereen as soon as he got out of the car. He made a quick dash to the front door and burst into the house. L.S., sitting on the couch with Jenna and Ann-Marie snoozing on either side of him, looked up, startled.

"Did you have a nice time, Andrew?" Great-aunt Euelene, sitting in the rocking chair under a heap of babies, smiled at him.

"Yes, quite nice, thank you."

The rest of the mob poured through the front door; the women dispersed to their young ones, who were sprawled in sleep in various positions on Great-aunt Euelene, or arrayed on the floor in front of L.S.

"L.S. entertained the younguns all evening with one story after another," Great-aunt Euelene said. "Just sent them off to dreamland with all his tales."

After the little ones were settled in their beds, the adults met in the dining room for a late-night snack of dessert leavings. As much as he wanted to have a bite to eat, Andrew pleaded tiredness and went upstairs to bed.

Once in Jereen's room, he stripped off his jeans and that wretched shirt he'd been forced to wear, and stretched out on the all too feminine bed. He would wait until later to get underneath the covers. L.S. came in after awhile and plopped down onto the trundle bed.

"Did you have a good time?" he asked Andrew.

"It was all right."

L.S. grunted, turned to Andrew as if to say something. His eyes suddenly narrowed and he tugged at something between the mattress and boxspring of Andrew's bed. He pulled out a magazine which was folded open and peered at the page.

"What are you reading?" Andrew asked.

L.S. grunted, turned the page. "Some story about a kid named Roger."

Andrew sat bolt upright; L.S.'s eyes widened in bewilderment, then recognition.

"It's *you*—it's you in the magazine!"

Andrew lunged towards him, but L.S. was too quick—he sprang out of bed and quickly thumbed through the rest of the article as Andrew scrambled across the trundle bed and tumbled to the floor.

"Give me that!" Andrew lunged at him, but L.S. turned sideways and blocked his thrust.

"*Give it to me!*" Andrew was distressed at the hysteria in his voice. Even though he knew millions had read about his life, he still felt as if he were being violated. L.S. looked startled, then held out the magazine to him.

Andrew snatched it out of his hand and flung it onto his bed.

"I'm sorry—I didn't mean to do anything to hurt you," L.S. mumbled.

"It's all right," Andrew said sharply. He turned away, not wanting L.S. to see his discomposure. He not only was irked that L.S. had read about him, but that Jereen had, too.

"You want the lights out?" L.S. asked.

"Yes please."

L.S. turned out the lights and got into the trundle bed. The moonlight illuminated his face; Andrew could see that L.S. was staring up at the ceiling and biting his lip. Then he spoke.

"Do you ever think about your father? I mean, think about him a lot?"

"Yes, I do," Andrew whispered.

L.S. grunted, then turned over, away from Andrew. He pulled the sheet up over his head, and Andrew heard the sound of soft, gulped sobs.

Before they left the next day, they were treated to a performance by Jereen's singing pig, Otis, who snorted out the chorus to *In the Fuehrer's Face* as Jereen sang the verses.

"It didn't take me long to teach him the routine," Jereen said as she dropped a corn cob to her talented porcine protege. "Otis has no doubt figured out that being the life of the party ensures that he won't ever be the main course! Besides, he earns me money for college. He performs at the county fair every year."

Andrew couldn't help but smile; then a thought hit him. "My father—" he began, then clamped his mouth shut. He realized that what he was going to say was rather insulting. Besides, he felt a little uncomfortable talking about his father in front of Jake's family.

"What?" Jereen asked.

"Oh, nothing," Andrew said.

"Oh, please tell me!"

"Well, don't be offended. I just thought of it just now, that's all."

Jereen looked at him pleadingly, and he began, "My father said—or rather he told me that it was an American saying—" Even the memory of that bit of advice brought a smile to his face. "He said, 'Never teach a pig to sing; it—it—'" He found himself fumbling.

"It wastes your time and annoys the pig," Jereen finished with a smile. "Well, I don't think Otis is annoyed—" She dropped another corncob into the feed trough. "Just keep singing, Otis, and you'll get to live forever, or at least into senility and old age—how's that?"

"So you're going to go to college?" Andrew asked Jereen. They were in her room; Andrew had been packing and had opened the door to a tentative knock. Jereen said she'd wanted to get something from her jewelry box. After withdrawing a necklace with a heart-shaped locket, she turned to Andrew, as if expecting him to say something.

So he did, after a few seconds of racking his brain for a safe topic.

She smiled at his question, then answered, "For as long as I can remember, I've always wanted to be a doctor. I know that sounds completely outrageous. I mean, it's almost impossible for a woman to get into medical school, and first there's college. My father said he'd help me in whatever way he can to pay for my college education, but I don't want to take too much from him. I'll have to work for two years, I figure, to save up enough money."

Andrew nodded. Another reason for him to dislike her—she wanted to be a doctor!

"Andrew, are you ready?" his mother called.

"Coming."

Jereen held up the locket to him.

"Could you please fasten this for me?"

He took the necklace. She turned and stood close to him, her shoulder blades brushing against his chest. She was wearing a dress of midnight blue, and it suddenly seemed to Andrew the most erotic color he'd ever seen. As she bent her head forward and lifted her hair, his hands began to tremble; somehow he managed to work the tiny clasp into the catch.

"Got it?" she asked.

"Uh-huh," he breathed.

She reached up to check the clasp; her fingers touched his for a second, maybe longer. "Thanks," she whispered.

Then she was gone.

There was a flurry of farewells: Jake and Andrew's mother were hugged and kissed and hugged again; Andrew and L.S. were hugged by all the little ones and had their backs slapped by everyone older than ten.

"Alice, I have an idea," Jake said.

"What?"

He whispered something in her ear. She smiled, and nodded.

"Come on, Jereen!" Jake called.

"What?" Jereen asked.

"A little farewell present." He grinned and escorted her to the car.

Andrew and L.S. walked to the car; L.S. said "After you," as they got to the door. Andrew stood stock still, and L.S. nudged him. "Get in," he whispered.

So it was again that Andrew found himself next to Jereen. Jake was talking in low tones to Wannie; she got into the car and sat on the other side of Jereen.

Well, at least she's not jammed up beside me....

Andrew tried to sit as close to L.S. as possible, so that there would be an obvious space between him and Jereen, in case Jake happened to take an interest in just how close they were sitting to one another.

Andrew's mother sat in the front seat, between Wayne and Jake. Wayne drove in silence for awhile, then glanced at Jake.

"Did you hear that Nate got the Navy Cross?" he asked.

"Yeah," Jake answered quietly.

"Nate—he was your fellow barnstormer, wasn't he?" Andrew's mother asked Jake.

Jake nodded. "He taught me how to fly." He gazed skyward, seemed to talk more to himself than to anyone in particular. "It was me, Nate, Casey, and Wanda, the wacky wing-walker."

"Wanda remarried. She's still living in Oregon," Wayne said. She had a baby girl eight months after Nate was killed. Her new husband adopted the baby and Nate Jr. From what I hear, they're doing all right. Casey died last year—I don't know if you heard."

"Cirrhosis, I'll bet," Jake said.

"Yep." Wayne turned onto the road leading to the airstrip. "Never did want to take anyone's advice about giving up the bottle. Well, here we are, folks."

Wayne got their things out of the trunk as Andrew's mother and Jake studied their maps together. Then, as Jake did the preflight checklist on the Skyfarer with L.S., Andrew's mother went through the routine on the Reliant with Jereen. Andrew helped Wayne load the luggage into the Reliant, as he didn't want to be seen anywhere near Jereen.

Wayne shook hands with Andrew and L.S.

"Thank you very much for the clothes," L.S. said to Wayne.

Wayne laughed. "With twin boys, there's always a double heap of outgrown clothes—

glad you could use them. Best of luck to you, L.S." He gave L.S. a friendly slap on the shoulder, then did the same with Andrew.

Andrew said a polite farewell to Wannie and Wayne, then got in the backseat of the Reliant. He figured L.S. would at least enjoy the view up front.

Andrew's mother whispered something to L.S.; he nodded, and sat in the backseat. Before Andrew could ask what the form was, Jereen got into the plane and sat next to Andrew's mother.

Andrew was horrified. Was Jereen going with them?

"It was Jake's idea, darling," Andrew's mother smiled. "Since the Skyfarer is so slow, he figured it would be nice if I took Jereen for a spin while he got a head start." She turned to Jereen and explained the preflight routine as Jake took off.

Andrew, sitting behind his mother, could not help but notice the rapture on Jereen's face as the Reliant sped down the airstrip and got airborne. She gazed out the window as the plane banked, then smiled as they headed for the Jay farm.

"Ooh—I'd almost forgotten how *wonderful* this is!" Jereen waved excitedly to the cluster of people standing outside the house; Andrew's mother waggled her wings and then buzzed low over the top of the barn. As the Reliant soared upward, Jereen laughed with delight.

"So Jake used to take you for a spin?" Andrew's mother asked.

Jereen nodded. "In a two-seater Steerman. He took Becky, once—" she broke off, embarrassed.

"His old girlfriend?" Andrew's mother queried.

Jereen nodded. "She threw up, though. Jake never took her up again." She looked joyfully at Andrew's mother. "I'm glad she puked. If she had loved flying, he probably would have married her. I'm glad he married you, instead."

Andrew's mother smiled at her, then looked ahead to plan out her landing. Jereen's ecstatic gaze travelled back to Andrew; he hoped his mother didn't notice, but L.S. did. He winked at Andrew.

Andrew turned away and looked out the window.

Wish that silly girl hadn't tossed her cookies!

The Reliant skimmed the surface of the desolate ground, then graced the airstrip in a perfect three-point landing. As the plane slowed to a halt, Jereen leaned over and threw her arms around Andrew's mother. She then turned around.

"Byc L.S.! Best of luck to you!" She grabbed his hand and squeezed it. L.S. smiled at her. "The best to you, too." He glanced at Andrew.

Now Jereen's gaze was on him. She reached, clasped his hand, held it for a moment. "Good-bye, Andrew," she whispered.

"Bye." He could barely get the word out.

She hopped out and ran to her parents as Andrew's mother took the Reliant to the sky again. Andrew tried to fix his sight on the horizon, but his eyes were drawn to the ground. Jereen spun round and round, her hands held high in joyful farewell, her dress of dark blue fashioning a striking roundel against the brown Nebraska earth.

They caught up with Jake. He led them out over the Platte River, a broad, muddy watercourse that looked as unprepossessing as the drab land around it. It had to be about the ugliest river in the world, Andrew decided. They flew over a massive rock formation called Courthouse Rock.

"Jake said that this was an important landmark that guided the pioneers on their way to Oregon," Andrew's mother said. "He said the Oregon Trail was two thousand miles long. Can you imagine, travelling that vast distance in a covered wagon?"

L.S., sitting in the front seat, shook his head in wonder. Andrew grunted. This buggerall was getting *awfully* tiresome.

They turned south, then landed to refuel. Wannie had packed them a lunch of ham sandwiches and cornbread, so they feasted on that as they waited for Jake to arrive. He landed just as they'd finished eating. As he gobbled a sandwich, he and Andrew's mother consulted their maps again.

"Might be a storm coming across the Rockies," Jake said. He pointed out some emergency airstrips on the map. "Let's stick close together. At the first sign of trouble, I'll waggle my wings and you make for the nearest one, all right?"

They parted with the usual quick kiss and got airborne. Andrew's mother noted when they crossed the Colorado border.

"Didn't you tell me that Mr. Nugent visited Colorado?" Andrew's mother asked him.

Andrew grunted in reply, then slumped back in his seat. His mother pointed out some nondescript rock outcropping to L.S.

"I think I'll nap for a bit, Mum," Andrew said. "I...um, I—

"What?" his mother asked.

"I, um, didn't sleep very well last night." He feigned a yawn, lolled his head, and, resting his head against the back of the seat, closed his eyes.

The truth was, he really *hadn't* slept well, and a genuine drowsiness overtook him as the Reliant circled around and around and *around* that cursed Skyfarer.

"Andrew!" his mother called. "Heads up! We're coming in for a landing."

Andrew shook his head and rubbed his eyes. No longer did the sun shine brightly overhead; it was cloaked in a dusty haze. Menacing dark clouds were creeping towards it.

"Can you still see the Skyfarer?" Andrew's mother asked L.S.

"Yes—he's almost out of sight, though," L.S. answered.

"That must be it," Andrew's mother said, peering at the ground. "Not much of an airstrip, but it'll do. This one definitely calls for a three-point landing." Without another word, she set the plane down and taxied quickly off the airstrip.

"Andrew, L.S.—let's get this plane tied down before the wind picks up."

They got out and proceeded to fasten the Reliant to Mother Earth. L.S. got a good-sized rock and pounded the stakes into the hard land. The clank of stone against metal seemed somehow obscene in this vast stillness, but as L.S. hammered the last few blows, they heard another noise: *Hoofbeats.*

Looking up, Andrew saw four riders on horseback thunder to a halt about fifty feet from the Reliant. They were dressed in dusty brown clothing and wore battered cowboy hats. Grimy red bandannas were wrapped around their faces; only a slit of shadow showed along their eyes. The horses snorted and fidgeted as the riders looked—stared?—*glared?*—at Andrew's mother.

She drew L.S. and Andrew close to her.

"Hullo!" she called. Her voice had a slightly higher pitch. "Sorry, we had to make an emergency landing because of the storm. Would you know where we might find lodgings for the night?"

Bloody hell, Andrew thought. These desperados are going to rob us, kill us, cut us up into little bits and feed us to the horses, and she's inquiring about *accommodations?* He peered at the sky—no sign of the Skyfarer.

Should have known the bastard would desert us at the first sign of trouble!

Chapter 47

*T*he riders glanced at one another, then slowly took off their hats and pulled down their bandannas. The one on the far left revealed a cascade of long grey curls which tumbled down around a tanned face with a wide smile. A lilting female voice—with a distinctly *British* accent—called out:

"I say—what part of England are you from?"

Andrew's mother let out a peal of laughter, then called: "Northumberland, originally." She darted over to the woman, with Andrew and L.S. in tow.

"I'm Alice Givens, pleased to meet you."

I *thought* I detected a trace of Northumbria," the woman chuckled. She extended her hand to Andrew's mother. "Vera Fair—formerly of Derbyshire, but for the past thirty years from the great state of Colorado. Welcome—you're just in time for tea!"

Andrew's mother gave her a dazzling smile, then introduced Andrew and L.S.; Vera, in turn, introduced the other riders, who were her "hands." Two of them, Carson and Reno, were black; the other, Dartt, was pure Comanche Indian, Vera said with pride. Dartt's brothers were in the Army, and had served as "code-talkers" during the war in Europe.

"They radioed information and instructions between units, in the Comanche language." Dartt explained. "If the Germans tried to listen in, they wouldn't have any idea what language they were hearing, much less what was being said."

The Skyfarer buzzed overhead.

"That's my husband, Jake," Andrew's mother told Vera. "We're ferrying these planes out to California. We've come all the way from New Jersey."

"Both of you pilots, how grand!" Vera exclaimed.

The Skyfarer touched down. Jake hopped out and Andrew's mother ran over to help him tie down the plane. That done, she took Jake's hand and pulled him over to Vera.

"Darling, we've been invited for tea!" Introductions were made all around again; then Vera assigned each of her hands to convey Andrew, Jake, and L.S. back to her ranch.

"You ride with me, my dear," she told Andrew's mother. "You've got to catch me up on all the latest from England!" She helped Andrew's mother up onto her horse. Andrew rode with Dartt, Jake with Carson, and L.S. with Reno.

The dust was starting to kick up and Andrew pressed his face against Dartt's back.

"You doing all right back there?" Dartt asked.

"Uh-huh," Andrew replied. He still couldn't quite believe he was riding with a real live Indian. The Indians were always the bad guys in the movies, wild savages who'd just as soon scalp you as shake your hand. And here he was, on horseback with this solicitous young man who was, right now, his shelter from the storm. Over the wind, he could hear the excited chatter of his mother and Vera. Vera revealed that she came to Colorado after getting fed up with the "tiresome" life of social engagements that was her lot in England: "I was expected to choose a husband from among the most appalling assortment of twits and fools you could ever imagine. I fled to America on holiday and when I found a man who had more sense than all of them put together, I asked him to marry me!"

Andrew's mother shrieked with laughter, then spoke to Vera in a low voice. Andrew couldn't hear what she said, but he did hear a hearty chuckle from Vera. "We're very much alike, my dear," she said to Andrew's mother. "Well, Sherman and I were married for twenty-five wonderful years. He died ten years ago, and now my hands and I keep the ranch going."

They arrived at the "castle keep," as Vera called it, which consisted of the house, a long rambling structure which housed everyone who worked the ranch, plus several outbuildings. Carson took a wagon back to the planes to collect their luggage. Vera ushered them into the house and called out, "Consuela! Set another four places, *por favor*. We've got company!"

She showed them upstairs to their rooms and told them they could wait out the storm with her for as long as need be. After everyone had been seated around the dining room table, Vera introduced her other hands: Paco and Cruz, of Mexican origin, and two Chinese brothers, Tommy and Kit Cheung. Tea was unlike any Andrew had ever experienced. The table was laden with platters of all sorts of strange-looking things: tortillas, burritos, enchiladas, quesadillas, tacos, dishes of salsa. He found that the food was very spicy, but quite good.

"Your boy's really getting into those enchiladas!" Vera smiled at Andrew's mother. "He'll never be happy with Shepherd's Pie again! My nephew came over here from England several years ago with a friend, and the two of them said they'd never had anything so good."

"Mr. Nugent, my housemaster at school visited Colorado, too," Andrew said. "He told us all about it, and brought us back leather and tools to make things."

"Did you say Nugent?" Vera asked.

"Yes."

"My nephew's friend was named Nugent—Douglas Nugent. He was a housemaster at a boy's school and he took back leather and tools with him. Could that have been him?"

Andrew paused. Though Mr. Nugent had been his housemaster for four years, he had no idea what his first name was.

"Yes, his name was Douglas," Andrew's mother affirmed.

Vera's face broke into a broad smile. "Consuela, please get me that old photo album—the one that has the pictures of Julian and Douglas in it."

Consuela got up and pulled a leather-bound album from one of the bookshelves and gave it to Vera. Vera flipped through the pages and handed the open album to Andrew.

"That's him!" Andrew exclaimed. He gazed at the picture of Mr. Nugent, sitting tall in the saddle on a dappled horse, and looking ever so comical wearing a cowboy hat. He handed the album back to Vera.

"He was such a nice young man." Vera looked at the picture; her eyes narrowed a bit and her lips pursed into a tight line. Then she spoke in a soft voice.

"It's terrible what happened to him, isn't it?"

"What?" Andrew felt his heart do a somersault. He looked at his mother. She looked a little guilty, and her eyes held a sort of strained sorrow. She took a deep breath, glanced at Vera.

"I didn't tell Andrew," she said.

"What?" Andrew tried to keep his voice even, but the hysteria seemed to leak out of him.

"Excuse us, please." Andrew's mother got up, walked over to Andrew, and touched his arm. He rose to his feet, felt his knees tremble as they walked out of the room. He was afraid to say anything, afraid his voice would split with terror again. He stumbled up the stairs after her, followed her into the room she was sharing with Jake. She sat on the bed.

"What—what happened?" he asked.

"Andrew, there was a V-2 attack on your school. Mr. Nugent lost his legs, and some of the students were killed. I thought it best not to write to you about it, darling. I wanted to tell you in person, but then, I had to tell you about Thomas and Mrs. Tuttle and you were so upset...." She bit her lip.

He looked through the dormered window at the storm raging outside. The rain was by now pelting the windows, a savage accompaniment to the tears rolling down his cheeks.

They stayed with Vera for two more days while the storm raged. Jake and L.S. kept busy helping out with repair work that needed to be done in the outbuildings; Andrew and his mother pitched in to do some of the household chores. Andrew's mother told Vera of L.S.'s circumstances, and Vera suggested that L.S. stay with her.

"Looks like he'd take to ranching just fine. If he would like to finish out the trip to California, there'll be a job waiting for him. He can also do his schooling here. Cruz and Hector are doing a high school correspondence course in the evenings, and I'm tutoring them. Be glad to take on another pupil."

L.S. was quite excited by the thought of having a career as a cowboy, after he got a chance to see California, of course.

The third day brought clear blue skies and a round of farewells. Andrew's mother took Vera, Consuela, and the hands, three at a time, for rides in the Reliant while Jake went on ahead.

After the last goodbyes were said, they made their way south over the vast, table-top flat plain, the wall of the Rocky Mountains to their right. Andrew's mother exclaimed over and *over* about what an *incredible* sight they were.

They landed in New Mexico and stayed at a motor court on the shore of a lake. The shower in Andrew's and L.S.'s room emitted pathetic dribbles of rusty water, so they made flying leaps off the dock into the deep blue lake and splashed around until they were thoroughly exhausted. Then they stretched out on the dock and let the sun scorch them dry.

"Well, today's the big day," Jake said as he and Andrew's mother consulted their maps. "I figure this pass is about the best bet. There's an airstrip here, in case we need it. Wish me luck."

Andrew's mother gave him a quick kiss, then another more lingering one. "That's for luck. Don't worry, you'll make it." She helped Jake clear out the Skyfarer of every last bit of extraneous weight: coffee cups, thermos, Irvine jacket, litter, rags. Jake stripped down to his shorts and tee shirt and got into the plane.

They'd gotten into the habit of L.S. sitting in the front seat in the mornings, Andrew in the afternoons. L.S. went through the pre-takeoff check with Andrew's mother as the Skyfarer lifted off the runway.

Hope he crashes into the side of a mountain....

"Safety belts, boys?" Andrew's mother queried.

"Check!"

All I want is to see that Skyfarer in little pieces....

"Tally-ho, here we go!"

They caught up with the Skyfarer in no time; then Andrew's mother went ahead, threading her way through the mountain passes.

From time to time she consulted the map lying on L.S.'s lap. The Skyfarer plodded behind them, straining to gain altitude.

"Well, this looks like the one," she said. She waggled her wings and flew over a gap between two ridges.

"Boys, how's the Skyfarer doing?"

Hope it's about to be have a very close encounter with that peak....

"He's almost there," L.S. said.

Andrew's mother banked the Reliant into a 180-degree turn so that she could have a full view of the Skyfarer's progress. As they were so much higher than the Skyfarer, it wasn't easy to tell if it was going to make it or not.

"No, Jake," Andrew's mother whispered.

The Skyfarer made a quarter turn just before the gap. Andrew's mother pursed her lips, glared at the jagged landscape below. The Skyfarer made a wide circle, then another, as it struggled to climb above the rocky spires. It aimed again for the gap.

"Come on, Jake, you can do it," Andrew's mother murmured.

"Come on, Jake," L.S. echoed.

Come on, Jake—let's see you and your pathetic little aircraft in little bits on the side of that ridge....

Andrew's mother held her breath, then groaned as the Skyfarer again shied away from the gap.

"He just can't get enough altitude," Andrew's mother muttered. She flew back across the gap and tagged alongside Jake. She made a thumbs-down gesture and then a palms up motion: Why don't you land?

Jake shook his head, replied with an adamant thumbs up, then an index finger pointed up: *One more time.*

Andrew's mother flew alongside him, gently increasing in altitude, as if to urge the Skyfarer upward. She remained on the east side of the crest as Jake aimed towards the gap again. This time it was plain to see that the third time wouldn't be a charm.

"Oh Jake, don't try it...." she breathed.

Go ahead, go for it, you bastard....

The Skyfarer veered away and headed back to the Reliant. Jake frowned and made a dispirited thumbs down sign.

Well, what do we do now—since you can't get your wretched little aeroplane over the mountains?

Andrew's mother was silent as she headed towards the airstrip and brought the Reliant in for a landing. As she stood on the edge of the airstrip and waited for Jake, she glared at the sky. The Skyfarer touched down, bounced to a halt. Andrew's mother ran over to it and embraced Jake as he got out. She said something to him in a low voice. He shook his head. She answered him, her voice high and insistent this time. And now four words carried back to Andrew, four words spoken loudly and adamantly, four words that sent a chill through him:

"I can do it!"

No, Mum, NO!

Andrew could see that Jake was going from strong opposition to uncertainty to grudging acquiescence as Andrew's mother repeated her affirmation several more times.

Why don't you tell her no, you clot! You're the man—just put your foot down!

Now Andrew's mother was scampering over to him.

"I'm going to give it a go, Andrew. Jake will take you and L.S—"

"Mum, *no!* You don't have to—I mean, Jake couldn't do it, why do you think you—

"Because I'm twenty pounds lighter, that's why!" The determination in her eyes told him it was pointless to argue. Bloody hell, why did she have to be so spirited!

After the planes were refueled, Jake insisted on taking Andrew's mother up to give her some pointers on using the hand controls. That done, she dropped Jake off and took to the sky again. Jake ambled over to the Reliant.

"*My* turn to sit up front," L.S. winked at Andrew.

As long as Jake's flying the plane, it's always your turn to sit up front....

The Reliant seemed transformed in Jake's hands, like a rocket racing hell-bent across the heavens. Andrew's mother flew with such a light touch it almost seemed as if she were caressing the plane to its destination. Jake threw the Reliant about as if it needed to be goaded into obeying. He caught up with the Skyfarer; Andrew's mother smiled and made a V-for-Victory sign.

As they approached the gap, Andrew's throat tightened with fear.

I wished for that Skyfarer to end up in pieces on the side of a mountain...How could I know my mother would be inside?

An awful nausea rose within him.

What if God's like some dotty messenger boy who gets the orders bungled up?

Jake flew over the gap and banked around so that he could see the Skyfarer. It skimmed over a craggy ridge, then aimed at the break.

Please God, please...I take it all back...I just want to see that Skyfarer get across...Please!

"She's not going to make it," L.S. said.

Andrew closed his eyes.

Oh God, Please...Strike me dead with lightning...Take me, don't take her....

A low groan from Jake. Silence. Andrew opened his eyes but didn't dare look outside.

Please, somebody say something....

"Is she going to try again?" L.S. asked.

"Knowing her, she'll try a million times," Jake replied.

"What's she doing now?" L.S. said.

The Skyfarer was now some distance away, flying in a lazy circle over a low mountain. Jake stared intently at this strange behavior, then a smile broke across his face.

"She's catching a thermal—good girl!" He flew in a wide arc around the Skyfarer, like a mother bird urging her fledgling out of the nest. The Skyfarer seemed to float upwards, until it was even with the Reliant.

"Go for it, Alice—*GO!*" Jake jammed the throttle forward and the Reliant bolted towards the pass. The Skyfarer tagged along, lagging more and more behind but not losing altitude.

God please, let her make it....

A shrill whoop from L.S., a shout of joy from Jake.

"*She did it!*" Jake wheeled around in a three-quarter circle and flew alongside the Skyfarer. He waggled his wings, then made a V-for-Victory sign. Andrew's mother answered back: V-for-Victory. She grinned at Andrew. He put his hand, still shaking, up to the window and made a V. It wasn't until Jake flew on ahead that he slumped back in his seat, utterly drained.

"Here she comes!" L.S. called.

The Skyfarer touched down and sped down the runway, whipping past Andrew, Jake, and L.S. They ran up onto the runway and dashed behind it. It seemed to Andrew that he was flying as he outdistanced L.S., then Jake. If all of his running were for this one moment, to be the first to greet his mother, then it was all worth it.

He flung himself into his mother's arms; she chortled and shrieked and cried his name. He wanted to say so much to her, but the words jumbled in his mouth, so he just held her close.

Dad would be so proud of you....

Jake was by her side now; she was hugging and kissing him, then embracing L.S., who was sputtering with joy.

Jake stepped back from her and assumed a very formal demeanor. "May I be permitted the honor of tying down your plane, my dear?

"Delighted!" Andrew's mother exclaimed.

Jake anchored the Skyfarer, then put his arm around Andrew's mother. "Well, after lunch, how about a scenic tour over the Grand Canyon?

"Sounds smashing!" Andrew's mother put one arm around Jake, the other around Andrew, and walked between them to the hangar. L.S. walked alongside Andrew and beamed at her. She smiled at him, then at Jake. An enigmatic looked crossed her face. It was a sort of faraway gaze, happy, but somewhat pensive.

"What?" Jake asked.

"I was just thinking," she murmured.

"About what?"

She looked as if she were about to say something, then looked dreamily into the distance.

Jake slowed, looked at her worriedly. She smiled reassuringly at him, then took a deep breath. "I was just thinking that it was a good thing we didn't have to do this a few months from now."

"What do you mean?" Jake asked.

Disengaging her arm from Andrew's shoulder, she turned to Jake and whispered something in his ear.

"*WHAT!*" he hollered. "Are you sure?" His face was taut with shock.

"Not certain," she replied gently. "We're going to visit Marlys in Los Angeles. I could see her father."

Jake was breathing heavily now, and the shock on his face was overlaid something else: *Fear*.

Andrew wondered what in the world his mother could have said to Jake to produce a reaction like that. And what did it all have to do with Marlys's father?

"Now, what were you saying about this man with no legs who was a fighter pilot?" L.S. asked Jake.

"His name was Douglas Bader," Jake spoke loudly over the din of conversation at the airfield diner. "He lost his legs in a flying accident in the early thirties, so he was discharged from the RAF. After being fitted with artificial legs, he was determined to get back in. He proved he could fly, but he got turned down every time. When the war came along he rattled enough cages and was let back in, and within a few months he was commanding a squadron. Bader was one helluva pilot, too. He could make these tight turns that would nearly black his wingmen out; the doctors figured that since he didn't have any legs, and nowhere for the blood to go, the G-forces didn't affect him as much—"

"Pardon me, but are you Mr. Gibbons?" A man in a wheelchair approached their table.

"The name's Jake Givens," Jake said with a smile. "You must be Philip Poole."

"Givens!" The man shook Jake's hand heartily. "I knew a Givens once, when I was a student at Rutgers. Couple who ran a boarding home in New Brunswick. I lived there for four years."

"Lois and Gene Givens?" Jake asked.

"Why, yes! Jake! You were knee-high to a grasshopper, then—and the house mascot!" He shook his head in wonder. "We all used to give you airplane rides—how you loved them. Do you remember?"

Jake grinned. "Those were my earliest memories. I guess that's why I wanted to fly more than anything."

"I'll be dammed! And you flew my plane to me—any trouble getting it over the Rockies?"

"Piece of cake," Andrew's mother chirped.

"My wife took care of that," Jake said proudly. He introduced Andrew's mother, then Andrew and L.S.

"This calls for a celebration!" Philip exclaimed. "What say you and me go up for a spin, then you all can come home with me!"

Philip's home turned out to be a palatial estate overlooking the Pacific Ocean.

"Made my fortune in manufacturing aircraft propellers," Philip said to Jake, as he showed them to the guest house. "You and your family are welcome to stay here as long as you want. We usually have guests here only in the wintertime." He introduced them to his wife, Tia, who was a pilot also. She happily chatted with Andrew's mother about flying.

The guest house was situated next to a huge sunken swimming pool. "You boys look like you could use a swim," Philip laughed. Andrew and L.S. quickly changed into swim trunks and jumped into the cool waters.

Supper was served outside on the "veranda" by the pool. The maid, Inga, attended them. She was movie-star beautiful, with platinum blond hair and a thick Norwegian accent. Philip urged Andrew and L.S. to help themselves to oranges off the trees which were liberally planted all around. As Andrew plucked one he thought back to that day, so long ago at Armus House, when he'd dreamt of sitting under an orange tree and picking as many oranges as he wanted.

The next day Marlys arrived, and she and Andrew's mother reminisced happily about their times in the ATA, while Andrew and L.S. swam in the pool. Jake had taken Philip out flying; Andrew was delighted to see Marlys again and happy not to have to suffer Jake's company.

"Have you heard from Kaz?" he asked her.

Marlys shook her head. "I wrote to her in Pennsylvania, but my letter came back—no forwarding address."

Philip and Jake came back in the late afternoon, and Tia invited Marlys to stay for dinner. Over dessert, Marlys recounted the hilarious trick she, Irene, Kaz, and Andrew had played on Freddie. Andrew's mother laughed wildly; she seemed not a little astounded by their charade.

"Didn't Kaz tell you about it?" Marlys asked her.

"No, she didn't. How did you find out about Freddie's nefarious plans?"

"Oh, Andrew overheard Freddie plotting with his friend Maurice. Freddie threatened him not to tell, and that was why we had to hatch up our little plot."

"Freddie threatened you?" Andrew's mother turned to Andrew; her voice was not so happy now.

Andrew shrugged. "It turned out all right." He wished Marlys hadn't brought the subject up. His mother gave him a worried look, then turned to Marlys again. They talked more about their experiences in the ATA, and Marlys talked about her budding charter business: "Pilot to the Stars," she boasted.

It was getting late, and Marlys excused herself, saying she had an early flight the next morning. Before she left she told Andrew's mother, "I'll pick you up at noon tomorrow."

Andrew's mother smiled a funny smile at Jake, and Andrew wondered what it was about her meeting with Marlys that had produced that enigmatic expression on her face.

Later, as he was getting ready for bed, there was a tap at his door.

"Andrew?" his mother called.

"Come in."

His mother entered. On her face was that look of consternation again. "Andrew—" she began. She glanced at L.S. "Come with me, Andrew." She took his hand and silently led him to the room she shared with Jake.

Jake was not there, thank goodness; Andrew had some idea of what was on her mind, and he didn't want Jake to be around.

She sat on the bed, and patted the space next to her. When Andrew sat down, she said, "Now, what is this about Freddie threatening you?"

Although he expected to be confronted, he hadn't thought out exactly how he would soft-pedal things.

"He, um—he just got a little nasty, and said it wouldn't be right for me to tell."

"I never thought that *you* could be so swayed as to Freddie's ideas about right and wrong," she said sarcastically.

"He—he—"

"What?"

"He said—" Andrew was perturbed that his voice had risen half octave. "He said he would...bother you if I told."

"*Bother* me?"

He felt the tears well up in his eyes. "Yes."

Her arms went around him. "Oh, darling! Why did you feel that you needed to protect me? And why didn't you come to me?"

"I didn't want you to worry."

She tightened her embrace and whispered. "Andrew, it's my *job* to worry."

It's not your job to worry if you're flying planes....

All of a sudden her body stiffened, as if she'd been struck. She coaxed his face towards hers and fixed him with a stern glare.

"Did Freddie ever threaten *you?*"

714

Her question took him by surprise.

"Uh—uh—yuh—n—no—*NO!*"

"Andrew, *don't lie to me*!" She shook him savagely. "*Did he ever threaten you?*"

He sputtered, then choked, then the words poured out of him like vomit. He blurted out all about the veiled threats, about the hypodermic, about the marbles and the bleach and the knife. She listened, horrified, then embraced him as he collapsed in sobs against her.

"Andrew—*Andrew!* Why didn't you come to me!" Her voice was ravaged with hysteria.

He started clutching at her and screaming.

"*It was my fault—my fault! You crashed because I was so mean to you—when you and Jake—you were upset because of me—I said all those awful things—*"

Then she was clutching at him and he heard her cries lace with his.

He awoke, and saw his mother asleep beside him. She looked so fragile and vulnerable in sleep, and the memory of that dreadful scene the night before began to torment him.

All I wanted to do was protect her, keep her from worry and care....

She stirred, and her eyes fluttered open. She stared at him, silent, and in her eyes was a look he'd never seen before: a kind of deep sorrow and agony, but traced with a sort of resolve and—could it be—gratefulness? She scooted up to a sitting position and threw her arms around him.

"I want to tell you something," she said softly.

"I'm sorry," he whispered.

She hugged him fiercely. "Oh, Andrew, it's not for you to be sorry!" She took a deep breath, drew away a bit and gazed at him again.

"I want to tell you about what happened to me in the court of Elizabeth the Queen."

"*What?*"

She laughed that wonderful lilting laugh he loved so much. "It was the strangest thing—I was in a Spitfire, making an emergency landing because the engine had quit. I was skimming across Nicholsons's Pasture and all of a sudden the plane lurched and my head slammed against the canopy, and I woke up to find myself in the court of Elizabeth the Queen. I was one of her ladies-in-waiting, Bess's favorite, in fact, because I was a relative of hers, on the Howard side. It was so exciting being at court, but I had the strangest feeling I didn't belong. You see, every so often this little boy would appear, and he'd take my hand and say, 'Sorry mum, please come back!' No one else could see him except me. Everyone would look at me rather oddly when this happened, and I was so afraid I'd be accused of consorting with familiar spirits—after all, they *did* burn witches in those days. But I'd feel the boy's hand in mine, and I'd try to follow him, but then I'd get lost from him. Everything would go dark, and my legs would feel so heavy, as if I were trying to run underwater. Then I'd find myself back at court, but the feeling that I didn't belong would be even stronger. Then, after awhile, the boy would appear again...." Her voice trailed off; she smiled at Andrew, then continued.

"I finally vowed that I would go with him, no matter how terrifying things got. This time he held onto my hand ever so tightly, and he pleaded: 'Come back, come back, please mum, come back!' Then I felt another hand, and I heard someone say my name, and all of a sudden I realized who I was and what had happened. I felt these two hands pulling me, heard these two voices pleading with me, and then I opened my eyes and found myself in hospital, and you and Jake were with me."

The tears streamed down her cheeks. "You brought me back, Andrew!"

Andrew slumped against her. "When I heard the engine cut out—I was so afraid—it was all my fault because I'd been—"

"Andrew!" She whispered. "I didn't crash because of you. It was engine failure, didn't I tell you?"

"I just didn't want you to worry—ever!" he moaned.

Her kisses fluttered over his face and her hands stroked his hair. "It's all right now, it's all right. Everything's all right."

"I didn't want Freddie to bother you. I know it was wrong for me to keep quiet about his plans, but I didn't want him to...to—"

"Andrew!" She clasped his face in her hands. "You didn't need to worry about Freddie bothering me. He was a bit of a nuisance at times, but I took care of that!"

"You did?"

His mother nodded. "It was just after you'd recovered from pneumonia. I'd gone to Armus House for a bath and a change of clothes. Freddie didn't know you were on the mend, and he tried to 'comfort' me. Well, I decked him with a left hook!"

"You *decked* him?"

"Yes. I didn't mean to, but he tried to get his arms around me, and I just wanted to make it clear I didn't like his attention. Your father taught me to box, you know."

Andrew threw his arms around her. "He told me. Oh, Mum, he'd be so proud of you!"

They went outside and found Jake taking a picture of L.S., who was lounging in one of the floating chairs in the pool. He had an ear-splitting grin on his face as Inga handed him a glass of orange juice. Jake snapped the picture, then winked at Andrew's mother.

"L.S. wants to send some photos to his mother to show her how much he's enjoying California—especially the part about the white woman serving *him!*"

Andrew's mother threw back her head and shrieked with glee.

"What time are you seeing Marlys's father?" Jake asked her.

"One o'clock."

There it was again—that enigmatic look on his mother's face. Jake's expression was just as inscrutable: Andrew couldn't tell if he was perturbed or pleased.

"Philip got me a job flying some bigwigs all up and down the coast for the next two weeks," Jake told her. "He said you all could stay here while I'm gone—is that okay?"

"Okay!" Andrew's mother parodied his American accent and gave him a swift kiss. "I'd better get freshened up. Marlys will be here soon." She turned to Andrew. "Why don't you join L.S. in the pool, darling?"

Marlys and his mother returned just before dinnertime, giggling like schoolgirls. Andrew was sunbathing by the pool and kept his eyes shut when he heard them approach. It sounded as if they were catching up on ATA gossip, because his mother lowered her voice and said something about "it" happening in an Anson, and that this wasn't the first time "it" had happened.

"I didn't know they had Ansons back then," Marlys said.

"No, that time it was in a Giant Moth, and it was all because Sparky forgot—" His mother lowered her voice even more, and Andrew couldn't make out what she was saying. Then she laughed and said loudly, "Well, all Sparky remembered was that Roger had sent him to get something that started with an *F*, and so he got flowers!"

The mention of his father's name startled Andrew. He looked up and saw Jake striding over from the main house.

"Alice?"

Andrew's mother ran into his arms. Jake gave her a quizzical look, and she smiled the most dazzling smile at him. Jake seemed momentarily stunned, then pulled her into the guest house.

Andrew had been floating all day on a cloud of rapture after the wonderful time he'd had with his mother that morning, but now the cloud evaporated and he fell to earth.

Bloody hell—why can't he leave her alone!

Jake left the next day, for his stint of flying "bigwigs," and Andrew enjoyed a blissful two weeks alone with his mother.

It just doesn't get any better than this, Andrew thought, as he bounded out of the pool and picked an orange off a tree. L.S. was away too, though Andrew would not have minded his company. Marlys knew a casting coordinator and had gotten L.S. a job as an extra in a film.

"Sorry, Andrew," she'd told him. "Wish I could have gotten you a role, but you're not the right color!"

Though L.S. enjoyed his stint as a "movie star," he was often bored by all the waiting between shoots. When one of the stage crew twisted his ankle, L.S. was hired as a quick replacement and found that more to his liking. He came home on his last day to report that he'd been offered a job as a stagehand, with first dibs on any opportunities to work as an extra.

"The job doesn't start until September," he told Andrew's mother. "I'm not sure if I'll take it, but I've found someone I could stay with if I do—that is, when I start earning money. And I can go to night school, too, and get my high school diploma."

"Well, my young man, it looks as if you'll have to choose between being a cowboy or a movie star," she teased. "Philip just got Jake a job flying a Grumman Duck up to Alaska. Why don't you come with us while you make up your mind? We might do a bit of sightseeing while we're up there. I've heard Alaska is ever so lovely!"

They took off for Alaska on a clear day, and flew northward under a flawless sky of dazzling blue. Jake planned to do the trip in two days, stopping off in southern Washington for the night.

"I'd like to take you all on the scenic route," he said.

The Duck was a flying boat, which thrilled Andrew's mother to no end, as the women in the ATA had not been allowed a Class 6 rating. She insisted on doing the first leg, up the coast.

"Type-catcher." Jake grinned as Andrew's mother inspected the wing floats.

The Duck was also amphibious, with retractable landing gear in the hull, so it could be used on land or water. Since Jake had a water rating, he would do the last leg up to Anchorage where the Duck would be landed on water.

Andrew's mother flew the first leg, sitting high up in the pilot's seat at the top of the Duck. Andrew sat with L.S. in the bench seat in the belly of the plane, next to L.S.; Jake sat cross-legged on the floor, facing them. There was a small window in the door, so that they had a view of the scene below. After taking off, Andrew's mother skimmed along the shore. She glanced down at Jake and grinned.

"Go ahead—you've been dying to do it!" Jake laughed.

Andrew's mother shouted with triumph and veered out to sea.

"Okay," Jake said after the coast had nearly disappeared on the horizon, "Let's take her back in."

"Aye-aye, captain!" Andrew's mother steered the duck back to land.

As Andrew's mother flew north, Jake chatted with L.S., telling one flying story after another, though nothing about himself: No barnstorming tales, Battle of Britain sagas, or Hurricat stories. Andrew occasionally listened in as Jake traced their route on the map; most of the time he daydreamed about being back in England.

"...So they had this whole squadron of colored fighter pilots?" L.S. asked Jake.

"A whole *group*—the 332nd Fighter Group—it had four squadrons," Jake replied. "They called themselves the Red Tail Angels because the tails of their P-51s were painted red. They were also known as the Tuskegee Airmen, since that's where they trained. And they were the best fighter group in the Fifteenth Air Force—they never lost a single plane they were charged with protecting."

After flying over the Golden Gate Bridge, Andrew's mother landed to refuel. They had lunch, then Jake took over the controls and headed inland. Andrew's mother sat next to Andrew on the bench seat while L.S. settled himself on the floor, opposite them.

"I'd like you all to get a look at the Cascades," Jake called down to them. "The Rockies and the Sierras are majestic, but the Cascades are the most beautiful I've ever seen."

They flew around Mount Shasta, a broad, towering sentinel, mottled with snow.

"There's something really incredible coming up; it would be even better if you'd all close your eyes and open them when we're right overhead."

Andrew slouched back in his seat, trying to ignore L.S.'s *oohs* and *ahs*.

Just a bunch of silly mountains and stupid lakes....

"Okay, close your eyes," Jake said. "It'll just be a few minutes."

All right—how about if I just keep them closed....

"Okay—open," Jake said.

Andrew's mother gasped with astonishment as she looked out the window.

"Why, it looks as if God scooped out a bit of ocean and put it in a mountain!"

Andrew looked out the window. There below was a lake of stunning sapphire blue, set in what looked like a crater. Rising Phoenix-like in the middle of it was a sort of miniature peak, stubbled with a few trees.

"It's called Crater Lake," Jake said. "This all used to be a mountain called Mount Mazama. It blew about nine thousand years ago and left a crater. The lake is almost two thousand feet deep in spots. That's Wizard Island, in the middle, and over there is Phantom Ship. He flew lower and pointed at jagged rock formation that looked for all the world like a ghost ship skimming the azure surface.

"It's an ancient rock formation, even older than Mount Mazama," Jake said. "It was hidden when the mountain formed around it, and uncovered when Mount Mazama erupted."

"Oh, darling, it's the loveliest thing I've ever seen!" Andrew's mother beamed at Jake.

Jake made another circuit of the lake, then flew on. He pointed out other peaks of the Cascades, which were slung down the spine of the range like a string of pearls against a background of dark green velvet.

"...Mount Thielsen, Diamond Peak, Bachelor Butte, Broken Top, The Sisters—Faith, Hope, and Charity."

"Faith, Hope, and Charity," Andrew's mother mused. "The names of the three Glouster Gladiator biplanes that defended Malta." She looked down at the mountains. "Which is which?"

"I don't know—they're usually called North, Middle, and South Sister," Jake said. "Nate and I climbed all three of them one summer." He flew a figure eight around the mountains, tying off South Sister from her other siblings, then pointed to a meadow with three lakes on the eastern flank of South Sister.

"Those are Green Lakes. We camped there. The southern lake is perfect for swimming—feels like you're floating in heaven."

Green Lakes! And they were *green*, a lovely sea-green, and they were beautiful and peaceful—just as Gerry had said.

"It's one thing to fly over mountains. It's another thing to climb them and stand on top of the world." Jake had a faraway look in his eyes. "I always wanted to come here with—" He caught himself, pursed his lips together and squinted at the land below. Andrew's mother laid her hand on his. "Maybe we'll climb them together someday, Alice," he said softly.

Jake wanted to show them the Oregon desert, so they flew east. The thick forest carpet scraggled into dots of juniper and bitterbrush, which grew progressively farther and farther apart until the landscape turned to a barren dusty brown.

"It's amazing—you can go from rain forest to desert in just a few minutes," Jake said. "Now you're going to see something spectacular!"

A wondrous sight came into view: an area of softly rounded hills and gentle ridges, dabbled with serrated bands of red, yellow, green, and blue.

"The Painted Hills," Jake announced. He then explained how this radiant display had all come about: Long ago this region had been the site of volcanic activity and, from time to time, showers of pumice and ash had deposited various mixtures of minerals and soil upon the young land. Later, lava flows wrinkled and shrouded these differently-hued layers, and earthquakes heaved the strata into ripples and folds. Wind and water added the final polish, carving the lumpy landscape into beribboned sculptures that sparkled in the blazing sun. To Andrew, the lustrous colors glissading down the flanks of the low buttes gave the appearance of gaily striped square-dancing skirts flared against a tawny backdrop. It seemed incongruous, and somewhat disturbing, that this exquisite beauty could be born of such violent and destructive forces.

Jake circled around the scene a few times, then headed west, following a highway that aimed straight for the mountains.

"Mount Jefferson up ahead. To the north is Mount Hood." He veered north from the road to inspect some lakes.

"Look!" Andrew's mother exclaimed.

On a dusty road below lay two smashed vehicles, looking like crunched-up toy cars. Three blood-soaked bodies were scattered around the wreck; a few other people lurched around and looked skyward.

Andrew saw L.S. lean forward as if he were about to be sick. His breath came out in low moans; then he pressed his face into his knees. Jake, up in the pilot's seat and staring at the horrid scene below, was oblivious to L.S.'s distress, as was Andrew's mother, who was staring, horrified, out the window.

"Oh dear, can't we do something?" Andrew's mother cried.

"We can't land here, but we can make sure that they get help." Jake headed back to the main road.

"Wonderful—there's an ambulance coming down the highway," Andrew's mother breathed.

The ambulance stopped at the intersection of the highway and the dirt road, which was a four-way junction, then turned south.

"Bloody hell—it's going the wrong way!" Andrew's mother exploded.

Jake didn't say a word. He put the plane into a dive and swooped low over the ambulance. He buzzed the wayward vehicle again, then waggled his wings and headed north.

"It's turning around," Andrew's mother said.

Jake flew back to the site of the crash and circled overhead until the ambulance arrived at the scene.

"Your good deed for the day, darling." Andrew's mother smiled at Jake.

L.S. gasped, then dissolved into wails of anguish.

"L.S.—what's wrong?" Jake turned to him.

L.S. kept his face pressed into his knees, said softly, "I'm all right." He stayed in the same position, looking as if he were asleep, or in prayer.

After they landed in Washington, Jake took L.S. out for dinner. Andrew was concerned about L.S., but glad to have the time alone with his mother. They got some sandwiches at a deli and ate a picnic supper at a park near their hotel.

Jake met them as they were walking back to the hotel and told them that L.S. had turned in early.

"What was the matter with him?" Andrew's mother asked.

Jake shook his head angrily. "L.S. and his father were in a car wreck a few years ago. His father was a schoolteacher, and was driving to the next town to get some used text-books. They were hit head-on by some drunk in a pickup. The ambulance came, but it was for whites only and the attendants wouldn't take L.S. and his father to the hospital—took the drunk, though. By the time help came, L.S.'s father was—" He swallowed, cleared his throat, then continued, his voice choked with rage. "He was dead, Alice. He died in L.S.'s arms. Oh God, what a thing for a kid to have to go through—" He broke off again, gazed at Mount Hood in the distance.

Andrew's mother slipped her arm around his waist and they walked in silence to the hotel.

They were seated in a restaurant in Anchorage. Andrew wrote Effie Mae's address on a postcard of Mount McKinley; his mother scanned a local newspaper. They'd just delivered the Duck, and Jake had immediately gotten two more ferry jobs: flying a Bellanca Skyrocket to Vancouver, and a Lockheed Electra from there to Fairbanks.

Andrew's mother gasped. "Andrew, look!" She pointed to a article on the front page. It was titled: *Bush Pilot Saves Life of Boy Mauled by Bear.*

Andrew's read the article:

Prompt action by a Kelso bush pilot saved the life of an eight-year-old boy, Brian Lytle, who was mauled by a bear last Saturday at his family's home near Kelso. Francis "Kaz" Kazmierski, who was flying in the area and heard the distress call put out by the boy's father, made a quick landing and flew the boy to Fairbanks, where he was transported to Saint Joseph's Hospital. Lytle is listed in critical condition but is expected to recover. Doctor Louis Nowotny credits Kazmierski's quick response as being crucial: "Twenty more minutes, and that boy would have been dead."

His mother shook her head in wonder. "Kaz—a bush pilot!"

"Let's go see her!" Andrew said.

"That's a wonderful idea!" Andrew's mother turned to Jake. "How about stopping off tomorrow in Kelso, darling?"

Jake consulted a map. "Sure, let's get an early start. I'd like to make Vancouver in one day. If you'd like, I'll leave you there—I know you and Kaz have got a lot of catching up to do."

"Super!" Andrew's mother said.

Andrew was pleased: two days away from Jake!

L.S. decided to stay in Kelso with them. After supper, Andrew's mother tried to contact Kaz, but without success:

"I had to talk by radio to some chap at the airfield there. The reception was ghastly, but I was able to find out that Kaz is in Nome and won't be back until tomorrow after-noon. You can drop us off in Kelso and we'll wait until she arrives."

Andrew's mother flew the Skyrocket to Kelso and happily noted the fact in her log book. After giving her a good-bye kiss, Jake soared off to Vancouver.

They had breakfast at a roadhouse, then went for a walk, enjoying the crisp morning air. Andrew's mother noticed a Stearman doing aerobatics above and explained the vari-ous maneuvers to L.S. Andrew decided to check back at the airfield, which only a short distance away. Perhaps Kaz might have arrived early.

"Hullo—do you know when Frances Kazmierski will be arriving?"

The man at the desk didn't look up at him. "Just got in—down the hall, first door on the right."

Andrew went down the corridor and opened the first door on the right. He saw three men sitting at a table, all holding fans of cards in their hands.

"Oh, sorry," Andrew said. "I was looking for Kaz."

He quickly shut the door. Perhaps the man had meant the first door on the *left*. An-drew crossed the hall and peered into the room: It was a sort of storeroom, with shelves around the perimeter. There seemed to be a small alcove off to one side; perhaps Kaz was there. He took a step towards it, called, "Kaz?"

He heard the door click shut but before he could turn around, someone grabbed him from behind and clapped a hand over his mouth. He struggled, but the hand pressed more tightly to his face and a strong arm held him fast.

Chapter 48

"*A*ndrew! It's me—Kaz."

Andrew broke free, spun around.

"Kaz! You're a m—"

Kaz clapped her hand over his mouth again. Andrew gently pulled her wrist away.

"Why are you dressed as a *man?*" he hissed.

Kaz stood before him, looking mortified, as if someone had caught her without her clothes on. Andrew realized now: She'd been one of the "men" at the poker table. Her hair was cropped very short; in her Irvine jacket and trousers she looked just like "one of the guys."

"It was the only way I could get a job as a pilot," she said, as if she were apologizing. "What are *you* doing here, Andrew?"

"We flew into Anchorage yesterday. Mum saw the article in the newspaper about you, and Jake dropped us off here. He's flying a Skyrocket down to Vancouver."

"Where's your mother?"

"Outside—I'll get her."

"Wait...Tell her about me first. I can't risk anyone finding out."

Andrew was suddenly overcome with sadness. It was awful that Kaz should have to masquerade as a man, just to get a job. He gave her a hug and tried to blink away his tears.

"Hey Andrew—it's still me," Kaz assured him.

"I know."

"You'd better get to your mother before she comes in here, okay?"

"All right." He gave her another hug and dashed outside.

His mother was quite astounded by his report; so was L.S. He led them to the store-room.

"Alice..." Kaz held her hands out, as if begging forgiveness. Andrew's mother wrapped her arms around her.

"Kaz—it's so good to see you!"

"Sorry it's under these circumstances."

"Wouldn't matter if you'd turned into a little green man from Mars!"

"He's with you?" Kaz nodded at L.S.

"Yes, he is," Andrew's mother said. "Tell you about it over lunch, all right? We've got a *lot* of catching up to do!"

"...so the only jobs for women pilots were as stewardesses." Kaz spoke in a low voice as she stirred her coffee. Fortunately, the roadhouse was almost empty and the cook was clattering loudly in the kitchen.

"Would you like more coffee, Kaz?" A waitress, young and blond and buxom, smiled sweetly at Kaz.

"Uh, yeah. Alice, more coffee for you?"

"Yes please."

The waitress eyed Andrew's mother as she poured the coffee. "Looks like you and Kaz are old friends."

"Oh, yes, we go back—" Andrew's mother waved her hands. "Years! We're both pilots, you see. We were in the Air Transport Auxiliary together. In England." She smiled at the waitress.

"England," the waitress echoed. She glanced back at Kaz.

"England," Kaz affirmed.

There was an uncomfortable silence. Kaz cleared her throat but didn't say anything.

Andrew's mother fluttered her hands. "Yes, we had all *sorts* of adventures together. Remember that turkey run to Ireland?" She raised her eyebrows at Kaz, then explained to the waitress: "We nipped over to Ireland, this was back in '43, to pick up some Christmas turkeys. We thought they would be butchered and plucked, but it turned out they were very much alive. So we loaded up the back of the Anson with these crated gobblers, and wouldn't you know, a few of them got loose over the Irish Sea. They were flapping all over the fuselage and making a hell of a racket. We couldn't catch them, so the pilot yells, "Hold onto your hats!" and puts the plane into a dive that leaves the birds plastered to the back of the plane! Poor things—even after we landed, they were paralyzed with terror. We gathered them up—it was like picking toys off the floor—and put them back in their cages. They didn't make a peep in protest!" Andrew's mother got a mischievous look on her face. "And *then* there was the time we were at that bash that one of those fighter squadrons from the Eighth Air Force gave, remember, Kaz?"

Kaz grunted nervously.

Andrew's mother turned to the waitress. "Well, I was with my husband, and—"

"You're married, then?" the waitress asked.

"Oh, yes, happily." Andrew's mother displayed her ring finger.

The waitress smiled.

Andrew's turned back to Kaz. "And *you* were with that nice-looking Norwegian! You two made the *cutest* couple—what ever happened?"

Kaz said evenly, "Well, you know, the war and all—things just didn't work out."

"Pity," Andrew's mother murmured. "I thought you two—"

"Hey Shirley—stop your yakkin' and give us some service!" a red-faced man hollered from one of the tables across the room.

"Keep your pants on, willya!" the waitress snapped. She smiled again at Kaz, then ambled over to her impatient customer.

"He wasn't my type," Kaz whispered.

Andrew's mother arched her eyebrows. "She likes you."

"Alice—*please!* I never—"

"Women *like* the quiet types, you know. Still waters run deep and all that."

"Kaz—howzitgoin?" A tall man with an amiable smile walked into the roadhouse and nodded at Kaz.

"Fine, Sam," Kaz replied. "Oh, uh, this is Alice Givens—we were in the ATA together. And this is her son, Andrew, and L.S., their friend. Alice—Sam Major. He's our one-day-a-week doctor, out of Fairbanks."

"Pleased to meet you," Sam said. "I come here more for the fishing than for the doctoring." He winked at Andrew's mother. "So you knew Kaz in the ATA? Must be quite a surprise seeing each other after all this time."

"Yes, it is." Andrew's mother seemed somewhat disconcerted.

Sam winked again at Andrew's mother, smiled at Kaz, then seated himself two tables down.

Kaz leaned forward and spoke softly to Andrew's mother. "He knows."

"About you?"

Kaz nodded. "I had to see him just after I got here—you know, medical, uh, visit, and he, um, he—he—" She turned very red.

Andrew's mother squeezed her hand and whispered, "*He* likes you too!"

Kaz turned even redder.

"Well," Andrew's mother said. "You never know how things might turn out."

"As it looks now," Kaz sighed, "They're not going to turn out very well. I'll only have this job for a few more months. The company is being sold."

"Couldn't *you* buy it, or get a loan?"

Kaz shook her head. "I'd have to disclose too much, you know. Oh well, at least I can always go back to building planes—maybe do a bit of instructing."

"How much does your boss want for the company?"

Kaz fished reached into her jacket pocket, pulled out a piece of paper, and handed to Andrew's mother. "The company has two planes: an American Pilgrim and a Fairchild 51. My boss just got this offer last week. He'd like more, but he'll take this if nothing else comes along."

"Hey, get your hands off me!" The waitress was struggling with a florid-faced, obviously inebriated customer, who was grabbing at her breasts. She broke free, but the man, guffawing loudly, lunged at her. She whipped a dishtowel off her shoulder and snapped it across his crotch. The man howled and doubled over. The man's companions, in various stages of intoxication, whistled and hooted.

"Shirley's got the fastest dishtowel in the West," Kaz said. She lowered her voice. "Should have tried that on Freddie."

"*Freddie!*" Andrew's mother smacked the table. "That's *it!* We'll use Freddie's money to buy the company!"

"What?" Kaz asked.

Andrew's mother laughed wildly. "Freddie left me a bit of money when he went to his reward. I *know* he intended it to stir up trouble—he indicated in his will that he left it to me as a token of his affection and esteem! I was so *incensed*—I couldn't make up my mind what to do with it, thought maybe I should donate it to build a dance hall for

American GIs or something. Anyway, I left it in a bank until I could decide. Oh, Kaz—this is *marvelous!*"

"Alice, you ought to use the money for yourself, or for Andrew, at least—"

"Oh, I don't need it, and Andrew's not only got the Howard family fortune to inherit, but the Hadley-Trevelyan Family Trust as well. No, I think this would be the perfect way to dispose of Freddie's money! I'd like to think he was rolling over in his grave! Now," She grinned at Kaz, "Since I'm going to buy the company, I need to check out those planes, first."

"Typecatcher," Kaz chuckled.

"...and it wasn't until Freddie died that I found out that he'd done quite well for Hadley-Trevelyan Family Trust."

Kaz had invited them to stay at her place, a two room apartment over the general store. Andrew, snuggled up on a cot borrowed from Sam, pressed his ear to the wall adjoining the bedroom, where his mother and Kaz were chatting. L.S. was already asleep on the sofa.

"...so he borrowed the money from the trust to finance his American investments—the provision was that the trust get half the profits. The solicitor that Roger's father had retained to manage the trust was quite clever—" Andrew's mother giggled, and went on. "And Freddie was clever about figuring that there was money to be made hand over fist in Yankland."

"I remember him saying that he was into liberty ships," Kaz said.

"Liberty ships weren't even half of it! You see, before the United States would release one penny in Lend Lease aid to England, practically all British assets in America had to be liquidated and the proceeds turned over to the US government. Many British companies were sold for a fraction of their value, and Freddie got in on the feeding frenzy, buying businesses through an American 'front man'."

"Boy, Freddie doesn't miss a trick!"

"He certainly doesn't. The trust is worth over ten million now."

"Ten million dollars?"

"Pounds!"

"Good grief, Alice—that's over forty million dollars! And Andrew's getting it all?"

"Jane, too."

"Oh, right. Whom did Freddie leave his personal fortune to?"

"He had a half-sister, Daphne. Poor girl, she was interned on Borneo by the Japanese and suffered terribly. Her husband and two daughters died. She came back to England just before I left for America and I put her up in Freddie's place in London—it's owned by the trust, actually. Daphne's using her inheritance to build orphanages and hospitals in Borneo...."

His mother's voice faded; Andrew only caught giggly snatches of something about "it" happening in the Anson, and something else about "French letters." The term was familiar, but he couldn't remember where he'd heard it before.

He rolled over and went to sleep.

It was early, Andrew sensed. He opened his eyes and looked at his watch: six-thirty. Turning over, he saw crumpled sheets on the sofa, but no sign of L.S.

He waited for awhile, then got up to see if L.S. was in the bathroom.

He wasn't. While Andrew stood pondering if he should wake his mother and tell her that L.S. had disappeared, he heard voices on the outside stairway: Kaz's and L.S.'s.

They came in; Kaz seemed surprised to see Andrew up so early.

"I hope I didn't wake you," she said. "I usually get up early and go out for some coffee. L.S. was already awake, so he came with me."

L.S. smiled at her. "I guess we should tell him," he said.

"Tell me what?" Andrew said.

Kaz beamed at L.S. "L.S. is staying with me. I'm going to teach him how to fly."

"You're going to learn how to *fly?*" Andrew exclaimed.

"Uh-huh." L.S.'s grin was threatening to split his face in two.

"*And* finish out high school," Kaz added. "That's the deal, remember?"

"Deal!" L.S. affirmed.

"That must be Jake," Andrew's mother said, pointing at the Electra that had just appeared on the horizon. She turned to Kaz. "I'll explain things to him—poor dear, he's already had one too many shocks this month. Good thing you'll be able to drop your ruse soon!"

Andrew thought he'd better make one last visit to the W.C. before getting airborne. Besides, he hated happy reunions, especially when they were between his mother and Jake.

She'll probably throw herself at him, as if they hadn't seen each other in weeks....

He was washing his hands when he heard voices outside the lavatory door.

"...So that English dame *bought* the company for Kaz?"

"Lock, stock, and barrel! I heard her husband's flying in to pick up her and the kid— wonder what he'll think of that! Boy, if I was him, I'd be pretty damned sore to find out my wife had blown the family fortune on some other guy!"

Jake was quite delighted to hear that L.S. would be staying with Kaz. He gave L.S. his extra Irvine jacket, then took everyone out to the roadhouse to celebrate. Over a dinner of moose steak, L.S. told Jake that hearing about the Tuskegee airmen had put the idea in his mind that he could also be a pilot.

"And if that man with no legs could fly a plane, I figured I could too!" He turned to Andrew's mother. "Watching you fly all the way across the country made me realize that being a pilot was what I wanted more than anything."

Kaz put them up again for the night, installing Andrew's mother and Jake in the bedroom. She wedged another borrowed cot between Andrew's cot and the sofa, and she and Andrew stayed up until the late hours reminiscing, with L.S. listening in.

"Remember the time I won all those Hershey's kisses?" Andrew said.

Kaz laughed. "Irene could never get over how good you were at bluffing. She was absolutely terrible! She always used to hum *Amy, Wonderful Amy* whenever she bluffed."

"She was killed too," Andrew said. "Amy Johnson, I mean."

Kaz sighed. "At least she died doing something she loved."

At their parting the next day, Andrew realized how close he'd grown to L.S., even though they had known each other barely a month. He felt as if he were saying good-bye to his best friend.

In a way, I am....

Andrew's mother flew the Electra to Fairbanks. There, Jake got another job ferrying a Staggerwing Beech to Wyoming. He was quite pleased with this particular job, as the cattle rancher to whom the plane was being delivered was willing to barter their ferry services for a 1940 air-conditioned Packard.

"We can drive back across the country, see the folks in Nebraska again, then visit with my Uncle Lee and his family in New York." Jake smiled at Andrew. "I know Lee-Ann will be happy to see you."

Andrew tried to hide his displeasure. While he welcomed the chance to see Lee-Ann, he was not thrilled with the prospect of an interminable cross-country excursion in close quarters with Jake. And he was even less pleased with the idea of seeing Jereen again.

Andrew's mother, of course, wanted the Staggerwing Beech in her logbook. Once airborne, however, she had a sudden attack of nausea and had to hand over the controls to Jake while she heaved up her breakfast in a canvas dufflebag. Jake looked quite worried, but she reassured him that this sort of thing had happened to her before. Andrew was bewildered: *Before?* He had *never* known his mother to get airsick.

The trip to Wyoming took the better part of two days; then they were off to Yellowstone Park in their newly acquired Packard. Andrew's mother at first was quite excited by the "marvelous" scenery, but presently her face took on an awful grey cast and she frantically motioned Jake to pull over to the side of the road. She scooted off into the brush, escorted by Jake, and Andrew again heard horrid retching noises. Jake had to practically carry her back to the car; she seemed almost in a daze, though she kept reassuring Jake that it had been like this "the other time."

The other time? Andrew wondered.

"Andrew, why don't you sit up front with me?" Jake said. "Let your mother lie down in the backseat." He turned to Andrew's mother. "We'll be there in an hour—can you hang on that long?"

Andrew's mother nodded weakly as she crawled into the car.

Bloody hell, Andrew thought as he sat up front with Jake. It's bad enough being in the same car with Jake, but sitting on the same seat....

He glared at his mother's inert form, then at Jake.

You bastard—don't you even care about her?

As they drove on, Andrew's ire turned to anguish.

What's the matter with her? She hasn't even moved! She's never, ever been ill, never even had a sniffle.

Even when Jake stopped for groceries, she didn't stir, didn't even open her eyes.

Andrew was tormented by the remembrance of a classmate from his first year at Askew Court. He couldn't recall the boy's name, but he did remember how the spirited, energetic child had suddenly grown listless and weak, then had been whisked away by his worried mother. A few months later Andrew found out that he had died of leukemia.

Then Andrew remembered: His mother had been very anxious to see Marlys's father in California.

Physician to the Stars, that's what Marlys had said her father was! Why would my mother want to see him, unless she was ill?

"We're here," Jake said softly.

Andrew looked at the what was to be their quarters for the next few days: a minuscule log cabin with a sagging front porch.

Andrew's mother lifted her head a bit, opened her eyes for a millisecond, then laid her head back on the seat and groaned.

"I'll get up in a minute, all right?" she whispered.

Jake handed the car keys to Andrew. "Could you please bring in the groceries, Andrew?" He got out, opened the back door, and gently lifted her off the seat.

"Oh darling, I'll be all right—just a minute—"

"Come on, put your arms around me." Jake pulled her out of the car and carried her to the cabin; her arms flopped uselessly around his shoulders. Andrew brought one of the sacks of groceries into the house and set it on the kitchen table. He saw that it contained a package of bacon, so he took it out and stashed it on top of the refrigerator. The kitchen was hot and fuggy, so he opened the window. Then he went to see to his mother.

"Okay, here we are—" Jake deposited Andrew's mother on a bed in one of the bedrooms. She crawled under the covers and closed her eyes again. Her mouth hung slack and her face was horribly pallid.

"Mum?" Andrew took her hand.

Without opening her eyes, she nodded her head, as if that would reassure him. "I'm all right," she said weakly.

"Come on, Andrew—let your mother rest." Jake laid his hand on Andrew's shoulder. Andrew wanted to fling it off but he was afraid it might cause his mother more distress.

Jake quietly closed the bedroom door and got the rest of the groceries out of the car. Andrew plopped down on the sofa and glared at the bedroom door. Every so often, he heard soft rattles and clunks in the kitchen.

"Andrew—supper." Jake stood before him.

It wouldn't do him any good to starve himself. But if Jake expected any show of appreciation....

Andrew threw him a contemptuous glance and stomped into the kitchen.

The table was already set with two plates, each holding half of a roasted chicken, some boiled potatoes, and corn.

"Would you like some milk?" Jake asked him.

Andrew grunted. Jake poured some milk into his glass.

They ate in silence.

729

Andrew scraped his plate clean. Still hungry, he got up and rummaged through the cupboards. He grabbed a package of soda crackers and tore it open.

"Andrew, those are for your mother," Jake said. "I bought you some cookies—"

"Who are *you* to boss me around?" Andrew snapped.

"Andrew—"

"What's the matter with my mother? Why aren't you doing anything about it?"

Jake blinked, bit his lip.

"You don't care about her! Why haven't you gotten her to a doctor? She's ill—she could be dying!"

"Andrew, she's going to be all right—"

"No she isn't—you *know* she isn't! If you don't do something, I'm going to call for an ambulance! You don't care about her, but I do! If my father were here, he'd—"

"Andrew, she's going to have a baby." Jake's words were measured and soft.

The words hit Andrew like a punch. He gasped, then choked on his own breath.

A baby!

He groaned, and turned over again. After Jake's appalling revelation, Andrew had stared at him, too stunned to speak.

I should have called him every name in the book...should have smashed his sodding face in....

Instead, he'd stumbled into the other bedroom and had slammed the door.

*Watch out for the guy with the ace up his sleeve...*that's what Ray said.

He tried to stifle the sob welling up within him.

That bastard! That fucking bastard! He's won!

She won't go back to my father, now that she's having Jake's child!

A loud clanging noise startled Andrew out of his slumber. It was dawn, and freezing cold. Just what he bloody needed, to be awakened at first sparrow-fart by rude goings-on.

He was still dressed in his jeans and tee shirt. He remembered crawling under the covers as dusk fell the night before; he'd been too distraught to even undress.

Just as well, he thought, throwing back the covers. There was some kind of awful racket coming from the kitchen now.

Probably Jake, celebrating....

He dashed across the living room, into the kitchen, and came face to face with a horrid, hairy beast with black, beady eyes.

A bear!

It was standing on its hind legs, grasping the package of bacon in its paws. Andrew lunged at it, but it turned and quickly wriggled out the window.

Bloody hell! I'm not going to let that animal steal our bacon!

He leapt out the window and followed the lumbering creature through a clump of trees. It wasn't going very fast. Andrew decided to make a wide arc and intercept it head-on.

He ran about twenty yards past the bear, then turned and made a forward attack, thrusting his hands out in front of him so that he could snatch the bacon and make a run for it.

Suddenly he was knocked to the ground and strong arms were locked around him. He struggled to break free.

"Andrew—leave it alone! What did you think you were going to do—wrestle a bear?" *Jake!*

His fury gave Andrew a burst of strength, and he broke free from Jake's hold. He stood and saw the bear shambling off into the forest.

Jake grabbed him around the waist and Andrew thrashed against him. They both fell to the ground. Andrew was past fury now: He kicked at Jake and tried to yell the most horrid oaths he could think of, but his voice came out as a wild shriek.

"Dammit, Andrew—you could have gotten yourself killed!" Jake winced as Andrew's kicks connected, but didn't break free. He pinned Andrew's shoulders to the ground.

Andrew twisted and broke free again; Jake fell to the ground with a thud.

"I don't need you—I can take care of myself!" Andrew stood and spun round. The bear had vanished. He turned back to Jake.

"*I don't need you to protect me!*"

Jake raised himself up on his elbows. He started to say something, then clamped his mouth shut. He gazed at Andrew, but it looked as if his mind were a million miles away.

Andrew turned and stamped back to the cabin.

His mother was staring into the kitchen, her eyes wide with consternation.

"Oh dear."

Following her gaze, Andrew saw that the kitchen was a shambles: All of the food Jake had stocked in the cupboards was scattered on the floor, along with broken dishes and garbage. Andrew hadn't even noticed the mess in his rush to retrieve their bacon.

"Alice?" Jake opened the front door.

"Jake—what happened?"

Jake ambled over to the kitchen, gave a soft grunt.

"Looks like a bear was here." He didn't so much as glance at Andrew.

"A *bear!* Oh Jake, how *ghastly!* We might have been torn to bits in our sleep!

Jake put his arm around her. "Sorry, I forgot to close the window last night. Why don't you lie down, and I'll clean things up and make breakfast."

"Andrew, quick! It's going off!" his mother cried.

"Step to the right a little, Andrew," Jake said, squinting through the camera.

"Andrew, *smile!*" his mother urged.

Old Faithful whooshed an explosion of vapor skyward as Andrew defiantly folded his arms and glowered at the camera. He was bloody well *not* going to smile.

Jake, sitting in a booth in a decrepit diner across from Andrew and his mother, crumpled the edges of the newspaper in his hands.

"*Shit*—they did it." He sounded as if he'd been punched in the stomach.

"You folks ready to order?" The waitress whipped a grubby pencil from behind her right ear.

"Oh God, Alice..." Jake shook his head. "I can't *believe* they really did it—"

"What, darling?"

Jake slowly dropped the newspaper onto the table. Andrew's mother turned it around, and now Andrew discerned what the gigantic headline read: *Hiroshima in Ruins.*

"What is it, Jake?"

Jake closed his eyes, blew out a slow breath.

"Whereyall been?" the waitress said. "That there's old news—happened three days ago. Some kinda new bomb, just blew that there Jap city clean off the map—"

"Hey Ruta!" The cook, listening to a tinny radio, bellowed from behind the grill. "We just dropped another one them 'tomic bombs—place called Naggi-saki."

"*Another* one?"

Jake slumped forward a bit, shook his head again. "*Shit*," he whispered. Andrew's mother reached for his hand.

"Oh, Alice—" Jake's voice was a soft moan. "What a time to bring a kid into the world."

Andrew's mother reached across the front seat and tooted the horn all the way up the drive to the farmhouse. Children sprayed out the front door; a clutch of floral print dresses rippled down the steps after them.

As Jake braked to a halt, Andrew hunched down in the backseat. He was in no mood to be sociable.

I'll just say I'm very tired from the long journey...just want to take a bit of a nap....

"Andrew—we're here!" His mother leaned back and gave him a gentle nudge.

He sat up, rubbed his eyes.

Maybe I can make a quick dash to the house and get away from everyone, especially—

He got out of the car and came face to face with Jereen. She took his arm, and spoke over the din.

"Hello—we're all so excited to hear the news! Let's get inside, ahead of the mob." As she ushered him into the house, she whispered conspiratorially, "We're giving your mother a surprise baby shower after dinner. My mom and Mel got together a whole bunch of used baby things, and Aunt Euelene even knitted some booties yesterday. Here, you sit here." She started to pull out a chair for him at the dining room table.

"Um—I'm feeling a bit tired." He smiled weakly. "It was such a long drive. I think I'll rest up first."

She laid her hand on his arm, gazed solicitously at him. "All right. You'll be in my room again—come on."

She led him upstairs, holding his hand tightly, as if he might fall. She pulled back the covers on her bed and fluffed the pillows.

"So L.S. is staying in Alaska with your friend?"

"Yes—he's going to learn how to fly."

"Good for him! He was so nice—I hope things turn out okay for him."

"Yes, um, I hope they do too." He sat down at the foot of the bed and took his shoes off. "Well, see you later."

She tilted her head slightly, as if to challenge his dismissal of her, then smiled and left without a word.

He tore off his clothes and flung them into the corner.

There was a tap on the door. "Andrew?"

Andrew dove onto the bed and scrambled under the covers as his mother came into the room.

Wish she would bloody knock first....

"Oh, darling, are you ill?" She sat down on the bed next to him. "Jereen said you didn't want to have dinner."

"I'm fine—just a little tired. I just want to rest a bit."

She pressed her hand to his forehead.

"I'm fine, Mum."

"Andrew—I thought you might like a bite to eat." Jereen stood at the door, a tray in her hands.

"Oh, Jereen, how *thoughtful* of you!" Andrew's mother exclaimed. "Andrew, would you be able to eat a little bit?"

He wasn't all that hungry, but he knew that if he refused, his mother would make a horrible fuss over him.

"All right—I guess I am a bit peckish."

Jereen beamed, then set the tray down on the nightstand.

"You'd better get downstairs," she said to Andrew's mother. "They aren't going to start dinner without the guest of honor." Jereen put her hand around her waist and walked out with her.

Jereen's abrupt departure took Andrew by surprise. He expected that she would stay with him awhile; oddly enough, he was a bit dismayed that she didn't.

All this time I was dreading seeing her...and now I want her to stay with me...Just as well—if she had lingered, Jake probably would have come storming up here, would have made one hell of a fuss if he'd found me lying here naked and chatting up his cousin....

He set the tray on his lap and proceeded to demolish the generous ham dinner.

"Andrew?"

The door opened and Jereen came in, carrying another tray.

"I thought you'd like some tea." She smiled shyly, and set the tray on the dresser. "Milk and sugar, right?"

"Um, yes, thank you." He noted that there were *two* cups on the tray.

"Gosh—already finished with your dinner! You must have been starving!"

"Well, um, I guess I was hungrier than I'd thought."

She smiled broadly, handed him his tea, then poured a cup for herself. She sat cross-legged at the foot of the bed, took a few sips of tea, then smiled at him again.

"How do you feel about your mother having a baby?"

He choked on his tea, coughed, choked again.

"Sorry—must have gone down the wrong way." He set his cup and saucer on the nightstand and wiped his eyes.

Instantly, she was beside him, gently patting his back. "Are you all right?"

"Fi—fine." He blinked, felt stinging tears leak past his eyelashes. Jereen took a napkin and blotted his eyes. Her face was very close to his now, moving closer.

"You're not very happy about it, are you?" she whispered.

He drew a deep breath. "It was just a bit of a surprise, that's all."

She gently stroked his cheek.

"I think there's more to it than that." She looked as if she were going to say something else, but instead looked away. Then she gathered up the dishes and left.

A soft clattering awoke him. He glanced at the alarm clock: five-thirty.

He got up and drew back the organdy curtains. Dawn was streaking across the sky and a lone figure was striding towards the house from the barn.

He dressed, then made his way down to the main kitchen. Phyl came in through the back door, dressed in overalls and a flannel shirt.

"Morning, Andrew."

"Good morning—you're up early."

"Been up for over two hours. Cows need to get milked, you know. Well, at least it's a nice morning for doing it."

He glanced out the kitchen window. It was a *beautiful* morning.

"I think I'll go out for a walk," he said. "Would you please tell my mother, when she gets up? I don't want her to worry."

"Sure."

Once outside, he padded around the house until he came to the driveway. It stretched out before him, straight like a runway. He turned onto it and started to walk down to the road, but it seemed as if something in the distance were urging him to go faster. He broke into a run; the morning breeze whipped against his face as he flew towards the rising sun.

"Got the cobwebs out, darling?" His mother greeted him with a cheery grin. She was seated at the dining room table with the rest of the Jay clan in attendance.

He went to her and gave her a kiss on the forehead. "Feeling better, Mum?"

"Oh yes, much! The baby shower last night really perked me up. Too bad you couldn't come, darling. It was so much fun!"

"Help yourself to breakfast, Andrew," Phyl said.

Jake, who was seated next to Andrew's mother, got up and motioned Andrew to his chair. "I'm going to help out Wayne and the boys today—see you later, Andrew."

"Yeah, fighter pilot turned field hand," Phyl laughed. "Hope driving a tractor isn't going to be too exciting for you, Jake!"

Andrew sat down and dished up a plate of eggs, biscuits, and ham. While he ate, his mother showed him all the marvelous things she'd gotten at the shower: baby clothes, crib linens, diapers, even a precious pair of rubber pants. Mel had given her a boxful of tiny baby dresses, one from each pair of twin outfits she'd sewn. Andrew's mother was especially delighted with a minuscule dress in bright green velvet.

"For their first Saint Patrick's Day," Mel pronounced. "Well, if this one's a boy, you can save the dresses for the next—or the one after that!"

Andrew shoveled in a final mouthful of scrambled eggs and took a gulp of tea. He stood.

"I think I'll go for another walk," he said.

He ambled in circles around the farm for most of the morning, and the rhythms of the workday provided a sort of distraction for his inner turmoil. The men were out in the "back forty," so Andrew, thankfully, had no sight of Jake. Phyl's older boys "slopped" the hogs and weeded the vegetable patch; the little ones fed the chickens and gathered up eggs. The women did the cooking and household chores, and Jereen helped to take care of the babies. She pressed Andrew into service in the bottle-holding department.

"See—" she nestled Jimmie into Andrew's arms. "Just hold him like a football—he fits right in the crook of your arm." She sat down next to Andrew and started feeding Ruth.

Jimmie sucked greedily on his milk and stared intently at Andrew's face. In an effort to make conversation, Andrew said, "Your mother's name, Wannie—is that short for Wanetta?"

"No, her real name is Tjuana. She was named after her mother, sort of. My grandmother's name was Juana."

"Juana—that's Spanish, isn't it?"

"Not always. My grandmother was half-English and half-Cheyenne."

"Cheyenne?"

"Cheyenne Indian."

"You're *Indian?*"

"Yes, one-eighth. Are you shocked?"

"Uh—well, no—"

"Yes, you are." She grinned. "Well, I'm one-eighth English too. My great-grandfather came from Nottinghamshire. Is that English enough for you?" Her dark eyes challenged him.

"It doesn't matter—I mean, I think it's—it's—"

"It's what?"

"It's all right...I mean, it's nice...It's very nice."

Jimmie started fussing.

"He needs to be burped—" Jereen set Ruth down in a dresser drawer lined with blankets. She laid a diaper on Andrew's shoulder and propped Jimmie against his shoulder. Taking Andrew's hand, she patted it gently against the tiny back. Jimmie gave a soft belch.

"Uh-oh—he's wet, too." Jereen took her baby brother, laid him on the dressing table and changed his diaper, giving the new one a practiced half-twist before pinning up the sides.

"Gives a little extra padding in the middle." She gave Jimmie a kiss.

After lunch, the babies were settled down for their naps. Since Jereen had a few hours free, she asked Andrew to walk with her along the creek:

"It's shaded with cottonwood trees, so it's not too hot."

With Jake safely away with the other "menfolk," Andrew considered that there would be no harm in spending the afternoon in Jereen's company.

For awhile, they walked in silence along the shaded banks. The gurgling of the creek and the rustling of leaves soothed him a little, but all too soon Jereen's nearness began to vex him.

Maybe I shouldn't have come with her....

She turned to him.

"I'm so glad you came out here—to Nebraska, I mean. I read the story about you in *Life*, and I really wanted to meet you. One time, my mother was on the phone to Aunt Lois. I'd just come in from putting Jimmie to bed, and she handed the phone to me. I heard your voice in the background and I blurted out, 'That's Andrew, isn't it?' Aunt Lois asked me if I wanted to talk to you, and I was so flustered, I just said, 'No, no, I don't.' I was so afraid, I didn't know what to say to you, I probably would have babbled all over the place like a complete idiot. Then I wanted to kick myself for blowing the chance to talk with you—I was up all night, wishing..." Jereen looked intently at him. "Wishing I could have another chance to talk to you. Wishing I could meet you—somehow." She smiled. "And here you are."

Crikey—here I am, thought Andrew. Her outburst was, to all intents and purposes, a declaration of love, and he was completely flummoxed as to how to deal with it. It was all so bizarre—she had stayed up all night thinking of him, and he hadn't even known she existed!

If this were the movies, I'd take her in my arms and kiss her....

Her smile flattened into a nervous line.

I can't have anything to do with her—she's Jake's cousin!

She bit her lip, glanced away, as if she couldn't bear see the rejection in his eyes. Then she spoke.

"I know you're angry about your mother having a baby—and you're afraid, too."

He shook his head vehemently. "How could I be afraid of a baby!" he scoffed. "It's not...I mean—" He groaned, closed his eyes, and turned away.

She laid her hand on his arm.

"I felt the same way when I found out my mother was pregnant with Jolene. I was afraid that I would be pushed aside—that the baby would take my mother's love away from me. But when Jolene was born, I couldn't help but love her, and her birth didn't affect my parents' love for me—"

"That's *different*!" Andrew shot back. He instantly regretted his outburst, realized he'd have to explain. He lowered his voice and tried not to sound upset. "You're all one big happy family—I mean, just having another baby really wouldn't change things. With me, it's different. Jake's not my father—"

"Wayne's not my father, either," she said gently, almost apologetically. "I mean, my biological father." She pressed her fingers more tightly against his arm. "I'm not sure if I should be telling you this—please don't tell my mother, or anyone, that I've said anything to you about it."

"What?"

She looked fearful, bit her lip, then spoke.

"My mother wasn't married when I was born—she was only fifteen. My earliest memories are of the two of us living together in one tiny room. I remember it being so cold in winter that the blankets froze to the walls. My mom worked as a waitress, so after paying the rent and buying groceries, there wasn't much left over. I wore hand-me-down feedsack dresses. When I first started school, I got teased, and I felt so ashamed...." She gazed at a crow spiraling lazily overhead, then went on. "Then my mother married Wayne and I came to live here. Wayne adopted me, and everyone else was so wonderful—Phyl and Mel made the prettiest dresses for me, Boyd and Blaine watched out for me at school, and I even had my own room. Jake was especially nice. He was living out here then and he used to take me up for rides in the Stearman. I was a little in love with him—well, a *lot* in love with him." She blushed. "We called each other "J.J.," because both our initials are J and J—Jacob Jay and Jereen Juana." Her expression turned serious again; Andrew felt somehow that he should comfort her.

"I know how you must feel about things," he said. "I mean, about your parents not being married when you were born. My parents weren't—I mean, they had to get married because of me. I was born six months after their wedding." The words spilled out of him so easily; he then realized it was the first time he'd divulged this deep, dark secret to anyone. Suddenly, he felt very frightened. Why had he told *her?*

"Please don't tell my mother," he said quickly. "She doesn't know that I know. I heard my father's cousin talking about it—" His voice caught in his throat. "I wish I'd never found out—I always thought they loved each other so much—"

"Andrew, I don't think your parents got married because of you. I know your mother, and I know she wouldn't have let herself be forced into doing something just because she had to. Maybe you don't see because you're too close to her, but I see, and I know she's not the type of person to let others push her around. She loved your father—I *know* that—and she married him because she loved him, not because of you!"

She turned away, then spoke in a dull, soft voice. "It's different with me. I never knew my father, or anything about him—I don't even know his name. But I don't think he and my mother loved each other. One time, I asked my mother about him and she said he died before I was born, and then she started crying. I never asked her about him again."

Andrew saw that her face was wet with tears and felt even worse. He had tried to comfort her, but had instead opened a terrible wound. He laid his hand on her shoulder; she was still for a moment, and he was afraid he'd committed another sin. He drew his hand away; in a motion echoing his, she moved towards him, pressed her face to his chest. And then, before he realized what he was doing, he had his arms around her.

He recalled that when he used to go for walks with his father along the chalk cliffs at Beachy Head, he'd always insisted that his father hold his hand. Though he'd never once, in those days, entertained any thoughts of self-destruction, he'd been terribly afraid he might be seized by some irrational impulse to dash off and fling himself over the edge of the precipice.

Oh Dad—I wish you'd been holding my hand...I never meant to do this....

They'd walked in silence back to the house. Everything was the same as it had been before: the vibrant blue sky overhead, the vast, shimmering landscape all around, the distant shrieks of children and chickens and crows...but it had all changed, somehow. Before, he was just a traveller passing through; now, he felt somehow bound up in this place.

As if I'd always been a part of it, and a part of her, too...and she a part of me.

He felt almost lightheaded, as if he were floating along on the terrifyingly wonderful sensations spinning through him.

And when he saw Jake striding towards them, he fell to earth with a crash.

"Just heard the news!" Jake called. "Japan's agreed to surrender!"

Jereen broke into a run. Andrew crossed his arms and walked slowly, letting Jereen get far in front of him.

Don't want Jake to think that I've anything to do with her....

But Jereen was by Jake's side now, and looking happily in Andrew's direction. Jake smiled at him, but Andrew knew it was only for Jereen's sake.

He'll lay into me later, that's for sure....

He made it a point to sit by his mother at dinner and carefully avoided even making eye contact with Jereen. He thought of going up to his room afterwards, but he was afraid Jereen might follow him so he sat with his mother in the parlor. He was just about to go up to his room when Phyl came in and announced that the party was about to start.

"Party?" he said.

"Yeah—it's Jereen's and Jake's birthday both, so it's a double celebration. Jereen's wearing her birthday suit—come on!"

"Her *birthday* suit!" Andrew's mother exclaimed.

"It's a Cheyenne wedding dress. It belonged to her great- grandmother," Phyl said.

He followed his mother to the dining room, which was festooned with streamers and paper flowers. Jereen and Jake stood together, both presiding over a gigantic sheet cake. Jereen was wearing a long fringed dress of white buckskin; the yoke was adorned with a brilliant stripe of beadwork in red, blue, and yellow that continued down the sleeves. She wore a matching beadwork necklace and earrings; her hair was twined with strands of beads in white and blue. To Andrew, she looked lovelier than ever, especially when she smiled at him.

Everyone sang *Happy Birthday,* Jake and Jereen blew out the candles, then sat down.

Andrew's mother read aloud the birthday greetings squiggled on the cake: "*Jake—30 Minus 3, Old Man* and *Happy Sweet 16, Jereen.*"

Andrew tried to hide his shock.

Sixteen!

As soon as he was able to make an unobtrusive exit, he got away. He spent the better part of an hour lying in the bathtub, then made a quick dash to his room. Without bothering to turn on the lights, he quickly undressed and got into bed.

There was a tap on the door. He heard Jereen softly calling his name but he didn't answer.

For the next few days he tried to avoid Jereen as much as possible: No sitting by her at mealtimes, no helping out with the babies, no walks—except by himself, and at times he knew she'd be busy with other things. In the mornings and late afternoons he went running; during the times he was obliged to be in the house he spent by his mother's side.

On the night before they were to leave, his mother was telling him a bedtime story about her experiences in the ATA. There was a tap on the door.

"Alice?" It was Jereen. "May I come in?"

"Certainly," Andrew's mother said.

Jereen came in, bearing a package wrapped in light blue tissue paper. "I just finished making this—it's a little something for the baby." She handed the package to Andrew's mother.

Andrew's mother eagerly tore the wrappings and pulled out a small crocheted afghan in pale green and yellow.

"Oh Jereen, it's *lovely!*" Andrew's mother gave her a hug.

"Alice!" Jake's voice, calling from downstairs.

"Yes—what is it?"

"Can you come down here for a minute?"

Andrew's mother left; to Andrew's dismay, Jereen didn't.

She sat down on the bed next to him.

"You've been avoiding me," she said in a low voice. "Why?"

Please Mum, please come back!

"What makes you think that?" he asked.

"I know you have. Have I done something wrong?"

"No—I mean, I haven't been avoiding you, so you haven't done anything wrong—"

Bloody hell—what's taking her so long?

"It seems that I have. The other day, when you put your arms around me, I thought that you...cared."

"I do care, I mean, but we can't be—I mean, we can be...friends, you know."

"*Friends?*" She seemed stricken.

He closed his eyes, turned away. "I can't, I mean we can't—"

"Why?"

"Because you're two years older than me, that's why!" He turned back to her. "I know it's not your fault, but it's not right—"

"Why? What difference does it make? Look at your mother and Jake—she's *six* years older than him!"

"*Exactly!*" The word was out of his mouth before he realized what he'd said.

She moved a little away from him, fixed him with a perturbed stare, as if weighing his soul. Then she said, "I don't think this is about me at all."

She got up and left.

His mother never did come back, and for that, he was glad. It wouldn't do for her to see how upset he was.

If only I'd never come on this bloody trip!

If only I'd never been sent to America!

They left early the next day, so as to make it to Iowa before nightfall. Andrew's mother had called Irene's parents and asked if they might visit, and the Bocks had invited them to stay overnight.

Irene's parents were just as gregarious and bubbly as Irene had been. Mrs. Bock, upon learning that Andrew's mother was expecting, produced a newly made crib quilt in a "Log Cabin" design.

"I've got five grandbabies on the way," she laughed. "I just keep making quilts and the babies keep a-comin'!"

Andrew looked closely at the quilt; something seemed familiar about it. Then he realized: Each block contained two small inner squares, one a rosebud print, the other navy blue. He pointed to the rosebud print.

"Irene had a dress like that."

Mrs. Bock nodded. "Yes, it's from her dress. Do you know what that is?" She pointed to the other square.

Andrew's mother gazed at the dark blue block.

"It's ATA blue, isn't it?"

Mrs. Bock nodded again, a little more slowly this time.

"When Irene had her uniform made, she persuaded the tailor to give her the scraps of material left over. She sent it to me, so that I could sew a little bit of ATA blue into all my baby quilts. She wrote, 'I want all my nieces and nephews to think of their Aunt Irene flying a Spitfire when they go to sleep.'"

They motored on to Lee's place in New York. Lee-Ann flew out the front door as they pulled up in the drive and flung herself into Andrew's outstretched arms. She was even taller than before and there was a joy about her that Andrew found comforting. He looked up and saw Grandfather Givens standing over him. The old man grinned, then turned to greet Jake.

"Let me introduce myself to you, grandson—I'm your granddad!"

Jake, smiling, presented Andrew's mother, who gave Grandfather Givens a kiss on the cheek and told him he would have another great-grandchild in January.

Hearing the news, Lee and Mac and Velma proceeded to make a grand fuss over Jake and Andrew's mother. Andrew was irked.

The sod—he fathered a child on her so she wouldn't go back to my father!

Lee-Ann was tugging him around to the back of the house so that he could see her "Lassie-dog."

"My mommy gived her to me on my daddy's birthday."

Lee-Ann and her "Lassie-dog" (which was, of course, named Lassie) kept Andrew out of Jake's way during the two days they spent at Lee's. Even though he figured that Jake would wait until they were back in New Jersey before laying into him about Jereen, Andrew didn't want to tempt fate by spending any unnecessary time around him.

On the way back to New Jersey, a horrible thought occurred to him:

What if my mother chooses to stay in America when I go back to England?

As they approached Scotch Plains, he was faced with an even more awful prospect:

What if she makes me stay in America with her?

Lois burst out the front door as the Packard pulled up the drive. She hugged and kissed and hugged Andrew's mother again, then did the same with Jake, and the same again with Andrew.

"I'm going to be a grandmother—again!" she exclaimed to Andrew. Then she gave him another hug. "I can't help but think of you as my first grandchild."

A mountain of mail was waiting for Andrew, so he went up to his room after supper and sorted through it. Besides the deluge of fan mail there was a letter from Lynette, one from Erich, and one from Sarge's mother. Lynette waxed ecstatic about her job at *Life*, Erich wanted to find his family, but hoped he might be able to stay in America, somehow. Mrs. Ferguson was quite overwhelmed by the trust fund that had been set up for Debbie, and thanked Andrew over and over for his thoughtfulness in seeing to Debbie's welfare.

There was also a letter from Peter:

Dear Andrew,

Madison had six puppies I got to keep one his name is Lanc we got a boat and we are going down to the Bahamas Daddy is going to be a pilot with the airlines Lanc and Diane are coming too.

Your friend,
Peter

P.S. Mummy had a baby it's coming too.

"Boy or girl?" Andrew's mother laughed as she read the letter. "Liz and Diane will certainly have their hands full on this voyage, what with a baby, a puppy, and our intrepid master Peter!"

The next evening, the whole Casini clan came to dinner, even Danny, who'd just gotten out of the Seabees.

"Seabees—now what does that mean?" Andrew's mother asked Danny.

"Construction Battalion, according to the US Navy, but everyone else knows it means Confused Bastards," Danny grinned.

"*Danny!*" Mrs. Casini exclaimed.

"Sorry, Ma. Well, most of the time we were—confused I mean. We built anything and everything: airstrips, docks, roads, fuel tanks, barracks, hospitals. We could turn jungle into an airstrip in eight days—on Guam we paved a hundred miles of road in thirteen weeks. We sewed tents, repaired watches—one guy even used a quarter to make a star for a General. Lotsa times we were surveying land while the shooting was still going on. We even joined in the fighting when the Marines needed a little help!"

"Don't ever say that around Eddie Kosanovic," Jake laughed. "He joined the Marines, didn't he?"

There was an uncomfortable silence. Shannon finally cleared his throat and said, "Um, Eddie was killed at Iwo Jima."

Jake reddened, mumbled, "Sorry," then dished up some more corn relish. The conversation turned to the subject of Mr. and Mrs. Casini's thirty-fifth wedding anniversary, which was coming up in a few weeks.

"What's the secret of such a long and happy marriage?" Andrew's mother asked Fiona.

"Mis-communication," Danny said.

"*Mis*-communication?" Andrew's mother asked.

"Yeah," Danny replied. "Whenever my parents got into an argument, Dad would yell in Italian, Ma would scream Gaelic curses at him, and since neither one could understand the other, no one got their feelings hurt!"

After dinner, Andrew sought out Shannon in private. He felt he owed Shannon an apology for his churlishness after that mishap at the race.

Shannon seemed touched and surprised at Andrew's fumbling attempts at repentance. Laying his hand on Andrew's shoulder, he said, "Even if you never race again, don't give up running, okay?"

There was a knock at the door. Lois went to answer it. Sarah, Alida, and several other women filed in, all bearing presents wrapped in paper with baby motifs.

"Surprise!" Alida yelled.

Andrew's mother gasped, then broke into a delighted chortle.

There was a woman with them whom Andrew thought looked vaguely familiar, but he couldn't quite place her: She was quite beautiful, with dark hair and dark eyes, and elegantly dressed in a pale blue suit with a matching silk blouse and hat.

"Andrew!" the woman called. Then Andrew realized who she was:

"Lucia!" He ran over to greet her.

Andrew's mother came over to them and exclaimed over how well Lucia looked, and *especially* exclaimed over the huge diamond ring on Lucia's finger.

"I am married to a colonel in the American Army Air Forces," Lucia told her. She lowered her voice. "I met him on the voyage to America. An American GI was being—

um, how you say—rowdy to me. You know, slapping my bottom, saying rude things. I said to him, 'Get your hands off me, buster, or your ass is grass—'" She winked at Andrew. "Like Irene said to Freddie, remember? Well, this colonel came up to me and to this GI, and I thought this GI would die with fright. Then the colonel apologized to me for this man, and asked me to have dinner with him. And so...." She fluttered her hand.

"Oh, Lucia—how *marvelous!*" Andrew's mother squealed.

More people streamed in—it seemed as if half of Scotch Plains had shown up for the occasion. Andrew fumed:

Bet they never had a party like this for me: After all, it's bad form to celebrate when there's a bastard on the way....

He made his way upstairs. As he got to the landing, he heard low voices in the upstairs hall: Jake's and Danny's.

"...and since I've been out of touch so long, I don't know what happened to everyone," Jake was saying. "I just don't want to mention someone's name and have everyone give me a funny look, know what I mean?"

"Yeah," Danny said. He cleared his throat. "Well, Dwight Keppler—he was on a tanker that got torpedoed in the Atlantic. And Tony Mucciano—he was shot down in a B-17 over Germany. Bud Derensky was killed at Anzio, Sammy Weiss on Guadalcanal, Jamie Cox and Liam Mackey somewhere in France. That's all I know about."

Andrew got to the top of the stairs just as Danny finished with his grim inventory.

"Okay, thanks," Jake whispered. He glanced at Andrew, and Andrew saw in his eyes that same look he'd seen almost two years ago, on that first train ride to New Jersey:

Fear.

He had no stomach for celebrating, so he lay in bed, trying to ignore the clamor over all those silly little presents.

Bet Jake is just gloating—as if getting someone pregnant were the most magnificent thing someone could do....

"Andrew?" The door opened and Lois came in, bearing a tray with a piece of cake and a cup of tea. "The *last* thing a fourteen-year-old boy is interested in is a baby shower, right?"

"Oh, I um—um, sorry, I mean, I was just a little tired, that's all." His voice broke, and he didn't know why. He was as touched by Lois's concern as he was dismayed by the celebration.

"Andrew, what's the matter?" Lois set the saucer and cup on the dresser and put her arms around him.

How could he tell her he was upset that she was to be a grandmother—a *real* grandmother?

"I'm just upset. I mean, I guess I'm going back to England, and I'll miss you...."

"Oh, Andrew—" As she crushed him against her breast, he thought, *I really would be upset if I had to leave her....*

"I'd miss you too, Andrew," Lois soothed. "But maybe you'll be staying here—who knows? Jake is trying to get a job with the airlines. Now drink your tea and eat your cake."

At least Jake's efforts in trying to find employment seemed to occupy him, for he didn't approach Andrew about Jereen. Andrew, though glad that Jake had a temporary diversion, nonetheless dreaded the confrontation sure to take place when Jake found gainful employment.

Please God, please don't let him get a job....

Jake trudged into the living room, plopped down on the sofa, grimaced and loosened his tie.

"How did it go?" Andrew's mother was by his side in a flash.

Jake shook his head wearily. "Same old story—they'd prefer someone with a four-engine rating—"

"Darling, I just can't *believe* they wouldn't jump at someone with your experience—"

"Experience in fighters doesn't count—it's probably more of a drawback. They'd rather hire guys who flew bombers or transports. I guess they think fighter pilots are too twitchy to make good airline pilots." Jake groaned, slumped back and stared at the ceiling. "They're probably right."

Andrew, stretched out on the floor listening to *Terry and the Pirates*, tried to hide his elation.

I hope my mother sees him for the pathetic excuse for a man he is—imagine, he can't even get a job! How does he expect to provide for that child he's bringing into the world—live off my mother's money? Hope she wakes up to the realization that he's no good and takes me back to England!

"The college money I set aside for you is still in the bank, Jake." Mr. Givens passed the basket of rolls to Lois. "I never spent a dime of it. You could go back to Rutgers, finish off your degree. Alice and Andrew could live here, okay? I know how much you love flying, but this way you'd have something to fall back on, at least."

Jake carefully smoothed a blob of gravy over his slice of roast beef. His shoulders slumped ever so slightly, then he looked wistfully at his father.

"Thanks Dad, but—" He closed his eyes, cleared his throat.

"Okay, I know," Mr. Givens said gently.

Andrew heard the clank of the mail slot and ran to inspect the day's correspondence.

Maybe today I'll get a letter from Dad...He's probably sent off a letter to Greycliff, and Grandmother Howard will forward it here....

He sorted though the mail. There was a package from Barbara, and a letter with an Alaska postmark.

"Letter from Kaz, Mum." Andrew handed his mother the letter, then opened the package.

"More fan mail, Andrew?" Lois chuckled.

Andrew's mother opened Kaz's letter. Her eyebrows raised as she read it.

"How's your company doing, Alice?" Lois asked. "Now, what did you decide to call it, again?"

"Kaz-Al Airways," Jake said. "Al for Alaska or Alice, whatever you prefer." He smiled at Andrew's mother.

Andrew's mother reported from Kaz's letter: "Well, Kaz dropped her ruse. She threw a party at the roadhouse to celebrate the new company, and when everyone had had enough to drink she dropped the bomb on them. No one was outraged, since she'd already proven she could do the job, *and* since she'd flown in the very best liquid entertainment money could buy." She smiled and read on. "She just got a few freight contracts, too. She uses the Pilgrim for the heavy hauling; it's about the largest single-engine aircraft there is and has been adequate, up until now. She really needs to get a twin-engined plane to keep up with all the work."

"Shouldn't be too hard to find a plane, cheap, what with all the surplus aircraft there is around," Jake said.

"Well, it seems as if Kaz is so frightfully busy she doesn't have the time to look," Andrew's mother said. "She'd like to hire another pilot, too, one with a twin-engine and instrument rating, but one who would be able to handle bush flying. She says most of the bush pilots are former barnstormers—they really know how to handle themselves in emergencies." Andrew's mother smiled at Jake. "Know anyone who might be interested, darling?"

Jake took a deep breath. "I'm not sure if you'd like living in Alaska—"

"Darling, I'd *love* it! What they say is true: After you've seen Alaska, everything else pales by comparison!"

Andrew spent the rest of the day, and most of the following night, in a maelstrom of despair.

Alaska!

"Eight thousand for a Gooneybird?" Jake shifted the receiver from his right ear to his left. "Yeah, that's a great price...It's in good condition, right?...Okay, I'll come down and take a look at it."

Alice's mother smiled as Jake put down the receiver. "Found your plane, darling?"

"Yeah," Jake replied. "A surplus C-47. I used to fly them, when they were called DC-3s."

"A Dakota?"

"Yeah—have you flown them?"

"*Bags* of them. And it's a good deal, you say?"

"Sounds like it, but I have to take a look at it."

"Well, why don't we both take a look at it? I'd like to finish out the American chapter of my logbook with a spin in a Dakota!"

"So Miz Thompson's boy, Billy, he get back from all those years in that Jap prison camp and find out his wife done left and marry herself to somebody else." Sarah threw down two cards; Alida dealt her two more. Sarah grunted and shifted her cards around. "Well, everyone, even Miz Thompson, think he was dead—didn't hear hide nor hair of Billy all this time. When Billy find out 'bout his wife, he just take off, don't say where he going, jus' leave his momma a letter saying he want to forget and start over. Miz Thompson jus' beside herself—she take to her bed and moan she lose her son all over again. I spend all last Friday mopping her brow, didn't get a stitch of work done." She threw down three pennies.

Maybe that's what's happened to Dad. Maybe that's why he hasn't written to me. He found out about Mum and now he's too upset about things...Perhaps he thinks I don't love him anymore either....

"Andrew, your turn," Alida said.

Andrew stared at his cards: Four of a kind—queens.

"Fold," he said.

"Mom?" Jake rummaged through the top drawer of the sideboard. "Where's my savings passbook?"

"In the bottom right drawer of the secretary, at the back, behind the utility bills." Lois replied.

Jake went to the secretary, pulled out his passbook, glared in consternation at the battered pages. "Dad was right," he muttered to Andrew's mother. "I should have joined up with the Americans. I'd probably have enough to buy that C-47. Well, time to go down to my friendly banker and talk about a loan—"

"Darling—" Andrew's mother laid her hand on Jake's shoulder. "Let me buy—"

"No." Jake shook his head furiously. He turned to her. "You already bought the company. That's more than enough."

Andrew knew what he had to do.

Mum will certainly be going up to Alaska with Jake. There's no way I can keep her from running off after that wretched sod...After all, it's her choice, and I have my choice, too....

I won't go with her, no matter what. I need to be in England, to look for my father. He's there now, surely, trying to put his life back together. He needs me...just as much as I need him.

Jake trudged into the living room.

"How did it go with your friendly banker?" Andrew's mother asked.

Jake looked down at the floor.

"Oh dear," Andrew's mother said. She went to Jake.

Jake shrugged apologetically. "Try to convince a New Jersey banker that financing a plane for a bush outfit in Alaska is a great idea, *and* that an ex-fighter pilot is a good credit risk...."

"Darling, please—"

"No—I don't want you putting out any more money on my account."

Lois brought out a chocolate cake topped with twenty-seven flaming candles. "Happy Belated Birthday Jake!" she chirped.

Mr. Givens placed an envelope by Jake's plate.

Jake opened the envelope and withdrew a card. A piece of paper fluttered down to his lap. He picked it up, showed it to Andrew's mother. "From Dad. It's a check—there's no amount, though." He looked, bewildered, at his father.

"You fill in however much you need for that plane," Mr. Givens said. "It's from the money I put aside for your college education. I always wanted you to have a future, and I guess your future is in Alaska, not here."

Jake seemed to be in a daze as he looked at his father, then down at the check.

"Happy Birthday, Son," Mr. Givens smiled.

The next evening, Andrew was lying in bed when he heard a knock on the door. Jake called his name.

Now he's going to lay into me about Jereen....

He sat straight up, crossed his arms defiantly. "Come in," he said, trying to sound annoyed. He was dismayed that his voice quavered with fear.

His mother and Jake walked in.

"Time for a family conference, Andrew," his mother said.

Uh-oh...He told her about things, and she, no doubt, believes his wild accusations against me....

"Andrew—" His mother sat down next to him and took his hand. "Jake and I have talked things over, and we've decided—" She glanced at Jake and smiled. "Well, it was Jake's idea, really. What with him going up to Alaska, it would probably be best if you and I went back to England until after the baby's born. We'll fly back to England next Tuesday. Jake is coming along; he'll stay for a few days, then go on to Alaska."

"I'd be so worried about your mother if she were staying in Alaska with me," Jake said. "The only way to the hospital in Fairbanks is by plane, and it's not always possible to fly, especially in winter. It would really put my mind at ease if she were in England—after all, it only takes a few minutes to drive to town from Greycliff, just in case she needed to go to a hospital."

"You worry so, darling!" Andrew's mother squeezed Jake's hand. "I had Andrew at home, without a bit of trouble. This new little one—" She patted her belly, "Is going to take after his—or her—brother." She grinned at Andrew. "My two children already have something in common."

Andrew, though enormously relieved that this had not been a bloody confrontation over Jereen, was irked by the mysterious bond he was supposed to have with this interloper.

I don't have, and never will have, anything in common with Jake's child!

That night, he dreamt he was back at Kaz's place, hearing the giggly chatter of his mother in the next room:

It happened in the Anson... last time it was in a Giant Moth... French letters, but Sparky got flowers instead....

Andrew sat bolt upright, wide awake.

Bloody hell!

He recalled his father mentioning that Sparky had been a bit forgetful—but *this!*

I was not only conceived out of wedlock, but accidentally, too, and in a Giant Moth of all places! And all because someone forgot to buy rubbers!

He managed not to gape at his mother during breakfast.

And this new one got started in an Anson! But at least people won't be wagging their tongues about it being born too soon after the wedding!

As he sorted through his things, deciding what to pack for his trip back to England, he grew a little more philosophical about things.

Well, the past is past, and nothing can be done about it. Anyway, I'm going back to England with Mum, and without Jake. Couldn't expect things to turn out any better. Jake doesn't seem to be upset with me about Jereen—maybe I was just being paranoid about him suspecting that there was something between us. Not to worry—in less than a week, I'll be home.

"Andrew, may I come in?" It was Lois.

"Sure."

"I was wondering if I could swipe one of your pillows. What with your mother and Jake here, I'm out of spares."

"Sure." Andrew handed her one of his pillows.

"I'm fixing up the back room," Lois told him. "I just got a call this morning from Jereen. She's coming here for a visit—she'll be here tomorrow afternoon."

Just like in the horror movies, Andrew thought. Just when you think everything is going to be all right....

"Andrew?" His mother called from the bottom of the stairs. "Someone here to see you."

He trudged down the steps. At the landing he glanced down at the front entryway.

"Miriam!" He took the rest of the steps at a full gallop.

"Hello! I just found out you were back. I was down at the pharmacy and Mr. Givens mentioned you'd gotten in the other day."

"Sorry, I was going to call, but...." He thought quickly; he very well couldn't explain why his mind had been so muddled. "Well, things have just been so busy."

He noticed his mother's quizzical look. "Oh," he said, "This is my mother. Mum, this is Miriam."

"Pleased to meet you, Miriam." Andrew's mother extended her hand and smiled. "Andrew wrote to me about you."

"Miriam!" Lois called. "You're just in time for fresh peach pie—got the peaches right off the tree this morning."

"Sounds lovely!" Miriam said.

Over peach pie Miriam asked Andrew's mother about her ferrying duties and told her that Andrew used to "brag and brag" about her flying planes in the ATA. Andrew's mother seemed quite pleased with her interest and chatted happily about her flying experiences. After she left, Andrew's mother remarked that Miriam seemed like a very sweet girl. Andrew blushed to think that his mother might suspect there was something more to their friendship than...well, than just being friends.

Which there wasn't, of course.

The next day after lunch, Miriam came by again. This time she asked Andrew if they might go for a walk together. Knowing that Jereen would be arriving that afternoon, he thought it would be nice if he and Miriam went for a nice, *long* walk. He told his mother they would be back by dinnertime.

As they walked through the fields south of town, Miriam asked him about his summer. Andrew told her all about L.S., Vera, Philip, Kaz, and Lee-Ann. Miriam was happy to hear that Lee-Ann was doing so well. Then she bit her lip, and smiled shyly.

"My brother Josh and some of his friends are going to the shore for a few days. Josh's girlfriend's family has a cottage near the beach, and she invited me to come along. She said I could bring a friend. Would you like to come? We'll be leaving the day after tomorrow and coming back Monday. I know you're leaving for England on Tuesday, but we'll be back Monday afternoon, Monday evening at the latest. Do you think your mother would mind if you came? That is, I mean, if you want to come...."

He nearly tripped with excitement.

Perfect! Good old Miriam—trust her to come through for me! I'd only be around Jereen for a bit this evening...I could probably stay out all day tomorrow...Then leave for the shore the next morning, be away from here, thank God...Nip in Monday evening and be gone the next day....

He smiled at Miriam. "Of course I'd like to come."

She smiled back at him.

One more worry out of the way—I'll be miles away from Jereen! That's the ticket—a nice holiday at the beach. Perfect way to end my sojourn here: enjoy a few days of sunshine and sand and surf, then buzz off to England, leaving any entanglements behind.

Piece of cake!

Chapter 49

*H*e thought it might not be a bad idea to return home with Miriam.

Jereen ought to be here by now....

As Andrew walked up the front steps he heard Jereen's voice.

In fact, it would be an even better idea to ask Mum right now about going to the shore with Miriam....

"Mum, I'm home!" He held the front door open for Miriam.

"Hullo! Did you two have a nice walk?" Andrew's mother called from the dining room.

"Yes, *marvelous!*" Andrew took Miriam's hand and walked into the dining room. He saw Jereen, who was sitting up very straight at the table. Her mouth was set in a straight line; her eyes held a kind of stunned misery as she looked at Miriam.

Andrew considered that a show of manners wouldn't hurt.

We can all be civilized about this, can't we?

"Oh, hi Jereen. This is my friend, Miriam." He smiled at Miriam as he said her name. "Miriam, this is Jake's cousin, Jereen, from Nebraska."

"Hello," Jereen said softly.

"Nice to meet you," Miriam replied.

Andrew turned to his mother. "Miriam invited me to go to the shore with her. She's going with her brother and some of his friends the day after tomorrow. We'll be back Monday afternoon." He tried to sound glib about the whole plan, as if he always went on holiday with Miriam.

Andrew's mother raised her eyebrows at him, then fixed Miriam with a questioning stare.

"My brother's girlfriend's family has a cottage near the beach," Miriam said to her. "I can give you their name and phone number if you'd like to contact them."

"Yes, I'd appreciate that," Andrew's mother said pleasantly, but firmly.

Lois got a pad of paper and pencil from the sideboard and gave them to Miriam. While Miriam was writing, Andrew repeated to his mother, "We'd be back Monday, Mum."

His mother nodded absently.

"Well, I'd better be going," Miriam said.

"I'll walk you home." Andrew put his arm around her shoulder as he escorted her outside.

His mother didn't mention anything about his hoped-for holiday at supper. Lois and Jake tried to engage Jereen in conversation about her train journey; Jereen answered their questions in a flat, strained voice.

After supper, his mother motioned Andrew upstairs to his room. She sat down on his bed and patted the space beside her. Her eyes were grave and troubled, and he wondered if she were trying to ease her denial of his request.

"Mum, I promise everything will be all right if you let me go to the shore with Miriam—"

She nodded and said, "All right. Miriam's friends are long-time customers of Jake's father. He knows them quite well and assured me they're good people."

He'd expected an argument and was a little astonished to have gotten his way so easily. He smiled at his mother, but she seemed even more troubled than ever.

"Mum?"

She grabbed his hand.

"I've been meaning to talk to you about this, Andrew—I'm not sure if this is a good time. I thought I should tell you before we left for England, but not at the very last minute. But since we're going to leave just after you get back from the shore, well...." She squeezed Andrew's hand tightly. "Oh darling, I was hoping that things would turn out all right, that I would have heard something by now, but—

"What?"

She regarded him with a sorrowful gaze.

"It's about your Aunt Jane."

"Aunt Jane? She's coming back to England, isn't she? You said she would be coming back—"

"Andrew, she's not coming back."

"What do you mean?"

"Andrew, Jane went to France."

"I know that. You told me she went to France, after the Invasion—"

"No," his mother softly said. "*Before.*"

An awful feeling of dread and horror descended upon him. His mother's voice sounded very far away, as if she were speaking at the other end of a tunnel.

"Andrew, she went to France as a British agent. She seems to have...well, no one knows what happened, but she, um...she hasn't...turned up—"

"*NO!*" He flung her hand out of his and backed away from her, as if by distancing himself from her he could nullify this horrible revelation.

"Andrew—"

"*NO!* It's not true! I wrote to her in my cipher—only she knows—"

"Andrew, she told me about the cipher."

It was all very clear now.

"You wrote the letters," he breathed.

His mother nodded. "She told me as much as she could about things I ought to know. Filled out a whole copybook, in fact. And she signed her name on every sheet in a ream of typing paper, for me to use when I typed the letters. Andrew, darling, she couldn't tell you where she was going. She wasn't supposed to tell anyone, in fact. She only told me. Not even Gram or Gwen knew—"

"No—*NO!*" He threw himself face-down against the bed, smothering his tears in his pillow. His mother gently rubbed his back. He lay very, very still.

If only she'd go away....

And after awhile, she did.

"Andrew?" Jereen's voice, soft and solicitous.

He heard the door creak open, felt her sit down on the bed beside him. She laid her hand on his back.

"Your mother told us about your aunt. Andrew, I'm so sorry—"

"*Why did she do it?*" He screamed the words against the pillow.

"I don't know," she said quietly.

He wanted to throw himself into her arms. Perhaps that would ease the anguish he felt, chase the horror away.

Perhaps not, though.

And it wouldn't do for Jake to walk in and find me in a compromising position with his cousin. I don't even dare turn and face her....

Her hand gently moved over his back in a wavy, soothing course. She said nothing more, but her soft breathing seemed to him a prayer for all to come right.

"Andrew, phone for you." Lois held the receiver in one hand, the coffeepot in the other.

Andrew swallowed his mouthful of scrambled eggs as he got up from the dining room table, and took the receiver from Lois's outstretched hand. He didn't need eyes in the back of his head to know that Jereen was looking intently at him. She had stayed with him a long, long time the evening before, just stroking his back. As darkness fell, his anguish had become a soul-consuming blackness that had blotted out all else. He could not have cared less if Jake had burst into the room and made a scene about things. Then he'd fallen asleep, with Jereen still by his side. When he awoke at dawn, he found a single red rose lying on his dresser. There was no accompanying note from the giver, but of course he didn't need one.

"Andrew—" It was Miriam. "Could you meet me in the grape arbor?" She sounded upset.

"Is everything all right? I mean—" He lowered his voice. "About us going away."

"That's what I need to talk to you about, but not now. Meet me in the grape arbor in ten minutes, okay?"

He returned to the dining room. Not bothering to sit, he gulped down the last of his tea. Then he said, "I'll be back in a bit."

"Where are you going, darling?" his mother asked.

All right, since you asked....

"To see Miriam."

Miriam was sitting on the wrought iron bench, knotting her hands together and chewing her lip.

"Miriam—is everything all right?"

She seemed both relieved and apprehensive. He sat down beside her. "What's wrong?"

She rolled her eyes, sighed. "My mother wants to meet you. She wants to meet your mother, too—Andrew, I'm sorry—"

"Well, there's nothing wrong with that. I've never met your mother anyway, and I'm sure that Mum—"

"Andrew, it's not that...simple."

"What do you mean?"

She looked away, then spoke in a low, tense voice.

"My mother has always been...well, she's always needed something to drink when she gets upset about things, which is about all the time now. That's why I never went home after school. She was either passed out or in a rage." She turned back to Andrew.

"Most of her family was in Germany. She had ten brothers and sisters. Only she and another brother came to America with their parents, thirty years ago, because they were the youngest. Andrew, she had over a hundred relatives—brothers, sisters, nieces, nephews, cousins. We haven't heard from one of them—not one! Eva wrote last month, and she's still searching, but it doesn't look—I mean—" She closed her eyes. "They're all dead, Andrew."

A tear slid down her cheek. Andrew gently brushed it away. She sniffled, clutched his hand. "My mother's taking things very hard, and I'm afraid—well, she's already downed half a bottle of gin, watered-down. I can't put too much water in it, or she'll notice." She took a deep breath.

"When would be a good time for us to come over? I'll tell my mother—I know she'll understand."

"Oh, Andrew, I don't want to put you through—"

"You're my friend, and I really want to go on holiday with you." He smiled.

She looked at him gratefully. "She's probably still okay now—I mean, she needs a whole lot more before she gets, um, really bad. If you came over soon, she'll be okay, sort of—I mean, not a problem. A *big* problem, I mean."

He stood and laid his hand on her shoulder.

"We'll be right over."

He explained the situation to his mother, and she was both understanding and sympathetic.

"Poor girl, she must have had a hard time of it."

As they walked up the front steps of the Kantor residence, Andrew heard a deep, petulant voice:

"Miriam, when you said a boy, I thought you meant a nice *Jewish* boy."

"Mama, he's not like the others. Everyone made fun of him because he was different."

Andrew's mother glanced at him, concern in her eyes.

"It was a little bad at first, Mum, but things are fine now," he said quietly.

He knocked on the door. It opened and Miriam stood there, stiff and solemn, as if she were greeting mourners at a funeral.

"Hullo," Andrew said breezily. He ushered his mother in. Miriam dashed ahead, motioned them into the dining room. Her mother, seated at the table, did not rise to meet them, but merely nodded in their direction.

"Pleased to meet you, Mrs. Kantor," Andrew's mother chirped. She seated herself in the chair next to Miriam's mother. "I'm Alice Givens, Andrew's mother."

"You said his last name was Hartley-something," Mrs. Kantor protested to Miriam.

"Hadley-Trevelyan. Andrew's father was killed. I've remarried," Andrew's mother explained.

"His father was a pilot in the Royal Air Force—remember I told you?" Miriam gently said to her mother. "He was killed in the Battle of Britain."

Mrs. Kantor nodded. "Those English, they fought that sonofabitch Hitler before anyone else." She looked at Andrew's mother, took her hand. "You poor thing. It must have been awful, losing your husband and being left alone with a child."

Andrew's mother smiled. "Fortunately, Andrew was not a difficult child. I'm very proud of him, and very happy with the way he's turned out, though things have not been easy for him."

Mrs. Kantor patted her hand, then turned to Miriam.

"Miriam dear, will you show Andrew the garden?"

Miriam jumped up and motioned Andrew out through the French doors at the back.

When they were outside, Andrew whispered, "I think things are going all right."

Miriam seemed frozen in a panicked daze. He laid his hand on her arm. She didn't seem to notice his touch, but stood very still, like a rabbit alert to the scent of danger on the wind. Andrew heard his mother's lilting replies accenting Mrs. Kantor's deep, raspy voice, but couldn't make out what was being said.

"Andrew! Miriam!" His mother came out onto the terrace and waved happily to them. Andrew took Miriam's hand and led her to his mother. His mother winked at him, then drew him into the house.

"It's been a pleasure meeting you," Andrew's mother said to Mrs. Kantor.

"A pleasure meeting you, too." Mrs. Kantor smiled at her, then nodded at Miriam. Miriam ushered them to the front door. "What should Andrew bring besides swim trunks and a change of clothes?" Andrew's mother asked Miriam.

"Um, sleeping bag and pillow," Miriam replied. "The boys are going to sleep outside on the deck, girls in the house."

"Jake has some old camping equipment. He must have a sleeping bag Andrew can use. Well, good day Miriam."

"Good day," Miriam said. "And thank you very much."

"Not at all," Andrew's mother grinned.

As they were walking home, Andrew took his mother's hand.

"Thanks Mum."

She smiled at him, then pursed her lips and gave him a stern look. "I expect you to behave like a gentleman, Andrew. Do you know what I mean?"

He wanted to insist that his relationship with Miriam was entirely platonic, but was afraid he might somehow bungle things by doing so. So he nodded his head and said, "Yes, Mum."

Focusing on Miriam's distress had taken his mind off of his Aunt Jane for awhile, but his anguish returned as he packed his clothes into Jake's old dufflebag.

Why did she do it? Why did she have to go off and do something so appallingly dangerous? She could have stayed in England, done work that was just as vital—translating messages, that sort of thing.

Why?

He didn't expect Jereen to be up so early.

"I made you some tea," she said softly as he came into the kitchen.

"Oh, um, thanks."

"I hope you have a nice time. It must be wonderful—at the shore, I mean. I've never even seen the ocean."

"You haven't?" It seemed strange to him that someone could spend their whole life without ever seeing the sea.

His mother came into the kitchen. "All ready, darling?"

"Yes, Mum."

"Now don't get too much sun—don't want you getting sun poisoning on us."

"Yes, Mum." He *hated* it when his mother fussed over him.

"Do you need any money, darling?"

"Uh, no—I'm bringing some." He didn't want to disclose to his mother just how much he was bringing: the grand sum of thirty-five dollars, all that he'd saved from his job at the pharmacy. He wasn't sure if the itinerary for the holiday included anything that involved a substantial monetary outlay; still, he wanted to be prepared.

There was a soft tap at the back door. He went to answer it.

"Morning, Andrew," Miriam said. "I didn't want to wake everyone else. Oh, hello Mrs. Givens."

"Hullo, Miriam."

Andrew turned around and saw that Jereen had vanished.

Andrew's mother helped him tote his things out to the car. Miriam introduced her and Andrew to the others who were going along: her brother, Josh; Josh's girlfriend, Marcie; Marcie's older sister, Ellen, and younger brother, Paul; and Paul's girlfriend, Esther.

Andrew squeezed into the backseat with Miriam. Next to them were Paul and Esther; Marcie and Ellen sat up front with Josh, who drove. The talk was light and cheery for awhile, then everyone settled into quietness as they motored to the coast. Esther snuggled against Paul, who put his arm around her and murmured something into her ear. Andrew sat, his arms pressed tightly to his sides, wedged between Miriam and the door. He was reminded of sitting in the bomb shelter, being jammed in, elbow to elbow, with the other boys.

The car turned a sharp corner and he fell towards Miriam; instinctively, he grabbed her shoulder. The car swerved a bit in the opposite direction and she fell against him.

She didn't move away when the car straightened out, but smiled at him, and then rested her head against his chest.

He wasn't sure at what point it happened—maybe it had been happening all along, ever since they'd met.

I'm in love with her....

Josh pulled up to a tiny cottage on a sand-dusted street. There was a small patch of sand that made for a front yard; behind the house was a slightly larger stretch of sand, overlaid with wooden decks that led to a dock on the bay. The distant roar of the surf seemed both soothing and exhilarating at the same time.

It's the same ocean I crossed almost two years ago. And I was so sure, then, that I'd be miserable here....

As he toted his things inside he saw that the interior of the cottage was one room, with a minuscule kitchen and a tiny lavatory to one side. A ladder ran up to a sleeping loft.

"Boys sleep outside on the deck," Josh said. "But keep your stuff in the house until tonight. Shower's outside."

Ellen fixed them a lunch of sandwiches and fruit cocktail; then they changed into swimsuits and walked to the beach, which was only a few blocks away.

The beach was unlike any Andrew had ever seen in England, with hot pale sand and a shoreline stretching straight for miles. Brightly colored umbrellas dotted the sand, children skittered in and out of the water, and gulls screeched and dipped over the waves. He dashed across the burning sand with Miriam and flung himself into the surf.

On the other side, the waves are crashing on English shores....

Miriam bobbed up beside him. She was wearing a two-piece bathing suit, as were most of the other girls on the beach. It was the latest fashion, considered quite patriotic as a matter of fact, because it used less cloth that the old one-piece style. Never before in his life had Andrew seen so much female flesh in one place; he felt as if he'd wandered into a vast, open-air girls' locker room by mistake. Perhaps the shortages and scarcities of wartime life weren't all that bad, he thought. Then Miriam turned to him as a wave crashed against them; they were thrown against each other and her arms went round him as the current pulled them towards shore.

"If we'd had our own country, it wouldn't have happened." Josh tossed his sleeping bag onto the deck.

"We need a land of our own," Paul agreed. "We've spent the last two thousand years wandering; at best, getting kicked out from one country after another, at worst...Well, just look at the pictures in the newspapers. It'll happen again if we don't do something."

"It couldn't happen here," Ellen said.

"Who knows? America wouldn't take Jewish refugees trying to escape from Germany in the '30s—sent 'em straight back to Germany," Paul countered.

Miriam fluffed Andrew's pillow as he untied the knot on the cord around Jake's sleeping bag. She seemed a little embarrassed by the talk, as if dirty family secrets were being aired. She glanced apologetically at Andrew.

I know what it was like to be a stranger in a strange land. I know what it's like to long for my home, for the place where I belong...Everyone needs a country to call his own....

He laid his hand on Miriam's shoulder.

"They're right," he said softly.

They spent the next day at the beach. Andrew and Miriam took their blanket and towels farther down the beach, away from everyone else. They tumbled in the surf, delighting in being spit out again and again onto the shore by mischievous waves. With the foam spraying over them, they would smile at one another, then race back into the tempestuous sea.

They returned to the cottage with the others in the late afternoon. Marcie and Ellen began to cook up a fish dinner. They were going to boil potatoes, but when Andrew told them about fish and chips they decided to try frying potato wedges instead, and the results were quite good.

"Dinner English-style," Miriam pronounced.

Ellen scooped another batch of potatoes onto the serving platter. "We'll have chocolate-covered strawberries later on. Do they have those in England, Andrew?"

"I suppose. We have strawberries, but I've never had chocolate-covered ones. We don't have much chocolate in England."

"Well, you're in for a treat," Marcie promised.

After dinner, Miriam suggested to Andrew that they sit outside.

"To watch the sunset," she smiled. She took some towels and spread them on the dock.

As they sat together, Miriam grazed her finger along his shoulder. "You've got a pretty bad sunburn," she murmured. The gray eyes, solemn and serene, focused intently on his pink skin.

He felt the color rising to his face; good thing the blushy sunburn on his cheeks camouflaged the flustery feelings kicking around within him.

The finger slowed in its course, veered southward in a meandering pattern; four other fingers followed in the wandering journey across his flesh. He watched, held his breath, felt splayed fingers press against his chest, felt his heart hammering like distant crumping explosions jarring him at the secret center of his soul, wondered if she could feel the uneasy thumping also...

How could she not feel it?

"Hey you guys! Wanna come inside and help out with the chocolate covered strawberries?"

Josh's voice was close, very close, too close. A hand grabbed his shoulder and Andrew lurched, more from shock and fear than from pain, though a stinging sensation shot through him, momentarily banishing the stirrings within.

"Josh! Andrew's got a sunburn—be careful!"

"Oh, gee, sorry—" Withdrawing his hand, Josh eyed Andrew with an amused stare, then shook his head in mock exasperation. "These blue-eyed goys—let 'em out in the sun for a minute and they burn to a crisp!"

"Josh!" Miriam looked mortified.

Andrew blushed furiously; he wondered if Miriam noticed. Then again, his face was so red anyway. Miriam looked at him; Andrew held his breath again. "They're not," she said.

"Not what?" Josh asked.

"His eyes." Miriam said. "They're not blue—they're hazel, with blue sparkles." Though she was addressing Josh, her eyes fixed Andrew in a steady gaze.

Josh peered at Andrew's eyes. "Hazel with blue sparkles—if you say so!" His eyebrows shot up; Andrew wondered if he were being given some sort of secret signal, or being teased.

Josh turned to Miriam. "You ought to soak your blue-eyed goy in some cold water—that'll take the heat away. There's a tin tub in the shed. Marcie's got some kind of minty lotion or stuff—that'll help too. I'll get it." He sauntered backed to the cottage. Andrew watched him, afraid to look at Miriam. Then he felt a gentle pressure on his arm. He glanced at Miriam, noticed her shy smile. He racked his brain for something to say.

"What's a goy?" he finally asked.

Stupid, stupid question, a voice within him sneered.

Miriam rolled her eyes in apology and embarrassment.

"It's a...it's not a very nice word that means someone who isn't Jewish." She bit her lip.

"Oh."

"Josh was just teasing—he didn't mean to be unkind." She took a breath, bit her lip again. "He likes you, really." The lips formed a smile, and the gray eyes twinkled with mirth.

Andrew was tempted to ask, *Do you like me, too?* It would be a glib, easy way to break through the unease that had thrown an almost suffocating fog around him.

"Here's the magic potion, guys—hey, Miriam, haven't you dunked your fellah in some cold water yet?" Josh handed off a bottle of some pale green substance to Miriam, then ambled over to the shed.

He returned, hoisting a huge tin tub on one shoulder. "Here you go—" He set the tub down at Miriam's feet, winked at her, and strolled off.

Miriam looked at Andrew, pursed her lips—whether from embarrassment or anticipation or determination to get on with the task at hand, Andrew could only guess. She walked over to the faucet, turned it on, and carried the hose, spurting water, to Andrew. A look of mischief crossed her face.

Placing her forefinger over the end of the hose, she leveled it at Andrew's midsection and sprayed jets of water on his chest and stomach. He gasped, and a burst of laughter convulsed him as the squirts of stinging cold water blasted against his flesh. Miriam's squeals of delight counterpointed his husky chortles; he turned, and the spray of water ceased.

Glancing back at Miriam, he saw that her face had lost its mischievousness, though it still beamed with pleasure and plans. She dropped the end of the hose so that the water gushed against the sandy ground, and a serious, sensual look drifted across her face. Raising the hose so that water splurged upwards like a fountain, she stood a moment, gazing into his eyes as if asking for some sort of permission. Then she aimed the hose just below his neck and gently splashed the cold water onto his shoulders.

The water coursed down his chest and arms, feeling so soothingly cool as it banished every vestige of discomfort and brought forth the familiar, unsettling stirrings.

"Why don't you get into the tub," she said softly.

He complied, lounging nervously back into the tub as she doused the water over him. He noticed the subtle change in her expression as the stream of water moved from his neck and shoulders, where her face was utter concentration, to his waist, where something sublimely mysterious and pleasureful hinted within the dark gray eyes.

The tub filled, slowly, inexorably, and Andrew wished for some sort of divine intervention to arrange for a hole of sufficient size in the bottom to ensure that Miriam's task might never be accomplished.

I wish that this could last forever...If only I didn't have to go back to England!

"A penny for your thoughts," she said.

He was struck by the vision of his younger self pleading with his mother to take him back to England, of that petulant little boy cajoling and threatening and angrily proclaiming that he would rather eat Hitler's underwear than feel nothing short of glee in shaking the dust off his heels in his departure of this place. Now, seeing Miriam's face shining with hope and joy, a wave of dismay swept through him.

If only I didn't have to leave!

The words were almost on his lips; he swallowed, searched for something to say. Every possibility that occurred to him seemed either trite or scarily serious.

If only I could be with you, just like this...always!

His silence did not seem to perturb her; those gray eyes continued to hold him in a steady gaze. The sound of water sloshing over the brim of the tub jolted him back to reality. Miriam hopped up, walked briskly to the faucet, turned it off. Watching her, Andrew noticed the slim legs and purposeful swing to her arms, all businesslike and unfussy, yet suffused with a covert sensuousness that was for his eyes alone.

If only I could look at you, like this...forever!

"Feeling better?"

Better is not the word for it, he thought.

"Yes, better." His voice had a disconcerting quaver to it.

"Good," she said crisply. She sat down, not more than a foot from the tub, and rocked on her haunches, gazing at him.

He felt the color rise to his face again. Sliding back into the tub, he closed his eyes as the cool water submerged his shoulders. Then he felt a sort of wavy motion in the water and a trickle of water coursing down his legs. As he opened his eyes he saw Miriam dipping her hands into the tub and pouring the water onto him.

"Your legs and feet are a little burned, too."

"Hmm—" he nodded, afraid his voice might betray him.

"Here, why don't you put your legs in the tub and I'll splash some water on your shoulders."

Raising himself to a sitting position, Andrew drew his legs into the tub. Miriam moved behind him, dipping her hands into the water and drenching his back and shoulders with sploshes of cool water. She was very near, unbearably near to him, though he couldn't even see her, save for the tips of her fingers that appeared now and then over his shoulders.

Suddenly she came into full view in front of him. He realized his teeth were chattering, but whether from cold or nervousness or anticipation, he couldn't quite tell.

"Your lips are a little blue. Better get out before you freeze to death." She reached over, grabbed a towel that had been lying on the deck, and held it up for him.

He pushed himself out of the tub and stood a little unsteadily, shaking with cold. Then he felt soft terrycloth enclosing his shivering form. Gentle hands patted and stroked through the plushy fabric, and then arms enfolded him, soothing his shaking.

"Sorry, I'm just a bit cold," he whispered.

Her response was to hug him more tightly. He felt the soft curve of her body press against him and tried to stifle the moan that escaped his lips nonetheless.

She gave no indication that she'd heard, but continued to hold herself motionless against him. His trembling subsided, but the thumping of his heart seemed to batter wildly against his chest, so loud that it filled his ears and pounded his brain.

But that was the least of his problems right now.

"Um, I think I'd better lie down for a bit," he said.

Making a quick quarter-turn, he flung the towel off and onto the dock, then threw himself down just as the towel hit the wooden boards. Needless to say, it was untidily arranged, and though a long wrinkle chafed him from his chest to his thigh, he didn't dare move. His cheeks were beet-red now, he knew, so he buried his face into the towel.

Then he felt a tender, gliding caress on his back, cool and slippery, smelled something wonderfully minty as her lotion-slicked hands slid in easeful circles against his skin. Her splayed fingers grazed over his shoulder blades, down his spine; her hands then separated and skimmed along the waistband of his bathing trunks, then brushed up his sides to regroup at his shoulders and repeat their tender rangings across the expanse of his acquiescing flesh.

"Hey you guys!" Ellen's voice rang across the ruffly breeze. "Chocolate covered strawberries are up—come and get 'em!"

Andrew twisted his head around, as if to consult Miriam on whether they should accept such a tempting offer, though it was completely out of the question for him even to sit up, let alone stand and walk to the house.

Miriam tilted her head, awaiting his suggestion as to what they should do.

"I think I'll just lie here for a bit. We can get some later, all right?"

Her face scrunched into an expression of amusement, as if he'd cracked a joke.

"There probably won't be any left in a few minutes. I'll get us some." She stood up, then sauntered to the house. Halfway there, she turned, tilted her head, and a teasingly joyous smile broke across her face.

"Don't run away on me, now!"

His response was an involuntary grin that belied the churnings within him. "Wouldn't dream of it!"

She stood for a moment, facing him, and her smile melted into graceful curve of delight. Then she continued towards the house in that jaunty, decisive walk. He watched her for a moment, then, realizing he should take advantage of the fact that her back was turned, he arched up a bit, smoothed out the towel beneath him, and quickly settled down again.

As Miriam entered the house, the murmur of conversation rose in pitch and intensity, punctuated with indistinct exclamations. Andrew snuzzled his face into the towel again, afraid that even a curious look through a window might completely unnerve him. A wave of terror swept though him at the thought that someone (or everyone!) might tromp out to investigate his unsociable behavior.

Soft footfalls, then Miriam's voice.

"Ever had chocolate covered strawberries before?"

"Hmm—no, never."

"Well, you're in for a treat." She grabbed a towel and spread it out next to Andrew. Dropping down beside him, she lounged sideways, facing him, resting her weight on one arm. She set a saucer of ten chocolate-encased strawberries between them, plucked one, and held it inches away from his lips.

If it weren't for the war, if my father were around, he would surely have told me what to do in a situation like this!

He opened his mouth and she popped the chocolate-garnished treat onto his tongue. Her fingers momentarily brushed against his lips. The rich chocolate, mingled with tangy, luscious fruit, burst on his taste buds and swirled in delightful orbits through his mouth. He smiled as the succulent concoction melted into nothingness and all that was left was the lingering memory of the exquisite flavor.

If it weren't for the war, I wouldn't even be here....

"It's good," he whispered.

Stupid, stupid, STUPID thing to say!

Her eyes crinkled with delight.

"I can't believe you've *never* had chocolate covered strawberries!" Her voice had an enchanting lilt to it.

"My father and I once had peaches and chocolate. It was very good—not as good as this, though."

Her eyes twinkled with pleasure. "Peaches and chocolate—that sounds like an interesting combination!"

"Um, yes—it was. My father—" He caught himself, not sure if his reminiscences were appropriate for this occasion. For that matter, he was entirely confounded as to exactly what in the world *was* appropriate for this occasion.

"Your father?" A look of extraordinary intensity swept across her face, as if he had said exactly the right thing.

"Yes, um—he...we were having a picnic, and he'd brought along chocolate and peaches. He said that a lot of things that are different go together even better than if they were alone."

"They do?"

"Uh...." He looked at her, took a deep breath. "Yes, they do," he said quietly.

That alluring smile appeared again, but she said nothing.

Loud laughter—Josh's. Low, amused words—Paul's. Marcie, Ellen, and Esther giggling in approval, their muted voices flitting from the cabin, dancing across the bleached deck.

If only he could chat up a girl so easily! He envied Josh and Paul their ease in gabbing with the opposite sex. But then, they were Americans and such things, of course, came naturally to them. They knew exactly what to say, exactly how to act, exactly how to dazzle girls with that cocky yet self-effacing brashness that seemed to be the birthright of every Yank.

Blasts of laughter and giggles again.

Panic and self-doubt tore through him. He was a lost voyager, a plane caught between layers of cloud. Childhood was behind him, adulthood ahead of him, but compass points were of no comfort without a map to guide him home.

Miriam continued to gaze at him, and her benevolent smile was a beacon in the mist.

She had been his friend and guide through all the chaos and misery in this new land. Funny, he had known her barely two years, yet it seemed as if she had always been with him. In a way, it was almost the same as it had been at the beginning: He, a scared British boy in a strange land; she, the bold New Jersey schoolgirl holding out her hand in friendship.

But it was not the same.

They were no longer children.

He picked up a chocolate covered strawberry and held it to her lips. She opened her mouth and he placed it inside. His hand trembled a bit; he breathed a silent prayer that she wouldn't notice.

Her face filled with bliss as she savored his offering, then she took another strawberry and presented it to him. This time her fingers lingered on his lips for an all-too-brief moment. He reciprocated, and this time his hands didn't tremble quite so much.

As they worked their way down to the final two strawberries, Andrew's senses reeled with rapture. He delighted in the sight of her, how her sun-burnished face seemed to glow with a wonderful ecstasy, how her heat-frizzled hair lay in a gauzy halo about her head, how the water droplets on her skin glistened in the fading light. He heard the piercing caws of sea gulls, the gentle lap of water against the dock, the low conversation from the house. He smelled the mint and salt air, tasted the tangy fruit and chocolate still lingering on his tongue, sensed her thigh press against his and her toes playfully stroke his heel and felt exquisite, excruciating sensations rocking him to the core....

Her face, expectant and serene, basked in the flare of the setting sun. She reached her hand towards his, and he hesitated for a moment—a moment which seemed like an eternity.

Then he laced his fingers in hers.

Miriam insisted that he wear a shirt at the beach the next day, only allowing him to take it off when he went into the water. She also covered his legs with a towel as they lay on the blanket.

"I don't want to return you to your mother tomorrow, with you looking like a baked lobster," she told him.

That night, Josh suggested that they all go to the amusement park: "To celebrate our last night here." Ellen said she would stay home and read.

"You young folks go and enjoy yourself," she urged.

"What is this *young folks* talk! So your hair's turning gray and your teeth are falling out?" Marcie chided.

"Well, I'd rather not be a fifth wheel," Ellen said. "Or in this case, a seventh wheel."

Josh took her arm. "When that guy of yours gets back from the Pacific, I'll horn in on one of your dates, just to even things up, okay?"

"What's going on with Lev nowadays?" Paul asked.

"He's in Indochina," Ellen said. "Before the war ended, he was helping to coordinate military efforts between the native Indochinese and the American army. I don't think he's going to be back for awhile. It sounds as if keeping the peace is going to be harder than fighting the war. Lev says he hopes things work out with the Indochinese getting their independence from France."

"They're not the only ones who want a country of their own," Paul observed.

They rode to the amusement park; again, Andrew sat in the backseat with Miriam, Paul, and Esther. At the entrance, Josh draped one arm across Miriam's shoulder, the other across Andrew's.

"Mama said I should keep an eye on you two, but I don't think you guys need a babysitter." He winked at them, then walked off with Marcie and Ellen. "Behave yourselves! Meet you at the car at ten!" he called.

So now we're alone together....

At least he'd thought to bring some money with him.

What would I need it for in England, anyway?

He took Miriam's hand and walked with her down the noisy, crowded boardwalk. There were all sorts of games of chance and skill with garish prizes displayed above the booths: stuffed animals, giant pennants and pinwheels, gaudy trinkets. Andrew watched Miriam's face as she scanned the offerings; he noted how her smile widened at various items: a patchwork alligator, a calico bear, a bright blue kangaroo, a purple lion. He delighted in peeling the bills from the thick wad of dollars he'd brought along and plunking them down onto the counters of the gaming establishments. Miriam won the kangaroo by tossing pennies onto oil-slicked saucers. Andrew took possession of the bear by flinging darts at a map of Europe: ten hits on Nazi Germany won the prize. They acquired the alligator and the kangaroo by downing Messerschmidts and Zeroes in a shooting gallery.

"Hey, Andrew and Miriam just won the zoo!" Josh came up to them, his arms around Marcie and Ellen. "Here, I'll take your animals out to the car."

They off-loaded their garish menagerie into Josh's arms, then strolled past booths of various wares. They came upon a woman jewelry-maker, and Andrew bought Miriam a necklace of black velvet cord with a tiny blue-painted wooden bird dangling from it.

They rode the merry-go-round, screamed their lungs out on the roller coaster, swerved and crashed the bumper cars.

"Let's ride the Ferris wheel," Miriam suggested.

They stood in line, which was not really a proper queue, but an organized mob. Ordinarily, Andrew would have been irked, but he found the press of people around quite enjoyable. He put his arm around Miriam's shoulder to shield her from the jostling crowd.

She nestled against him.

Is she just grateful that I'm protecting her, that I've bought her some nice things....Is she merely being kind in pretending to like the attention....

Does she feel about me the way I feel about her?

It was their turn to board. He helped Miriam up onto the chair, then sat beside her. He wondered if he were sitting too close to her and if she would mind if he put his arm around her. They soared upward, then stopped at the top of the wheel as the operator loaded the last chair at the bottom. Their chair swayed alarmingly; without a second thought, Andrew put his arm around her shoulder. She moved a little closer to him. They plummeted down to earth and soared up again, then down again and up, like an interlinked series of take-offs and landings. The calliope music rushed through Andrew's brain, beating time to his heart, and the lights of the amusement park sparkled all around like multi-colored stars in a benign heaven. He loved the way the different colors reflected on her face, loved the salty scent of her hair, loved the sensation of her body close to his.

How could I have been around her all this time and not have felt what I feel for her now?

They stopped about a third of the way up, facing outward towards the sea as the operator began off-loading the chairs.

It wouldn't be fair to let things go any further... We might not ever see each other again after tomorrow....

Miriam nuzzled her face into his neck.

"I'm leaving in two days," he said as he looked out at the sea. He wasn't sure if it was a protest or an apology.

"I know," she whispered.

And then he kissed her.

Or rather, she kissed him.

What actually happened was that he turned to her and then froze, terrified that what he was about to do was horribly wrong.

You don't just kiss someone, then leave....

Then her lips were on his.

The chair began to move and instead of startling them apart, the motion seemed to urge them together. They soared upward, over the top, dropped down, stopped halfway to the bottom. Their kiss turned into a kind of lingering caress; her lips nuzzled against his and his breath came out in astonished gasps as wondrous, alarming sensations shot through him.

How can I bear to leave her?

The Ferris wheel stopped and started several more times. New passengers boarded the chairs, and each slam of the gate seemed to crash at Andrew's soul:

Why is life always full of parting and pain?

He broke away from her as their chair stopped at the bottom, then grabbed her hand as if to apologize. She didn't seem perturbed.

They walked quietly through the exit and, as if by mutual agreement, found themselves at the back of the line again. She pressed against him, his arms went around her, and the crowd crushed around them. Never before had Andrew found mobs so...wonderful. There were other couples around them, in various stages of lovemaking: some giggling in each other's ears, some embracing, some kissing with open-mouthed passion. He wondered if any of them felt what he felt now: that sublime, soaring sensation of all coming right.

They slowly moved to the front of the line; Andrew would have been quite happy to wait for all eternity. Then they were loaded onto the Ferris wheel again, and once more their lips met as they flew toward the sky.

They walked along the beach afterwards, feeling the wet sand slap at their heels and the waves tug at their ankles. At first they just held hands, but then his arm went around her shoulder and her arm went around his waist, and it all seemed so natural and right, as if they were an old married couple with a lifetime of memories behind them.

They kissed again; compared to sitting side by side on the Ferris wheel this one was enough to send Andrew's senses careening to new heights of ecstasy. Her arms locked around him and her hips snuggled against his.

Everything about her is so right...It's as if she's my other half, fitting against me so perfectly, knowing me so deeply, loving me more than I could love my own life....

They arrived at the car at ten-thirty; to Andrew's relief no one seemed curious or peeved by their lateness. It started to rain and they piled into the car.

On the way back to the cottage the rain turned into a downpour. Even in their quick dash to the door, they managed to get soaking wet.

"Looks like the guys get to sleep inside tonight!" Josh cracked as they got indoors. He winked at Miriam. "Just don't mention it to Mama."

Ellen heated up some apple cider as the boys took turns changing in the lavatory and the girls changed in the loft. Miriam climbed down the ladder, dressed in an oversized tee-shirt and baggy shorts. Andrew thought she would not have looked any lovelier than if she'd been wearing a Paris gown. They sat together on the floor, huddled under an old blanket, sipping their cider and listening to the excited chatter of the others. Marcie and Esther exclaimed over the stuffed animals; Josh and Paul laughed about the rides. When Ellen retired to the loft, everyone else began arranging their bedding. Miriam had brought a quilt and blanket, and she laid her quilt and Andrew's sleeping bag side by side in one corner of the room. Andrew wondered if Josh would protest, but then saw that Marcie was doing the same thing with her's and Josh's bedding in another corner. Esther was similarly occupied in a third corner with Paul looking on. Josh turned out the light, and the darkness seemed to Andrew a comfort, rather than a fearsome thing. The gentle hammering of rain on the roof drowned out the random sounds of everyone settling to sleep.

I guess I'm sleeping with a girl...sort of!

"Good night," Miriam whispered. She gently kissed him once, then again, then snuggled into his embrace and fell asleep in his arms.

He was still asleep when he sensed a sort of commotion near him. At first he thought that Lindy was attacking him, but then he realized where he was and whom he was with. He opened his eyes to find Miriam thrashing about. Her eyes were still closed in sleep. Then she started moaning, a soft, low croon of distress. He gently patted her face and whispered her name.

Her eyes fluttered open and she uttered a soft cry of—it sounded like a cross between anguish and relief. She slumped against him, and his arms went around her.

How good it feels to hold her in my arms....

He kissed her forehead, then embraced her again. She drew back. Distress and sorrow flooded her face as she gazed at him.

Oh God...She's going to say she's sorry it all happened....

The words seemed to rush out of him, like horses bursting forth from a starting gate. "I love you."

She regarded him with a look of wonder and rapture, then her arms went round him and her lips pressed against his ear.

"I love you too, Andrew," she whispered.

"You were having a nightmare, weren't you?"

Miriam kicked a chunk of sand as they walked along the beach. They were the only two people on the sandy expanse; the sun, low in the eastern sky, sent faint dawn rays across the gray sea.

He had wanted to lie by her side all morning, but had been compelled to find out what had troubled her sleep. He sensed, somehow, that she'd had this nightmare before.

She gazed ahead, as if seeing something beyond the benign seascape before them.

"It always starts like this. I'm walking along, sometimes at the shore, sometimes...somewhere else. A dusty road, a path, a meadow. At first I feel happy...Last night I dreamt I saw you running towards me, and I was so filled with joy that I'd be with you in a few seconds, and then it happened."

"What?"

"The bodies appeared, like they always do. Stacks and stacks of bodies, piled up like logs all around, and I ran and ran, trying to find my way out, trying to find my way to you...." She turned to him, pressed her face against his chest.

"I felt so awful, so guilty. I felt that it was wrong for me to be alive when everyone else was dead. I felt even worse because I'd been with you, and I was so happy, and I felt I had no right to feel that way—I had no right to even be alive—" Her voice cracked with anguish, then soft sobs convulsed her body.

"Miriam—oh, Miriam—" He wrapped his arms around her and shook her in his embrace, trying to jostle the demons away. He wanted to crush her into himself, as if by merging their two souls he could banish all the guilt and pain she felt.

"Miriam, you mustn't feel that way; you mustn't even *think* that! You have every right to be alive, to be happy, and so did they. It's not wrong that you're alive—it's wrong that they're dead! Please believe that."

She drew back and regarded him uneasily with a grief-swollen face, as if his implorings were too outrageous to be believed. He wanted to tell her how precious she was to him, how sublimely happy she'd made him, but he realized he would be travelling on a track of faulty reasoning: *You deserve to be alive because of what you mean to me.*

What about those who died unloved and unmourned, and even unknown? Does that mean their lives were worth any less?

But all he knew was that he'd never experienced such happiness before, that he'd never known such distress at another's torment.

She's all the world to me....

He pressed her to himself again.

"I can only imagine how you must feel," he said. "Losing so many of your family like that." The horror bubbled up in him like vomit as he thought of his aunt. "My Aunt Jane went off to France. I didn't know it at the time. I thought she just went away to do translating or secretarial work. My mother told me that she went to France as a British agent, and she's—" His voice broke in anguish. "She hasn't turned up. She would have made it back to England if she were still alive—"

Bloody hell! I've tried to comfort her and I'm blubbering like a baby!

Miriam threw her arms around his neck and pressed her face against his. Their tears mingled together, and his lips gently swept over her face. The salt taste of her skin seemed strangely familiar; then he remembered:

When I was sick with pneumonia....When Dad came to me and he cried as he was holding me and I tasted his tears....

Their lips met, and their kiss was not so much an expression of affection as it was an embodiment of all the pain and grief and desperate hope he felt, and knew that she felt too.

I've never needed anyone the way I need her...It would kill me to be parted from her! If only I could stay!

Of course he couldn't stay.

I need to find my father...He needs me as much as I need him... When I find him, though, maybe we could come here....

The plans whirled through his mind as they motored back to Scotch Plains. Everyone else was quiet, and the rush of air past the open windows seemed to cleanse his mind and sharpen his focus.

Yes...I need to find him. And when I do, I'll help him put his life back together again. Even if Mum chooses to stay with Jake, Dad and I will have each other, and some way, somehow, Miriam and I will be together.

Miriam snuggled against him. He stroked her hair, brushed a gentle kiss across her forehead.

We'll be together....

"Here's the trunk key." Josh handed his keychain to Andrew. It was dark, but the air was still sultry with the day's heat.

Andrew got out, stretched his legs to get the kinks out, and walked to the back of the car. Miriam followed him. He opened the trunk; the crunch of the key turning in the lock seemed to have a depressing finality.

I have to say goodbye to her....

Scattered over the bedding and luggage were the stuffed animals they'd won. He picked up the bear and nuzzled it in Miriam's face. She emitted a soft cry, something between a giggle and a sigh, then put her arms around his neck.

The trunk's open...No one can see us....

As he kissed her, her body seemed to dissolve into his, as if she were trying to find her way into his soul.

"Oh Miriam, I love you," he breathed.

"I love you too, Andrew."

The light from the house bathed her face with a radiance that made her look lovelier than ever. He wanted to tell her that he wished he didn't have to leave, but that would make their parting all the more painful.

"I'll come back—I promise," he said gently.

Should I ask her to wait for me?

"I'll wait for you, Andrew." She kissed him, cupping his face in her hands. "I'll wait for you."

He shut the trunk, then walked with her around the car. Handing the keys to Josh, he said, "Bye—and thanks for a lovely time, all of you."

"So long—and take it easy, Andrew," Josh said. Everyone echoed his farewell.

He held the door open for Miriam, then watched as the car sped off into the darkness.

As he walked into the house, Lois called to him from the dining room.

"We're all sitting down to dessert, Andrew. You're just in time for blackberry cobbler."

All? Only his mother, Lois, and Mr. Givens were seated at the dining room table. He'd planned on making a quick dash up to his room, but since Jereen wasn't there, he thought it might not be a bad idea to have a bite to eat before turning in.

And Jake isn't here, either—bloody marvelous!

He set his things by the couch and ambled into the dining room.

"How was your holiday, darling?" his mother asked.

"Smashing—just smashing." He smiled as he sat down at the table.

"Looks like you got a little sun," Lois observed.

"Oh dear, he did," Andrew's mother fretted.

"I'm fine, Mum," Andrew said.

"Are you sure, darling? If you feel the least bit ill, we ought to take you to a doctor—"

"I'm *fine*, Mum." He attacked his blackberry cobbler, hoping that a display of voracious appetite might quell his mother's concern.

"Jake! Isn't Jereen coming down for dessert?" Lois asked.

Jake walked into the dining room and sat down next to Andrew's mother.

"She's a little tired—just wanted to turn in early," Jake said. He glanced at Andrew, then looked at Andrew's mother. She gazed lovingly at him and took his hand. He smiled shyly back at her, squeezed her fingers.

She really loves him, and he loves her....

It was as if he were seeing the two of them for the first time, without the memory of his father to color his perception of the scene. Still basking in the love he'd just found for himself, he couldn't help but feel a quiet joy at the happiness his mother knew.

She already believed my father was dead when she fell in love with Jake...It isn't as if Jake caused her to betray my father...After all, he came along after my father went missing....

He smiled at Jake. Jake glanced again at him, did a double-take. His eyes registered a stunned bewilderment.

Andrew stood. "I guess I'd better get packing. Night, Mum." He walked over to his mother and gave her a kiss on the forehead. He nodded at Jake. "Good night, Jake."

Jake blinked, then swallowed. "Night, Andrew," he croaked.

As Andrew was sorting through his clothes, he heard a knock on his door.

"Come in," he said breezily, thinking it was his mother. He opened the bottom drawer of his dresser, shuffled through his jeans.

"Hi Andrew." Jereen stood in the doorway, holding a blue-gray wooly bundle. She closed the door behind her and presented the bundle to Andrew.

"I made it for you," she said. "It's a sweater, in RAF blue. I wanted you to have something warm to wear when you got back to England. Jake told me that winters could be very damp and chilly there. Here, try it on. If it doesn't fit, I'll alter it before you go."

Andrew pulled the sweater over his head, smoothed it over his waist and extended his arms. The cuffs came exactly to his wrist bone, and the fit of the sweater was perfect: snug, but not too tight.

"It fits perfectly, and it seems quite warm. Thank you ever so much," he said with a smile.

She bit her lip, smiled, then looked a bit worried. "Do you really like it?"

"Of course I do," he assured her. Funny, he'd been dreading seeing her again; he was surprised at how nonchalant and cheerful he managed to sound. He was even more surprised at the delightful, alarming sensations kicking around inside of him.

"It's smashing," he said.

She smiled again, then looked at the pictures of the airplanes. Pointing to the Hurricane, she asked, "Is that a Spitfire?"

"No, that's a Hurricane. My father flew Hurricanes."

She nodded, stared at the picture for awhile, then said quietly, "Did they ever find him?"

Startled by her question, he stammered, "N—no, no, they didn't."

"So he's missing."

"Um, yes—you could say that."

She fixed him with a pointed stare. "Do you think he's still alive?"

"Uh, perhaps, I mean, it—it's possible."

She continued to stare at him, like a headmaster grilling a student on an exam.

"Do *you* think he's still alive?"

His voice caught in his throat; he coughed, took a deep breath, and shrugged.

"Do you think he's still alive?" she asked again.

An awful fear gripped him.

If I deny it, it would be the same as denying him. It's one thing to keep my faith a secret; it's another thing to lie about it....

He closed his eyes.

"Yes," he whispered.

He wondered how she would take his declaration. He opened his eyes. She took a step towards him, pressed her hand to his chest.

"Now I know," she said gently. "If you believe your father's alive, then I can only imagine what you must think of Jake—and of me. That's why you don't want anything to do with me. It would be like betraying your father, wouldn't it?"

He felt as if he were standing on a precipice; one breath, one blink, could send him hurtling to hell.

She moved still closer, her body almost touching his.

"What was he like?" Her voice was a soft, breathy murmur.

"He...he was—" Andrew swallowed. "He was good...and kind...caring, and strong...and brave."

She gazed at him as he spoke, as if engraving his words on her soul. She tilted her head, smiled.

"What did he look like?"

He tried to recall: He saw dark hair, gray eyes, but nothing else. Blank, a complete blank, where his father's face should be. It was like forgetting someone's name, only this was infinitely more awful.

I can't remember him....

His voice came out in panicky gasps.

"I can't—can't—can't remember—I can't remember!"

He had that horrible feeling of the world flying apart, of all order and reason disintegrating.

Then Jereen's arms were around him.

"I'm sorry—oh, Andrew—I'm so sorry...."

He thought he would dread her touch, and now he found it the most comforting thing in the world.

Voices on the stairs: Jake's parents. Their voices grew louder; Andrew froze as he heard them right outside his door. The soft click of a door shutting, their voices soft and muffled now. Jereen stepped back from him, then turned, opened the door—and left.

He plopped down on his bed, utterly drained, yet wretchedly uneasy. He wanted to scream, but he knew that would only bring his mother running.

More voices: his mother's and Jake's.

"He didn't look well. Perhaps we ought to call the doctor," his mother said.

"He's fine—probably just a little worn out, that's all," Jake said.

Silence.

Andrew got up, tore off the sweater and tossed it onto his dresser, then pulled off his tee shirt and flung it at the corner. After peering out into the hallway to make sure the coast was clear, he walked to the bathroom. He brushed his teeth and splashed cold water on his face. As he blotted his face dry, he looked through the window to the sleeping porch. The canvas bed was set up on the porch.

Maybe I'd sleep better outside....

He went out on the porch, stretched out on the canvas bed, and looked up at the stars.

Like I used to do with Dad....

What if we passed each other on the street? I wouldn't know him, and he wouldn't know me, either....

A soft click, a squeak. The door opened and Jereen stood before him. She was dressed in a light-colored pajama top and shorts.

She sat down at the foot of the bed, clasped her hands together.

"I'm sorry—"

"No, it's not your fault," he said.

She laid her hand on his ankle.

"You'll remember—I *know* you will! It's been a long time since you've seen him. Doesn't your mother have any pictures of him?"

"Everything was destroyed when our home was bombed—almost everything. There aren't any photos left...."

"You'll remember! Just don't try so hard! It'll come to you, when you least expect it."

Her hand moved up his jeans, skirted his hip. She scooted up so that she was sitting by his waist. Her fingers grazed across the bare flesh of his stomach, his chest, his shoulder.

"You have a bad burn," she murmured. "I'll get something for it."

She left, and after a minute returned with a small bottle. She poured some of the contents into her hand, slathered her palms together, then soothed something cool and fragrant onto his chest. The scent seemed familiar, like an old friend.

Lavender...like Aunt Jane used to wear....

"Turn over—I'll put some on your back," Jereen said.

He was glad for the suggestion. The familiar stirrings were threatening to make themselves highly visible.

How can I feel for her what I felt for Miriam?

Her hands gently worked over his back, soothing the balm into his tender skin.

She'd better not ask me to turn over....

"Please don't stop," he whispered.

"Wouldn't dream of it," she said.

He was in that horrid mob again. Everyone was yelling *Sieg Heil*, and Andrew knew *he* was coming.

If only I could kill him....

There was some kind of contraption being wheeled down the street. Andrew at first thought it was a sort of movable stage, with several people dancing on it. Then he saw that the people weren't dancing—they were twitching. Their feet were dangling a few inches off the ground, their heads were at odd angles, their faces were a horrid, dusky blue. Ropes, attached to a beam overhead, were knotted around their necks. One of them was a man wearing an RAF uniform. He had dark hair....

DAD!

Someone put a hand over his mouth. He tried to scream....

Strong arms were around him....

"Andrew!"

He tried to break free and realized he wasn't standing; he was lying down, and it was dark, not light.

"Andrew—you were having a nightmare." Jereen held him fast. "It's all right—it's all right...." Her lips pressed against his ear.

He groaned, came to full consciousness.

"Did you dream about your father?"

He must have called out in his sleep.

"Yes," he moaned.

She clasped him more tightly; then he realized he was crying. Her lips slowly moved across his cheek, gently kissed his tears, then grazed across his mouth. He gasped with shock—and pleasure. Her mouth pressed hard on his and her fingers fluttered over his cheeks and eyelids. She coaxed his lips apart, and her kiss turned into a sort of half-caress, half-exploration, as her tongue moved inside him.

Oh God—if she doesn't stop I'm going to have some explaining to do....

She gently eased away from him, then snuggled back into his embrace.

"I had a dream about your father," she said.

"My father?"

"Uh-huh. Just now—before you woke up from your nightmare." She looked up at him and smiled. "I dreamt you were a little boy, and you were holding a model plane above your head. It had roundels on the wings—I think it was a Hurricane. Your father took your picture, then he smiled at me. He had the kindest eyes, and the nicest smile. I felt....so happy, just being with him. Oh, Andrew—I wish I could tell you what he looked like! I'll never forget his face!"

"I'm so afraid he might not get in touch with me," he said. "If he finds out that my mother's gotten remarried, he might think that...I don't want to see him—"

"Andrew, why don't you write to the RAF when you get back to England? Someone must know something about what happened to him. If he's still alive, they'll be able to tell you how to contact him!"

Her suggestion made sense—a lot of sense.

Funny it should come from someone who's related to the man who took my father's place....

He held her close to him, and this time his lips sought hers.

"Andrew—wake up."

He opened his eyes, saw that it was morning. Jereen was sitting up beside him.

"I'll go back in first." She stood, peered around the edges of the curtain of the glass-paned door, then slipped inside.

My God—did we spend the whole night together?
God stone the crows! I've slept with two different girls, two nights in a row....
Well, it's a good thing no one saw us....

He went to his room. He was still a bit groggy, so he decided to lie down and catch a few winks.

Just a few....

"Andrew!" His mother's voice chimed from downstairs. "Breakfast—chop chop! We've got a plane to catch today!"

He bounced out of bed, grabbed a shirt, and buttoned it as he dashed down the stairs. Everyone was seated in the dining room.

"Eggs Benedict this morning, Andrew," Lois announced. "A special farewell breakfast!" She dished up two portions on Andrew's plate. His mother, sitting beside him, beamed.

"Andrew darling, just imagine! Tomorrow this time we'll be in England."

He nodded as he shoveled a chunk of yolk-coated muffin into his mouth. Looking across the table, he saw Jereen looking intently, lovingly at him.

He felt a hot-red flush creep up his neck and explode on his face.

"Oh, dear, you really *are* red." His mother's smile had turned to a puzzled frown.

"I—I'm fine, just fine." His voice came out as a squeaky croak.

His mother pressed her hand to his forehead.

"You're warm, too." She turned to Lois. "He does look a bit redder than he did last night, doesn't he?"

Lois squinted at him. "Now that you mention it—"

"I'm fine!" Andrew insisted.

"Oh, dear, we don't want you coming down with sun poisoning. Maybe we should call a doctor—" Andrew's mother bent a little closer to him. She sniffed, then stared at him, bewildered.

"Andrew, what have you got on?"

Bloody hell! This is bloody unbearable...her hovering about...me, smelling like a whorehouse and blushing like a bride!

"I'm fine. I'm really all right, Mum—" He bolted from the table and sprinted across the living room. "I think I'll finish packing."

"But darling, aren't you going to eat your Eggs Benedict?" his mother wailed.

"I'll grab a bite to eat later on," he yelled as he dashed up the stairs.

Once in his room, he furiously cleaned out his dresser drawers: shirts, jeans, underwear, socks—all went on a heap on his bed.

There was a tap at the door.

"I'm all *right*, Mum!" he called.

The door slowly opened.

"Hi," Jereen said quietly.

He swallowed, nodded. His voice wouldn't even come.

She shut the door. Her eyes held a sort of desperate plea.

What does she want from me?

She took a step towards him.

She's Jake's cousin! I can't let myself fall in love with her!

She took another step.

He felt as if he were falling—falling into his deepest fears, falling into what he knew was certain damnation, falling into the chasm of his dreadful desires....

And then he was in her arms, and her mouth was on his. Her breath, hot and sweet, seemed to shoot through him. Her body pressed so tightly against him it seemed as if they would melt together.

He pressed against her, hoping that would stop the awful trembling of his knees.

He lurched forward a bit; she pitched back. They tottered, then tumbled onto the bed. She ended up on top of him, whether by accident or design, Andrew could only guess. She writhed against him and her mouth clamped down on his; then she began that terrifyingly wonderful exploration. He drew a slow gasp as her languorous, urgent kisses urged him to an unbearable ecstasy.

She pushed herself up a bit, hovering over him with her arms locked straight; her legs wrapped around his thighs and her hips nuzzled against his.

Doesn't she know what she's doing to me?

She sat up straighter, so that her weight brought pressure to bear. His body convulsed with the shock of his own desire. He groaned; she snuggled against him, then smiled.

Without a word, she started unbuttoning his shirt.

He felt as if he were a Christmas present being unwrapped.

She undid the last button, pulled his shirt out of his jeans, ran her fingers over his chest as she stared raptly at him.

"I know your father is the most important person in the world to you," she said softly. "And I know that you'd rather die than do anything that you thought might...betray him. You'll always be your father's son, and I'll always be Jake's cousin, and I know—" She pressed her lips together. Her eyes brimmed with tears; she blinked, and they splashed down her cheeks.

"I know you can't love me, because of that." Her voice came out as a hiss of despair. She swallowed, closed her eyes.

He reached up, touched his fingers to her cheek.

She opened her eyes. "You're leaving today," she whispered. "I might not ever see you again. You might not even *want* to see me again—I'll understand if you don't. But we can...be together...*now.*"

Together?

"You're not leaving for an hour—that's more than enough time," she said. She ran her fingers across his shoulders, down his chest, over the waistband of his jeans. He shuddered, and moaned—a soft, low crooning wail of horror and rapture.

"*Andrew!*" His mother's voice, strident with an edge of hysteria, and her footsteps, quick and purposeful on the stairs.

"...I *know* something's wrong with him!"

Jereen seemed to fly across the room, like Peter Pan, Andrew thought, even as his mind reeled with terror. She quickly locked the door; Andrew jumped to his feet and furiously buttoned his shirt. Too late, he realized he'd gotten the buttons all wrong.

"*Andrew!* His mother was rattling the doorknob now. Jereen grabbed the sweater off the dresser and tossed it at him.

"Put this on!"

He quickly pulled the sweater on.

"Andrew—*open this door!*"

Jereen unlocked the door.

"I'm sorry—I must have locked the door," she said to Andrew's mother. "I wanted to give Andrew a sweater I made for him—see?"

His mother took a step towards him, peered at the sweater, then eyed him worriedly.

His mind was a fog of fear but he realized, to his horror, that his body was still...reacting pleasurably.

Oh God, if she sees....

He tore off the sweater and stuffed it in his lap.

"Andrew! What's the matter with you?"

He inched away from her, holding the sweater tight to his groin. Looking past her shoulder, he saw Jake, staring at him.

He knows...He knows!

"Andrew—let me see it!" His mother tugged at the sweater, but Andrew held it fast. "Andrew!"

He clambered backwards and fell off the other side of the bed with a mighty *thunk.*

"Andrew!" His mother raced around the bed to his side. He flung the sweater at her and scrambled under the bed.

"*ANDREW!*" She grabbed his ankles and started pulling him out.

"What's the matter?" Lois's voice, loud and agitated.

Andrew grasped the bedpost.

"Oh my God, he's *deranged!*" his mother shrieked. "Pry his fingers loose! Quickly! He's got sun poisoning!"

"Sun poisoning?" Lois started to work Andrew's fingers loose.

"Some sort of delayed heatstroke!" his mother yelled.

"Alice, he's okay," Jake said. "There's no such thing as delayed heat—"

"What the hell is going on?" Mr. Givens ran up the stairs.

"Mom, he's all right!" Jake's hands were on Lois's, trying to pry her hands off of Andrew's.

Bloody hell...he knows!

"Will somebody tell me what the *hell* is going on?" Mr. Givens bellowed.

Andrew kicked at his mother's hands. She screamed, then shrieked, "*Sun poisoning! Delayed heatstroke!*"

"He's okay!" Jake yelled. "Alice—Mom, he's okay!"

Jereen was crying, Mr. Givens roared his query again, Lois jabbered something incoherent.

"He's all *right!*" Jake yelled. "Andrew—are you all right?"

Dead silence. Andrew realized that his immediate concern had...subsided.

"Are you okay?" Jake softly asked.

"Yes," Andrew replied.

"He's okay," Jake declared. "Come on—he's okay. Let him—let him get, uh, finished packing. Okay? Come on, everyone, let's leave him alone for awhile. He's fine."

Andrew heard the patter of exiting feet, heard the door close. He sighed in relief.

"Andrew?" Jake spoke barely above a whisper. Andrew saw his shoes through the gap between the bottom of the bedspread and the floor.

Oh God...He's going to kill me. He got everyone out so he could kill me....

"Andrew, it's a little dusty under the bed. We're not leaving for another hour, so why don't you take a shower? There probably won't be much hot water left because everyone's been taking showers all morning, but a cold shower might feel pretty good right now, okay?"

Why is he acting so nice to me if he's going to kill me?

"Okay—see you downstairs," Jake said. Andrew saw his feet leave the room and the door shut behind him.

"Come on." Jake's voice was distant, muffled. "Let's go downstairs. He'll be all right." Andrew waited...waited. Not a sound.

He slithered out from under the bed, picked through the pile of garments, and got a change of clothes.

A cold shower sounds like a bloody good idea....

"Darling—all packed?" Andrew's mother set down her coffee cup, smiled brightly at him.

"Um—uh, no—I'll finish up—" Andrew turned to go back up the stairs.

"I'll take care of that." Jake stood, nodded amiably at Andrew. As he walked past Andrew, he gently squeezed his shoulder.

What the bloody hell is going on?

"I made you some more Eggs Benedict, Andrew," Lois said. She indicated Andrew's place.

"Thanks," Andrew said. He sat down, began to eat. Jereen was sitting across from him, but he didn't dare so much as glance at her.

Everyone acted as if nothing had happened. Andrew's mother chatted with Lois about the journey.

"It took us several days to come here by ship. We'll be back across the Atlantic in less than a day."

"You flew when you went back to England after leaving Andrew here, didn't you? Lois asked.

"Yes, I came over as a war bride, returned as a ferry pilot. We snagged a ride with Atlantic Ferry Service on a Liberator going to Prestwick."

Andrew shoveled in his last bite of Eggs Benedict. Without a word, he stood, then walked quickly upstairs. As he got to the top of the stairs he saw Jake setting his suitcase in the hallway.

"I packed your wooden box in, too," Jake said. "I left a change of clothes on top of the dresser. You might want to pack it in your mother's carry-on bag, okay?"

Andrew nodded.

"Well, we'll be leaving in a few minutes."

Andrew felt something brush against his leg, heard a throaty meow.

"Hey—" Jake picked Lindy up and handed him to Andrew. "Lindy wants to say goodbye to you." He scratched Lindy's ears. "I think he's going to miss you."

Andrew clasped Lindy to him. Jake picked up the suitcase.

"I'll put this in the car. See you downstairs."

He's not going to kill me here...now. He's just biding his time. That's why he's being so nice....

Jereen sat beside him as they rode to the station. Andrew glared out the window.

I'm not going to so much as blink at her. Jake's going to lay into me anyway, but I'm not going to give him any more ammunition....

Mercifully, they didn't have to wait long for the train; mercifully, Lois occupied Andrew's attention. Andrew allowed himself to be fussed over, and hugged, and fussed over again. Dear, sweet Lois—he *was* going to miss her.

As the train pulled in, Andrew suddenly experienced a sharp pang.

I'm leaving them—I won't see them when I wake up tomorrow, won't hear Lois's cheery "Good Morning," won't see Mr. Givens's gentle smile....

Lois was hugging him fervently, and Andrew returned her embrace, nuzzling his face into her shoulder. Mr. Givens put his arm around Andrew's shoulder; Andrew turned to him and fell against him. He felt strong arms go round him, felt his heart ache at the thought of being parted from this man who had been so much like a father to him.

As his mother and Jake bid farewell to Jake's parents, Andrew slipped into the train. He saw Jereen through the window, saw the look of dismay and yearning on her face.

He turned away and sat on the opposite side of the aisle, setting his gaze away from her.

The plane made a wide arc over New York harbor. Andrew gazed down at the toy-like ships and tiny boats skimming over the shimmering expanse, at the skyscrapers of Manhattan looking like fanciful blocks neatly arranged. There was the Statue of Liberty, a friendly figurine on a scrap of green, holding her torch high in welcome.

Funny—she looked so scary when I first saw her....

They were over New Jersey now. Below were grid-like streets lined with neat houses, so benign and unassuming in their orderliness, interspersed with baseball diamonds, cemeteries, and tree-dotted parks.

It all looks so beautiful from up here....

In the distance were the Watchung Mountains, from which General George Washington had looked out over enemy British troops. On the now placid plains below, battles had been fought between the soldiers of the King and men who wanted to be free.

Could General Washington have ever imagined that, a century and a half later, a British subject would look on this nation, this nation now drenched in prosperity and peace, as his own?

This bold, wild, hard land had claimed him, shamed him, harrowed him, embraced him, judged him, redeemed him. And what he had so feared, when he first saw that stern face of liberty, did not seem to be such a fearful thing, after all.

The plane soared out to sea and the land raced away from him until it was a thin purple line on the horizon and finally disappeared in the distance.

"A penny for your thoughts," his mother said.

Andrew spoke softly. "I was just thinking—it's a good thing Hitler's dead."

Her face scrunched in puzzlement.

He smiled.

"I'd have to eat his underwear, wouldn't I?"

"Andrew—wake up! We're over England!" His mother gently shook him.

He sat straight up, rubbed the sleep from his eyes, looked out the window at the brilliant green, crazy-quilt landscape below. In the distance were the white cliffs of Dover, edging the shores of this blessed emerald realm.

It all seems so fantastic, he thought. Just click your heels together and you're home.

He was like a drunken man in London, reeling and gaping with each wonderful sight: Big Ben, red double-decker busses, Underground symbols, even the letter boxes still garnished with lurid yellow gas-detecting paint. There were heaps of rubble too, and desolate tracts of land also, more so than Andrew remembered from his last visit to London. The V-1s and V-2s had certainly done their work.

But it's all so beautiful!

He drank in the sounds, the Cockney and Oxbridge speech, the occasional West County accent. He bought a stack of picture postcards to send to his friends and pen-pals, and took particular care in selecting a giant one of Big Ben to send to Effie Mae.

They stayed with Daphne, Freddie's sister, who was living in Freddie's old place (or rather, the Hadley-Trevelyan Trust's place, Andrew remembered). Andrew had been a little surprised at the sight of her: For a half-sister, she looked alarmingly like Freddie, with the same dimpled chin and narrow eyes. But when she smiled at Andrew and gently embraced him as his mother introduced him and Jake, he felt a strange sense of wonder and ease about her.

She's not like Freddie at all....

There was a picture on the corner table in the sitting room: a younger, carefree Daphne, standing next to a handsome, kindly-faced young man. In front of them were two small, curly-haired girls caught, mid-giggle, by the camera's eye.

He wondered for a moment where the rest of this happy family was, then remembered overhearing his mother telling Kaz that Daphne's husband and daughters had died on Borneo.

Looking more closely at Daphne, he detected the subtle ravages of suffering: the terrible thinness, the lines of sadness around her eyes, the way she seemed to be so grateful at hearing every kind and pleasant word.

Her roommate, Pamela, served them lunch. Daphne had an appointment with her solicitor in the afternoon (to see to disbursing more of her inheritance to building another orphanage on Borneo), so Andrew's mother thought it would be a good idea to go out to dinner.

They were walking through Piccadilly when Andrew's mother stiffened. Her mouth dropped open and her eyes bulged in amazement.

Then she bolted.

"Ro—" Her voice was lost in the clamor of traffic. She charged ahead, threading her way through the mob, dashing across an intersection. It was then that Andrew saw the object of her pursuit: a man in an RAF uniform, walking purposefully ahead.

"*DAD!*" Andrew took off after her, his heart hammering wildly.

My God, he thought. Finding Dad on a busy street! *Mum* finding Dad on a busy street! He raced ahead.

She called out to him! She still loves him! She still loves him!

He made a mad leap into the intersection, then felt something snag him back to the sidewalk.

What the hell—

Jake was holding him fast. A taxi whizzed by.

"Andrew—you could have gotten yourself kil—"

Andrew thrashed wildly, trying to break Jake's grip.

"Let me go! Let me *go!* You're not my father—" He took a wild swing, connected with Jake's jaw, broke free. He raced through the traffic, heard horns blaring, scrambled across the hood of an infuriatingly slow lorry.

"DAD!"

He saw the look of astonishment and joy on his mother's face as she embraced his father. His father's back was to him, but Andrew had no doubt that there was rapture in his eyes.

She still loves him!

He was now only about twenty feet away from them.

I can't believe this is happening. Imagine—finding Dad on a busy street! What do I say to him? He won't even recognize me....

His mother was jabbering wildly, ecstatically. Andrew couldn't make out what she was saying.

He slowed.

I should let them have a few moments together. I've waited for this moment for years— a few more minutes won't matter. We have the rest of our lives....

Jake was beside him now, looking bewildered. Andrew suddenly felt a little sorry for him.

This is the happiest moment of my life; it's probably the saddest of his. He'll get over it, find someone else. Things will work out for him, somehow, some way....

The sounds of traffic, the jostle of the pedestrians rushing by seemed a million miles away. He felt suspended in space, saw nothing save his parents, now standing only a few feet away from him, heard nothing, save the sound of his own heartbeat as he walked slowly forward.

Chapter 50

"**A**ndrew!" his mother exclaimed. "It's your Uncle Robert! Can you believe it!"

As Uncle Robert turned and nodded at him, Andrew felt his soul shatter into a million pieces. He wanted to scream out his anguish, but instead nodded back at Uncle Robert.

"Nice to see you."

"You've grown a bit, Andrew," Uncle Robert said.

"It's all that *marvelous* food he got in America!" Andrew's mother gushed. "We just flew in this morning, in fact. Andrew was staying with Jake's parents and—" Jake walked up to them. "Jake! Can you believe it? It's Robert! I just saw him—darling, what happened to your lip? It's bleeding!"

Jake rubbed his hand across his mouth, inspected the crimson streak. "Sorry, I bumped into someone."

Uncle Robert took a handkerchief from his front pocket and handed it to Jake.

"Thanks," Jake said. He blotted his lip. Andrew's mother turned back to Uncle Robert.

"Robert, darling, we *must* keep in touch. I'm going to be staying at Greycliff—" She patted her belly. "Until the little Givens arrives this January. Please Robert, give me your address. We mustn't lose track of one another."

Uncle Robert looked quickly away. It was only then that Andrew realized he had not smiled once. His eyes held a haunted look, like Daphne's, and his face was haggard and lined. His frame, though gaunt, seemed encumbered with an unaccustomed load of flesh, as if it had once been even more emaciated.

Andrew's mother rummaged through her purse and pulled out a small notepad and pencil.

"Here Robert, I want you to write down your address. And you must come up to Greycliff sometime. The country air will do you good." She smiled and laid her hand on Uncle Robert's shoulder as he wrote.

"Good—I'll be pestering you to come for a visit."

Uncle Robert handed her back the notepad and pencil. She put them in her purse, then threw her arms around him.

"We're family, Robert. We always will be. Now, I'll be in touch."

Uncle Robert nodded again, looked wary.

"Robert, darling, I *mean* it," Andrew's mother said. She kissed him on the cheek.

Uncle Robert cleared his throat, said, "All right." Then he walked away.

Andrew's mother stared after him, then shook her head sadly.

"Poor dear. He was shot down over France just before Gwen was killed, and spent two years in a prison camp. He didn't even know about her until he got back to England."

Andrew was glad his mother was preoccupied. He didn't want her to see his tears.

His mother came into his room as he was getting ready for bed.

"Would you like a bite to eat before turning in, darling? Daphne has some tea and biscuits for snack."

"No, thank you. I'm a bit tired." Andrew kicked his shoe off into the corner.

"You seem a bit on the quiet side. Is anything wrong?"

Andrew shook his head. "I'm just tired, that's all. I guess all the excitement of being back has finally caught up with me."

As his mother kissed him goodnight, a strand of red hair fell across her cheek. He reached up, brushed it back.

Red hair....

In his mind's eye, he saw a shock of red hair, a smile, a model Giant Moth.

"What ever happened to Sparky?"

His mother made a soft sound that sounded like a cross between a sigh and a murmur, then spoke.

"Sparky was captured in the fall of Singapore. He was in a Japanese prison camp and was put to work on the Burma railway, along with so many others. He died...." Her voice trailed off.

Now he felt that his tears could come. His mother seemed a bit startled.

"I'm surprised you even remember him, darling."

He pressed his face against her shoulder.

"It's just...everything."

"...and Colin Kirknewton's father was killed in France."

Mr. Nugent poured Andrew's tea, as Andrew reflected on their squalid surroundings: a "prefab," a serviceable dwelling that could be quickly built and easily festooned with all the amenities of civilization. In reality it was little more than a flimsy box of wood, and tackier by far than any clapboard cottage Andrew had ever seen in America. They had mushroomed by the thousands upon the English countryside, profaning an already desecrated landscape with their sullen tawdriness, like blemishes on scarred flesh. The interior, with its cheap paneling and cast-off furniture, was a shoddy reproach to all the wisdom and grace and dignity that Andrew's former housemaster embodied. Mr. Nugent's quarters at Armus Court, though unassuming, had the elegance of age and the comfortable patina of furnishings and bric-a-brac that seemed a living, breathing part of the whole. This place was a travesty, an embarrassment, like seeing the King in a shabby hotel.

Mr. Nugent's roommate, Julian, came in with a plate of scones.

"Thank you Julian," Mr. Nugent said.

Julian nodded, disappeared back into the kitchen.

"What happened?" Andrew asked.

Mr. Nugent grew immensely saddened as he spoke.

"Colin's father was in a regiment that held up an SS company while the bulk of the British army retreated to Dunkirk. When they ran out of ammunition, they decided to surrender. The SS marched them into a pit and machine-gunned them. Only two men out of ninety-nine survived."

Andrew nodded, reached for a scone, munched it in silence. Then he asked, "What about Keith Vincent-Hill's father? I remember he was shot down over Germany."

Mr. Nugent looked even more sorrowful. "He returned, after spending five years in a prison camp, but—" Mr. Nugent took a deep breath. "Keith was killed, when the V-2 hit the dormitory."

Andrew was about to take a sip of tea; his cup clattered against the saucer.

"Wh—why—I mean, I thought that everyone in my class would have gone on to public school by then—"

"Keith got pneumonia, just like you. The Luftwaffe unleashed another aerial offensive in early 1944, and we had a few air raids in February. Keith had a cold that went into pneumonia after we spent a freezing night in the bomb shelter. He was out of school the rest of the year, and fell so far behind in his studies that he had to come back here to repeat his last year."

Andrew didn't want to ask his next question, but he knew he had to.

"Is everyone else all right?"

Mr. Nugent cleared his throat, then spoke in a low voice that crackled with grief.

"Harry Peal was killed in the summer of 1944. He and his mother and two sisters, when their home was hit by a buzz bomb. Charles Provis—"

"He went to America, didn't he?" Andrew couldn't bear to hear another name in this grim rollcall; somehow he thought that by refuting Mr. Nugent he could reverse whatever terrible fate had befallen Charles.

"Charles sailed on the *City of Benares*, with many other children who were being evacuated from Britain during that first summer of the war. The ship was torpedoed...." Mr. Nugent's voice faded. He swallowed. "There were seventy-seven children drowned."

Andrew resisted the urge to slump back in his chair and moan in anguish. Poor, poor, Charles—so terrified of being subjugated and starving, and never dreaming he would meet with death by cold drowning.

Julian brought in a plate of sliced pears. He glanced at Andrew, then looked sadly at Mr. Nugent.

"Julian, sit with us." Mr. Nugent said.

Julian set the pears on the table, pulled out a chair, and sat down. He smiled at Andrew.

"My Aunt Vera wrote me that you and your mother, um, dropped in on her. She mentioned that you were with a friend, and that she offered him a job. Did he take it?"

Andrew shook his head. "No, L.S. decided to stay in Alaska. He's learning to fly."

"How grand!" Julian exclaimed. "I've heard Alaska has the most incredible scenery."

"Yes, um, it's very nice," Andrew replied. He gazed outside as he nibbled on a slice of pear.

"Well," Mr. Nugent said loudly, as if trying to banish the demons of death by a show of spunkiness. "Tomorrow I'm getting my legs. Then I'll be able to walk about, just like before. I won't be able to teach this year, but perhaps next...." He pushed his wheelchair back from the table, reached into the cupboard behind him, withdrew a magazine, and handed it to Andrew. Andrew had to steel himself not to show revulsion at the sight of the bandaged stumps—all that remained of the legs that had gone on so many ramblings around Askew Court.

"Your mother sent this to me while I was in hospital. She enclosed a note with it, saying 'Guess who?'" Mr. Nugent showed the magazine to Andrew.

Andrew looked: It was the issue of *Life* with him on the cover.

"It really cheered me to read about you and about how well you were doing in America," Mr. Nugent said. "I couldn't believe how much you'd grown."

Andrew nodded. It seemed strange to see himself, smiling like that. He felt as if he would never be able to smile again.

Until Dad comes home....

"Darling, there's nothing left of Armus House, just piles of rubble. Why do you insist on seeing it?"

Andrew couldn't tell her why. Even *he* didn't know why he wanted to see it.

Andrew's mother looked at Jake, as if asking him how she should deal with the situation.

Bloody hell! Why does she always have to defer to him!

"I...I just want to see it. *It's important.*" He spoke the last two words slowly, deliberately.

His mother arched her eyebrows.

"It wouldn't be any trouble to go to Berkshire," Jake said.

"Are you sure?" Andrew's mother asked.

"Of course," Jake replied. "It's lovely country. I could go for a walk while you two...uh, visit." He smiled at Andrew.

"Well, all right," Andrew's mother said.

Andrew was relieved that he didn't have to battle Jake, but also irked that his opinion seemed to carry so much weight.

When he's gone, it'll just be my mother and me...until my father comes home, of course.

Andrew stared at the scene: two heaps of rubble in an empty land.

How can so much life and love and laughter be reduced to this?

He kicked aside a piece of wood molding, scanned the detritus that was once Armus House. Some blots of red, splashed against a jumble of tiles, caught his eye. Walking over, he saw a tangle of roses growing up through the wreckage.

He tugged at the thorny stems, managed to tear a few blooms loose. The thorns gashed his flesh, and his blood smeared against the red petals—not that it mattered.

Looking over his shoulder, he saw his mother and Jake picking through the rubble.

His mother straightened up, stared at him. He held the flowers up, as if in explanation, then turned and walked to Charlie's grave.

Arriving at the cemetery, he saw that there were three new headstones in the family plot: Aunt Gwen's, Gram's, and Freddie's. He was relieved to see that there was no memorial stone for his father.

Perhaps Mum couldn't bring herself to put one in....

The iron fence around Charlie's grave was gone; Andrew supposed that it had been melted down into a cannon or a battleship. Somehow, some way, he would see that it was replaced.

He held the roses to one of the angel faces smiling out from the headstone, then laid them on the ground.

At least Charlie has his two sisters with him now....

On the train ride up to Northumberland, Andrew stared numbly at the landscape blurring by.

Fifty million people killed in this war—that's what they're saying...Fifty million dead after six years of this stupid, bloody, brutal, hateful business....

He tried to recollect what he'd said to El, something about the sacrifice being...worth it. Or something like that.

He couldn't remember. And it wouldn't help if he could, anyway. The rhythmic clatter of the train wheels seemed to hammer at him as his mind tumbled with the names and faces of the people whose lives were squandered in this ghastly madness.

Audrey, Irene, Aunt Gwen, Aunt Jane, Gram, Thomas, Mrs. Tuttle, Mr. Beaton, Gerry, Sarge, J.D., Cowboy, Wheeler, Davy, Grover, Murph, Clint, Charles, Harry, Keith...Dickie—I only saw him for a few seconds, but I'll never forget him, never stop dreaming about him. Sparky—I barely remember him, but I'll never forget him either. Even the people I never knew at all: Lee-Ann's father, Colin's father, Bob and Harry's parents, Barbara's brother, Alida's husband, Sarah's son, Antoinette's family, Miriam's relatives, Daphne's husband and daughters—their deaths have torn into my heart too....

His existence, his elegy, his epitaph: sadness after sadness, grief upon grief, all a bloody heap of waste and woe, all to no purpose save that of leaving him immured in desolation, flayed with bitterness, impaled by despair. He felt as if every death, every loss had punched a hole into the fabric of his life, again and again, leaving only ragged fragments and threads to hold his soul together. There was only one thing that would keep him from crumbling to bits entirely.

I need to see my father's face....

I need for him to come back!

Greycliff came into view. Andrew never thought he would love the sight of the place, but now it seemed to be the most beautiful building in the world.

Even before Alfred braked the car to a halt, Andrew was out the door and running up the steps. Grandmother Howard, looking tinier than ever, came out through the massive front doorway.

Andrew threw himself into her arms.

She gasped in astonished delight, then Andrew realized...He had never rushed into her embrace like that.

She looked up at him, smiled, hugged him again.

Now Andrew's mother was dashing up the steps, Jake by her side. Grandmother embraced her and asked, "Are you feeling well, dear? When I got your letter telling the good news, I feared that you might have taken ill while you were travelling across America. I remember how sick you were with Andrew."

"Oh, nothing serious—just a touch of tummy trouble for a few days," Andrew's mother smiled.

Andrew was peeved by his mother's dismissal of her (and his) ordeal.

Just a touch of tummy trouble? She was spewing her brains out for the longest time, and then had to be carried out of the car....

Grandmother gave Jake a hug, then ushered them all inside. Andrew couldn't help but look at the huge canvas of his uncles. Strange, they looked so young....

Mrs. Beaton met them and enfolded Andrew in a crushing embrace.

"My, Andrew—you've done a wee bit of growing, haven't you!"

Maria stepped forward, and Andrew's mother exclaimed over the wedding band on her finger.

"She's Maria McDermott, now," Mrs. Beaton said.

"Not Maria Annunziatta anymore," Maria laughed as she led them to the dining room.

"And there's a wee McDermott on the way," Mrs. Beaton chuckled, patting Maria's belly.

"My husband was demobbed last month," Maria said. "He is back in America, in Richmond, Virginia," Maria said. "I have to wait for passage to go to the United States, because all of the soldiers are going home first."

They were introduced to the new servants: Birdie, who was upstairs maid, and Felicity, the tween maid and laundress.

"There's help to be had," Grandmother said to Andrew's mother, after Birdie and Felicity had departed. "Felicity does most of the downstairs work. Dear Maria really needs her rest. Birdie and Felicity were in the Women's Land Army, so they've taken over the gardening too, as Alfred isn't able to get around very well now. We had a marvelous crop of vegetables this summer."

Andrew knew that Mrs. Beaton had tried to have a grand meal for their arrival; even so, it would have been considered poor fare in America.

After eating, he excused himself to go up to his room, citing tiredness from the journey. The truth was, he'd had as much of Jake's company as he could stand. In London, he had tried to avoid being by himself, knowing that Jake would certainly lay into him if he caught him alone. So he'd stayed around his mother as much as possible, which meant invariably tolerating Jake's company too. Now that he was at Greycliff, he could make use of its vast size and maze of rooms to keep his distance from Jake.

The tin soldiers and glum teddy bears still stood guard over the fraying books. Funny, he didn't sense any malevolent spirits lurking about, just a terrible sadness and desolation.

Jake's voice:

"Andrew—may I come in?"

Andrew kicked off his shoes and dove under the bedcovers.

Let him think I've collapsed from exhaustion....

"Andrew?"

He heard the door squeak open, heard footsteps, felt a hand on his back. He kept very still, then realized he wasn't even breathing. He drew a deep, slow breath, muzzled his face against the mattress.

The hand was withdrawn, and Jake's footsteps faded out the door.

Mercifully, Jake stayed for only four more days. During that time, Andrew went "ranging" through the Northumberland hills or ran to town. At Greycliff, he managed to stick close to his mother. When she took her late afternoon nap, he stayed by his grandmother's side or followed Mrs. Beaton around the kitchen. When Alfred finally drove Jake to town to catch the train, Andrew heaved a sigh of relief. Now he could sit down and do the task he'd been putting off, for fear of Jake finding him alone and awake. Not only that: He felt as if it would somehow be sacrilegious, or profane, for him to address himself to this particular matter when Jake was at such close quarters. It would be like trying to sing *God Save the King* while someone next to you was singing *Deutschland Uber Alles*.

His journey up to Northumberland had been filled with such dread and despair, but now he realized he shouldn't have been dismayed or surprised at it all. Even though he'd tried to prepare himself, the physical devastation of his country had come as a shock, and had no doubt precipitated his spiral into darkness. But even in the black night of his soul, he could still desire, crave, cry out; and that salvo of longing was slowly transforming itself into a redoubt of hope.

As soon as the car was out of sight, Andrew sat down at the desk in his room, took a clean sheet of writing paper from the drawer, and wrote:

Dear Sirs:

My father, Roger Hadley-Trevelyan, served in your squadron during the summer of 1940. He was shot down over the sea and never found, and I hope that he may have survived. Perhaps he was captured or spent the war years in hiding. If he has returned to England, he probably has heard that my mother has remarried.

If my father has been in contact with anyone in his squadron, I would like for him to know that my mother's husband has left for Alaska, and my mother and I are staying at Greycliff. I would very, very much like to see my father again. Please tell him that.

Thank you very much.

Andrew Hadley-Trevelyan

He addressed the letter to his father's squadron, and posted it the next time he went to town.

He expected that his mother would make preparations for him to go away to public school. Time passed, and she said nothing about the subject, so he decided to put forth a request to her. It was a preposterous idea, he knew; still, all she could do was to tell him that he was being silly and pack him off to boarding school.

He lingered at breakfast one morning, refilled his mother's tea, then took her hand in his and said, "We've spent so much time apart, and I was wondering...Could I stay here with you, go to school in town, instead of going away to boarding school? Just for this year, all right?"

He'd expected a gentle refusal, or tender dissuasion; he was astounded when her face broke into a broad smile and she embraced him.

"I think that's a marvelous idea, darling!"

So he was enrolled in the state school in town. It was strange, being in a classroom and not being pegged as the "kid who talks funny," though he'd unwittingly picked up some American expressions such as "Okay" and "Hi" which produced some raised eyebrows, but nothing more. He soon learned, or rather, relearned, to say "All right" and "Hullo."

Another bonus of going to school in town was that he could run to school and back every day, a total distance of twelve miles. Alfred said he would drive Andrew to town when the weather was nasty; however, Andrew never found the weather disagreeable enough to require being transported. Even a few raindrops made the run all the more refreshing. He always brought a change of clothes in his rucksack, and took a shower and changed at school before classes. His mother had gotten him an extra set of textbooks, so he wouldn't have to carry any books to and fro from school.

One day a red M.G. pulled along beside him as he was running to town. He had just passed the south road and had only a mile to go before arriving at school.

"Hullo—you're Alice Givens's son, aren't you?" The voice was pleasant and alert, even at this early hour of the morning.

Andrew slowed his pace, peered at the smiling face behind the wheel.

"I'm Dr. Blake. I remember seeing you once, but you were a wee one at the time. You probably don't remember me."

"Um—" Andrew slowed to a trot. "No, sorry—" He smiled, for the face was so much like his father's, pleasant and happy and kind. The hair was a lighter brown, but the eyes were gray.

"Would you like a lift?"

"No, uh—um—" Andrew kept his pace up, "I really—do—like—to run."

"Jolly good for you!" The car accelerated, then slowed.

"I say, if you'd like to have a bite to eat, you're welcome to stop at my place. It's two doors down from the hospital. My housekeeper, Mrs. Witherby, does up a fine breakfast, although you'll have to bear the company of my junior partner, Dr. Mead. He's insufferably pompous, as all new doctors are, but harmless, I can assure you."

"Oh...Isn't Dr. Baxter still practicing?"

"No, he's retired and living in a cottage out in the country. He keeps busy, though, growing roses and teaching English to German POWs. Anyway, why don't you stop by before going to school and have a spot of tea?"

Andrew consulted his watch. "Well, I'm running a bit late and I need to shower before school—"

"Tomorrow then? You can wash up at my place. I'll tell Mrs. Witherby to fix up a good breakfast for you. How does that sound?"

Andrew felt a heady rush as six miles of heart-pumping exertion burst into the sublime rapture he always felt at the end of a run.

"Sounds grand!"

It was only after awhile that he realized his grandmother had hired Birdie and Felicity more for their strong backs and love of the outdoors than for their domestic skills. The war might be over, but wartime shortages remained, and probably would for a long time to come. Grandmother Howard was never one to dictate policy, but it was clear that she preferred a full larder to polished woodwork. Birdie and Felicity were happy to oblige, and thus spent most of their time working the land. To them, dirt was a partner in production, not an enemy. Andrew helped out as much as he could in the afternoons and on weekends, and a few times stayed home from school to lend a hand when the workload was especially heavy. He found that he took to fieldwork quite well, and he realized that helping Lois in her garden had given him an aptitude and affection for gardening. He also discovered that he enjoyed the women's easygoing and sometimes ribald attitude towards him. The bonds of class fell away as the three of them worked their hands into the soil and hauled their bounty into Mrs. Beaton's kitchen. The women teased him about his love life, and speculated on which of their former colleagues in the Land Army might make a suitable match for him. Sometimes their excogitations were quite explicit, almost indecent. Despite Andrew's confusion in that sphere, he enjoyed their brash banter.

It did not shock him in the least to find his mother helping Mrs. Beaton in the kitchen (after all, she *had* been to America), but he almost fell to the floor one day in astonishment at the sight of Grandmother Howard hunched over the sink, washing and peeling vegetables and chatting amiably with Mrs. Beaton, as if she had been a scullery maid all her life. His grandmother sensed his confoundment, and smiled triumphantly as if to say, "No use protesting, young man. I've already made up my mind about this!"

Still, for everyone's "pitching in," the lion's share of the work was done by the former Land Girls. The war had turned a lot of things topsy-turvy, and not all for the worst. Andrew reflected how strange and wonderful it was that these two sturdy, saucy young women would keep Greycliff from want in the coming winter.

"Hullo—you must be Andrew!" A tiny, bird-like woman met him at the door. Though small in stature, her voice boomed like Churchill's.

"Andrew! Come in! We're just sitting down to breakfast." Dr. Blake's voice called from a room down the passageway.

Andrew followed Mrs. Witherby to a small dining room. Dr. Blake and another man, younger and freckle-faced, were seated at the table. The younger man was stabbing at a platter of sliced ham.

"My partner, Dr. Mead." Dr. Blake nodded at his colleague. "He received a pig a few months ago in payment for delivering twins; that's why we have such a grand breakfast. Dr. Mead, this is Andrew Hadley-Trevelyan, Mrs. Givens's son."

"Pleased to meet you, Andrew," Dr. Mead said.

Mrs. Witherby brought in a plate of scones, then sat down to eat.

"Your mother's having a baby soon, isn't she, Andrew?" she asked Andrew.

"Um, yes, she is." Andrew avoided her stare, reached for a scone. He buttered one, took a bite. "These are very good."

Mrs. Witherby glanced at Dr. Blake.

"You were in America during the war, weren't you?" Dr. Mead asked him.

"Only for two years. I went over in the fall of 1943. I was *here* during the Blitz." Andrew realized he'd sounded a bit defensive. He smiled at Dr. Mead. "It was all right, in America, I mean. But I'm glad to be back in England."

"What was America like?" Mrs. Witherby asked.

Andrew shrugged. "Oh, different."

"Well, I give you a lot of credit for having survived it," Dr. Mead said. "Imagine, a whole nation full of overpaid, over-sexed—

"That will be quite enough, Dr. Mead," Dr. Blake said.

"Are the women like that, too? Over-sexed, I mean?" Dr. Mead winked at Andrew.

"Really, Dr. Mead!" Mrs. Witherby exclaimed. "Andrew wouldn't know—he's only fourteen!"

"Darling—mail from America for you!"

As Andrew walked into the morning room, his mother, lying on the sofa, held out two letters for him. Andrew glanced at the return addresses: one was from *M. Kantor*, the other from *JJJ*.

"Thanks, Mum." He took the letters from her.

"Did you have a nice run, darling?"

"Very nice." He gave her a kiss on the cheek.

"I got a letter from Lois, also," his mother said. "She misses you terribly, and sends her love."

"I miss her, too. Well...I think I'll go upstairs and read these."

"We'll be having tea in a bit. Alfred's lit a fire in the dining room fireplace. It's getting a bit nippish."

"I'll be down straightaway."

He always liked to go through the kitchen and take the backstairs up to the nanny's alcove that adjoined his bedroom.

As he walked through the dining room, he saw that the fire was roaring. He walked over to it, then looked over his shoulder to make sure no one was looking.

He took Jereen's letter and threw it onto the flames.

That night, as he reread Miriam's letter, he ached to hold her in his arms.

The letter was brief, only one page, but he didn't mind. He knew Miriam was not one to waste time and paper writing about trivial things. The last fourteen words spoke volumes, and filled his soul with joy and longing:

I love you. I miss you. I can't wait to be with you again.

He got a letter from Lois the following week. She gave him the sad news that Lindy had died:

....some kind of cancer, the vet said. He didn't seem to be suffering, but was very, very weak—he could barely lift his head, and there was nothing the vet could do for him. I brought him home and made him a special bed in the corner of the kitchen. I stroked his ears, like you used to do, and he purred and closed his eyes and then he was gone....

More letters came from Jereen, two or three a week, at least. It had gotten to be an almost automatic routine: He'd see the *JJJ* on the return address, saunter into the dining room, and toss her missive into the fire.

He hated to see his mother's formerly slim frame taking on the shape of a barrage balloon. What was even worse was that she would every so often gaze rapturously at her protruding belly.

Bet she never did that when she was carrying me! After all, I was an accident, and they had to get married because of me....

He dreamt he was with Miriam and they were walking along the beach. It was night: All he could see was her face, lit with moonlight. He kissed her and felt that rapturous shock of delight course through him. She sighed with pleasure, then kissed him back, and he felt her body close to his...Now her mouth was pressing hard against his and he felt those wonderfully familiar stirrings again....

Then she spoke.

"I know you can't love me because I'm Jake's cousin...But we can be together...."

He drew back and saw that it was not Miriam in his arms, but Jereen.

Dr. Blake stretched out his fingers, then laid them against the table.

"So you think it's wrong to be in love with two different people?"

"Well, it is, isn't it?" Andrew was startled, but relieved, that Dr. Blake had seen so clearly through his dilemma.

It *was* wrong, wasn't it?

"So there are two different girls that you feel strongly about. It feels like love in both cases, but are your feelings for them exactly the same?"

"Sort of, but not really. Miriam was my friend for so long and things got sort of, um—"

"The friendship grew into love."

"Yes, I suppose you could say that."

"Happens all the time," Dr. Blake smiled.

"But with Jereen, it was different—I just saw her, and...and—"

"It was love at first sight."

"But that's impossible! How could I feel—how could I want her, when I didn't even know her, and she didn't know me?"

"But you *do* want her, and she *did* know you, in a way. You said you found the magazine article about you under her bed?"

"Yes, but what would that have to do with things?"

"Everything. She fell in love with you, or with the image of you, so to speak."

"But she didn't even *know* me!"

"She thought she did. Jereen felt as if she knew you because of the story about you. She built up in her mind an image of what she thought you were like, and fell in love with that image. And when she finally met you, that image became you, and so she fell in love with you."

"But that doesn't explain what I feel for her."

"Well, you're just responding to her feelings. That happens all the time, too."

"But it's not *right!*"

He was dismayed at his outburst, and knew he would have to explain.

"It's...it's just that this love at first sight...and her being in love with me because of the magazine article and all...and me feeling for her—"

"Is there anything, else, Andrew?" Dr. Blake asked gently.

He'd wanted honest answers from Dr. Blake, and realized now that honesty went both ways.

"She's Jake's cousin."

Dr. Blake regarded him thoughtfully.

"And you think it's wrong for you to like Jereen because she's Jake's cousin?"

"Well—I think he might be upset."

"Jake?"

"Uh-huh."

Dr. Blake cupped his chin in his hand. "Well, I haven't met Jake, so I wouldn't know. You know what I think—" He stared intently at Andrew. "*You're* upset with *yourself.* That might explain why you feel so strongly about her."

Andrew was thoroughly flummoxed.

"Wh—what do you mean? How can I feel so strongly about someone when I'm upset...upset about how I feel...about her, I mean?"

"Did you ever hear about Romeo and Juliet?"

"Shakespeare? What's that got to do with—"

"Forbidden love—probably the most potent aphrodisiac known to man."

"But it's not as if someone has forbidden us. I mean, I think Jake's upset with me, but he's never said anything, and no one's forbidden us—I mean, forbidden me...about us, I mean—"

"Oh, but someone *has* forbidden you."

"What do you mean—who?"

"*You.*"

Andrew grunted, folded his arms and stared at the tablecloth.

Dr. Blake cleared his throat.

"Would you like my honest opinion, Andrew?"

"Yes," Andrew said softly.

Dr. Blake seemed lost in thought for a moment, then he spoke.

"I may be looking at things through the lens of my own experience. You see, I was married."

"Oh, I'm sorry. I mean, was she killed?"

Dr Blake shook his head. "No, but the marriage didn't survive. She was from a, well, very modest background, and I think that she was more in love with the idea of being married to a doctor than she was in love with me. When the war came and I was away, well, in some cases, absence makes the heart grow fonder. In other cases—"

"Did she take up with a Yank?" Andrew's voice had an edge of bitterness.

Dr. Blake looked sharply at him, then said gently, "That's not the point."

"I'm sorry." Andrew saw the wounded look in Dr. Blake's eyes, and said quietly, "I'm sorry—I really am." He knotted his hands into fists, pressed them together.

Dr. Blake gave him an odd look, as if he were seeing beyond the silence and anger. He took a deep breath, then said, "I'm sure Jereen is a very nice girl, but it seems that your relationship with Miriam is built on the solid foundation of friendship. You said Miriam was the only one who was nice to you on your first day of school in America. She saw a lonely, frightened boy, and reached out her hand in friendship. I would think that that's a stronger basis for a relationship than for someone to fall in love with you because your picture was on the cover of a magazine."

He arrived home to find another letter from Jereen, which, as usual, went into the fire.

"Wonderful news, Andrew!" his mother said to him over tea. "I got a letter from Jake. He's coming at the end of November."

Andrew tried to keep his expression even.

Hell, hell, bloody hell!

He was running home one rainy Friday afternoon when he heard what sounded like a soft squeak. He jumped over the body of a gray tabby cat, crushed by a car or some other vehicle. The squeak was louder now. He stopped, and listened. The squeak came again, stridently sustained. The patter of the rain made it a little difficult to hear but Andrew started in the general direction from where it seemed to be coming from. He came upon a hollowed-out tree stump; peering within the cavity he saw the inert bodies of three gray kittens. The squeak came again, from the tangle of tall grass beyond.

Andrew listened closely, then heard the squeak again; only this time he could discern that it was a high-pitched meow. He worked his hands through the grass and parted the blades to reveal a tiny gray tabby lurching its way forward, meowing piteously.

He picked it up and saw that its eyes were closed; it couldn't have been more that a few days old. Its fur was draggled and sopping wet. It meowed again, and Andrew gently placed it inside his jacket. The creature squirmed and nuzzled at him. It must be starved, he realized.

Holding the bundle against him, he ran home and burst through the kitchen door.

"Mrs. Beaton—quick!" He withdrew the furry form from his jacket. "It's starving— it needs milk—something!"

"What a dear little thing!" Mrs. Beaton exclaimed.

"I heard it while I was running. Its mother was run over by a car—"

The kitten opened its mouth very wide and meowed loudly.

"Aye, it's a demanding one," Mrs. Beaton chuckled. She got a bottle of milk from the refrigerator, poured a little into a pan on the stove, and lit the burner. She gave Andrew an old dishtowel, and Andrew snuggled the crying bundle of fur in it. After a few minutes, Mrs. Beaton dipped her finger in the milk and said, "I think that's about right." She set the pan on the counter. Andrew got a spoon out of the drawer and ladled out a bit of milk. Holding the kitten in his arms, he tilted the spoon into its mouth. The kitten gulped the milk, then gagged and sneezed.

"It can't drink it!" Andrew cried. He dipped his finger in the milk and put it to the tiny pink mouth. The kitten sucked at his finger, then meowed loudly as the droplet disappeared.

"We need something to feed it with," he said.

Mrs. Beaton pursed her lips, shook her head.

"I know!" Andrew exclaimed. "An eye dropper! Do you have one?"

Mrs. Beaton rummaged through one of the drawers. "Ah—here's one!" she said, pulling out an ancient glass dropper with a brown rubber bulb. She handed it to Andrew. He quickly filled it with milk, gently placed it in the mouth wide open with hunger, and dribbled the milk in. The kitten sucked greedily and started to purr in a high-pitched thrumming sound.

Andrew filled the dropper again and gave the kitten another slow squirt of milk. He could feel the tiny belly bulging to taut fullness. After a few more dropperfuls, the kitten suckled a little less greedily, then curled up in a tight little coil of fur which had a silvery sheen in the light.

"I think he's a silver tabby," Andrew said.

Alfred came into the kitchen.

"Andrew's brought home a wee friend," Mrs. Beaton announced.

Alfred smiled. "What are you going to call him, Andrew?"

Andrew stroked the furry body.

"I'm going to call him Lindy."

Mrs. Beaton lifted up the tiny, tiger-striped tail.

"It looks as if *he* is a *she*," she said.

"Well, then—" Andrew thought quickly.

"Linda—I'll name her Linda."

Andrew made Linda a bed out of a shoebox lined with one of his old flannel shirts. As he placed the box near the stove, he wondered how Grandmother would feel about having this newcomer at Greycliff. To his joy, she was enchanted with the dainty feline, as was Andrew's mother.

"Arthur had a cat," Grandmother murmured, as she gazed at Linda.

"Arthur?" Andrew asked.

"Your uncle. He was the older one. William was the younger."

Andrew had never heard his grandmother speak of her two dead sons. Andrew's mother arched her eyebrows, and her mouth made a small *o*. Evidently, she had never heard her mother speak of the dead boys, either.

Grandmother looked at Mrs. Beaton and a sort of understanding passed between them.

Later, Andrew asked Mrs. Beaton what she knew of Arthur's cat.

Mrs. Beaton seemed a bit reluctant to speak.

"Did something happen to it?" he asked.

Mrs. Beaton stroked Linda's sleeping form as she spoke.

"Your grandfather was very upset when he found out that Arthur had a pet cat. He seemed to think it was...unmanly for a boy to like cats. He had the poor thing drowned, when Arthur went away to school." She shook her head sorrowfully.

"Arthur never forgave him for that."

Andrew brought Linda up to his room at bedtime. He put her box on the floor by his bed so that he could hear her when she awakened and needed to be fed, which was quite often that night. It was a good thing the following day was a Saturday, for Andrew couldn't have made it through a schoolday with as little sleep as he'd gotten. He snoozed most of Saturday, and Birdie and Felicity gave Linda her meals.

After he returned to school, Birdie and Felicity offered to take turns doing the night feedings. Andrew persuaded his Grandmother to give them the day off after they had been up the night before.

Andrew got in one afternoon just as Linda needed to be fed. As he was giving Linda the last dropperful of milk, his mother came into the kitchen.

"Andrew, something for you arrived in the mail today. When you've got Linda settled, come up to my room."

Andrew settled Linda in her bed and followed his mother upstairs. As he noticed how she lumbered up the steps, pausing for a moment on each rise to catch her breath, he ruefully remembered how she used to be able to dash up the stairs like a gazelle.

Plodding into her room, she pointed at a large cardboard box. Andrew looked inside, and saw the "England" quilt Lois had given him for his first Christmas in America. He lifted it up, ran his hands over the White Cliffs of Dover.

"Lois also sent your guitar, darling," Andrew's mother handed it to Andrew. "And all the things from the baby shower, too. Look!" She pulled out Mrs. Bock's log cabin quilt and another crib quilt with the Givens home appliqued on it.

"Isn't this *lovely?*" she exclaimed. "Lois made it—see? There's Lindy on the front porch."

Andrew looked: There was Lindy, embroidered for posterity on the front steps of white muslin. A bright yellow velvet sun shone above the pleasant house rendered in light blue corduroy.

"...and Fiona Casini crocheted this little cap...." Andrew's mother pulled out a minuscule white hat and gave it to Andrew. "And here are the dresses from Mel, and the booties Aunt Euelene knitted, and Sarah made these adorable little undershirts, and Maybelle made this snowsuit, and Lucia gave this beautiful satin teddy bear and here's diapers and bottles and all these precious little outfits—can you imagine that you were once this small?" She held up a tiny sailor suit.

"Yes, um—" Andrew clutched his England quilt and guitar to his chest. He smiled at them; better to let his mother think he was pleased to have his treasured possessions again, rather than upset to see all these wretched baby accoutrements.

"Well," he said, turning to leave, "I think I'll go practice a few chords."

The next afternoon he happened to be walking by the study when the phone rang. Felicity was polishing the conservatory floor and Andrew saw no reason to stand on convention and expect the servants to answer the phone every time. He sauntered into the study and picked up the receiver.

"Hullo?"

"Good day—" A male voice, firm and authoritative, spoke on the other end. "May I speak with Mrs. Alice Hadley-Trevelyan?"

"Uh—um, yes, just a minute." He dashed up to his mother's room, all the while wondering who this mysterious caller was, and why he was asking for Mrs. Alice *Hadley-Trevelyan.*

"Mum—phone for you."

His mother plodded down the stairs after him. He raced ahead to the study, picked up the receiver, said, "She's coming—just a minute."

Andrew's mother wheezed into the study, took the receiver from his outstretched hand, and sank onto the sofa.

"Hello?" she said.

The voice on the other end crackled. Andrew's mother said, "It's Alice Givens now— you see, I've remar—" She bent forward, pressed the receiver tight to her ear. A look of stunned astonishment swept across her face, and she spoke one word:

"*Alive?*"

Andrew's knees nearly buckled; he sat down on the edge of the sofa, almost afraid to believe....

My father's come back!

Chapter 51

*A*ndrew's mother listened, as if in a trance, to the crackling voice emanating from the receiver. She then nodded furiously, grabbed at a pencil and a pad of paper lying on the desk, and scribbled something on it.

"Yes, yes—I'll be down tomorrow," she said. "Yes...yes, thank you." She hung up the receiver, gazed ahead, then put her hands up to her mouth and closed her eyes.

"Mum—" Andrew touched her arm.

He's been found, hasn't he? Please, please don't be upset—everything's going to be all right....

His mother grabbed his hands, shook her head slowly, as if she still couldn't believe the news. He squeezed her fingers, trying to impart to her the joy he felt.

"Andrew—" She squeezed his hand back. "It's Jane. She's been found—*alive.*"

"A—A—Aunt Jane's been *found?*" His voice broke, and he hoped his mother would think that it was with astonishment, which it was, in a way. He had resigned himself to the idea that Aunt Jane was gone for good...and now *this!* It was like seeing someone rise from the grave.

How could she be alive? Why did she wait so long to contact us?

His mother took a deep breath, then spoke in a strained voice.

"Andrew, she's...she's not...herself. She was discovered in a concentration camp. They didn't know who she was, because she's suffering from some sort of—" She shook her head furiously, as if she didn't want to believe what she was about to reveal. "She's got some sort of amnesia. She doesn't recognize anyone, doesn't remember anything, doesn't even speak...."

Andrew threw his arms around her as she broke down.

"I'm just so glad she's alive, Andrew, but...."

"I know," Andrew whispered, as the anguish within him burst into a choked sob.

His mother wiped her eyes. "I said I'd come down to London tomorrow to...to see her...."

Andrew drew back, looked into her eyes brimming with sorrow and wonder.

"I'm coming with you," he said.

"...she was identified by another SOE agent." The doctor walked slowly down the hall, holding Aunt Jane's chart to her chest as if it were a shield. A nurse drew her aside and whispered something to her. The doctor nodded, grunted, and walked back to Andrew's mother. Andrew stood by his mother's side, to all intents and purposes invisible in this medical maelstrom.

The doctor lowered her eyes. "In interviews with other prisoners, there was something said about medical experiments, but the information was rather garbled. It couldn't be established if your sister-in-law was a victim of these experiments, whatever they were, or only witnessed them. We couldn't detect any physical injury. Well, she was brought here, and it so happened that one of the nurses here is married to your late husband's armorer, and she recognized the name. We tried contacting your husb—pardon me, your late husband's relatives, but, um...."

"Yes, they're all gone," Andrew's mother said.

"We made inquiries at the estates near your late husband's home, and one of the neighbors remembered your maiden name and that you were from Northumberland. It took a bit of tracking, but we managed to find you. Sorry, we didn't know you'd remarried. I hope that your new husband won't be upset about you seeing to your late husband's sister."

Andrew's mother shook her head in fierce protest. "No, of course not! He—" She glanced at Andrew, as if suddenly remembering his presence. "He won't mind at all," she said quietly.

The doctor walked into a narrow corridor, eyed the numbers on the doors as she walked past them. She slowed, then stopped at a door.

"There's a chance she might recognize you, but please don't be upset if she doesn't. She didn't remember any of her associates in SOE, but then, she didn't know them all that long. Perhaps seeing family members might—" She shrugged. "Might jostle her memory. There's no way of telling; we've seen other victims of this sort of thing in the same state as your sister-in-law. It's a condition that we are unable to...well, we're at a loss as to how to treat it. Perhaps being in a familiar environment, with people she knows...."

Andrew's mother put her hand on Andrew's shoulder. "Andrew is Jane's nephew. He's her only living relative."

"She might not recognize me, Mum. I've changed so much. She'd probably remember you."

The doctor pursed her lips, then spoke in a quiet voice. "She may not know either of you. I want you to be prepared for that."

Andrew's mother nodded. The doctor opened the door.

The sunlight silhouetted the thin, fragile figure sitting in profile in a straight-backed chair.

"Jane," the doctor said softly.

Andrew took a few cautious steps forward, until he was standing in front of his aunt. "Aunt Jane, it's me—Andrew."

She fixed him with an expressionless stare.

"Jane," Andrew's mother whispered.

The doll-like eyes gazed at Andrew's mother for a moment, then wandered, then stared again at the blank wall ahead.

Andrew's mother stepped in front of her, then knelt and clasped her hands.

"Jane, it's Alice. Andrew and I came to take you up to Greycliff. Remember, you were there—just after Andrew was born."

Aunt Jane seemed to look through her, as if she were air, and gave no sign that she had even heard her voice.

Andrew knelt beside his mother, then reached up and touched his aunt's face.

"Don't worry, Aunt Jane. We're going to take you home."

Upon hearing about Aunt Jane, Daphne offered to accompany them up to Greycliff. The doctor gave them last minute instructions:

"She is able to take care of herself, to an extent. She seems to be on the level of a three or four year old. She can get dressed and undressed, see to bodily functions, and wash herself. Give her a small basin of water and a washcloth. Don't ever try to get her into a bathtub—she nearly killed one of the nurses who tried to bathe her. Showers frighten her, too. She eats very little, and hoards her food. We had to feed her intravenously when she first arrived; she was only seventy pounds. Other than that, all I can say is be patient with her, talk to her, tell her about the past. Perhaps a word, an old photograph might jog her memory. Don't pressure her to remember, just act as if you expect that she'll come round. Even if she doesn't seem to be acknowledging you, just talk to her. Perhaps on some level, she's taking it in. I think she needs to feel safe, first. This state seems to be a kind of protective shell. I'll give you the name of some doctors in Northumberland whom you can contact should you need to."

The ride to Northumberland was uneventful. Andrew's mother booked a first-class compartment and seated Aunt Jane so that she could look out the window.

"The scenery might do her some good," she reasoned.

Aunt Jane stared out at the countryside and towns racing by as if she were looking at a blank wall; no comprehension or recognition flickered in the china-blue eyes. Daphne seemed especially drawn to her, and gently placed her hand on her arm. Daphne said nothing but her silence was comforting, all the same. After awhile, Andrew tried talking to his aunt about happier times in France and at Armus House, but he might as well have been talking to a mannequin. He fell silent for awhile; then Daphne asked him about America. As he answered her questions, he found it easier to chat about his life there. He remembered how his mother had told him that she had, in a way, been aware of his presence and entreaties when she'd been in a coma, and he hoped that Aunt Jane was hearing him on some level.

Alfred met them at the station and drove them to Greycliff. Andrew's mother went in first to inform Grandmother and the servants as to what to expect, then led Aunt Jane inside.

"Hello, Jane dear," Grandmother said, as if Aunt Jane were returning to Greycliff after a short holiday. "I'll put you in the room you stayed in when you were here before, when you and your mother visited just after Andrew was born."

Andrew was glad to find out that Aunt Jane's room was next to his. He took her hand and led her on a tour through the house. Linda scampered after them, alternately nosing into new places, biting Andrew's heels, or chasing her tail.

The doctor was right: Aunt Jane didn't eat very much. She usually consumed only about a third of her meal, then carried her plate up to her room. When Andrew went in to bid her good night, he saw no sign of the uneaten meal. The next day, though, Birdie reported that it was under the bed and what should she do about it? Andrew's mother told her to leave it there. It was Maria's idea to leave some food out on the dining room table at all times: biscuits, fruit, scones, bits of smoked salmon.

"If she knows the food is always there, she might not feel she needs to save it all the time."

Andrew hated to go back to school and leave his aunt, but was assured by his mother and the servants that they could watch over her as well as he could. When he went to Aunt Jane's room to kiss her goodbye, he found Linda curled up on her lap. He took his aunt's hand and stroked it along the furry back, then held her finger to Linda's throat so that she could feel the gentle purring.

"See—Linda likes to be petted." He gave his aunt a kiss on the cheek. "I'll be back this afternoon, and we'll have tea together—all right?"

He met with Dr. Blake, as usual, and told him about Aunt Jane. Dr. Blake couldn't shed any more light on her condition.

"I suppose what you're doing is probably the best thing," he said.

All day in school, Andrew wondered if somehow, some way, a miracle might greet his arrival at home. He bounded up the front steps, hoping against hope that his aunt might greet him with her arms opened wide and her face shining with remembrance.

"Your aunt is in her room," Grandmother said as he walked into the front hall. "She seems to prefer being there. Why don't you bring her down for tea? Your mother's still taking her nap. I'm afraid she exhausted herself talking to Jane all morning."

Andrew went up to his aunt's room and found her sitting in the wing-backed chair by her bed. Linda was curled up on her lap, asleep. He went over to Aunt Jane, gave her a kiss on the cheek.

"So, you've been keeping my cat company, haven't you? Come on—" He gently picked Linda up and took his aunt's hand. "Let's go down for tea."

He'd gotten into the habit of practicing his guitar when he got home from school. Linda seemed to enjoy these musical sessions; she would sit at rapt attention on the sofa, facing him while he sat on the windowseat beneath the bay window in his room. Andrew thought it might be a good idea to include Aunt Jane in his audience, so he led her to his room and sat her on the sofa next to Linda. Aunt Jane sat, still and silent, while Andrew practiced his chords and played one tune after another.

Perhaps, some way, some how, my music will help her to find her way back....

"Andrew—package from Barbara," his mother called as he came through the dining room doorway. She shook the box and soft rustly sounds issued from within. "More fan mail, from the sound of it."

Andrew took the box from her hands.

"I also got a letter from Jake today," his mother said. "Business is fairly booming: Lots of people moving up to Alaska, so he and Kaz have been quite busy. Still, he'll be able to get the time off to visit us next month. L.S. just turned eighteen and got his commercial license, so he can help out with the work now. He's making the short hops in the Fairchild; he also flies co-pilot in the Dakota. One can fly a Dakota alone, but it's nice to have another hand with the landing gear."

Aunt Jane was already seated at the dining room table. Andrew went over to her, kissed her cheek, and asked her how her day had been. He was greeted with a blank stare and silence, as usual, so he sat down next to her and gave her a running commentary on the fare for tea.

"Mrs. Beaton's made a carrot flan again, and raisin cookies—sorry, biscuits. I can't help talking in American, so you'll just have to bear with me."

"Jake's going to stop off in Nebraska first." Andrew's mother poured Aunt Jane's tea. "Then he'll go to New Jersey, to celebrate—now what is it again? That holiday with all the food."

"Thanksgiving," Andrew said glumly.

"Right!" Andrew's mother took a bite of carrot flan. "Then he'll come here."

The knot in Andrew's stomach quashed his desire for any food. He pushed his plate away, took a sip of tea, and opened the package from Barbara.

"A marvelous collection of pretty stationery," Andrew's mother observed.

"Hmmm...." Andrew sifted through the pastel and floral-decorated envelopes. A few of them were heavily perfumed, and the scent wafted through the room.

The knot in his stomach untangled itself as an idea took shape in Andrew's mind.

I have another month before Jake arrives.

Yes...that should be more than enough time to get things all arranged....

After doing his homework he took a few sheets of blank paper from his desk and set to work.

I'll write three, four letters a night, and a score or so this weekend. That ought to be more than enough....

He picked out a letter from the box and read it. The writer was Laurena, from San Diego, California. He chewed his pen for a bit, then wrote:

Dear Laurena,

Thank you for your letter. It was very nice, and I hope you'll write to me again. My real name is Andrew Hadley-Trevelyan, and I'm back in England now. I miss America ever so much, and hope to be able to go on holiday in the United States someday soon.

I visited California this past summer. My mother and her husband flew some planes from the East coast out to California, and I got to see the Pacific ocean for the first time. It's ever so grand....

He urged Laurena to write him soon, then wrote three more letters: to Donna in Boston, Massachusetts; to Carlene in Anchorage, Alaska; and to Diane in Sommerville, New Jersey. It was a good thing he had visited or flown over so many states in his travels back and forth across America, for he could slip in a word to that effect in the

801

letters he wrote, pointing out that he'd been over or through or near the particular state in which the letter writer happened to live.

He posted the letters after school the next day, then ran home, exhilarated and invigorated as he contemplated his scheme working out as planned.

He arrived home to find a letter from Miriam. He tore the letter out of the envelope as he ran up the backstairs and plopped down on his bed to read it. He could wait to greet Aunt Jane—not that it would take very long to read Miriam's letter, or matter much if it did.

He almost shouted with glee as he scanned Miriam's letter.

Perfect!

Good old Miriam! She really knows how to come through!

Of course, he would wait until Jake arrived before divulging the contents of Miriam's letter to his mother. It would be just perfect to have Jake be a witness to what he planned to say.

If he has any intention of tearing into me because of Jereen, this will certainly quash his wretched little notion.

He was feeling so cocky that he spoke boldly to Grandmother Howard after supper that night. His mother had retired early again; it seemed that she could barely get through the day, even with an afternoon nap.

That sodding bastard's not around to see what he's done to her...a few seconds of pleasure for him, and she's suffering the consequences!

He scooped out a serving of Portman pudding for his grandmother, smiled as he handed it to her, then dished out a helping for Aunt Jane. No problem that she was here; he might as well have been talking in Greek for all that it mattered.

He took a helping of pudding for himself and ate a few bites. Then he looked at Grandfather Howard's portrait at the far end of the room and shook his head, as if pitying the old man.

"I wonder how he'd feel, knowing my mother had married an American."

Grandmother Howard gave him a curious glance; then a slow smile spread across her face.

"Your mother wasn't exactly one for doing things to please her father. She was seated in the very chair you're sitting in now when she announced to your grandfather that she was already married to your father, and that you were on the way."

Andrew choked on a mouthful of pudding.

"I thought when my parents got married she was—I mean, my grandfather was at their wedding, wasn't he? I saw him in their wedding photograph."

"No, that ceremony was just for show, to mollify your grandfather. Your parents were married a few days after your mother's eighteenth birthday."

"You mean I wasn't—um—they were married in *April*, then?"

His grandmother nodded and smiled. "In a Giant Moth—at five thousand feet!"

Mrs. Beaton came in with a plate of sliced apples. She chuckled at grandmother's declaration and added, "And you, young man, got your start in a Giant Moth, too!"

"*Mrs. Beaton!*" Grandmother's eyes bulged with mortification, then she giggled. "I don't think this is a proper topic for Andrew's tender ears, Mrs. Beaton."

"Oh—*tch!*" Mrs. Beaton exclaimed. "Andrew's been to America—he no doubt has a fairly good idea of what it's all about, don't you, Andrew?"

Andrew held his napkin up to his mouth, hoping that would hide the blush he felt creeping up his cheeks.

"Aye, young man," Mrs. Beaton continued, "You got your start up there—" She pointed her finger towards the window, at the sky. "It was when your mother and father went on holiday to Eastbourne, the summer after they were married. I can still see your mother sitting right there, proud and defiant, telling your grandfather that you were on the way. When she said that you'd been conceived a mile above the earth in a Giant Moth, I thought your grandfather was going to have a stroke!"

Grandmother smiled at Mrs. Beaton, as if bidding her to go on.

Mrs. Beaton beamed with mirth. "And when your grandfather said he would disown her if she didn't break off her marriage and, well, send you off after you were born, she marched right out, with just the clothes on her back."

"He came round, though," Grandmother added.

"Aye, he did. But he didna smile at the wedding."

"But everyone *else* did," Grandmother said.

At breakfast the next morning, Andrew gave his mother a hug.

"What's that all about young man?" she laughed.

"Oh...nothing," he said.

Letters from America arrived, two or three a day, but Andrew didn't open them. Since his mother always took a nap in the afternoon and the mail was usually delivered while she was asleep, she wouldn't have any idea as to how much mail he got every day.

He stashed the letters in the bottom drawer of his desk, to await Jake's arrival.

Andrew's heart hammered as he ran home. Jake would have already arrived at Greycliff.

Not to worry—everything's going to go according to plan.

He dashed in through the back door. Mrs. Beaton was beating the clotted cream.

"Andrew! Just in time, you are. Everyone's sitting down for tea—Jake just arrived."

"Why don't you tell them to start without me?" Andrew said. "I'm going to change first. I'll be down in a sec." He bent down, rubbed Linda's ears, then ran up the backstairs. After changing into a pair of jeans and a sweater, he got the stack of letters out of his desk drawer and sauntered down to the dining room. As much as he tried to brace himself, the scene that greeted him was unnerving and loathsome. At the head of the table sat his mother, ensconced in a lushly cushioned chair like some bloated faerie queen. Jake, by her side, played the toadying consort, gazing upon her swollen form with possessive arrogance. Andrew fumed. Jake's sole claim on her devotion was his propensity to rise to whatever occasion promised the most in terms of future rewards; now the manifestation of his lecherous and self-aggrandizing proclivities infested Andrew's mother like some renegade tumor. The creature within her was Jake's royal flush, his promise of wealth and stature, his prerogative to challenge what was Andrew's birthright.

Andrew fought back his disgust and nodded at Jake.

"Hullo, did you have a nice trip?"

"Yes, very nice," Jake replied.

Andrew tossed the stack of letters by his plate as he sat down. His mother's eyes widened.

"Oh, just some letters from some girls in America," Andrew said. He took the top envelope and slit it open with his finger.

His mother glanced at Jake, then looked back to Andrew.

"That's wonderful, darling. Are these the girls who have written to you because of the magazine article?"

Andrew nodded. "Mostly. I'm also writing to Miriam, too. In fact, I got a letter from her the other day, and she's planning on coming here next summer."

His mother arched an eyebrow. "*Here?*"

"Well, she's going to Switzerland, actually. Her cousin Eva is living there. She found one of her sisters, Hannah. Hannah was in a concentration camp, and one of the other women there inherited an estate in Switzerland from her uncle, and so Hannah and some other women who were in the concentration camp are living there now, and Eva is too. Anyway, Miriam is going to spend the summer with Eva and Hannah, but she wants to come here, first." He spooned some clotted cream over his bowl of plums, ate a few bites, then said, "I really *do* miss her—we were *such* good friends. Anyway, she'll be stopping off in London and she can take the train up here. And then we could go on to Switzerland together." He said the last sentence very casually, as if, surely, that would be the most natural thing to do.

His mother stared at him, then carefully laid her fork by her plate.

"Andrew, your going to Switzerland is entirely out of the question. You're coming to Alaska with me for the summer."

"*Alaska!*" Andrew's voice dripped with disdain. "That's *ridiculous!* I mean, I'm going to be going to public school here next fall, aren't I? It wouldn't make any sense to go all the way off to Alaska, then come back here. On the other hand, Switzerland isn't very far. Miriam and I could fly there in a few hours and—"

"Andrew, distance is not the point." His mother glanced at Jake. "We're your family, and—"

"You're going to have the baby—you don't need me." He didn't look at his mother as he grabbed a scone. "I'd really rather be with Miriam." He buttered his scone, took a bite, brushed the crumbs off his plate. He dared not meet his mother's gaze.

"Andrew," she said sternly. "You're talking nonsense. I will *not* have you going off to Europe! It's a dreadful place—millions and millions of homeless, starving, desperate people wandering around. It's positively *ghastly*—"

"We're going to *Switzerland*, Mum. They weren't at war, you know."

"That's *not* the point, Andrew. You're only a child, and you're not going to—"

"It's because she's Jewish, isn't it! If she weren't Jewish you wouldn't mind—"

"It would make no difference if she were Christian, Hindu, or tree-worshipping Druid!" His mother's voice was shrill with outrage. "You are *not* to go traipsing across the continent with a young lady—"

"You didn't see anything wrong with dumping me in America, did you?" Andrew hollered. "I was all by myself—"

"You were with Jake's parents and it was for your own good. There was a war on—"

"Well, the bloody war's over, didn't you know?"

"Andrew—"

"Hitler shot himself." Andrew narrowed his eyes at his mother and spoke in a low, even voice. "It was in all the papers—"

"Andrew, that will be *quite* enough—"

"No, it *won't* be quite enough!" Even as he shouted at his mother, Andrew was dismayed that his playacting had gotten out of hand. Still, he couldn't stop himself: He'd unwittingly dislodged a few pebbles of resentment which had turned into avalanche of fury and recrimination.

"I am *not* a child, and you *can't* order me around anymore! I've had bloody enough of being dragged all over this bloody world, and I won't stand for it anymore! I'll stay here then, with Aunt Jane. She's my family now!"

He heard a sharp intake of breath from his mother. Against his will, his eyes met hers, and he saw the hurt and bewilderment and fear in them. She clutched at Jake's arm, looked desperately at him, like a drowning swimmer reaching out to a rescuer.

Her turning to Jake was the one thing he couldn't bear.

I've mucked it up...I've mucked everything up....

He got up, stumbled out of the dining room, through the kitchen, and up the back stairs to his room.

As he was lying on his bed, Linda came to him and curled up on his chest. Her tail lashed against his nose. He turned her around, so he could stroke her ears and watch her face, content in sleep.

There was a tap at his door. Terror knifed through him.

What if it's Jake? He'll lay into me for sure now....

Another tap.

He'll scream his bloody brains out at me. Well, I'll scream back—he can't order me about either!

"Andrew?" His mother's voice.

She opened the door.

Andrew sat bolt upright. Linda dug her claws into his chest.

"Ow—Linda, sorry—" He gently disengaged Linda's claws from his skin, then saw that his mother was standing over him. She'd been crying, he could tell.

"Oh, Mum—" He threw himself into her arms. "I'm sorry—I didn't mean it...."

She embraced him and broke into sobs.

"Oh Andrew—" She drew back, gazed at him tenderly, then hugged him again. "You're not a little boy anymore."

He hugged her back.

"I still need you," he whispered.

She nuzzled her face into his shoulder and sniffled. Then she gazed at him, her eyes red-rimmed and brimming with tears. "I just want what's best for you, you know that, don't you?"

"I know. I'm sorry for everything. I know it was best for me to be in America, and it wasn't all that bad—"

"Oh Andrew—"

"It really wasn't."

"Yes, I know." She smiled at him. "It looks as if you've got some very dear friends."

He nodded. "I was thinking—I could just meet with Miriam here, and then come to Alaska, all right?" I would so like to see Kaz and L.S., and be with you, too, until I have to go back to school. Maybe I could stop off in New Jersey. I'd like to see Lois and Mr. G.—I miss them ever so much. And Lynette and Sarah and Shannon and Collie and Miss Fitt, also, and perhaps Lee-Ann and Mac might be able to come down for a visit...."

She hugged him again.

"That sounds like a good plan to me."

"...so when Mom went to Nebraska last month, she was going to stop off in Kansas and see Debbie and Mrs. Ferguson." Jake ladled a spoonful of peas on his plate. "A few days before she arrived, Debbie's grandmother was killed in an car accident. Sarge's brothers were all there for the funeral, and they didn't know what to do about Debbie. None of them were married, or even in a permanent living situation; they were all going to college. They were going to send her to a cousin in Arizona who was a widow with six kids of her own. Well, Mom just fell in love with Debbie, and it didn't take much to convince Sarge's brothers that Debbie would be much better off with her and Dad. After all, they'd already seen the magazine story about Andrew." Jake smiled at Andrew.

"And they're in the process of adopting her—isn't that wonderful, Andrew?" Andrew's mother beamed at him.

"Oh, that's grand!" Andrew exclaimed. He was glad that there were no aftershocks from his outburst.

And I did manage to convince Jake that I want nothing to do with his cousin. He wouldn't dare lay into me now....

"Tell Andrew the other good news, Jake," Andrew's mother urged.

"It's your doing, too, Andrew," Jake said happily. "Mom and Dad are also adopting Harry and Bob. When their sister's husband came home, he wanted to go to college. The government's got this G.I. Bill that gives American servicemen money for school— Sarge's brothers are on it too. Well, anyway, Gert was going to send the boys back to

England because they couldn't live with her and her husband at college, and her mother-in-law was moving down to Florida. The boys were pretty upset about leaving. Harry came to work one day almost in tears. It seems they were going to be sent to live with an uncle whom they'd stayed with after their mother was killed. Guy was kinda rough on them—"

"Harry said his uncle used to 'knock 'em about,' didn't he Jake?" Andrew's mother said.

"Yeah—" Jake shook his head as he passed a bowl of suet pudding to her. "Poor kids—for them, coming to America was about the only good thing to happen to them, what with the war and all. Well, Dad told Mom about the boys having to go back to England, and Mom just about burst with excitement. She said the boys could live with her and Dad. They're in your room, Andrew, and their adoption is in the works, too. Mom is just in seventh heaven—" Jake grinned at Andrew. "She was desolate after you left and now she's got a houseful of younguns!"

"And it's all because of you, Andrew." Andrew's mother beamed at him. "You knew Sarge, and you hired Harry, and now Jake's parents have a family again."

"Yeah, they do." Jake smiled as he took out his wallet. He pulled out a snapshot and handed it to Andrew. "Our family portrait."

Andrew looked at the snapshot: It had been taken on the front porch of the Givens home. Jake and Mr. Givens stood on either side of Lois, who held Debbie in her arms. Harry stood in front of Mr. Givens, Bob in front of Jake. Lois's face seemed about to split with joy, and everyone else was all smiles, too. Andrew peered at Debbie.

She looks so much like Sarge....

"And that's not all," Andrew's mother said. "Harry's got the store going 'gangbusters' as they say. Tell him, Jake."

"Harry sort of took over as store manager; he puts in just a few hours a week, actually. Dad wants him to concentrate on his schooling. But business is booming, to put it mildly. First of all, Harry persuaded Dad to expand. The hardware store next door was moving out to Route 22, and Harry convinced Dad that he should buy the building. So now the pharmacy is three times the size it was. Harry got all the business records together so that my Dad could go down to the bank and get a loan, then he designed the new store and hired a carpenter to do the work."

"And a good job he did on that score," Andrew's mother proclaimed.

"Yeah," Jake said. "Harry got a couple of carpenters to give bids on the remodeling and Dad, being the typical thrifty New Englander, was going to go with the lowest bid. Harry did some checking, and discovered that the guy didn't have any credible references. As Harry told my dad, 'You'll get a bargain if all you want is a lot of talk.' The next lowest bid came from a carpenter who did good work; Harry got Mom to drive him around and check out the jobs he'd done. Harry told Dad he'd be better off going with this guy, so Dad took his advice. And Harry was right. Mr. Bischoff, the hardware store owner, hired the guy Harry had warned my Dad not to hire to do the interior work on his new store. Bischoff had nothing but problems. The guy either didn't show up for work or showed up drunk, and that put the opening of the store off by two weeks. And in the retail business time is money, and Bischoff lost bags of it. And on top of everything, the workmanship was terrible. Bischoff is going to have to have most of the work done all over again." He shook his head. "Anyway, our guy did a terrific job. You wouldn't recognize the pharmacy—it looks like a palace compared to the old place."

"And Harry's managing all the ordering, too," Andrew's mother said.

Jake nodded and, between mouthfuls of suet pudding and stewed apples, talked of Harry's amazing business acumen.

"Dad had always ordered from a regular supplier. The guy did all right for Dad, I suppose. He'd come in to the store, see what was needed, and have it shipped. Dad really didn't have the time to see to all that, and Maybelle was too busy running the store to deal with it either. Well, Dad's supplier was retiring, so instead of going with his replacement, Harry checked into things and found he could really save ordering directly from the wholesalers. Like he could get candy for half the price by ordering it in twenty pound sacks from the candy company. Lots of other stuff too." He smiled and took a sip of tea. "I went out to lunch with Harry and a guy from a toothpaste company, and it was amazing to see that kid wheel and deal and get a good price on a case of toothpaste. Well, Harry's got all the ordering and inventorying down to an exact science. He's even taking some business and bookkeeping classes at school, and set up a new accounting system for the store. He hired a couple of new boys to do the delivering and some cashiers and clerks from his business classes. Maybelle's retiring, and the store needs a lot more than one clerk, now—lots more. Our banker stopped by our grand opening, and told my Dad that he'd better watch out—Harry's going to make him a millionaire."

"Oh yes, the grand opening!" Andrew's mother exclaimed. "Look, Andrew—" She got up and took a newspaper from the china cupboard and handed it to Andrew.

It was an issue of the *Courier News* with Jake's picture on the front page. He had been photographed standing at the cash register in Mr. Givens's store. The title of the accompanying article read: *Battle of Britain Pilot Turned Salesclerk at Local Pharmacy.*

"I helped out with the grand opening of the new store," Jake said. "One of my friends from high school is a reporter for the *Courier News*, and he wanted to do an article about me because I was in the RAF and in the Battle of Britain and all. I didn't know why he thought that would be an interesting story. I mean, there were lots of guys in the Battle of Britain—"

"Not many Americans though," Andrew's mother said.

Jake shrugged. "Well, maybe about a dozen of us—I don't know for sure. Anyway, I said I'd be happy to do the story if he'd put in a mention about the opening of our new store. I figured might as well get some free publicity out of it. Well, it was a mob scene at the pharmacy that day—Dad did more business in that one day than he usually does in a month! We just about sold out the store—good thing Harry had ordered a whole bunch of stuff. I worked the cash register all day, met lots of old friends from school, saw lots of new faces too. Central Jersey is really growing—lots of building going on, loads of people settling in and starting families. Harry figured that we ought to take advantage of all that growth."

"Bob's done his bit, too," Andrew's mother added.

"He's too young to work at the store," Jake explained. "But he found out an Army surplus store was selling a load of metal cases really cheap, and he got this idea of buying them up and outfitting them as first aid kits. Mom got some first aid booklets from the Red Cross, and Bob filled the cases with bandages and tape and all sorts of stuff from the store. He even thought up a slogan: 'Get one for your home, and one for your car.' The kits went like hotcakes—we sold over a hundred at the grand opening. Bob added on fifty cents to the cost of the cases and the supplies as his own profit, so he made a pretty tidy sum on it all. Well, between Harry's shrewd management and Bob's first aid kit project, business has been so good that Dad's hired a part-time pharmacist to help out and give him a few days off a week—one of my friends from Rutgers, in fact. Now Dad's got weekends and Mondays off, and he'll have a few weeks' vacation in summer, too. It's good to see him take it easy and enjoy life after all those years of working so hard. He and my mom have been able to go places and do things with the boys and Debbie. In the spring, Dad's going to take Harry and Bob to a Yankees' game— the boys are really excited about that. And they all want to come up to Alaska next summer, too." He scraped his plate and remarked to Andrew's mother, "Those boys are something. Wasn't it Hitler who said that England was only a nation of shopkeepers?"

"That was Goebbels," Grandmother said.

"Well, the Nazis were right about one thing," Andrew's mother laughed. "We *are* a country of shopkeepers, aren't we?"

Jake chuckled. "The Germans should have known not to tangle with a nation of shopkeepers—better to have the shopkeepers on your side!"

After supper, they sat in the morning room and listened to the BBC for awhile. Linda started playing with Jake's shoelaces. He picked her up.

"You look like someone I knew," Jake said, holding her up to his eyes. He laid her in his lap and tickled her tummy. She writhed in ecstasy, then curled up and went to sleep on his lap.

"She's a nice cat, Andrew," Jake said.

Andrew nodded. He was irked that Linda had taken so readily to Jake.

"Well..." Andrew stood. "I'll take Aunt Jane up to her room. She looks a bit tired."

He took his aunt by the hand and led her up the stairs.

After taking Aunt Jane to her room, Andrew brought his guitar in and played for her awhile. When her head started to nod, he led her to her bed and tucked her in. That done, he went back to his room and did some homework. He thought his mother would come upstairs after awhile; when she didn't, he decided to go downstairs and bid her goodnight. As he approached the morning room, he heard Jake's voice.

"...and we found out that my cousin Eric, Uncle Oak's son, was dead. He'd been captured on Bataan, survived the Death March, then was sent to work on the Burma railway. The Japanese put the survivors of the railroad on a transport to Japan, and the transport was torpedoed by an American sub. Eric and most of the other prisoners were killed. God, after having gone through Bataan and the railway...."

Jake's voice faded; Andrew's mother murmured something. Jake spoke again.

"Eric and I were pretty close—we were the only Givens grandsons. Uncle Lee and Uncle Reed had all girls, so Eric and I used to hang out with each other when the family got together at Thanksgiving. Well, I found out from Uncle Lee that my father and Oak had had a falling-out of sorts—over me. Evidently, Oak had thought my father had done the wrong thing by going off to college against my grandfather's wishes, and he told my father that he'd gotten paid back for his wrongdoing—by my running off to join the RAF. My dad didn't speak to Oak for almost six years because of that. But when my father heard about Eric he went up to see Oak, and they made their peace. I'm just so glad things have turned out so well for my father, after all he and my mom have been through."

"Don't be so hard on yourself, darling." Andrew's mother said. "You weren't all that terrible a son."

"Well, I know I gave my dad a hard time, but there was something else I found out about. One day I dropped in at the store to see about having lunch with Dad. Maybelle said he'd already gone out to lunch, so I walked down to the coffee shop to catch up with him. He wasn't there, so I started to walk back to the store. I happened to look across the street and saw Dad walking out of the florist's shop, with a bunch of flowers in his hands. I thought they were for Mom, even though I've never known him to buy flowers for her. But then he got in the car and drove off—in the opposite direction from home! He didn't see me, and all I could think was—God, I didn't even want to think it. So this taxi's coming down the street and I flagged it down and jumped in and yelled, 'Follow that car!' Sounds like something out of a bad movie, but I was just sick at the idea of Dad seeing...someone, even though I couldn't believe it. Well, Dad headed south of town, and then he pulled into the cemetery. I was so relieved, but then I started racking my brains trying to think of whose grave he was going to lay the flowers on. No one from our family is buried there. His car stopped, and he got out and went over to this headstone and put the flowers down. I got out of the taxi and went over and...and—"

"What darling?" Andrew's mother asked.

"I looked at the headstone. There were three names on it: Eugene Givens, born 1923, Joel Givens, born 1925, and Grace Givens, born 1926. The boys died a few days after birth; the girl was born dead. I looked at my father, and he put his arms around me...."

There was a long silence, and Andrew thought he'd better go away in case his mother and Jake should walk out. Then Jake's voice came again, soft with wonder and anguish.

"I had two brothers and a sister I never knew about! Eugene was born the summer we moved to Scotch Plains, when I was four. All I remember of that time is being so mad at my father for moving us away from New Brunswick; I had no idea my mother was expecting. In 1925 my parents started sending me out to Nebraska for the summer, so that's why I didn't know about the other two—they were born while I was away. God, it must have been a horrible thing for my parents, to lose three children like that! My father told me that Sarah was a great help to my mother when all this happened. You know, Alice, for the first time, I really understood my father. No wonder he tried so hard to get me to follow him in the business—I was the only one left...."

Silence again, then Jake's voice, husky and strained.

"I asked my father if he knew...what happened to them. He said the boys turned yellow and died, and the girl was born already dead. There was something wrong with their blood, the doctor said. My father said this thing ran in my mother's family. My mother's aunt, the one she inherited the house in New Brunswick from, had nine children die from it. Not everyone in Mom's family had it, though. One of her sisters had her first child okay, the second one died, but the third and fourth were just fine. And I was okay—whatever affected my brothers and sister didn't affect me. I called Sam Major about it. He's one pretty sharp doctor and I figured he'd know something. He told me it sounded like Rh Disease. They just discovered all about it a few years ago. It's a kind of blood type—"

"Like Type A and Type B and Type O?" Andrew's mother asked.

"Sort of—but this is a different system entirely."

"Dear me, why do they have to make things so complicated?"

"Well, it's not the scientists who make things complicated—they just figure things out. The disease has been around forever but they just found out what causes it. If the mother's blood is negative for this Rh factor, and she's pregnant with a child that is positive for the factor, the mother's blood attacks the baby's blood."

"So you must be negative for this Rh factor if you didn't get this disease."

"No, I'm positive. The first child is usually okay; it's when the baby's blood mixes with mother's at birth that the problem starts. The next child is affected if it's Rh positive. Sam contacted our family doctor and asked him to order some tests on us, and that confirmed it. My dad and I are Rh positive. Mom is Rh negative, and has the antibody against the Rh factor. That's what killed my brothers and sisters. I was really worried that it would somehow affect our child, but Sam said that the fact that it runs in my family wouldn't affect the baby. There would only be a problem if you're Rh negative. Do you know if anyone in your family has had this problem?"

"No, but then I didn't have any sisters or aunts or cousins. I should think not, though. My mother had my brothers and me and we didn't suffer from this thing."

"Well, all the same, I'd like you to ask Dr. Blake about it, and have him order some blood tests. It would really put my mind at ease."

"All right. I have an appointment tomorrow. Why don't you come along? Dr. Blake is ever so nice, and he said he wanted to meet you."

"Okay."

"I was just thinking...."

"What?"

"Your parents lost two sons and a daughter. I know you can't ever replace a life with a life, but they do have their family back, in a way—three sons and a daughter."

"You're right, they do. I've never seen the two of them so happy. And the boys and Debbie are great kids. It's nice to have brothers and a sister after so many years of being an only child. I told Dad if he ever needed me to come back to New Jersey to run the store, for any reason, that I'd be happy to do it, but he told me not to worry. Harry's got the store set up so it can run itself, practically. It's amazing! That kid is so happy managing the store, and I couldn't stand the thought of having anything to do with it. And my Dad wants the boys—Debbie too—to go to college, and Harry and Bob are just ecstatic at the thought. Harry wants to study business and Bob wants to be a pharmacist. In England, they would have to leave school at the age of fourteen; college would be out of the question for them. When I think of how I hated college, it makes me feel kind of ashamed."

"You're a skilled pilot, darling. Don't think that isn't worth something."

"Well, I'm just glad that everything's turned out so great—for everyone. I can't get over it—Dad even brags to his friends that I'm a bush pilot! I never imagined, not even in my wildest dreams, that things would turn out so well. And I have you, too—I can't wait when we're all together. You can't imagine how much I miss you."

"Oh yes I can!"

Andrew pressed his ear to the door. Sighs, giggles, and low moans emanated from within.

God stone the crows! What are they going to do in there—fuck all over the floor?

He stomped up the stairs.

And her—seven months pregnant! Don't they have any decency?

As he reached the top of the stairs, something his mother said to Jake hit him like a punch.

Dr. Blake is ever so nice, and he said he wanted to meet you.

Andrew groaned aloud.

Bloody, bloody, bloody hell!

I should have kept my big mouth shut. Now Dr. Blake is going to tell Jake everything!

No sense stopping by Dr. Blake's today, Andrew thought. Today—or ever!

As he ran home from school, he saw two figures walking through the meadow behind Greycliff's old stable. He cut across the front field, and as he rounded the back side of the stable, he saw Jake, holding Aunt Jane's arm as they walked along. He could hear Jake's voice but couldn't make out what he was saying.

What does he have to say to her anyway? And why doesn't he leave her alone?

As he strode across the meadow, his fury increased.

He won't be happy until he's taken everything from me. He took my mother, then my cat, now Aunt Jane....

"Andrew!" Jake turned and smiled at Andrew. "I was just taking your aunt out for a walk. I thought the fresh air might do her some good."

Andrew wanted to lash out at him, but thought better of it.

After all, Dr. Blake probably told him how I feel about Jereen. He'd just tear into me....

He glared at Jake as he took his aunt's hand.

"Come on, Aunt Jane. I'll take you home."

"Andrew!" Dr. Blake dashed across the street to the schoolyard. "You haven't stopped by the last few days—I was wondering how you were."

"Oh, I'm fine," Andrew replied. "It's been getting darker in the mornings, so I start out a little later, when there's more light. I have a bite to eat and a quick shower at school."

"Well, do stop by sometime—perhaps after school, then. I usually break for tea in the afternoon about this time."

Andrew nodded noncommittally, then broke into a run.

For the next few days, Andrew managed to keep his distance from Jake, and avoided being alone as much as possible. He'd bring his aunt into his room when he was studying and sit her on the sofa facing the front bay window in his room. There was a lovely view of the front lawn and of the distant hills to the west, and the setting sun made a goldeny haze which Andrew thought was very peaceful. The front drive arched a graceful parabola from the main road and, even though the shrubs lining it were badly in need of pruning, it still had a grandeur and loveliness that Andrew found soothing. His grandfather's words rang in his ears:

Someday, this will all be yours....

It *will* be mine, Andrew thought. *All* mine. And if Jake thinks any of his wretched offspring will inherit so much as a clot of ground of this place, he's got another thing coming.

If only Jake had chosen to leave on a weekday, Andrew would not have had to endure his company just before his departure. However, Jake had decided to go to London on Saturday morning so Andrew was forced to bear his presence at breakfast. He knew his mother expected him to be appropriately cordial in making small talk with Jake and wishing him safe journey. At least Jake did most of the talking.

"L.S. really wants to see you again, Andrew. He asks about you all the time."

"His mother and sisters are staying with him and Jake and Kaz," Andrew's mother added.

"In fact—" Jake reached for another scone. "I gave Savannah and the girls a lift from Nebraska. They'd traveled by bus from Daniel, and my folks had invited them to stay the night. It turned out to be at the same time I was flying the Gooneybird out to Alaska, and I'd planned to stop in Nebraska for the night, too. Savannah and the girls were going to continue on by bus all the way to Seattle, and then go by boat up to Anchorage, where Kaz was going to fetch them. But since I was flying the plane up to Kelso anyway, I persuaded them to sign on as passengers. We had a wonderful flight: beautifully clear weather all the way, and the scenery was just incredible! Savannah and the girls were just amazed at the sight of Mt. McKinley."

"Savannah made the most darling baby things and sent them with Jake," Andrew's mother said to Andrew. "Four flannel sleeping gowns with matching receiving blankets. Two of the gowns and blankets are grey-blue, with the RAF insignia embroidered on the gowns, and the other two sets are navy blue, with ATA wings. You ought to come up to my room after breakfast and see them, Andrew. Oh, and Kaz sent some little fur booties—they're just adorable!"

Andrew grunted as he swallowed a mouthful of porridge.

"Well—" Jake stood and gave Andrew's mother a kiss on the cheek. "I've got some last minute packing to do. You have another cup of tea—I'll be right down."

Andrew poured his mother a cup of tea as Grandmother spooned some more porridge into Aunt Jane's bowl. Aunt Jane was eating a little more heartily, and she no longer squirreled away food in her room.

If only her mind could be as healthy and whole as her body, Andrew thought. He added a dollop of jam to her porridge and stirred it in. He smiled at her as she ate, hoping against hope to see a flash of remembrance in those dull eyes.

Perhaps someday she'll come back....

He heard Jake descend the stairs.

Good! In a few more minutes he'll be gone....

Jake walked into the room. He went to Aunt Jane, bent over, and gave her a gentle hug. Then he helped Andrew's mother to stand and walked with her into the front hall. Andrew and his grandmother followed them.

Mrs. Beaton, Maria, Birdie, and Felicity were lined up in the hall, and they each wished Jake safe journey. Grandmother gave him a hug. Jake then turned to Andrew.

Andrew stepped back and nodded.

"Safe journey."

Hope you go down in flames....

"Thanks," Jake smiled. "You take care of yourself, Andrew."

The sight of Jake's back going out the front door was the sweetest thing Andrew had seen in a long time. No matter that his mother was going with Jake to the station.

As long as she's saying goodbye to him, it's just fine with me!

Andrew breathed a silent sigh of relief as the door closed. He decided to go into the morning room to listen to the BBC.

Nice to be alone...to relax, without worrying about that wretched sod catching me alone.

As he turned on the radio he heard Alfred start the car.

The most beautiful sound I've ever heard....

He stretched out in the easy chair, put his hands behind his head and closed his eyes.

"Andrew?"

At the sound of Jake's voice, Andrew lurched upwards, like a plane doing a short field take-off.

Jake took a step towards him. Andrew noticed that he wasn't smiling.

Oh God, oh God, oh God...He's going to lay into me, after all!

Chapter 52

*J*ake took a step towards Andrew.
All right, let's have it out then....

For someone who was about to deliver a thrashing, Jake seemed oddly unsure of himself. He bit his lip, hesitated, then reached into his breast pocket.

"I stopped in Nebraska before I went to New Jersey." Jake withdrew an envelope and held it out to Andrew. "Jereen wanted me to give this to you."

Andrew was too stunned to move, or even speak. Jake continued to hold the envelope in his hand. After what seemed like a long, long time, he placed it on the table by the door, turned, and walked out.

Andrew stumbled towards the table, tore open the letter and started reading it. He was halfway through the letter before he realized he hadn't even thought to destroy it. He could almost feel Jereen standing by his side as he read her words:

Dear Andrew,

I've written so many letters to you, and I've hoped and prayed that you would answer me. Every day when I come home from school I hold my breath as I sort through the mail, hoping to see a letter from you, and I try not to feel despair when there isn't. As you read this now, know that I am thinking about you, for hardly a minute goes by when you are not in my thoughts.

I wish that things could have turned out better between us. I know that you're angry with me because of what happened. Perhaps I shouldn't have come to you that morning, but I couldn't help myself. I couldn't bear the thought of you being upset with me, and I thought you were, but I just made things worse. I'm sorry!!!!!

I'm not sure of this, and let me know if I'm wrong—PLEASE!!!!! I believe you're upset about things because you think that Jake is angry with you for what happened. He isn't!!!!! He was upset with me, because he knew how I feel about you, and he knows I'm responsible for what happened. While you were taking a shower, he told me that if he ever thought I'd do anything to hurt you, he'd protect you. He said, "I'm Andrew's stepfather first, your cousin second." If you don't believe me, ask him!!!!! Andrew, he saw us together on the sleeping porch that morning. He woke me, because he didn't want anyone else to find us. Don't you think he would have made a scene if he'd been mad about things? Or said something to you later about it? Well, did he? He cares about you, Andrew—can't you believe that?

I wish you could love me. I wish you could realize that you wouldn't be betraying your father by loving me. I wish we could work past what happened, and somehow start over again. I used to think that my mom marrying Wayne and my being a part of the Jay family was the most wonderful thing that ever happened to me, but I'd give it all up if we could be together. I'd give up <u>everything</u>, if I could only be with you, even for a minute. Please write—every day that I don't hear from you, I die a little more.

> Love, love, love
> Jereen

Andrew closed his eyes and groaned.

I'd always thought that falling in love would be a wonderful thing, like it was with Mum and Dad. Why did things have to get so bloody mucked up with me?

He refolded the letter and put it in his pocket. He'd destroy it later. He knew he couldn't bear one more thing right now, and even the act of throwing Jereen's missive on the flames would shatter him completely.

He was sure of one thing, though: Anything that caused this much pain couldn't be right.

Even though it was Saturday, he ran to town anyway, hoping that his exertion might somehow exorcise the demon he felt within. He pushed himself past what he knew his body could endure, and felt as if he were racing against time: He didn't want to meet up with his mother returning from town.

One word, one look from her—I'd die, just die, but I want to do that anyway....

His chest hurt horribly, and his lungs screamed with pain, but he didn't stop.

Maybe my heart will just burst...then I won't have to feel this anguish.

He walked back to Greycliff and found a pile of mail waiting for him. Hidden within the pastel and scented letters with American postage was a plain, white envelope bearing a British stamp and a return address in London.

His heart pounded as he dashed up to his room. Once within, he tore open the envelope with shaking hands. He sank down on the bed and read the handwritten note.

Dear Andrew,

Your letter eventually found its way to me. I was in your father's squadron, and served with him during the Battle of Britain. I would like very much to meet with you. I will be travelling to Scotland for Christmas holidays, and will stop by and see you on the afternoon of 23 December. If this is inconvenient for you, please write to me and I'll try to arrange another time.

I look forward to meeting you.

> Len Kenyon-Wright

He tried to suppress his ecstasy as he sat down to supper that night. His mother gave him a penetrating look, though.

"I had a very nice run this morning." He passed her a platter of Egg and Rice Loaf. She took a portion for herself, then gave Aunt Jane a serving.

"So Jake is coming here for Christmas?" Grandmother asked Andrew's mother.

"If all goes well. He and Kaz and L.S. have been quite busy, but he ought to be able to get the time off."

With every silver lining there's a cloud, Andrew thought. Still, at least Jake wasn't angry with him, though Andrew still found it hard to believe that Jake would be on his side about things. He passed the plate of sardine fritters to his mother.

Why would he care so much about me?

When he went to lay out his clothes for the next day, he thought he ought to destroy Jereen's letter.

He'd thrown his clothes in the corner when he'd changed to go for his run. He picked up his trousers, thrust his hand in one pocket, then the other.

The letter wasn't there.

Maybe I dropped it somewhere while I was dashing through the house, Andrew thought.

He made his way down the backstairs and grabbed a torch from the kitchen.

No sense attracting attention to my quest by turning on all the lights....

He walked slowly through the kitchen, dining room, and morning room, sweeping the beam across the floor. Since he couldn't even remember whether he'd dashed up the backstairs or the main stairs after reading Jereen's letter, he made a thorough sweep of the front hallway and both staircases. He was near despair as he walked down the upstairs hallway to his room when he spied a folded piece of paper on the linen chest outside Aunt Jane's room.

He picked it up and saw to his relief that it was Jereen's letter.

But how did it get on top of the chest? If it had fallen out of his pocket, someone must have picked it up and set it there.

Who?

Perhaps one of the maids put it there...or maybe Aunt Jane.

As he walked to his room, he tried to push back the awful realization that began beating down the door of desperate denial.

It was Mum....

She knows!

He groaned into his pillow, turned over onto his back, stared at the ceiling for the hundredth time.

So....she knows. So what of it? If she confronts me with it, I'll tell her that Jereen means nothing to me. I'll joke about all the letters I've gotten from girls who want to "take me round the world," then reassure her that just because a girl throws herself at me doesn't mean I'm going to reciprocate.

817

Saturday, December 22nd.

His mother and grandmother wanted to go to town to do some last minute Christmas shopping, and Mrs. Beaton realized she was out of nutmeg and rice for the Norfolk Pudding, so Alfred took them to town. Birdie and Felicity had been given the week off to visit with their families for the holidays, and Maria was napping. So Andrew had the house to himself, more or less. Aunt Jane was home, of course, but her presence was innocuous.

After recovering Jereen's letter, Andrew had waited for the other shoe to drop, but his mother had said nothing. His worry over the situation gradually faded as his anticipation of Len's visit grew. He tried to contact Len in London, but was told there was no telephone number listed under that name.

He was in the morning room, listening to the BBC, when the phone rang. He picked up the receiver.

"Hullo?"

"Overseas call from Jacob Givens for Alice Givens," a female voice piped.

"She's not here."

He heard some muffled thunks and clicks, then the operator's voice came again. "Is there anyone there who can take the call then? I'm told it's urgent."

Bloody hell! Why does he have to ruin a perfectly nice day!

"I'll take it."

More thunks and clicks, then Jake's voice punctuating an annoying barrage of static:

"Hi Andrew—could you please give your mother a message?"

Andrew let a few seconds go by, then curtly said, "All right."

"Thanks...I wasn't sure if I could get a flight out, but I did. I'm in New York, and I'll be flying out this afternoon and arriving in England tomorrow morning. I'll try to get a sleeper up to Northumberland, so I hope to be in Christmas Eve morning. If I can't swing that, I'll take a day train and arrive there in the late afternoon or evening. Tell your mother that, okay?"

Andrew didn't answer.

"Andrew—did you hear me?"

"Yes, I did." Andrew said the words slowly, as if he were talking to a dim-witted child.

"Um—uh, okay. Okay, then. Well, um, tell your mother I'll be coming in on BOAC Flight 51 and I'll be in the day after tomorrow, okay?"

"All right."

"And, um, tell your mother, uh, tell her...."

Who do you think I am—your damned messenger boy?

"What?" Andrew snapped.

"Uh—just tell her I'll see her, then. I'll see you all for Christmas, okay?"

"Mmm...right."

"Yeah, okay...um, bye."

Andrew slammed the receiver down.

He gave the message to his mother when she returned home.

"Flight 51," she mused. "We were married on May first. Did he say anything else?"

"No, just that he's coming in Christmas Eve."

He awoke the next morning just as dawn was breaking across the sky.

In less than twelve hours I'll know where he is...He's waiting for me...He just needs to find out that I really do want to see him....Maybe I'll see him on Christmas day—he was always one to make a delightful surprise out of everything!

He knew that Grandmother expected everyone to attend Christmas services in town, but he was afraid that he would miss Len if they lingered. So he pleaded that he hadn't sleep well the night before and he thought he might be coming down with something. He pointed out that he could just as well remember the spirit of Christmas without infecting a church full of worshippers.

After everyone had left, he went up to his room, wrapped himself in a blanket and perched himself in the windowseat, so he'd have a full view of any car coming up the drive. He tried to pass the time by reading, but he just couldn't get his mind focused on the book in front of him.

A few hours later, a car came down the road, but it was only Alfred bringing everyone back from church. Andrew went downstairs to greet them. His mother furrowed her brow in worry and pressed her hand to his forehead.

"Darling, if you're not feeling well, I'll have Maria bring you up some lunch. Maybe we should have you see Dr. Blake. As a matter of fact, we ran into him at church and he asked how you were doing. He's on his own for the Christmas holidays; Dr. Mead is visiting his family in Brighton. We could invite Dr. Blake here for lunch and have him take a look at you—"

"Oh, no, Mum, I'm fine now. I think I dozed a bit while you were away, and I'm feeling much better now."

Andrew hoped that his mother would take her usual afternoon nap, so that he wouldn't have to explain Len's presence to her.

Grandmother wouldn't nose into the reasons for Len's visit, so as long as his mother was asleep he wouldn't have to do any explaining whatsoever.

We could go to town perhaps...I'm sure Len would understand why we have to keep things secret from Mum.

His mother lingered at lunch though, and Andrew was afraid that Len might show up early. He finally took her hand and said, "You look a little tired, Mum. Why don't you rest for awhile?"

"Andrew—you worry so!" she giggled as she followed him up the stairs. She paused, placed her hand on her belly. "I'm not sure if this little one's going to let me get any rest. He's kicking up a storm—here—" She took Andrew's hand and placed it on the gigantic mound. Andrew felt a little jab from within.

"Boy or girl, I think I'm going to have a prizefighter," she laughed.

Like to give the little bugger a bloody good thump to quiet him down....Should have expected that Jake's child would try to muck things up....

He led his mother to her room, pulled back the covers for her, and drew the drapes shut. "Get your rest now," he said gently.

She smiled at him, then closed her eyes.

Perfect!

He went into his room and settled himself on the windowseat.

What if he doesn't come? What if he comes after Mum wakes up?

He closed his eyes, and pressed his hands to his face to try to calm himself. After taking a few deep breaths, he opened his eyes.

There was a car in the drive.

He raced downstairs, flung open the front door.

A man, casually dressed in brown wool trousers and a tweed jacket, walked up the steps and nodded at Andrew.

"Len?" Andrew asked.

The man smiled. "Hullo, Andrew."

Andrew knew it would be impolite not to invite Len in and offer him some refreshment.

"Here, come inside," Andrew whispered, holding the door open. "Please be quiet—my mother's sleeping."

"Oh dear, I was hoping to see her," Len said.

"Um, well, perhaps when we get back." Andrew realized that he would have some explaining to do, since he'd written that Jake and his mother were apart.

Later, though.

He smiled at Len. "Would you like some tea?"

"Oh, no thank you. I just got a bite to eat in town. I was thinking we might go for a walk."

"Oh, that's *perfect!* I mean, that sounds like a very nice idea. I'll go get my jacket, all right?" Andrew sprinted into the kitchen, grabbed his jacket from the peg by the back door, and returned to the front hall. As he put his jacket on he said, "I tried to contact you in London, but your telephone wasn't listed."

"Oh, sorry—I live with my sister. The phone's under her name."

Andrew opened the door. "There's a very nice walk to the top of the hill."

"Andrew?"

His mother stood at the top of the stairs. Andrew's heart sank.

"Alice?" Len's eyes widened as Andrew's mother maneuvered her grotesquely swollen form down the stairs.

"*Len!* I didn't know you were coming."

"Well, aah, Andrew wrote to me—that is, to the RAF, asking about his father... Len glanced at Andrew, then looked back at Andrew's mother. "Alice, is everything all right?"

"My stepfather's in Alaska, flying as a bush pilot," Andrew said quickly. "My mother's here because of the—the baby and we're all going out to Alaska this summer."

Andrew's mother descended the last few steps, all the while staring at Andrew.

"Le— Len was going to tell me about Dad." Andrew looked quickly at Len. "We were just going out for a walk."

Len glanced at Andrew, and his eyes flashed with understanding. "Yes—ahh—to chat about old times, about Andrew's father."

Instead of mollifying Andrew's mother, the whole exchange seemed to alarm her even more. She glanced sharply at Andrew, then at Len.

Damn! Now I've got a whole lot of explaining to do!

Andrew's mother lurched over to Len and put her hand on his arm.

"Alice—is anything wrong?" Len asked.

She looked at Andrew again. Andrew felt a chill go up his spine.

Suddenly, her expression changed. Her features softened, and she smiled at Len, then at Andrew. Her face seemed to glow with a serenity Andrew had never seen before.

"No, everything's fine," she said. "Why don't you two go for your walk? Take your time—I'll have tea waiting when you get back."

Thoroughly bewildered, but enormously relieved, Andrew tugged Len out the door. It occurred to him that he should reassure Len that everything was all right between his mother and Jake, but he didn't want to get his foot any further into his mouth than it already was. When they were a good distance from the house, he said, "My father."

Len looked down at the ground, took a deep breath, then looked at Andrew. "You're very much like him, Andrew."

He turned away and continued walking. Andrew followed him until they were at the top of the hill. As he looked out at the sea, Len quietly said, "He worried about you so." He continued looking into the distance.

"Five and a half years ago." Len shook his head. "It seems like yesterday. Your father came back to our squadron at the end of June, just before the Germans began their attack on England. I came back two weeks later. I had dislocated my shoulder when I crash-landed during the evacuation of Dunkirk, so I was out of action for over a month."

"Things were rather quiet during that time, after Dunkirk, or so I've heard. Hitler thought Britain would 'realize the hopelessness of her position,' so he tarried for over a month as he sent peace feelers out. That month gave us a blessed respite: a chance to get aircraft into production, train pilots, get ready for the attack we knew would come when Hitler realized we weren't going to capitulate to him."

"During that time, though, the morale in Fighter Command was low. We'd fought hard over Dunkirk and lost eighty pilots there, but many of the soldiers and sailors believed we didn't do anything to protect them. One of our chaps was shot down and made his way to the beach to be evacuated. When the soldiers found out he was a pilot, they groused that for all the good the RAF was doing he might as well be on the ground. Trouble was, they couldn't see us through the thick black smoke over the port, and often we were miles away, shooting down the dive bombers and bombers before they got to the beaches. Still, it stung us to hear the reproach, 'Where *was* the bloody RAF?'"

"That's what this soldier said, when my mother and I were in a restaurant," Andrew said. "I got in to a fight with him—"

Len grinned and put his hand on Andrew's shoulder. "Yes—your mother told your father about that. He was ever so delighted and he told us all that you had struck a blow for Fighter Command's honor. It cheered us up, it did."

"In early July, the Luftwaffe started bombing the Channel convoys. The ships weren't important; Goering wanted to draw our fighters into battle, to destroy them. We knew what the game was about. The politicians, though, thought we should keep the Channel open at all costs—for morale."

"That's stupid," Andrew said. "Why didn't they ship all the stuff by rail?"

Len smiled. "Wish we'd had people with your sense in power then. Park and Dowding knew they had to keep Fighter Command from being decimated. We'd lost over three hundred pilots in the battle for France and at Dunkirk, and were down to only eleven hundred pilots. Fighter Command "borrowed" pilots from Bomber and Coastal Commands, and Dowding got Churchill to release pilots from the other services—the Fleet Air Arm and Army Cooperation. We got some Polish, Czech, and French pilots, too. We couldn't afford to lose any more men in silly skirmishes. And the Channel patrols were exhausting. Even though it didn't seem as if Fighter Command saw much action during that time, it was a bloody tiring and nerve-racking business flying patrol. You never knew when a 109 would come out of the sun at you. Park kept in close touch with his squadrons in 11 Group. He got an earful from your father and from our squadron leader, probably from all the other squadron commanders as well. They finally managed to get the politicians to see sense. The convoys were suspended in early August—just in time."

"The Germans launched "Eagle Day" on August 13th. Hitler was determined to annihilate the RAF, so the Luftwaffe attacked our airfields. Goering thought he could destroy Fighter Command's defenses in southern England in four days, and completely wipe out the RAF in a month. He was a bit cocky on the timing, but he damn near came close to demolishing Fighter Command. It was men like your father who made the difference."

"Your father was too old to be a squadron leader, but he was the one who really led us, trained us, got us in to fighting form. Our squadron leader was a young chap, but at least he had the sense to let your father take charge of things, though your father never intruded on the S.L.'s role. They worked well together: Your father had the knowledge, the experience, the wits as to what air combat was all about. He'd been in France; he knew what we were up against and wanted us to have every advantage. He knew that our tactics were twenty years out of date, and saw to it the we got rid of those absurd Fighting Area Attacks and stupid vics and those ridiculous wingtip-to-wingtip formations. He had us reharmonize our guns to 250 yards—we'd had them at 400 yards, and at that distance it wasn't easy to hit a bomber, let alone a 109. 'Get in close, and you can't miss,' your father used to say. He also told us we had to learn from the enemy: He had us fly 'Fingers-Four,' like the Germans."

"Fingers-Four?" Andrew asked.

Len held out his right hand and spread his fingers. "Four aircraft: Flight leader—" he wiggled his middle finger. "His wingman—" He wiggled his index finger, then his ring finger and pinkie. "Element leader, his wingman—all spaced about two hundred yards apart and staggered in height so they could maneuver more easily, and be able to spot the enemy instead of having to watch each other's wingtips. Your father drilled us, trained us, hammered us with advice." Lens eyes took on a faraway look, as if he were hearing a voice out of the past. "'Keep turning, never fly straight and level for more than a few seconds in an engagement, never dive or climb in front of a 109, never fly with wet boots—your feet'll freeze to the rudder pedals. Wear your goggles and gloves, always keep a sharp lookout—beware the Hun in the sun. Get in as close as you can, hit hard, get out.' Your father bought rear-view mirrors and had them installed in our Hurricanes, also bought us silk scarves so we wouldn't chafe our necks as we looked around for Jerry planes."

"At least we had RDF, Radio Direction Finding—you probably know it as radar. It gave us a decisive advantage, for we knew when the Jerries were coming. We only had about a twenty minute warning at most, though—barely enough time to get a fighter up to altitude to intercept the German planes. But it was enough. Goering also made the mistake in putting too much faith in planes that proved to be absolute disasters in the Battle of Britain: the Stuka and the ME-110. The Stuka was slow and very vulnerable in a dive—a piece of cake to shoot down. We had quite a few successful "Stuka Parties," as we used to call them. The ME-110, though fast in level flight, was very unmaneuverable, and we could pot them without any trouble either. But the ME-109—*that* was our worry. It was faster than the Hurri, and had a better rate of climb than even the Spit. The 109 had fuel-injection too, so the engine didn't quit in a dive. And the Germans had more of them than we had Hurris and Spits. Even after the Stukas and 110s were withdrawn from the Battle, the Luftwaffe, with its bombers and 109s, still outnumbered us by about three to one."

"By the end of August, things were desperate. It wasn't that we were short of planes; Lord Beaverbrook was in charge of aircraft production and he had the factories cranking fighters out pretty quickly. You'd lose a Hurri or a Spit, and you'd get a new one right away, spanking new and better than the one that was shot down. But the pilot sent to replace the man that was lost—if you were lucky enough to get a replacement—didn't have the experience, the skill to survive. The operational training time was cut from six months to two weeks. Some of the chaps came to us with just ten hours in a Hurricane, and their level of gunnery skill was dreadful. Some pilots had fired their guns in practice only a few times—they couldn't hit a bull's arse with a fiddle. One of our replacements drove in one day—didn't even get his things out of his car when we were scrambled. He was shot down, lost at sea, with his things still packed in his car."

"Churchill liked to paint a glowing picture of that time—called us undaunted and unwearied. Undaunted—hell! We were always overwhelmed and outnumbered: It always was four against twenty, eight against fifty, a squadron against a hundred Jerries. We knew Dowding was inflexible on the matter of keeping reserves in the North and Midlands. Though he was pressured by the politicians and others in the RAF, he would not allow the defenses in the rest of England to be weakened. It was a wise policy but, at the time, it seemed as if there were always so many of the enemy, and so few of us— at least Churchill was right about that! By that time we were losing about one hundred and twenty pilots a week—about ten percent of our total force, and the training schools were only turning out half as many replacements. It was only a matter of time before Fighter Command would simply run out of pilots. And it was the loss of experienced pilots that really took a toll. In one week, we lost eighty percent of our squadron commanders."

"The more experienced pilots that were left had the worst of it. We were nursing the newcomers, flying more sorties—four, five, sometimes six a day. Even when we weren't engaging, the constant strain of keeping a lookout, knowing that every second might be your last and you'd probably never even see the Jerry that hit you was enough to shred our nerves to pieces. Even when we weren't flying and were waiting to be scrambled, we didn't have a moment's peace. Any second the phone could ring, the signal for a scramble. We were so twitchy, we'd jump at the sound of bicycle bells."

"As for being unwearied, we were so bloody tired all the time that we were like walking dead men. We were lucky if we got a few hours sleep a night. Often we slept out under our planes, or in the cockpits. One morning in the mess, one of our pilots keeled over in a dead sleep—his face fell right into his plate of scrambled eggs. Funny thing about it was, we were all so punchy with exhaustion no one even raised an eyebrow. Another time, your father landed after an engagement. He taxied his plane to a halt, but didn't get out. I ran over, thinking he might be wounded, and found him fast asleep in his seat."

"By the end of August, our squadron was pretty well decimated. We'd lost more than half our pilots—Barky, Roddy, Ginger, Doc—they were all killed. Doc was shot to death as he parachuted down—the Germans had no compunctions about machine gunning our lads dangling from their parachutes. They knew, as well as we did, that it was the pilots that mattered, and they were determined to eliminate as many of us as they could."

"Roddy had to bail out over the Channel. He died of hypothermia or drowning—there wasn't a scratch on his body when it washed up on shore a week later. Ginger and Barky were shot down in flames, and died of burns. Our airfield was under constant attack—no one was safe, even on the ground. Two of our new pilots—I don't even remember their names—were killed when the lorry they were riding in was strafed."

"At the beginning of September, we were ordered up north to rest and re-form. It was Dowding's policy to rotate the squadrons between groups, sending the battle-weary squadrons in 10 Group and 11 Group in the south up to 12 Group in the Midlands or 13 Group in the North. Ideally, a squadron was to stay in the front line for about six weeks before it was moved to a quieter area so that replacements could be trained and the veterans given a rest. Our squadron had been in the thick of things for over two months and we were long overdue for a break—the few of us who were left were utterly exhausted and demoralized."

"But Dowding couldn't rotate his squadrons fast enough to keep up with the losses, and the more experienced pilots were pulled to plug the gaps in the squadrons sent back to the south. Because I had gotten back to the squadron in late July, I was ordered to stay with our replacement squadron, which wasn't up to full strength yet. Your father, since he'd been in the fighting in France and through Dunkirk with only a few weeks' rest, was to go up north with the rest of our squadron—" Len looked at Andrew, then spoke softly. "He volunteered to stay."

"I know," Andrew whispered. "He called me..." He turned away, shouted at the sea in the distance, "I just need for him to know that I didn't mean...what I said...I need...I need—"

"I heard your father talking on the phone to you, Andrew. He was saying over and over, 'I love you too, Andrew, I love you too,' and then he was calling your mother's name—evidently there was a problem with the connection, because he was yelling 'I can hear you—can you hear me?' Then he hung up. He told me that you'd been crying, 'I love you Dad.'"

"He heard—" Andrew gasped, then swallowed. "He heard me telling him that I loved him...."

"He tried to call you," Len said. "But he couldn't get through. Then we were scrambled. When we got up to altitude, we saw a horrifying sight: a sea of German planes, two miles high, twenty miles broad, and forty miles long. Over a thousand fighters and bombers—headed straight for London. The planes were stacked up in layers to thirty thousand feet. It was like looking up an escalator at Picadilly Circus."

"That was the miracle Dowding had been hoping for. Though it was the beginning of terrible times for the people of London, it was Fighter Command's—and England's—salvation. At the time though, we thought it was the end—for us, at least."

Andrew looked at Len, knowing, dreading, what Len would say next. Yet, in the deepest center of his soul, a tiny spark of peace glowed.

I can bear it now....

"We mixed it up," Len said. "Your father shot down two Heinkels, I got one, then we had to land to refuel and re-arm. There was a second wave, so we went up again right away. Your father got a Ju-88, then was bounced by a 109. He veered away, towards the Channel. Over the R/T I heard him call that he'd been hit and that he was paralyzed. His plane flew straight and level, towards the sea. I only had a few seconds' glimpse of it because I was caught in a dogfight with two 109s. My wingman had already been shot down and I was sure that I had bought it too, so I dove on a Dornier—I figured I might as well take one with me. The next thing I knew, I was lying on my back in someone's back garden, with my parachute billowing around me. A friendly WVS worker gave me a lift back to base."

"I found out that your father's plane was tracked on RDF and that his signal disappeared over the Channel." Len looked intently at Andrew. Then he lowered his eyes and said, "Even though he'd been in the new squadron only a few days, everyone took his death very hard; me, even more so." He took a deep breath, and shook his head slowly.

"But Jake...He was devastated."

"*What?*" Andrew blurted. "*Jake* knew my *father?*"

Len's eyes widened. He looked warily at Andrew for a moment, then said, "Jake was your father's wingman, and his best friend. You didn't know?"

Chapter 53

*T*he world seemed to spin for an instant. Andrew had the disconcerting sensation that the very foundations of his life were being jumbled up, as if an earthquake had shaken loose all the underpinnings that had kept his soul intact. Suddenly he experienced a rock-solid clear-sightedness and certainty about everything.

It all makes sense now....

He looked at Len.

"It was all my fault."

Len gave him a puzzled look.

"Jake was afraid I'd blame him," Andrew said.

Len stared at him, then looked off into the distance again.

"I wasn't there when Jake arrived at the squadron—he came a few days after your father returned. Your father usually took all the new pilots up, to check them out and give them a few pointers. Your father told me that he knew right off that Jake was a natural—he had that instinct for flying that all of us wish we had, but few of us possess. Your father told me, 'Get yourself a good wingman, but keep your hands off Charlie.' Your father called him Charlie. Dunno why."

"After his brother," Andrew said. "He died the day after he was born, and my father—" He gasped as the realization hit him. "August 14th! August 14th, 1918! That's the day Charlie died, and that's the day Jake was born!"

Len smiled, and nodded. "Your father was the only one who called him Charlie. I sensed it was a...personal thing, so I didn't, just called him Jake. Almost everyone else in the squadron, though, called him Yank—short for 'Roger's Barnstorming Yank.' Some of them took a dim view of his flying experience, thought it was rather disreputable sort of thing to do, but Jake could fly circles around every one of them. He and your father were quite a team—never saw anything like it. It seemed as if they were somehow connected—they acted together in perfect harmony, like two halves of the same whole. They enjoyed trading off with each other: Sometimes Jake would be the leader and your father his wingman. Their favorite routine was for one of them to dive on a Jerry bomber and draw the rear gunner's attention, then the other would swoop up from below and shoot up the fuel tanks. Between the two of them, they accounted for half the squadron's score." Len looked up and scanned the sky, as if searching for a high-flying plane.

"On that day, they went up together, as they always did. Jake got hit, and was leaking coolant. He started into a dive and called out over the R/T that he was going to get back to base. Your father saw a 109 going after him and yelled at him to bail out. Jake answered that he could make it, then your father screamed, "Don't be a bloody fool—

ditch the kite! That's an order!" Jake bailed out and a second later his plane was blown to bits. Your father saw another 109 going after Jake as he was parachuting down and shot it out of the sky."

"Only half the squadron made it back. When your father went up again, he had to take an inexperienced wingman, who was killed right off. Then your father...." Len cleared his throat.

"Jake landed miles away—he didn't get back to the squadron until after dark. When he heard what happened to your father, he went bloody berserk. He blamed himself for not being there to protect your father, but took his fury out on the Luftwaffe. Up until then, I believe he rather thought it was all sort of a game, even though he'd racked up a respectable score. He used to laugh that it was like shooting crows on his uncle's farm. But now he was a man possessed. He never laughed, never even cracked a smile, did absolutely crazy things. He'd fly sideways through bomber formations, and loved nothing better than a screaming, head-on firing pass. He never, *never* once pulled away. When other pilots ran out of ammunition, they sensibly headed back to base. Jake...well, Jake just got creative. He loved to ram the Jerries—you could do that in a Hurri, it was such a sturdy kite. He brought down several planes without firing a shot. One time he charged a 109—it veered off, slammed into a Dornier, and both planes went tumbling down. When we got back to base there was an argument amongst the other pilots as to whether Jake should be given credit for the Dornier, since it was technically brought down by the 109. Jake couldn't care less. He said, 'I don't care how many I've shot down, I only care about how many are left.'"

"I tried to get the squadron leader to ground Jake—he was just bloody bonkers. The S.L. said crazy or not, Jake's shooting down more Jerries than anyone else, so he stays. I didn't expect Jake to survive. No one even wanted to be his wingman because he was so wild. Didn't matter, we were so short of pilots anyway, and I don't think Jake really wanted to have someone protecting him."

"September seventh seemed to us like the end of the world, and the Germans were convinced they'd destroyed Fighter Command. But in attacking London the Luftwaffe took the pressure off our airfields, and we were able to turn the tide in the days after that. When the Germans sent over another huge formation on September 15th they were properly routed, and Hitler called off the invasion."

"The Germans don't like to admit that we won the Battle of Britain. They claim they withdrew their forces and changed their plans. But in simply continuing to exist, Fighter Command won, hands down. It was the turning point of the whole war, for if Fighter Command had been defeated, England most certainly would have been invaded and occupied by the Nazis, and everything, *everything*, would be different. No Stalingrad, no El Alamien, no Normandy—the Third Reich would be ruling the world now. Churchill said a few thousand airmen made the difference—he exaggerated that a bit. I don't think there were more than eight hundred fighter pilots in the RAF who had an even chance of going up in a Spit or Hurri and coming back alive. And when the figures were tallied, it turned out that only about five hundred pilots, out of three thousand, had shot down any Jerries at all. It was men like your father, men like Jake, who made the difference."

Len fell silent. Andrew sensed he needed to be alone with his thoughts. A chill wind blasted their backs. Finally, Len spoke.

"Jake was nearly killed just as the Luftwaffe ceased daylight operations. The Blitz was just a petulant gesture; the Germans knew they'd lost, but were determined to wreak havoc on the civilian population, and so began the night attacks on the cities."

"It was the last day of September, and the Luftwaffe sent over one last big daylight raid over southern England. They paid heavily for it, for Fighter Command was now stronger than ever. Jake, as usual, started getting inventive when he ran out of ammunition. He flew in between two Heinkels and tore a wing off each of them—tore his own wings off too. The Heinkels rolled into each other and burst into flames, and some of the exploding debris caught Jake's plane on fire. He bailed out in flames and landed in the Channel.

"Luckily, he was picked up by a fishing boat. He spent several months in hospital, getting plastic surgery on his hands. Your mother visited him all during that time, and afterwards, too. At first, I think it was out of kindness, but that kindness turned into love, though Jake was bloody terrified of having anything to do with her. Thought he'd be betraying your father...."

"She's persistent, though," Andrew smiled.

Len laughed. "Yes, that she is. Took her over two years to bring him round, but she did. I was best man at their wedding."

A dark cloud rolled in overhead. Len reached into his pocket and pulled out an envelope.

"I was unofficial squadron photographer." He gave the envelope to Andrew.

Andrew withdrew a small stack of snapshots. Leafing through them, he saw flashes of daily life at a fighter base: pilots lounging in deck chairs in the sun, standing by their planes, describing aerial maneuvers with hands poised in arcs of flight and expressions of triumph and glee on their faces. He scrutinized one photo showing a pilot—Andrew was amazed at how *young* he looked—holding a piece of tailplane with a swastika on it.

"He doesn't look much older than me," Andrew murmured.

Len nodded. "That's Roddy—he was just nineteen. Strange—most of the chaps in our squadron weren't even old enough to vote, but they were old enough to give their lives to defend their country."

Andrew put the photo to the back of the pile and saw, in the next picture, his father's face smiling out at him. There was another face smiling at him, too—Jake's. The two of them stood facing the camera; Andrew's father had his arm around Jake's shoulder, and Jake's arm was around Andrew's father in a reciprocal gesture. Their free hands were held up in a V-for-Victory sign.

"They got two Ju-88s that day," Len said.

"I remember—" Andrew said. "I remember him now. I was so afraid I'd forgotten his face." He looked at Len. "Did my father say anything? Anything else, after...at the end, I mean—did he say anything about me?"

Len grunted, narrowed his eyes in consternation. "Well, he must have been a bit delirious from pain and shock. I don't believe he was thinking clearly."

"What did he say?"

Len cleared his throat. "He said...*March forth*. Mind you, he was never the bombastic type—far from it. *March forth* is something you'd rather expect from Winnie when he'd worked himself into a froth." He cracked an embarrassed smile.

"March fourth is my birthday," Andrew breathed.

"Ah, so he *was* thinking of you."

A stiff wind nearly tore the photos from Andrew's hand. He grasped them tightly.

"You can keep these." Len looked up at the sky. "We'd better be getting back."

They walked in silence back to the house. As Andrew opened the front door, his mother came into the entryway. Her eyes spoke a question.

Andrew smiled at her.

"I need to be on my way," Len said. "There's a storm coming in, and I'd like to make Scotland before nightfall."

"Another time, then?" Andrew's mother asked.

"Certainly, another time. Bye, Andrew. Happy Christmas."

"Happy Christmas."

"Happy Christmas, Len," Andrew's mother said.

After Len had closed the door behind him, Andrew took the photo of his father and Jake and showed it to his mother.

"Now you know," she said softly.

"Jake didn't want me to tell you." Andrew's mother paused on the stairs, took a breath, and climbed the last three steps to the top.

"I understand," Andrew said.

His mother turned and smiled at him, then her face abruptly grew serious. "He was so afraid of you—afraid you'd blame him. He blamed himself for a long, long time."

She placed her hand on her belly as she lumbered down the hall. Andrew followed her into her room. She sank down on her bed and swung her feet up, then lay back on the pillows and held her arms wide. Andrew nestled into her embrace.

"He heard me, Mum."

His mother gave him a puzzled look.

"Dad—he heard me. The last time I talked with him, on the phone. I thought the connection had been cut, but he heard me telling him that I loved him."

She looked at him, finally understanding.

"So that's what's been bothering you all these years."

Chapter 54

*A*lfred narrowed his eyes in consternation at the small stubby pine tree at the crest of the hill.

"Not as grand as we used to have at Greycliff, but I suppose it'll do."

"It'll do just fine," Andrew said.

They walked up the hill. The frozen grass crunched sweetly underfoot; the sky, hanging heavy with ragged grey clouds, looked like hammered pewter. Lois would say *It was coming up a storm.*

But it's all so lovely, Andrew thought.

It's all so lovely when you're not mired in guilt and fear and despair.

He helped Alfred wrest the chopped pine tree into the house.

"In the drawing room, as usual, Alfred," Grandmother said.

"I'll get the decorations from the storeroom." Mrs. Beaton bustled up the back stairs.

"I'll help." Andrew followed her.

Mrs. Beaton huffed up to the third floor, which Andrew had never seen before. The stairs led to a warren of narrow corridors and tiny rooms. "Used to be the servants' quarters," Mrs. Beaton said. She stopped at one door, reached for a key on top of the doorframe, unlocked the door, and stepped inside.

The wan afternoon light filtered in through dust-filmed windows. After sorting through trunks and boxes, Mrs. Beaton located two large boxes covered in faded red gabardine.

Andrew stepped forward to pick up the boxes. As he lifted the first one from the pile, he spied a leather case behind it with the letters *R.H.* stenciled on the top. He pulled out the case, set it on the floor, and opened the latches.

There was a funny sort of canvas contraption inside the case: It was rather like a rucksack, but had two holes in the bottom and a hole on each side. Andrew lifted it out and saw a large brown envelope. He picked up the envelope and opened the flanges on the flap. As he pulled out a large photograph, he drew a sharp breath.

His father smiled out at him again, only this time he was not clad in an RAF uniform. He was dressed casually, and wore the rucksack device around his chest; inside it was a smiling baby.

"*Me!*" Andrew breathed.

Mrs. Beaton chuckled. "Your father had one of the maids sew up this sling out of one of his old rucksacks. The summer after you were born, your parents stayed here. Your grandfather was off in India. Almost every day your father and mother would take you out "ranging," as they called it. Your father carried you in this." She pointed at the rucksack, then gazed at the photograph. "Your father was always in such a jolly mood, but he positively glowed with rapture when he held you in his arms. He was here when you were born, and he spent all that day—and the next several days, in fact, until he had to go back to Oxford—sitting in your mother's room, holding you in his arms. I used to bring him his tea and, if your mother was asleep, I'd sit with him a bit and hold you while he drank his tea. He used to whisper this poem to you—just two lines, I can't remember them exactly. Something about spring."

"I can't imagine a dawn in spring, without my heart awakening," Andrew softly said.

"Yes—that's it!" Mrs. Beaton exclaimed. "Oh, he had the most joyful look on his face when he said it! I thought he would split in two with happiness. When I reminded him that it wasn't exactly spring yet, your father laughed and said, 'I hereby proclaim that forever more, March fourth shall be the first day of spring!'"

Andrew put the photograph and rucksack back in the case, then carried it with one of the boxes down to the drawing room. Mrs. Beaton followed, carrying the other box.

Alfred had already set up the tree, and Maria and Grandmother were fluffing out the branches. Andrew's mother was lounging on one of the sofas. Andrew set the box near the tree, and brought the case to her. Her eyes widened with astonishment.

"I thought we'd lost that!" she cried.

Andrew opened the case and showed her the rucksack and photo.

"Oh, what a happy summer that was!" she said. "And you were the happiest baby! You used to smile just seeing your father's face, even hearing his voice!"

Grandmother looked at the photo and smiled. "It *was* a happy time," she said. "Let's put that in a frame and set it on the table by the tree." She walked over to the mantle, picked out a sepia portrait set in a large, ornate frame. "I think this is Cousin Cedric—I'm not sure. In any case, he's been peering out at the world long enough." She unfastened the back of the frame, withdrew the picture, and replaced it with the photograph.

"There!" she said, setting it on the table. "Well, let's get this tree decorated."

Andrew realized it was the first Christmas he'd ever spent at Greycliff. He happily set to hanging the ornaments on the tree, with Maria, Mrs. Beaton, and Alfred helping. His mother and grandmother sorted through the boxes and handed out the ornaments. Linda eyed the tree with button-round eyes, then padded over and batted a gold-filigreed angel dangling from one of the lower branches.

"Linda—here," Andrew said. "I'll give you your own Christmas plaything." He took a little silver bell off the tree and tied it to the end of a poker. He set the poker in the metal ash bucket, so that the bell hung just within Linda's reach.

"Linda can provide us with Christmas music while we do the tree," he said.

As they put the finishing touches on the tree, Mrs. Beaton said, "I'll put us on some tea." After she'd left, Andrew's mother motioned to Alfred. He went over to her, and she whispered something in his ear. He nodded, and left the room. He returned after a few minutes, bearing an armload of gaily wrapped packages.

"I thought it would be nice to put out a few presents now," Andrew's mother said.

Alfred spread the presents under the tree. Andrew went over and looked at them, and saw that two of the gifts were for him. One, wrapped in white and gold striped paper, was quite large, about half the size of a steamer trunk. Picking it up, he found it to be quite light, though. His name was written on a small envelope attached to the top of the package. The handwriting was familiar—he tugged off the envelope, opened it, and pulled out a small card. It read:

Dear Andrew,

I made this for you—I hope it keeps you warm on those chilly Northumberland nights. I know you probably don't ever want to see me again, and I understand, but I wanted you to have this. Merry Christmas.

Love,

Jereen

"It arrived from Nebraska the other day," Andrew's mother said.

Andrew grazed his fingers over the white and gold bands.

"Maria and Alfred, would you please help Mrs. Beaton with tea?" Andrew's mother asked.

"I'll help too," Grandmother said quietly.

After Maria, Alfred, and Grandmother had filed out, Andrew's mother looked at Andrew and said, "Why don't you open it?"

Andrew tore back the wrappings, then lifted the lid off the box within. He pulled out a granny afghan with squares of light blue, grey-blue, and navy blue, with a black border.

"RAF and ATA colors," his mother said. "It's lovely."

"It is," Andrew whispered. He gazed at the offering which had been lovingly created by the girl who'd laced herself into his soul.

"She's a very nice girl," Andrew's mother said.

Andrew nodded, then looked at his mother. She smiled.

"Miriam's a very nice girl, too." She opened her arms to him.

He flew into her embrace.

"It must be so very confusing and overwhelming for you," she murmured. "When I was your age, I was riding horses and climbing trees. You've grown up so very fast, what with the war and all. I guess I should have expected it, but...." She hugged him tightly.

"I'll always need you," he said. "Always."

She drew back and looked into his eyes. "I don't purport to be the world's greatest expert on matters of the heart, Andrew. If I were you, I'd have an awfully hard time trying to sort things out. They're both wonderful girls."

Andrew sighed. "I wish that I were two people, or that they were one girl."

His mother laughed gently. "That's the way of it sometimes. But you know, you're several years away from having to make a serious decision about things. A lot can happen during that time. And I know, when the time comes to make a choice, you'll be able to see your way clear. Who knows? Anything can happen! Life is full of wonderful surprises. You might even meet someone else. Anything is possible."

Andrew started to groan, but it bubbled into a laugh. "Oh God—I'd truly be a basket case if that happened!"

His mother laughed too, then said, "Well, don't fret about it. I know that things will turn out all right for you. But if you ever want to talk about things...." She took a deep breath. "I know that you've kept some things from me, because you didn't want me to worry."

"Well, with the war...and you were flying. I didn't want you to be...distracted."

"I know. But the war's over—you don't need to worry anymore."

He bit his lip. "And I didn't want you to be upset, either...about, um, things."

"Well, don't be afraid to talk to me, Andrew, about...things. I'm not all that easily shocked, you know." She gazed at Andrew, her face full of joy and delight; then to his astonishment, she burst into tears.

"Oh Andrew, for so long I've wanted to tell you how I felt about Jake, and how I felt about your father; to draw you into my heart, so that you could see that the love I felt for Jake did not diminish what I felt—what I still feel—for your father. I didn't know how to explain it, how to make you see that I could love your father so much, and love Jake too. Oh my darling, there were times when even I couldn't make sense of how I felt; it was such an illogical tangle of desire and fear and guilt. But now you understand. You understand...."

He put his arms around her, and held her close. It was strange: He felt as if he were a parent comforting a distressed child. Neither of them said anything for awhile. The silence was occasionally broken by the sound of Linda swatting her bell. Then Andrew spoke.

"When you and Jake...I mean, when did you know how you felt about him?"

His mother's voice was quavery, yet joyful. "I think it grew out of knowing how much your father cared for him. The first time I met Jake was when he came to your father's memorial service. He didn't come willingly; his squadron leader had grounded him because he was shooting at parachuting Jerries, which was against regulations. The S.L. *ordered* Jake to come to your father's service. Even so, the adjutant had to practically drag him into the chapel. When I saw Jake, I went over to him and took his hand. I wanted to tell him how much your father cared for him, but he started crying and then bolted out the door. I couldn't bear the thought of him tearing himself apart with guilt, and I knew your father would have felt the same way too. When Jake was in hospital, after he'd gotten his hands burnt, I often stayed with him. I sensed that his agony was much more than the physical suffering he was going through. It was as if your father's spirit were inside of me, filling me with a longing for Jake to break free of that terrible guilt, for him to be whole again. But gradually I started having...different, new emotions towards him. I was afraid, at first, and I thought I could never love anyone as I had loved your father. Andrew, I loved your father, fell madly in love with him, the first time I saw him."

Andrew's mother seemed to be in a joyous trance; she talked as if she were caught up in some epiphany, as if she were alone, crying out her rapture and sorrow to a formless world.

"I saw him, at my engagement party; his face floating in a sea of other faces, all of which I knew already, but it was as if he were the only one in the room. And at that moment, I knew there would never be anyone else—even though I was standing next to the man I had promised to marry. And I thought I should shatter to pieces if this stranger didn't feel for me what I felt for him. I tried to act calm as I asked him to dance; I was sure everyone in the room could hear my heart beating. And he said *Yes*, and I died with joy in his arms."

She noticed Andrew's smile, and laughed. "A bolt out of the blue, that's the way of it sometimes. With Jake, it was a joy distilled from struggle and pain—for both of us. I was afraid of him, he was afraid of me; and to make matters worse, I had competition— her name was Ursula. Quite a ravishing beauty, but shallow as a puddle after a thirty-second rainsquall. She never came to visit Jake when he was in hospital. Then, that horrible day when we were bombed in London, I'd just gotten dug out when Jake appeared on the scene. He and a friend were in London for the day. Dr. McIndoe used to send his burn patients, when they were well enough, to walk around London."

"So they could get used to being stared at," Andrew whispered.

"Well," his mother went on. "Jake and his friend pitched right in and started digging through the rubble. Jake was the one who carried you out to me. When I saw the look of relief on his face, and the love in his eyes as he looked at you, it was then that I knew I loved him."

She gazed at the star at the top of the tree.

"A few months after we were married, Jake woke up in the middle of the night, screaming your name. Then he said you *had* to go to America. He wouldn't tell me why, but I knew he was sure the Germans were up to something. When the V-2 rockets fell, he told me that he already knew about them because he'd done aerial reconnaissance of the German rocket installations. He also knew, or rather figured out, about work the Germans were doing on the atomic bomb. He didn't tell me about *that* until after we'd heard about Hiroshima. He was terrified for you, Andrew. He'd lost your father, and he didn't want to lose you, too."

Andrew was struck by a thought.

"Jake's father—he knew, didn't he? About my father and Jake, I mean."

His mother nodded. "He knew. The day before Jake and I were to leave to come back to England, his father stormed home from church because he'd somehow found out about Jake coming in Saturday night in such a...state. I think one of the parishioners must have told him. I don't know what caused Jake's lapse. He never told me, but I knew it had something to do with his feelings about your father. He never wanted his parents to know about things—maybe it was just the stress of keeping it all in. Lois and I were so afraid there was going to be a bloody row when Jake's father went in to talk with Jake, but Jake, thank God, told his father everything." She shook her head in wonder. "I still can't believe how it all turned out. Jake was positively terrified at seeing his father again. He'd run off, you know, against his father's wishes, to join the RAF. But he wanted you safely in America, and that was why he had to return home. And it all worked out so wonderfully...." She wrapped her arms even more tightly around Andrew. "And now it's all come full circle, and you know, too."

"I can't wait to see him tomorrow." Andrew looked at the gifts under the tree, and realized he had not gotten a present for Jake.

"I know!" he exclaimed. "I'll put the picture of him and my father in a frame!"

"Perfect!" his mother said. "Well, let's take care of that later, all right?" She nodded at Andrew's other present, a flat package wrapped in red.

Andrew went over to it and opened it. Within was a framed certificate with the seal of England printed at the top. Below were the words:

This scroll commemorates
Flight Lieutenant R. Hadley-Trevelyan
Royal Air Force
held in honour as one who
served King and Country in
the world war of 1939-1945
and gave his life to save
mankind from tyranny. May
his sacrifice help to bring
the peace and freedom for
which he died.

Peace and freedom, Andrew thought. After all these years, I finally have them.

Grandmother gave him a small silver frame which had held a silhouette of Great-aunt Clarice. Andrew placed the photo of his father and Jake within, and wrapped it in dark blue paper embossed with silver angels.

He stayed up late with his mother and Grandmother and Aunt Jane and the servants. As Linda batted her bell and stalked the packages under the tree, Andrew played Christmas carols on his guitar. He wasn't sure, but he thought that there was a hint of brightness in Aunt Jane's eyes.

The brightness faded, and Aunt Jane's head began to nod. Andrew helped her up to her room and tucked her into bed. He heard his mother retiring and was just about to say goodnight to her when he remembered something.

He ran to his room and got his father's book of poems. As he carried it down the hall, he opened it to his father's poem.

"Here." He handed the book to his mother. "Dad left this, when he went away."

His mother read aloud: "*I've tried for many an hour and minute, to think of this world without me in it....*"

As she read the rest of the poem, Andrew felt a sublime peace settle on him.

"I used to think he was...you know, speaking to me, when I read that," he said to his mother.

"Well, I think he was." His mother turned the page, blinked, then said, "Have you read this?" She handed the book to Andrew.

Andrew breathed with amazement as he scanned the lines. He read aloud:

All life, all love's his fee
Whose perished fire conserves my spark,
Who brought the brightening day for me
And for himself, the dark.

Suddenly he felt overwhelmed by a suffocating, desolate sadness as he thought of his father, lying in cold darkness in a Hurricane coffin at the bottom of the sea.

I know that he wouldn't want me to be sad forever, but this tangle of grief and grate-fulness will always be a part of me....

He kissed his mother goodnight, then patted her belly and whispered, "Good night to you too, little one. Your daddy is coming tomorrow."

He dreamt he was walking outside in the sunlight and saw Charlie's grave in the distance. Two figures were sitting on the grass in front of it. As he ran towards it, he saw that one of the figures was his father; the other man, dressed in an RAF uniform, had his back to Andrew.

"Charlie—look who's here!" his father called. The other man turned, and Andrew saw that it was Jake.

He'd had this dream before, sort of, only then Aunt Gwen and Aunt Jane were in it also.

When I ran from Armus House, after Freddie's threats, and fell asleep by Charlie's grave...It was Jake who was Charlie in the dream then, too....

A Hurricane flew overhead, then swooped down upon them and scattered a shower of brightly-wrapped candy. Andrew's father laughed as the candy pelted down around them. Soon they were encased within a riot of color, and Andrew felt his father's arms go round him, felt himself being lifted up. His father brushed a kiss across his forehead, then Andrew felt another pair of arms enfold him.

He turned and saw that he was in Jake's arms. Andrew's father looked at Jake, nod-ded once, smiled a sad, grateful smile, then stepped back into the whirlwind of color.

Andrew felt Jake's arms tighten around him. He pressed his face into Jake's shoul-der, then awoke to the darkness of his room.

He looked out his window, and saw that it was snowing.

He was awakened again by the faint morning light. Wrapping Jereen's afghan around him, he padded over to the window. The snowfall had stopped and the world was swathed in white. The newness of the winter landscape seemed a fitting touch to all the astounding revelations of the previous day.

Like a clean slate, Andrew thought, as he bounded down the backstairs. We can start over, Jake and I....

Mrs. Beaton greeted him in the kitchen, which was bathed in candlelight.

"Morning to you Andrew! Looks like we're going to have an old fashioned Christmas." Thrusting a mug of tea into his hands, she nodded at Linda, who was perched up on a cupboard and peering out a window at the frosty vista.

"I let her out a bit ago. She put one paw in the snow and raced back inside. I've fixed her up a litter box in the tool closet."

Andrew reached over and rubbed Linda's back. She made a funny little sound that was a cross between a purr and a meow, then arched her back and closed her eyes in bliss.

"Morning Andrew! My, you're up early." Andrew's mother shuffled into the kitchen. "Looks like the electricity is out," she said.

"Phone too," Mrs. Beaton said.

"Oh, dear—Jake's arriving today. Well, he can get a taxi from town. Let's get the house all done up in grand Christmas style for him."

"Super idea!" Andrew said. "I'll finish up my Christmas wrapping, then we can put all the gifts under the tree."

"And get out all the candles and scatter them throughout the house," Mrs. Beaton said. "A candlelit Christmas—oh, it'll be lovely!"

After breakfast, Andrew wrapped the presents he'd bought: a quilted treasure box for his mother; a lap blanket for Aunt Jane; a sweater for his grandmother; slippers for Mrs. Beaton, Maria, Birdie, and Felicity; some leather driving gloves for Alfred. He'd also bought Linda a gray felt mouse and a rag ball. He put the gifts under the tree and added them to the packages his mother and grandmother had already piled under the branches. Mrs. Beaton served them elevensies as they sat around the tree.

"I think I'll try to see if I can get the battery wireless working," Andrew's mother said. "They'll be playing Christmas carols on the BBC; we can drink our wassail and eat the plum pudding while we listen to the music."

"Remember Razz and his ragtime Christmas carols?" Grandmother asked. "Oh, that was a wonderful Christmas!"

"It was," Andrew's mother agreed. "But this one will be the best of all, because we'll all be together."

After they'd had lunch, Mrs. Beaton got the battery wireless from the upstairs storeroom and set it on the dining room table. Andrew's mother got to work on it. Andrew gazed at her as she probed through the wires and tubes; he thought she looked so beautiful as she pursed her lips and squinted at the metal and glass innards of their link with the outside world.

"There." She dialed the knobs and a hum issued from the radio.

The *Hallelujahs* of Handel's Messiah blared out, reminding Andrew of that Christmas of five years ago.

Andrew looked up and saw Aunt Jane standing in the doorway.

"Remember when you took me to church and we listened to that?" he asked her.

Aunt Jane stood, motionless as a memorial, then turned and walked away.

"Don't give up hope, darling," his mother said gently. "She'll come round—don't you worry."

The radio emitted a barrage of screeches and blasts of static. Andrew's mother fiddled with the dial and adjusted the aerial, but to no avail. "I think one of the connections broke—I'll get some wire," she said.

She got up and plodded out. Andrew adjusted the aerial some more, then tapped the top of the radio. He heard a faint voice emanate from the radio, then crackle into static. He tapped the radio again. At that moment his mother walked in, and a loud voice issued from the radio:

....authorities have determined that a mid-air collision with a light plane was responsible for yesterday's tragic crash of BOAC Flight 51. The flight, which originated from New York, crashed yesterday morning near London, killing all aboard—

Andrew's mother cried out in a horrid, animal-like wail, then crumpled to the floor like a marionette with its strings cut.

"Alice—?" Grandmother rushed into the room.

Andrew ran to his mother's side.

"Jake's plane—it crashed—he—he's—" Andrew choked on the cry of horror forcing its way from his throat.

Grandmother took one look at his face. "Oh my God," she whispered. Then she knelt down by Andrew's mother and patted her face.

"Alice—*Alice!*"

Andrew's mother opened her eyes, but they were unseeing, vacant eyes, eyes like Aunt Jane's.

"Mum!" Andrew cried.

His mother's eyes rolled back; she clutched her belly and moaned. The moan turned into a loud cry that sounded like the up-and-down wail of an air-raid Alert.

"Oh God, oh no—it's coming!" Grandmother said.

"What—what—*WHAT?*" Andrew gasped, even as the terrifying realization hit him. *It can't be coming...It's too soon....*

"Andrew—tell Alfred to go to town and get Dr. Blake," Grandmother yelled, her voice shrill with panic.

Andrew sprang forward like a racer from a starting block. He lurched down the corridor to the kitchen and flew into Mrs. Beaton, who was bustling along from the other direction.

"Andrew, what—" she cried.

"It's Mum—the baby—Alfred—the car—the car—the—the—Dr. Blake—"

Mrs. Beaton turned round and scurried back to the kitchen. Andrew heard her jabbering loudly to Alfred. By the time Andrew got to the kitchen, Alfred had already grabbed his coat and was dashing out the door.

Andrew sank down onto a chair and pressed his face against the polished oak of the kitchen table.

Oh God—why did you have to do this to her? Hasn't she had enough already?

He heard a worried sigh from Mrs. Beaton.

"Alfred should have gotten the car out by now," she murmured.

Andrew looked out the window, saw that the garage door was opened. He stood, then stumbled to the back door. He grabbed his jacket off the peg, jammed his arms into the sleeves, and exploded out the door.

As he ran to the garage, he breathed a silent prayer that he would hear the sound of the engine starting.

Please, please, please...just start that bloody damned car!

As he dashed into the garage, Andrew knew his worst fears had come true when he heard a soft click, then another, issue from the car. He pounded on the hood with his fists.

Alfred rolled down the window. "Battery's dead," he said sorrowfully.

Andrew gave one last furious punch to the wretched contraption, then spun round. He knew what he had to do.

I've done it over a hundred times...So what if there's a little snow on the ground....

He broke into a run. As he veered around the house and dashed down the front drive, his mind pounded with a drumming despair.

It's all for nothing...Mum's going to die, like Lynette's mother and Sarge's wife...The baby's going to die too, like Baby Charlie and Jake's brothers and sister....

He screamed as he ran, trying to banish the tormenting thoughts. He had to, *had* to get Dr. Blake.

I can't let it happen...Lois lost all those babies, then Jake...can't let her lose her grandchild too....

At least the snow wasn't all that deep, and it was a rather fluffy, dry snow which offered no resistance to his pummelling stride.

Almost like running in a cloud....

He could see the south road ahead. Good—he was almost into town.

Just another mile...then I'll be at Dr. Blake's....

He shut his eyes for a few seconds. As he opened them, he saw a flash of red turning onto the south road.

Oh God, oh no...it can't be...Why the hell is he heading out that way? It's Godallbloody Christmas Eve, for Christ's sake....

Andrew watched in horror as the M.G. sped down the south road.

And Dr. Mead's away, too....

The horrible thoughts hammered away at him.

She's going to die...the baby too...

Andrew suddenly realized that about three hundred yards separated him from the south road. The M.G. was about a half mile away, and it would have to negotiate a series of curves before it reached the point directly opposite Andrew's position.

I could cut across that pasture...intercept the car....

He leapt over the stone fence edging the road and sped across the pasture. The ground was rutty and he had to watch his footing. The pasture dipped down into a ravine; Andrew flung himself down the side and scrambled out.

Now he could hear the M.G. He was running in a parallel course to the south road now, as a thick tangle of bushes blocked him from cutting across to it. There was a path a little ahead which led up to the road.

He looked over his shoulder to check how much distance he had on the M.G. At that moment a calm, steady voice broke across his panicked mindspin.

Never look back...Remember, never look back....

As Andrew's head snapped forward, he saw—one step ahead of him—a hole the size of a wheelbarrow.

Bloody hell....

He leapt over the hole and, as his feet smacked the ground, the irony of it all struck him like a thunderclap.

I told Shannon there wouldn't be a next time....

He sped along the path up to the road, made another flying leap over the stone fence, and landed in the middle of the road.

The M.G. was about a hundred and fifty feet away, and bearing down on him at a fast clip. Andrew faced the car and waved his arms.

The car didn't slow down.

No matter...if he hits me, he'll have to stop in at Greycliff to explain....

He waggled his arms frantically and shouted, even though he was sure Dr. Blake couldn't hear him. God—he'd never deliberately stood in the path of an oncoming car.

Is this what it feels like to do a head-on, firing pass?

He heard the screech of brakes, like a scream of death from the sky.

For the second time in my life, I know what it sounds like to die....

Chapter 55

*A*ndrew came to consciousness to find himself draped over the hood of the M.G. The hot metal stung his cheek.

If I can still feel, I must be alive....

"My God, Andrew—are you all right?" Dr. Blake's hands fluttered over his back.

"*Mum....*" Andrew's voice came out as a cross between a croak and a bleat. He pulled himself across the hood to the passenger side and tugged at the door handle. It was locked, and he frantically tried to work it open. He had an insanely horrid fear that Dr. Blake would think he was mad and drive off, leaving him to his ravings on the snow-covered lane.

He felt Dr. Blake's arms around his shoulders, then felt the welcome crush of warm leather against his face. As the car sped along, Andrew closed his eyes and remembered another horrible time, another journey, when he'd agonized for his mother's life.

Only that time, it was Alfred and Grandmother with me, and we were racing away from Greycliff, trying to find her....

As the car slowed, he opened his eyes and saw Greycliff come into view.

Dr. Blake glanced at Andrew as he braked the M.G. Then he grabbed his bag and dashed into the house.

Andrew slumped against the dash.

I'm too late, too late...Mum is going to die, and so is the baby....

"Andrew!" Maria ran down the front steps. "Come inside, come on." She opened the door and tugged Andrew out of the car. He stumbled up the steps behind her and lurched inside.

A horrific howl issued from the dining room. Andrew felt his knees go to jelly. He grabbed onto one of the ornate tables lining the hall.

"Andrew, come on, don't worry now—" Mrs. Beaton came to his side and put her arms around him.

"She's dying—sh—she's dy—" The words choked in his throat.

"No she's not—it's called labor, and it's how you came into the world, too."

"It's too *soon—the baby's going to die, too—*"

"Andrew, your mother's all right." Dr. Blake came into the hall.

Another howl issued from the dining room.

"She's *not!* She's going to d—"

Dr. Blake pulled Andrew from Mrs. Beaton's grasp and hustled him up the stairs. "Come on—you need to get those wet clothes off, or you'll catch your death of cold."

Maria scurried ahead of them and led the way to Andrew's room. Dr. Blake steered Andrew down the hall after her.

"Doctor's orders." Dr. Blake sorted through Andrew's drawers and pulled out a pair of pajamas. "Dry clothes, bed rest, and a cup of hot chocolate. I'll have Mrs. Beaton bring it up to you." He tossed the pajamas to Andrew and disappeared out the door.

Andrew's mind was spinning, but he had enough of his wits still about him to know he needed to get out of his wet clothes. But *pajamas?* He was bloody well not going to go to sleep! He changed into a pair of jeans and a sweater.

"Andrew, are you decent?" Mrs. Beaton's voice drifted up from the backstairs.

"Um—yes—"

Mrs. Beaton came in through the nanny's alcove and handed Andrew a mug of hot cocoa. "Drink up—you've worn yourself out and you need your strength back."

Andrew didn't bother to sit down; he gulped down the cocoa and thrust the empty mug back at Mrs. Beaton.

"I'd better go downstairs." He started through the nanny's alcove.

"You'd better go to *bed*." Mrs. Beaton grabbed his arm and pulled him back. "You've already done your bit, Andrew. Let Dr. Blake take care of things now—you'll just fret yourself to a frazzle and get in the way. Come on, now—"

"*But Mum—*"

"There's nothing you can do now, except rest up and let Dr. Blake do his job."

She led him to his bed and pulled the covers back. "Just a wee bit of rest—I'll bring you up some tea later." She sat down in the rocking chair, folded her arms, and glared at him.

Andrew had never known Mrs. Beaton to resort to physical force, but he knew that now was not the time to test her capabilities. He closed his eyes.

As soon as she's gone, I'll go back downstairs....

His bed seemed to undulate a bit, like the gentle motion of a ship at sea. His arms and legs felt like lead weights—even forcing his eyelids open took more exertion than his run to town had required.

Mrs. Beaton was still in the rocking chair. She looked a little blurry, though. He closed his eyes again.

Just a few more minutes, then I'll get up and go downstairs to Mum....

He awoke, got out of bed, and walked down the hall and into his mother's room. His mother was asleep in bed.

"Hullo, old chap!"

Andrew turned.

There was his father, sitting in a rocking chair by the window. He held a newborn baby.

"I can't imagine a day in spring, without my heart awakening," his father whispered as he gazed lovingly at the child in his arms.

"That's *me!*" Andrew cried.

His father nodded, then stood and presented the baby to him.

Andrew sank down in the chair and looked down at the sleeping infant.

"Is that really me?" he asked, touching the baby cheek.

His query met with an alarming silence. He looked up.

His father was gone.

He heard a sound like a high-pitched yell, and glanced down. The baby was crying: Its face was beet-red and contorted with dreadful unhappiness.

Andrew was frantic. What could he do to stop the terrible cries? He tried gently bouncing the infant, but it arched its back and screeched even louder.

Suddenly, everything went dark and silent, and he no longer felt the child in his arms. He tumbled over and over in the blackness, then felt that woozy, rocking feeling again before he lost consciousness.

"Andrew—what are you doing there?" Dr. Blake's voice broke through the fog.

As Andrew jerked awake, he realized he'd been lying on the sofa in front of the bay window. Somehow he'd gotten there from his bed. Then he remembered his dream.

I must have been sleepwalking....

As Andrew turned round, he saw Dr. Blake walking over to him. He cradled a small bundle to his chest.

"Here's your sister, Andrew." Dr. Blake placed the bundle in Andrew's arms.

"Don't be afraid—she's not made of glass." Dr. Blake shifted the baby into the crook of Andrew's arm. "Just support her head like this. Her neck muscles aren't very strong."

This was no dream, Andrew realized, though it seemed somehow...unreal. He'd *never* seen a baby so little; not even Jereen's baby brother and Mel's twins had been this small. She was dressed in the grey-blue gown Savannah Olney had made, and wrapped in the log-cabin quilt sewn by Mrs. Bock. Andrew carefully peeled back the quilt and studied the tiny creature with the doll-like face. A thatch of red hair swept down to the delicate eyelids, which were fringed with fine lashes and closed in slumber. A nub of a nose was underlined by a wisp of a mouth with lips like slivers of rose petals. Two minuscule hands with impossibly tiny fingers peeked out from the grey-blue sleeves. At the sight of the RAF wings embroidered on the chest, Andrew breathed a soft groan of anguish.

"He won't know her! He won't ever know her. Oh God—I'd give anything to have him back!"

The tiny eyes popped open and stared at him. Andrew was terror-stricken.

"Oh no, *oh no*—she's looking at me! What do I do?"

"Look back." Dr. Blake stroked the tiny wrist and spoke in a low, crooning voice. "See little one? There's your brother. You gave him quite a scare yesterday. He ran to get me, ran five miles, that he did."

"She's so *little*," Andrew breathed. "Are you sure she's all right? She was born too soon—She's not going to—" the word caught in his throat.

Like Baby Charlie, he thought.

"Not to worry," Dr. Blake smiled. "I'd wager she's a good six pounds."

Andrew squinted at the little chest. Alarm rose within him.

"She's breathing too fast—I've never seen anyone breath that fast! Something's wrong—she's having trouble—babies who are born too soon don't breath right—"

"Don't worry, Andrew, she's doing just fine. She was a little early, but none the worse for wear. She did give your mother a hard time, though. Acted for all the world like she was ready to make a grand entrance at any minute, but then decided to stay put. It was getting close to midnight and she probably realized she was going to be born on Christmas day. I don't think she liked the thought of having her birthday forever jumbled up with the holiday madness—isn't that right, little one?" Dr. Blake touched his finger to her temple. "Well, I had to pluck her from her cozy little nest, before her mother got too tired of the whole business. A few minutes after midnight, it was—hope she didn't wake you. This little lassie's a real Spitfire—she's got a good lusty set of lungs and sang her own Christmas carol as she came into the world. Thought she would wake the whole house." He looked at Andrew. "It was a good thing you got me. I really had the easy part of it, just waiting to give a few minutes' assistance. You ran five miles of snow-covered road, then stood in front of a car." He brushed his fingers over the feathery auburn hair. "You're a lucky little lady—you have a brother who loves you very much."

Andrew closed his eyes in shame.

"I fell asleep—after you left. I wanted to be awake, for Mum...for *her*...."

"Andrew, I put a bit of sedative in your chocolate. I knew that you'd worry yourself into a tailspin. You needed your rest."

Another alarm jangled in him.

"I heard Jake talking about some kind of disease that was in his family. His brothers and sister died. She doesn't have it, does she?"

Dr. Blake shook his head. "No, your mother is Rh positive, so there's no problem with that."

Andrew heaved a sigh of relief and touched his finger to the tiny hand. The matchstick fingers curled around his knuckle, and the deep blue eyes stared intently at him.

"Looks like she's already wrapped herself around your heart," Dr. Blake said.

Andrew lifted the child to his face and brushed a kiss across her forehead.

My sister....

"She looks like you, Andrew."

Andrew lowered his sister a bit and looked into her gaze. The penetrating newborn eyes tore into his soul.

"She has Jake's eyes," he whispered.

"As I recall, mum, Miss Alice gave all the baby things away after they found out—"
Mrs. Beaton's head snapped around as Andrew came into the kitchen.

"Oh dear," Grandmother said. "I'd thought she at least would have kept the cradle."

"No mum—she gave that away, too—remember?"

Grandmother heaved a sigh. "Well, I don't know what we're going to do for a bed for this baby. Where is she going to sleep tonight?"

"I know," Andrew said. "We can use one of my dresser drawers. I'll line it with a blanket and put it next to my bed."

"Perfect!" Dr. Blake exclaimed. "It's not the first time a makeshift bed has been used for a Christmas baby. Tell you what, Andrew—you see to the bed, and I'll see to help-ing Alfred start the car."

Andrew dashed up the backstairs, relieved that he had something to occupy him. He couldn't bear to let his mind dwell on the horrible fact that Jake was gone, gone for good.

If only I could have told him....

He slowed his steps as he walked through the nanny's alcove. His sister was asleep on his bed. Dr. Blake had rolled the quilts into cylinders and placed them on either side of her. Andrew stood for a moment and stared at her face, placid in sleep.

She doesn't have a care in the world...Thank God for that!

He set to work, pulling out the large bottom drawer of his dresser and clearing out his sweaters. Then he folded the afghan Jereen had crocheted and placed it in the drawer. It had a nice, cushy feel to it. He took a towel and placed it on top, then covered the whole works with one of the navy blue receiving blankets Savannah had made. The flan-nel would be gentle against his sister's skin.

Mrs. Beaton came in from the hall, bearing a pile of baby clothes.

"Since you're going to be setting up the nursery in here, I thought I'd bring all these baby things in."

"Thank you, Mrs. Beaton." Andrew jumped up and cleared off his desk. "We can use this for a changing table, and I'll clear out the bookcase for her clothes and things."

Mrs. Beaton nodded, then walked out and returned with another armload of clothes and diapers. Andrew stacked them on the bookshelves, then turned to Mrs. Beaton.

"Why did my mother give my baby things away? Didn't they want to have any more children?"

Mrs. Beaton looked a little embarrassed. She took a deep breath and said, "They couldn't have any more, Andrew."

"*Couldn't?* But Mum just—just had—"

"*They* couldn't have any more." Mrs. Beaton knelt down, folded the receiving blan-kets Savannah had sewn, and stacked them on the bottom shelf.

"Your father got the mumps at the end of your first summer. Oh, he looked so comi-cal, with his cheeks puffed out like a chipmunk! He was just wretched, though, not with being ill, but with having to be quarantined from you. Your mother used to bring you outside and hold you up under his window so he could at least see you. He recovered, and we thought that was the end of it. But then—" Mrs. Beaton looked at Andrew. "Your parents wanted more children—your mother said she wanted a housefull. But it wasn't to be. The doctor told them it was because of your father having the mumps. That sort of thing...happens to a man, you see."

Andrew nodded.

Mrs. Beaton placed the gowns next to the blankets.

"Your parents hadn't planned on starting a family right away, but you came along. Later your mother said to me, 'Thank God things didn't work out as we'd planned. If Roger and I had waited to start a family, we never would have had any children at all. Every time I look at Andrew, I'm so grateful for life's surprises.'"

After Dr. Blake got the car going, he made sure Mrs. Beaton had enough tinned milk on hand for the day, and promised to pick up some more in town.

"I should check in at the surgery and see to any calls I might have, maybe catch a few winks of sleep. I'll be back this evening at teatime."

He looked in on Andrew's mother just before he left, and allowed Andrew to see her too. Before Andrew went in to her, Dr. Blake took him aside.

"Your mother is physically all right, but she's going to need a lot of time before she's over this. I wish you could have had some chance at a normal childhood after so many years of war, but I'm afraid your mother is going to need your strength now. If you need any help, anyone to talk with, don't hesitate to come to me."

"Thank you," Andrew said. He wanted to apologize to Dr. Blake for his standoffishness as of late, but knew that would be best saved for another time.

His mother was in the billiard room, where she had labored and given birth. Andrew took slow, light steps across the room to the massive bed. His mother's form looked so frail and small in the huge expanse of linens, like a bird nesting on an aerodrome.

Even in slumber, her face was sad and strained.

If only I could somehow make everything all right for her!

"There's something wrong with her—I know there is!" Andrew insisted to Mrs. Beaton. "She's sleeping too much."

"Andrew—don't worry! That's what babies do most of the time."

"Please, Mrs. Beaton, please come up and make sure she's all right."

Mrs. Beaton chuckled as she wiped her hands off on her apron.

"All right, Andrew."

Andrew dashed up the stairs ahead of her.

"See?" He pointed at his sister, fast asleep in her bed.

Mrs. Beaton bent over and peered at her.

"Oh, what a bonny lass!" she whispered. She straightened up and smiled at Andrew. "She's all *right*, Andrew. Now, why don't you come downstairs and have elevensies? You need to eat, and you didn't have breakfast—"

"No, I'm not hungry. I ought to stay with her—"

"Andrew, you fret so! She's fine!"

Andrew knelt down and gently pulled the receiving blanket up to his sister's neck.

"She needs a Christmas," he whispered.

He enlisted Maria to help him wrap up the baby things. As he handed each item to her, he reflected on how everything had been so lovingly bestowed by the people from across the sea, people who had become so very dear to him. Then he realized: He had not gotten anything for her.

He carried the packages down to the drawing room and scattered them in front of the tree. Then he saw it: The small blue package garnished with silver angels.

It'll be hers now....

He set the package in with the other gifts for his sister, and returned upstairs. As he entered his room, he noticed his treasure box.

There's something else I can give her too....

He opened the box and sifted though the letters from his father. He would know which one it was by the postmark—there! He withdrew the letter from the envelope and read it. Good—that was the one! He refolded the letter, placed it back in the envelope, and handed it to Maria.

"Could you please wrap this up in that blue paper with the silver angels?"

Maria nodded. As she cut the paper, she asked, "Did you know what your mother wanted to name her?"

Andrew shook his head. "No." He looked at his sister, who was now busily nuzzling her lips together, even as she slept. "She ought to have a name, even if it's only temporary." He brushed back a wisp of red hair from forehead.

"Let's call her Jake Junior, all right? You don't have to be a boy to be called Junior."

"Jake Junior, that's very nice." Maria reached for the green velvet dress. "Shall I wrap this too?"

"No. It's a nice Christmas color, even though it's supposed to be for Saint Patrick's Day. When she wakes up, let's dress her in this, so she can wear it when we give her her Christmas gifts."

Maria smiled and set the dress aside. She picked up the booties Aunt Euelene had knitted. "She can wear these too."

"She should have something on her head as well. The drawing room is a bit chilly. Here—" Andrew sorted through the pile of items on the floor, pulled out the little cap Fiona Casini had crocheted and one of the little undershirts Sarah had made. "And she should have these on, too."

Just as Maria had finished wrapping all the baby things, Jake Junior started to fuss.

"She must be hungry," Andrew said. He ran down the backstairs and asked Mrs. Beaton to heat up a bottle. As he dashed back up to his room, Jake Junior's cries grew louder and more demanding.

"Hurry, Mrs. Beaton, *hurry!*" Andrew hollered.

"Andrew—can't rush boiling water!" Mrs. Beaton called.

"She's wet, too." Maria felt inside Jake Junior's gown.

"I'll take care of that." Andrew draped his England quilt over the dresser and lifted his sister out of her bed.

"Andrew!" Maria giggled. "Do you know how to change a baby?"

Andrew laid Jake Junior down on the dresser. "I've watched. I think I can manage."

Maria handed him a diaper and watched as Andrew pulled up Jake Junior's gown and took off her rubber pants and wet diaper. He maneuvered the clean diaper under her, gave it a twist in the middle, and pinned up the sides, being careful to place his hand under the pin so she wouldn't get stuck.

"First-rate job!" Maria shook her head in wonder. "This is the first time in my life I've seen a *man* change a nappie!"

Andrew blushed as he arranged his sister's gown down over her bottom.

"And here's the milk for that wee one." Mrs. Beaton strode into the room, bearing a bottle. "Now that Andrew's taken care of one end, let's take care of the other. Sit you down, Andrew, and give your sister her lunch."

Andrew carried his sister over to the sofa and sat down. Mrs. Beaton handed him the bottle and he put the nipple to Jake Junior's mouth. She sucked greedily at it, making funny little squeaks and grunts as she drank. The grunts increased in intensity; then she sputtered and gasped. Andrew pulled the nipple from her mouth, and she responded with a loud wail.

"I think she needs to be burped," Mrs. Beaton said. "Here, I'll do—"

"No, I can manage." Andrew handed Mrs. Beaton the bottle, shifted Jake Junior to his shoulder and patted her back. She stiffened, then let out a delicate belch. A bit of milk dribbled from her mouth; Maria grabbed a clean diaper and blotted it.

Andrew cradled his sister back into his arms again and continued feeding her. When she was finished, he burped her again. She made a contented, squeaky sigh, then scrunched down and snuggled her face against his chest.

"Oh Mrs. Beaton, she's so *beautiful!*" he whispered. "She's the most beautiful baby in the world, isn't she?"

Mrs. Beaton smiled. "Well, that would be hard to judge. Your father used to insist that *you* were the most beautiful baby in the world."

Andrew brushed his cheek against the silken strands of auburn hair. "Let's get her dressed for Christmas, all right?"

While Maria brought the packages downstairs and told Grandmother to be ready in the drawing room, Mrs. Beaton helped Andrew get Jake Junior into her outfit. Andrew was amazed that the dress, which had looked so ridiculously little, enveloped his sister's tiny form like a field tent. He put on her booties and cap, then wrapped her in a lacy white blanket Alida had made.

"She's a bonny lass, that's for certain," Mrs. Beaton said. "And with that red hair to go with her green dress, she's all decked out in Christmas colors."

Andrew carried Jake Junior down to the drawing room where Grandmother was seated on the sofa. As he placed his sister in his grandmother's arms, he said, "Happy Christmas, little one." Then he set to unwrapping her gifts and presenting them to her as Maria and Mrs. Beaton and Alfred looked on.

"Here's a quilt from Grandmother Lois in New Jersey—see? There's Lindy on the front porch. He died, but we have Linda now—she's a silver tabby, just like him. Here's some fur booties from Kaz, and a gown with ATA wings on it from L.S.'s mother. And here's a quilt from Irene's mother in Iowa—those little blue squares are ATA blue. Irene was a pilot in the ATA, just like our mother."

As he showed his sister the quilt, her eyes widened. Andrew smiled. He laid the quilt down, and noticed all the other scraps of fabric in the design: gingham and dotted swiss and seersucker and various floral prints. He thought it was so marvelous that someone could take cast-off pieces of cloth and design something so beautiful.

And that's what I can make of my life, too—take the shredded bits and threads and try to put them together into a tapestry that's even more wonderful than the whole cloth ever was....

He saved his gifts to his sister for last. As he held the picture of his father and Jake up to her eyes, he said, "They were best friends, your father and mine. I'll tell you all about them someday. And this is what my father said about your father." He opened his father's letter.

"He's a splendid chap, Charlie is—" Andrew glanced at his sister. "My father called him Charlie, because he was like a brother to him. He looked back at the letter and read, *"Flies like a bird, and is the sort of fellow you can trust implicitly."*

He showed the letter to his sister. She looked a little baffled, then blew a bubble out of her mouth.

"Well, I'll read it to you again—every day, all right? Now, it's time for your first Christmas song." Andrew put the letter down and reached for his guitar. Kneeling in front of his sister, he played *O Little Town of Bethlehem*. He had chosen it because he thought the part about *hopes and fears of all the years* seemed so appropriate to this occasion.

I'd learned to play my heart so well, and never realized that I was only trying to keep my desperate hopes and dreadful fears from tearing me apart....

As he fingered the last note, Jake Junior closed her eyes in sleep.

"Oh, no—I've tired her out!" Andrew put his guitar down and stroked her cheek.

"Don't worry, Andrew, you've given her a very nice Christmas," Grandmother said.

Andrew folded the blanket around his sister.

"Did Mum look like that, when she was little?"

Grandmother nodded. "Down to the last wisp of red hair. Red hair runs in my family. My aunt, my father's sister, had a flaming crown of it. Red like a Brown, everyone used to say."

"Your maiden name was Brown?" Andrew asked. "I never knew." He fingered a strand of his sister's hair. "She's Brown and Howard and Jay and Givens—what'll be her first name, I wonder?"

Grandmother shook her head. "I know that if she'd had a boy, your mother wanted the name Arthur William, after her two brothers. I know she can't remember them, but they loved her so. Your grandfather was away in India when she was born, but William and Arthur were here, Arthur home from Oxford, and William being tutored here because he had troubles with his schoolwork. He was left-handed, and his teachers at school made a fuss over it. William hated school because of that, so I arranged for him to be tutored here. Good thing your grandfather was away most of the time. He used to get ever so angry whenever he saw William writing with his left hand. Well, I never expected to have a child so late in life, and I didn't think your mother would even survive. You see, after William and Arthur, I'd had four more children, all boys. They all died soon after they were born, weak little things they were. So when your mother was born, I didn't hold out much hope of her surviving either, especially since she was born a little early, too. But when I heard her cry, a piercing, angry wail, I thought, well, maybe this one just might pull through."

Andrew held his breath, afraid that even a sigh would shatter his grandmother's reverie. Her outpouring of her most private griefs had stunned him. Imagine—he'd had four other uncles!

"William and Arthur were positively enchanted with her." His grandmother smiled. "I don't think Nanny McPhee did a stitch of work—William and Arthur were only too happy to give her a bottle, soothe her to sleep, sit and rock her for hours on end. Alice smiled when she was barely a month old, smiled at the sound of her brothers' voices— didn't she, Mrs. Beaton?"

"Aye, she did," Mrs. Beaton affirmed.

"She learned to walk when she was only eight months old, on Christmas day it was, here in this room. Arthur held her up and William knelt a few feet away and held his arms out to her. She toddled over to him and shrieked with glee as she fell into his arms, then William laughed and turned her around and sent her back to Arthur. Oh, that was a happy Christmas, wasn't it, Mrs. Beaton?"

"Aye," Mrs. Beaton agreed. "A happy Christmas, that indeed."

Jake Junior made a squeaky sigh and pressed her hands to her cheeks, as if clasping her face in consternation. Grandmother kissed her forehead.

"Happy Christmas, little one," she whispered.

Andrew carried his sister out to the front hall and stood under the painting of his uncles.

"Here's your niece." He held his sister up to the faces he used to fear so much. "She looks like her mother, don't you think?"

He looked at Arthur first, his mother's dear oldest brother who had a pet cat too, then at William, who also had to endure Grandfather Howard's fury over being left-handed.

Funny, Andrew thought. I used to think they looked so mean. If only I could have known them....

He looked at his sister.

Her father will only be a memory to her, just as my uncles are only a memory to me.

He'd planned on putting his sister to bed and going downstairs for lunch, but found he couldn't bear to let her out of his arms. So he sat down on the sofa in his room and held her as she slept. He loved to watch the sudden changes in her expression: At times her face was so serene and her body so still that she looked like a porcelain doll in a shop window—all she needed was a price tag hanging from her wrist to complete the effect. At other times she would wrinkle her nose, furrow her brow, or billow her mouth like a goldfish—sometimes all at the same time. Every so often the baby eyelids would pop open and she would regard him with a curious half-demanding, half-acquiescent gaze. Then Andrew would find himself falling into the depths of those deep blue pools, find himself submerged in that bold, complaisant newborn stare.

A little Anglo-American chimera, he thought.

She'll belong to both worlds, the old and the new. Will she be wild and brash and bold like a Yank, or as proud and strong and determined as the island race of her mother? Perhaps both—how strange that will be, having someone who's so much like me, so much a part of me, be so foreign! Yet I'm an Anglo-American chimera too. A part of me will always think American, feel American, be American....

"Andrew—brought you some lunch." Mrs. Beaton set a tray down on the Queen Anne table by the sofa. "Here, let me hold her for a bit while you eat." She sat down next to Andrew.

"Oh, I can eat and hold her at the same time," Andrew said.

"Give her here." Mrs. Beaton held her arms out. "I don't want you getting crumbs up her nose or spilling hot tea all over her. Eat, and then you can have her back."

Andrew reluctantly handed his sister to Mrs. Beaton and grabbed a sandwich.

"Don't wolf your food down, now," she admonished. "Here, I'll hold her so you can see her." She tilted Jake Junior up so that Andrew had a better view of her.

"You're just like your uncles, you are. They couldn't bear to have your mother out of sight. They were fine lads, they were. You'd have gotten on famously with them."

"I think so, too," Andrew agreed. He ate his Norfolk pudding, then took a sip of tea.

"It's a little hot—I'll drink it later." He put the cup back in the saucer and reached for his sister.

"Andrew, I don't want you drinking your tea and holding her at the same time."

"I promise, I won't. I'll put her in her bed, all right?"

"All right." Mrs. Beaton handed Jake Junior to him. "I'll take your tea things later." She took the tray and departed.

The baby eyes opened for a moment and Andrew found himself falling again into that newborn gaze. He felt himself floating, soaring, in the universe of those eyes: eyes knowing and unknowing, stern and benevolent....

Jake's eyes....

I wonder how she'll feel about me when she finds out how badly I treated her father? I can't bear her not knowing—keeping it from her would be like living a lie. I'll have to tell her how wonderful he was, how he tried to be a father to me, how I repaid him with hatred. And if she hates me for it, then, that's only what I deserve. I couldn't bear to have her forgive me, but I'll love her, love her, love her until the day I die....

"*Andrew!* You haven't touched your tea!" Mrs. Beaton cried.

"Sorry," Andrew said. "I really wasn't all that thirsty."

"Well, I can't blame you for being distracted. I'll fix you up another cup. Oh, here's some of the baby things; Maria's bringing up the rest. Where do you want me to put this picture of Jake and your father?"

"On the window seat, thank you. Then I can look at it while I'm holding her."

Maria came in and stacked the rest of the Jake Junior's gifts in the bookcase, then asked Andrew where she should put the letter. Andrew told her to put it in his box, for safekeeping. As soon as Maria and Mrs. Beaton had left, Jake Junior began to stir. Andrew felt her diaper—it was damp.

"Time for another change, little one," he said.

She quieted down while he pinned a dry diaper on her, but as he pulled her rubber pants up she began howling again. He put her in her bed and ran down the backstairs.

"Mrs Beaton—quick! Heat up another bottle—she's hungry again!"

"All right, Andrew."

"Please hurry—*please*! She's *crying*!"

"Yes, I hear. I'll just use the tea water to get the bottle warmed up in a jiff."

As Andrew ran up the backstairs the wailing ceased. He dashed through the nanny's alcove, thinking something dreadful must have happened.

Maybe she stopped breathing....

Then he heard a curious sound...like singing.

As he burst into his room, he drew a sharp, startled breath. There, leaning over Jake Junior, was Aunt Jane. And she was *singing!*

In French!

Andrew recognized the song: It was the lullaby she'd sung to him after he'd fainted, when he'd found his father bloodsoaked in the drawing room.

He stood, transfixed for a brief moment, then dropped to his knees.

As Aunt Jane turned to him, Andrew saw her eyes flicker with...he wanted to think it was remembrance, but it looked more like alarm.

He embraced her. "Do you remember when you sang that to me? After I saw Dad, when he was all bloody and I thought he was dead? Remember? I wet my pants, and I was so ashamed. You didn't tell anyone, I know. You got me clean clothes, then took me to see Dad. Aunt Gwen was bandaging him up—don't you remember?"

He saw the agitation and panic in her eyes: She looked like a student at an oral examination who'd forgotten all the answers. Then she closed her eyes and slumped against him.

"It's all right," he murmured. "I know you'll be able to remember. You're just tired. Come on, I'll put you to bed."

He picked his aunt up and carried her to his room. He was surprised by her incredible lightness. Though she did not protest, she looked at him warily.

"I've changed, haven't I? I was only eleven years old the last time you saw me. Remember when you told me you were going away and we looked out at the stars together? I'm fourteen now, and I know I've grown an awful lot, so you probably don't recognize me." He gently laid her on the bed, and arranged the bedclothes around her.

"Get some rest now, Aunt Jane." He kissed her on the cheek. "You'll remember, I know you will."

She closed her eyes and her body sagged against the bed. He stroked her hair, then kissed her again.

You'll remember...maybe not today, or tomorrow, but you'll come back to us!

As he dashed down the hall, he heard Jake Junior clamoring to be fed. No doubt about it, she had a lusty set of lungs!

"Mrs. Beaton—*Mrs. Beaton!* She's *starving!* Please hurry!" He ran down the backstairs and into the kitchen. Mrs. Beaton was just taking the bottle out of the pan. She sprinkled a few drops of milk on her wrist, then handed it to him.

"Thanks awfully!" He ran up to his room, scooped up his sister from her bed, and sat down on the sofa.

"Here, it's all right now." He gave her the bottle. "It's all right—there."

Jake Junior sucked hungrily, opening and closing her eyes as she did so, as if the effort of consuming a few ounces of milk had taxed every bit of her strength. Then her eyes stayed open. As she stared at Andrew, he again felt himself caught in her spell.

He went willingly into her enchantment, for it kept the savage despair and pain at bay. It was the same anguish all over again: The memory of those last awful words, spoken in anger: As it had been with his father, so it was now with Jake, only this time there was no redeeming hope that Jake would return.

If only I'd had the chance to tell him...the last thing he heard from me was the receiver slamming down....

He looked at the picture on the windowseat, saw the smiling faces of the two men who had cared so much for him, and for one another.

"They were best friends, your father and mine." He looked into his sister's eyes, trying to banish that gut-tearing desolation within him.

At least I had the remembrance of my father—she won't even have that...And she's been lost to Jake, too. He won't see her grow up, won't see that first smile, hear that first word, feel her arms around him....

He groaned, glanced back at the photo, tried to blink back the tears as he looked at Jake's face.

He was my father's best friend...He could have given me so many memories of my father, and now he's gone too....

Suddenly, it seemed that his father was smiling out at him, as if he *knew....*

It's my turn now...It's my turn to give Jake's child the memory of her father.

As he watched his sister greedily draining her bottle, Andrew realized that his father's legacy had not been extinguished by Jake's death; it had merely taken a strange, circuitous route. The child Jake had left behind would be the instrument of Aunt Jane's healing and recovery; indeed, this tiny baby had already kindled the spark of remembrance within the dark night of Aunt Jane's shattered spirit. And Aunt Jane, who had been closer to Andrew's father than anyone, who had known his heart and felt his thoughts, would, when she found her way out of the darkness, give to Andrew the gift of knowing, really *knowing,* his father. Andrew knew that his own remembrances, though valid, had been filtered through the sieve of a child's narrow view. To know the man his father was: That was the one thing Andrew wanted more than anything, and the child in his arms had the power to make that all come about.

Full circle, he realized.

And I'm the last link in the chain. The child that Jake left will bring Aunt Jane back, Aunt Jane will give me the remembrance of my father, and I'll give my sister the memory of her father.

Jake Junior sputtered and gulped. Andrew set the bottle down and laid her against his shoulder.

"All right, little one. I know there's a bubble in there." He patted her back and was rewarded with a respectable burp.

"Good girl—do you want to finish your bottle now?" As he cradled her in his arms and put the bottle to her mouth again, he saw the red M.G. come up the drive. Dr. Blake had kept his word.

He turned back to his sister and gave her the rest of her milk. "Good girl," he murmured as she finished the last drops out of the bottle. He burped her again, then put his feet up against the windowseat. He laid his sister against his thighs so that she was facing him.

"Now that I've got your undivided attention, little one, I'm going to tell you about your father." He brought his face very close to hers.

"He would be so very proud of you, and you of him. He was the best father a little girl could want. He was strong and brave and bright and kind and good—" Andrew took a deep breath. "And I'm going to make sure you know that. You'll know—you'll know, because I'll tell you every day. I'll never stop telling you—never."

His sister yawned, then closed her eyes in sleep.

"All right, little one, go to sleep. When you wake up, I'll tell you again—you had the best daddy in the world." His voice dropped to a whisper. "You had the best daddy in the world."

He kissed her forehead, then laid her against his shoulder. As he looked up, he caught a flicker of movement in the window, a reflection of sorts...

It couldn't be—his mind was playing tricks on him.

He turned around, and gasped. He was so stunned he couldn't even speak.

Finally his voice found him.

"I thought you were dead!"

Chapter 56

*J*ake lurched forward.

"I missed the plane." His explanation was spoken in a husky, flat voice. It almost sounded like an apology.

Realizing that his jaw was still hanging slack from shock, Andrew slowly closed his mouth. Other than that, he didn't—couldn't—move a muscle. He was afraid if he so much as blinked, Jake would disappear in a puff of smoke.

Jake, his eyes fixed on the bundle in Andrew's arms, cautiously moved forward, like a soldier picking his way through a minefield. He had the glazed, haggard stare of someone who had lived through a battle. Arriving at Andrew's side, he gazed down at the sleeping face of his child. Andrew reached up with his free hand and touched Jake's sleeve; only then, feeling the smooth wool of his coat and the reassuringly solid flesh underneath, did he take his eyes off Jake. He gazed for a moment at his sister, then looked back at Jake.

"Here's your daughter," he softly said.

Jake swayed slightly, then moved to the windowseat. He sank down onto it, his hands clutching the front edge of the cushion, all the while staring in stunned disbelief at the sleeping infant. His hands suddenly sprang open, as if in surprise; one of them reached forward, stopped halfway, then drew back, hitting the corner of the framed picture and knocking it to the floor. It lay face-down; Jake bent over to pick it up. As he turned it over and looked at the photo, his eyes widened with fright. He glanced sharply at Andrew, as if expecting a blow.

"Len was here," Andrew said. "He told me about my father." His voice dropped to a whisper. "And about you."

Closing his eyes, Jake slumped backward, rocking his head slowly from side to side, as if in mourning. Andrew's voice failed him again as he witnessed this outpouring of pain and grief. He reached forward and laid his hand on Jake's arm. Jake, as if stung, snapped forward, his eyes now open wide like a madman's.

"If only I hadn't bailed out—"

"If you hadn't bailed out, you would have been killed too." Andrew didn't mean for his voice to sound so crisp and sharp, but the stinging words seem to jolt Jake out of his torment. Jake looked at Andrew, stunned; then a wave of guilt washed across his face. Andrew pressed his fingers against his arm.

"He gave you an order. He would have been ever so upset if you'd disobeyed him."

The dark gray eyes looked at Andrew, as if seeking absolution, and Andrew was reminded of Lee-Ann, journeying to him for forgiveness. He had felt unworthy of the esteem in which she'd held him, and he experienced the same stab of unease now, seeing Jake's anguish and knowing that he alone held the power to banish the crushing guilt his father's friend had carried for all these years. His fingers tightened around Jake's arm.

"It's not your fault," he whispered.

The gray eyes blinked, blinked again.

"It's not your fault," Andrew repeated. "He saw your chute open. He got the 109 that was going after you. He knew you were all right—" His voice broke; he swallowed, took a deep breath. "He wanted you to be all right." He looked at Jake, and his words came out as a plea. "It's *not* your fault."

Jake stared at Andrew, as if seeing him for the first time. Then he looked at the photo.

"I still miss him." The words were moaned, not spoken distinctly.

"I know."

They looked at each other, unspeaking, and Andrew felt the silence enfold them like a sheltering cloak. He had a wonderful soaring sensation within; he felt lighter than air, like a plane being embraced by the sky. If fate somehow decreed them to spend eternity bound together in this communion of silence, he would see it as a blessing. And yet, he felt compelled to speak.

"I was so afraid I'd forgotten him. I couldn't even remember what he looked like, couldn't remember what it was like being with him. It was as if I'd gotten lost from him, and he'd gotten lost from me. All I remembered was what I said, the last time—" He felt his voice disappear into that void of anguish.

Andrew felt Jake's hand reach for his; their fingers laced together, like those of a drowning swimmer and lifeguard—only they were both rescued and rescuer in this bond of redemption. Looking at the snapshot of his father and Jake—seeing his father's face smiling out at him from across the years, and Jake's face basking in the affirmation of his best friend—Andrew felt such a rapture of soul that his father had left this man to be his companion and guide.

"I thought that was what he remembered of me, at the end. Now I know, I know he heard me saying I loved him. That's what he remembered when—"

Andrew swallowed, felt the tears coursing down his cheeks.

Jake looked at him, then his eyes took on a faraway gaze.

"When I was flying over Normandy, I kept looking out ahead, expecting to see him...wishing I could see him...out ahead and just above, like it was when I flew as his wingman. I kept thinking how he should have been able to see what I saw that day. Because he saw what happened at Dunkirk, and he should have been able to see the—"

"Reciprocal course." Andrew said the words gently, as if murmuring a prayer.

Jake looked down and nodded, as if the weight of those two words was too much to bear. "That's what he always used to say." He was silent for a moment, then spoke softly, almost as if he were confessing a sin. "I wasn't at Dunkirk. I was still in training."

"I know."

Jake swallowed.

"The guys in our squadron who were there, who saw the British army being tossed into the sea, and saw the German planes going in for the kill—" He took a deep breath.

"It was something that went so deep with them, it was like a fist, deep down inside, wanting to put things right again. I wish he could have known, somehow, that things did get put right. He died, not knowing—" Jake's jaws clenched, and his eyes took on that faraway look again. "He should have been there." His voice had an odd, flat tone. "He should have been able to see—"

"You were there for him." Andrew looked directly into Jake's eyes. "You were there for him, and...I think he knew, somehow, that everything would be all right." He bit his lip. "Mum said you knew about the rockets, and about the work the Germans were doing, trying to make an atomic bomb. She said you were afraid for me, that you wanted me out of England, so I'd be safe."

"I wish I could have told you why. It must have been awful for you, not understanding—"

Andrew smiled. "Can't go around telling military secrets." Then he felt an awful heaviness settle on him. "I knew I would have been there at my school—when the rocket hit. I would have been there—"

Jake shook his head, as if he didn't want to acknowledge an unpleasant truth. "You wouldn't have been there. You would have been at another school, a public school. Don't torture yourself thinking that you—"

"I would have been there," Andrew said firmly. "One of the boys in my class was killed. He had to stay back because he got ill. I know, I *know* I would have been there." He closed his eyes as yet another appalling realization hit him. "Mum took me to Greycliff after I met you...*because* of you. I would have been at Armus House...I would have been—" His voice caught again. Jake looked away, as if he'd done something wrong, then turned to contemplate the child in Andrew's arms.

They were both silent for awhile and, as if by mutual agreement, they regarded Jake Junior, now busily nuzzling her lips together as she slept with utmost concentration. Jake shifted position; Andrew was suddenly afraid he might bolt. Instead, Jake reached into his back pocket and pulled out his wallet.

Why would he check his wallet at a time like this? Andrew watched, dumbfounded, as Jake pulled forth some scraps of paper. Thumbing through the pile, Jake withdrew what looked like a card, folded in half. Wordlessly, he handed it to Andrew.

Opening it, Andrew saw a snapshot of his younger self, holding aloft the model Hurricane on his ninth birthday. He touched his finger to the little-boy face, felt the joy of that childhood long since banished by the grim shadow of war. His father had captured that moment for Andrew to hold in his hand, as he had clasped a future shining with promise and hope—

A future he will never know.

Andrew looked at his sister, saw her future full of love and joy and marvelous possibilities: a gift from his father, across the abyss of five horrific years of war.

All life, all love's his fee....

Jake's soft voice broke his reverie. "He had it tacked up above his bed—we shared a room, when we weren't sleeping outside under our planes, that is. He always looked at it before turning out the light. Afterwards—" Jake cleared his throat. "I found it, under his bed, after they'd...um...cleared away his things. I meant to give it to your mother, but then I had my accident. After that, I...well, I never did get around to giving it back." His eyes took on that faraway gaze again as he looked at the photo. "It was all I had left of him."

Andrew handed the photo back to him. They were silent again. Jake stared at Jake Junior, as if he were looking at her for the last time and trying to memorize her features. Then he spoke.

"I ran into Dr. Blake in town—well, he almost ran into me, to be exact. He was on his way out here, and he nearly had a heart attack when he saw me. He told me about yesterday, about you running to get him and standing in the road to make him stop. He said if it hadn't been for you, that—" His voice dropped to a strangled whisper. "Both of them might not have—"

Andrew gazed at Jake Junior. "She's mine too, you know."

Jake looked at him wonderingly.

Full circle, Andrew thought. My father saved Jake, Jake saved me, I saved my sister, and my sister delivered me into the love my father and Jake had for one another.

"I wish he could see her, somehow," Andrew said. "I wish she could somehow know him."

Jake nodded, his eyes shining.

In the midst of this wondrous peace, Andrew felt stabbed by an awful realization.

This is what war is all about. It tears life from the living, and the living from their futures. The fifty million who perished have been wrenched from the generations not yet born. We who have survived must stand in the breach, and remake the future with the remnants of the past. It is given to us to remember, and to speak of our remembrance.

He squeezed Jake's hand.

"I was so afraid I would forget him, forget what he was like. Now I remember...I knew him as my father, though. You were his friend. You knew him better than anyone else. Maybe sometime you can tell me about him." His eyes sought Jake's: a plea.

Jake blinked, then closed his eyes and nodded. Andrew smiled, so that when Jake's eyes opened they would meet with grateful joy.

"Not now, though." Andrew stood. "Right now—" He sat by Jake and lifted the child up to meet Jake's gaze. "Right now, you have to meet your daughter." He gently maneuvered her into Jake's arms. "That's it—you hold her sort of like a football...Just make sure to support her head; her neck muscles aren't very strong." He positioned Jake's left arm under her head and back, and his right hand under her bottom. "See—" He stroked his finger against her cheek. "Snug as a bug in a rug."

For all of Andrew's coaching, Jake held her stiffly and gingerly, as if she were made of dynamite. Andrew marvelled that a man who could fly sideways through a formation of German bombers and steer head-on into an ME-109 could be so terrified of a six-pound infant. He tried a little more encouragement.

"That's right, just relax. She won't break." He continued caressing her cheek, and the baby eyes popped open. "See, your daddy's here. He's so happy to see you—" Andrew noticed Jake's eyes, wide with wonder and terror. "You're doing just fine. See—she likes you."

Jake managed a nervous grin. "It's really scary. Parenthood, I mean."

Andrew smiled broadly. "You've had lots of practice. This one will be a *lot* easier—promise! A piece of cake!"

Jake laughed softly. "Well, on occasion, you *might* be able to get away with calling war a piece of cake." He shook his head. "I'm not so sure about parenthood."

Andrew traced his forefinger down to the baby fist, which opened and gripped his finger tightly. "I've been calling her Jake Junior. I didn't know what you and Mum planned on naming her."

Jake shrugged. "We didn't talk about that yet. I guess we were going to discuss it, after Christmas, I mean." He was silent for a moment, then said, "You name her, Andrew. You should be the one to give her a name."

His request caught Andrew by surprise. Him—name a *child? Jake's* child? His hand closed around his sister's. He looked at Jake, as if asking a favor.

"Lois—that's a nice name, I think. What do you think?"

"Lois is a very nice name," Jake whispered.

"Lois it is." Andrew leaned over, brushed his lips against her forehead. Straightening up, he said, "I don't know about a middle name."

Jake gazed lovingly at Lois. "I'll choose her middle name." The gaze transferred to Andrew. "Andrea. Lois Andrea Givens." He pronounced her name quietly, as a benediction. The newborn eyes regarded him with that curious half-demanding, half-acquiescent gaze, then fluttered shut.

For the second time that day, Andrew was caught speechless. He could only nod. If he tried to say a word, he knew he would crumple to pieces. All he could do was try to breathe away the sob welling up within him.

Jake looked back again at Lois, not seeing only his daughter, Andrew sensed, but as if he were looking at forever and seeing the years ahead, bright with hope and happiness and peace. The tears welled up within Jake's dusky eyes, then coursed through dark lashes and traced their way down unshaven cheeks. A rogue droplet splashed down onto the face of the sleeping infant; she winced, but did not turn her head—like a child catching raindrops on her face in a summer shower.

Andrew reached his hand to Jake's cheek and brushed aside the entourage of tears following their leader down the stubbly expanse. "You're getting the baby wet," he said gently. The feel of the bristly skin seemed strangely compelling; he had a curious sense of deja-vu.

This had happened before.

"It was you!" he cried, his voice a choked whisper. "It was you, with me, when I was in hospital, when I had pneumonia. *It was you!*

Shame and terror flowed over Jake's face.

Andrew's fervent strokings turned into a caress. "It was you," he said gently. "I thought you were my father—you were holding me—I felt your arms around me, felt the tears on your face, and I was filled with the most incredible joy. You said you wanted me to get well—"

Jake closed his eyes.

"You said you wanted me to get well," Andrew repeated. And I did—*I did*! Oh Jake, how frightening it must have been for you!" His fingers brushed across Jake's closed eyelids, as if soothing a child to sleep.

Jake's eyes flickered open, full of worry now.

"You were there for him," Andrew whispered. "Just as you were there for him at Normandy. You were always there for him, all the time."

The worry was replaced by uneasy wonderment, as if Jake were afraid to believe what he was hearing.

"You were always there for him," Andrew told him. "I just didn't realize it." He pursed his lips together for a moment, afraid to say what had to be said, even more afraid not to say the words that were choking their way into his throat and out of his mouth.

"Oh Jake, I'm sorry—I'm sorry for everything. It was me—it was *me*—it wasn't you!" As the sob welled up within him again, he bent over and pressed his face into his sister's dress. He felt within him an almost physical sensation of a strange sort of incredible warmth, as the ice of fear and anger melted and sprang forth into a fountain of joy. Then he felt Jake's hand stroking his hair, his shoulders, his back; felt suspended in time and space, sensing only the enfolding love around him.

If I died now, and spent all eternity captured in this moment, only this moment, it would be more than heaven could ever be.

He lifted his head to gaze again at the face of his sister.

"Lois Andrea Givens," he murmured. "Mum will be so pleased, don't you think?"

Jake's head snapped back and consternation filled his face. "Your mother...oh gosh, Dr. Blake is waiting downstairs. He said he would tell her about me, before I go in— don't want to startle her—" He started to hand Lois back to Andrew.

Andrew passed her back to Jake. "No. You stay with her. As for telling Mum, I'd like to be the one to do that—all right?"

Jake looked at him, his eyes shining. "All right." His voice was almost a croak.

Andrew gave his sister a gentle kiss on the forehead, then stood. He touched Jake's shoulder, and felt as if he should say something, but the silence seemed to say it all.

He walked to the door, then turned and stood for a moment to look at Jake, holding Lois Andrea Givens in his arms, father and daughter bathed in the pale gray light of the winter afternoon.

A Brief History of the Air Transport Auxiliary

By E.M. Singer
with
Philip Rogers,
ATA Association Representative
for North American Membership

*T*he Air Transport Auxiliary began with an idea: In 1938, Gerald d'Erlanger, director of British Airways, foresaw a problem: An inevitable war with Germany would lead not only to the suspension of many overseas routes, but also to the impounding of civil aircraft by the British government. The result: Commercial pilots would have no planes to fly, and nowhere to go. In addition, there were many private pilots who faced the same predicament. In the event of war, the government would severely restrict—if not prohibit entirely—flying activities by amateurs, and impound their aircraft as well. Some of these commercial and civilian pilots could, and would, be absorbed into the Royal Air Force. But many capable and experienced pilots, because of their age and in some cases because of physical limitations, would not be considered suitable for operational service in the RAF.

But d'Erlanger believed that war would create a demand for the services these pilots could provide, such as transporting dispatches, mail, supplies, medical officers, ambulance cases, and the occasional VIP. He contacted the Parliamentary Under Secretary for Air, Harold Balfour, and the Director General of Civil Aviation, Sir Francis Shelmerdine, and proposed the creation of a pool of peace-time civil pilots who could employ their aviation skills in service of their country.

As he was the one with the idea, he was given the job: to contact holders of "A" (private) licenses with at least 250 hours of flying time, and make arrangements to interview and flight-test these candidates with the goal of incorporating them into this newly created organization, which was given the working name "Air Transport Auxiliary."

About a hundred pilots responded to the offer, and they came from all walks of life: doctors, lawyers, stockbrokers, artists, innkeepers, journalists, factory managers, farmers. War broke out on September 3, 1939, just as the first of these men were arriving at a base in the west of England for vetting.

Thirty were selected out of this group. At this time, it was decided to create two ranks in the ATA: that of Second Officer, for those whose abilities limited them to flying light single-engined aircraft, and that of First Officer, for those with over 500 hours experience and who could pilot twin-engined aircraft. The uniform would be dark blue, consisting of trousers, a forage cap, light blue RAF shirt, black tie, and a single-breasted jacket bearing the ATA insignia: a circlet enclosing the letters "ATA," superimposed on a set of wings. Gold bars on the shoulders would indicate rank. (Eventually there would be also Third Officers, Flight Captains, and three ranks of Commanders. Gerald d'Erlanger held the rank of Commodore.) At this stage, the ATA was under the direction of National Air Communications and the Director-General of Civil Aviation, with British Airways responsible for clerical, personnel, and administrative services.

As England geared up to wartime standing, the ATA was given the urgent task of ferrying trainers, fighters, and bombers from storage units to RAF squadrons. Before the war, the RAF had thought it could handle all its own ferrying duties. But it was becoming apparent, even during the "Phony War," that more aircraft would be required to have a viable air force. The resultant workload was beyond the capacity of the RAF ferry pilots. If the war heated up, this situation would become a crisis. In addition, many more RAF pilots would be needed to fly operationally, and off-loading ferrying duties onto civilian aviators would free more Service pilots to Fighter, Bomber, and Coastal Commands.

Since most of the ATA pilots were limited to flying light single-engined training aircraft, it was decided to give them "conversion" courses to the single-engined fighters (primarily Hurricanes and Spitfires) and multi-engine types. This they would do, for the moment, at RAF Central Flying School in Upavon. The ATA would be now be operationally under the control of the Air Ministry, in effect the RAF, but British Airways would still oversee its administrative and clerical functions.

With the ever-increasing demand for ferrying services, the Under Secretary of State for Air proposed that the ATA open its ranks to women. There was a snag, though. The ATA was now operating out of RAF Ferry Pools, its pilots working alongside RAF transport pilots, and the Air Ministry was opposed to the posting of women pilots to RAF units. Politically and culturally, there was opposition as well, the arguments falling broadly along two lines:

1. Aviation was an unsuitable profession for a woman.
2. Women pilots would be taking flying jobs away from men.

The view taken by C.G. Grey, editor of the Aeroplane, was typical of the sentiment of the time:

> *We quite agree...that there are millions of women in the country who could do useful jobs in war. But the trouble is that so many of them insist on wanting to do jobs which they are quite incapable of doing. The menace is the woman who thinks that she ought to be flying a high-speed bomber when she really has not the intelligence to scrub the floor of a hospital properly, or who wants to nose round as an Air Raid Warden and yet can't cook her husband's dinner. There are men like that so there is no need to charge us with anti-feminism. One of the most difficult types of man*

with whom one has to deal is that which has a certain amount of ability, too much self-confidence, an overload of conceit, a dislike of taking orders and not enough experience to balance one against the other by his own will. The combination is perhaps more common amongst women than men. And it is one of the commonest causes of crashes, in aeroplanes and other ways.

Many people, men and women, voiced their protests to these attitudes, and worked vigorously to promote the idea utilizing women for ferrying duties, but none with as much energy and determination as Pauline Gower, a commercial pilot with over 2000 hours' experience, and a commissioner in the Civil Air Guard. In the latter role she had been responsible for overseeing the training and licensing of pilots in civilian flying clubs. Her tireless efforts are too extensive to chronicle here. Three books provide excellent accounts of her work and accomplishments: *A Harvest of Memories*, by Pauline's son, Michael Fahie, *The Forgotten Pilots*, by ATA pilot Lettice Curtis, and *Spreading My Wings*, by ATA pilot Diana Barnato Walker.

Because of Pauline's zealous efforts, the decision was made in November of 1939 to form a Pool of eight women pilots to ferry Tiger Moths, which were small, slow single-engined open cockpit trainers. As it was in the case of Gerald d'Erlanger, the one who proposed the idea was the one who got the job, and Pauline was appointed commander of this first batch of women flyers. Like d'Erlanger, she would hold this post throughout the war.

The women would be based at Hatfield, just north of London, and would fly their planes from the nearby deHavilland factory to training airfields and storage units. As it turned out, these destinations would be located for the most part in northern England and Scotland. As it also turned out, this task would be done in the middle of winter. There were two reasons why the women were given this task:

1. Nobody else wanted it.
2. Light trainers would be cheapest to replace if broken by a woman. As Pauline herself remarked on this attitude: *"(It's assumed) the hand that rocked the cradle wrecked the crate."*

On January 1, 1940, the ATA officially accepted the "First Eight" into service: Winifred Crossley, Margaret Cunnison, Margaret Fairweather, Mona Friedlander, Joan Hughes (the youngest, at 20), Gabrielle Patterson, Rosemary Rees, and Mirion Wilberforce. All these women were highly experienced, each having more than 600 hours of flying time, and seven were rated flying instructors. Pauline, at 29, was younger than most of the women she commanded. Yet she was a natural leader, and capably shouldered the responsibilities of her office.

Pauline had an iron will and a fierce determination to see women accepted on an equal basis with men. She was a mover and a shaker, but never was pushy or overbearing. She was gracious, tactful, gently persuasive, friendly, warm, and kind. She got things accomplished because people respected and admired her. Among all the ATA pilots I have talked with, men and women, not one has said a negative thing about her.

This was the first time in history (in England, or anywhere else in the world) that women would be officially employed in ferrying military aircraft, and despite the almost overwhelming hardships of that first winter, they would do a sterling job of it. They knew that the fate of hundreds of women pilots, who desperately longed to be also allowed into the ATA's ranks, depended on them. Of their own feelings at being tendered such a heavy responsibility, Pauline joked that in their case ATA stood for "Always Terrified Airwomen." Their spotless and efficient record made an impression of those with the power to make things happen, and more women were accepted into the ATA.

As with the men, they came from all walks of life. Some were accomplished athletes: a skiing instructor, an international ice-hockey player, a ballet dancer. Several were mothers (and there was one grandmother!). They were wealthy socialites and working girls, whose pre-war occupations included stunt-pilot, mathematician, map-maker, architect, typist, actress, and world famous record-setting endurance pilot (Amy Johnson, who was killed on a ferry trip in January, 1941).

A few weeks after the First Eight were installed at Hatfield, another separate, all-civilian ATA Ferry Pool was formed at White Waltham, west of London. It would clear aircraft factories in the Midlands and southern England, and eventually become the administrative headquarters and conversion school for the ATA.

While the women were courting hypothermia on their trips north, the male ATA pilots, who by now numbered one hundred and fifty-seven, were kept busy ferrying RAF planes from factories and storage units to operational airfields. They also collected impounded civilian aircraft.

In May, 1940, the German army broke through the French lines and swept across France to the Channel. The British Expeditionary Force and the French First Army were cut off from the rest of France's military forces and forced towards the coast. The men of the ATA were given an urgent task: to fly much needed Fairey Battles to RAF bases in France. This would be the first time ATA pilots would fly to the continent, and it would be an all too brief endeavor. Probably none of them could imagine, at that time, that they would not see France again for another four years.

Even though the pilots were given just a moment's notice to collect their planes and fly straightaway to France, by the time they arrived the tactical situation had deteriorated catastrophically. One group of pilots was stranded overnight. The next morning, with the German army only twelve hours away, they were pressed into service flying Hurricanes *back* to England. These planes would be needed in the coming Battle of Britain. The men of the ATA would continue their work throughout that desperate summer, ferrying Hurricanes and Spitfires to Fighter Command squadrons as aerial battles waged in the skies over England.

At this time, the women pilots were not allowed to ferry operational aircraft. Flying fighter planes was considered beyond a woman's physical and psychological capabilities, though some of the non-operational single-engined planes they flew were almost as powerful, and their handling almost as complex, as the Hurricanes and Spitfires they dreamed of flying. In the meantime, Pauline worked tirelessly to get her women recognized as competent to ferry more advanced aircraft, and finally the decision was made to allow women to fly Lysanders, which were light Army Co-op planes designed for short take-offs and landings, and twin-engined non-operational aircraft, such as Oxfords and Dominies. This was a step, a small one, but a significant gain none the less. This was followed another modest victory: For the first time, women would train at the RAF Central Flying School in Upavon.

With the end of the Blitz in May, 1941, the RAF went fully on the offensive—just in time for summer, the peak period for aerial operations. The ferrying demands for fighters and bombers would soon be far beyond the capacity of the male ATA pilots, so the women were at last cleared to fly Class 2 Aircraft, Hurricanes and Spitfires.

Four of the First Eight, Winnie Crossley, Margie Fairweather, Joan Hughes, and Rosemary Rees, took that first leap on July 19, 1941. Each did a short solo flight in a Hurricane, at their home base at Hatfield. Several more women checked out on Hurricanes over the next few weeks.

In September 1941, eleven women ferry pilots moved to Hamble, then an all-male Pool, to clear Spitfires from the Vickers Supermarine factory at Southhampton, on the south coast of England. They would also move Oxfords and Blenheims from other local plants, and ferry naval aircraft to and from the Royal Naval Air Stations in the area. All of the men, except for four, were posted to other Pools. The four remaining men stayed for awhile to ferry aircraft the women were not yet qualified to fly, and to provide orientation to the women, giving technical pointers and introducing them to the maintenance units, factories, RAF squadrons, and naval bases. Margot Gore was appointed Pool Commander, and the men readily accepted their status under her direction, a rare thing in those days.

In the early days of the ATA, the training on unfamiliar types was largely informal, mainly because the early joiners were highly experienced and versatile, and usually needed only a few pointers when they were assigned a plane they had not flown before. Sometimes pilots did go through standard training courses on more advanced classes of aircraft, such as at the RAF Central Flying School. Often, though, when faced with an unfamiliar type, a pilot would snag someone who had flown that particular aircraft and ask for information and helpful hints, or buttonhole one of the groundcrew for particulars.

With the ever-increasing workload and influx of new pilots, who were for the most part less experienced than the pilots who had joined early on, it became necessary to a institute a systematic training program for pilots as they progressed to more advanced types of aircraft. There had been several unpleasant incidents in which inexperienced pilots mistook one control for another. For instance, in the Blenheim, it was very easy to confuse the emergency fuel cut-off for the pitch control (they were located very close together, behind the pilot's head.) Thus was born the ATA Conversion School, where pilots would be trained to fly various classes of aircraft.

Types of aircraft were organized into the following categories:

Class 1: Single-engined light aircraft (Primarily trainers)
Class 2: Single-engined operational aircraft (Mostly fighters, such as Hurricanes, Spitfires, F4U Corsairs, and P-51 Mustangs.)
Class 3: Twin-engined light aircraft
Class 4: Twin-engined operational aircraft (Mostly medium bombers)
Class 5: Four-engined aircraft (Heavy bombers, such as Lancasters, Stirlings, B-17 Fortresses, and B-24 Liberators)
Class 6: Flying boats (PBY Catalinas, Sunderlands)

Classes 2 and 4 also had plus ratings, for more difficult types within that class. Class 2 Plus included P-40 variants, Tempests, Typhoons, and P-39 Airacobras; Class 4 Plus included Hudsons, Mosquitos, rare or older twin-engined types, and twins with tricycle undercarriages, such as A-20 Havocs (which were also B-20 Bostons), P-38 Lightnings, B-26 Mauraders, and B-25 Mitchells.

Pilots were given classroom courses, then flying instruction —first dual, then solo— usually on only one or two representatives of each type. They were then expected to be able to ferry any aircraft in that class.

However, planes in the same class might have wildly varying control configurations and operational setting. So the Ferry Pilots Notes were created: 4x6 cards, bound on two rings, that contained everything a pilot needed to know about flying that particular aircraft—usually all on just one card, front and back. Settings and configurations were clearly indicated, as well as pertinent aircraft speeds: takeoff, climbing, cruising, landing, and (last but not least) *stalling* speed. Pilots also had access to maker's handling notes, which were generally on eight to twelve pages and contained more detailed information. (Most pilots reported, however, that there rarely was time to swot up these handling notes before a flight, and the cards did the job just as well.)

Even within a particular type, there might be wide variations. In Mosquitos, the rudder trim controls migrated from the dash to the ceiling in later models. Also, the Mosquito's control column was configured differently in the bomber and fighter versions. The Spitfire went through twenty-four Marks, its engine rating going from 1030 horsepower to over 2000. Probably the most notorious intra-type modification was the "backwards" throttle on some P-40 Tomahawks originally destined for the French Air Force, well remembered by every ferry pilot who had to deal with it. These planes had been manufactured in the United States, to French specifications, which directed that the throttle be pushed forward to decrease power and pulled back to increase power, opposite to the way British and American planes operated. France capitulated before these aircraft could be delivered, so they were re-routed to England. To the pilots of the ATA, flying these planes was akin to driving a car in which one pressed down on the gas pedal to slow down, and eased off the pedal to speed up!

After their conversion courses, pilots would be "seconded" to a Pool in a trainee capacity to gain experience in that particular class, then reassigned, usually to their "Home" Pool, to handle regular ferrying duties.

The success of the Conversion School, and the versatility of ATA pilots, is demonstrated by Lettice Curtis, who was the first woman to fly four-engined bombers. (Twelve women eventually attained a Class 5 Ranking). In a single day, she flew two Class 1 Aircraft, a Spitfire (Class 2), a Mitchell and a Mosquito (Class 4), and a Stirling (Class 5). Her experience was not unusual: Class 5 pilots were expected, at a moment's notice, to fly any one of one hundred and forty-four types of aircraft. Class 4-Plus pilots were capable of flying one hundred and thirty-three different types.

As the ATA grew, it became too unwieldy for British Airways (now BOAC) to effectively administer, and the ferrying responsibilities too complex for the Air Ministry to handle. So during 1940 and 1941 it gradually was turned over to the Ministry of Aircraft Production, the civilian organization created by Winston Churchill in 1940 to streamline and maximize production and distribution of aircraft needed for the war effort. (RAF Fighter Command Chief Sir Hugh Dowding gave credit to the MAP for providing the steady stream of Hurricanes and Spitfires that won the Battle of Britain).

ATA Ferry Pools were sited near aircraft factories they were responsible for clearing. As various types of aircraft became obsolete, the Pools situated near the factories manufacturing them would be relocated to sites closer to those making newer types. By 1942 there were fourteen Ferry Pools, which were designated by numbers:

No. 1   White Waltham
No. 2   Whitchurch, Bristol
No. 3   Hawarden, near Chester
No. 4   Prestwick, Scotland
No. 5   Luton, later Thame
No. 6   Ratcliffe, Leicester
No. 7   Shelburn-in-Elmet, Leeds
No. 8   Sydenham, Belfast
No. 9   Aston Down, near Stroud
No. 10 Lossiemouth, Scotland
No. 12 Cosford, near Wolverhampton
No. 14 Ringway, Manchester
No. 15 Hamble, Southampton
No. 16 Kirkbride, Solway Firth

Eventually the ATA would have twenty-two Ferry Pools. Some Pools, like Hamble, Cosford, and Hatfield (which in 1942 moved to Luton) were all-women Ferry Pools. Most of the others were "mixed," with men and women pilots working side-by-side.

Ferry movements were complicated by the fact that England was under aerial attack throughout most of the war. It was difficult to relocate major factories, or camouflage them. (The Germans knew where they were, anyway.) With aircraft factories under constant attack, it was vital to get planes out of harm's way as soon as they were flyable. So maintenance units, or MUs, were built, where the fine work (installing armament and radios, and making other minor modifications) could be carried out under safer conditions.

MUs were smaller units, and could be easily hidden around the countryside. The use of MUs followed, on a grander scale, the general principle of "dispersal" as practiced at RAF bases: Scattering aircraft around as much as possible and also camouflaging them, so as to minimize losses in the event of aerial attack. This protection came at a cost to ATA resources: A plane needed to be ferried twice in its journey from factory to RAF base, so ATA movements were doubled from the start. If the planes were damaged in combat and could not be repaired at squadron workshops, they were ferried back to the MUs, or in some cases to factories, for repair. (If the planes were flyable, that is, and often they were barely airworthy, another challenge to ferry pilots.)

Regarding the enormous amount of ferrying work carried out by the ATA, Commodore d'Erlanger once remarked to a group of visiting dignitaries: "Every machine you see in the sky has been, or will be, flown at some period of its life by a pilot of the ATA."

Some MUs took over various existing structures for their work: workshops, garages, barns, and sheds. Other MUs were built from scratch, and an ingenious way was found to camouflage them. A site was found near the edge of a forest or within a clump of trees. Construction workers would chop out the foliage in a central area; then tie ropes to the tops of trees at the edge of this newly-made clearing, pull them down away from the perimeter, and anchor them to the ground. That done, the workers would build the workshops and other structures inside the clearing. When this work was finished, they would cut the ropes holding down the bordering trees, and these trees would snap right up to provide cover for the new MU.

The airstrips of these MUs were in adjacent fields or bits of open land. They were usually rough, and very short. ATA pilots had to do three-point landings in order to get their planes down with a minimum amount of runway.

In the early years of the ATA, ferry pilots invariably had to get back to their bases using ground transport, which usually meant a slow, tiring journey by train. Often they would ferry planes over great distances, making the return trip excruciatingly long. (A rail system in a war zone is a model of inefficiency and discomfort.) With the desperate shortage of pilots, the time wasted in travelling by rail meant a critical drain in ferrying resources. So two solutions were found.

The first was the taxi program. The ATA acquired several planes to transport ferry pilots to the factories or maintenance units to pick up their planes, then collect them at their destinations. Some of these taxi aircraft were small, single-engined transports which could hold a few pilots, such as Puss Moths, Stinsons, Airspeed Couriers, and American Fairchilds. These were not satisfactory for the most part, for often several pilots at a time would need transport to the same factory. The Avro Anson, a twin-engined aircraft, proved perfect for taxiing duties. The Anson was designed as a bomber, but by the time the war was in full swing it was apparent that it was too underpowered for an operational role. Fortunately, "Annie" found a new life with the ATA: It could officially hold seven or eight pilots (and many times ten or twelve squeezed in).

The second innovation was the institution of a relay system for ferrying planes. For longer ferrying journeys, instead of one pilot delivering a plane to its final destination, he or she would drop it off at the next Ferry Pool along the way. A pilot from that Pool would ferry it along to the next Pool, and so on until the plane reached the end of its journey.

ATA pilots faced serious risks in performance of their ferrying duties. They were not trained to be instrument rated, so bad weather was a constant danger. Although they had to abide by very detailed bad weather flying restrictions, the changeable English weather made for rather dicey decision-making. Sometimes a few degrees' drop in temperature could turn clear skies into a cloud-filled nightmare. Barrage balloons and friendly fire from anti-aircraft batteries were also a hazard. Pilots were not allowed to mark their maps with the location of defensive positions, lest their maps fall into enemy hands.

In the early years of the war the RAF did not have complete air superiority over England, and attacks by German planes were a continual threat. Some of the Ansons were fitted with guns (which only fired backwards) but the vast majority of times pilots flew unprotected. The planes ferried by ATA pilots were more often than not devoid of armament; if they had guns or cannon, they were unloaded anyway.

In February of 1943, a taxi Anson filled with twelve ATA pilots and flown by Jim Mollison, Amy Johnson's husband, was attacked by a Messerschmidt 110. Jim made a dash into a cloud and lost the unfriendly pursuer, then put down at White Waltham.

ATA pilots flew without radio, and often with no more sophisticated equipment other than a compass and gyro.

Besides pilots, every ATA Ferry Pool had a ground staff, consisting of administrative officers in command, meteorological information, operations, maps, and signals. There were also secretaries, typists, drivers, and custodial and canteen staff. Finally there were ground engineers and mechanics, who performed superbly in keeping the aircraft ferried by the ATA in flying condition. The ATA developed its own handling notes for maintaining and repairing aircraft; these instructions were considered to be so clear and comprehensive that they were adopted by the RAF for its own riggers and fitters. Women served as mechanics, and in every other capacity as ground staff.

There were, in addition to pilots, other flying personnel in the ATA. The organization had its own Flight Engineers, among them four women, one of whom was killed in service.

The ATA also utilized Air Training Corps Cadets, boys from sixteen to eighteen years of age. They were initially brought in to help out in cleaning airplanes, as there was a severe shortage of hanger staff. As a reward they were given the occasional flight. Once airborne, they would often be given the task of winding undercarriages. Many planes at this time had manually operated landing gear, and the work in raising and lowering them was much appreciated by ATA aircrews. The Cadets were issued RAF-blue uniforms with appropriate insignia, which made them the envy of their peers.

They did such sterling work that they were offered permanent jobs with the ATA. Some worked in the post department, sorting mail and acting as runners for urgent messages. They delivered aircraft spare parts and other equipment, travelling by car or by plane. Some worked as despatch riders and were given motorcycles for their duties. They also acted as escorts and orderlies to visiting dignitaries, among whom were the King and Queen and Eleanor Roosevelt.

As the ferrying demands grew, the ATA actively recruited pilots to handle the workload, and limitations that might bar a pilot from service in peacetime were no barrier when every capable aviator was sorely needed. Most of the men who flew were in their thirties, forties, and fifties. Many physically challenged pilots also found employment with the ATA. There were a few men who were color-blind, and one who suffered from narcolepsy, who but for the unfortunate tendency to nod off at the most inappropriate times was quite a good pilot. (On his ferrying trips he would take along an "assistant" to shake him awake if he happened to fall asleep at the controls.) There were several one-armed pilots, and a one-armed, one-eyed pilot, Stuart Keith-Jopp, who was one of the first thirty men to join the ATA at its inception. He was also over fifty years old, a veteran of World War I, and an extraordinarily skilled and capable pilot who flew with the ATA until the war's end.

Many foreign pilots also found employment in the ATA. In this aspect, the ATA was known as the "Flying Legion of the Air," as pilots from thirty other countries served in the organization. There were pilots from almost every occupied nation in Europe, most of whom escaped just ahead of invading Nazis. Soon after her country was occupied by Germany, Anna Leska of Poland managed to snatch a Polish Air Force plane at an airfield guarded by German soldiers, and fly it to Rumania. She made her way to France, then to England, where she joined the ATA and rose to the rank of First Officer.

The thirty countries who contributed pilots to the ATA were: Argentina, Armenia, Australia, Austria, Belgium, Bermuda, Canada, Ceylon, Chile, China, Cuba, Czechoslovakia, Denmark, Ethiopia, Ireland, Estonia, France, Holland, India, Malaya, Mauritius, New Zealand, Norway, Poland, the Soviet Union (one Russian pilot was seconded from the RAF), South Africa, Spain, Switzerland, Thailand, and the United States.

The Americans formed the largest foreign contingent in the ATA. One hundred and fifty-four American men served, many of them joining before America officially entered the war. Since the ATA was a civilian organization, these men did not violate the American Neutrality Laws by joining it, even though they ferried military aircraft. (Americans who joined the RAF were considered to be breaking the law, and risked criminal penalties such as prison terms and loss of citizenship.) One American woman joined the ATA before the U.S. officially entered the war, and in 1942 Jacqueline Cochran, the record-setting American aviator, recruited twenty-five more. Almost all of these women made the journey to England by ship, when the U-Boat threat was at its height. Crossing the Atlantic during that time was an act of courage in itself.

With America's entry into the war and the aerial battles over Germany at a fever-pitch, the demands for aircraft ferrying increased dramatically. After scrounging every available female, foreign, handicapped and over-aged pilot, the ATA still faced a serious personnel shortfall. Jacqueline Cochran had been asked to provide two hundred American women for ATA duty. This she would not do, for Jackie had a dream of her own: to start up a women's ferrying program in the U.S. For that she would need a sizable pool of experienced pilots, and two hundred was too tall an order. Twenty-five would have to do. (Jackie would realize her dream: Her organization, the Women's Airforce Service Pilots, would employ over a thousand American women in ferrying aircraft within the continental United States.)

If the ATA could not find pilots, it would create them, and thus the *ab initio* program was born. Most of these novices came from the Women's Auxiliary Air Force (WAAFs), from non-flying RAF personnel, and from the ATA's ground staff. They did their initial training at Barton-in-the-Clay, in Bedfordshire, then moved to Thame in Oxfordshire for their Class 2 Conversion Course. (The Class 2 training had been shifted to Luton in 1942, then to Thame in the summer of 1943 because White Waltham had become so congested with training classes and ferrying movements. White Waltham continued as a training center for twin and four-engined aircraft.)

Also during the summer of 1943, the women ATA pilots, who had previously earned 20% less then male pilots, were at last given equal pay. By now they were ferrying all classes of aircraft, with the exception of Class 6 flying boats. The women faced the same dangers as the men, the same long, grueling hours of flying, the same discomforts. Pauline Gower and some of the men on the Senior Staff of the ATA took their case to the MAP, to the Treasury, to Parliament, and finally won. Pauline's son Michael has done an extensive amount of research on the subject and, as far as he can tell, the ATA was the first major organization or corporation to treat men and women equally as a matter of policy.

After the Normandy Invasion, the ATA was given the task of helping to ferry aircraft to the continent. At first, ATA pilots delivered aircraft to Ground Support Units (GSUs) at White Waltham and Aston Down, from where they were off-loaded onto the RAF and delivered to France by RAF ferry pilots. In September, two male ferry pilots, Hugh Bergal and Maurice Harle, a Frenchman, delivered two Spitfires to an RAF airstrip near Dieppe. Thereafter, male pilots of the ATA made regular deliveries to the continent.

With the return to the continent, and the Allied front line moving constantly eastward, supply considerations became a critical issue. The ATA's original purpose had been the transporting of supplies and personnel, but the demands of war soon made the task of ferrying aircraft its almost sole priority. After four years the ATA returned to its initial role as a transport service, and the Ansons filled the bill perfectly. ATA Ansons carried ammunition, small arms, mortar bombs, petrol, radios, spare parts, food, newspapers, and medical supplies. They also ferried passengers: military personnel, civilian VIPs, medical teams, wounded servicemen, ENSA entertainers. On the return trips, freed Allied POWs and war orphans were transported to England.

For the first time, Ansons were fitted with radio, and the ATA was given the call-sign *Ferdinand*. Shortly thereafter, in the proud tradition of aircraft nose art, the overseas Ansons were emblazoned with the Walt Disney character Ferdinand the Bull.

The women at this time were not officially allowed to ferry to the continent, though in late September of 1944 Diana Barnato Walker managed to fly a Spitfire to Brussels, following her husband, a Wing Commander in the RAF, in another Spitfire. At the time she was on a short leave from the ATA. Her husband Derek got permission from the

Headquarters of the Second Tactical Air Force of the RAF to allow her to travel to Brussels. (In the autumn of 1943, RAF Fighter Command was split into the Second Tactical Air Force, which was to assist on offensive operations over the continent, and the Air Defense of Great Britain, which was charged with defending the skies over England.)

In December, 1945, ATA women pilots were officially cleared to fly to the continent. In the final days of the war some made it to Berlin. Also during this time a few women were given the opportunity to ferry the new Meteor jets.

But the women of the ATA knew their days as professional aviators were numbered. With the war winding down, their services would no longer be needed. And with the huge surplus of pilots created by the war effort, their opportunities would be limited. Once again, women pilots would be viewed as "taking jobs away from men."

A few women managed to carve out professional and commercial roles. In 1963 Diana Barnato Walker became the first British woman to break the sound barrier, in a Lightning jet fighter. Margot Duhalde found employment as a commercial pilot in her native Chile. Monique Agazarian started her own air charter business in England. Nancy Miller, along with her husband, founded a helicopter service in Alaska. Jackie Sorour of South Africa ferried surplus RAF aircraft to countries in the Middle East and Far East. Edith Stearns became a flight instructor. But most of the women found the employment doors closed.

They refused to be grounded. They would fly whenever they could, wherever they could, for as long as they could. Ann Welch travelled around the world, taking part in glider competitions. Roberta Leveaux also flew gliders, then turned to Ultralights, and in her seventies spent hours soaring above the Arizona desert. Some women, like my mother-in-law, taught their children to fly.

Tragically, the one person who did so much to promote the cause of women pilots did not live long enough to thoroughly indulge her passion for flying. Pauline Gower died in 1947, shortly after giving birth to twin boys.

The ATA began as a way to give unemployed and idle pilots a chance to do their "bit" in the event of war. It became a huge organization, whose work was vital to the war effort.

ATA pilots delivered 308,567 aircraft, of 147 different types, logging a total of 742,614 flying hours. The ATA's total pilot complement comprised 1152 men and 166 women; 129 men and 14 women were killed in service. Thirty-six pilots, among them two women, received Certificates of Commendation from the British government. Four women pilots, Pauline Gower, Margot Gore, Joan Hughes, and Rosemary Rees, were awarded MBEs (Members of the British Empire). Other aircrew included 151 flight engineers, 19 radio officers, and 27 ATC Cadets.

As this century draws to a close, most of the former ATA pilots are now in their late seventies and eighties. Many have grandchildren who are the same age that they themselves were when they flew over a war-torn England. Many are no longer here. Each year the ATA Association Newsletter chronicles the thinning of the organization's ranks

At this time, the American contingent of the ATA Association is headed by Philip Rogers, a "youngster" of 73. He was one of the Cadets, those eager teenagers who happily washed planes and cranked undercarriages in exchange for a few hours of "airtime" a week. He became a pilot in the RAF, then went on to become a flying instructor with the Oxford University Auxiliary Air Squadron. Another former Cadet, Eric Viles, leads the British contingent of the ATA Association.

For all the pilots, from those who joined the ATA as seasoned aviators with hundreds of hours of flying time, to the "infants" of the ab initio program, and for the flight engineers and Cadets who also took to the skies, the ATA's motto would became a lifelong aspiration: *Aetheris Avidi*—Eager for the Air.

E.M.S.

August, 1999

It was not until I eventually joined the RAF, after nearly four years in the Army, that I began to realize what the ATA pilots had accomplished, particularly the flying of operational types in poor weather, without radios, or approach aids. When I graduated from Flight School, at Feltwell in Norfolk, it was a requirement that we be Instrument Rated, and that Rating was required to be kept current throughout my eight years in the RAF. Not being able to radio ahead, to find out if the weather was getting worse or better, not being able to rely upon a radar approach system, or other approach aids, in English weather, and with plenty of barrage balloons to look out for; ferrying over 300,000 aircraft during WWII, in such conditions, was perhaps their greatest achievement.

During my time (as a Cadet) with the ATA from July '43 to February '45, I thought flying in poor weather was normal. By the time I started my RAF career, I had a very healthy respect for the weather, and made sure I always had communication with Air Traffic.

One last comment: I am sure that my experience in the ATA was a major contribution to graduating at the top of the class at Flight School, and more importantly, becoming an "Old" pilot!

P.R.

August, 1999

Recommended Reading:

Spreading My Wings, by Diana Barnato Walker (Patrick Stephens Ltd., Sparkford 1994)
Brief Glory, by E.C. Cheesman (Harborough Ltd., Leiscester 1946)
The Forgotten Pilots, by Lettice Curtis (Nelson Saunders Ltd., Buckinghamshire 1971)
A Harvest of Memories, by Michael Fahie (GMS Enterprises, Peterborough, 1995)

Author's Notes

*I*n writing this story, I have sought above all to accurately convey the history and workings of the Air Transport Auxiliary, especially in regards to the women ferry pilots. During WWII, the press tended to play up the glamorous angle of women pilots in newsreel images and photos showing them climbing, with casual, confident smiles, into Hurricanes and Spitfires. This wartime propaganda obscured the struggle that these women faced to be accepted, and the passage of time has veiled the long, hard road of the physical and psychological challenges they had to travel. The "First Eight" knew that the hopes and dreams of so many other women pilots were travelling with them on those bleak, frozen journeys to the North in their tiny biplanes; not only in England, but in the rest of the world as well. The ATA was the direct forerunner of the WASP program in the United States; Jacqueline Cochran was able to present the sterling record of the women ATA pilots to the US Army Air Forces, and thus get the go-ahead to organize American women into their own ferrying service. And once the "genie" was uncorked, there was no going back. Eventually women gained entry into commercial, professional, and military aviation, and finally into America's space program, because of these "First Eight" and the ATA women ferry pilots who followed them.

I have chosen to place Alice into the ATA in early 1941; not that hers would be a "typical" experience of women ferry pilots—there really was not what could be termed a typical experience. The early joiners were light-years ahead of their later counterparts in experience and skill, and needed little formal training as they progressed to more advanced aircraft types. By March of 1941, the ATA Conversion School was getting underway, and the women who joined at that time were the first to fully benefit from this organized system of classroom and in-flight instruction. As the war progressed, and the doors were opened to women with little or no flying experience at all, the small cozy, group of women aviators became a sizeable force. Alice would thus be "in the middle" of this transition, being closely acquainted with the early joiners, and knowing of their struggles, and also at the forefront of the throng of women who sailed through the conversion programs later on. If I couldn't present a "typical" experience of a woman ferry pilot, I could at least offer one that would be fairly comprehensive in conveying the varied experiences of women ATA aviators.

In this, I have tried to be as faithful to the historical record as possible. There are two aspects in which my story plays hard and loose with the facts: The first is in placing the Class 2 training at White Waltham in early 1943. By that time the Class 2 conversion courses had moved to Thame, after being transferred to Luton from White Waltham in early 1942. There was really no way that I could contrive to have Andrew meet the American women ferry pilots except by overstriking reality in this instance.

The second aspect is in regards to the amount of information that Alice communicates to Andrew about aircraft and other technical matters. ATA pilots were charged with secrecy, just as if they had been in the military. Their mail was censored, and they were not even allowed to have cameras on base. In conveying the story though Andrew's eyes, there would not have been very much to tell about the ATA had I not given in to dramatic license on this score. For that matter, there are others in my cast of characters who are absolute blabbermouths as to matters they should be keeping quiet about. Andrew is intuitive, but not telepathic, and the only way to present this information is by suspending this particular prohibition within the confines of my story.

One last word: The "ever so nice" American Ferry Pool commander at Lossiemouth is Ed Heering, who was the only American to head an ATA Ferry Pool. He not only commanded Lossiemouth, he designed it, and oversaw its construction. After the war, every male head of a ATA Ferry Pool received an OBE from the British government. The two women who commanded Ferry Pools received MBEs. Ed, because he commanded what was technically considered a Sub-Pool, received nothing. When this matter is mentioned to him, he invariably dismisses it with a casual wave of his hand, and a gentle smile: "We Americans aren't concerned about things like that." At an ATA reunion a few years ago, the British contingent of the ATA Association presented him with a lovely framed photograph of an aerial view of Lossiemouth; he was touched beyond words, and considered it honor enough. Yet there are many of those in the American contingent who would like to see Ed receive some sort of official recognition from Great Britian for his service. It would be a fitting tribute not only to him, but to all the Americans who served in the ATA, and who formed the largest foreign contingent in the organization: One pilot in seven was American.

It has been over a half-century since the books were closed on the most devastating conflict in history; courage and sacrifice were ordinary virtues in those days. In the flood of honors at the war's end, it was understandable for many to get lost in the shuffle. Still, it would be a welcome and appropriate gesture, after all these years, to see this oversight redressed.

Ensinger